STAR TREK®

THE ORIGINAL SERIES

OMNIBUS

STAR TREK
THE ORIGINAL SERIES
OMNIBUS

STAR TREK created by Gene Roddenberry. Special Thanks to Risa Kessler and John Van Citters of CBS Consumer Products for their invaluable assistance.

www.IDWPUBLISHING.com   ISBN: 978-1-60010-712-2   16 15 14 13   2 3 4 5

IDW
Operations: Ted Adams, Chief Executive Officer • Greg Goldstein, Chief Operating Officer • Matthew Ruzicka, CPA, Chief Financial Officer • Alan Payne, VP of Sales • Lorelei Bunjes, Dir. of Digital Services • AnnaMaria White, Marketing & PR Manager • Marci Hubbard, Executive Assistant • Alonzo Simon, Shipping Manager • Angela Loggins, Staff Accountant • Cherrie Go, Assistant Web Designer • Editorial: Chris Ryall, Publisher/Editor-in-Chief • Scott Dunbier, Editor, Special Projects • Andy Schmidt, Senior Editor • Bob Schreck, Senior Editor • Justin Eisinger, Editor • Kris Oprisko, Editor/Foreign Lic. • Denton J. Tipton, Editor • Tom Waltz, Editor • Mariah Huehner, Associate Editor • Carlos Guzman, Editorial Assistant • Design: Robbie Robbins, EVP/Sr. Graphic Artist • Neil Uyetake, Art Director • Chris Mowry, Graphic Artist • Amauri Osorio, Graphic Artist • Gilberto Lazcano, Production Assistant • Shawn Lee, Production Assistant

Originally published as STAR TREK: KLINGONS: BLOOD WILL TELL Issues #1–5; STAR TREK: YEAR FOUR Issues #1–6; STAR TREK: ALIEN SPOTLIGHT Issues GORN, VULCANS, ORIONS, and ROMULANS; and STAR TREK: YEAR FOUR—THE ENTERPRISE EXPERIMENT Issues #1–5.

Collection Edits by Justin Eisinger and Mariah Huehner
Collection Design by Shawn Lee
Collection Cover by The Sharp Brothers

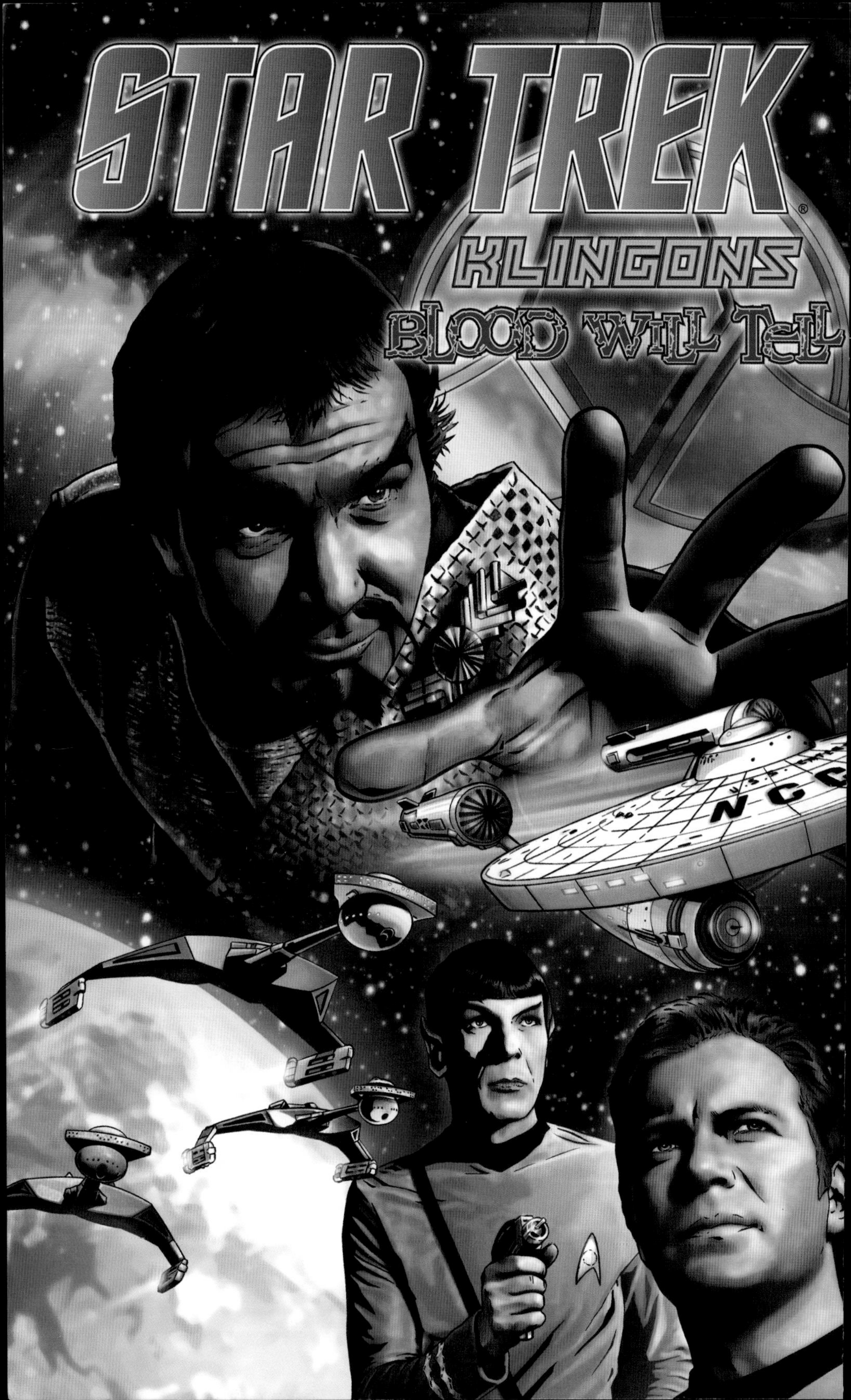
STAR TREK®
KLINGONS
BLOOD WILL TELL
NCC

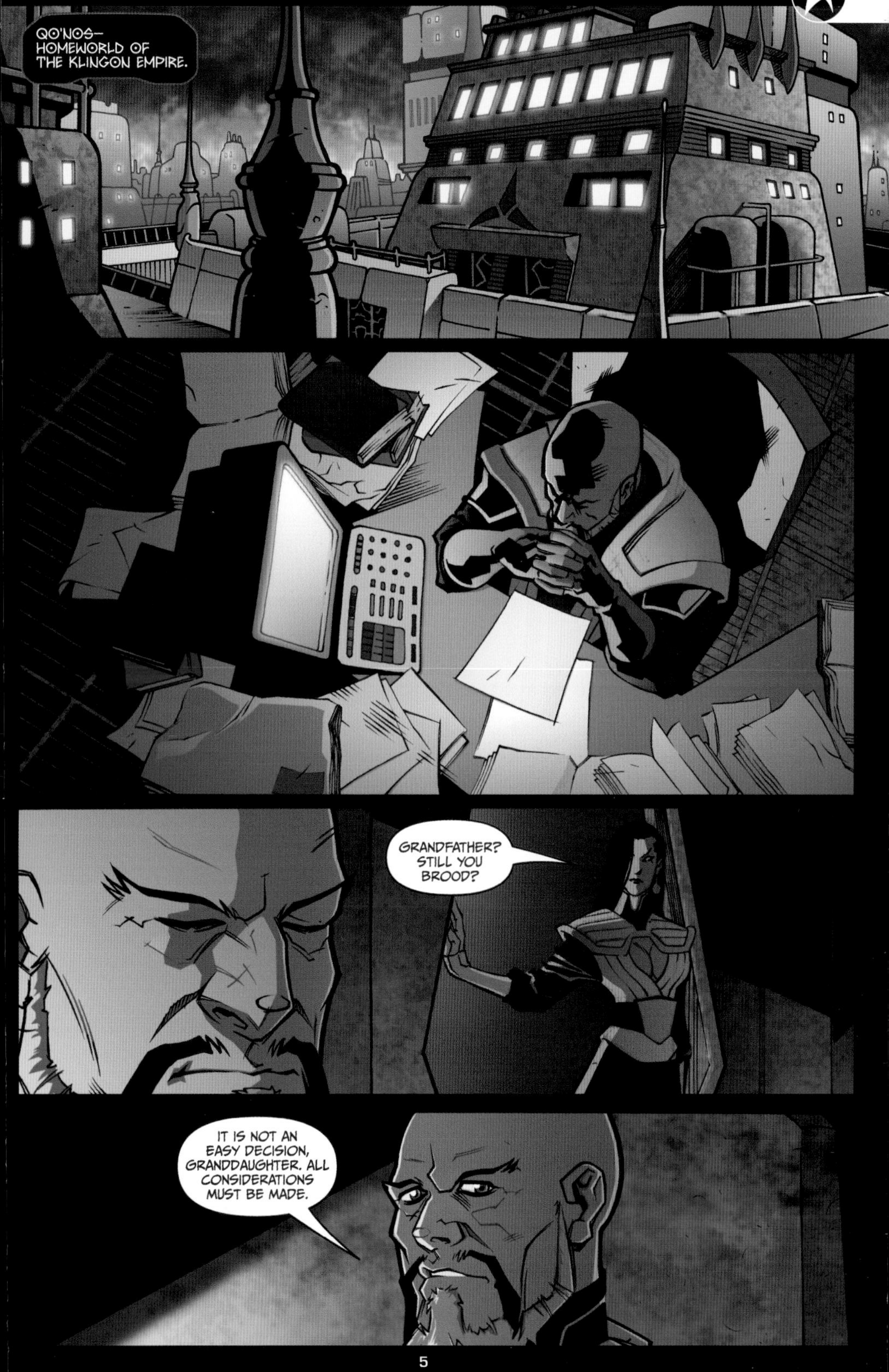
QO'NOS—
HOMEWORLD OF
THE KLINGON EMPIRE.
GRANDFATHER? STILL YOU BROOD?
IT IS NOT AN EASY DECISION, GRANDDAUGHTER. ALL CONSIDERATIONS MUST BE MADE.

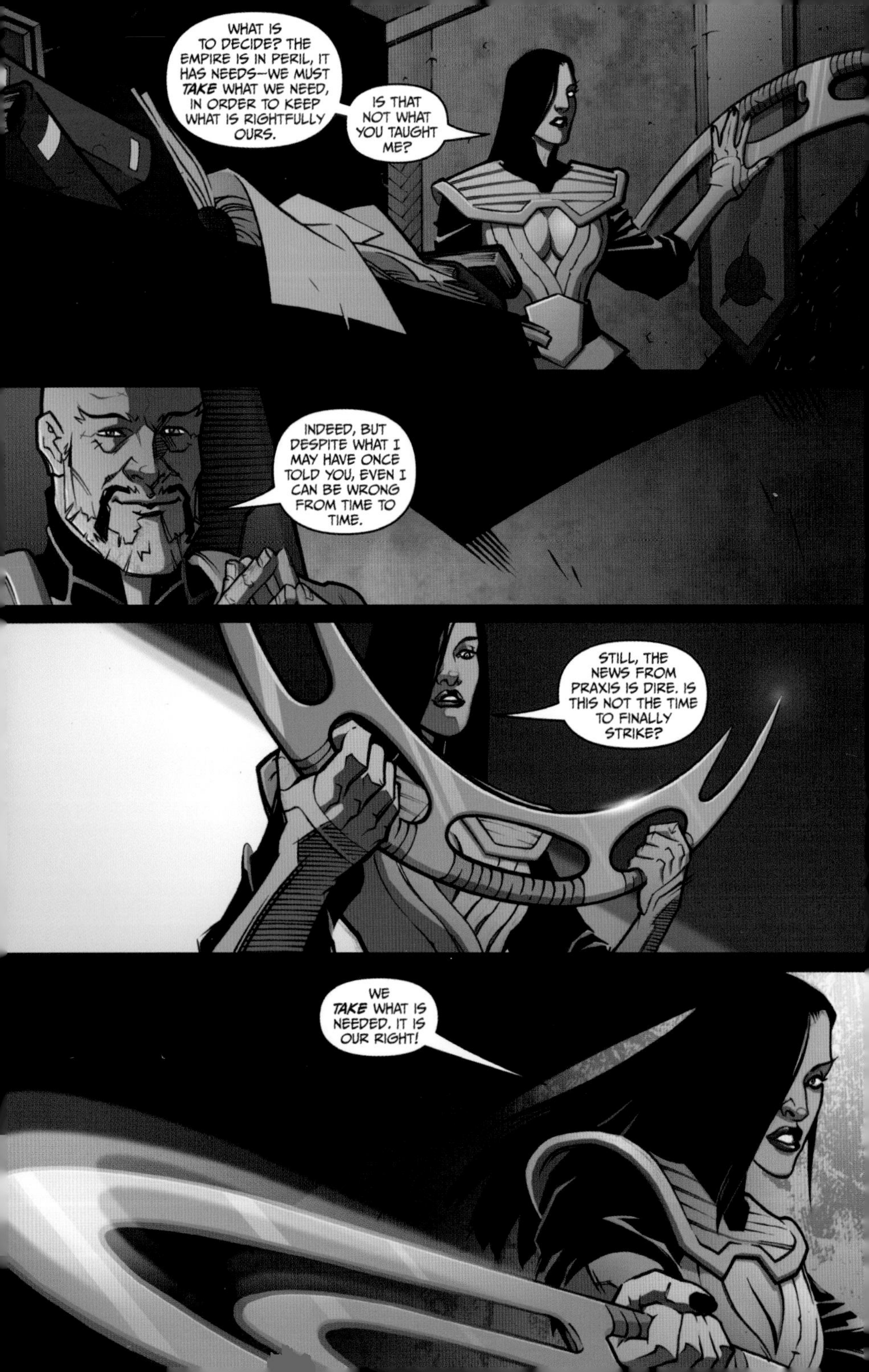
WHAT IS TO DECIDE? THE EMPIRE IS IN PERIL, IT HAS NEEDS—WE MUST *TAKE* WHAT WE NEED, IN ORDER TO KEEP WHAT IS RIGHTFULLY OURS.
IS THAT NOT WHAT YOU TAUGHT ME?
INDEED, BUT DESPITE WHAT I MAY HAVE ONCE TOLD YOU, EVEN I CAN BE WRONG FROM TIME TO TIME.
STILL, THE NEWS FROM PRAXIS IS DIRE. IS THIS NOT THE TIME TO FINALLY STRIKE?
WE *TAKE* WHAT IS NEEDED. IT IS OUR RIGHT!

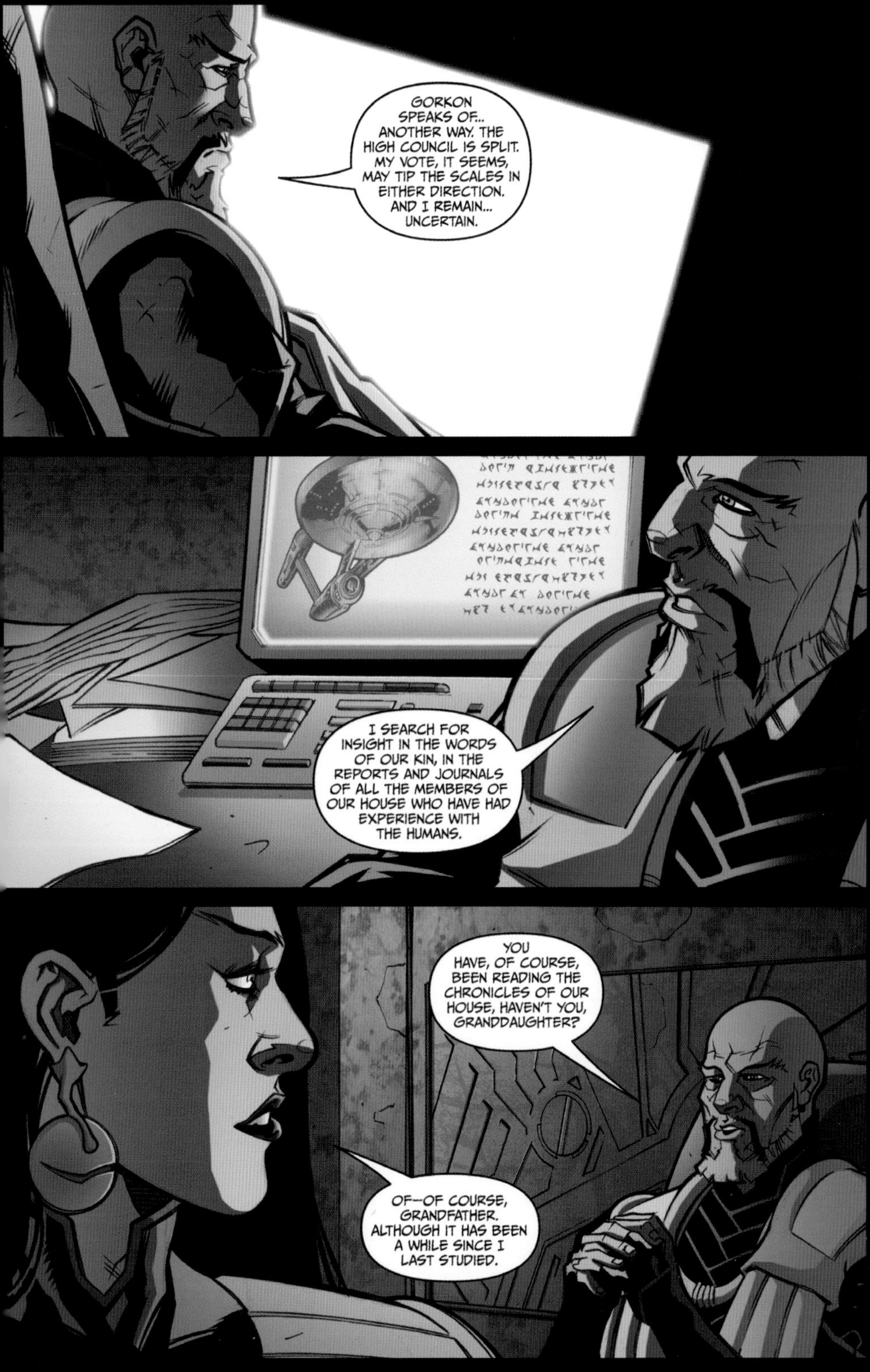
GORKON SPEAKS OF.. ANOTHER WAY. THE HIGH COUNCIL IS SPLIT. MY VOTE, IT SEEMS, MAY TIP THE SCALES IN EITHER DIRECTION. AND I REMAIN... UNCERTAIN.
I SEARCH FOR INSIGHT IN THE WORDS OF OUR KIN, IN THE REPORTS AND JOURNALS OF ALL THE MEMBERS OF OUR HOUSE WHO HAVE HAD EXPERIENCE WITH THE HUMANS.
YOU HAVE, OF COURSE, BEEN READING THE CHRONICLES OF OUR HOUSE, HAVEN'T YOU, GRANDDAUGHTER?
OF--OF COURSE, GRANDFATHER. ALTHOUGH IT HAS BEEN A WHILE SINCE I LAST STUDIED.

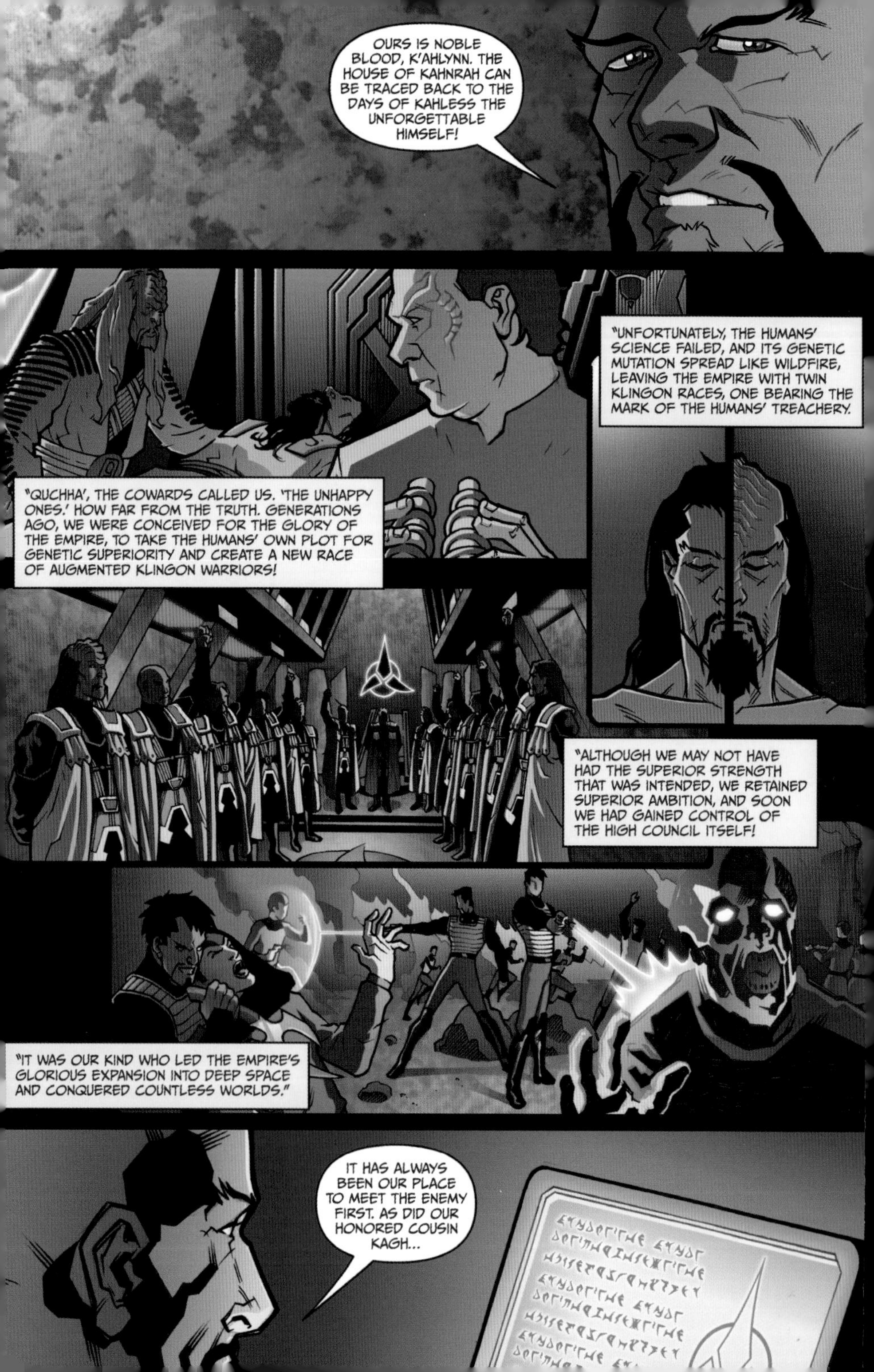
OURS IS NOBLE BLOOD, K'AHLYNN. THE HOUSE OF KAHNRAH CAN BE TRACED BACK TO THE DAYS OF KAHLESS THE UNFORGETTABLE HIMSELF!
"QUCHHA', THE COWARDS CALLED US. 'THE UNHAPPY ONES.' HOW FAR FROM THE TRUTH. GENERATIONS AGO, WE WERE CONCEIVED FOR THE GLORY OF THE EMPIRE, TO TAKE THE HUMANS' OWN PLOT FOR GENETIC SUPERIORITY AND CREATE A NEW RACE OF AUGMENTED KLINGON WARRIORS!
"UNFORTUNATELY, THE HUMANS' SCIENCE FAILED, AND ITS GENETIC MUTATION SPREAD LIKE WILDFIRE, LEAVING THE EMPIRE WITH TWIN KLINGON RACES, ONE BEARING THE MARK OF THE HUMANS' TREACHERY.
"ALTHOUGH WE MAY NOT HAVE HAD THE SUPERIOR STRENGTH THAT WAS INTENDED, WE RETAINED SUPERIOR AMBITION, AND SOON WE HAD GAINED CONTROL OF THE HIGH COUNCIL ITSELF!
"IT WAS OUR KIND WHO LED THE EMPIRE'S GLORIOUS EXPANSION INTO DEEP SPACE AND CONQUERED COUNTLESS WORLDS."
IT HAS ALWAYS BEEN OUR PLACE TO MEET THE ENEMY FIRST. AS DID OUR HONORED COUSIN KAGH...

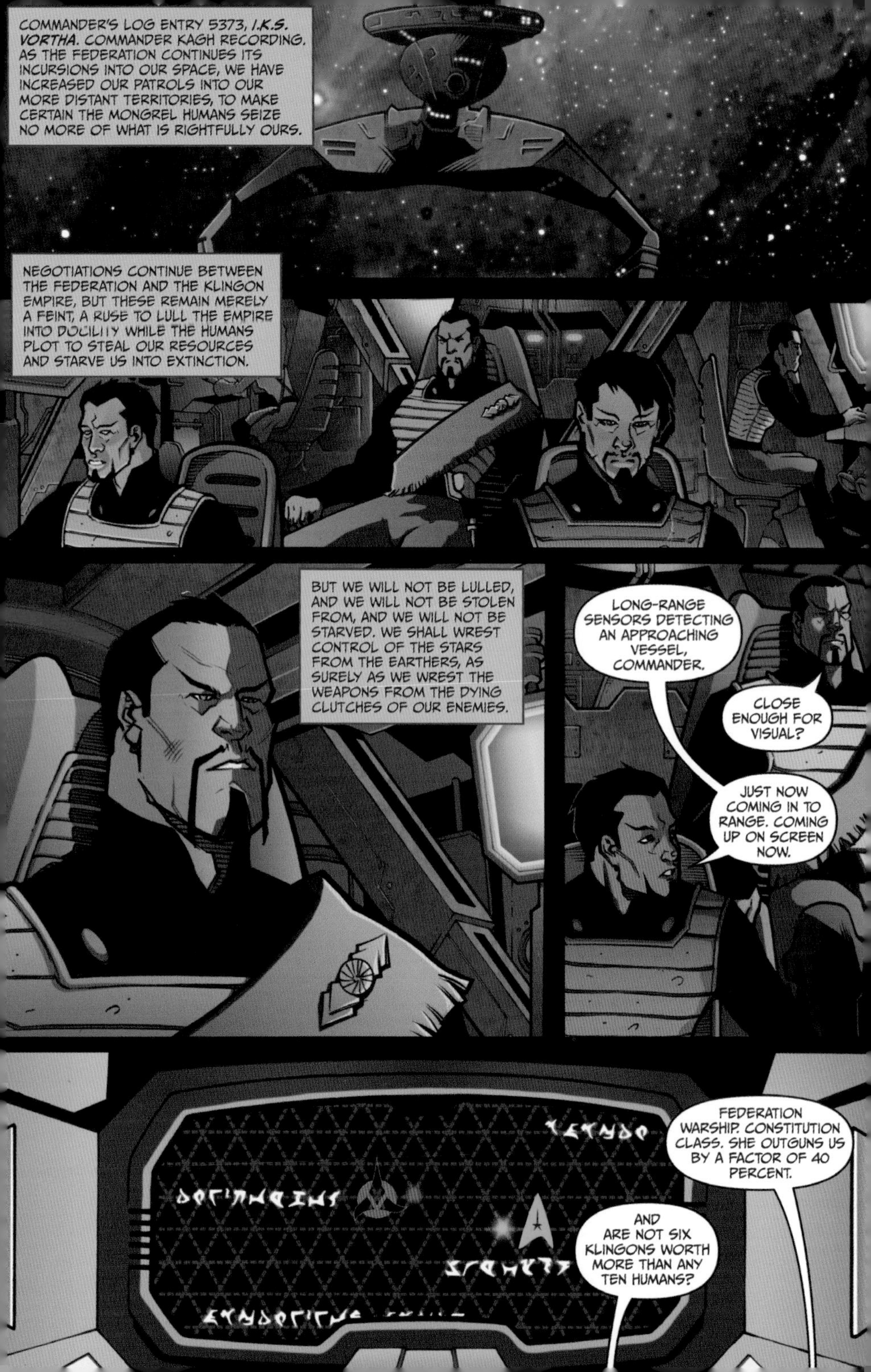
COMMANDER'S LOG ENTRY 5373, *I.K.S. VORTHA*. COMMANDER KAGH RECORDING. AS THE FEDERATION CONTINUES ITS INCURSIONS INTO OUR SPACE, WE HAVE INCREASED OUR PATROLS INTO OUR MORE DISTANT TERRITORIES, TO MAKE CERTAIN THE MONGREL HUMANS SEIZE NO MORE OF WHAT IS RIGHTFULLY OURS.
NEGOTIATIONS CONTINUE BETWEEN THE FEDERATION AND THE KLINGON EMPIRE, BUT THESE REMAIN MERELY A FEINT, A RUSE TO LULL THE EMPIRE INTO DOCILITY WHILE THE HUMANS PLOT TO STEAL OUR RESOURCES AND STARVE US INTO EXTINCTION.
BUT WE WILL NOT BE LULLED, AND WE WILL NOT BE STOLEN FROM, AND WE WILL NOT BE STARVED. WE SHALL WREST CONTROL OF THE STARS FROM THE EARTHERS, AS SURELY AS WE WREST THE WEAPONS FROM THE DYING CLUTCHES OF OUR ENEMIES.
LONG-RANGE SENSORS DETECTING AN APPROACHING VESSEL, COMMANDER.
CLOSE ENOUGH FOR VISUAL?
JUST NOW COMING IN TO RANGE. COMING UP ON SCREEN NOW.
FEDERATION WARSHIP. CONSTITUTION CLASS. SHE OUTGUNS US BY A FACTOR OF 40 PERCENT.
AND ARE NOT SIX KLINGONS WORTH MORE THAN ANY TEN HUMANS?

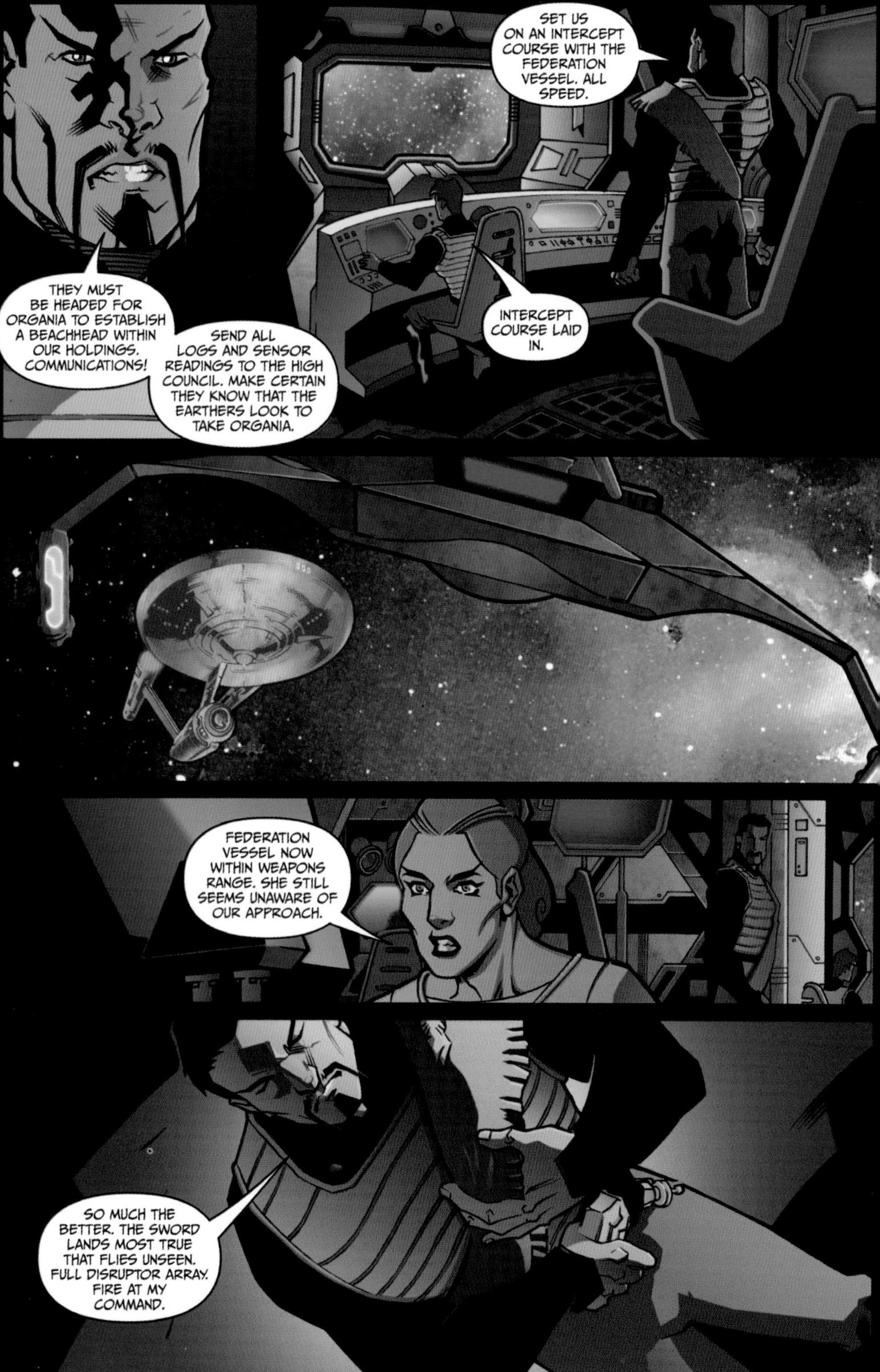
THEY MUST BE HEADED FOR ORGANIA TO ESTABLISH A BEACHHEAD WITHIN OUR HOLDINGS. COMMUNICATIONS!
SEND ALL LOGS AND SENSOR READINGS TO THE HIGH COUNCIL. MAKE CERTAIN THEY KNOW THAT THE EARTHERS LOOK TO TAKE ORGANIA.
SET US ON AN INTERCEPT COURSE WITH THE FEDERATION VESSEL. ALL SPEED.
INTERCEPT COURSE LAID IN.
FEDERATION VESSEL NOW WITHIN WEAPONS RANGE. SHE STILL SEEMS UNAWARE OF OUR APPROACH.
SO MUCH THE BETTER. THE SWORD LANDS MOST TRUE THAT FLIES UNSEEN. FULL DISRUPTOR ARRAY. FIRE AT MY COMMAND.

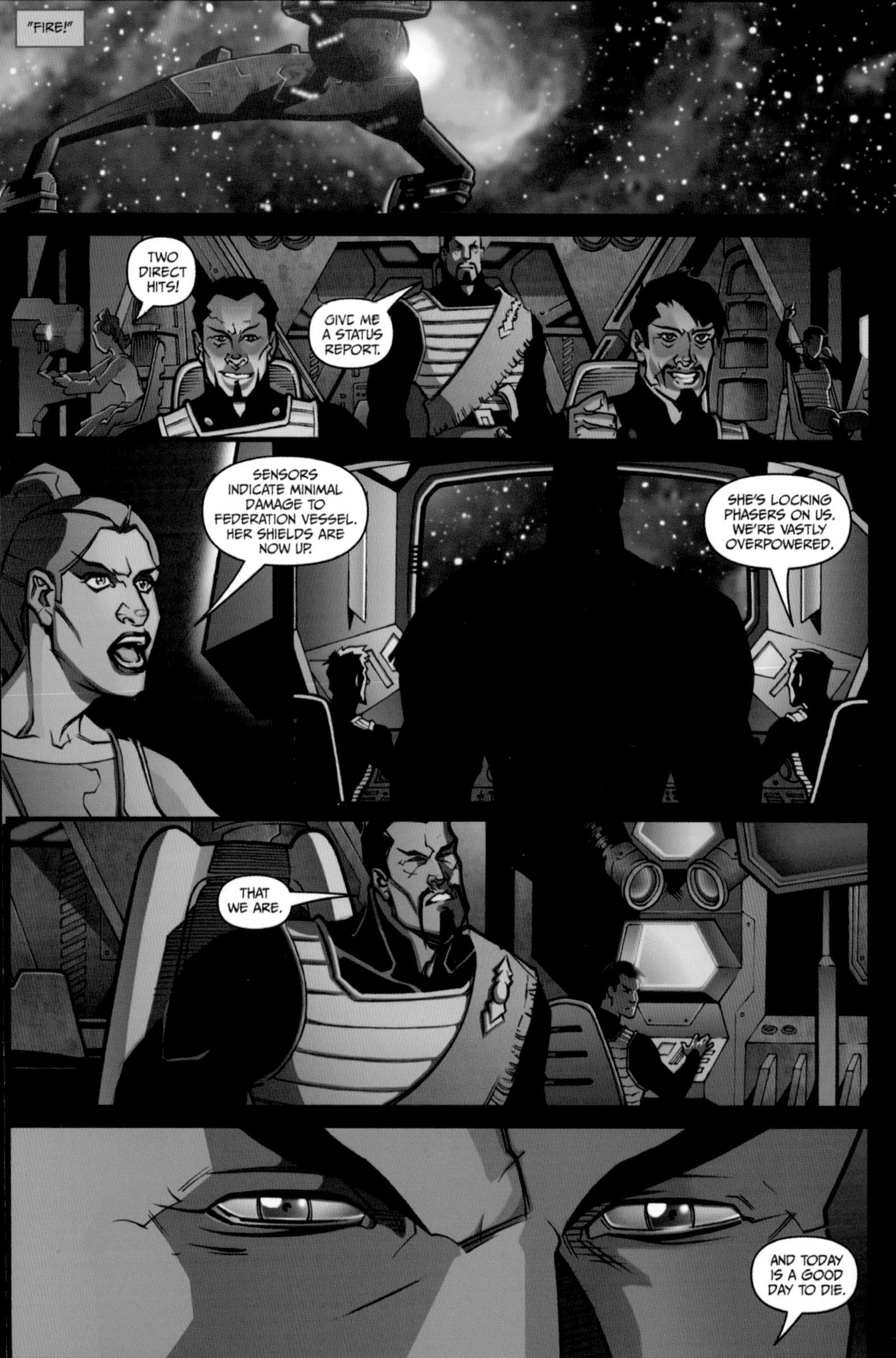
"FIRE!"
TWO DIRECT HITS!
GIVE ME A STATUS REPORT.
SENSORS INDICATE MINIMAL DAMAGE TO FEDERATION VESSEL. HER SHIELDS ARE NOW UP.
SHE'S LOCKING PHASERS ON US. WE'RE VASTLY OVERPOWERED.
THAT WE ARE.
AND TODAY IS A GOOD DAY TO DIE.

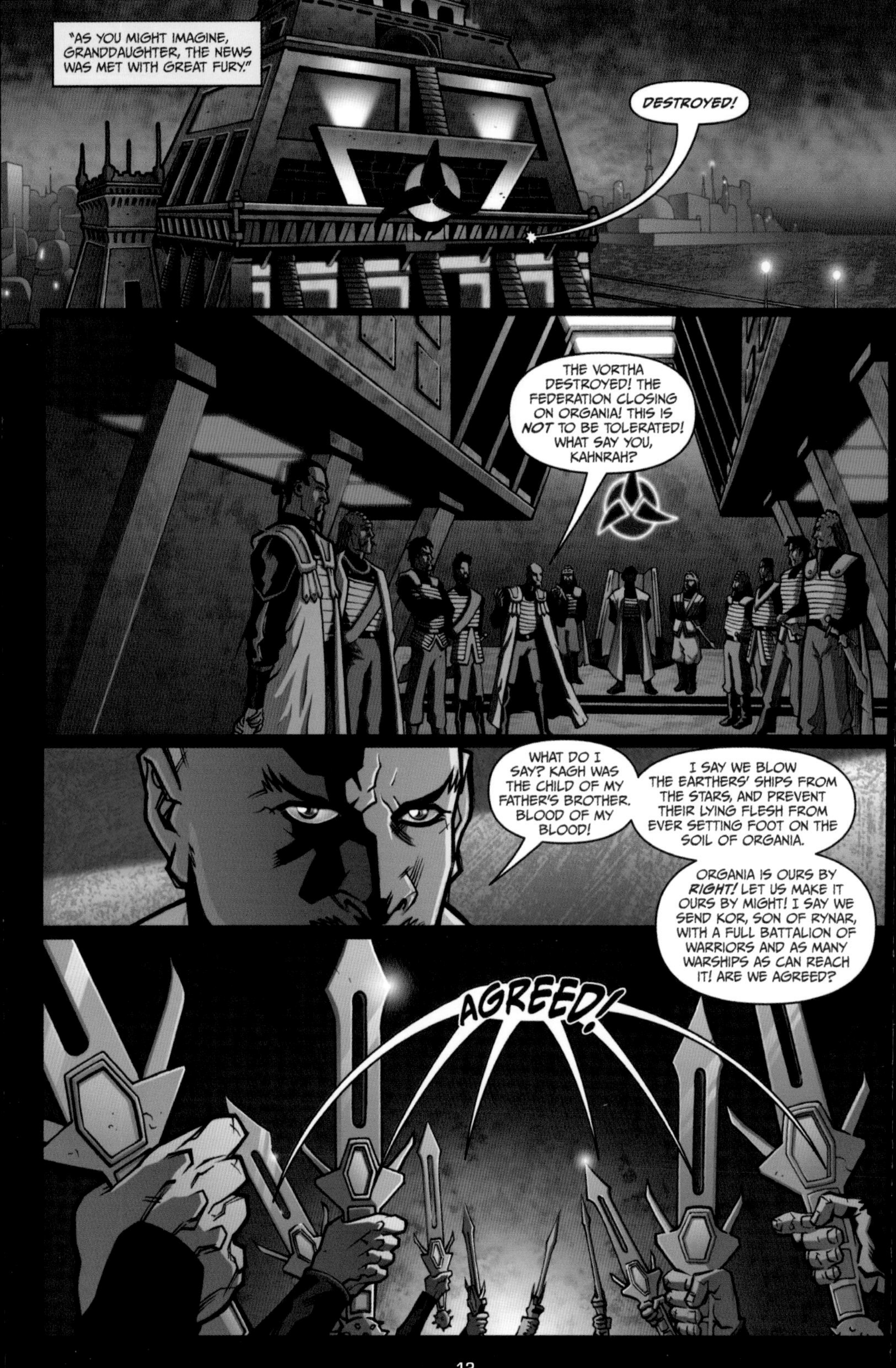
"AS YOU MIGHT IMAGINE, GRANDDAUGHTER, THE NEWS WAS MET WITH GREAT FURY."
DESTROYED!
THE VORTHA DESTROYED! THE FEDERATION CLOSING ON ORGANIA! THIS IS NOT TO BE TOLERATED! WHAT SAY YOU, KAHNRAH?
WHAT DO I SAY? KAGH WAS THE CHILD OF MY FATHER'S BROTHER. BLOOD OF MY BLOOD!
I SAY WE BLOW THE EARTHERS' SHIPS FROM THE STARS, AND PREVENT THEIR LYING FLESH FROM EVER SETTING FOOT ON THE SOIL OF ORGANIA.
ORGANIA IS OURS BY RIGHT! LET US MAKE IT OURS BY MIGHT! I SAY WE SEND KOR, SON OF RYNAR, WITH A FULL BATTALION OF WARRIORS AND AS MANY WARSHIPS AS CAN REACH IT! ARE WE AGREED?
AGREED!

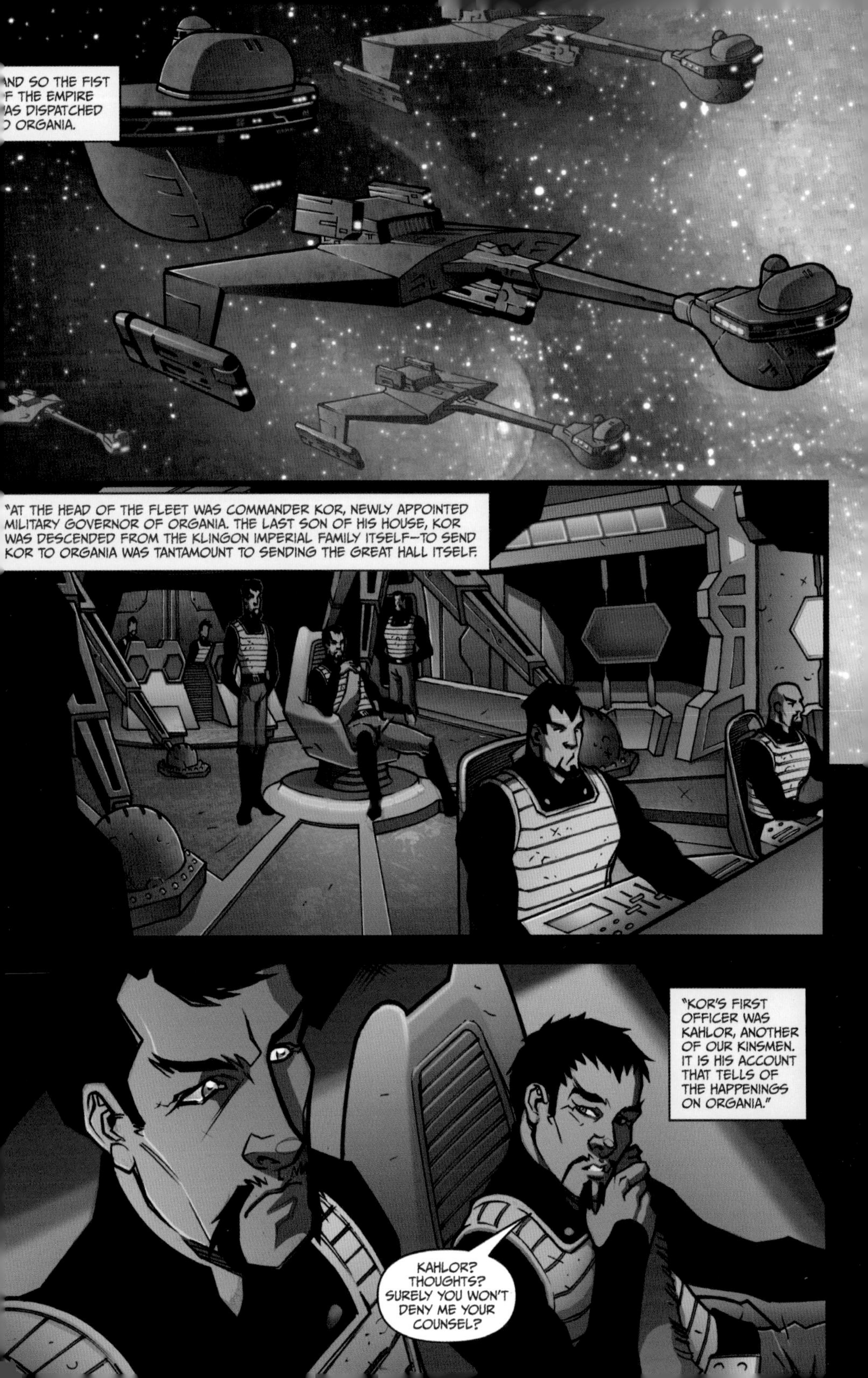
AND SO THE FIST OF THE EMPIRE WAS DISPATCHED TO ORGANIA.
"AT THE HEAD OF THE FLEET WAS COMMANDER KOR, NEWLY APPOINTED MILITARY GOVERNOR OF ORGANIA. THE LAST SON OF HIS HOUSE, KOR WAS DESCENDED FROM THE KLINGON IMPERIAL FAMILY ITSELF—TO SEND KOR TO ORGANIA WAS TANTAMOUNT TO SENDING THE GREAT HALL ITSELF.
"KOR'S FIRST OFFICER WAS KAHLOR, ANOTHER OF OUR KINSMEN. IT IS HIS ACCOUNT THAT TELLS OF THE HAPPENINGS ON ORGANIA."
KAHLOR? THOUGHTS? SURELY YOU WON'T DENY ME YOUR COUNSEL?

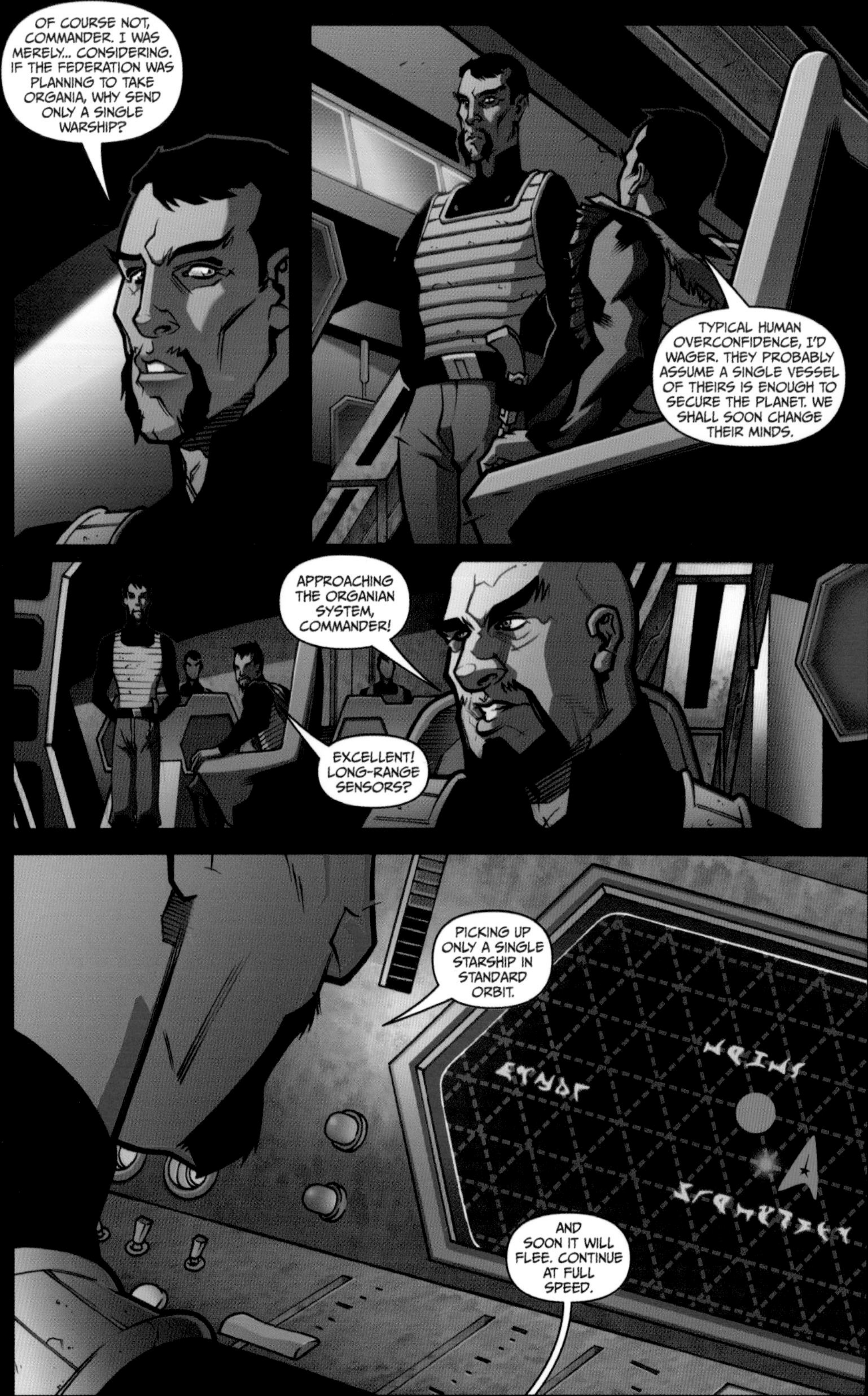
OF COURSE NOT, COMMANDER. I WAS MERELY... CONSIDERING. IF THE FEDERATION WAS PLANNING TO TAKE ORGANIA, WHY SEND ONLY A SINGLE WARSHIP?
TYPICAL HUMAN OVERCONFIDENCE, I'D WAGER. THEY PROBABLY ASSUME A SINGLE VESSEL OF THEIRS IS ENOUGH TO SECURE THE PLANET. WE SHALL SOON CHANGE THEIR MINDS.
APPROACHING THE ORGANIAN SYSTEM, COMMANDER!
EXCELLENT! LONG-RANGE SENSORS?
PICKING UP ONLY A SINGLE STARSHIP IN STANDARD ORBIT.
AND SOON IT WILL FLEE. CONTINUE AT FULL SPEED.

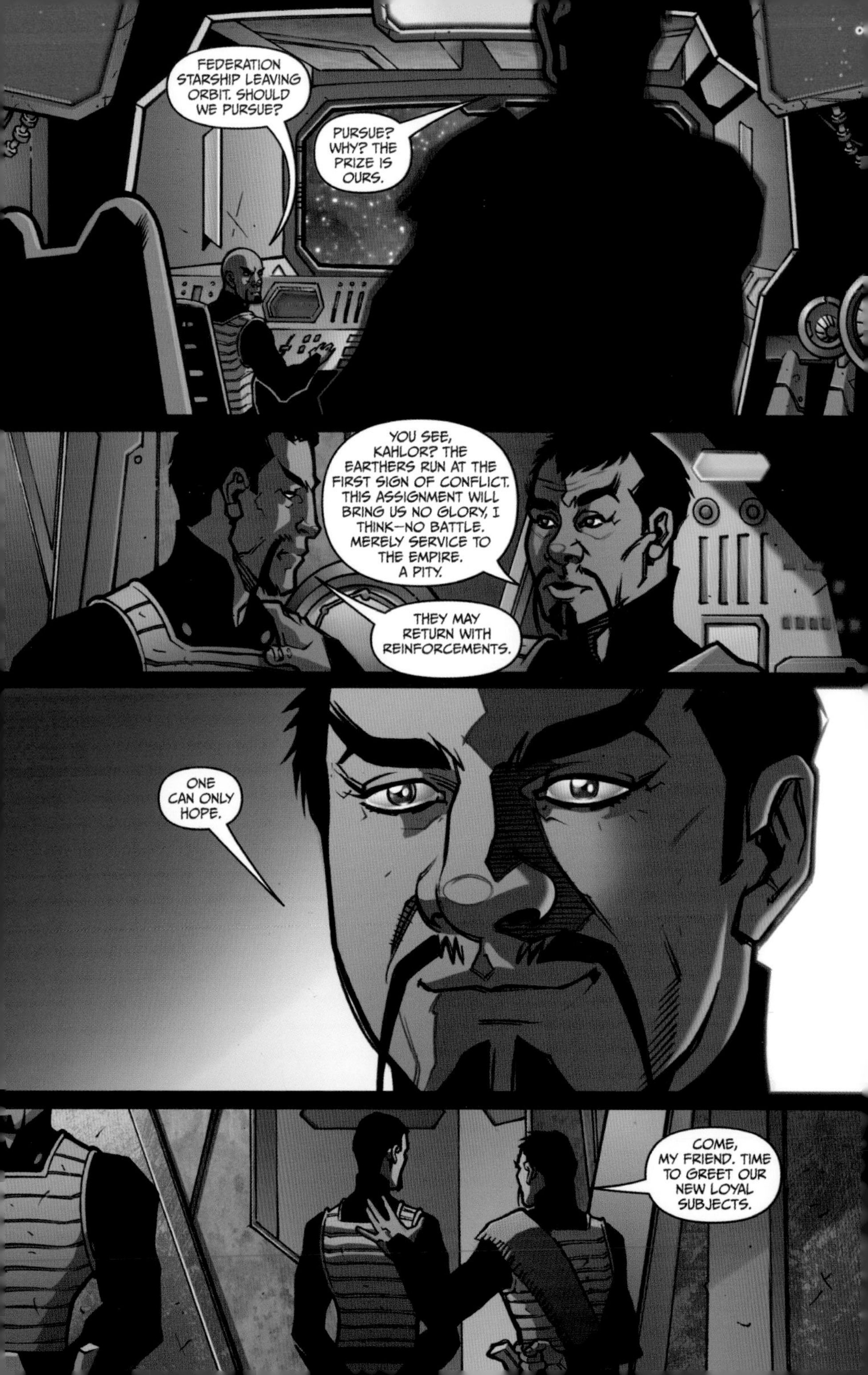
FEDERATION STARSHIP LEAVING ORBIT. SHOULD WE PURSUE?
PURSUE? WHY? THE PRIZE IS OURS.
YOU SEE, KAHLOR? THE EARTHERS RUN AT THE FIRST SIGN OF CONFLICT. THIS ASSIGNMENT WILL BRING US NO GLORY, I THINK—NO BATTLE. MERELY SERVICE TO THE EMPIRE. A PITY.
THEY MAY RETURN WITH REINFORCEMENTS.
ONE CAN ONLY HOPE.
COME, MY FRIEND. TIME TO GREET OUR NEW LOYAL SUBJECTS.

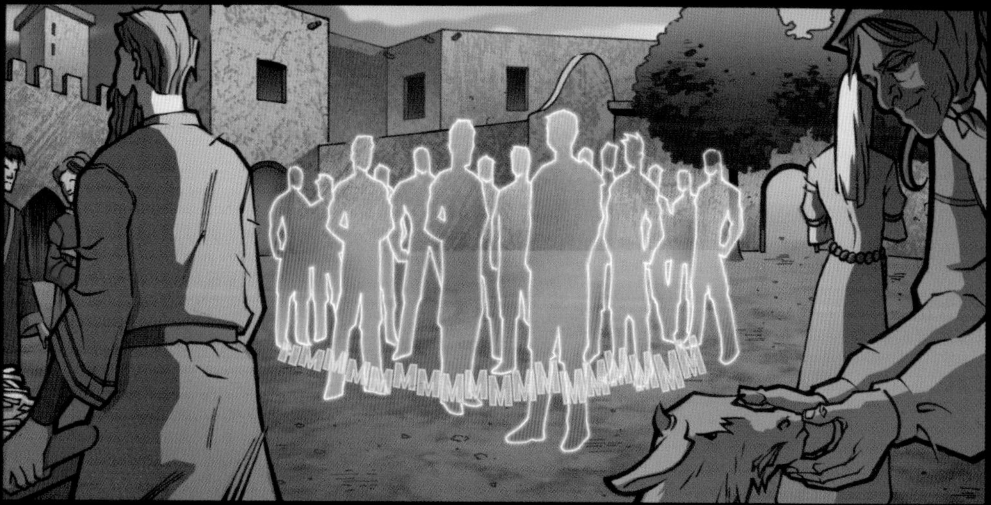

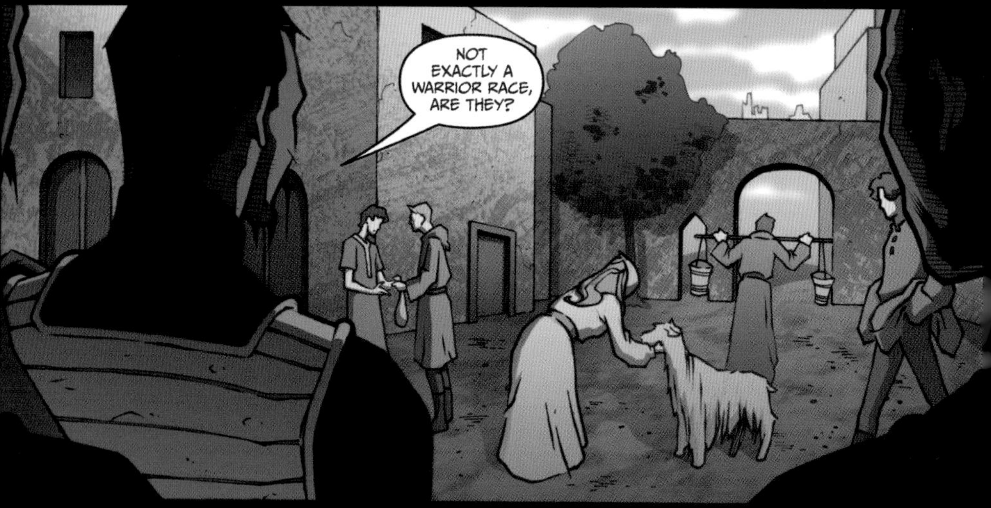
NOT EXACTLY A WARRIOR RACE, ARE THEY?

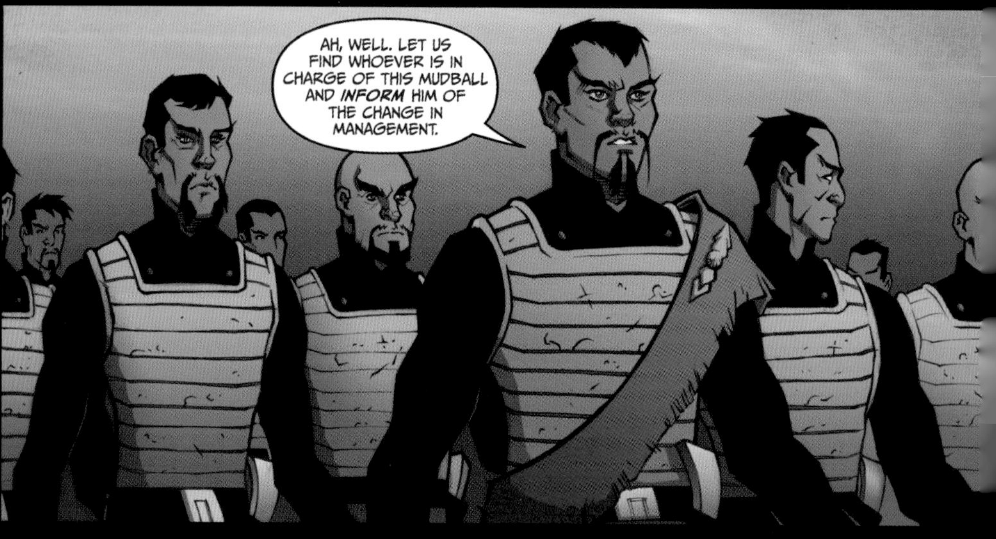
AH, WELL. LET US FIND WHOEVER IS IN CHARGE OF THIS MUDBALL AND *INFORM* HIM OF THE CHANGE IN MANAGEMENT.

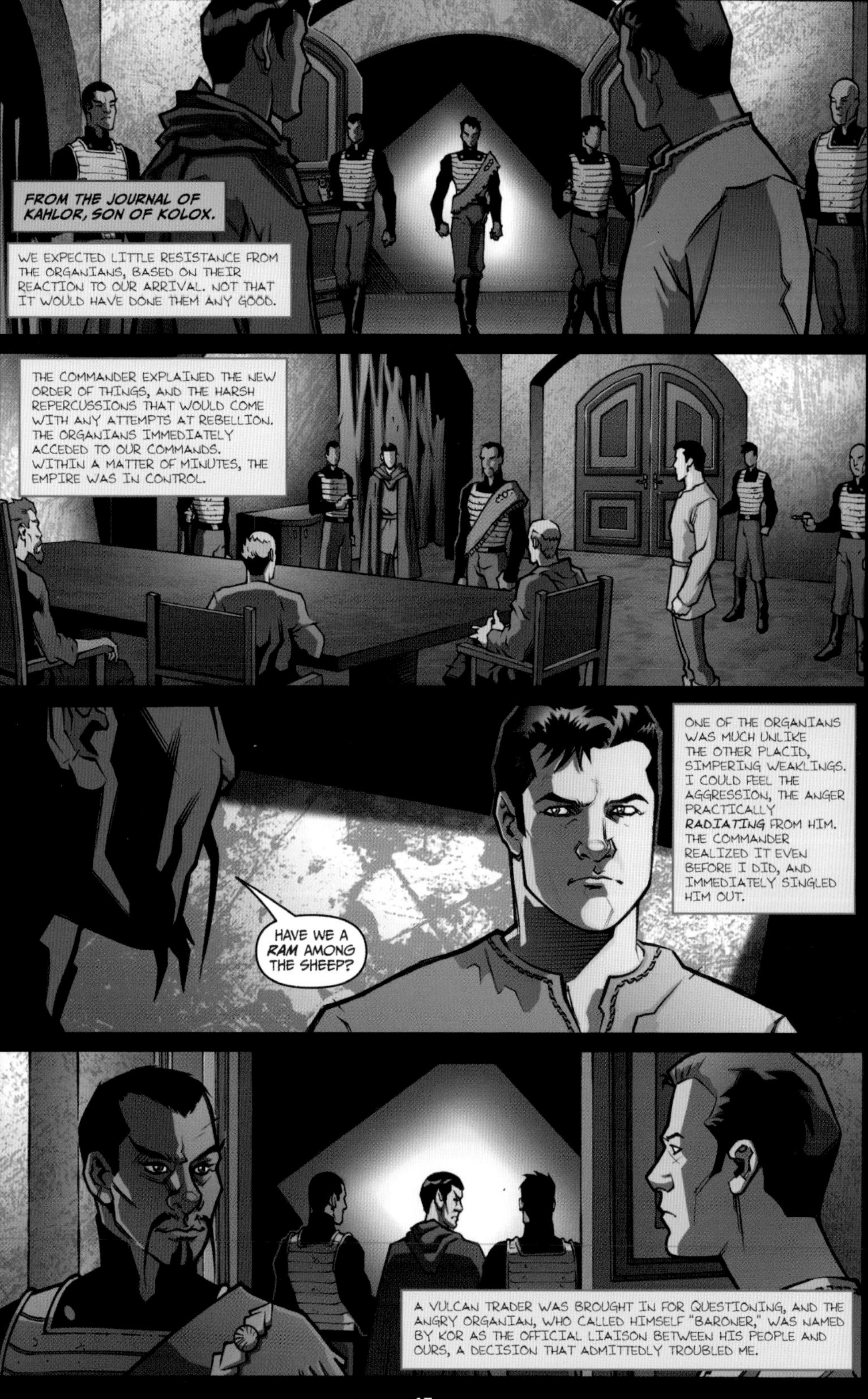
FROM THE JOURNAL OF KAHLOR, SON OF KOLOX.
WE EXPECTED LITTLE RESISTANCE FROM THE ORGANIANS, BASED ON THEIR REACTION TO OUR ARRIVAL. NOT THAT IT WOULD HAVE DONE THEM ANY GOOD.
THE COMMANDER EXPLAINED THE NEW ORDER OF THINGS, AND THE HARSH REPERCUSSIONS THAT WOULD COME WITH ANY ATTEMPTS AT REBELLION. THE ORGANIANS IMMEDIATELY ACCEDED TO OUR COMMANDS. WITHIN A MATTER OF MINUTES, THE EMPIRE WAS IN CONTROL.
ONE OF THE ORGANIANS WAS MUCH UNLIKE THE OTHER PLACID, SIMPERING WEAKLINGS. I COULD FEEL THE AGGRESSION, THE ANGER PRACTICALLY RADIATING FROM HIM. THE COMMANDER REALIZED IT EVEN BEFORE I DID, AND IMMEDIATELY SINGLED HIM OUT.
HAVE WE A RAM AMONG THE SHEEP?
A VULCAN TRADER WAS BROUGHT IN FOR QUESTIONING, AND THE ANGRY ORGANIAN, WHO CALLED HIMSELF "BARONER," WAS NAMED BY KOR AS THE OFFICIAL LIAISON BETWEEN HIS PEOPLE AND OURS, A DECISION THAT ADMITTEDLY TROUBLED ME.

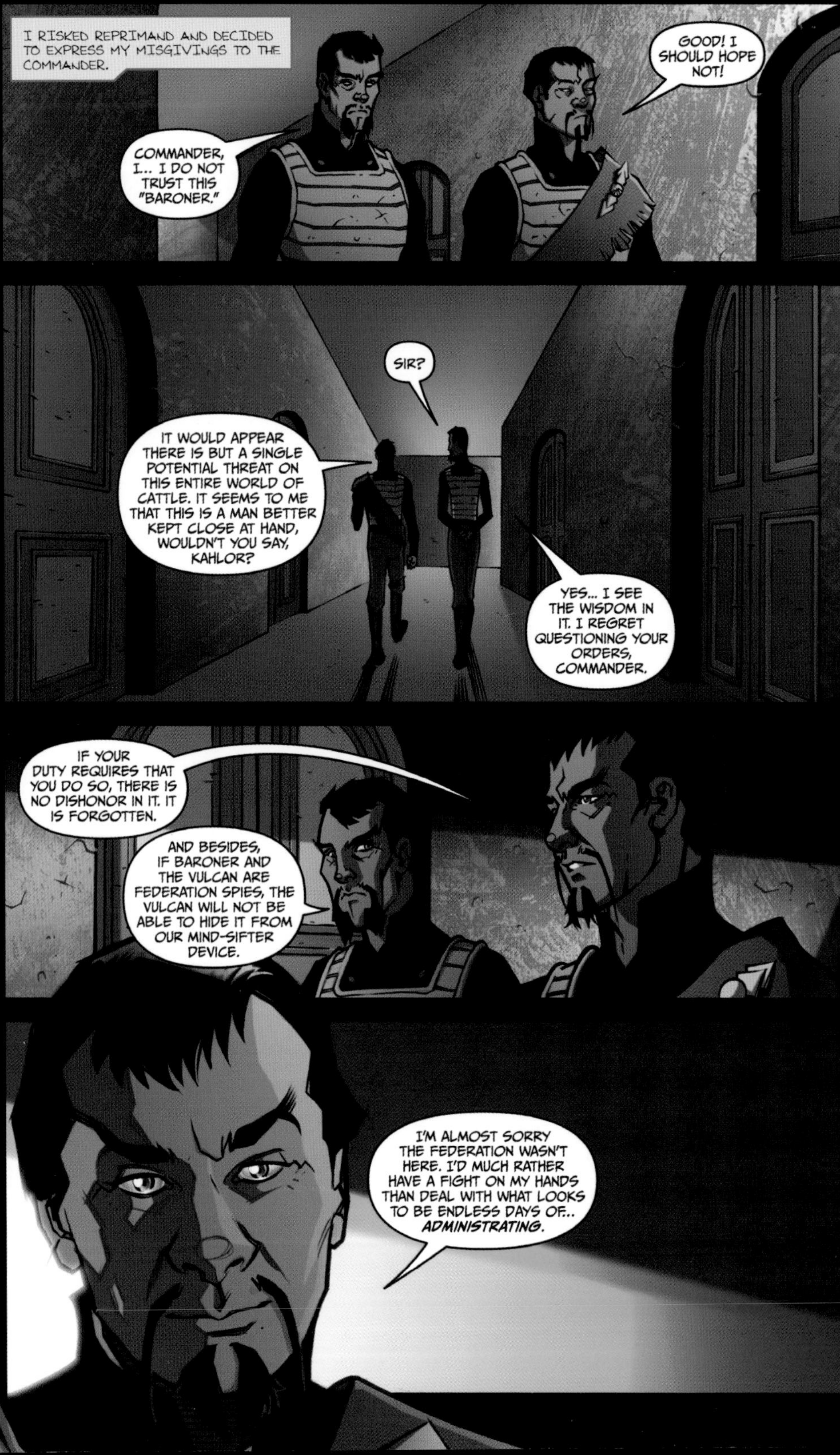

I RISKED REPRIMAND AND DECIDED TO EXPRESS MY MISGIVINGS TO THE COMMANDER.
COMMANDER, I... I DO NOT TRUST THIS "BARONER."
GOOD! I SHOULD HOPE NOT!
SIR?
IT WOULD APPEAR THERE IS BUT A SINGLE POTENTIAL THREAT ON THIS ENTIRE WORLD OF CATTLE. IT SEEMS TO ME THAT THIS IS A MAN BETTER KEPT CLOSE AT HAND, WOULDN'T YOU SAY, KAHLOR?
YES... I SEE THE WISDOM IN IT. I REGRET QUESTIONING YOUR ORDERS, COMMANDER.
IF YOUR DUTY REQUIRES THAT YOU DO SO, THERE IS NO DISHONOR IN IT. IT IS FORGOTTEN.
AND BESIDES, IF BARONER AND THE VULCAN ARE FEDERATION SPIES, THE VULCAN WILL NOT BE ABLE TO HIDE IT FROM OUR MIND-SIFTER DEVICE.
I'M ALMOST SORRY THE FEDERATION WASN'T HERE. I'D MUCH RATHER HAVE A FIGHT ON MY HANDS THAN DEAL WITH WHAT LOOKS TO BE ENDLESS DAYS OF... *ADMINISTRATING*.

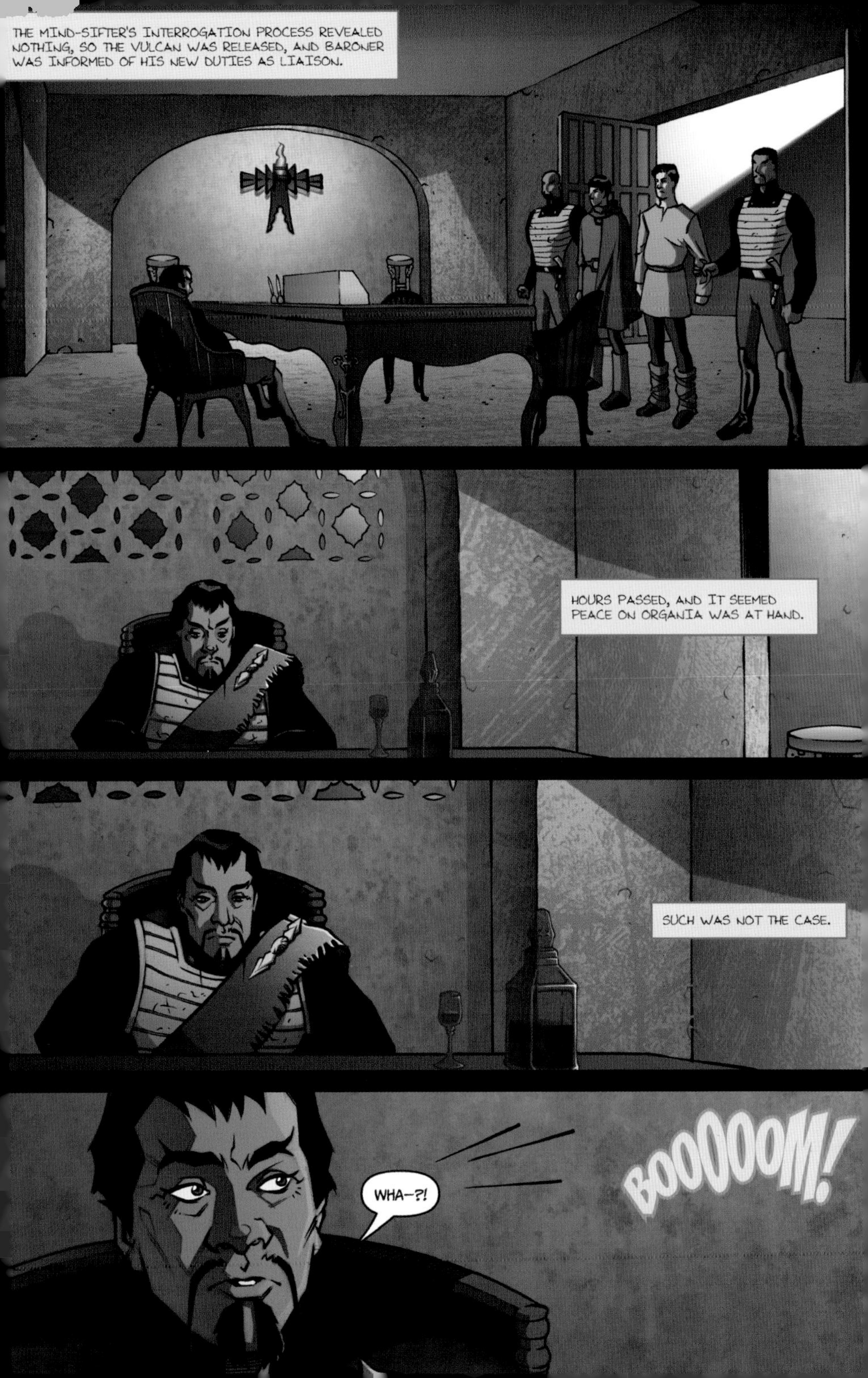
THE MIND-SIFTER'S INTERROGATION PROCESS REVEALED NOTHING, SO THE VULCAN WAS RELEASED, AND BARONER WAS INFORMED OF HIS NEW DUTIES AS LIAISON.
HOURS PASSED, AND IT SEEMED PEACE ON ORGANIA WAS AT HAND.
SUCH WAS NOT THE CASE.
BOOOOOM!
WHA-?!

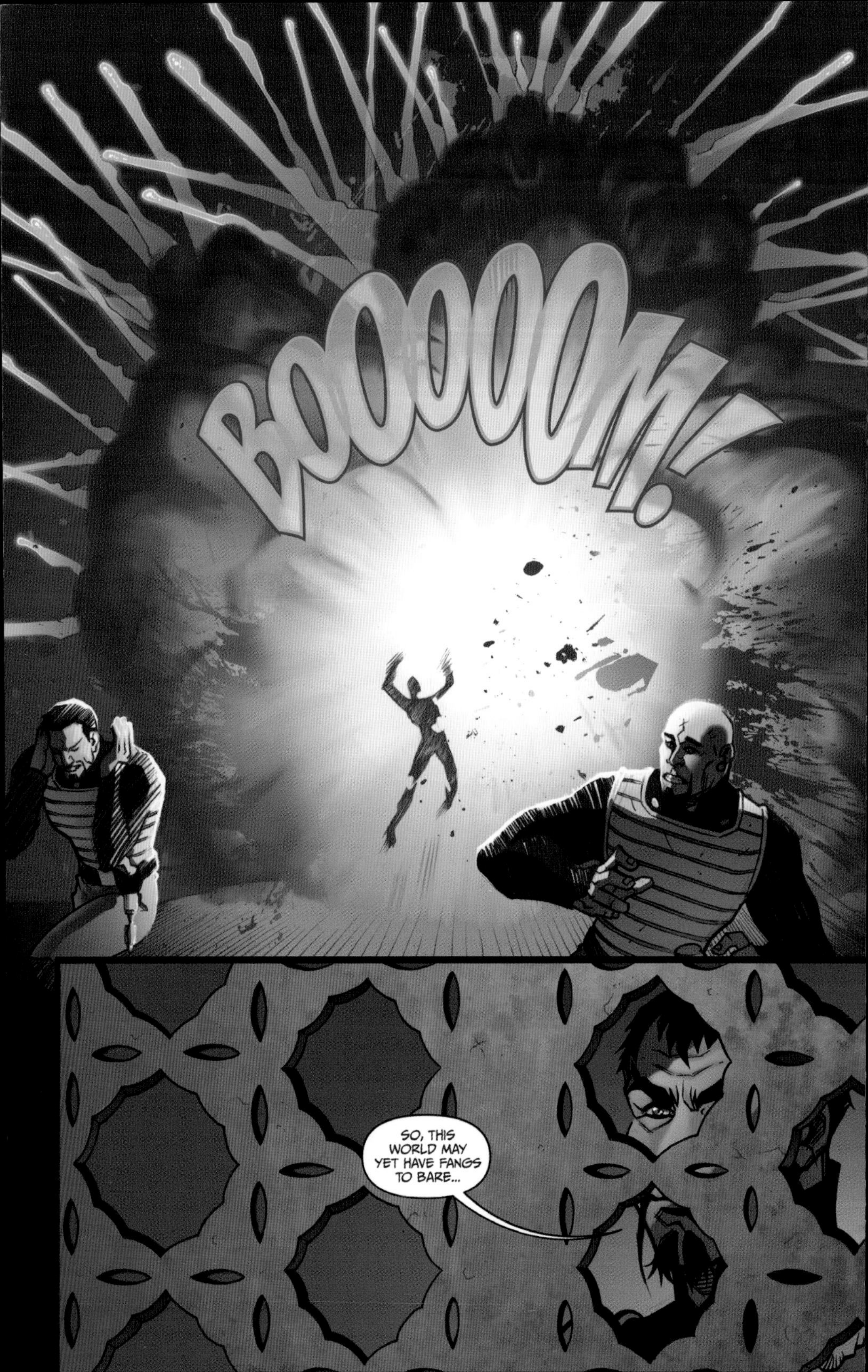
BOOOOOM!
SO, THIS WORLD MAY YET HAVE FANGS TO BARE...

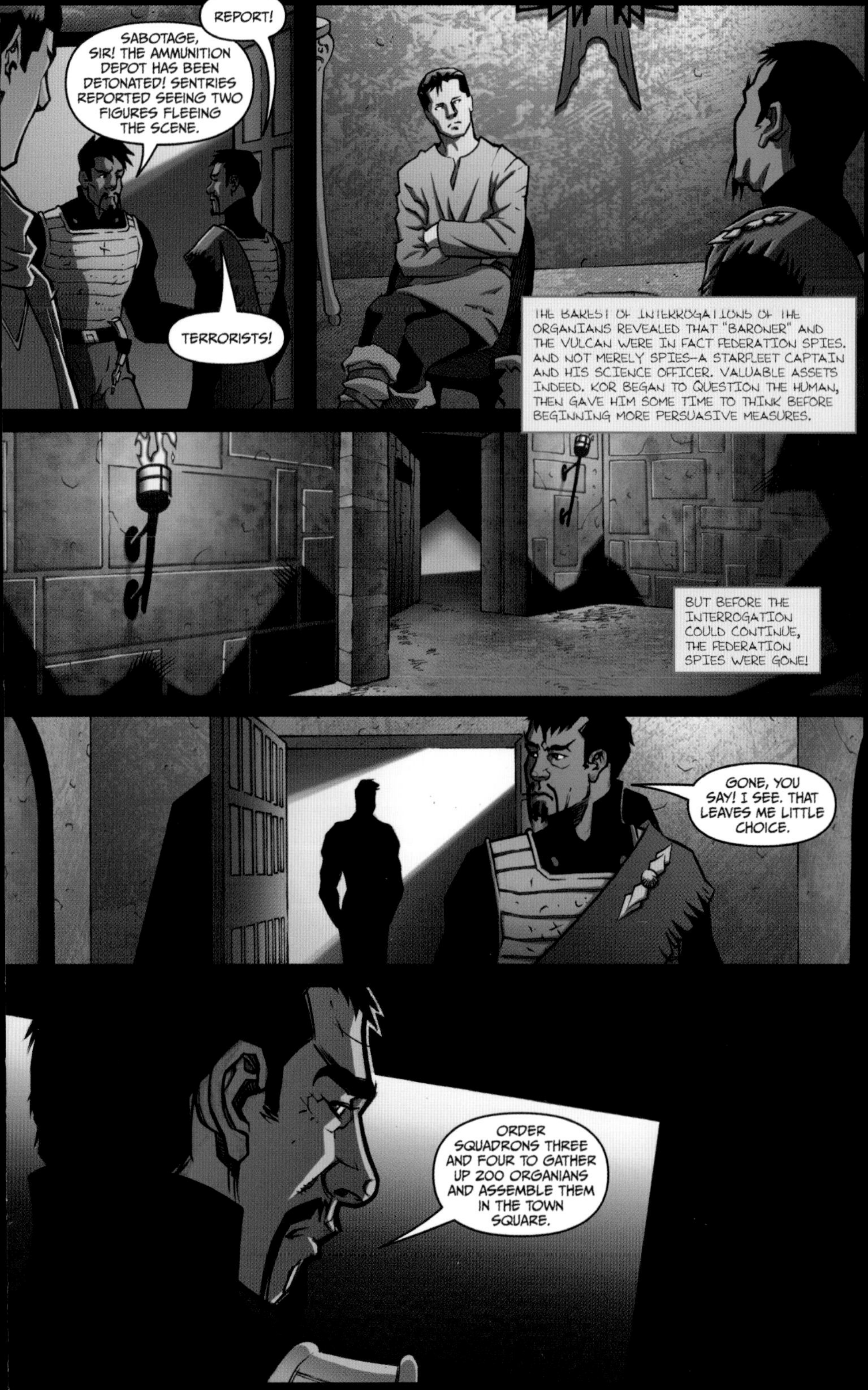
REPORT!
SABOTAGE, SIR! THE AMMUNITION DEPOT HAS BEEN DETONATED! SENTRIES REPORTED SEEING TWO FIGURES FLEEING THE SCENE.
TERRORISTS!
THE BAREST OF INTERROGATIONS OF THE ORGANIANS REVEALED THAT "BARONER" AND THE VULCAN WERE IN FACT FEDERATION SPIES. AND NOT MERELY SPIES--A STARFLEET CAPTAIN AND HIS SCIENCE OFFICER. VALUABLE ASSETS INDEED. KOR BEGAN TO QUESTION THE HUMAN, THEN GAVE HIM SOME TIME TO THINK BEFORE BEGINNING MORE PERSUASIVE MEASURES.
BUT BEFORE THE INTERROGATION COULD CONTINUE, THE FEDERATION SPIES WERE GONE!
GONE, YOU SAY! I SEE. THAT LEAVES ME LITTLE CHOICE.
ORDER SQUADRONS THREE AND FOUR TO GATHER UP 200 ORGANIANS AND ASSEMBLE THEM IN THE TOWN SQUARE.

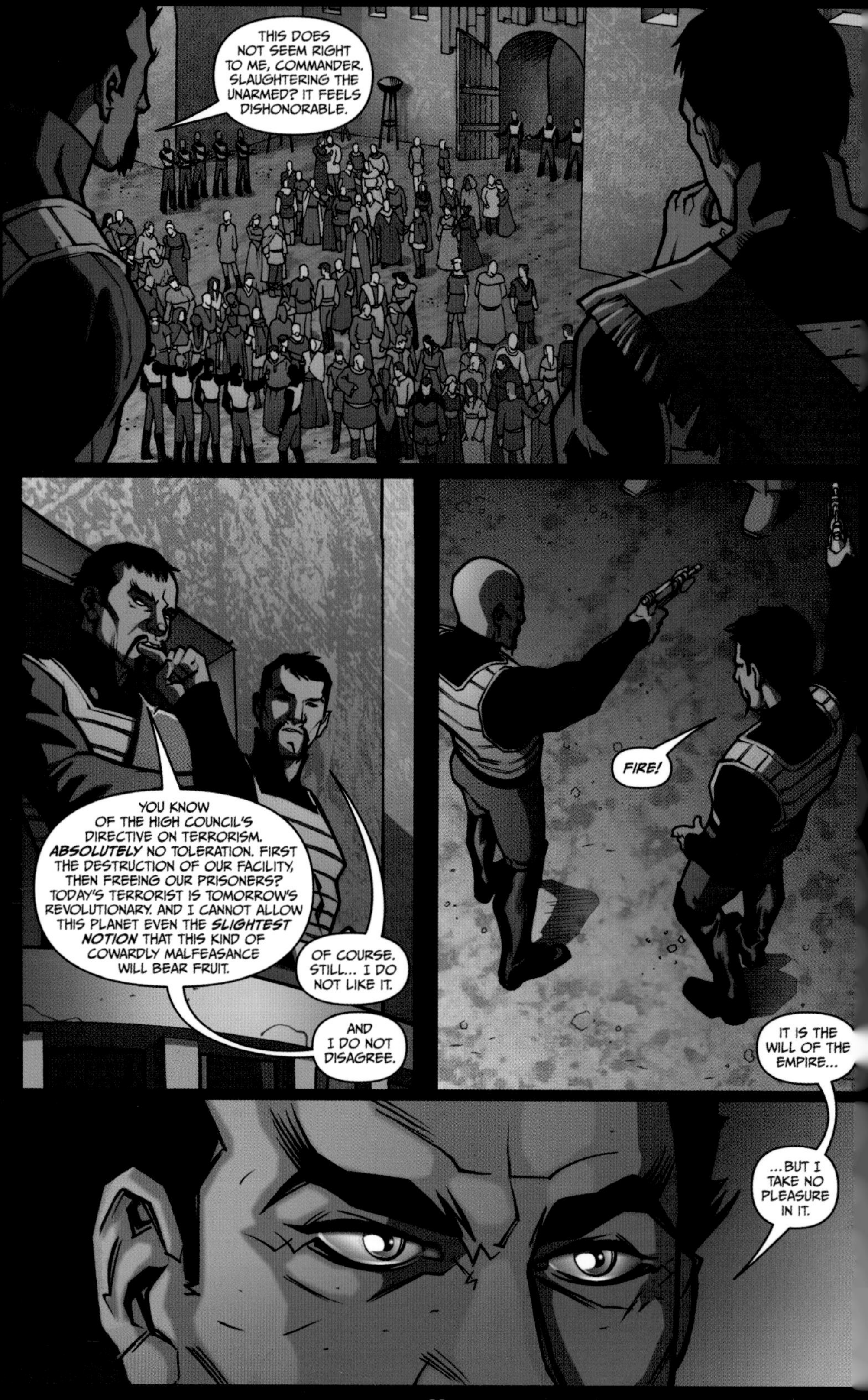
THIS DOES NOT SEEM RIGHT TO ME, COMMANDER. SLAUGHTERING THE UNARMED? IT FEELS DISHONORABLE.
YOU KNOW OF THE HIGH COUNCIL'S DIRECTIVE ON TERRORISM. ABSOLUTELY NO TOLERATION. FIRST THE DESTRUCTION OF OUR FACILITY, THEN FREEING OUR PRISONERS? TODAY'S TERRORIST IS TOMORROW'S REVOLUTIONARY. AND I CANNOT ALLOW THIS PLANET EVEN THE SLIGHTEST NOTION THAT THIS KIND OF COWARDLY MALFEASANCE WILL BEAR FRUIT.
OF COURSE. STILL... I DO NOT LIKE IT.
AND I DO NOT DISAGREE.
FIRE!
IT IS THE WILL OF THE EMPIRE...
...BUT I TAKE NO PLEASURE IN IT.

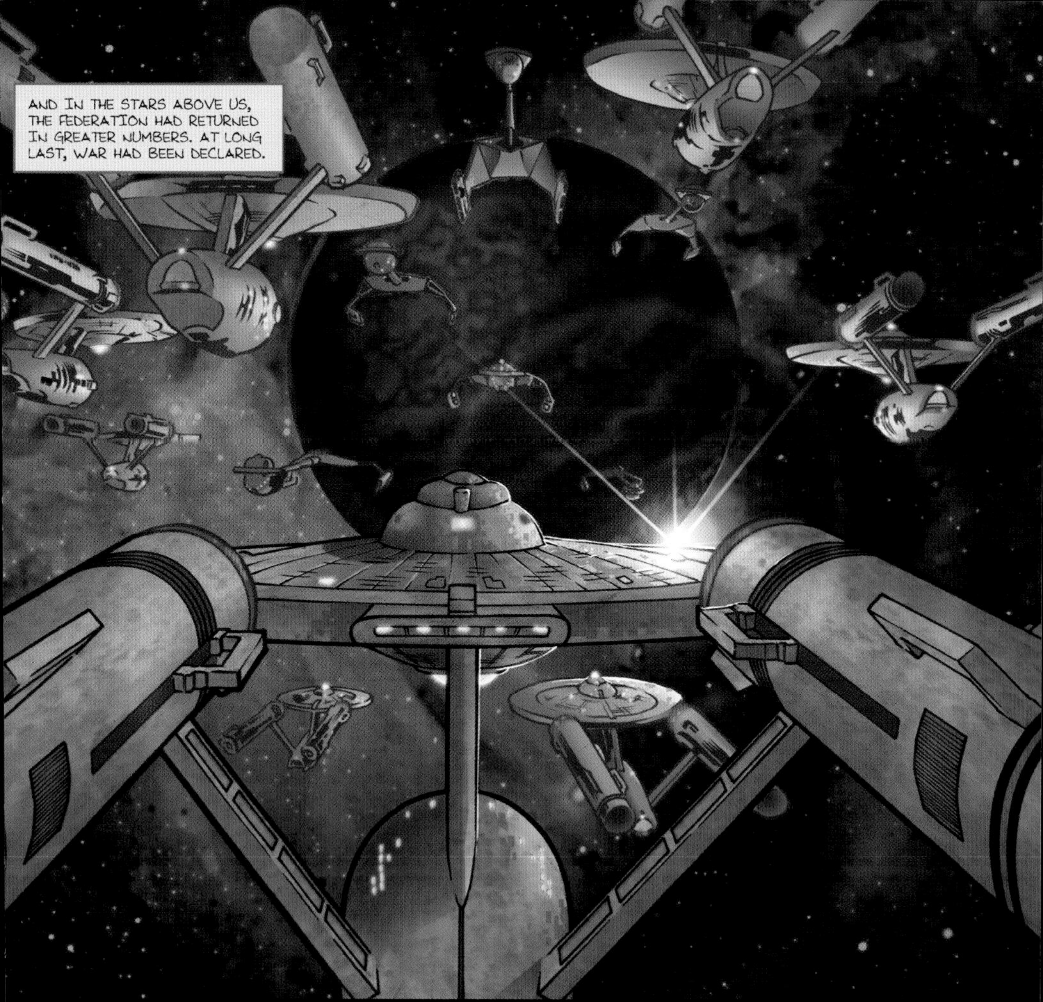
AND IN THE STARS ABOVE US, THE FEDERATION HAD RETURNED IN GREATER NUMBERS. AT LONG LAST, WAR HAD BEEN DECLARED.

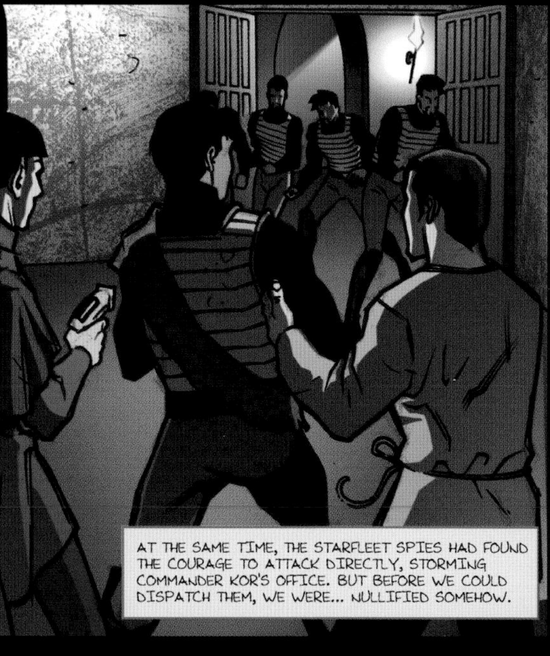
AT THE SAME TIME, THE STARFLEET SPIES HAD FOUND THE COURAGE TO ATTACK DIRECTLY, STORMING COMMANDER KOR'S OFFICE. BUT BEFORE WE COULD DISPATCH THEM, WE WERE... NULLIFIED SOMEHOW.

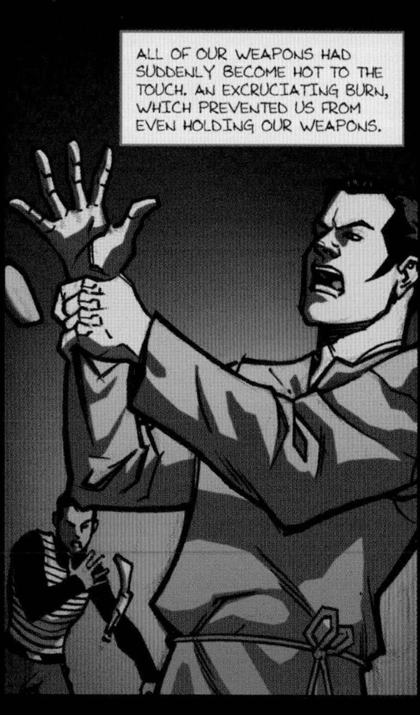
ALL OF OUR WEAPONS HAD SUDDENLY BECOME HOT TO THE TOUCH. AN EXCRUCIATING BURN, WHICH PREVENTED US FROM EVEN HOLDING OUR WEAPONS.

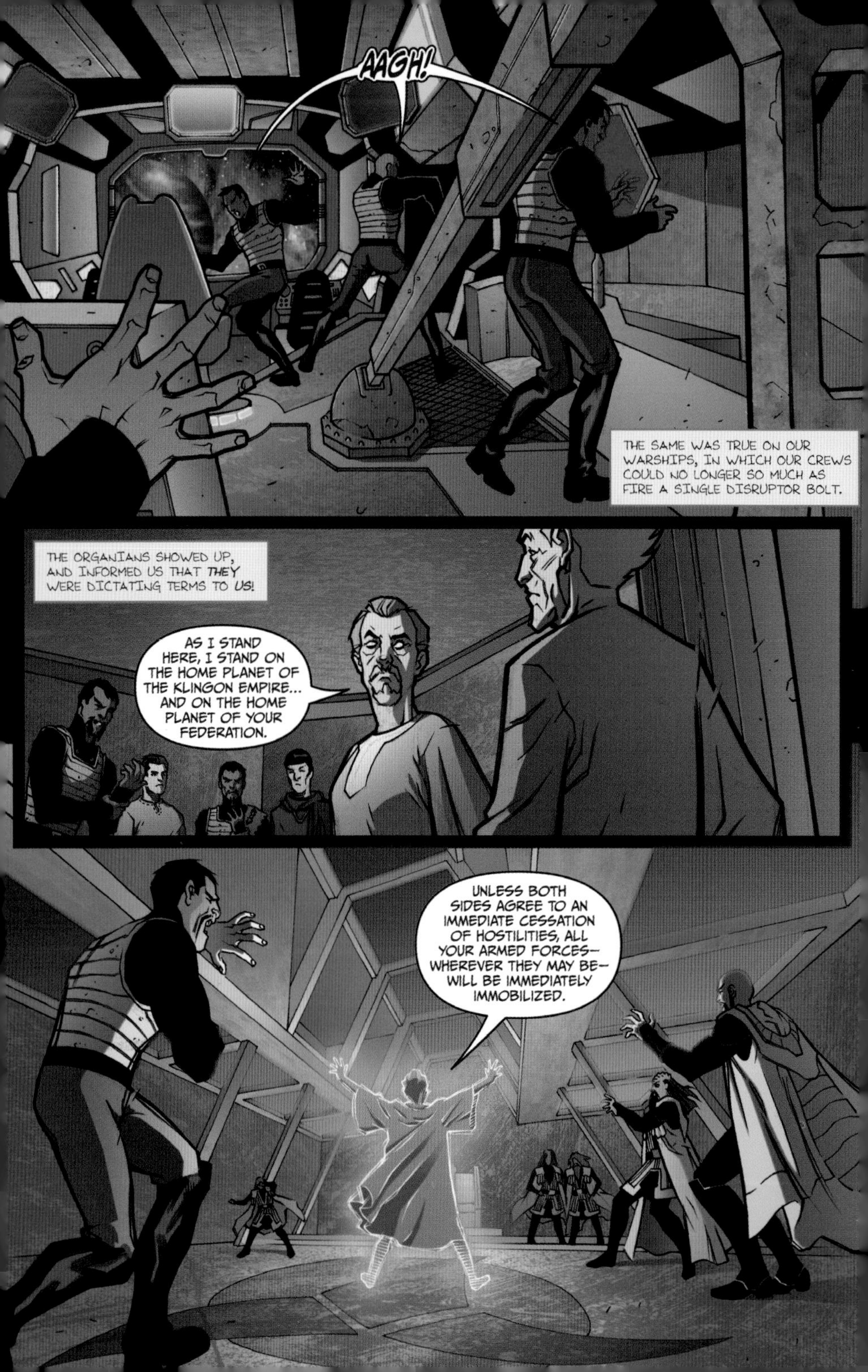
AAGH!
THE SAME WAS TRUE ON OUR WARSHIPS, IN WHICH OUR CREWS COULD NO LONGER SO MUCH AS FIRE A SINGLE DISRUPTOR BOLT.
THE ORGANIANS SHOWED UP, AND INFORMED US THAT THEY WERE DICTATING TERMS TO US!
AS I STAND HERE, I STAND ON THE HOME PLANET OF THE KLINGON EMPIRE... AND ON THE HOME PLANET OF YOUR FEDERATION.
UNLESS BOTH SIDES AGREE TO AN IMMEDIATE CESSATION OF HOSTILITIES, ALL YOUR ARMED FORCES— WHEREVER THEY MAY BE— WILL BE IMMEDIATELY IMMOBILIZED.

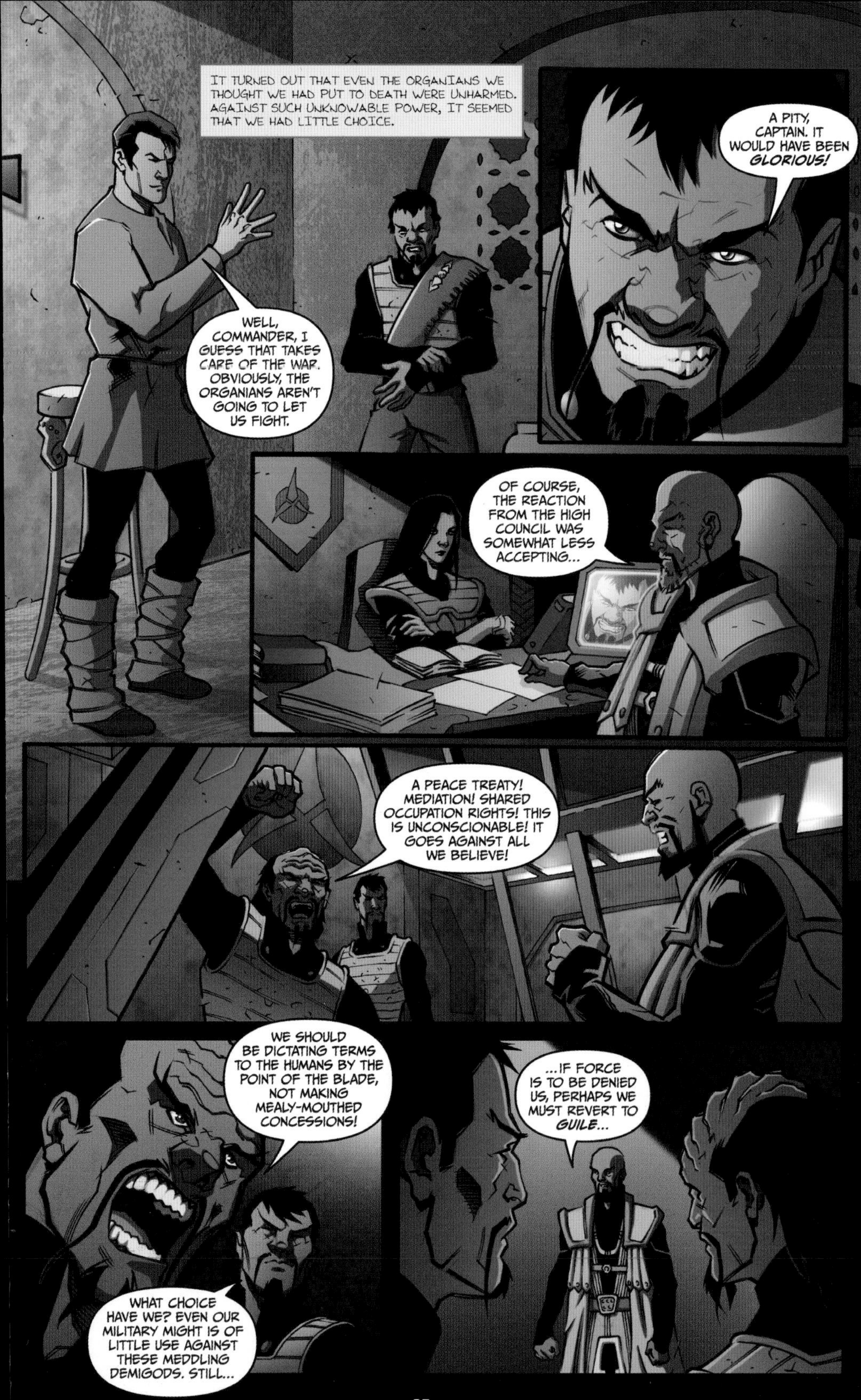
IT TURNED OUT THAT EVEN THE ORGANIANS WE THOUGHT WE HAD PUT TO DEATH WERE UNHARMED. AGAINST SUCH UNKNOWABLE POWER, IT SEEMED THAT WE HAD LITTLE CHOICE.
WELL, COMMANDER, I GUESS THAT TAKES CARE OF THE WAR. OBVIOUSLY, THE ORGANIANS AREN'T GOING TO LET US FIGHT.
A PITY, CAPTAIN. IT WOULD HAVE BEEN *GLORIOUS!*
OF COURSE, THE REACTION FROM THE HIGH COUNCIL WAS SOMEWHAT LESS ACCEPTING...
A PEACE TREATY! MEDIATION! SHARED OCCUPATION RIGHTS! THIS IS UNCONSCIONABLE! IT GOES AGAINST ALL WE BELIEVE!
WE SHOULD BE DICTATING TERMS TO THE HUMANS BY THE POINT OF THE BLADE, NOT MAKING MEALY-MOUTHED CONCESSIONS!
WHAT CHOICE HAVE WE? EVEN OUR MILITARY MIGHT IS OF LITTLE USE AGAINST THESE MEDDLING DEMIGODS. STILL...
...IF FORCE IS TO BE DENIED US, PERHAPS WE MUST REVERT TO *GUILE*...

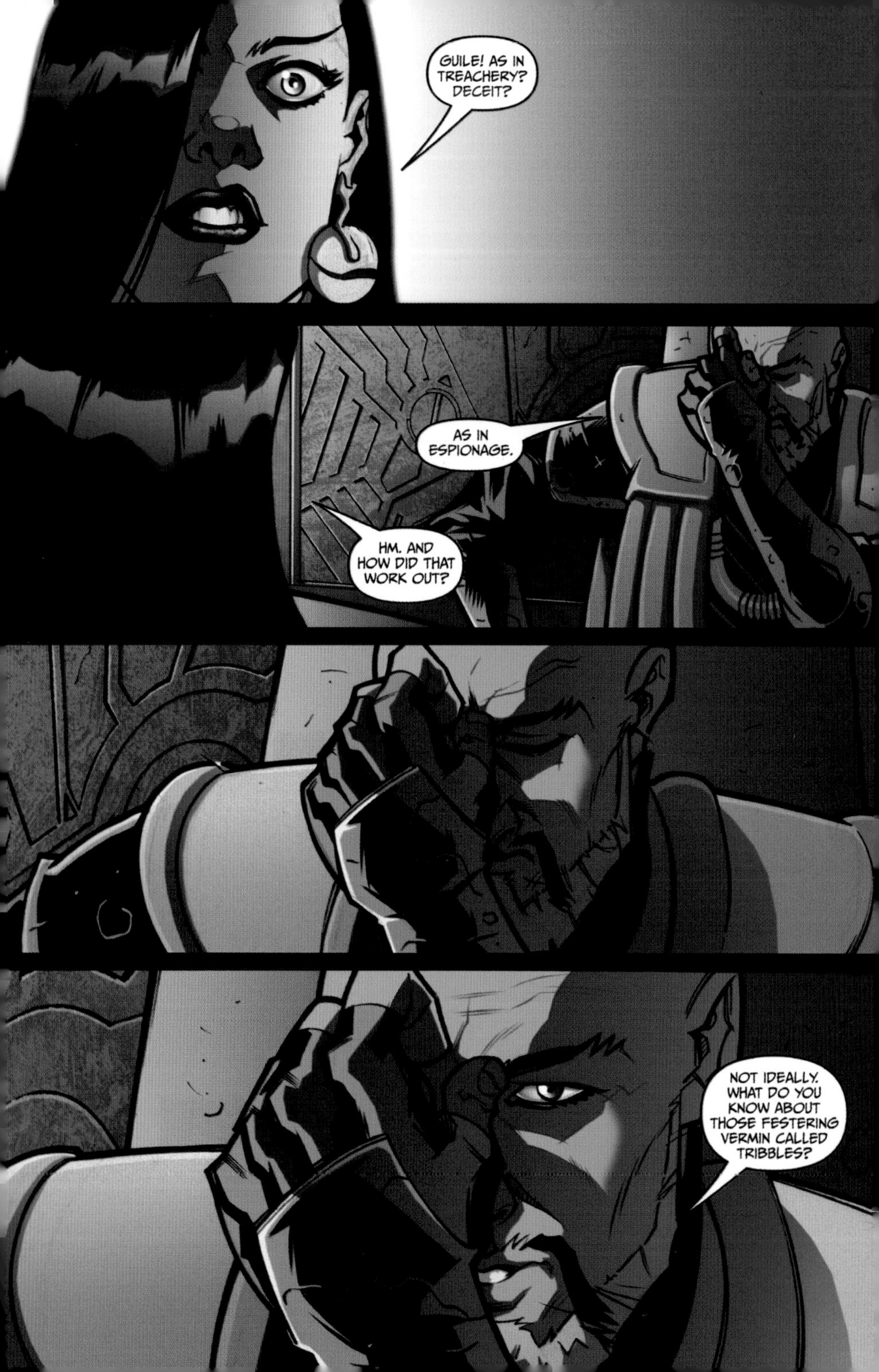
GUILE! AS IN TREACHERY? DECEIT?
AS IN ESPIONAGE.
HM. AND HOW DID THAT WORK OUT?
NOT IDEALLY. WHAT DO YOU KNOW ABOUT THOSE FESTERING VERMIN CALLED TRIBBLES?

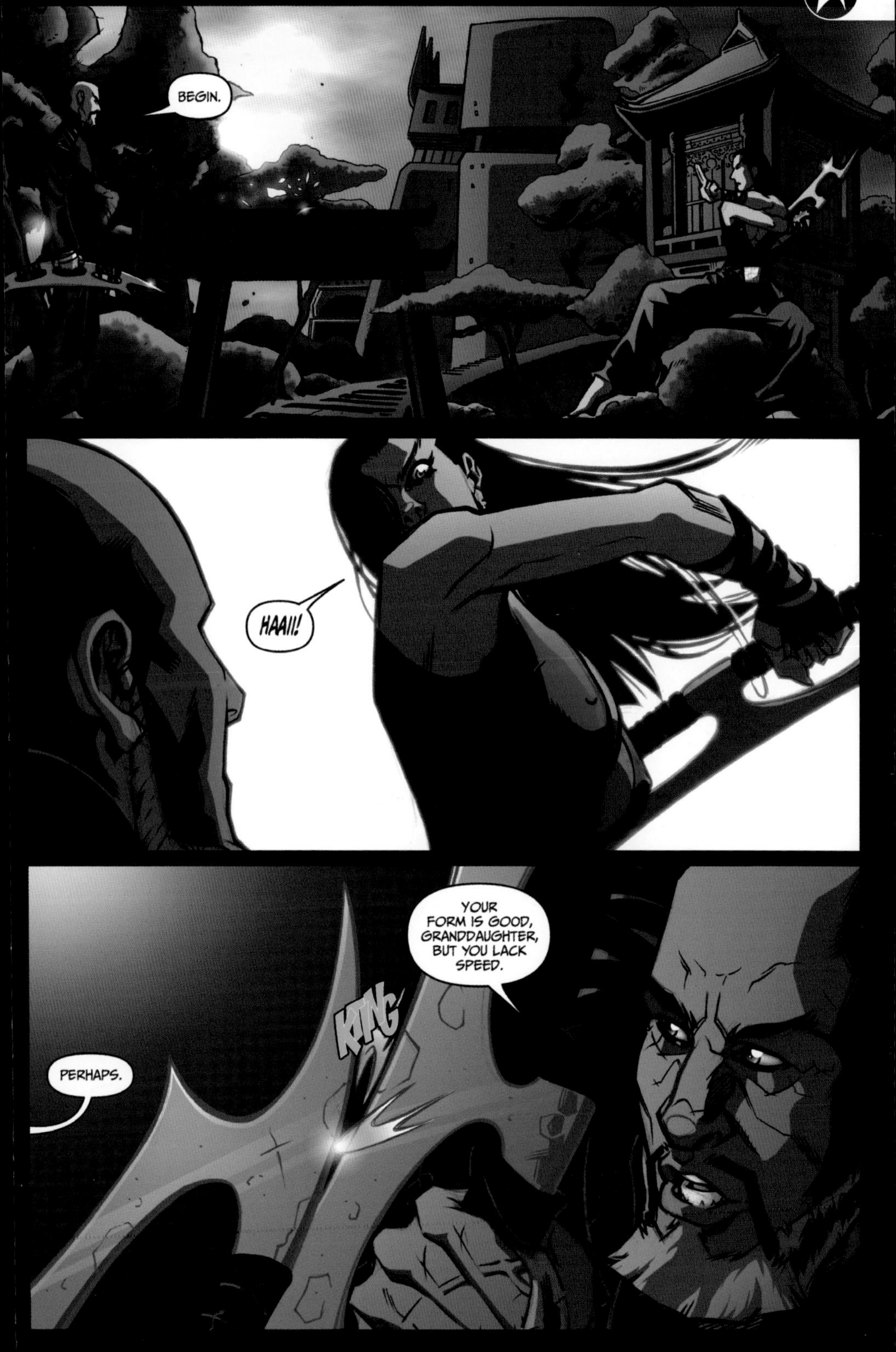
BEGIN.
HAAII!
YOUR FORM IS GOOD, GRANDDAUGHTER, BUT YOU LACK SPEED.
KTING
PERHAPS.

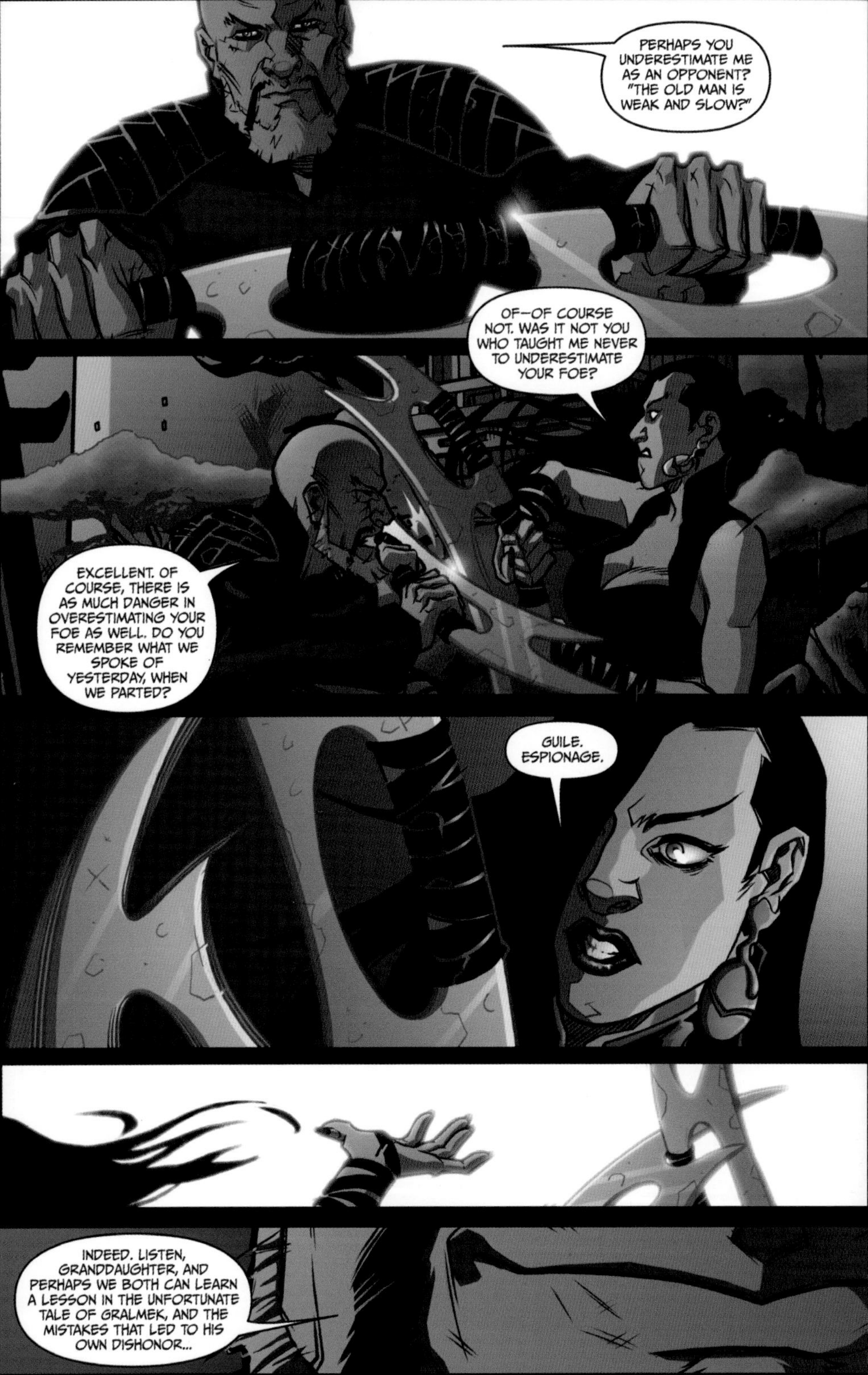
PERHAPS YOU UNDERESTIMATE ME AS AN OPPONENT? "THE OLD MAN IS WEAK AND SLOW?"
OF—OF COURSE NOT. WAS IT NOT YOU WHO TAUGHT ME NEVER TO UNDERESTIMATE YOUR FOE?
EXCELLENT. OF COURSE, THERE IS AS MUCH DANGER IN OVERESTIMATING YOUR FOE AS WELL. DO YOU REMEMBER WHAT WE SPOKE OF YESTERDAY, WHEN WE PARTED?
GUILE. ESPIONAGE.
INDEED. LISTEN, GRANDDAUGHTER, AND PERHAPS WE BOTH CAN LEARN A LESSON IN THE UNFORTUNATE TALE OF GRALMEK, AND THE MISTAKES THAT LED TO HIS OWN DISHONOR...

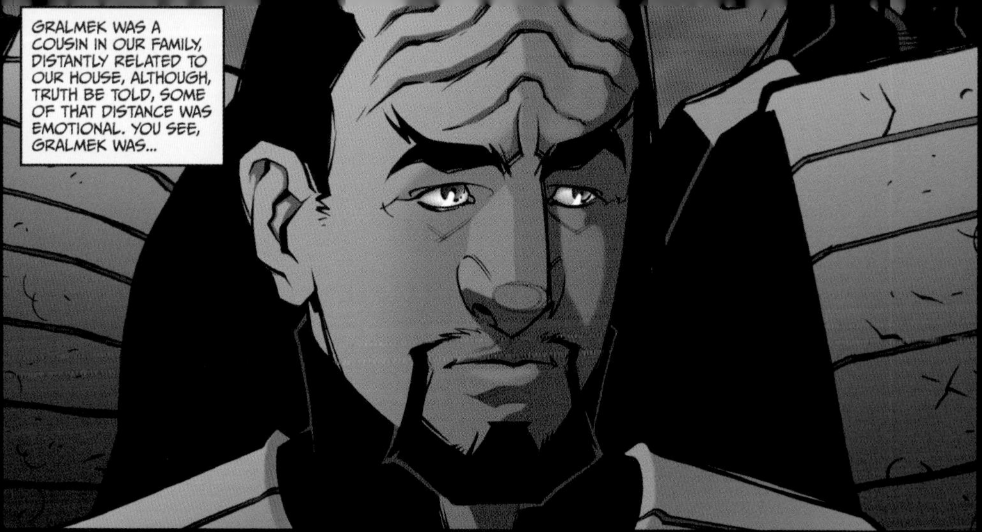
GRALMEK WAS A COUSIN IN OUR FAMILY, DISTANTLY RELATED TO OUR HOUSE, ALTHOUGH, TRUTH BE TOLD, SOME OF THAT DISTANCE WAS EMOTIONAL. YOU SEE, GRALMEK WAS...

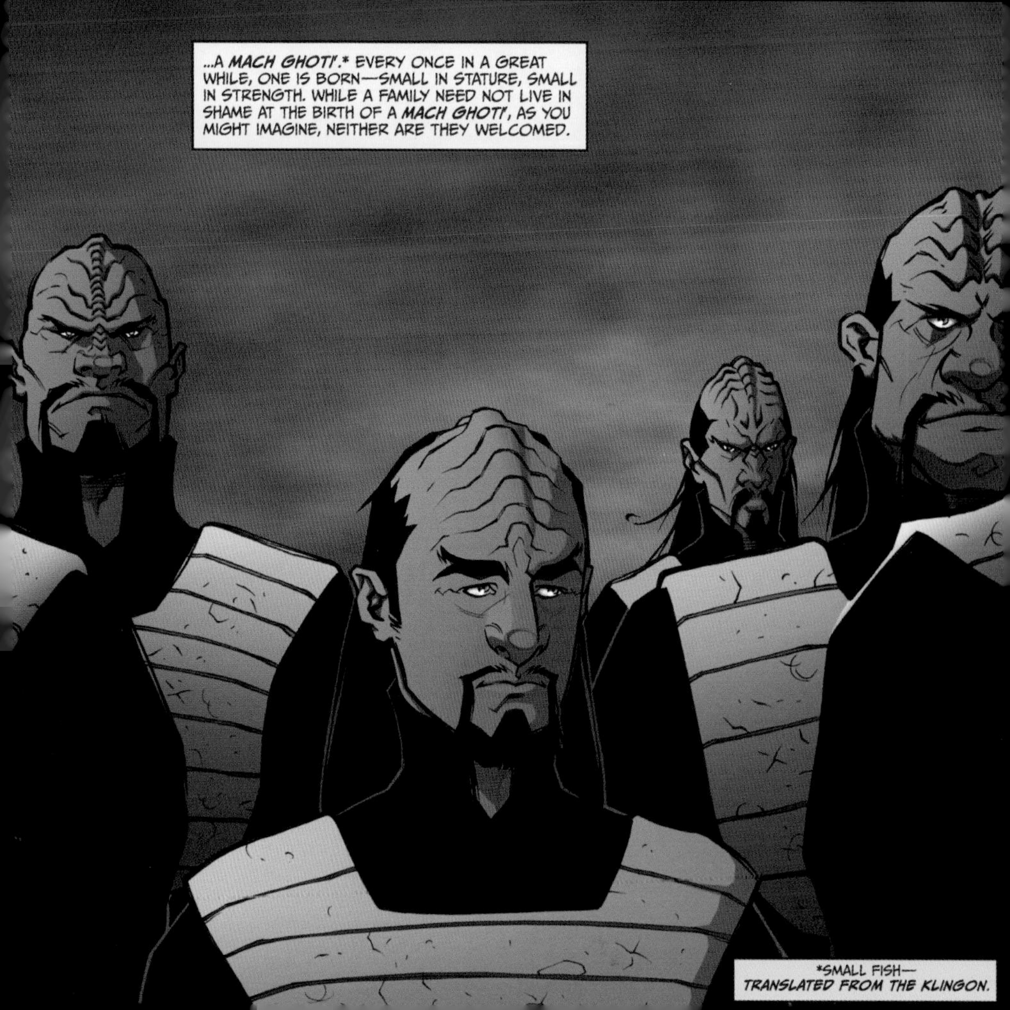
...A *MACH GHOTI'*.* EVERY ONCE IN A GREAT WHILE, ONE IS BORN—SMALL IN STATURE, SMALL IN STRENGTH. WHILE A FAMILY NEED NOT LIVE IN SHAME AT THE BIRTH OF A *MACH GHOTI'*, AS YOU MIGHT IMAGINE, NEITHER ARE THEY WELCOMED.
*SMALL FISH— *TRANSLATED FROM THE KLINGON.*

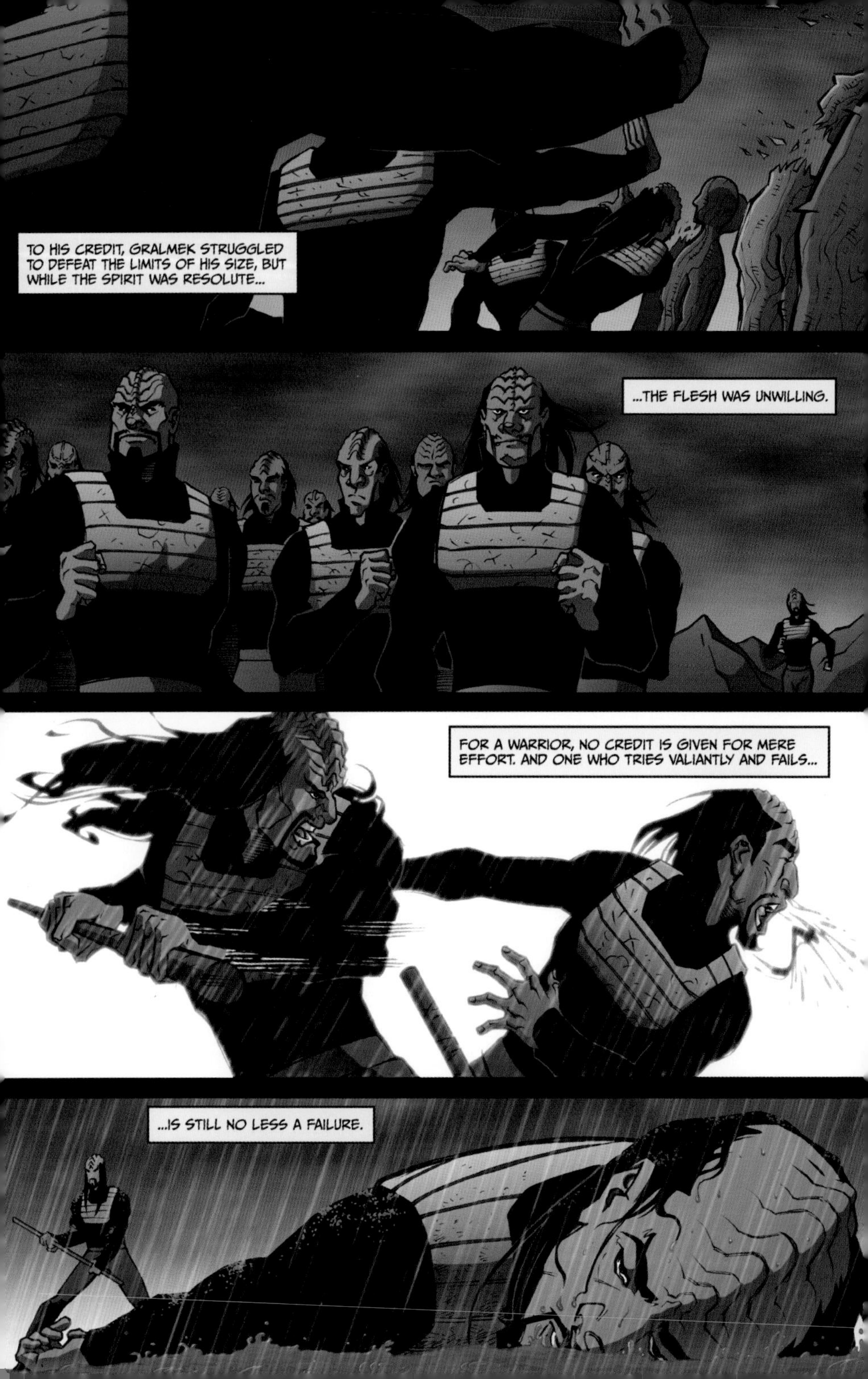
TO HIS CREDIT, GRALMEK STRUGGLED TO DEFEAT THE LIMITS OF HIS SIZE, BUT WHILE THE SPIRIT WAS RESOLUTE...
...THE FLESH WAS UNWILLING.
FOR A WARRIOR, NO CREDIT IS GIVEN FOR MERE EFFORT. AND ONE WHO TRIES VALIANTLY AND FAILS...
...IS STILL NO LESS A FAILURE.

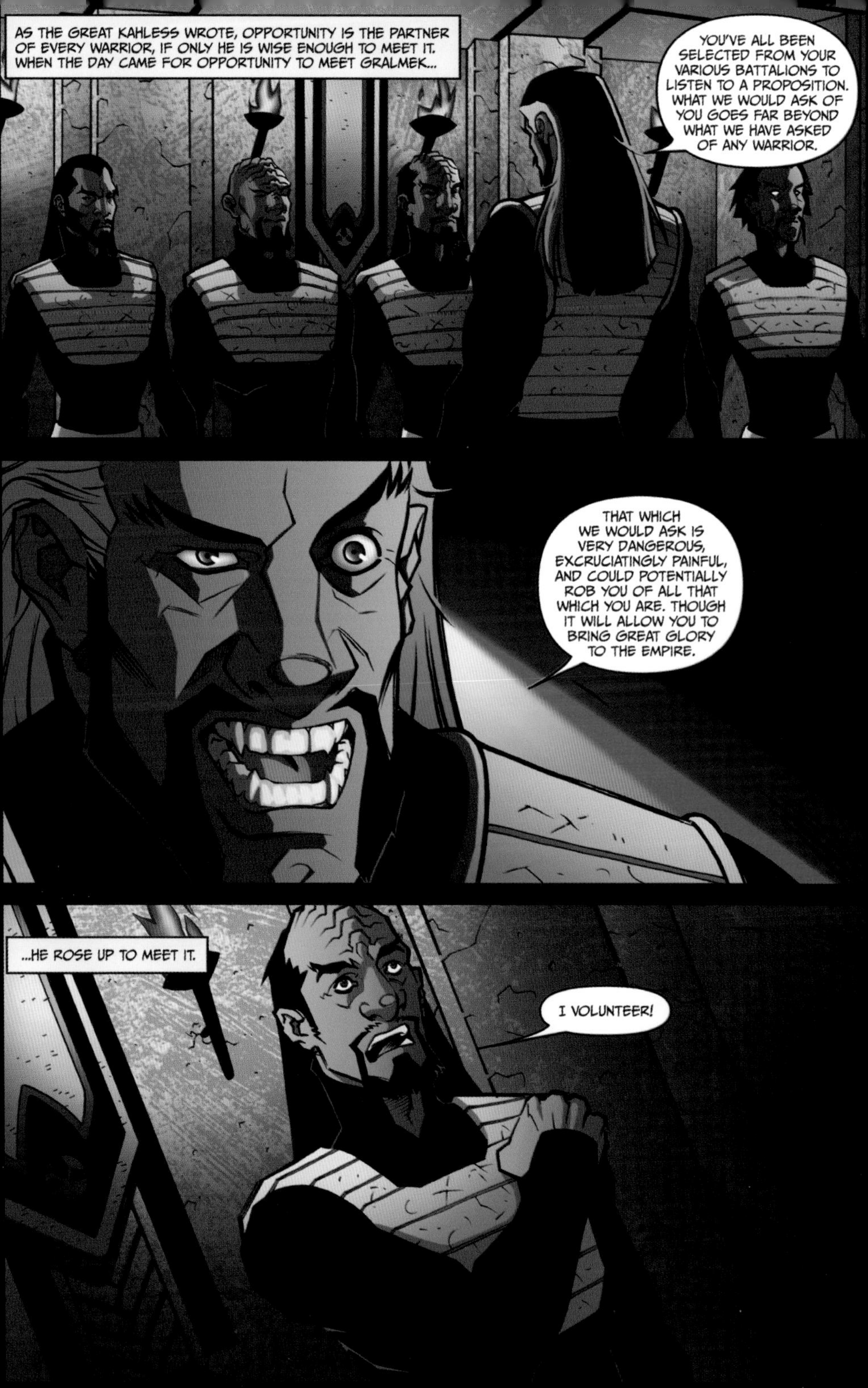
AS THE GREAT KAHLESS WROTE, OPPORTUNITY IS THE PARTNER OF EVERY WARRIOR, IF ONLY HE IS WISE ENOUGH TO MEET IT. WHEN THE DAY CAME FOR OPPORTUNITY TO MEET GRALMEK...
YOU'VE ALL BEEN SELECTED FROM YOUR VARIOUS BATTALIONS TO LISTEN TO A PROPOSITION. WHAT WE WOULD ASK OF YOU GOES FAR BEYOND WHAT WE HAVE ASKED OF ANY WARRIOR.
THAT WHICH WE WOULD ASK IS VERY DANGEROUS, EXCRUCIATINGLY PAINFUL, AND COULD POTENTIALLY ROB YOU OF ALL THAT WHICH YOU ARE. THOUGH IT WILL ALLOW YOU TO BRING GREAT GLORY TO THE EMPIRE.
...HE ROSE UP TO MEET IT.
I VOLUNTEER!

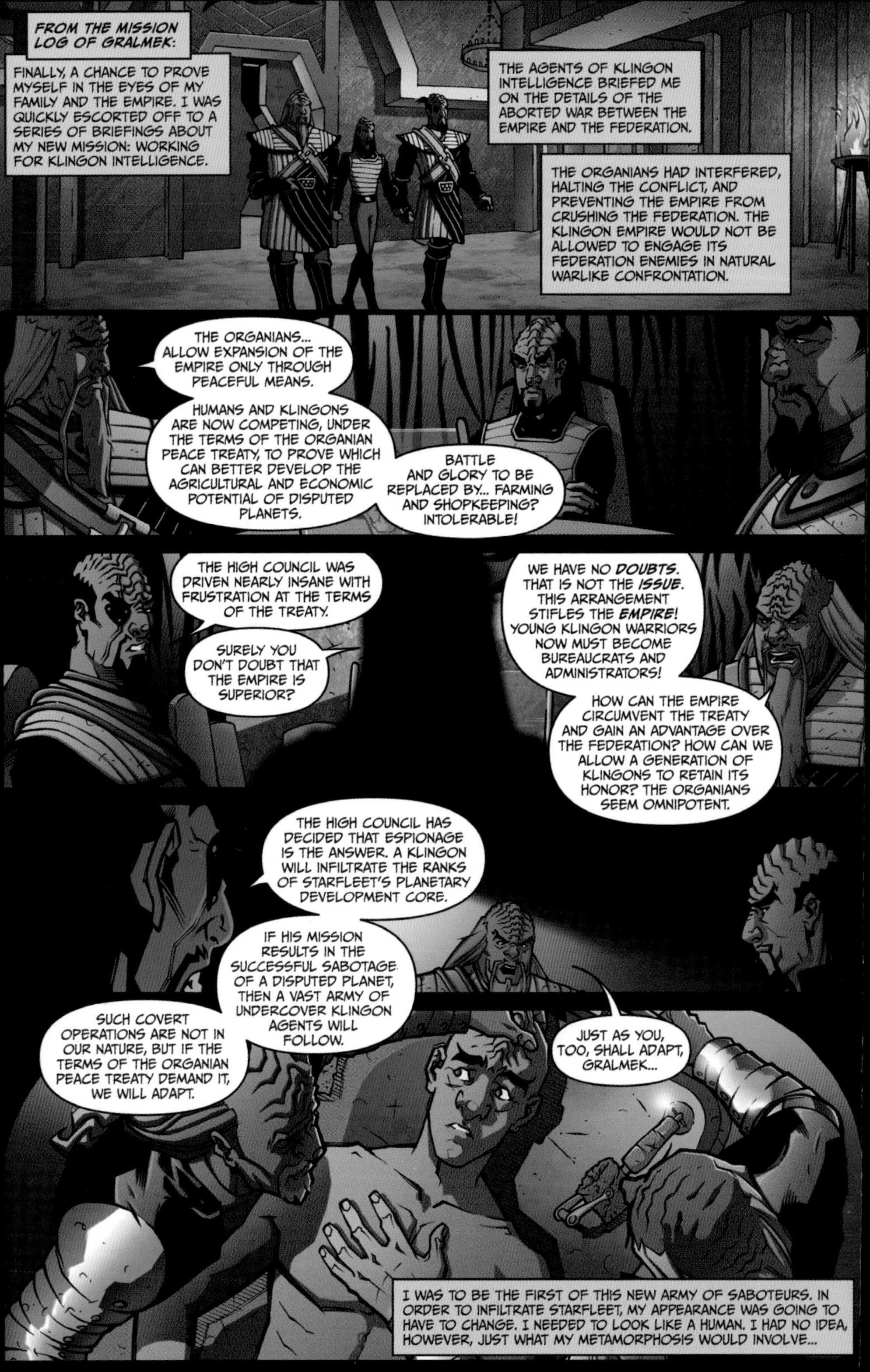
FROM THE MISSION LOG OF GRALMEK:
FINALLY, A CHANCE TO PROVE MYSELF IN THE EYES OF MY FAMILY AND THE EMPIRE. I WAS QUICKLY ESCORTED OFF TO A SERIES OF BRIEFINGS ABOUT MY NEW MISSION: WORKING FOR KLINGON INTELLIGENCE.
THE AGENTS OF KLINGON INTELLIGENCE BRIEFED ME ON THE DETAILS OF THE ABORTED WAR BETWEEN THE EMPIRE AND THE FEDERATION.
THE ORGANIANS HAD INTERFERED, HALTING THE CONFLICT, AND PREVENTING THE EMPIRE FROM CRUSHING THE FEDERATION. THE KLINGON EMPIRE WOULD NOT BE ALLOWED TO ENGAGE ITS FEDERATION ENEMIES IN NATURAL WARLIKE CONFRONTATION.
THE ORGANIANS... ALLOW EXPANSION OF THE EMPIRE ONLY THROUGH PEACEFUL MEANS.
HUMANS AND KLINGONS ARE NOW COMPETING, UNDER THE TERMS OF THE ORGANIAN PEACE TREATY, TO PROVE WHICH CAN BETTER DEVELOP THE AGRICULTURAL AND ECONOMIC POTENTIAL OF DISPUTED PLANETS.
BATTLE AND GLORY TO BE REPLACED BY... FARMING AND SHOPKEEPING? INTOLERABLE!
THE HIGH COUNCIL WAS DRIVEN NEARLY INSANE WITH FRUSTRATION AT THE TERMS OF THE TREATY.
SURELY YOU DON'T DOUBT THAT THE EMPIRE IS SUPERIOR?
WE HAVE NO *DOUBTS*. THAT IS NOT THE *ISSUE*. THIS ARRANGEMENT STIFLES THE *EMPIRE*! YOUNG KLINGON WARRIORS NOW MUST BECOME BUREAUCRATS AND ADMINISTRATORS!
HOW CAN THE EMPIRE CIRCUMVENT THE TREATY AND GAIN AN ADVANTAGE OVER THE FEDERATION? HOW CAN WE ALLOW A GENERATION OF KLINGONS TO RETAIN ITS HONOR? THE ORGANIANS SEEM OMNIPOTENT.
THE HIGH COUNCIL HAS DECIDED THAT ESPIONAGE IS THE ANSWER. A KLINGON WILL INFILTRATE THE RANKS OF STARFLEET'S PLANETARY DEVELOPMENT CORE.
IF HIS MISSION RESULTS IN THE SUCCESSFUL SABOTAGE OF A DISPUTED PLANET, THEN A VAST ARMY OF UNDERCOVER KLINGON AGENTS WILL FOLLOW.
SUCH COVERT OPERATIONS ARE NOT IN OUR NATURE, BUT IF THE TERMS OF THE ORGANIAN PEACE TREATY DEMAND IT, WE WILL ADAPT.
JUST AS YOU, TOO, SHALL ADAPT, GRALMEK...
I WAS TO BE THE FIRST OF THIS NEW ARMY OF SABOTEURS. IN ORDER TO INFILTRATE STARFLEET, MY APPEARANCE WAS GOING TO HAVE TO CHANGE. I NEEDED TO LOOK LIKE A HUMAN. I HAD NO IDEA, HOWEVER, JUST WHAT MY METAMORPHOSIS WOULD INVOLVE...

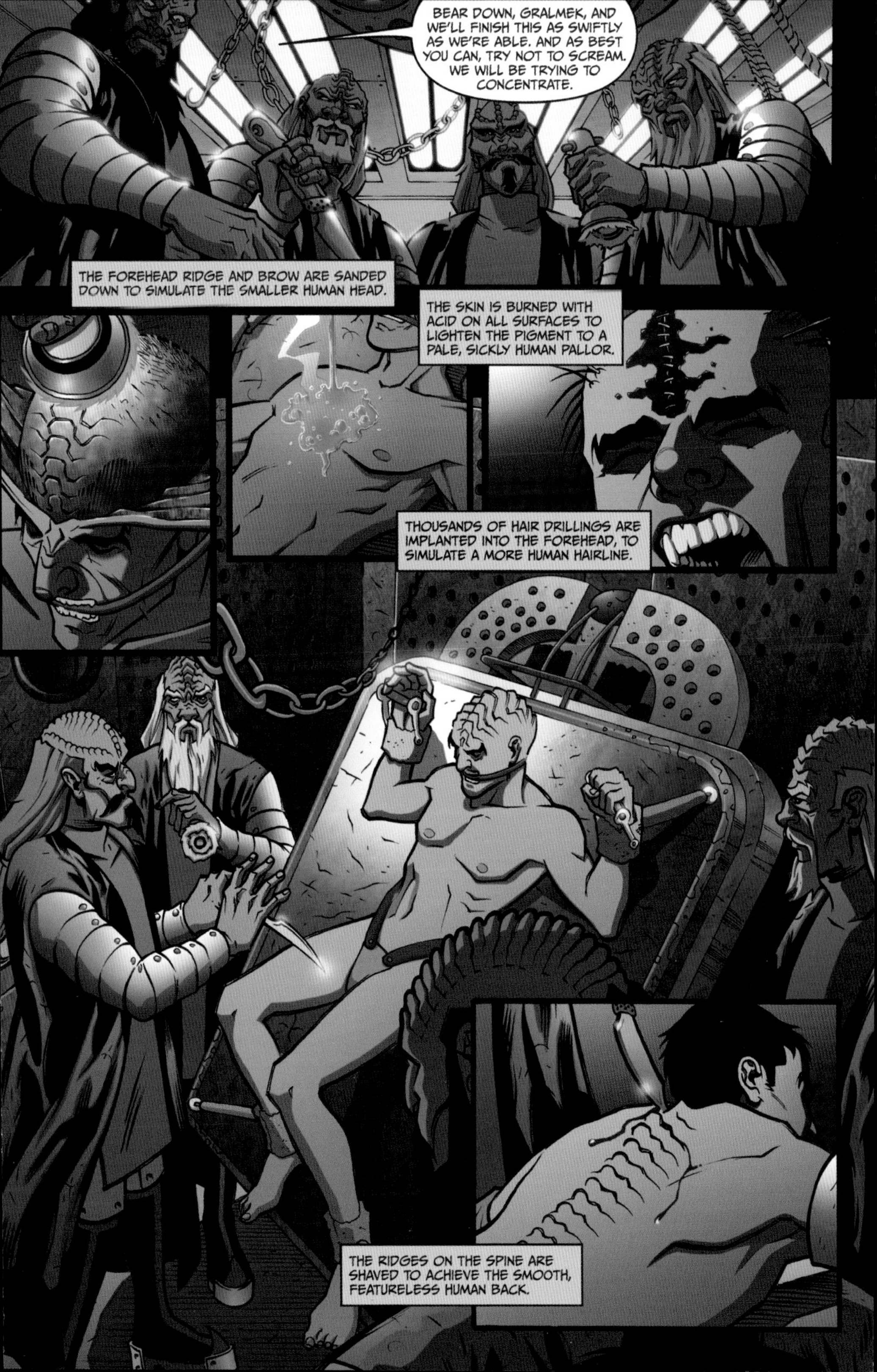
BEAR DOWN, GRALMEK, AND WE'LL FINISH THIS AS SWIFTLY AS WE'RE ABLE. AND AS BEST YOU CAN, TRY NOT TO SCREAM. WE WILL BE TRYING TO CONCENTRATE.
THE FOREHEAD RIDGE AND BROW ARE SANDED DOWN TO SIMULATE THE SMALLER HUMAN HEAD.
THE SKIN IS BURNED WITH ACID ON ALL SURFACES TO LIGHTEN THE PIGMENT TO A PALE, SICKLY HUMAN PALLOR.
THOUSANDS OF HAIR DRILLINGS ARE IMPLANTED INTO THE FOREHEAD, TO SIMULATE A MORE HUMAN HAIRLINE.
THE RIDGES ON THE SPINE ARE SHAVED TO ACHIEVE THE SMOOTH, FEATURELESS HUMAN BACK.

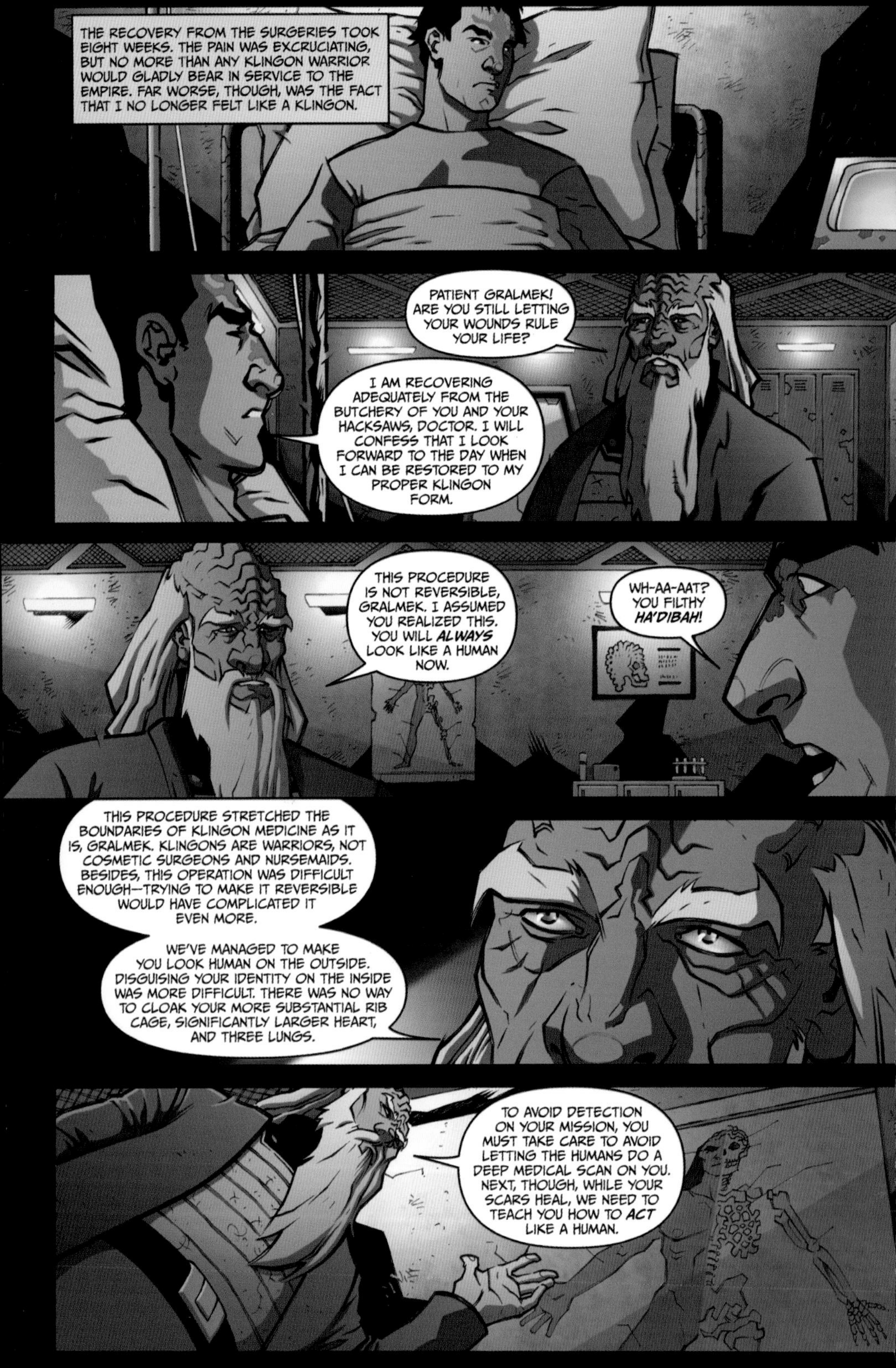
THE RECOVERY FROM THE SURGERIES TOOK EIGHT WEEKS. THE PAIN WAS EXCRUCIATING, BUT NO MORE THAN ANY KLINGON WARRIOR WOULD GLADLY BEAR IN SERVICE TO THE EMPIRE. FAR WORSE, THOUGH, WAS THE FACT THAT I NO LONGER FELT LIKE A KLINGON.
PATIENT GRALMEK! ARE YOU STILL LETTING YOUR WOUNDS RULE YOUR LIFE?
I AM RECOVERING ADEQUATELY FROM THE BUTCHERY OF YOU AND YOUR HACKSAWS, DOCTOR. I WILL CONFESS THAT I LOOK FORWARD TO THE DAY WHEN I CAN BE RESTORED TO MY PROPER KLINGON FORM.
THIS PROCEDURE IS NOT REVERSIBLE, GRALMEK. I ASSUMED YOU REALIZED THIS. YOU WILL *ALWAYS* LOOK LIKE A HUMAN NOW.
WH-AA-AAT? YOU FILTHY *HA'DIBAH*!
THIS PROCEDURE STRETCHED THE BOUNDARIES OF KLINGON MEDICINE AS IT IS, GRALMEK. KLINGONS ARE WARRIORS, NOT COSMETIC SURGEONS AND NURSEMAIDS. BESIDES, THIS OPERATION WAS DIFFICULT ENOUGH--TRYING TO MAKE IT REVERSIBLE WOULD HAVE COMPLICATED IT EVEN MORE.
WE'VE MANAGED TO MAKE YOU LOOK HUMAN ON THE OUTSIDE. DISGUISING YOUR IDENTITY ON THE INSIDE WAS MORE DIFFICULT. THERE WAS NO WAY TO CLOAK YOUR MORE SUBSTANTIAL RIB CAGE, SIGNIFICANTLY LARGER HEART, AND THREE LUNGS.
TO AVOID DETECTION ON YOUR MISSION, YOU MUST TAKE CARE TO AVOID LETTING THE HUMANS DO A DEEP MEDICAL SCAN ON YOU. NEXT, THOUGH, WHILE YOUR SCARS HEAL, WE NEED TO TEACH YOU HOW TO *ACT* LIKE A HUMAN.

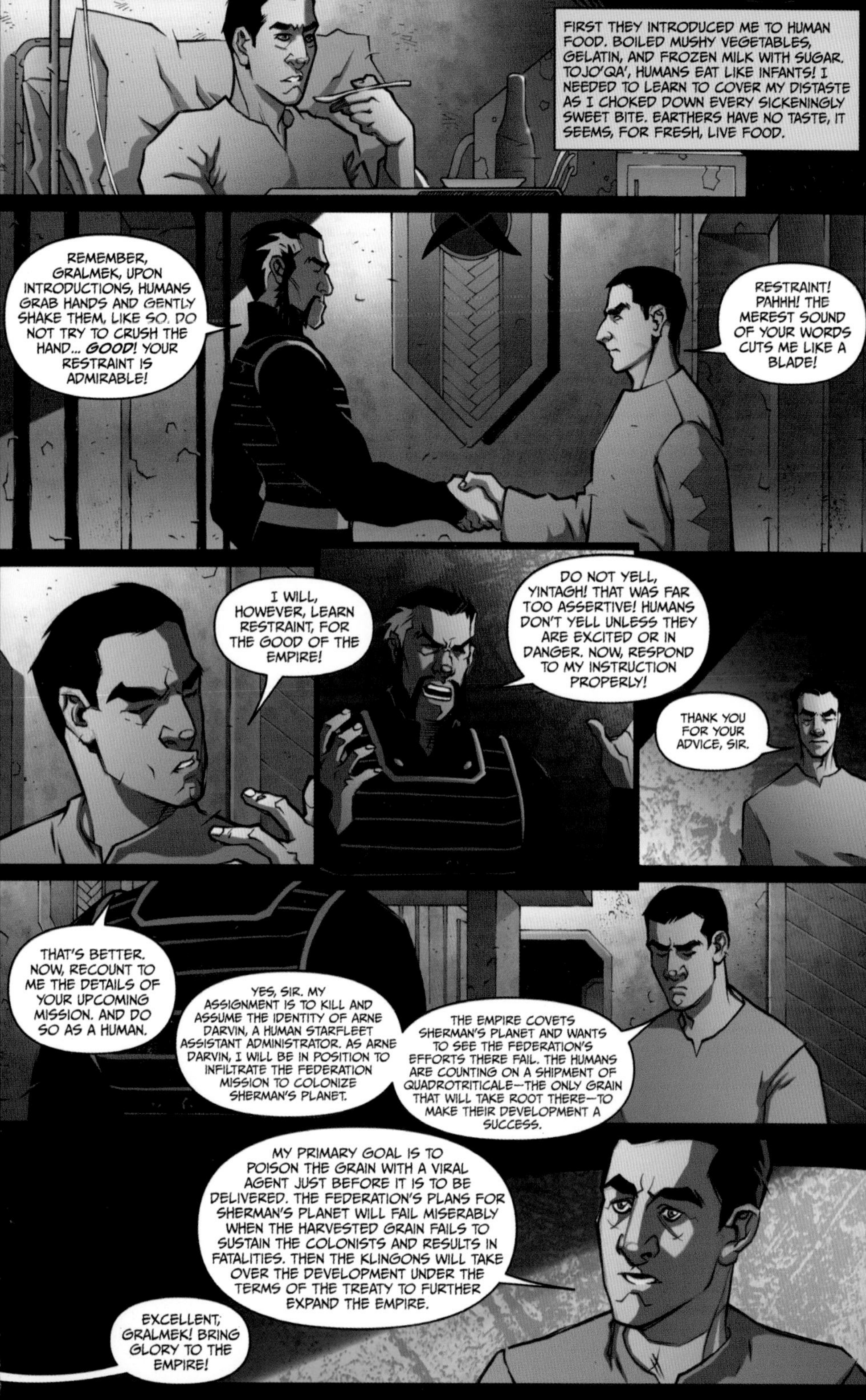
FIRST THEY INTRODUCED ME TO HUMAN FOOD. BOILED MUSHY VEGETABLES, GELATIN, AND FROZEN MILK WITH SUGAR. TOJO'QA', HUMANS EAT LIKE INFANTS! I NEEDED TO LEARN TO COVER MY DISTASTE AS I CHOKED DOWN EVERY SICKENINGLY SWEET BITE. EARTHERS HAVE NO TASTE, IT SEEMS, FOR FRESH, LIVE FOOD.
REMEMBER, GRALMEK, UPON INTRODUCTIONS, HUMANS GRAB HANDS AND GENTLY SHAKE THEM, LIKE SO. DO NOT TRY TO CRUSH THE HAND... GOOD! YOUR RESTRAINT IS ADMIRABLE!
RESTRAINT! PAHHH! THE MEREST SOUND OF YOUR WORDS CUTS ME LIKE A BLADE!
I WILL, HOWEVER, LEARN RESTRAINT, FOR THE GOOD OF THE EMPIRE!
DO NOT YELL, YINTAGH! THAT WAS FAR TOO ASSERTIVE! HUMANS DON'T YELL UNLESS THEY ARE EXCITED OR IN DANGER. NOW, RESPOND TO MY INSTRUCTION PROPERLY!
THANK YOU FOR YOUR ADVICE, SIR.
THAT'S BETTER. NOW, RECOUNT TO ME THE DETAILS OF YOUR UPCOMING MISSION. AND DO SO AS A HUMAN.
YES, SIR. MY ASSIGNMENT IS TO KILL AND ASSUME THE IDENTITY OF ARNE DARVIN, A HUMAN STARFLEET ASSISTANT ADMINISTRATOR. AS ARNE DARVIN, I WILL BE IN POSITION TO INFILTRATE THE FEDERATION MISSION TO COLONIZE SHERMAN'S PLANET.
THE EMPIRE COVETS SHERMAN'S PLANET AND WANTS TO SEE THE FEDERATION'S EFFORTS THERE FAIL. THE HUMANS ARE COUNTING ON A SHIPMENT OF QUADROTRITICALE—THE ONLY GRAIN THAT WILL TAKE ROOT THERE—TO MAKE THEIR DEVELOPMENT A SUCCESS.
MY PRIMARY GOAL IS TO POISON THE GRAIN WITH A VIRAL AGENT JUST BEFORE IT IS TO BE DELIVERED. THE FEDERATION'S PLANS FOR SHERMAN'S PLANET WILL FAIL MISERABLY WHEN THE HARVESTED GRAIN FAILS TO SUSTAIN THE COLONISTS AND RESULTS IN FATALITIES. THEN THE KLINGONS WILL TAKE OVER THE DEVELOPMENT UNDER THE TERMS OF THE TREATY TO FURTHER EXPAND THE EMPIRE.
EXCELLENT, GRALMEK! BRING GLORY TO THE EMPIRE!

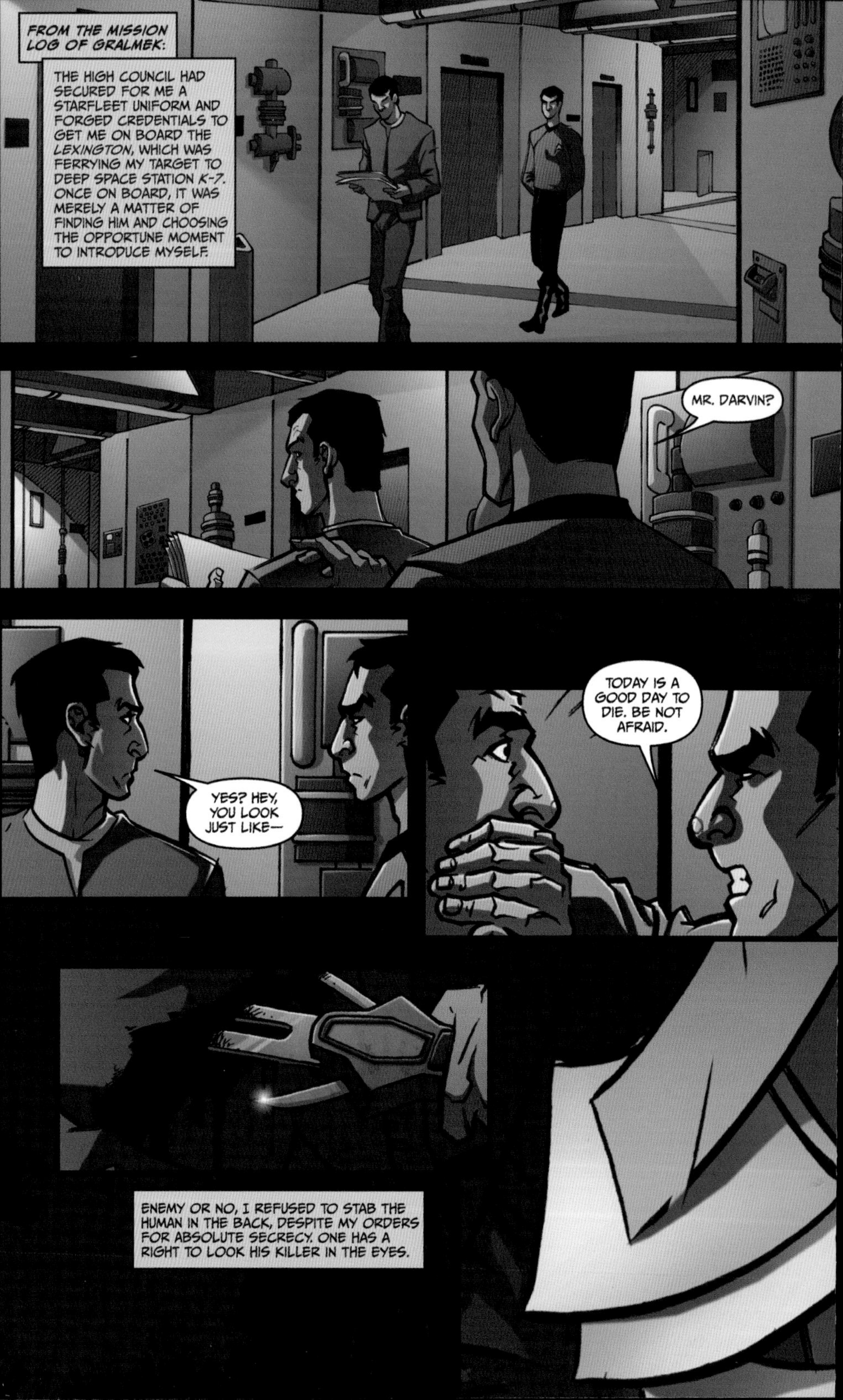
FROM THE MISSION LOG OF GRALMEK:
THE HIGH COUNCIL HAD SECURED FOR ME A STARFLEET UNIFORM AND FORGED CREDENTIALS TO GET ME ON BOARD THE *LEXINGTON*, WHICH WAS FERRYING MY TARGET TO DEEP SPACE STATION *K-7*. ONCE ON BOARD, IT WAS MERELY A MATTER OF FINDING HIM AND CHOOSING THE OPPORTUNE MOMENT TO INTRODUCE MYSELF.
MR. DARVIN?
YES? HEY, YOU LOOK JUST LIKE—
TODAY IS A GOOD DAY TO DIE. BE NOT AFRAID.
ENEMY OR NO, I REFUSED TO STAB THE HUMAN IN THE BACK, DESPITE MY ORDERS FOR ABSOLUTE SECRECY. ONE HAS A RIGHT TO LOOK HIS KILLER IN THE EYES.

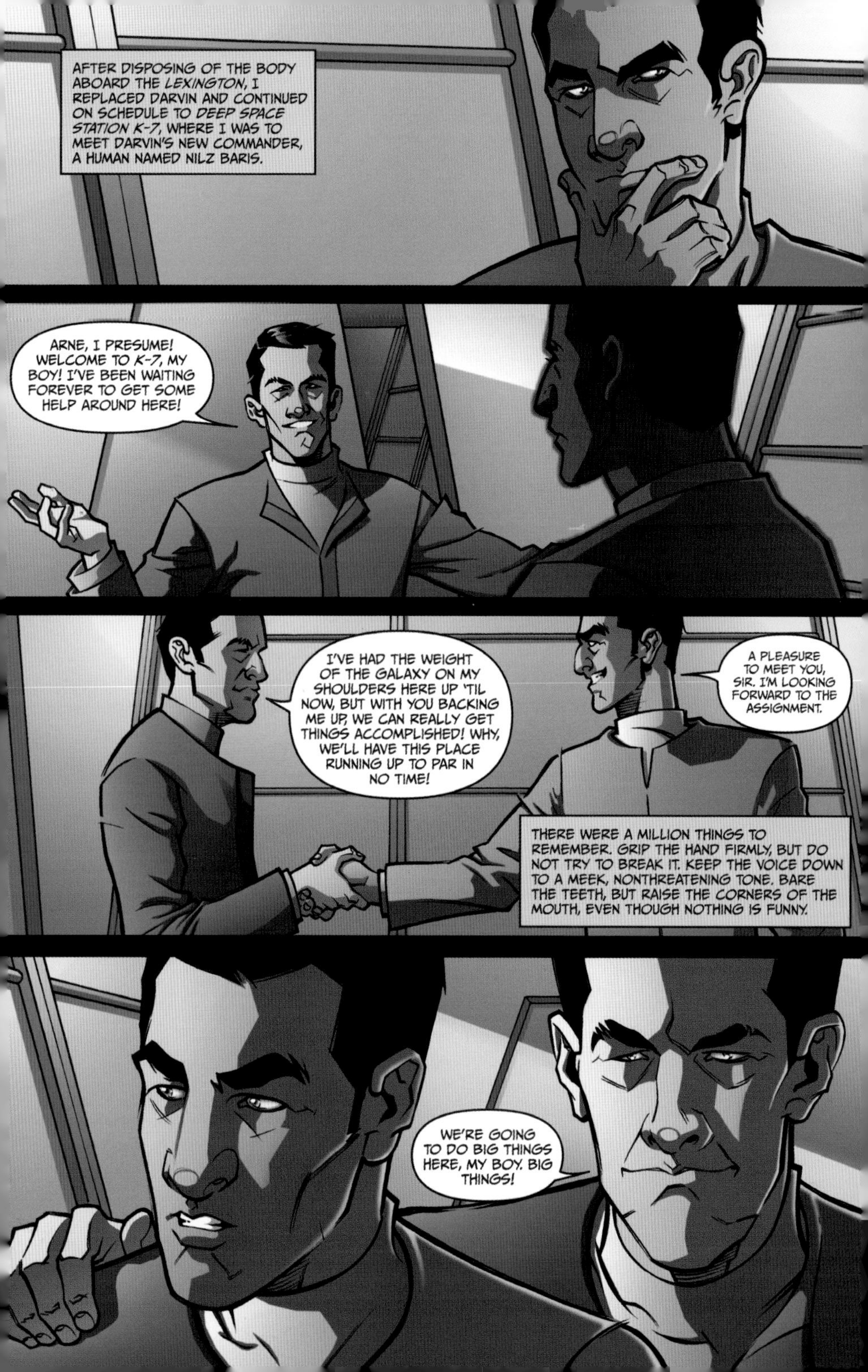
AFTER DISPOSING OF THE BODY ABOARD THE *LEXINGTON*, I REPLACED DARVIN AND CONTINUED ON SCHEDULE TO *DEEP SPACE STATION K-7*, WHERE I WAS TO MEET DARVIN'S NEW COMMANDER, A HUMAN NAMED NILZ BARIS.
ARNE, I PRESUME! WELCOME TO *K-7*, MY BOY! I'VE BEEN WAITING FOREVER TO GET SOME HELP AROUND HERE!
I'VE HAD THE WEIGHT OF THE GALAXY ON MY SHOULDERS HERE UP 'TIL NOW, BUT WITH YOU BACKING ME UP, WE CAN REALLY GET THINGS ACCOMPLISHED! WHY, WE'LL HAVE THIS PLACE RUNNING UP TO PAR IN NO TIME!
A PLEASURE TO MEET YOU, SIR. I'M LOOKING FORWARD TO THE ASSIGNMENT.
THERE WERE A MILLION THINGS TO REMEMBER. GRIP THE HAND FIRMLY, BUT DO NOT TRY TO BREAK IT. KEEP THE VOICE DOWN TO A MEEK, NONTHREATENING TONE. BARE THE TEETH, BUT RAISE THE CORNERS OF THE MOUTH, EVEN THOUGH NOTHING IS FUNNY.
WE'RE GOING TO DO BIG THINGS HERE, MY BOY. BIG THINGS!

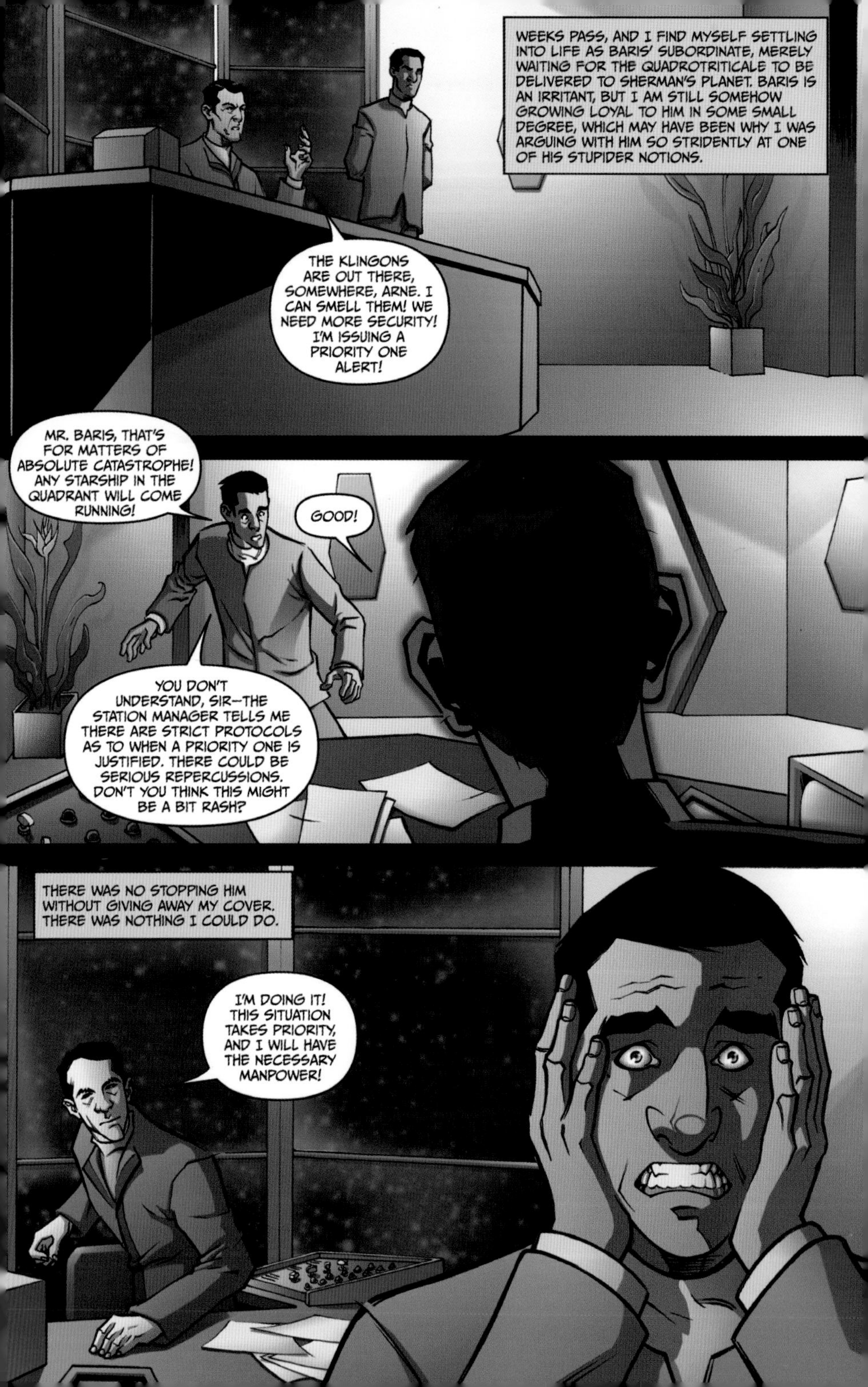
WEEKS PASS, AND I FIND MYSELF SETTLING INTO LIFE AS BARIS' SUBORDINATE, MERELY WAITING FOR THE QUADROTRITICALE TO BE DELIVERED TO SHERMAN'S PLANET. BARIS IS AN IRRITANT, BUT I AM STILL SOMEHOW GROWING LOYAL TO HIM IN SOME SMALL DEGREE, WHICH MAY HAVE BEEN WHY I WAS ARGUING WITH HIM SO STRIDENTLY AT ONE OF HIS STUPIDER NOTIONS.
THE KLINGONS ARE OUT THERE, SOMEWHERE, ARNE. I CAN SMELL THEM! WE NEED MORE SECURITY! I'M ISSUING A PRIORITY ONE ALERT!
MR. BARIS, THAT'S FOR MATTERS OF ABSOLUTE CATASTROPHE! ANY STARSHIP IN THE QUADRANT WILL COME RUNNING!
GOOD!
YOU DON'T UNDERSTAND, SIR—THE STATION MANAGER TELLS ME THERE ARE STRICT PROTOCOLS AS TO WHEN A PRIORITY ONE IS JUSTIFIED. THERE COULD BE SERIOUS REPERCUSSIONS. DON'T YOU THINK THIS MIGHT BE A BIT RASH?
THERE WAS NO STOPPING HIM WITHOUT GIVING AWAY MY COVER. THERE WAS NOTHING I COULD DO.
I'M DOING IT! THIS SITUATION TAKES PRIORITY, AND I WILL HAVE THE NECESSARY MANPOWER!

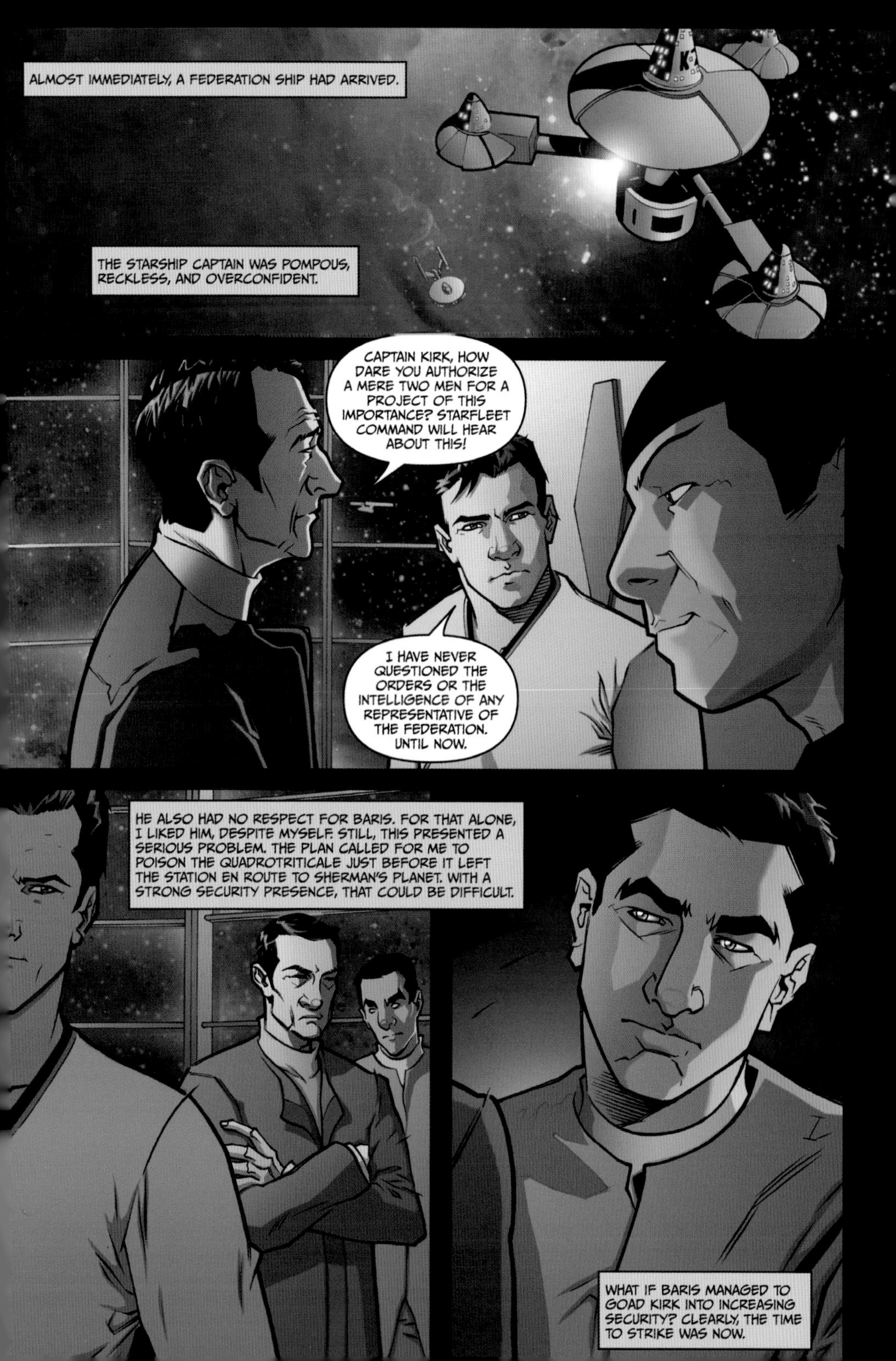

ALMOST IMMEDIATELY, A FEDERATION SHIP HAD ARRIVED.
THE STARSHIP CAPTAIN WAS POMPOUS, RECKLESS, AND OVERCONFIDENT.
CAPTAIN KIRK, HOW DARE YOU AUTHORIZE A MERE TWO MEN FOR A PROJECT OF THIS IMPORTANCE? STARFLEET COMMAND WILL HEAR ABOUT THIS!
I HAVE NEVER QUESTIONED THE ORDERS OR THE INTELLIGENCE OF ANY REPRESENTATIVE OF THE FEDERATION. UNTIL NOW.
HE ALSO HAD NO RESPECT FOR BARIS. FOR THAT ALONE, I LIKED HIM, DESPITE MYSELF. STILL, THIS PRESENTED A SERIOUS PROBLEM. THE PLAN CALLED FOR ME TO POISON THE QUADROTRITICALE JUST BEFORE IT LEFT THE STATION EN ROUTE TO SHERMAN'S PLANET. WITH A STRONG SECURITY PRESENCE, THAT COULD BE DIFFICULT.
WHAT IF BARIS MANAGED TO GOAD KIRK INTO INCREASING SECURITY? CLEARLY, THE TIME TO STRIKE WAS NOW.

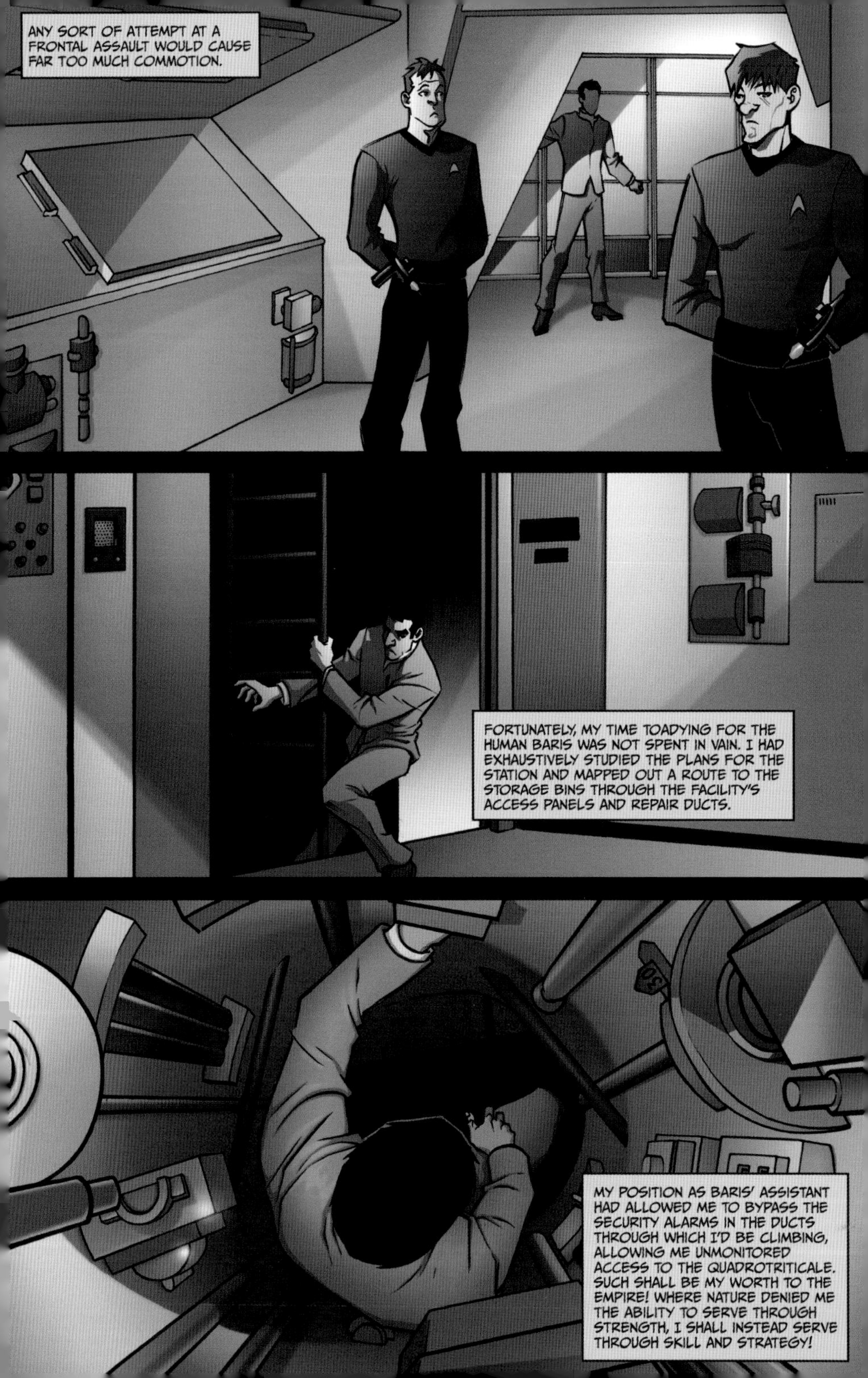
ANY SORT OF ATTEMPT AT A FRONTAL ASSAULT WOULD CAUSE FAR TOO MUCH COMMOTION.
FORTUNATELY, MY TIME TOADYING FOR THE HUMAN BARIS WAS NOT SPENT IN VAIN. I HAD EXHAUSTIVELY STUDIED THE PLANS FOR THE STATION AND MAPPED OUT A ROUTE TO THE STORAGE BINS THROUGH THE FACILITY'S ACCESS PANELS AND REPAIR DUCTS.
MY POSITION AS BARIS' ASSISTANT HAD ALLOWED ME TO BYPASS THE SECURITY ALARMS IN THE DUCTS THROUGH WHICH I'D BE CLIMBING, ALLOWING ME UNMONITORED ACCESS TO THE QUADROTRITICALE. SUCH SHALL BE MY WORTH TO THE EMPIRE! WHERE NATURE DENIED ME THE ABILITY TO SERVE THROUGH STRENGTH, I SHALL INSTEAD SERVE THROUGH SKILL AND STRATEGY!

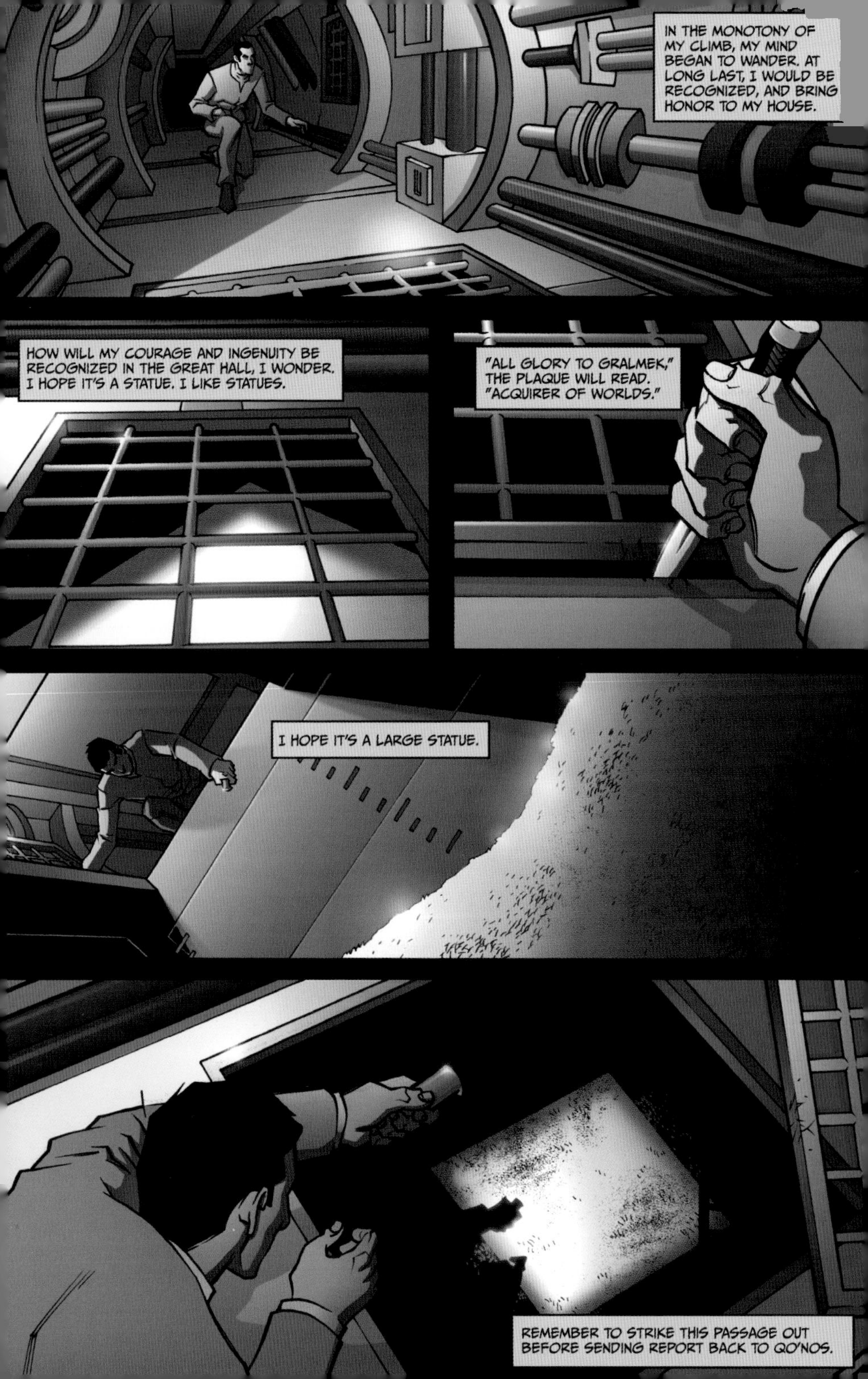
IN THE MONOTONY OF MY CLIMB, MY MIND BEGAN TO WANDER. AT LONG LAST, I WOULD BE RECOGNIZED, AND BRING HONOR TO MY HOUSE.
HOW WILL MY COURAGE AND INGENUITY BE RECOGNIZED IN THE GREAT HALL, I WONDER. I HOPE IT'S A STATUE. I LIKE STATUES.
"ALL GLORY TO GRALMEK," THE PLAQUE WILL READ. "ACQUIRER OF WORLDS."
I HOPE IT'S A LARGE STATUE.
REMEMBER TO STRIKE THIS PASSAGE OUT BEFORE SENDING REPORT BACK TO QO'NOS.

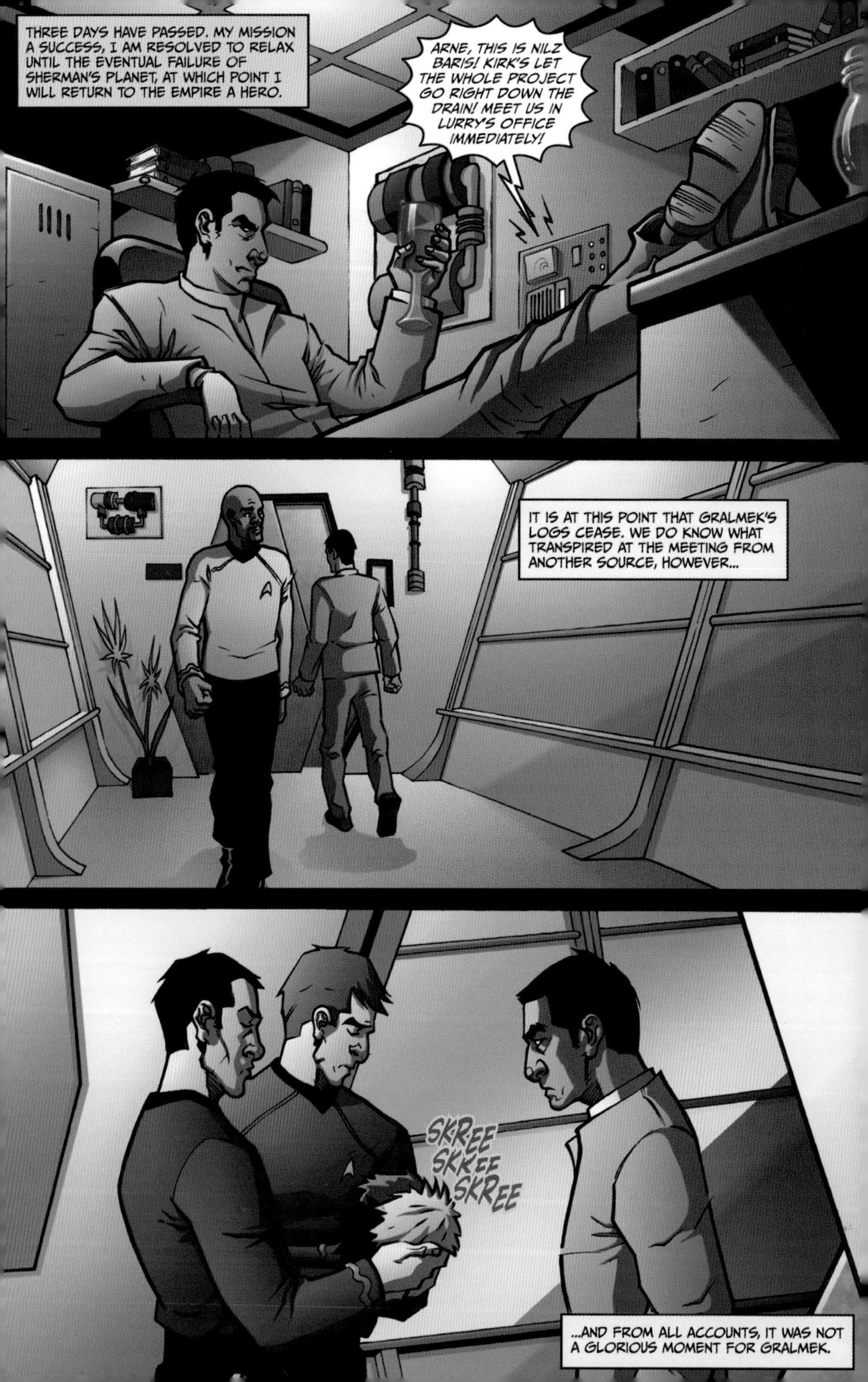
THREE DAYS HAVE PASSED. MY MISSION A SUCCESS, I AM RESOLVED TO RELAX UNTIL THE EVENTUAL FAILURE OF SHERMAN'S PLANET, AT WHICH POINT I WILL RETURN TO THE EMPIRE A HERO.
ARNE, THIS IS NILZ BARIS! KIRK'S LET THE WHOLE PROJECT GO RIGHT DOWN THE DRAIN! MEET US IN LURRY'S OFFICE IMMEDIATELY!
IT IS AT THIS POINT THAT GRALMEK'S LOGS CEASE. WE DO KNOW WHAT TRANSPIRED AT THE MEETING FROM ANOTHER SOURCE, HOWEVER...
SKREE SKREE SKREE
...AND FROM ALL ACCOUNTS, IT WAS NOT A GLORIOUS MOMENT FOR GRALMEK.

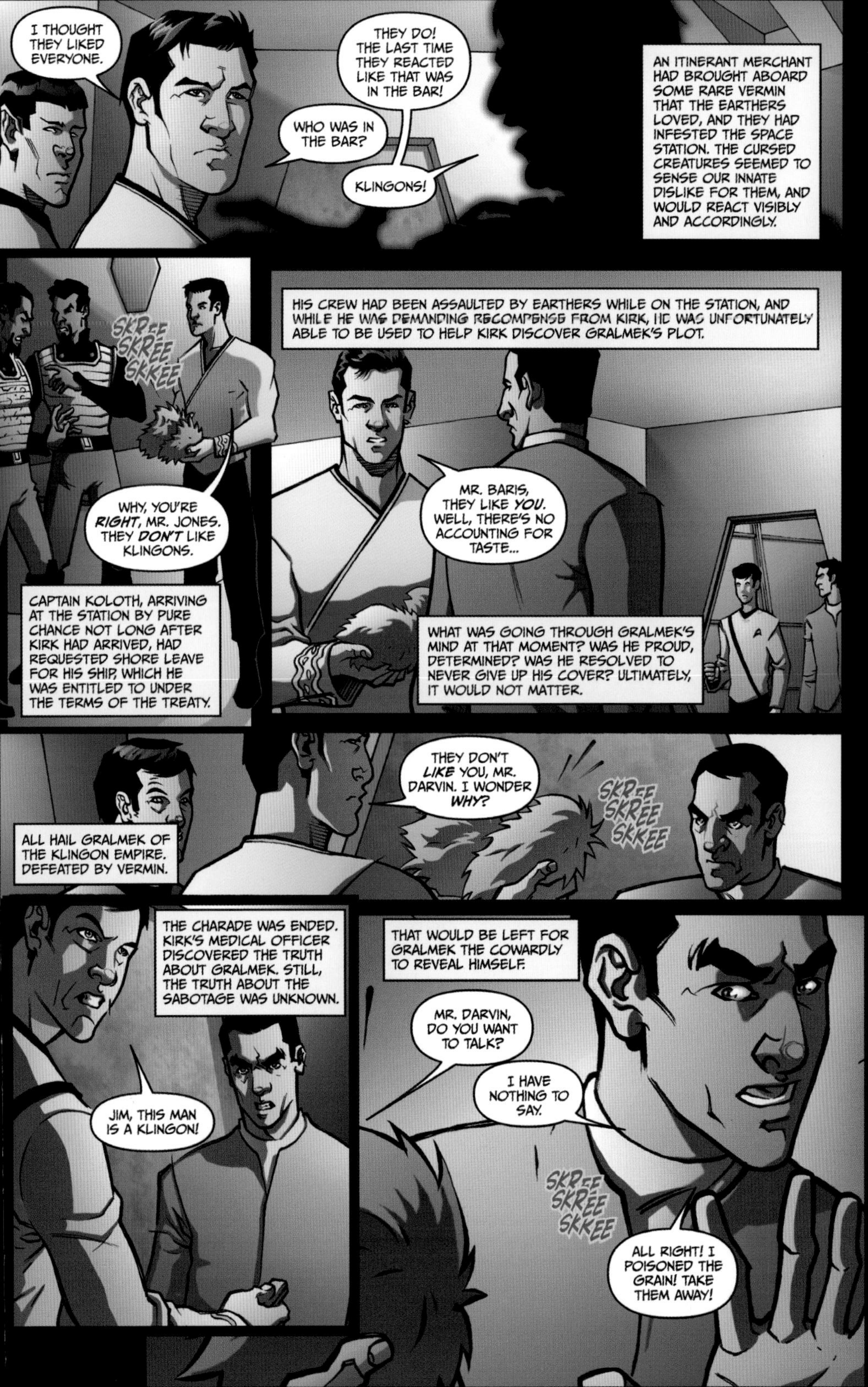
I THOUGHT THEY LIKED EVERYONE.
THEY DO! THE LAST TIME THEY REACTED LIKE THAT WAS IN THE BAR!
WHO WAS IN THE BAR?
KLINGONS!
AN ITINERANT MERCHANT HAD BROUGHT ABOARD SOME RARE VERMIN THAT THE EARTHERS LOVED, AND THEY HAD INFESTED THE SPACE STATION. THE CURSED CREATURES SEEMED TO SENSE OUR INNATE DISLIKE FOR THEM, AND WOULD REACT VISIBLY AND ACCORDINGLY.
SKREE SKREE SKKEE
WHY, YOU'RE RIGHT, MR. JONES. THEY DON'T LIKE KLINGONS.
CAPTAIN KOLOTH, ARRIVING AT THE STATION BY PURE CHANCE NOT LONG AFTER KIRK HAD ARRIVED, HAD REQUESTED SHORE LEAVE FOR HIS SHIP, WHICH HE WAS ENTITLED TO UNDER THE TERMS OF THE TREATY.
HIS CREW HAD BEEN ASSAULTED BY EARTHERS WHILE ON THE STATION, AND WHILE HE WAS DEMANDING RECOMPENSE FROM KIRK, HE WAS UNFORTUNATELY ABLE TO BE USED TO HELP KIRK DISCOVER GRALMEK'S PLOT.
MR. BARIS, THEY LIKE YOU. WELL, THERE'S NO ACCOUNTING FOR TASTE...
WHAT WAS GOING THROUGH GRALMEK'S MIND AT THAT MOMENT? WAS HE PROUD, DETERMINED? WAS HE RESOLVED TO NEVER GIVE UP HIS COVER? ULTIMATELY, IT WOULD NOT MATTER.
ALL HAIL GRALMEK OF THE KLINGON EMPIRE. DEFEATED BY VERMIN.
THEY DON'T LIKE YOU, MR. DARVIN. I WONDER WHY?
SKREE SKREE SKKEE
THE CHARADE WAS ENDED. KIRK'S MEDICAL OFFICER DISCOVERED THE TRUTH ABOUT GRALMEK. STILL, THE TRUTH ABOUT THE SABOTAGE WAS UNKNOWN.
JIM, THIS MAN IS A KLINGON!
THAT WOULD BE LEFT FOR GRALMEK THE COWARDLY TO REVEAL HIMSELF.
MR. DARVIN, DO YOU WANT TO TALK?
I HAVE NOTHING TO SAY.
SKREE SKREE SKKEE
ALL RIGHT! I POISONED THE GRAIN! TAKE THEM AWAY!

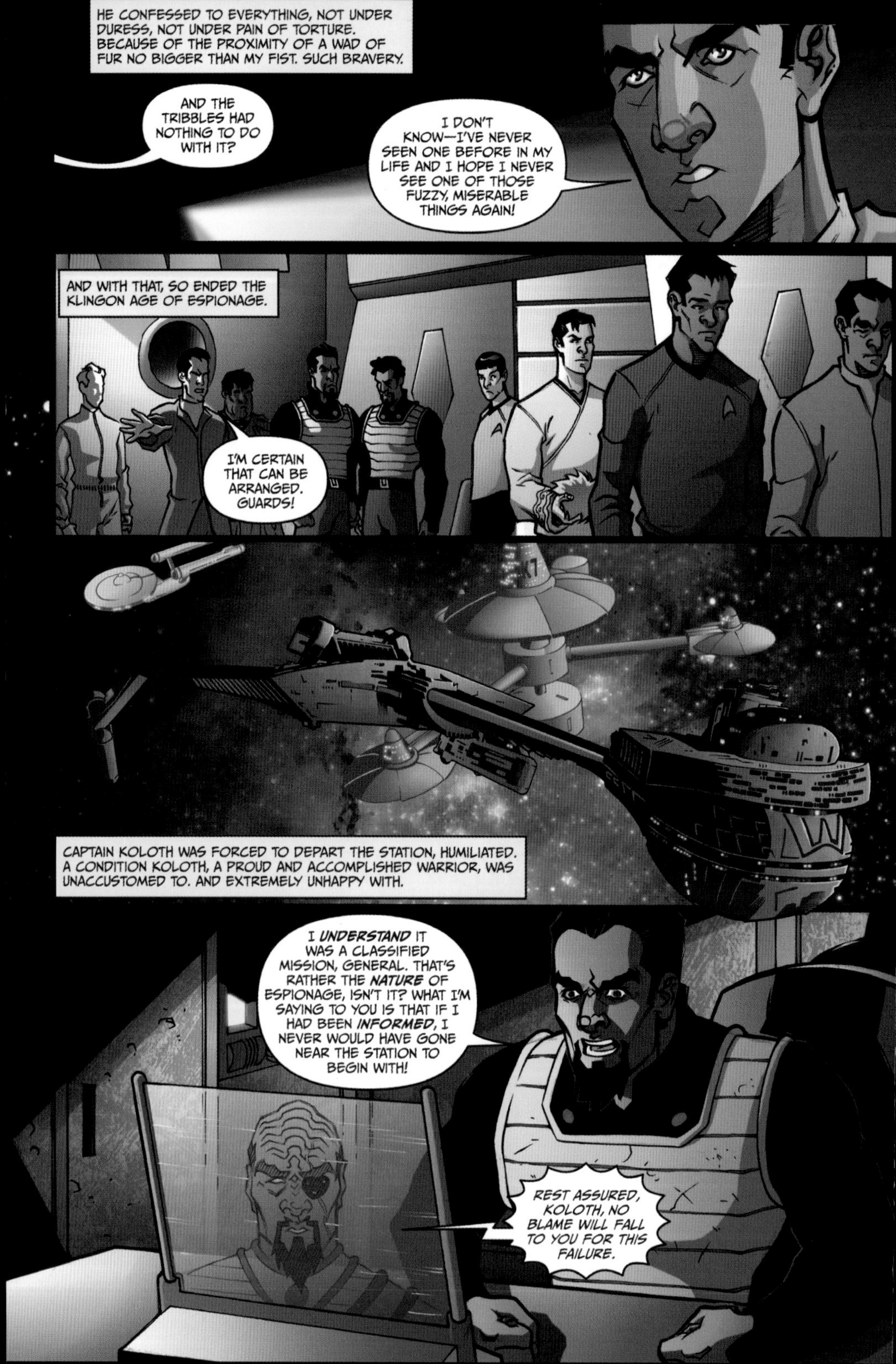
HE CONFESSED TO EVERYTHING, NOT UNDER DURESS, NOT UNDER PAIN OF TORTURE. BECAUSE OF THE PROXIMITY OF A WAD OF FUR NO BIGGER THAN MY FIST. SUCH BRAVERY.
AND THE TRIBBLES HAD NOTHING TO DO WITH IT?
I DON'T KNOW—I'VE NEVER SEEN ONE BEFORE IN MY LIFE AND I HOPE I NEVER SEE ONE OF THOSE FUZZY, MISERABLE THINGS AGAIN!
AND WITH THAT, SO ENDED THE KLINGON AGE OF ESPIONAGE.
I'M CERTAIN THAT CAN BE ARRANGED. GUARDS!
CAPTAIN KOLOTH WAS FORCED TO DEPART THE STATION, HUMILIATED. A CONDITION KOLOTH, A PROUD AND ACCOMPLISHED WARRIOR, WAS UNACCUSTOMED TO. AND EXTREMELY UNHAPPY WITH.
I UNDERSTAND IT WAS A CLASSIFIED MISSION, GENERAL. THAT'S RATHER THE NATURE OF ESPIONAGE, ISN'T IT? WHAT I'M SAYING TO YOU IS THAT IF I HAD BEEN INFORMED, I NEVER WOULD HAVE GONE NEAR THE STATION TO BEGIN WITH!
REST ASSURED, KOLOTH, NO BLAME WILL FALL TO YOU FOR THIS FAILURE.

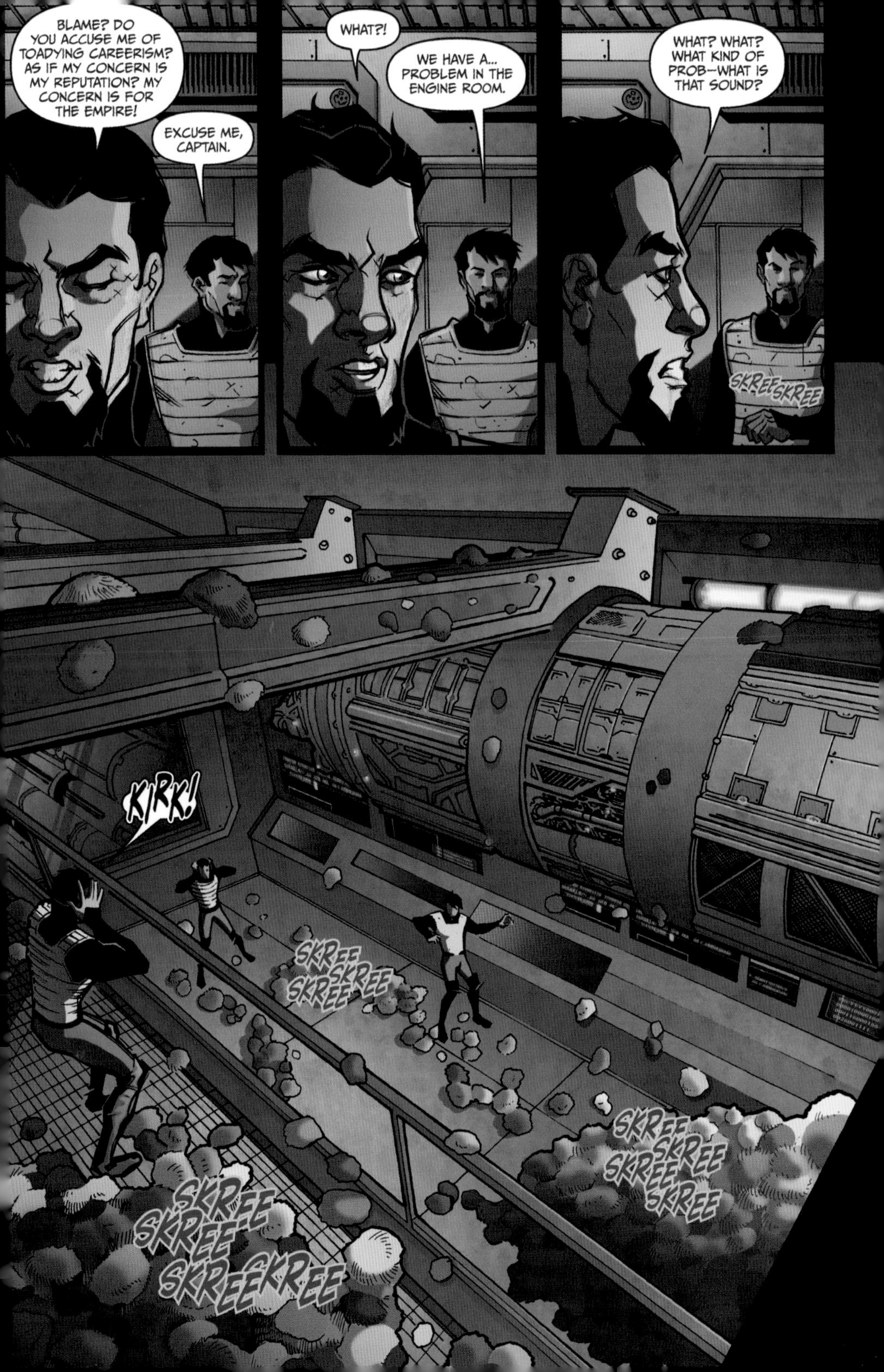
BLAME? DO YOU ACCUSE ME OF TOADYING CAREERISM? AS IF MY CONCERN IS MY REPUTATION? MY CONCERN IS FOR THE EMPIRE!
EXCUSE ME, CAPTAIN.
WHAT?!
WE HAVE A... PROBLEM IN THE ENGINE ROOM.
WHAT? WHAT? WHAT KIND OF PROB—WHAT IS THAT SOUND?
SKREESKREE
KIRK!
SKREE SKREE SKREE
SKREE SKREE SKREE SKREE
SKREE SKREE SKREESKREE

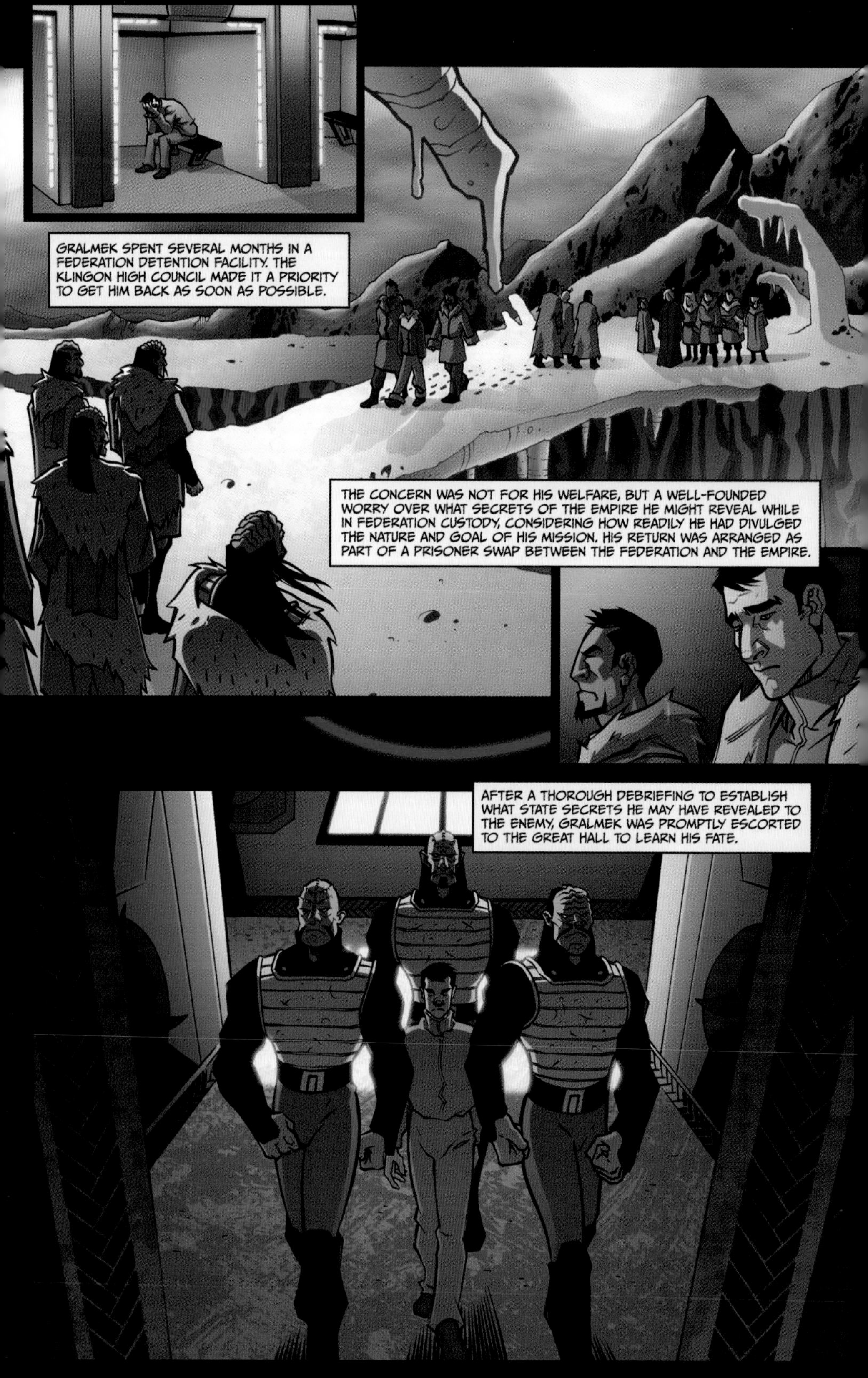

GRALMEK SPENT SEVERAL MONTHS IN A FEDERATION DETENTION FACILITY. THE KLINGON HIGH COUNCIL MADE IT A PRIORITY TO GET HIM BACK AS SOON AS POSSIBLE.
THE CONCERN WAS NOT FOR HIS WELFARE, BUT A WELL-FOUNDED WORRY OVER WHAT SECRETS OF THE EMPIRE HE MIGHT REVEAL WHILE IN FEDERATION CUSTODY, CONSIDERING HOW READILY HE HAD DIVULGED THE NATURE AND GOAL OF HIS MISSION. HIS RETURN WAS ARRANGED AS PART OF A PRISONER SWAP BETWEEN THE FEDERATION AND THE EMPIRE.
AFTER A THOROUGH DEBRIEFING TO ESTABLISH WHAT STATE SECRETS HE MAY HAVE REVEALED TO THE ENEMY, GRALMEK WAS PROMPTLY ESCORTED TO THE GREAT HALL TO LEARN HIS FATE.

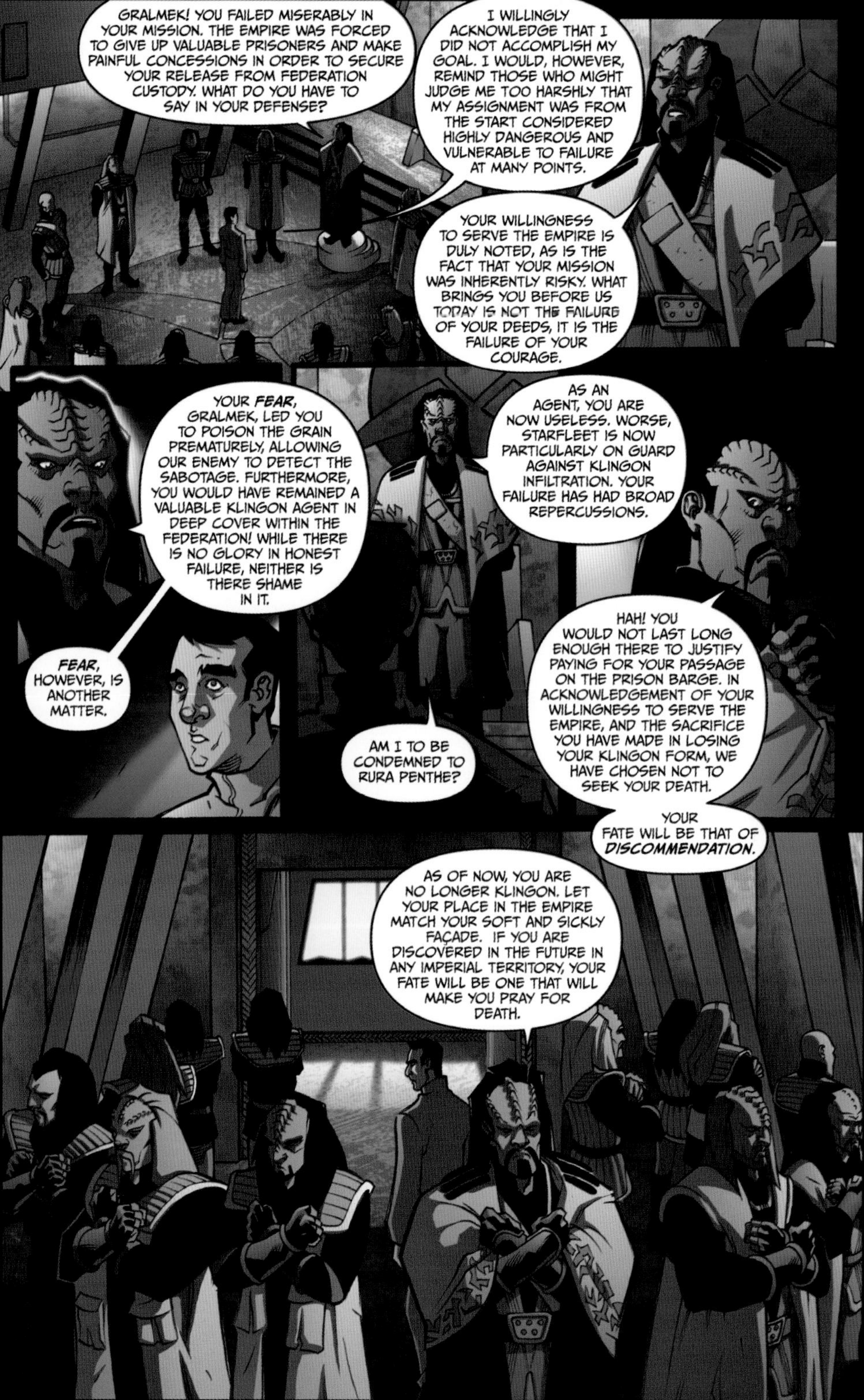
GRALMEK! YOU FAILED MISERABLY IN YOUR MISSION. THE EMPIRE WAS FORCED TO GIVE UP VALUABLE PRISONERS AND MAKE PAINFUL CONCESSIONS IN ORDER TO SECURE YOUR RELEASE FROM FEDERATION CUSTODY. WHAT DO YOU HAVE TO SAY IN YOUR DEFENSE?
I WILLINGLY ACKNOWLEDGE THAT I DID NOT ACCOMPLISH MY GOAL. I WOULD, HOWEVER, REMIND THOSE WHO MIGHT JUDGE ME TOO HARSHLY THAT MY ASSIGNMENT WAS FROM THE START CONSIDERED HIGHLY DANGEROUS AND VULNERABLE TO FAILURE AT MANY POINTS.
YOUR WILLINGNESS TO SERVE THE EMPIRE IS DULY NOTED, AS IS THE FACT THAT YOUR MISSION WAS INHERENTLY RISKY. WHAT BRINGS YOU BEFORE US TODAY IS NOT THE FAILURE OF YOUR DEEDS, IT IS THE FAILURE OF YOUR COURAGE.
YOUR *FEAR*, GRALMEK, LED YOU TO POISON THE GRAIN PREMATURELY, ALLOWING OUR ENEMY TO DETECT THE SABOTAGE. FURTHERMORE, YOU WOULD HAVE REMAINED A VALUABLE KLINGON AGENT IN DEEP COVER WITHIN THE FEDERATION! WHILE THERE IS NO GLORY IN HONEST FAILURE, NEITHER IS THERE SHAME IN IT.
FEAR, HOWEVER, IS ANOTHER MATTER.
AS AN AGENT, YOU ARE NOW USELESS. WORSE, STARFLEET IS NOW PARTICULARLY ON GUARD AGAINST KLINGON INFILTRATION. YOUR FAILURE HAS HAD BROAD REPERCUSSIONS.
AM I TO BE CONDEMNED TO RURA PENTHE?
HAH! YOU WOULD NOT LAST LONG ENOUGH THERE TO JUSTIFY PAYING FOR YOUR PASSAGE ON THE PRISON BARGE. IN ACKNOWLEDGEMENT OF YOUR WILLINGNESS TO SERVE THE EMPIRE, AND THE SACRIFICE YOU HAVE MADE IN LOSING YOUR KLINGON FORM, WE HAVE CHOSEN NOT TO SEEK YOUR DEATH.
YOUR FATE WILL BE THAT OF ***DISCOMMENDATION.***
AS OF NOW, YOU ARE NO LONGER KLINGON. LET YOUR PLACE IN THE EMPIRE MATCH YOUR SOFT AND SICKLY FAÇADE. IF YOU ARE DISCOVERED IN THE FUTURE IN ANY IMPERIAL TERRITORY, YOUR FATE WILL BE ONE THAT WILL MAKE YOU PRAY FOR DEATH.

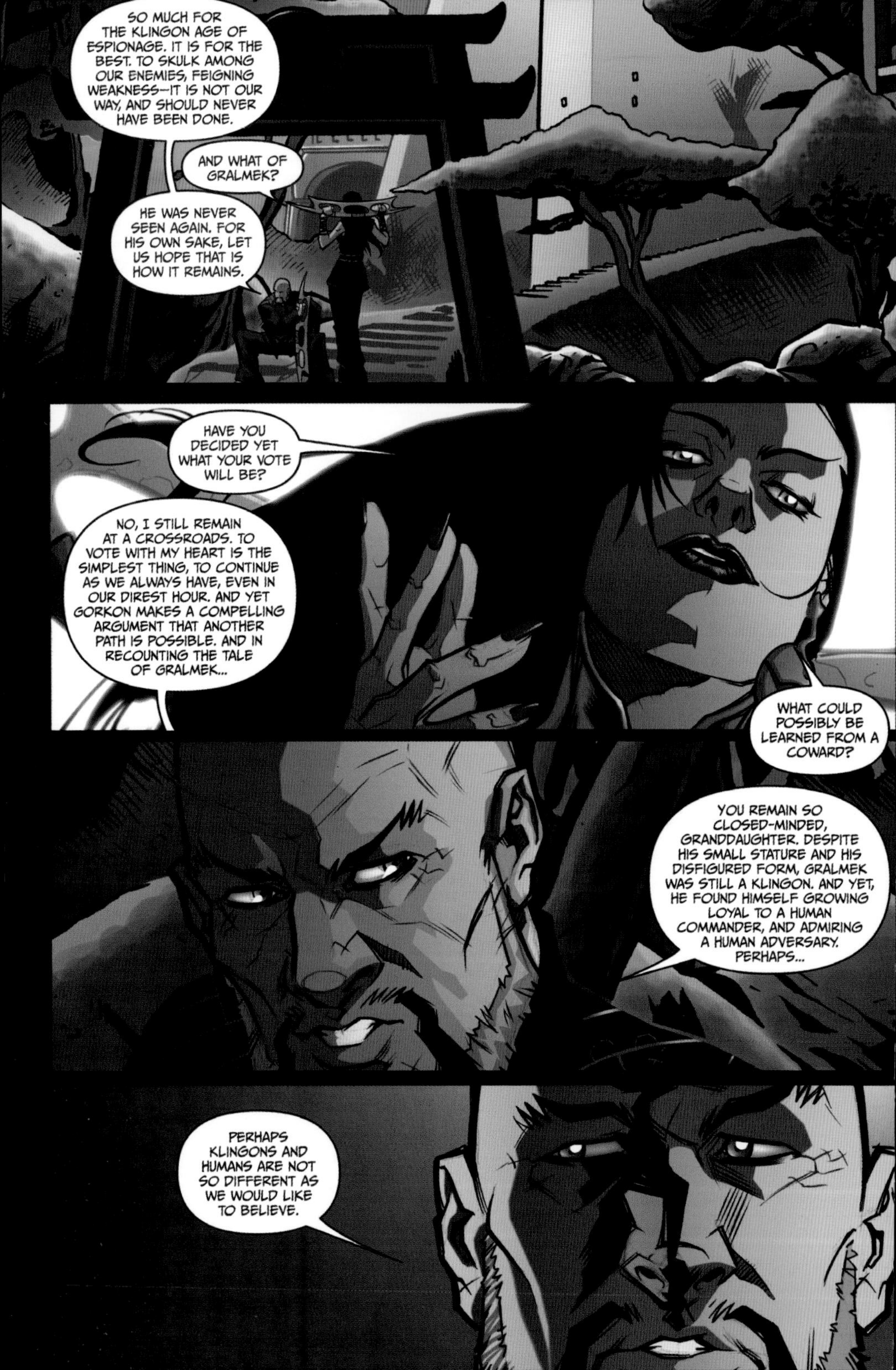
SO MUCH FOR THE KLINGON AGE OF ESPIONAGE. IT IS FOR THE BEST. TO SKULK AMONG OUR ENEMIES, FEIGNING WEAKNESS--IT IS NOT OUR WAY, AND SHOULD NEVER HAVE BEEN DONE.
AND WHAT OF GRALMEK?
HE WAS NEVER SEEN AGAIN. FOR HIS OWN SAKE, LET US HOPE THAT IS HOW IT REMAINS.
HAVE YOU DECIDED YET WHAT YOUR VOTE WILL BE?
NO, I STILL REMAIN AT A CROSSROADS. TO VOTE WITH MY HEART IS THE SIMPLEST THING, TO CONTINUE AS WE ALWAYS HAVE, EVEN IN OUR DIREST HOUR. AND YET GORKON MAKES A COMPELLING ARGUMENT THAT ANOTHER PATH IS POSSIBLE. AND IN RECOUNTING THE TALE OF GRALMEK...
WHAT COULD POSSIBLY BE LEARNED FROM A COWARD?
YOU REMAIN SO CLOSED-MINDED, GRANDDAUGHTER. DESPITE HIS SMALL STATURE AND HIS DISFIGURED FORM, GRALMEK WAS STILL A KLINGON. AND YET, HE FOUND HIMSELF GROWING LOYAL TO A HUMAN COMMANDER, AND ADMIRING A HUMAN ADVERSARY. PERHAPS...
PERHAPS KLINGONS AND HUMANS ARE NOT SO DIFFERENT AS WE WOULD LIKE TO BELIEVE.

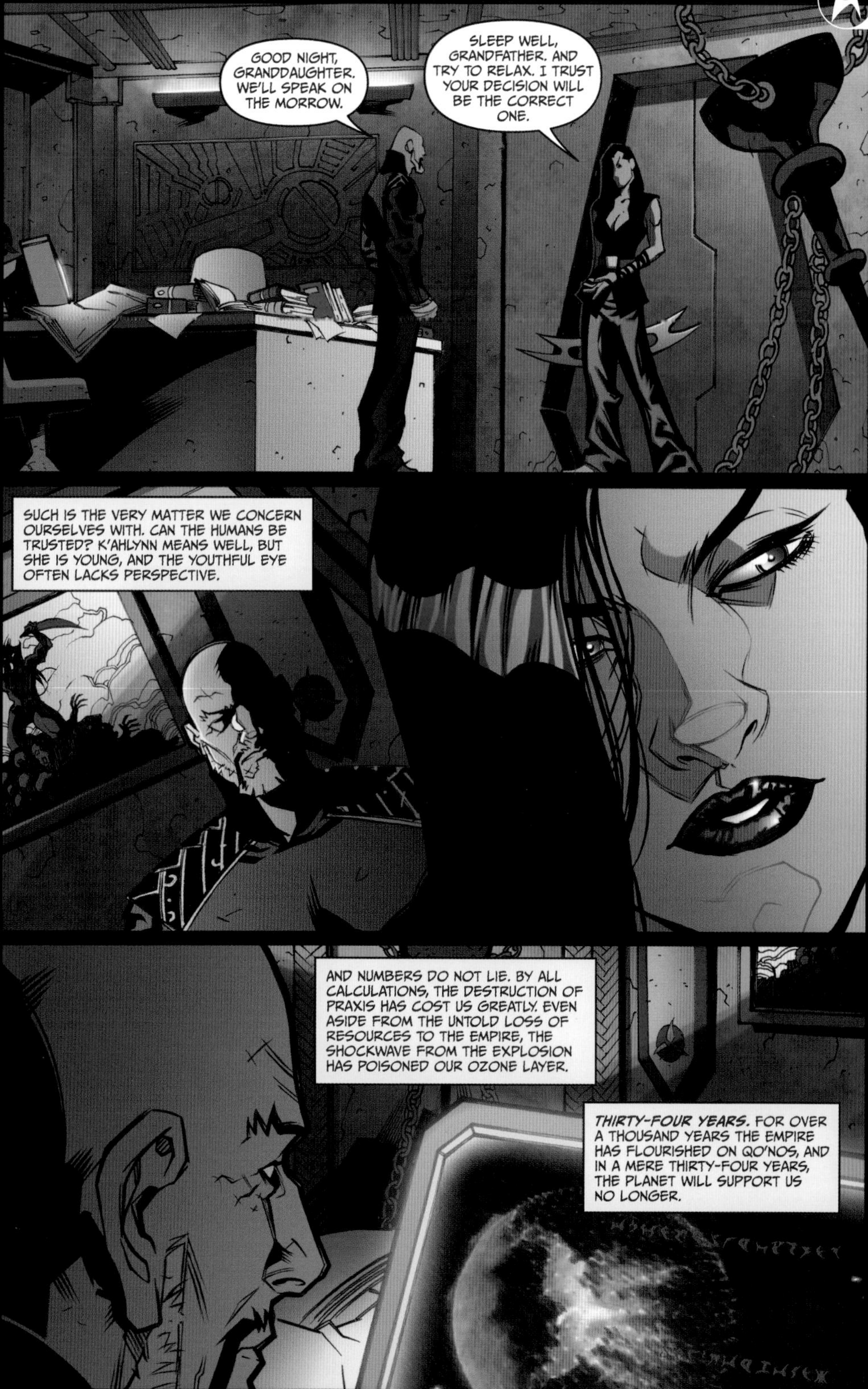
GOOD NIGHT, GRANDDAUGHTER. WE'LL SPEAK ON THE MORROW.
SLEEP WELL, GRANDFATHER. AND TRY TO RELAX. I TRUST YOUR DECISION WILL BE THE CORRECT ONE.
SUCH IS THE VERY MATTER WE CONCERN OURSELVES WITH. CAN THE HUMANS BE TRUSTED? K'AHLYNN MEANS WELL, BUT SHE IS YOUNG, AND THE YOUTHFUL EYE OFTEN LACKS PERSPECTIVE.
AND NUMBERS DO NOT LIE. BY ALL CALCULATIONS, THE DESTRUCTION OF PRAXIS HAS COST US GREATLY. EVEN ASIDE FROM THE UNTOLD LOSS OF RESOURCES TO THE EMPIRE, THE SHOCKWAVE FROM THE EXPLOSION HAS POISONED OUR OZONE LAYER.
THIRTY-FOUR YEARS. FOR OVER A THOUSAND YEARS THE EMPIRE HAS FLOURISHED ON QO'NOS, AND IN A MERE THIRTY-FOUR YEARS, THE PLANET WILL SUPPORT US NO LONGER.

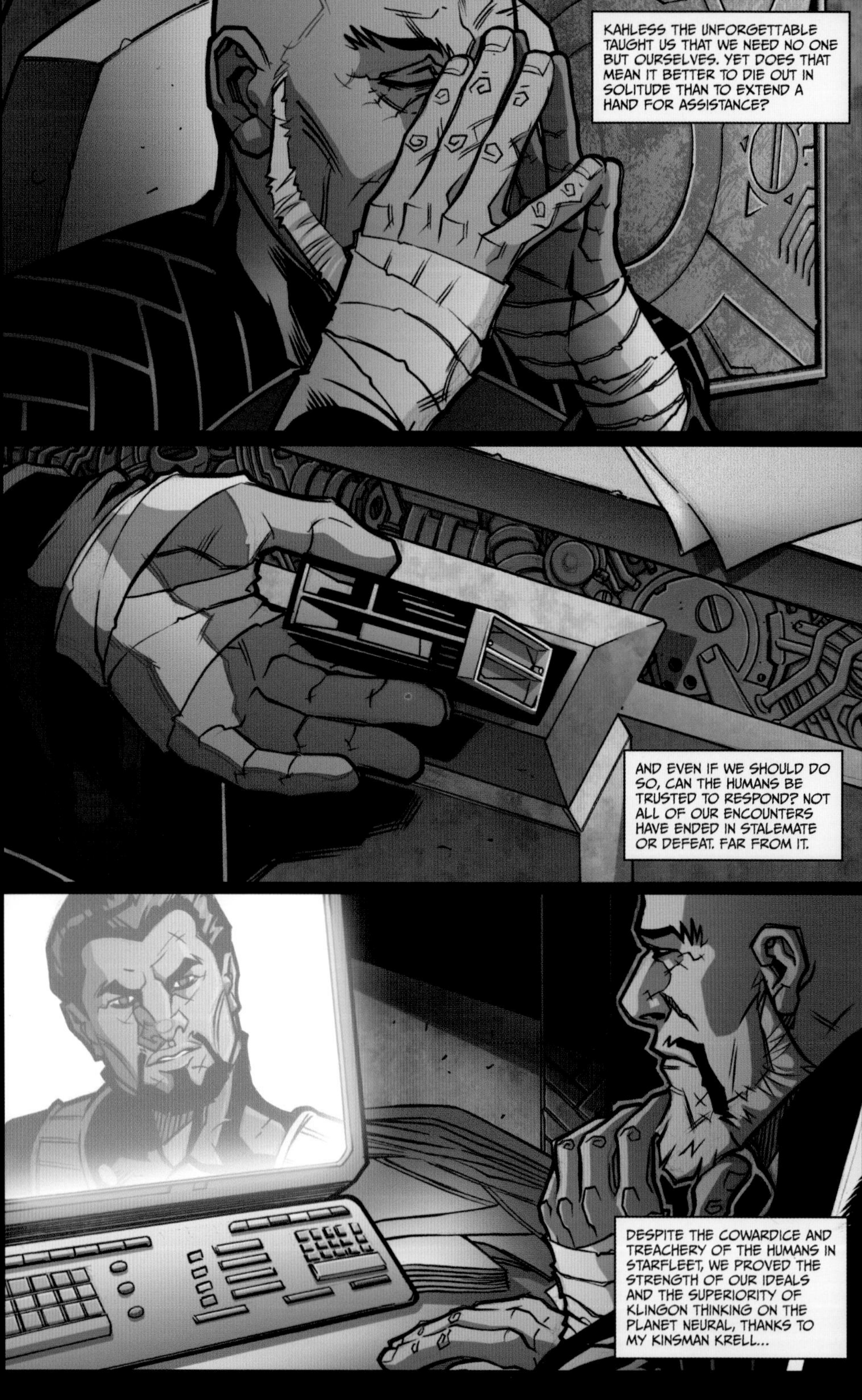
KAHLESS THE UNFORGETTABLE TAUGHT US THAT WE NEED NO ONE BUT OURSELVES. YET DOES THAT MEAN IT BETTER TO DIE OUT IN SOLITUDE THAN TO EXTEND A HAND FOR ASSISTANCE?
AND EVEN IF WE SHOULD DO SO, CAN THE HUMANS BE TRUSTED TO RESPOND? NOT ALL OF OUR ENCOUNTERS HAVE ENDED IN STALEMATE OR DEFEAT. FAR FROM IT.
DESPITE THE COWARDICE AND TREACHERY OF THE HUMANS IN STARFLEET, WE PROVED THE STRENGTH OF OUR IDEALS AND THE SUPERIORITY OF KLINGON THINKING ON THE PLANET NEURAL, THANKS TO MY KINSMAN KRELL...

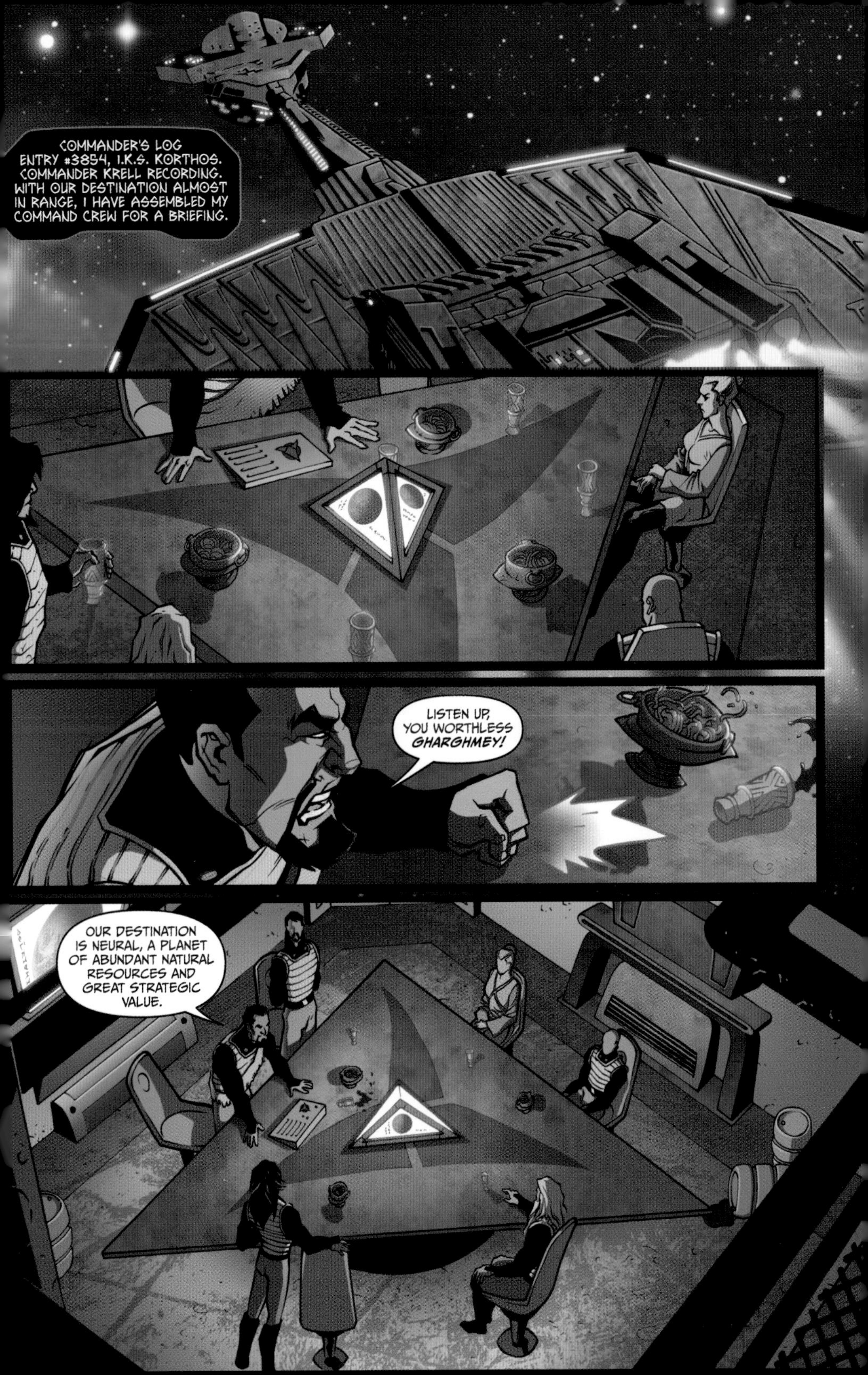
COMMANDER'S LOG ENTRY #3854, I.K.S. KORTHOS. COMMANDER KRELL RECORDING. WITH OUR DESTINATION ALMOST IN RANGE, I HAVE ASSEMBLED MY COMMAND CREW FOR A BRIEFING.
LISTEN UP, YOU WORTHLESS *GHARGHMEY!*
OUR DESTINATION IS NEURAL, A PLANET OF ABUNDANT NATURAL RESOURCES AND GREAT STRATEGIC VALUE.

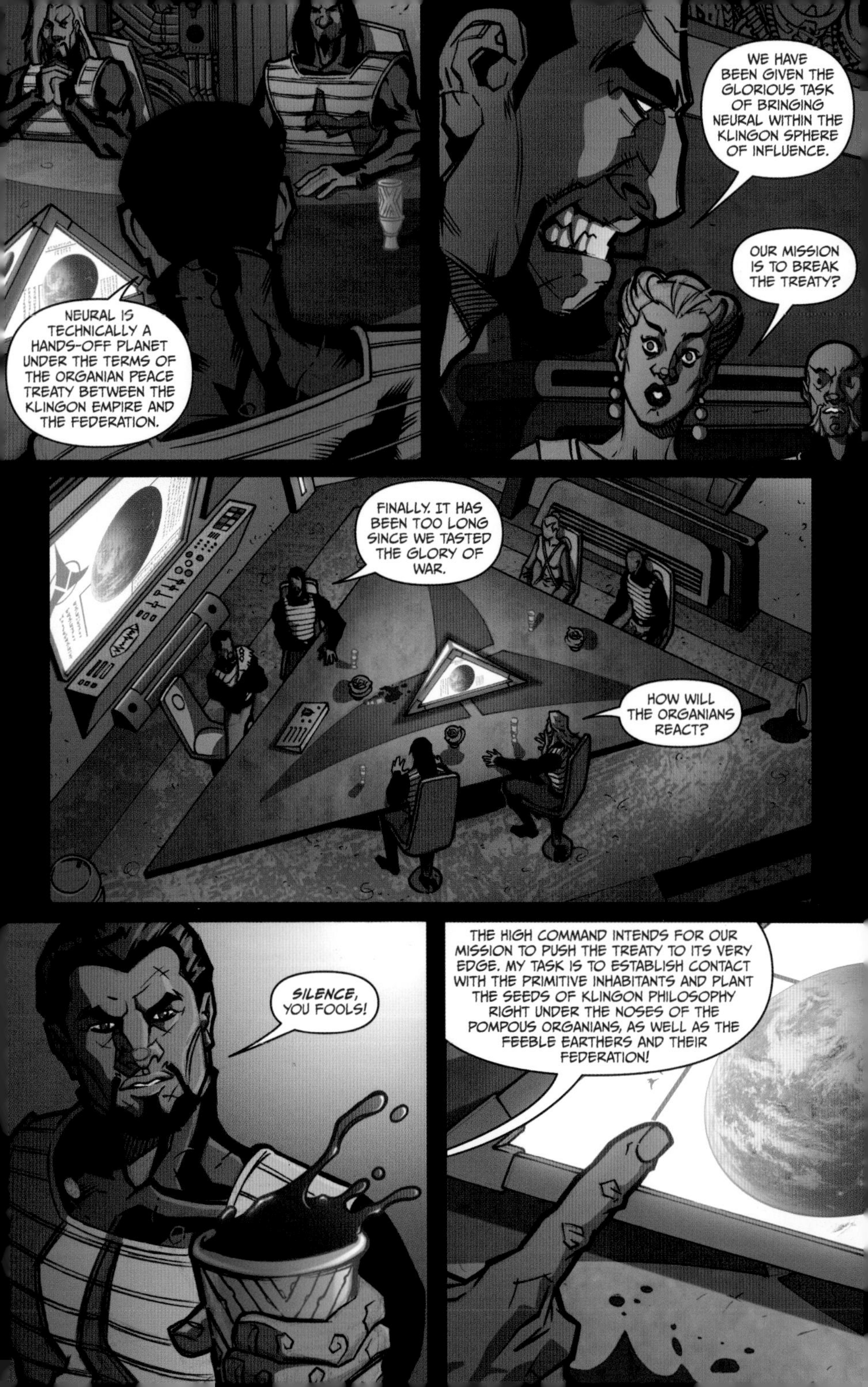
NEURAL IS TECHNICALLY A HANDS-OFF PLANET UNDER THE TERMS OF THE ORGANIAN PEACE TREATY BETWEEN THE KLINGON EMPIRE AND THE FEDERATION.
WE HAVE BEEN GIVEN THE GLORIOUS TASK OF BRINGING NEURAL WITHIN THE KLINGON SPHERE OF INFLUENCE.
OUR MISSION IS TO BREAK THE TREATY?
FINALLY. IT HAS BEEN TOO LONG SINCE WE TASTED THE GLORY OF WAR.
HOW WILL THE ORGANIANS REACT?
SILENCE, YOU FOOLS!
THE HIGH COMMAND INTENDS FOR OUR MISSION TO PUSH THE TREATY TO ITS VERY EDGE. MY TASK IS TO ESTABLISH CONTACT WITH THE PRIMITIVE INHABITANTS AND PLANT THE SEEDS OF KLINGON PHILOSOPHY RIGHT UNDER THE NOSES OF THE POMPOUS ORGANIANS, AS WELL AS THE FEEBLE EARTHERS AND THEIR FEDERATION!

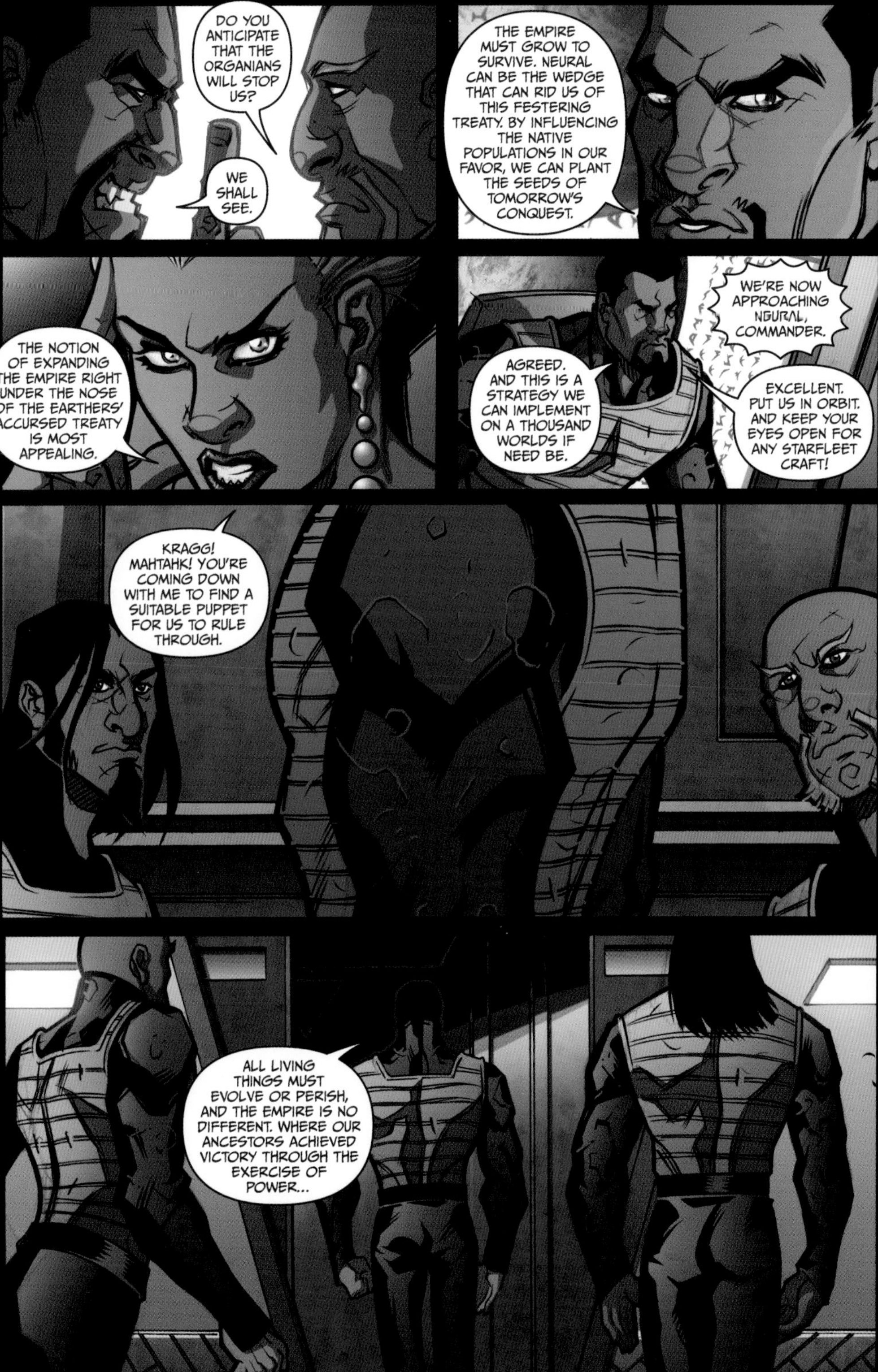
DO YOU ANTICIPATE THAT THE ORGANIANS WILL STOP US?
WE SHALL SEE.
THE EMPIRE MUST GROW TO SURVIVE. NEURAL CAN BE THE WEDGE THAT CAN RID US OF THIS FESTERING TREATY. BY INFLUENCING THE NATIVE POPULATIONS IN OUR FAVOR, WE CAN PLANT THE SEEDS OF TOMORROW'S CONQUEST.
THE NOTION OF EXPANDING THE EMPIRE RIGHT UNDER THE NOSE OF THE EARTHERS' ACCURSED TREATY IS MOST APPEALING.
AGREED. AND THIS IS A STRATEGY WE CAN IMPLEMENT ON A THOUSAND WORLDS IF NEED BE.
WE'RE NOW APPROACHING NEURAL, COMMANDER.
EXCELLENT. PUT US IN ORBIT. AND KEEP YOUR EYES OPEN FOR ANY STARFLEET CRAFT!
KRAGG! MAHTAHK! YOU'RE COMING DOWN WITH ME TO FIND A SUITABLE PUPPET FOR US TO RULE THROUGH.
ALL LIVING THINGS MUST EVOLVE OR PERISH, AND THE EMPIRE IS NO DIFFERENT. WHERE OUR ANCESTORS ACHIEVED VICTORY THROUGH THE EXERCISE OF POWER...

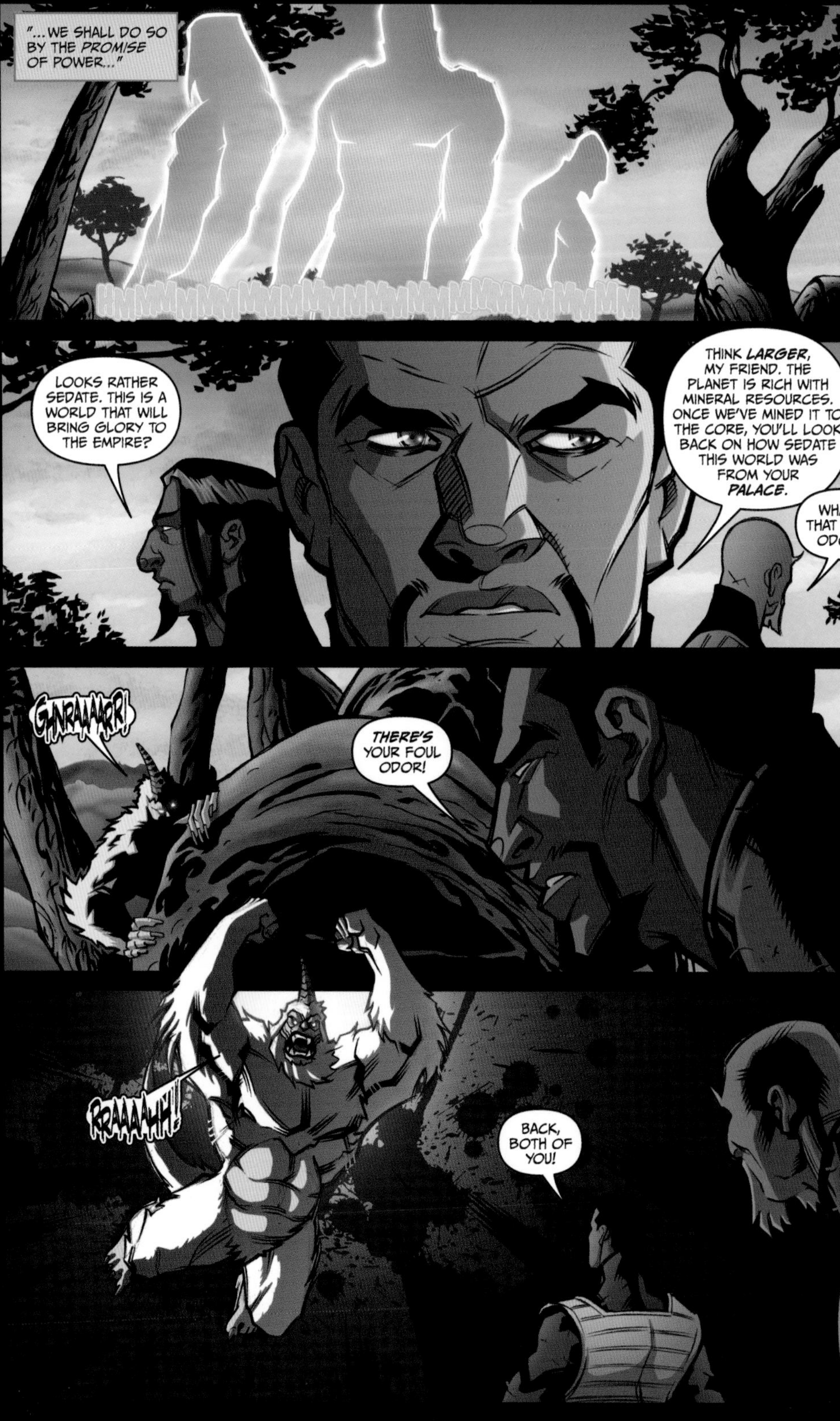
"...WE SHALL DO SO BY THE PROMISE OF POWER..."
HMMMMMMMMMMMMMMMMMMMMMMMMMMMMM
LOOKS RATHER SEDATE. THIS IS A WORLD THAT WILL BRING GLORY TO THE EMPIRE?
THINK LARGER, MY FRIEND. THE PLANET IS RICH WITH MINERAL RESOURCES. ONCE WE'VE MINED IT TO THE CORE, YOU'LL LOOK BACK ON HOW SEDATE THIS WORLD WAS FROM YOUR PALACE.
WHAT'S THAT FOUL ODOR?
GHNRAAAARR!
THERE'S YOUR FOUL ODOR!
RRAAAAHH!
BACK, BOTH OF YOU!

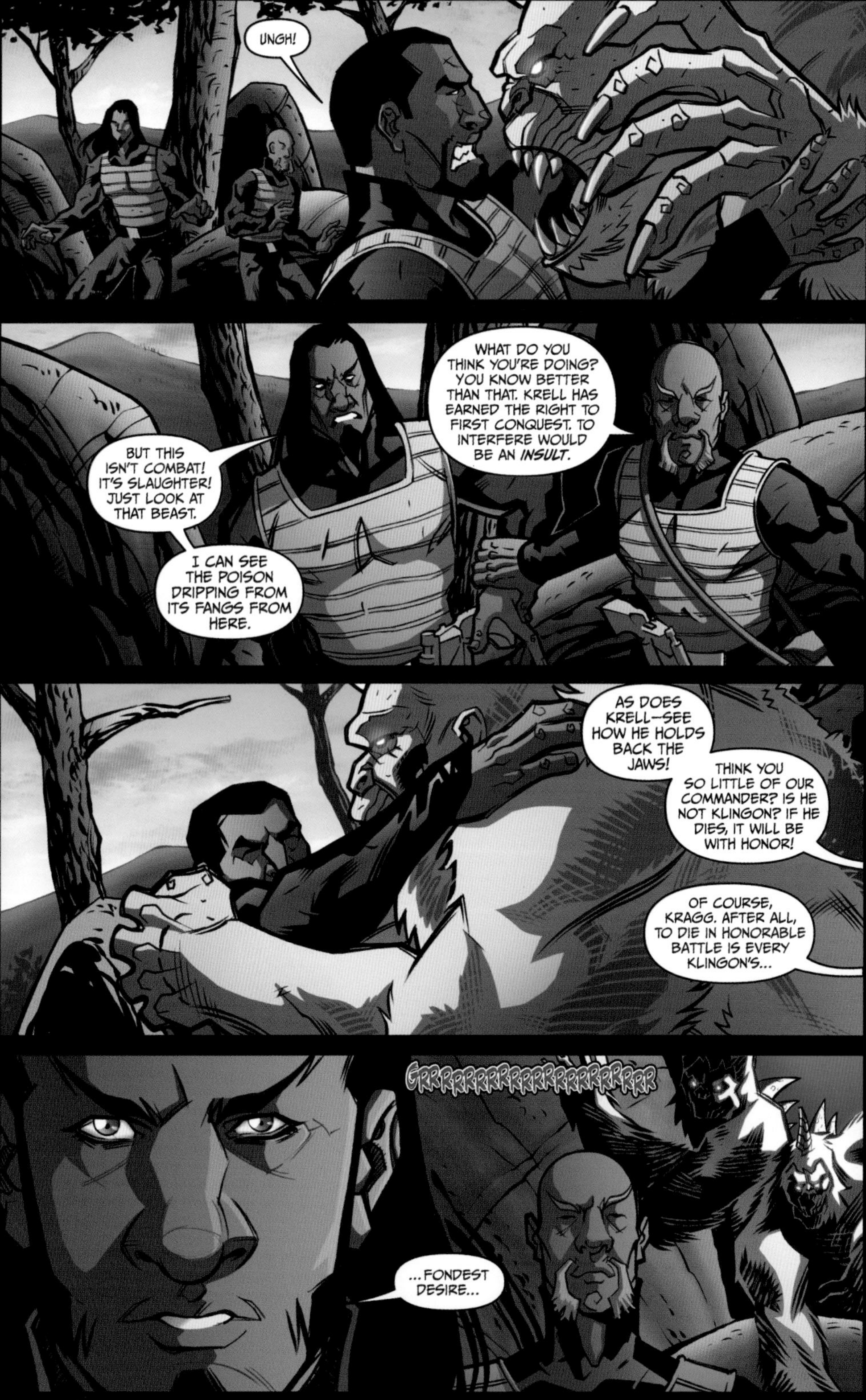
UNGH!
BUT THIS ISN'T COMBAT! IT'S SLAUGHTER! JUST LOOK AT THAT BEAST.
I CAN SEE THE POISON DRIPPING FROM ITS FANGS FROM HERE.
WHAT DO YOU THINK YOU'RE DOING? YOU KNOW BETTER THAN THAT. KRELL HAS EARNED THE RIGHT TO FIRST CONQUEST. TO INTERFERE WOULD BE AN *INSULT*.
AS DOES KRELL—SEE HOW HE HOLDS BACK THE JAWS!
THINK YOU SO LITTLE OF OUR COMMANDER? IS HE NOT KLINGON? IF HE DIES, IT WILL BE WITH HONOR!
OF COURSE, KRAGG. AFTER ALL, TO DIE IN HONORABLE BATTLE IS EVERY KLINGON'S...
GRRRRRRRRRRRRRRRRRRRR
...FONDEST DESIRE...

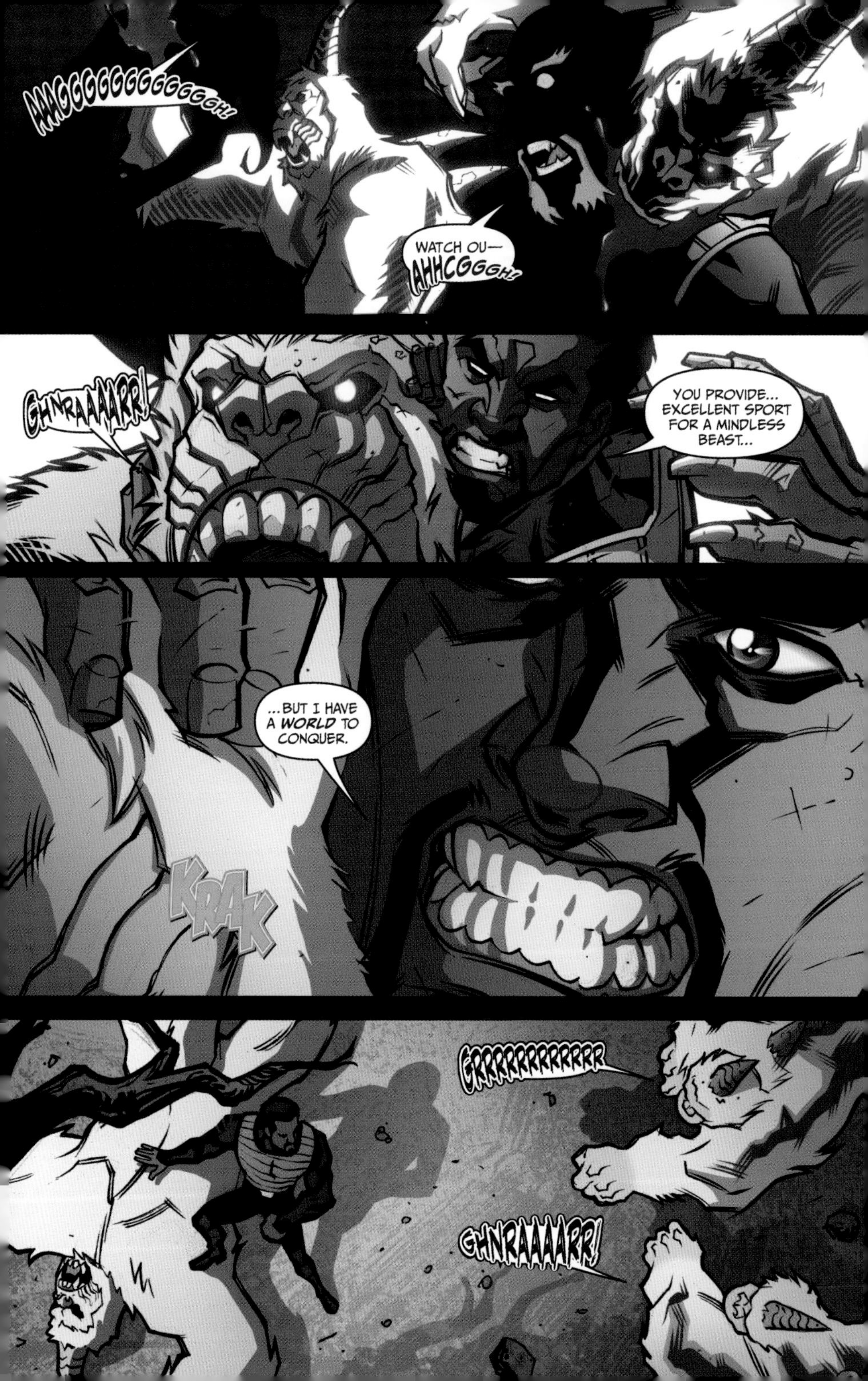
AAAGGGGGGGGGGGGH!
WATCH OU— AHHCGGGH!
GHNRAAAARR!
YOU PROVIDE... EXCELLENT SPORT FOR A MINDLESS BEAST...
...BUT I HAVE A WORLD TO CONQUER.
KRAK
GRRRRRRRRRRR
GHNRAAAARR!

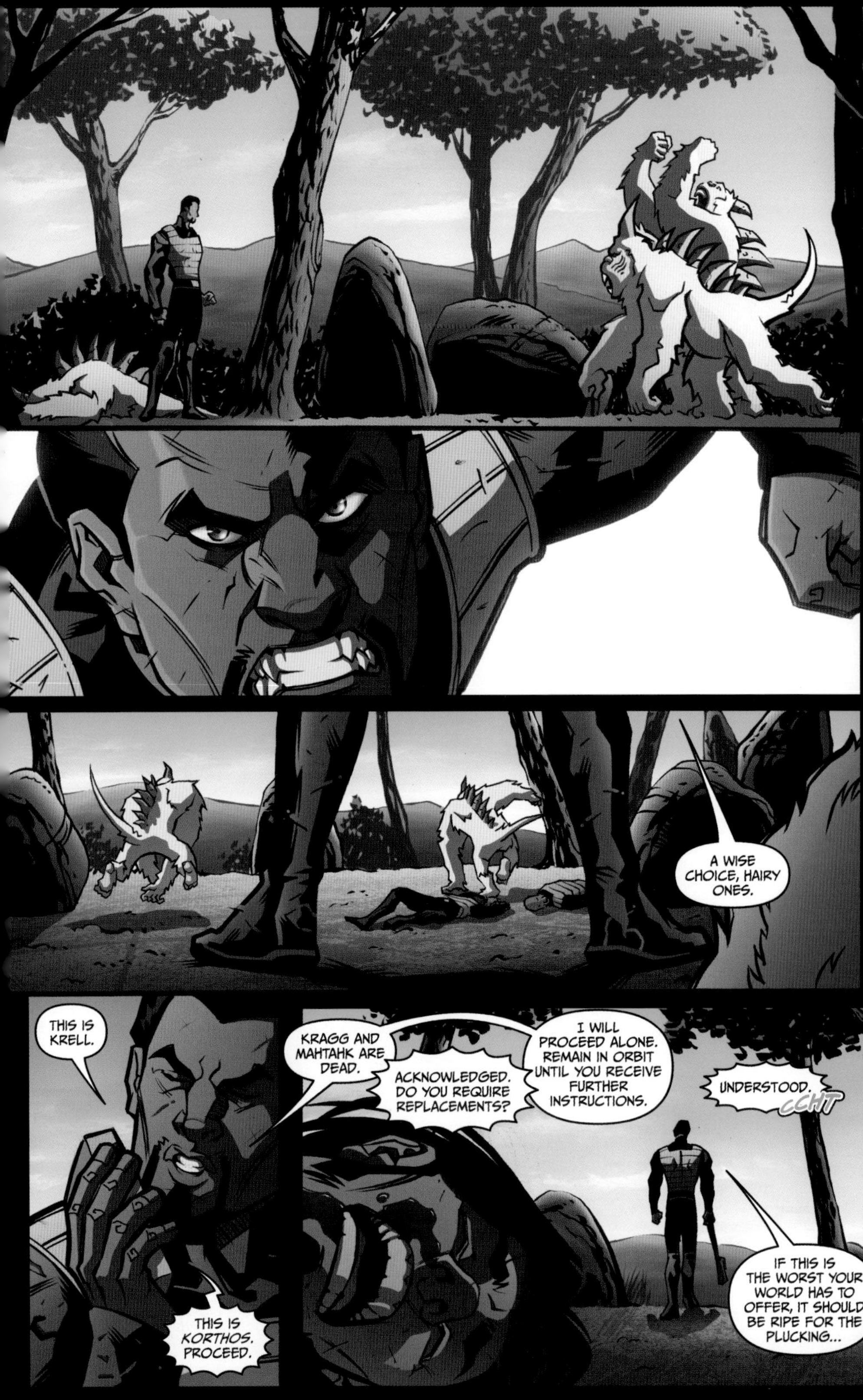

A WISE CHOICE, HAIRY ONES.
THIS IS KRELL.
KRAGG AND MAHTAHK ARE DEAD.
ACKNOWLEDGED. DO YOU REQUIRE REPLACEMENTS?
I WILL PROCEED ALONE. REMAIN IN ORBIT UNTIL YOU RECEIVE FURTHER INSTRUCTIONS.
UNDERSTOOD.
CCHT
THIS IS KORTHOS. PROCEED.
IF THIS IS THE WORST YOUR WORLD HAS TO OFFER, IT SHOULD BE RIPE FOR THE PLUCKING...

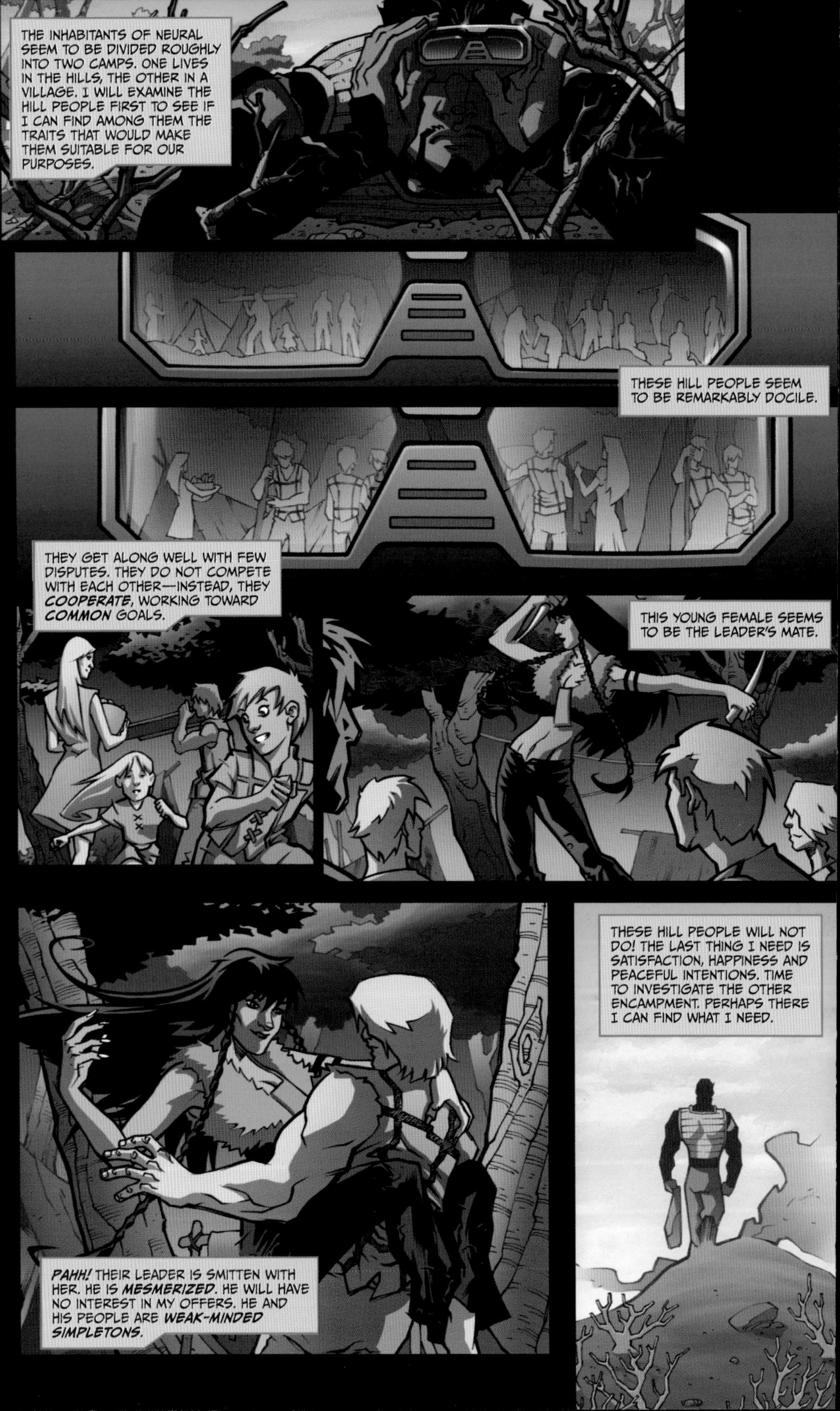
THE INHABITANTS OF NEURAL SEEM TO BE DIVIDED ROUGHLY INTO TWO CAMPS. ONE LIVES IN THE HILLS, THE OTHER IN A VILLAGE. I WILL EXAMINE THE HILL PEOPLE FIRST TO SEE IF I CAN FIND AMONG THEM THE TRAITS THAT WOULD MAKE THEM SUITABLE FOR OUR PURPOSES.
THESE HILL PEOPLE SEEM TO BE REMARKABLY DOCILE.
THEY GET ALONG WELL WITH FEW DISPUTES. THEY DO NOT COMPETE WITH EACH OTHER—INSTEAD, THEY COOPERATE, WORKING TOWARD COMMON GOALS.
THIS YOUNG FEMALE SEEMS TO BE THE LEADER'S MATE.
PAHH! THEIR LEADER IS SMITTEN WITH HER. HE IS MESMERIZED. HE WILL HAVE NO INTEREST IN MY OFFERS. HE AND HIS PEOPLE ARE WEAK-MINDED SIMPLETONS.
THESE HILL PEOPLE WILL NOT DO! THE LAST THING I NEED IS SATISFACTION, HAPPINESS AND PEACEFUL INTENTIONS. TIME TO INVESTIGATE THE OTHER ENCAMPMENT. PERHAPS THERE I CAN FIND WHAT I NEED.

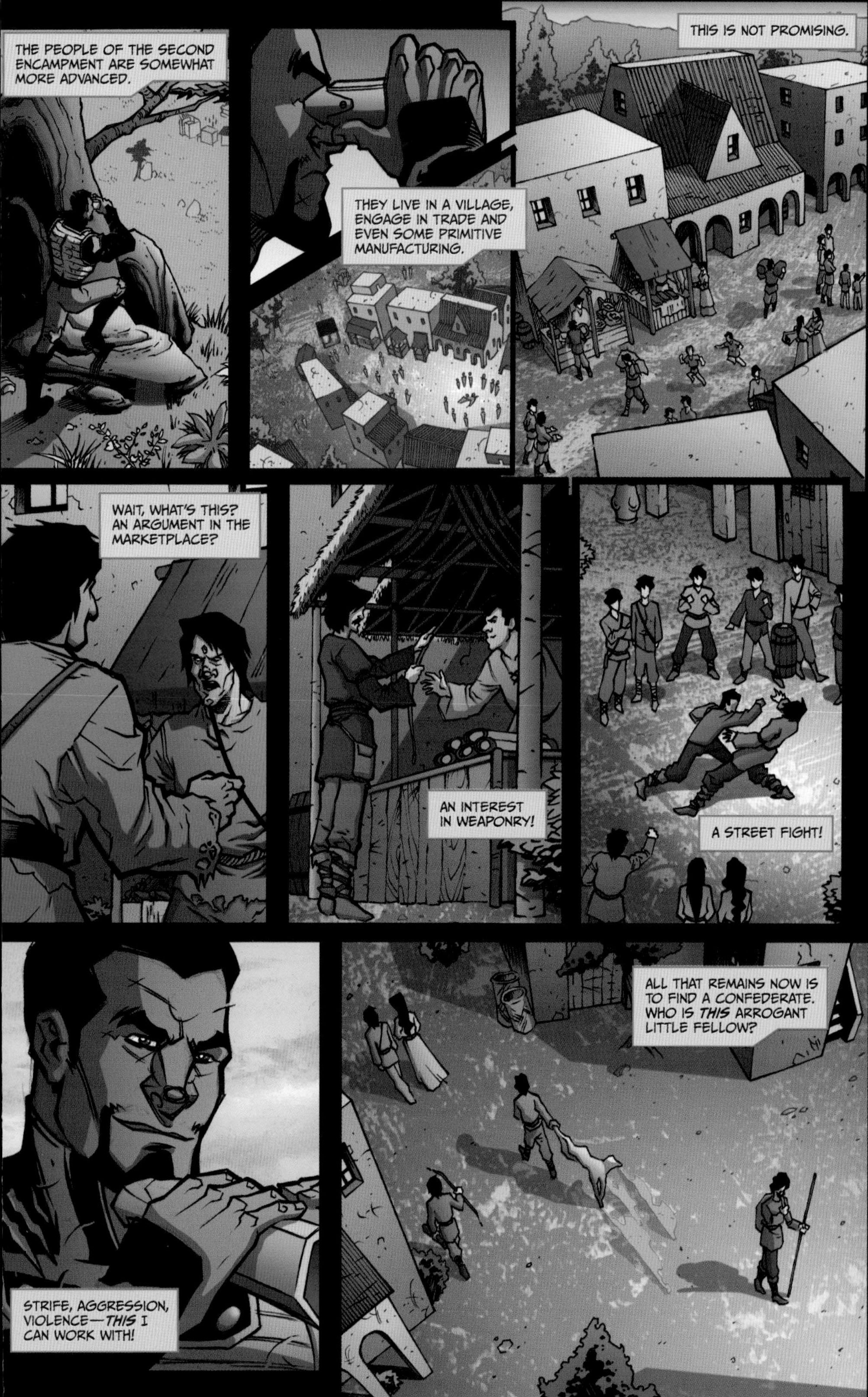
THE PEOPLE OF THE SECOND ENCAMPMENT ARE SOMEWHAT MORE ADVANCED.
THEY LIVE IN A VILLAGE, ENGAGE IN TRADE AND EVEN SOME PRIMITIVE MANUFACTURING.
THIS IS NOT PROMISING.
WAIT, WHAT'S THIS? AN ARGUMENT IN THE MARKETPLACE?
AN INTEREST IN WEAPONRY!
A STREET FIGHT!
STRIFE, AGGRESSION, VIOLENCE—*THIS* I CAN WORK WITH!
ALL THAT REMAINS NOW IS TO FIND A CONFEDERATE. WHO IS *THIS* ARROGANT LITTLE FELLOW?

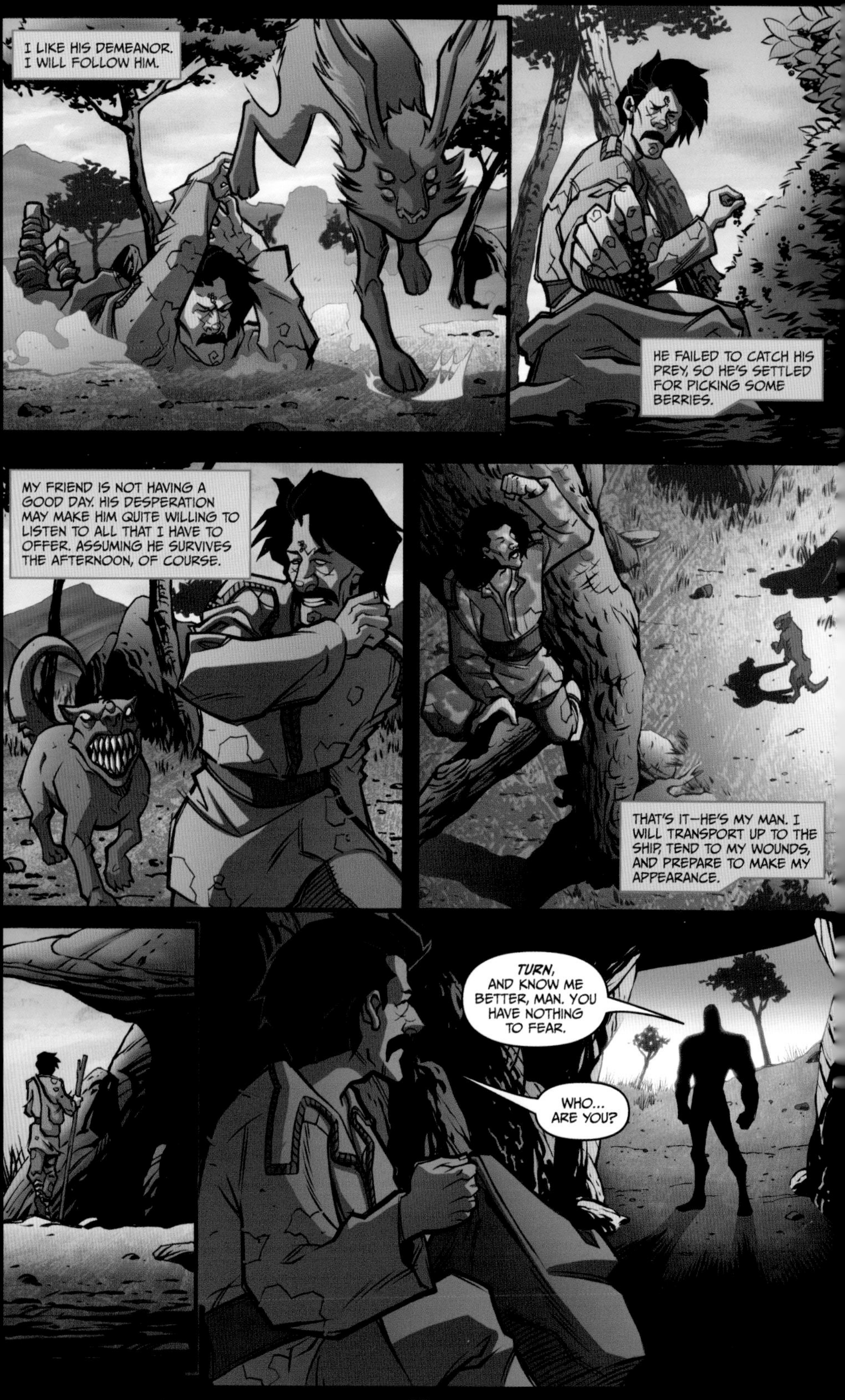
I LIKE HIS DEMEANOR. I WILL FOLLOW HIM.
HE FAILED TO CATCH HIS PREY, SO HE'S SETTLED FOR PICKING SOME BERRIES.
MY FRIEND IS NOT HAVING A GOOD DAY. HIS DESPERATION MAY MAKE HIM QUITE WILLING TO LISTEN TO ALL THAT I HAVE TO OFFER. ASSUMING HE SURVIVES THE AFTERNOON, OF COURSE.
THAT'S IT—HE'S MY MAN. I WILL TRANSPORT UP TO THE SHIP, TEND TO MY WOUNDS, AND PREPARE TO MAKE MY APPEARANCE.
TURN, AND KNOW ME BETTER, MAN. YOU HAVE NOTHING TO FEAR.
WHO... ARE YOU?

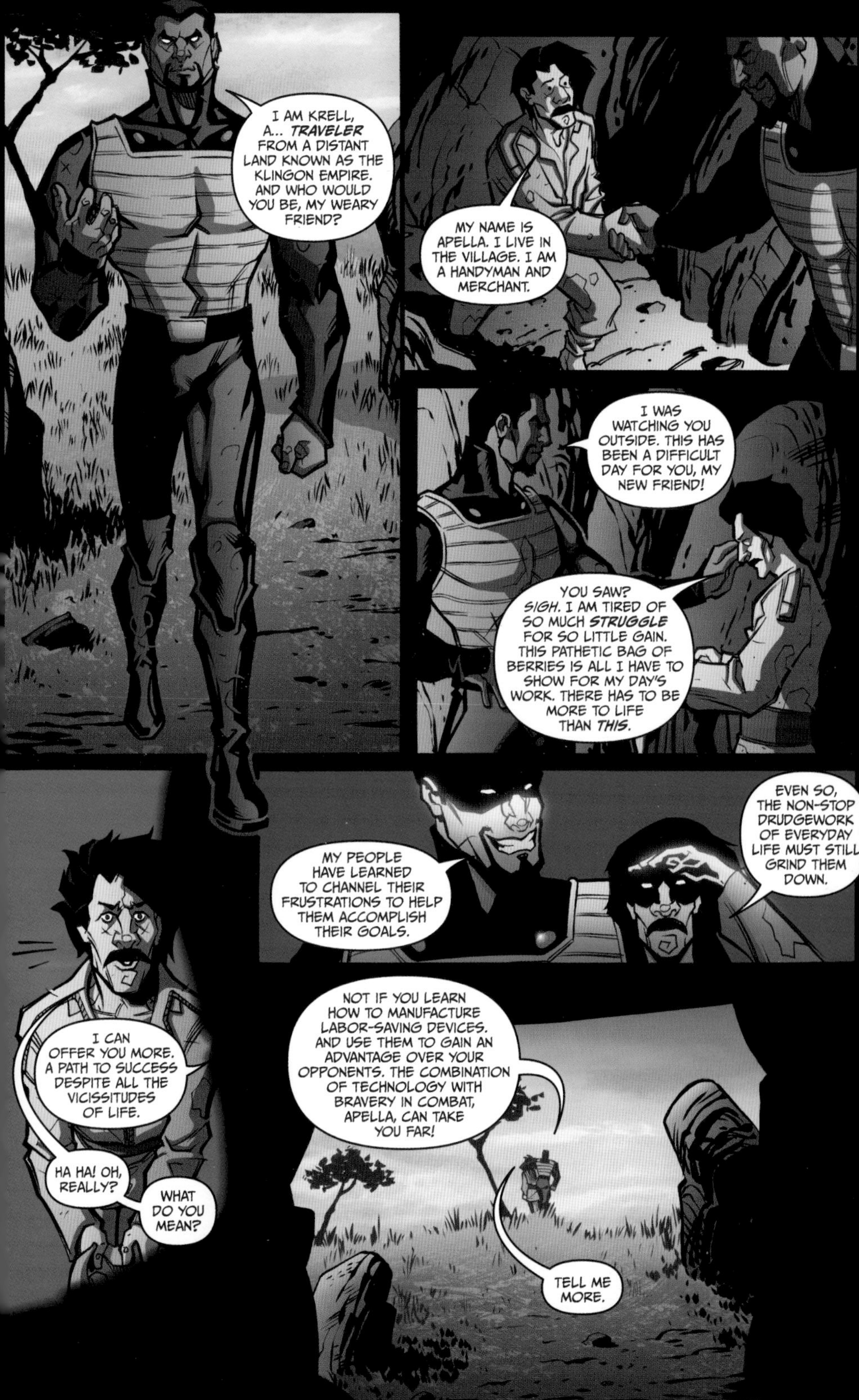
I AM KRELL, A... TRAVELER FROM A DISTANT LAND KNOWN AS THE KLINGON EMPIRE. AND WHO WOULD YOU BE, MY WEARY FRIEND?
MY NAME IS APELLA. I LIVE IN THE VILLAGE. I AM A HANDYMAN AND MERCHANT.
I WAS WATCHING YOU OUTSIDE. THIS HAS BEEN A DIFFICULT DAY FOR YOU, MY NEW FRIEND!
YOU SAW? SIGH. I AM TIRED OF SO MUCH STRUGGLE FOR SO LITTLE GAIN. THIS PATHETIC BAG OF BERRIES IS ALL I HAVE TO SHOW FOR MY DAY'S WORK. THERE HAS TO BE MORE TO LIFE THAN THIS.
MY PEOPLE HAVE LEARNED TO CHANNEL THEIR FRUSTRATIONS TO HELP THEM ACCOMPLISH THEIR GOALS.
EVEN SO, THE NON-STOP DRUDGEWORK OF EVERYDAY LIFE MUST STILL GRIND THEM DOWN.
I CAN OFFER YOU MORE. A PATH TO SUCCESS DESPITE ALL THE VICISSITUDES OF LIFE.
HA HA! OH, REALLY?
WHAT DO YOU MEAN?
NOT IF YOU LEARN HOW TO MANUFACTURE LABOR-SAVING DEVICES. AND USE THEM TO GAIN AN ADVANTAGE OVER YOUR OPPONENTS. THE COMBINATION OF TECHNOLOGY WITH BRAVERY IN COMBAT, APELLA, CAN TAKE YOU FAR!
TELL ME MORE.

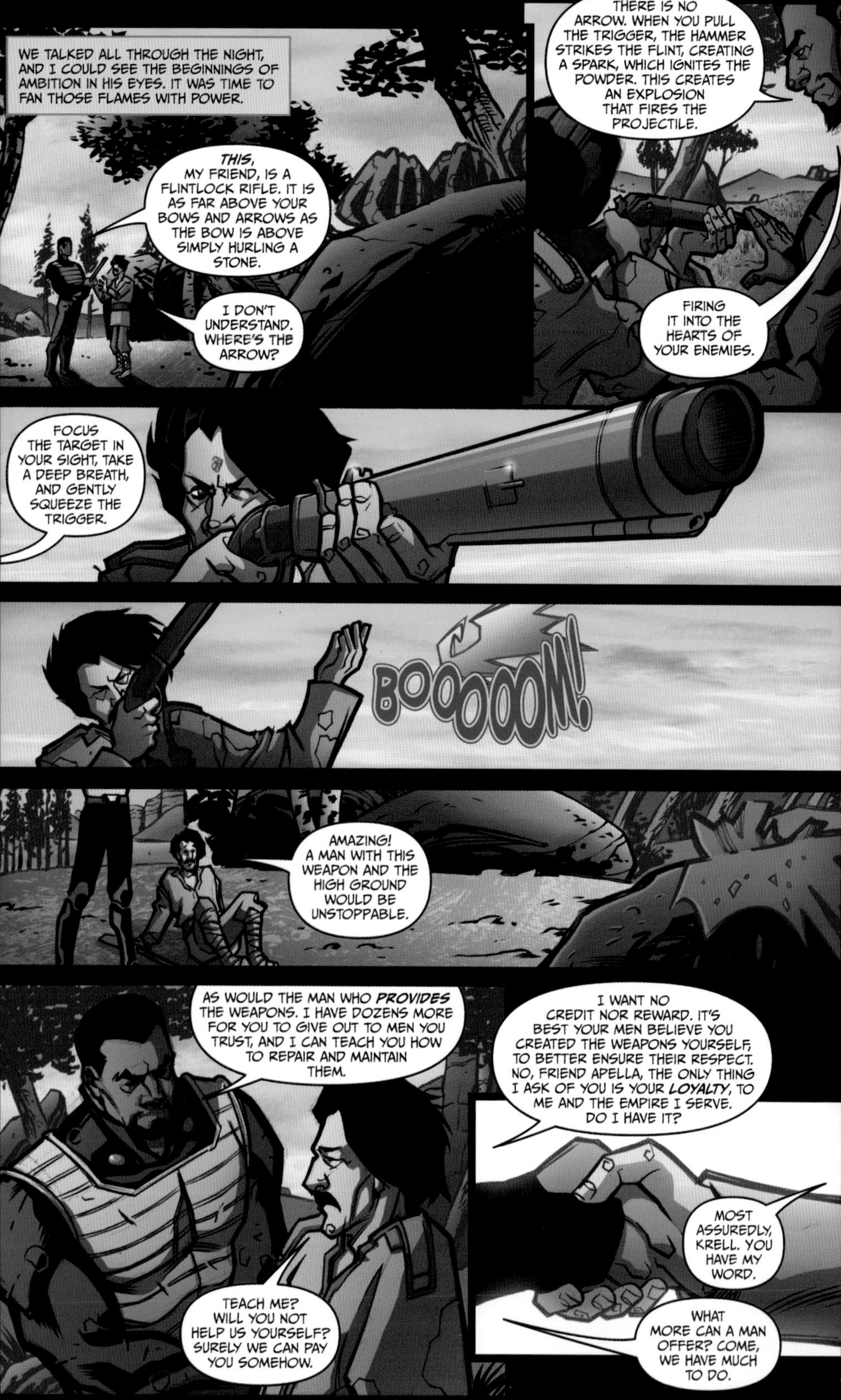
WE TALKED ALL THROUGH THE NIGHT, AND I COULD SEE THE BEGINNINGS OF AMBITION IN HIS EYES. IT WAS TIME TO FAN THOSE FLAMES WITH POWER.
THIS, MY FRIEND, IS A FLINTLOCK RIFLE. IT IS AS FAR ABOVE YOUR BOWS AND ARROWS AS THE BOW IS ABOVE SIMPLY HURLING A STONE.
I DON'T UNDERSTAND. WHERE'S THE ARROW?
THERE IS NO ARROW. WHEN YOU PULL THE TRIGGER, THE HAMMER STRIKES THE FLINT, CREATING A SPARK, WHICH IGNITES THE POWDER. THIS CREATES AN EXPLOSION THAT FIRES THE PROJECTILE.
FIRING IT INTO THE HEARTS OF YOUR ENEMIES.
FOCUS THE TARGET IN YOUR SIGHT, TAKE A DEEP BREATH, AND GENTLY SQUEEZE THE TRIGGER.
BOOOOOM!
AMAZING! A MAN WITH THIS WEAPON AND THE HIGH GROUND WOULD BE UNSTOPPABLE.
AS WOULD THE MAN WHO PROVIDES THE WEAPONS. I HAVE DOZENS MORE FOR YOU TO GIVE OUT TO MEN YOU TRUST, AND I CAN TEACH YOU HOW TO REPAIR AND MAINTAIN THEM.
TEACH ME? WILL YOU NOT HELP US YOURSELF? SURELY WE CAN PAY YOU SOMEHOW.
I WANT NO CREDIT NOR REWARD. IT'S BEST YOUR MEN BELIEVE YOU CREATED THE WEAPONS YOURSELF, TO BETTER ENSURE THEIR RESPECT. NO, FRIEND APELLA, THE ONLY THING I ASK OF YOU IS YOUR LOYALTY, TO ME AND THE EMPIRE I SERVE. DO I HAVE IT?
MOST ASSUREDLY, KRELL. YOU HAVE MY WORD.
WHAT MORE CAN A MAN OFFER? COME, WE HAVE MUCH TO DO.

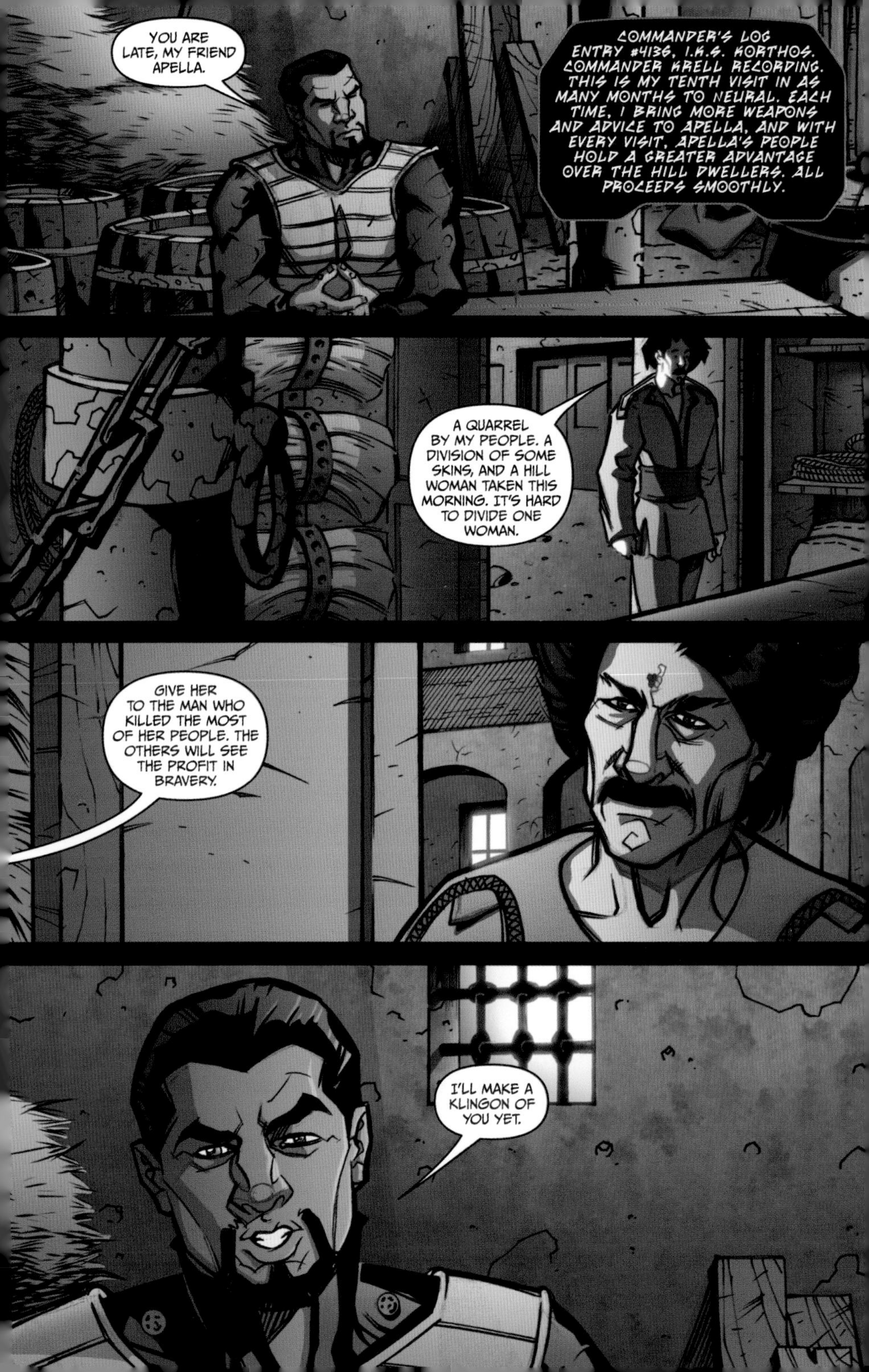
YOU ARE LATE, MY FRIEND APELLA.
COMMANDER'S LOG ENTRY #4136, I.K.S. KORTHOS. COMMANDER KRELL RECORDING. THIS IS MY TENTH VISIT IN AS MANY MONTHS TO NEURAL. EACH TIME, I BRING MORE WEAPONS AND ADVICE TO APELLA, AND WITH EVERY VISIT, APELLA'S PEOPLE HOLD A GREATER ADVANTAGE OVER THE HILL DWELLERS. ALL PROCEEDS SMOOTHLY.
A QUARREL BY MY PEOPLE. A DIVISION OF SOME SKINS, AND A HILL WOMAN TAKEN THIS MORNING. IT'S HARD TO DIVIDE ONE WOMAN.
GIVE HER TO THE MAN WHO KILLED THE MOST OF HER PEOPLE. THE OTHERS WILL SEE THE PROFIT IN BRAVERY.
I'LL MAKE A KLINGON OF YOU YET.

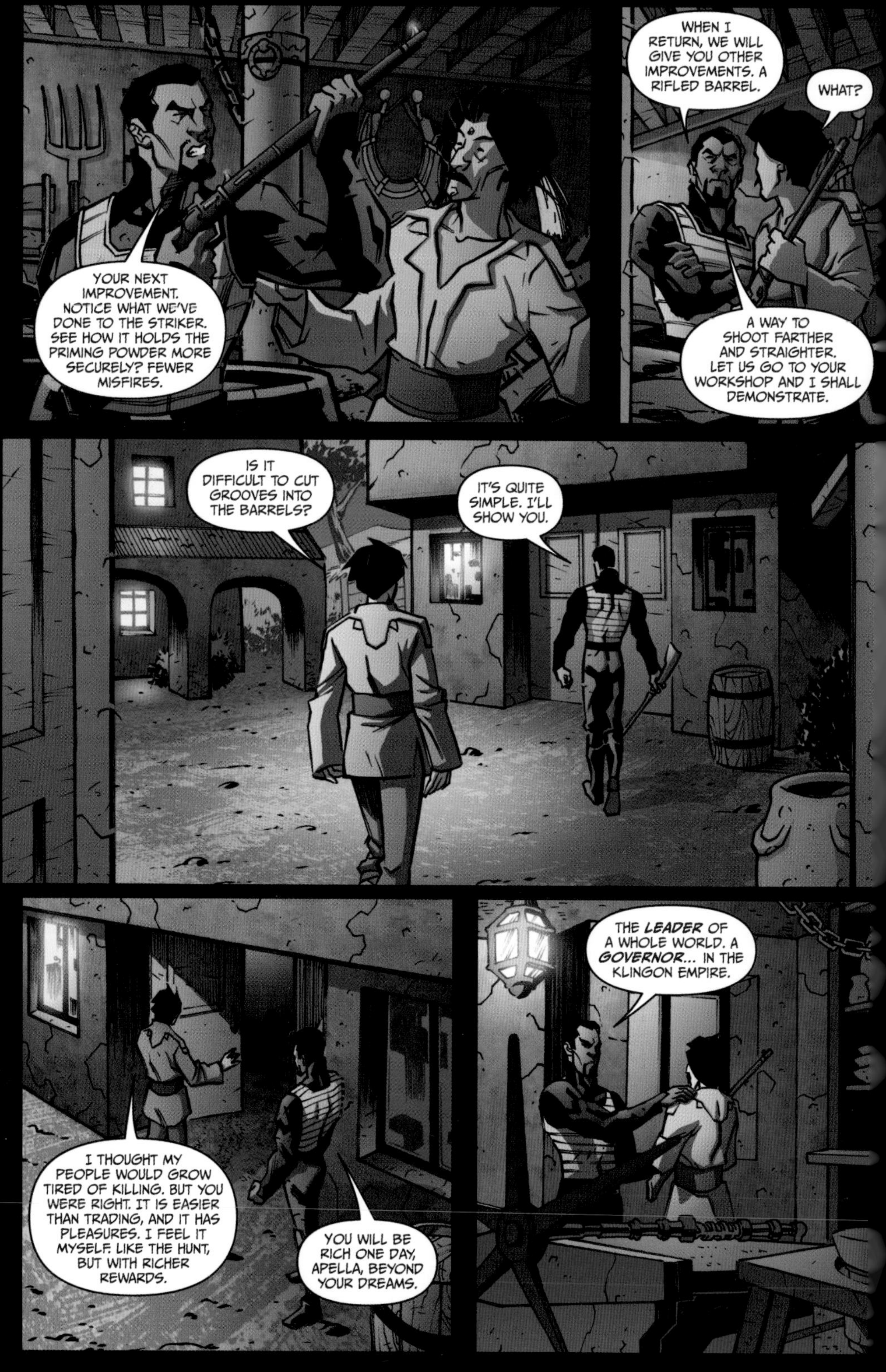
YOUR NEXT IMPROVEMENT. NOTICE WHAT WE'VE DONE TO THE STRIKER. SEE HOW IT HOLDS THE PRIMING POWDER MORE SECURELY? FEWER MISFIRES.
WHEN I RETURN, WE WILL GIVE YOU OTHER IMPROVEMENTS. A RIFLED BARREL.
WHAT?
A WAY TO SHOOT FARTHER AND STRAIGHTER. LET US GO TO YOUR WORKSHOP AND I SHALL DEMONSTRATE.
IS IT DIFFICULT TO CUT GROOVES INTO THE BARRELS?
IT'S QUITE SIMPLE. I'LL SHOW YOU.
I THOUGHT MY PEOPLE WOULD GROW TIRED OF KILLING. BUT YOU WERE RIGHT. IT IS EASIER THAN TRADING, AND IT HAS PLEASURES. I FEEL IT MYSELF. LIKE THE HUNT, BUT WITH RICHER REWARDS.
YOU WILL BE RICH ONE DAY, APELLA, BEYOND YOUR DREAMS.
THE *LEADER* OF A WHOLE WORLD. A *GOVERNOR*... IN THE KLINGON EMPIRE.

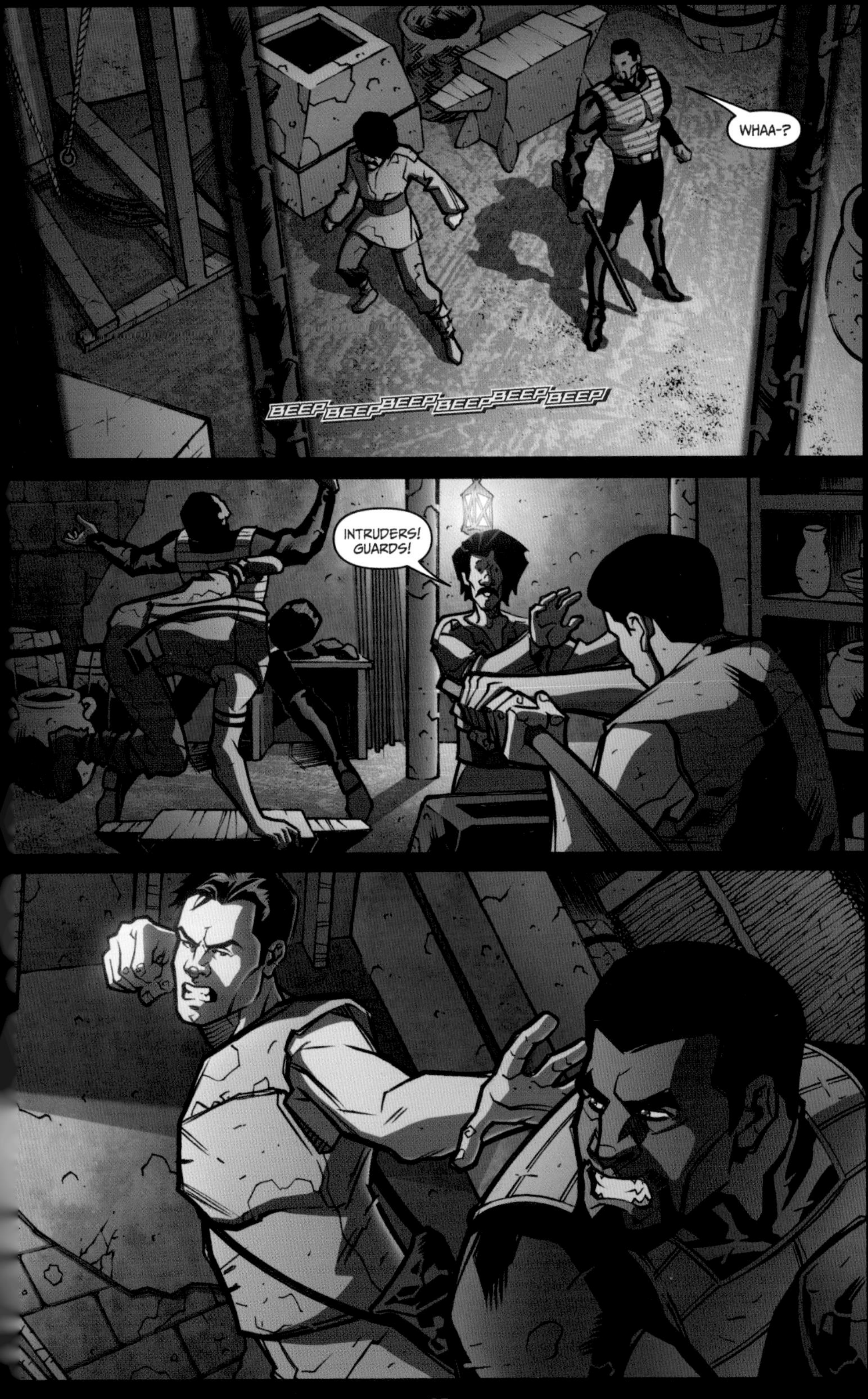
WHAA-?
BEEP BEEP BEEP BEEP BEEP BEEP
INTRUDERS! GUARDS!

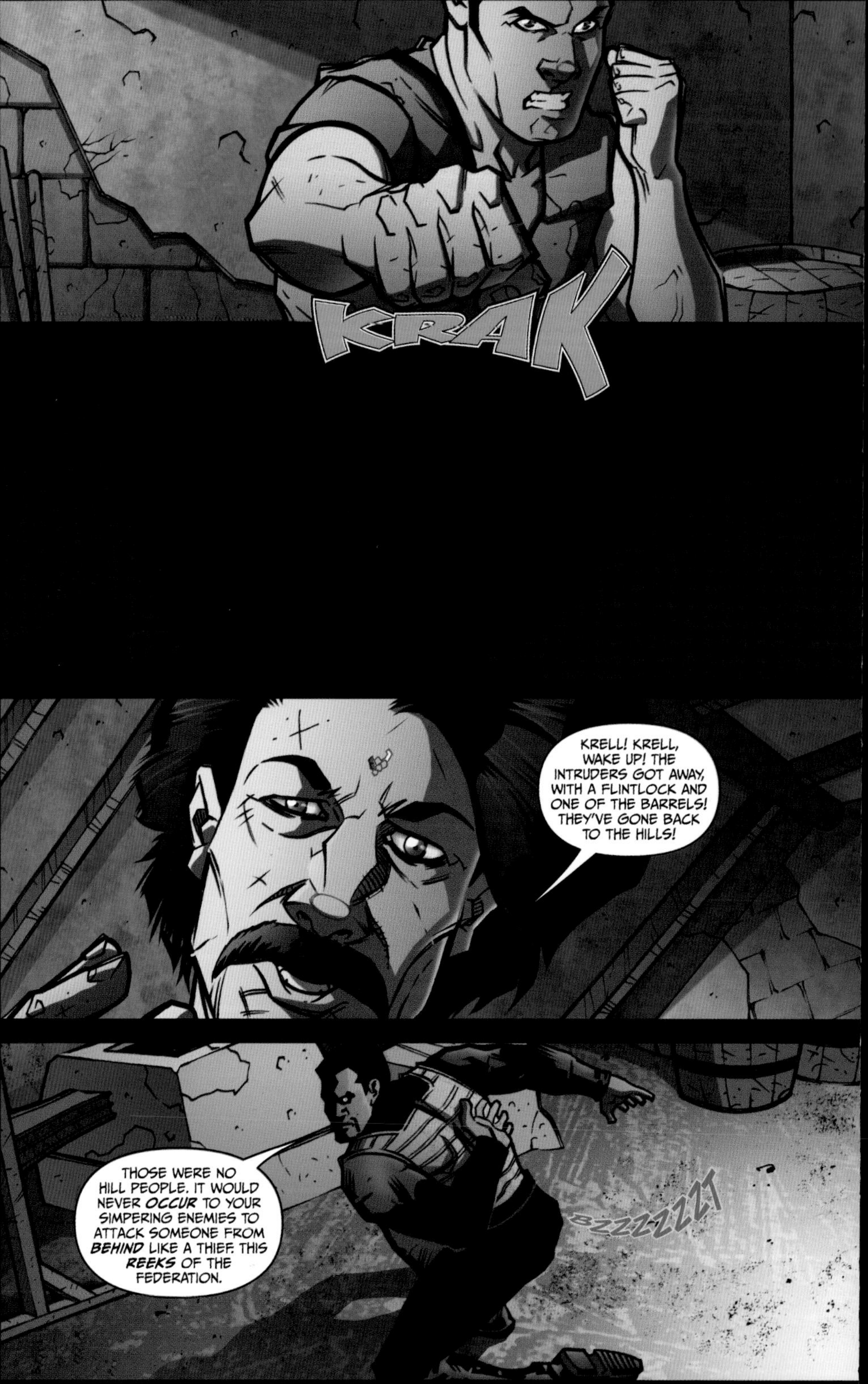
KRAK
KRELL! KRELL, WAKE UP! THE INTRUDERS GOT AWAY, WITH A FLINTLOCK AND ONE OF THE BARRELS! THEY'VE GONE BACK TO THE HILLS!
THOSE WERE NO HILL PEOPLE. IT WOULD NEVER *OCCUR* TO YOUR SIMPERING ENEMIES TO ATTACK SOMEONE FROM *BEHIND* LIKE A THIEF. THIS *REEKS* OF THE FEDERATION.
BZZZZZZT

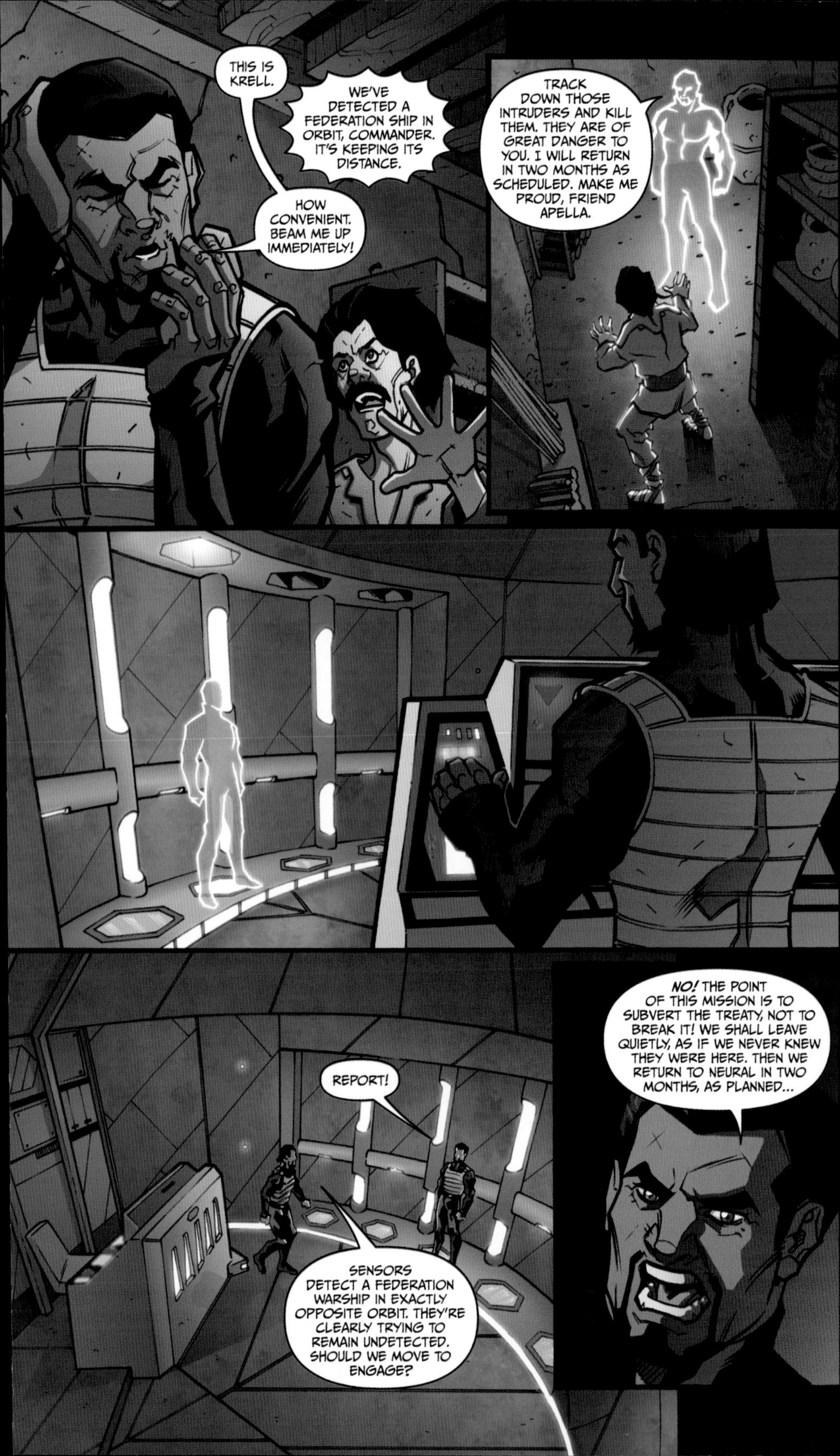

THIS IS KRELL.
WE'VE DETECTED A FEDERATION SHIP IN ORBIT, COMMANDER. IT'S KEEPING ITS DISTANCE.
HOW CONVENIENT. BEAM ME UP IMMEDIATELY!
TRACK DOWN THOSE INTRUDERS AND KILL THEM. THEY ARE OF GREAT DANGER TO YOU. I WILL RETURN IN TWO MONTHS AS SCHEDULED. MAKE ME PROUD, FRIEND APELLA.
REPORT!
SENSORS DETECT A FEDERATION WARSHIP IN EXACTLY OPPOSITE ORBIT. THEY'RE CLEARLY TRYING TO REMAIN UNDETECTED. SHOULD WE MOVE TO ENGAGE?
NO! THE POINT OF THIS MISSION IS TO SUBVERT THE TREATY, NOT TO BREAK IT! WE SHALL LEAVE QUIETLY, AS IF WE NEVER KNEW THEY WERE HERE. THEN WE RETURN TO NEURAL IN TWO MONTHS, AS PLANNED...

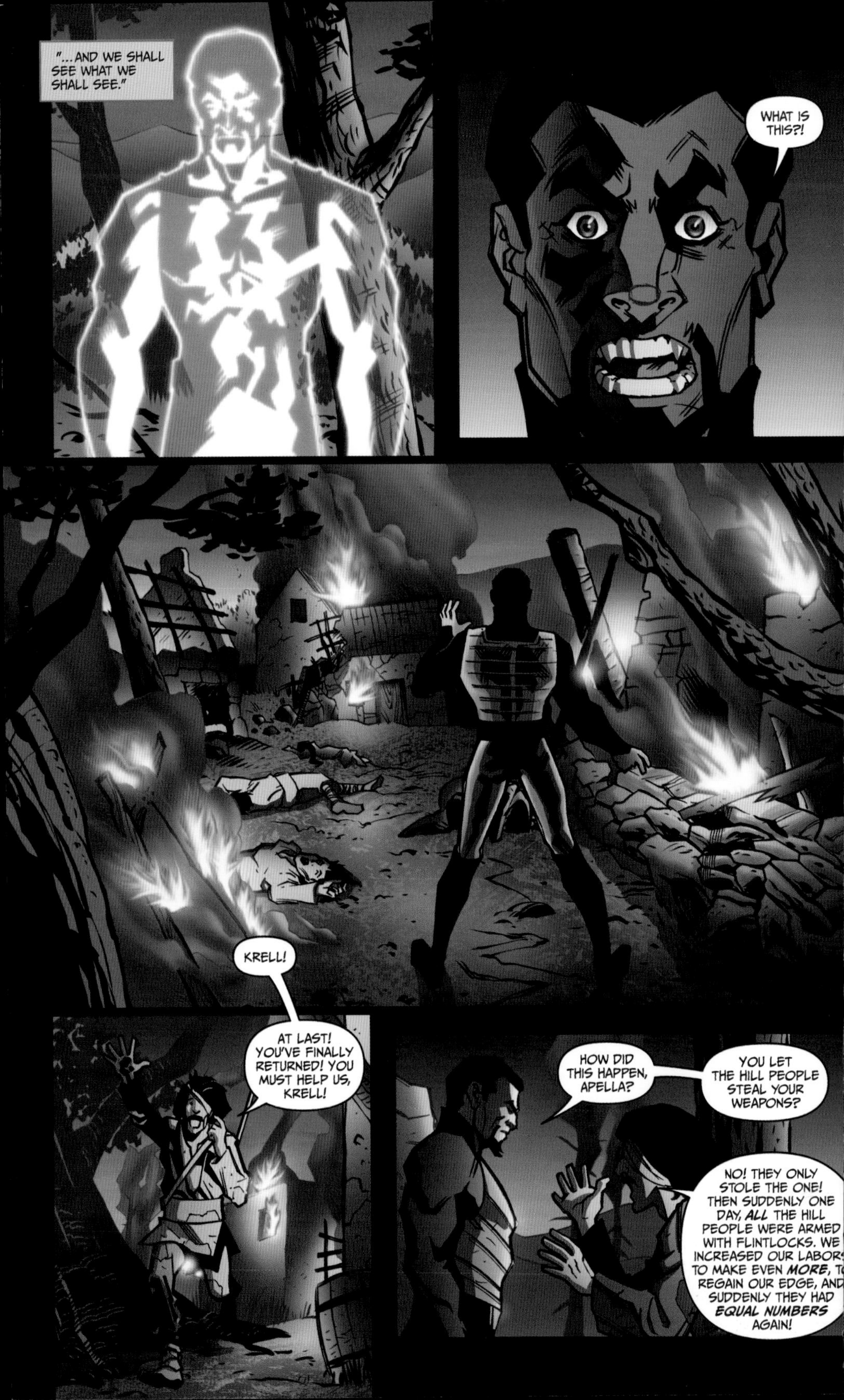
"...AND WE SHALL SEE WHAT WE SHALL SEE."
WHAT IS THIS?!
KRELL!
AT LAST! YOU'VE FINALLY RETURNED! YOU MUST HELP US, KRELL!
HOW DID THIS HAPPEN, APELLA?
YOU LET THE HILL PEOPLE STEAL YOUR WEAPONS?
NO! THEY ONLY STOLE THE ONE! THEN SUDDENLY ONE DAY, ALL THE HILL PEOPLE WERE ARMED WITH FLINTLOCKS. WE INCREASED OUR LABORS TO MAKE EVEN MORE, TO REGAIN OUR EDGE, AND SUDDENLY THEY HAD EQUAL NUMBERS AGAIN!

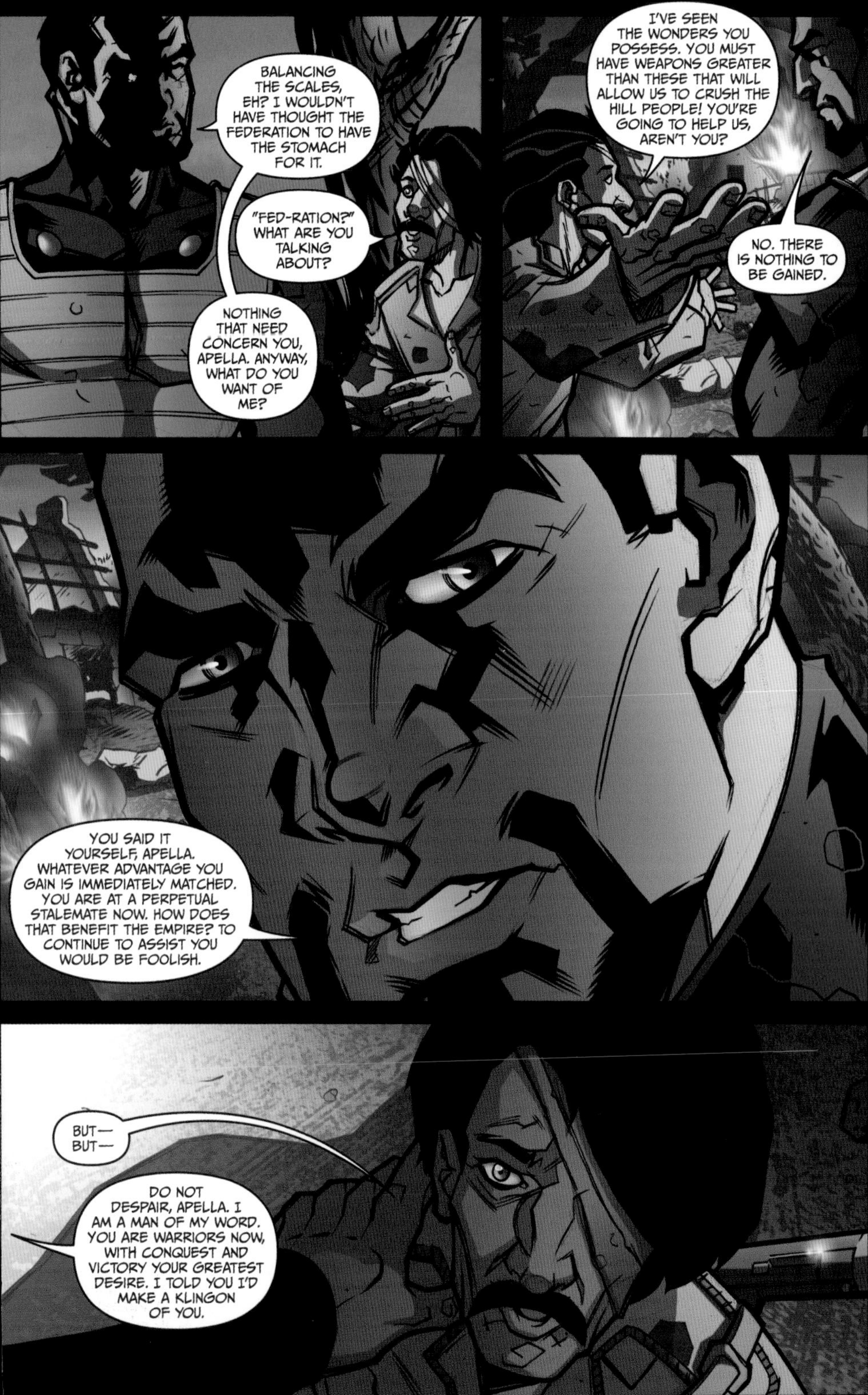
BALANCING THE SCALES, EH? I WOULDN'T HAVE THOUGHT THE FEDERATION TO HAVE THE STOMACH FOR IT.
"FED-RATION?" WHAT ARE YOU TALKING ABOUT?
NOTHING THAT NEED CONCERN YOU, APELLA. ANYWAY, WHAT DO YOU WANT OF ME?
I'VE SEEN THE WONDERS YOU POSSESS. YOU MUST HAVE WEAPONS GREATER THAN THESE THAT WILL ALLOW US TO CRUSH THE HILL PEOPLE! YOU'RE GOING TO HELP US, AREN'T YOU?
NO. THERE IS NOTHING TO BE GAINED.
YOU SAID IT YOURSELF, APELLA. WHATEVER ADVANTAGE YOU GAIN IS IMMEDIATELY MATCHED. YOU ARE AT A PERPETUAL STALEMATE NOW. HOW DOES THAT BENEFIT THE EMPIRE? TO CONTINUE TO ASSIST YOU WOULD BE FOOLISH.
BUT— BUT—
DO NOT DESPAIR, APELLA. I AM A MAN OF MY WORD. YOU ARE WARRIORS NOW, WITH CONQUEST AND VICTORY YOUR GREATEST DESIRE. I TOLD YOU I'D MAKE A KLINGON OF YOU.

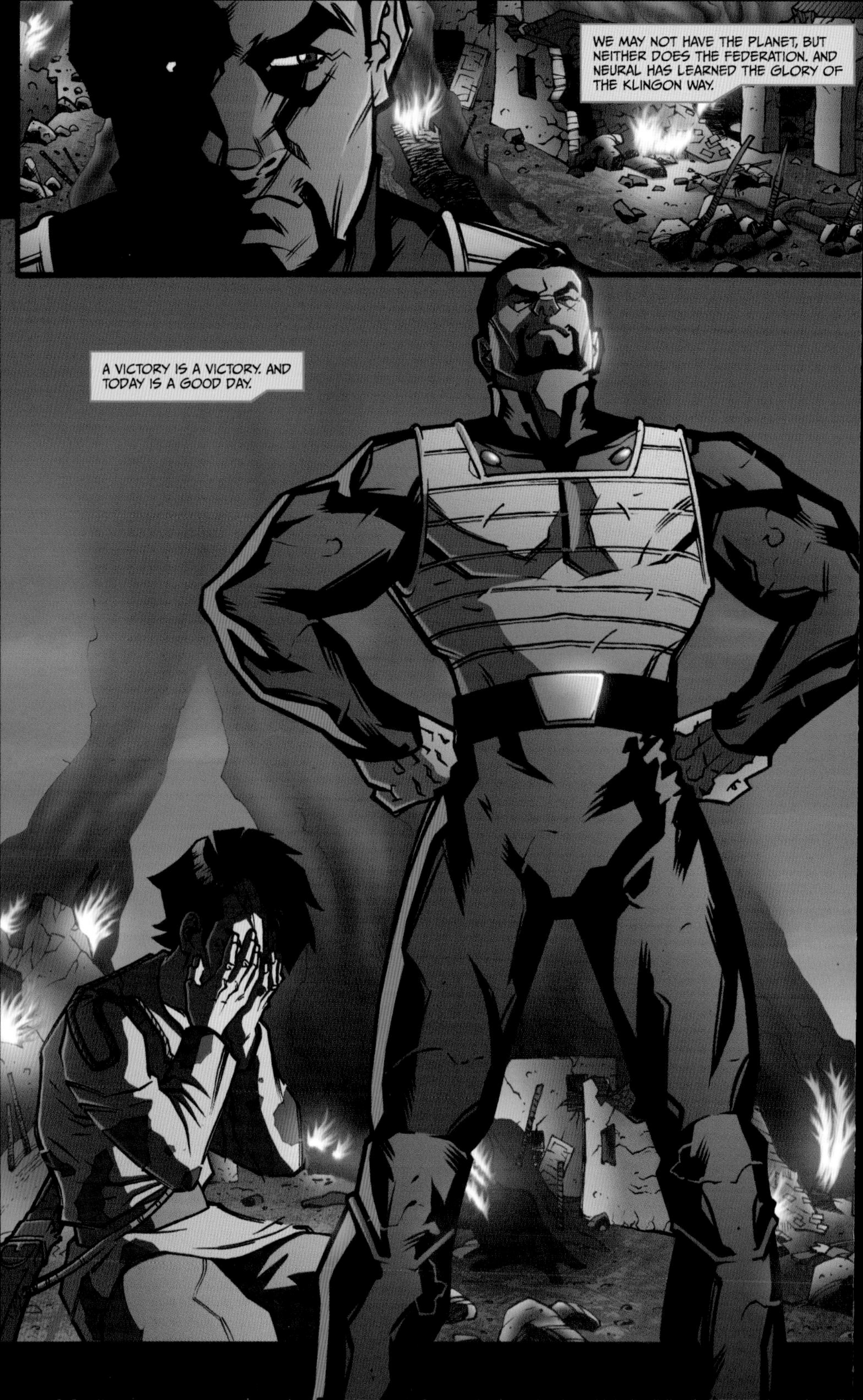
WE MAY NOT HAVE THE PLANET, BUT NEITHER DOES THE FEDERATION. AND NEURAL HAS LEARNED THE GLORY OF THE KLINGON WAY.
A VICTORY IS A VICTORY. AND TODAY IS A GOOD DAY.

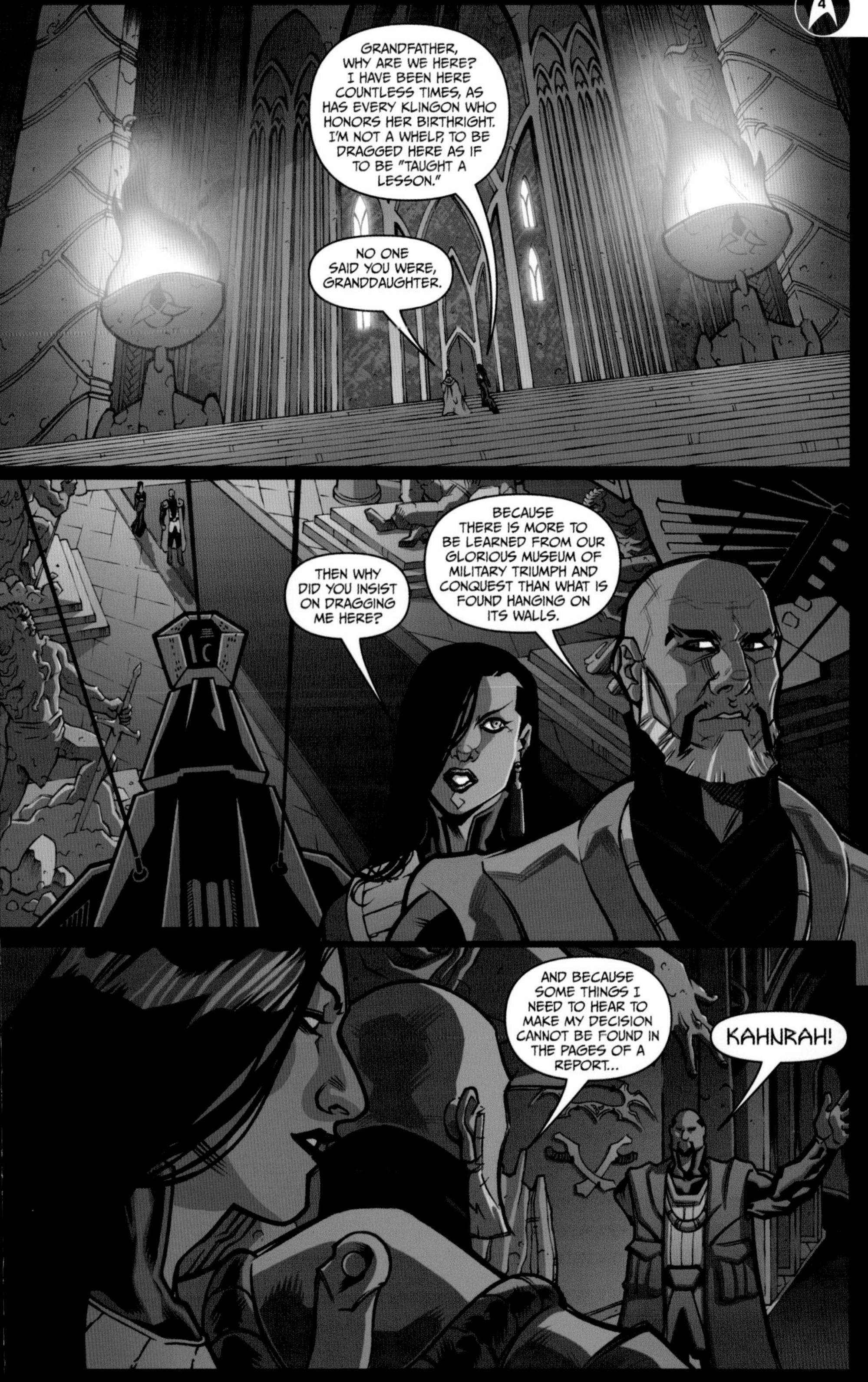
GRANDFATHER, WHY ARE WE HERE? I HAVE BEEN HERE COUNTLESS TIMES, AS HAS EVERY KLINGON WHO HONORS HER BIRTHRIGHT. I'M NOT A WHELP, TO BE DRAGGED HERE AS IF TO BE "TAUGHT A LESSON."
NO ONE SAID YOU WERE, GRANDDAUGHTER.
THEN WHY DID YOU INSIST ON DRAGGING ME HERE?
BECAUSE THERE IS MORE TO BE LEARNED FROM OUR GLORIOUS MUSEUM OF MILITARY TRIUMPH AND CONQUEST THAN WHAT IS FOUND HANGING ON ITS WALLS.
AND BECAUSE SOME THINGS I NEED TO HEAR TO MAKE MY DECISION CANNOT BE FOUND IN THE PAGES OF A REPORT...
KAHNRAH!

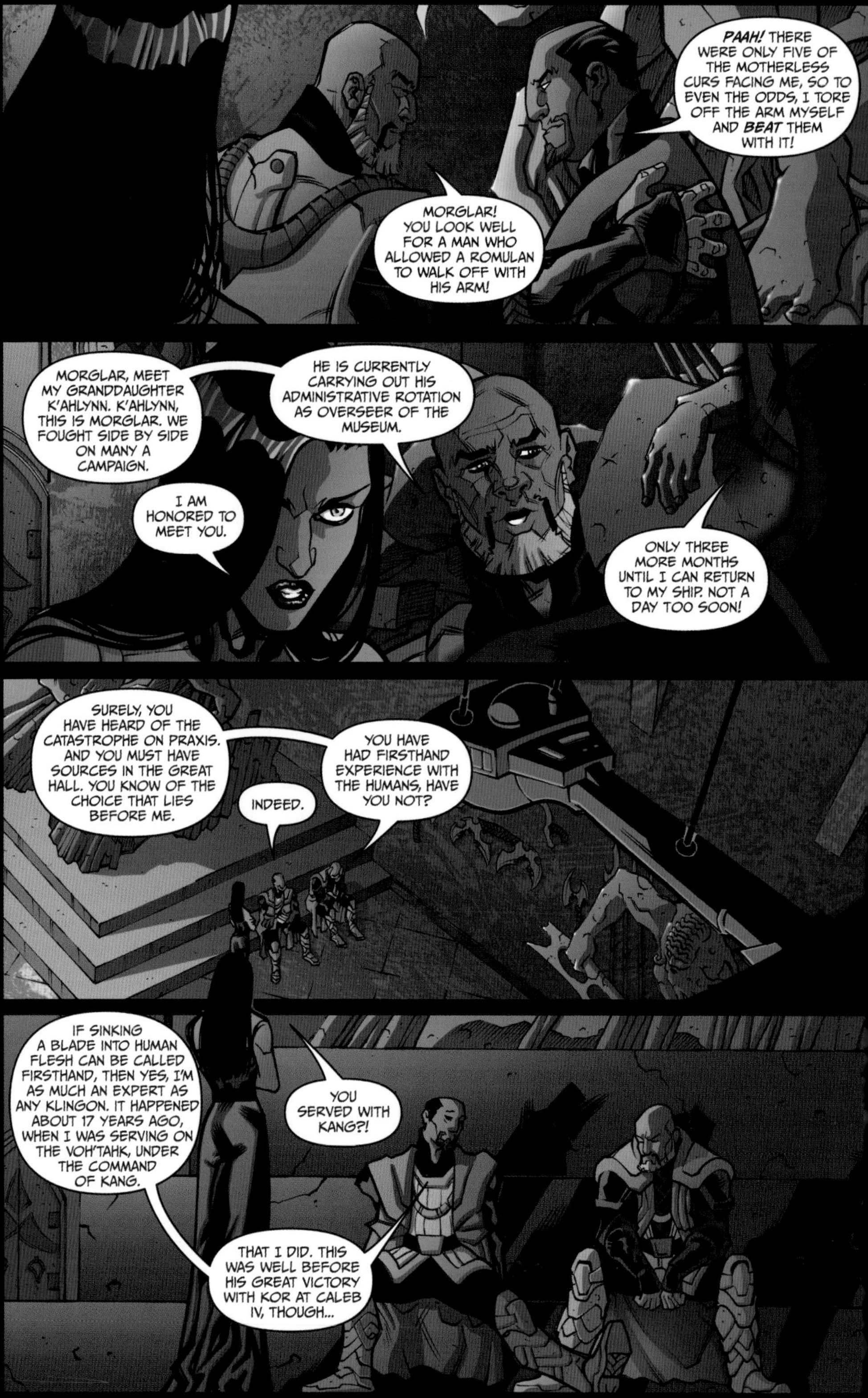
PAAH! THERE WERE ONLY FIVE OF THE MOTHERLESS CURS FACING ME, SO TO EVEN THE ODDS, I TORE OFF THE ARM MYSELF AND BEAT THEM WITH IT!
MORGLAR! YOU LOOK WELL FOR A MAN WHO ALLOWED A ROMULAN TO WALK OFF WITH HIS ARM!
MORGLAR, MEET MY GRANDDAUGHTER K'AHLYNN. K'AHLYNN, THIS IS MORGLAR. WE FOUGHT SIDE BY SIDE ON MANY A CAMPAIGN.
HE IS CURRENTLY CARRYING OUT HIS ADMINISTRATIVE ROTATION AS OVERSEER OF THE MUSEUM.
I AM HONORED TO MEET YOU.
ONLY THREE MORE MONTHS UNTIL I CAN RETURN TO MY SHIP. NOT A DAY TOO SOON!
SURELY, YOU HAVE HEARD OF THE CATASTROPHE ON PRAXIS. AND YOU MUST HAVE SOURCES IN THE GREAT HALL. YOU KNOW OF THE CHOICE THAT LIES BEFORE ME.
INDEED.
YOU HAVE HAD FIRSTHAND EXPERIENCE WITH THE HUMANS, HAVE YOU NOT?
IF SINKING A BLADE INTO HUMAN FLESH CAN BE CALLED FIRSTHAND, THEN YES, I'M AS MUCH AN EXPERT AS ANY KLINGON. IT HAPPENED ABOUT 17 YEARS AGO, WHEN I WAS SERVING ON THE VOH'TAHK, UNDER THE COMMAND OF KANG.
YOU SERVED WITH KANG?!
THAT I DID. THIS WAS WELL BEFORE HIS GREAT VICTORY WITH KOR AT CALEB IV, THOUGH...

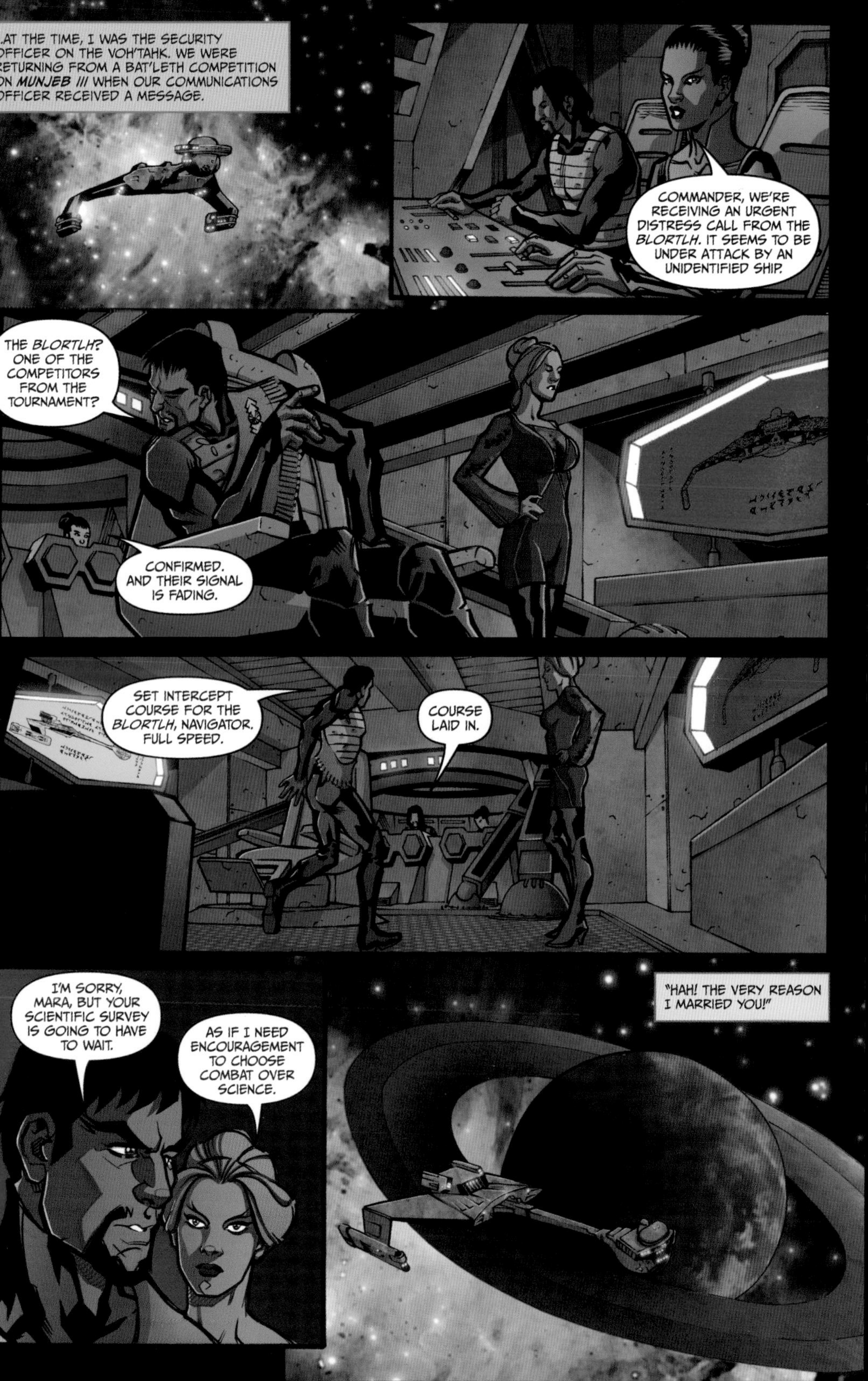
AT THE TIME, I WAS THE SECURITY OFFICER ON THE VOH'TAHK. WE WERE RETURNING FROM A BAT'LETH COMPETITION ON *MUNJEB III* WHEN OUR COMMUNICATIONS OFFICER RECEIVED A MESSAGE.
COMMANDER, WE'RE RECEIVING AN URGENT DISTRESS CALL FROM THE *BLORTLH*. IT SEEMS TO BE UNDER ATTACK BY AN UNIDENTIFIED SHIP.
THE *BLORTLH*? ONE OF THE COMPETITORS FROM THE TOURNAMENT?
CONFIRMED. AND THEIR SIGNAL IS FADING.
SET INTERCEPT COURSE FOR THE *BLORTLH*, NAVIGATOR. FULL SPEED.
COURSE LAID IN.
I'M SORRY, MARA, BUT YOUR SCIENTIFIC SURVEY IS GOING TO HAVE TO WAIT.
AS IF I NEED ENCOURAGEMENT TO CHOOSE COMBAT OVER SCIENCE.
"HAH! THE VERY REASON I MARRIED YOU!"

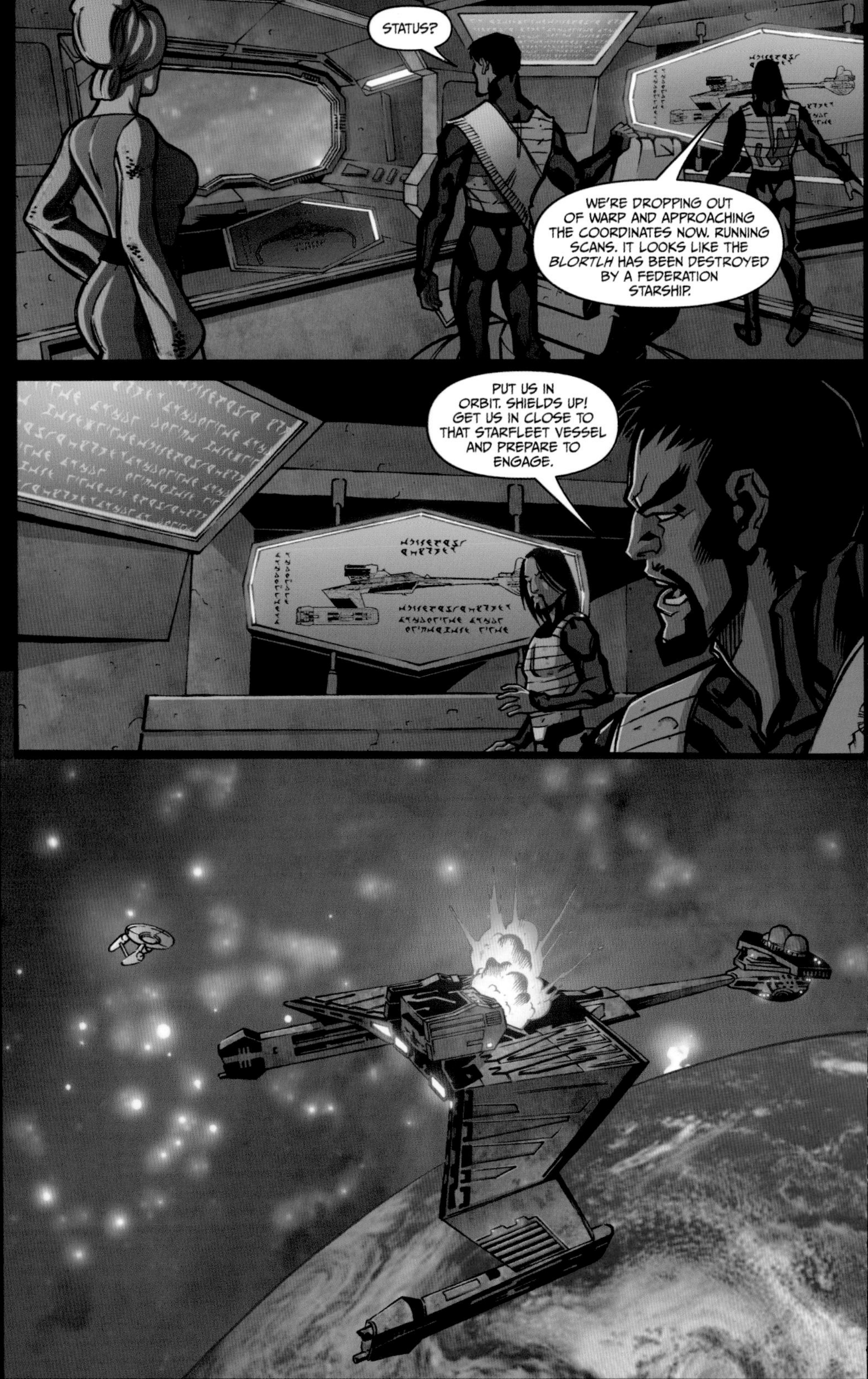
STATUS?
WE'RE DROPPING OUT OF WARP AND APPROACHING THE COORDINATES NOW. RUNNING SCANS. IT LOOKS LIKE THE *BLORTLH* HAS BEEN DESTROYED BY A FEDERATION STARSHIP.
PUT US IN ORBIT. SHIELDS UP! GET US IN CLOSE TO THAT STARFLEET VESSEL AND PREPARE TO ENGAGE.

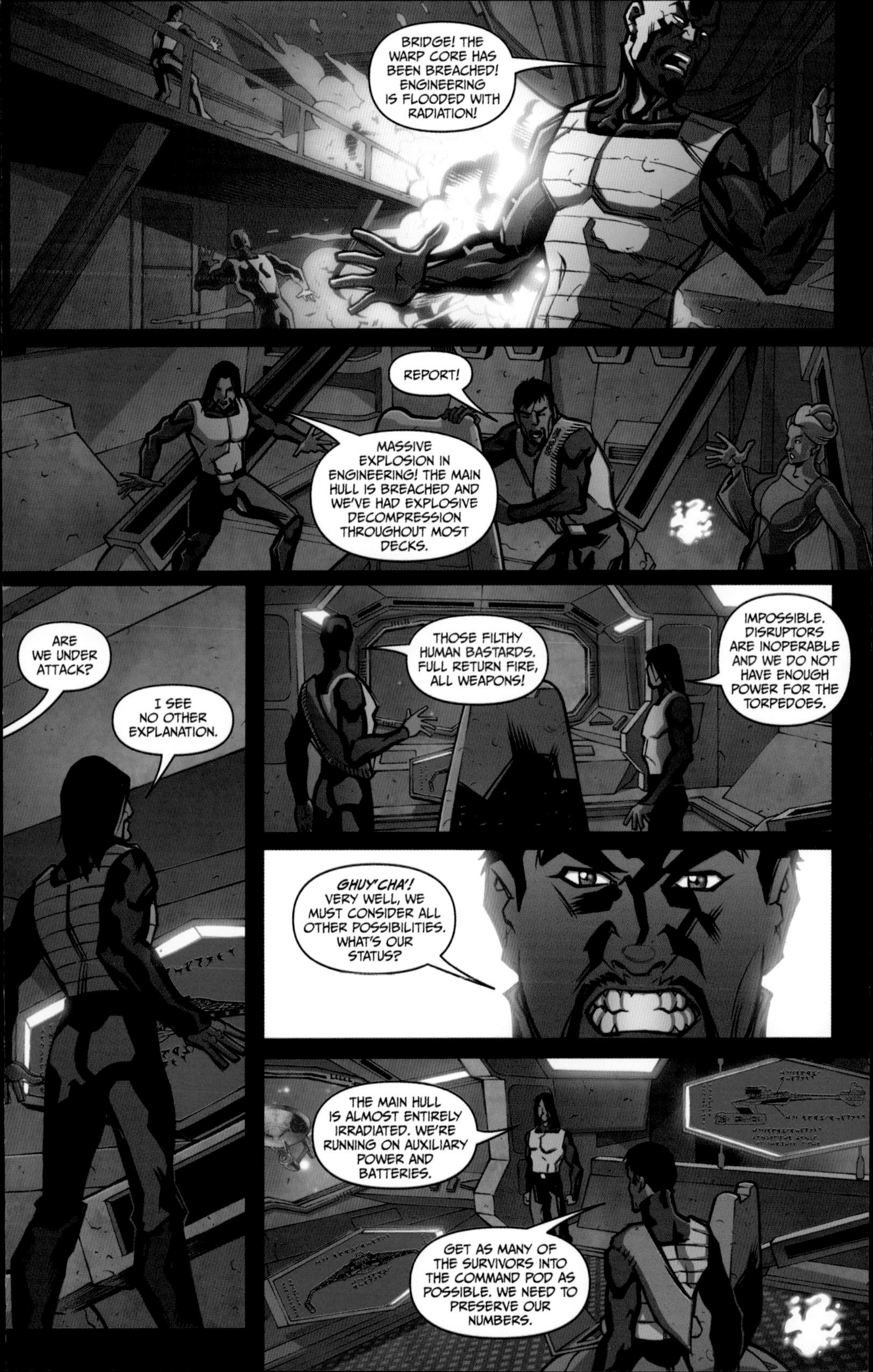
BRIDGE! THE WARP CORE HAS BEEN BREACHED! ENGINEERING IS FLOODED WITH RADIATION!
REPORT!
MASSIVE EXPLOSION IN ENGINEERING! THE MAIN HULL IS BREACHED AND WE'VE HAD EXPLOSIVE DECOMPRESSION THROUGHOUT MOST DECKS.
ARE WE UNDER ATTACK?
I SEE NO OTHER EXPLANATION.
THOSE FILTHY HUMAN BASTARDS. FULL RETURN FIRE, ALL WEAPONS!
IMPOSSIBLE. DISRUPTORS ARE INOPERABLE AND WE DO NOT HAVE ENOUGH POWER FOR THE TORPEDOES.
GHUY'CHA'! VERY WELL, WE MUST CONSIDER ALL OTHER POSSIBILITIES. WHAT'S OUR STATUS?
THE MAIN HULL IS ALMOST ENTIRELY IRRADIATED. WE'RE RUNNING ON AUXILIARY POWER AND BATTERIES.
GET AS MANY OF THE SURVIVORS INTO THE COMMAND POD AS POSSIBLE. WE NEED TO PRESERVE OUR NUMBERS.

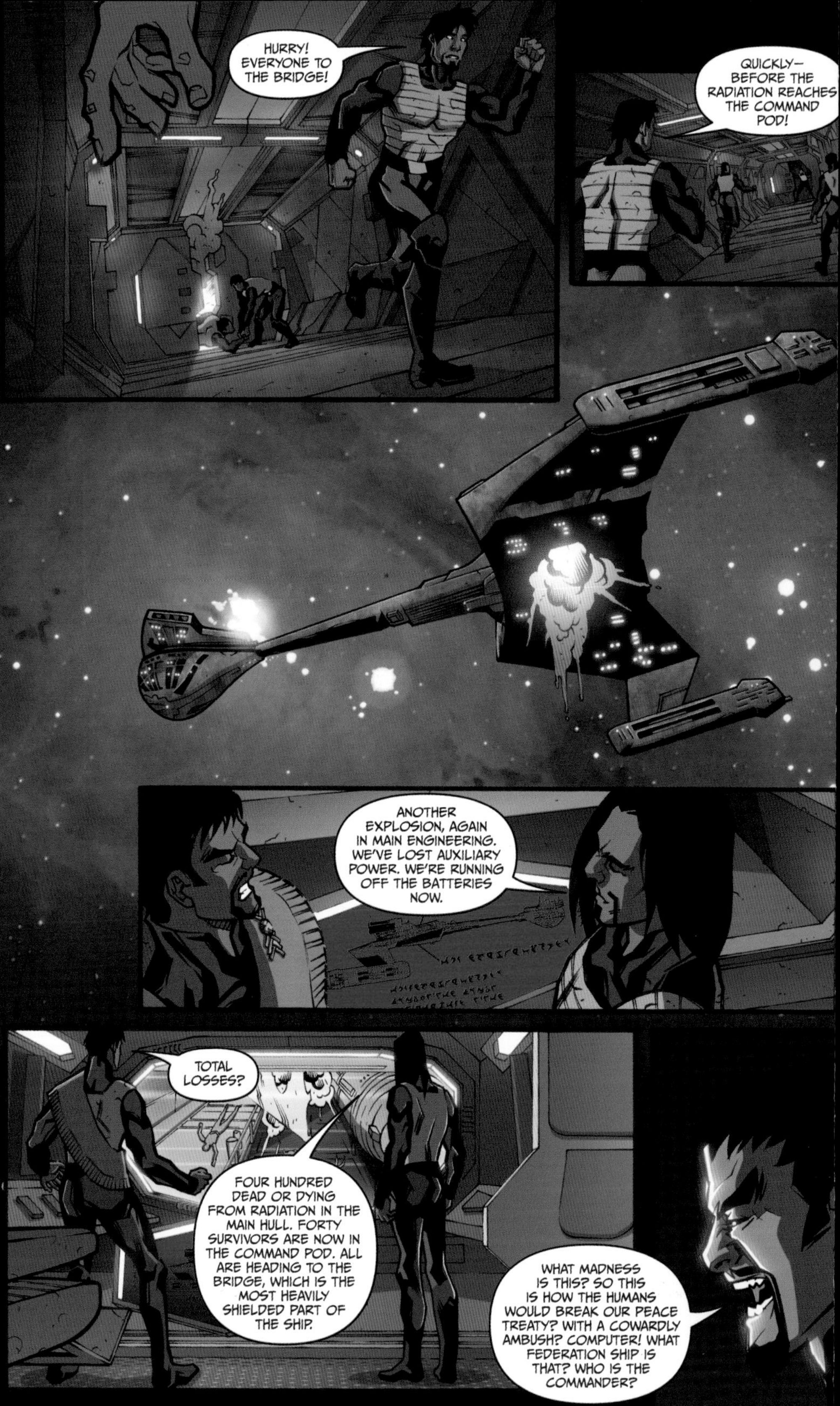
HURRY! EVERYONE TO THE BRIDGE!
QUICKLY— BEFORE THE RADIATION REACHES THE COMMAND POD!
ANOTHER EXPLOSION, AGAIN IN MAIN ENGINEERING. WE'VE LOST AUXILIARY POWER. WE'RE RUNNING OFF THE BATTERIES NOW.
TOTAL LOSSES?
FOUR HUNDRED DEAD OR DYING FROM RADIATION IN THE MAIN HULL. FORTY SURVIVORS ARE NOW IN THE COMMAND POD. ALL ARE HEADING TO THE BRIDGE, WHICH IS THE MOST HEAVILY SHIELDED PART OF THE SHIP.
WHAT MADNESS IS THIS? SO THIS IS HOW THE HUMANS WOULD BREAK OUR PEACE TREATY? WITH A COWARDLY AMBUSH? COMPUTER! WHAT FEDERATION SHIP IS THAT? WHO IS THE COMMANDER?

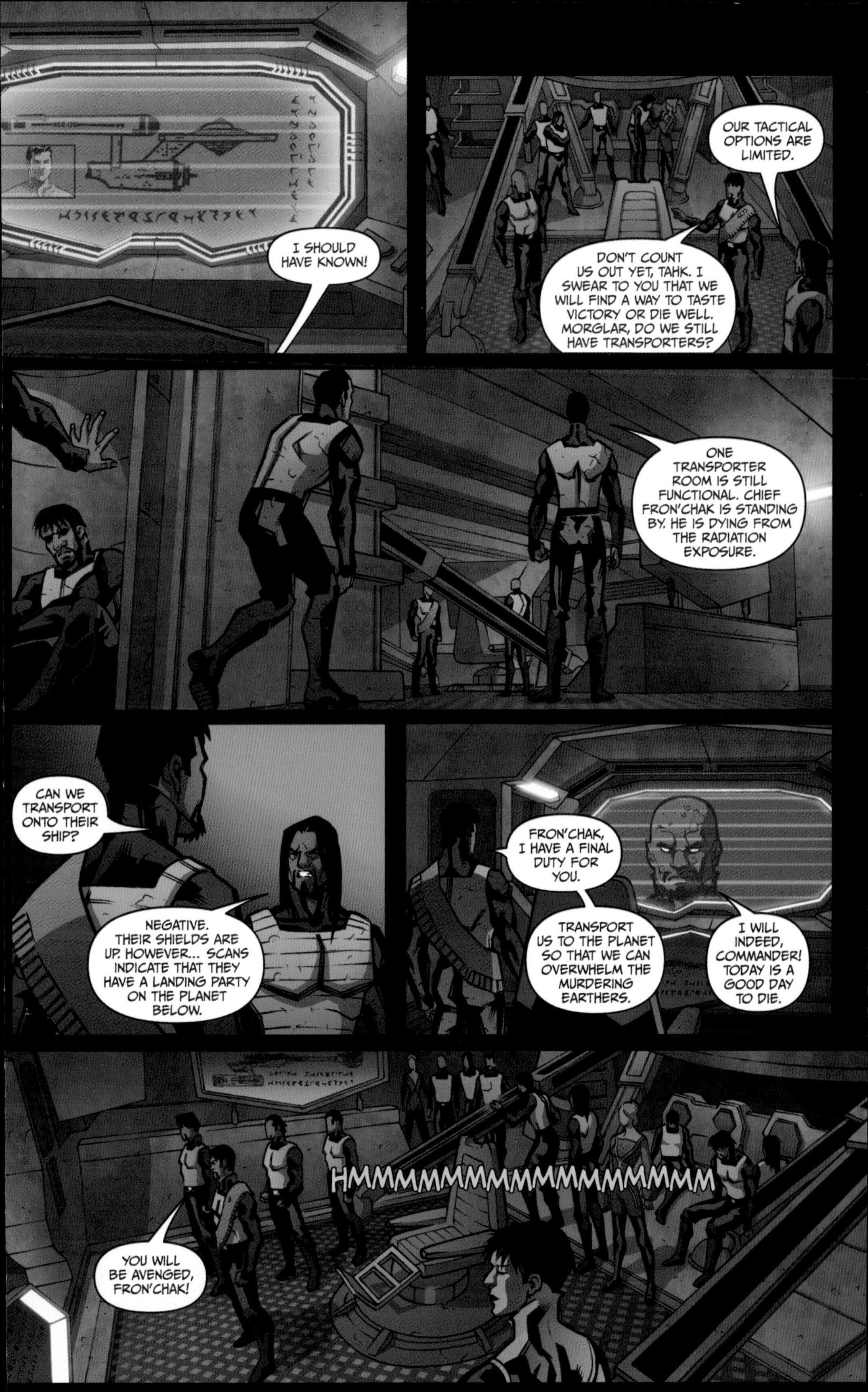

I SHOULD HAVE KNOWN!
OUR TACTICAL OPTIONS ARE LIMITED.
DON'T COUNT US OUT YET, TAHK. I SWEAR TO YOU THAT WE WILL FIND A WAY TO TASTE VICTORY OR DIE WELL. MORGLAR, DO WE STILL HAVE TRANSPORTERS?
ONE TRANSPORTER ROOM IS STILL FUNCTIONAL. CHIEF FRON'CHAK IS STANDING BY. HE IS DYING FROM THE RADIATION EXPOSURE.
CAN WE TRANSPORT ONTO THEIR SHIP?
NEGATIVE. THEIR SHIELDS ARE UP. HOWEVER... SCANS INDICATE THAT THEY HAVE A LANDING PARTY ON THE PLANET BELOW.
FRON'CHAK, I HAVE A FINAL DUTY FOR YOU.
TRANSPORT US TO THE PLANET SO THAT WE CAN OVERWHELM THE MURDERING EARTHERS.
I WILL INDEED, COMMANDER! TODAY IS A GOOD DAY TO DIE.
HMMMMMMMMMMMMMMMMMMM
YOU WILL BE AVENGED, FRON'CHAK!

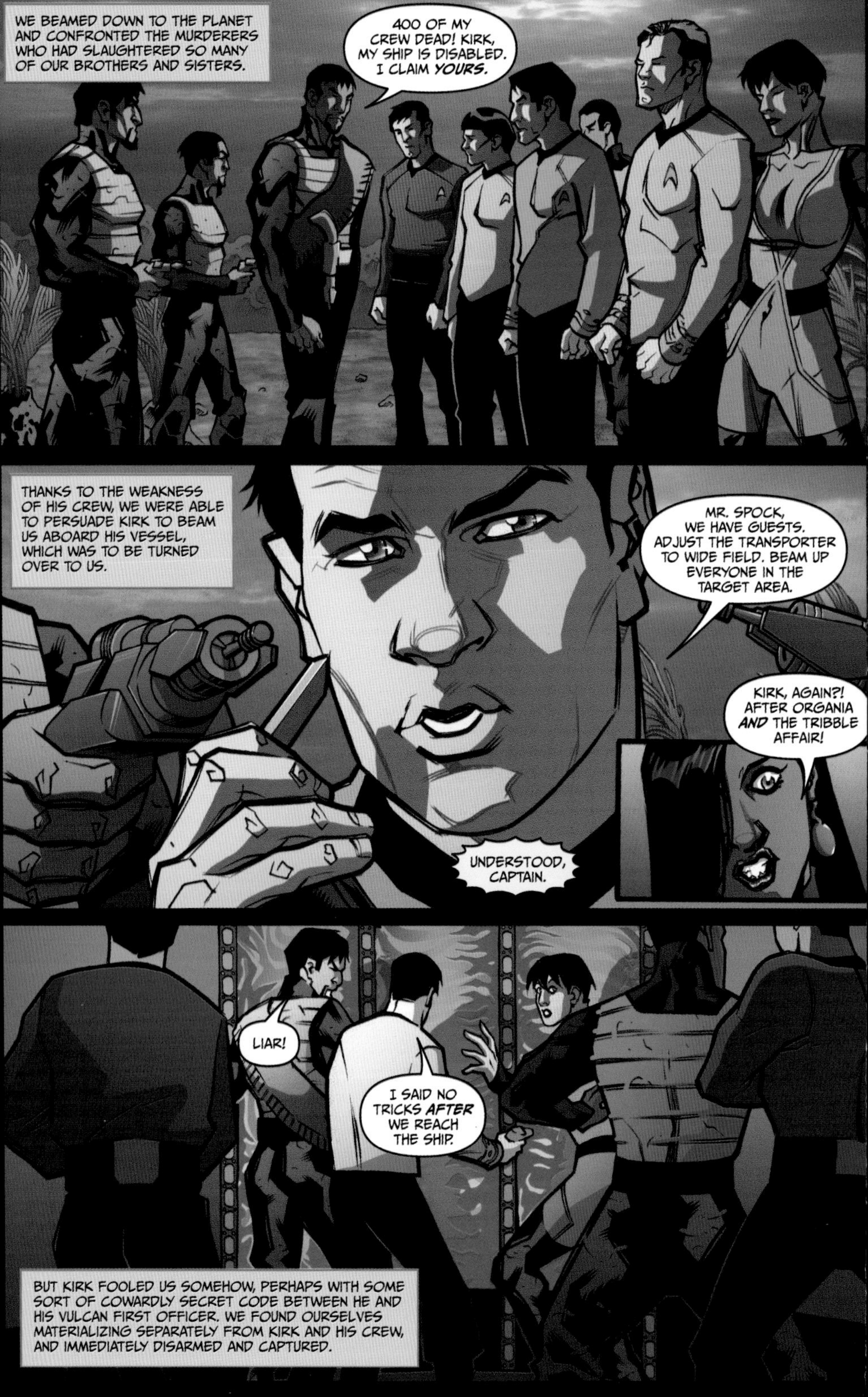
WE BEAMED DOWN TO THE PLANET AND CONFRONTED THE MURDERERS WHO HAD SLAUGHTERED SO MANY OF OUR BROTHERS AND SISTERS.
400 OF MY CREW DEAD! KIRK, MY SHIP IS DISABLED. I CLAIM *YOURS.*
THANKS TO THE WEAKNESS OF HIS CREW, WE WERE ABLE TO PERSUADE KIRK TO BEAM US ABOARD HIS VESSEL, WHICH WAS TO BE TURNED OVER TO US.
MR. SPOCK, WE HAVE GUESTS. ADJUST THE TRANSPORTER TO WIDE FIELD. BEAM UP EVERYONE IN THE TARGET AREA.
KIRK, AGAIN?! AFTER ORGANIA *AND* THE TRIBBLE AFFAIR!
UNDERSTOOD, CAPTAIN.
LIAR!
I SAID NO TRICKS *AFTER* WE REACH THE SHIP.
BUT KIRK FOOLED US SOMEHOW, PERHAPS WITH SOME SORT OF COWARDLY SECRET CODE BETWEEN HE AND HIS VULCAN FIRST OFFICER. WE FOUND OURSELVES MATERIALIZING SEPARATELY FROM KIRK AND HIS CREW, AND IMMEDIATELY DISARMED AND CAPTURED.

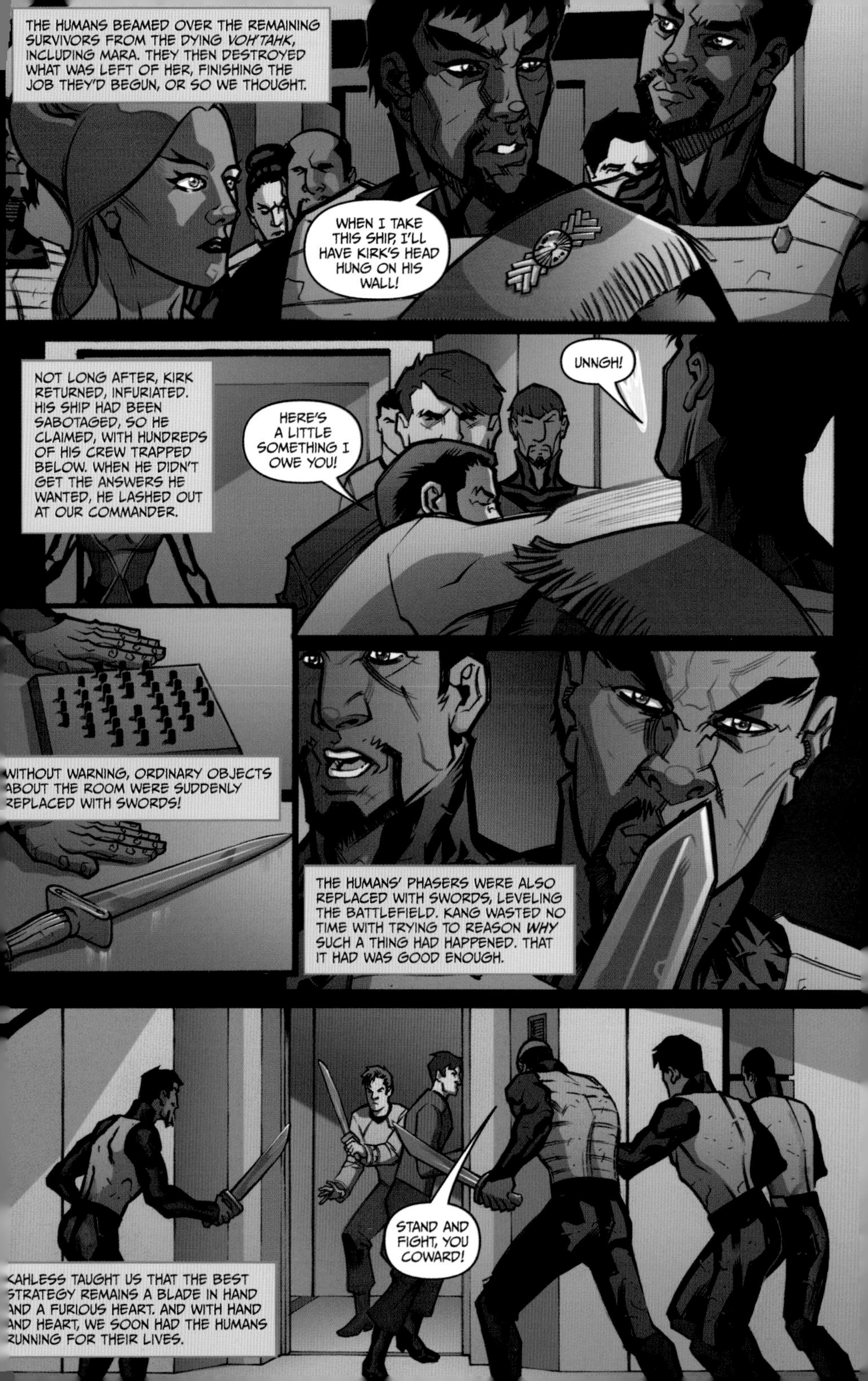
THE HUMANS BEAMED OVER THE REMAINING SURVIVORS FROM THE DYING *VOH'TAHK*, INCLUDING MARA. THEY THEN DESTROYED WHAT WAS LEFT OF HER, FINISHING THE JOB THEY'D BEGUN, OR SO WE THOUGHT.
WHEN I TAKE THIS SHIP, I'LL HAVE KIRK'S HEAD HUNG ON HIS WALL!
NOT LONG AFTER, KIRK RETURNED, INFURIATED. HIS SHIP HAD BEEN SABOTAGED, SO HE CLAIMED, WITH HUNDREDS OF HIS CREW TRAPPED BELOW. WHEN HE DIDN'T GET THE ANSWERS HE WANTED, HE LASHED OUT AT OUR COMMANDER.
HERE'S A LITTLE SOMETHING I OWE YOU!
UNNGH!
WITHOUT WARNING, ORDINARY OBJECTS ABOUT THE ROOM WERE SUDDENLY REPLACED WITH SWORDS!
THE HUMANS' PHASERS WERE ALSO REPLACED WITH SWORDS, LEVELING THE BATTLEFIELD. KANG WASTED NO TIME WITH TRYING TO REASON *WHY* SUCH A THING HAD HAPPENED. THAT IT HAD WAS GOOD ENOUGH.
STAND AND FIGHT, YOU COWARD!
KAHLESS TAUGHT US THAT THE BEST STRATEGY REMAINS A BLADE IN HAND AND A FURIOUS HEART. AND WITH HAND AND HEART, WE SOON HAD THE HUMANS RUNNING FOR THEIR LIVES.

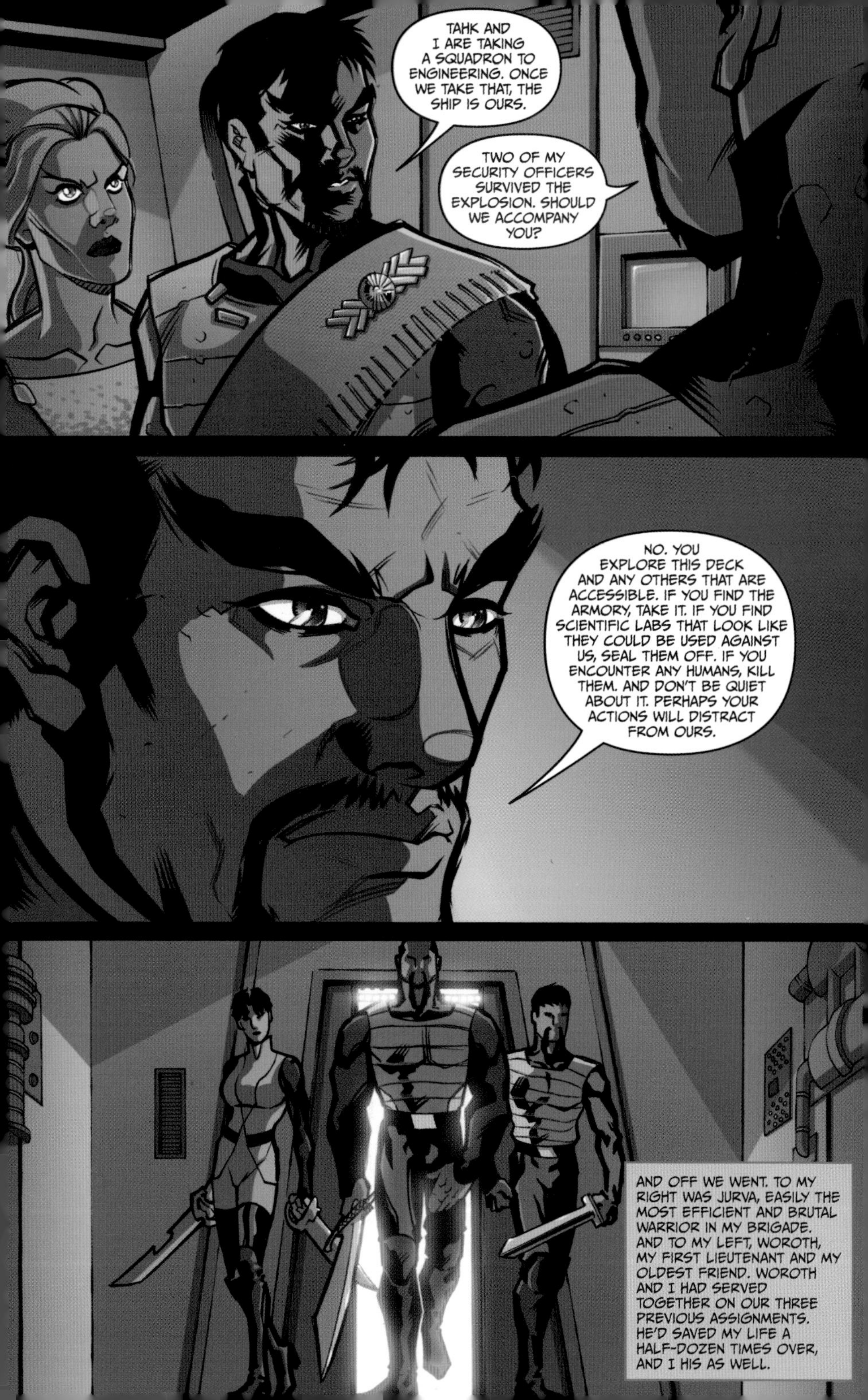
TAHK AND I ARE TAKING A SQUADRON TO ENGINEERING. ONCE WE TAKE THAT, THE SHIP IS OURS.
TWO OF MY SECURITY OFFICERS SURVIVED THE EXPLOSION. SHOULD WE ACCOMPANY YOU?
NO. YOU EXPLORE THIS DECK AND ANY OTHERS THAT ARE ACCESSIBLE. IF YOU FIND THE ARMORY, TAKE IT. IF YOU FIND SCIENTIFIC LABS THAT LOOK LIKE THEY COULD BE USED AGAINST US, SEAL THEM OFF. IF YOU ENCOUNTER ANY HUMANS, KILL THEM. AND DON'T BE QUIET ABOUT IT. PERHAPS YOUR ACTIONS WILL DISTRACT FROM OURS.
AND OFF WE WENT. TO MY RIGHT WAS JURVA, EASILY THE MOST EFFICIENT AND BRUTAL WARRIOR IN MY BRIGADE. AND TO MY LEFT, WOROTH, MY FIRST LIEUTENANT AND MY OLDEST FRIEND. WOROTH AND I HAD SERVED TOGETHER ON OUR THREE PREVIOUS ASSIGNMENTS. HE'D SAVED MY LIFE A HALF-DOZEN TIMES OVER, AND I HIS AS WELL.

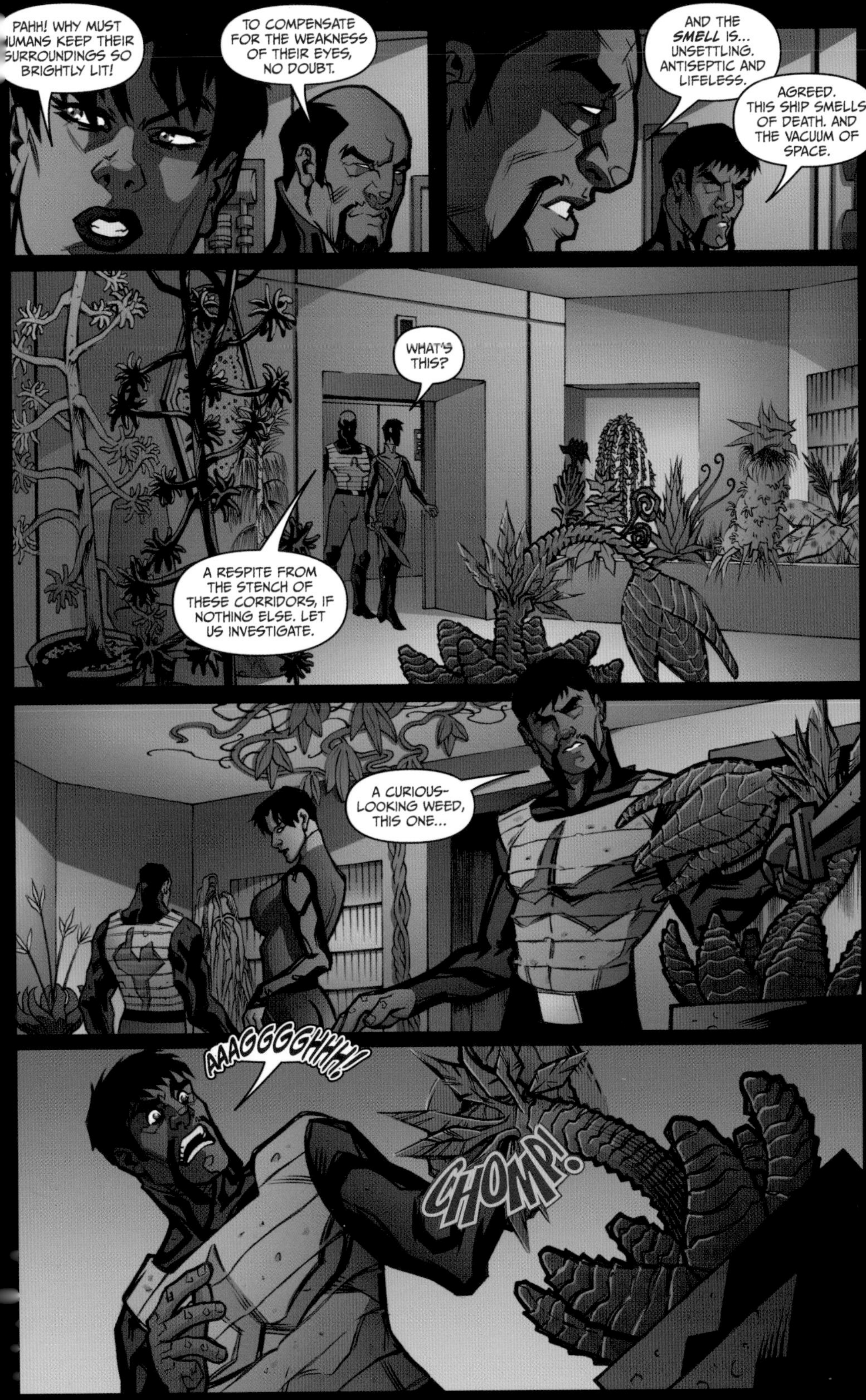
PAHH! WHY MUST HUMANS KEEP THEIR SURROUNDINGS SO BRIGHTLY LIT!
TO COMPENSATE FOR THE WEAKNESS OF THEIR EYES, NO DOUBT.
AND THE SMELL IS... UNSETTLING. ANTISEPTIC AND LIFELESS.
AGREED. THIS SHIP SMELLS OF DEATH. AND THE VACUUM OF SPACE.
WHAT'S THIS?
A RESPITE FROM THE STENCH OF THESE CORRIDORS, IF NOTHING ELSE. LET US INVESTIGATE.
A CURIOUS-LOOKING WEED, THIS ONE...
AAAGGGGHHH!
CHOMP!

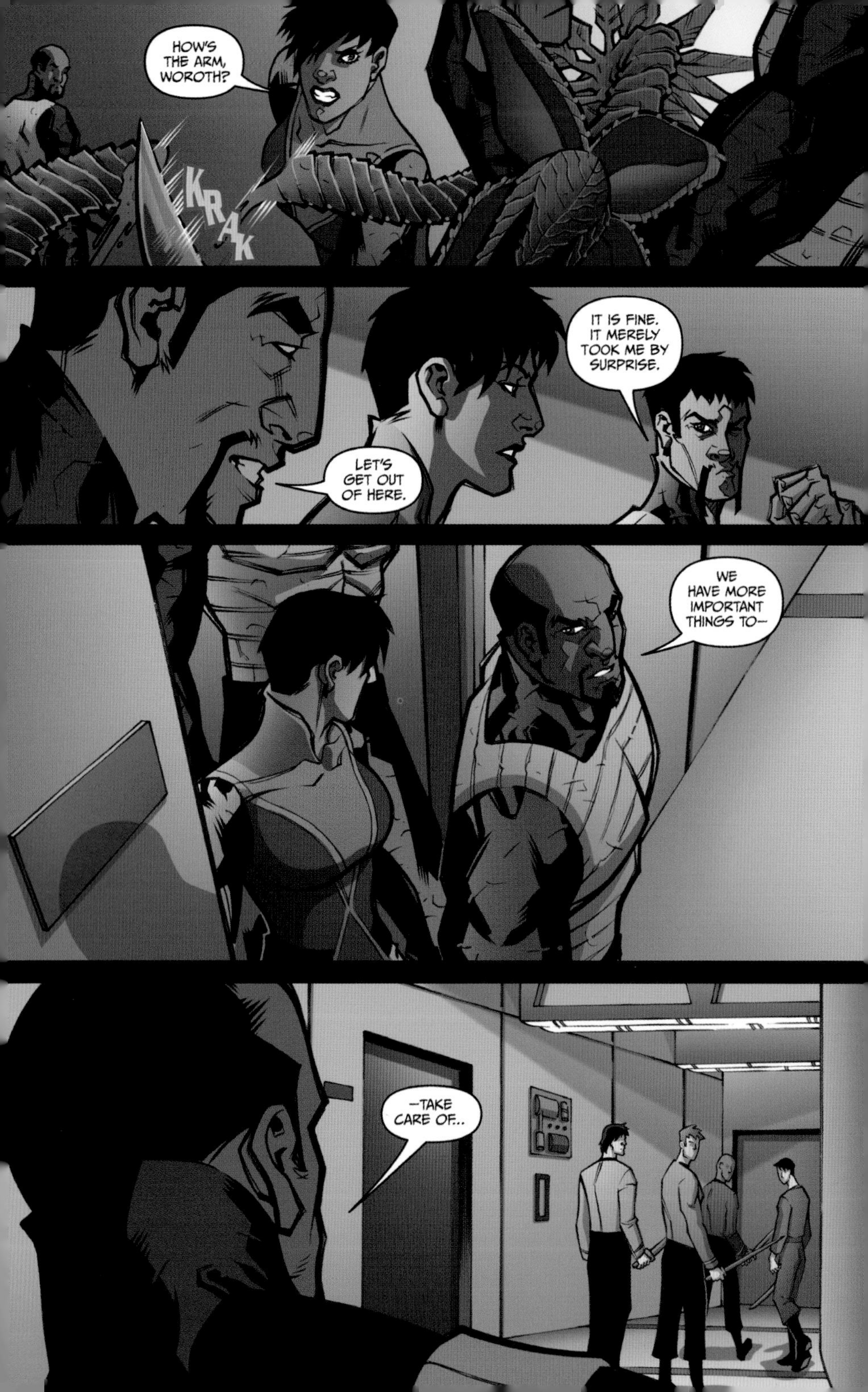
HOW'S THE ARM, WOROTH?
KRAK
IT IS FINE. IT MERELY TOOK ME BY SURPRISE.
LET'S GET OUT OF HERE.
WE HAVE MORE IMPORTANT THINGS TO—
—TAKE CARE OF...

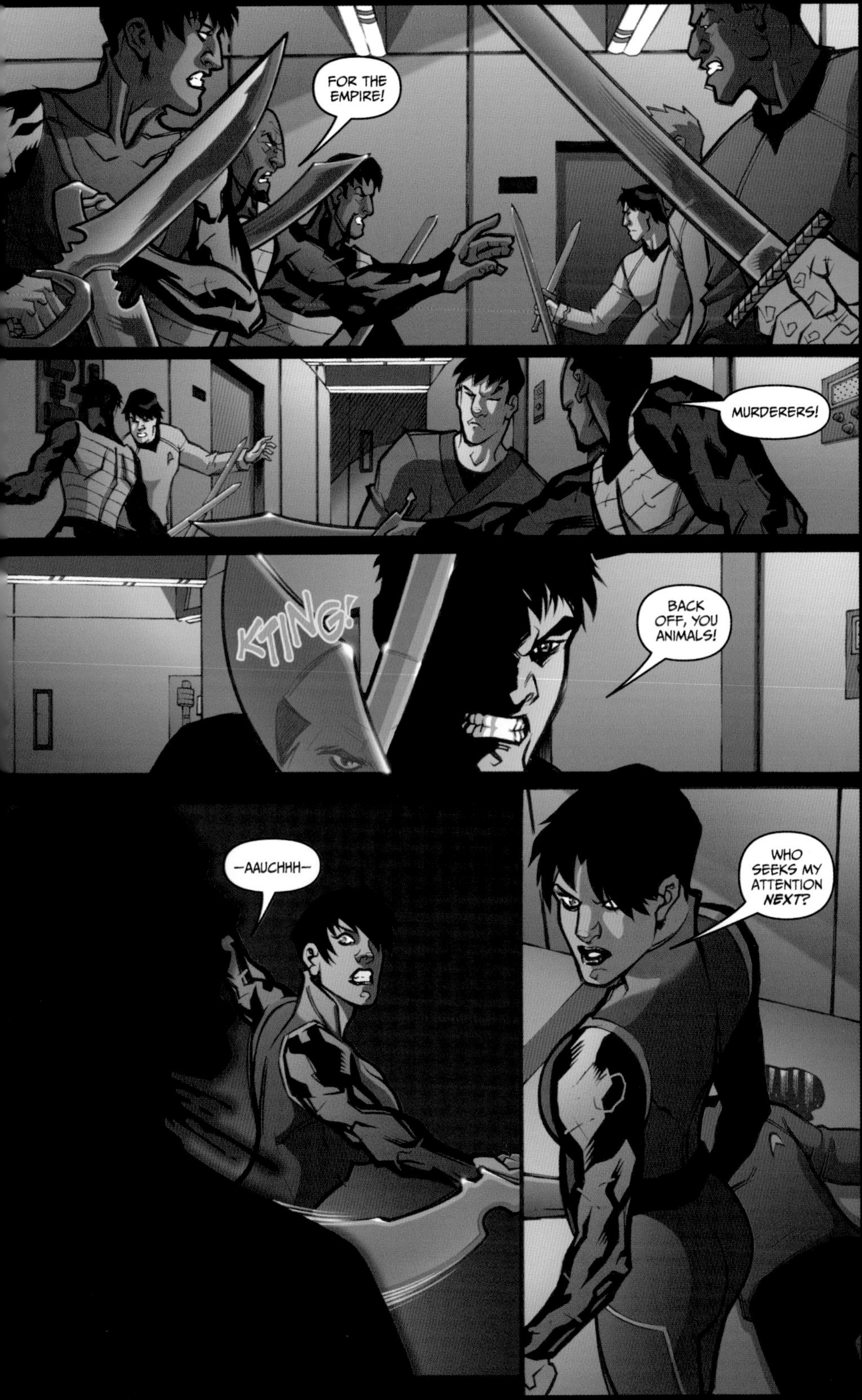
FOR THE EMPIRE!
MURDERERS!
KTING!
BACK OFF, YOU ANIMALS!
—AAUCHHH—
WHO SEEKS MY ATTENTION NEXT?

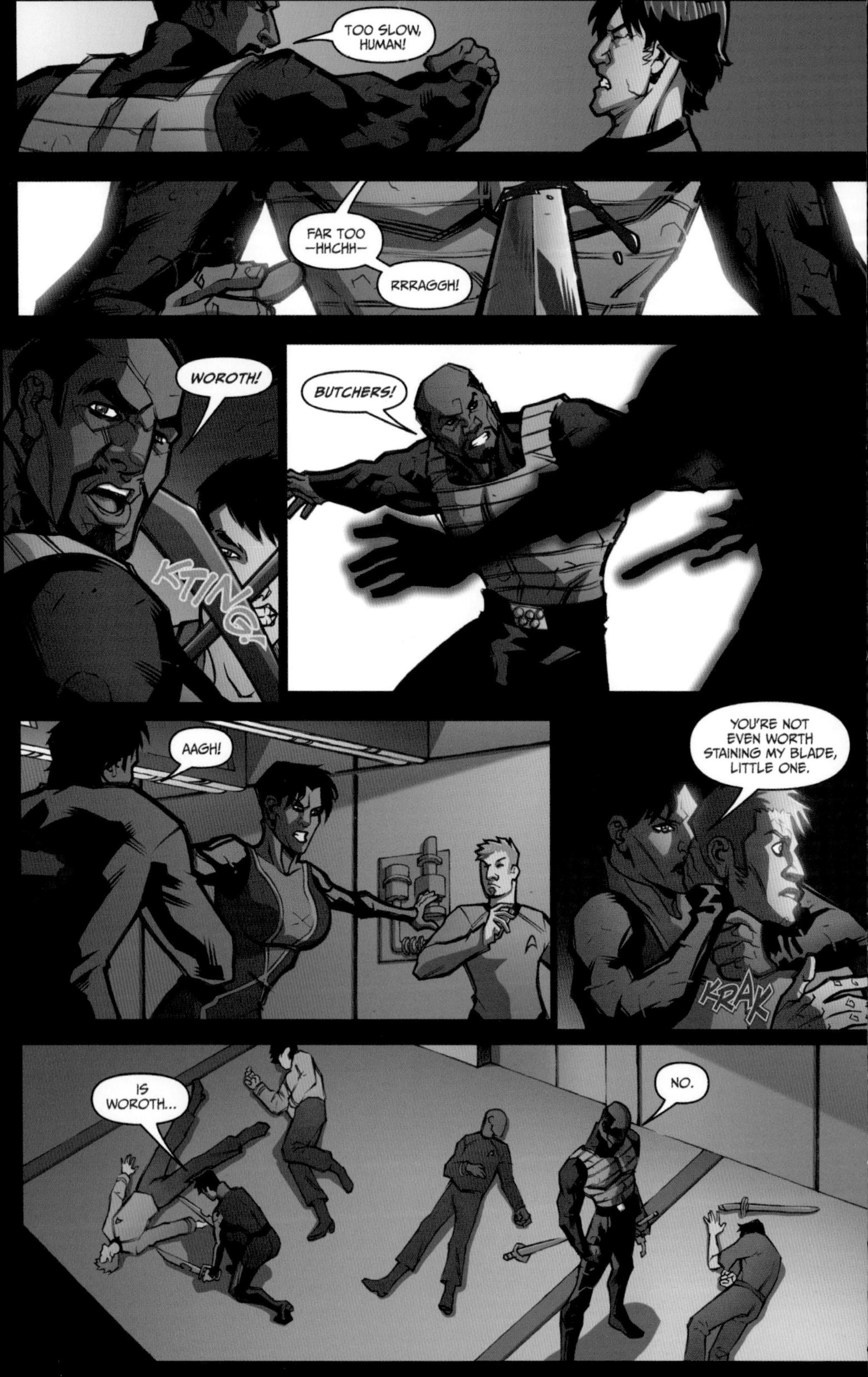
TOO SLOW, HUMAN!
FAR TOO —HHCHH—
RRRAGGH!
WOROTH!
KTING!
BUTCHERS!
AAGH!
YOU'RE NOT EVEN WORTH STAINING MY BLADE, LITTLE ONE.
KRAK
IS WOROTH...
NO.

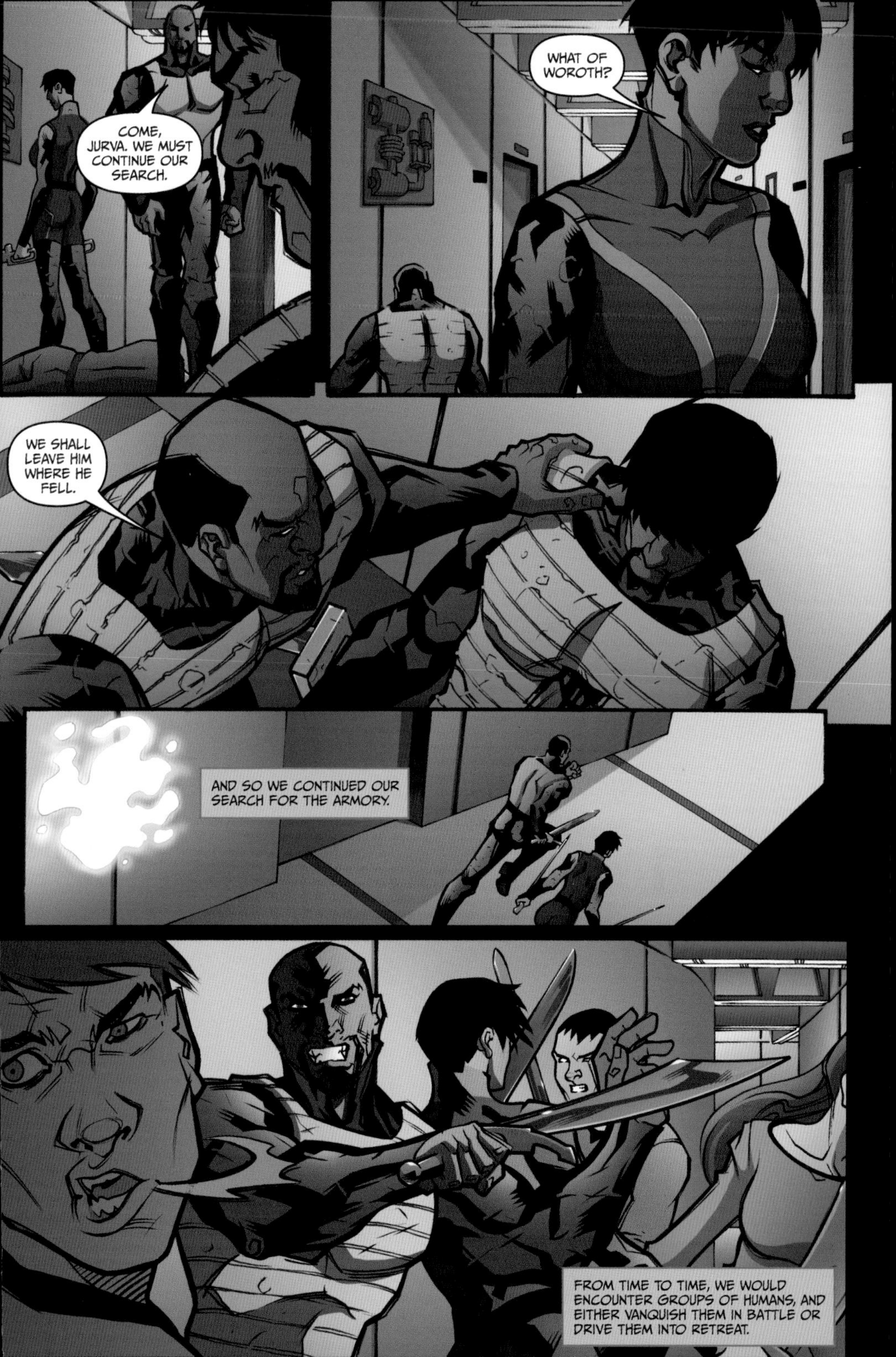
COME, JURVA. WE MUST CONTINUE OUR SEARCH.
WHAT OF WOROTH?
WE SHALL LEAVE HIM WHERE HE FELL.
AND SO WE CONTINUED OUR SEARCH FOR THE ARMORY.
FROM TIME TO TIME, WE WOULD ENCOUNTER GROUPS OF HUMANS, AND EITHER VANQUISH THEM IN BATTLE OR DRIVE THEM INTO RETREAT.

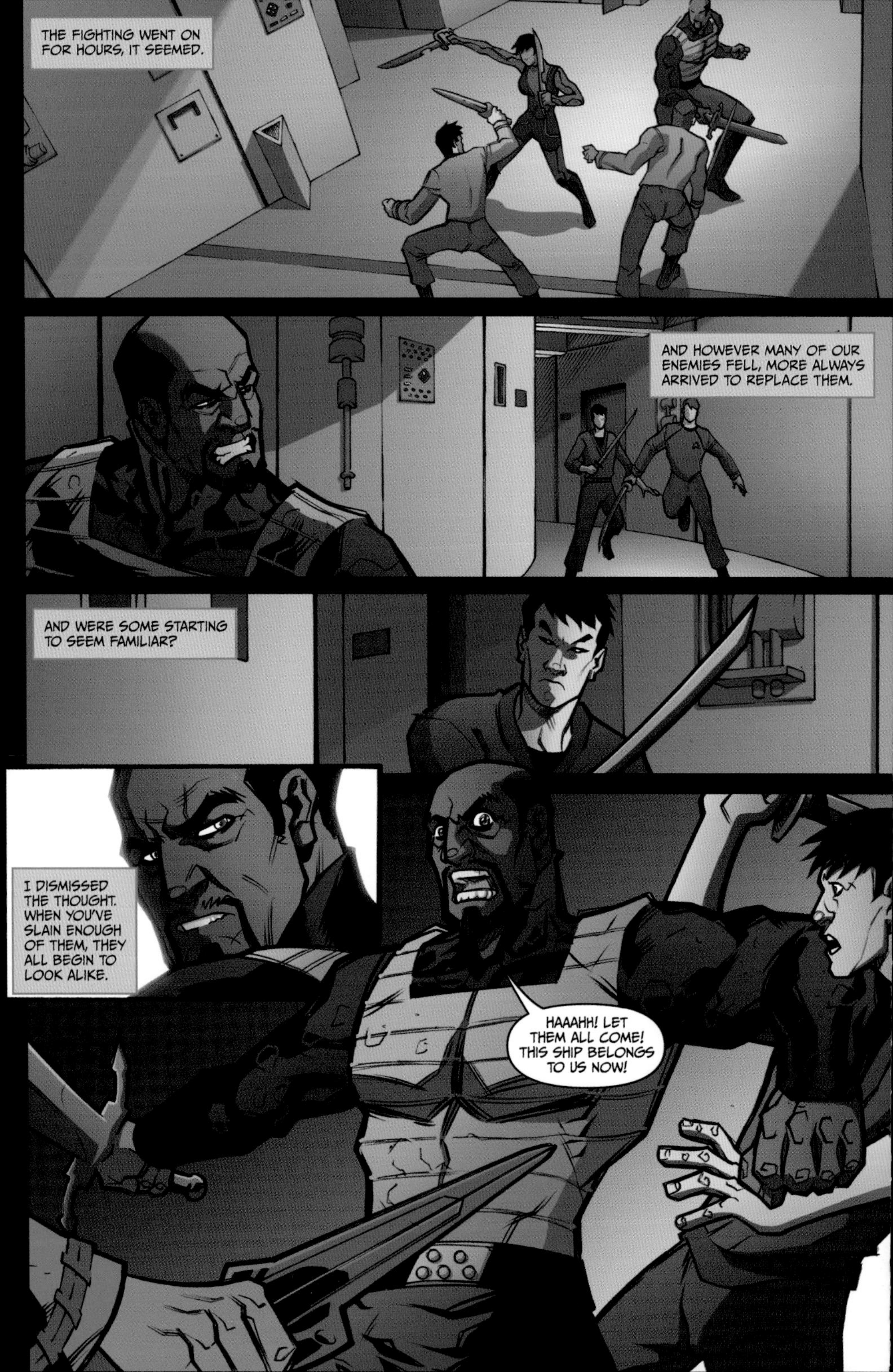
THE FIGHTING WENT ON FOR HOURS, IT SEEMED.
AND HOWEVER MANY OF OUR ENEMIES FELL, MORE ALWAYS ARRIVED TO REPLACE THEM.
AND WERE SOME STARTING TO SEEM FAMILIAR?
I DISMISSED THE THOUGHT. WHEN YOU'VE SLAIN ENOUGH OF THEM, THEY ALL BEGIN TO LOOK ALIKE.
HAAAAHH! LET THEM ALL COME! THIS SHIP BELONGS TO US NOW!

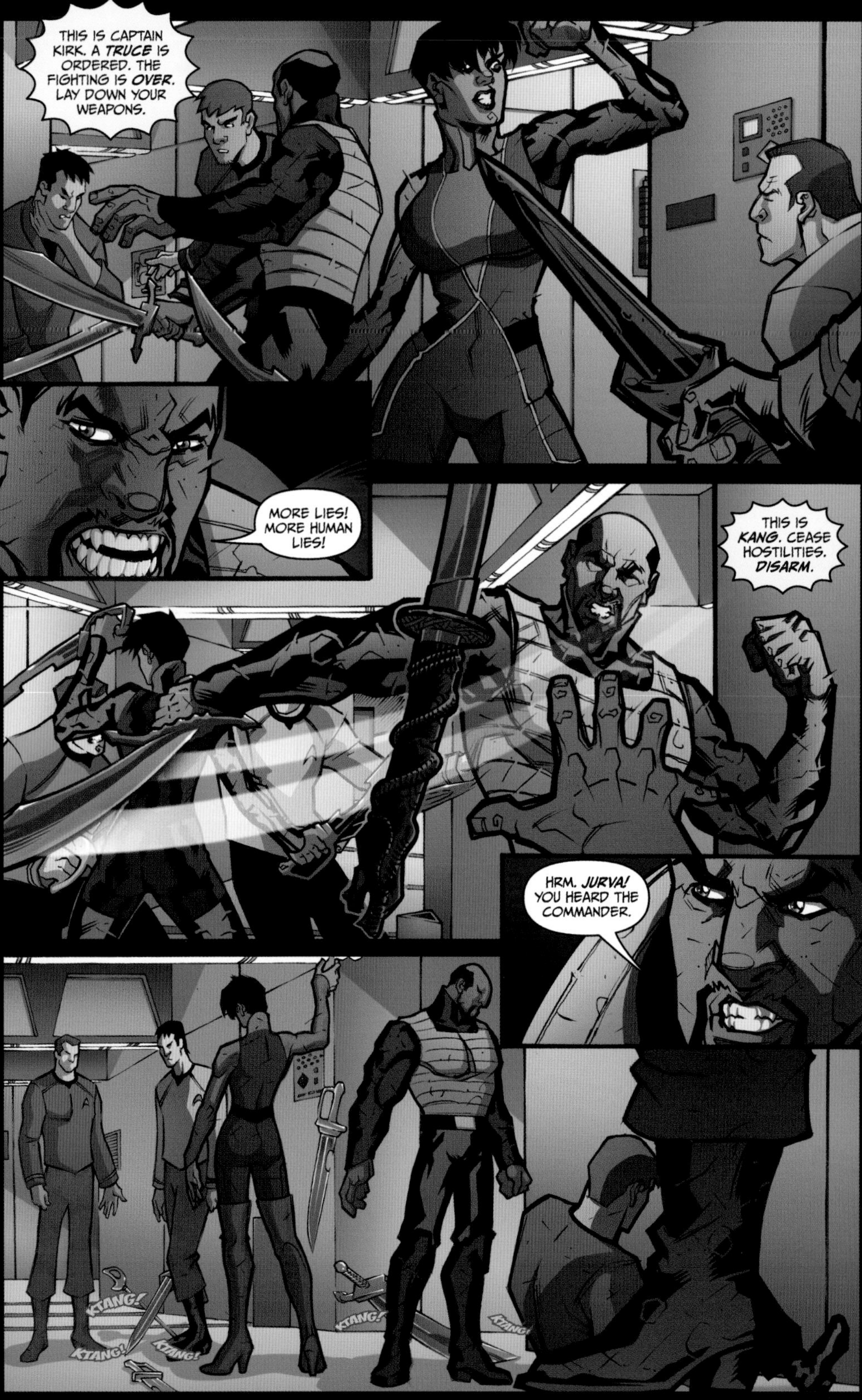
THIS IS CAPTAIN KIRK. A TRUCE IS ORDERED. THE FIGHTING IS OVER. LAY DOWN YOUR WEAPONS.
MORE LIES! MORE HUMAN LIES!
THIS IS KANG. CEASE HOSTILITIES. DISARM.
HRM. JURVA! YOU HEARD THE COMMANDER.
KTANG!
KTANG!
KTANG!
KTANG!
KTANG!

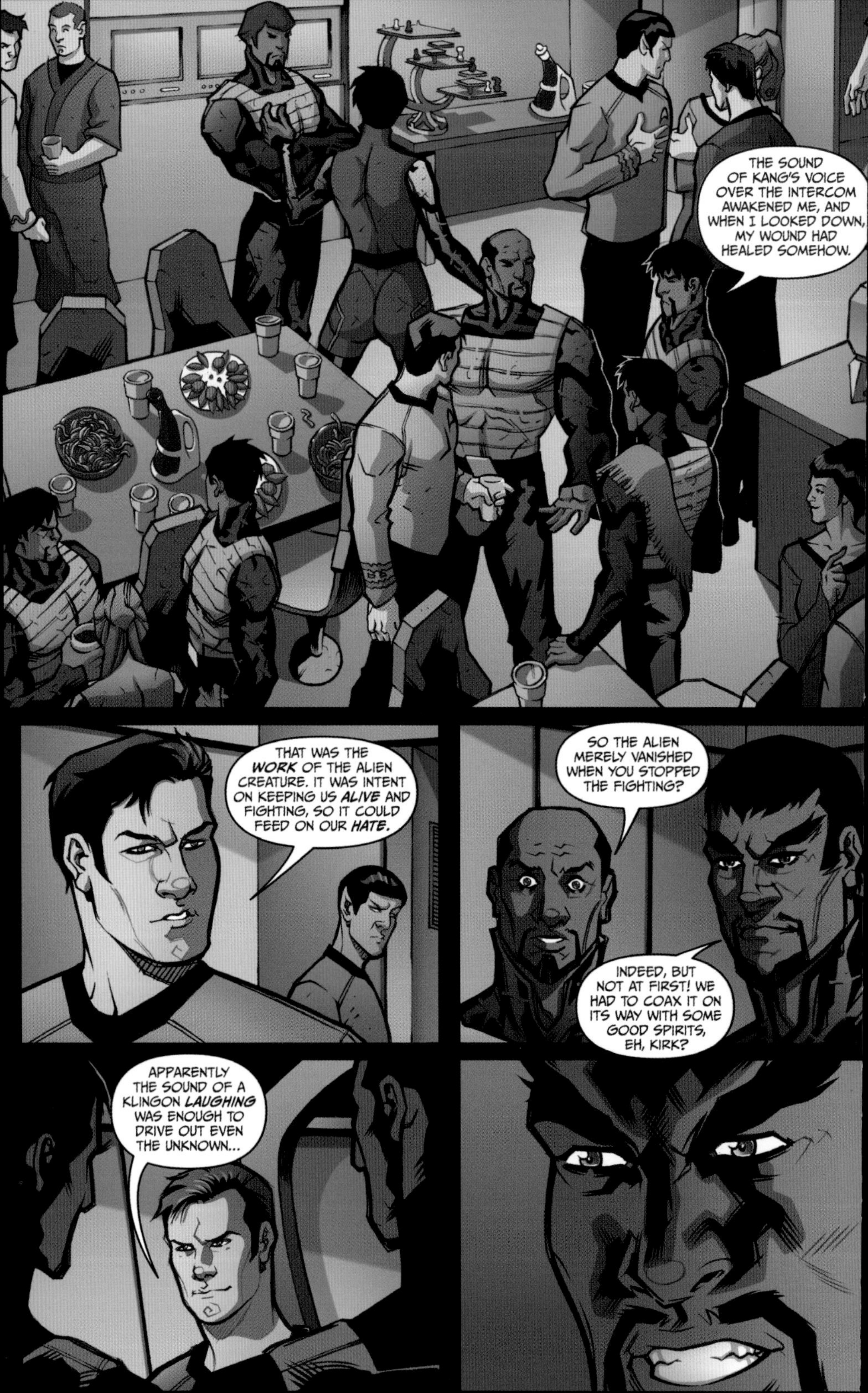
THE SOUND OF KANG'S VOICE OVER THE INTERCOM AWAKENED ME, AND WHEN I LOOKED DOWN, MY WOUND HAD HEALED SOMEHOW.
THAT WAS THE *WORK* OF THE ALIEN CREATURE. IT WAS INTENT ON KEEPING US *ALIVE* AND FIGHTING, SO IT COULD FEED ON OUR *HATE.*
SO THE ALIEN MERELY VANISHED WHEN YOU STOPPED THE FIGHTING?
INDEED, BUT NOT AT FIRST! WE HAD TO COAX IT ON ITS WAY WITH SOME GOOD SPIRITS, EH, KIRK?
APPARENTLY THE SOUND OF A KLINGON *LAUGHING* WAS ENOUGH TO DRIVE OUT EVEN THE UNKNOWN...

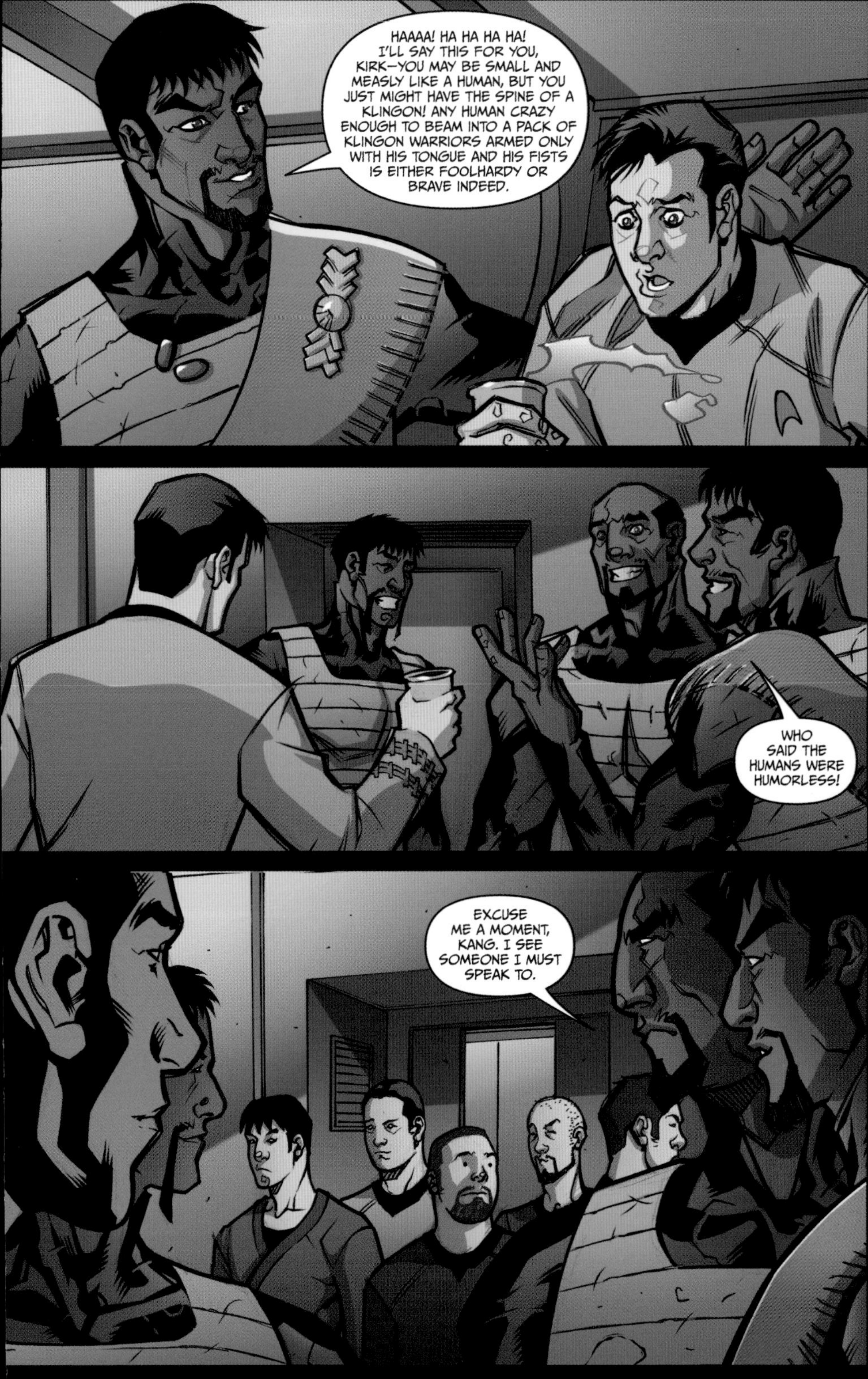
HAAAA! HA HA HA HA! I'LL SAY THIS FOR YOU, KIRK—YOU MAY BE SMALL AND MEASLY LIKE A HUMAN, BUT YOU JUST MIGHT HAVE THE SPINE OF A KLINGON! ANY HUMAN CRAZY ENOUGH TO BEAM INTO A PACK OF KLINGON WARRIORS ARMED ONLY WITH HIS TONGUE AND HIS FISTS IS EITHER FOOLHARDY OR BRAVE INDEED.
WHO SAID THE HUMANS WERE HUMORLESS!
EXCUSE ME A MOMENT, KANG. I SEE SOMEONE I MUST SPEAK TO.

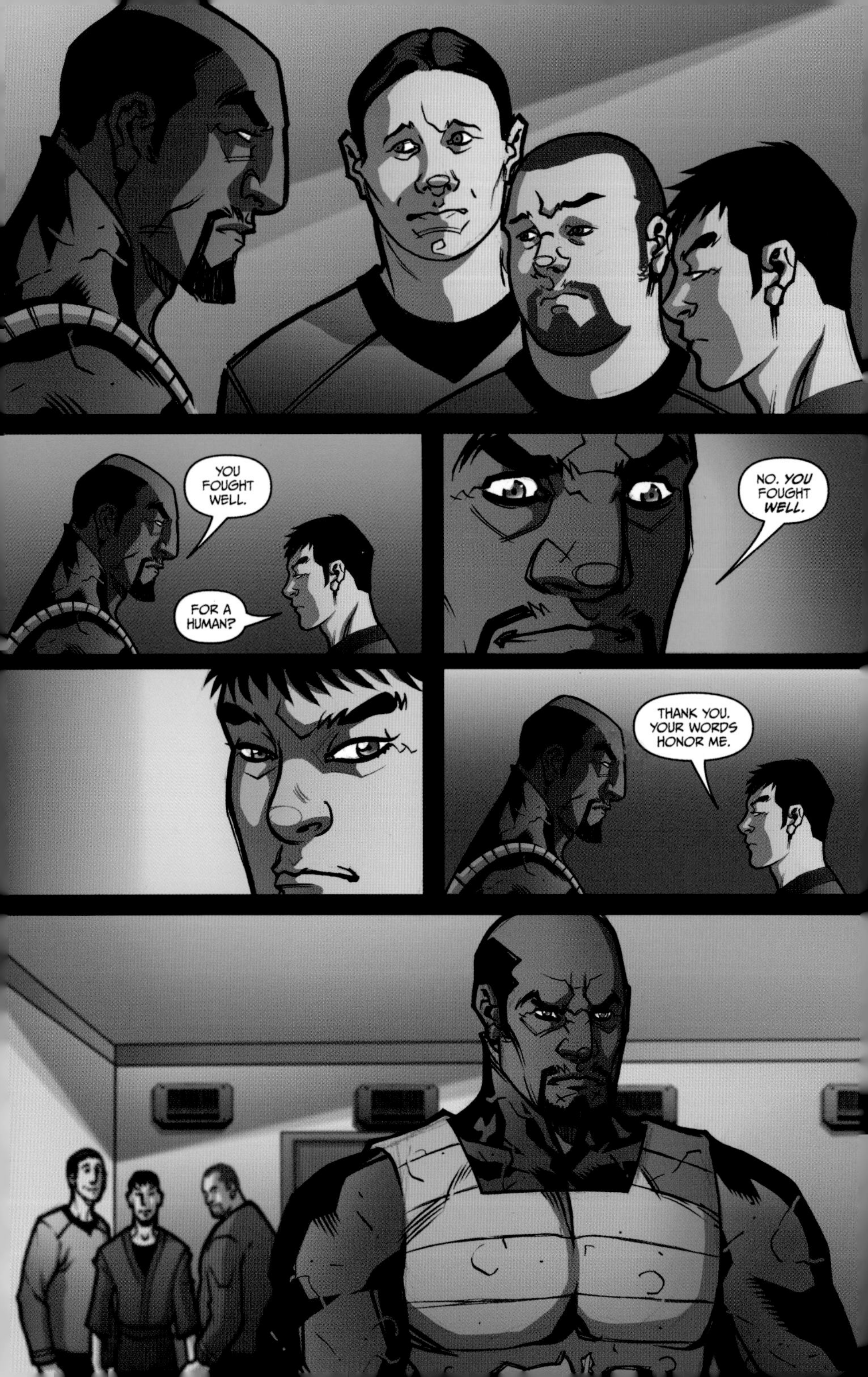
YOU FOUGHT WELL.
FOR A HUMAN?
NO. YOU FOUGHT WELL.
THANK YOU. YOUR WORDS HONOR ME.

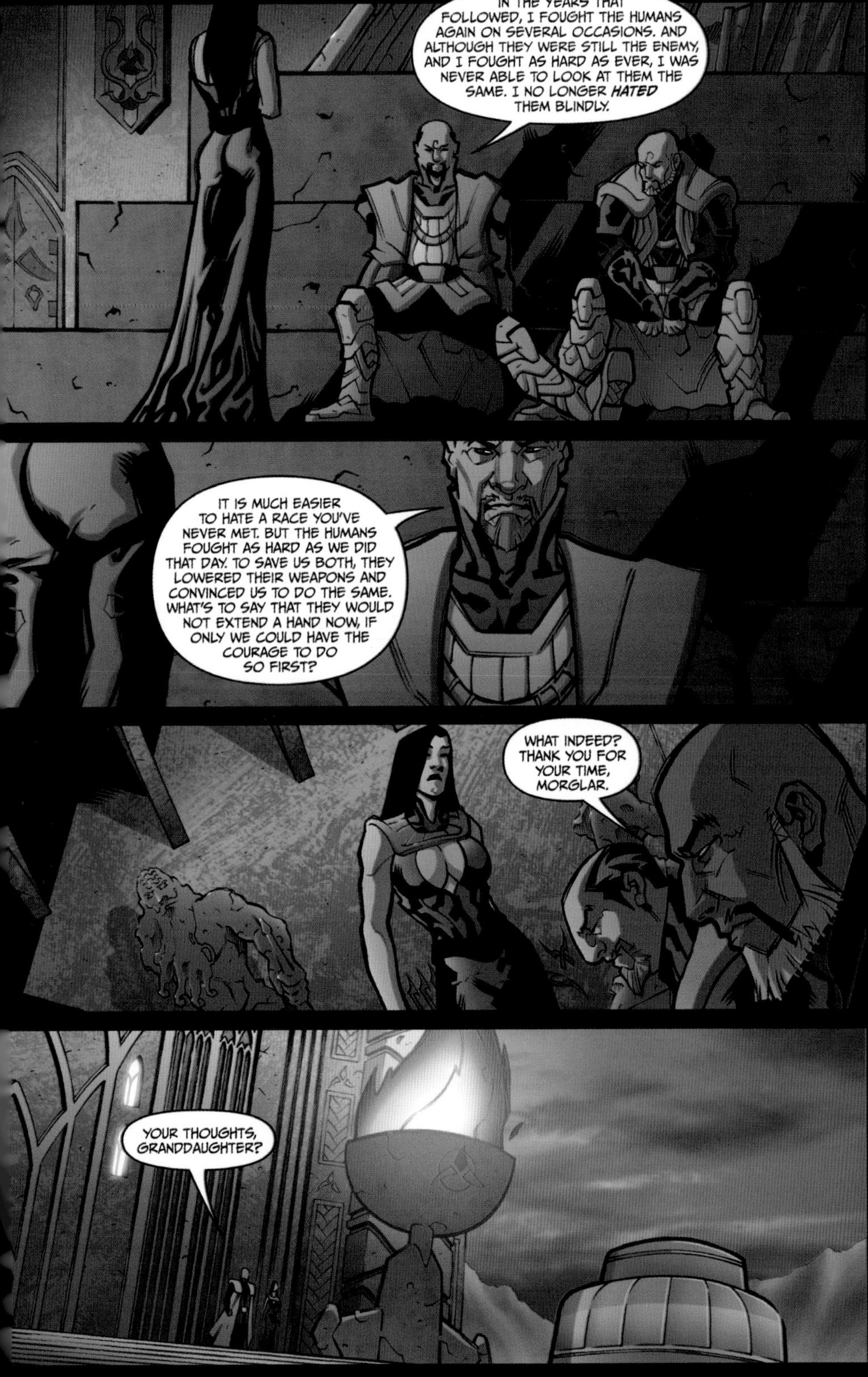
IN THE YEARS THAT FOLLOWED, I FOUGHT THE HUMANS AGAIN ON SEVERAL OCCASIONS. AND ALTHOUGH THEY WERE STILL THE ENEMY, AND I FOUGHT AS HARD AS EVER, I WAS NEVER ABLE TO LOOK AT THEM THE SAME. I NO LONGER *HATED* THEM BLINDLY.
IT IS MUCH EASIER TO HATE A RACE YOU'VE NEVER MET. BUT THE HUMANS FOUGHT AS HARD AS WE DID THAT DAY. TO SAVE US BOTH, THEY LOWERED THEIR WEAPONS AND CONVINCED US TO DO THE SAME. WHAT'S TO SAY THAT THEY WOULD NOT EXTEND A HAND NOW, IF ONLY WE COULD HAVE THE COURAGE TO DO SO FIRST?
WHAT INDEED? THANK YOU FOR YOUR TIME, MORGLAR.
YOUR THOUGHTS, GRANDDAUGHTER?

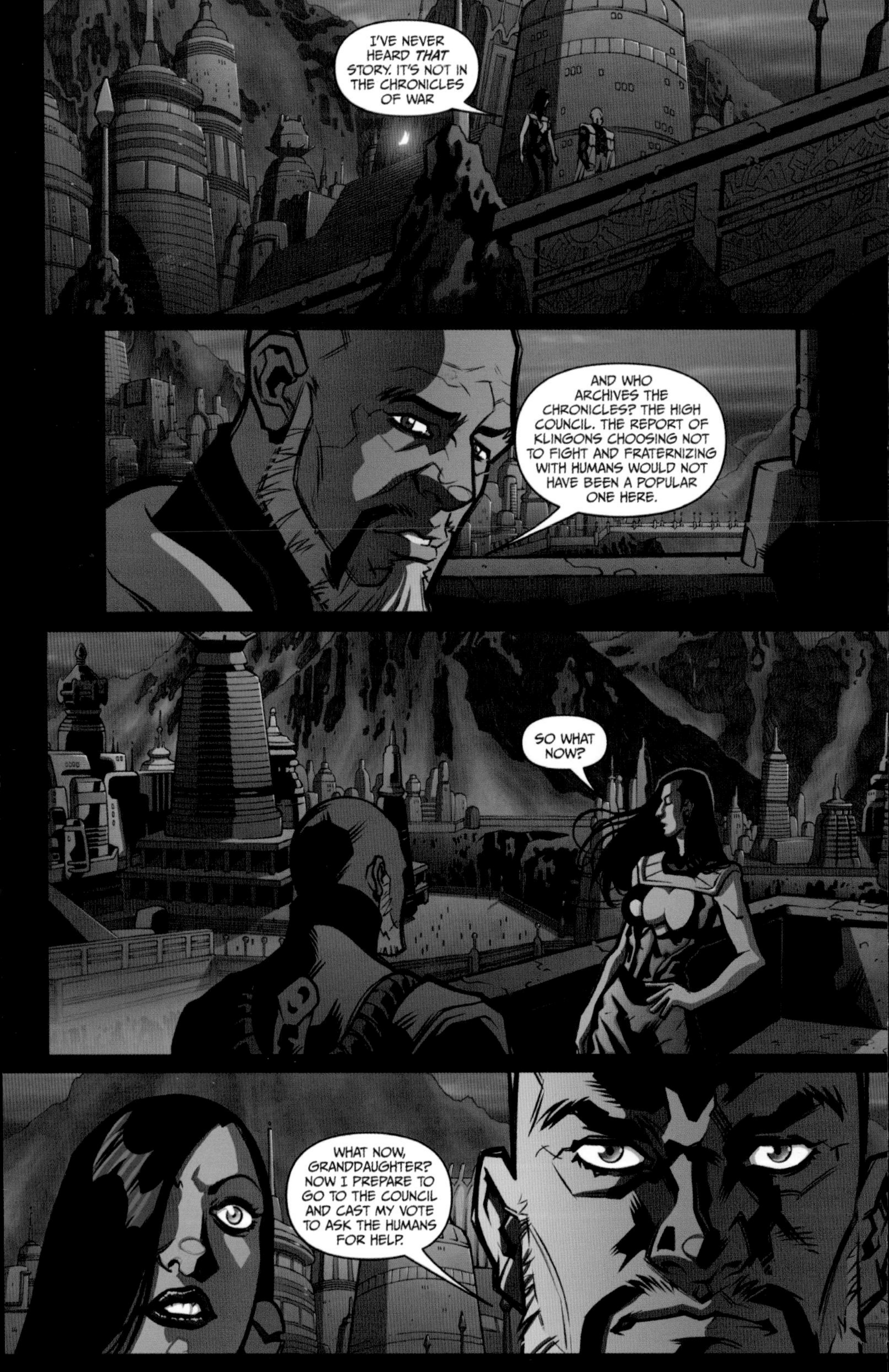
I'VE NEVER HEARD *THAT* STORY. IT'S NOT IN THE CHRONICLES OF WAR
AND WHO ARCHIVES THE CHRONICLES? THE HIGH COUNCIL. THE REPORT OF KLINGONS CHOOSING NOT TO FIGHT AND FRATERNIZING WITH HUMANS WOULD NOT HAVE BEEN A POPULAR ONE HERE.
SO WHAT NOW?
WHAT NOW, GRANDDAUGHTER? NOW I PREPARE TO GO TO THE COUNCIL AND CAST MY VOTE TO ASK THE HUMANS FOR HELP.

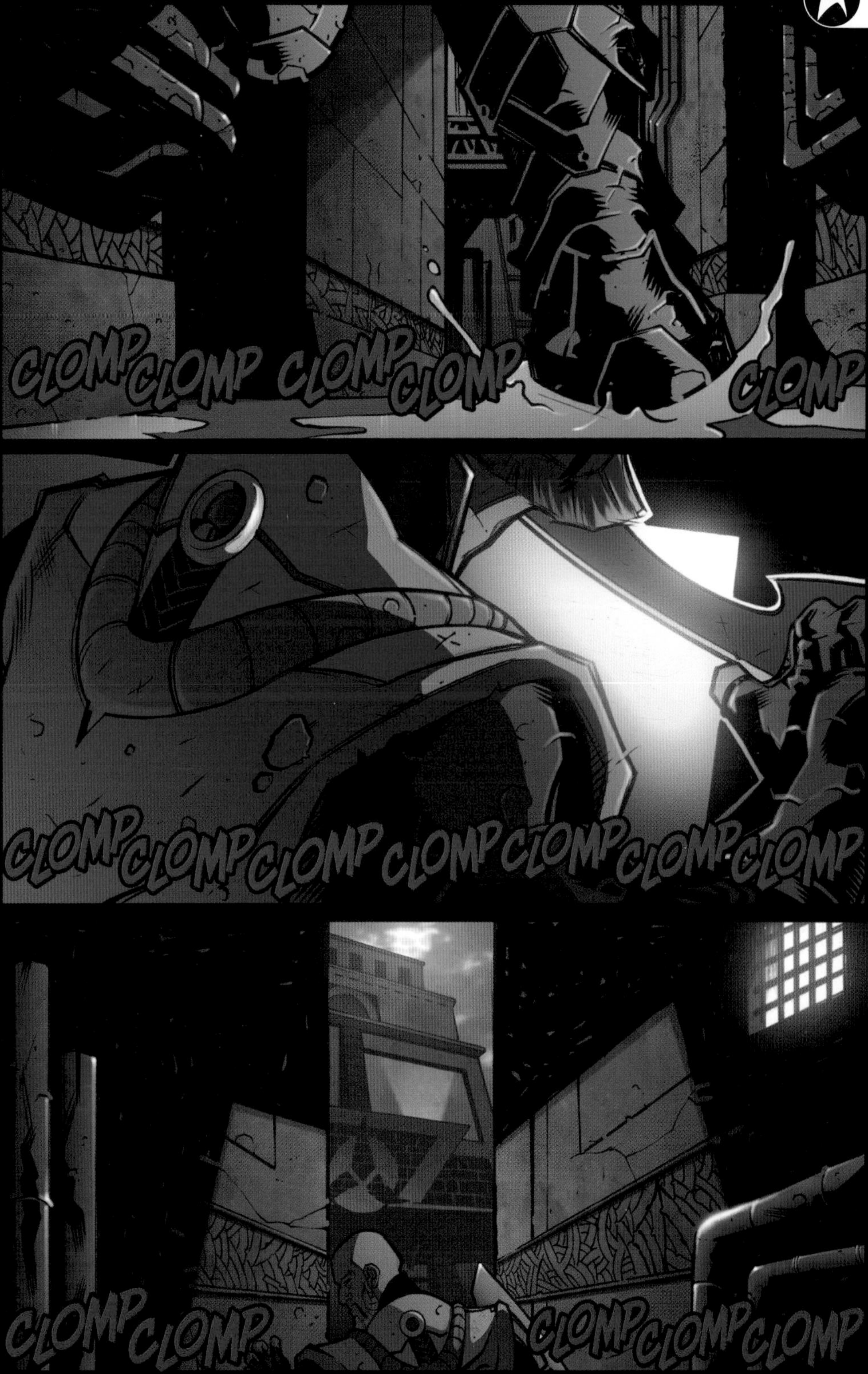
CLOMP CLOMP CLOMP CLOMP CLOMP
CLOMP CLOMP CLOMP CLOMP CLOMP CLOMP CLOMP
CLOMP CLOMP CLOMP CLOMP CLOMP

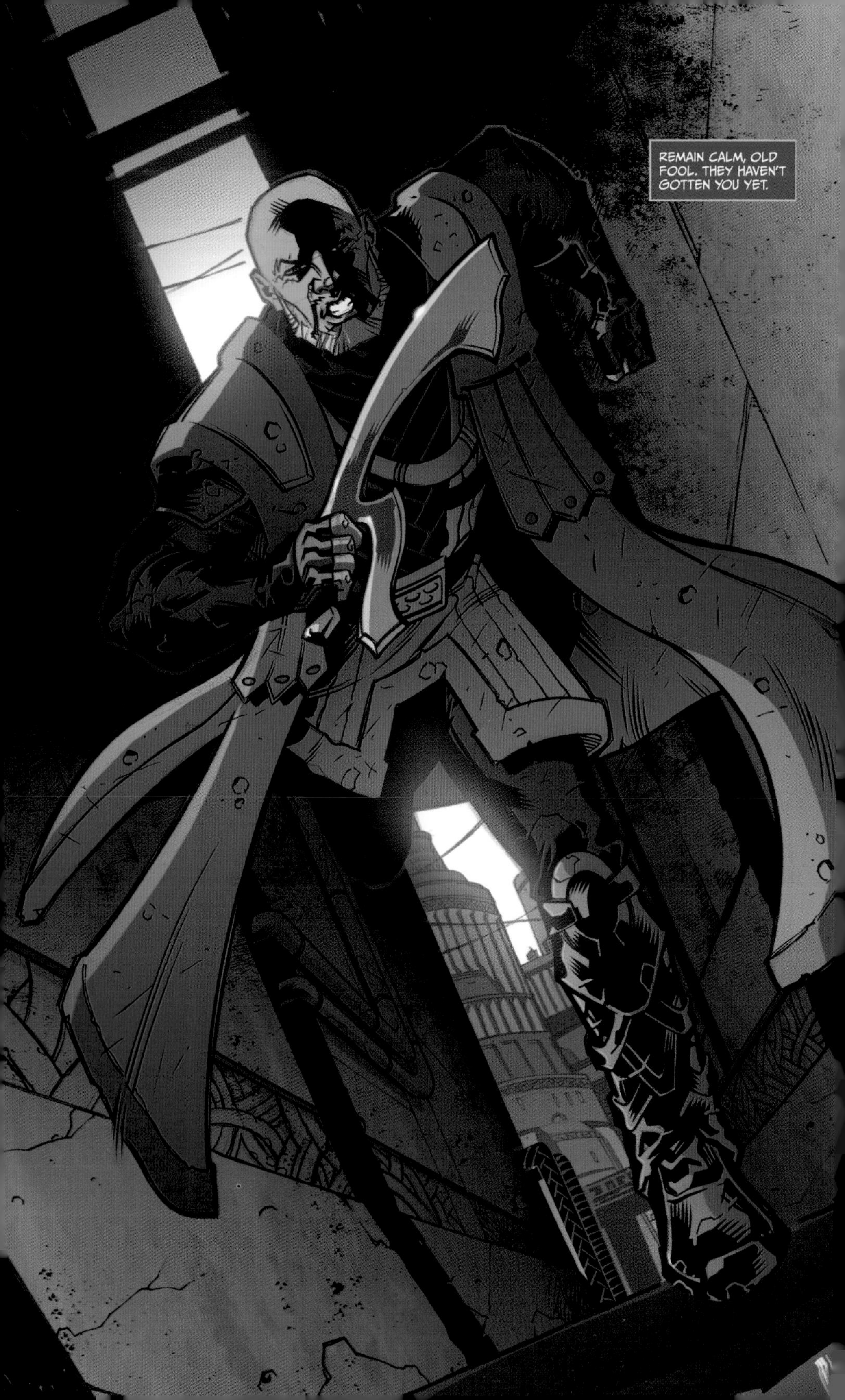
REMAIN CALM, OLD FOOL. THEY HAVEN'T GOTTEN YOU YET.

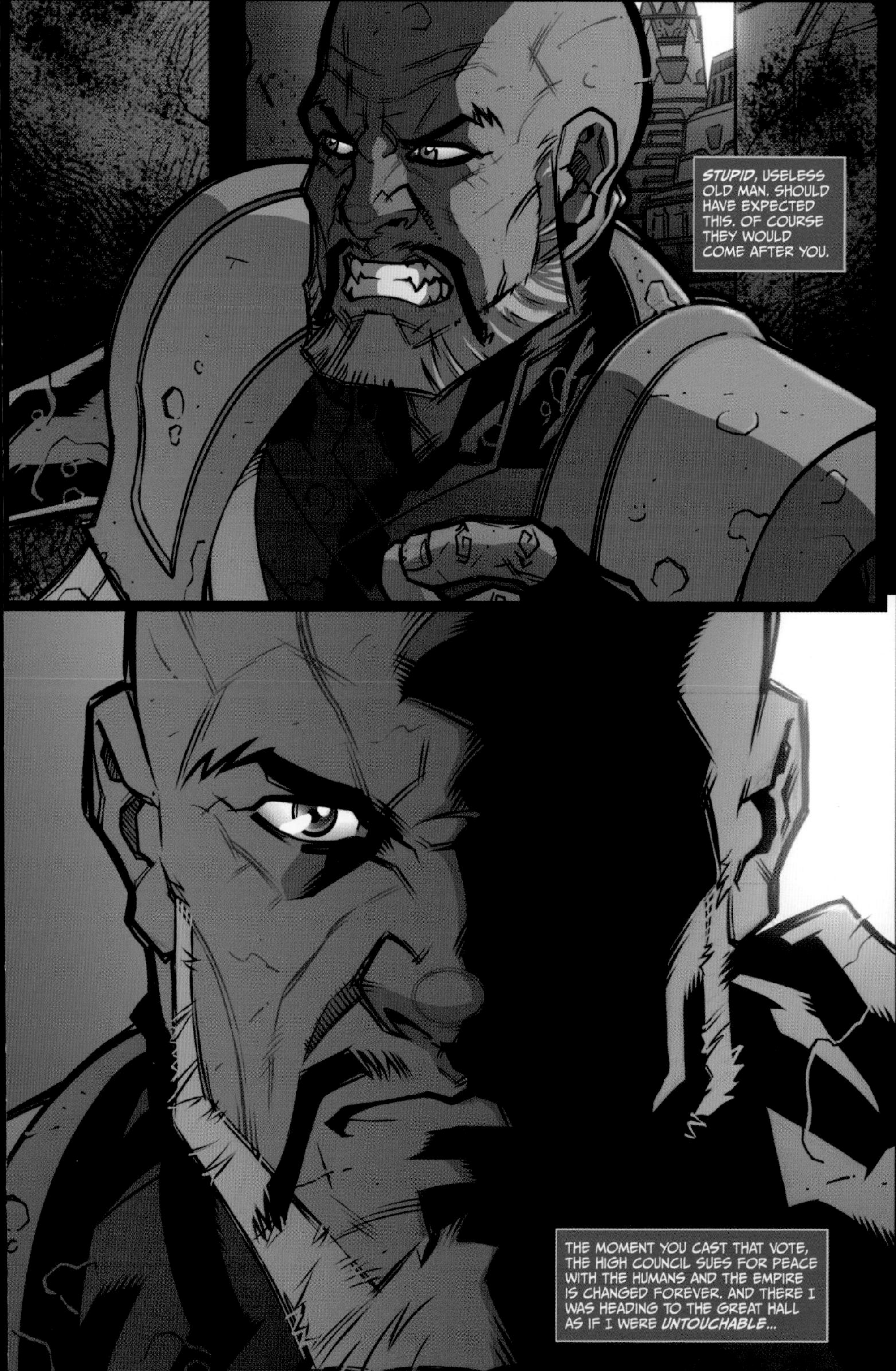
STUPID, USELESS OLD MAN. SHOULD HAVE EXPECTED THIS. OF COURSE THEY WOULD COME AFTER YOU.
THE MOMENT YOU CAST THAT VOTE, THE HIGH COUNCIL SUES FOR PEACE WITH THE HUMANS AND THE EMPIRE IS CHANGED FOREVER. AND THERE I WAS HEADING TO THE GREAT HALL AS IF I WERE UNTOUCHABLE...

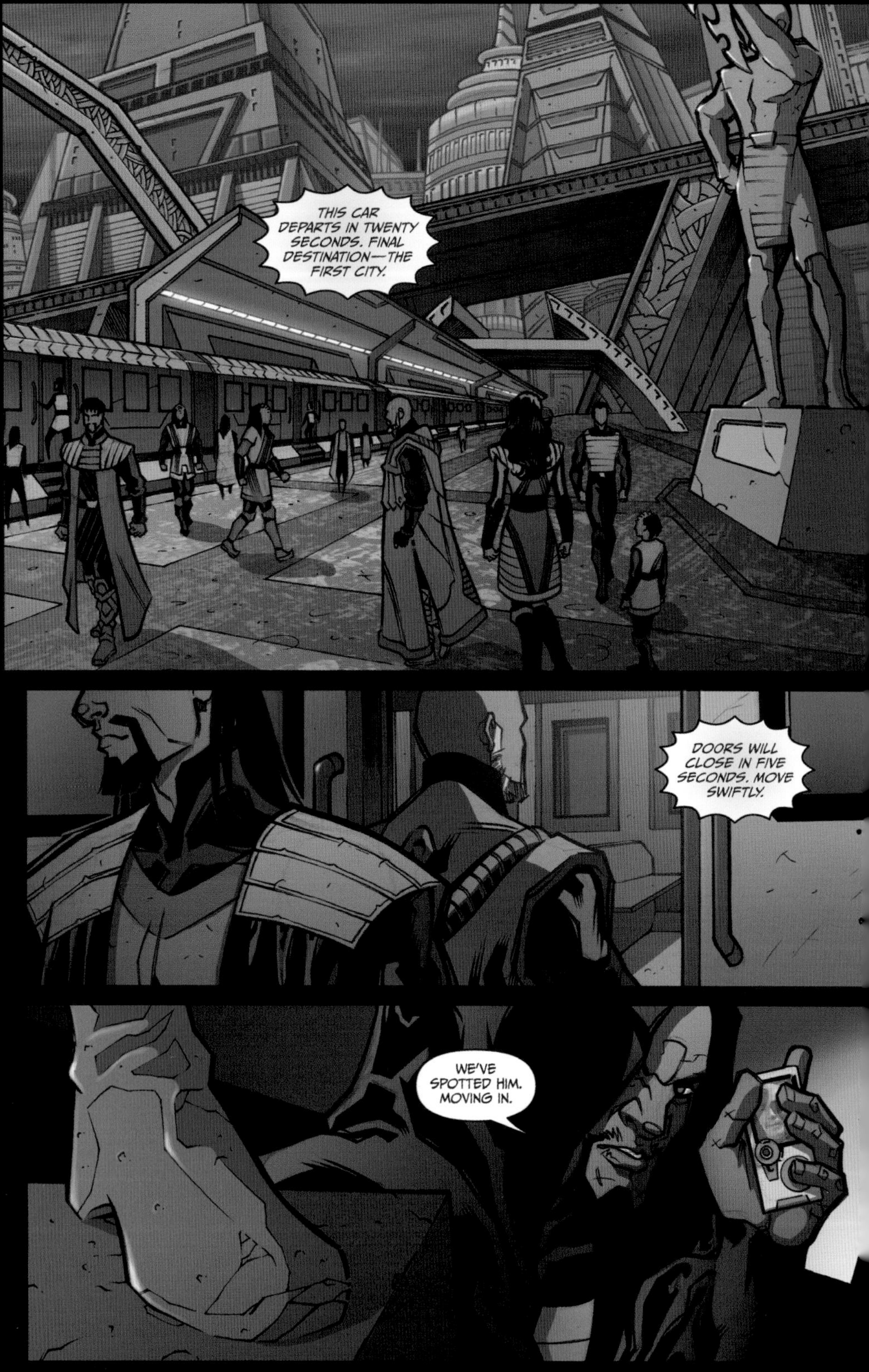
THIS CAR DEPARTS IN TWENTY SECONDS. FINAL DESTINATION—THE FIRST CITY.
DOORS WILL CLOSE IN FIVE SECONDS. MOVE SWIFTLY.
WE'VE SPOTTED HIM. MOVING IN.

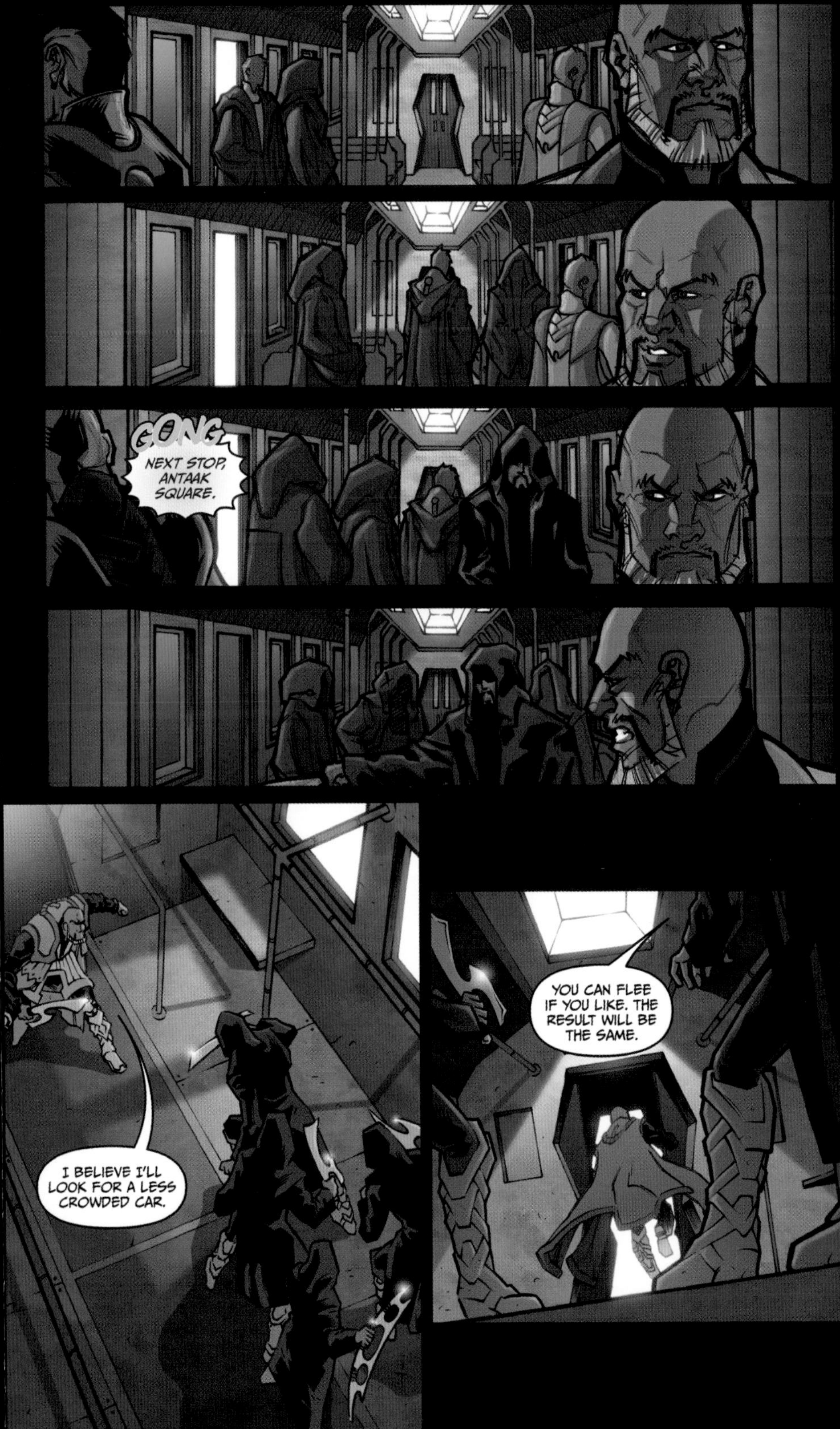
GONG
NEXT STOP, ANTAAK SQUARE.
I BELIEVE I'LL LOOK FOR A LESS CROWDED CAR.
YOU CAN FLEE IF YOU LIKE. THE RESULT WILL BE THE SAME.

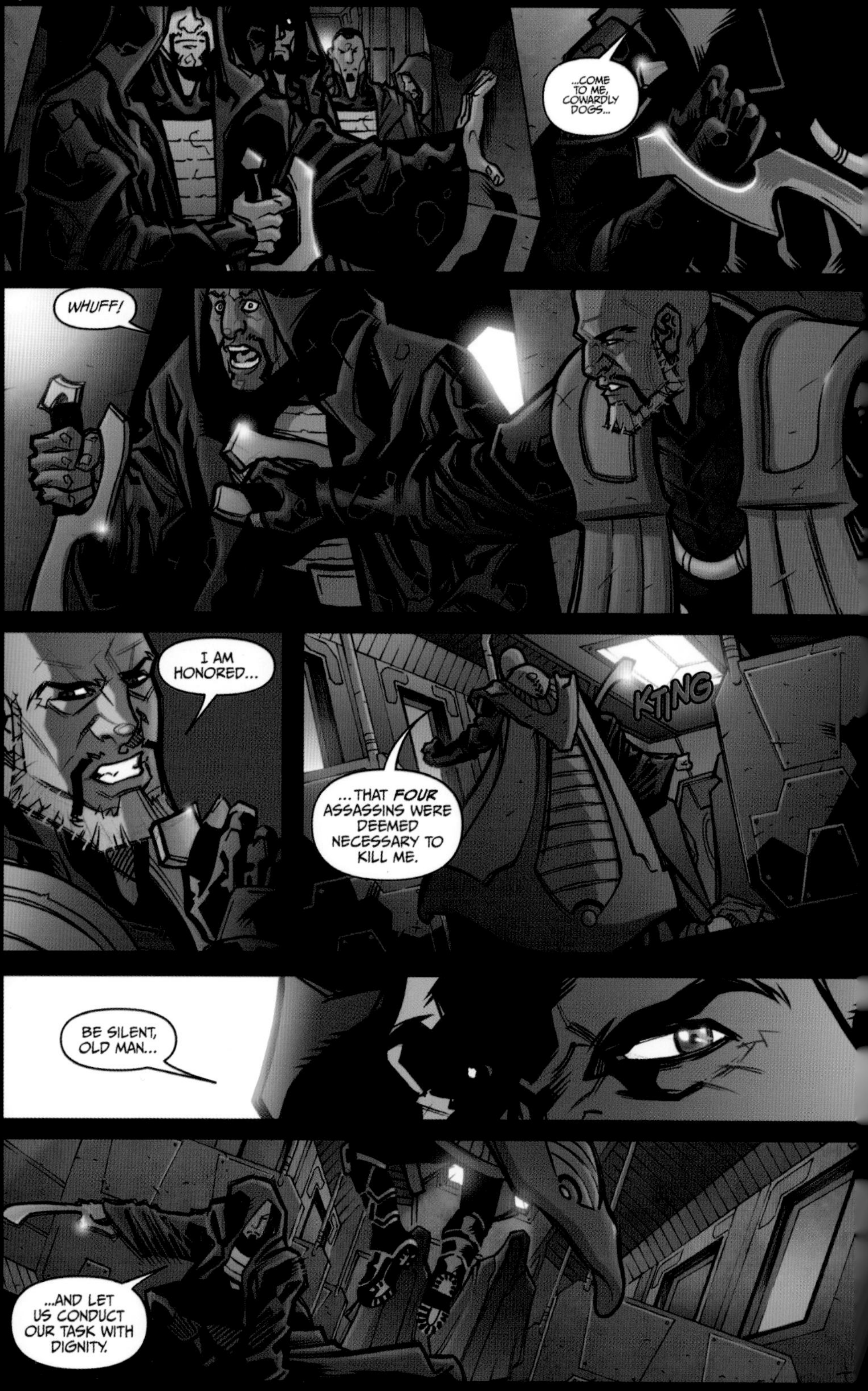
...COME TO ME, COWARDLY DOGS...
WHUFF!
I AM HONORED...
...THAT FOUR ASSASSINS WERE DEEMED NECESSARY TO KILL ME.
KTING
BE SILENT, OLD MAN...
...AND LET US CONDUCT OUR TASK WITH DIGNITY.

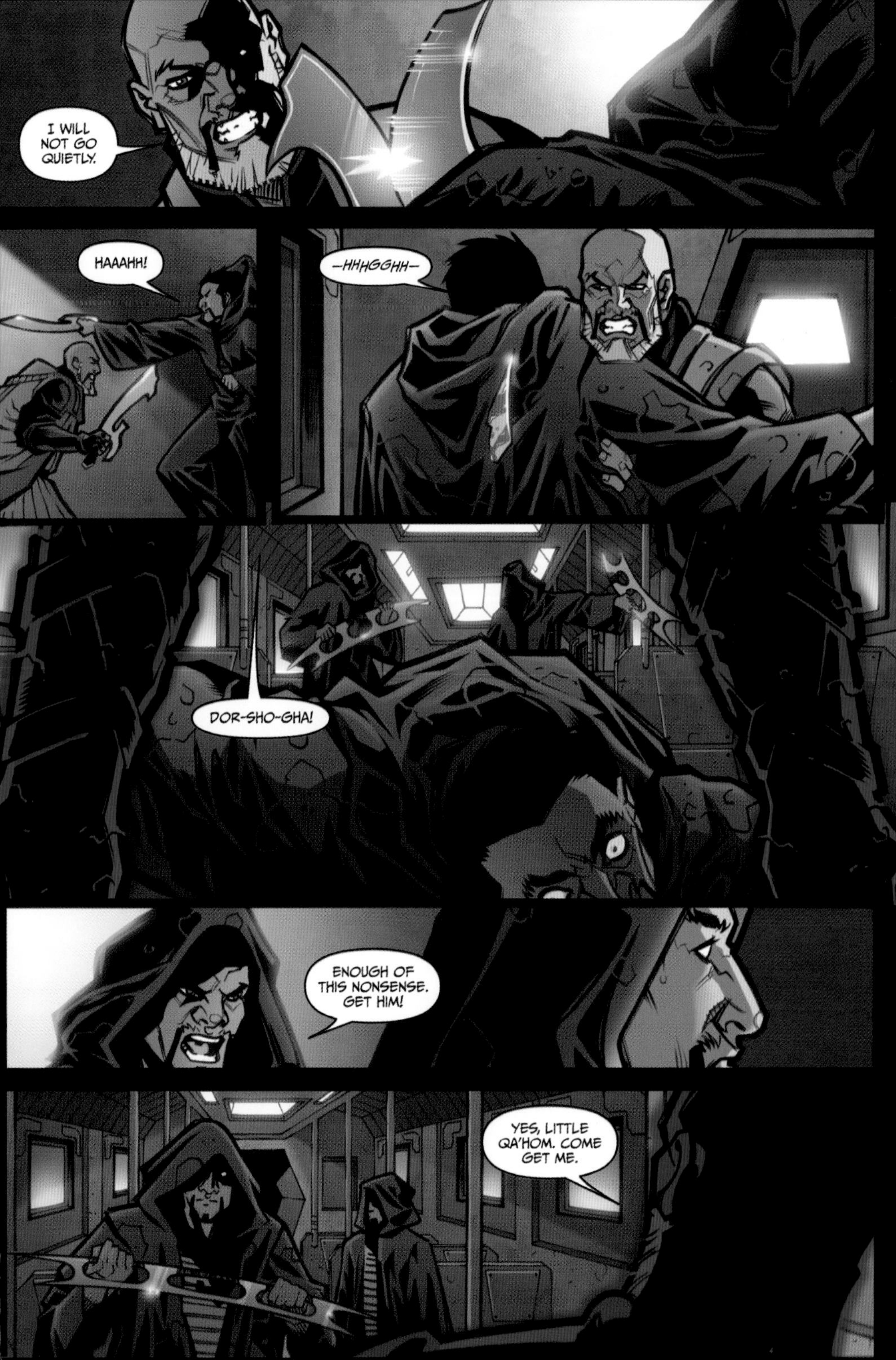
I WILL NOT GO QUIETLY.
HAAAHH!
—HHHGGHH—
DOR-SHO-GHA!
ENOUGH OF THIS NONSENSE. GET HIM!
YES, LITTLE QA'HOM. COME GET ME.

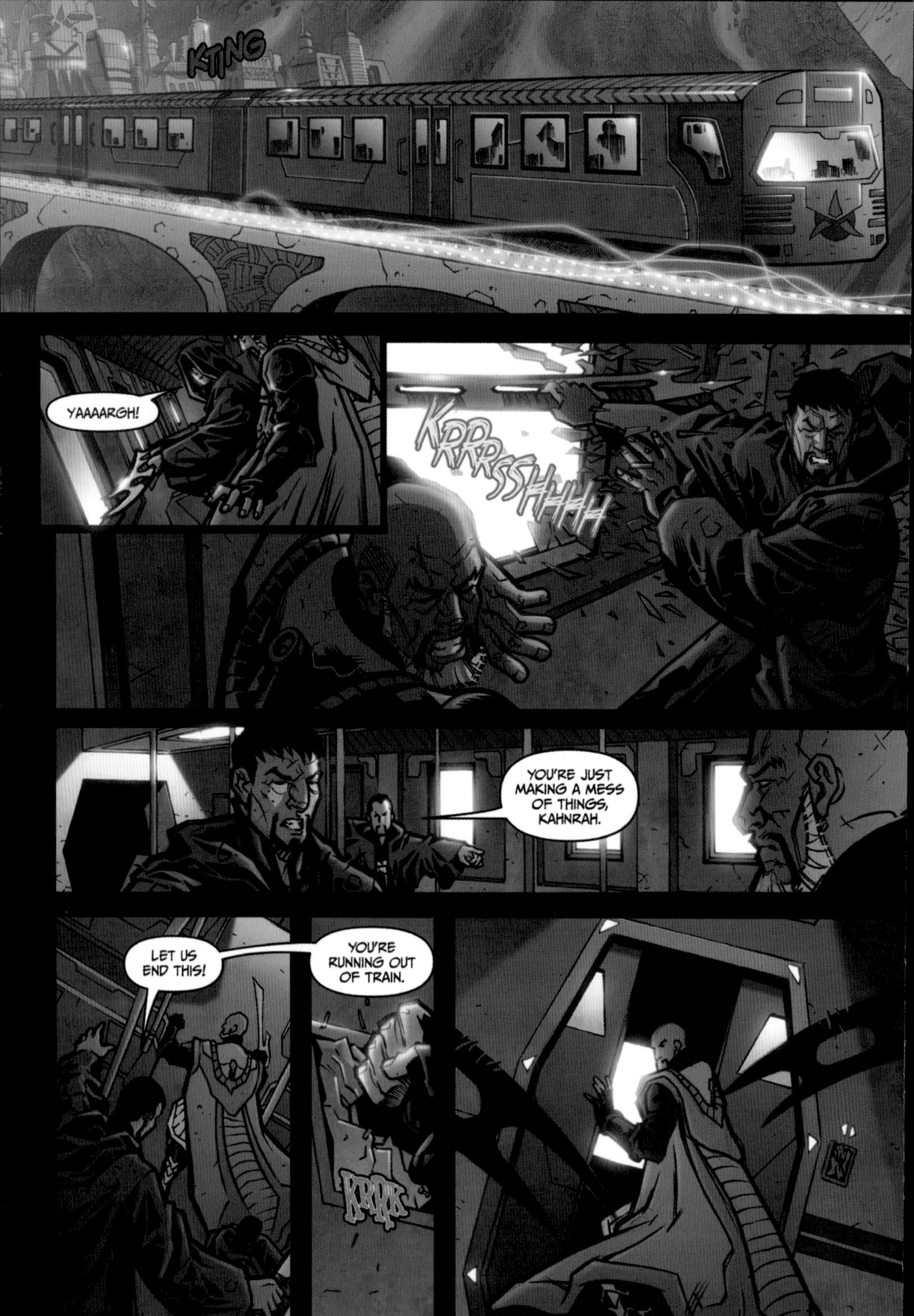
KTING
YAAAARGH!
KRRRRRSSHHHH
YOU'RE JUST MAKING A MESS OF THINGS, KAHNRAH.
LET US END THIS!
YOU'RE RUNNING OUT OF TRAIN.
KRRK

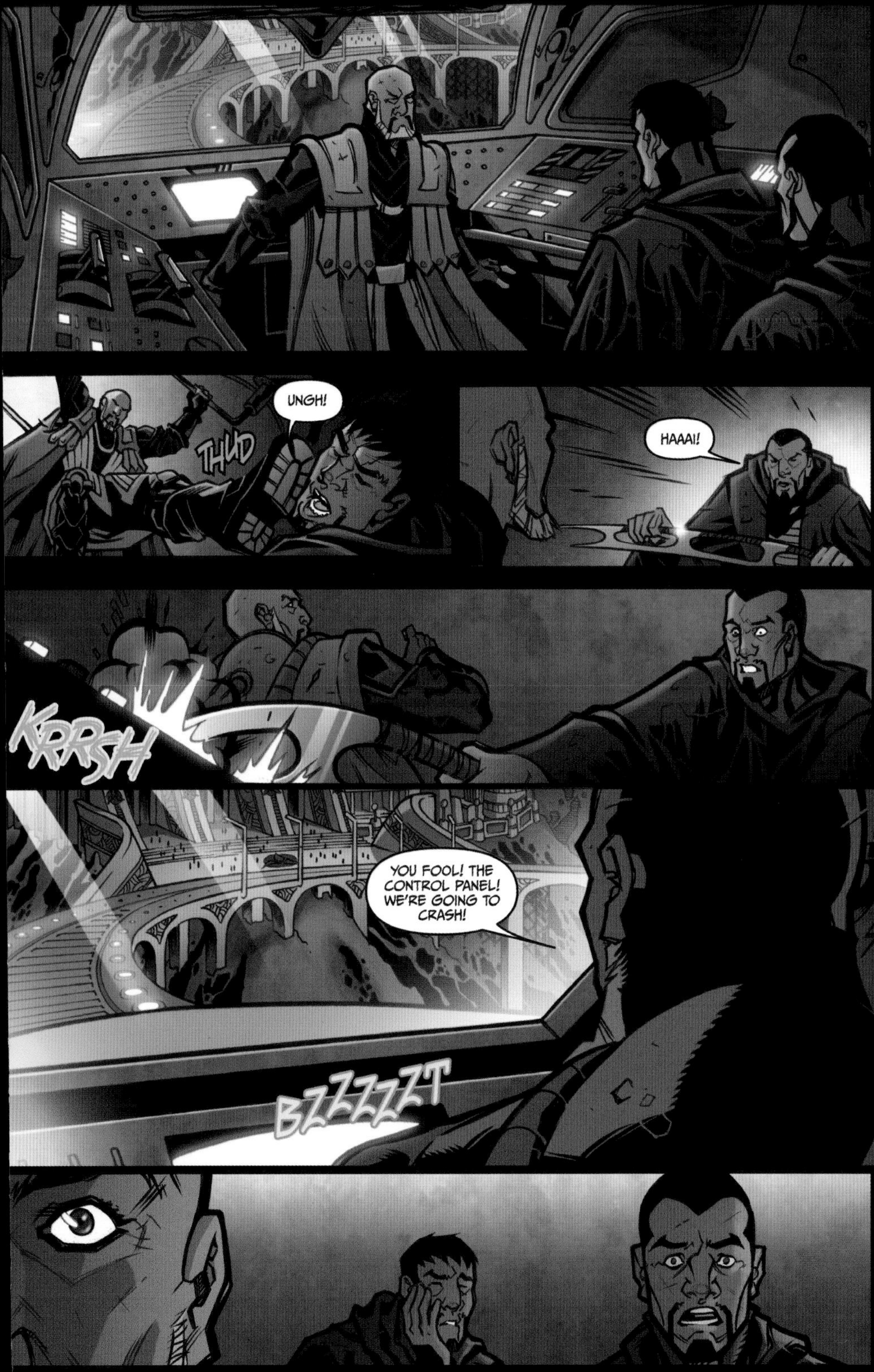
UNGH!
THUD
HAAAI!
KRRSH
YOU FOOL! THE CONTROL PANEL! WE'RE GOING TO CRASH!
BZZZZZT

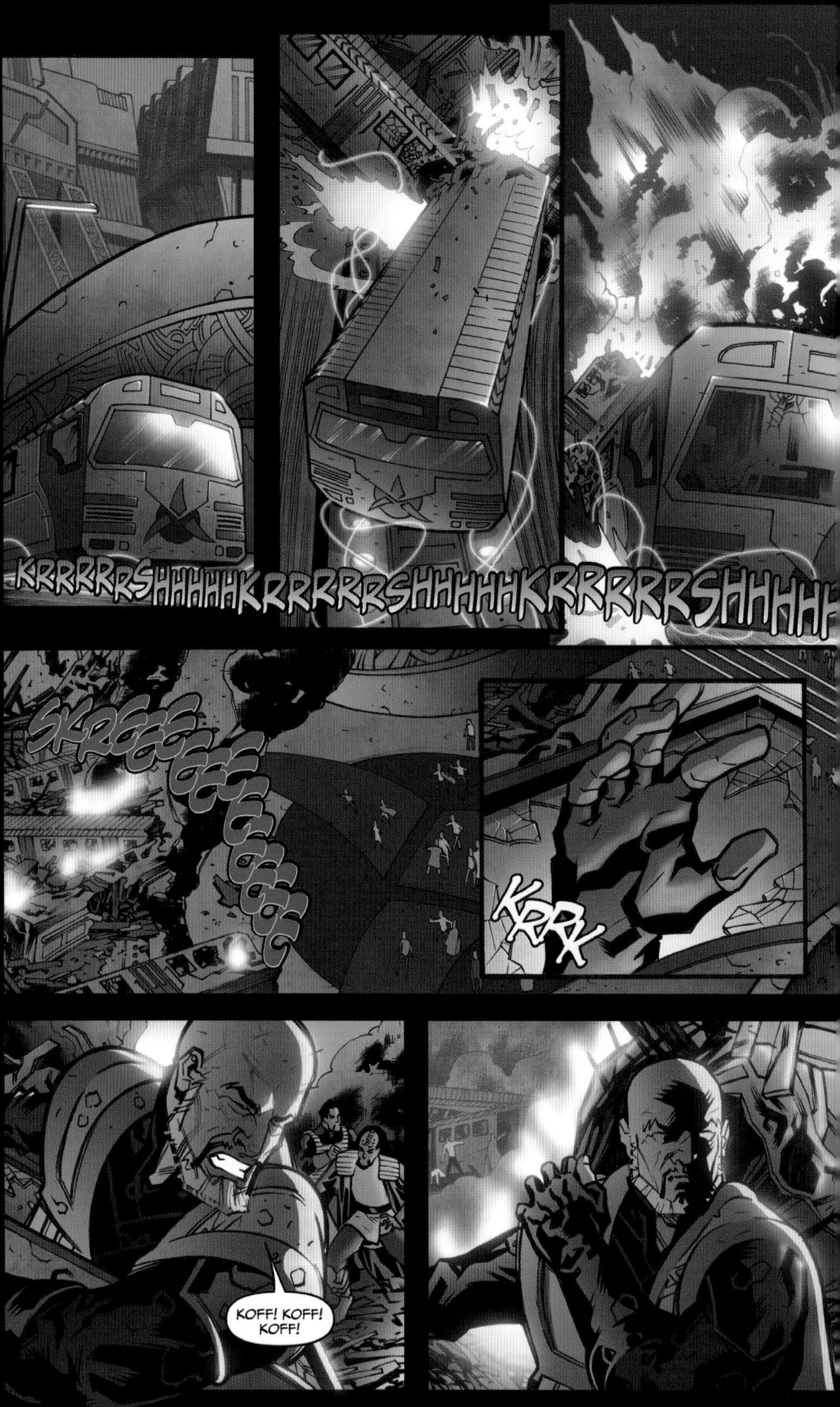
KRRRRRSHHHHHKRRRRRSHHHHHKRRRRRSHHHHH
SKREEEEEEEEEEEEE
KRRK
KOFF! KOFF! KOFF!

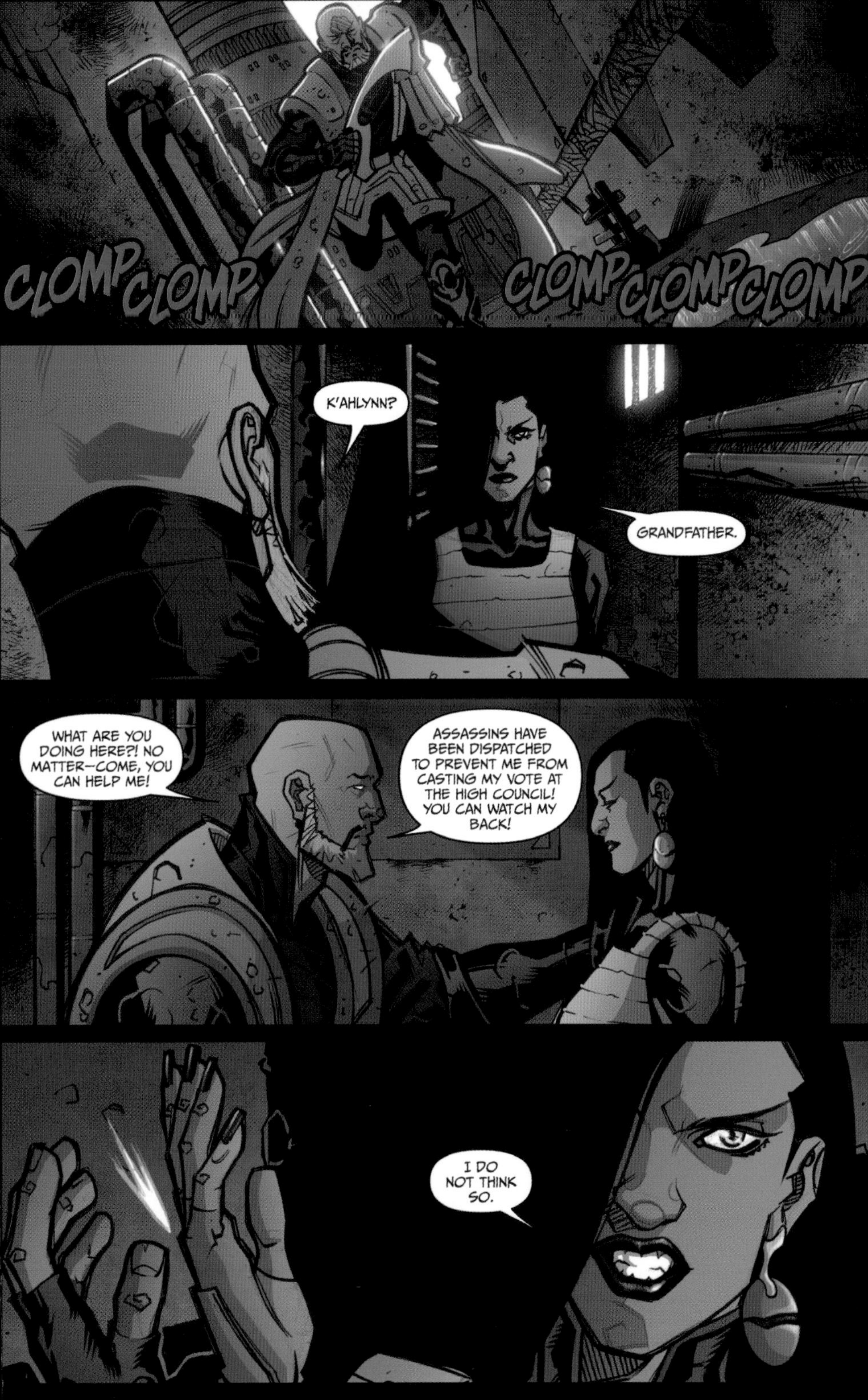
CLOMP CLOMP
CLOMP CLOMP CLOMP
K'AHLYNN?
GRANDFATHER.
WHAT ARE YOU DOING HERE?! NO MATTER—COME, YOU CAN HELP ME!
ASSASSINS HAVE BEEN DISPATCHED TO PREVENT ME FROM CASTING MY VOTE AT THE HIGH COUNCIL! YOU CAN WATCH MY BACK!
I DO NOT THINK SO.

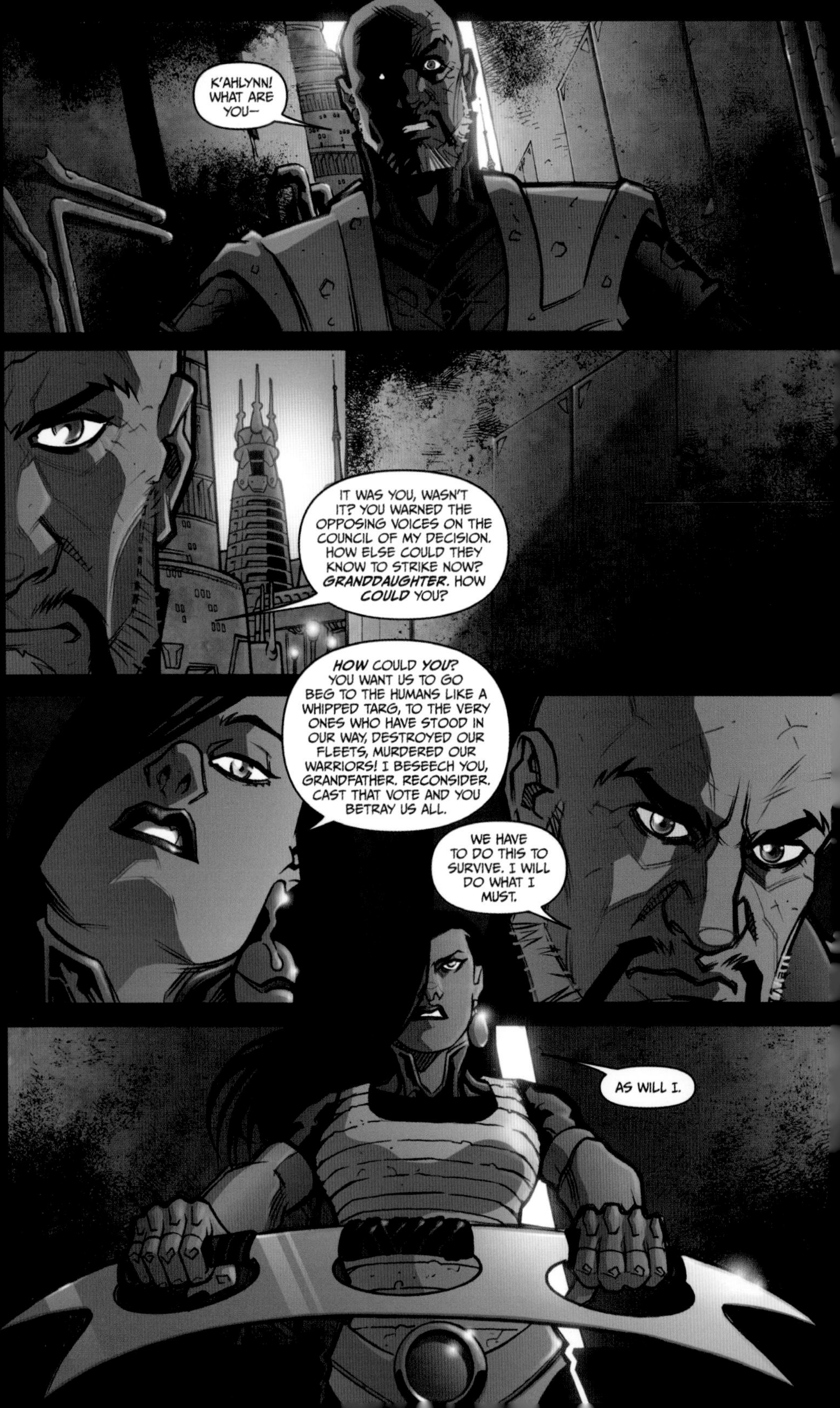
K'AHLYNN! WHAT ARE YOU—
IT WAS YOU, WASN'T IT? YOU WARNED THE OPPOSING VOICES ON THE COUNCIL OF MY DECISION. HOW ELSE COULD THEY KNOW TO STRIKE NOW? GRANDDAUGHTER. HOW COULD YOU?
HOW COULD YOU? YOU WANT US TO GO BEG TO THE HUMANS LIKE A WHIPPED TARG, TO THE VERY ONES WHO HAVE STOOD IN OUR WAY, DESTROYED OUR FLEETS, MURDERED OUR WARRIORS! I BESEECH YOU, GRANDFATHER. RECONSIDER. CAST THAT VOTE AND YOU BETRAY US ALL.
WE HAVE TO DO THIS TO SURVIVE. I WILL DO WHAT I MUST.
AS WILL I.

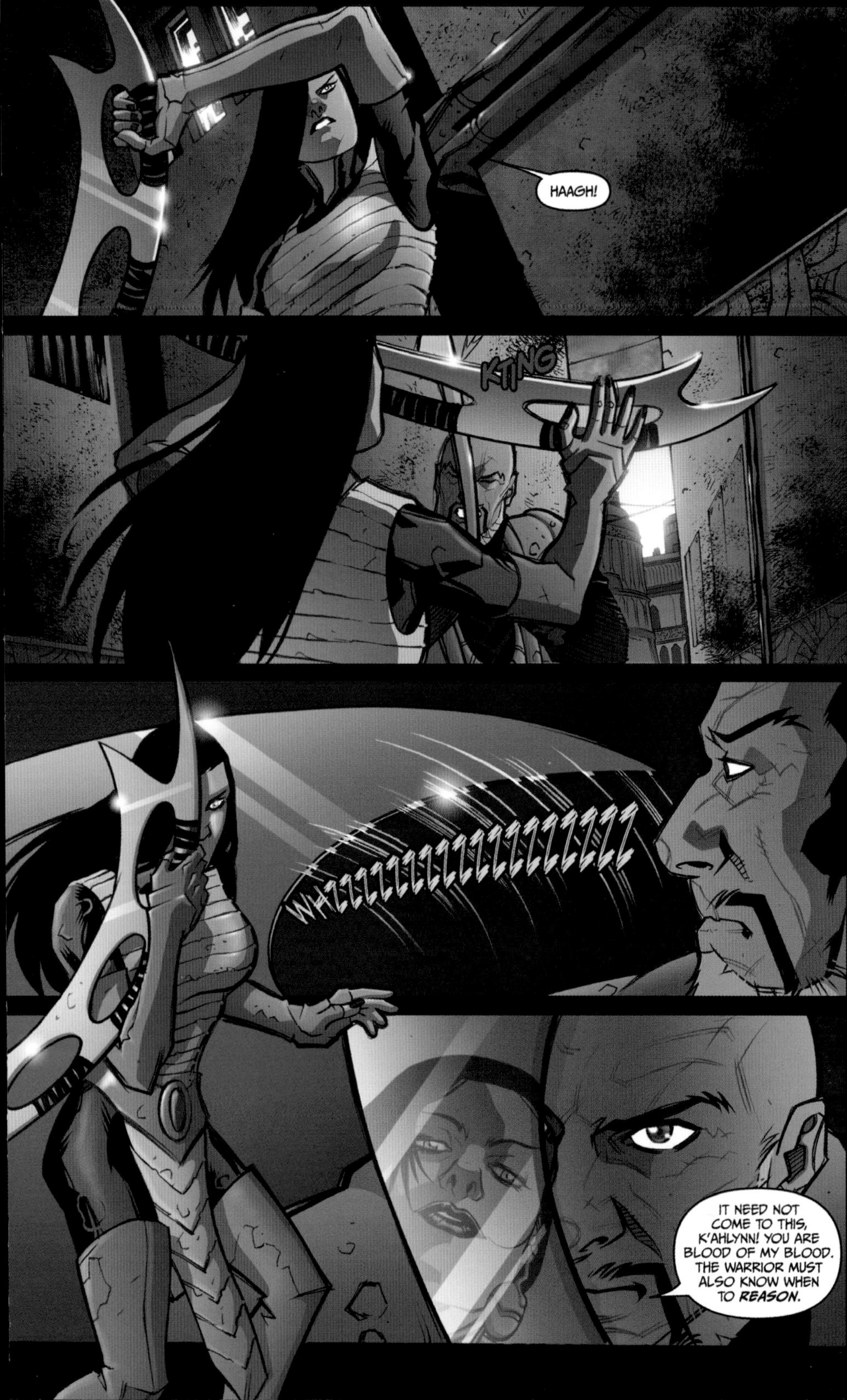
HAAGH!
KTING
WHZZZZZZZZZZZZZZZZZZZZZZZZZ
IT NEED NOT COME TO THIS, K'AHLYNN! YOU ARE BLOOD OF MY BLOOD. THE WARRIOR MUST ALSO KNOW WHEN TO **REASON**.

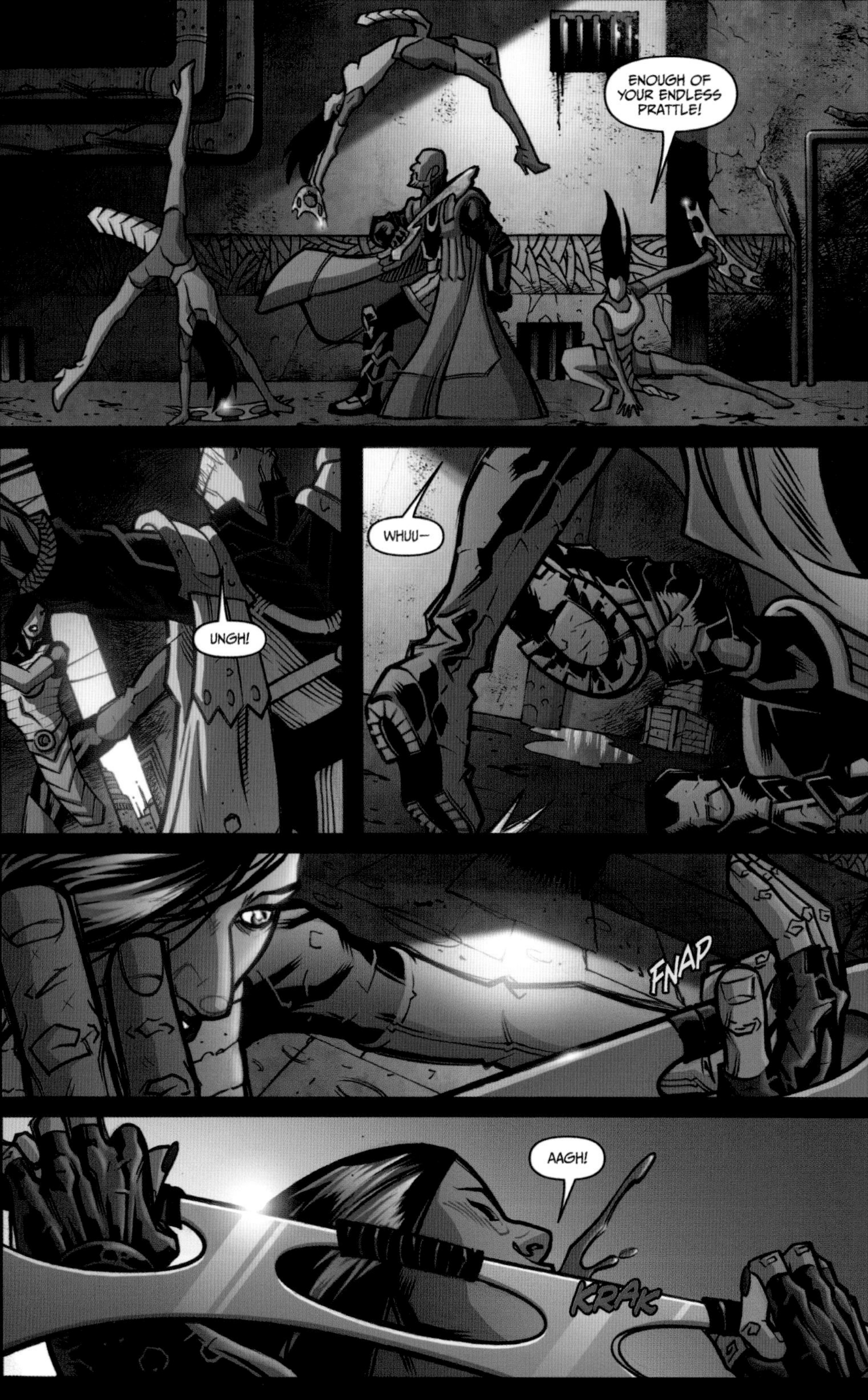
ENOUGH OF YOUR ENDLESS PRATTLE!
UNGH!
WHUU—
FNAP
AAGH!
KRAK

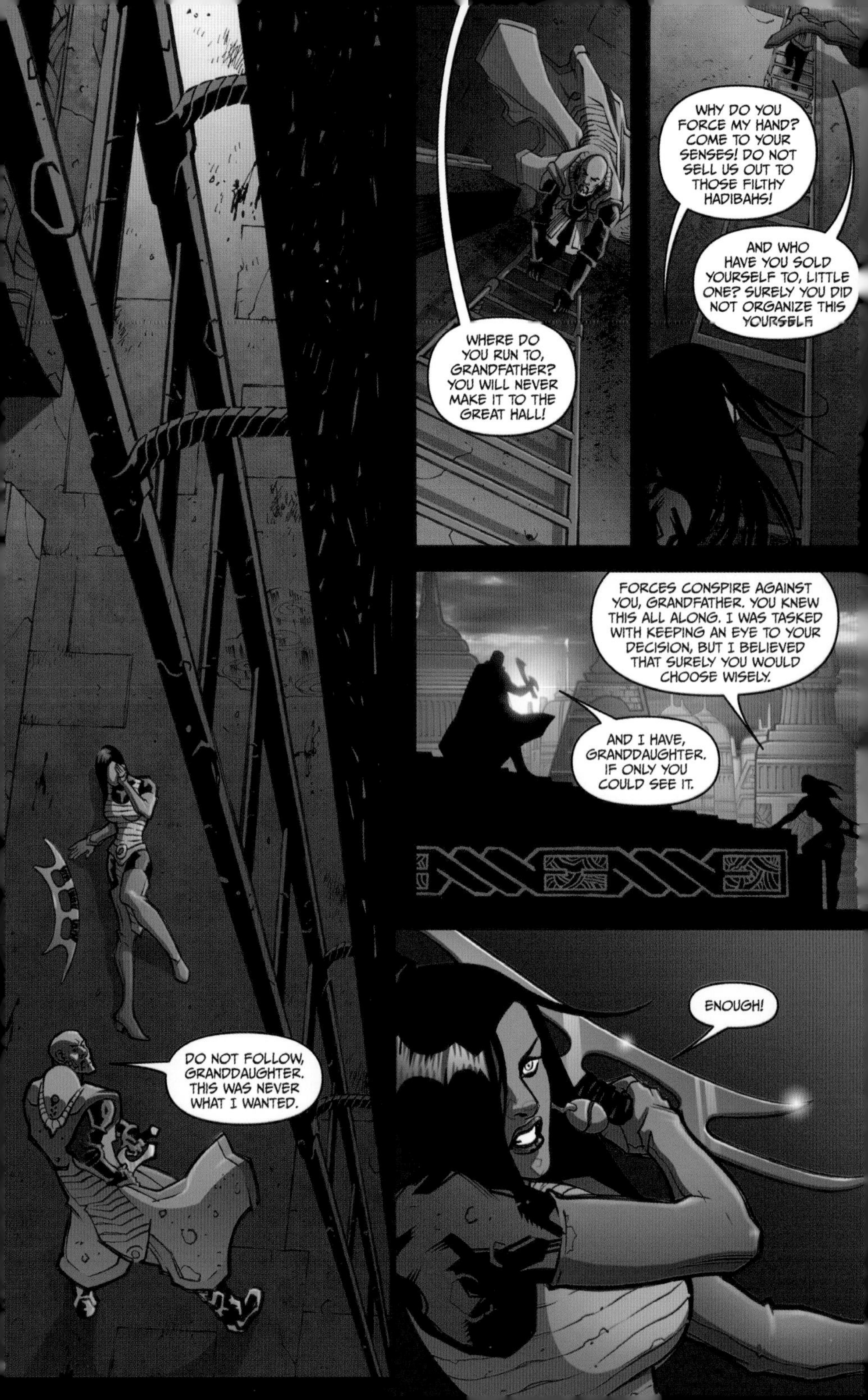
WHERE DO YOU RUN TO, GRANDFATHER? YOU WILL NEVER MAKE IT TO THE GREAT HALL!
WHY DO YOU FORCE MY HAND? COME TO YOUR SENSES! DO NOT SELL US OUT TO THOSE FILTHY HADIBAHS!
AND WHO HAVE YOU SOLD YOURSELF TO, LITTLE ONE? SURELY YOU DID NOT ORGANIZE THIS YOURSELF
FORCES CONSPIRE AGAINST YOU, GRANDFATHER. YOU KNEW THIS ALL ALONG. I WAS TASKED WITH KEEPING AN EYE TO YOUR DECISION, BUT I BELIEVED THAT SURELY YOU WOULD CHOOSE WISELY.
AND I HAVE, GRANDDAUGHTER. IF ONLY YOU COULD SEE IT.
ENOUGH!
DO NOT FOLLOW, GRANDDAUGHTER. THIS WAS NEVER WHAT I WANTED.

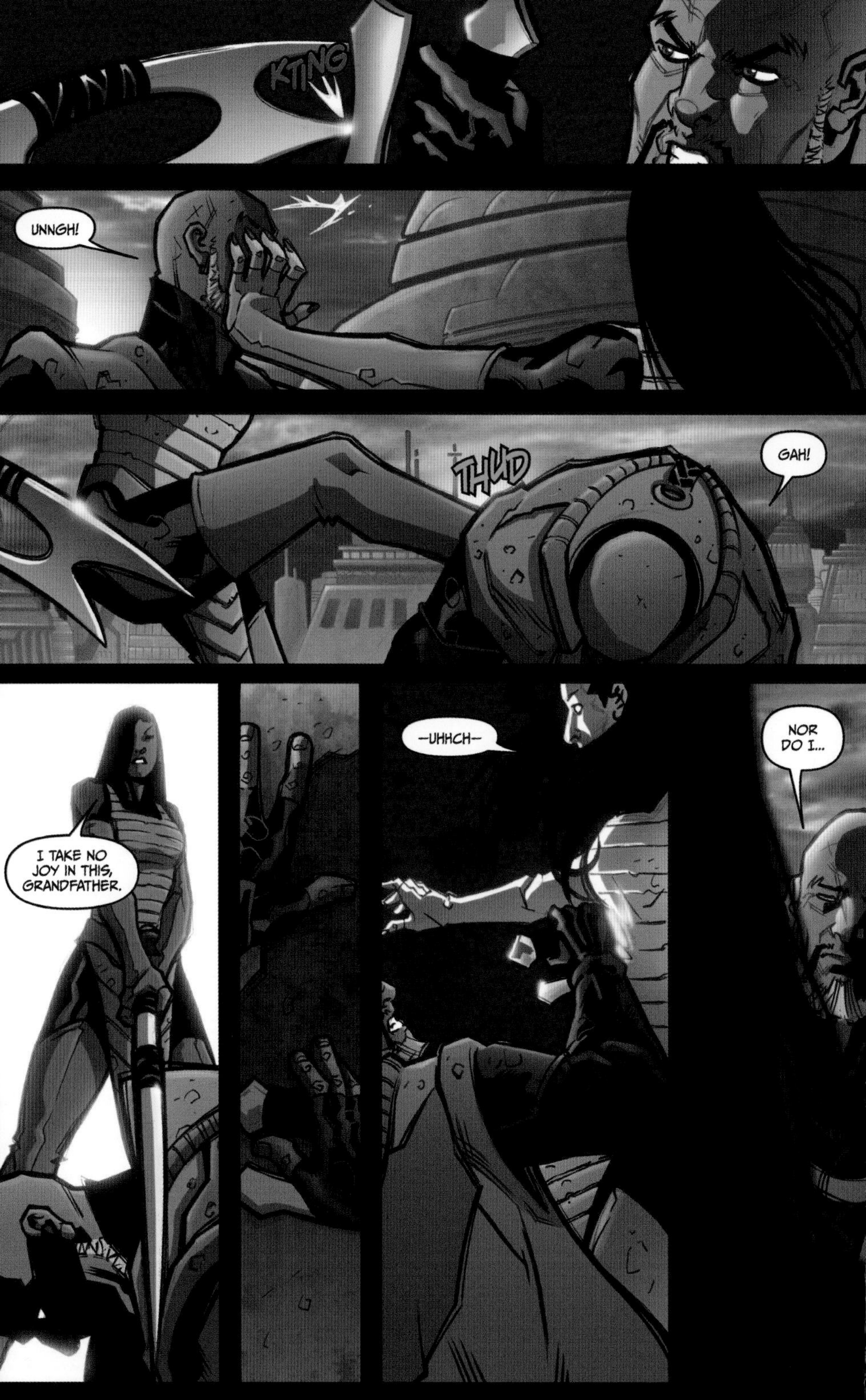
KTING
UNNGH!
THUD
GAH!
I TAKE NO JOY IN THIS, GRANDFATHER.
-UHHCH-
NOR DO I...

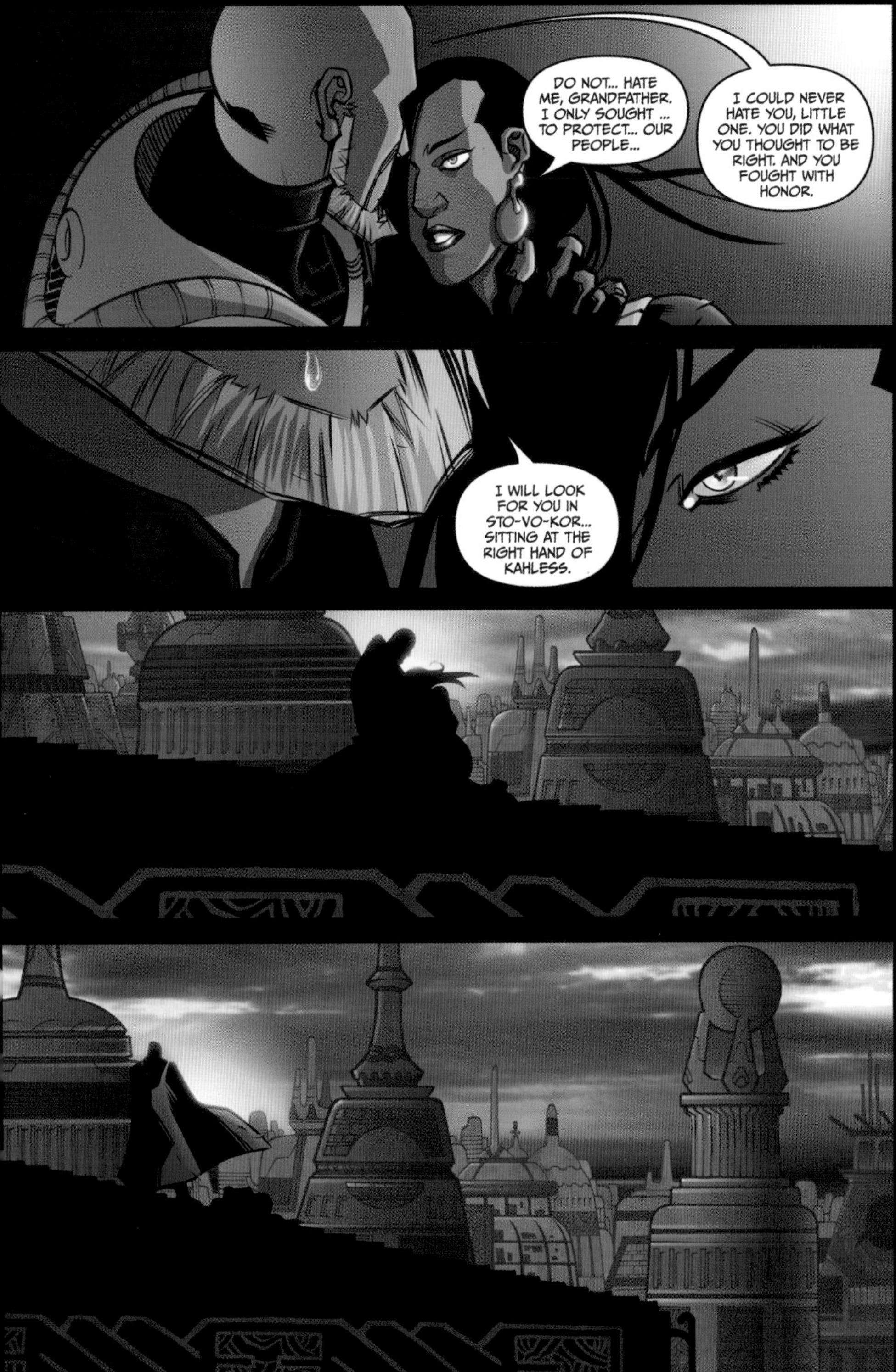
DO NOT... HATE ME, GRANDFATHER. I ONLY SOUGHT ... TO PROTECT... OUR PEOPLE...
I COULD NEVER HATE YOU, LITTLE ONE. YOU DID WHAT YOU THOUGHT TO BE RIGHT. AND YOU FOUGHT WITH HONOR.
I WILL LOOK FOR YOU IN STO-VO-KOR... SITTING AT THE RIGHT HAND OF KAHLESS.

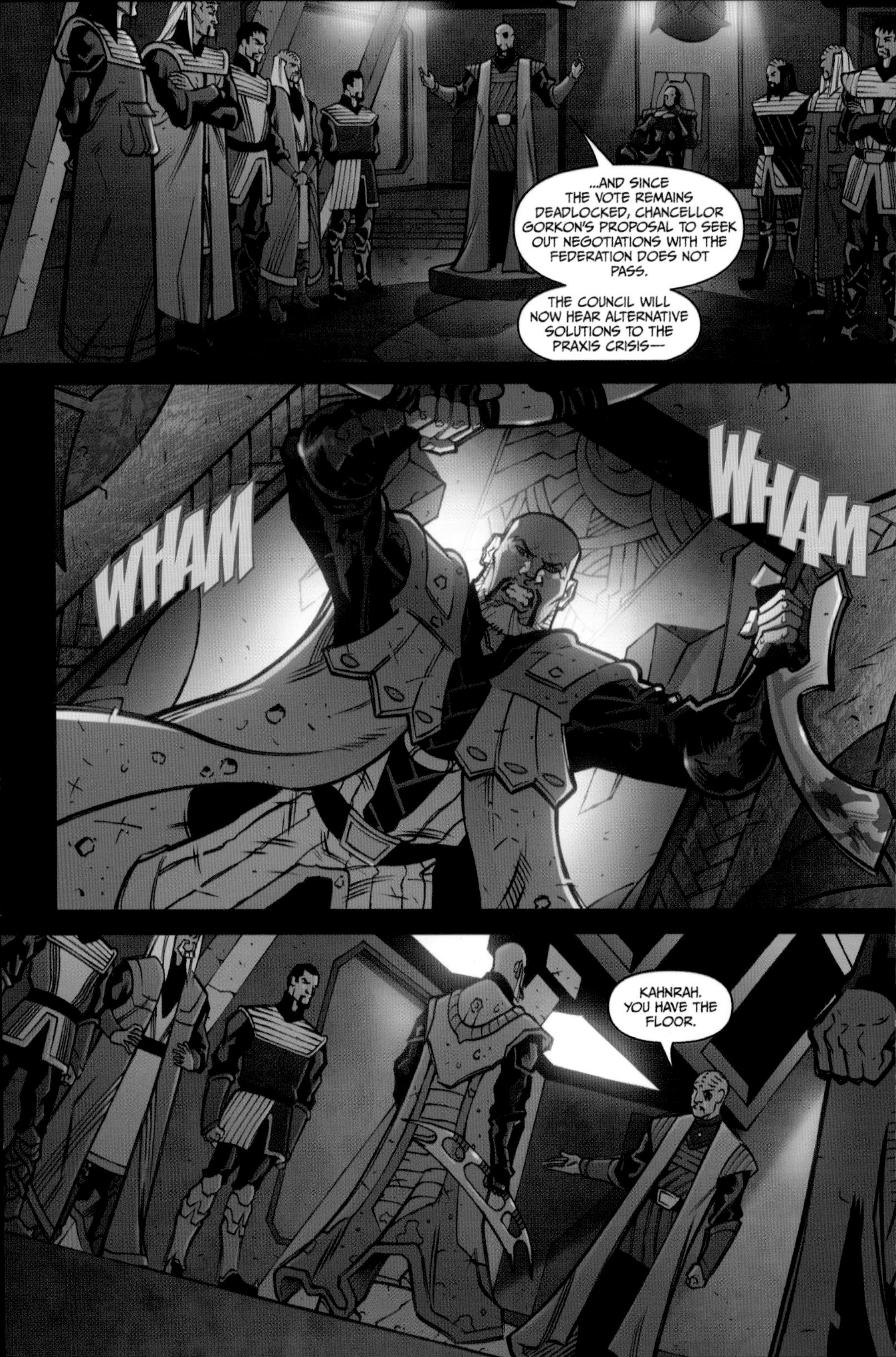
...AND SINCE THE VOTE REMAINS DEADLOCKED, CHANCELLOR GORKON'S PROPOSAL TO SEEK OUT NEGOTIATIONS WITH THE FEDERATION DOES NOT PASS.
THE COUNCIL WILL NOW HEAR ALTERNATIVE SOLUTIONS TO THE PRAXIS CRISIS—
WHAM
WHAM
KAHNRAH. YOU HAVE THE FLOOR.

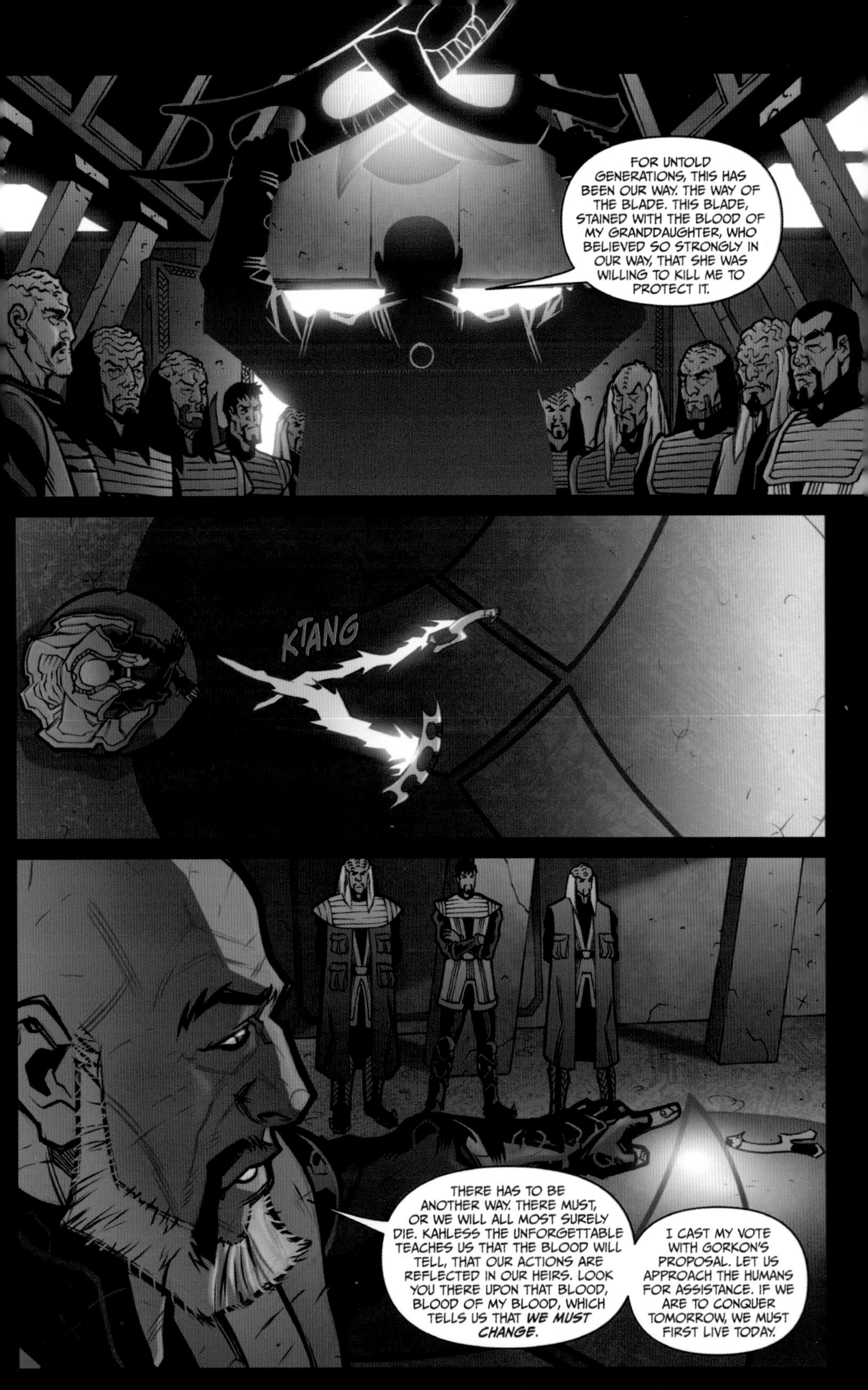
FOR UNTOLD GENERATIONS, THIS HAS BEEN OUR WAY. THE WAY OF THE BLADE. THIS BLADE, STAINED WITH THE BLOOD OF MY GRANDDAUGHTER, WHO BELIEVED SO STRONGLY IN OUR WAY, THAT SHE WAS WILLING TO KILL ME TO PROTECT IT.
KTANG
THERE HAS TO BE ANOTHER WAY. THERE MUST, OR WE WILL ALL MOST SURELY DIE. KAHLESS THE UNFORGETTABLE TEACHES US THAT THE BLOOD WILL TELL, THAT OUR ACTIONS ARE REFLECTED IN OUR HEIRS. LOOK YOU THERE UPON THAT BLOOD, BLOOD OF MY BLOOD, WHICH TELLS US THAT ***WE MUST CHANGE***.
I CAST MY VOTE WITH GORKON'S PROPOSAL. LET US APPROACH THE HUMANS FOR ASSISTANCE. IF WE ARE TO CONQUER TOMORROW, WE MUST FIRST LIVE TODAY.

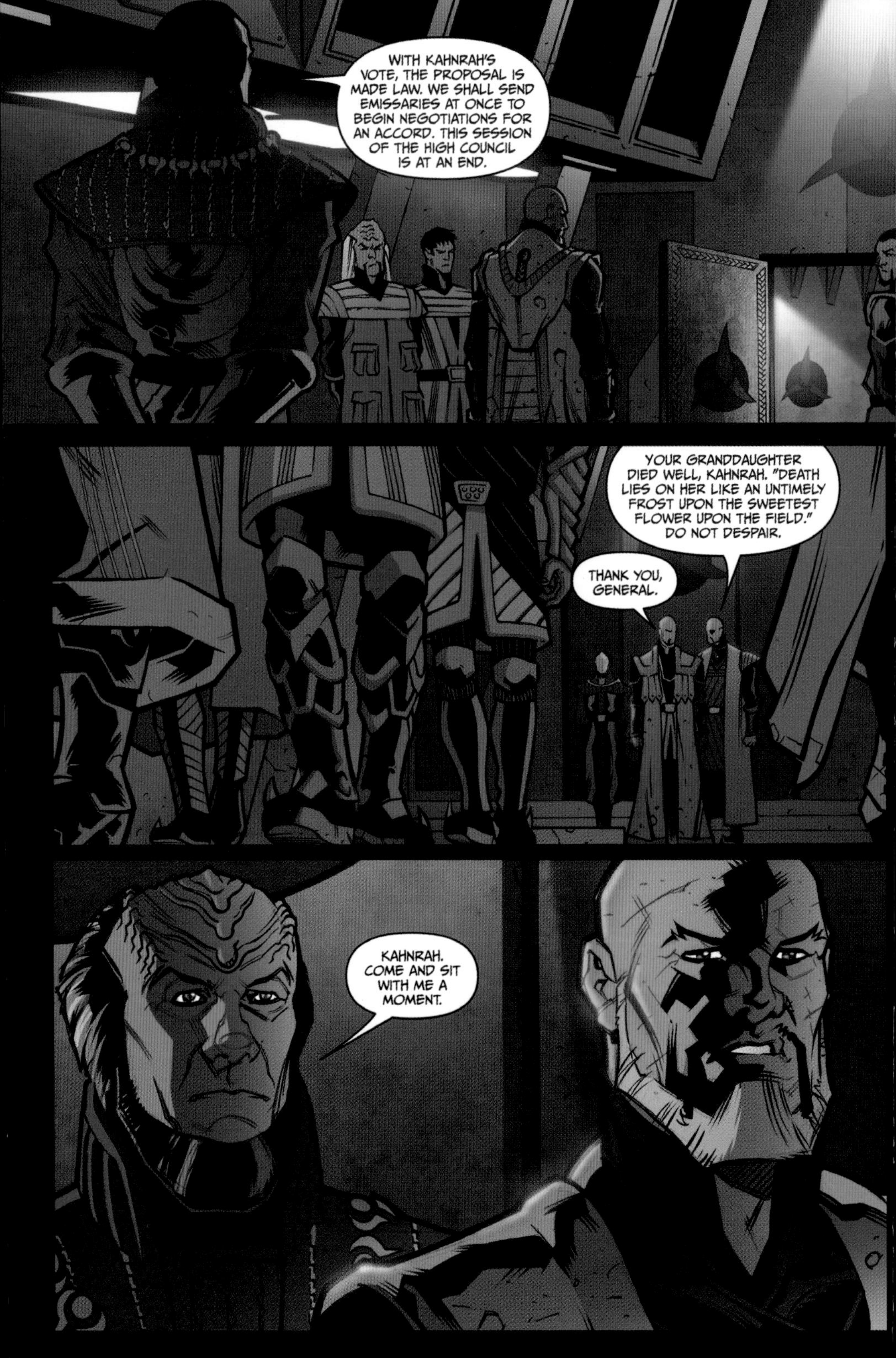

WITH KAHNRAH'S VOTE, THE PROPOSAL IS MADE LAW. WE SHALL SEND EMISSARIES AT ONCE TO BEGIN NEGOTIATIONS FOR AN ACCORD. THIS SESSION OF THE HIGH COUNCIL IS AT AN END.
YOUR GRANDDAUGHTER DIED WELL, KAHNRAH. "DEATH LIES ON HER LIKE AN UNTIMELY FROST UPON THE SWEETEST FLOWER UPON THE FIELD." DO NOT DESPAIR.
THANK YOU, GENERAL.
KAHNRAH. COME AND SIT WITH ME A MOMENT.

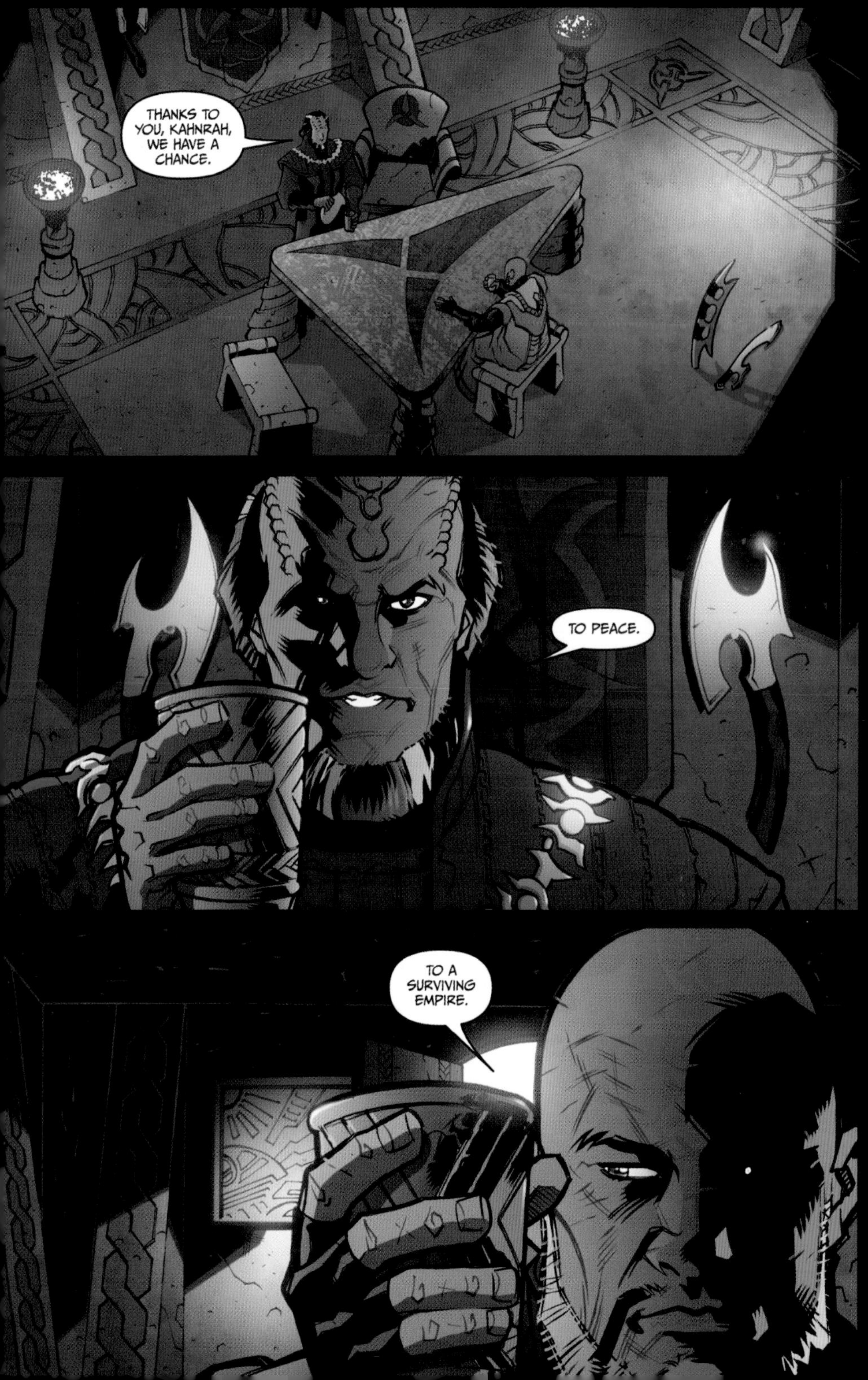
THANKS TO YOU, KAHNRAH, WE HAVE A CHANCE.
TO PEACE.
TO A SURVIVING EMPIRE.

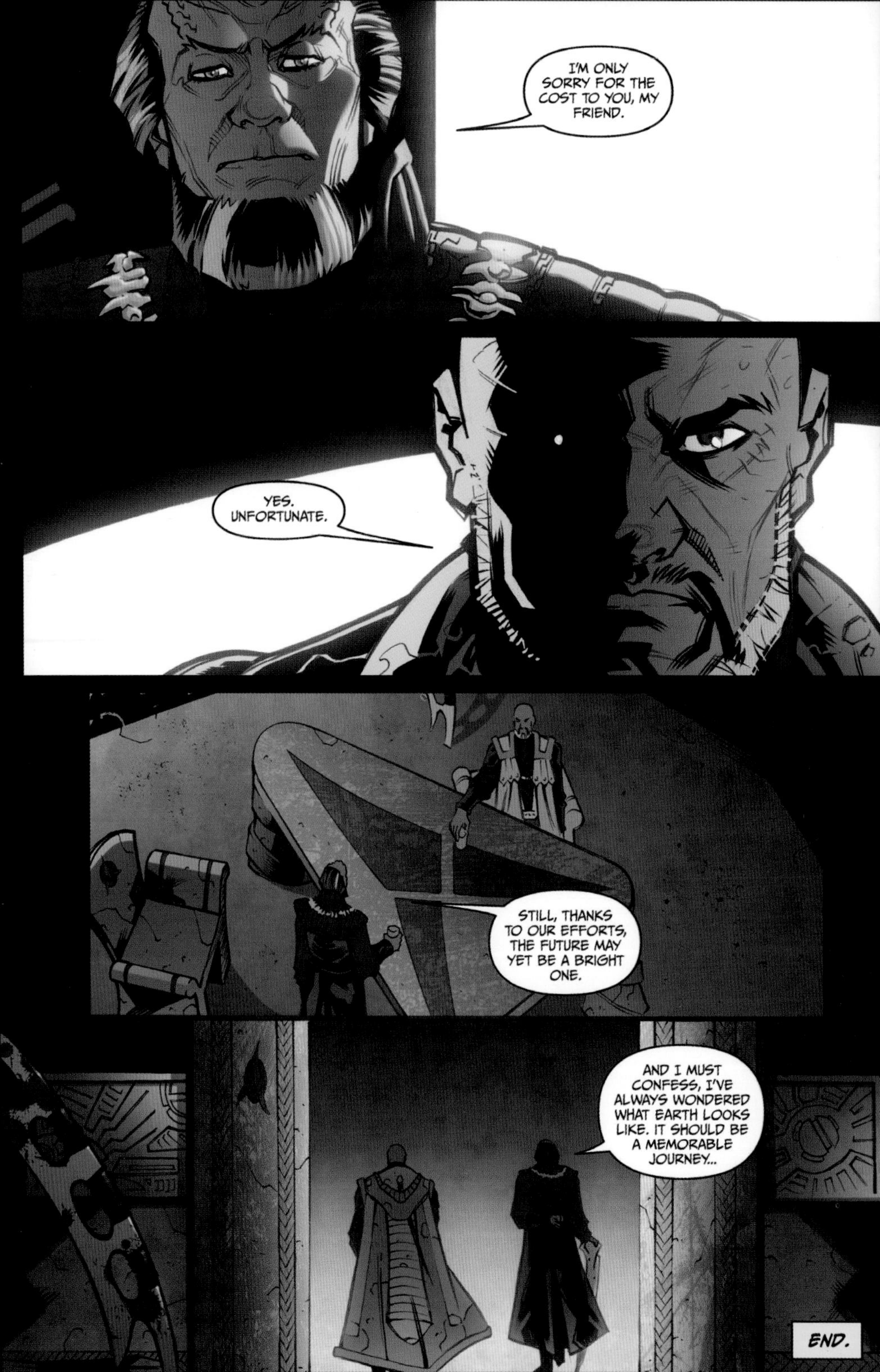
I'M ONLY SORRY FOR THE COST TO YOU, MY FRIEND.
YES. UNFORTUNATE.
STILL, THANKS TO OUR EFFORTS, THE FUTURE MAY YET BE A BRIGHT ONE.
AND I MUST CONFESS, I'VE ALWAYS WONDERED WHAT EARTH LOOKS LIKE. IT SHOULD BE A MEMORABLE JOURNEY...
END.

STAR TREK®

THE ORIGINAL SERIES

OMNIBUS

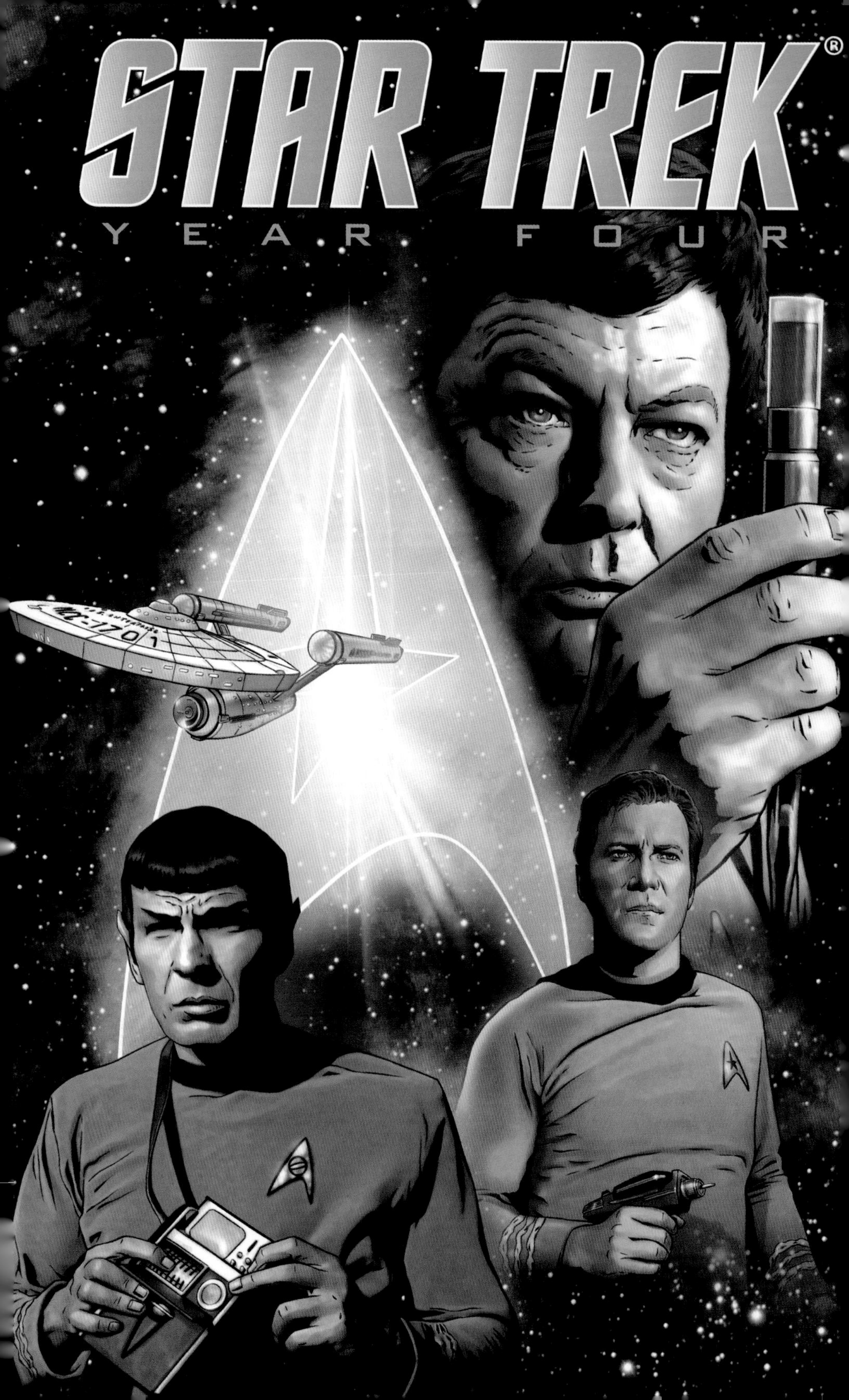
STAR TREK®
YEAR FOUR

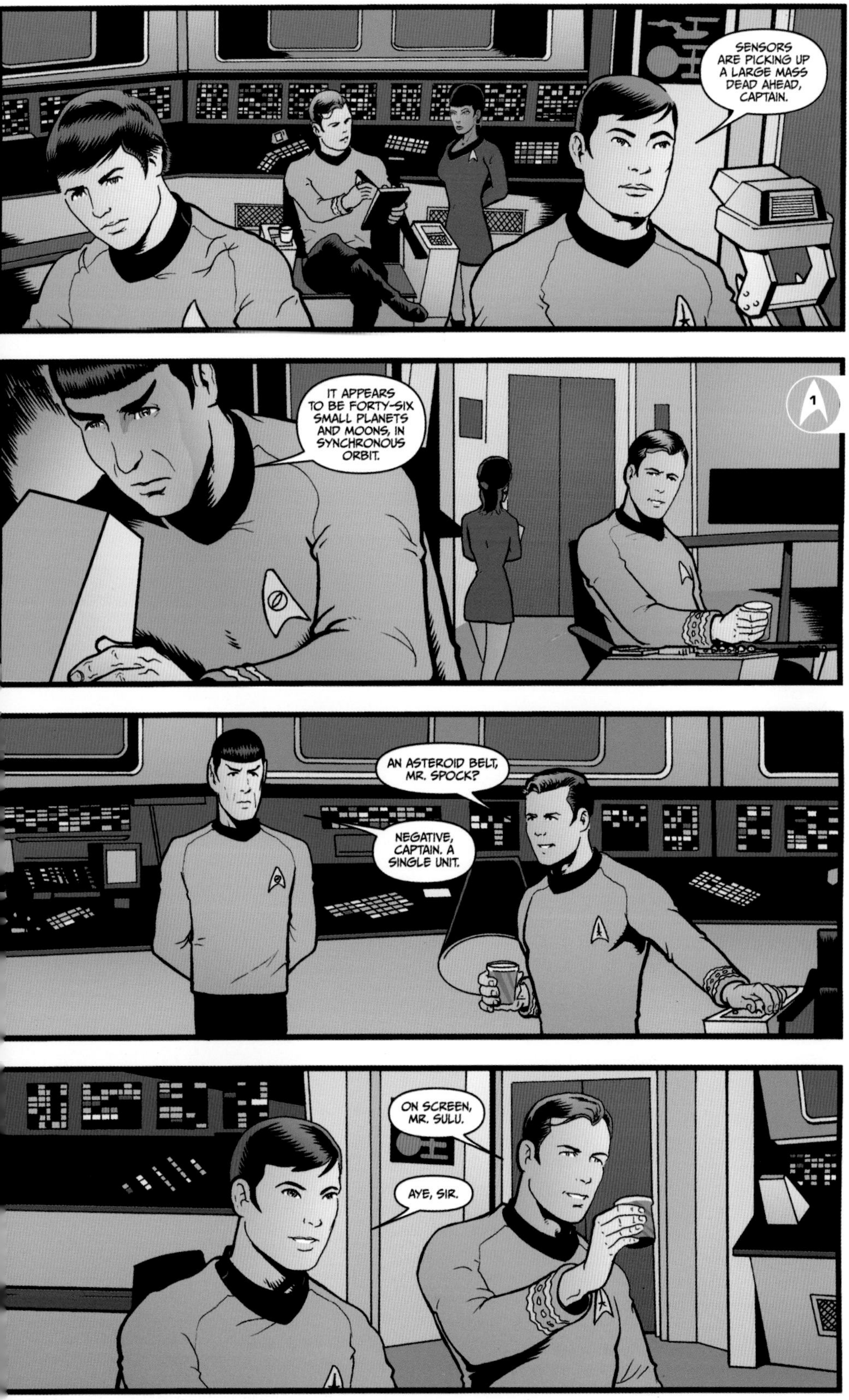
SENSORS ARE PICKING UP A LARGE MASS DEAD AHEAD, CAPTAIN.
IT APPEARS TO BE FORTY-SIX SMALL PLANETS AND MOONS, IN SYNCHRONOUS ORBIT.
AN ASTEROID BELT, MR. SPOCK?
NEGATIVE, CAPTAIN. A SINGLE UNIT.
ON SCREEN, MR. SULU.
AYE, SIR.

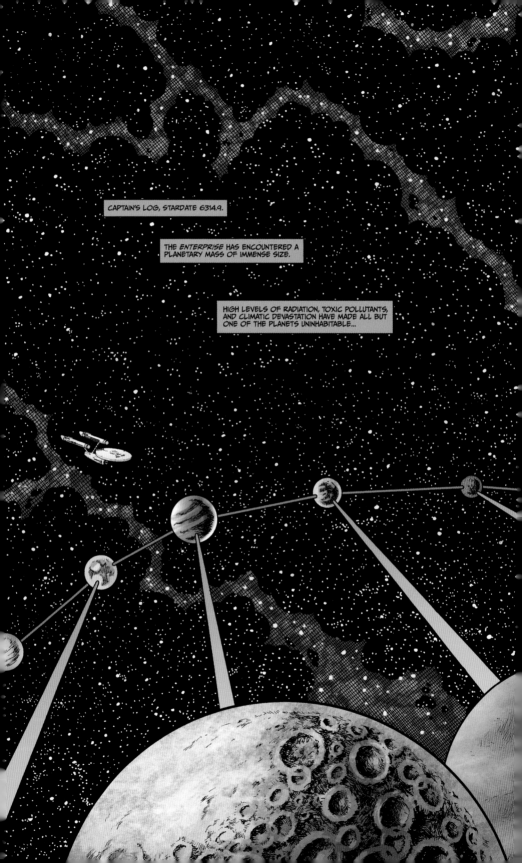

CAPTAIN'S LOG, STARDATE 6314.9.

THE *ENTERPRISE* HAS ENCOUNTERED A PLANETARY MASS OF IMMENSE SIZE.

HIGH LEVELS OF RADIATION, TOXIC POLLUTANTS, AND CLIMATIC DEVASTATION HAVE MADE ALL BUT ONE OF THE PLANETS UNINHABITABLE...

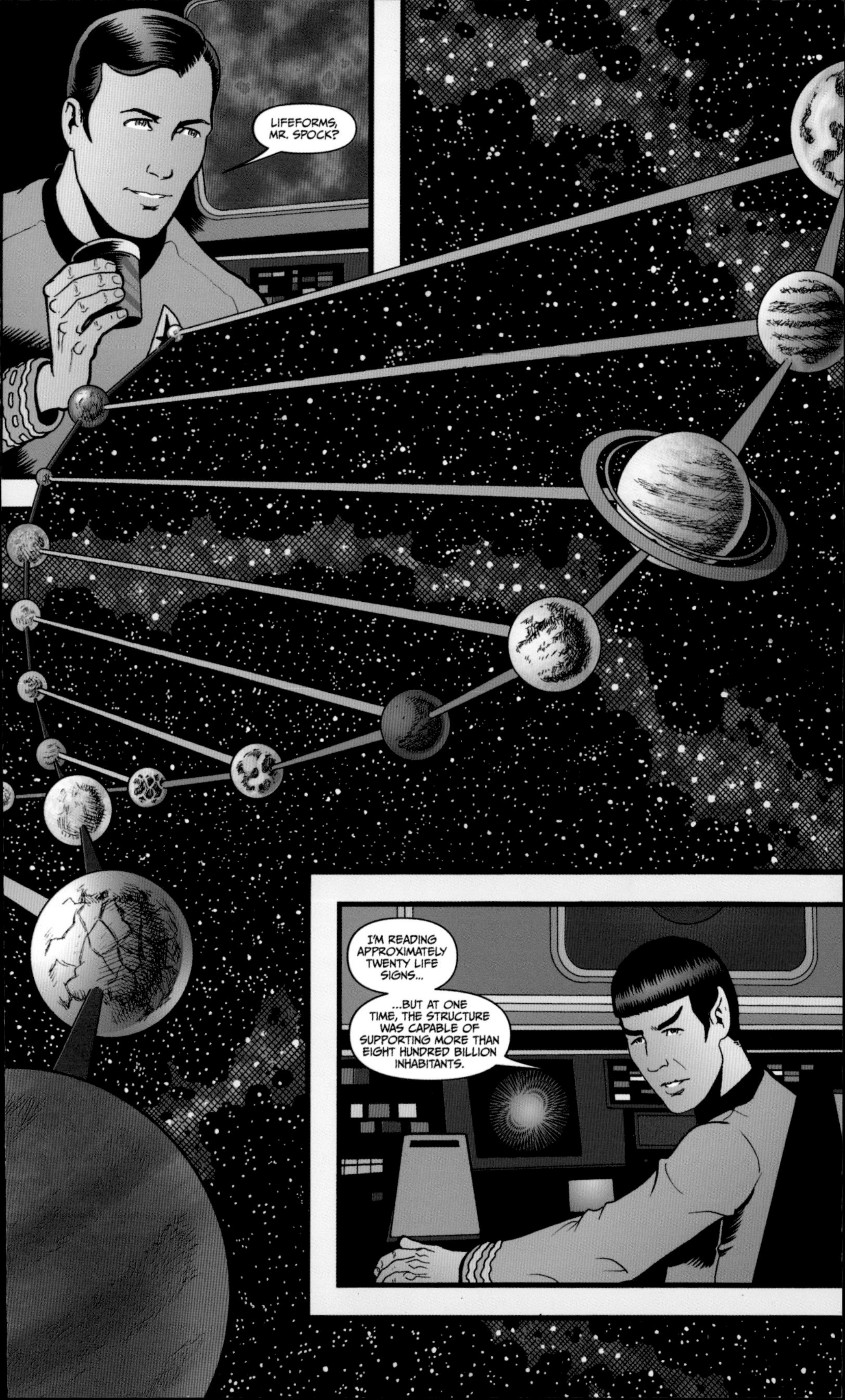
LIFEFORMS, MR. SPOCK?
I'M READING APPROXIMATELY TWENTY LIFE SIGNS...
...BUT AT ONE TIME, THE STRUCTURE WAS CAPABLE OF SUPPORTING MORE THAN EIGHT HUNDRED BILLION INHABITANTS.

...WE ARE BEAMING DOWN TO INVESTIGATE.

NHHHNNHHNNNNHHNNHHNNNHHNNNNHHH

EEEEEEEEEEE

I AM READING LIFE SIGNS WITHIN A TWENTY METER PERIMETER, CAPTAIN.

STAY HERE, ALONZO. USE YOUR COMMUNICATOR IF YOU SEE ANYTHING.

AYE, SIR.

SIR!

WELCOME TO THE STRAND, CAPTAIN KIRK!

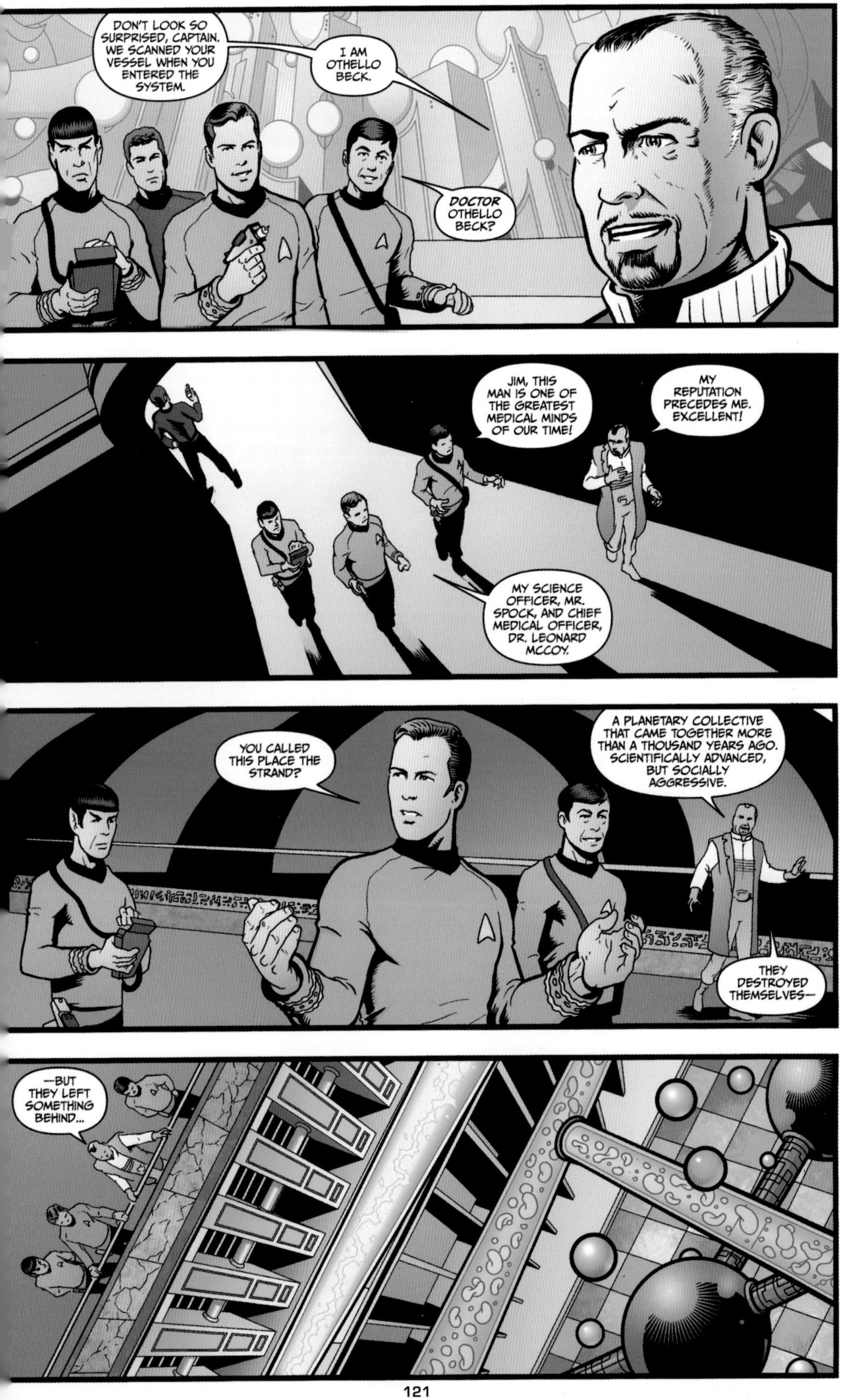
DON'T LOOK SO SURPRISED, CAPTAIN. WE SCANNED YOUR VESSEL WHEN YOU ENTERED THE SYSTEM.
I AM OTHELLO BECK.
DOCTOR OTHELLO BECK?
JIM, THIS MAN IS ONE OF THE GREATEST MEDICAL MINDS OF OUR TIME!
MY REPUTATION PRECEDES ME. EXCELLENT!
MY SCIENCE OFFICER, MR. SPOCK, AND CHIEF MEDICAL OFFICER, DR. LEONARD MCCOY.
YOU CALLED THIS PLACE THE STRAND?
A PLANETARY COLLECTIVE THAT CAME TOGETHER MORE THAN A THOUSAND YEARS AGO. SCIENTIFICALLY ADVANCED, BUT SOCIALLY AGGRESSIVE.
THEY DESTROYED THEMSELVES—
—BUT THEY LEFT SOMETHING BEHIND...

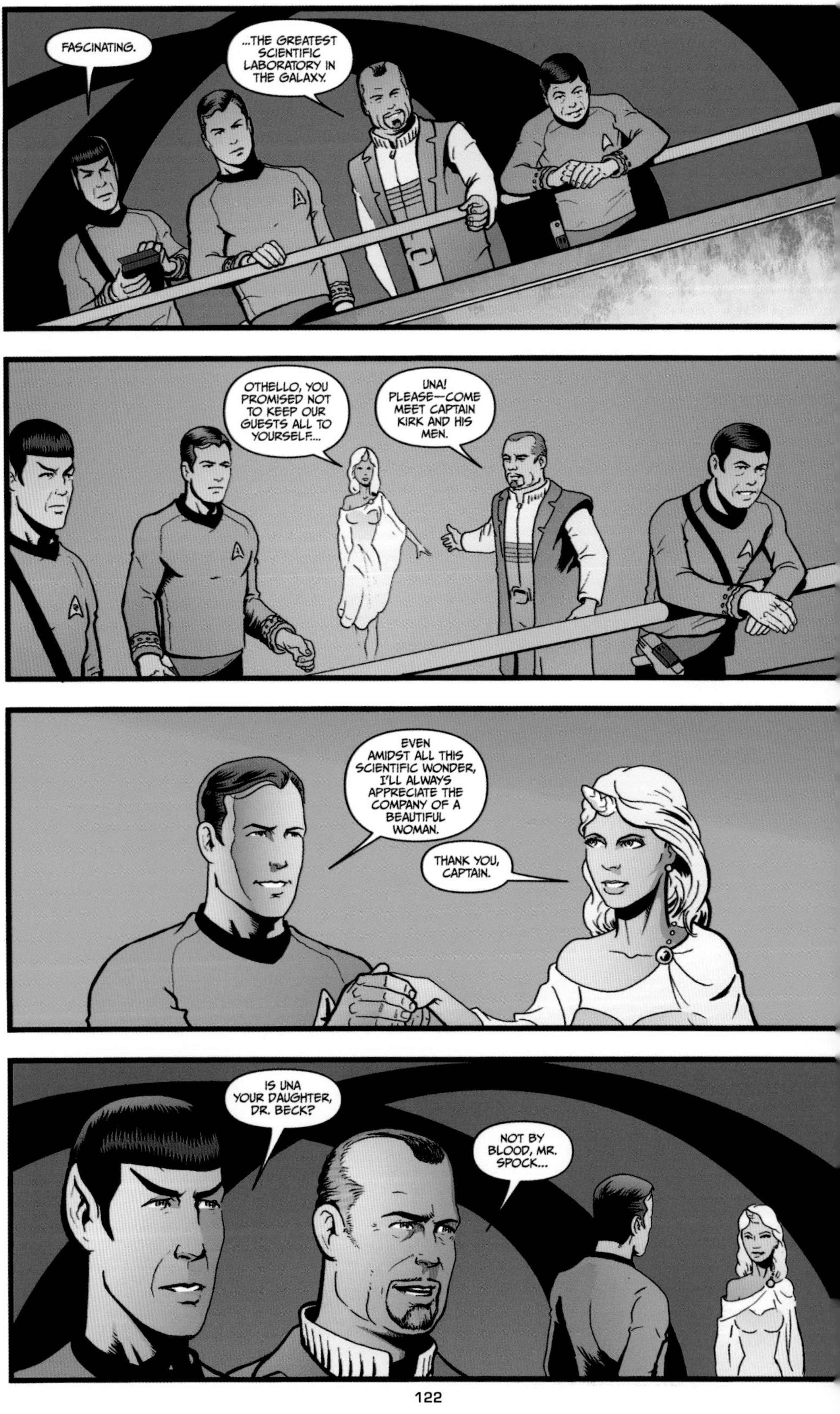
FASCINATING.
...THE GREATEST SCIENTIFIC LABORATORY IN THE GALAXY.
OTHELLO, YOU PROMISED NOT TO KEEP OUR GUESTS ALL TO YOURSELF...
UNA! PLEASE—COME MEET CAPTAIN KIRK AND HIS MEN.
EVEN AMIDST ALL THIS SCIENTIFIC WONDER, I'LL ALWAYS APPRECIATE THE COMPANY OF A BEAUTIFUL WOMAN.
THANK YOU, CAPTAIN.
IS UNA YOUR DAUGHTER, DR. BECK?
NOT BY BLOOD, MR. SPOCK...

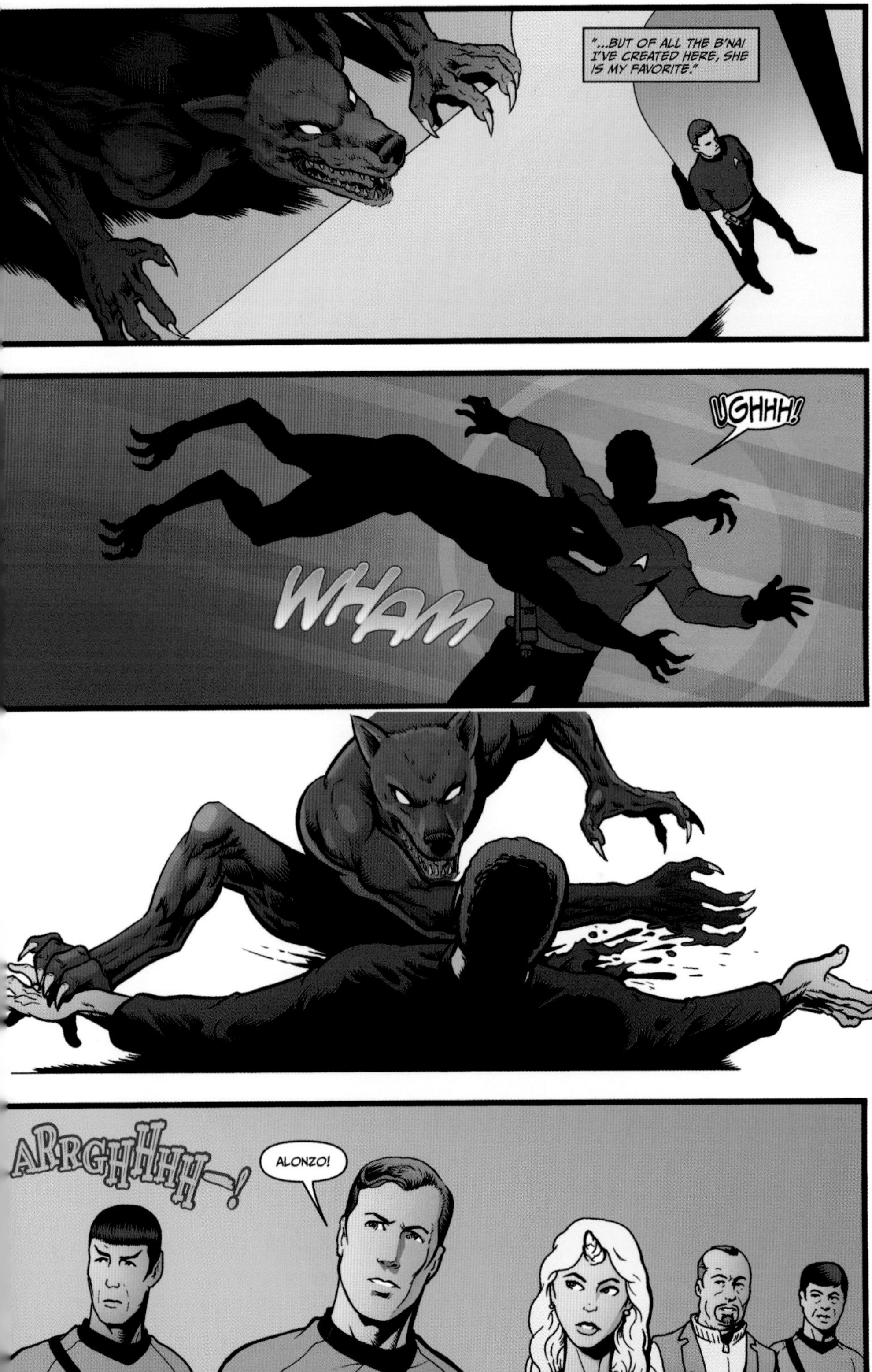
"...BUT OF ALL THE B'NAI I'VE CREATED HERE, SHE IS MY FAVORITE."
UGHHH!
WHAM
ARRGHHHH—!
ALONZO!

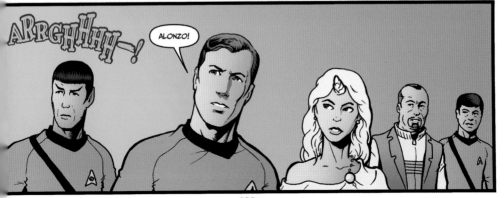

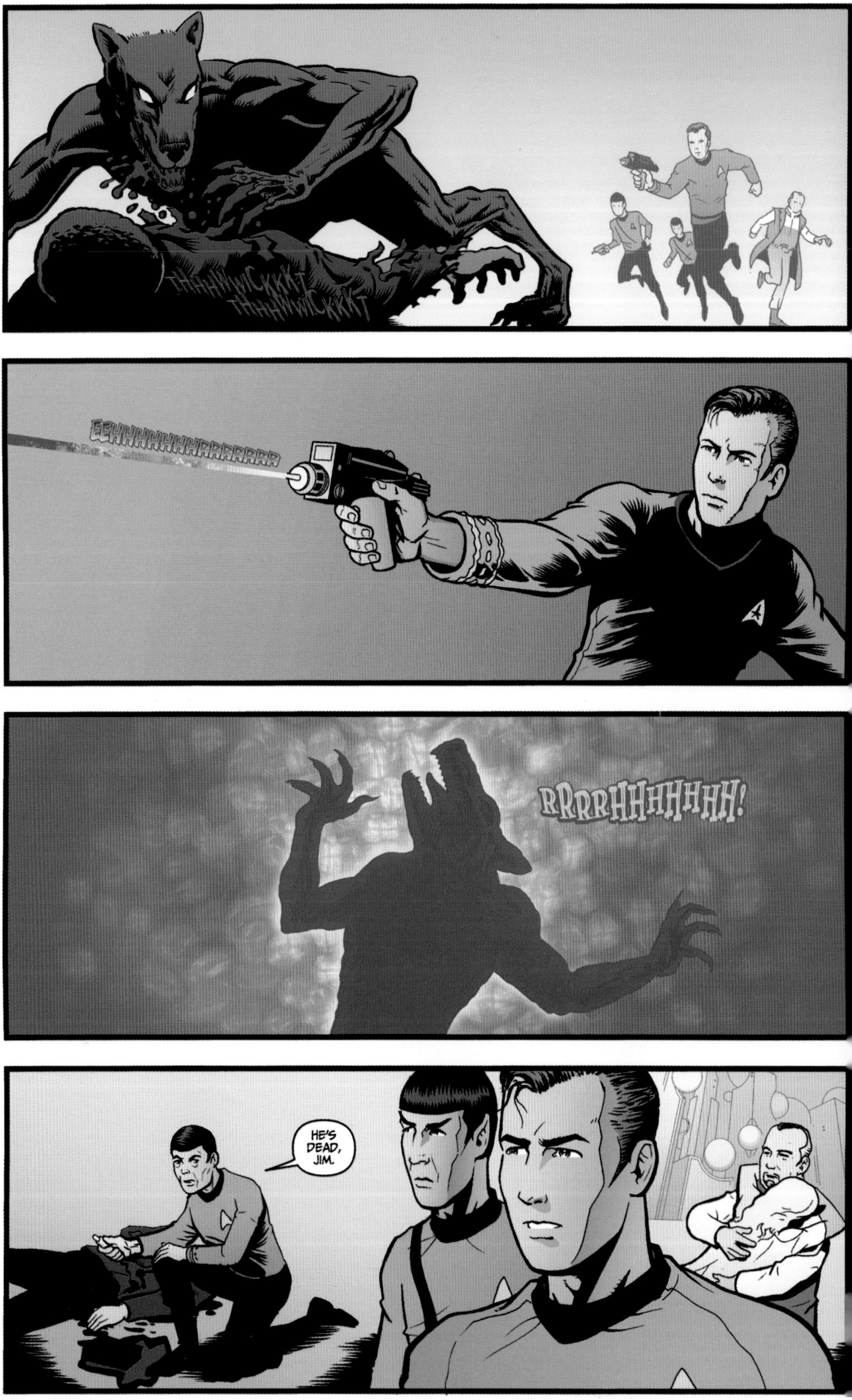
THHHWICKKKT
THHHWICKKKT
EEHHHHHHHHHRRRRRRRR
RRRRHHHHHHH!
HE'S DEAD, JIM.

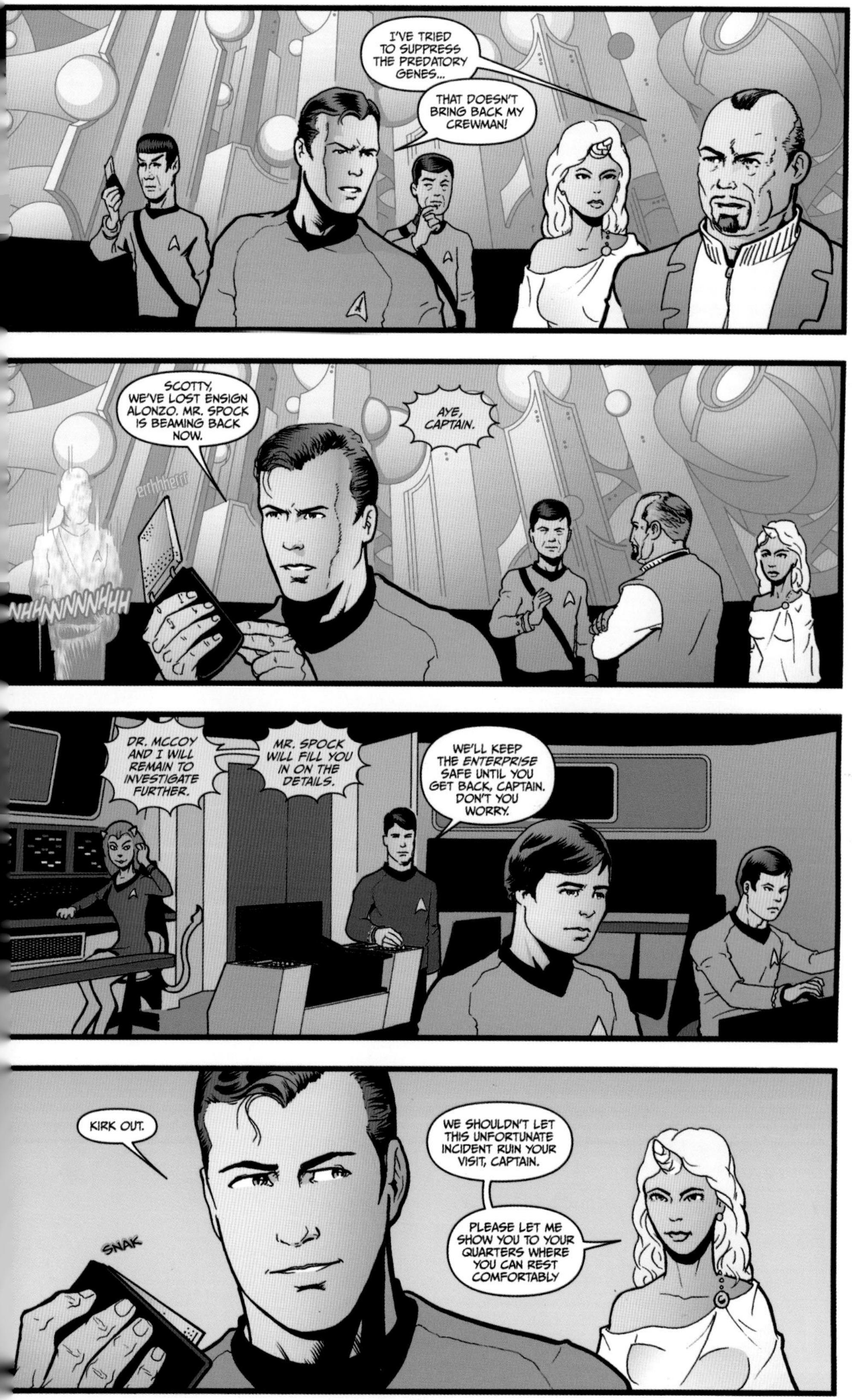
I'VE TRIED TO SUPPRESS THE PREDATORY GENES...
THAT DOESN'T BRING BACK MY CREWMAN!
SCOTTY, WE'VE LOST ENSIGN ALONZO. MR. SPOCK IS BEAMING BACK NOW.
AYE, CAPTAIN.
erhhherrr
NHHNNNNNHHH
DR. MCCOY AND I WILL REMAIN TO INVESTIGATE FURTHER.
MR. SPOCK WILL FILL YOU IN ON THE DETAILS.
WE'LL KEEP THE *ENTERPRISE* SAFE UNTIL YOU GET BACK, CAPTAIN. DON'T YOU WORRY.
KIRK OUT.
SNAK
WE SHOULDN'T LET THIS UNFORTUNATE INCIDENT RUIN YOUR VISIT, CAPTAIN.
PLEASE LET ME SHOW YOU TO YOUR QUARTERS WHERE YOU CAN REST COMFORTABLY

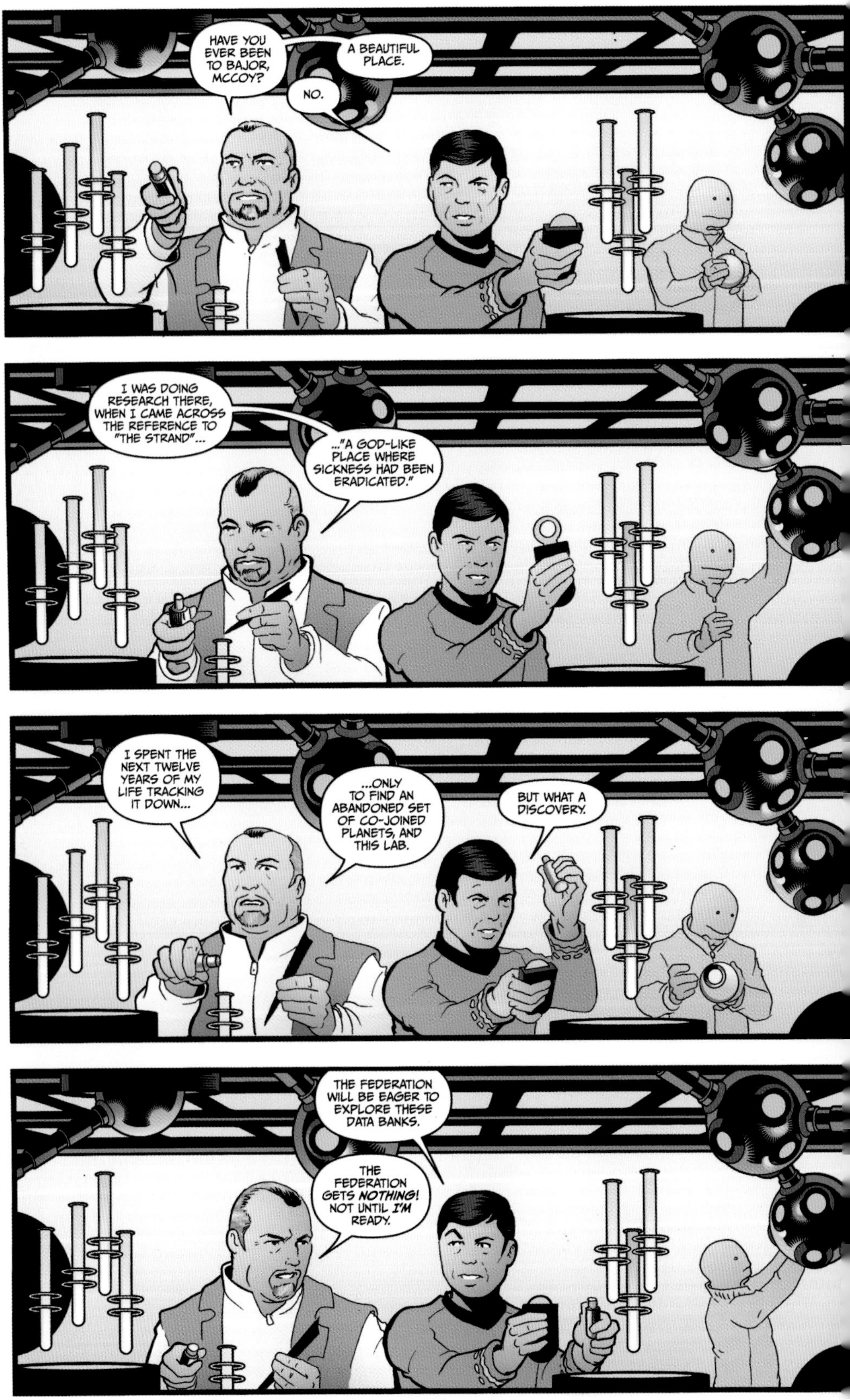
HAVE YOU EVER BEEN TO BAJOR, MCCOY?
A BEAUTIFUL PLACE.
NO.
I WAS DOING RESEARCH THERE, WHEN I CAME ACROSS THE REFERENCE TO "THE STRAND"...
..."A GOD-LIKE PLACE WHERE SICKNESS HAD BEEN ERADICATED."
I SPENT THE NEXT TWELVE YEARS OF MY LIFE TRACKING IT DOWN...
...ONLY TO FIND AN ABANDONED SET OF CO-JOINED PLANETS, AND THIS LAB.
BUT WHAT A DISCOVERY.
THE FEDERATION WILL BE EAGER TO EXPLORE THESE DATA BANKS.
THE FEDERATION GETS ***NOTHING***! NOT UNTIL ***I'M*** READY.

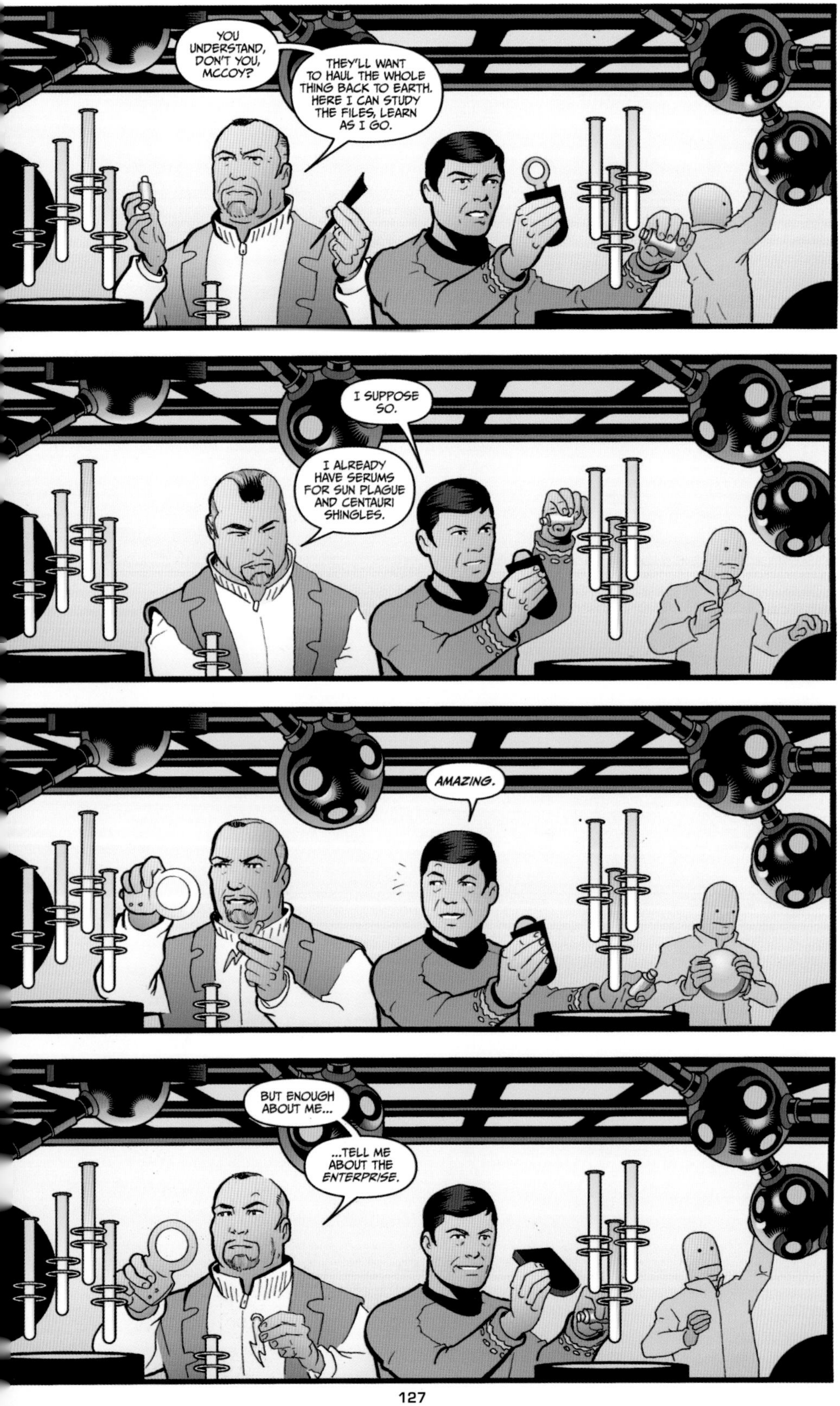

YOU UNDERSTAND, DON'T YOU, MCCOY?
THEY'LL WANT TO HAUL THE WHOLE THING BACK TO EARTH. HERE I CAN STUDY THE FILES, LEARN AS I GO.
I SUPPOSE SO.
I ALREADY HAVE SERUMS FOR SUN PLAGUE AND CENTAURI SHINGLES.
AMAZING.
BUT ENOUGH ABOUT ME...
...TELL ME ABOUT THE *ENTERPRISE*.

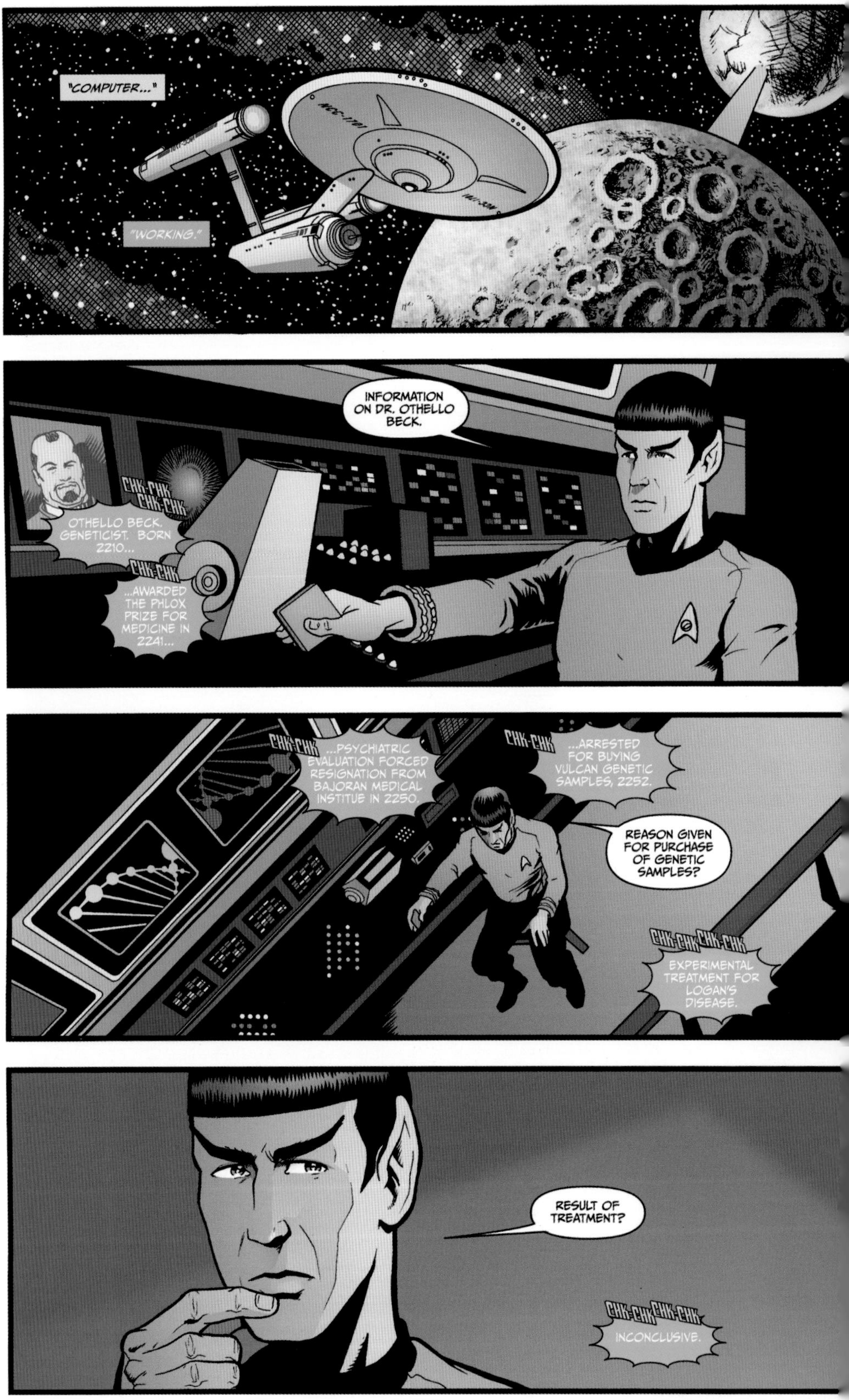
"COMPUTER..."
"WORKING."
INFORMATION ON DR. OTHELLO BECK.
CHK-CHK CHK-CHK
OTHELLO BECK. GENETICIST. BORN 2210...
CHK-CHK
...AWARDED THE PHLOX PRIZE FOR MEDICINE IN 2241...
CHK-CHK
...PSYCHIATRIC EVALUATION FORCED RESIGNATION FROM BAJORAN MEDICAL INSTITUE IN 2250.
CHK-CHK
...ARRESTED FOR BUYING VULCAN GENETIC SAMPLES, 2252.
REASON GIVEN FOR PURCHASE OF GENETIC SAMPLES?
CHK-CHK CHK-CHK
EXPERIMENTAL TREATMENT FOR LOGAN'S DISEASE.
RESULT OF TREATMENT?
CHK-CHK CHK-CHK
INCONCLUSIVE.

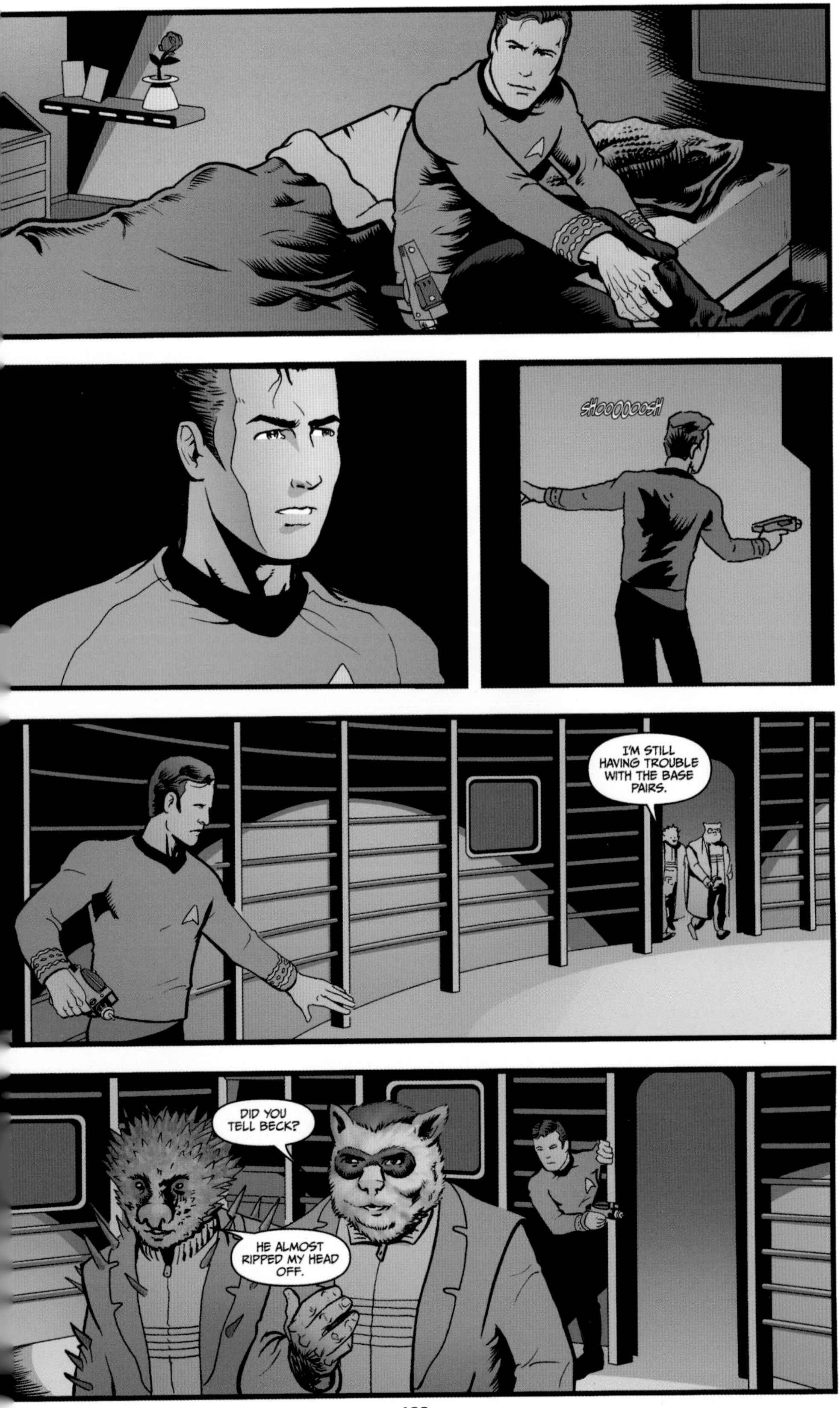
SHOOOOOOSH
I'M STILL HAVING TROUBLE WITH THE BASE PAIRS.
DID YOU TELL BECK?
HE ALMOST RIPPED MY HEAD OFF.

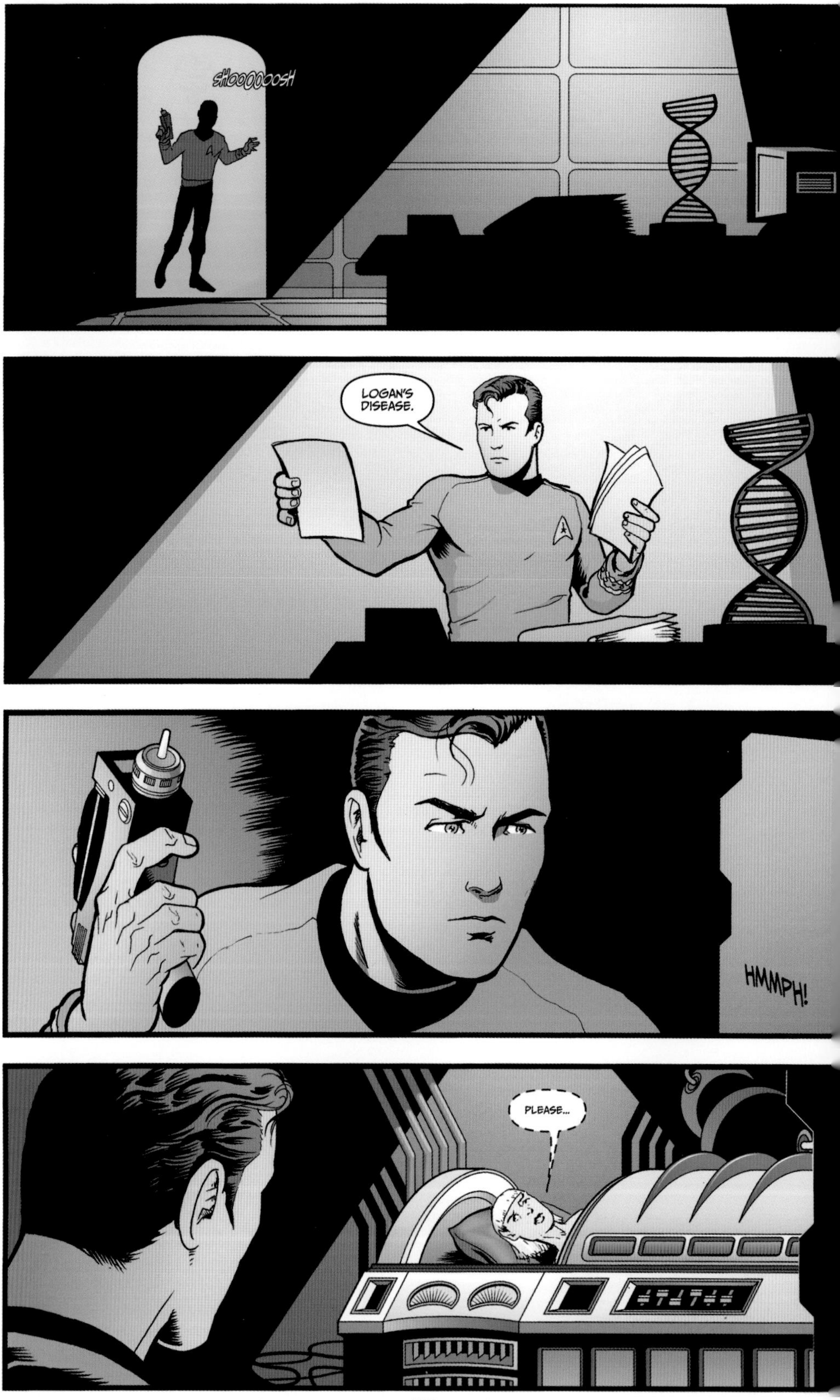
SHOOOOOOSH
LOGAN'S DISEASE.
HMMPH!
PLEASE...

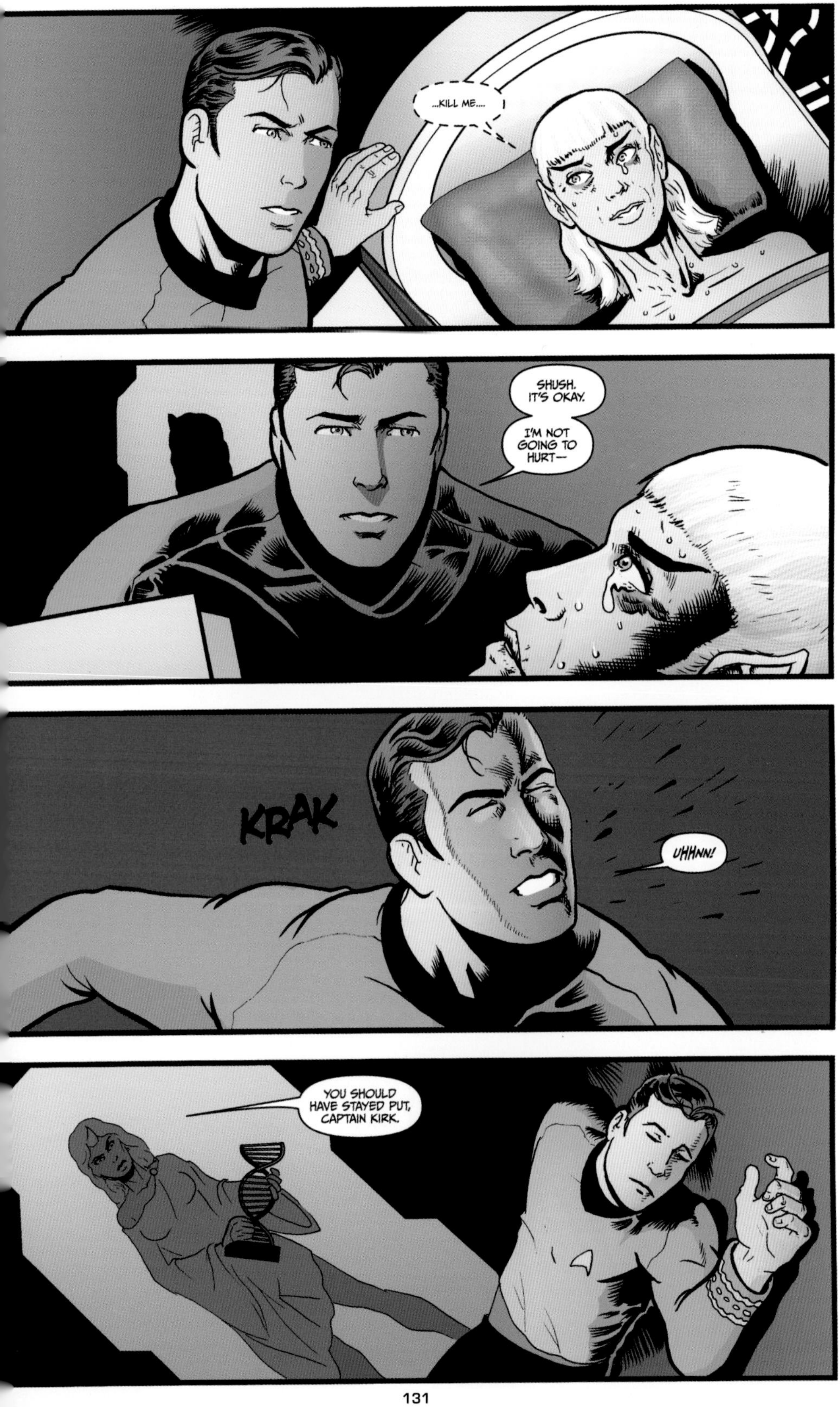
...KILL ME....
SHUSH. IT'S OKAY.
I'M NOT GOING TO HURT--
KRAK
UHHNN!
YOU SHOULD HAVE STAYED PUT, CAPTAIN KIRK.

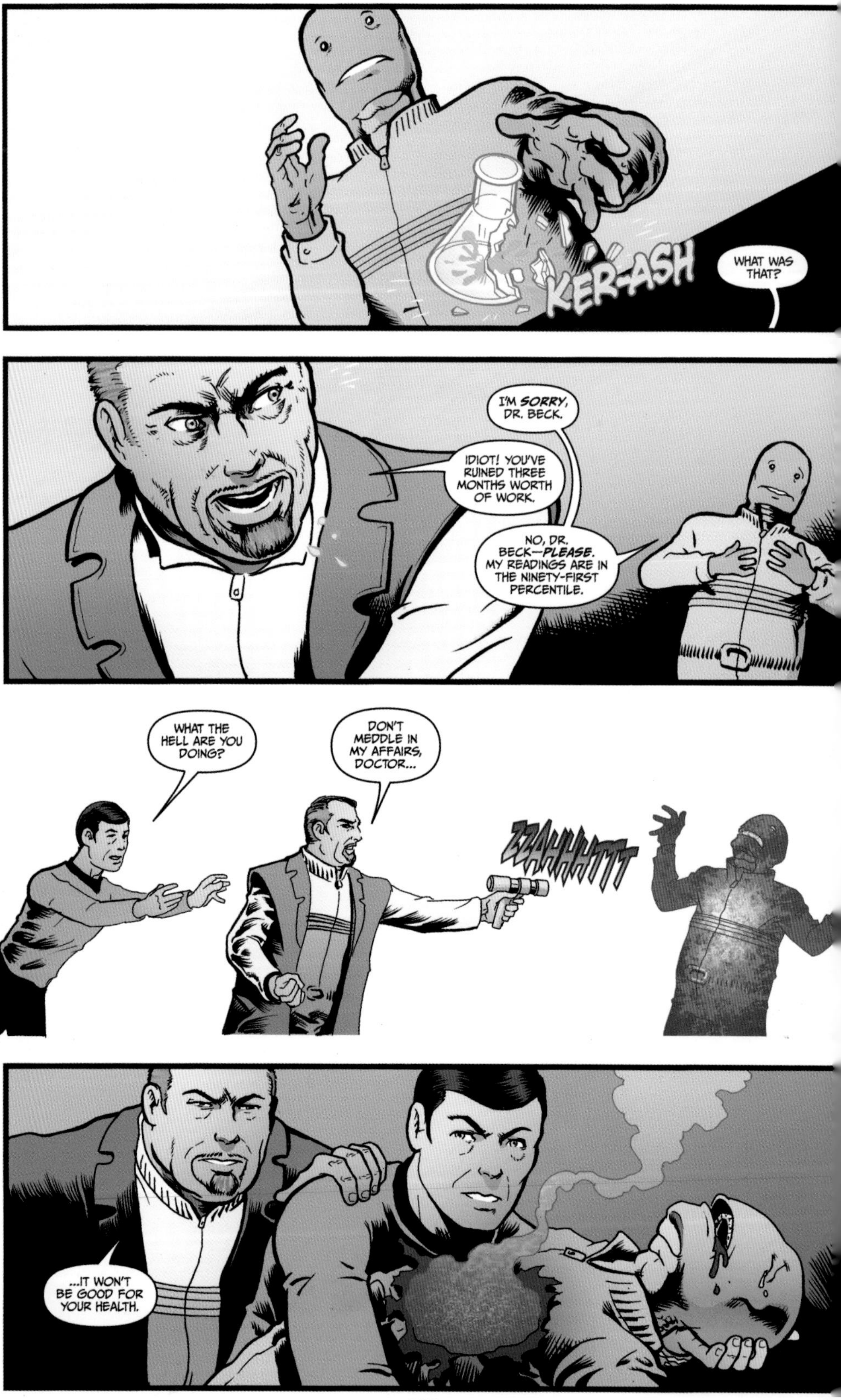
KER-ASH
WHAT WAS THAT?
I'M SORRY, DR. BECK.
IDIOT! YOU'VE RUINED THREE MONTHS WORTH OF WORK.
NO, DR. BECK—PLEASE. MY READINGS ARE IN THE NINETY-FIRST PERCENTILE.
WHAT THE HELL ARE YOU DOING?
DON'T MEDDLE IN MY AFFAIRS, DOCTOR...
ZZAHHHTTT
...IT WON'T BE GOOD FOR YOUR HEALTH.

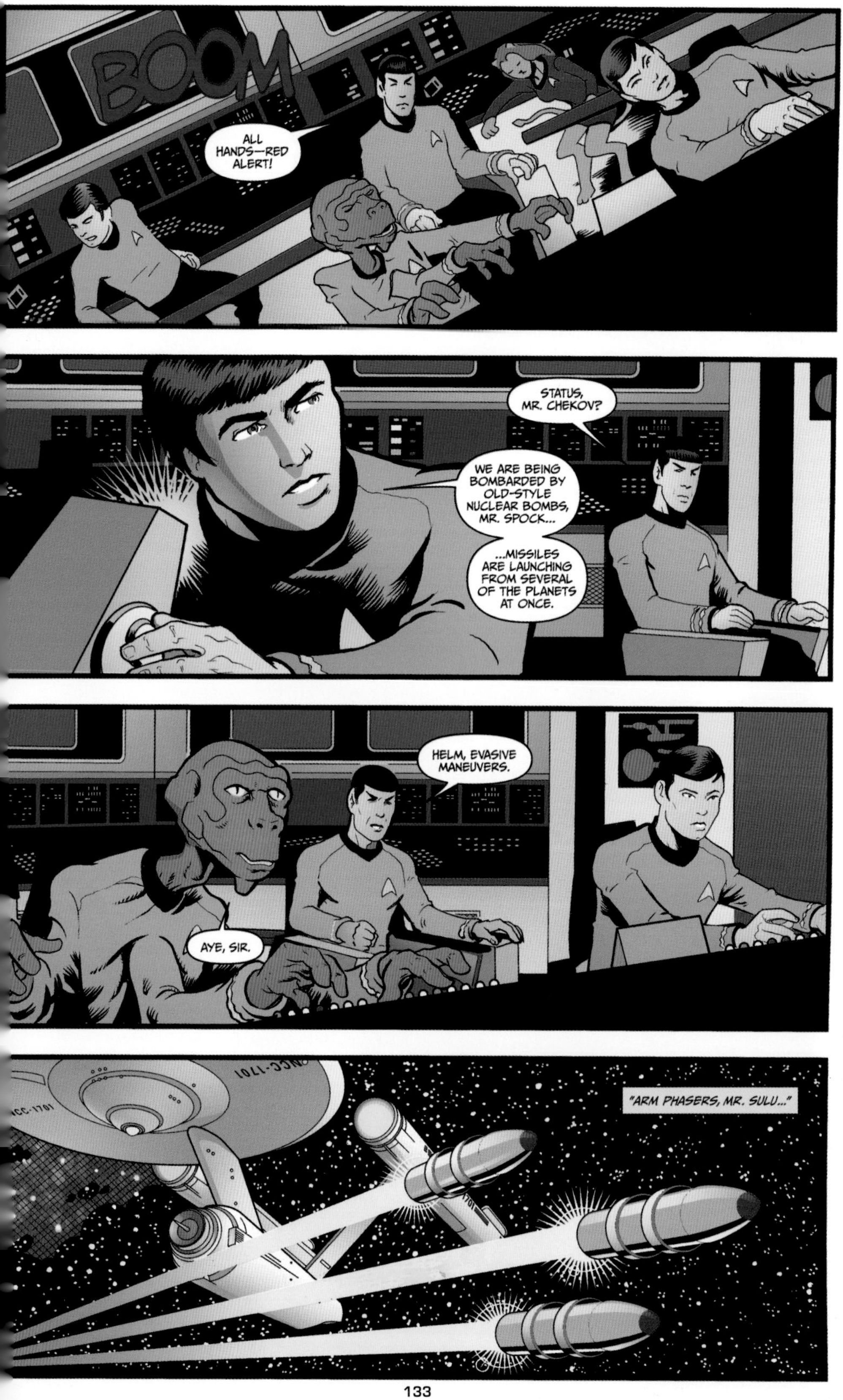
BOOM
ALL HANDS—RED ALERT!
STATUS, MR. CHEKOV?
WE ARE BEING BOMBARDED BY OLD-STYLE NUCLEAR BOMBS, MR. SPOCK...
...MISSILES ARE LAUNCHING FROM SEVERAL OF THE PLANETS AT ONCE.
HELM, EVASIVE MANEUVERS.
AYE, SIR.
NCC-1701
"ARM PHASERS, MR. SULU..."

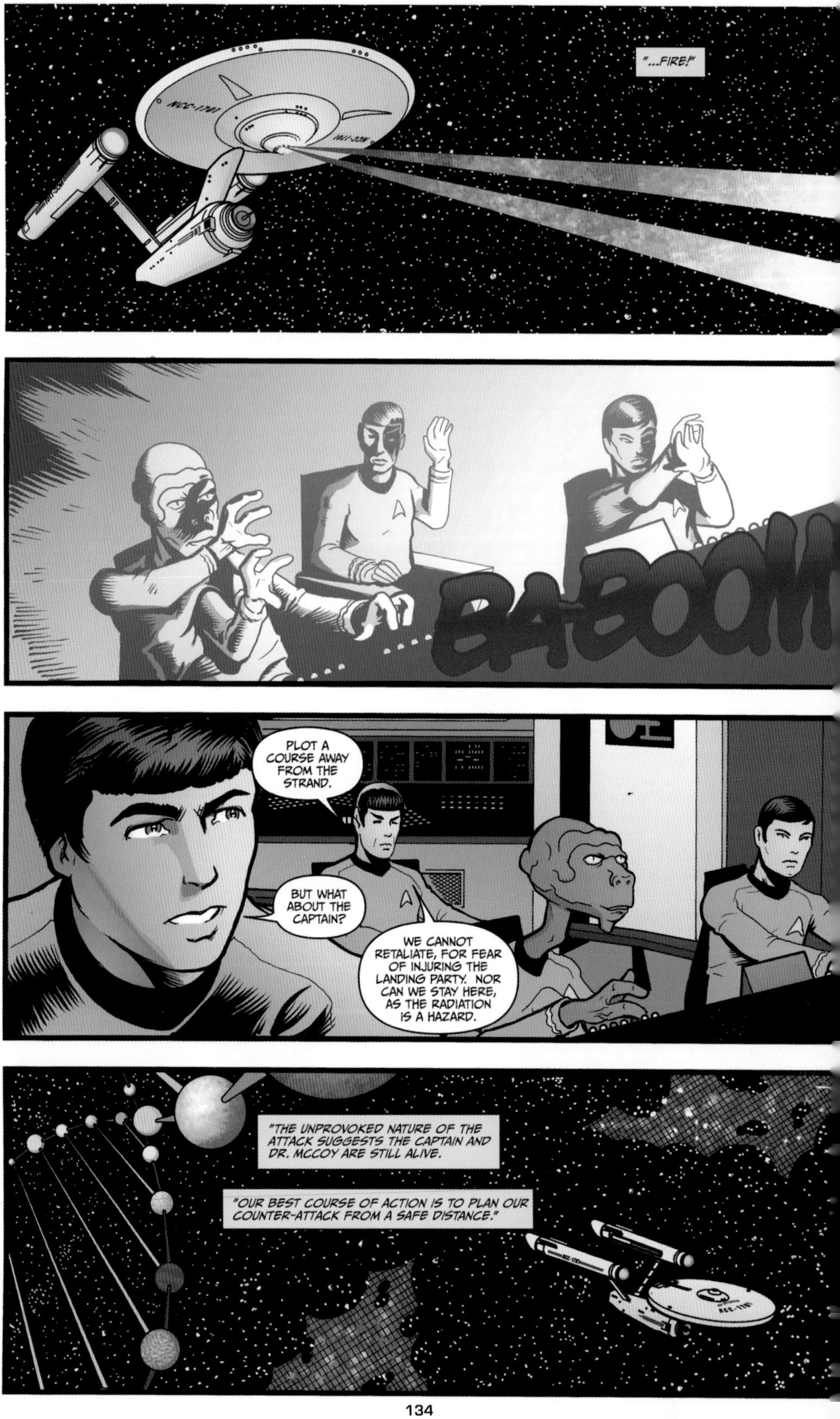
"...FIRE!"
BA-BOOM
PLOT A COURSE AWAY FROM THE STRAND.
BUT WHAT ABOUT THE CAPTAIN?
WE CANNOT RETALIATE, FOR FEAR OF INJURING THE LANDING PARTY. NOR CAN WE STAY HERE, AS THE RADIATION IS A HAZARD.
"THE UNPROVOKED NATURE OF THE ATTACK SUGGESTS THE CAPTAIN AND DR. MCCOY ARE STILL ALIVE.
"OUR BEST COURSE OF ACTION IS TO PLAN OUR COUNTER-ATTACK FROM A SAFE DISTANCE."

THEY PUT US IN HERE.

THERE ARE OUR COMMUNICATORS AND PHASERS...

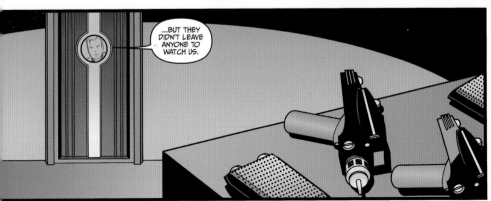

...BUT THEY DIDN'T LEAVE ANYONE TO WATCH US.

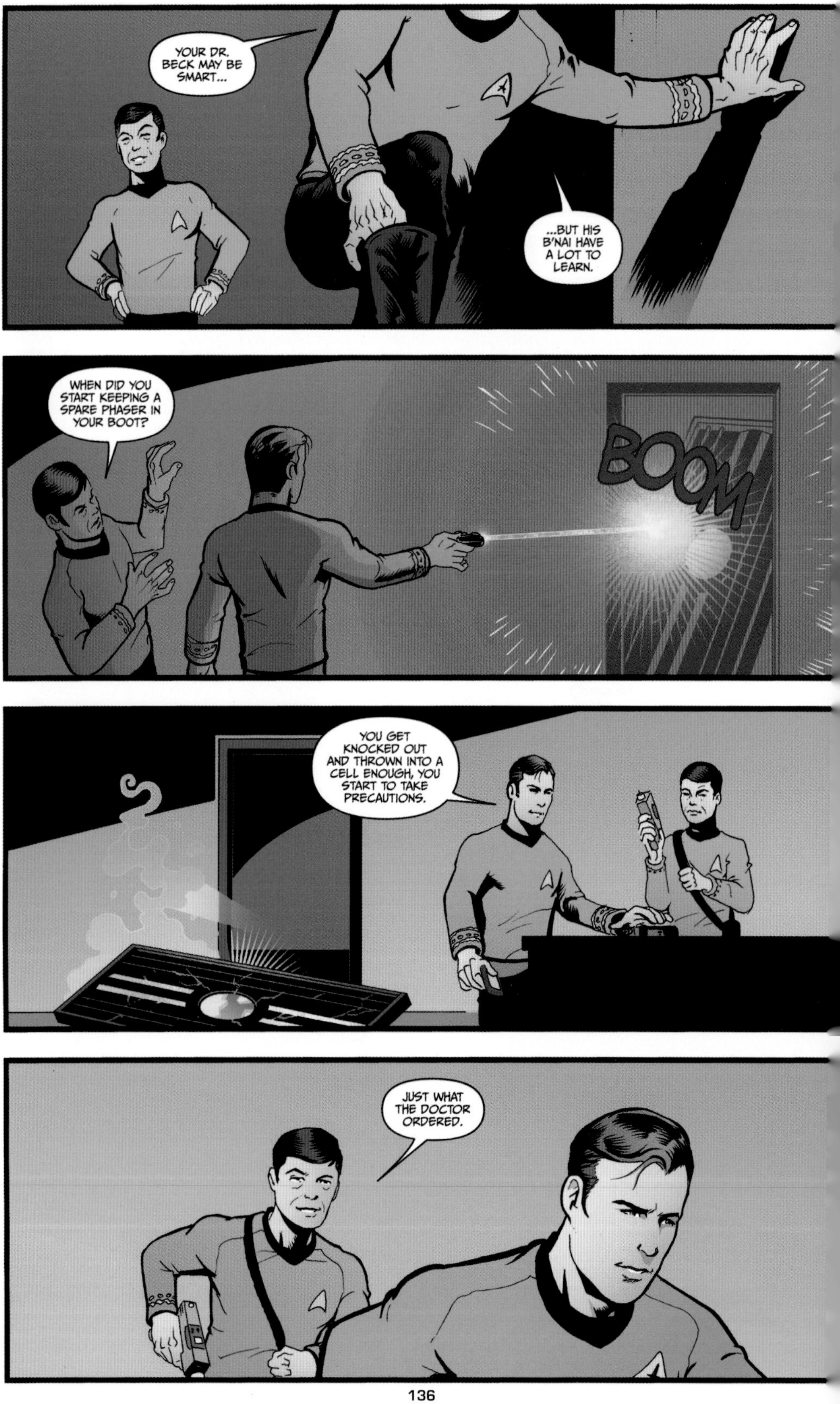
YOUR DR. BECK MAY BE SMART...
...BUT HIS B'NAI HAVE A LOT TO LEARN.
WHEN DID YOU START KEEPING A SPARE PHASER IN YOUR BOOT?
BOOM
YOU GET KNOCKED OUT AND THROWN INTO A CELL ENOUGH, YOU START TO TAKE PRECAUTIONS.
JUST WHAT THE DOCTOR ORDERED.

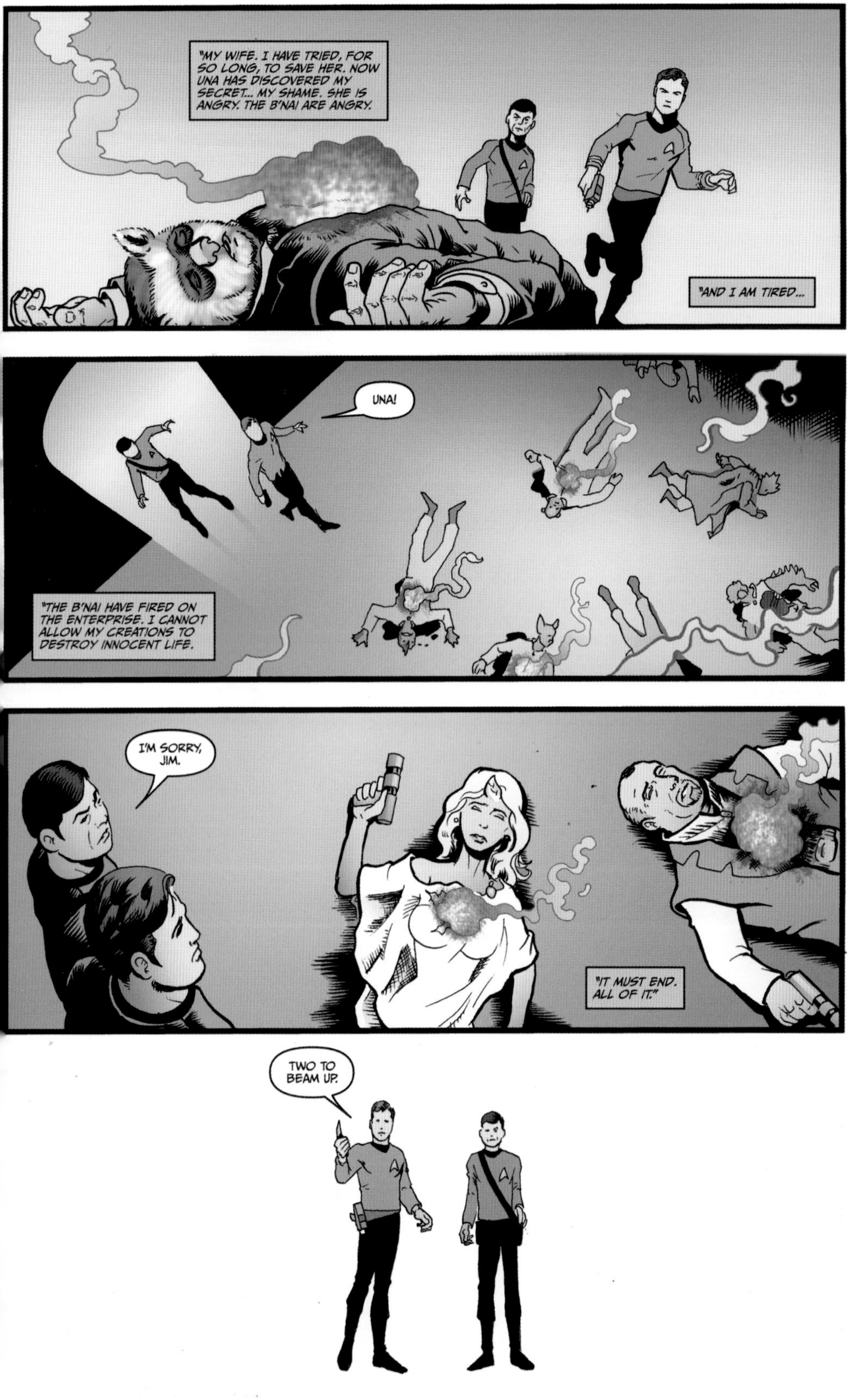
"MY WIFE. I HAVE TRIED, FOR SO LONG, TO SAVE HER. NOW UNA HAS DISCOVERED MY SECRET... MY SHAME. SHE IS ANGRY. THE B'NAI ARE ANGRY.
"AND I AM TIRED...
UNA!
"THE B'NAI HAVE FIRED ON THE ENTERPRISE. I CANNOT ALLOW MY CREATIONS TO DESTROY INNOCENT LIFE.
I'M SORRY, JIM.
"IT MUST END. ALL OF IT."
TWO TO BEAM UP.

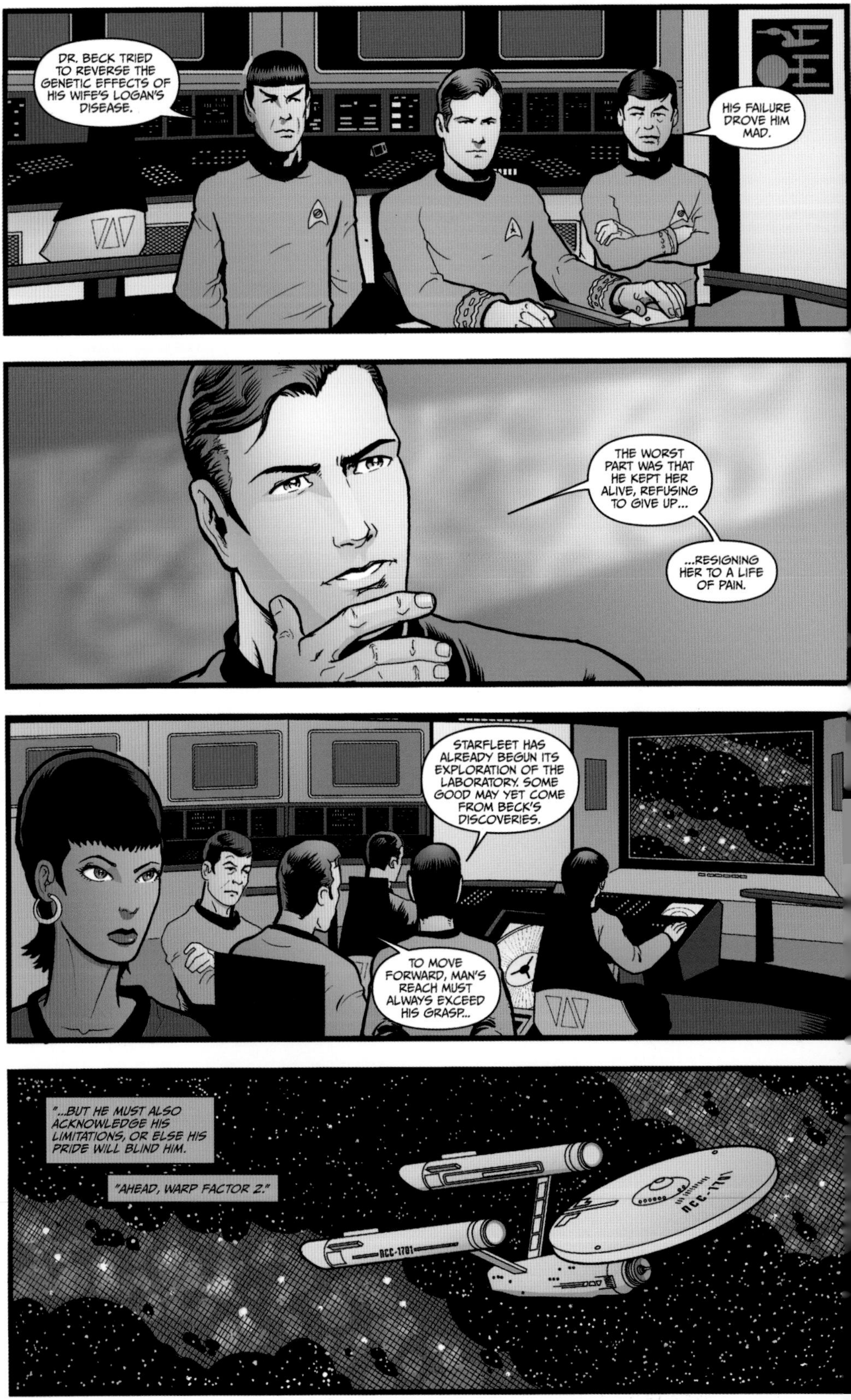
DR. BECK TRIED TO REVERSE THE GENETIC EFFECTS OF HIS WIFE'S LOGAN'S DISEASE.
HIS FAILURE DROVE HIM MAD.
THE WORST PART WAS THAT HE KEPT HER ALIVE, REFUSING TO GIVE UP...
...RESIGNING HER TO A LIFE OF PAIN.
STARFLEET HAS ALREADY BEGUN ITS EXPLORATION OF THE LABORATORY. SOME GOOD MAY YET COME FROM BECK'S DISCOVERIES.
TO MOVE FORWARD, MAN'S REACH MUST ALWAYS EXCEED HIS GRASP...
"...BUT HE MUST ALSO ACKNOWLEDGE HIS LIMITATIONS, OR ELSE HIS PRIDE WILL BLIND HIM.
"AHEAD, WARP FACTOR 2."

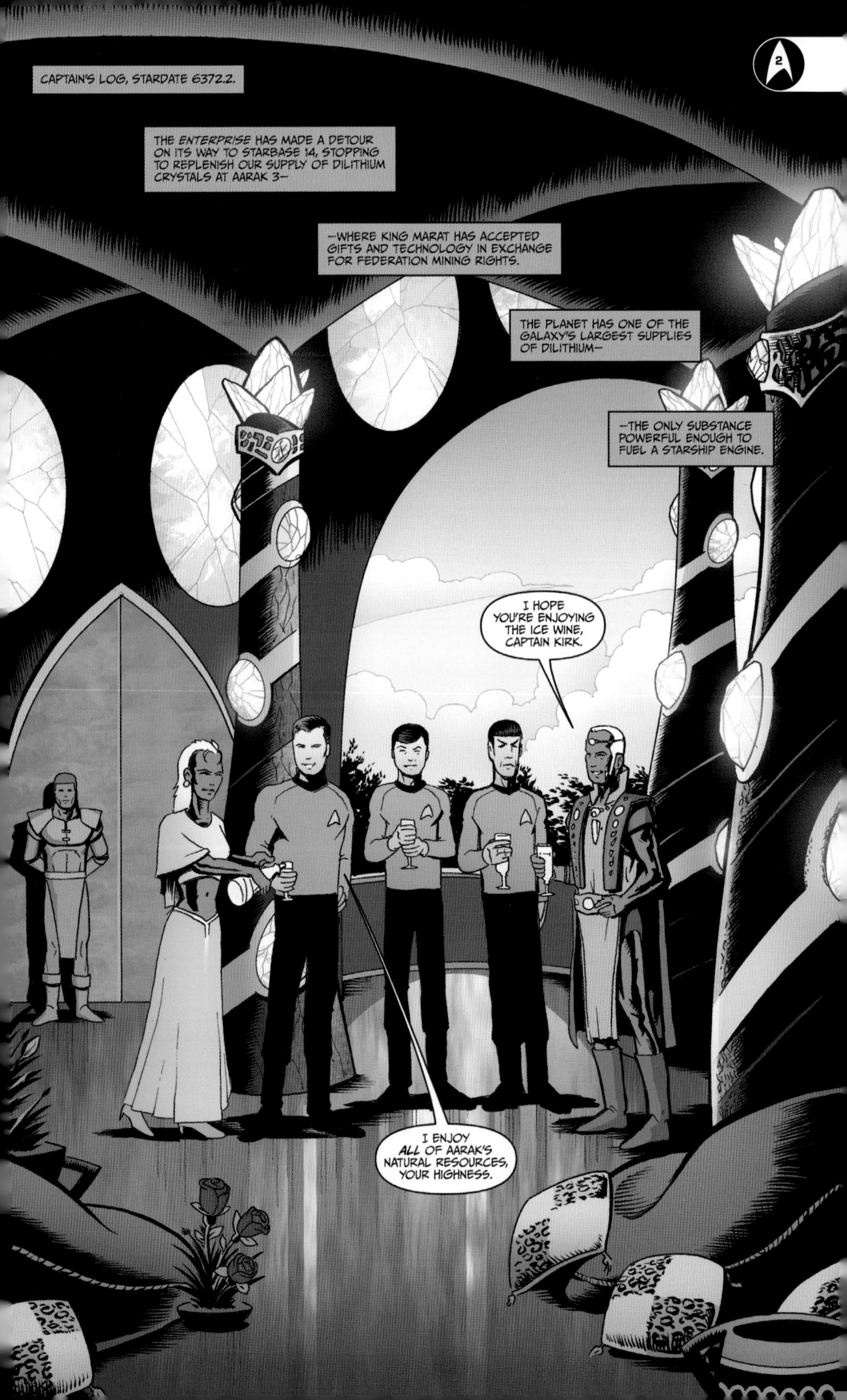
CAPTAIN'S LOG, STARDATE 6372.2.
THE *ENTERPRISE* HAS MADE A DETOUR ON ITS WAY TO STARBASE 14, STOPPING TO REPLENISH OUR SUPPLY OF DILITHIUM CRYSTALS AT AARAK 3—
—WHERE KING MARAT HAS ACCEPTED GIFTS AND TECHNOLOGY IN EXCHANGE FOR FEDERATION MINING RIGHTS.
THE PLANET HAS ONE OF THE GALAXY'S LARGEST SUPPLIES OF DILITHIUM—
—THE ONLY SUBSTANCE POWERFUL ENOUGH TO FUEL A STARSHIP ENGINE.
I HOPE YOU'RE ENJOYING THE ICE WINE, CAPTAIN KIRK.
I ENJOY *ALL* OF AARAK'S NATURAL RESOURCES, YOUR HIGHNESS.

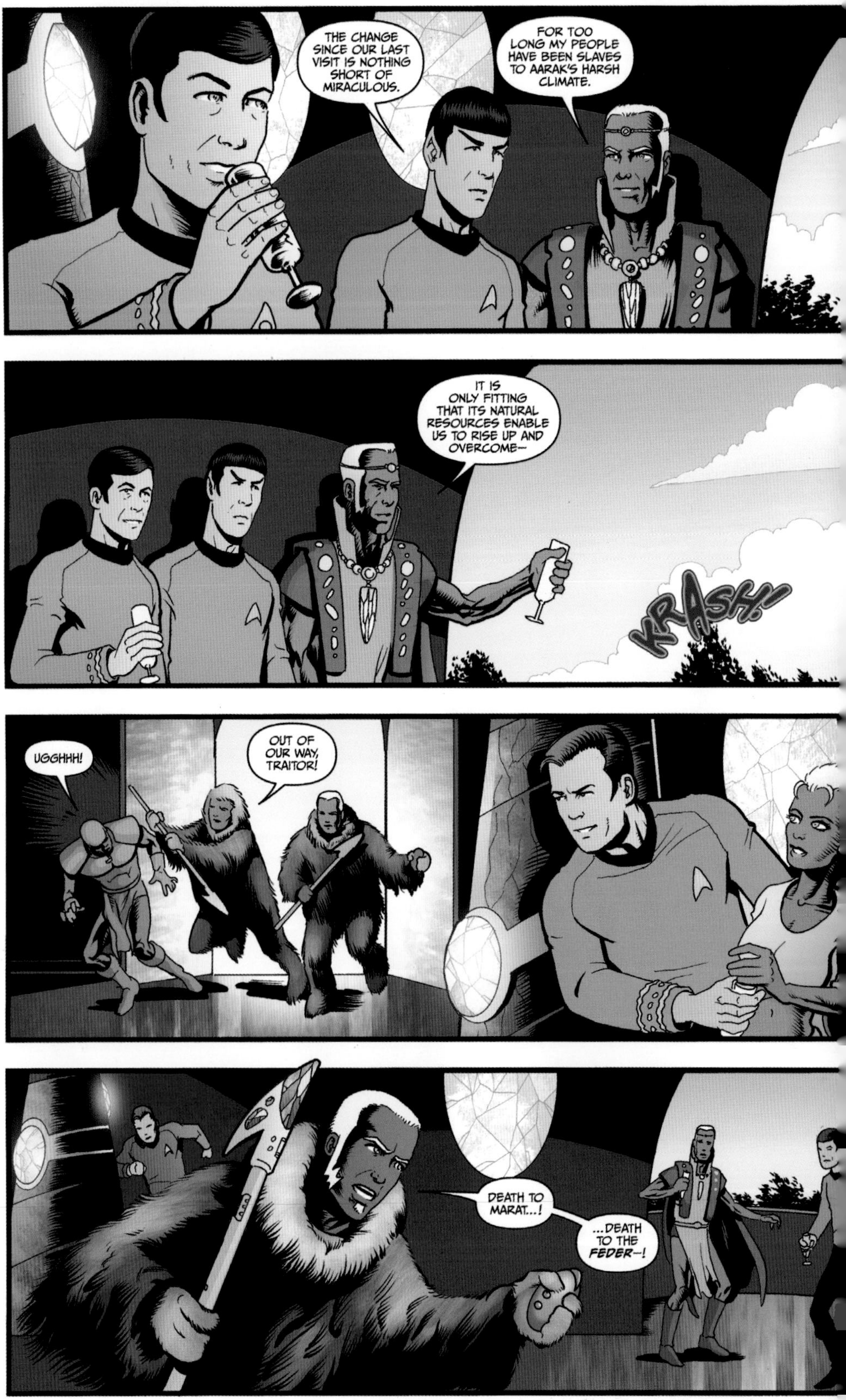
THE CHANGE SINCE OUR LAST VISIT IS NOTHING SHORT OF MIRACULOUS.
FOR TOO LONG MY PEOPLE HAVE BEEN SLAVES TO AARAK'S HARSH CLIMATE.
IT IS ONLY FITTING THAT ITS NATURAL RESOURCES ENABLE US TO RISE UP AND OVERCOME--
KRASH!
UGGHHH!
OUT OF OUR WAY, TRAITOR!
DEATH TO MARAT...!
...DEATH TO THE *FEDER*--!

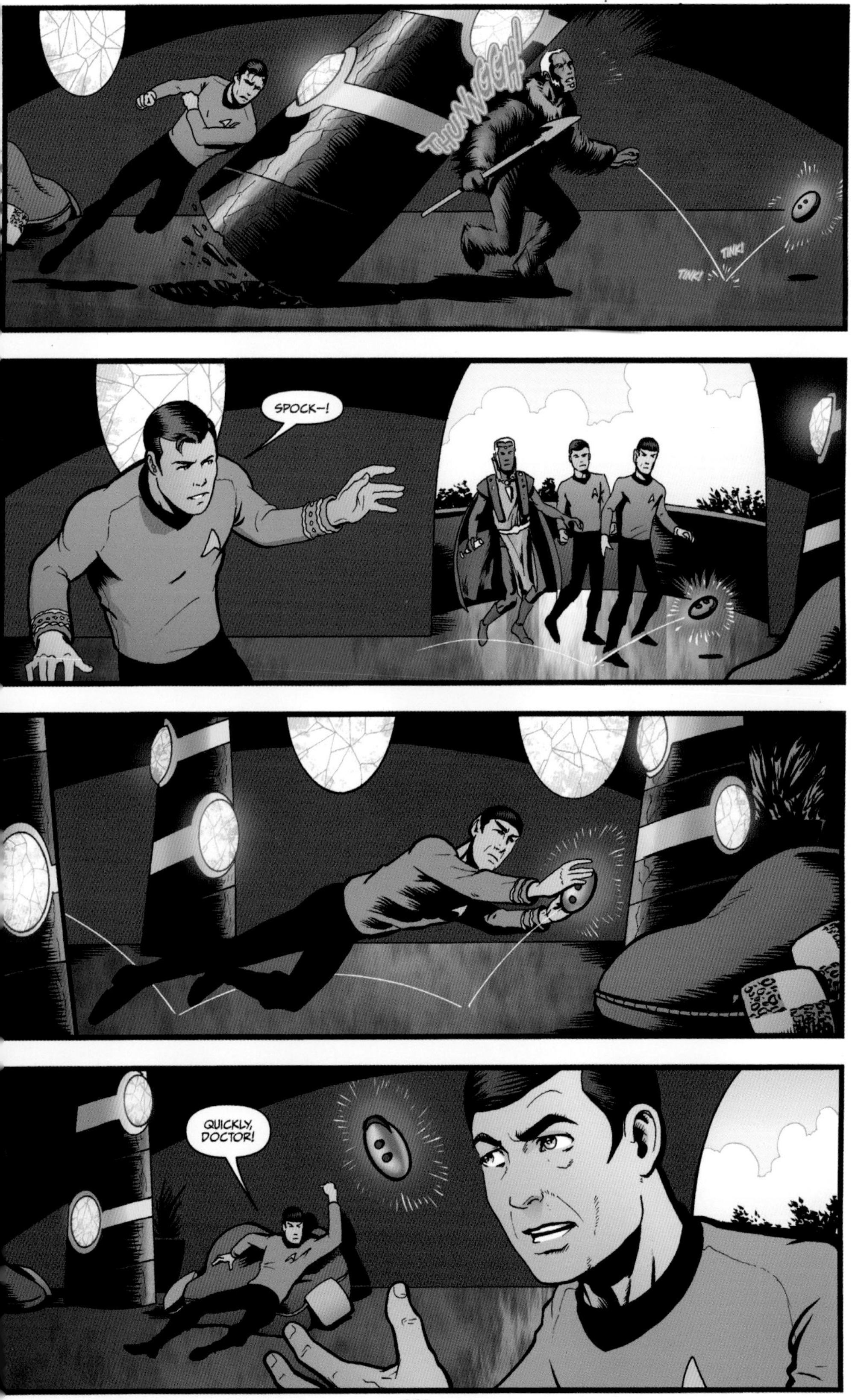
THUNNGGH!
TINK!
TINK!
SPOCK—!
QUICKLY, DOCTOR!

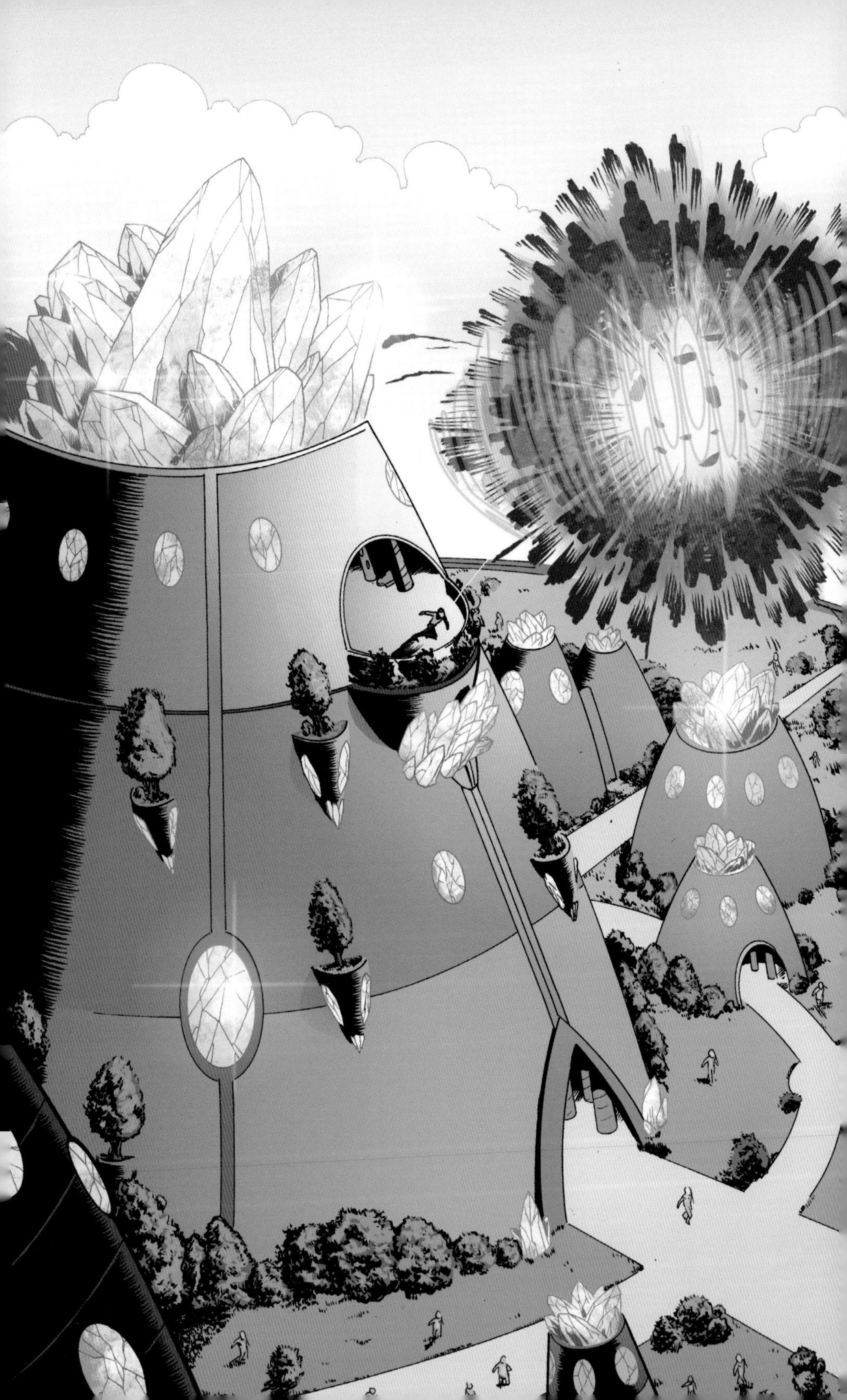

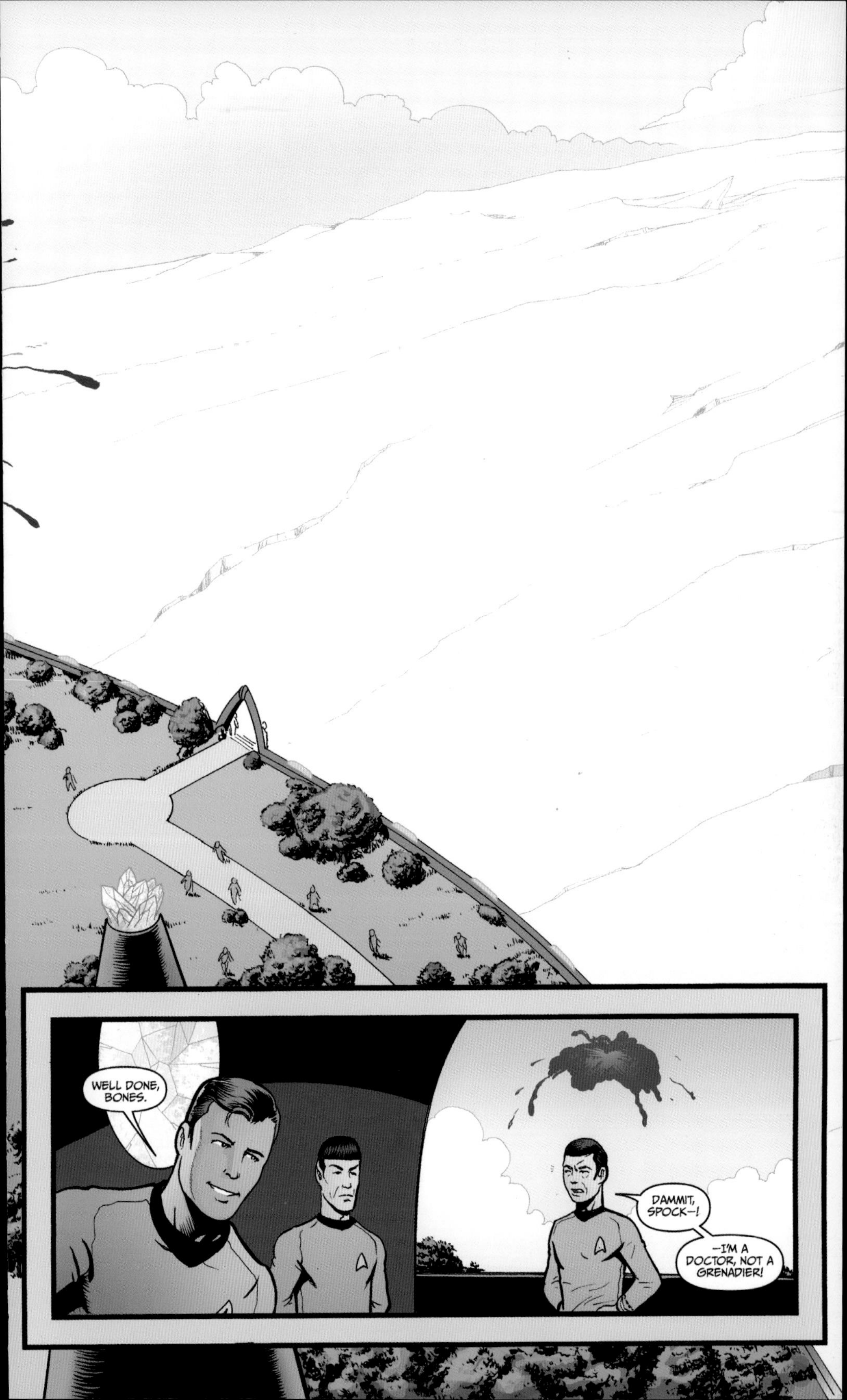
WELL DONE, BONES.
DAMMIT, SPOCK—!
—I'M A DOCTOR, NOT A GRENADIER!

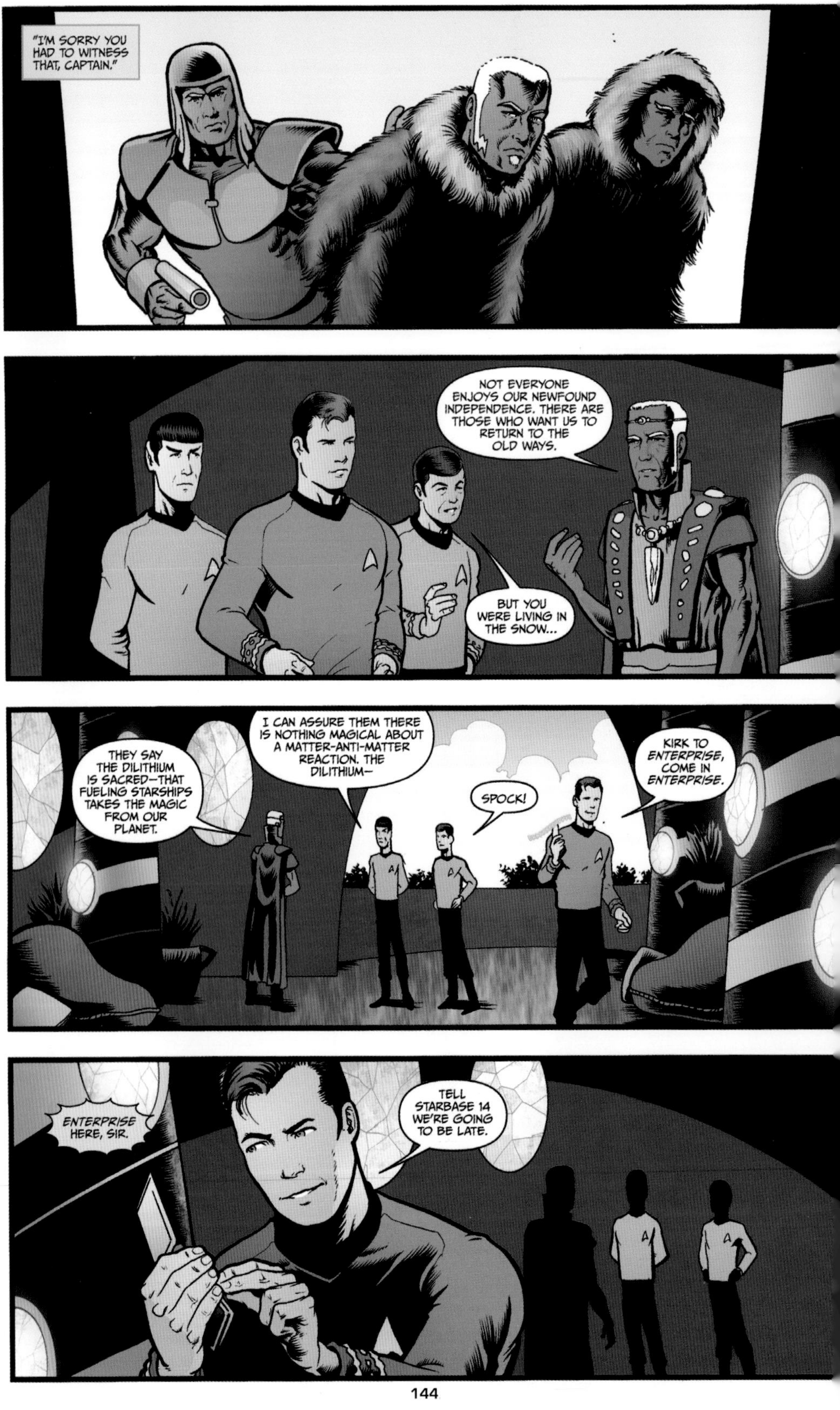
"I'M SORRY YOU HAD TO WITNESS THAT, CAPTAIN."
NOT EVERYONE ENJOYS OUR NEWFOUND INDEPENDENCE. THERE ARE THOSE WHO WANT US TO RETURN TO THE OLD WAYS.
BUT YOU WERE LIVING IN THE SNOW...
THEY SAY THE DILITHIUM IS SACRED—THAT FUELING STARSHIPS TAKES THE MAGIC FROM OUR PLANET.
I CAN ASSURE THEM THERE IS NOTHING MAGICAL ABOUT A MATTER-ANTI-MATTER REACTION. THE DILITHIUM—
SPOCK!
KIRK TO ENTERPRISE, COME IN ENTERPRISE.
ENTERPRISE HERE, SIR.
TELL STARBASE 14 WE'RE GOING TO BE LATE.

"THAT'S THE PROBLEM, RIGHT THERE."

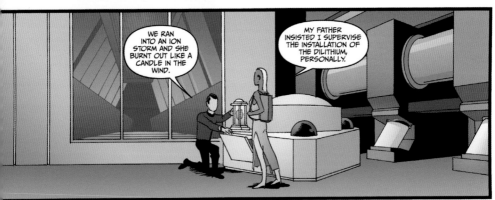

WE RAN INTO AN ION STORM AND SHE BURNT OUT LIKE A CANDLE IN THE WIND.

MY FATHER INSISTED I SUPERVISE THE INSTALLATION OF THE DILITHIUM, PERSONALLY.

SHE'S A BEAUTY.

ABOUT NINETY-SEVEN PERCENT PURITY, I'D SAY.

NINETY-SEVEN POINT FOUR...

...IT'S RARE TO SEE AN OFF-WORLDER WITH SUCH AN APPRECIATION FOR DILITHIUM

LIKE THE FIRST BIT OF LIGHT ON A SPRING MORNING.

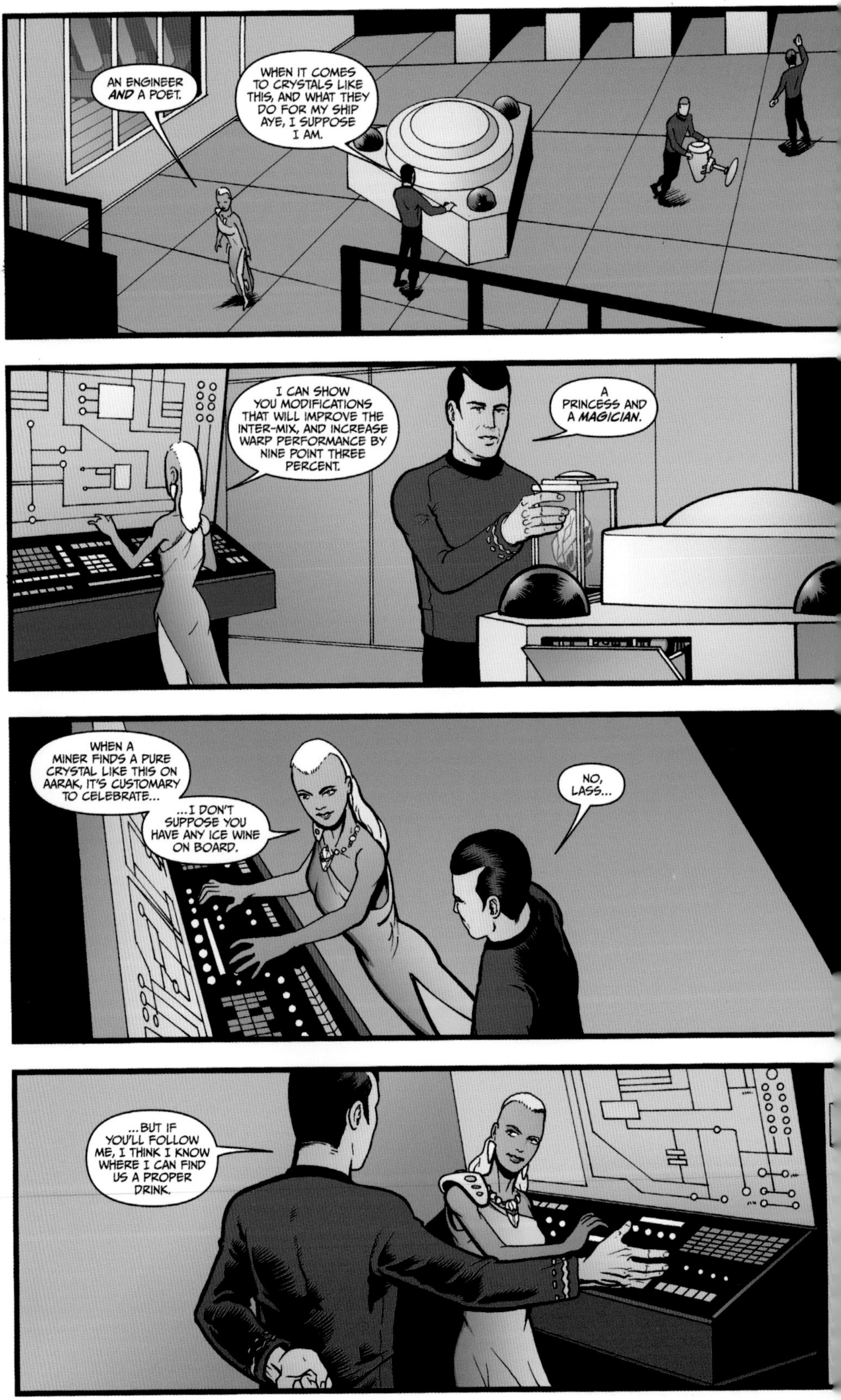
AN ENGINEER AND A POET.
WHEN IT COMES TO CRYSTALS LIKE THIS, AND WHAT THEY DO FOR MY SHIP AYE, I SUPPOSE I AM.
I CAN SHOW YOU MODIFICATIONS THAT WILL IMPROVE THE INTER-MIX, AND INCREASE WARP PERFORMANCE BY NINE POINT THREE PERCENT.
A PRINCESS AND A MAGICIAN.
WHEN A MINER FINDS A PURE CRYSTAL LIKE THIS ON AARAK, IT'S CUSTOMARY TO CELEBRATE...
...I DON'T SUPPOSE YOU HAVE ANY ICE WINE ON BOARD.
NO, LASS...
...BUT IF YOU'LL FOLLOW ME, I THINK I KNOW WHERE I CAN FIND US A PROPER DRINK.

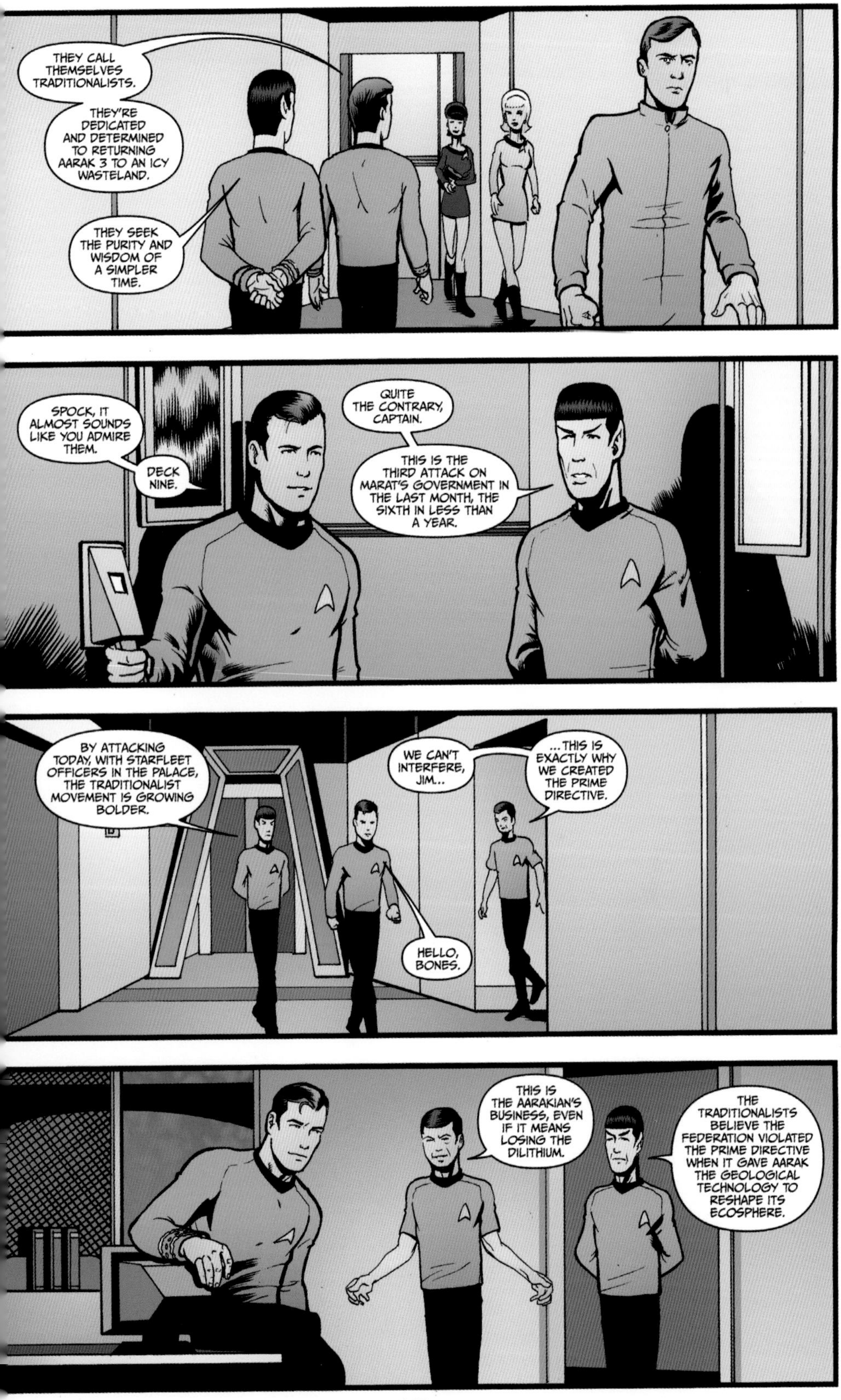
THEY CALL THEMSELVES TRADITIONALISTS.
THEY'RE DEDICATED AND DETERMINED TO RETURNING AARAK 3 TO AN ICY WASTELAND.
THEY SEEK THE PURITY AND WISDOM OF A SIMPLER TIME.
SPOCK, IT ALMOST SOUNDS LIKE YOU ADMIRE THEM.
DECK NINE.
QUITE THE CONTRARY, CAPTAIN.
THIS IS THE THIRD ATTACK ON MARAT'S GOVERNMENT IN THE LAST MONTH, THE SIXTH IN LESS THAN A YEAR.
BY ATTACKING TODAY, WITH STARFLEET OFFICERS IN THE PALACE, THE TRADITIONALIST MOVEMENT IS GROWING BOLDER.
HELLO, BONES.
WE CAN'T INTERFERE, JIM...
...THIS IS EXACTLY WHY WE CREATED THE PRIME DIRECTIVE.
THIS IS THE AARAKIAN'S BUSINESS, EVEN IF IT MEANS LOSING THE DILITHIUM.
THE TRADITIONALISTS BELIEVE THE FEDERATION VIOLATED THE PRIME DIRECTIVE WHEN IT GAVE AARAK THE GEOLOGICAL TECHNOLOGY TO RESHAPE ITS ECOSPHERE.

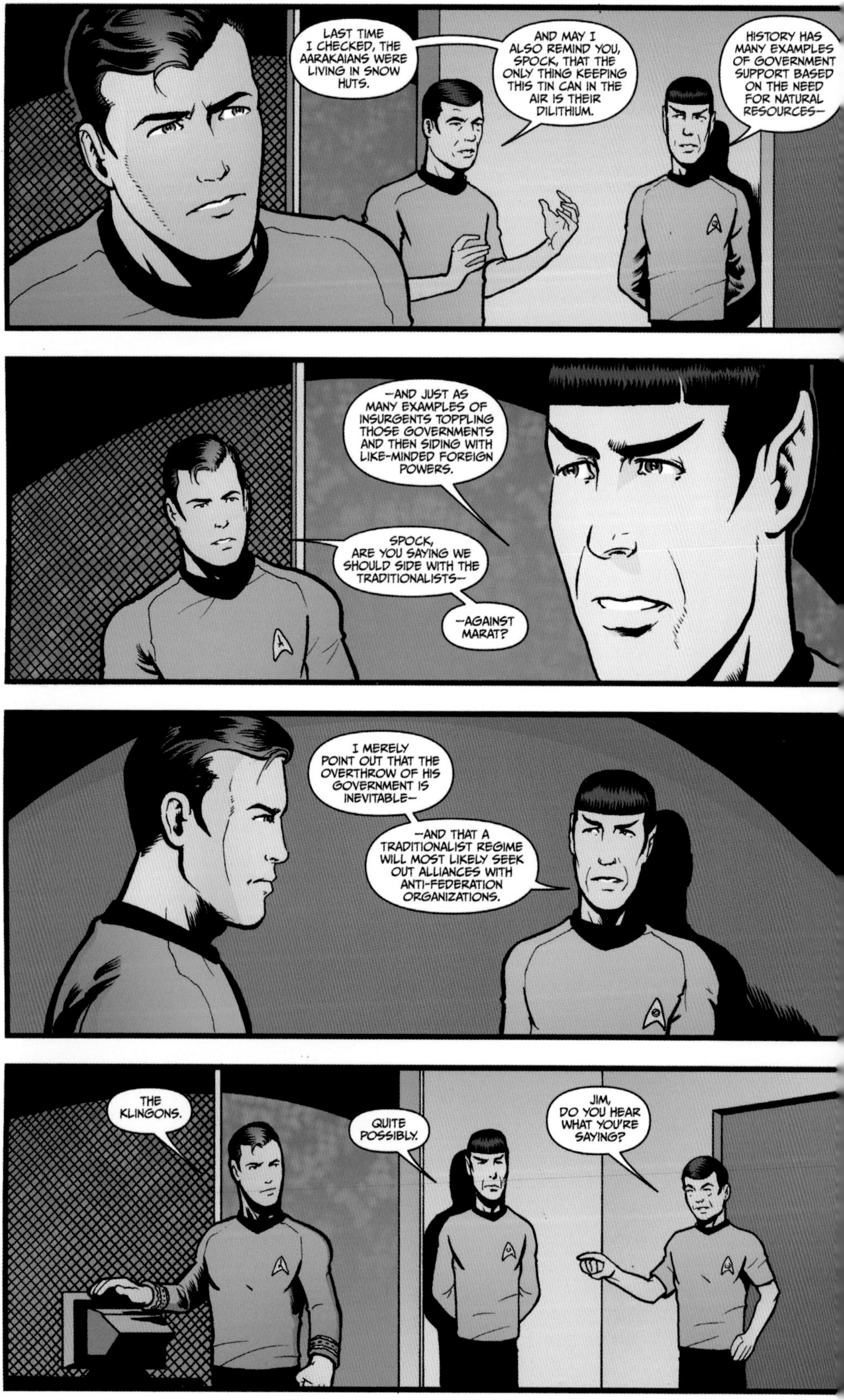
LAST TIME I CHECKED, THE AARAKAIANS WERE LIVING IN SNOW HUTS.
AND MAY I ALSO REMIND YOU, SPOCK, THAT THE ONLY THING KEEPING THIS TIN CAN IN THE AIR IS THEIR DILITHIUM.
HISTORY HAS MANY EXAMPLES OF GOVERNMENT SUPPORT BASED ON THE NEED FOR NATURAL RESOURCES--
--AND JUST AS MANY EXAMPLES OF INSURGENTS TOPPLING THOSE GOVERNMENTS AND THEN SIDING WITH LIKE-MINDED FOREIGN POWERS.
SPOCK, ARE YOU SAYING WE SHOULD SIDE WITH THE TRADITIONALISTS--
--AGAINST MARAT?
I MERELY POINT OUT THAT THE OVERTHROW OF HIS GOVERNMENT IS INEVITABLE--
--AND THAT A TRADITIONALIST REGIME WILL MOST LIKELY SEEK OUT ALLIANCES WITH ANTI-FEDERATION ORGANIZATIONS.
THE KLINGONS.
QUITE POSSIBLY.
JIM, DO YOU HEAR WHAT YOU'RE SAYING?

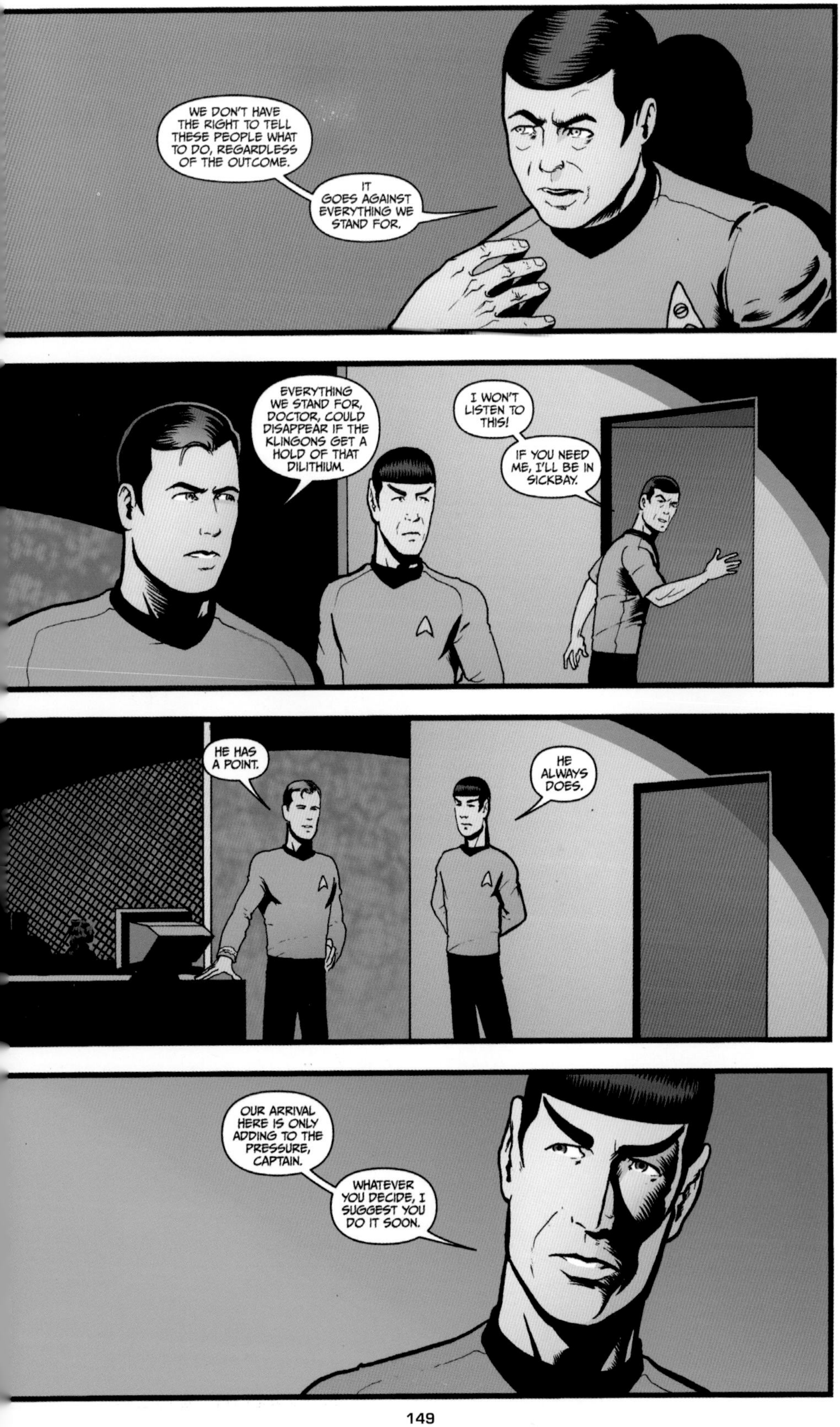
WE DON'T HAVE THE RIGHT TO TELL THESE PEOPLE WHAT TO DO, REGARDLESS OF THE OUTCOME.
IT GOES AGAINST EVERYTHING WE STAND FOR.
EVERYTHING WE STAND FOR, DOCTOR, COULD DISAPPEAR IF THE KLINGONS GET A HOLD OF THAT DILITHIUM.
I WON'T LISTEN TO THIS!
IF YOU NEED ME, I'LL BE IN SICKBAY.
HE HAS A POINT.
HE ALWAYS DOES.
OUR ARRIVAL HERE IS ONLY ADDING TO THE PRESSURE, CAPTAIN.
WHATEVER YOU DECIDE, I SUGGEST YOU DO IT SOON.

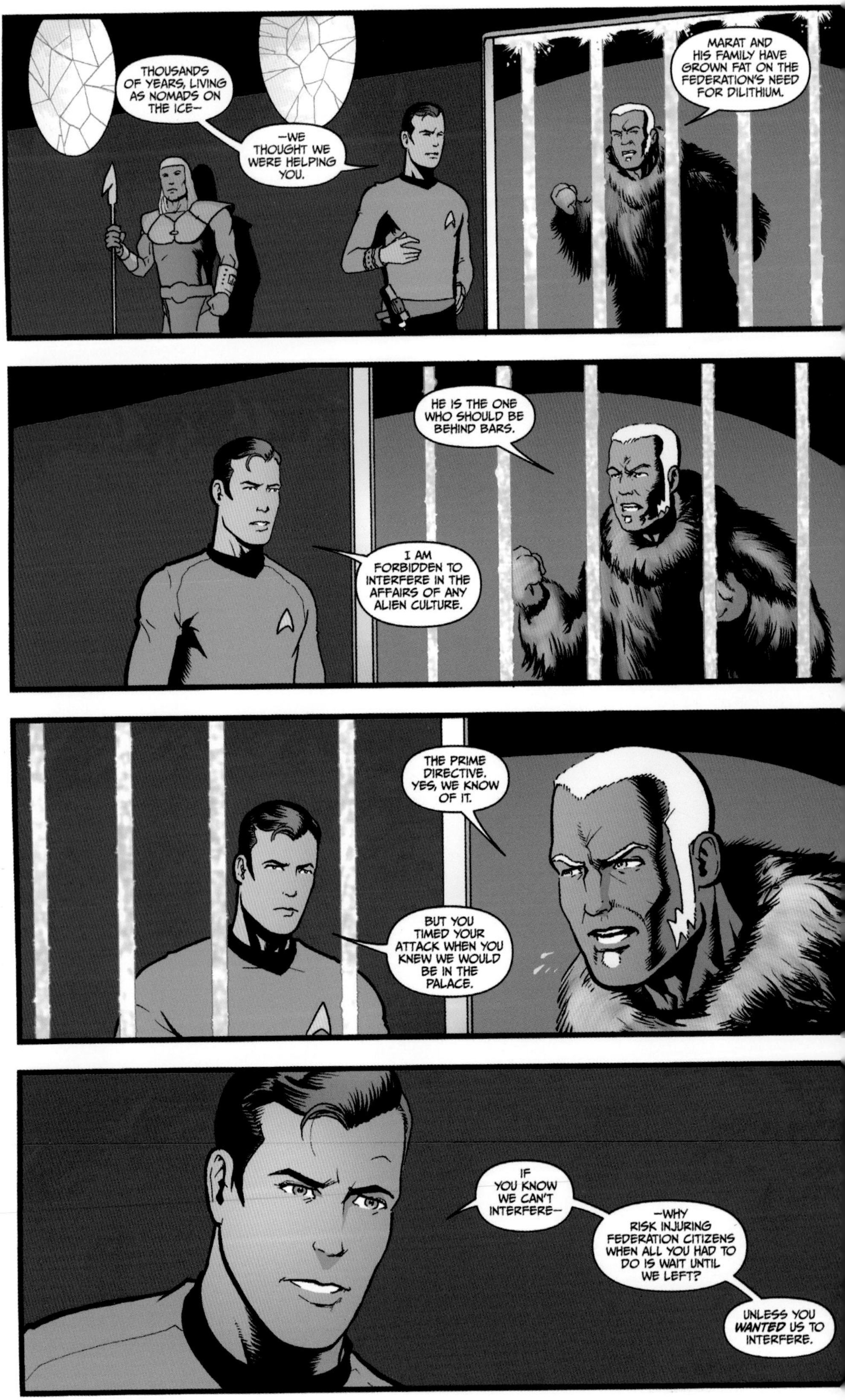
THOUSANDS OF YEARS, LIVING AS NOMADS ON THE ICE—
—WE THOUGHT WE WERE HELPING YOU.
MARAT AND HIS FAMILY HAVE GROWN FAT ON THE FEDERATION'S NEED FOR DILITHIUM.
HE IS THE ONE WHO SHOULD BE BEHIND BARS.
I AM FORBIDDEN TO INTERFERE IN THE AFFAIRS OF ANY ALIEN CULTURE.
THE PRIME DIRECTIVE. YES, WE KNOW OF IT.
BUT YOU TIMED YOUR ATTACK WHEN YOU KNEW WE WOULD BE IN THE PALACE.
IF YOU KNOW WE CAN'T INTERFERE—
—WHY RISK INJURING FEDERATION CITIZENS WHEN ALL YOU HAD TO DO IS WAIT UNTIL WE LEFT?
UNLESS YOU *WANTED* US TO INTERFERE.

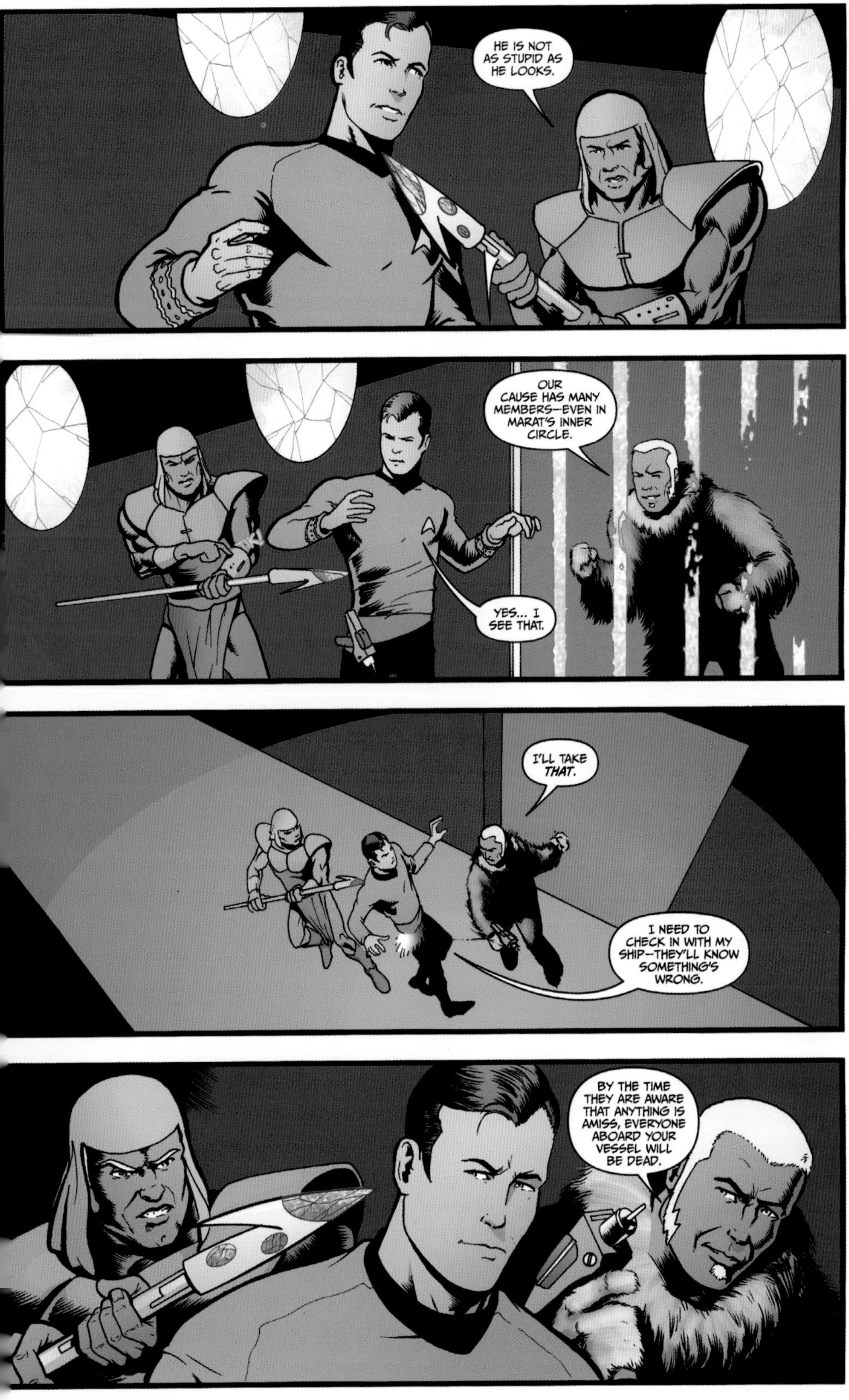
HE IS NOT AS STUPID AS HE LOOKS.
OUR CAUSE HAS MANY MEMBERS--EVEN IN MARAT'S INNER CIRCLE.
YES... I SEE THAT.
I'LL TAKE *THAT*.
I NEED TO CHECK IN WITH MY SHIP--THEY'LL KNOW SOMETHING'S WRONG.
BY THE TIME THEY ARE AWARE THAT ANYTHING IS AMISS, EVERYONE ABOARD YOUR VESSEL WILL BE DEAD.

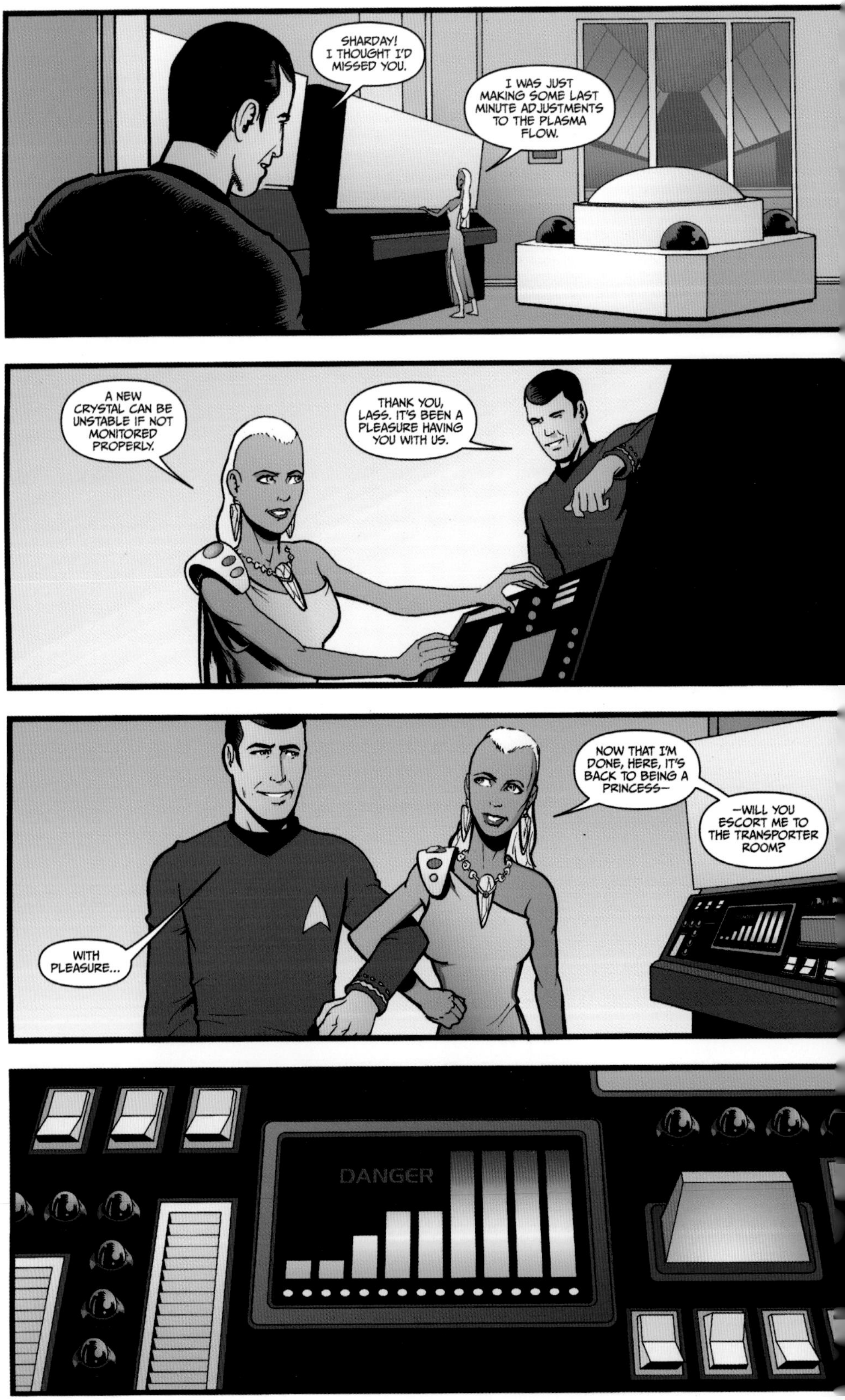
SHARDAY! I THOUGHT I'D MISSED YOU.
I WAS JUST MAKING SOME LAST MINUTE ADJUSTMENTS TO THE PLASMA FLOW.
A NEW CRYSTAL CAN BE UNSTABLE IF NOT MONITORED PROPERLY.
THANK YOU, LASS. IT'S BEEN A PLEASURE HAVING YOU WITH US.
NOW THAT I'M DONE, HERE, IT'S BACK TO BEING A PRINCESS—
—WILL YOU ESCORT ME TO THE TRANSPORTER ROOM?
WITH PLEASURE...
DANGER

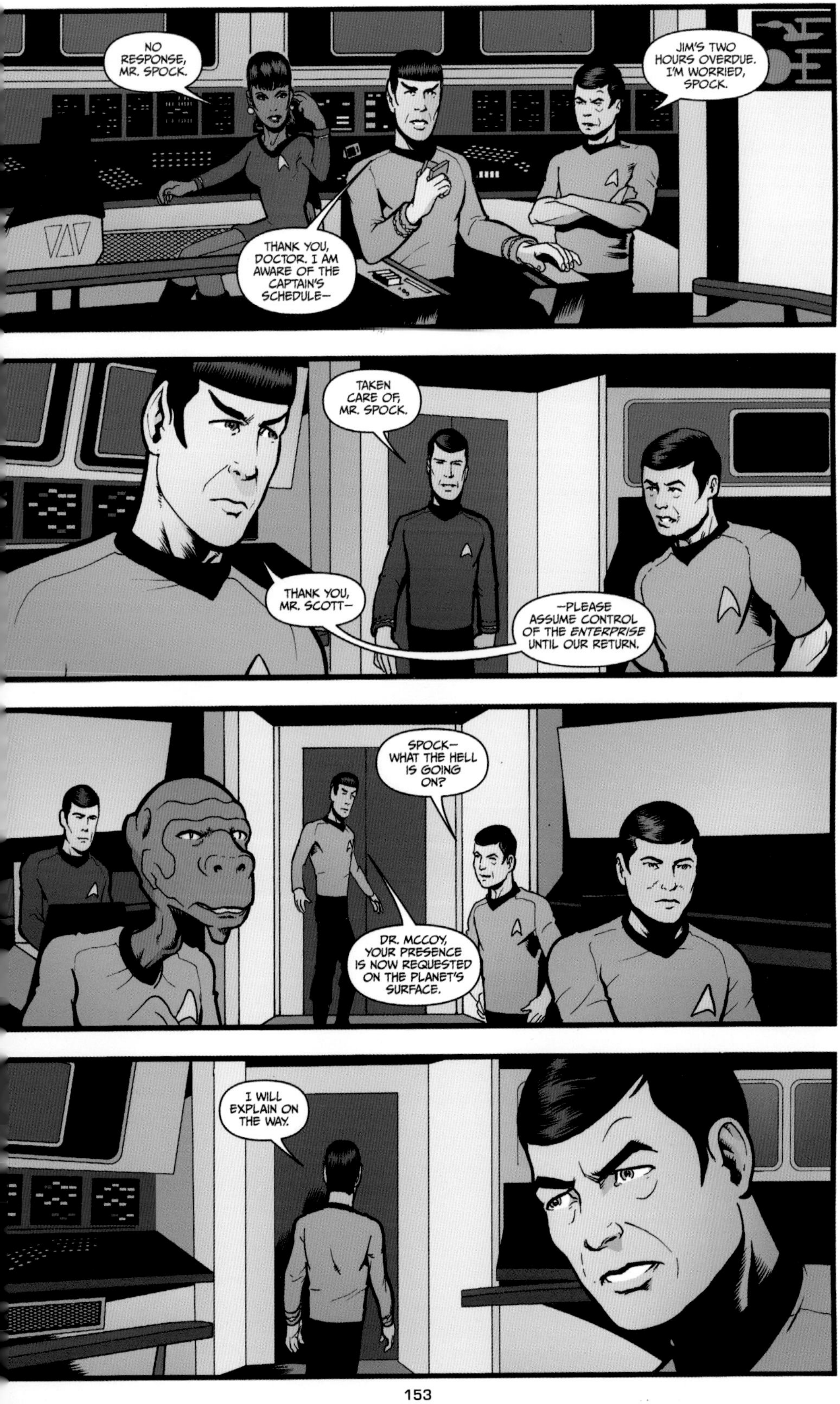
NO RESPONSE, MR. SPOCK.
JIM'S TWO HOURS OVERDUE. I'M WORRIED, SPOCK.
THANK YOU, DOCTOR. I AM AWARE OF THE CAPTAIN'S SCHEDULE—
TAKEN CARE OF, MR. SPOCK.
THANK YOU, MR. SCOTT—
—PLEASE ASSUME CONTROL OF THE *ENTERPRISE* UNTIL OUR RETURN.
SPOCK— WHAT THE HELL IS GOING ON?
DR. MCCOY, YOUR PRESENCE IS NOW REQUESTED ON THE PLANET'S SURFACE.
I WILL EXPLAIN ON THE WAY.

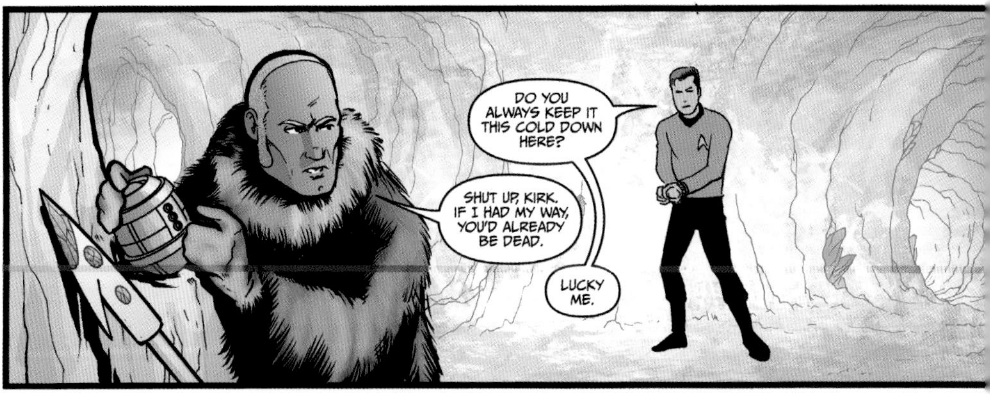
DO YOU ALWAYS KEEP IT THIS COLD DOWN HERE?
SHUT UP, KIRK. IF I HAD MY WAY, YOU'D ALREADY BE DEAD.
LUCKY ME.

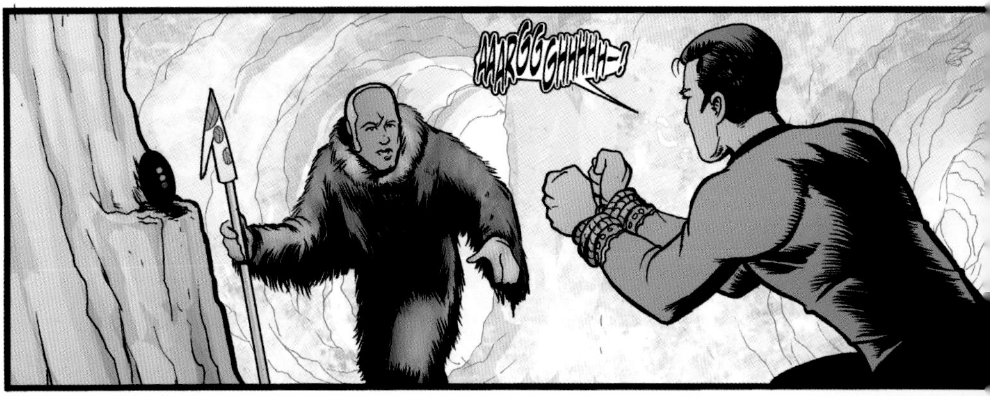
AAARGGGHHHHH--!

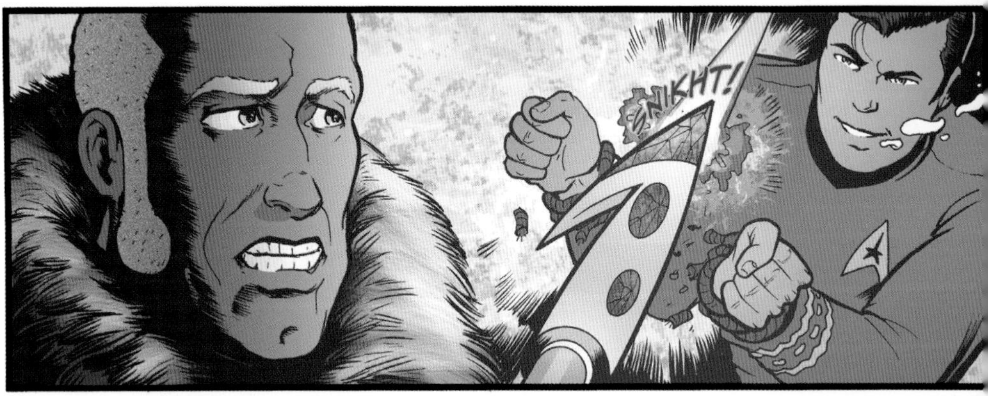
SNIKHT!

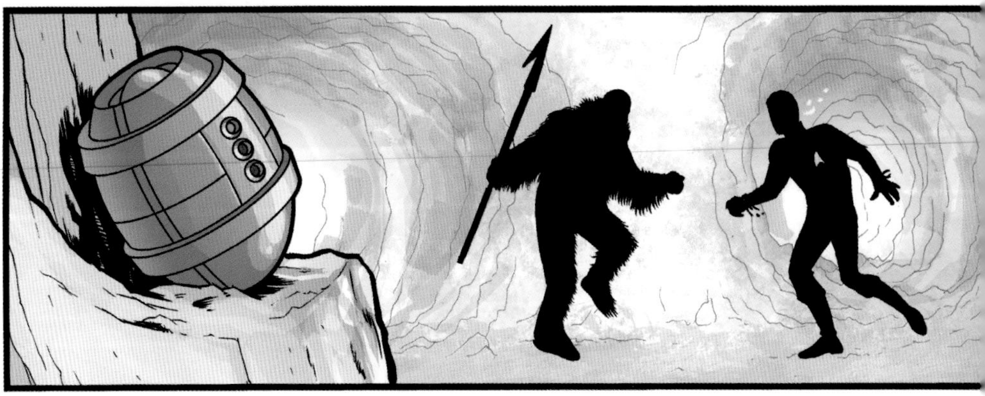

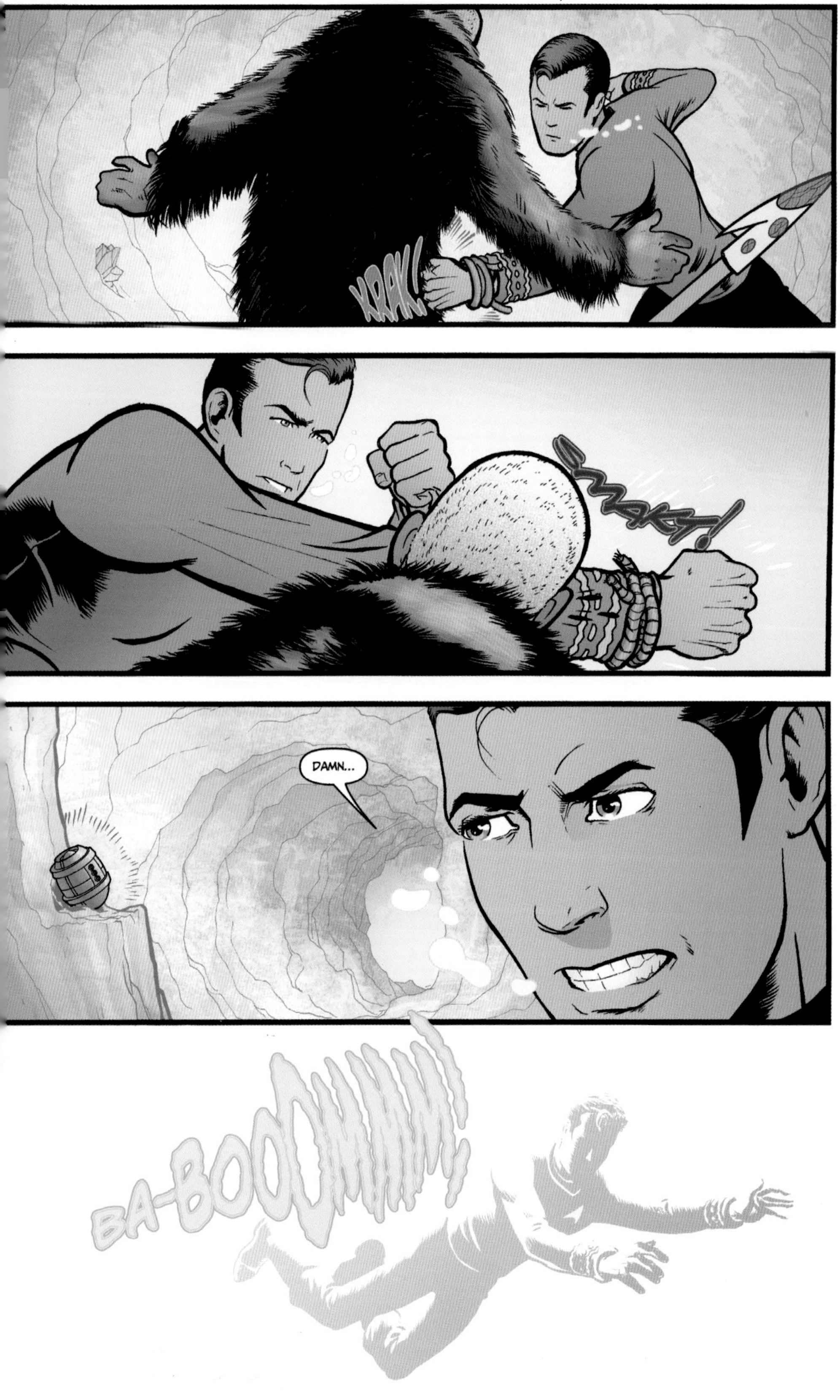
KRAK!
SMAKT!
DAMN...
BA-BOOMMMM!

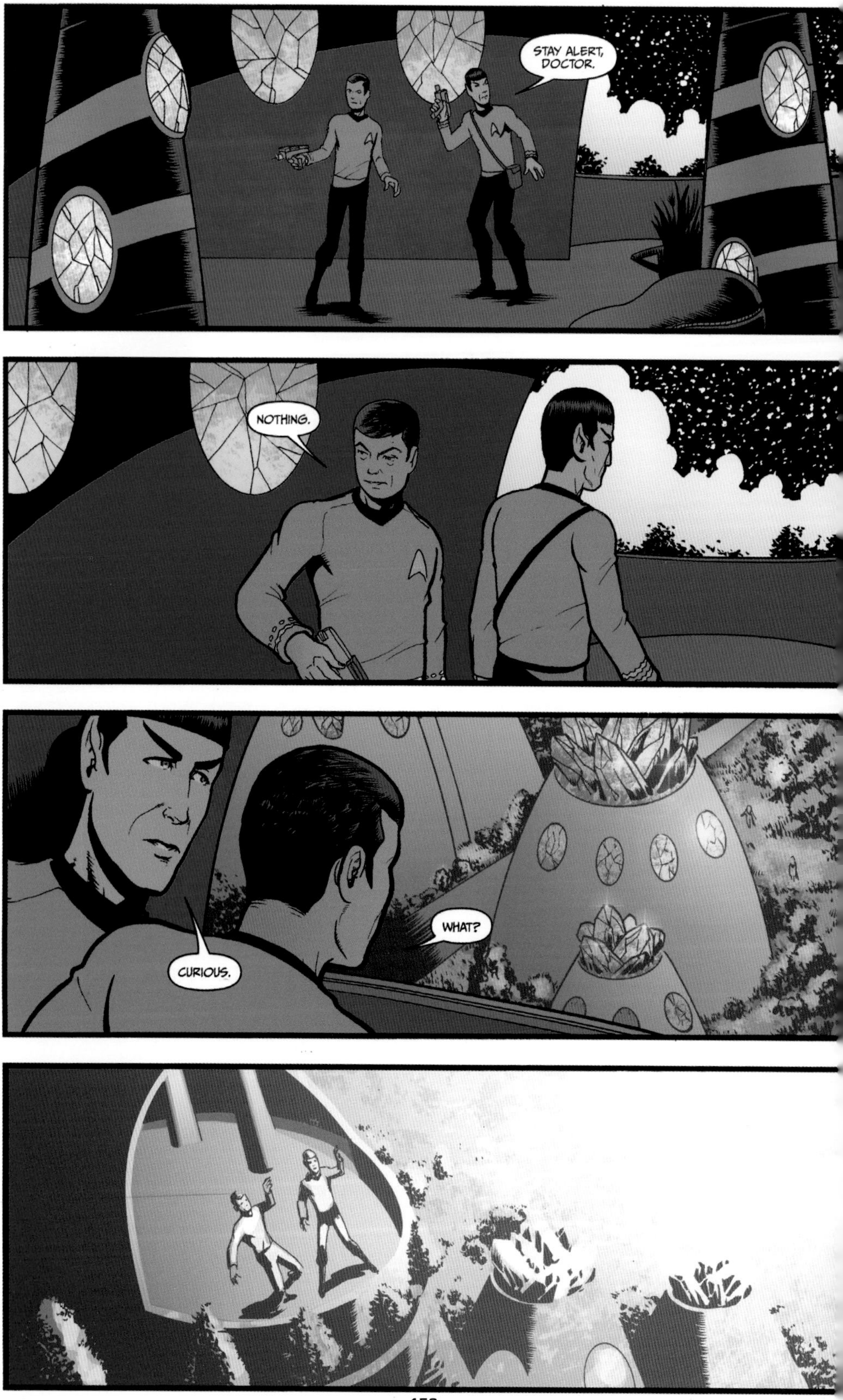

STAY ALERT, DOCTOR.
NOTHING.
CURIOUS.
WHAT?

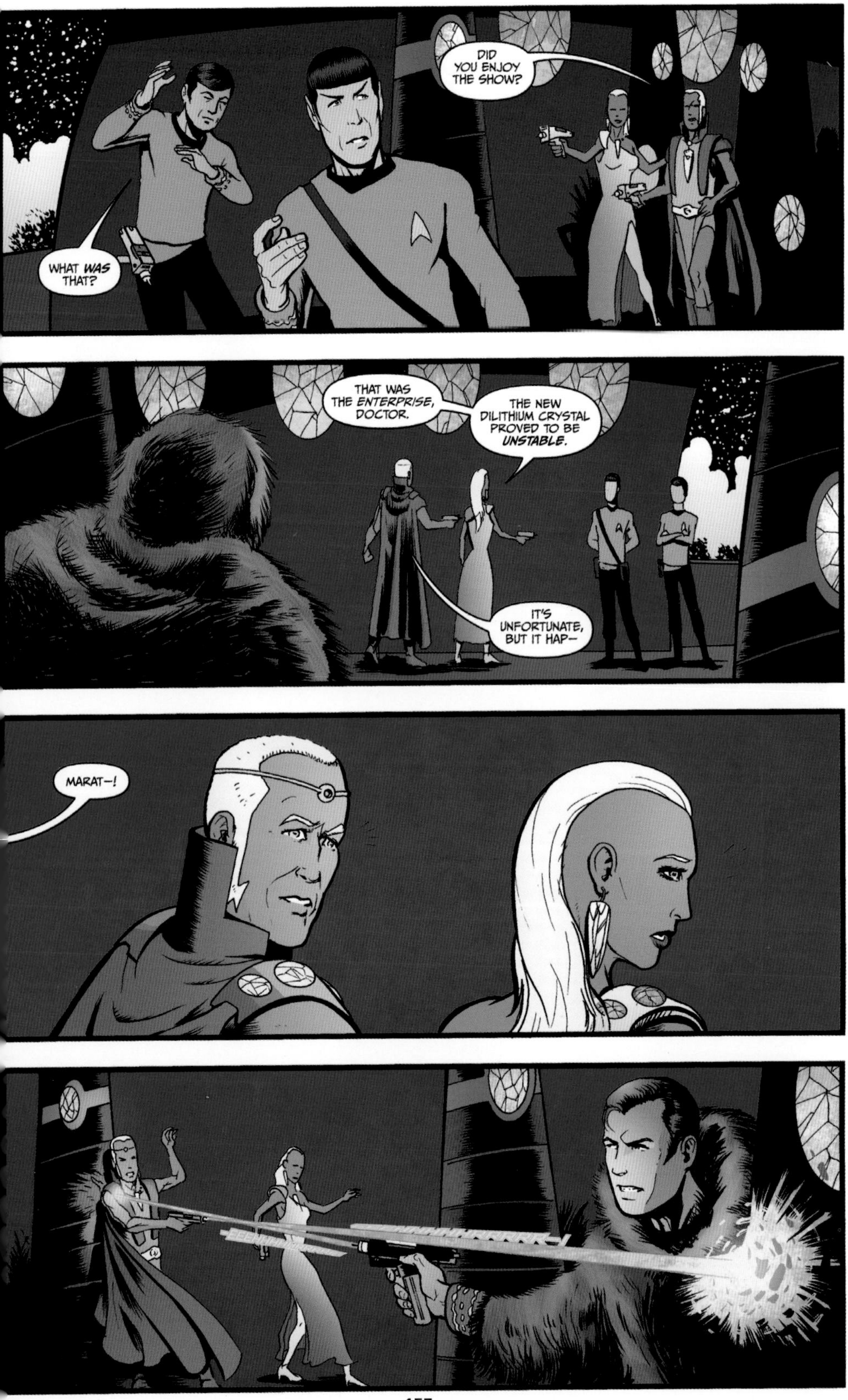
WHAT *WAS* THAT?
DID YOU ENJOY THE SHOW?
THAT WAS THE *ENTERPRISE*, DOCTOR.
THE NEW DILITHIUM CRYSTAL PROVED TO BE *UNSTABLE*.
IT'S UNFORTUNATE, BUT IT HAP—
MARAT—!

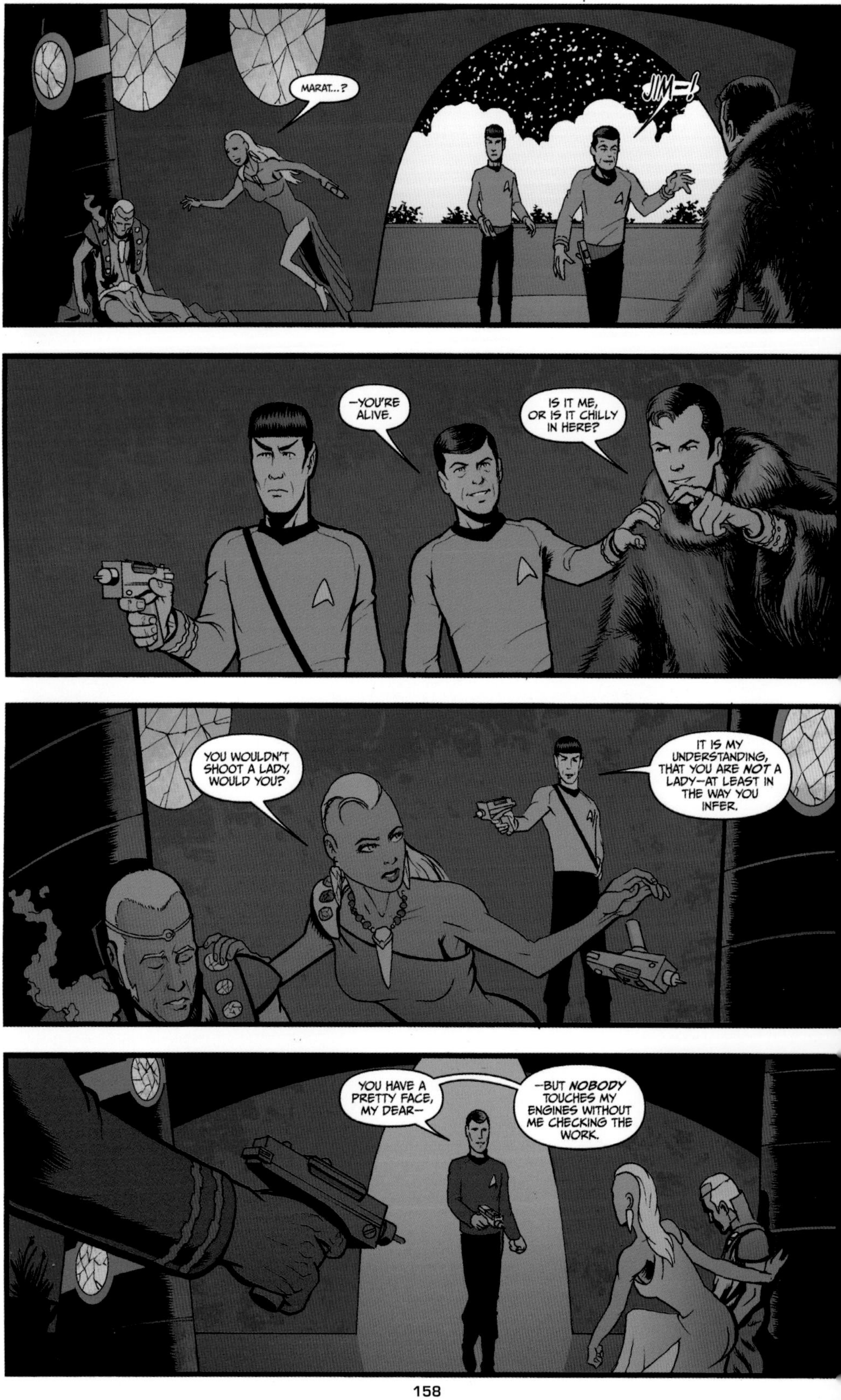
MARAT...?
JIM—!
—YOU'RE ALIVE.
IS IT ME, OR IS IT CHILLY IN HERE?
YOU WOULDN'T SHOOT A LADY, WOULD YOU?
IT IS MY UNDERSTANDING, THAT YOU ARE *NOT* A LADY—AT LEAST IN THE WAY YOU INFER.
YOU HAVE A PRETTY FACE, MY DEAR—
—BUT *NOBODY* TOUCHES MY ENGINES WITHOUT ME CHECKING THE WORK.

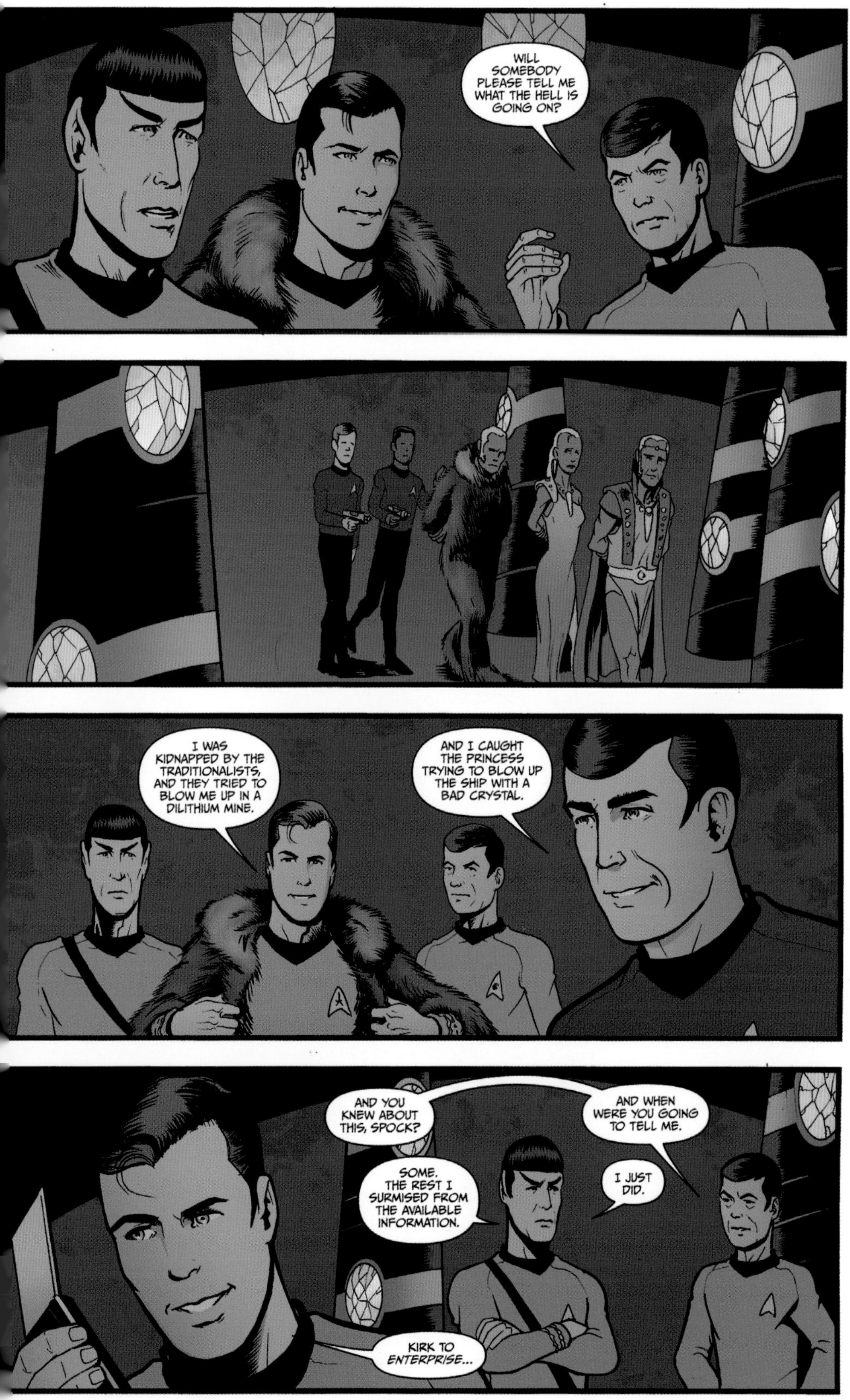
WILL SOMEBODY PLEASE TELL ME WHAT THE HELL IS GOING ON?
I WAS KIDNAPPED BY THE TRADITIONALISTS, AND THEY TRIED TO BLOW ME UP IN A DILITHIUM MINE.
AND I CAUGHT THE PRINCESS TRYING TO BLOW UP THE SHIP WITH A BAD CRYSTAL.
AND YOU KNEW ABOUT THIS, SPOCK?
AND WHEN WERE YOU GOING TO TELL ME.
SOME. THE REST I SURMISED FROM THE AVAILABLE INFORMATION.
I JUST DID.
KIRK TO *ENTERPRISE*...

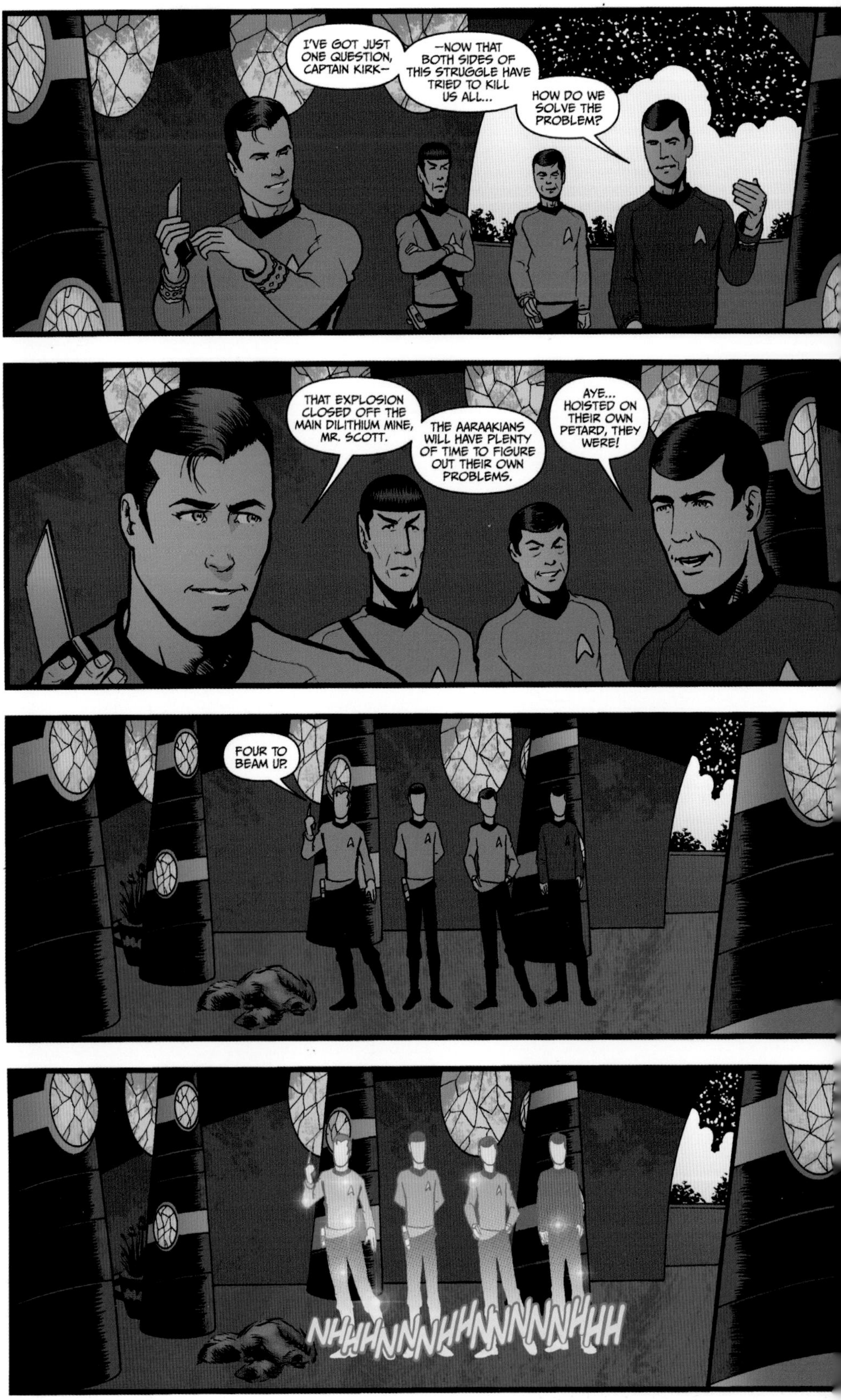
I'VE GOT JUST ONE QUESTION, CAPTAIN KIRK—
—NOW THAT BOTH SIDES OF THIS STRUGGLE HAVE TRIED TO KILL US ALL...
HOW DO WE SOLVE THE PROBLEM?
THAT EXPLOSION CLOSED OFF THE MAIN DILITHIUM MINE, MR. SCOTT.
THE AARAAKIANS WILL HAVE PLENTY OF TIME TO FIGURE OUT THEIR OWN PROBLEMS.
AYE... HOISTED ON THEIR OWN PETARD, THEY WERE!
FOUR TO BEAM UP.
NHHHNNNHHNNNNNHHH

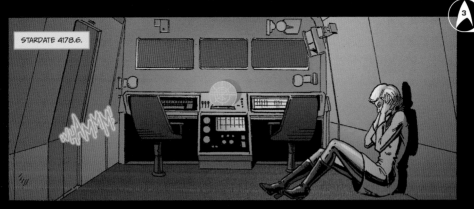

3

STARDATE 4178.6.

WHAMMM!

WHAMMM!
WHAMMM!

EEEHHHHHRRRRR!

STAY *AWAY* FROM ME!

SHE IS THE *LAST* ONE.

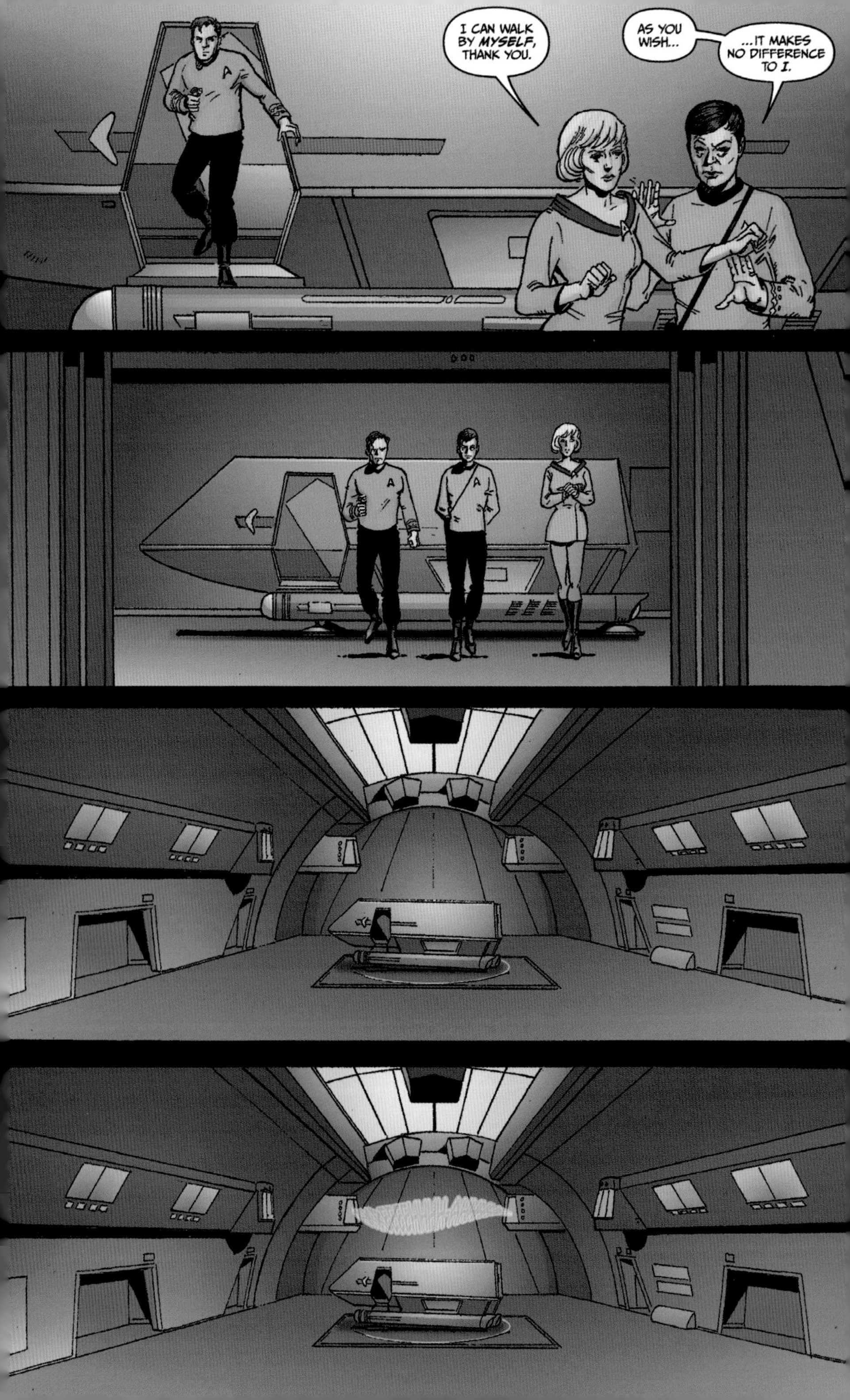
I CAN WALK BY MYSELF, THANK YOU.
AS YOU WISH...
...IT MAKES NO DIFFERENCE TO I.

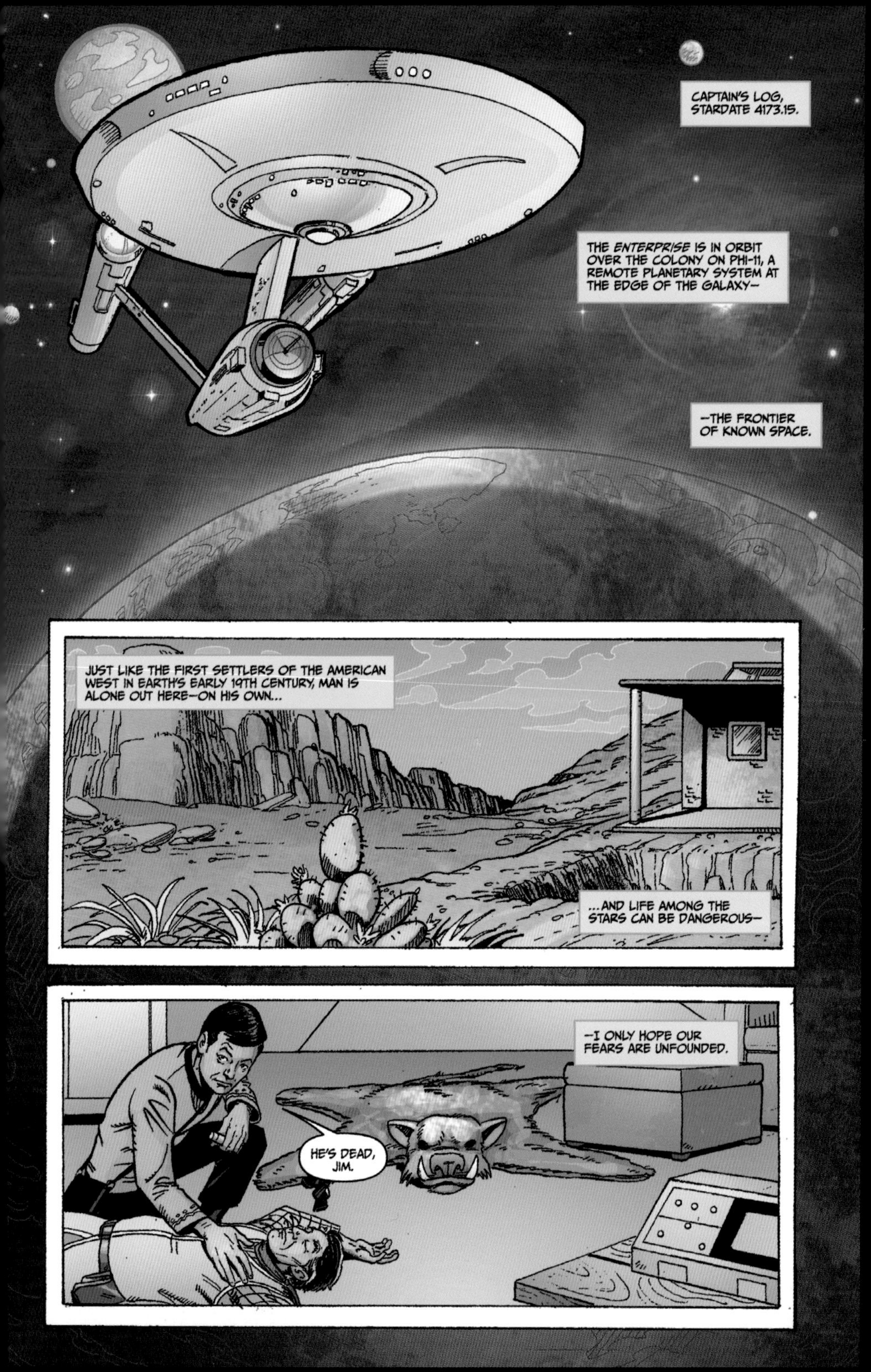

CAPTAIN'S LOG, STARDATE 4173.15.
THE *ENTERPRISE* IS IN ORBIT OVER THE COLONY ON PHI-11, A REMOTE PLANETARY SYSTEM AT THE EDGE OF THE GALAXY—
—THE FRONTIER OF KNOWN SPACE.
JUST LIKE THE FIRST SETTLERS OF THE AMERICAN WEST IN EARTH'S EARLY 19TH CENTURY, MAN IS ALONE OUT HERE—ON HIS OWN...
...AND LIFE AMONG THE STARS CAN BE DANGEROUS—
—I ONLY HOPE OUR FEARS ARE UNFOUNDED.
HE'S DEAD, JIM.

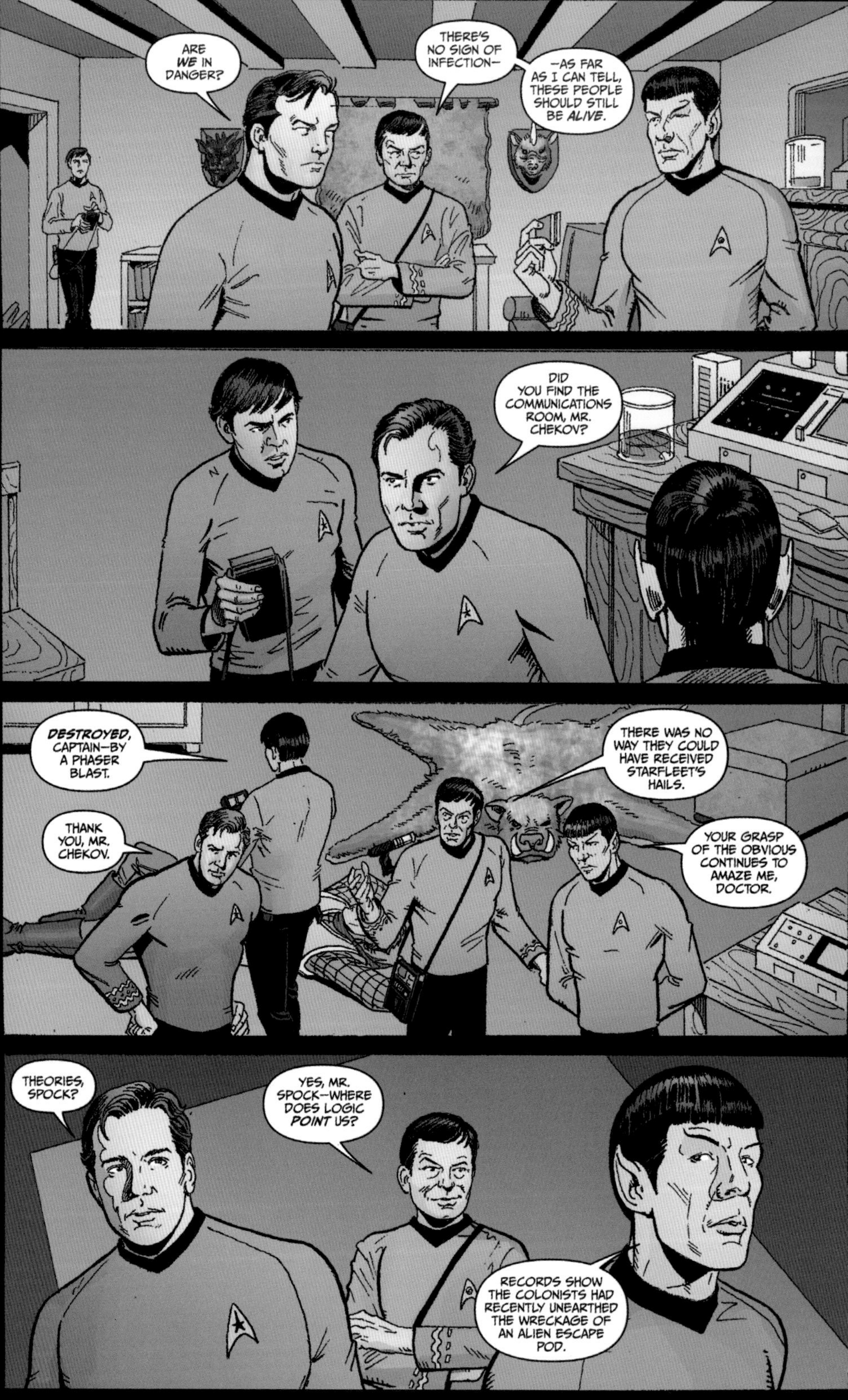
ARE *WE* IN DANGER?
THERE'S NO SIGN OF INFECTION—
—AS FAR AS I CAN TELL, THESE PEOPLE SHOULD STILL BE *ALIVE*.
DID YOU FIND THE COMMUNICATIONS ROOM, MR. CHEKOV?
DESTROYED, CAPTAIN—BY A PHASER BLAST.
THANK YOU, MR. CHEKOV.
THERE WAS NO WAY THEY COULD HAVE RECEIVED STARFLEET'S HAILS.
YOUR GRASP OF THE OBVIOUS CONTINUES TO AMAZE ME, DOCTOR.
THEORIES, SPOCK?
YES, MR. SPOCK—WHERE DOES LOGIC *POINT* US?
RECORDS SHOW THE COLONISTS HAD RECENTLY UNEARTHED THE WRECKAGE OF AN ALIEN ESCAPE POD.

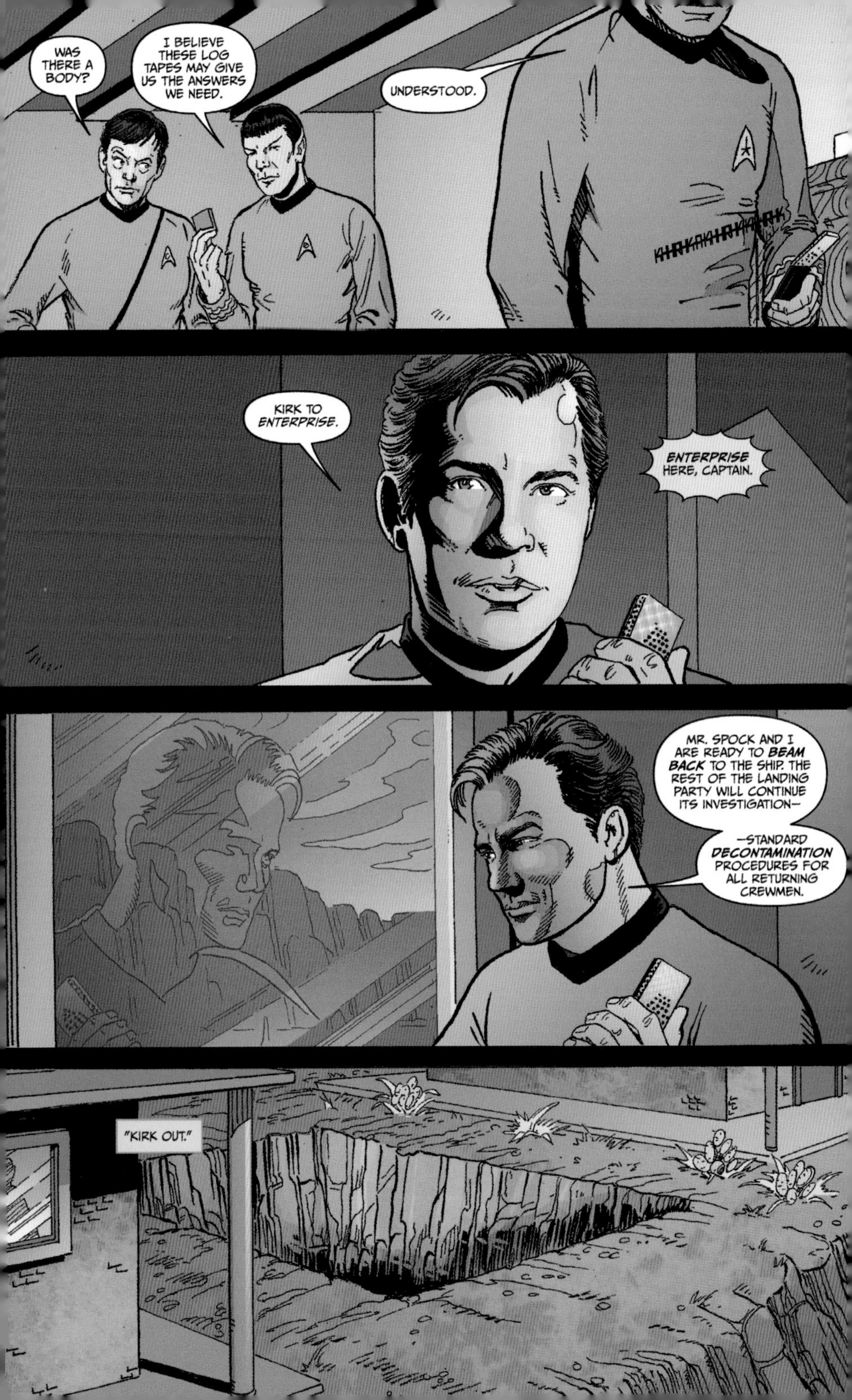
WAS THERE A BODY?
I BELIEVE THESE LOG TAPES MAY GIVE US THE ANSWERS WE NEED.
UNDERSTOOD.
KHRKKHRKKHRK
KIRK TO ENTERPRISE.
ENTERPRISE HERE, CAPTAIN.
MR. SPOCK AND I ARE READY TO BEAM BACK TO THE SHIP. THE REST OF THE LANDING PARTY WILL CONTINUE ITS INVESTIGATION—
—STANDARD DECONTAMINATION PROCEDURES FOR ALL RETURNING CREWMEN.
"KIRK OUT."

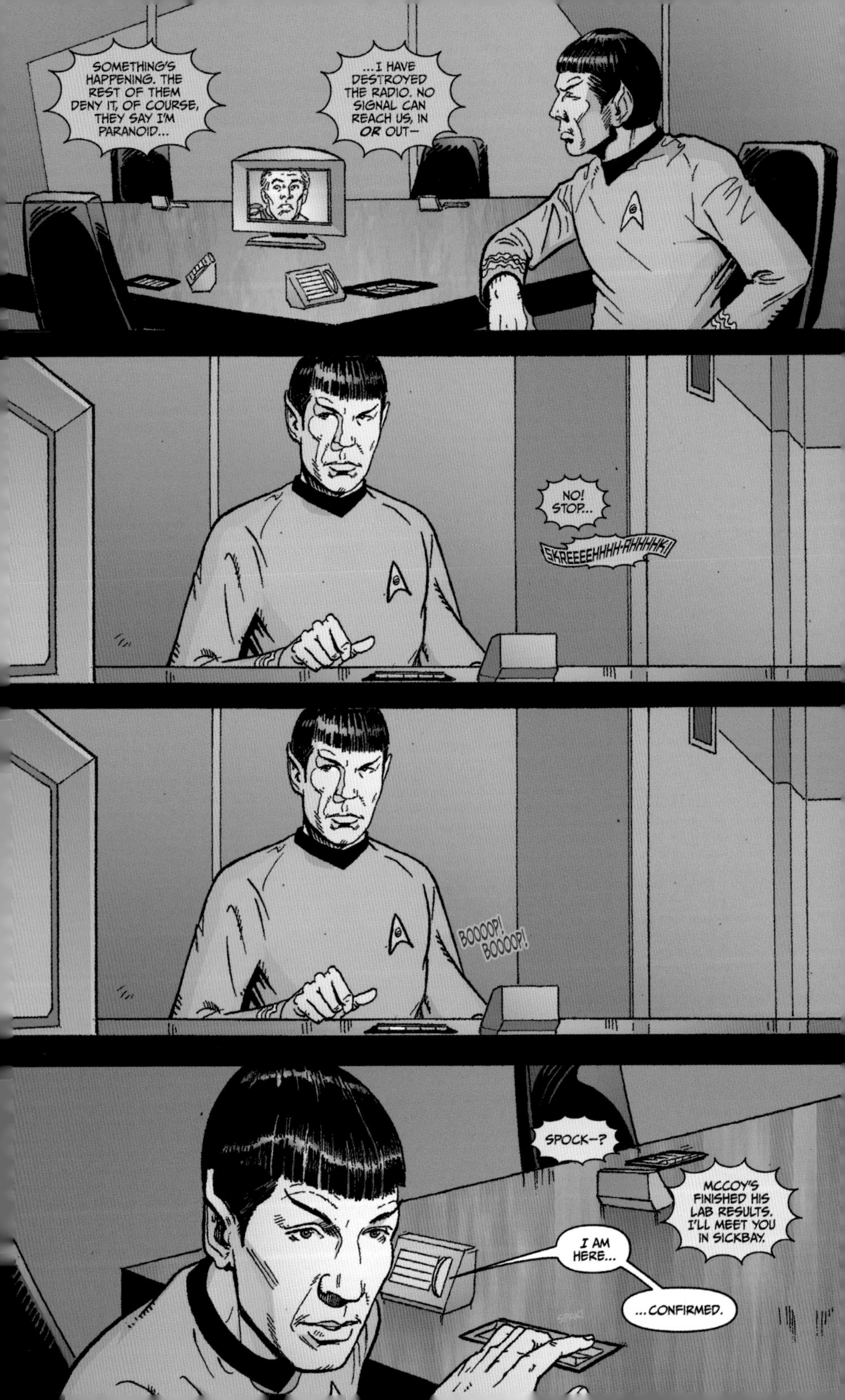
SOMETHING'S HAPPENING. THE REST OF THEM DENY IT, OF COURSE, THEY SAY I'M PARANOID...
...I HAVE DESTROYED THE RADIO. NO SIGNAL CAN REACH US, IN *OR* OUT--
NO! STOP...
SKREEEEEHHHH-AHHHHK!!
BOOOOP! BOOOOP!
SPOCK--?
McCOY'S FINISHED HIS LAB RESULTS. I'LL MEET YOU IN SICKBAY.
I AM HERE...
...CONFIRMED.

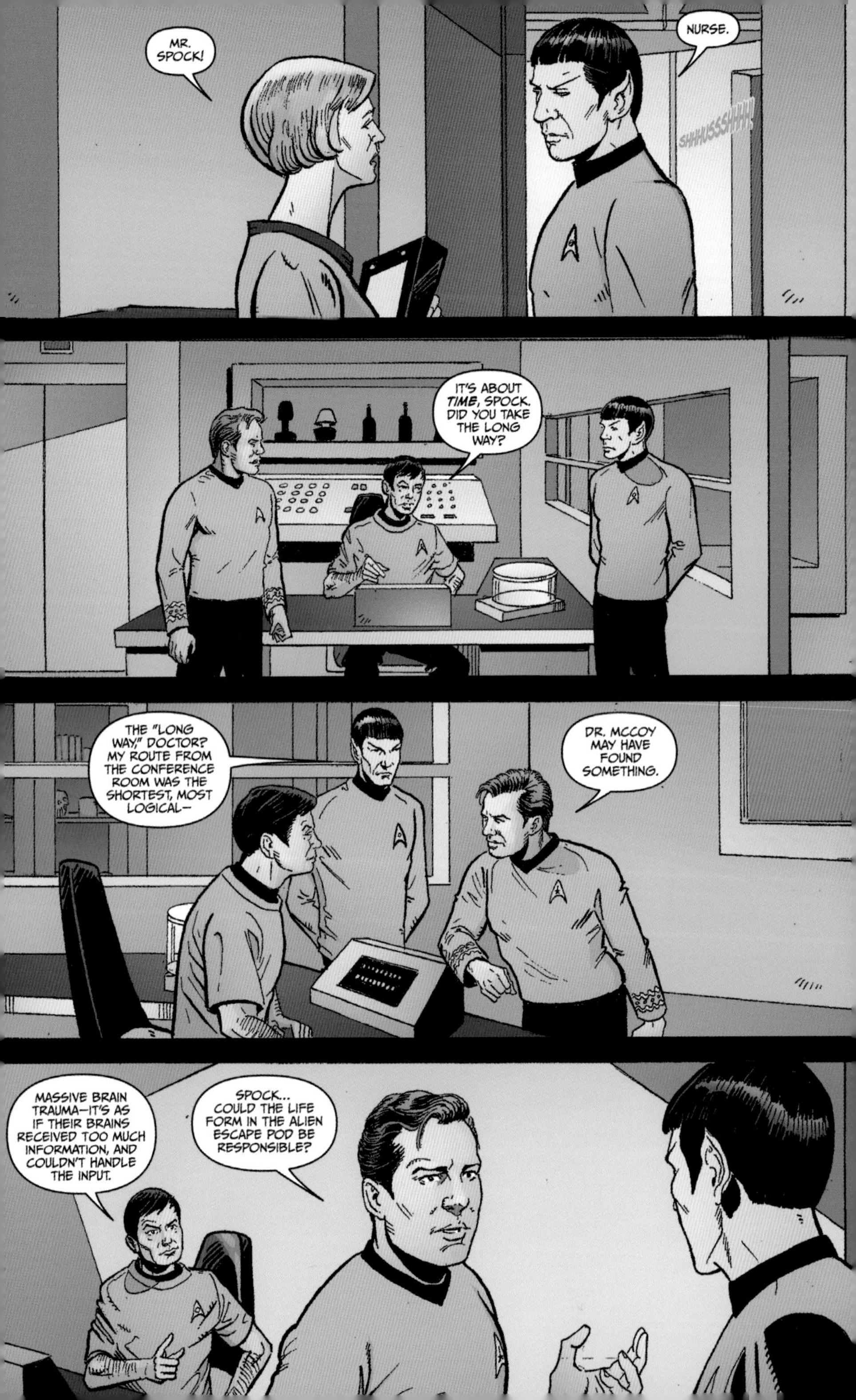

MR. SPOCK!
NURSE.
SHHHUSSSHHHH!
IT'S ABOUT TIME, SPOCK. DID YOU TAKE THE LONG WAY?
THE "LONG WAY," DOCTOR? MY ROUTE FROM THE CONFERENCE ROOM WAS THE SHORTEST, MOST LOGICAL—
DR. MCCOY MAY HAVE FOUND SOMETHING.
MASSIVE BRAIN TRAUMA—IT'S AS IF THEIR BRAINS RECEIVED TOO MUCH INFORMATION, AND COULDN'T HANDLE THE INPUT.
SPOCK... COULD THE LIFE FORM IN THE ALIEN ESCAPE POD BE RESPONSIBLE?

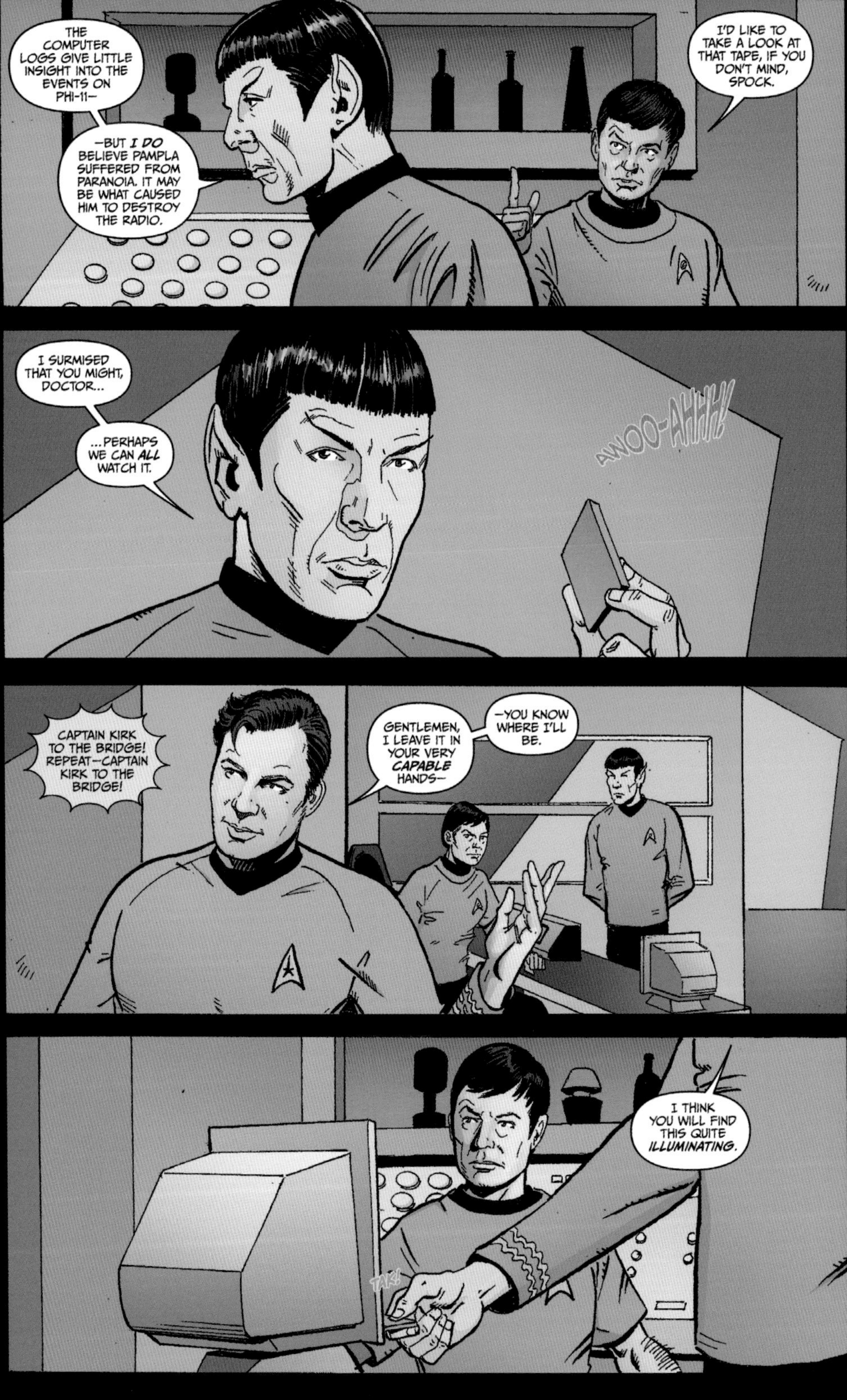
THE COMPUTER LOGS GIVE LITTLE INSIGHT INTO THE EVENTS ON PHI-11—
—BUT I DO BELIEVE PAMPLA SUFFERED FROM PARANOIA. IT MAY BE WHAT CAUSED HIM TO DESTROY THE RADIO.
I'D LIKE TO TAKE A LOOK AT THAT TAPE, IF YOU DON'T MIND, SPOCK.
I SURMISED THAT YOU MIGHT, DOCTOR...
...PERHAPS WE CAN ALL WATCH IT.
AWOO-AHHH!
CAPTAIN KIRK TO THE BRIDGE! REPEAT—CAPTAIN KIRK TO THE BRIDGE!
GENTLEMEN, I LEAVE IT IN YOUR VERY CAPABLE HANDS—
—YOU KNOW WHERE I'LL BE.
I THINK YOU WILL FIND THIS QUITE ILLUMINATING.
TAK!

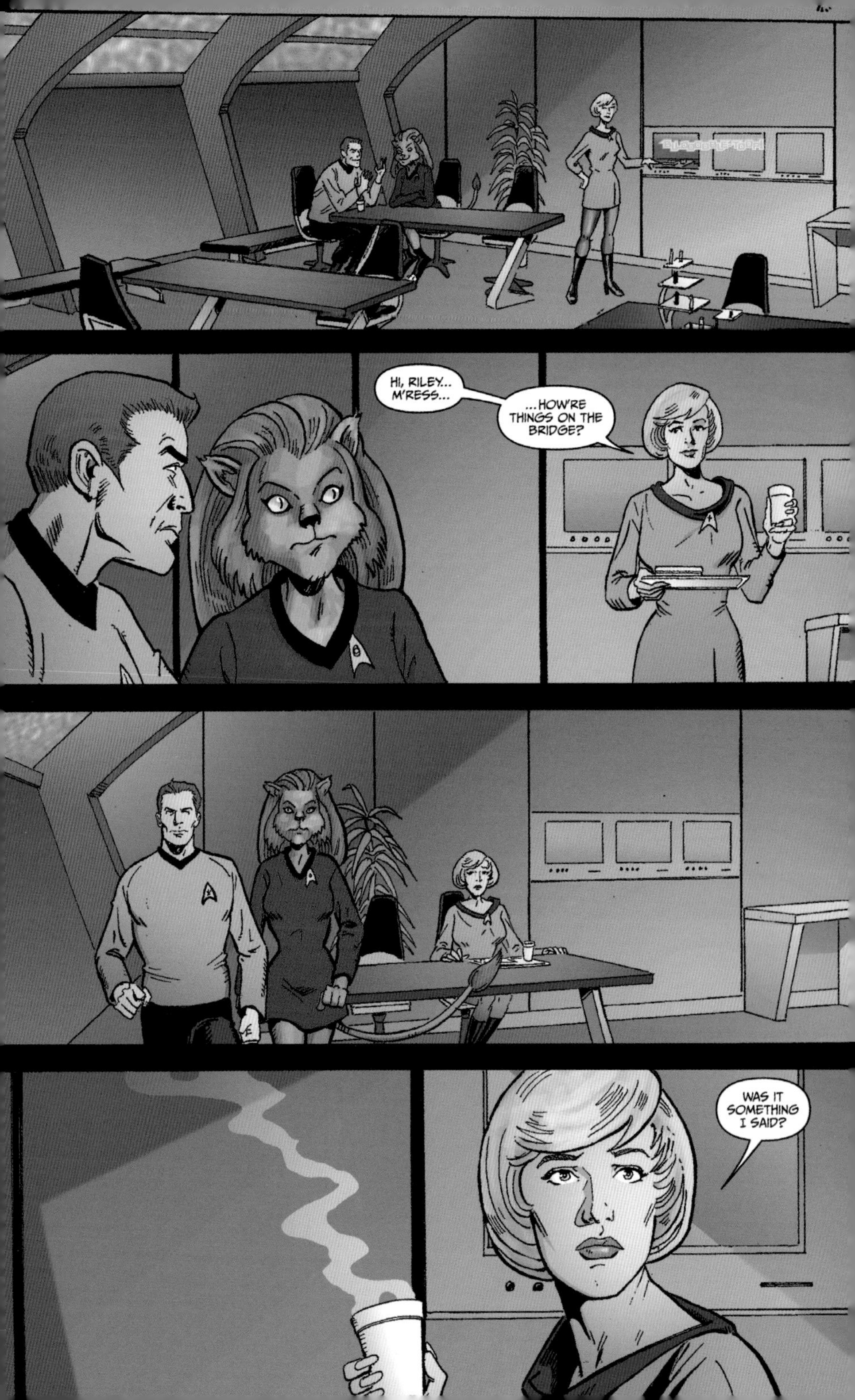
HI, RILEY... M'RESS...
...HOW'RE THINGS ON THE BRIDGE?
WAS IT SOMETHING I SAID?

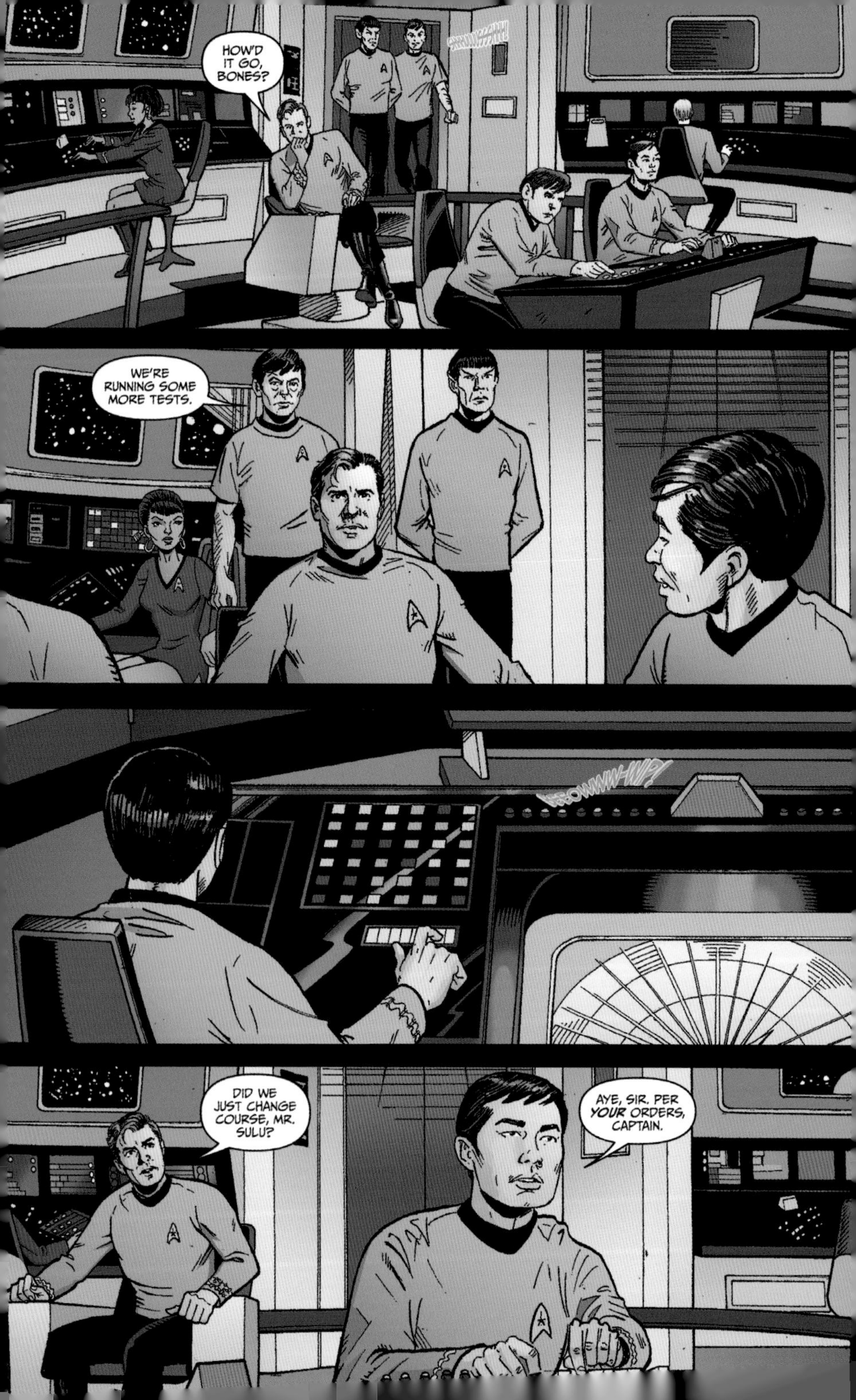
HOW'D IT GO, BONES?
WE'RE RUNNING SOME MORE TESTS.
DID WE JUST CHANGE COURSE, MR. SULU?
AYE, SIR. PER *YOUR* ORDERS, CAPTAIN.

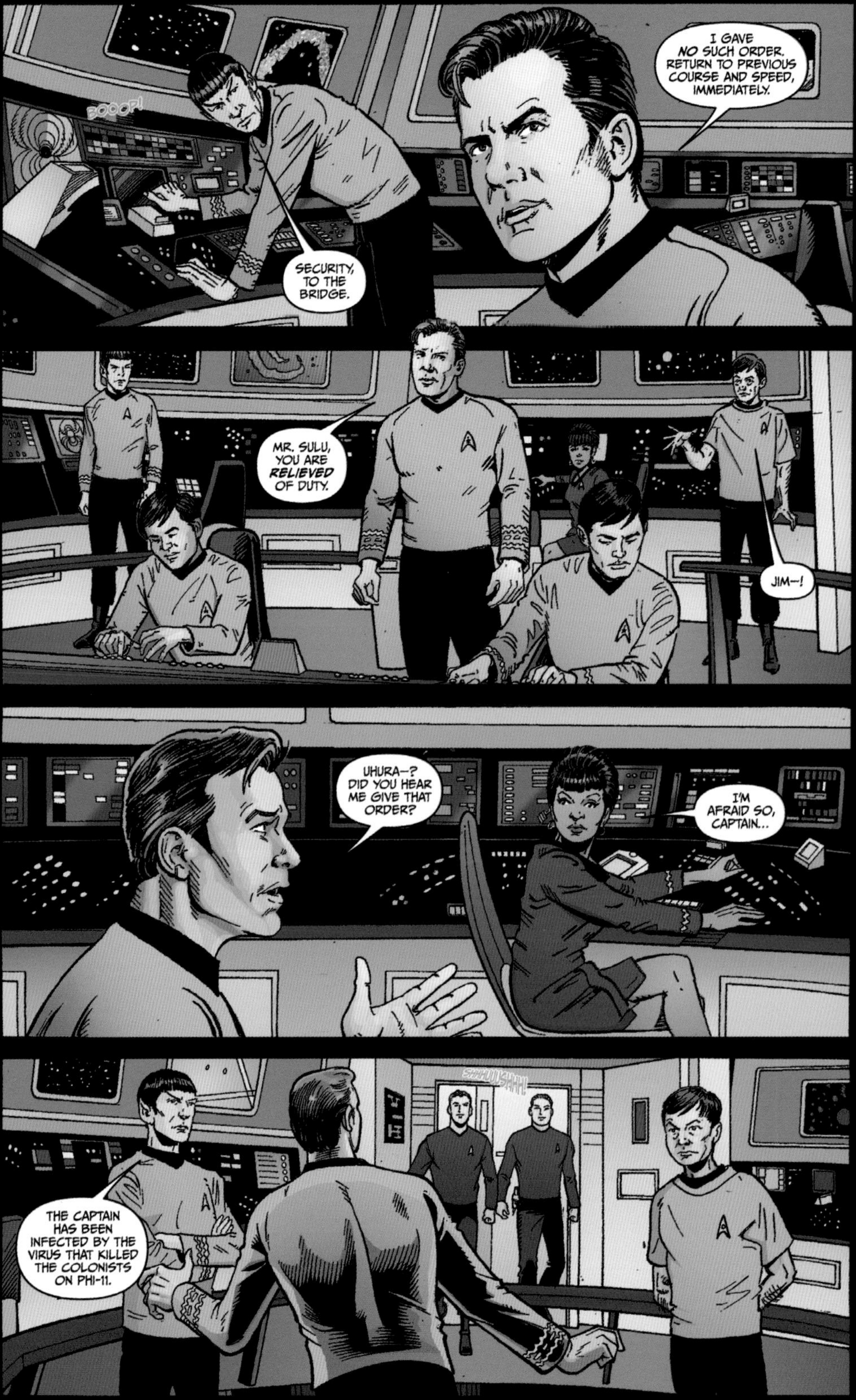
BOOOP!
I GAVE NO SUCH ORDER. RETURN TO PREVIOUS COURSE AND SPEED, IMMEDIATELY.
SECURITY, TO THE BRIDGE.
MR. SULU, YOU ARE RELIEVED OF DUTY.
JIM--!
UHURA--? DID YOU HEAR ME GIVE THAT ORDER?
I'M AFRAID SO, CAPTAIN...
SHHHUUUSHHH!
THE CAPTAIN HAS BEEN INFECTED BY THE VIRUS THAT KILLED THE COLONISTS ON PHI-11.

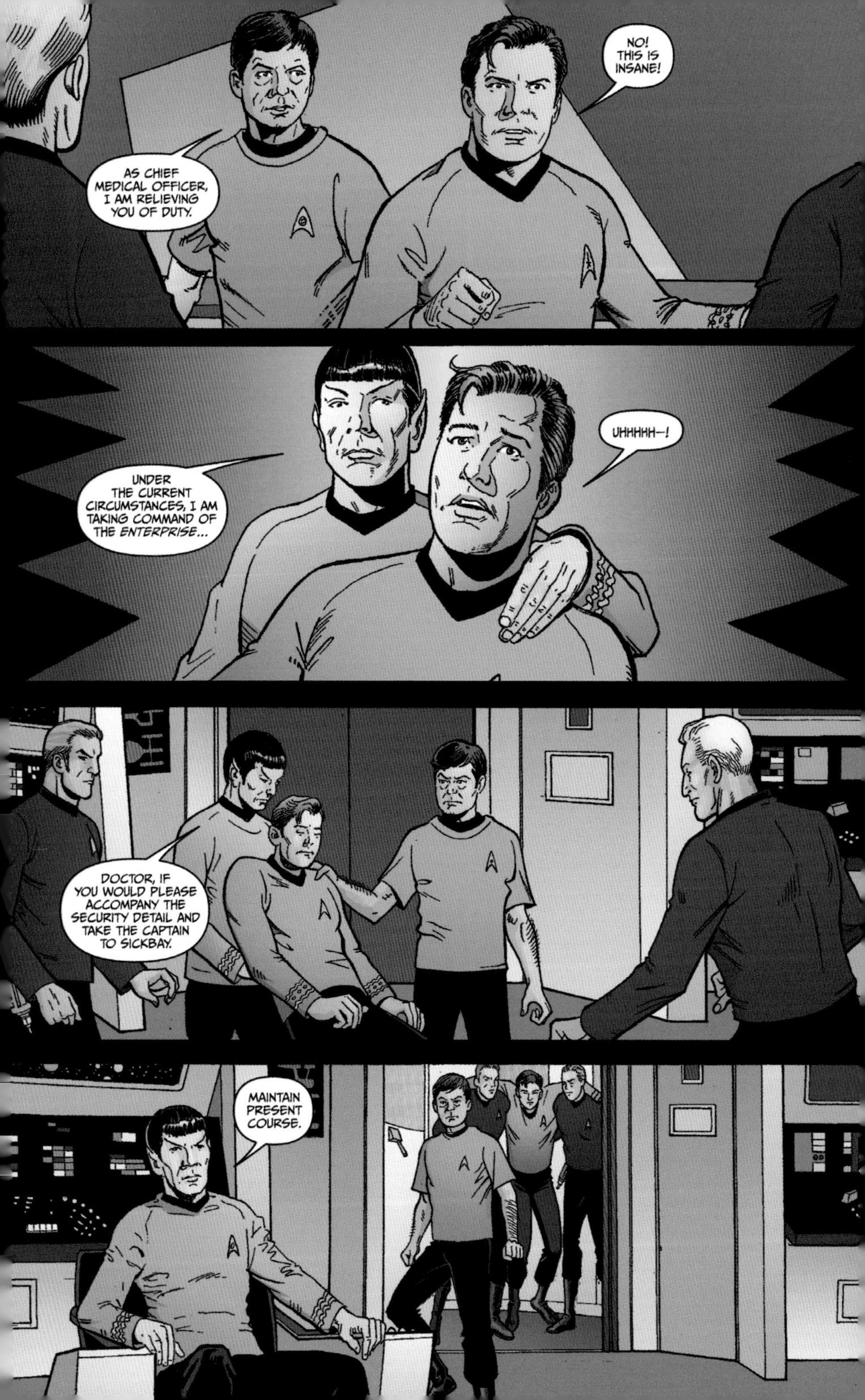
NO! THIS IS INSANE!
AS CHIEF MEDICAL OFFICER, I AM RELIEVING YOU OF DUTY.
UNDER THE CURRENT CIRCUMSTANCES, I AM TAKING COMMAND OF THE *ENTERPRISE*...
UHHHHH--!
DOCTOR, IF YOU WOULD PLEASE ACCOMPANY THE SECURITY DETAIL AND TAKE THE CAPTAIN TO SICKBAY.
MAINTAIN PRESENT COURSE.

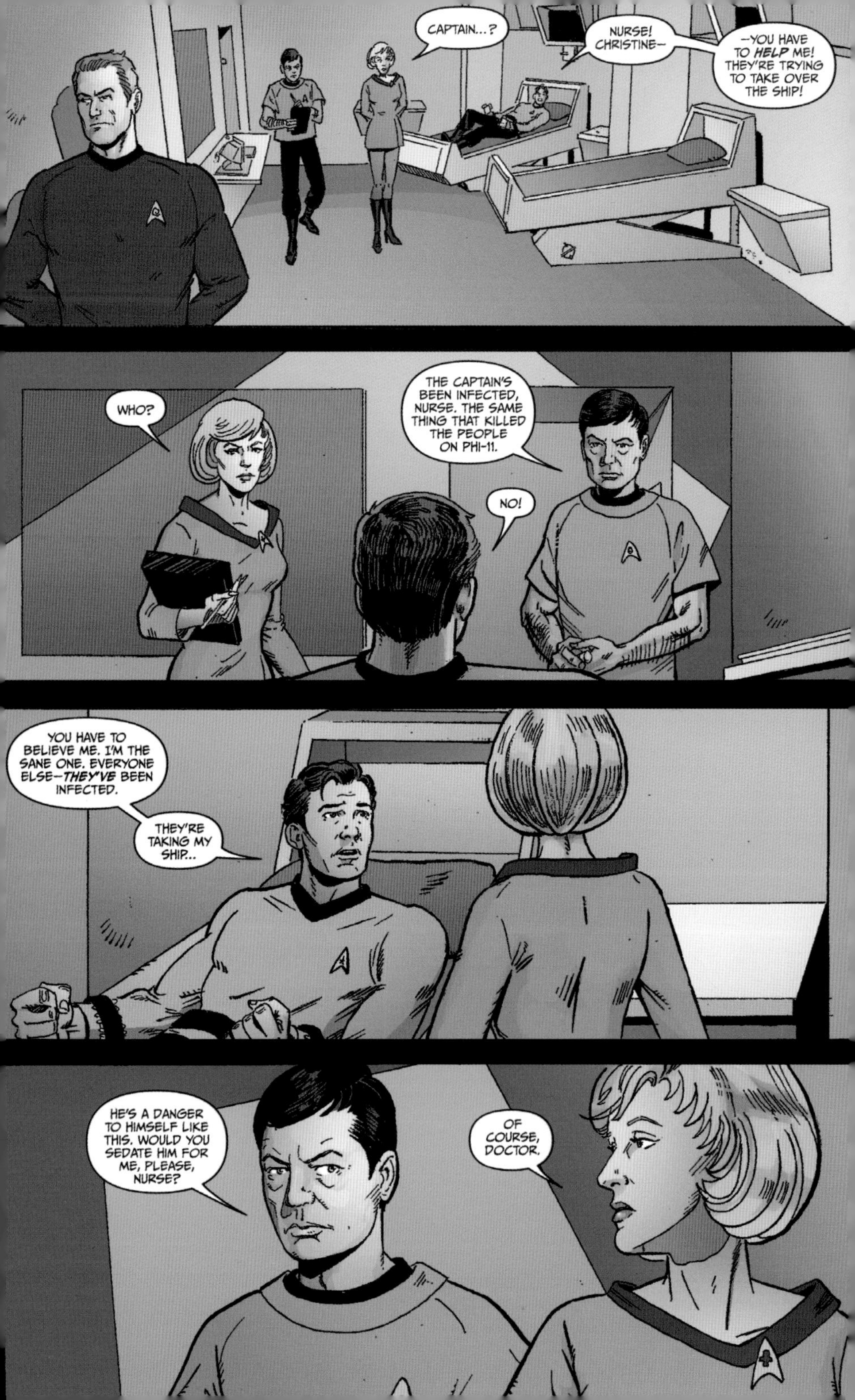
CAPTAIN...?
NURSE! CHRISTINE--
--YOU HAVE TO HELP ME! THEY'RE TRYING TO TAKE OVER THE SHIP!
WHO?
THE CAPTAIN'S BEEN INFECTED, NURSE. THE SAME THING THAT KILLED THE PEOPLE ON PHI-11.
NO!
YOU HAVE TO BELIEVE ME. I'M THE SANE ONE. EVERYONE ELSE--THEY'VE BEEN INFECTED.
THEY'RE TAKING MY SHIP...
HE'S A DANGER TO HIMSELF LIKE THIS. WOULD YOU SEDATE HIM FOR ME, PLEASE, NURSE?
OF COURSE, DOCTOR.

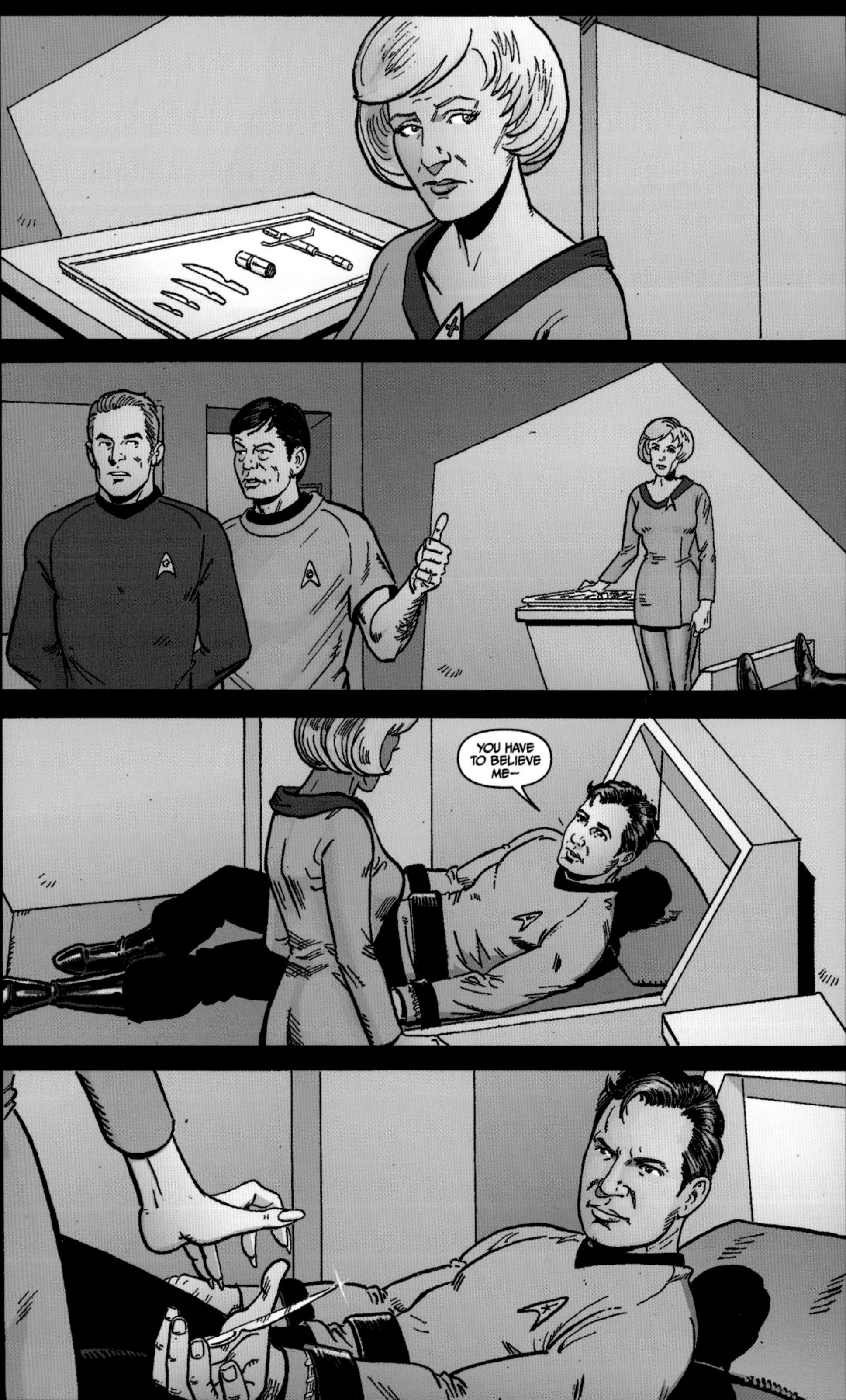
YOU HAVE TO BELIEVE ME—

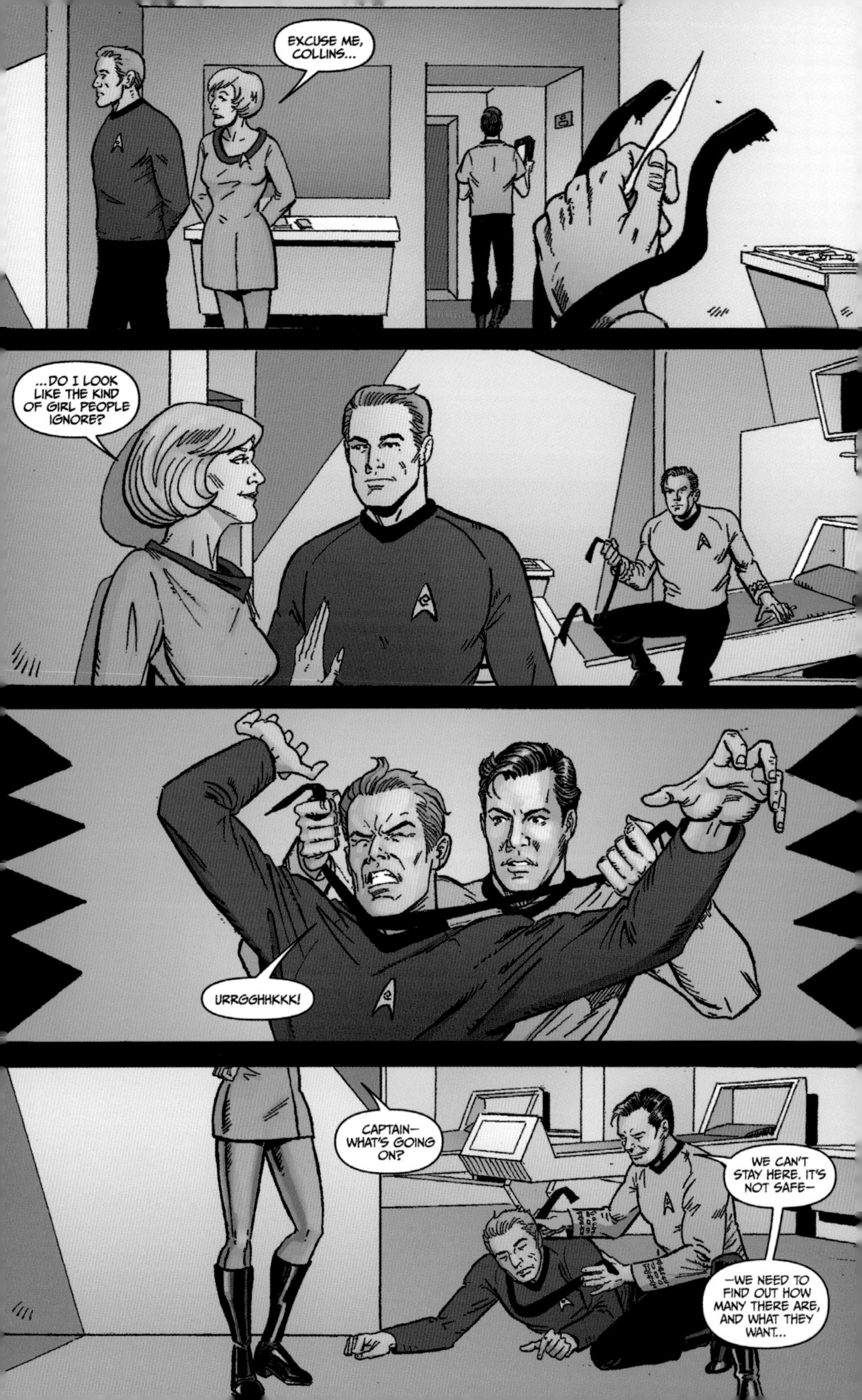
EXCUSE ME, COLLINS...
...DO I LOOK LIKE THE KIND OF GIRL PEOPLE IGNORE?
URRGGHHKKK!
CAPTAIN— WHAT'S GOING ON?
WE CAN'T STAY HERE. IT'S NOT SAFE—
—WE NEED TO FIND OUT HOW MANY THERE ARE, AND WHAT THEY WANT...

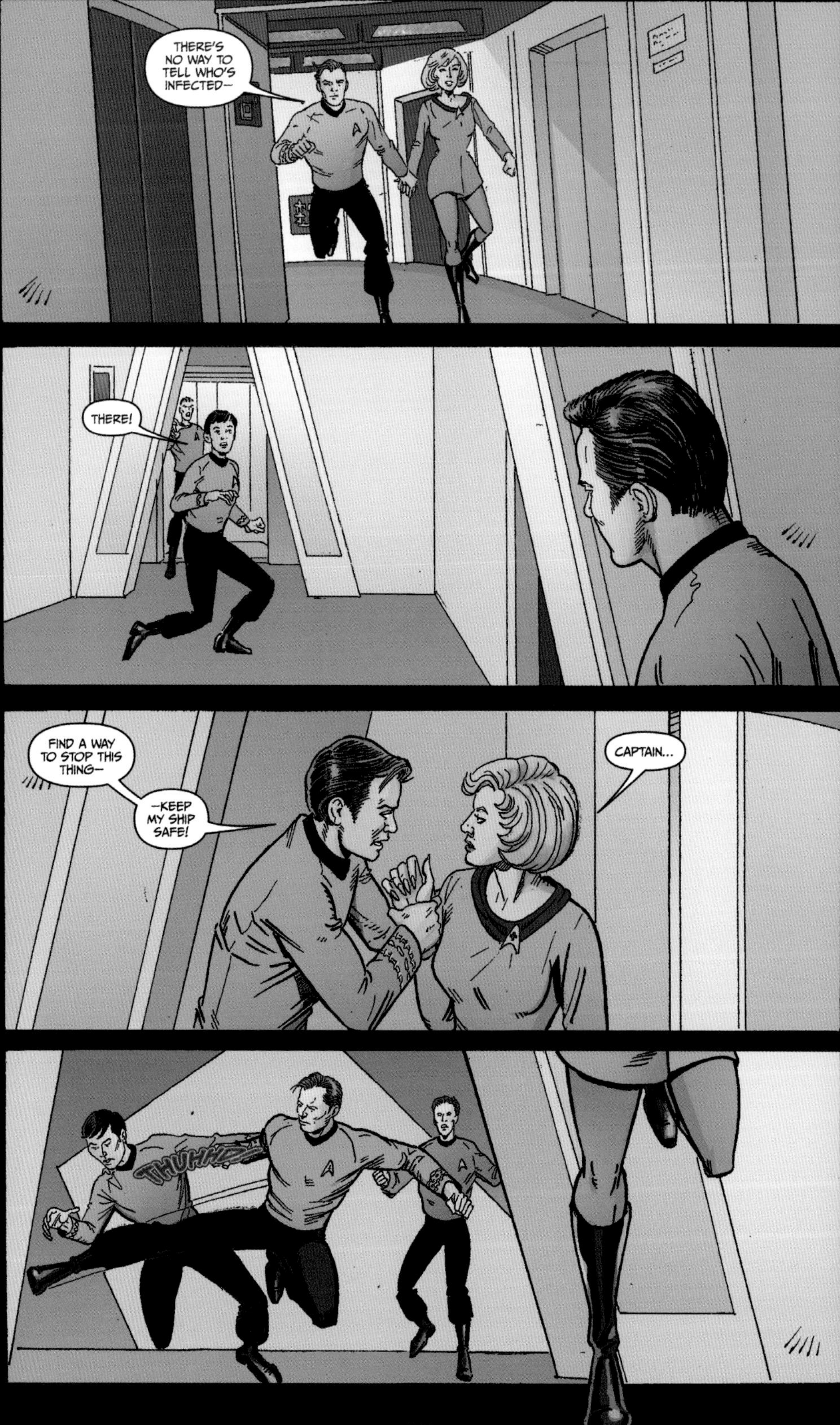
THERE'S NO WAY TO TELL WHO'S INFECTED—
THERE!
FIND A WAY TO STOP THIS THING—
—KEEP MY SHIP SAFE!
CAPTAIN...
THUHHD

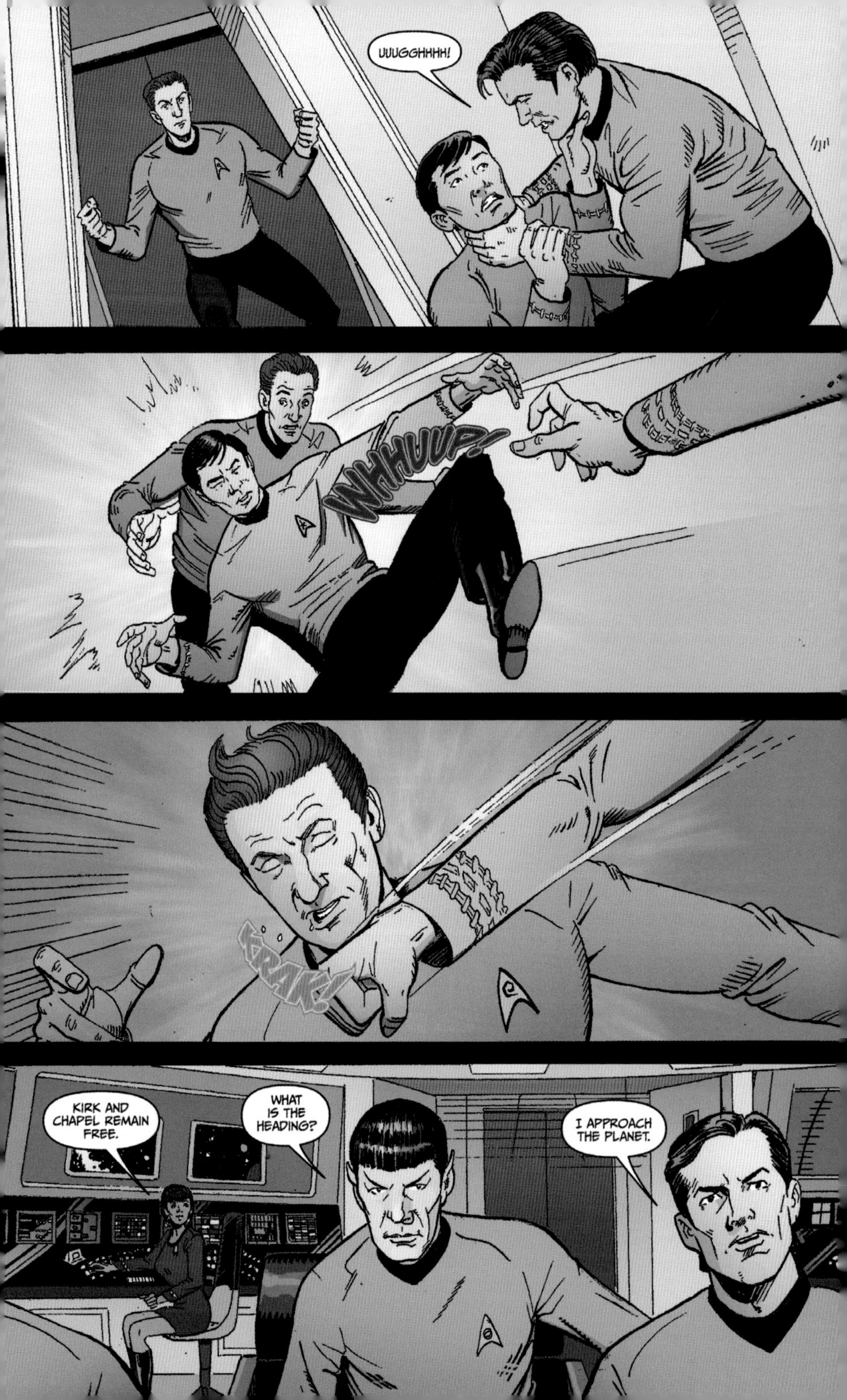
UUUGGHHHH!
WHHUUP!
KRAK!
KIRK AND CHAPEL REMAIN FREE.
WHAT IS THE HEADING?
I APPROACH THE PLANET.

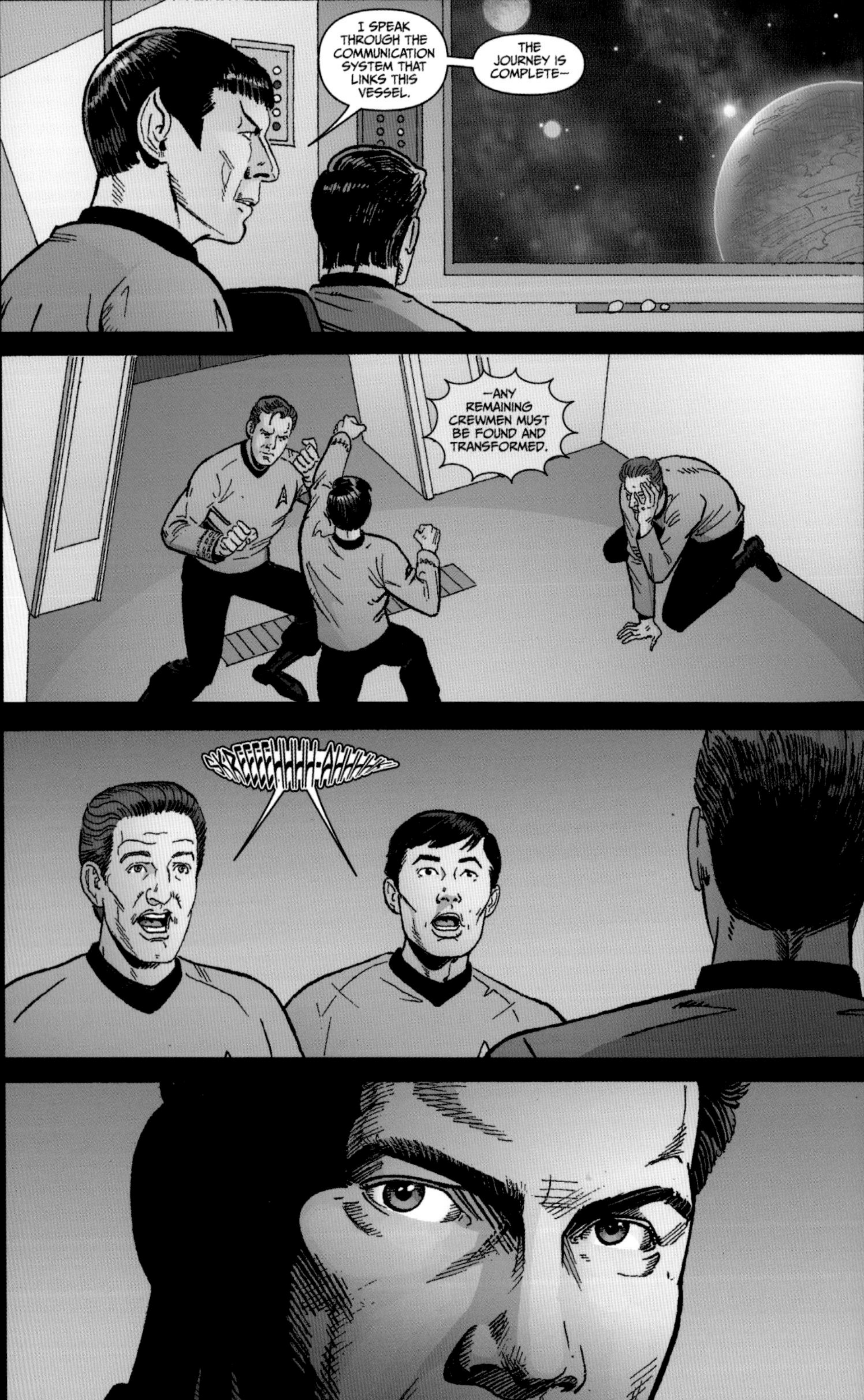
I SPEAK THROUGH THE COMMUNICATION SYSTEM THAT LINKS THIS VESSEL.
THE JOURNEY IS COMPLETE—
—ANY REMAINING CREWMEN MUST BE FOUND AND TRANSFORMED.
SKREEEEEHHHHH-AHHHH

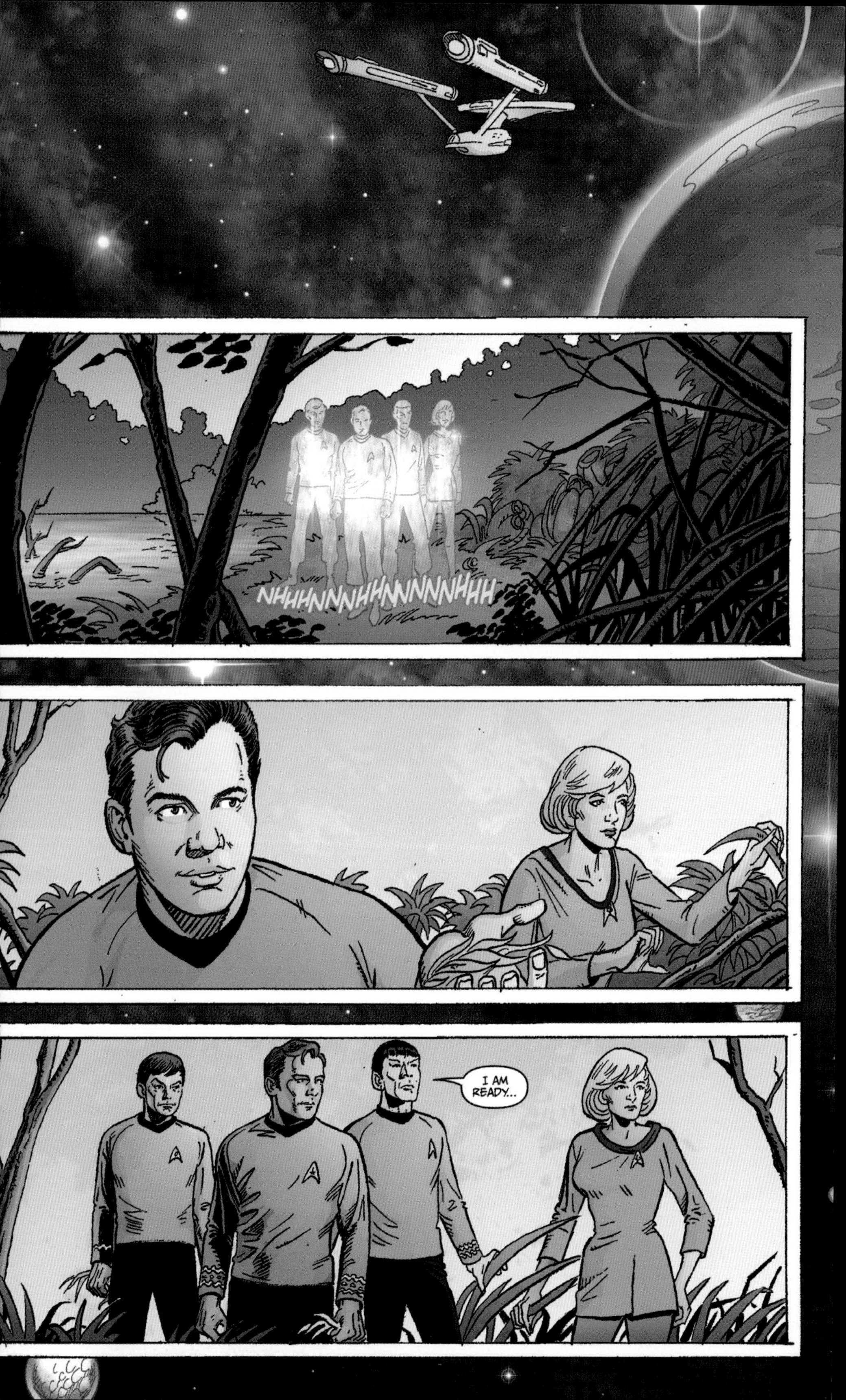
NHHHNNNHHHNNNNHHH
I AM READY...

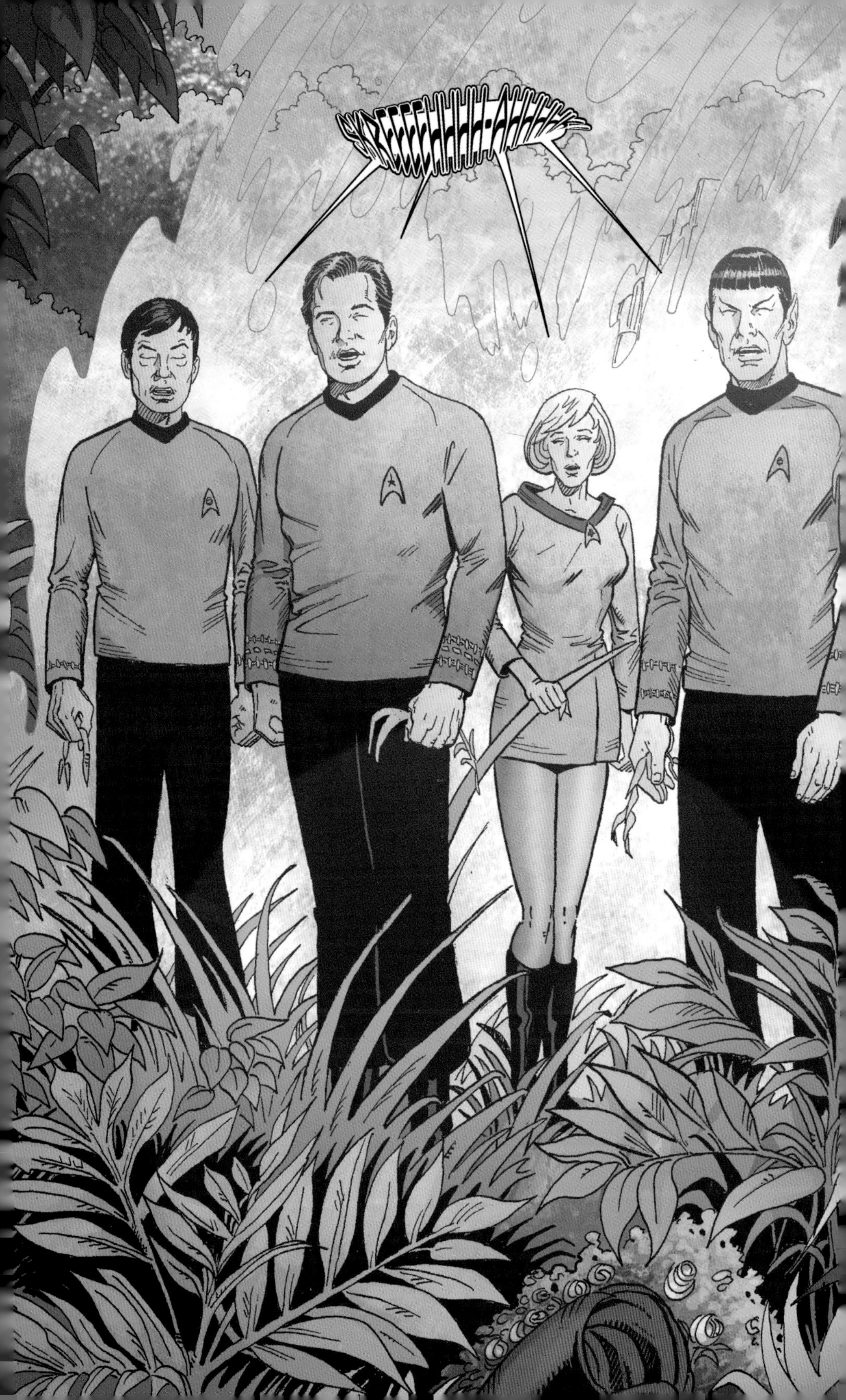
SKREEEEEHHHHH-AHHHHH

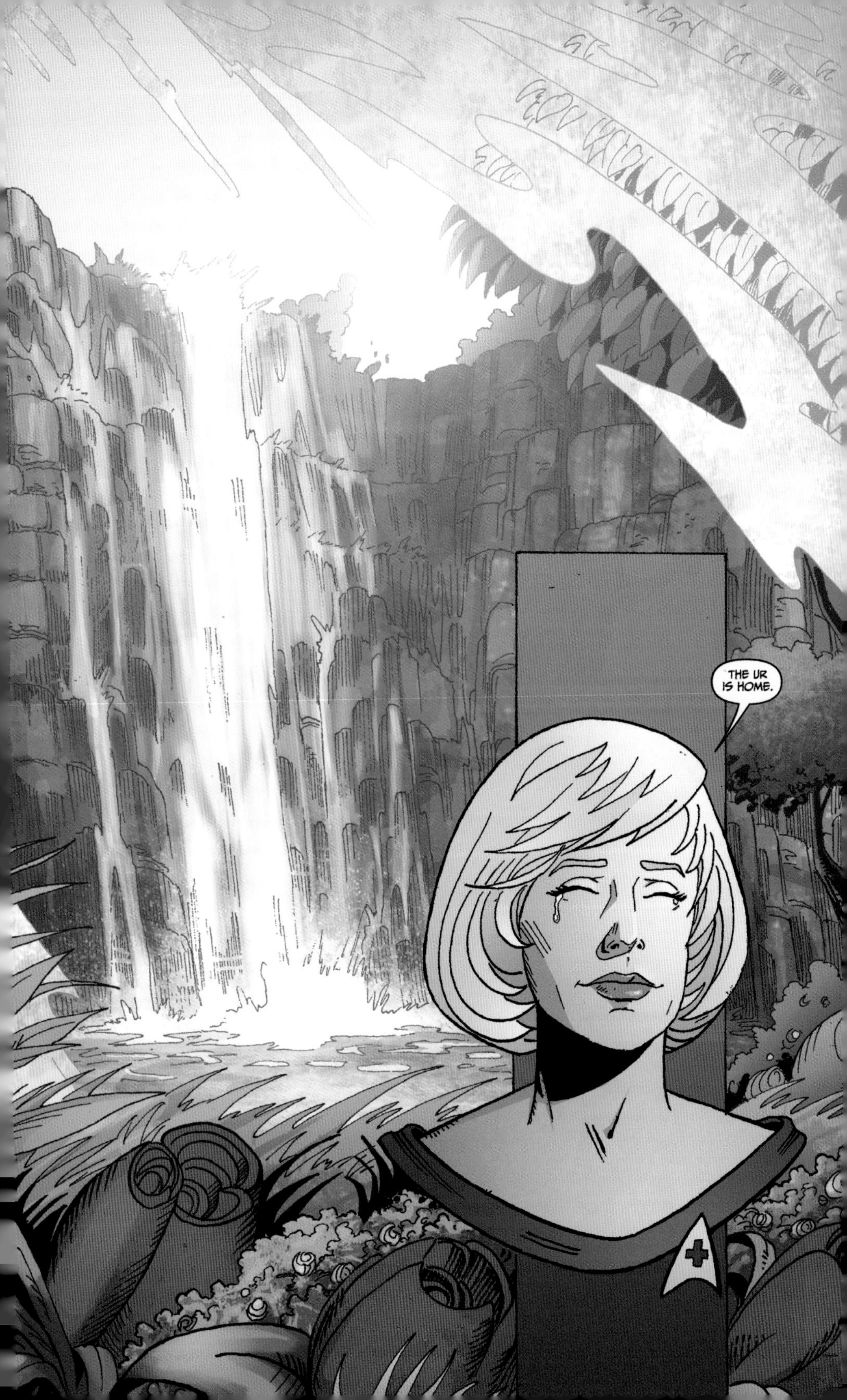
THE UR IS HOME.

CAPTAIN'S LOG, SUPPLEMENTAL.

THE UR IS A VIRAL LIFE FORM WITH A COMMUNAL SENTIENCE, INFECTING ITS CARRIERS THROUGH SOUND.

IT LAY DORMANT, IN THE BODY OF THE ALIEN PILOT ON PHI-11 FOR OVER A THOUSAND YEARS—

—UNFORTUNATELY, ITS UNFAMILIARITY WITH HUMAN PHYSIOLOGY KILLED THE COLONISTS...

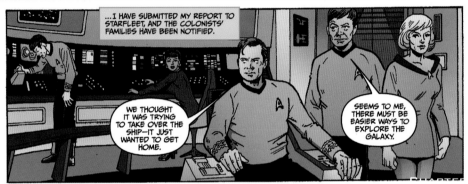

...I HAVE SUBMITTED MY REPORT TO STARFLEET, AND THE COLONISTS' FAMILIES HAVE BEEN NOTIFIED.

WE THOUGHT IT WAS TRYING TO TAKE OVER THE SHIP—IT JUST WANTED TO GET HOME.

SEEMS TO ME, THERE MUST BE EASIER WAYS TO EXPLORE THE GALAXY.

NOT FOR THE UR, DOCTOR.

WE STILL KNOW SO LITTLE.

THAT'S WHAT WE'RE HERE FOR, NURSE—

—OR WE'RE ALL OUT OF A JOB.

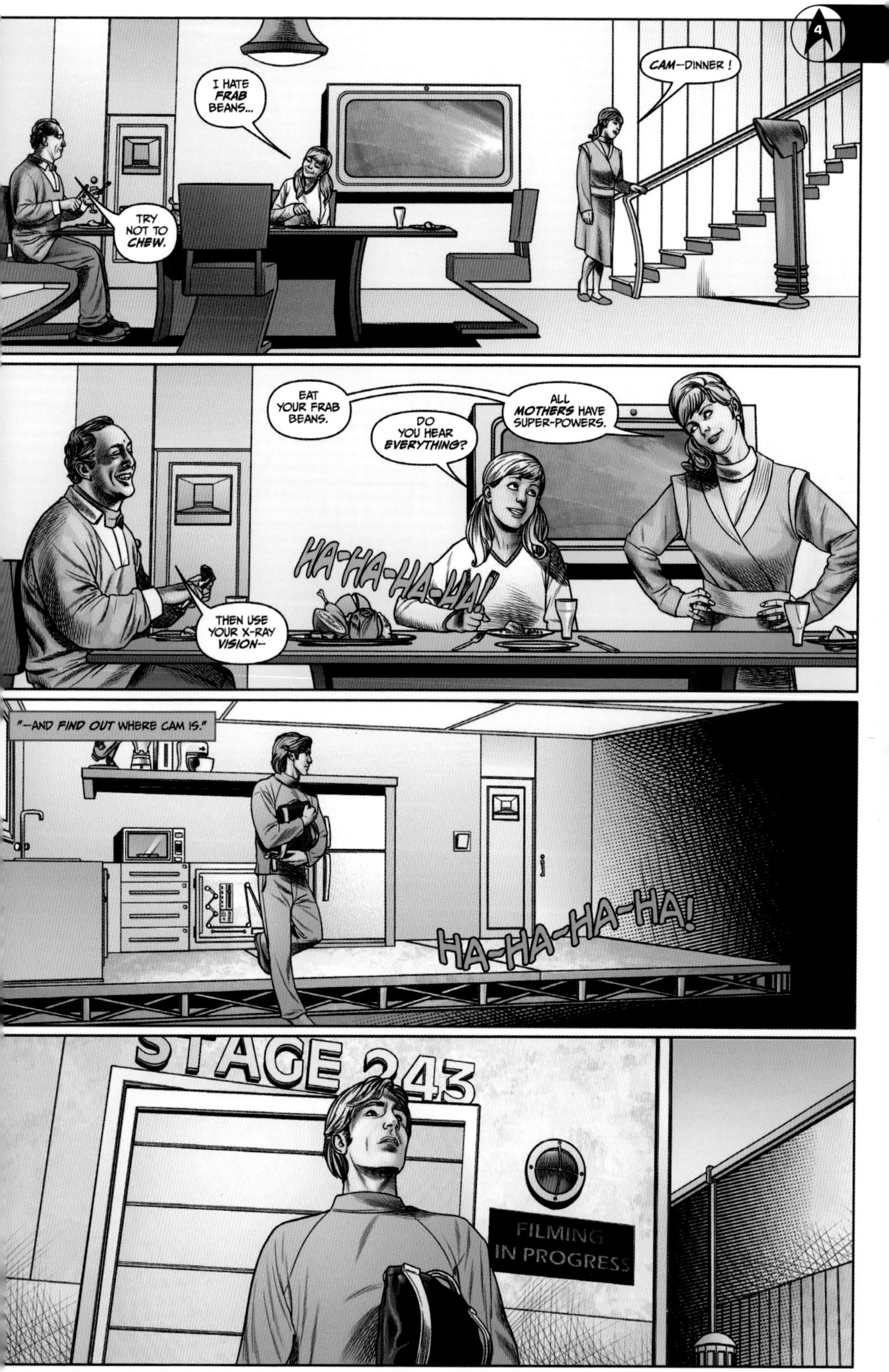
4
I HATE FRAB BEANS...
CAM—DINNER !
TRY NOT TO CHEW.
EAT YOUR FRAB BEANS.
DO YOU HEAR EVERYTHING?
ALL MOTHERS HAVE SUPER-POWERS.
HA-HA-HA-HA!
THEN USE YOUR X-RAY VISION—
"—AND FIND OUT WHERE CAM IS."
HA-HA-HA-HA-HA!
STAGE 243
FILMING IN PROGRESS

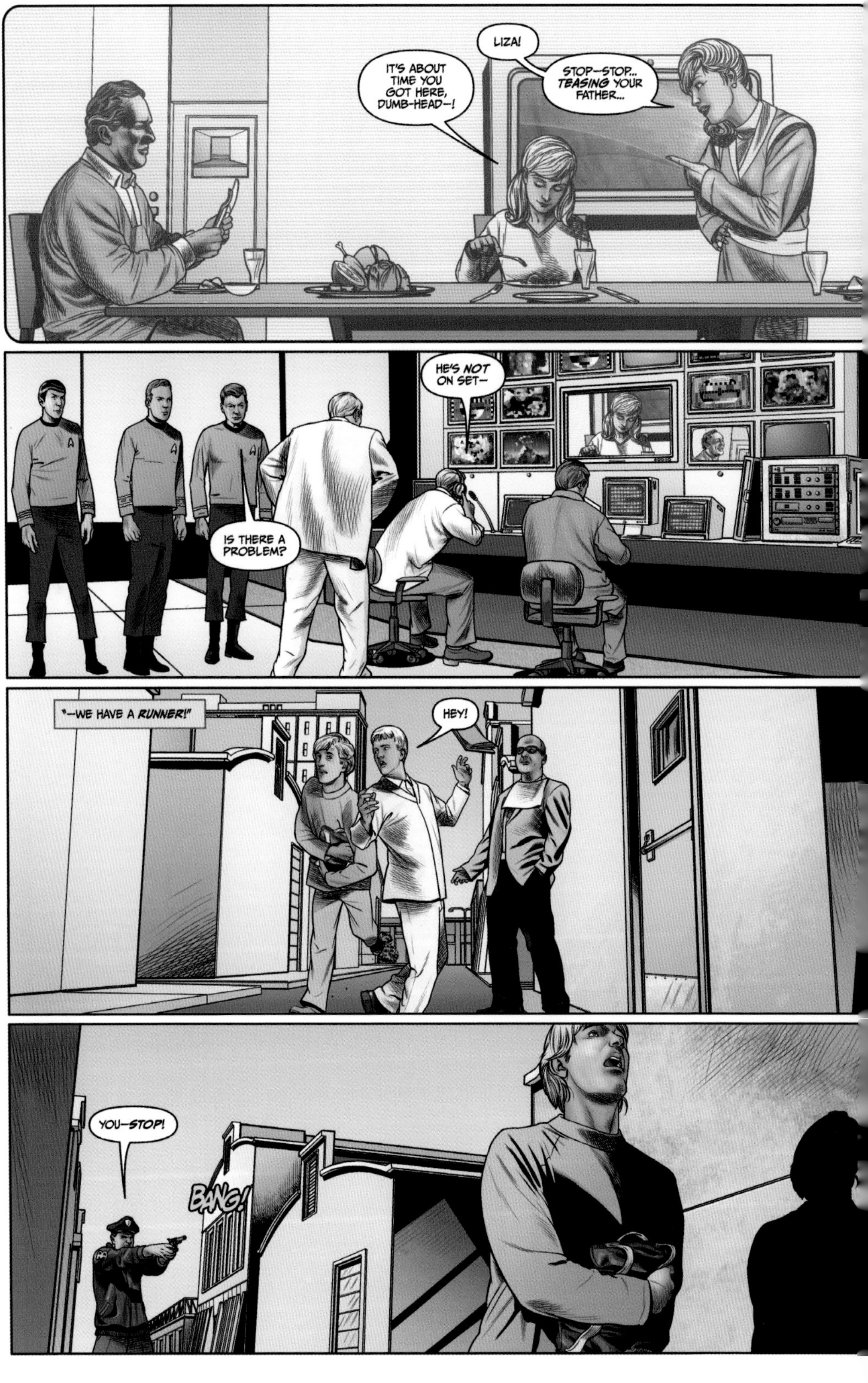

IT'S ABOUT TIME YOU GOT HERE, DUMB-HEAD--!
LIZA!
STOP--STOP... TEASING YOUR FATHER...
HE'S NOT ON SET--
IS THERE A PROBLEM?
"--WE HAVE A RUNNER!"
HEY!
YOU--STOP!
BANG!

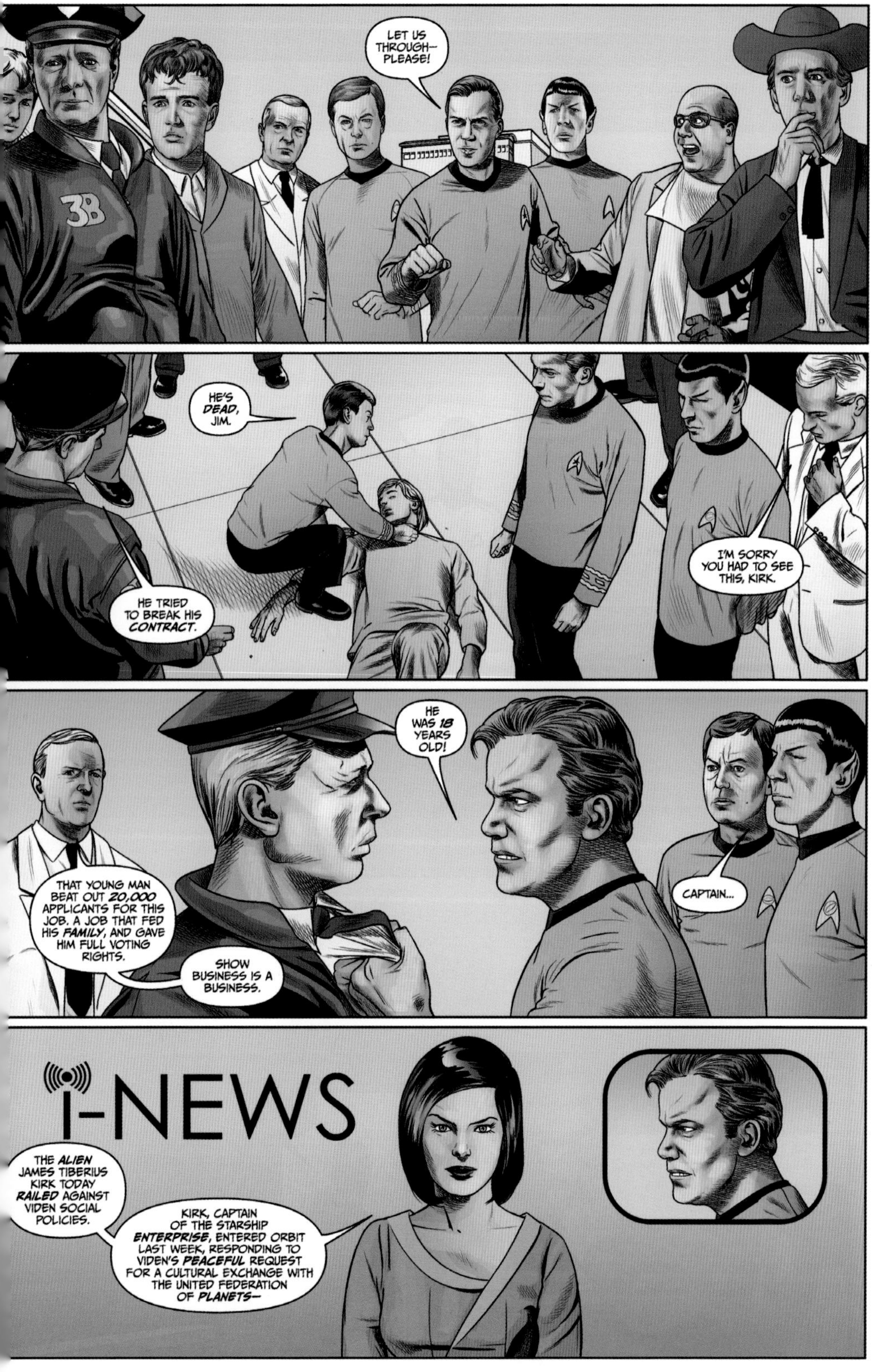
LET US THROUGH—PLEASE!
HE'S *DEAD*, JIM.
HE TRIED TO BREAK HIS *CONTRACT*.
I'M SORRY YOU HAD TO SEE THIS, KIRK.
HE WAS *18* YEARS OLD!
THAT YOUNG MAN BEAT OUT *20,000* APPLICANTS FOR THIS JOB. A JOB THAT FED HIS *FAMILY*, AND GAVE HIM FULL VOTING RIGHTS.
SHOW BUSINESS IS A BUSINESS.
CAPTAIN...
i-NEWS
THE *ALIEN* JAMES TIBERIUS KIRK TODAY *RAILED* AGAINST VIDEN SOCIAL POLICIES.
KIRK, CAPTAIN OF THE STARSHIP *ENTERPRISE*, ENTERED ORBIT LAST WEEK, RESPONDING TO VIDEN'S *PEACEFUL* REQUEST FOR A CULTURAL EXCHANGE WITH THE UNITED FEDERATION OF *PLANETS*—

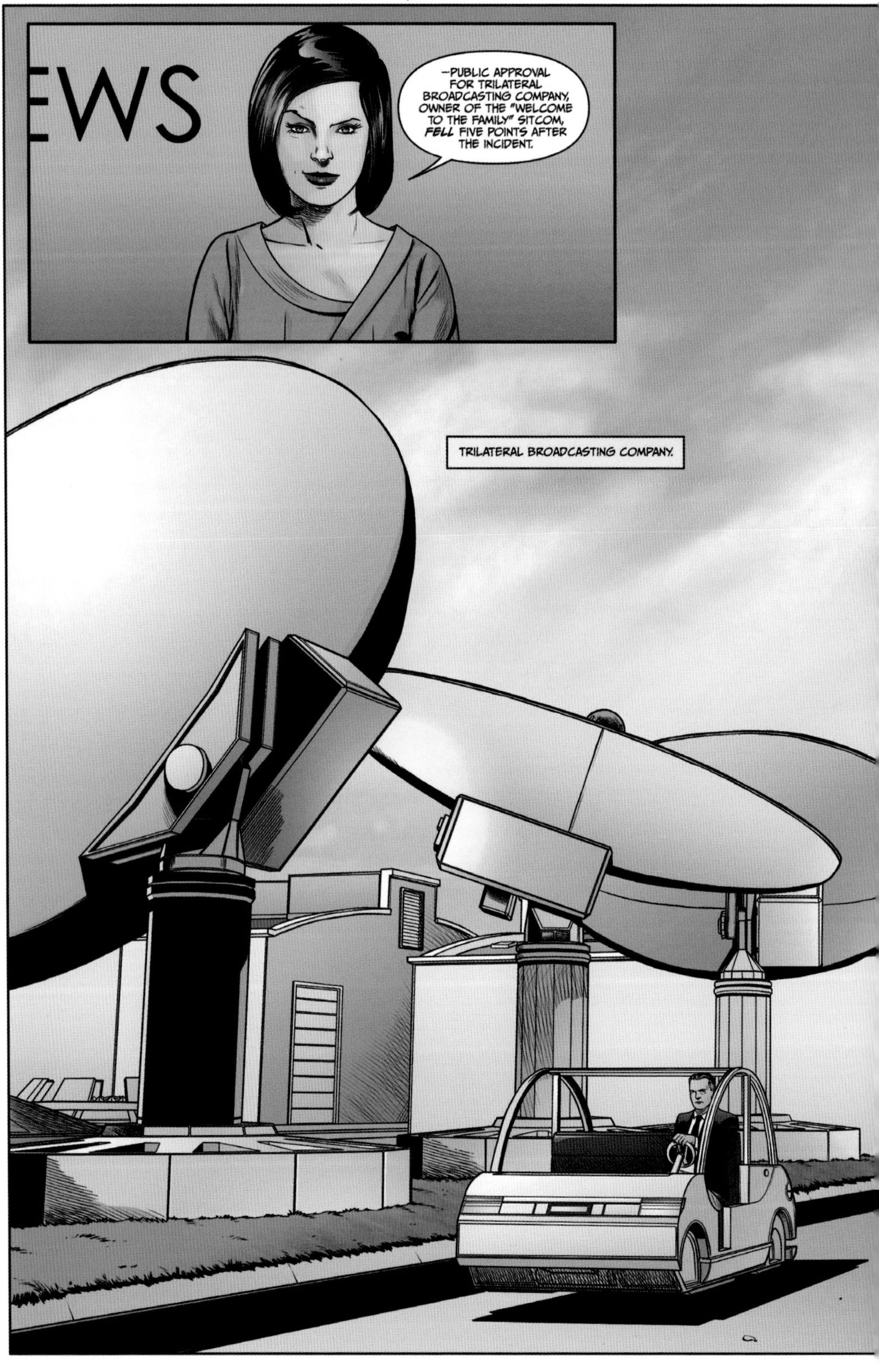
EWS
—PUBLIC APPROVAL FOR TRILATERAL BROADCASTING COMPANY, OWNER OF THE "WELCOME TO THE FAMILY" SITCOM, *FELL* FIVE POINTS AFTER THE INCIDENT.
TRILATERAL BROADCASTING COMPANY.

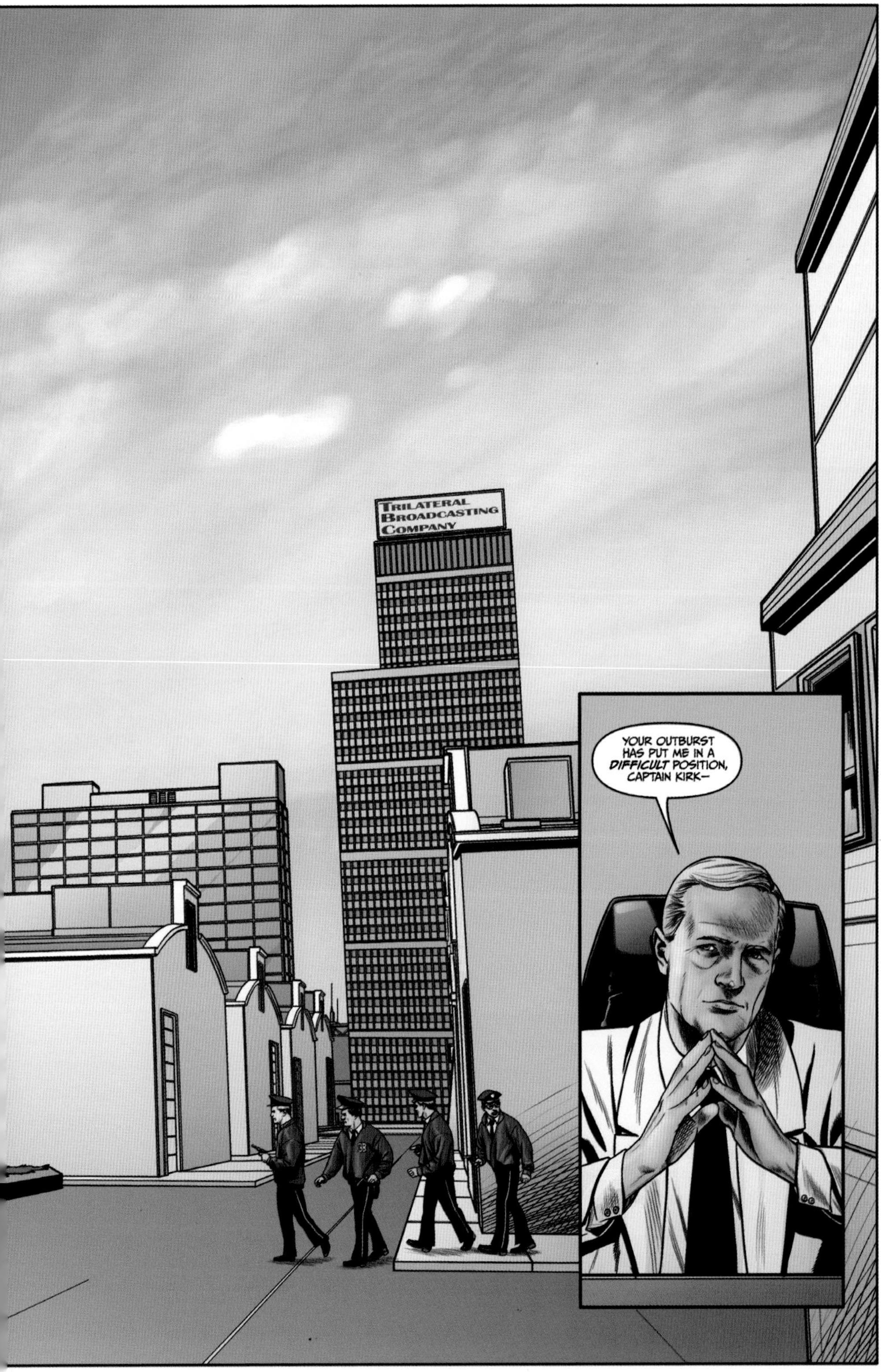
TRILATERAL BROADCASTING COMPANY
YOUR OUTBURST HAS PUT ME IN A *DIFFICULT* POSITION, CAPTAIN KIRK—

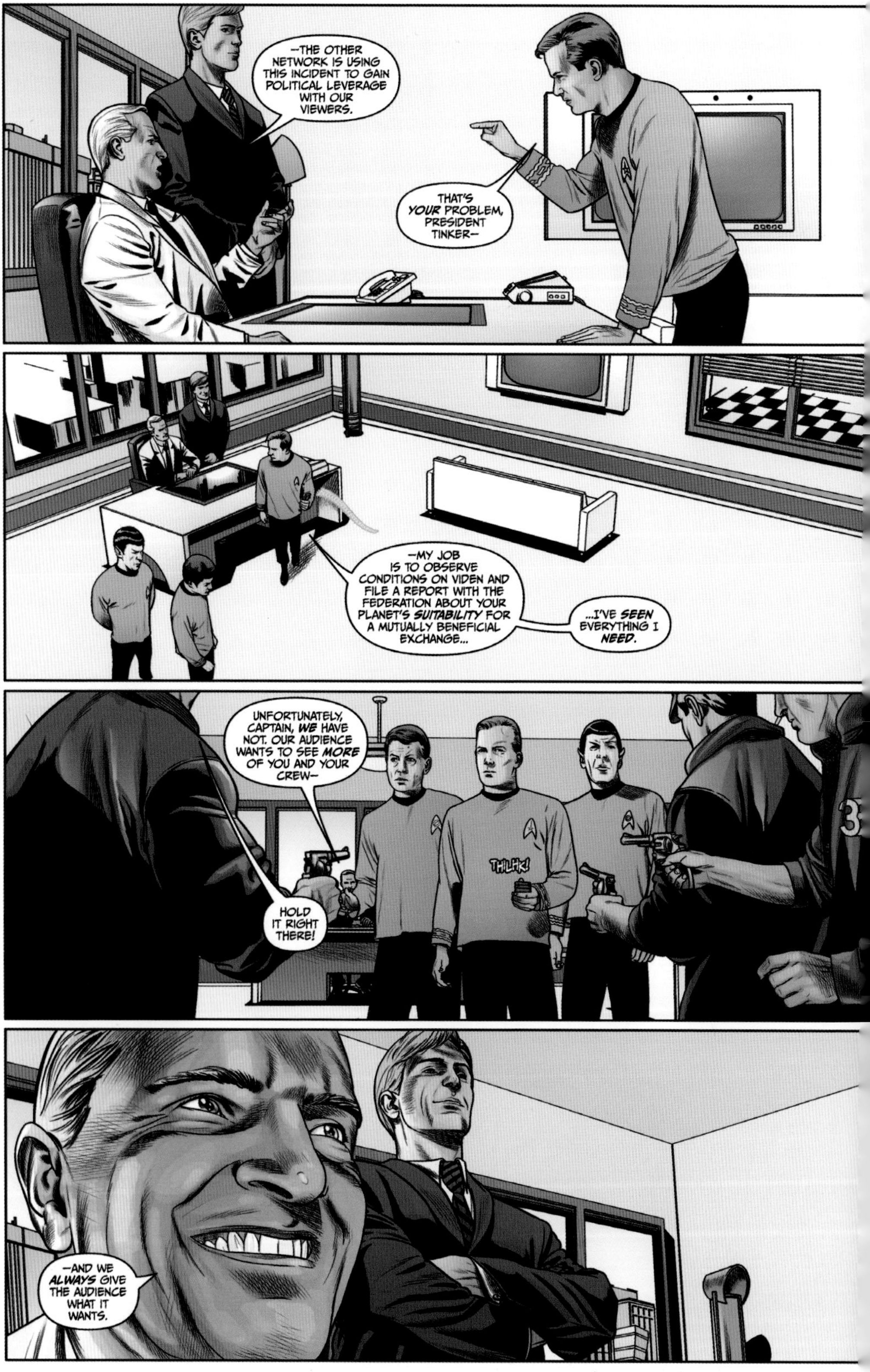
—THE OTHER NETWORK IS USING THIS INCIDENT TO GAIN POLITICAL LEVERAGE WITH OUR VIEWERS.
THAT'S *YOUR* PROBLEM, PRESIDENT TINKER—
—MY JOB IS TO OBSERVE CONDITIONS ON VIDEN AND FILE A REPORT WITH THE FEDERATION ABOUT YOUR PLANET'S *SUITABILITY* FOR A MUTUALLY BENEFICIAL EXCHANGE...
...I'VE *SEEN* EVERYTHING I *NEED*.
UNFORTUNATELY, CAPTAIN, *WE* HAVE NOT. OUR AUDIENCE WANTS TO SEE *MORE* OF YOU AND YOUR CREW—
THHLHK!
HOLD IT RIGHT THERE!
—AND WE *ALWAYS* GIVE THE AUDIENCE WHAT IT WANTS.

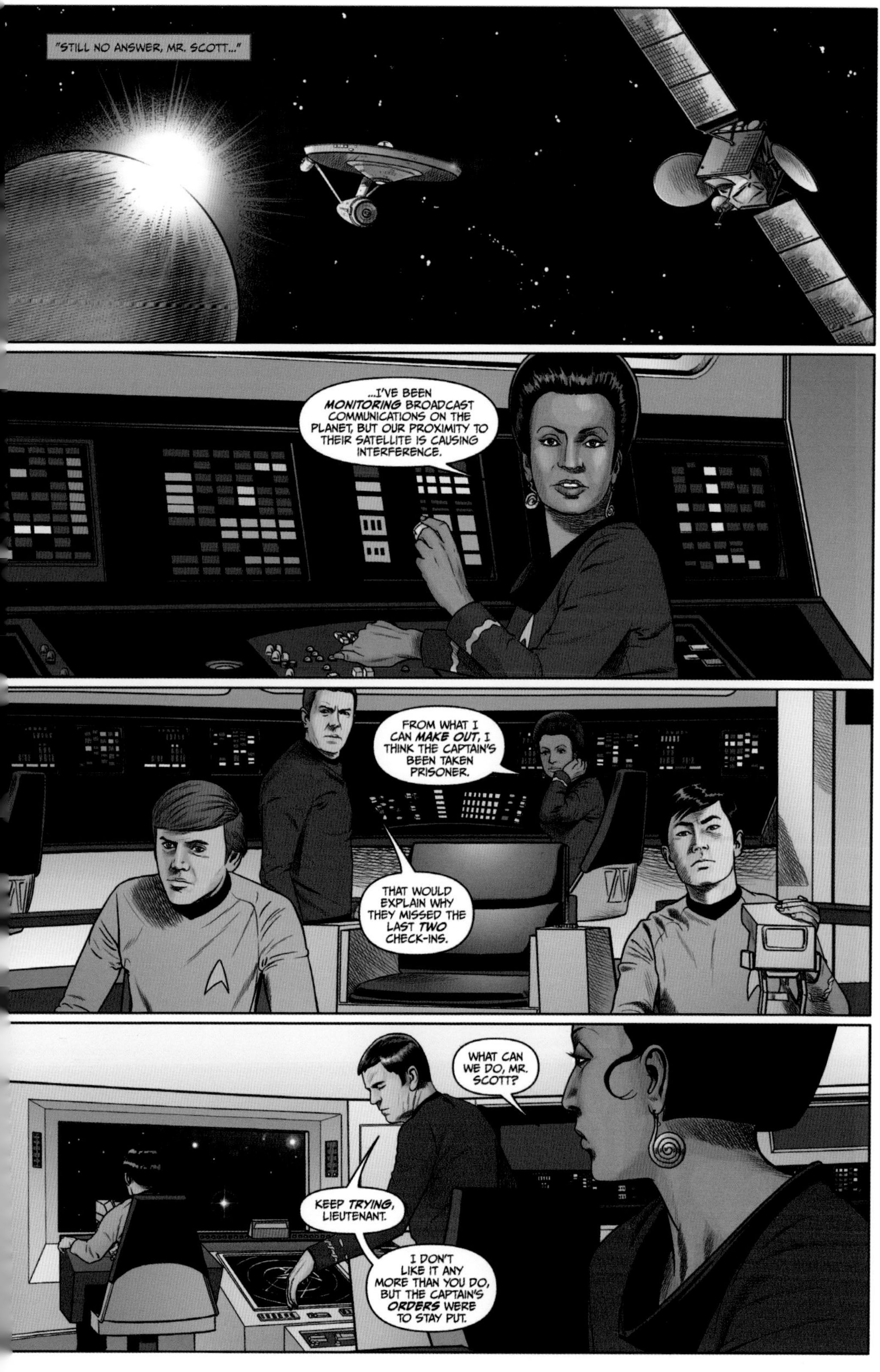
"STILL NO ANSWER, MR. SCOTT..."
...I'VE BEEN MONITORING BROADCAST COMMUNICATIONS ON THE PLANET, BUT OUR PROXIMITY TO THEIR SATELLITE IS CAUSING INTERFERENCE.
FROM WHAT I CAN MAKE OUT, I THINK THE CAPTAIN'S BEEN TAKEN PRISONER.
THAT WOULD EXPLAIN WHY THEY MISSED THE LAST TWO CHECK-INS.
WHAT CAN WE DO, MR. SCOTT?
KEEP TRYING, LIEUTENANT.
I DON'T LIKE IT ANY MORE THAN YOU DO, BUT THE CAPTAIN'S ORDERS WERE TO STAY PUT.

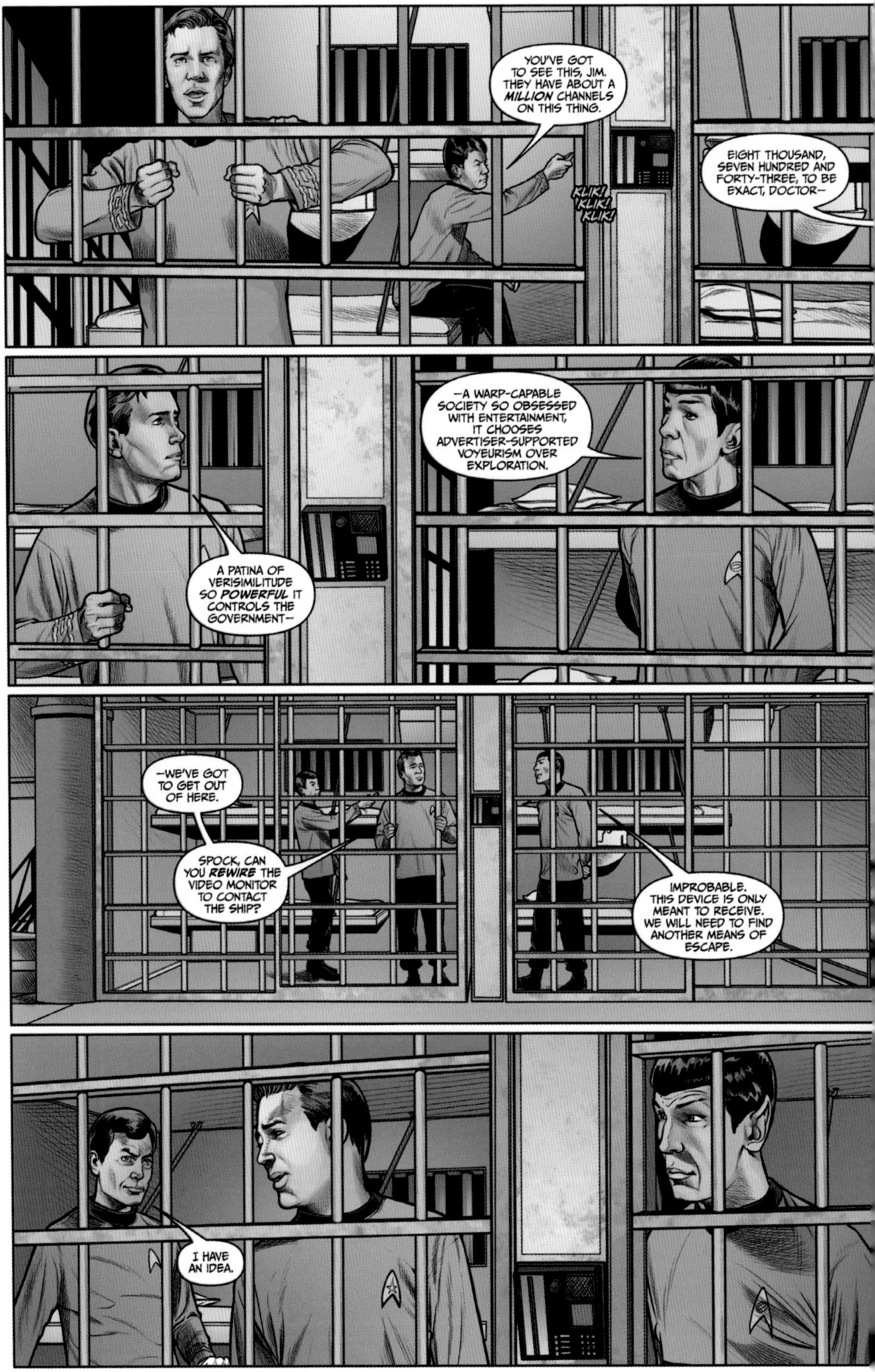
YOU'VE GOT TO SEE THIS, JIM. THEY HAVE ABOUT A MILLION CHANNELS ON THIS THING.
KLIK! KLIK! KLIK!
EIGHT THOUSAND, SEVEN HUNDRED AND FORTY-THREE, TO BE EXACT, DOCTOR—
—A WARP-CAPABLE SOCIETY SO OBSESSED WITH ENTERTAINMENT, IT CHOOSES ADVERTISER-SUPPORTED VOYEURISM OVER EXPLORATION.
A PATINA OF VERISIMILITUDE SO POWERFUL IT CONTROLS THE GOVERNMENT—
—WE'VE GOT TO GET OUT OF HERE.
SPOCK, CAN YOU REWIRE THE VIDEO MONITOR TO CONTACT THE SHIP?
IMPROBABLE. THIS DEVICE IS ONLY MEANT TO RECEIVE. WE WILL NEED TO FIND ANOTHER MEANS OF ESCAPE.
I HAVE AN IDEA.

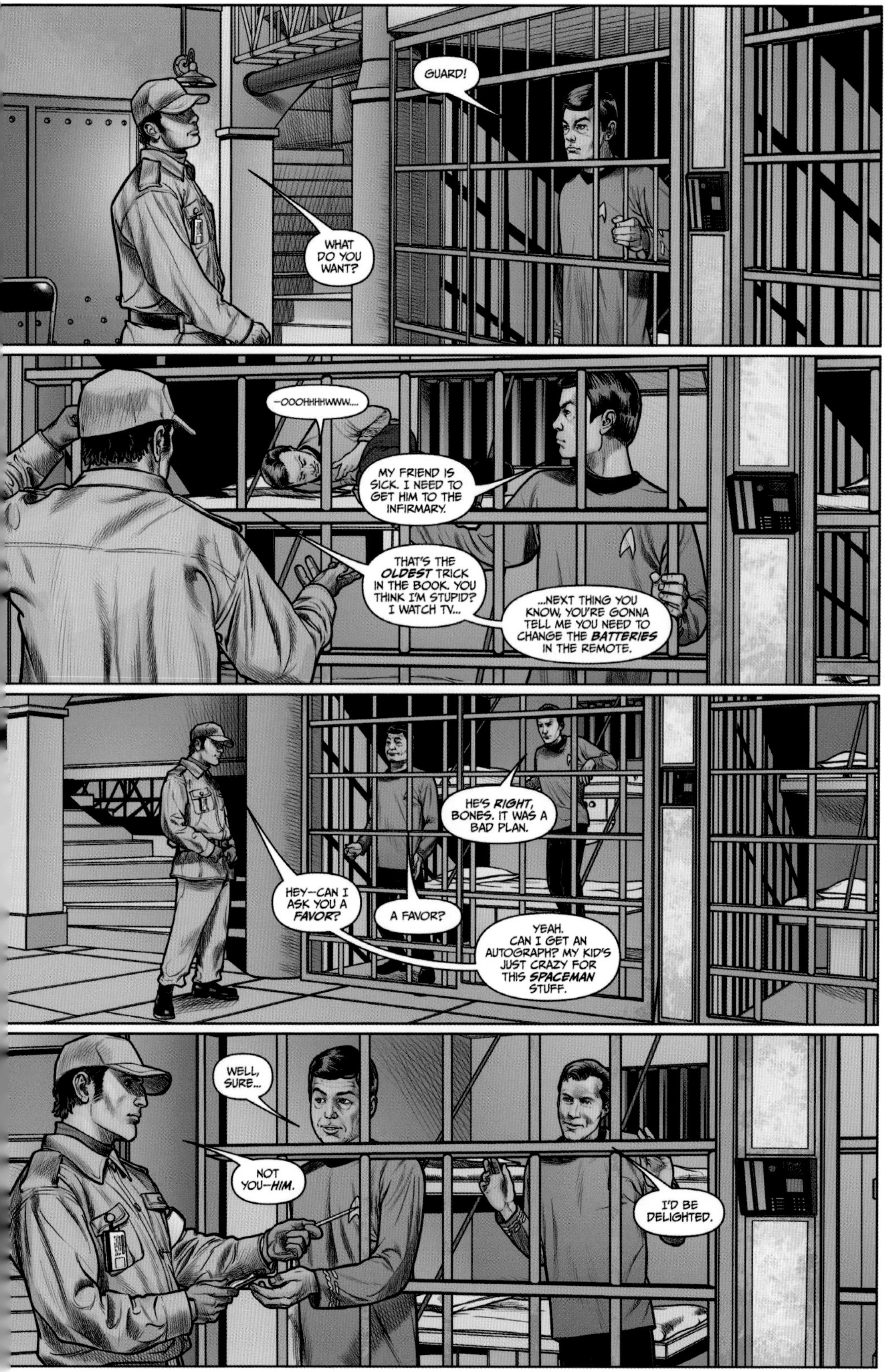
GUARD!
WHAT DO YOU WANT?
—OOOHHHHWWW....
MY FRIEND IS SICK. I NEED TO GET HIM TO THE INFIRMARY.
THAT'S THE OLDEST TRICK IN THE BOOK. YOU THINK I'M STUPID? I WATCH TV...
...NEXT THING YOU KNOW, YOU'RE GONNA TELL ME YOU NEED TO CHANGE THE BATTERIES IN THE REMOTE.
HE'S RIGHT, BONES. IT WAS A BAD PLAN.
HEY--CAN I ASK YOU A FAVOR?
A FAVOR?
YEAH. CAN I GET AN AUTOGRAPH? MY KID'S JUST CRAZY FOR THIS SPACEMAN STUFF.
WELL, SURE...
NOT YOU—HIM.
I'D BE DELIGHTED.

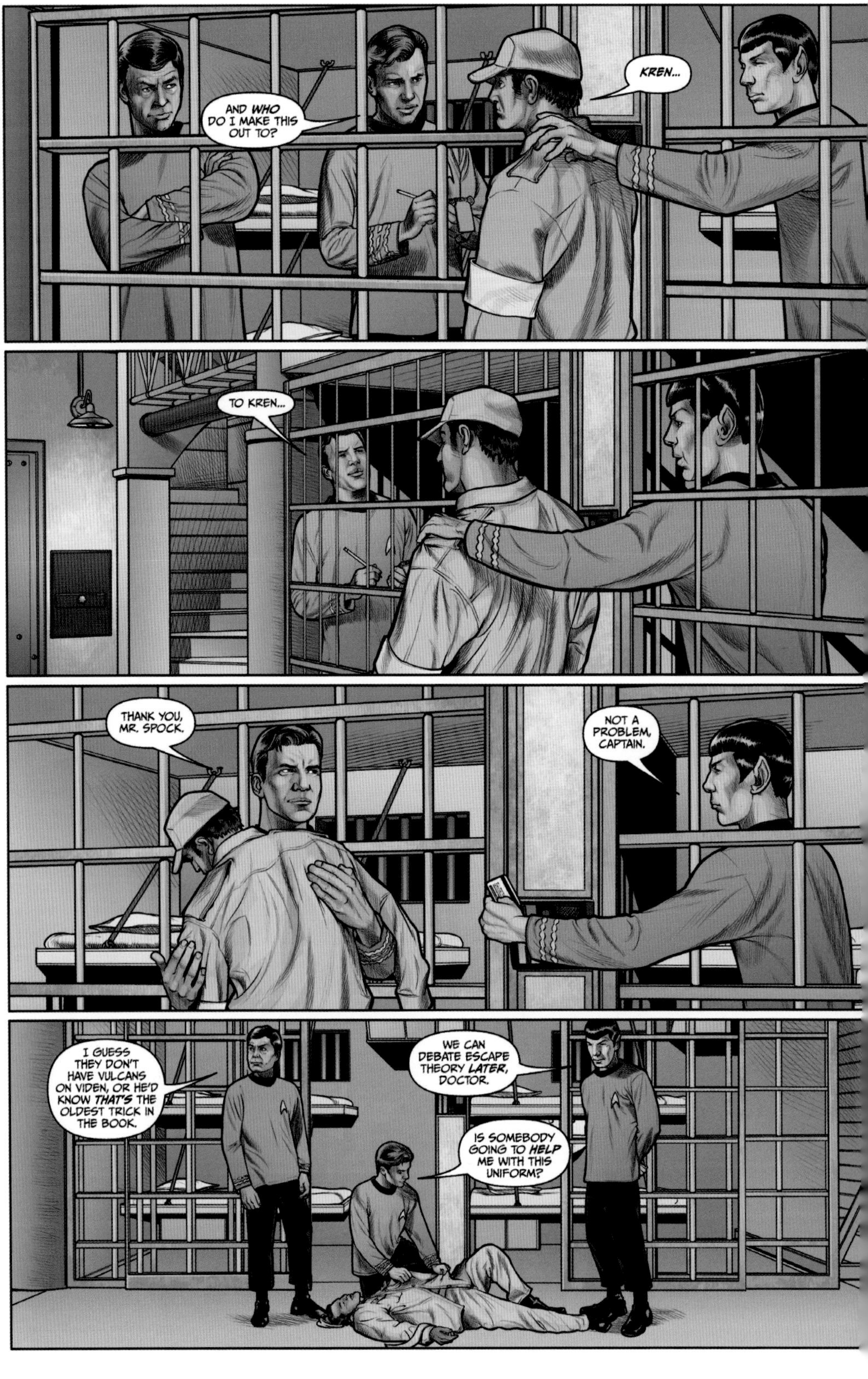

AND WHO DO I MAKE THIS OUT TO?
KREN...
TO KREN...
THANK YOU, MR. SPOCK.
NOT A PROBLEM, CAPTAIN.
I GUESS THEY DON'T HAVE VULCANS ON VIDEN, OR HE'D KNOW THAT'S THE OLDEST TRICK IN THE BOOK.
WE CAN DEBATE ESCAPE THEORY LATER, DOCTOR.
IS SOMEBODY GOING TO HELP ME WITH THIS UNIFORM?

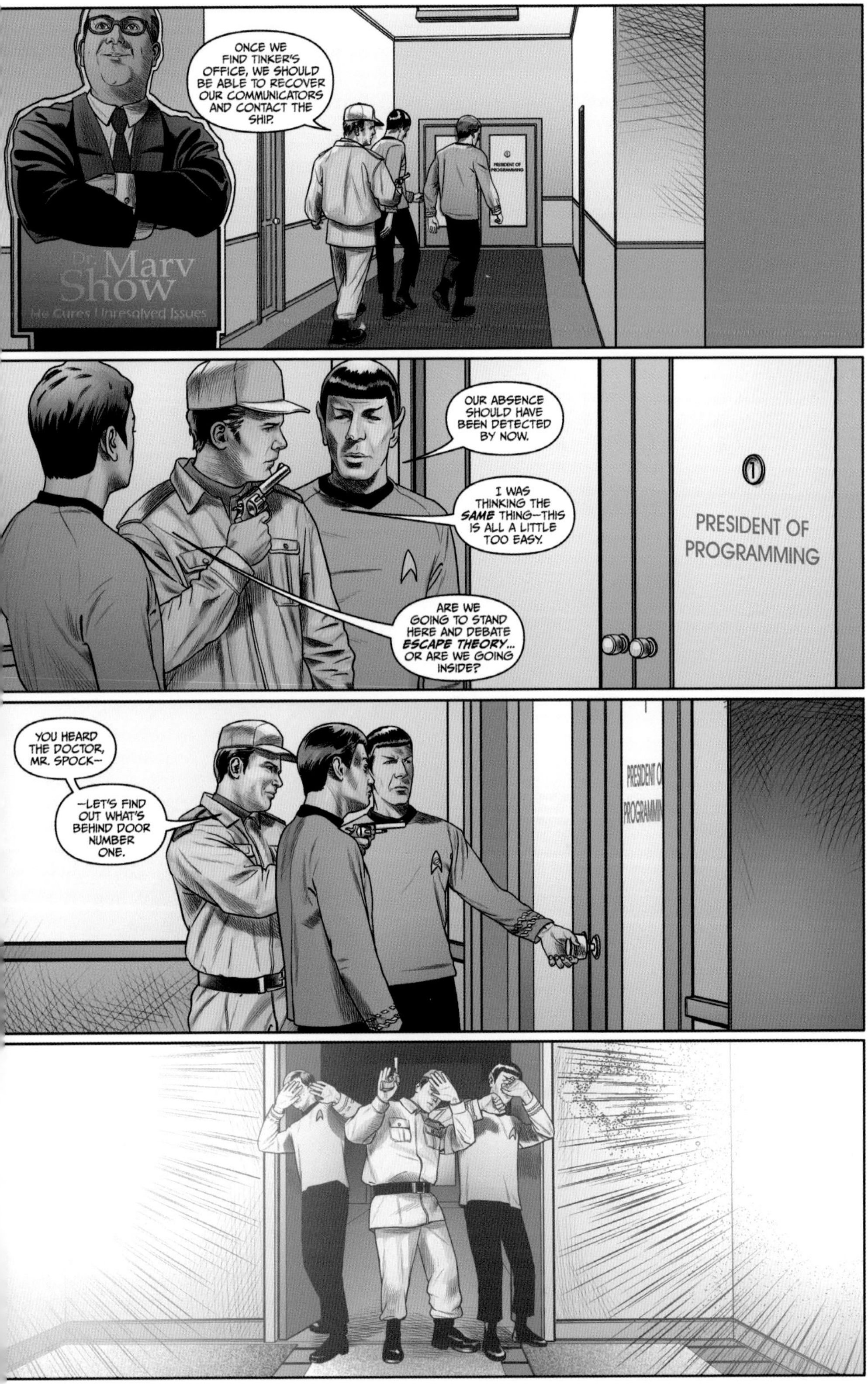
ONCE WE FIND TINKER'S OFFICE, WE SHOULD BE ABLE TO RECOVER OUR COMMUNICATORS AND CONTACT THE SHIP.
Dr. Marv Show
He Cures Unresolved Issues
PRESIDENT OF PROGRAMMING
OUR ABSENCE SHOULD HAVE BEEN DETECTED BY NOW.
I WAS THINKING THE SAME THING—THIS IS ALL A LITTLE TOO EASY.
ARE WE GOING TO STAND HERE AND DEBATE ESCAPE THEORY... OR ARE WE GOING INSIDE?
1
PRESIDENT OF PROGRAMMING
YOU HEARD THE DOCTOR, MR. SPOCK—
—LET'S FIND OUT WHAT'S BEHIND DOOR NUMBER ONE.

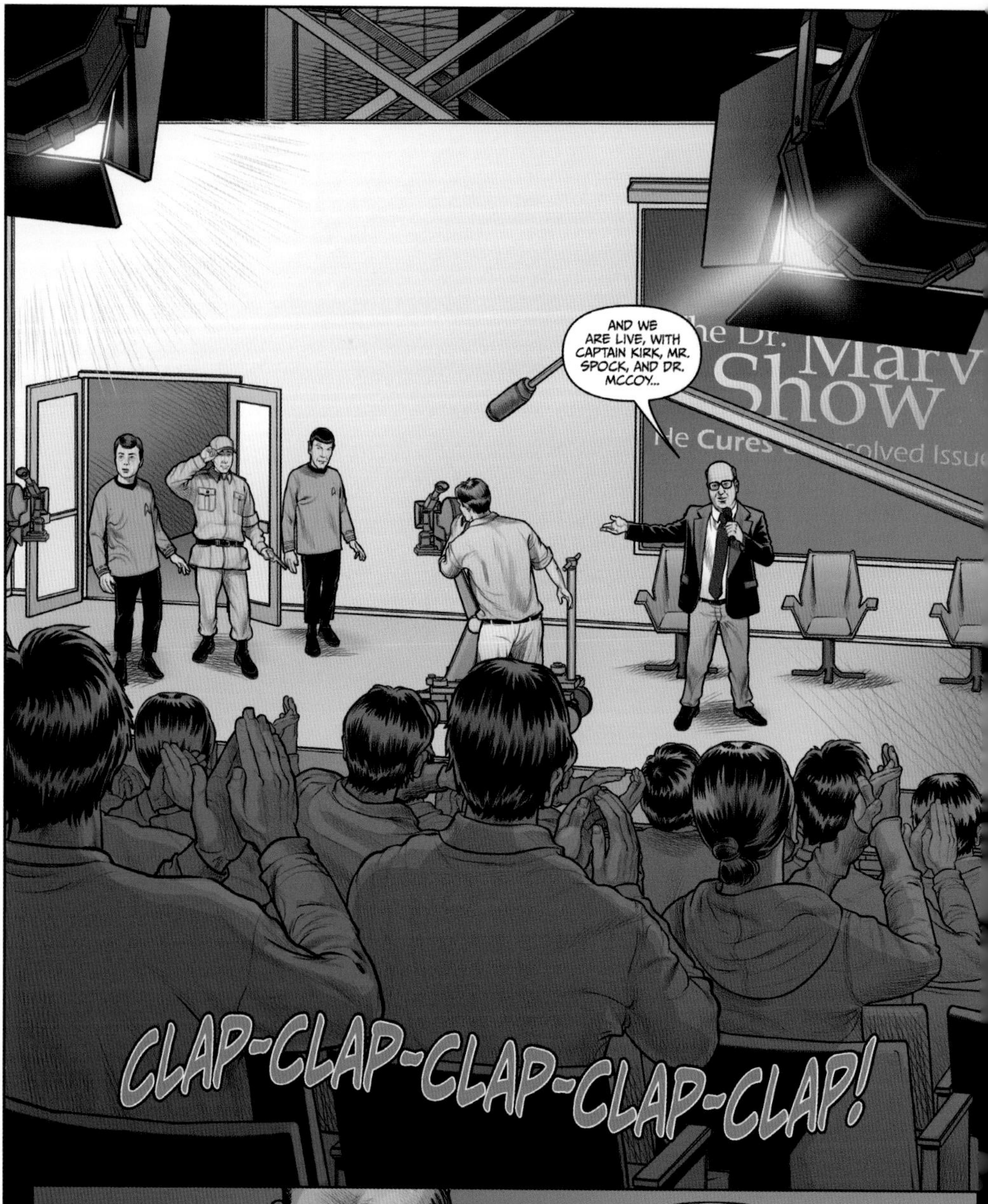
AND WE ARE LIVE, WITH CAPTAIN KIRK, MR. SPOCK, AND DR. MCCOY...
CLAP-CLAP-CLAP-CLAP-CLAP!

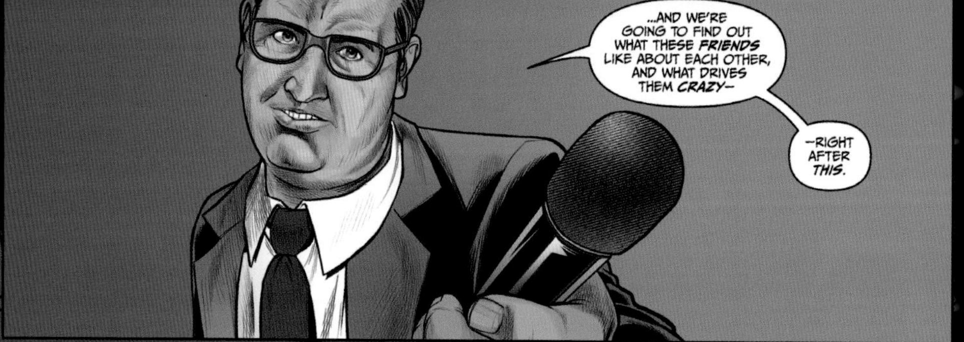
...AND WE'RE GOING TO FIND OUT WHAT THESE *FRIENDS* LIKE ABOUT EACH OTHER, AND WHAT DRIVES THEM *CRAZY*–
–RIGHT AFTER *THIS*.

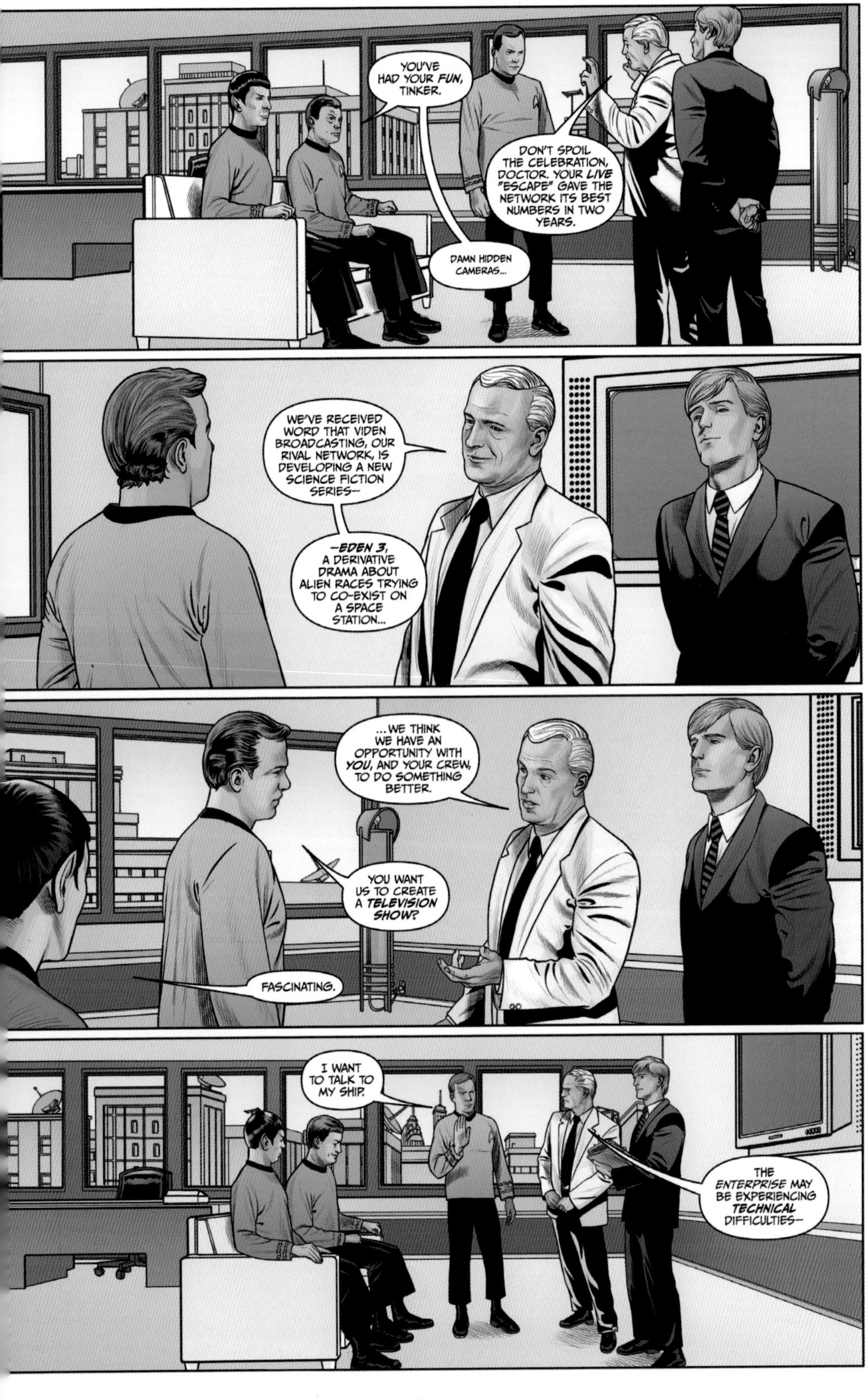
YOU'VE HAD YOUR FUN, TINKER.
DAMN HIDDEN CAMERAS...
DON'T SPOIL THE CELEBRATION, DOCTOR. YOUR LIVE "ESCAPE" GAVE THE NETWORK ITS BEST NUMBERS IN TWO YEARS.
WE'VE RECEIVED WORD THAT VIDEN BROADCASTING, OUR RIVAL NETWORK, IS DEVELOPING A NEW SCIENCE FICTION SERIES–
–EDEN 3, A DERIVATIVE DRAMA ABOUT ALIEN RACES TRYING TO CO-EXIST ON A SPACE STATION...
...WE THINK WE HAVE AN OPPORTUNITY WITH YOU, AND YOUR CREW, TO DO SOMETHING BETTER.
YOU WANT US TO CREATE A TELEVISION SHOW?
FASCINATING.
I WANT TO TALK TO MY SHIP.
THE ENTERPRISE MAY BE EXPERIENCING TECHNICAL DIFFICULTIES–

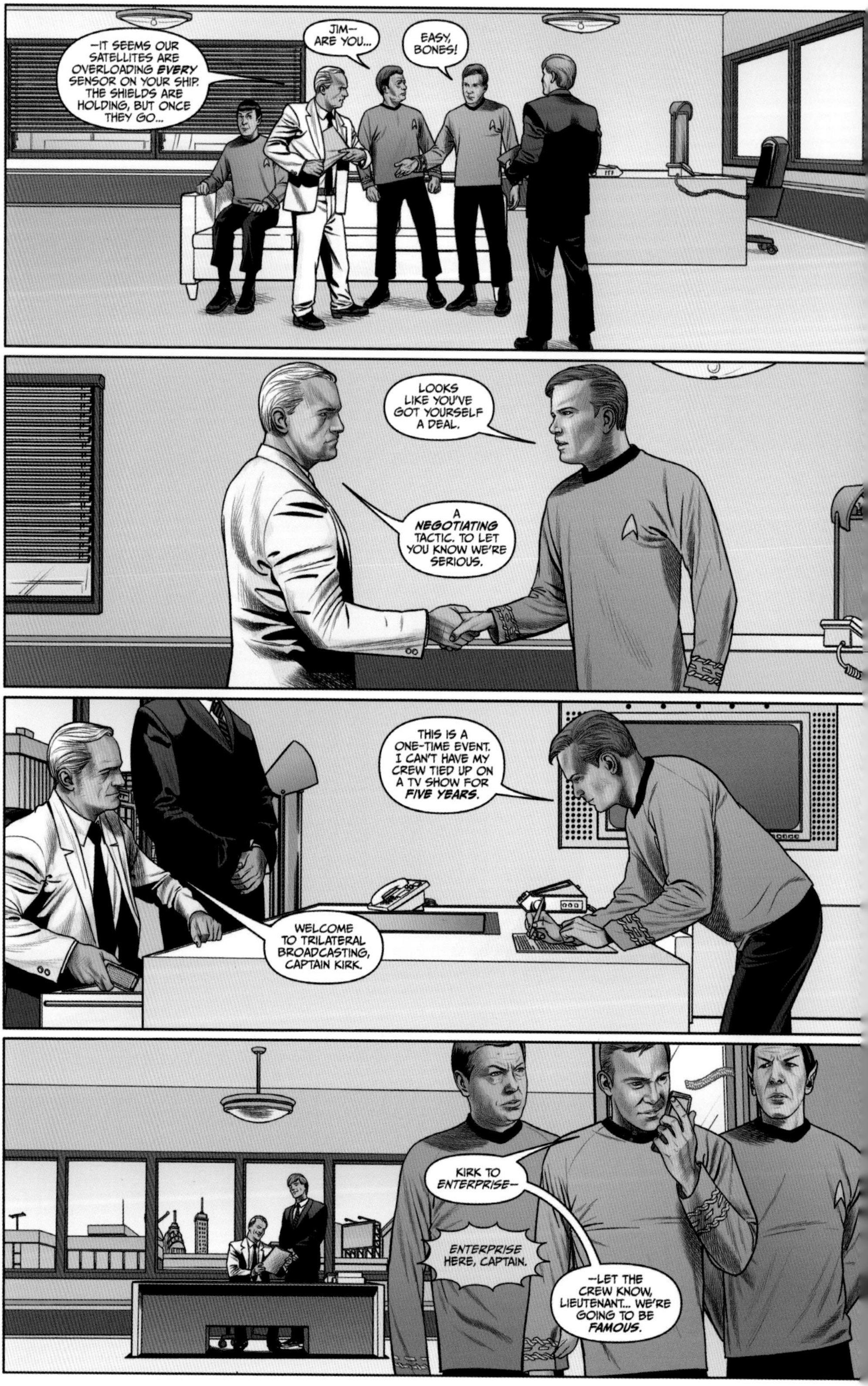
—IT SEEMS OUR SATELLITES ARE OVERLOADING EVERY SENSOR ON YOUR SHIP. THE SHIELDS ARE HOLDING, BUT ONCE THEY GO...
JIM— ARE YOU...
EASY, BONES!
LOOKS LIKE YOU'VE GOT YOURSELF A DEAL.
A NEGOTIATING TACTIC. TO LET YOU KNOW WE'RE SERIOUS.
THIS IS A ONE-TIME EVENT. I CAN'T HAVE MY CREW TIED UP ON A TV SHOW FOR FIVE YEARS.
WELCOME TO TRILATERAL BROADCASTING, CAPTAIN KIRK.
KIRK TO ENTERPRISE—
ENTERPRISE HERE, CAPTAIN.
—LET THE CREW KNOW, LIEUTENANT... WE'RE GOING TO BE FAMOUS.

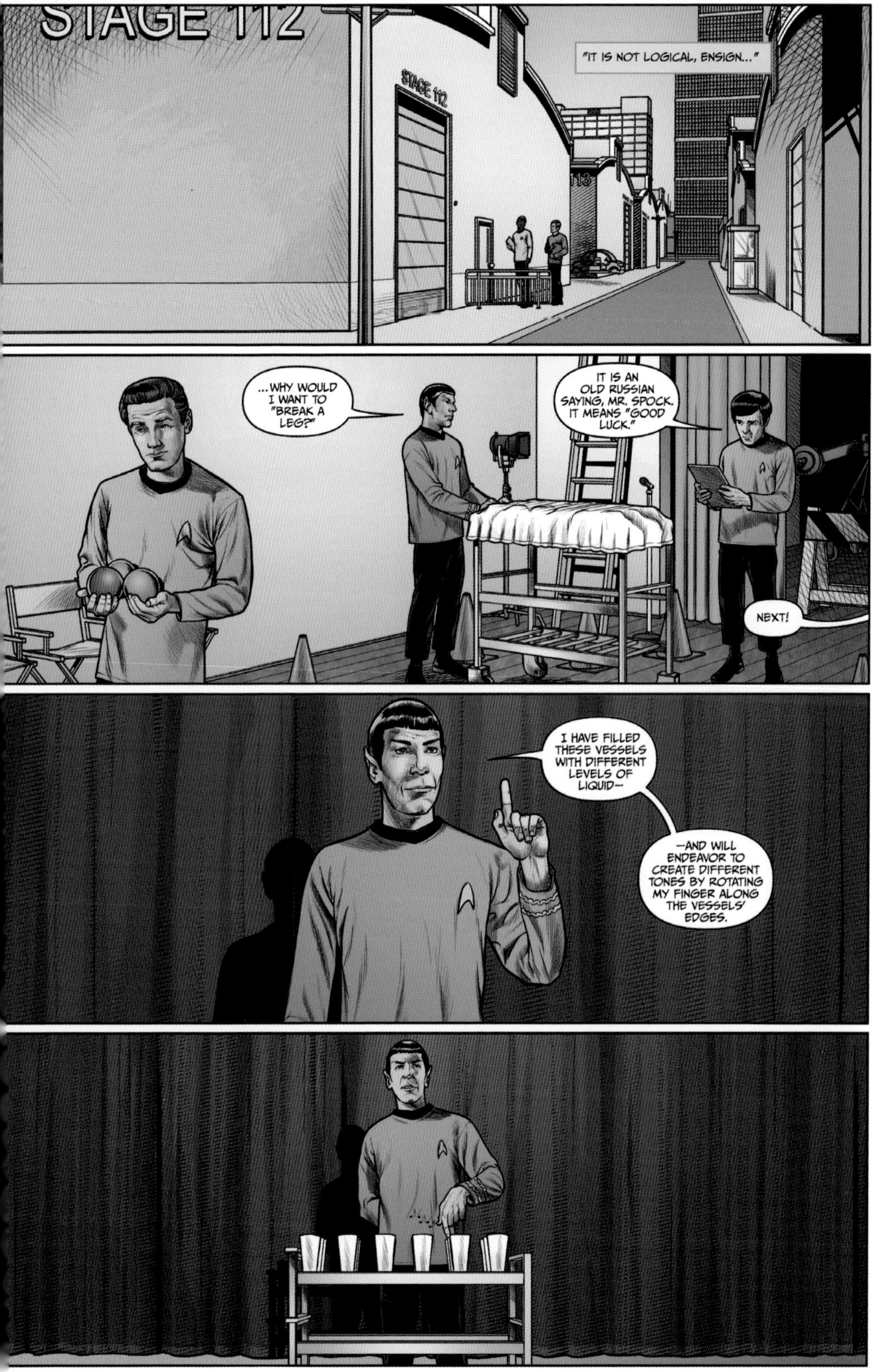
STAGE 112
STAGE 112
"IT IS NOT LOGICAL, ENSIGN..."
113
...WHY WOULD I WANT TO "BREAK A LEG?"
IT IS AN OLD RUSSIAN SAYING, MR. SPOCK. IT MEANS "GOOD LUCK."
NEXT!
I HAVE FILLED THESE VESSELS WITH DIFFERENT LEVELS OF LIQUID--
--AND WILL ENDEAVOR TO CREATE DIFFERENT TONES BY ROTATING MY FINGER ALONG THE VESSELS' EDGES.

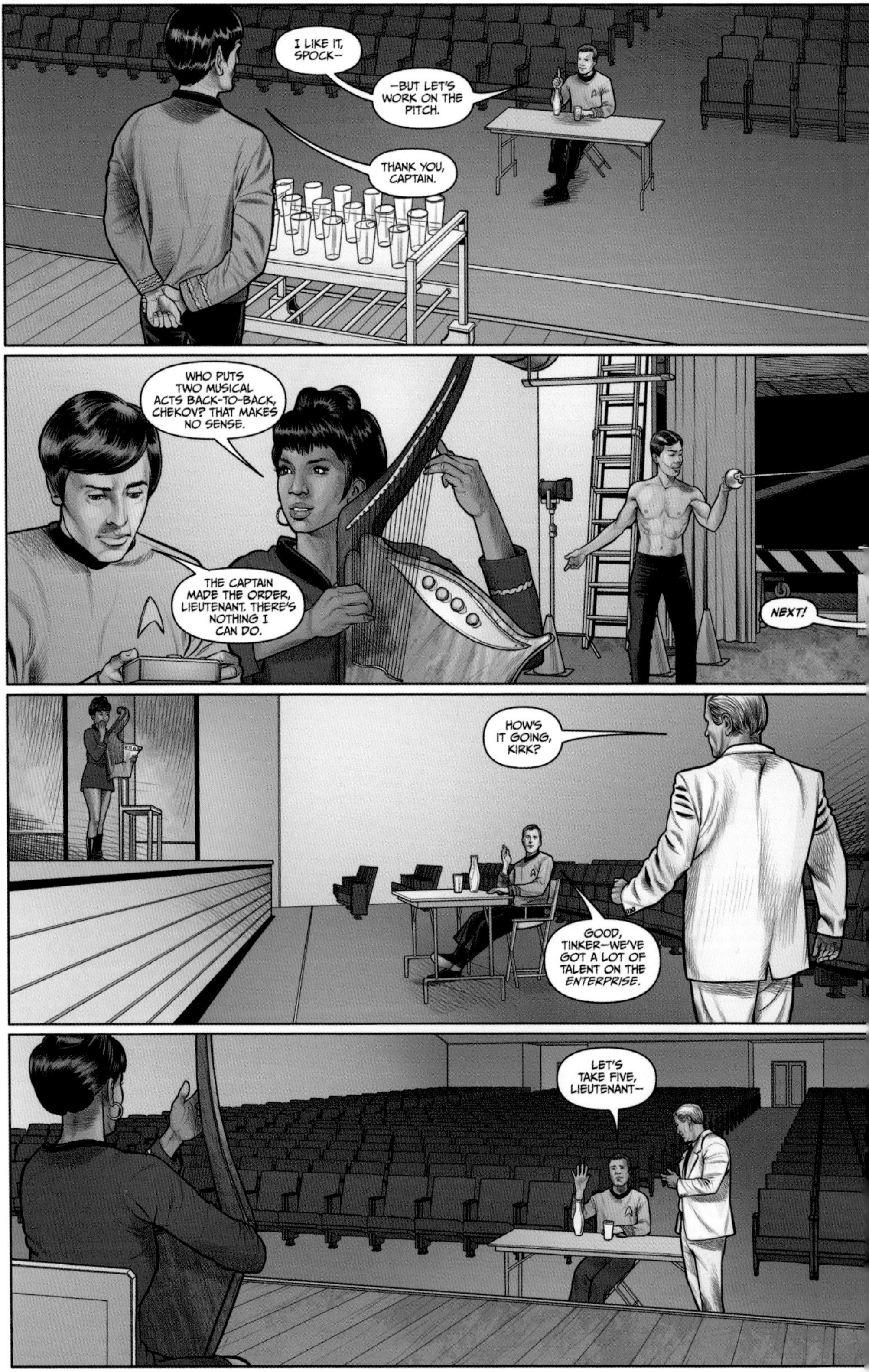
I LIKE IT, SPOCK--
--BUT LET'S WORK ON THE PITCH.
THANK YOU, CAPTAIN.
WHO PUTS TWO MUSICAL ACTS BACK-TO-BACK, CHEKOV? THAT MAKES NO SENSE.
THE CAPTAIN MADE THE ORDER, LIEUTENANT. THERE'S NOTHING I CAN DO.
NEXT!
HOW'S IT GOING, KIRK?
GOOD, TINKER--WE'VE GOT A LOT OF TALENT ON THE *ENTERPRISE*.
LET'S TAKE FIVE, LIEUTENANT--

MR. TINKER—!

WHAT IS IT, BRANDON?

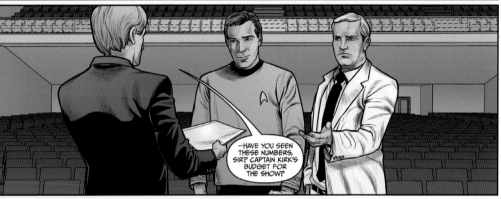

—HAVE YOU SEEN THESE NUMBERS, SIR? CAPTAIN KIRK'S BUDGET FOR THE SHOW?

KIRK, THIS IS ABSURD.

THAT'S WHAT WE NEED. THE CONTRACT SAID WE'D HAVE CREATIVE CONTROL.

THE FEDERATION'S PRODUCING FEE IS A LITTLE HIGH, BUT IT'S WHAT WE GET ON OTHER PLANETS.

WE CAN'T SELL ENOUGH AD TIME TO MAKE A PROFIT.

IS THAT A PROBLEM, GENTLEMEN?

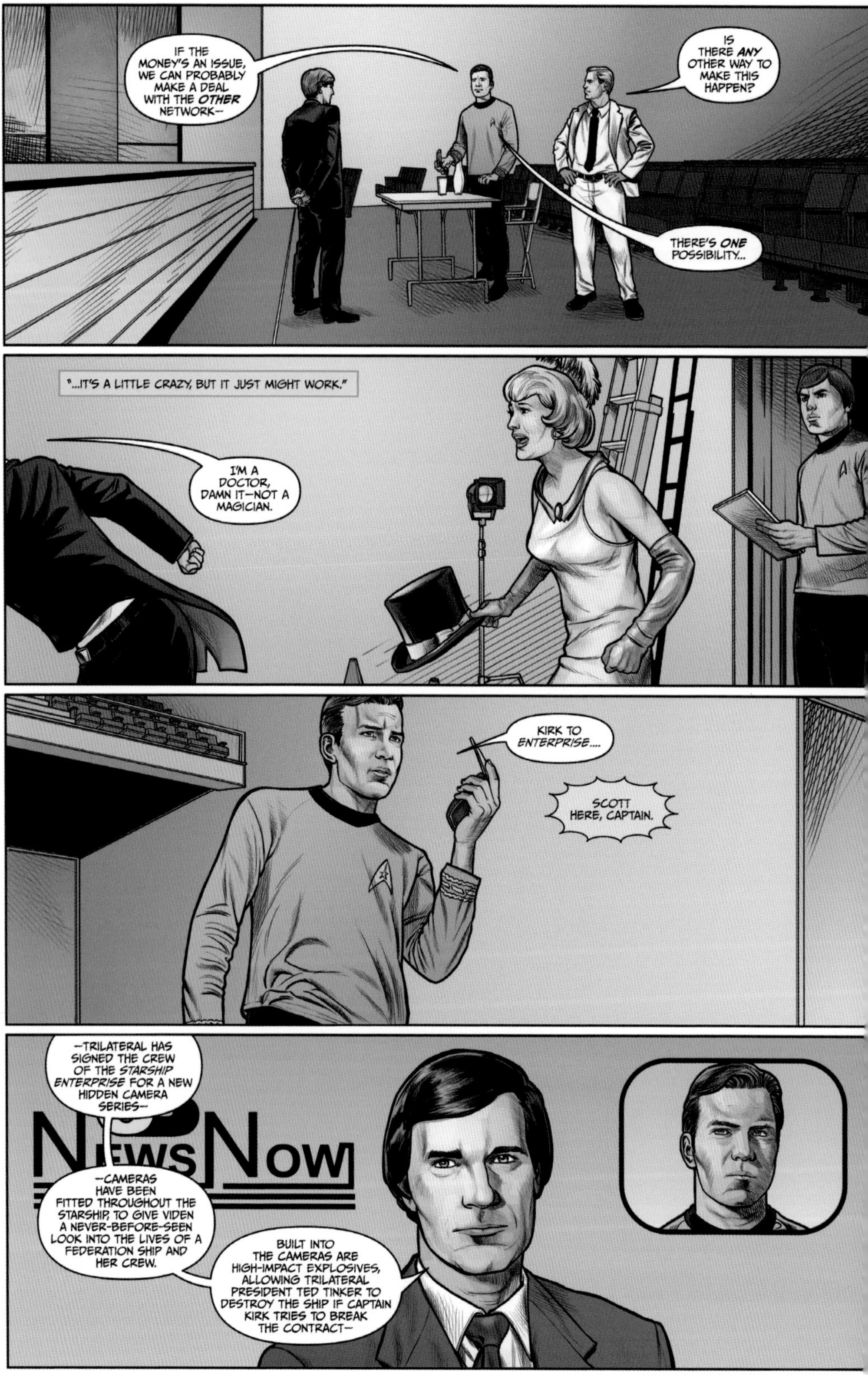
IF THE MONEY'S AN ISSUE, WE CAN PROBABLY MAKE A DEAL WITH THE *OTHER* NETWORK--
IS THERE *ANY* OTHER WAY TO MAKE THIS HAPPEN?
THERE'S *ONE* POSSIBILITY...
"...IT'S A LITTLE CRAZY, BUT IT JUST MIGHT WORK."
I'M A DOCTOR, DAMN IT--NOT A MAGICIAN.
KIRK TO *ENTERPRISE*....
SCOTT HERE, CAPTAIN.
--TRILATERAL HAS SIGNED THE CREW OF THE *STARSHIP ENTERPRISE* FOR A NEW HIDDEN CAMERA SERIES--
NEWS NOW
--CAMERAS HAVE BEEN FITTED THROUGHOUT THE STARSHIP, TO GIVE VIDEN A NEVER-BEFORE-SEEN LOOK INTO THE LIVES OF A FEDERATION SHIP AND HER CREW.
BUILT INTO THE CAMERAS ARE HIGH-IMPACT EXPLOSIVES, ALLOWING TRILATERAL PRESIDENT TED TINKER TO DESTROY THE SHIP IF CAPTAIN KIRK TRIES TO BREAK THE CONTRACT--

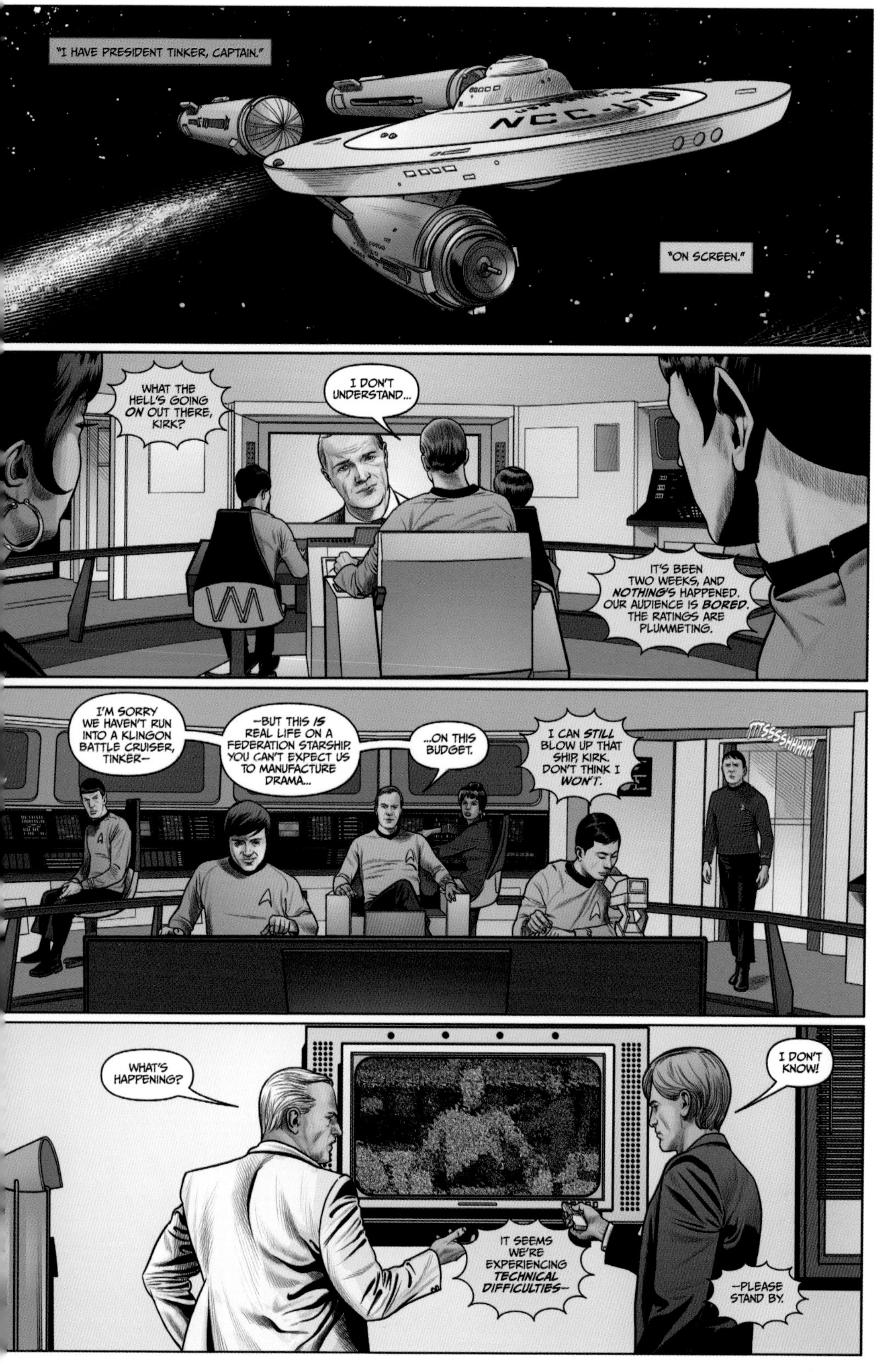
"I HAVE PRESIDENT TINKER, CAPTAIN."
NCC-1701
"ON SCREEN."
WHAT THE HELL'S GOING ON OUT THERE, KIRK?
I DON'T UNDERSTAND...
IT'S BEEN TWO WEEKS, AND NOTHING'S HAPPENED. OUR AUDIENCE IS BORED. THE RATINGS ARE PLUMMETING.
I'M SORRY WE HAVEN'T RUN INTO A KLINGON BATTLE CRUISER, TINKER--
--BUT THIS IS REAL LIFE ON A FEDERATION STARSHIP. YOU CAN'T EXPECT US TO MANUFACTURE DRAMA...
...ON THIS BUDGET.
I CAN STILL BLOW UP THAT SHIP, KIRK. DON'T THINK I WON'T.
TTTSSSSHHHHH!
WHAT'S HAPPENING?
I DON'T KNOW!
IT SEEMS WE'RE EXPERIENCING TECHNICAL DIFFICULTIES--
--PLEASE STAND BY.

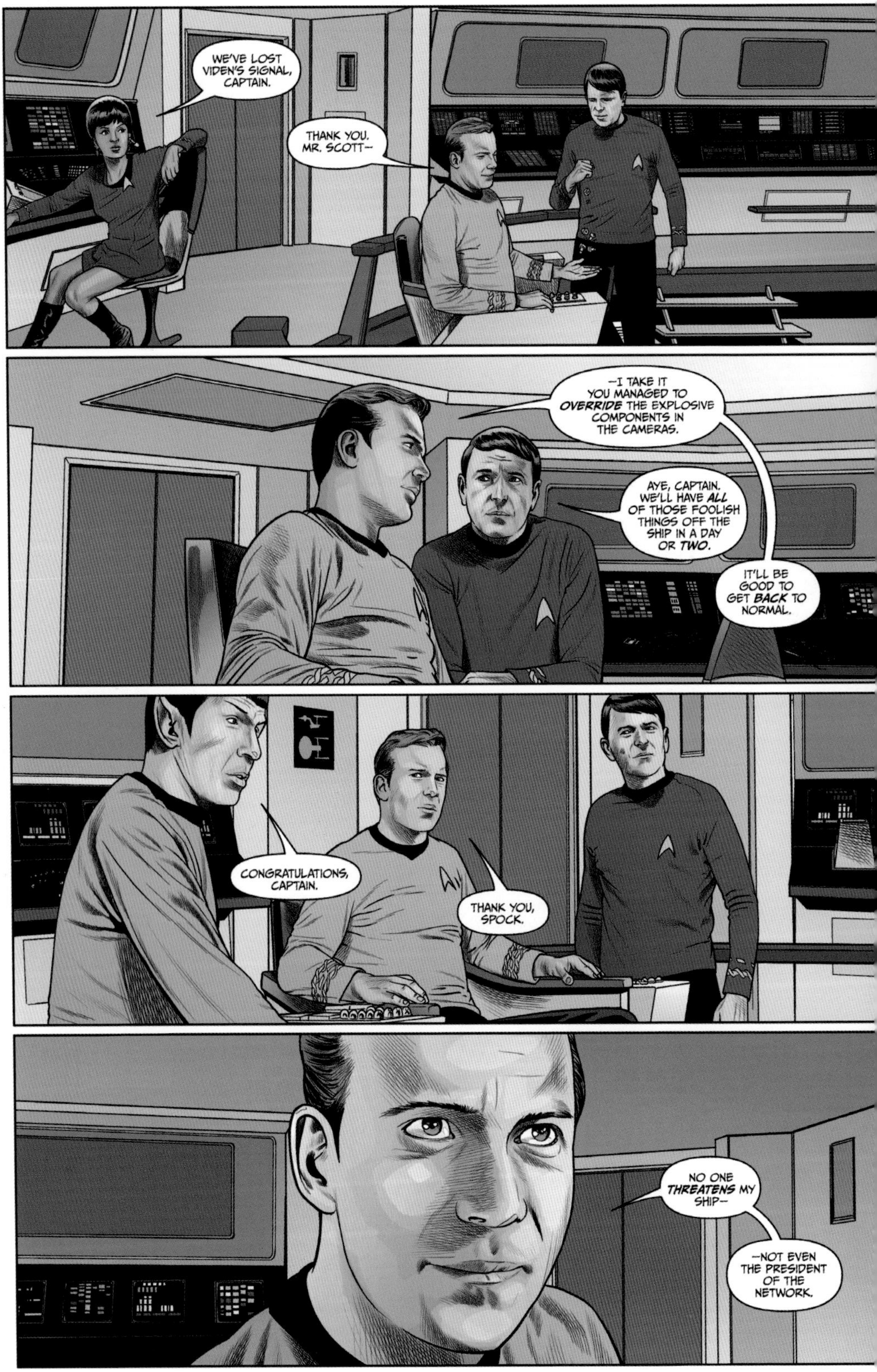
WE'VE LOST VIDEN'S SIGNAL, CAPTAIN.
THANK YOU. MR. SCOTT--
--I TAKE IT YOU MANAGED TO OVERRIDE THE EXPLOSIVE COMPONENTS IN THE CAMERAS.
IT'LL BE GOOD TO GET BACK TO NORMAL.
AYE, CAPTAIN. WE'LL HAVE ALL OF THOSE FOOLISH THINGS OFF THE SHIP IN A DAY OR TWO.
CONGRATULATIONS, CAPTAIN.
THANK YOU, SPOCK.
NO ONE THREATENS MY SHIP--
--NOT EVEN THE PRESIDENT OF THE NETWORK.

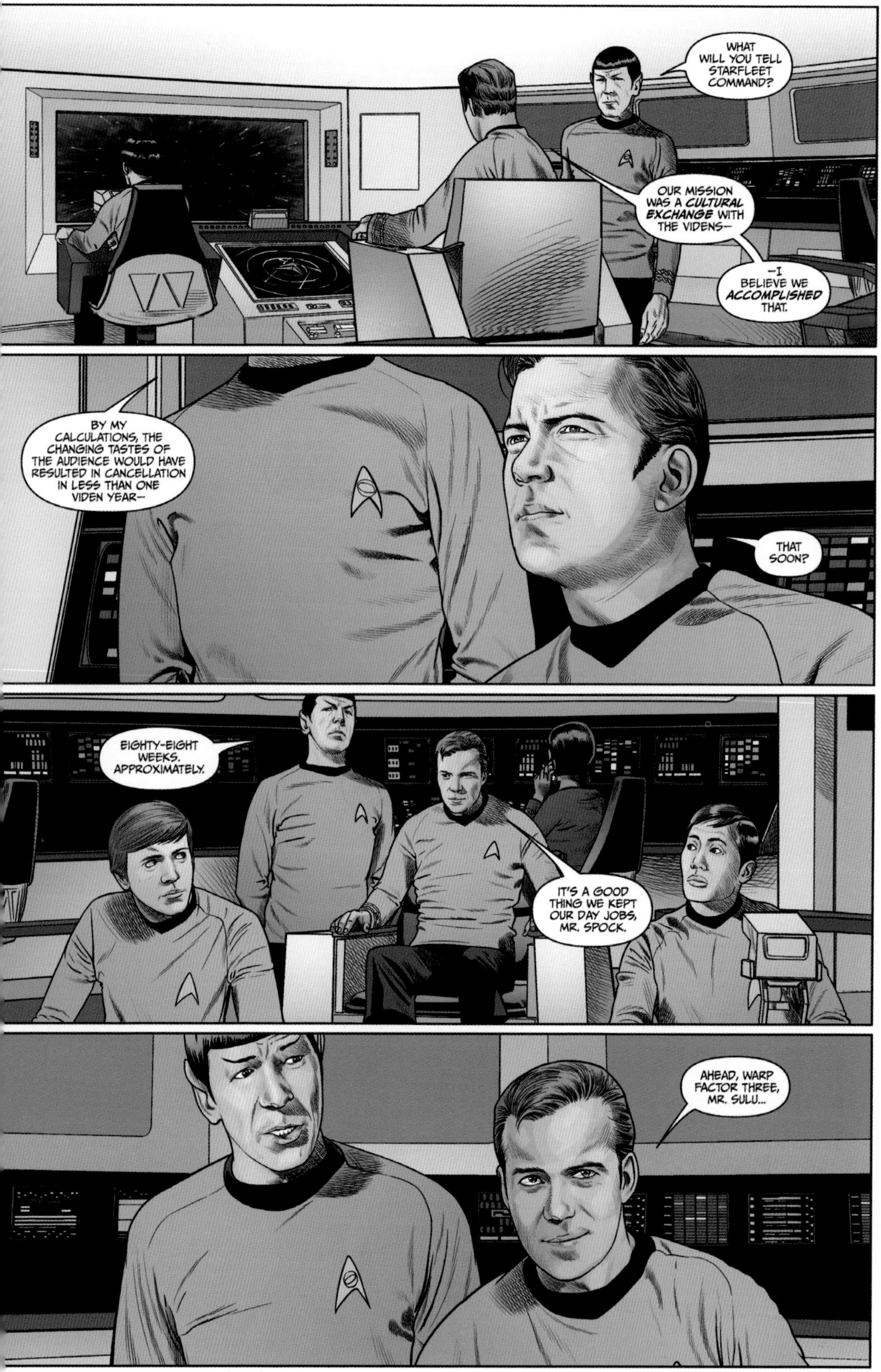
WHAT WILL YOU TELL STARFLEET COMMAND?
OUR MISSION WAS A *CULTURAL EXCHANGE* WITH THE VIDENS—
—I BELIEVE WE *ACCOMPLISHED* THAT.
BY MY CALCULATIONS, THE CHANGING TASTES OF THE AUDIENCE WOULD HAVE RESULTED IN CANCELLATION IN LESS THAN ONE VIDEN YEAR—
THAT SOON?
EIGHTY-EIGHT WEEKS. APPROXIMATELY.
IT'S A GOOD THING WE KEPT OUR DAY JOBS, MR. SPOCK.
AHEAD, WARP FACTOR THREE, MR. SULU...

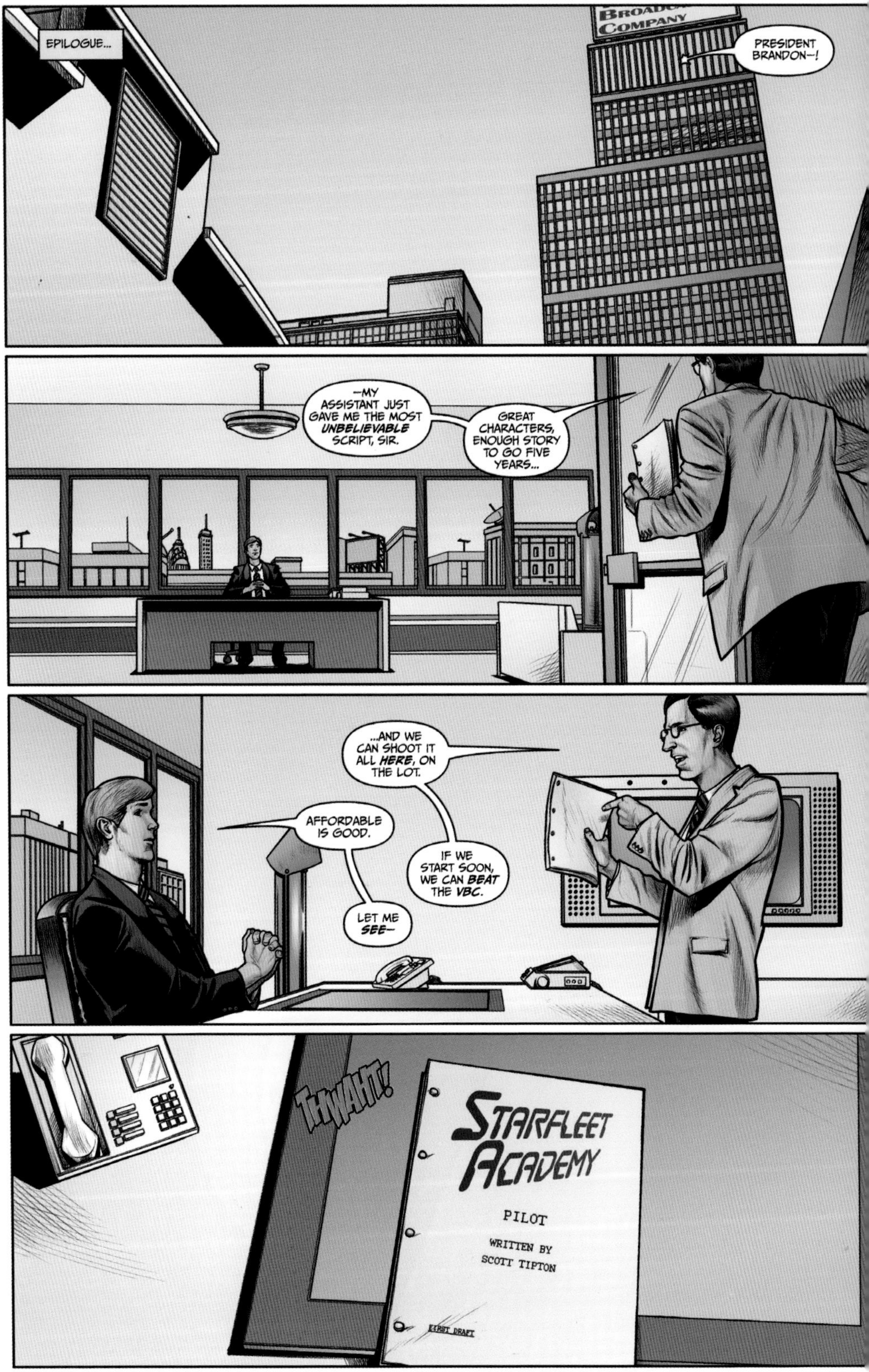
EPILOGUE...
BROADC... COMPANY
PRESIDENT BRANDON--!
--MY ASSISTANT JUST GAVE ME THE MOST *UNBELIEVABLE* SCRIPT, SIR.
GREAT CHARACTERS, ENOUGH STORY TO GO FIVE YEARS...
...AND WE CAN SHOOT IT ALL *HERE*, ON THE LOT.
AFFORDABLE IS GOOD.
IF WE START SOON, WE CAN *BEAT* THE *VBC*.
LET ME *SEE*--
THWAHT!
STARFLEET ACADEMY
PILOT
WRITTEN BY
SCOTT TIPTON
FIRST DRAFT

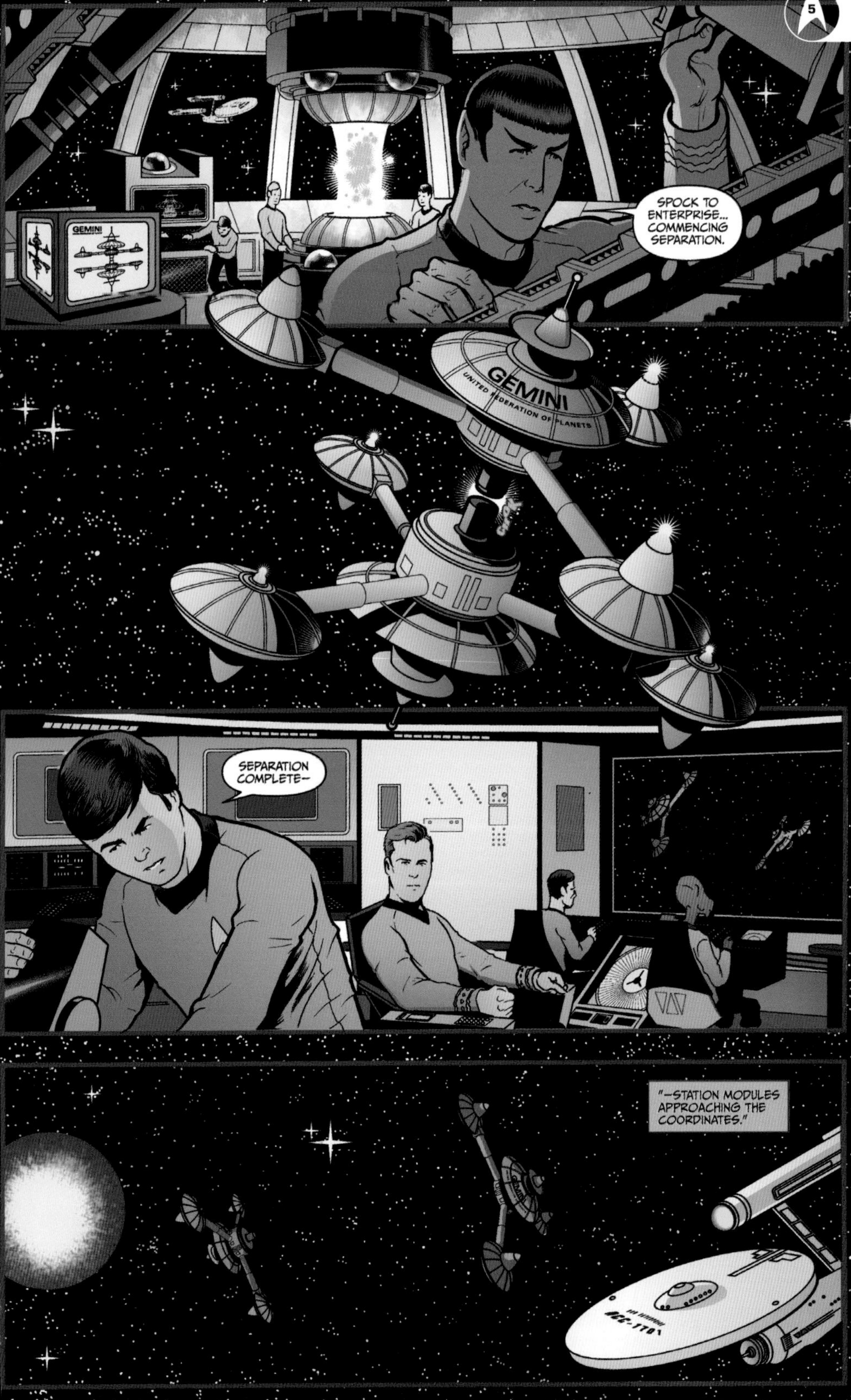
GEMINI
SPOCK TO ENTERPRISE... COMMENCING SEPARATION.
GEMINI
UNITED FEDERATION OF PLANETS
SEPARATION COMPLETE—
"—STATION MODULES APPROACHING THE COORDINATES."

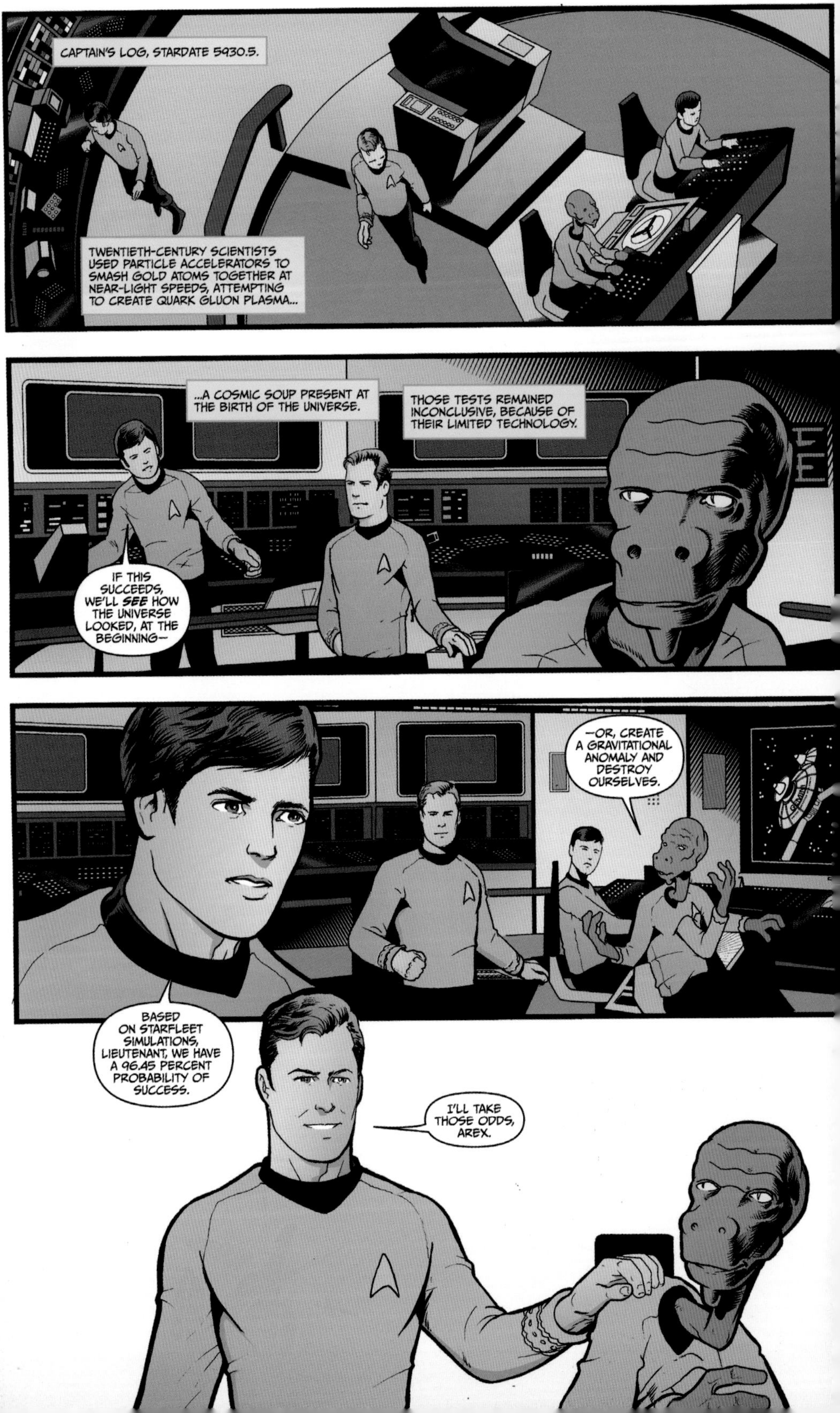
CAPTAIN'S LOG, STARDATE 5930.5.
TWENTIETH-CENTURY SCIENTISTS USED PARTICLE ACCELERATORS TO SMASH GOLD ATOMS TOGETHER AT NEAR-LIGHT SPEEDS, ATTEMPTING TO CREATE QUARK GLUON PLASMA...
...A COSMIC SOUP PRESENT AT THE BIRTH OF THE UNIVERSE.
THOSE TESTS REMAINED INCONCLUSIVE, BECAUSE OF THEIR LIMITED TECHNOLOGY.
IF THIS SUCCEEDS, WE'LL *SEE* HOW THE UNIVERSE LOOKED, AT THE BEGINNING—
—OR, CREATE A GRAVITATIONAL ANOMALY AND DESTROY OURSELVES.
BASED ON STARFLEET SIMULATIONS, LIEUTENANT, WE HAVE A 96.45 PERCENT PROBABILITY OF SUCCESS.
I'LL TAKE THOSE ODDS, AREX.

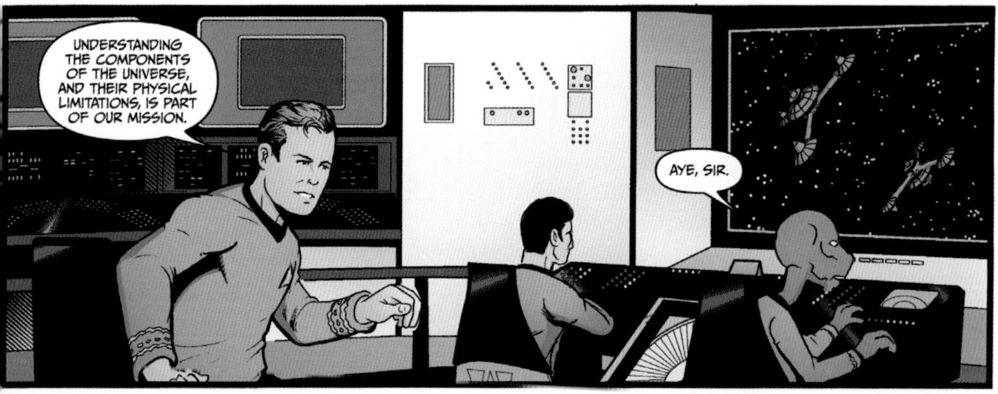

UNDERSTANDING THE COMPONENTS OF THE UNIVERSE, AND THEIR PHYSICAL LIMITATIONS, IS PART OF OUR MISSION.
AYE, SIR.

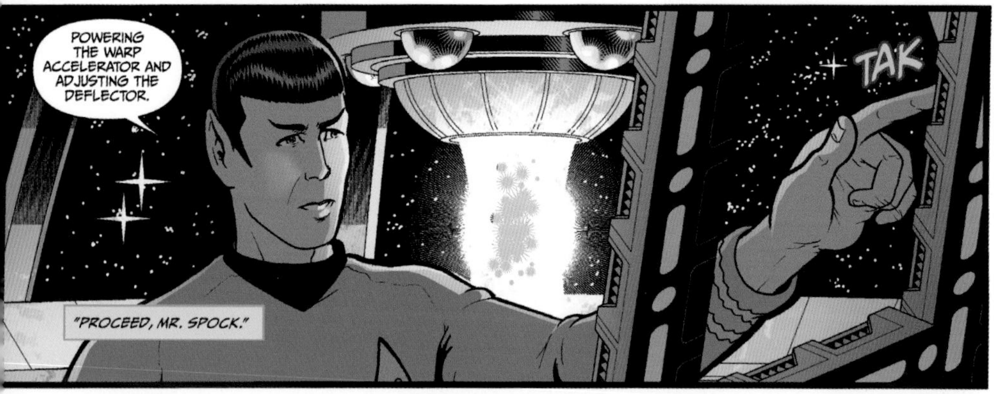

POWERING THE WARP ACCELERATOR AND ADJUSTING THE DEFLECTOR.
TAK
"PROCEED, MR. SPOCK."

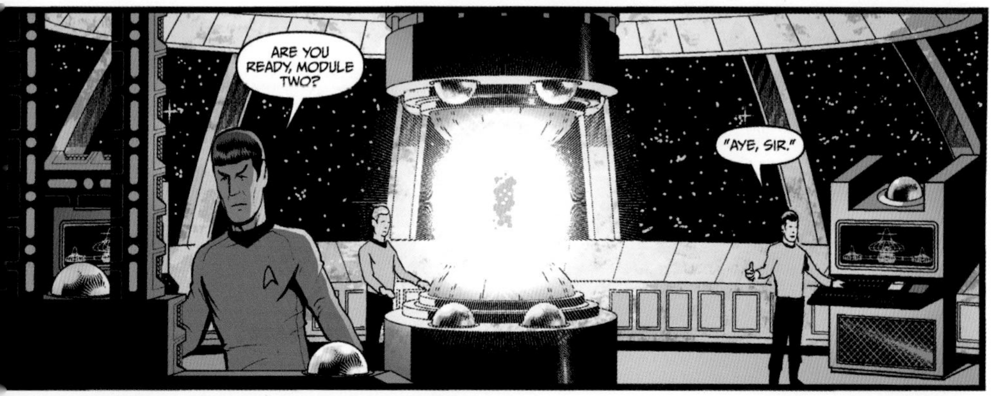

ARE YOU READY, MODULE TWO?
"AYE, SIR."

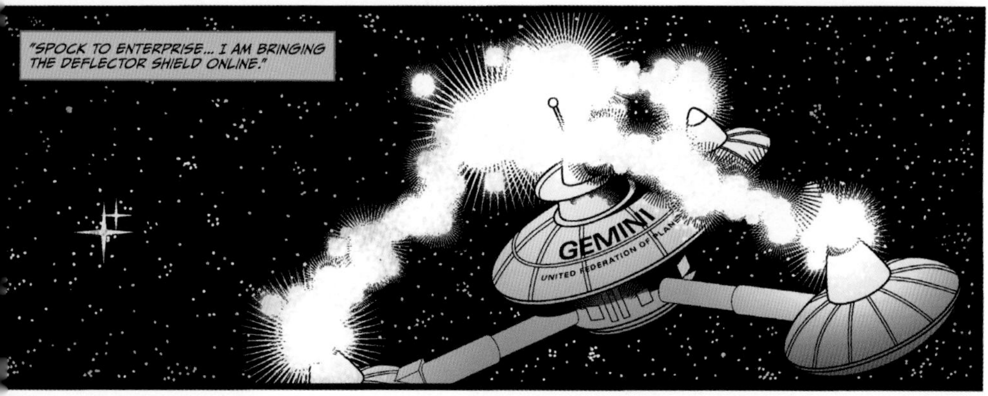

"SPOCK TO ENTERPRISE... I AM BRINGING THE DEFLECTOR SHIELD ONLINE."
GEMINI
UNITED FEDERATION OF PLANETS

ZZAAHHKK

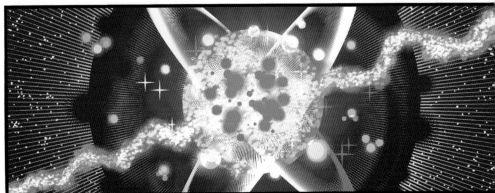

...IT'S BEAUTIFUL.

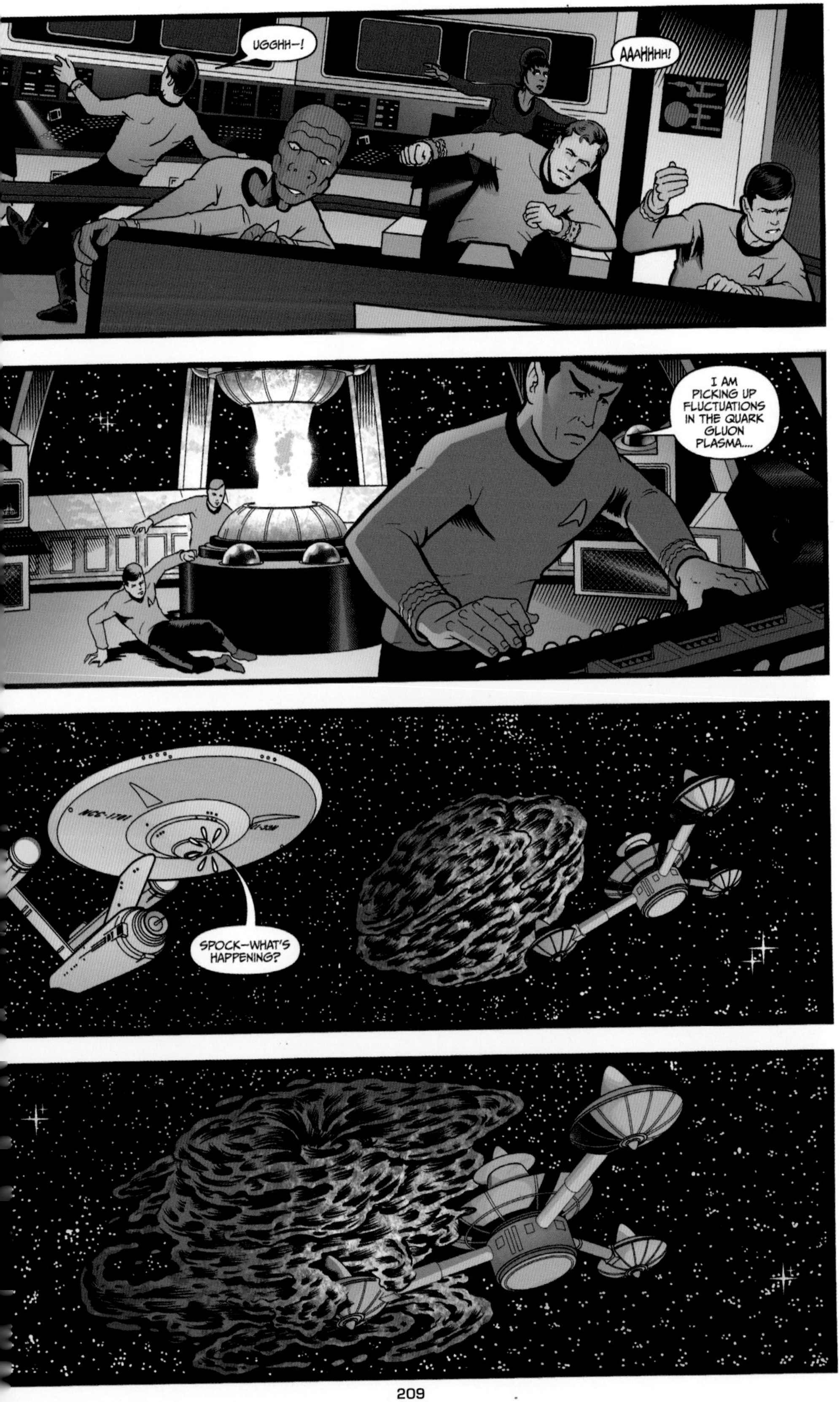
UGGHH—!
AAAHHHH!
I AM PICKING UP FLUCTUATIONS IN THE QUARK GLUON PLASMA....
NCC-1701
SPOCK—WHAT'S HAPPENING?

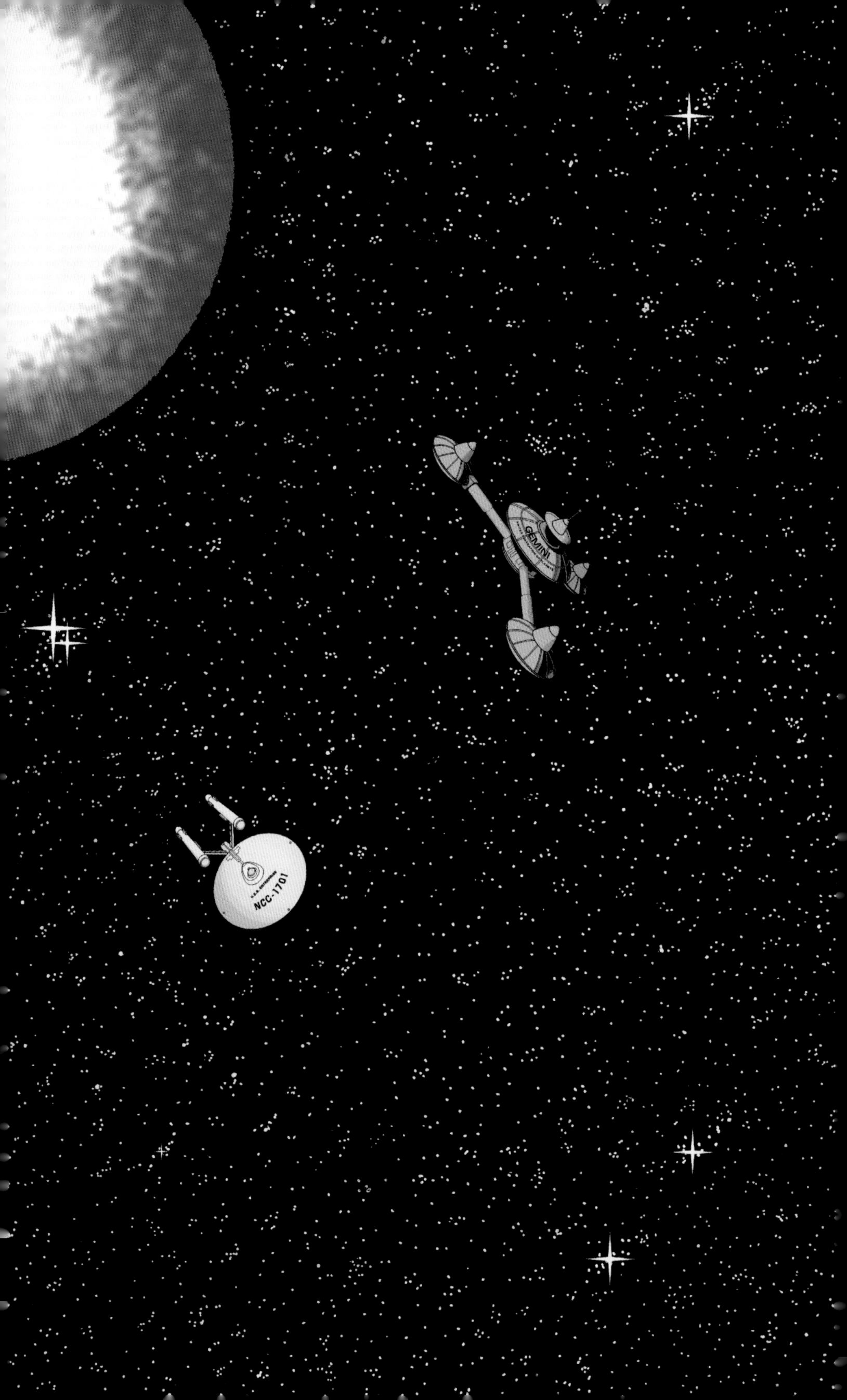
GEMINI
NCC-1701

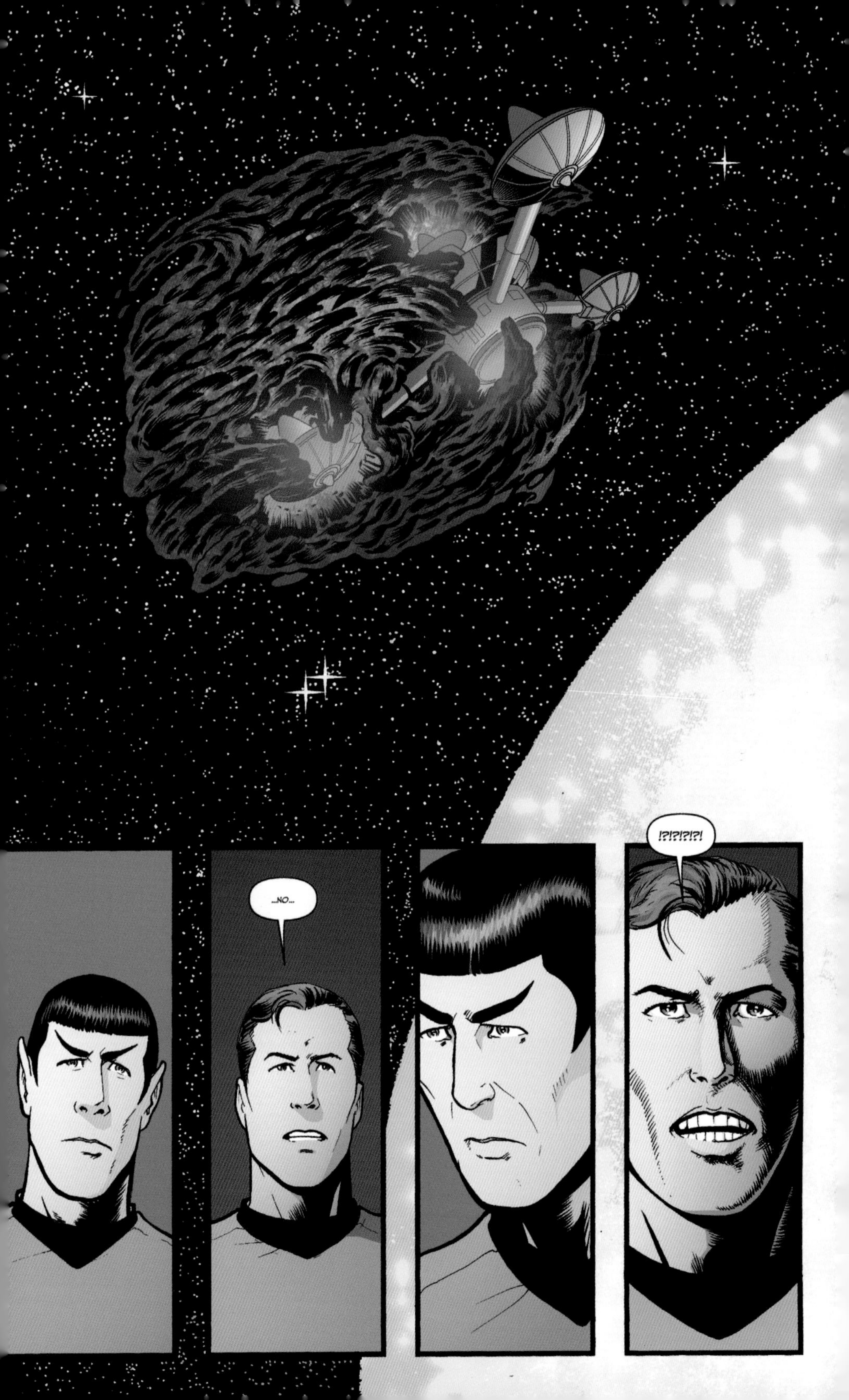
...NO...
!?!?!?!?!

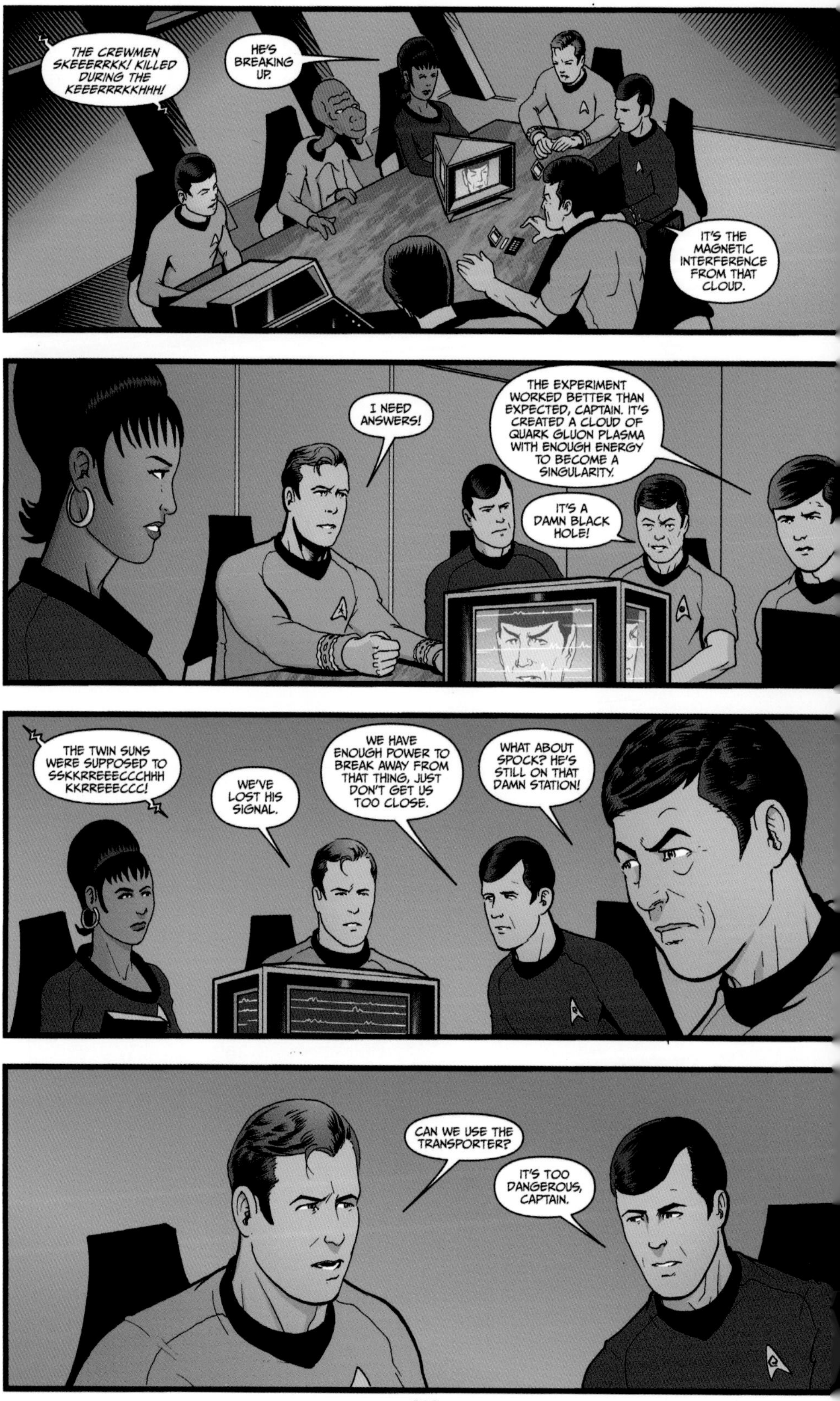
THE CREWMEN SKEEERRKK! KILLED DURING THE KEEERRRKKHHH!
HE'S BREAKING UP.
IT'S THE MAGNETIC INTERFERENCE FROM THAT CLOUD.
I NEED ANSWERS!
THE EXPERIMENT WORKED BETTER THAN EXPECTED, CAPTAIN. IT'S CREATED A CLOUD OF QUARK GLUON PLASMA WITH ENOUGH ENERGY TO BECOME A SINGULARITY.
IT'S A DAMN BLACK HOLE!
THE TWIN SUNS WERE SUPPOSED TO SSKKRREEECCCHHH KKRREEECCC!
WE'VE LOST HIS SIGNAL.
WE HAVE ENOUGH POWER TO BREAK AWAY FROM THAT THING, JUST DON'T GET US TOO CLOSE.
WHAT ABOUT SPOCK? HE'S STILL ON THAT DAMN STATION!
CAN WE USE THE TRANSPORTER?
IT'S TOO DANGEROUS, CAPTAIN.

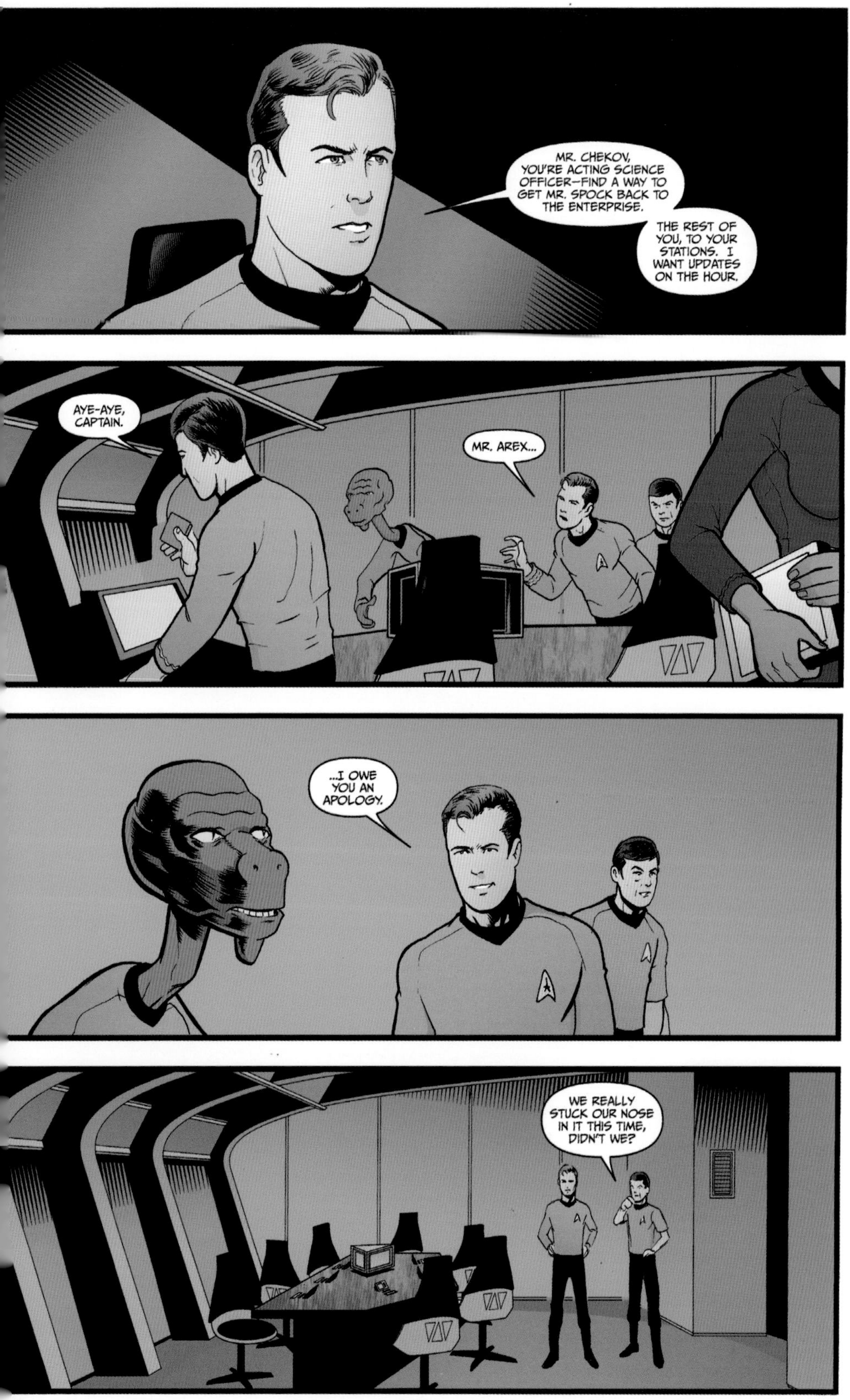
MR. CHEKOV, YOU'RE ACTING SCIENCE OFFICER—FIND A WAY TO GET MR. SPOCK BACK TO THE ENTERPRISE.
THE REST OF YOU, TO YOUR STATIONS. I WANT UPDATES ON THE HOUR.
AYE-AYE, CAPTAIN.
MR. AREX...
...I OWE YOU AN APOLOGY.
WE REALLY STUCK OUR NOSE IN IT THIS TIME, DIDN'T WE?

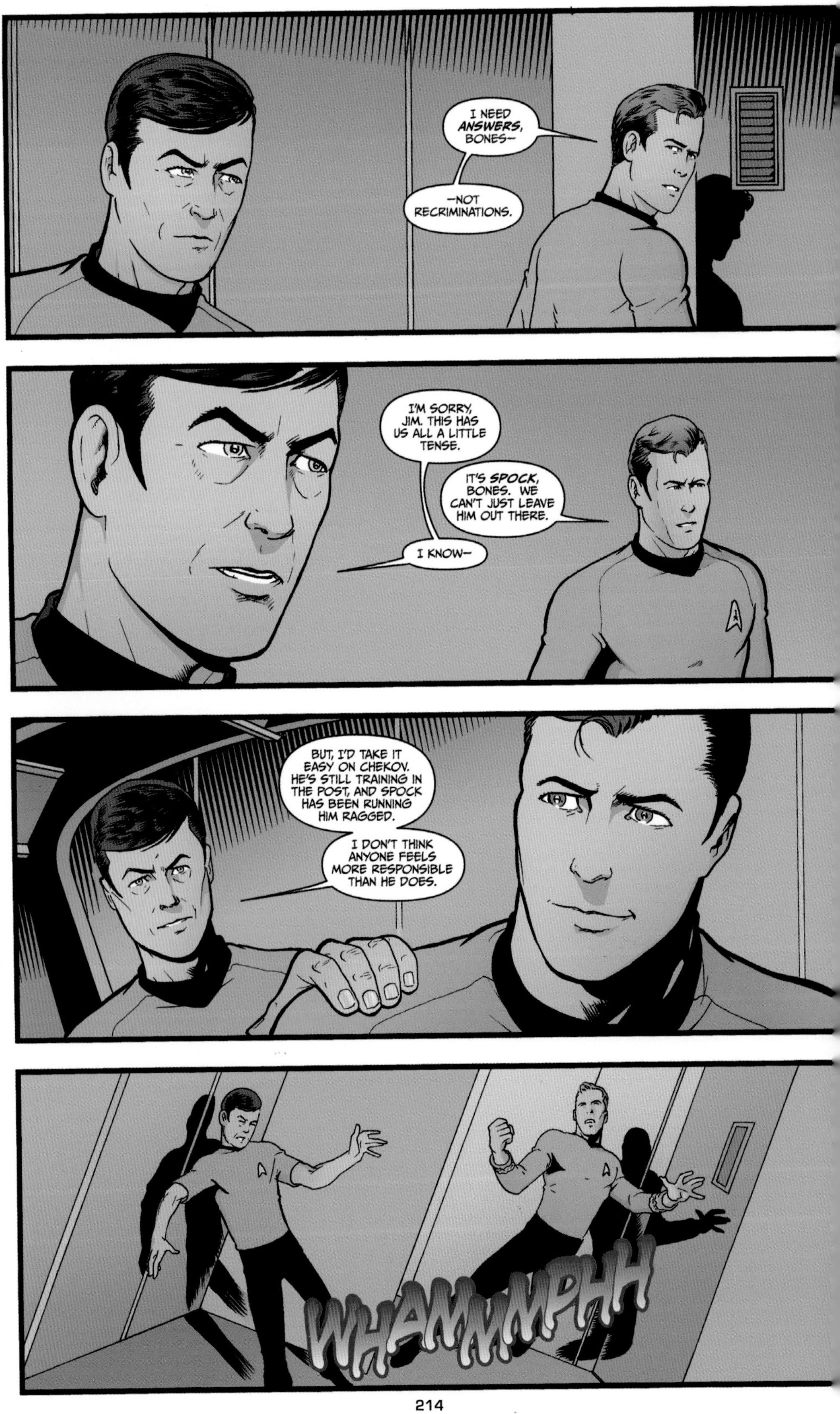
I NEED ANSWERS, BONES—
—NOT RECRIMINATIONS.
I'M SORRY, JIM. THIS HAS US ALL A LITTLE TENSE.
IT'S SPOCK, BONES. WE CAN'T JUST LEAVE HIM OUT THERE.
I KNOW—
BUT, I'D TAKE IT EASY ON CHEKOV. HE'S STILL TRAINING IN THE POST, AND SPOCK HAS BEEN RUNNING HIM RAGGED.
I DON'T THINK ANYONE FEELS MORE RESPONSIBLE THAN HE DOES.
WHAMMMPHH

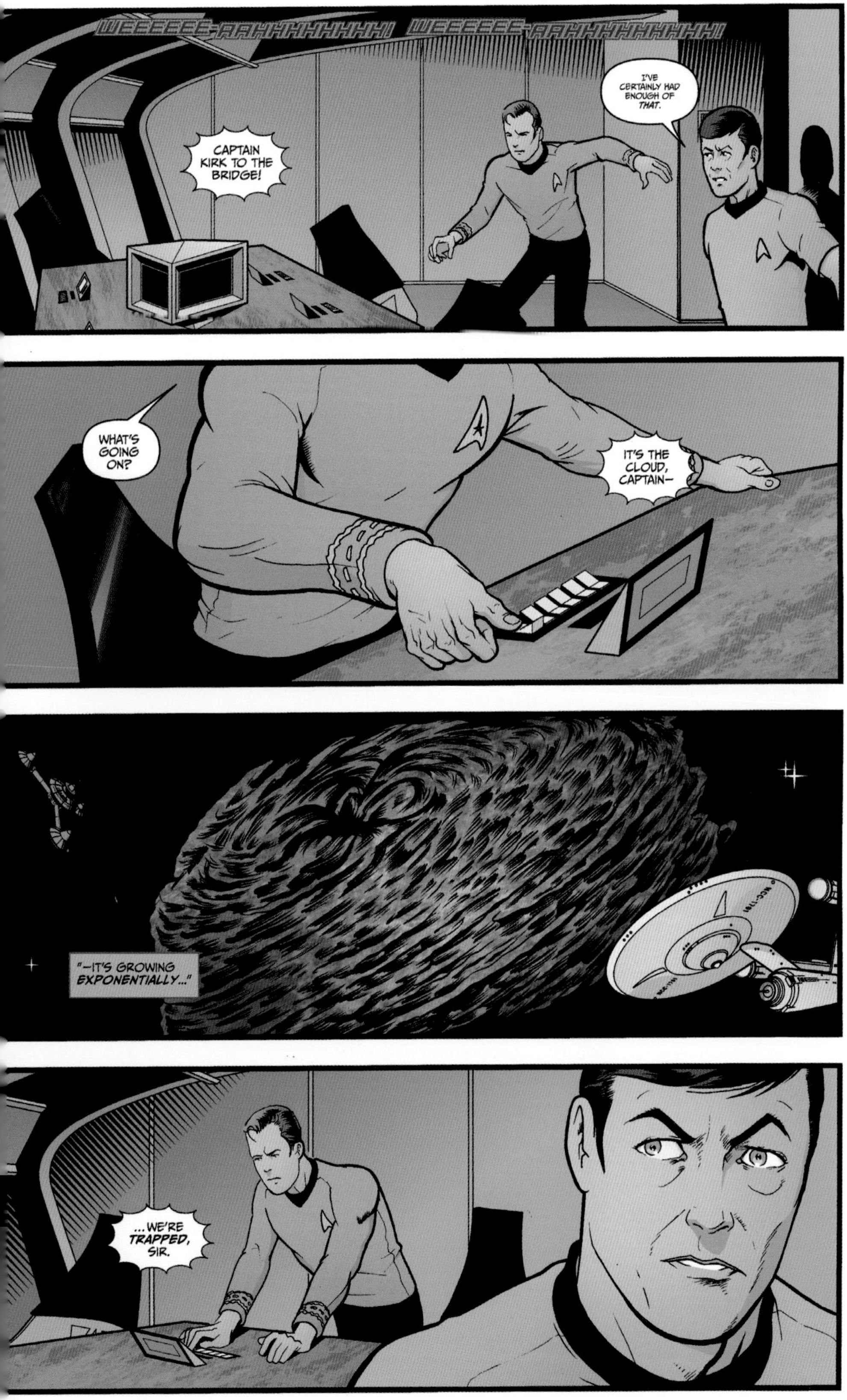
WEEEEEE-AAHHHHHHHH! WEEEEEE-AAHHHHHHHH!
CAPTAIN KIRK TO THE BRIDGE!
I'VE CERTAINLY HAD ENOUGH OF THAT.
WHAT'S GOING ON?
IT'S THE CLOUD, CAPTAIN–
"–IT'S GROWING EXPONENTIALLY..."
...WE'RE TRAPPED, SIR.

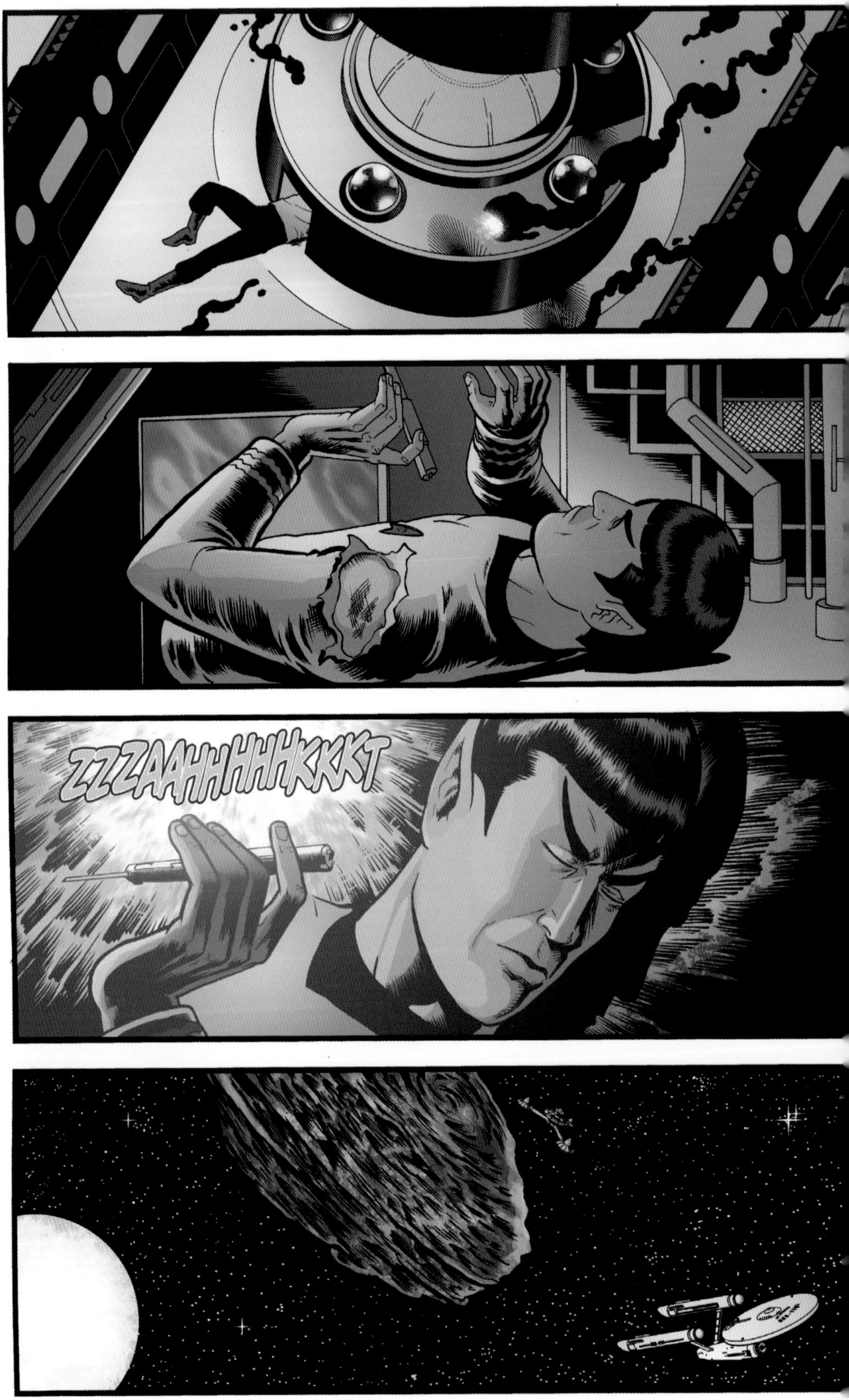
ZZZAAHHHHHKKKT

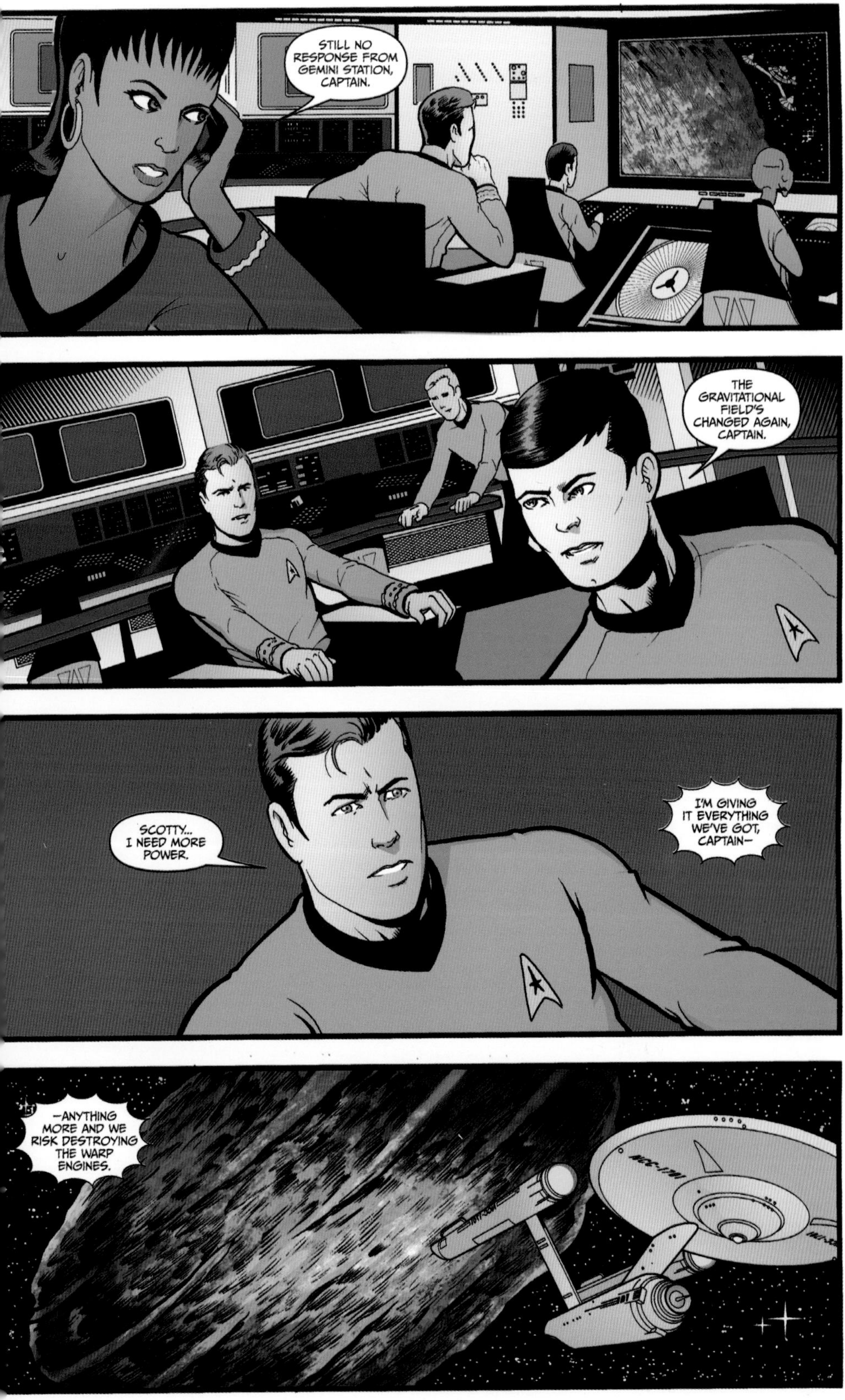
STILL NO RESPONSE FROM GEMINI STATION, CAPTAIN.
THE GRAVITATIONAL FIELD'S CHANGED AGAIN, CAPTAIN.
SCOTTY... I NEED MORE POWER.
I'M GIVING IT EVERYTHING WE'VE GOT, CAPTAIN—
—ANYTHING MORE AND WE RISK DESTROYING THE WARP ENGINES.

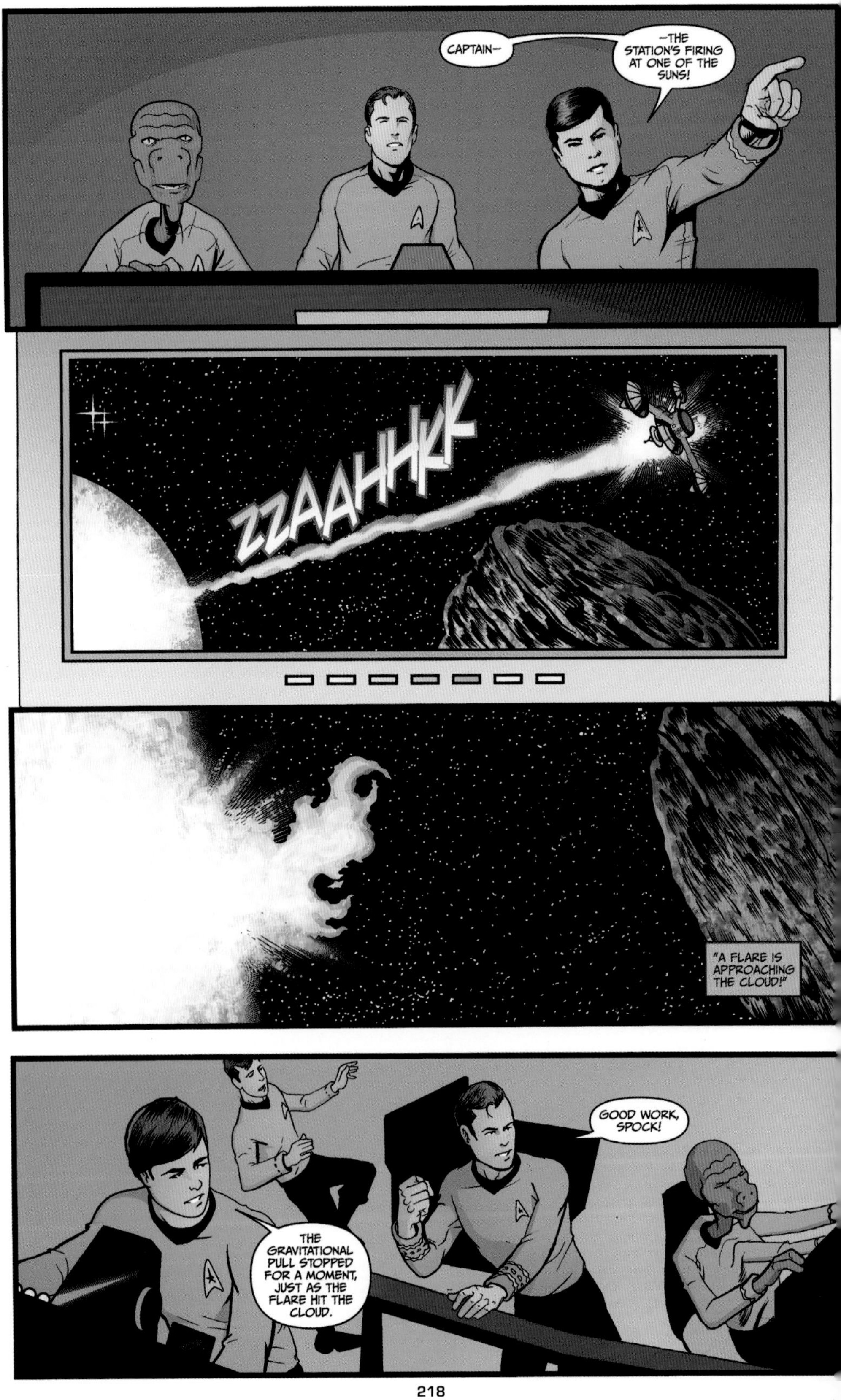

CAPTAIN—
—THE STATION'S FIRING AT ONE OF THE SUNS!
ZZAAHHKK
"A FLARE IS APPROACHING THE CLOUD!"
GOOD WORK, SPOCK!
THE GRAVITATIONAL PULL STOPPED FOR A MOMENT, JUST AS THE FLARE HIT THE CLOUD.

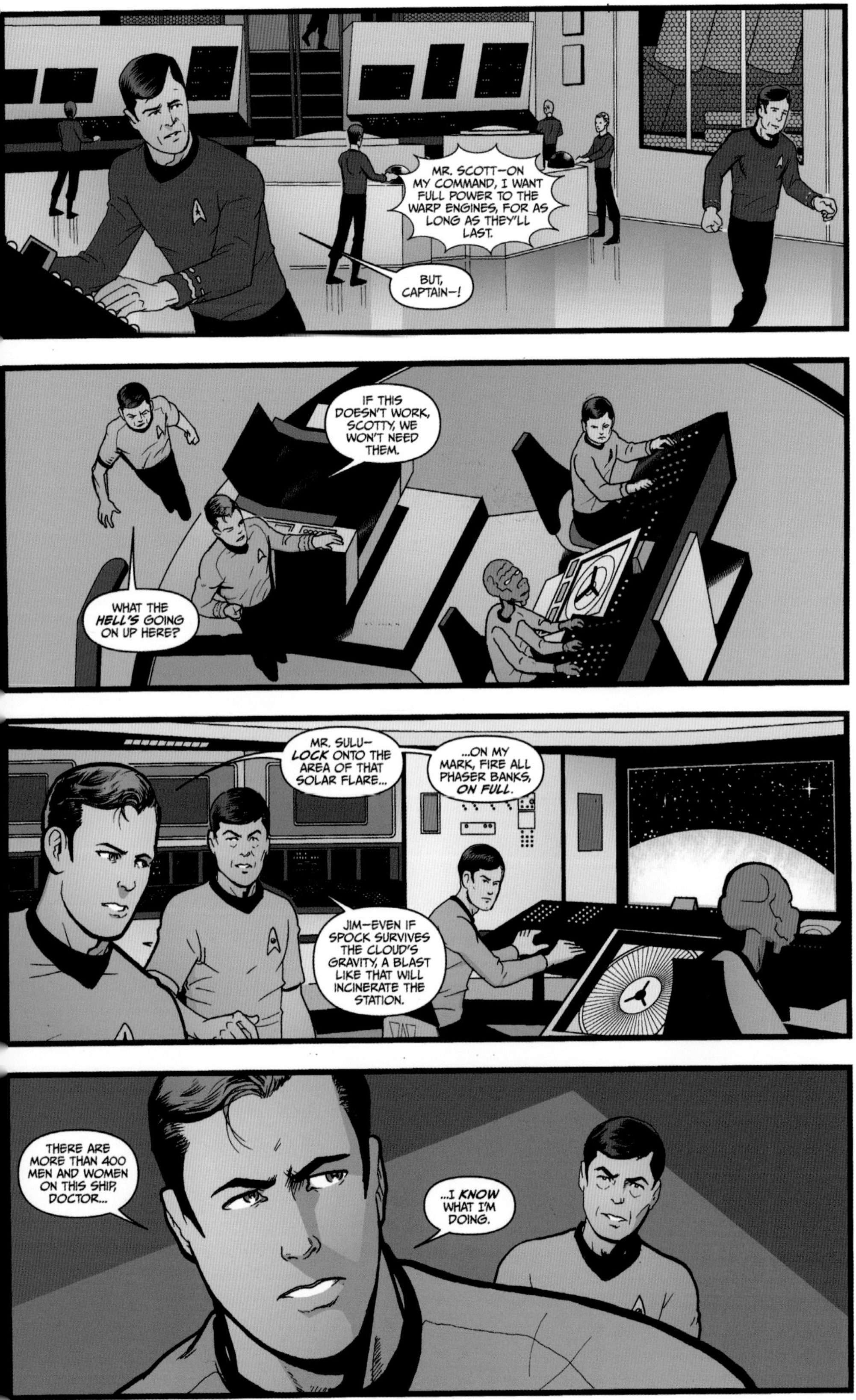
MR. SCOTT—ON MY COMMAND, I WANT FULL POWER TO THE WARP ENGINES, FOR AS LONG AS THEY'LL LAST.
BUT, CAPTAIN—!
IF THIS DOESN'T WORK, SCOTTY, WE WON'T NEED THEM.
WHAT THE *HELL'S* GOING ON UP HERE?
MR. SULU— *LOCK* ONTO THE AREA OF THAT SOLAR FLARE...
...ON MY MARK, FIRE ALL PHASER BANKS, *ON FULL*.
JIM—EVEN IF SPOCK SURVIVES THE CLOUD'S GRAVITY, A BLAST LIKE THAT WILL INCINERATE THE STATION.
THERE ARE MORE THAN 400 MEN AND WOMEN ON THIS SHIP, DOCTOR...
...I *KNOW* WHAT I'M DOING.

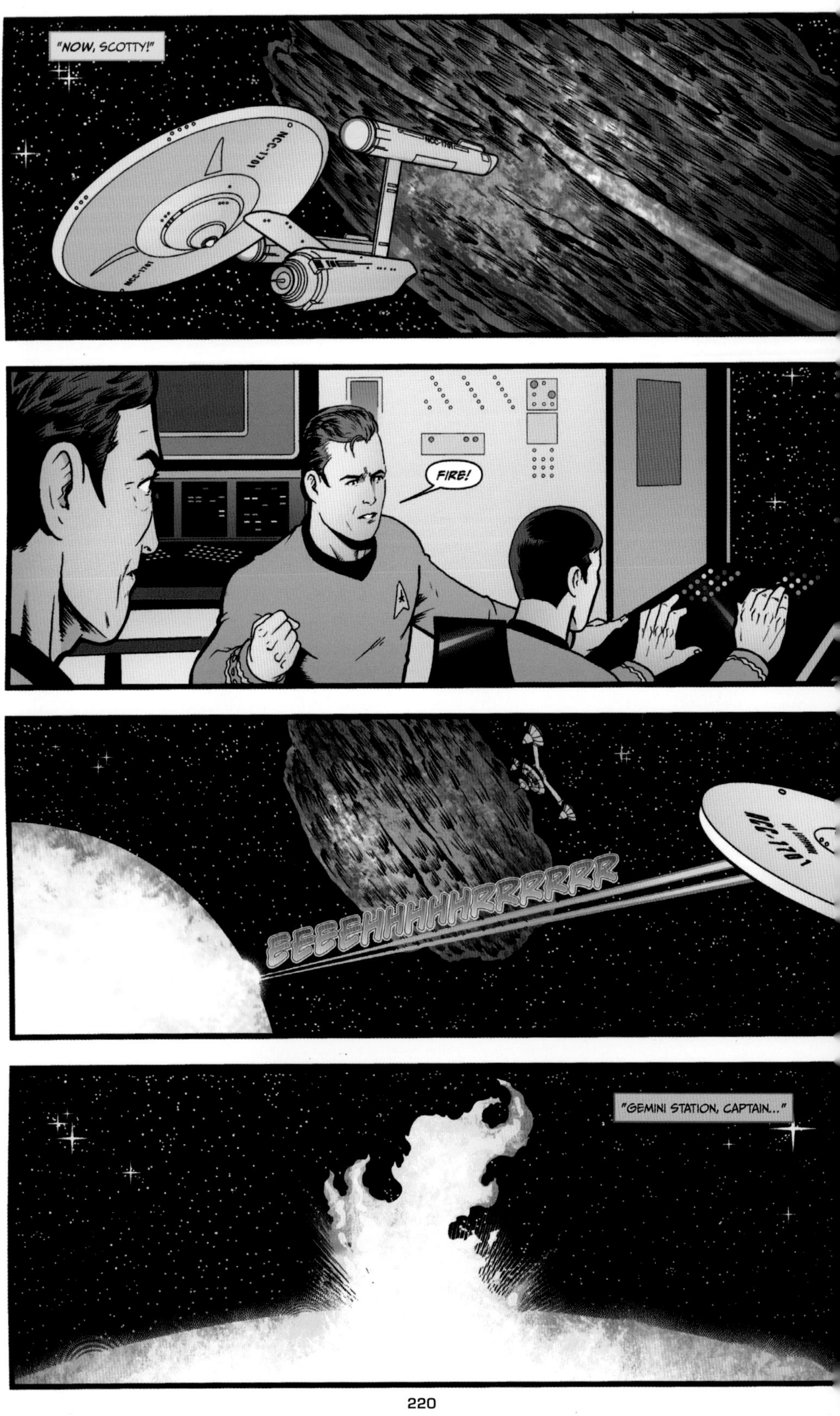
"NOW, SCOTTY!"
FIRE!
EEEEHHHHHRRRRRR
"GEMINI STATION, CAPTAIN..."

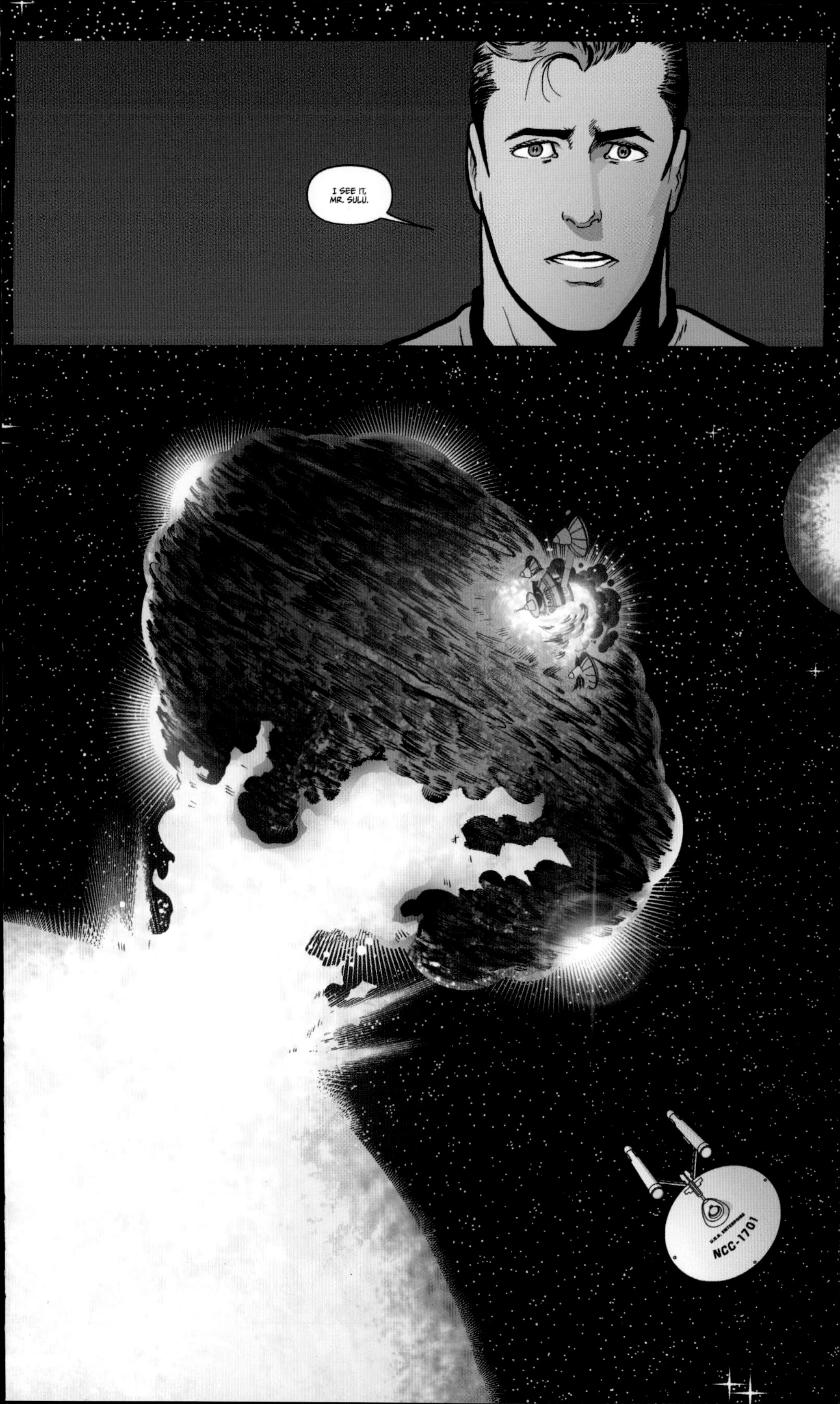
I SEE IT, MR. SULU.
NCC-1701

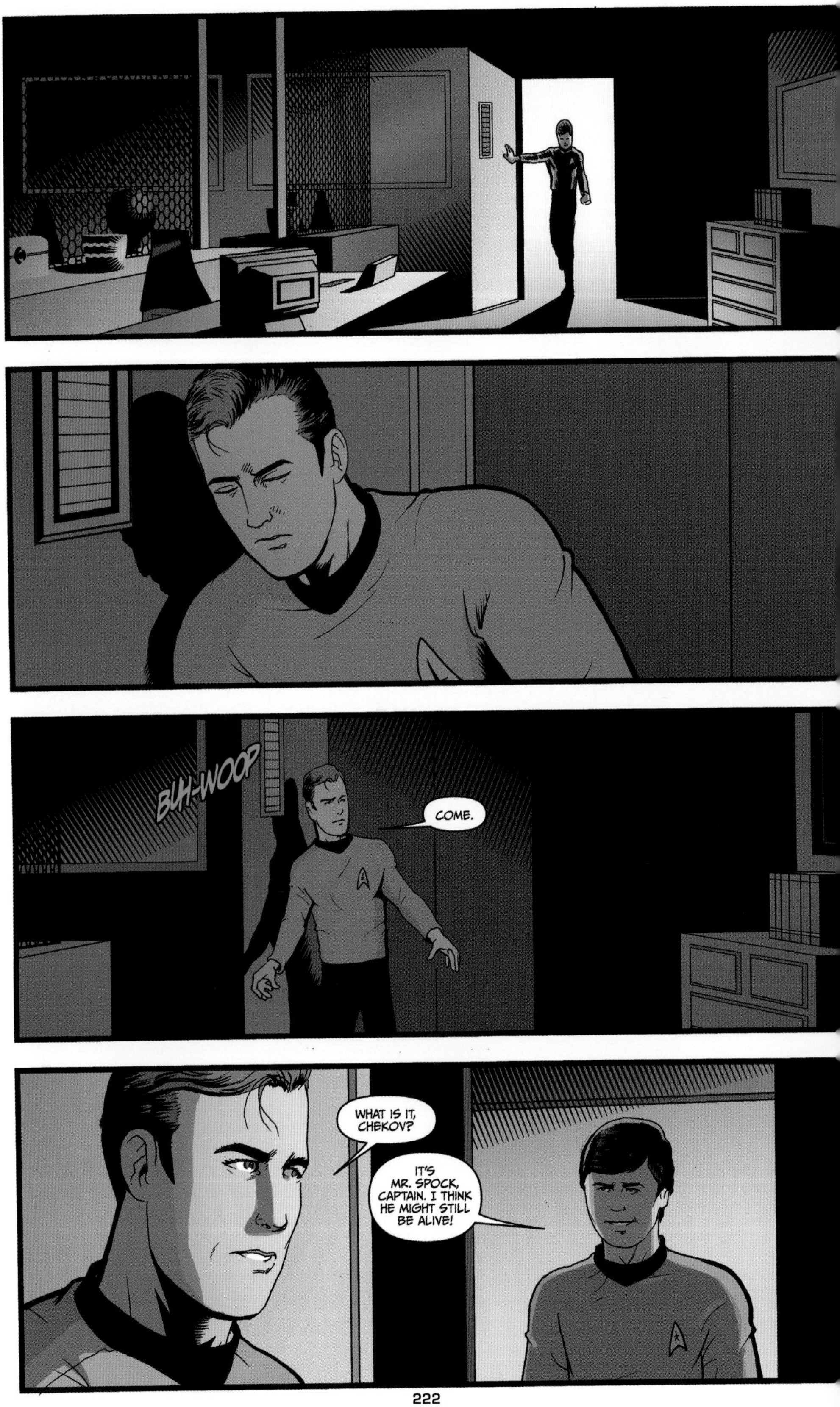
BUH-WOOP
COME.
WHAT IS IT, CHEKOV?
IT'S MR. SPOCK, CAPTAIN. I THINK HE MIGHT STILL BE ALIVE!

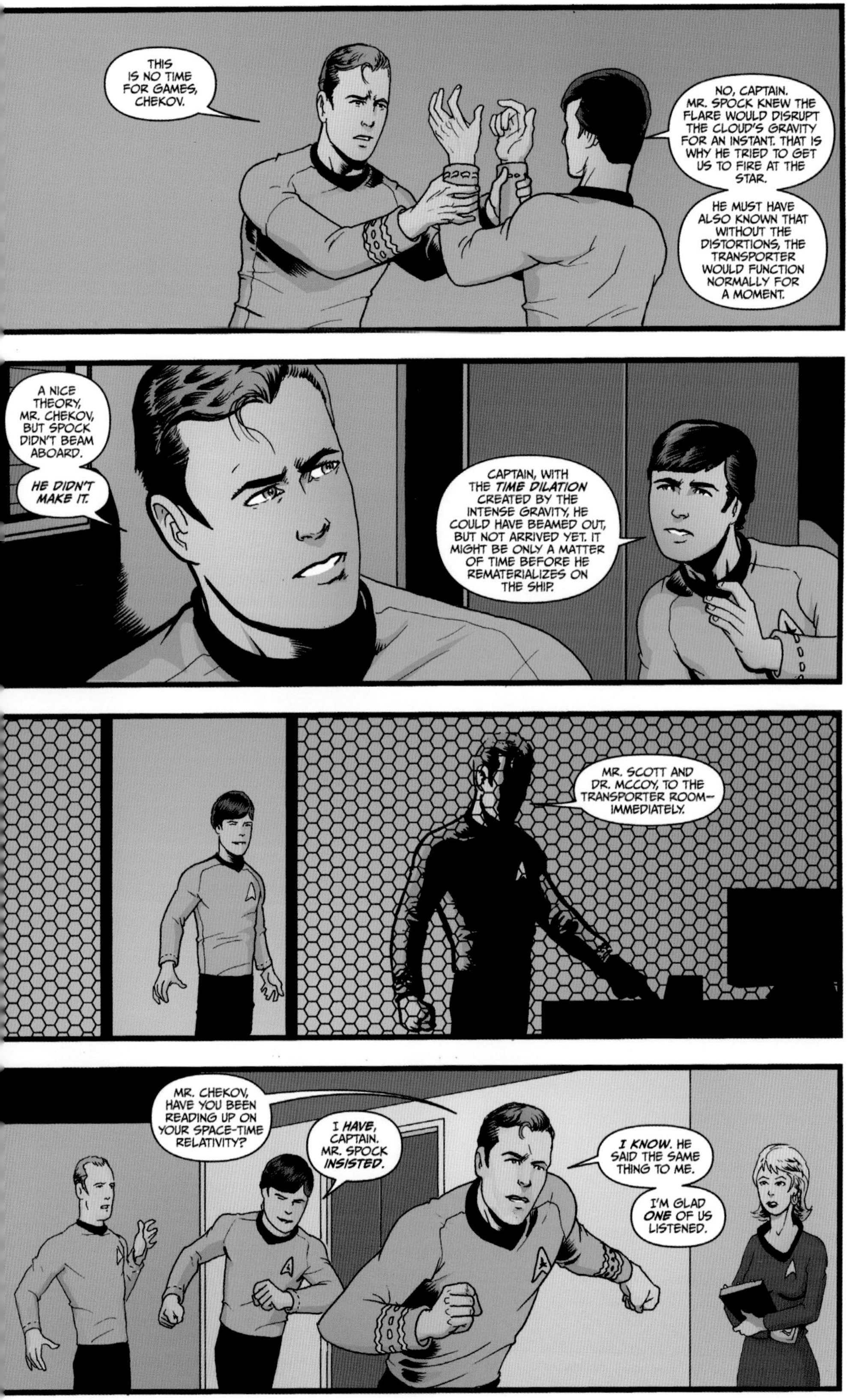

THIS IS NO TIME FOR GAMES, CHEKOV.
NO, CAPTAIN. MR. SPOCK KNEW THE FLARE WOULD DISRUPT THE CLOUD'S GRAVITY FOR AN INSTANT. THAT IS WHY HE TRIED TO GET US TO FIRE AT THE STAR.
HE MUST HAVE ALSO KNOWN THAT WITHOUT THE DISTORTIONS, THE TRANSPORTER WOULD FUNCTION NORMALLY FOR A MOMENT.
A NICE THEORY, MR. CHEKOV, BUT SPOCK DIDN'T BEAM ABOARD.
HE DIDN'T MAKE IT.
CAPTAIN, WITH THE *TIME DILATION* CREATED BY THE INTENSE GRAVITY, HE COULD HAVE BEAMED OUT, BUT NOT ARRIVED YET. IT MIGHT BE ONLY A MATTER OF TIME BEFORE HE REMATERIALIZES ON THE SHIP.
MR. SCOTT AND DR. MCCOY, TO THE TRANSPORTER ROOM— IMMEDIATELY.
MR. CHEKOV, HAVE YOU BEEN READING UP ON YOUR SPACE-TIME RELATIVITY?
I *HAVE*, CAPTAIN. MR. SPOCK *INSISTED*.
I KNOW. HE SAID THE SAME THING TO ME.
I'M GLAD *ONE* OF US LISTENED.

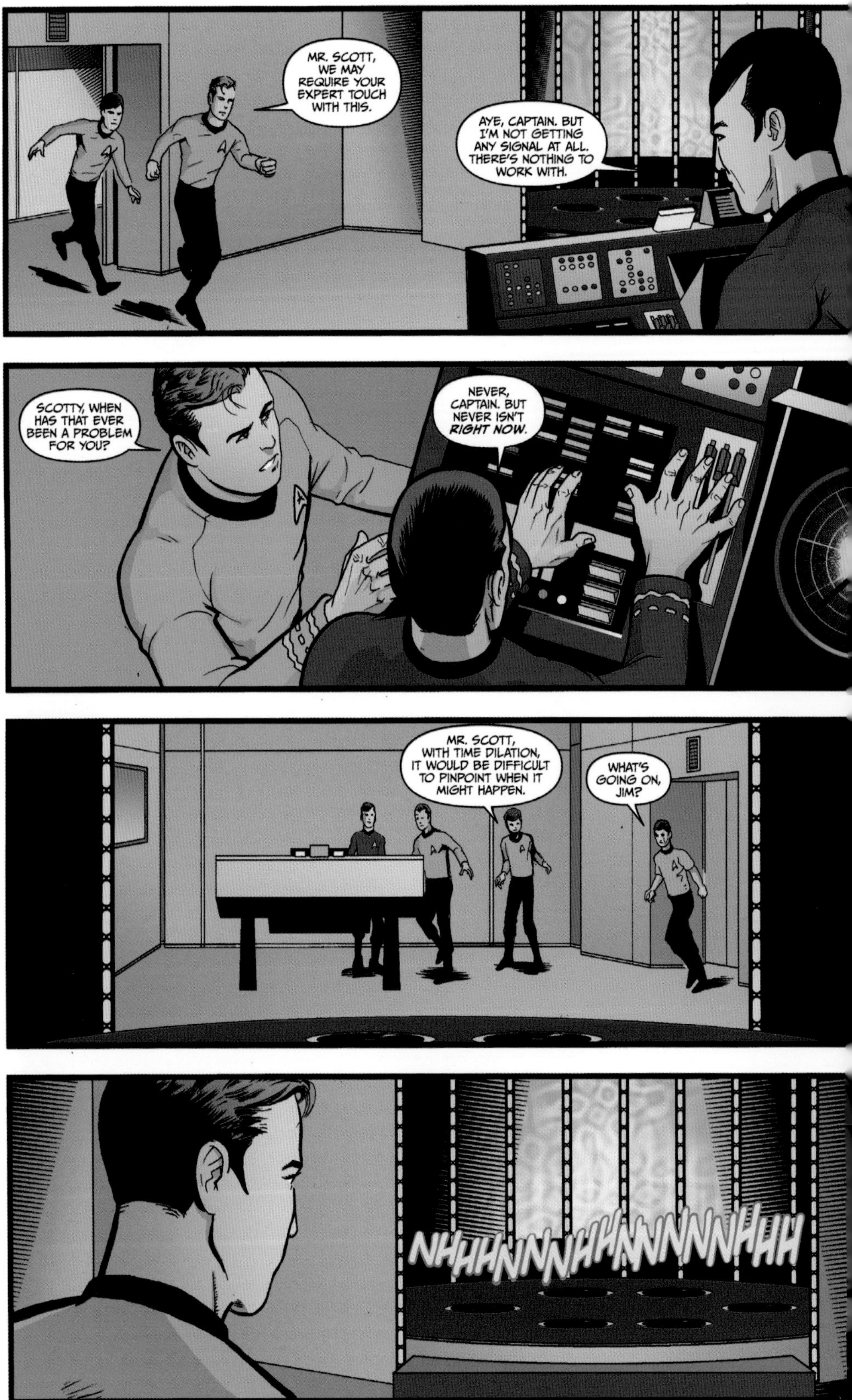
MR. SCOTT, WE MAY REQUIRE YOUR EXPERT TOUCH WITH THIS.
AYE, CAPTAIN. BUT I'M NOT GETTING ANY SIGNAL AT ALL. THERE'S NOTHING TO WORK WITH.
SCOTTY, WHEN HAS THAT EVER BEEN A PROBLEM FOR YOU?
NEVER, CAPTAIN. BUT NEVER ISN'T *RIGHT NOW*.
MR. SCOTT, WITH TIME DILATION, IT WOULD BE DIFFICULT TO PINPOINT WHEN IT MIGHT HAPPEN.
WHAT'S GOING ON, JIM?
NHHHNNNNHHHNNNNHHH

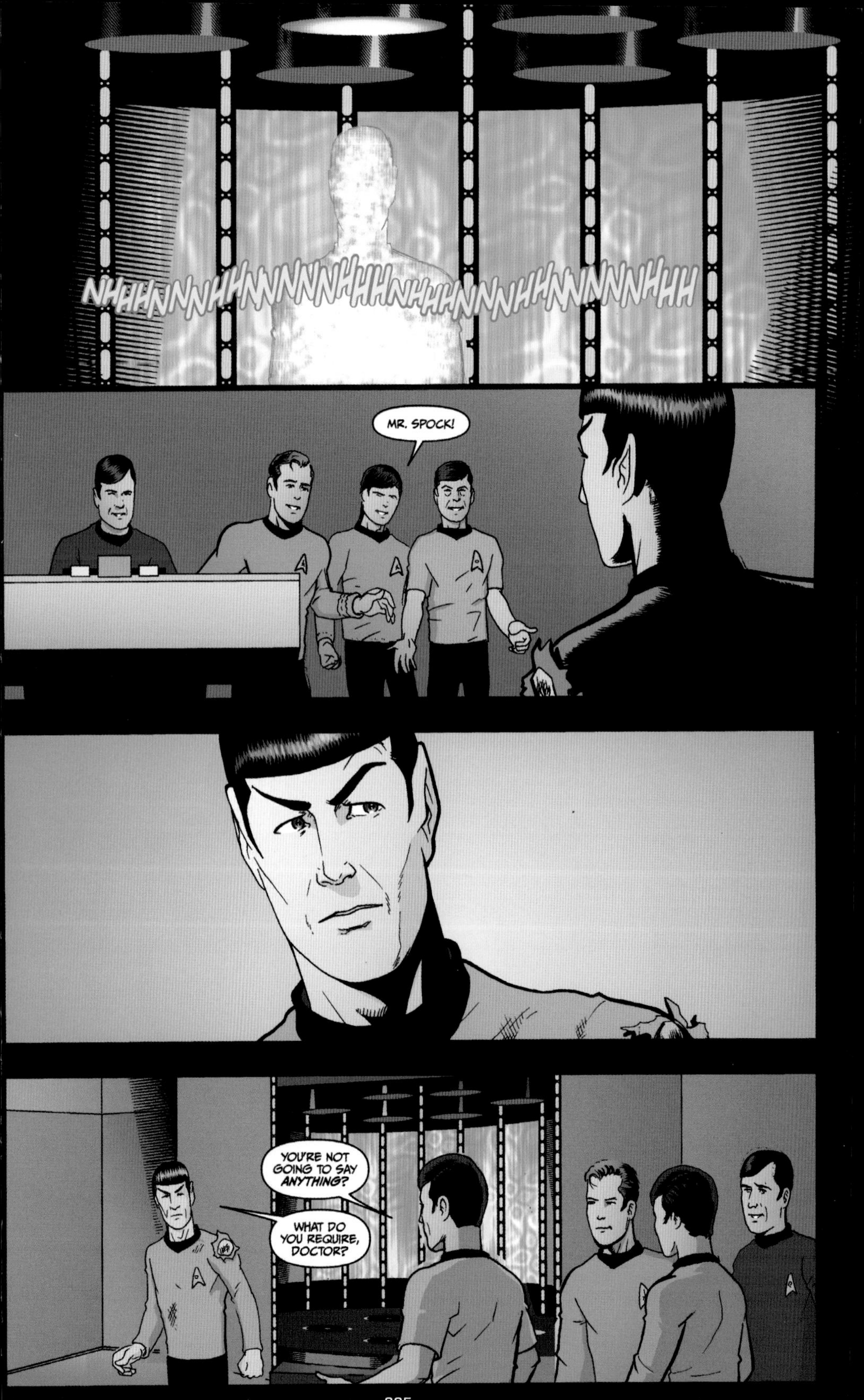
NHHHNNNHHNNNNNHHHHNHHHHNNNHHHNNNNNHHH
MR. SPOCK!
YOU'RE NOT GOING TO SAY *ANYTHING?*
WHAT DO YOU REQUIRE, DOCTOR?

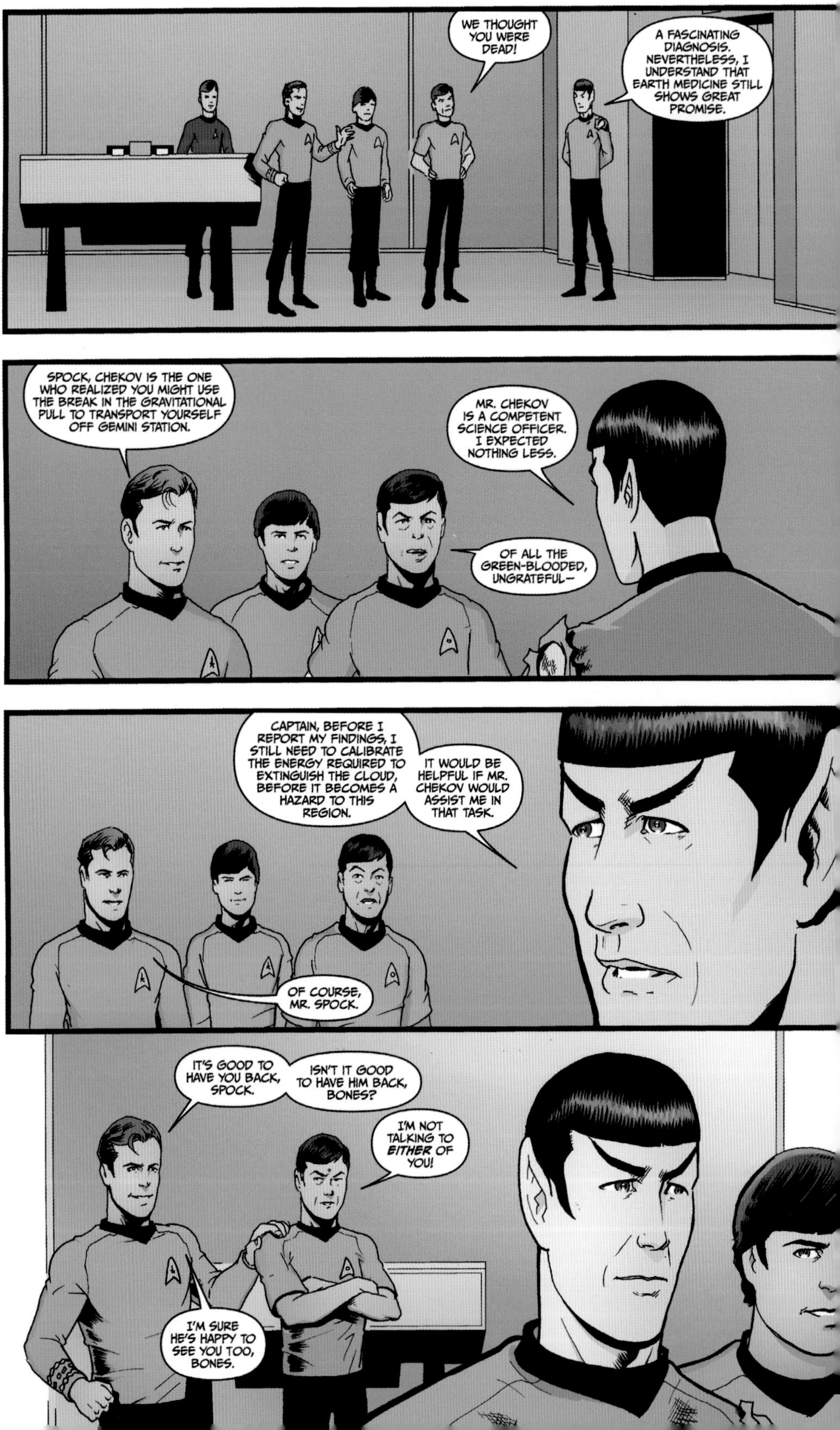
WE THOUGHT YOU WERE DEAD!
A FASCINATING DIAGNOSIS. NEVERTHELESS, I UNDERSTAND THAT EARTH MEDICINE STILL SHOWS GREAT PROMISE.
SPOCK, CHEKOV IS THE ONE WHO REALIZED YOU MIGHT USE THE BREAK IN THE GRAVITATIONAL PULL TO TRANSPORT YOURSELF OFF GEMINI STATION.
MR. CHEKOV IS A COMPETENT SCIENCE OFFICER. I EXPECTED NOTHING LESS.
OF ALL THE GREEN-BLOODED, UNGRATEFUL--
CAPTAIN, BEFORE I REPORT MY FINDINGS, I STILL NEED TO CALIBRATE THE ENERGY REQUIRED TO EXTINGUISH THE CLOUD, BEFORE IT BECOMES A HAZARD TO THIS REGION.
IT WOULD BE HELPFUL IF MR. CHEKOV WOULD ASSIST ME IN THAT TASK.
OF COURSE, MR. SPOCK.
IT'S GOOD TO HAVE YOU BACK, SPOCK.
ISN'T IT GOOD TO HAVE HIM BACK, BONES?
I'M NOT TALKING TO *EITHER* OF YOU!
I'M SURE HE'S HAPPY TO SEE YOU TOO, BONES.

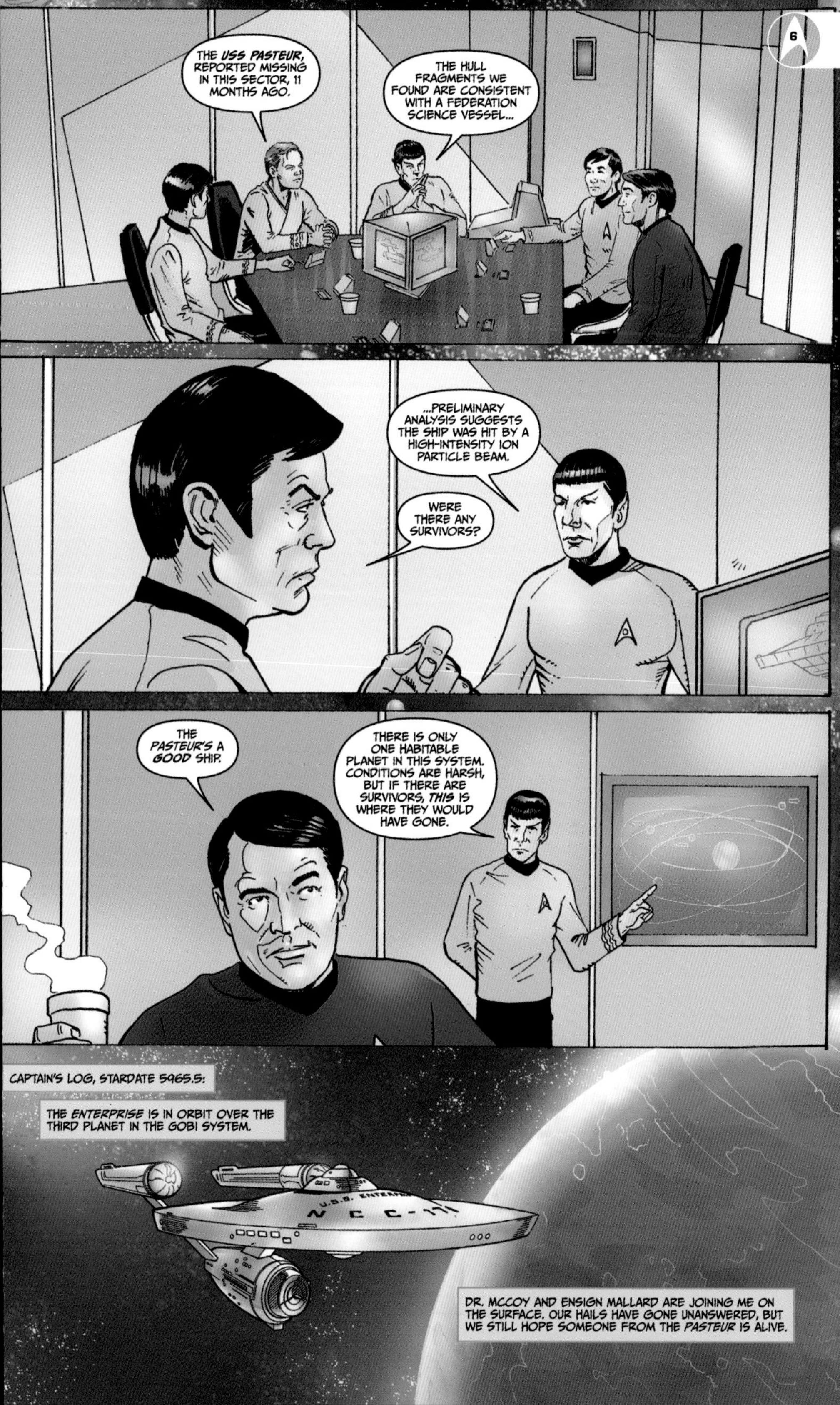
THE *USS PASTEUR*, REPORTED MISSING IN THIS SECTOR, 11 MONTHS AGO.
THE HULL FRAGMENTS WE FOUND ARE CONSISTENT WITH A FEDERATION SCIENCE VESSEL...
...PRELIMINARY ANALYSIS SUGGESTS THE SHIP WAS HIT BY A HIGH-INTENSITY ION PARTICLE BEAM.
WERE THERE ANY SURVIVORS?
THE *PASTEUR'S* A *GOOD* SHIP.
THERE IS ONLY ONE HABITABLE PLANET IN THIS SYSTEM. CONDITIONS ARE HARSH, BUT IF THERE ARE SURVIVORS, *THIS* IS WHERE THEY WOULD HAVE GONE.
CAPTAIN'S LOG, STARDATE 5965.5:
THE *ENTERPRISE* IS IN ORBIT OVER THE THIRD PLANET IN THE GOBI SYSTEM.
U.S.S. ENTERPRISE
NCC-1701
DR. MCCOY AND ENSIGN MALLARD ARE JOINING ME ON THE SURFACE. OUR HAILS HAVE GONE UNANSWERED, BUT WE STILL HOPE SOMEONE FROM THE *PASTEUR* IS ALIVE.

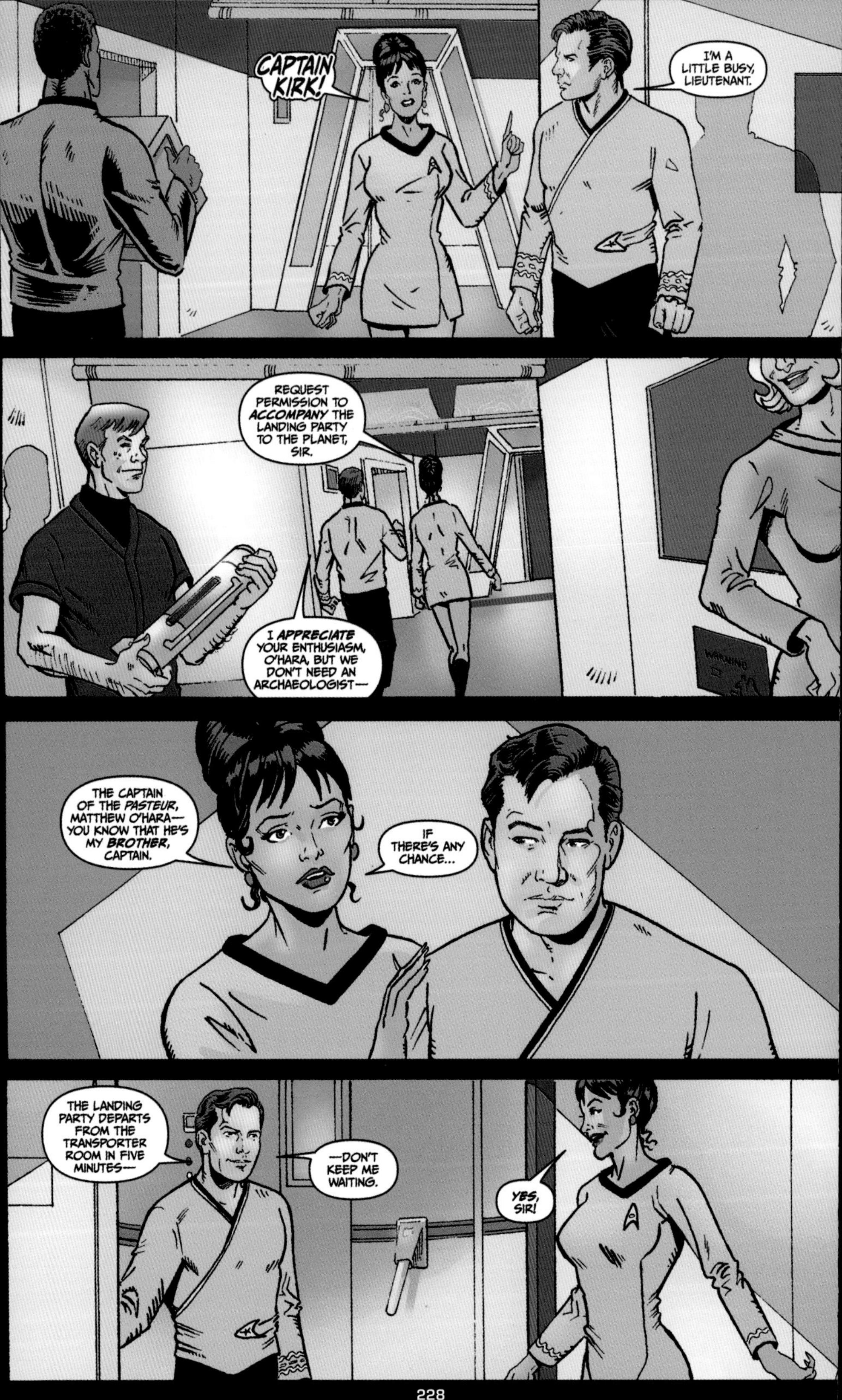
CAPTAIN KIRK!
I'M A LITTLE BUSY, LIEUTENANT.
REQUEST PERMISSION TO ACCOMPANY THE LANDING PARTY TO THE PLANET, SIR.
I APPRECIATE YOUR ENTHUSIASM, O'HARA, BUT WE DON'T NEED AN ARCHAEOLOGIST—
WARNING
THE CAPTAIN OF THE PASTEUR, MATTHEW O'HARA— YOU KNOW THAT HE'S MY BROTHER, CAPTAIN.
IF THERE'S ANY CHANCE...
THE LANDING PARTY DEPARTS FROM THE TRANSPORTER ROOM IN FIVE MINUTES—
—DON'T KEEP ME WAITING.
YES, SIR!

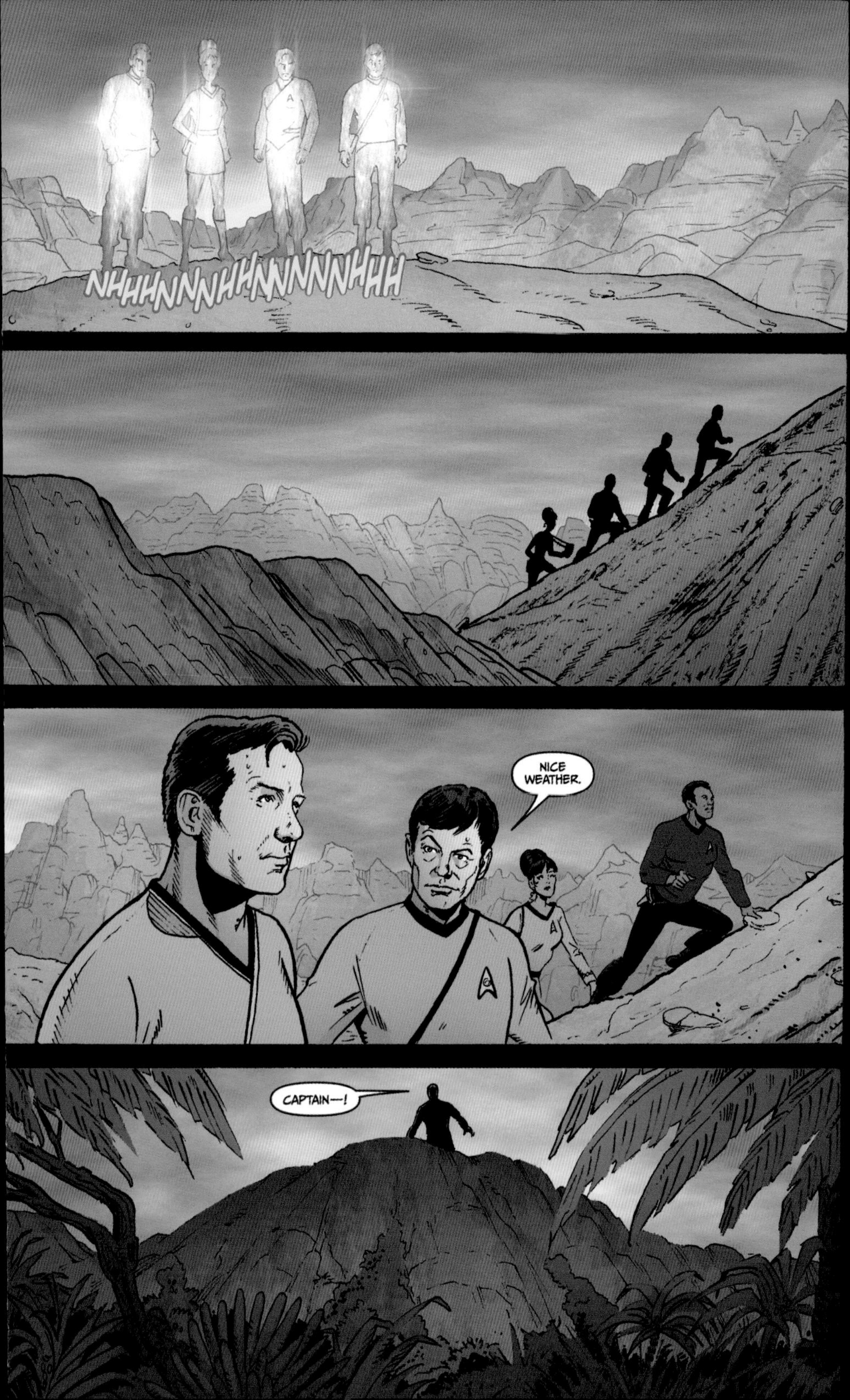
NHHHNNNNHHNNNNNHHH
NICE WEATHER.
CAPTAIN--!

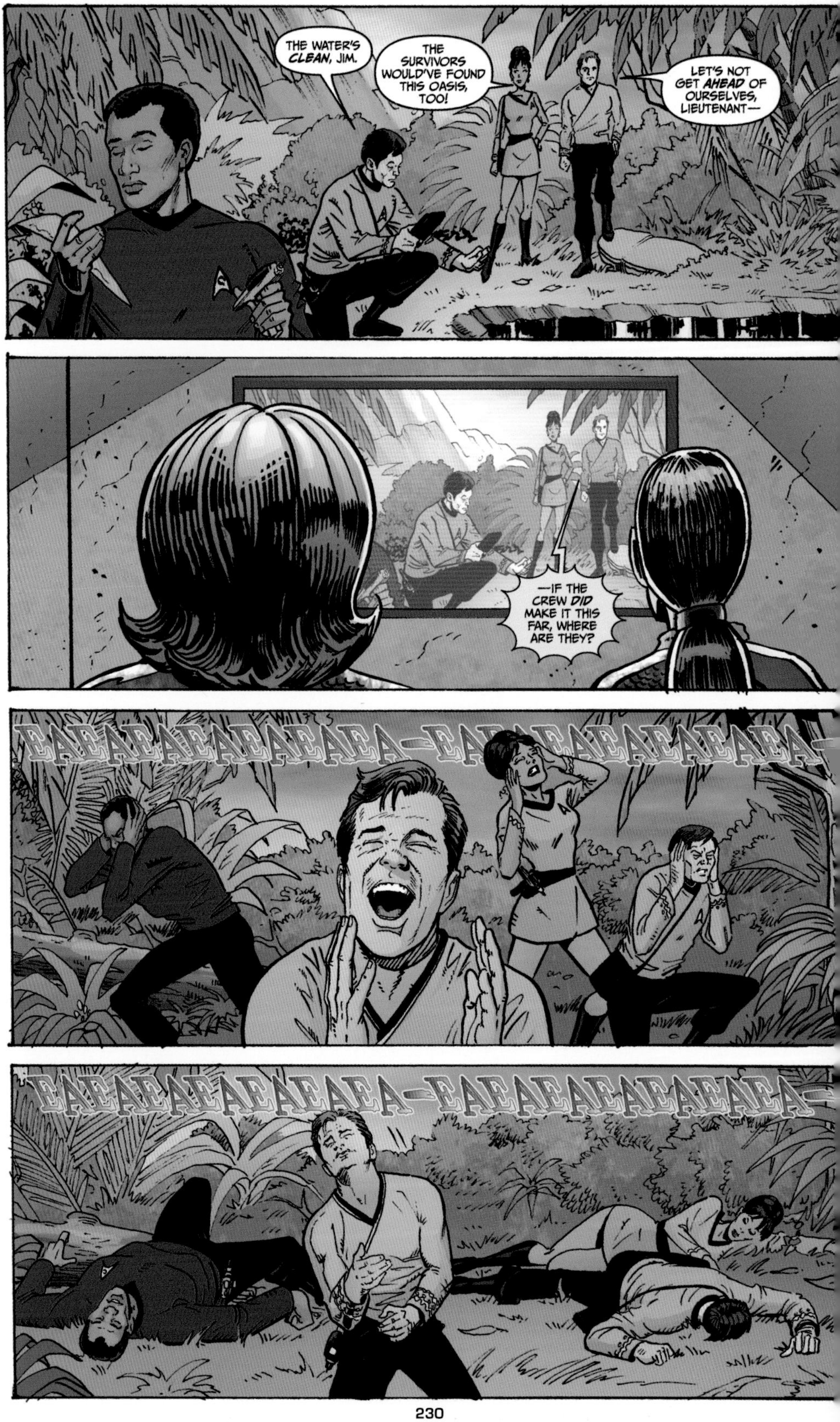
THE WATER'S *CLEAN*, JIM.
THE SURVIVORS WOULD'VE FOUND THIS OASIS, TOO!
LET'S NOT GET *AHEAD* OF OURSELVES, LIEUTENANT—
—IF THE CREW *DID* MAKE IT THIS FAR, WHERE ARE THEY?
EAEAEAEAEAEAEAEA—EAEAEAEAEAEAEAEA—
EAEAEAEAEAEAEAEA—EAEAEAEAEAEAEAEA—

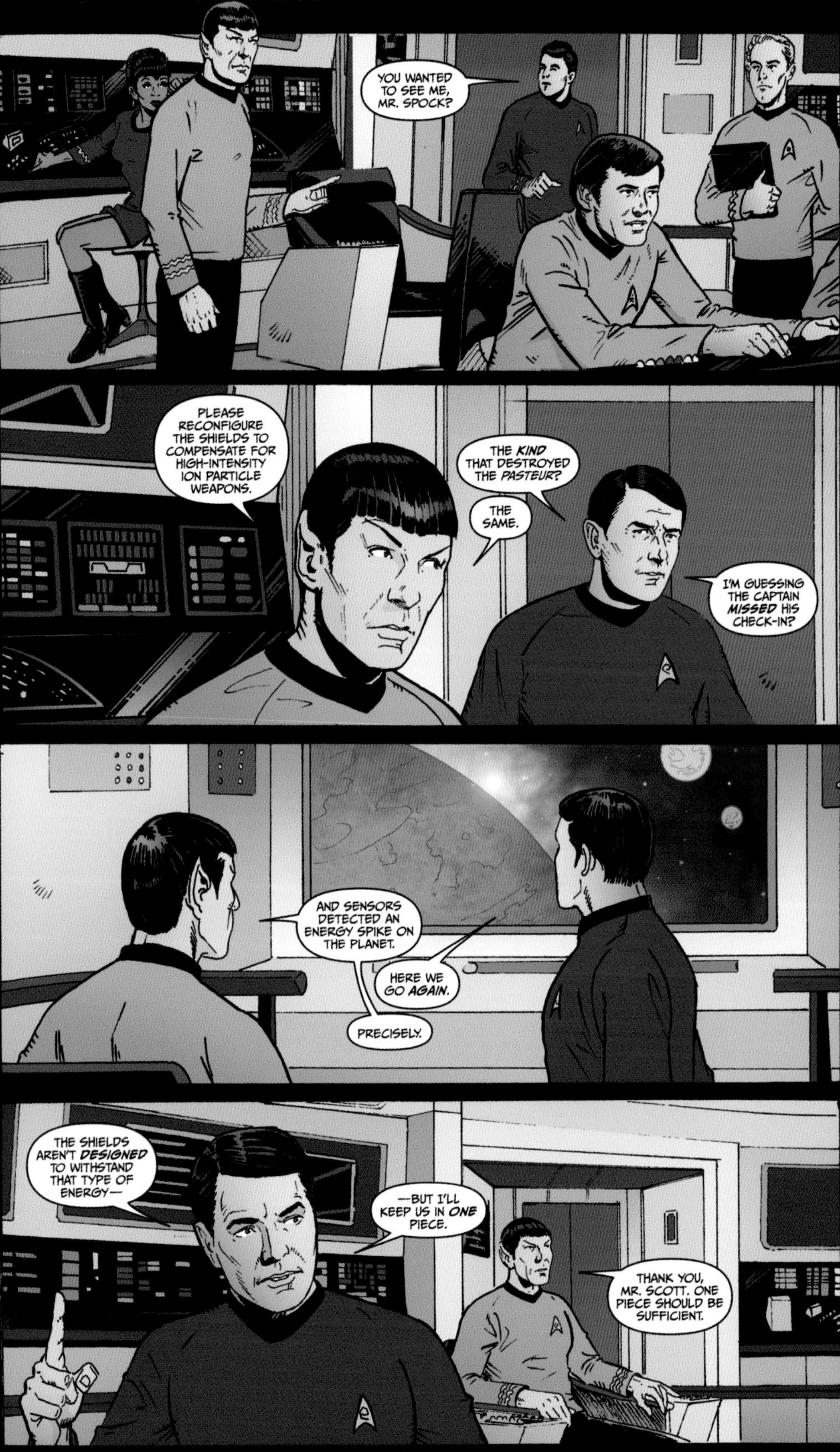

YOU WANTED TO SEE ME, MR. SPOCK?
PLEASE RECONFIGURE THE SHIELDS TO COMPENSATE FOR HIGH-INTENSITY ION PARTICLE WEAPONS.
THE *KIND* THAT DESTROYED THE *PASTEUR*?
THE SAME.
I'M GUESSING THE CAPTAIN *MISSED* HIS CHECK-IN?
AND SENSORS DETECTED AN ENERGY SPIKE ON THE PLANET.
HERE WE GO *AGAIN*.
PRECISELY.
THE SHIELDS AREN'T *DESIGNED* TO WITHSTAND THAT TYPE OF ENERGY—
—BUT I'LL KEEP US IN *ONE* PIECE.
THANK YOU, MR. SCOTT. ONE PIECE SHOULD BE SUFFICIENT.

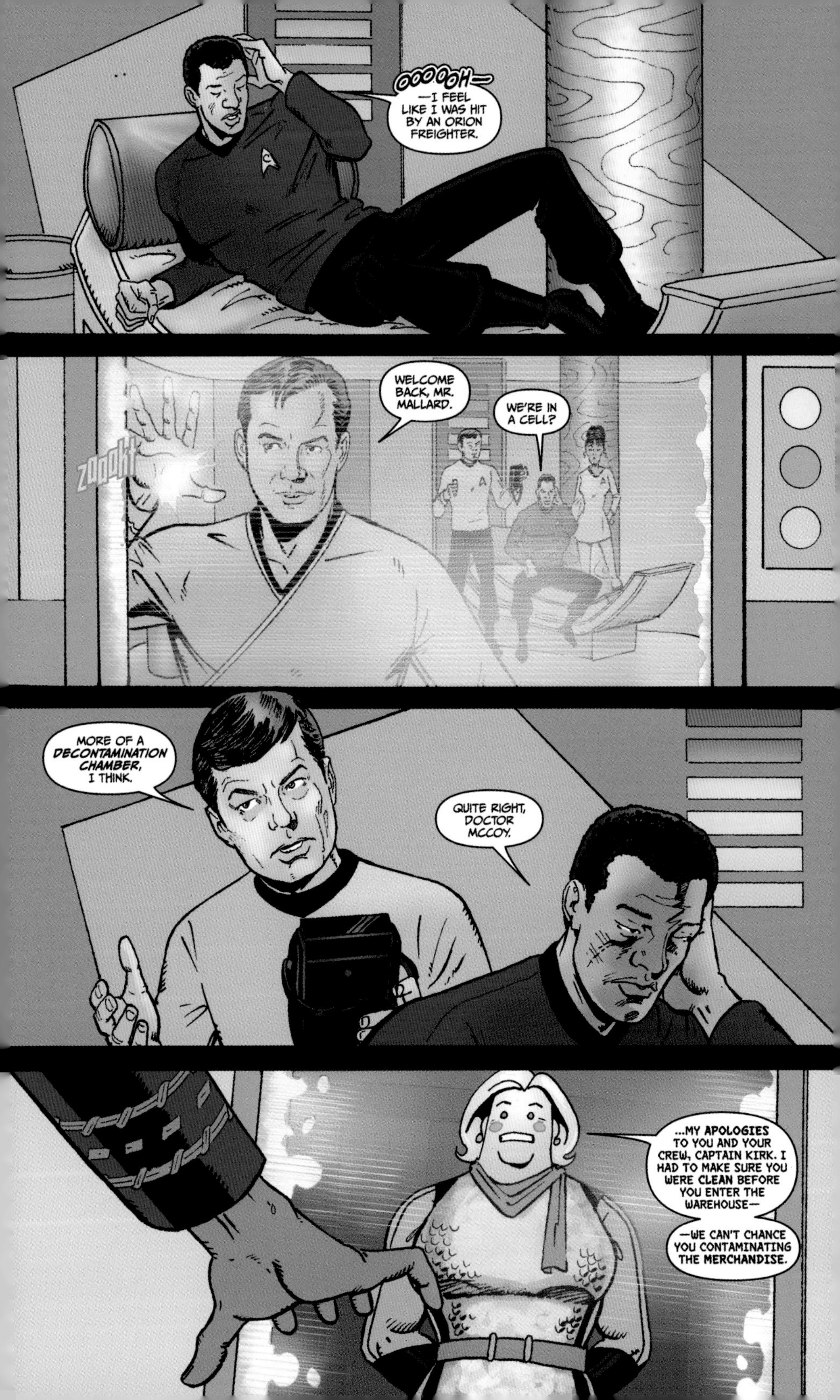
OOOOOOH—
—I FEEL LIKE I WAS HIT BY AN ORION FREIGHTER.
ZAAAKT
WELCOME BACK, MR. MALLARD.
WE'RE IN A CELL?
MORE OF A *DECONTAMINATION CHAMBER,* I THINK.
QUITE RIGHT, DOCTOR MCCOY.
...MY **APOLOGIES** TO YOU AND YOUR CREW, CAPTAIN KIRK. I HAD TO MAKE SURE YOU WERE **CLEAN** BEFORE YOU ENTER THE WAREHOUSE—
—WE CAN'T CHANCE YOU CONTAMINATING THE **MERCHANDISE.**

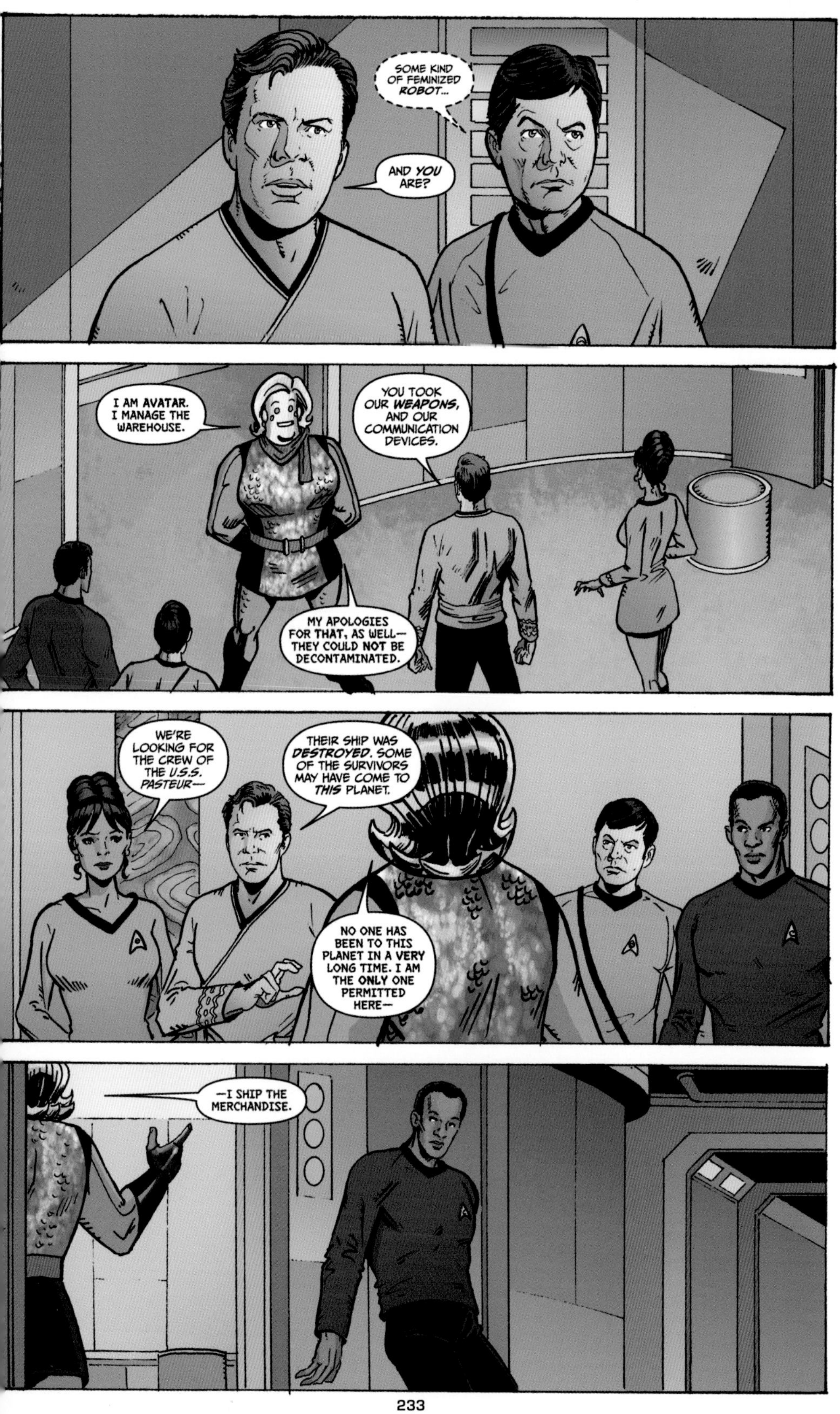
SOME KIND OF FEMINIZED *ROBOT*...
AND *YOU* ARE?
I AM AVATAR. I MANAGE THE WAREHOUSE.
YOU TOOK OUR *WEAPONS*, AND OUR COMMUNICATION DEVICES.
MY APOLOGIES FOR THAT, AS WELL— THEY COULD **NOT** BE DECONTAMINATED.
WE'RE LOOKING FOR THE CREW OF THE *U.S.S. PASTEUR*—
THEIR SHIP WAS *DESTROYED*. SOME OF THE SURVIVORS MAY HAVE COME TO *THIS* PLANET.
NO ONE HAS BEEN TO THIS PLANET IN A VERY LONG TIME. I AM THE **ONLY** ONE PERMITTED HERE—
—I SHIP THE MERCHANDISE.

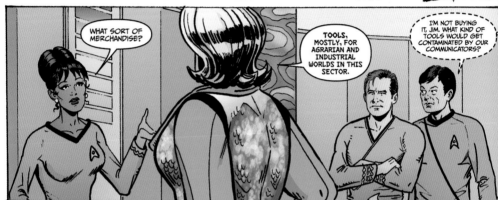

WHAT SORT OF MERCHANDISE?

TOOLS, MOSTLY, FOR AGRARIAN AND INDUSTRIAL WORLDS IN THIS SECTOR.

I'M NOT BUYING IT, JIM. WHAT KIND OF TOOLS WOULD GET CONTAMINATED BY OUR COMMUNICATORS?

AAAAAIGGHHH—!

SOMEONE'S BEEN A BAD BOY.

MALLARD!

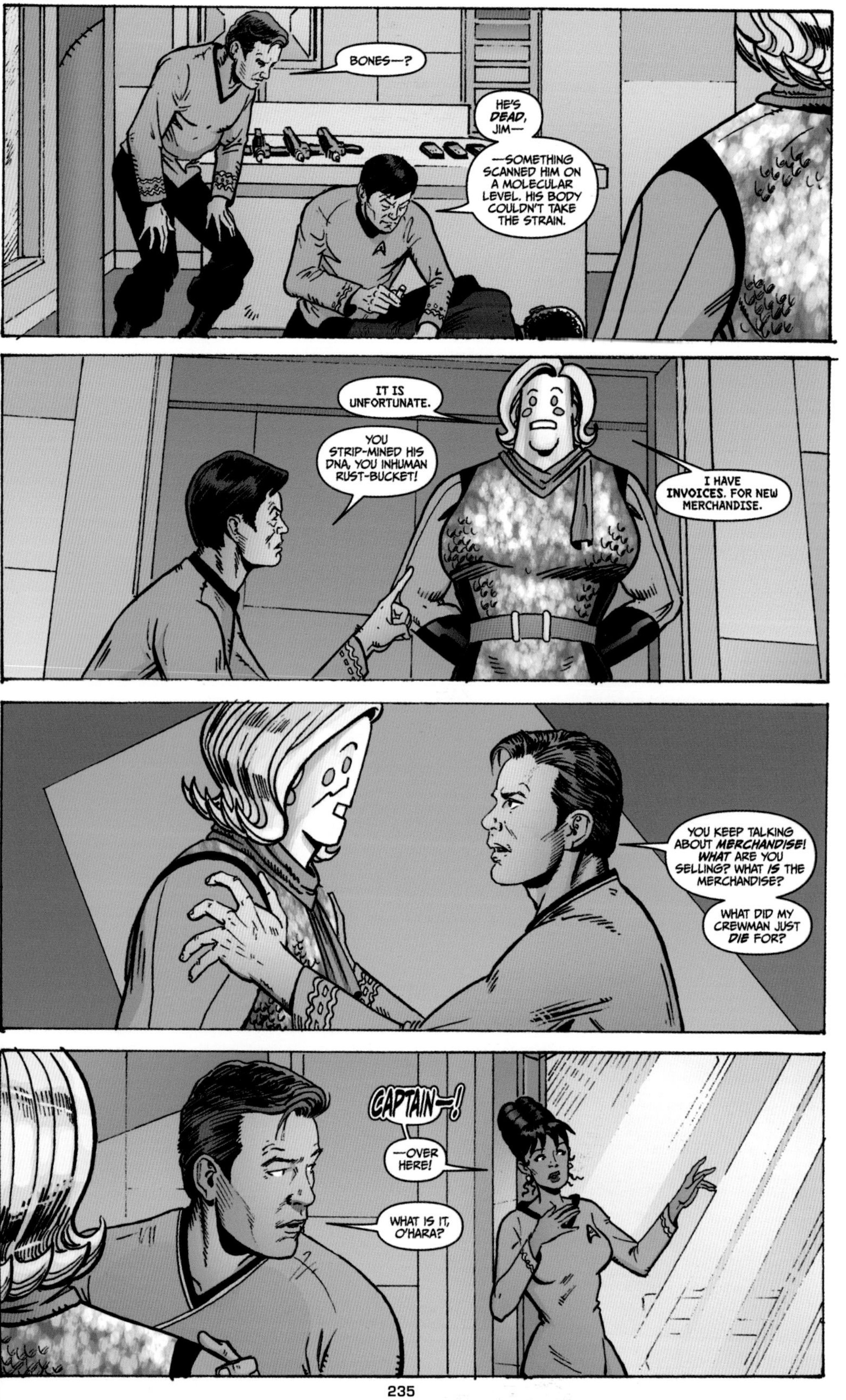
BONES—?
HE'S DEAD, JIM—
—SOMETHING SCANNED HIM ON A MOLECULAR LEVEL. HIS BODY COULDN'T TAKE THE STRAIN.
IT IS UNFORTUNATE.
YOU STRIP-MINED HIS DNA, YOU INHUMAN RUST-BUCKET!
I HAVE INVOICES. FOR NEW MERCHANDISE.
YOU KEEP TALKING ABOUT MERCHANDISE! WHAT ARE YOU SELLING? WHAT IS THE MERCHANDISE?
WHAT DID MY CREWMAN JUST DIE FOR?
CAPTAIN—!
—OVER HERE!
WHAT IS IT, O'HARA?

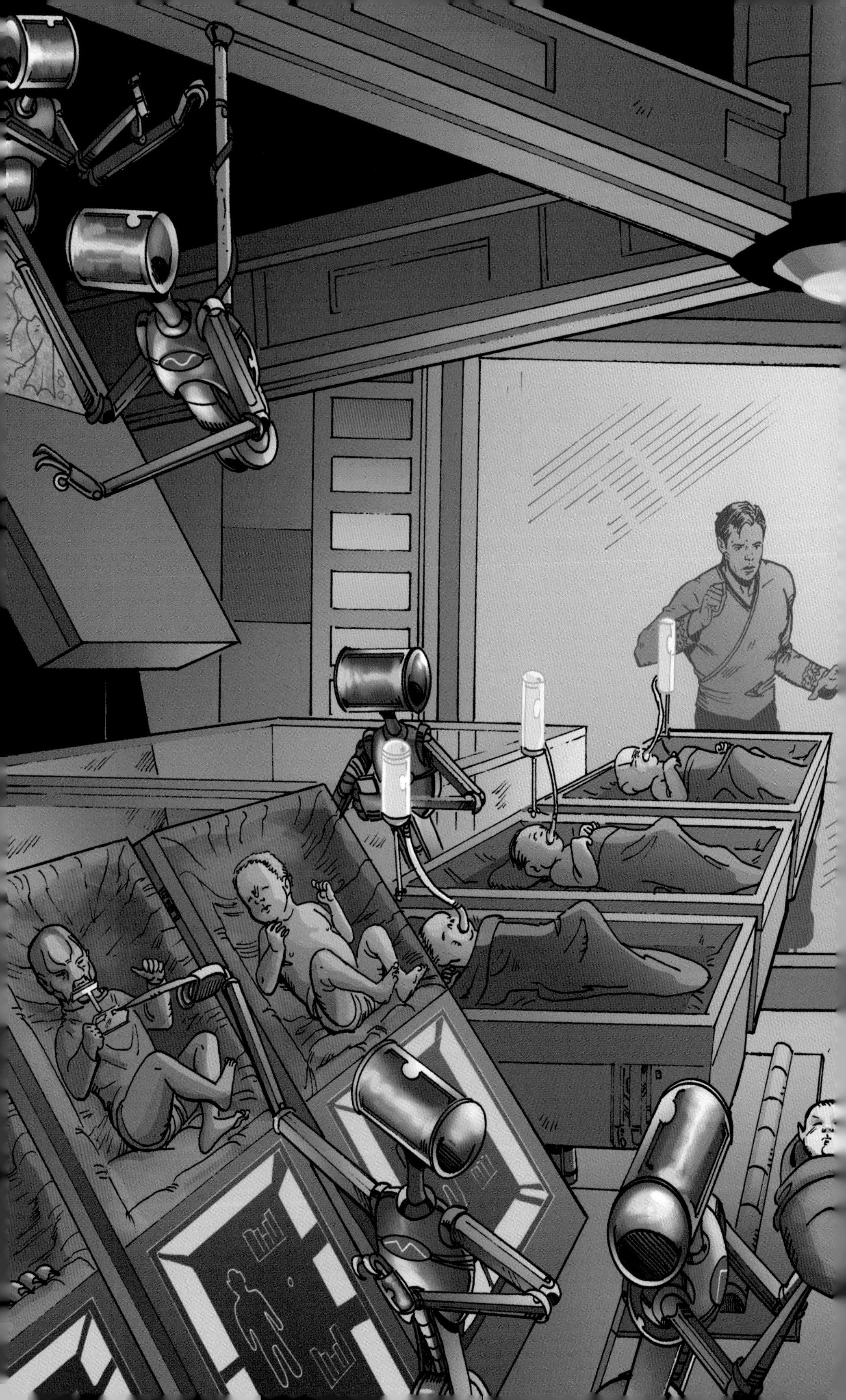

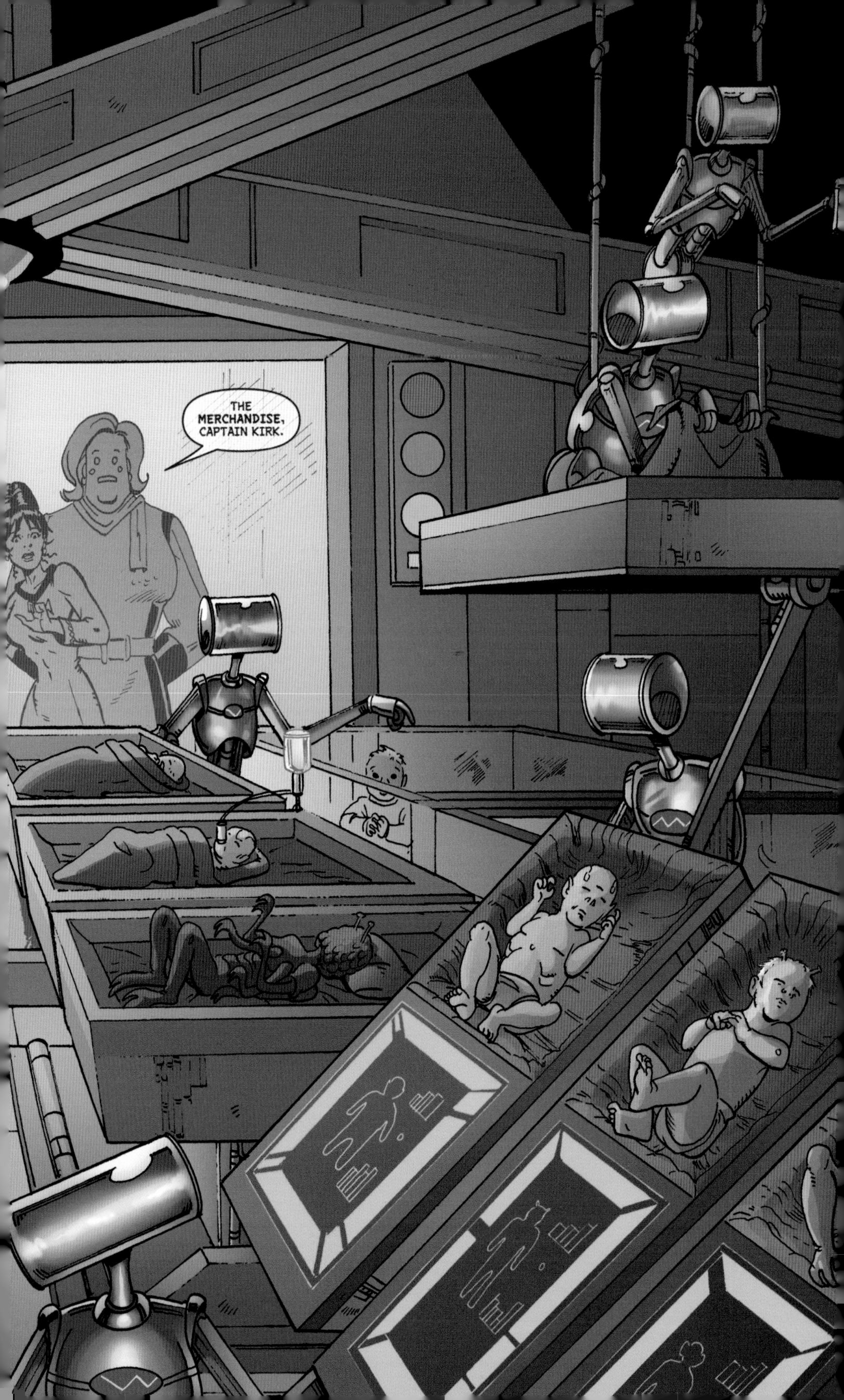
THE MERCHANDISE, CAPTAIN KIRK.

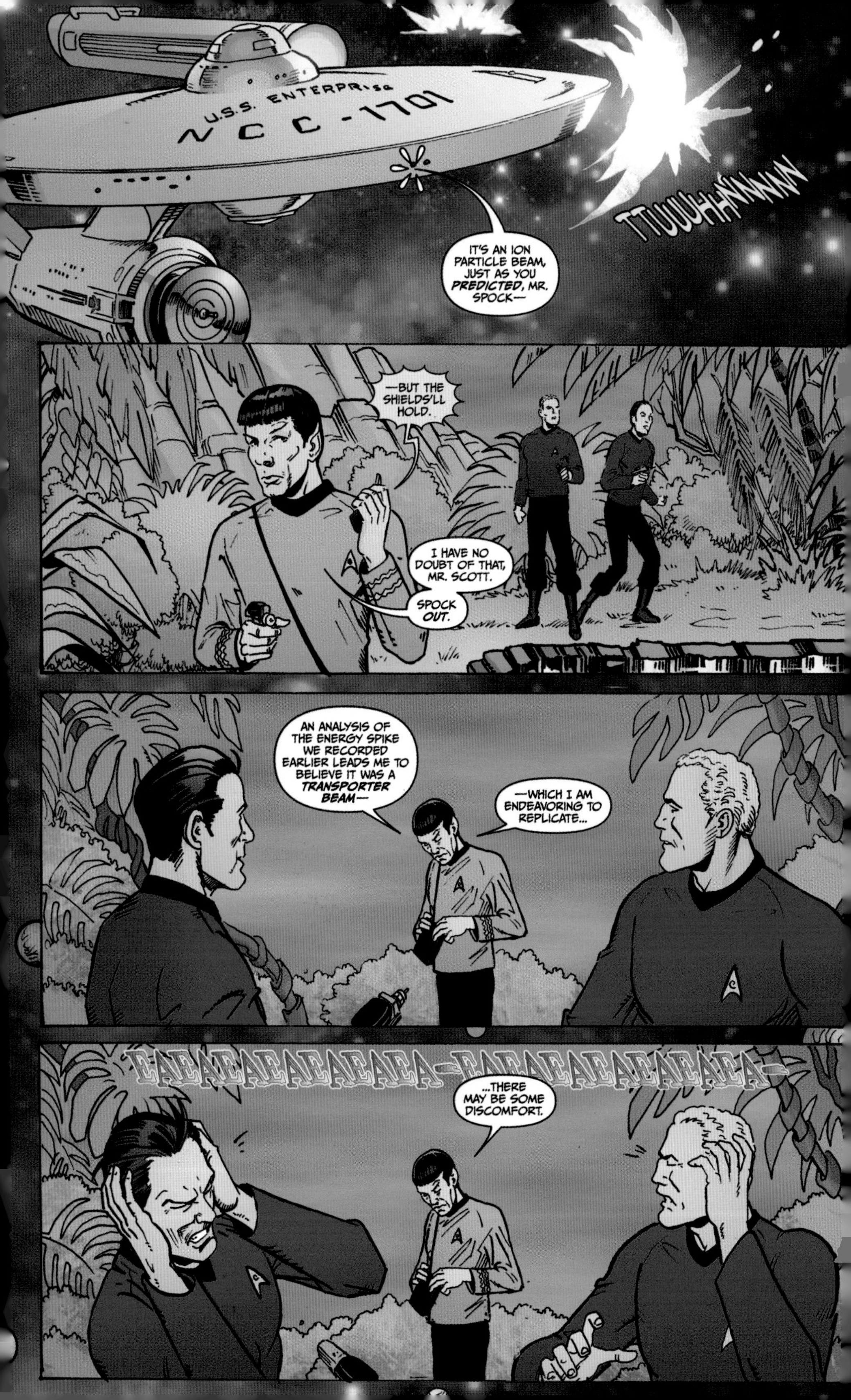

U.S.S. ENTERPRISE
NCC-1701
TTUUUHNNNNN
IT'S AN ION PARTICLE BEAM, JUST AS YOU PREDICTED, MR. SPOCK—
—BUT THE SHIELDS'LL HOLD.
I HAVE NO DOUBT OF THAT, MR. SCOTT.
SPOCK OUT.
AN ANALYSIS OF THE ENERGY SPIKE WE RECORDED EARLIER LEADS ME TO BELIEVE IT WAS A TRANSPORTER BEAM—
—WHICH I AM ENDEAVORING TO REPLICATE...
EAEAEAEAEAEAEAEA—EAEAEAEAEAEAEAEA—
...THERE MAY BE SOME DISCOMFORT.

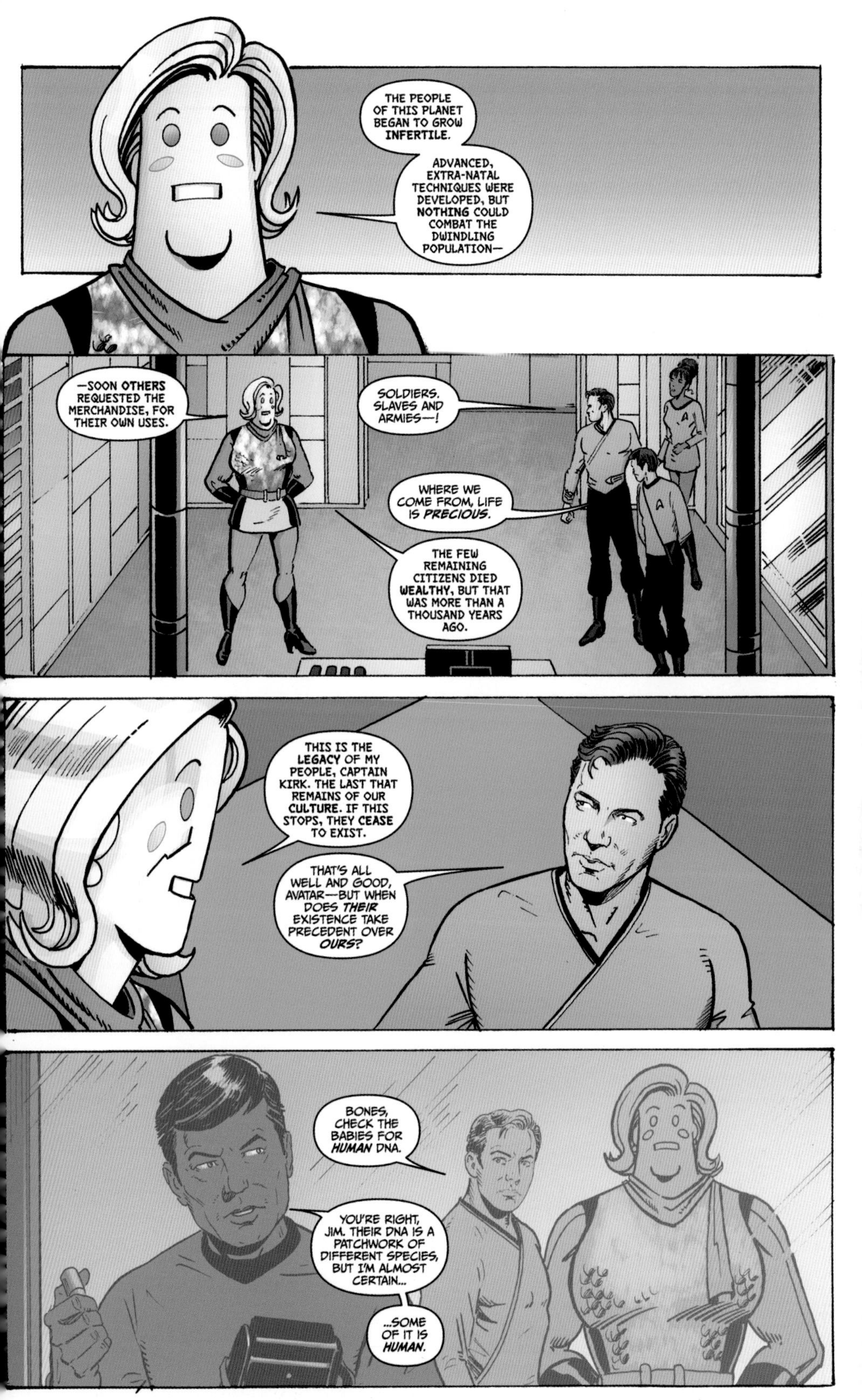
THE PEOPLE OF THIS PLANET BEGAN TO GROW INFERTILE.
ADVANCED, EXTRA-NATAL TECHNIQUES WERE DEVELOPED, BUT NOTHING COULD COMBAT THE DWINDLING POPULATION—
—SOON OTHERS REQUESTED THE MERCHANDISE, FOR THEIR OWN USES.
SOLDIERS. SLAVES AND ARMIES—!
WHERE WE COME FROM, LIFE IS PRECIOUS.
THE FEW REMAINING CITIZENS DIED WEALTHY, BUT THAT WAS MORE THAN A THOUSAND YEARS AGO.
THIS IS THE LEGACY OF MY PEOPLE, CAPTAIN KIRK. THE LAST THAT REMAINS OF OUR CULTURE. IF THIS STOPS, THEY CEASE TO EXIST.
THAT'S ALL WELL AND GOOD, AVATAR—BUT WHEN DOES THEIR EXISTENCE TAKE PRECEDENT OVER OURS?
BONES, CHECK THE BABIES FOR HUMAN DNA.
YOU'RE RIGHT, JIM. THEIR DNA IS A PATCHWORK OF DIFFERENT SPECIES, BUT I'M ALMOST CERTAIN...
...SOME OF IT IS HUMAN.

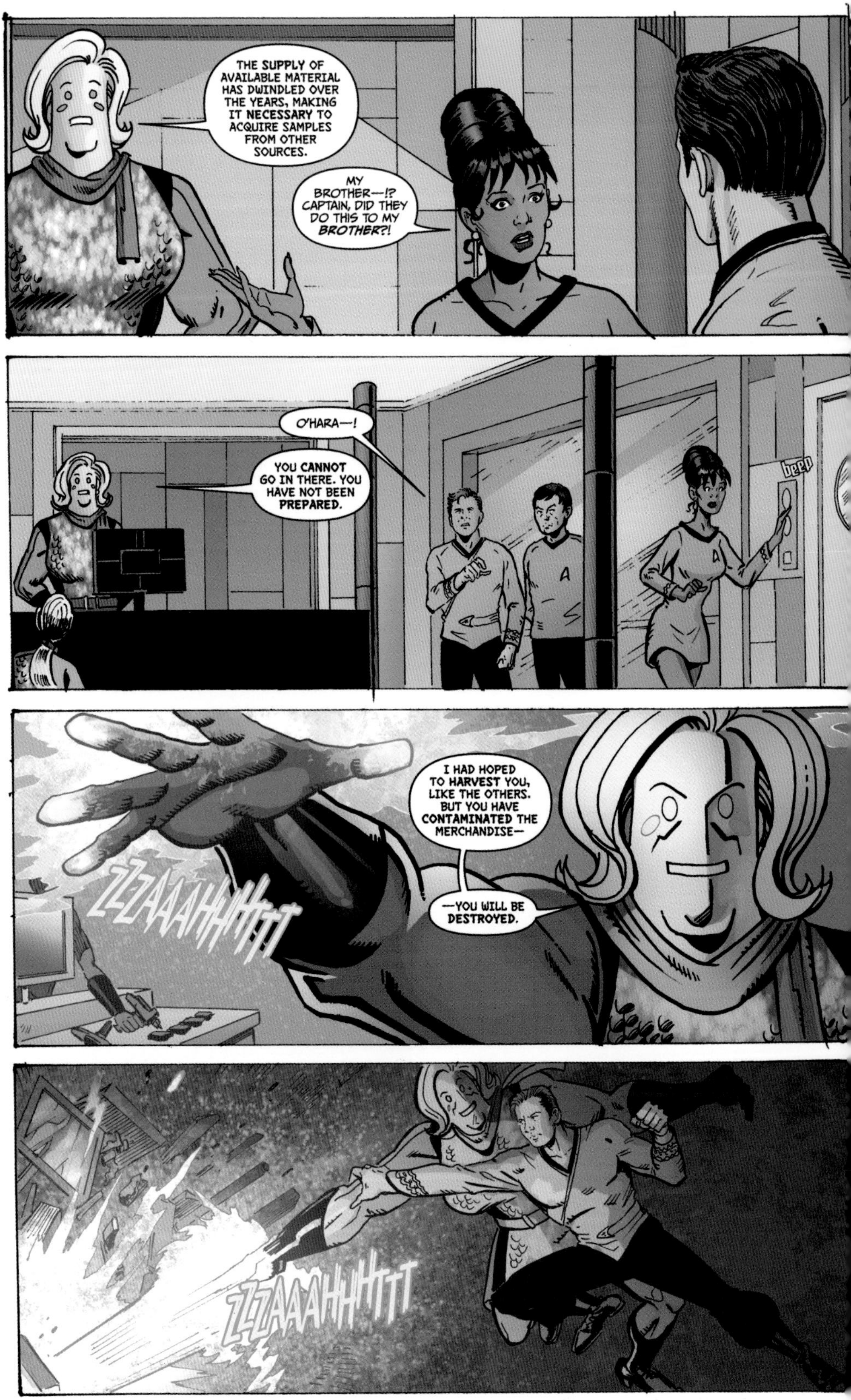
THE SUPPLY OF AVAILABLE MATERIAL HAS DWINDLED OVER THE YEARS, MAKING IT NECESSARY TO ACQUIRE SAMPLES FROM OTHER SOURCES.
MY BROTHER--!? CAPTAIN, DID THEY DO THIS TO MY *BROTHER*?!
O'HARA--!
YOU CANNOT GO IN THERE. YOU HAVE NOT BEEN PREPARED.
beep
I HAD HOPED TO HARVEST YOU, LIKE THE OTHERS. BUT YOU HAVE CONTAMINATED THE MERCHANDISE--
--YOU WILL BE DESTROYED.
ZZZAAAHHHTTTT
ZZZAAAHHHTTTT

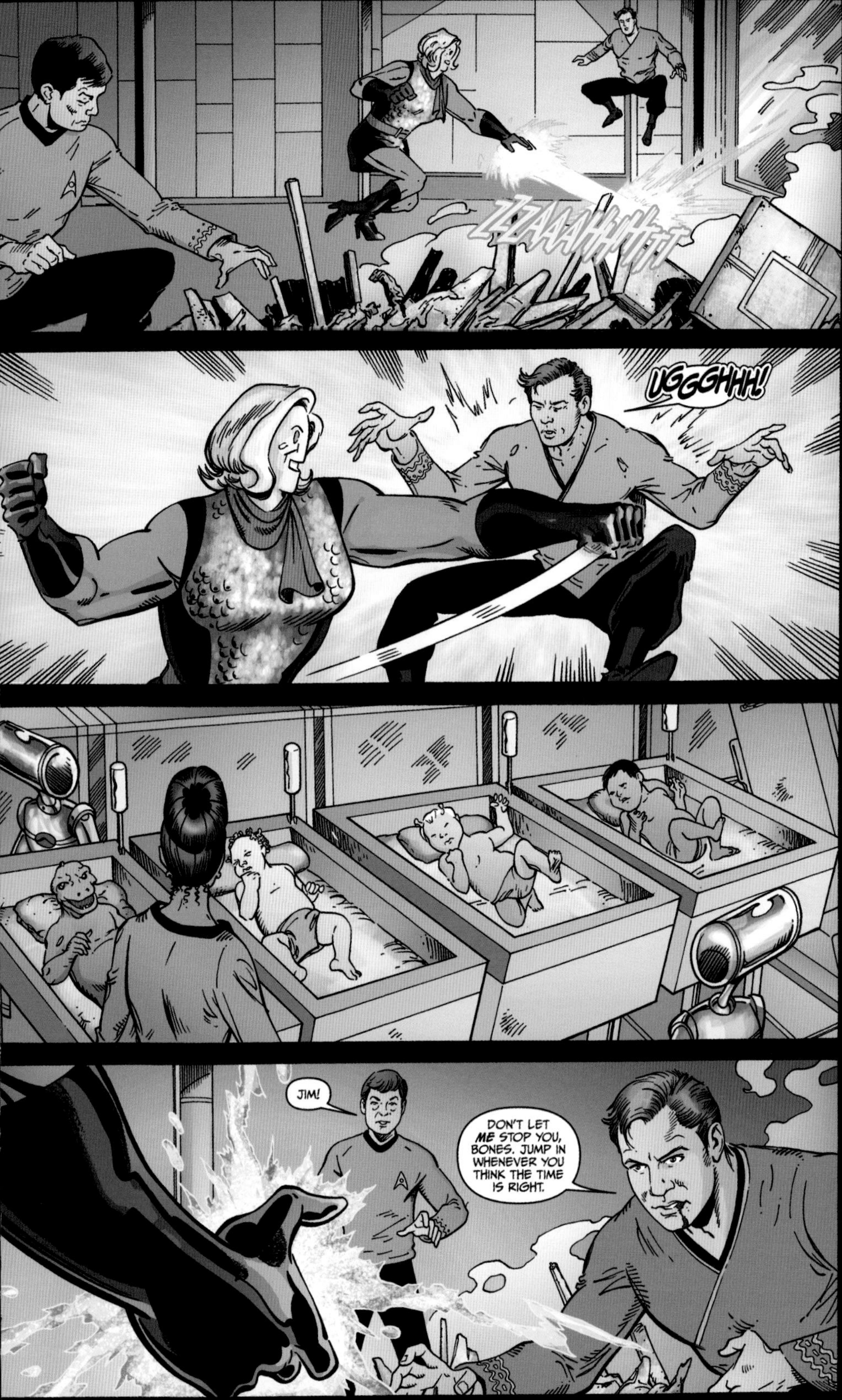
ZZAAAHHHTT
UGGGHHH!
JIM!
DON'T LET ME STOP YOU, BONES. JUMP IN WHENEVER YOU THINK THE TIME IS RIGHT.

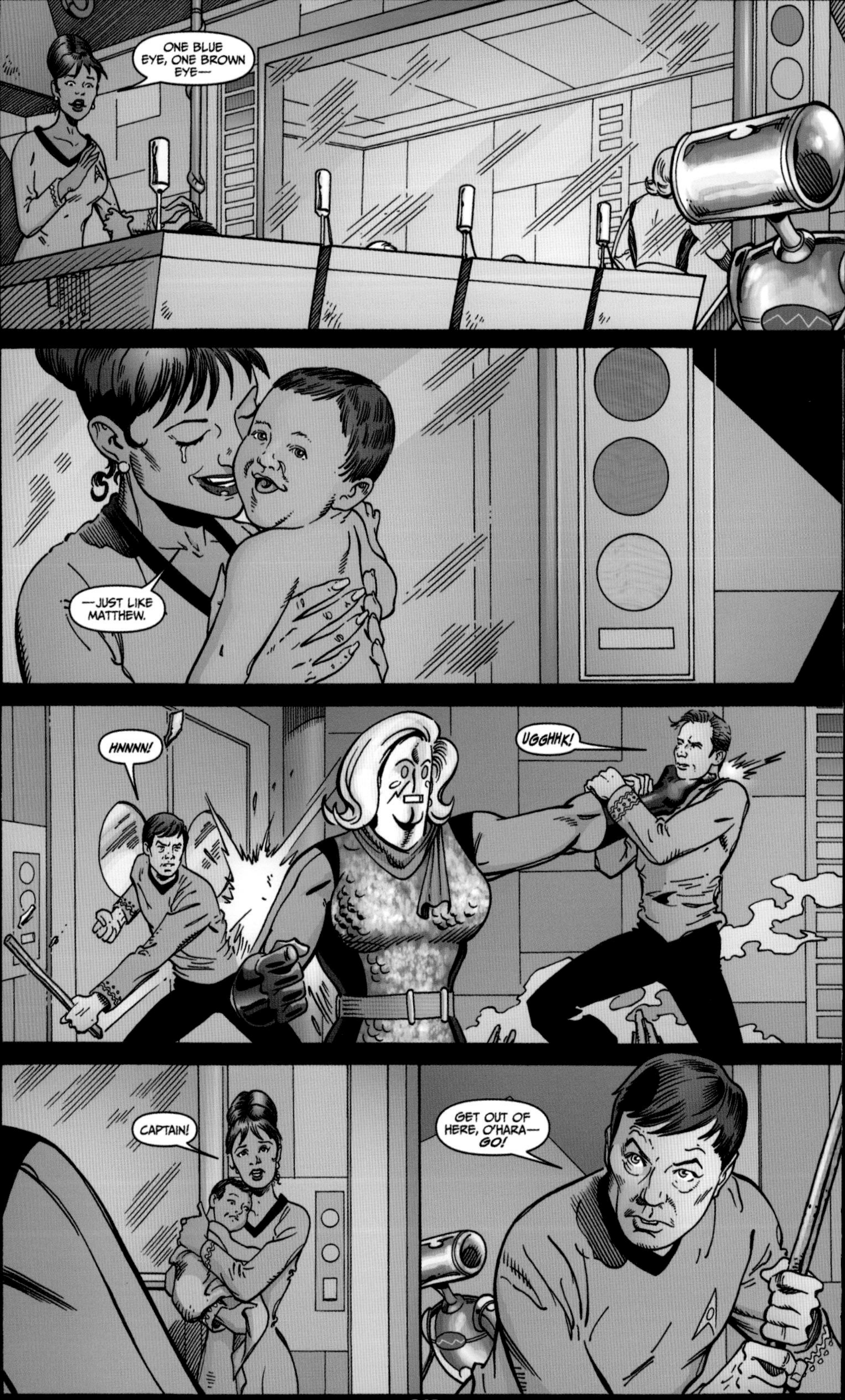
ONE BLUE EYE, ONE BROWN EYE—
—JUST LIKE MATTHEW.
HNNNN!
UGGHHK!
CAPTAIN!
GET OUT OF HERE, O'HARA— GO!

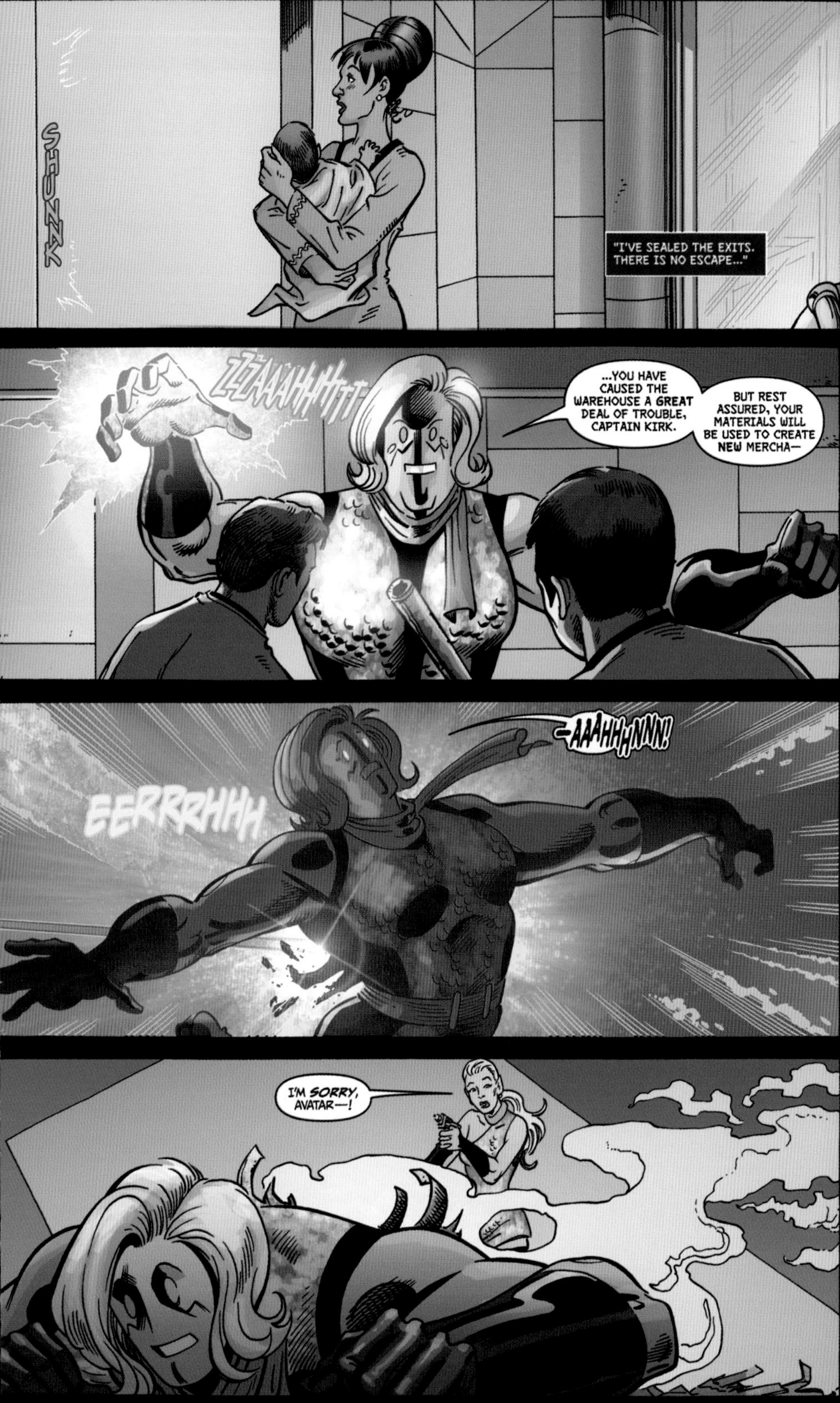
SHUNNK
"I'VE SEALED THE EXITS. THERE IS NO ESCAPE..."
ZZZAAAHHHTTT
...YOU HAVE CAUSED THE WAREHOUSE A GREAT DEAL OF TROUBLE, CAPTAIN KIRK.
BUT REST ASSURED, YOUR MATERIALS WILL BE USED TO CREATE NEW MERCHA—
—AAAHHHNNN!
EERRRRHHH
I'M SORRY, AVATAR—!

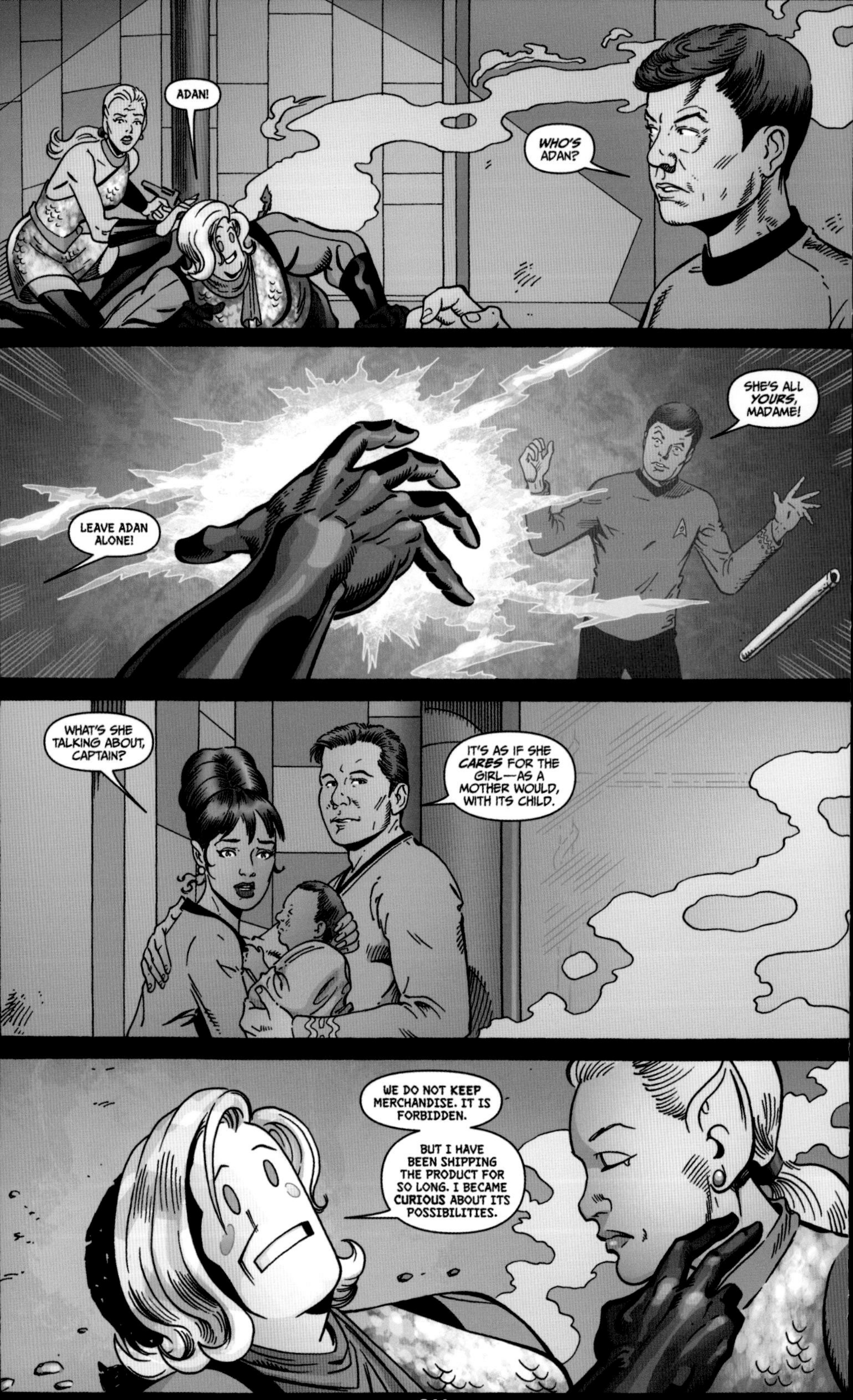

ADAN!
WHO'S ADAN?
SHE'S ALL YOURS, MADAME!
LEAVE ADAN ALONE!
WHAT'S SHE TALKING ABOUT, CAPTAIN?
IT'S AS IF SHE CARES FOR THE GIRL—AS A MOTHER WOULD, WITH ITS CHILD.
WE DO NOT KEEP MERCHANDISE. IT IS FORBIDDEN.
BUT I HAVE BEEN SHIPPING THE PRODUCT FOR SO LONG. I BECAME CURIOUS ABOUT ITS POSSIBILITIES.

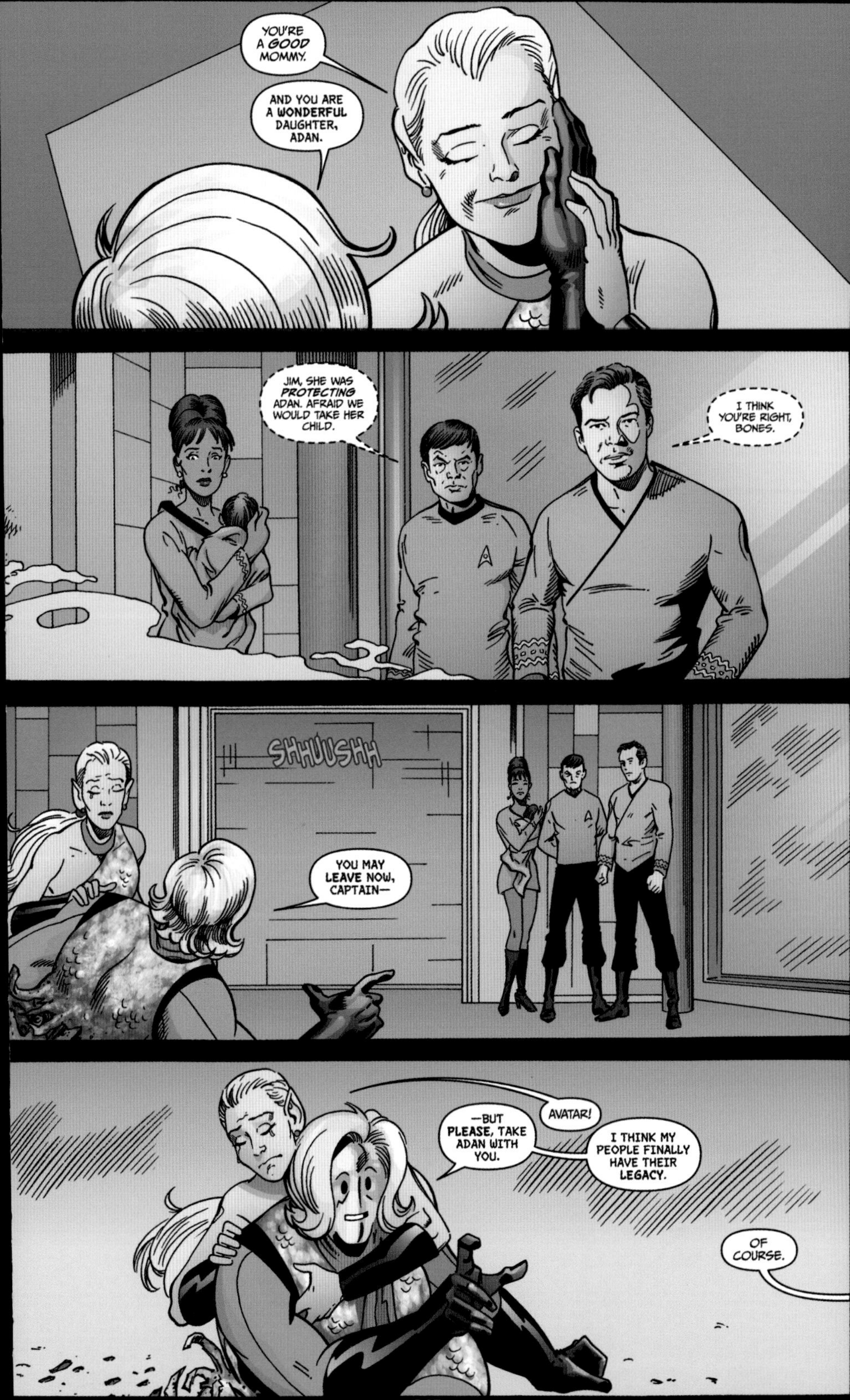
YOU'RE A GOOD MOMMY.
AND YOU ARE A WONDERFUL DAUGHTER, ADAN.
JIM, SHE WAS PROTECTING ADAN. AFRAID WE WOULD TAKE HER CHILD.
I THINK YOU'RE RIGHT, BONES.
SHHUUSHH
YOU MAY LEAVE NOW, CAPTAIN—
—BUT PLEASE, TAKE ADAN WITH YOU.
AVATAR!
I THINK MY PEOPLE FINALLY HAVE THEIR LEGACY.
OF COURSE.

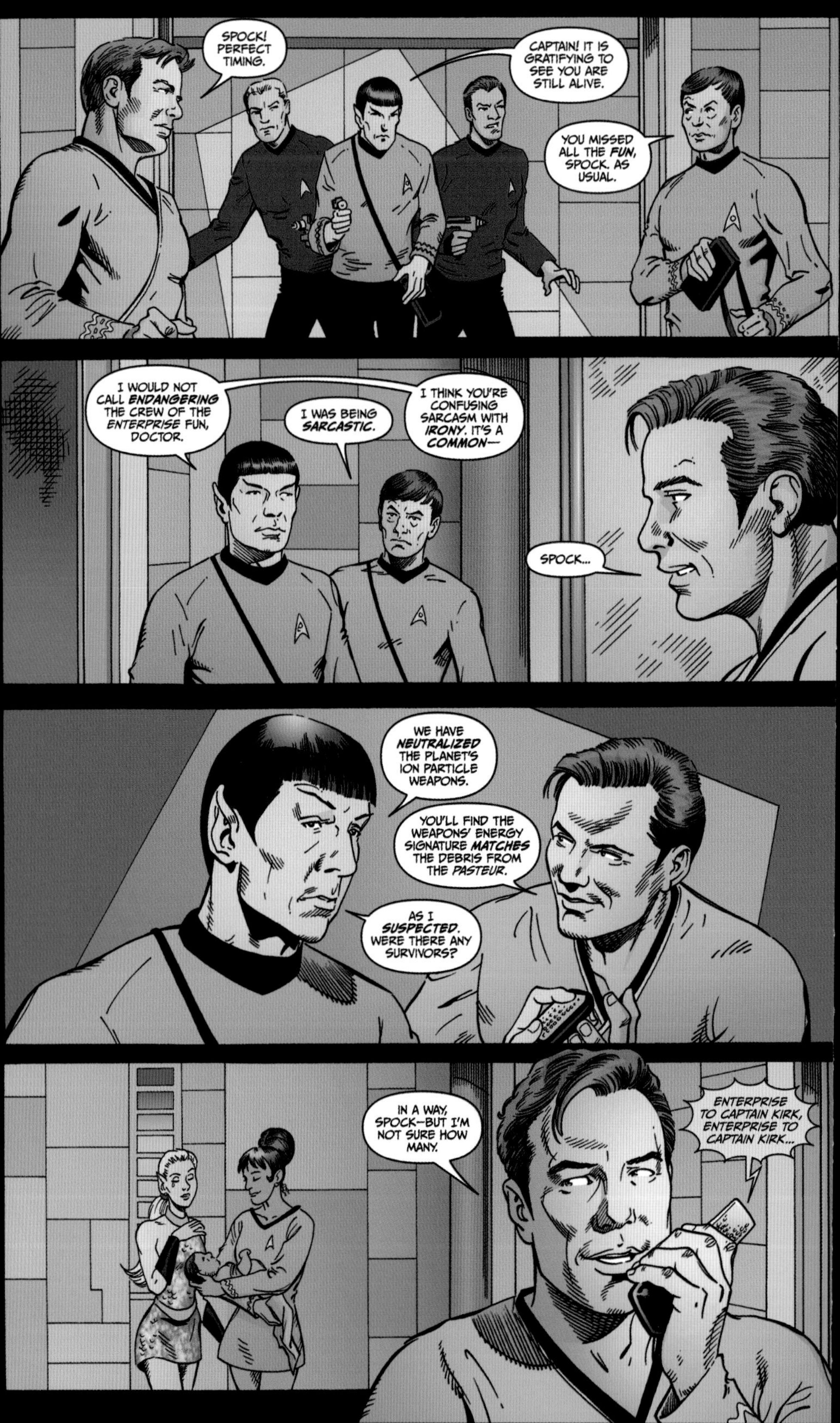
SPOCK! PERFECT TIMING.
CAPTAIN! IT IS GRATIFYING TO SEE YOU ARE STILL ALIVE.
YOU MISSED ALL THE *FUN*, SPOCK. AS USUAL.
I WOULD NOT CALL **ENDANGERING** THE CREW OF THE *ENTERPRISE* FUN, DOCTOR.
I WAS BEING ***SARCASTIC***.
I THINK YOU'RE CONFUSING SARCASM WITH ***IRONY***. IT'S A ***COMMON***--
SPOCK...
WE HAVE ***NEUTRALIZED*** THE PLANET'S ION PARTICLE WEAPONS.
YOU'LL FIND THE WEAPONS' ENERGY SIGNATURE **MATCHES** THE DEBRIS FROM THE *PASTEUR*.
AS I ***SUSPECTED***. WERE THERE ANY SURVIVORS?
IN A WAY, SPOCK--BUT I'M NOT SURE HOW MANY.
ENTERPRISE TO CAPTAIN KIRK, *ENTERPRISE* TO CAPTAIN KIRK...

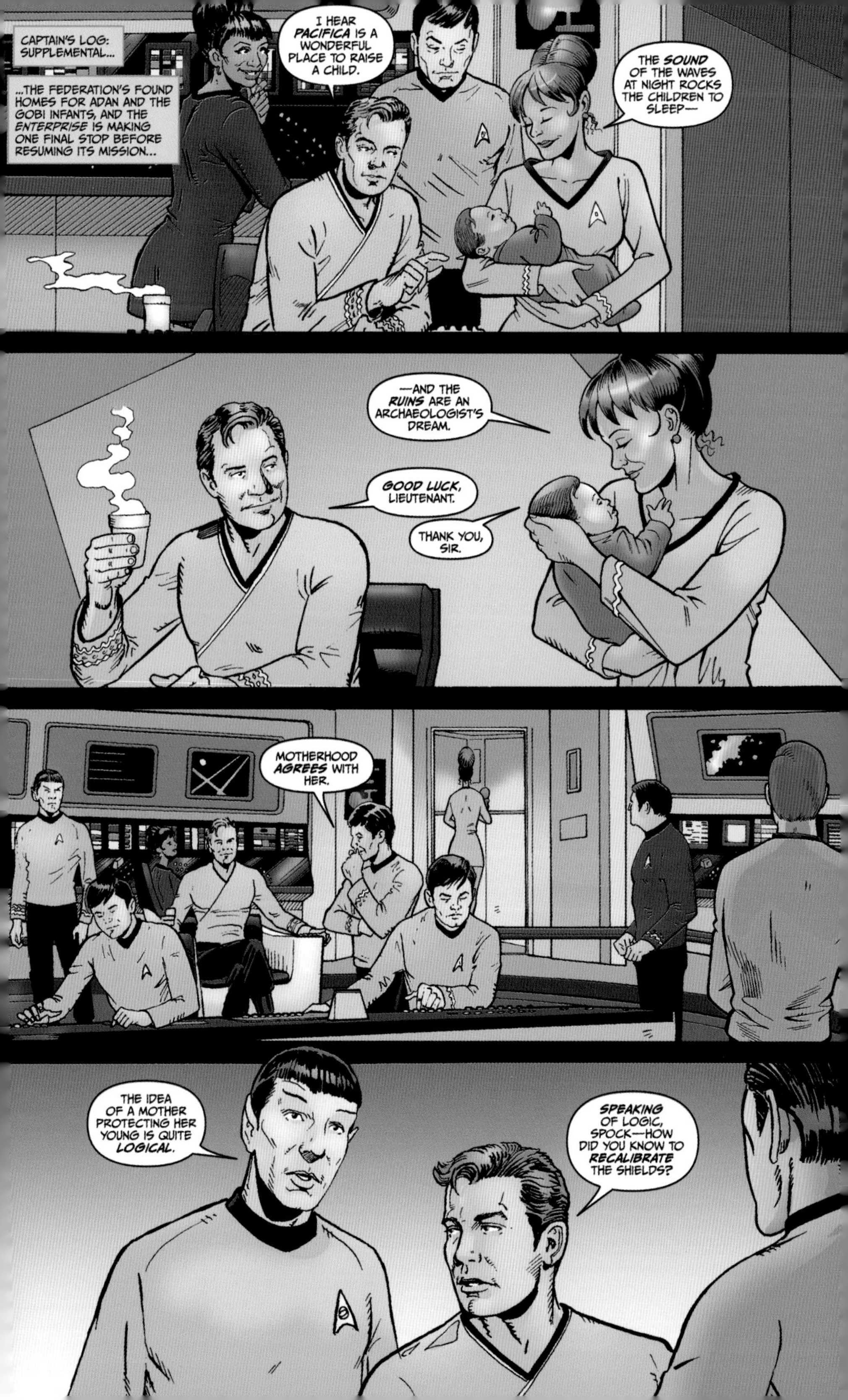
CAPTAIN'S LOG: SUPPLEMENTAL...
...THE FEDERATION'S FOUND HOMES FOR ADAN AND THE GOBI INFANTS, AND THE ENTERPRISE IS MAKING ONE FINAL STOP BEFORE RESUMING ITS MISSION...
I HEAR PACIFICA IS A WONDERFUL PLACE TO RAISE A CHILD.
THE SOUND OF THE WAVES AT NIGHT ROCKS THE CHILDREN TO SLEEP—
—AND THE RUINS ARE AN ARCHAEOLOGIST'S DREAM.
GOOD LUCK, LIEUTENANT.
THANK YOU, SIR.
MOTHERHOOD AGREES WITH HER.
THE IDEA OF A MOTHER PROTECTING HER YOUNG IS QUITE LOGICAL.
SPEAKING OF LOGIC, SPOCK—HOW DID YOU KNOW TO RECALIBRATE THE SHIELDS?

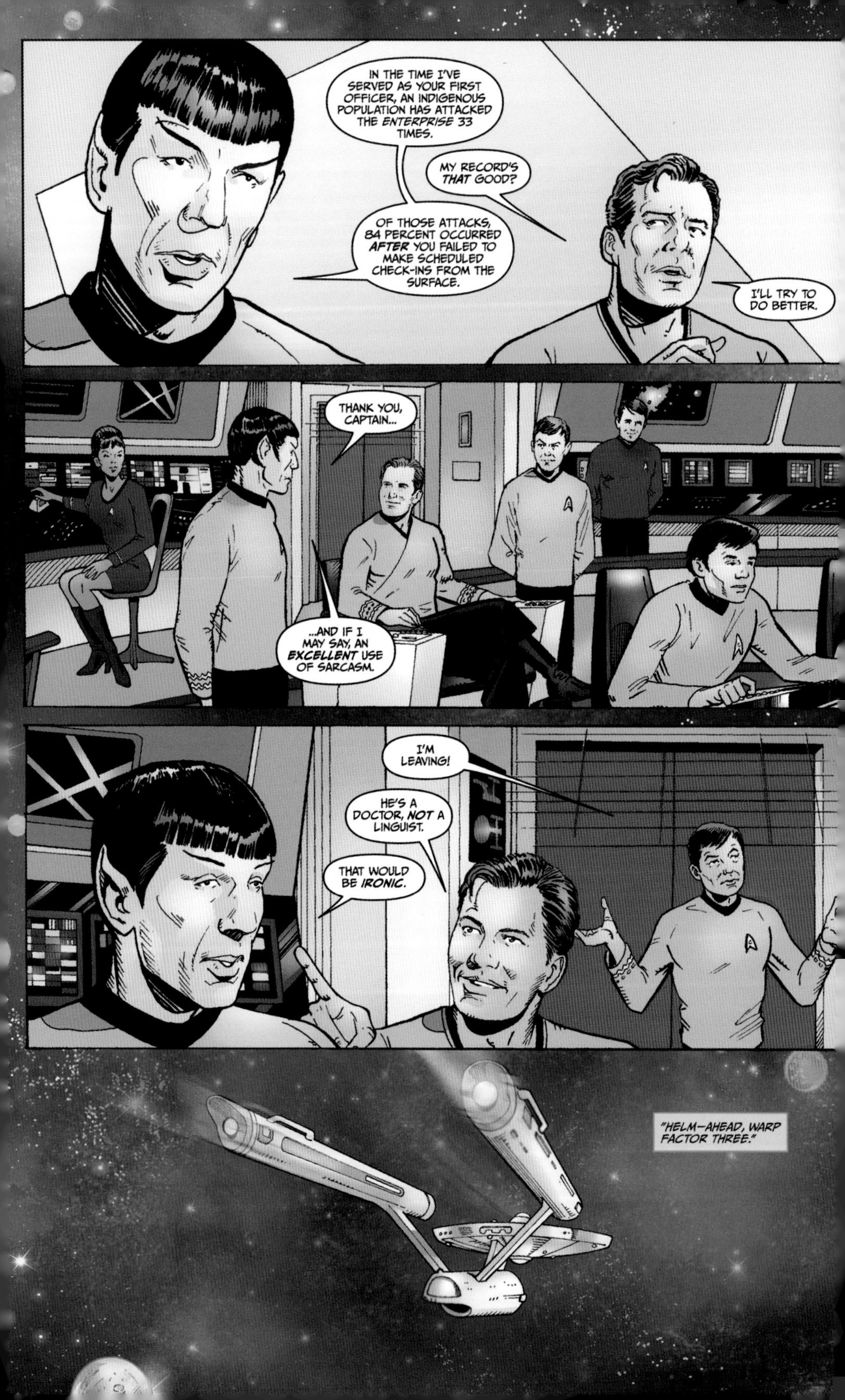
IN THE TIME I'VE SERVED AS YOUR FIRST OFFICER, AN INDIGENOUS POPULATION HAS ATTACKED THE ENTERPRISE 33 TIMES.
MY RECORD'S THAT GOOD?
OF THOSE ATTACKS, 84 PERCENT OCCURRED AFTER YOU FAILED TO MAKE SCHEDULED CHECK-INS FROM THE SURFACE.
I'LL TRY TO DO BETTER.
THANK YOU, CAPTAIN...
...AND IF I MAY SAY, AN EXCELLENT USE OF SARCASM.
I'M LEAVING!
HE'S A DOCTOR, NOT A LINGUIST.
THAT WOULD BE IRONIC.
"HELM—AHEAD, WARP FACTOR THREE."

STAR TREK®

THE ORIGINAL SERIES

OMNIBUS

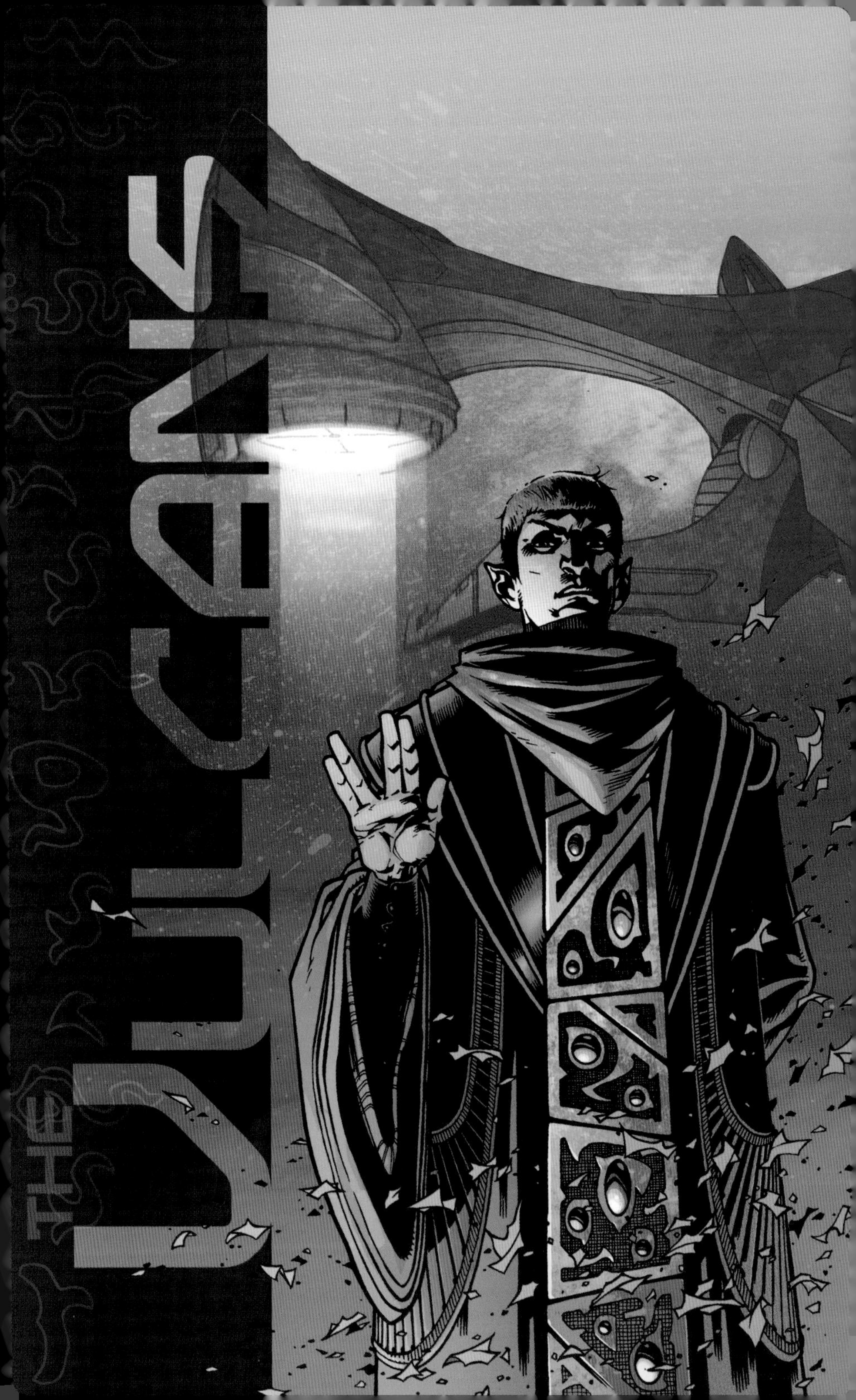
THE VULCANS

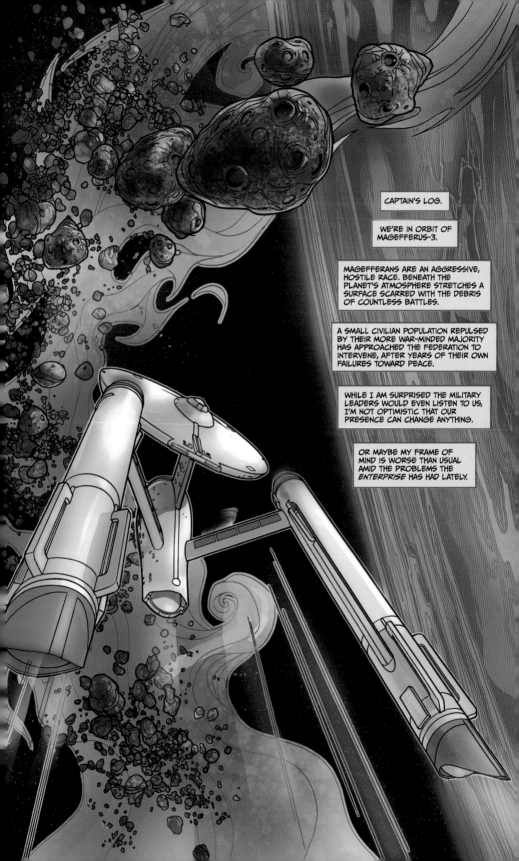

CAPTAIN'S LOG.

WE'RE IN ORBIT OF MAGEFFERUS-3.

MAGEFFERANS ARE AN AGGRESSIVE, HOSTILE RACE. BENEATH THE PLANET'S ATMOSPHERE STRETCHES A SURFACE SCARRED WITH THE DEBRIS OF COUNTLESS BATTLES.

A SMALL CIVILIAN POPULATION REPULSED BY THEIR MORE WAR-MINDED MAJORITY HAS APPROACHED THE FEDERATION TO INTERVENE, AFTER YEARS OF THEIR OWN FAILURES TOWARD PEACE.

WHILE I AM SURPRISED THE MILITARY LEADERS WOULD EVEN LISTEN TO US, I'M NOT OPTIMISTIC THAT OUR PRESENCE CAN CHANGE ANYTHING.

OR MAYBE MY FRAME OF MIND IS WORSE THAN USUAL AMID THE PROBLEMS THE *ENTERPRISE* HAS HAD LATELY.

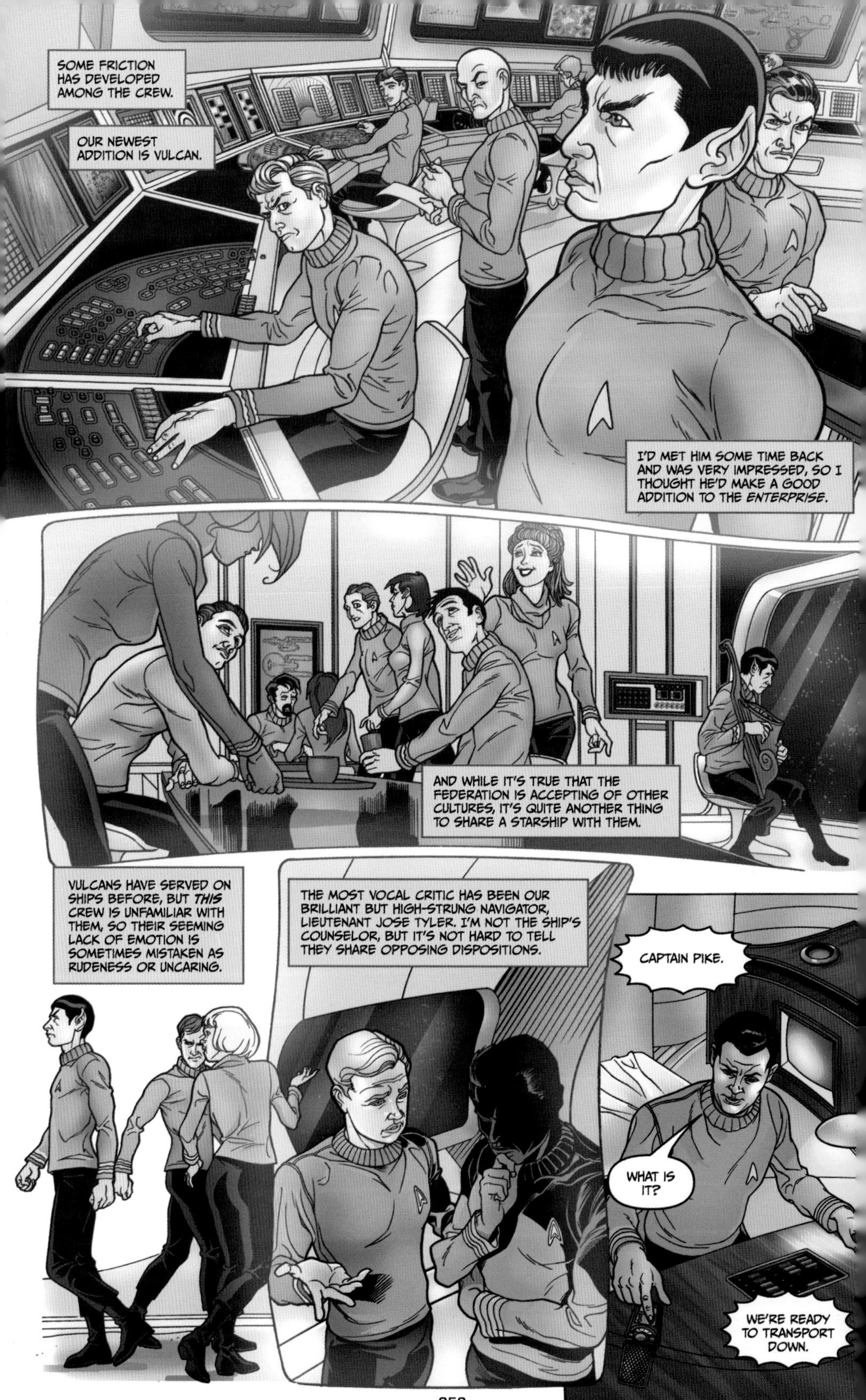

SOME FRICTION HAS DEVELOPED AMONG THE CREW.
OUR NEWEST ADDITION IS VULCAN.
I'D MET HIM SOME TIME BACK AND WAS VERY IMPRESSED, SO I THOUGHT HE'D MAKE A GOOD ADDITION TO THE *ENTERPRISE*.
AND WHILE IT'S TRUE THAT THE FEDERATION IS ACCEPTING OF OTHER CULTURES, IT'S QUITE ANOTHER THING TO SHARE A STARSHIP WITH THEM.
VULCANS HAVE SERVED ON SHIPS BEFORE, BUT *THIS* CREW IS UNFAMILIAR WITH THEM, SO THEIR SEEMING LACK OF EMOTION IS SOMETIMES MISTAKEN AS RUDENESS OR UNCARING.
THE MOST VOCAL CRITIC HAS BEEN OUR BRILLIANT BUT HIGH-STRUNG NAVIGATOR, LIEUTENANT JOSE TYLER. I'M NOT THE SHIP'S COUNSELOR, BUT IT'S NOT HARD TO TELL THEY SHARE OPPOSING DISPOSITIONS.
CAPTAIN PIKE.
WHAT IS IT?
WE'RE READY TO TRANSPORT DOWN.

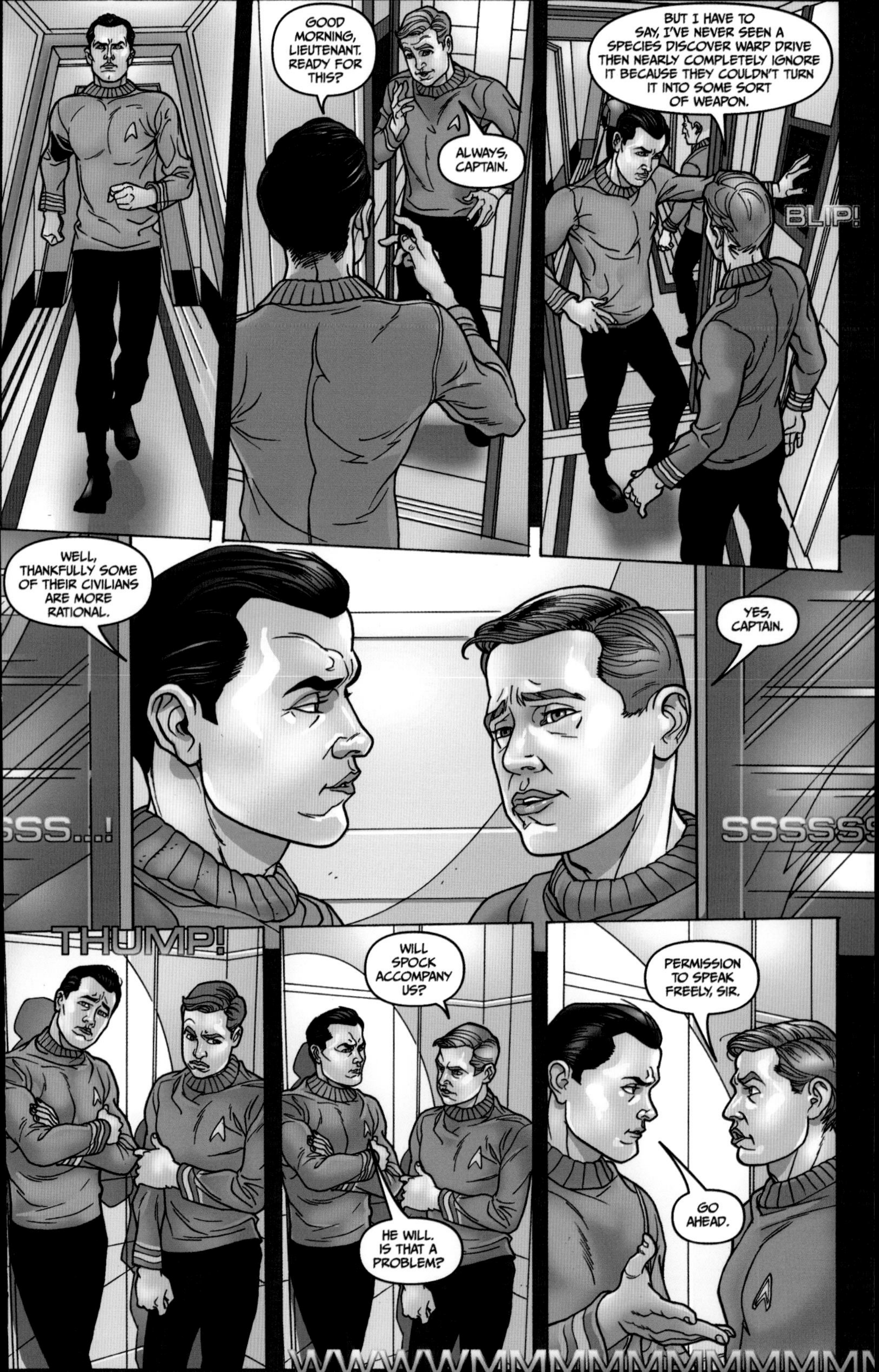
GOOD MORNING, LIEUTENANT. READY FOR THIS?
ALWAYS, CAPTAIN.
BUT I HAVE TO SAY, I'VE NEVER SEEN A SPECIES DISCOVER WARP DRIVE THEN NEARLY COMPLETELY IGNORE IT BECAUSE THEY COULDN'T TURN IT INTO SOME SORT OF WEAPON.
BLIP!
WELL, THANKFULLY SOME OF THEIR CIVILIANS ARE MORE RATIONAL.
YES, CAPTAIN.
SSS...!
SSSSSS
THUMP!
WILL SPOCK ACCOMPANY US?
HE WILL. IS THAT A PROBLEM?
PERMISSION TO SPEAK FREELY, SIR.
GO AHEAD.
WWWWWMMMMMMMMMMMM

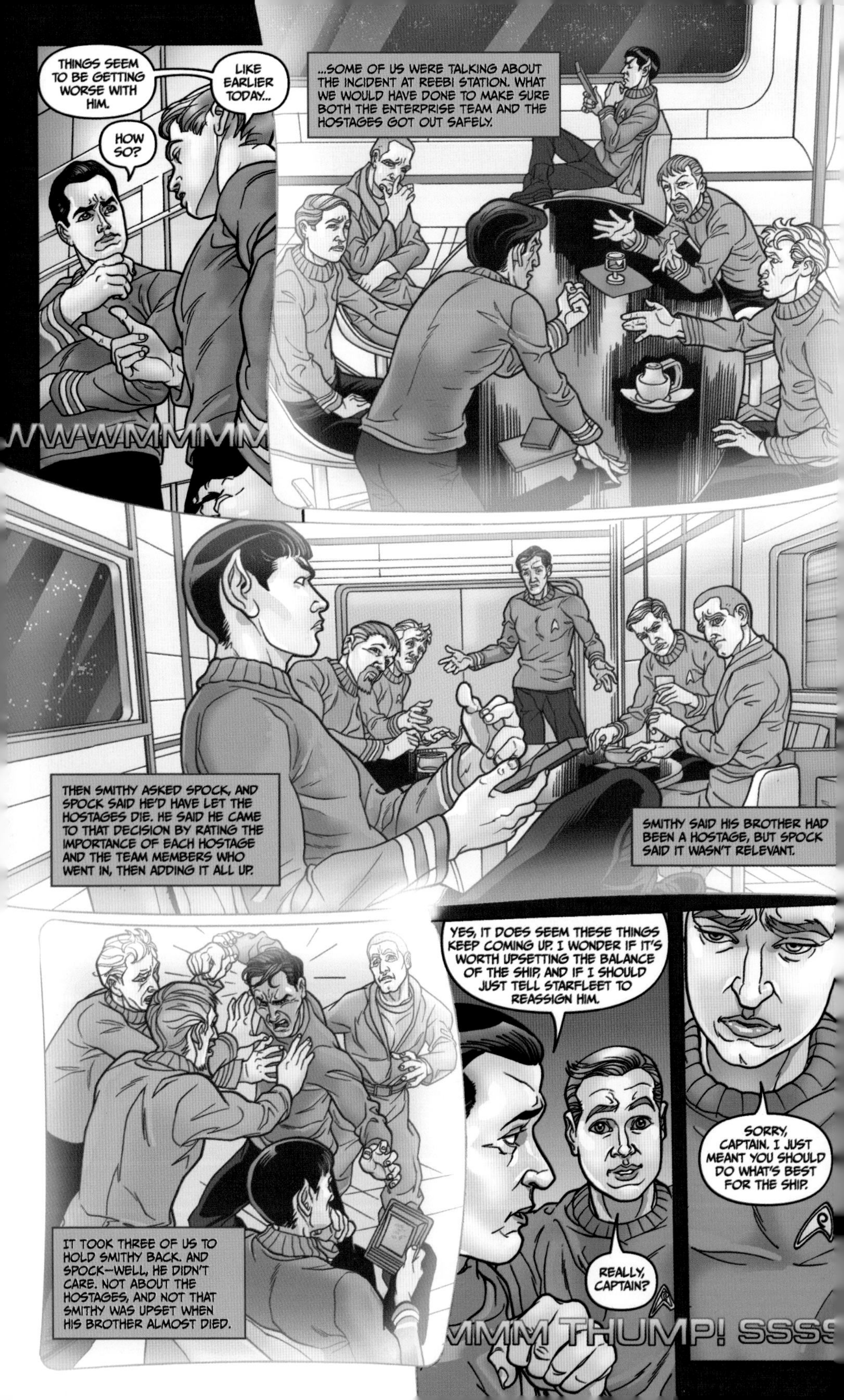
THINGS SEEM TO BE GETTING WORSE WITH HIM.
LIKE EARLIER TODAY...
HOW SO?
NWWWMMMMM
...SOME OF US WERE TALKING ABOUT THE INCIDENT AT REEBI STATION. WHAT WE WOULD HAVE DONE TO MAKE SURE BOTH THE ENTERPRISE TEAM AND THE HOSTAGES GOT OUT SAFELY.
THEN SMITHY ASKED SPOCK, AND SPOCK SAID HE'D HAVE LET THE HOSTAGES DIE. HE SAID HE CAME TO THAT DECISION BY RATING THE IMPORTANCE OF EACH HOSTAGE AND THE TEAM MEMBERS WHO WENT IN, THEN ADDING IT ALL UP.
SMITHY SAID HIS BROTHER HAD BEEN A HOSTAGE, BUT SPOCK SAID IT WASN'T RELEVANT.
IT TOOK THREE OF US TO HOLD SMITHY BACK. AND SPOCK--WELL, HE DIDN'T CARE. NOT ABOUT THE HOSTAGES, AND NOT THAT SMITHY WAS UPSET WHEN HIS BROTHER ALMOST DIED.
YES, IT DOES SEEM THESE THINGS KEEP COMING UP. I WONDER IF IT'S WORTH UPSETTING THE BALANCE OF THE SHIP, AND IF I SHOULD JUST TELL STARFLEET TO REASSIGN HIM.
REALLY, CAPTAIN?
SORRY, CAPTAIN. I JUST MEANT YOU SHOULD DO WHAT'S BEST FOR THE SHIP.
MMM THUMP! SSSS

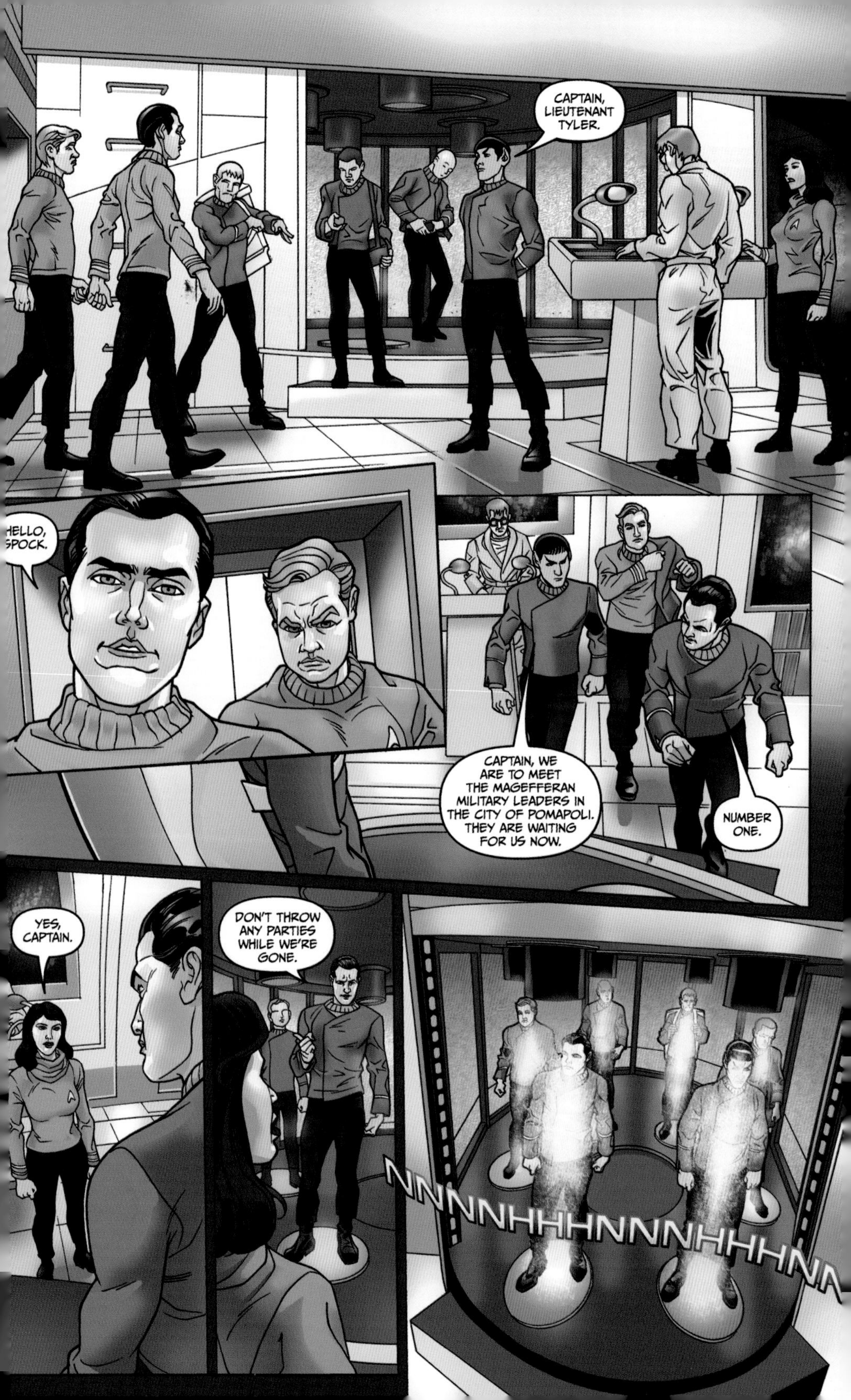
CAPTAIN, LIEUTENANT TYLER.
HELLO, SPOCK.
CAPTAIN, WE ARE TO MEET THE MAGEFFERAN MILITARY LEADERS IN THE CITY OF POMAPOLI. THEY ARE WAITING FOR US NOW.
NUMBER ONE.
YES, CAPTAIN.
DON'T THROW ANY PARTIES WHILE WE'RE GONE.
NNNNHHHNNNNHHHHNA

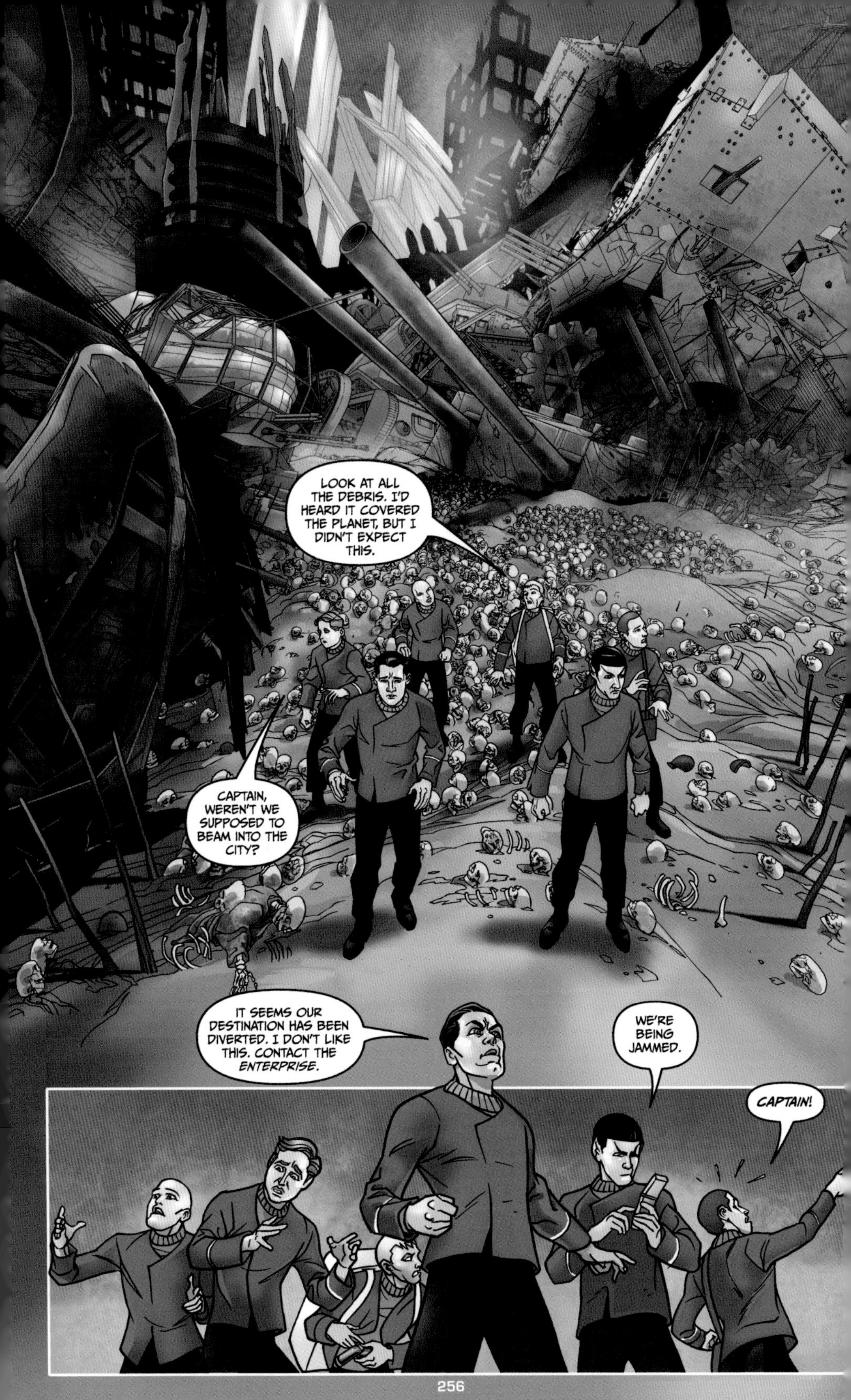
LOOK AT ALL THE DEBRIS. I'D HEARD IT COVERED THE PLANET, BUT I DIDN'T EXPECT THIS.
CAPTAIN, WEREN'T WE SUPPOSED TO BEAM INTO THE CITY?
IT SEEMS OUR DESTINATION HAS BEEN DIVERTED. I DON'T LIKE THIS. CONTACT THE *ENTERPRISE*.
WE'RE BEING JAMMED.
CAPTAIN!

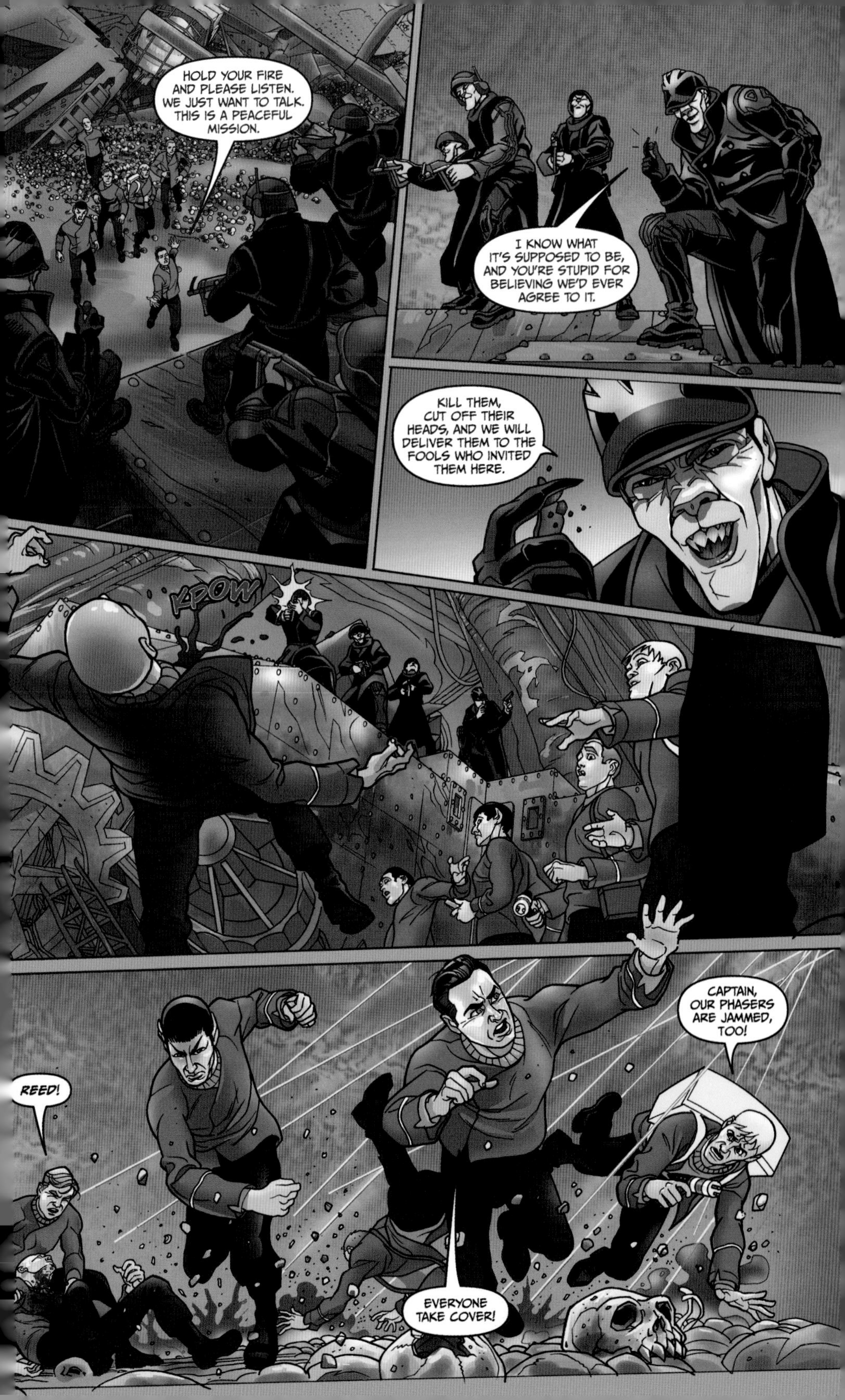
HOLD YOUR FIRE AND PLEASE LISTEN. WE JUST WANT TO TALK. THIS IS A PEACEFUL MISSION.
I KNOW WHAT IT'S SUPPOSED TO BE, AND YOU'RE STUPID FOR BELIEVING WE'D EVER AGREE TO IT.
KILL THEM, CUT OFF THEIR HEADS, AND WE WILL DELIVER THEM TO THE FOOLS WHO INVITED THEM HERE.
KPOW
CAPTAIN, OUR PHASERS ARE JAMMED, TOO!
REED!
EVERYONE TAKE COVER!

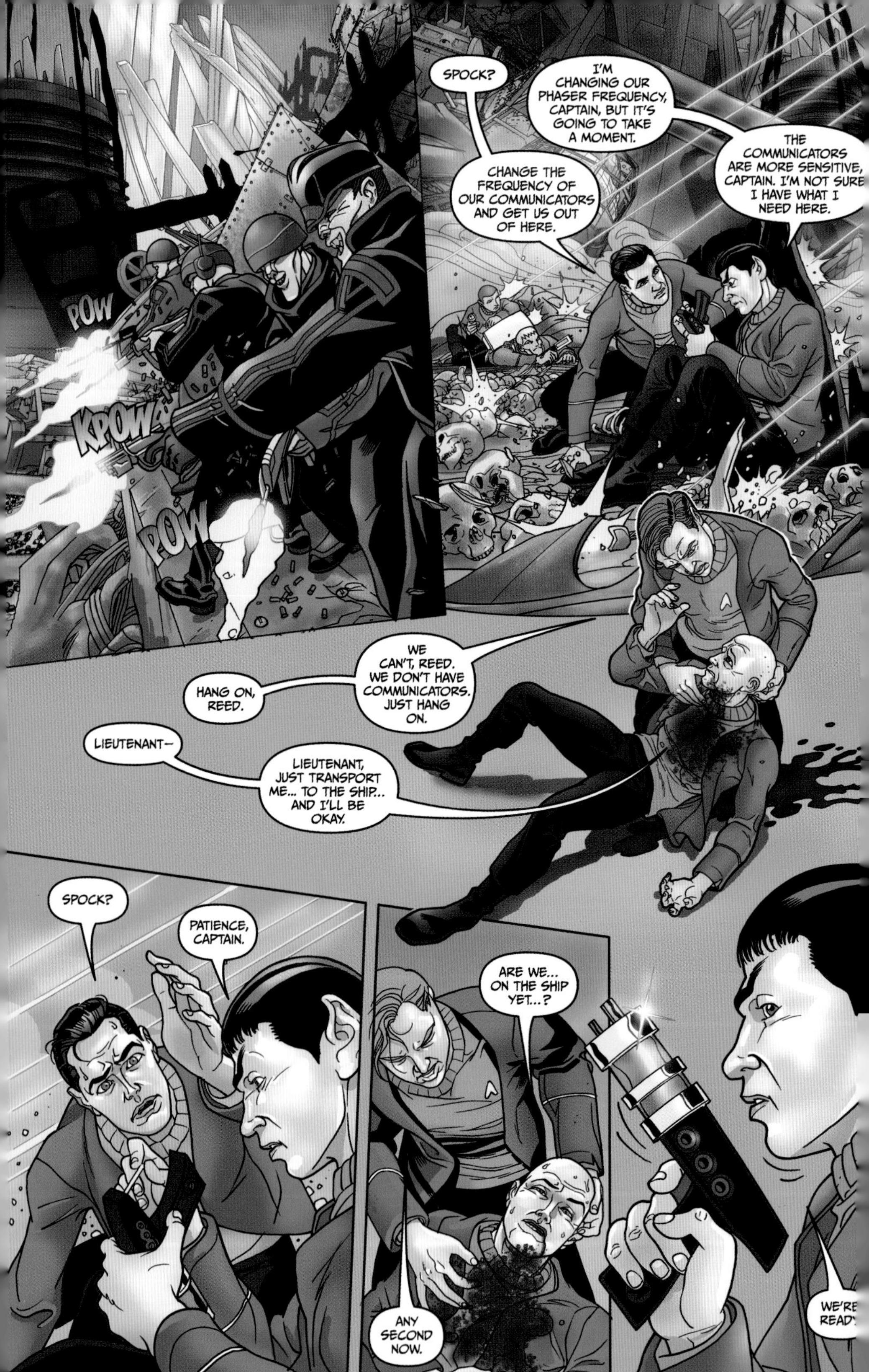

POW
KPOW
POW
SPOCK?
I'M CHANGING OUR PHASER FREQUENCY, CAPTAIN, BUT IT'S GOING TO TAKE A MOMENT.
CHANGE THE FREQUENCY OF OUR COMMUNICATORS AND GET US OUT OF HERE.
THE COMMUNICATORS ARE MORE SENSITIVE, CAPTAIN. I'M NOT SURE I HAVE WHAT I NEED HERE.
HANG ON, REED.
WE CAN'T, REED. WE DON'T HAVE COMMUNICATORS. JUST HANG ON.
LIEUTENANT--
LIEUTENANT, JUST TRANSPORT ME... TO THE SHIP... AND I'LL BE OKAY.
SPOCK?
PATIENCE, CAPTAIN.
ARE WE... ON THE SHIP YET...?
ANY SECOND NOW.

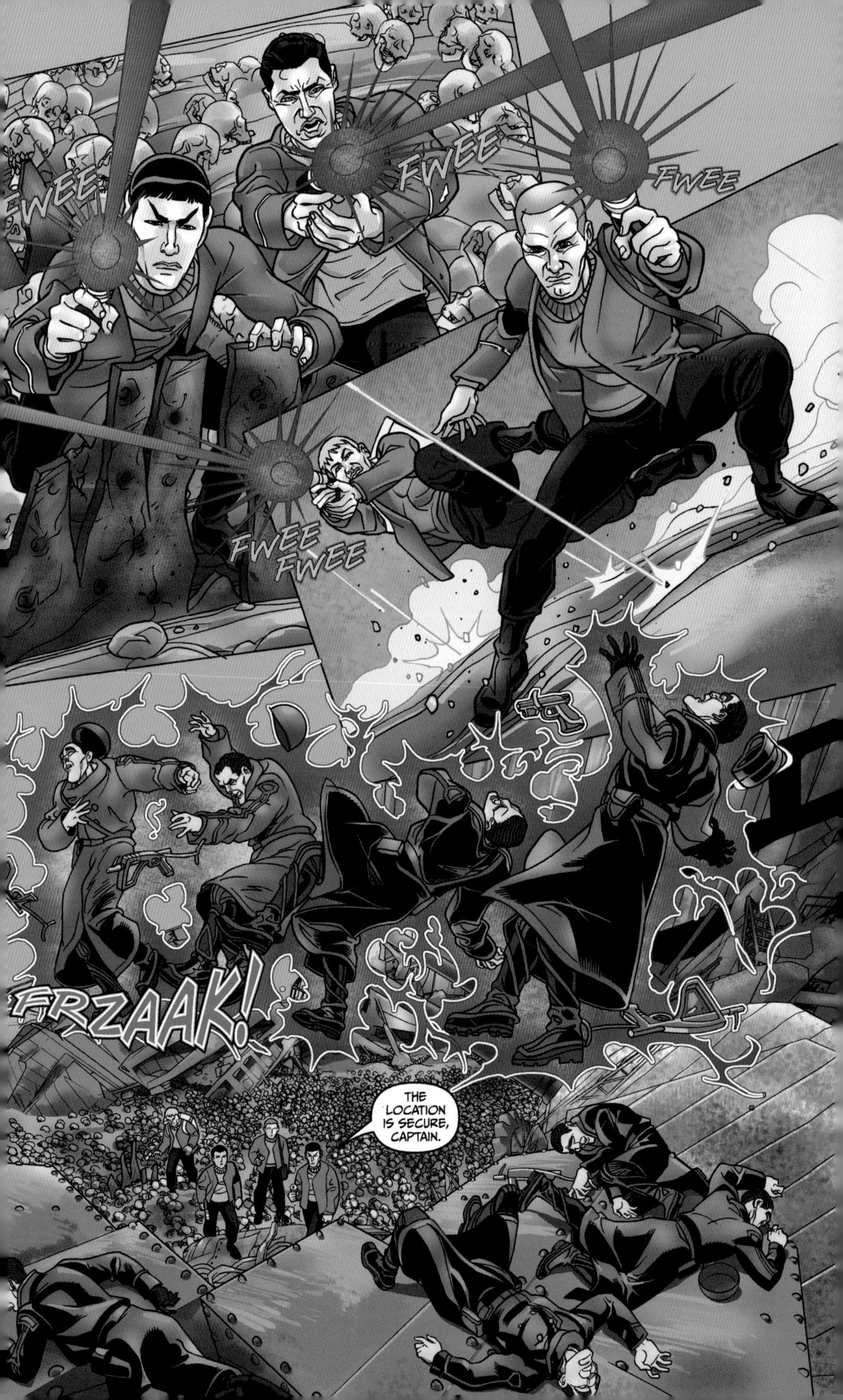
FWEE
FWEE
FWEE
FWEE
FWEE
FWEE
FRZAAK!
THE LOCATION IS SECURE, CAPTAIN.

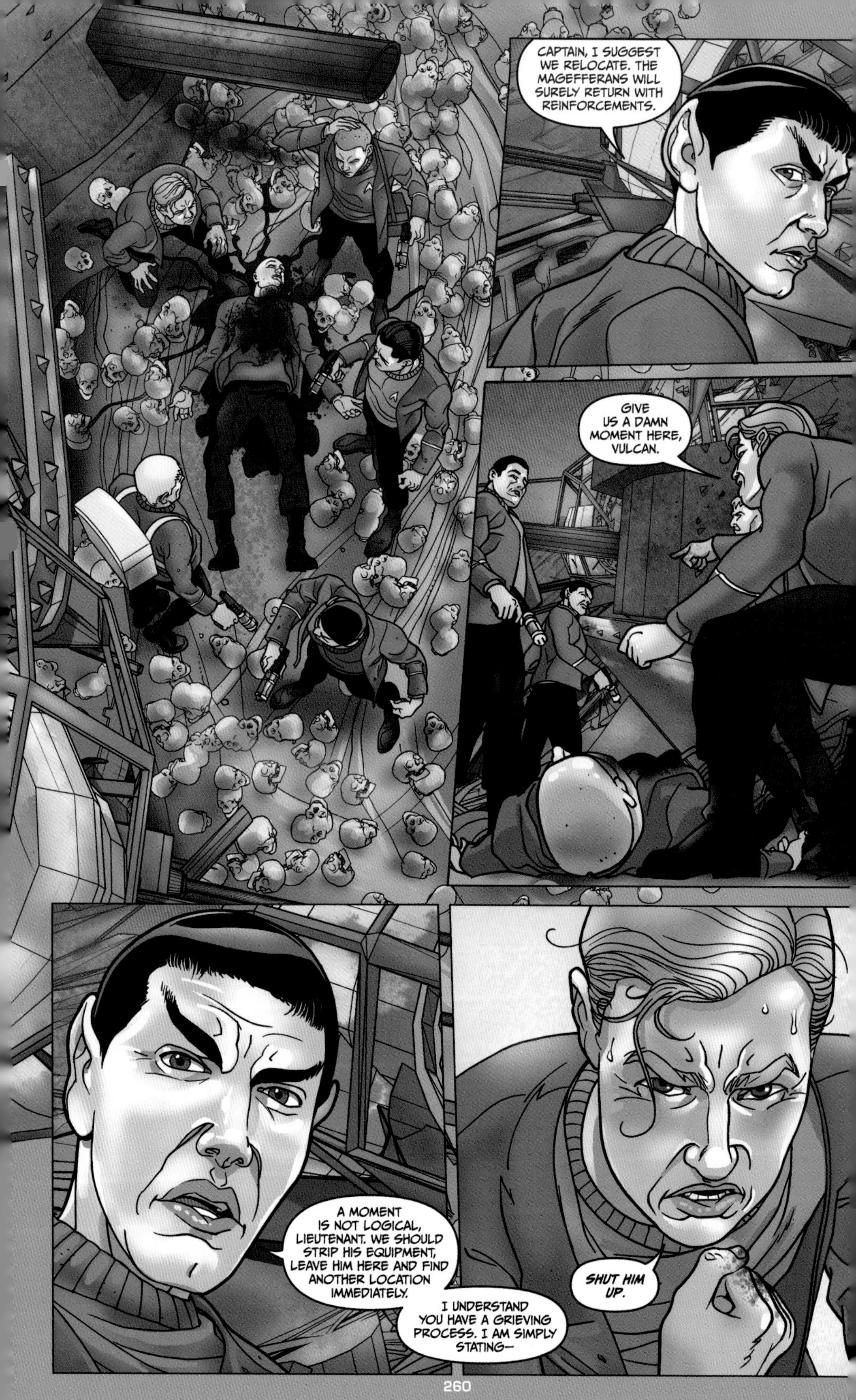
CAPTAIN, I SUGGEST WE RELOCATE. THE MAGEFFERANS WILL SURELY RETURN WITH REINFORCEMENTS.
GIVE US A DAMN MOMENT HERE, VULCAN.
A MOMENT IS NOT LOGICAL, LIEUTENANT. WE SHOULD STRIP HIS EQUIPMENT, LEAVE HIM HERE AND FIND ANOTHER LOCATION IMMEDIATELY.
I UNDERSTAND YOU HAVE A GRIEVING PROCESS. I AM SIMPLY STATING—
SHUT HIM UP.

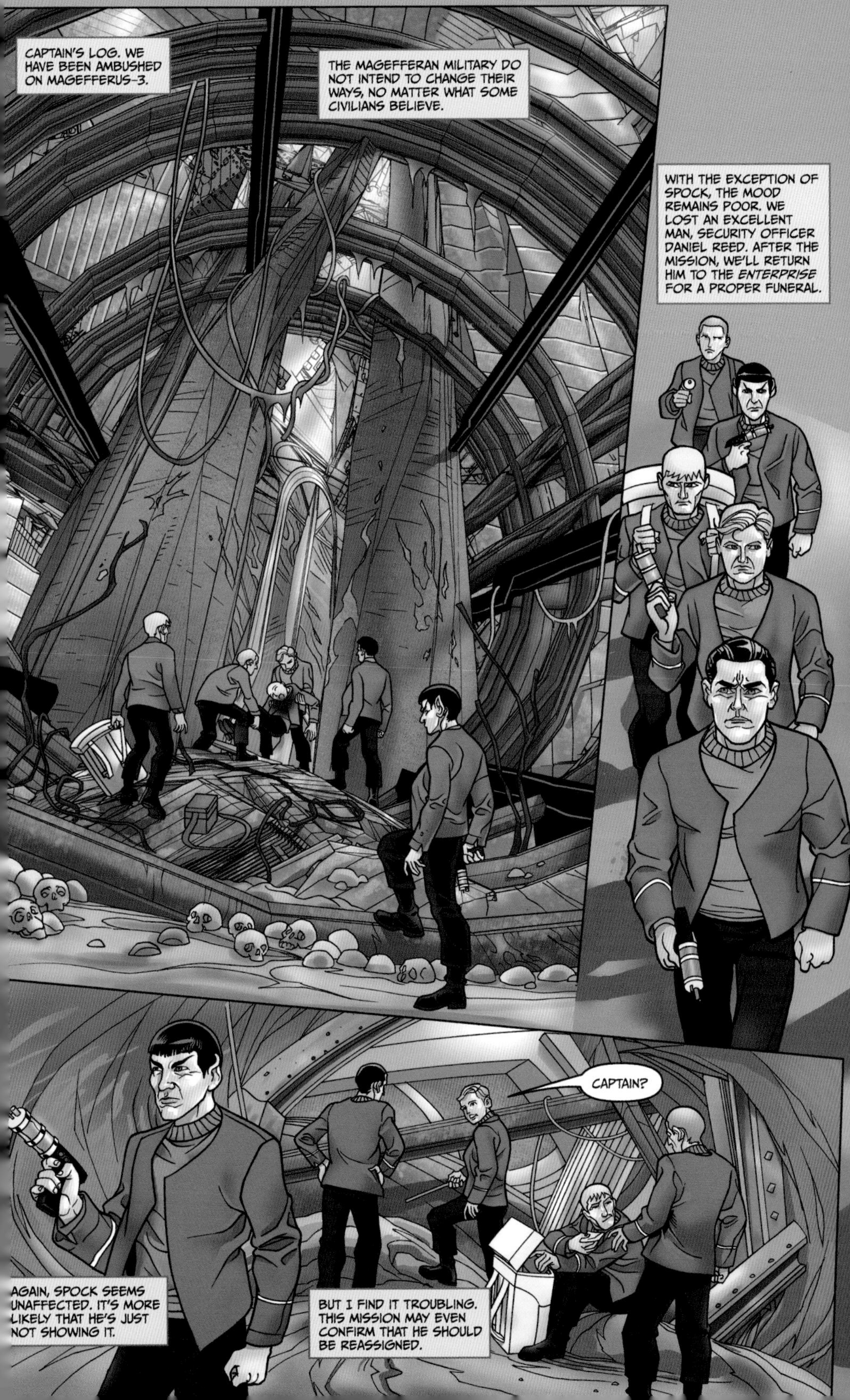
CAPTAIN'S LOG. WE HAVE BEEN AMBUSHED ON MAGEFFERUS-3.
THE MAGEFFERAN MILITARY DO NOT INTEND TO CHANGE THEIR WAYS, NO MATTER WHAT SOME CIVILIANS BELIEVE.
WITH THE EXCEPTION OF SPOCK, THE MOOD REMAINS POOR. WE LOST AN EXCELLENT MAN, SECURITY OFFICER DANIEL REED. AFTER THE MISSION, WE'LL RETURN HIM TO THE *ENTERPRISE* FOR A PROPER FUNERAL.
CAPTAIN?
AGAIN, SPOCK SEEMS UNAFFECTED. IT'S MORE LIKELY THAT HE'S JUST NOT SHOWING IT.
BUT I FIND IT TROUBLING. THIS MISSION MAY EVEN CONFIRM THAT HE SHOULD BE REASSIGNED.

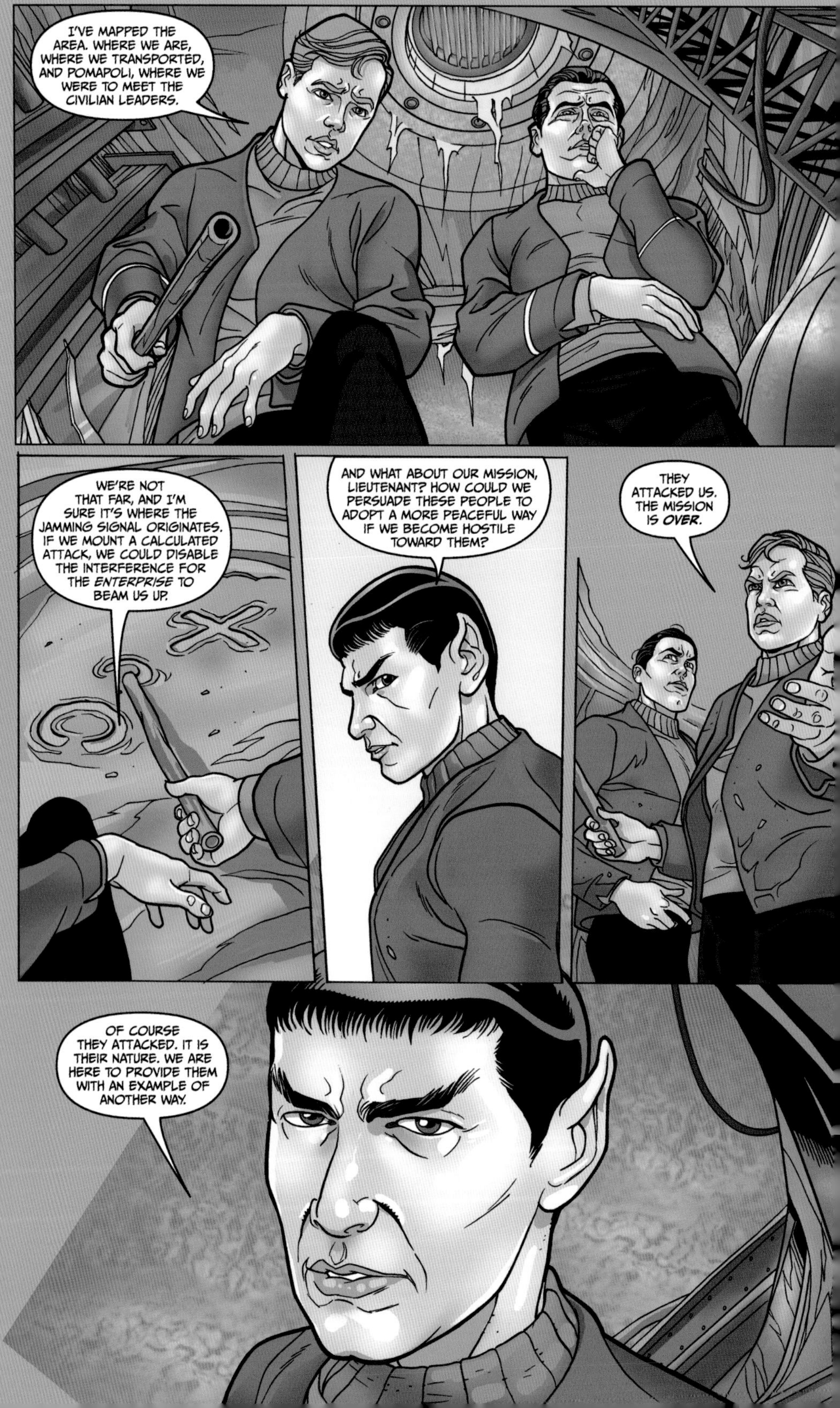
I'VE MAPPED THE AREA. WHERE WE ARE, WHERE WE TRANSPORTED, AND POMAPOLI, WHERE WE WERE TO MEET THE CIVILIAN LEADERS.
WE'RE NOT THAT FAR, AND I'M SURE IT'S WHERE THE JAMMING SIGNAL ORIGINATES. IF WE MOUNT A CALCULATED ATTACK, WE COULD DISABLE THE INTERFERENCE FOR THE *ENTERPRISE* TO BEAM US UP.
AND WHAT ABOUT OUR MISSION, LIEUTENANT? HOW COULD WE PERSUADE THESE PEOPLE TO ADOPT A MORE PEACEFUL WAY IF WE BECOME HOSTILE TOWARD THEM?
THEY ATTACKED US. THE MISSION IS *OVER*.
OF COURSE THEY ATTACKED. IT IS THEIR NATURE. WE ARE HERE TO PROVIDE THEM WITH AN EXAMPLE OF ANOTHER WAY.

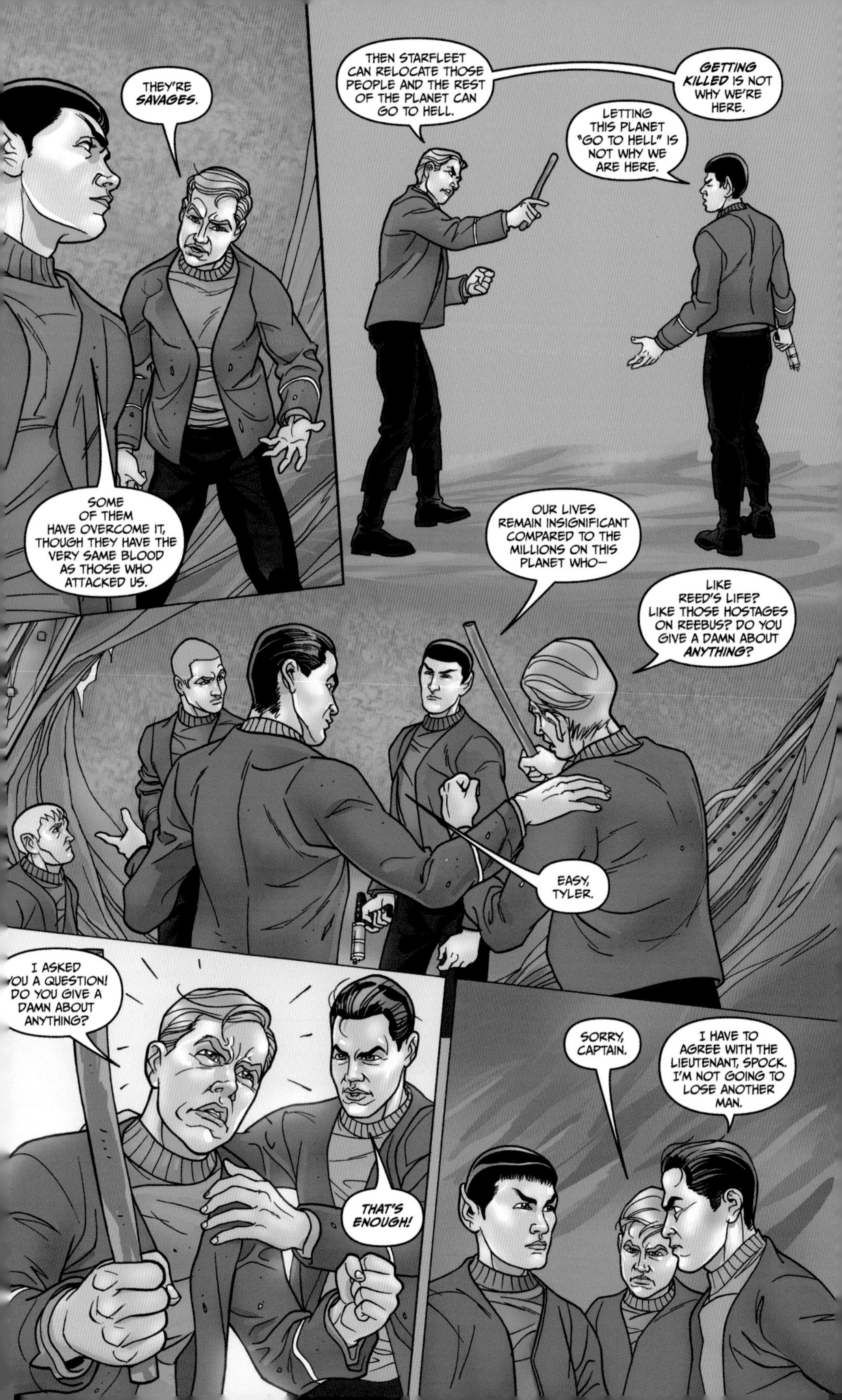
THEY'RE SAVAGES.
SOME OF THEM HAVE OVERCOME IT, THOUGH THEY HAVE THE VERY SAME BLOOD AS THOSE WHO ATTACKED US.
THEN STARFLEET CAN RELOCATE THOSE PEOPLE AND THE REST OF THE PLANET CAN GO TO HELL.
GETTING KILLED IS NOT WHY WE'RE HERE.
LETTING THIS PLANET "GO TO HELL" IS NOT WHY WE ARE HERE.
OUR LIVES REMAIN INSIGNIFICANT COMPARED TO THE MILLIONS ON THIS PLANET WHO—
LIKE REED'S LIFE? LIKE THOSE HOSTAGES ON REEBUS? DO YOU GIVE A DAMN ABOUT ANYTHING?
EASY, TYLER.
I ASKED YOU A QUESTION! DO YOU GIVE A DAMN ABOUT ANYTHING?
THAT'S ENOUGH!
SORRY, CAPTAIN.
I HAVE TO AGREE WITH THE LIEUTENANT, SPOCK. I'M NOT GOING TO LOSE ANOTHER MAN.

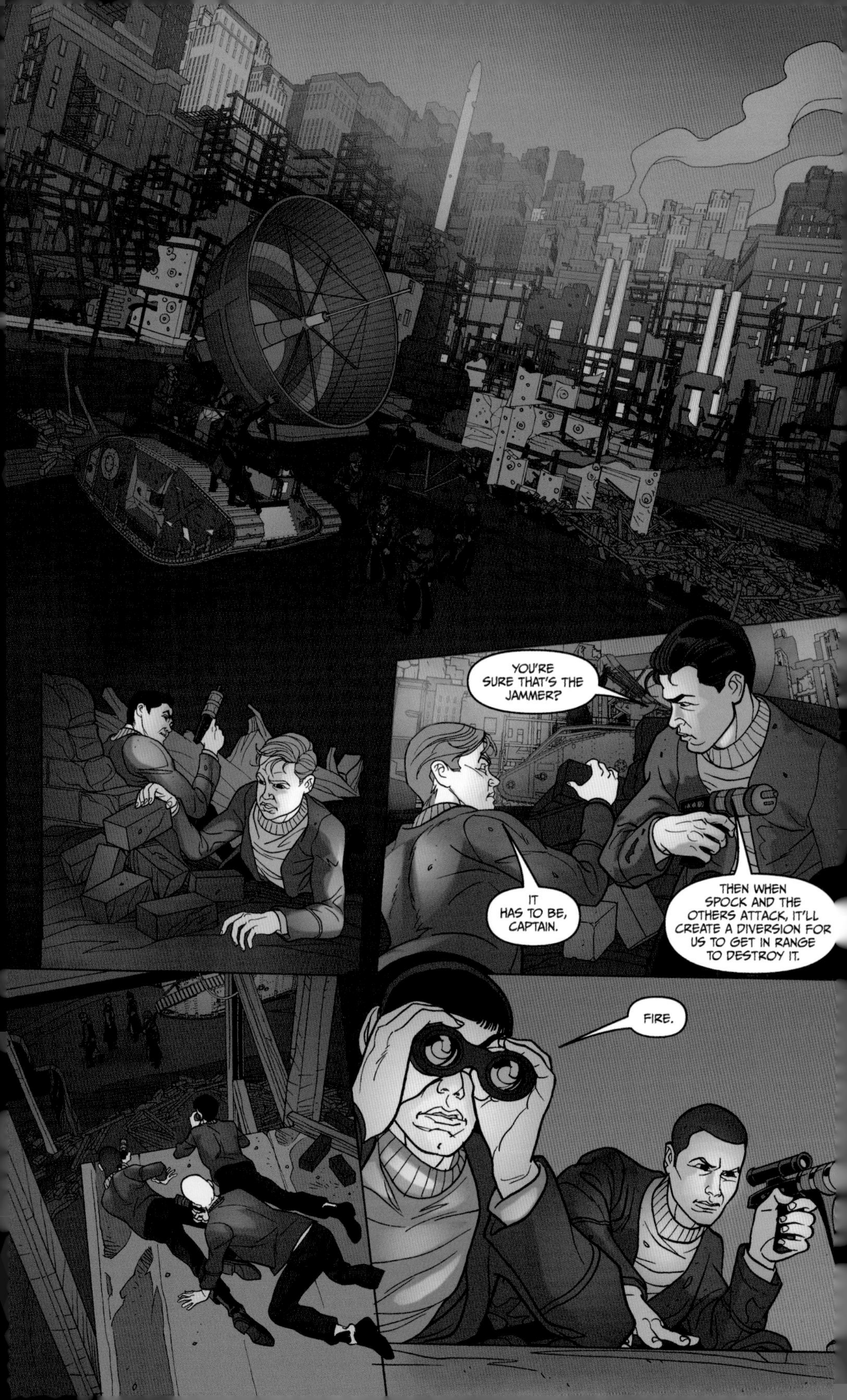
YOU'RE SURE THAT'S THE JAMMER?
IT HAS TO BE, CAPTAIN.
THEN WHEN SPOCK AND THE OTHERS ATTACK, IT'LL CREATE A DIVERSION FOR US TO GET IN RANGE TO DESTROY IT.
FIRE.

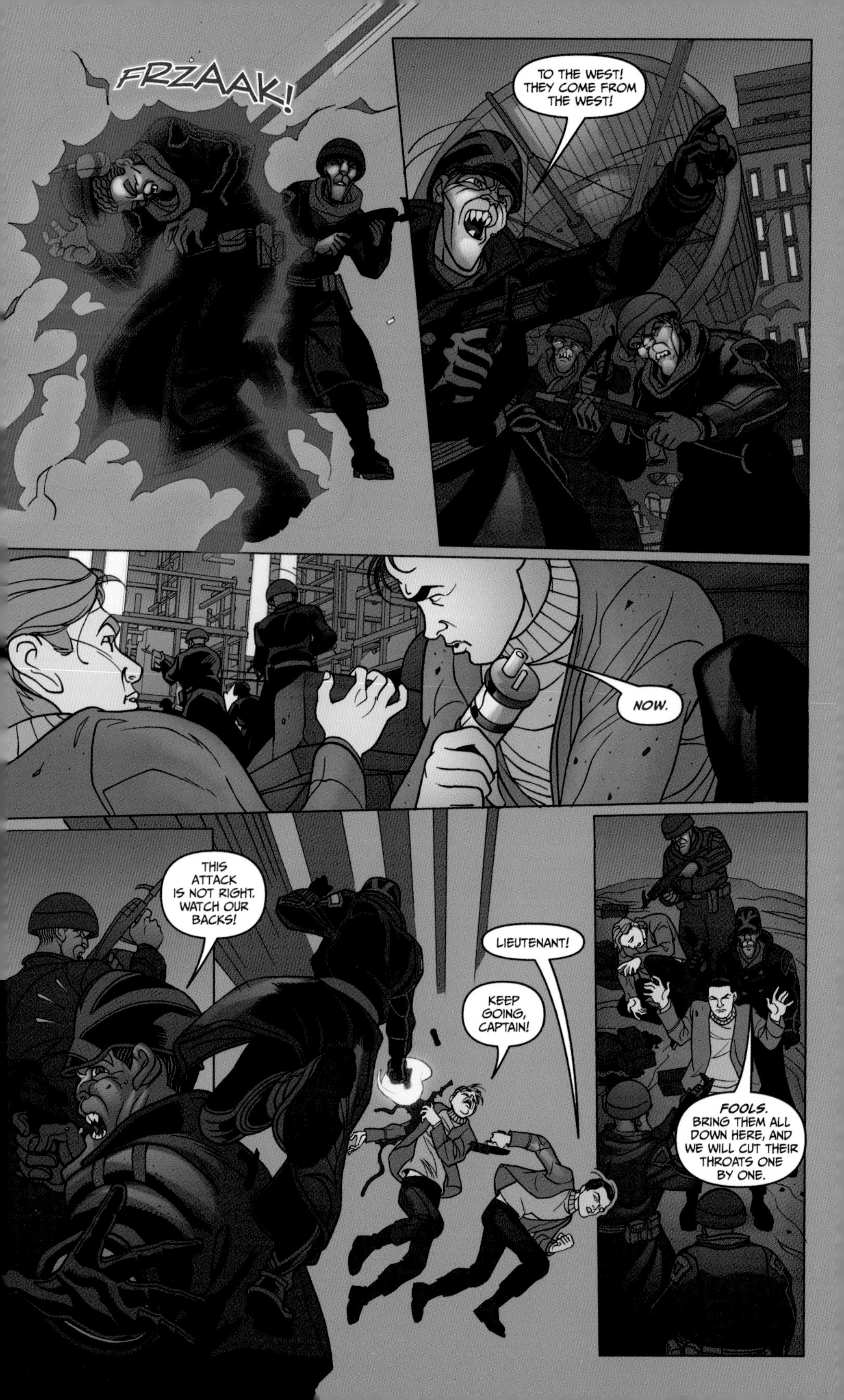
FRZAAK!
TO THE WEST! THEY COME FROM THE WEST!
NOW.
THIS ATTACK IS NOT RIGHT. WATCH OUR BACKS!
LIEUTENANT!
KEEP GOING, CAPTAIN!
FOOLS. BRING THEM ALL DOWN HERE, AND WE WILL CUT THEIR THROATS ONE BY ONE.

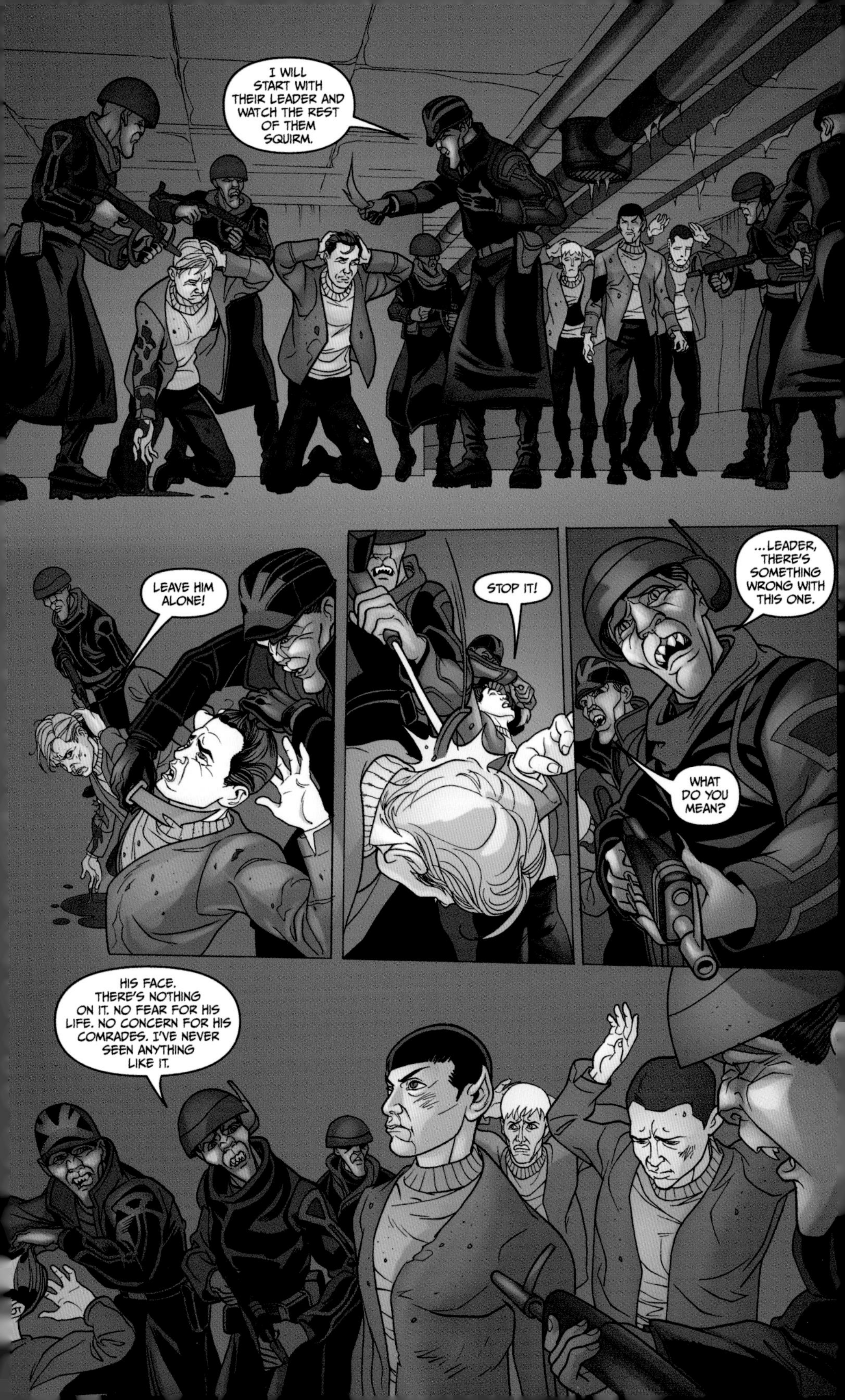
I WILL START WITH THEIR LEADER AND WATCH THE REST OF THEM SQUIRM.
LEAVE HIM ALONE!
STOP IT!
...LEADER, THERE'S SOMETHING WRONG WITH THIS ONE.
WHAT DO YOU MEAN?
HIS FACE. THERE'S NOTHING ON IT. NO FEAR FOR HIS LIFE. NO CONCERN FOR HIS COMRADES. I'VE NEVER SEEN ANYTHING LIKE IT.

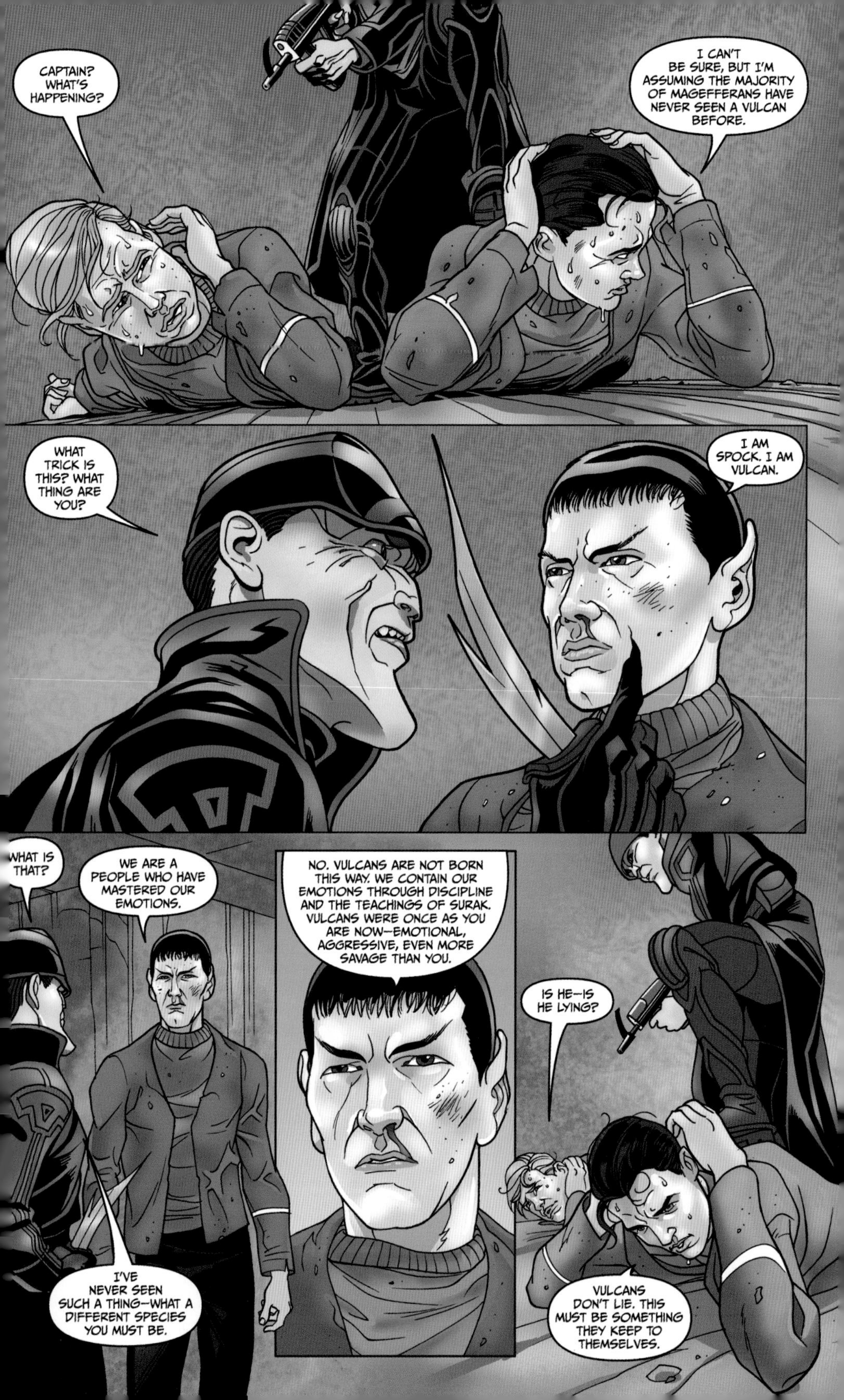
CAPTAIN? WHAT'S HAPPENING?
I CAN'T BE SURE, BUT I'M ASSUMING THE MAJORITY OF MAGEFFERANS HAVE NEVER SEEN A VULCAN BEFORE.
WHAT TRICK IS THIS? WHAT THING ARE YOU?
I AM SPOCK. I AM VULCAN.
WHAT IS THAT?
WE ARE A PEOPLE WHO HAVE MASTERED OUR EMOTIONS.
I'VE NEVER SEEN SUCH A THING--WHAT A DIFFERENT SPECIES YOU MUST BE.
NO. VULCANS ARE NOT BORN THIS WAY. WE CONTAIN OUR EMOTIONS THROUGH DISCIPLINE AND THE TEACHINGS OF SURAK. VULCANS WERE ONCE AS YOU ARE NOW--EMOTIONAL, AGGRESSIVE, EVEN MORE SAVAGE THAN YOU.
IS HE--IS HE LYING?
VULCANS DON'T LIE. THIS MUST BE SOMETHING THEY KEEP TO THEMSELVES.

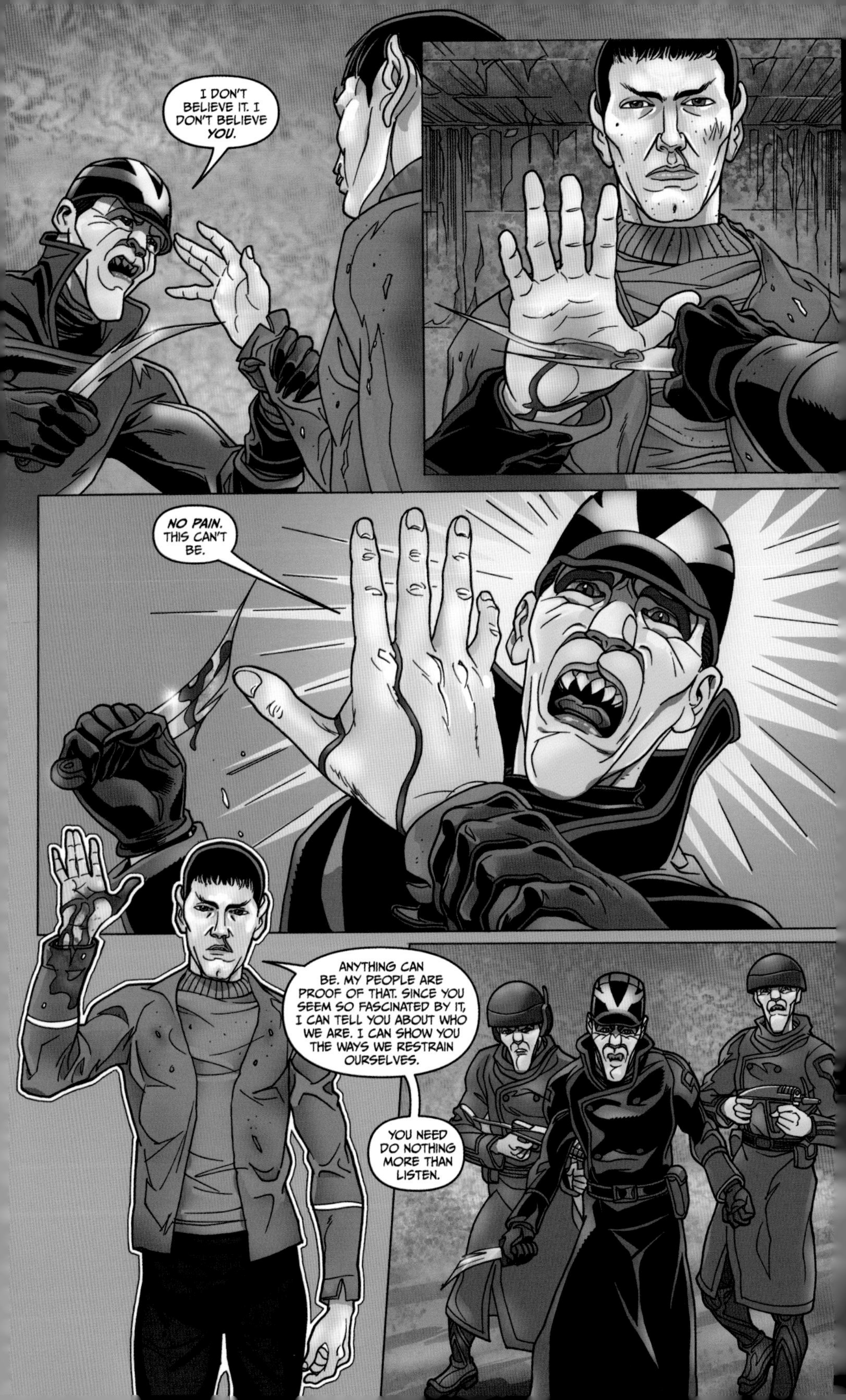
I DON'T BELIEVE IT. I DON'T BELIEVE *YOU*.
NO PAIN. THIS CAN'T BE.
ANYTHING CAN BE. MY PEOPLE ARE PROOF OF THAT. SINCE YOU SEEM SO FASCINATED BY IT, I CAN TELL YOU ABOUT WHO WE ARE. I CAN SHOW YOU THE WAYS WE RESTRAIN OURSELVES.
YOU NEED DO NOTHING MORE THAN LISTEN.

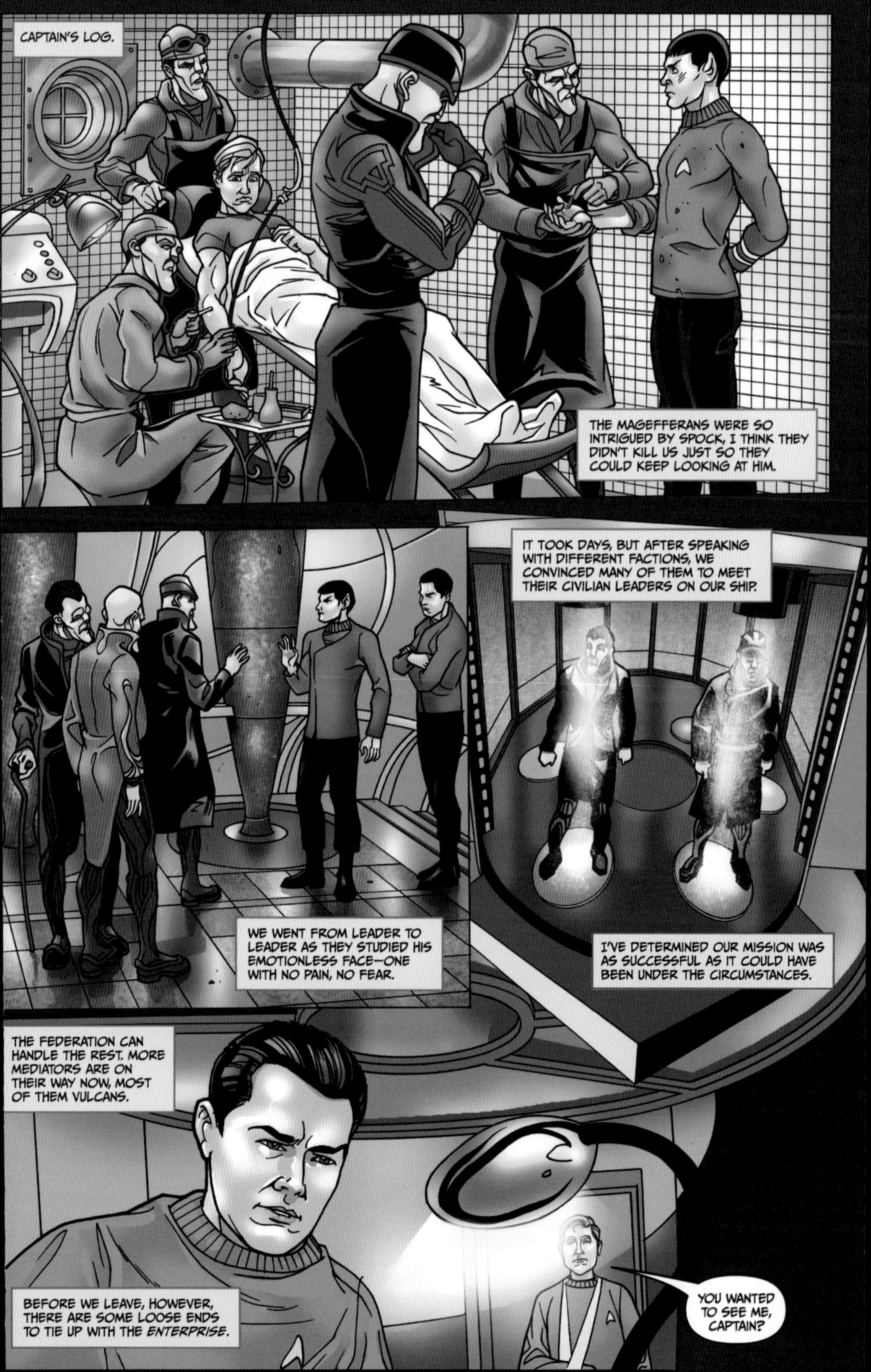
CAPTAIN'S LOG.
THE MAGEFFERANS WERE SO INTRIGUED BY SPOCK, I THINK THEY DIDN'T KILL US JUST SO THEY COULD KEEP LOOKING AT HIM.
IT TOOK DAYS, BUT AFTER SPEAKING WITH DIFFERENT FACTIONS, WE CONVINCED MANY OF THEM TO MEET THEIR CIVILIAN LEADERS ON OUR SHIP.
WE WENT FROM LEADER TO LEADER AS THEY STUDIED HIS EMOTIONLESS FACE—ONE WITH NO PAIN, NO FEAR.
I'VE DETERMINED OUR MISSION WAS AS SUCCESSFUL AS IT COULD HAVE BEEN UNDER THE CIRCUMSTANCES.
THE FEDERATION CAN HANDLE THE REST. MORE MEDIATORS ARE ON THEIR WAY NOW, MOST OF THEM VULCANS.
BEFORE WE LEAVE, HOWEVER, THERE ARE SOME LOOSE ENDS TO TIE UP WITH THE *ENTERPRISE*.
YOU WANTED TO SEE ME, CAPTAIN?

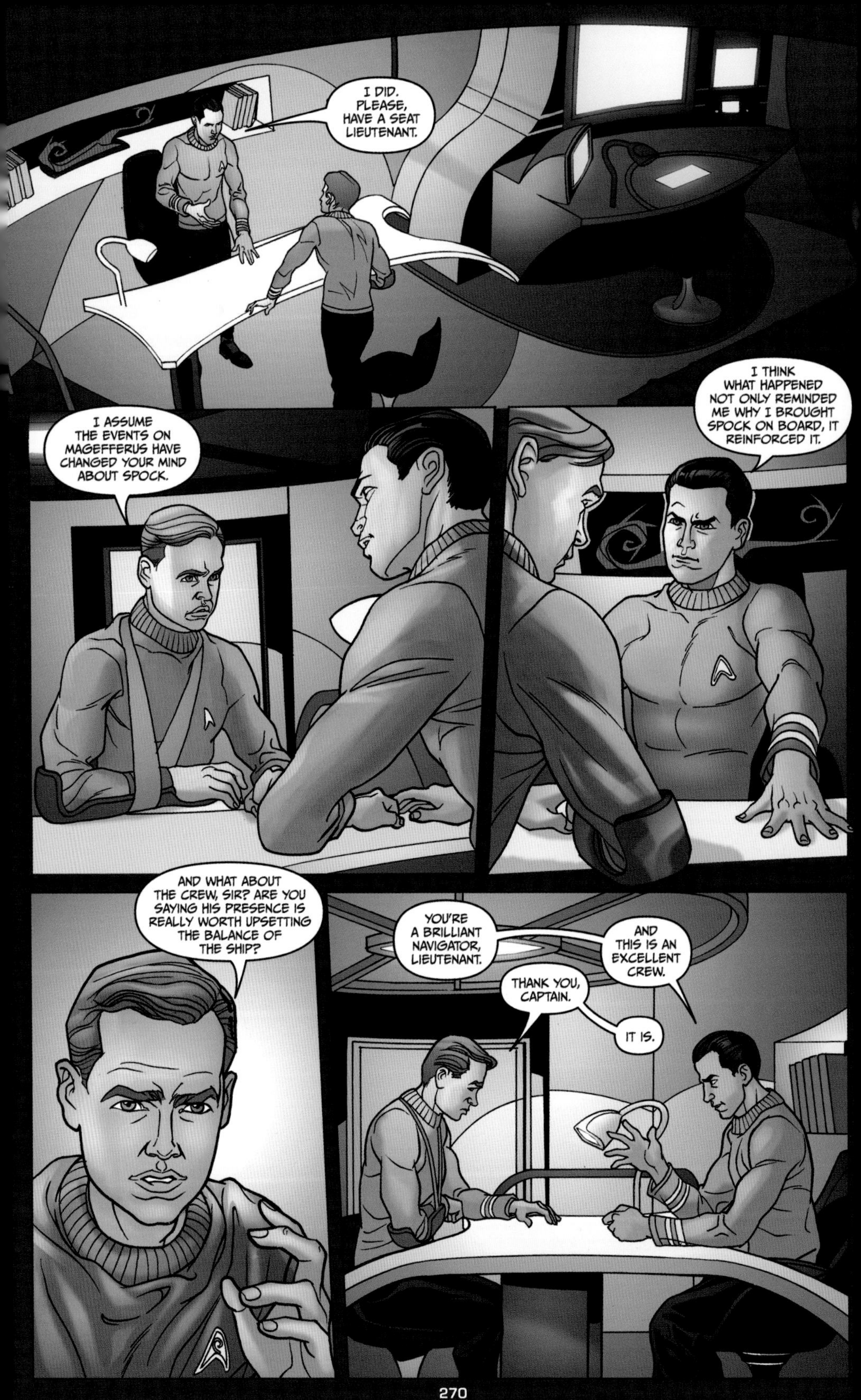
I DID. PLEASE, HAVE A SEAT LIEUTENANT.
I ASSUME THE EVENTS ON MAGEFFERUS HAVE CHANGED YOUR MIND ABOUT SPOCK.
I THINK WHAT HAPPENED NOT ONLY REMINDED ME WHY I BROUGHT SPOCK ON BOARD, IT REINFORCED IT.
AND WHAT ABOUT THE CREW, SIR? ARE YOU SAYING HIS PRESENCE IS REALLY WORTH UPSETTING THE BALANCE OF THE SHIP?
YOU'RE A BRILLIANT NAVIGATOR, LIEUTENANT.
AND THIS IS AN EXCELLENT CREW.
THANK YOU, CAPTAIN.
IT IS.

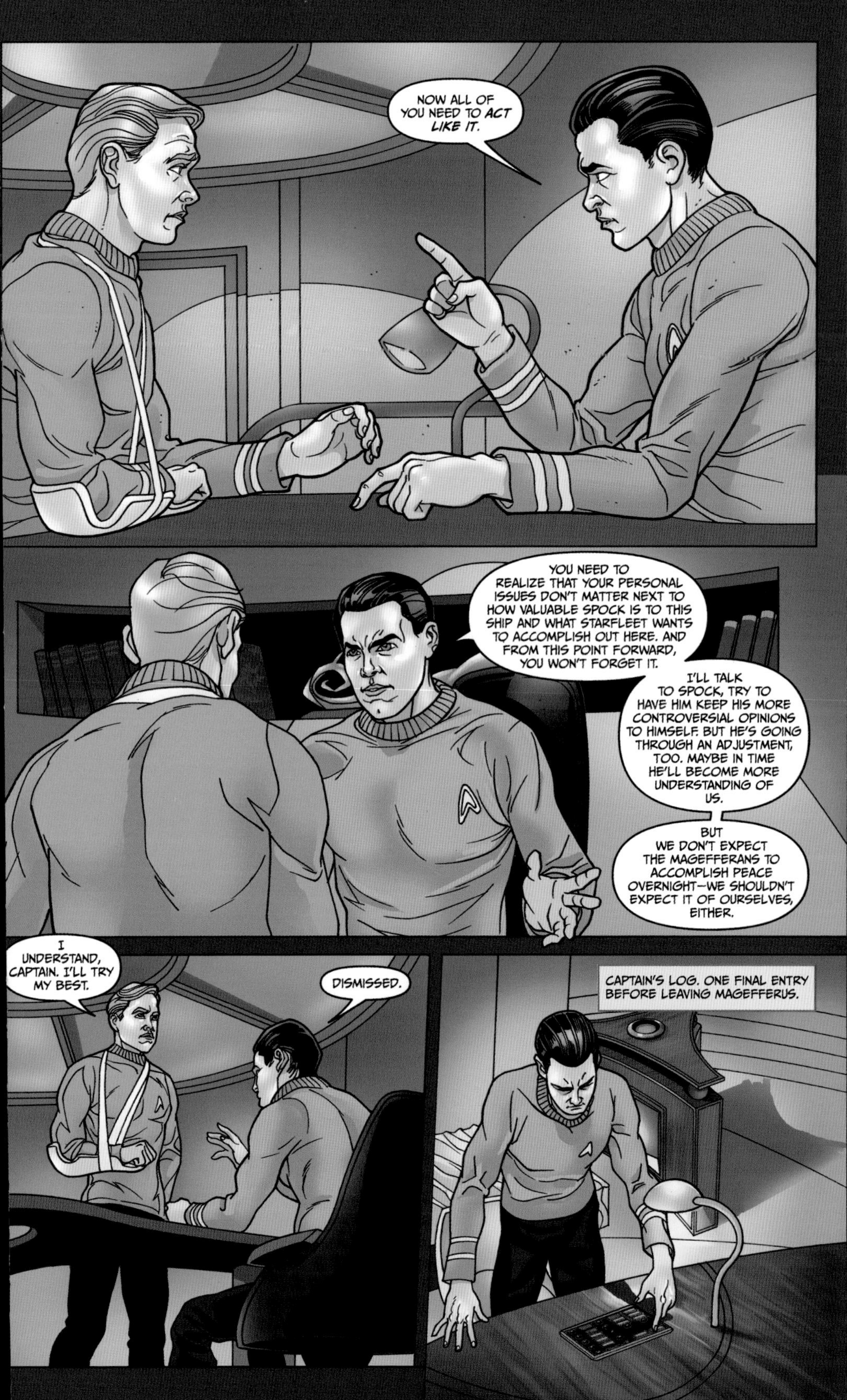
NOW ALL OF YOU NEED TO *ACT LIKE IT*.
YOU NEED TO REALIZE THAT YOUR PERSONAL ISSUES DON'T MATTER NEXT TO HOW VALUABLE SPOCK IS TO THIS SHIP AND WHAT STARFLEET WANTS TO ACCOMPLISH OUT HERE. AND FROM THIS POINT FORWARD, YOU WON'T FORGET IT.
I'LL TALK TO SPOCK, TRY TO HAVE HIM KEEP HIS MORE CONTROVERSIAL OPINIONS TO HIMSELF. BUT HE'S GOING THROUGH AN ADJUSTMENT, TOO. MAYBE IN TIME HE'LL BECOME MORE UNDERSTANDING OF US.
BUT WE DON'T EXPECT THE MAGEFFERANS TO ACCOMPLISH PEACE OVERNIGHT—WE SHOULDN'T EXPECT IT OF OURSELVES, EITHER.
I UNDERSTAND, CAPTAIN. I'LL TRY MY BEST.
DISMISSED.
CAPTAIN'S LOG. ONE FINAL ENTRY BEFORE LEAVING MAGEFFERUS.

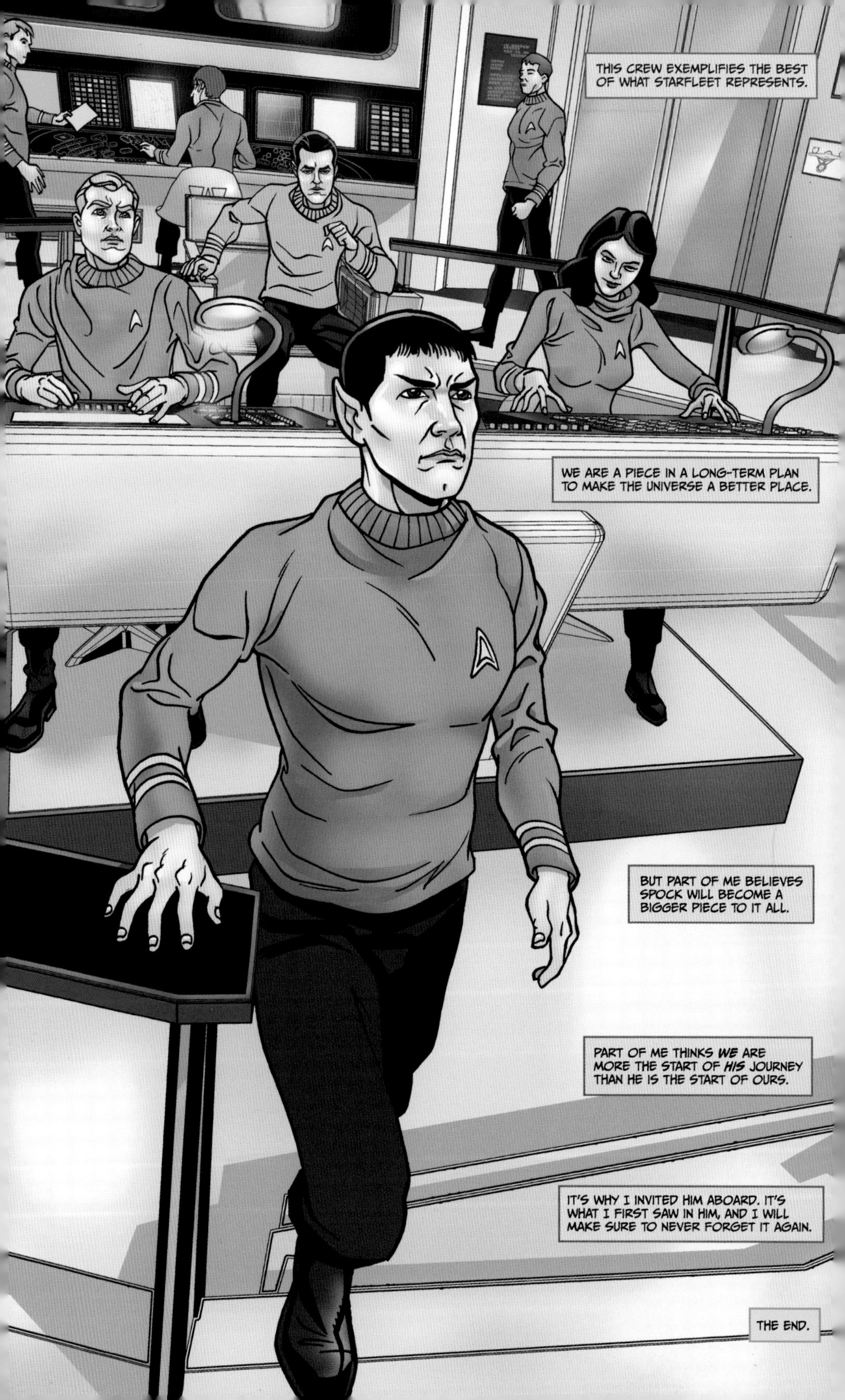
THIS CREW EXEMPLIFIES THE BEST OF WHAT STARFLEET REPRESENTS.
WE ARE A PIECE IN A LONG-TERM PLAN TO MAKE THE UNIVERSE A BETTER PLACE.
BUT PART OF ME BELIEVES SPOCK WILL BECOME A BIGGER PIECE TO IT ALL.
PART OF ME THINKS *WE* ARE MORE THE START OF *HIS* JOURNEY THAN HE IS THE START OF OURS.
IT'S WHY I INVITED HIM ABOARD. IT'S WHAT I FIRST SAW IN HIM, AND I WILL MAKE SURE TO NEVER FORGET IT AGAIN.
THE END.

STAR TREK ®

THE ORIGINAL SERIES

OMNIBUS

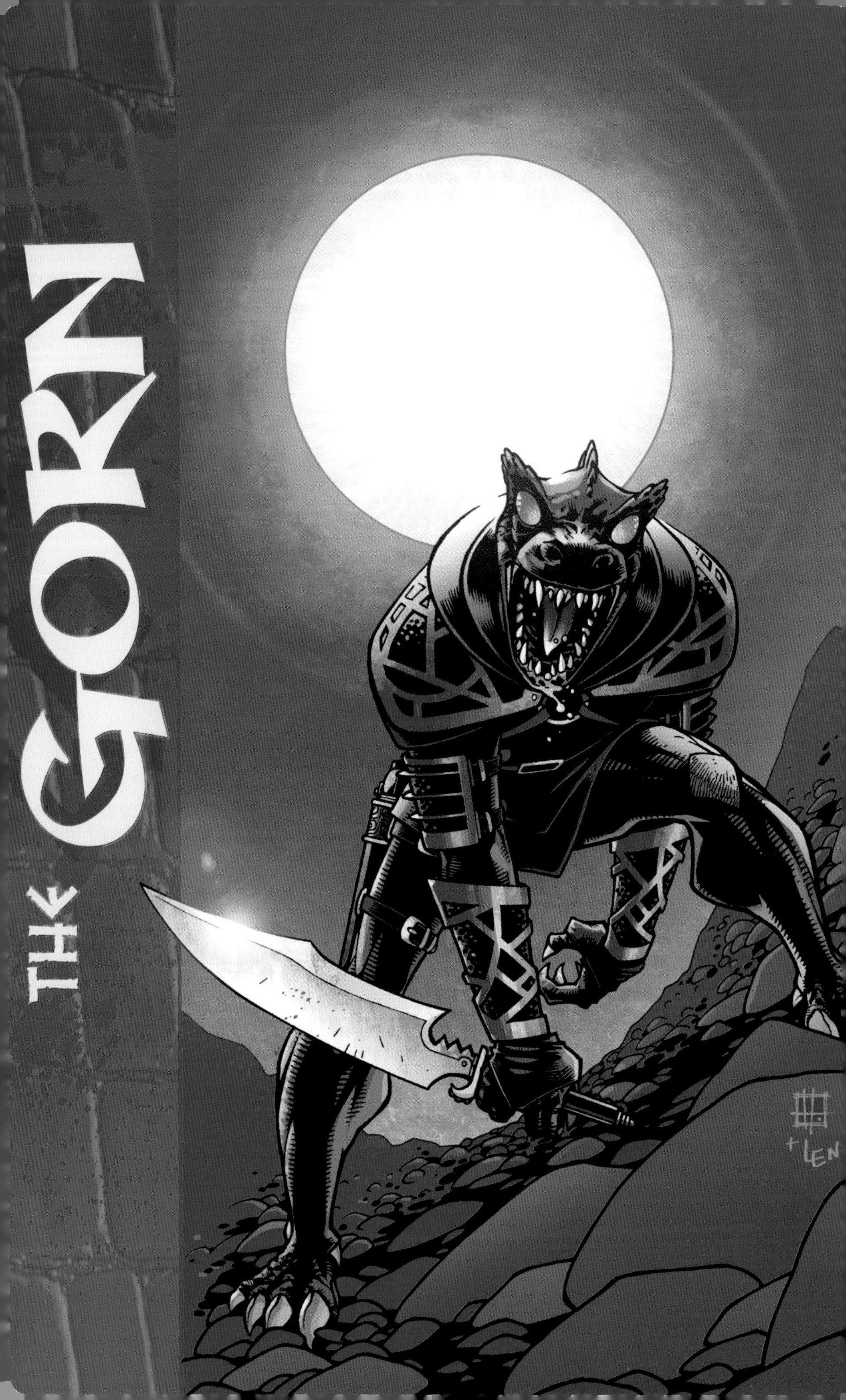
THE GORN

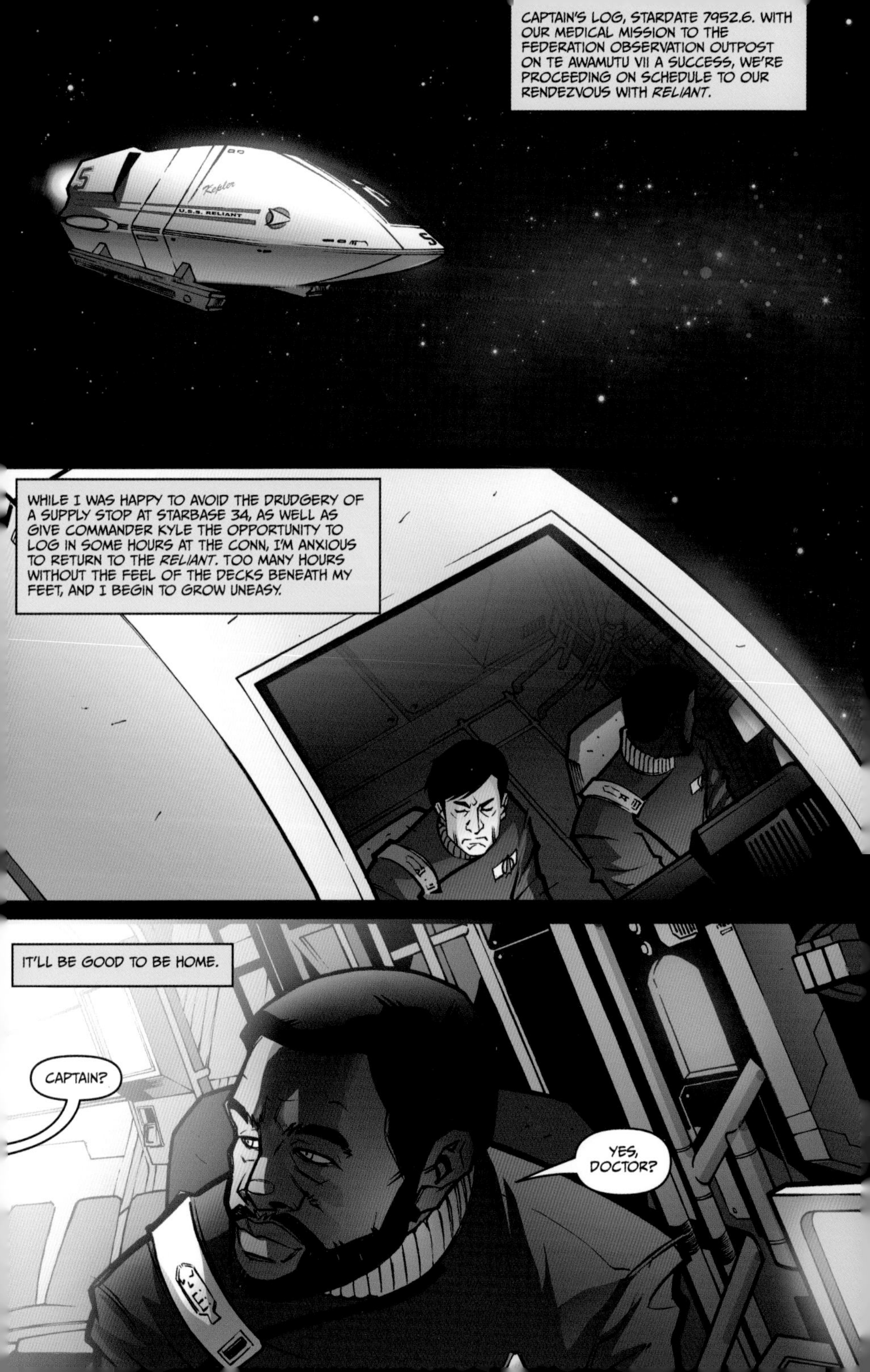

CAPTAIN'S LOG, STARDATE 7952.6. WITH OUR MEDICAL MISSION TO THE FEDERATION OBSERVATION OUTPOST ON TE AWAMUTU VII A SUCCESS, WE'RE PROCEEDING ON SCHEDULE TO OUR RENDEZVOUS WITH *RELIANT*.
Kepler
U.S.S. RELIANT
WHILE I WAS HAPPY TO AVOID THE DRUDGERY OF A SUPPLY STOP AT STARBASE 34, AS WELL AS GIVE COMMANDER KYLE THE OPPORTUNITY TO LOG IN SOME HOURS AT THE CONN, I'M ANXIOUS TO RETURN TO THE *RELIANT*. TOO MANY HOURS WITHOUT THE FEEL OF THE DECKS BENEATH MY FEET, AND I BEGIN TO GROW UNEASY.
IT'LL BE GOOD TO BE HOME.
CAPTAIN?
YES, DOCTOR?

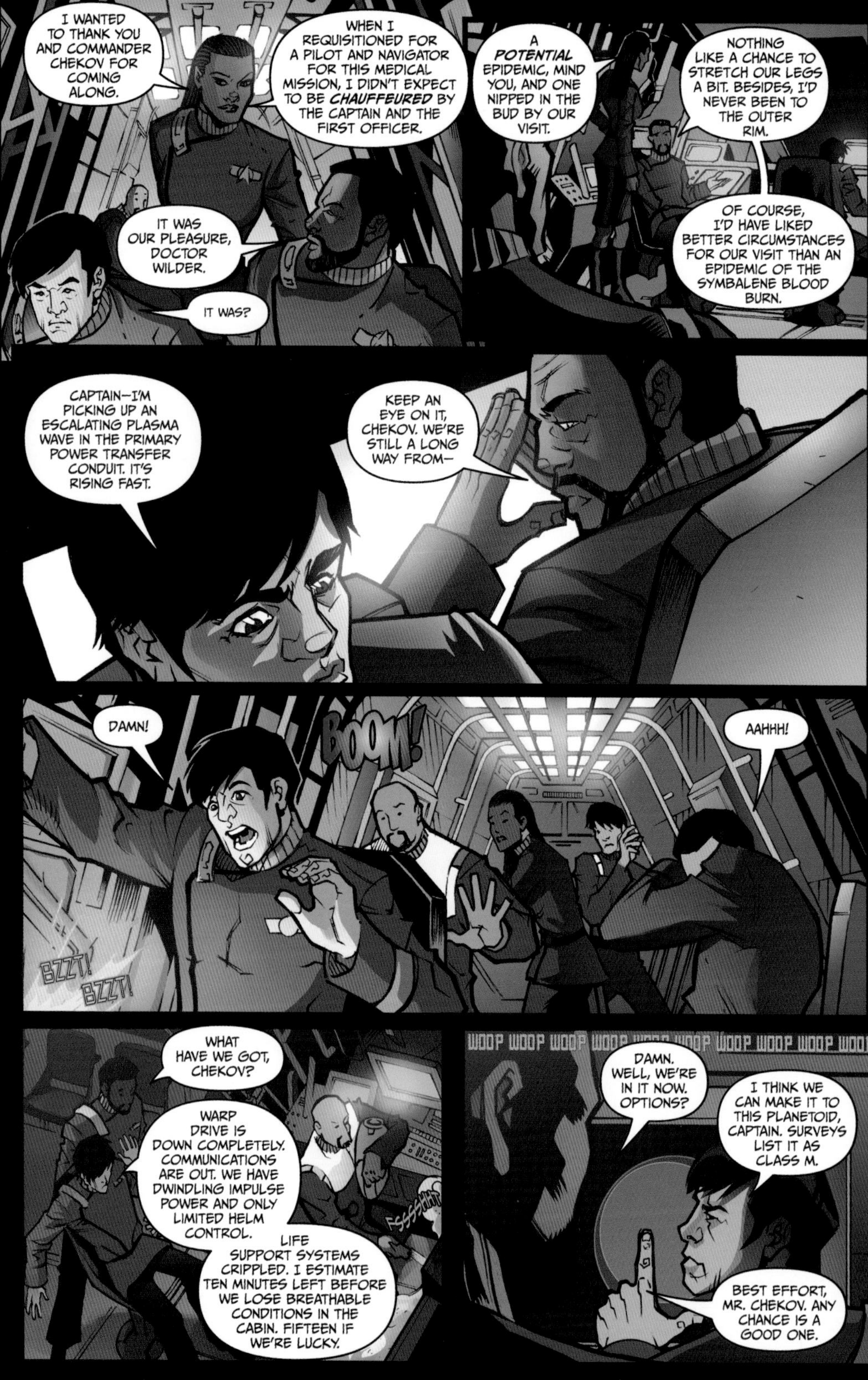

I WANTED TO THANK YOU AND COMMANDER CHEKOV FOR COMING ALONG.
WHEN I REQUISITIONED FOR A PILOT AND NAVIGATOR FOR THIS MEDICAL MISSION, I DIDN'T EXPECT TO BE *CHAUFFEURED* BY THE CAPTAIN AND THE FIRST OFFICER.
IT WAS OUR PLEASURE, DOCTOR WILDER.
IT WAS?
A *POTENTIAL* EPIDEMIC, MIND YOU, AND ONE NIPPED IN THE BUD BY OUR VISIT.
NOTHING LIKE A CHANCE TO STRETCH OUR LEGS A BIT. BESIDES, I'D NEVER BEEN TO THE OUTER RIM.
OF COURSE, I'D HAVE LIKED BETTER CIRCUMSTANCES FOR OUR VISIT THAN AN EPIDEMIC OF THE SYMBALENE BLOOD BURN.
CAPTAIN—I'M PICKING UP AN ESCALATING PLASMA WAVE IN THE PRIMARY POWER TRANSFER CONDUIT. IT'S RISING FAST.
KEEP AN EYE ON IT, CHEKOV. WE'RE STILL A LONG WAY FROM—
DAMN!
BOOM!
AAHHH!
BZZT! BZZT!
WHAT HAVE WE GOT, CHEKOV?
WARP DRIVE IS DOWN COMPLETELY. COMMUNICATIONS ARE OUT. WE HAVE DWINDLING IMPULSE POWER AND ONLY LIMITED HELM CONTROL.
LIFE SUPPORT SYSTEMS CRIPPLED. I ESTIMATE TEN MINUTES LEFT BEFORE WE LOSE BREATHABLE CONDITIONS IN THE CABIN. FIFTEEN IF WE'RE LUCKY.
FSSSSHHT
WOOP WOOP WOOP WOOP WOOP WOOP WOOP WOOP WOO
DAMN. WELL, WE'RE IN IT NOW. OPTIONS?
I THINK WE CAN MAKE IT TO THIS PLANETOID, CAPTAIN. SURVEYS LIST IT AS CLASS M.
BEST EFFORT, MR. CHEKOV. ANY CHANCE IS A GOOD ONE.

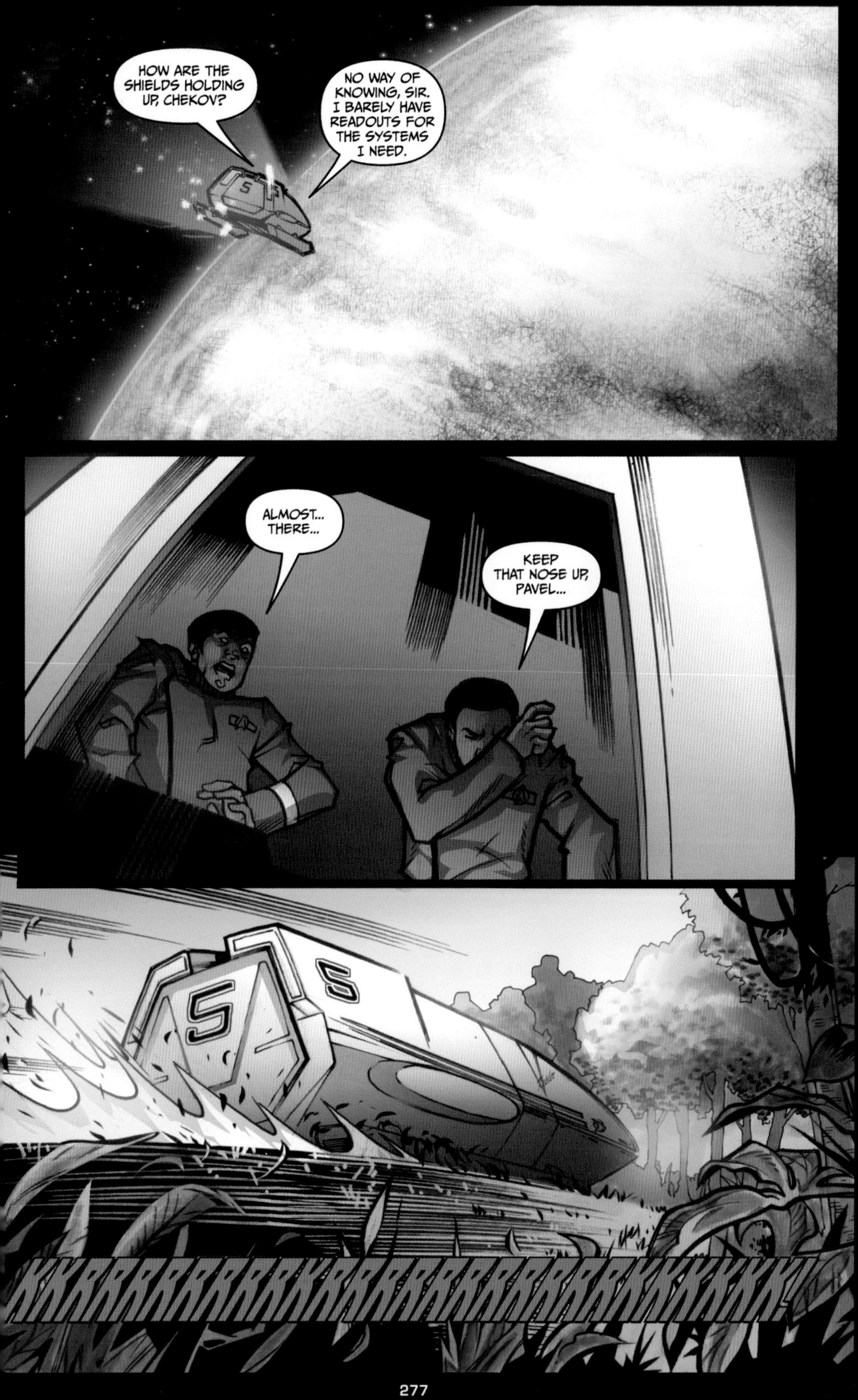
HOW ARE THE SHIELDS HOLDING UP, CHEKOV?
NO WAY OF KNOWING, SIR. I BARELY HAVE READOUTS FOR THE SYSTEMS I NEED.
ALMOST... THERE...
KEEP THAT NOSE UP, PAVEL...
KKRRRRRRRKRRRRRRRRRRRRRKKKKKK!

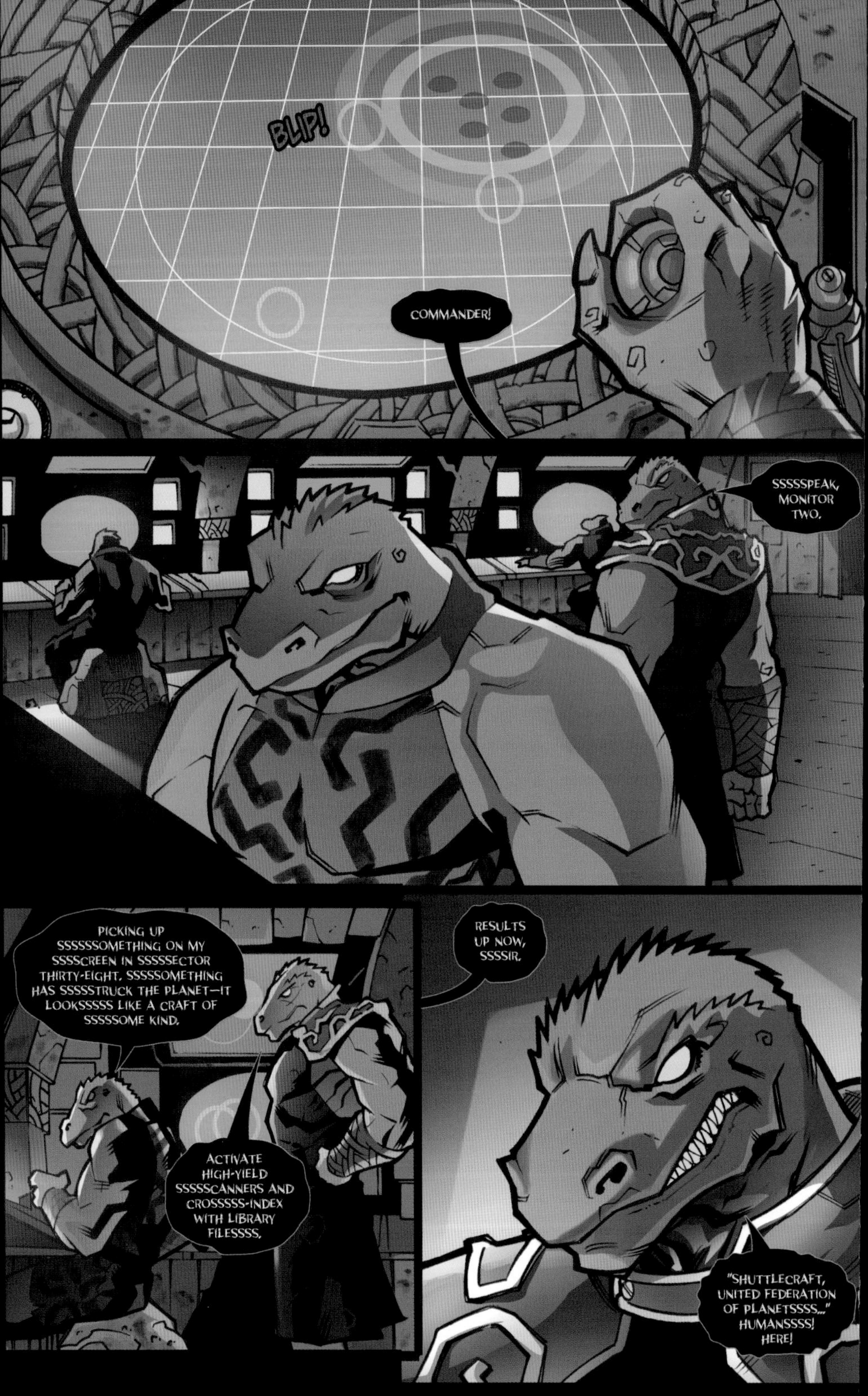
BLIP!
COMMANDER!
SSSSSPEAK, MONITOR TWO.
PICKING UP SSSSSSOMETHING ON MY SSSSCREEN IN SSSSSECTOR THIRTY-EIGHT. SSSSSOMETHING HAS SSSSSTRUCK THE PLANET—IT LOOKSSSSS LIKE A CRAFT OF SSSSSOME KIND.
ACTIVATE HIGH-YIELD SSSSSCANNERS AND CROSSSSS-INDEX WITH LIBRARY FILESSSS.
RESULTS UP NOW, SSSSSIR.
"SHUTTLECRAFT, UNITED FEDERATION OF PLANETSSSS..." HUMANSSSS! HERE!

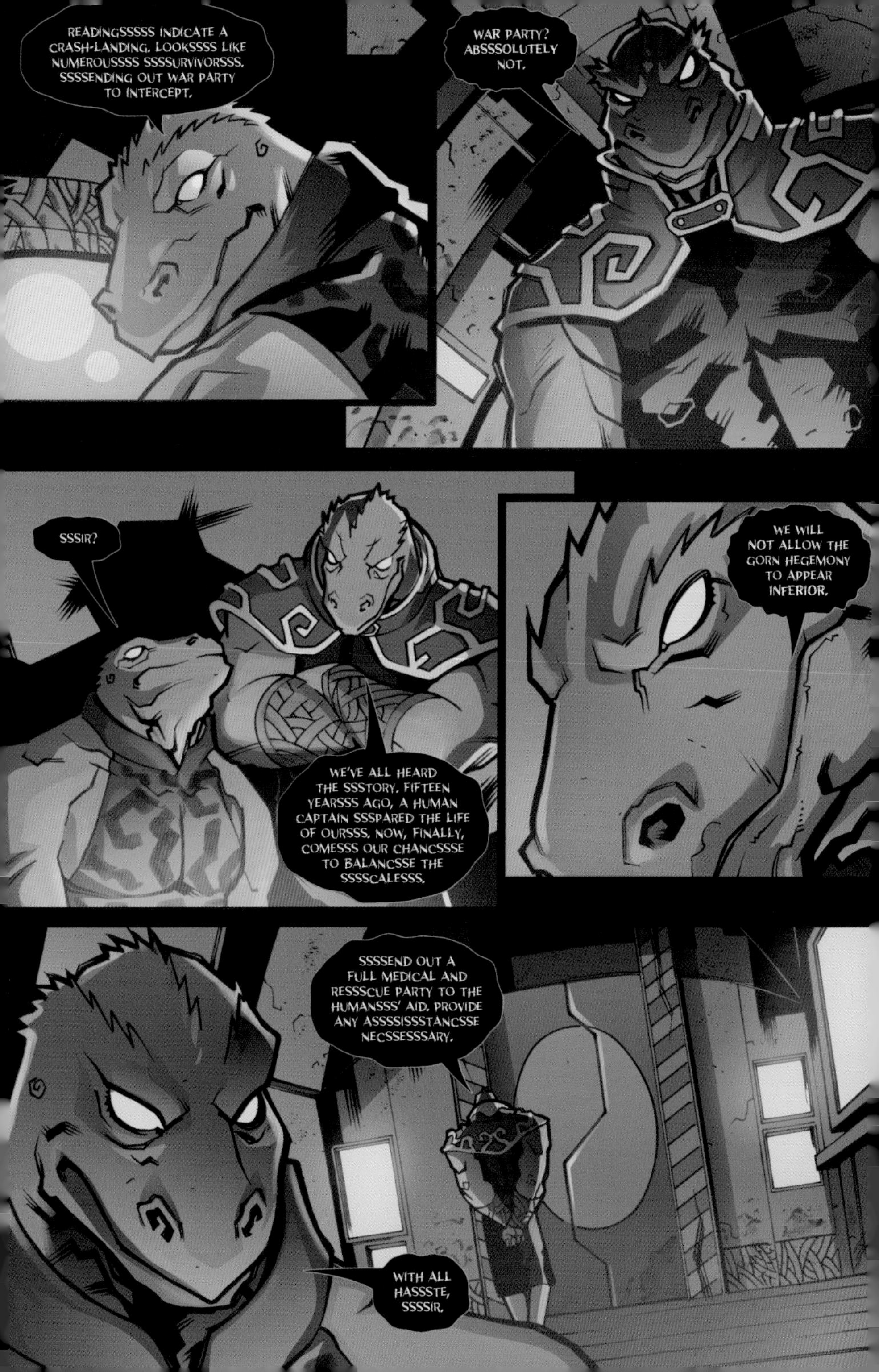
READINGSSSSS INDICATE A CRASH-LANDING. LOOKSSSS LIKE NUMEROUSSSS SSSSURVIVORSSS. SSSSENDING OUT WAR PARTY TO INTERCEPT.
WAR PARTY? ABSSSOLUTELY NOT.
SSSIR?
WE'VE ALL HEARD THE SSSTORY. FIFTEEN YEARSSS AGO, A HUMAN CAPTAIN SSSPARED THE LIFE OF OURSSS. NOW, FINALLY, COMESSS OUR CHANCSSSE TO BALANCSSE THE SSSSCALESSS.
WE WILL NOT ALLOW THE GORN HEGEMONY TO APPEAR INFERIOR.
SSSSEND OUT A FULL MEDICAL AND RESSSCUE PARTY TO THE HUMANSSS' AID. PROVIDE ANY ASSSSISSSTANCSSE NECSSESSSARY.
WITH ALL HASSSTE, SSSSIR.

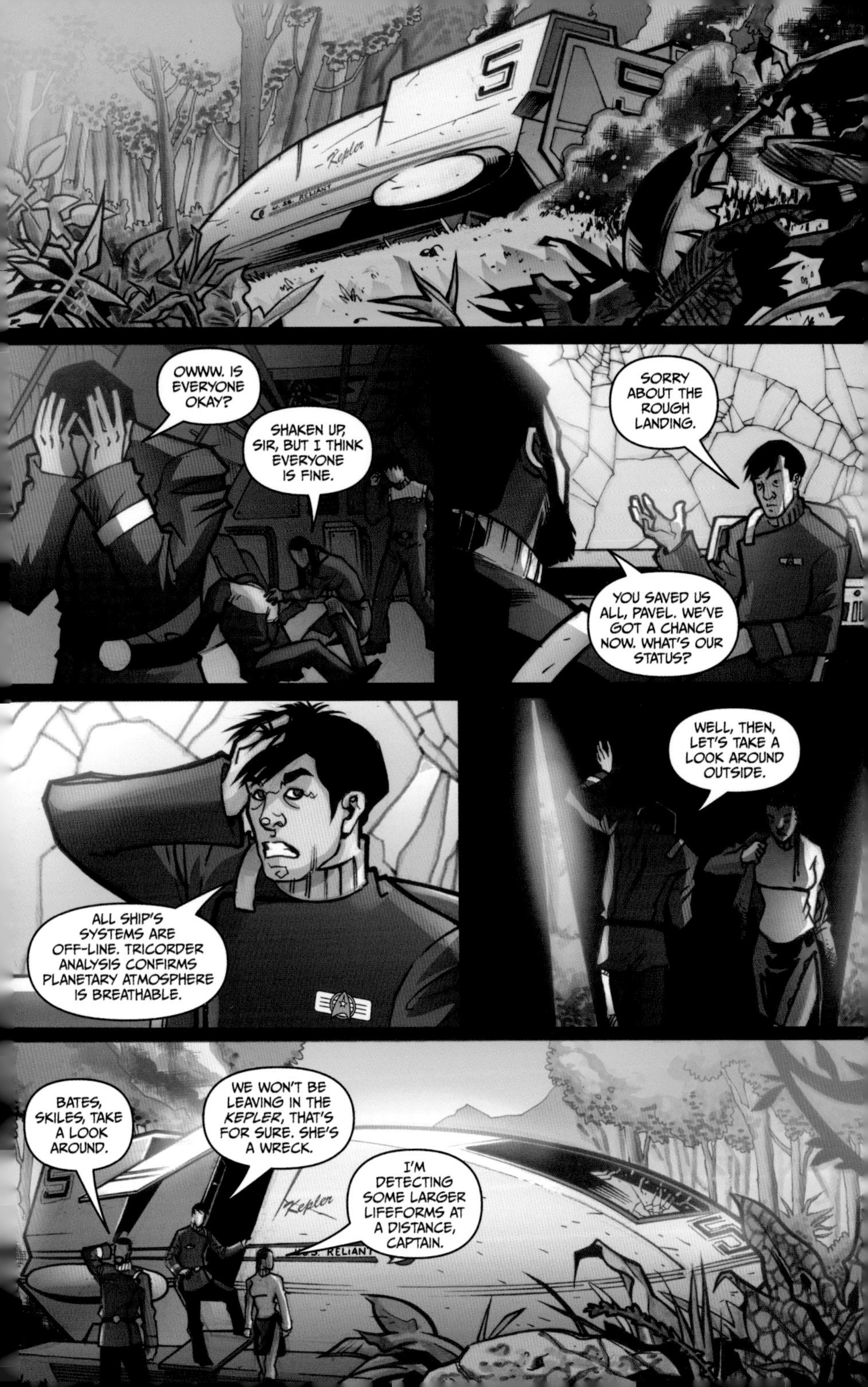

Kepler
U.S.S. RELIANT
OWWW. IS EVERYONE OKAY?
SHAKEN UP, SIR, BUT I THINK EVERYONE IS FINE.
SORRY ABOUT THE ROUGH LANDING.
YOU SAVED US ALL, PAVEL. WE'VE GOT A CHANCE NOW. WHAT'S OUR STATUS?
ALL SHIP'S SYSTEMS ARE OFF-LINE. TRICORDER ANALYSIS CONFIRMS PLANETARY ATMOSPHERE IS BREATHABLE.
WELL, THEN, LET'S TAKE A LOOK AROUND OUTSIDE.
BATES, SKILES, TAKE A LOOK AROUND.
WE WON'T BE LEAVING IN THE KEPLER, THAT'S FOR SURE. SHE'S A WRECK.
I'M DETECTING SOME LARGER LIFEFORMS AT A DISTANCE, CAPTAIN.
Kepler
U.S.S. RELIANT

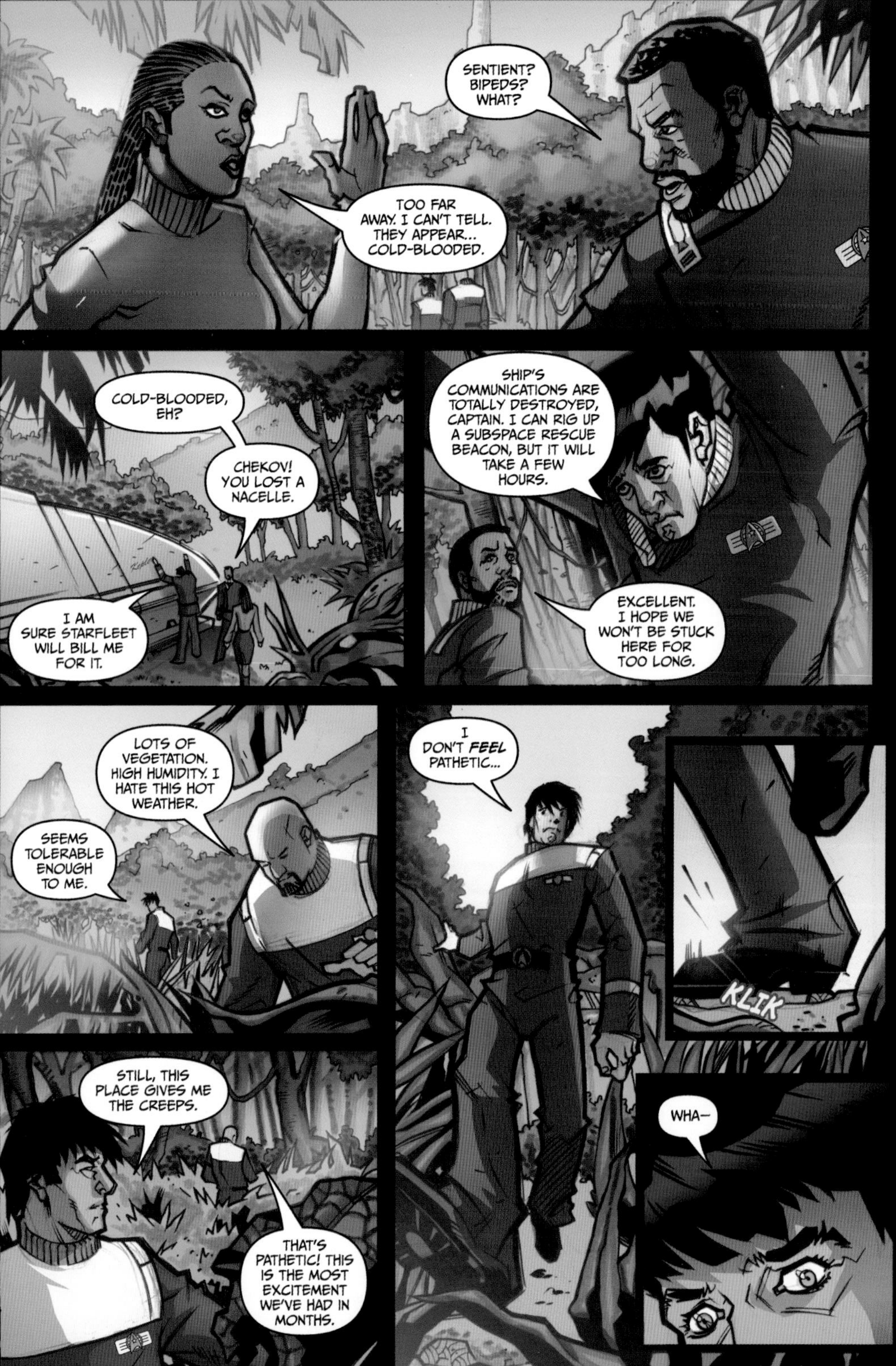
SENTIENT? BIPEDS? WHAT?
TOO FAR AWAY. I CAN'T TELL. THEY APPEAR... COLD-BLOODED.
COLD-BLOODED, EH?
CHEKOV! YOU LOST A NACELLE.
I AM SURE STARFLEET WILL BILL ME FOR IT.
SHIP'S COMMUNICATIONS ARE TOTALLY DESTROYED, CAPTAIN. I CAN RIG UP A SUBSPACE RESCUE BEACON, BUT IT WILL TAKE A FEW HOURS.
EXCELLENT. I HOPE WE WON'T BE STUCK HERE FOR TOO LONG.
LOTS OF VEGETATION. HIGH HUMIDITY. I HATE THIS HOT WEATHER.
SEEMS TOLERABLE ENOUGH TO ME.
STILL, THIS PLACE GIVES ME THE CREEPS.
THAT'S PATHETIC! THIS IS THE MOST EXCITEMENT WE'VE HAD IN MONTHS.
I DON'T FEEL PATHETIC...
KLIK
WHA-

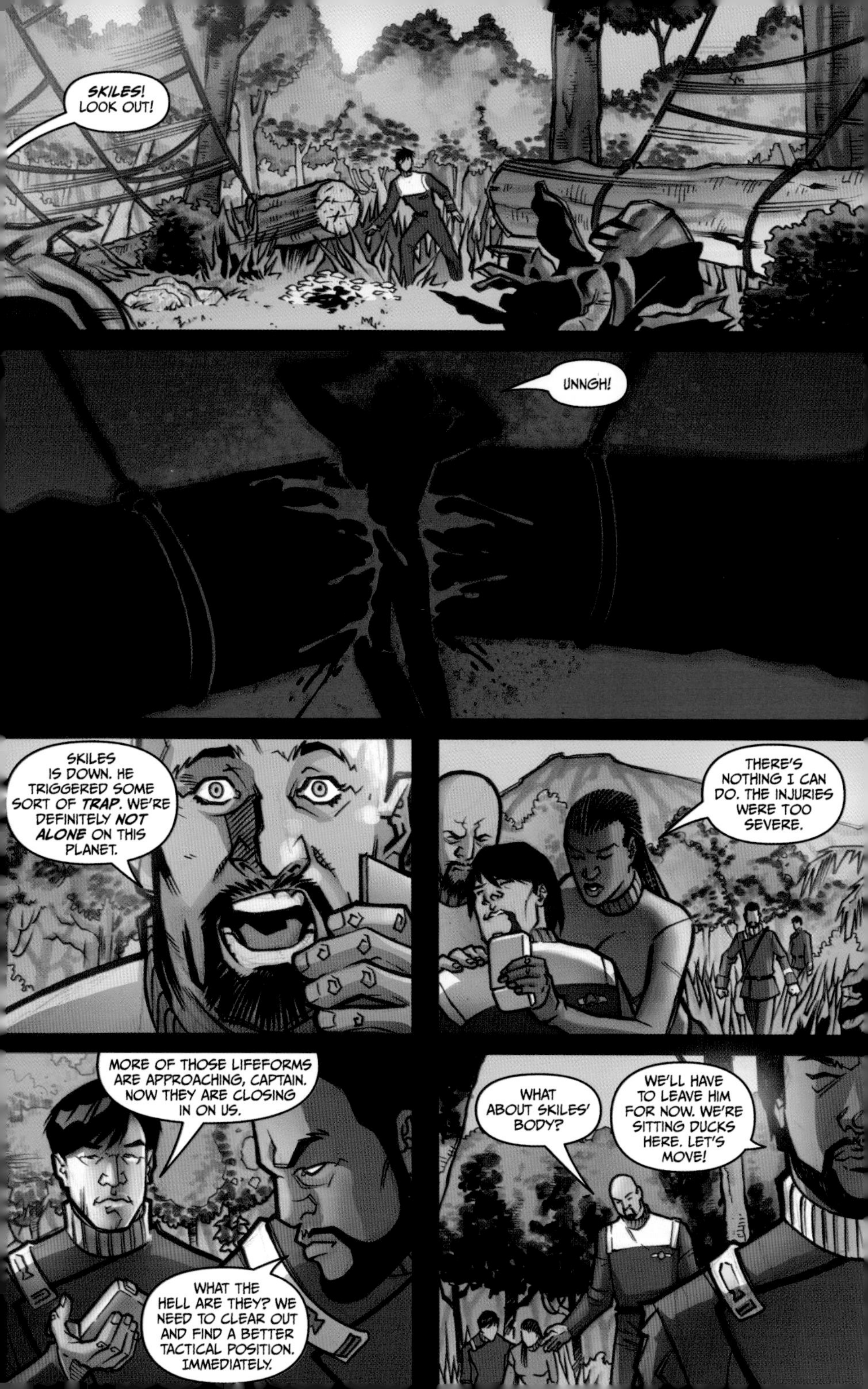
SKILES! LOOK OUT!
UNNGH!
SKILES IS DOWN. HE TRIGGERED SOME SORT OF TRAP. WE'RE DEFINITELY NOT ALONE ON THIS PLANET.
THERE'S NOTHING I CAN DO. THE INJURIES WERE TOO SEVERE.
MORE OF THOSE LIFEFORMS ARE APPROACHING, CAPTAIN. NOW THEY ARE CLOSING IN ON US.
WHAT THE HELL ARE THEY? WE NEED TO CLEAR OUT AND FIND A BETTER TACTICAL POSITION. IMMEDIATELY.
WHAT ABOUT SKILES' BODY?
WE'LL HAVE TO LEAVE HIM FOR NOW. WE'RE SITTING DUCKS HERE. LET'S MOVE!

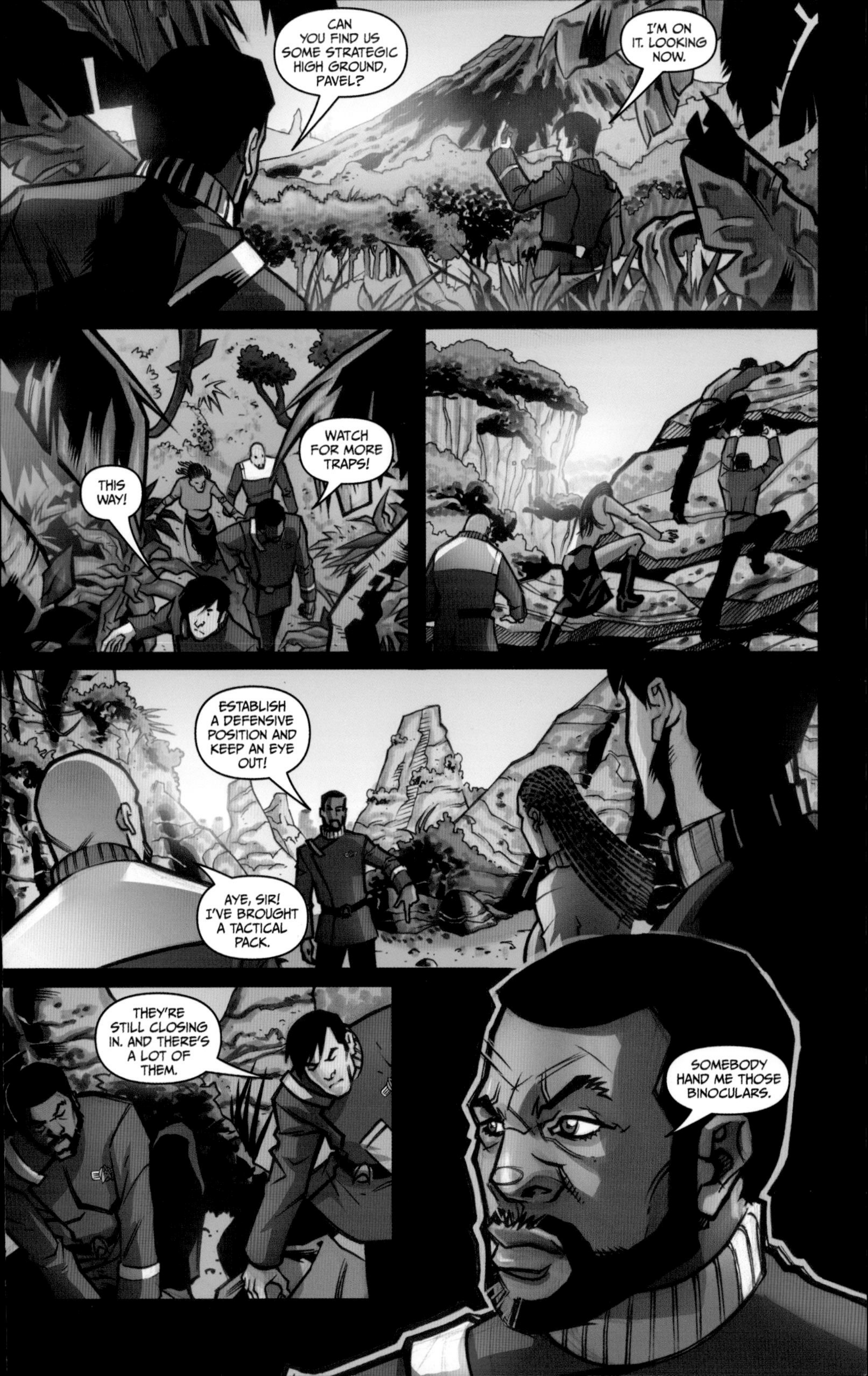
CAN YOU FIND US SOME STRATEGIC HIGH GROUND, PAVEL?
I'M ON IT. LOOKING NOW.
THIS WAY!
WATCH FOR MORE TRAPS!
ESTABLISH A DEFENSIVE POSITION AND KEEP AN EYE OUT!
AYE, SIR! I'VE BROUGHT A TACTICAL PACK.
THEY'RE STILL CLOSING IN. AND THERE'S A LOT OF THEM.
SOMEBODY HAND ME THOSE BINOCULARS.

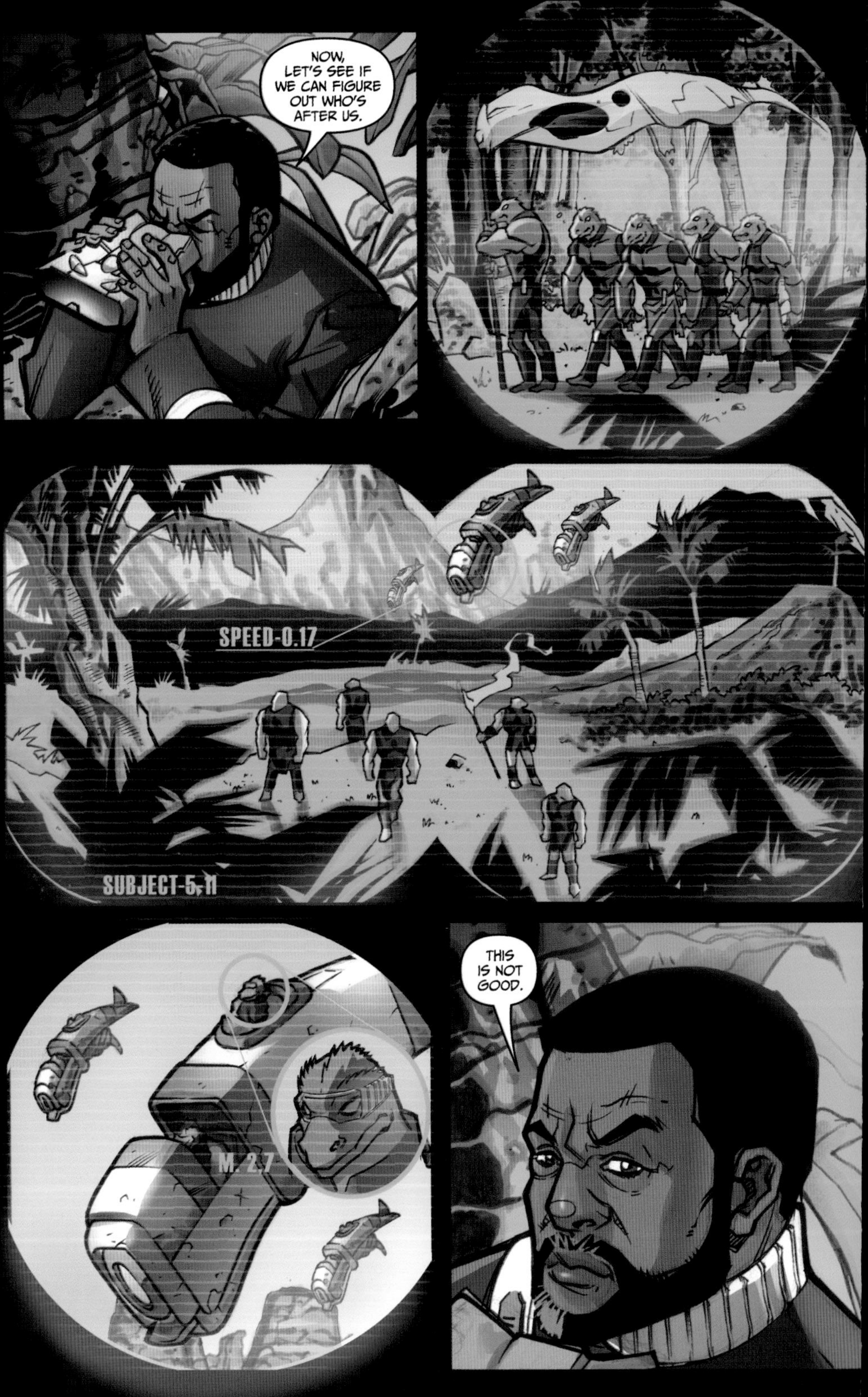
NOW, LET'S SEE IF WE CAN FIGURE OUT WHO'S AFTER US.
SPEED-0.17
SUBJECT-5.11
M. 2.7
THIS IS NOT GOOD.

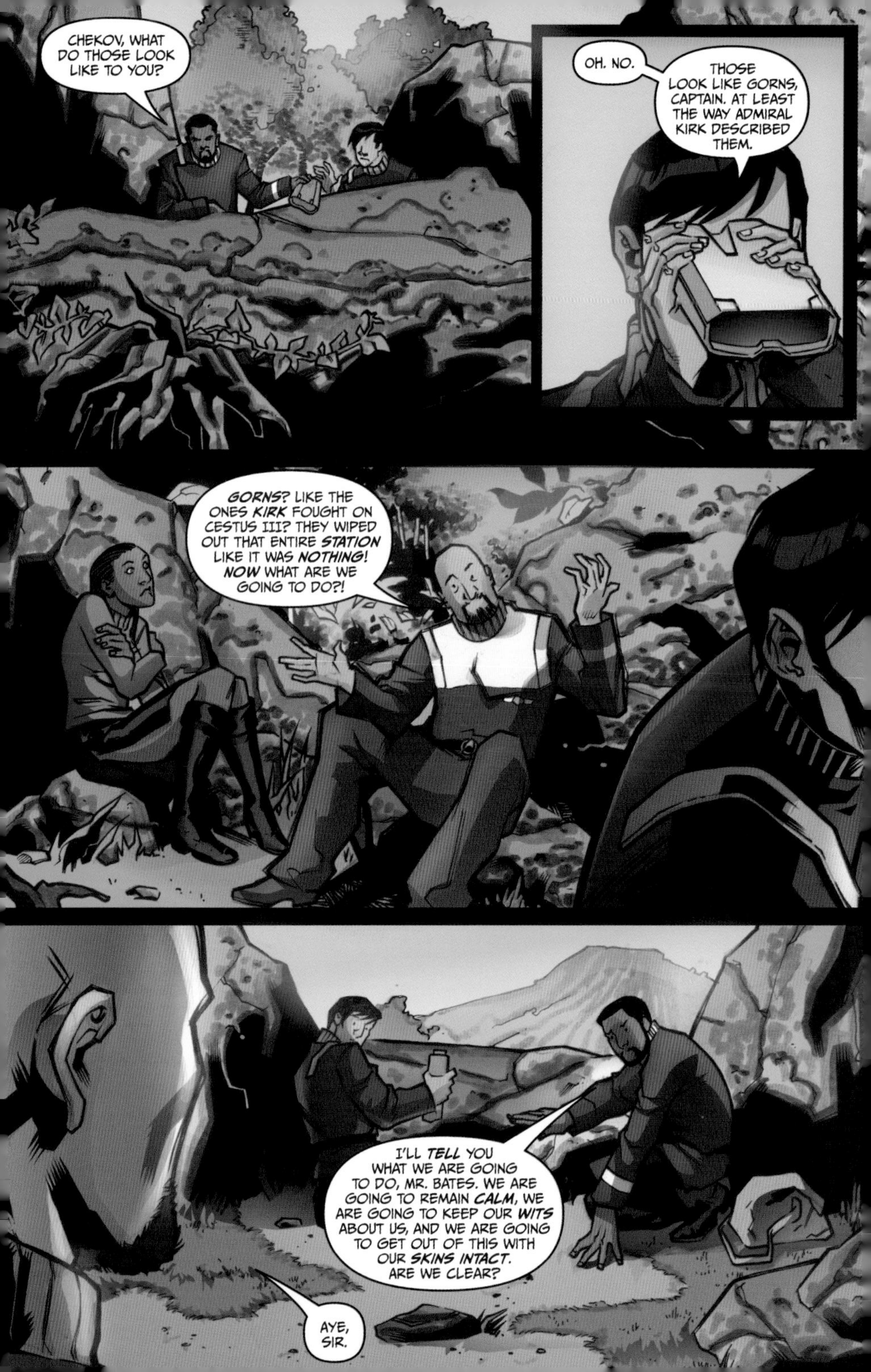
CHEKOV, WHAT DO THOSE LOOK LIKE TO YOU?
OH. NO.
THOSE LOOK LIKE GORNS, CAPTAIN. AT LEAST THE WAY ADMIRAL KIRK DESCRIBED THEM.
GORNS? LIKE THE ONES KIRK FOUGHT ON CESTUS III? THEY WIPED OUT THAT ENTIRE STATION LIKE IT WAS NOTHING! NOW WHAT ARE WE GOING TO DO?!
I'LL TELL YOU WHAT WE ARE GOING TO DO, MR. BATES. WE ARE GOING TO REMAIN CALM, WE ARE GOING TO KEEP OUR WITS ABOUT US, AND WE ARE GOING TO GET OUT OF THIS WITH OUR SKINS INTACT. ARE WE CLEAR?
AYE, SIR.

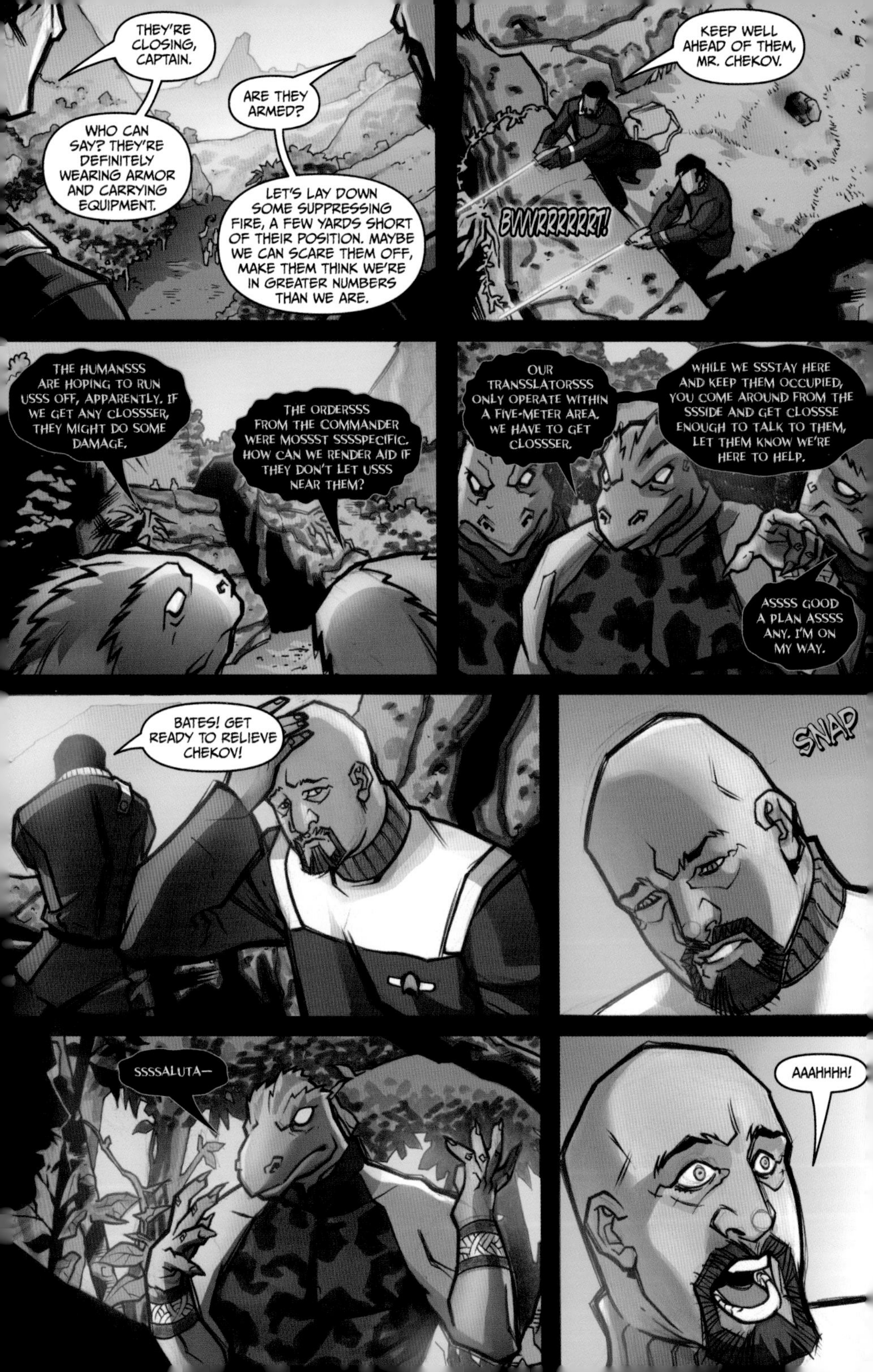
THEY'RE CLOSING, CAPTAIN.
ARE THEY ARMED?
WHO CAN SAY? THEY'RE DEFINITELY WEARING ARMOR AND CARRYING EQUIPMENT.
LET'S LAY DOWN SOME SUPPRESSING FIRE, A FEW YARDS SHORT OF THEIR POSITION. MAYBE WE CAN SCARE THEM OFF, MAKE THEM THINK WE'RE IN GREATER NUMBERS THAN WE ARE.
KEEP WELL AHEAD OF THEM, MR. CHEKOV.
BVVVRRRRRRRT!
THE HUMANSSS ARE HOPING TO RUN USSS OFF, APPARENTLY. IF WE GET ANY CLOSSSER, THEY MIGHT DO SOME DAMAGE.
THE ORDERSSS FROM THE COMMANDER WERE MOSSST SSSSPECIFIC. HOW CAN WE RENDER AID IF THEY DON'T LET USSS NEAR THEM?
OUR TRANSSLATORSSS ONLY OPERATE WITHIN A FIVE-METER AREA. WE HAVE TO GET CLOSSSER.
WHILE WE SSSTAY HERE AND KEEP THEM OCCUPIED, YOU COME AROUND FROM THE SSSIDE AND GET CLOSSSE ENOUGH TO TALK TO THEM, LET THEM KNOW WE'RE HERE TO HELP.
ASSSS GOOD A PLAN ASSSS ANY. I'M ON MY WAY.
BATES! GET READY TO RELIEVE CHEKOV!
SNAP
SSSSALUTA—
AAAHHHH!

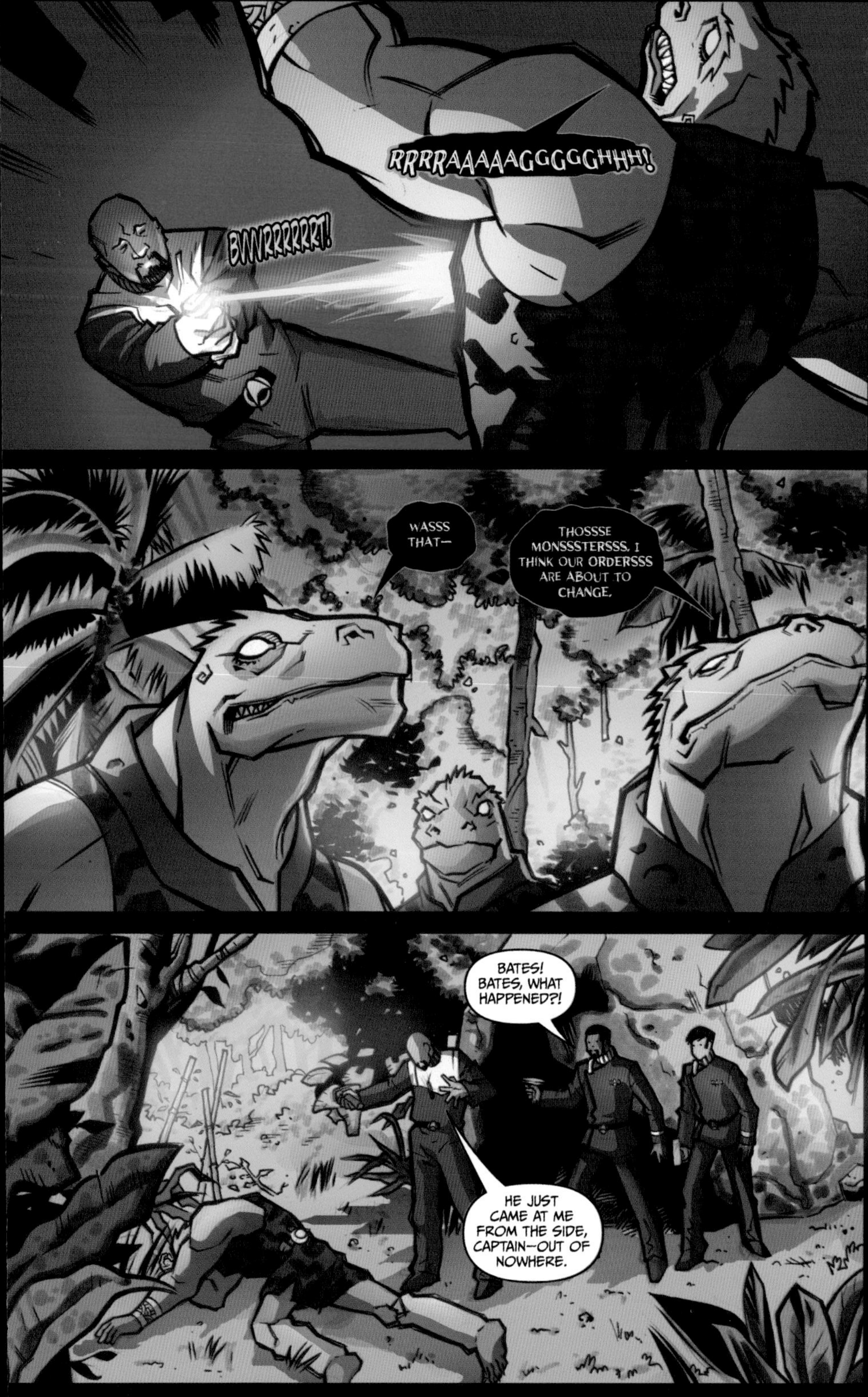

RRRRAAAAAGGGGGHHH!
BWWRRRRRRT!
WASSS THAT—
THOSSSE MONSSSTERSSS. I THINK OUR ORDERSSS ARE ABOUT TO CHANGE.
BATES! BATES, WHAT HAPPENED?!
HE JUST CAME AT ME FROM THE SIDE, CAPTAIN—OUT OF NOWHERE.

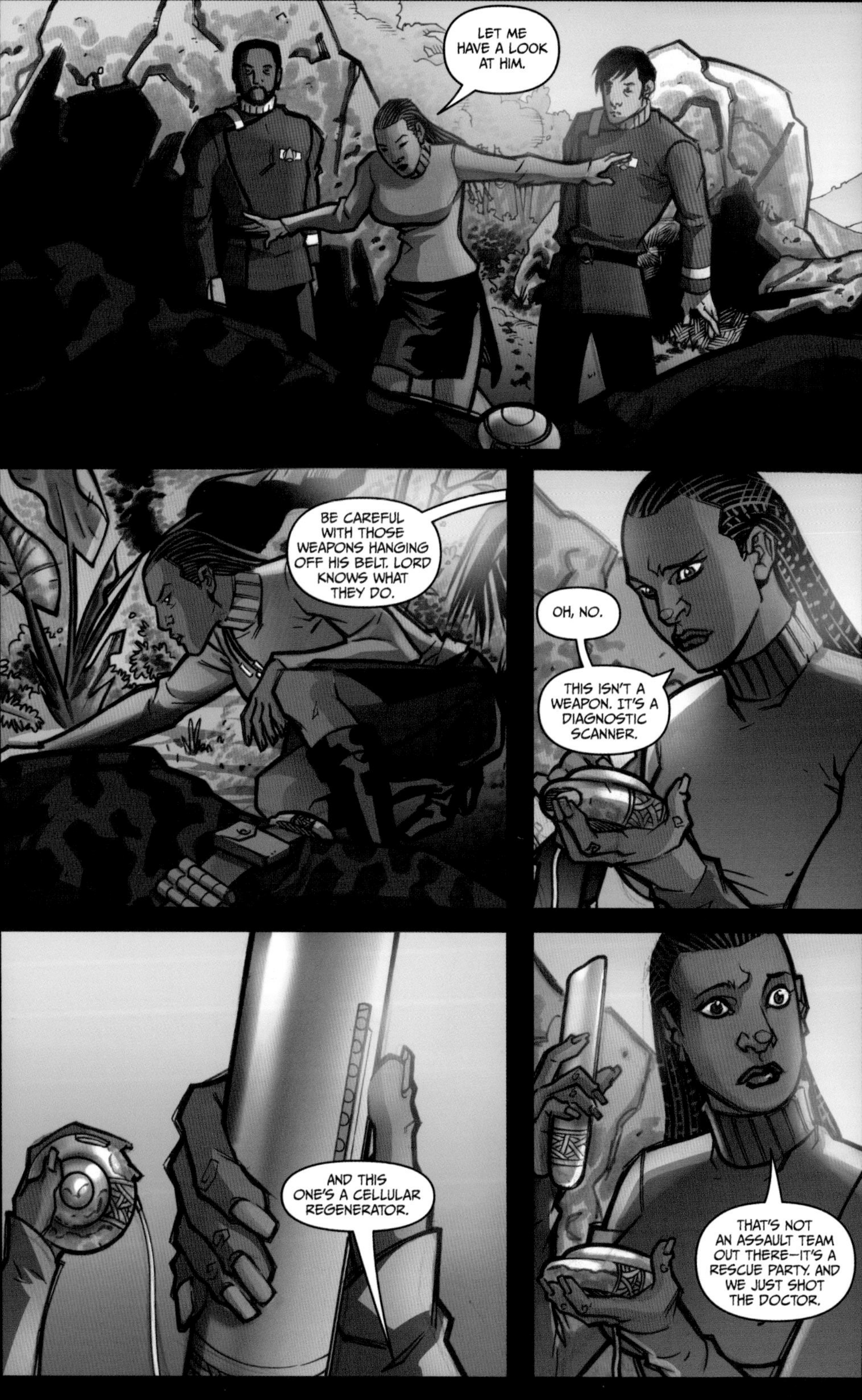
LET ME HAVE A LOOK AT HIM.
BE CAREFUL WITH THOSE WEAPONS HANGING OFF HIS BELT. LORD KNOWS WHAT THEY DO.
OH, NO.
THIS ISN'T A WEAPON. IT'S A DIAGNOSTIC SCANNER.
AND THIS ONE'S A CELLULAR REGENERATOR.
THAT'S NOT AN ASSAULT TEAM OUT THERE—IT'S A RESCUE PARTY. AND WE JUST SHOT THE DOCTOR.

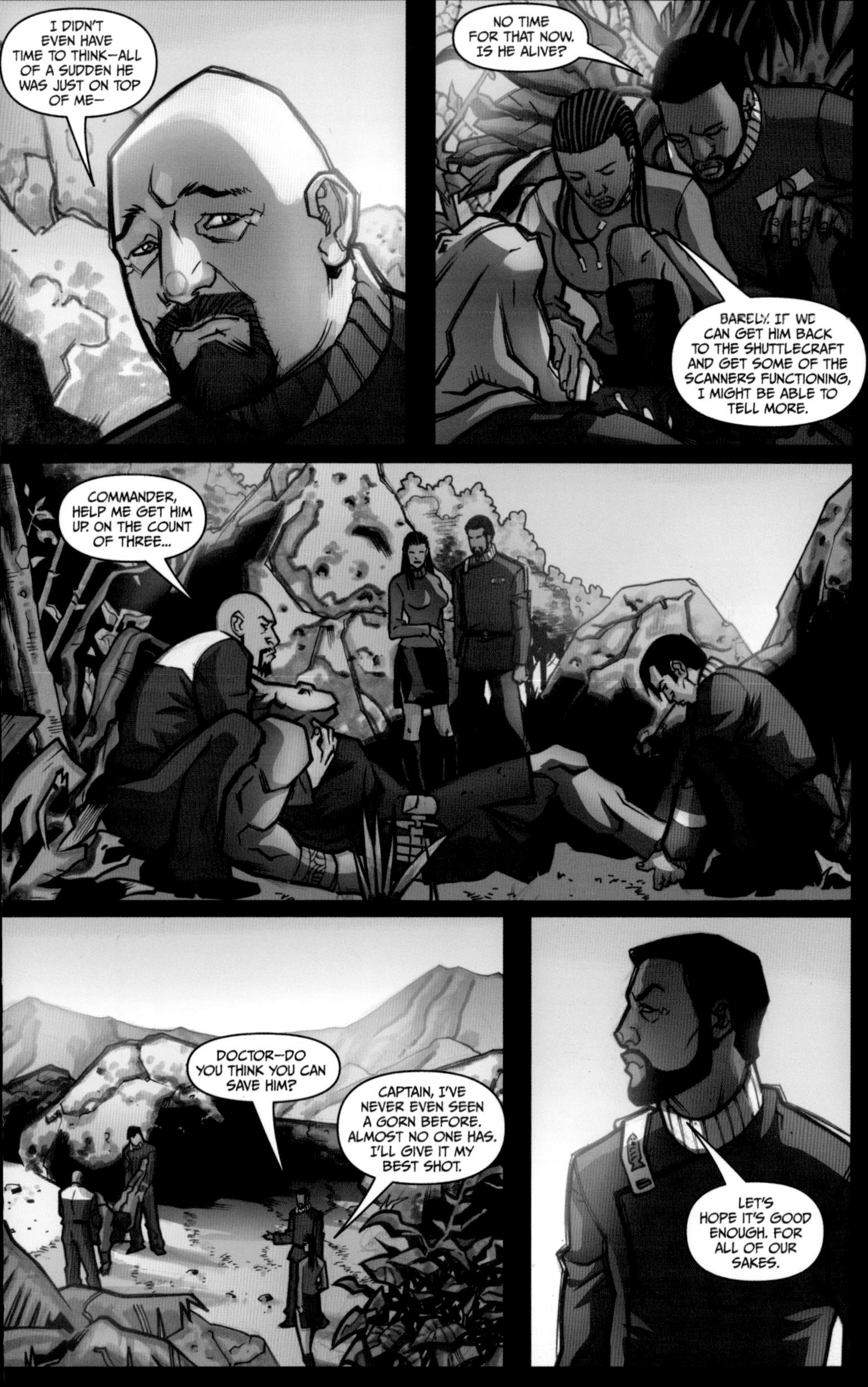
I DIDN'T EVEN HAVE TIME TO THINK—ALL OF A SUDDEN HE WAS JUST ON TOP OF ME—
NO TIME FOR THAT NOW. IS HE ALIVE?
BARELY. IF WE CAN GET HIM BACK TO THE SHUTTLECRAFT AND GET SOME OF THE SCANNERS FUNCTIONING, I MIGHT BE ABLE TO TELL MORE.
COMMANDER, HELP ME GET HIM UP. ON THE COUNT OF THREE...
DOCTOR—DO YOU THINK YOU CAN SAVE HIM?
CAPTAIN, I'VE NEVER EVEN SEEN A GORN BEFORE. ALMOST NO ONE HAS. I'LL GIVE IT MY BEST SHOT.
LET'S HOPE IT'S GOOD ENOUGH. FOR ALL OF OUR SAKES.

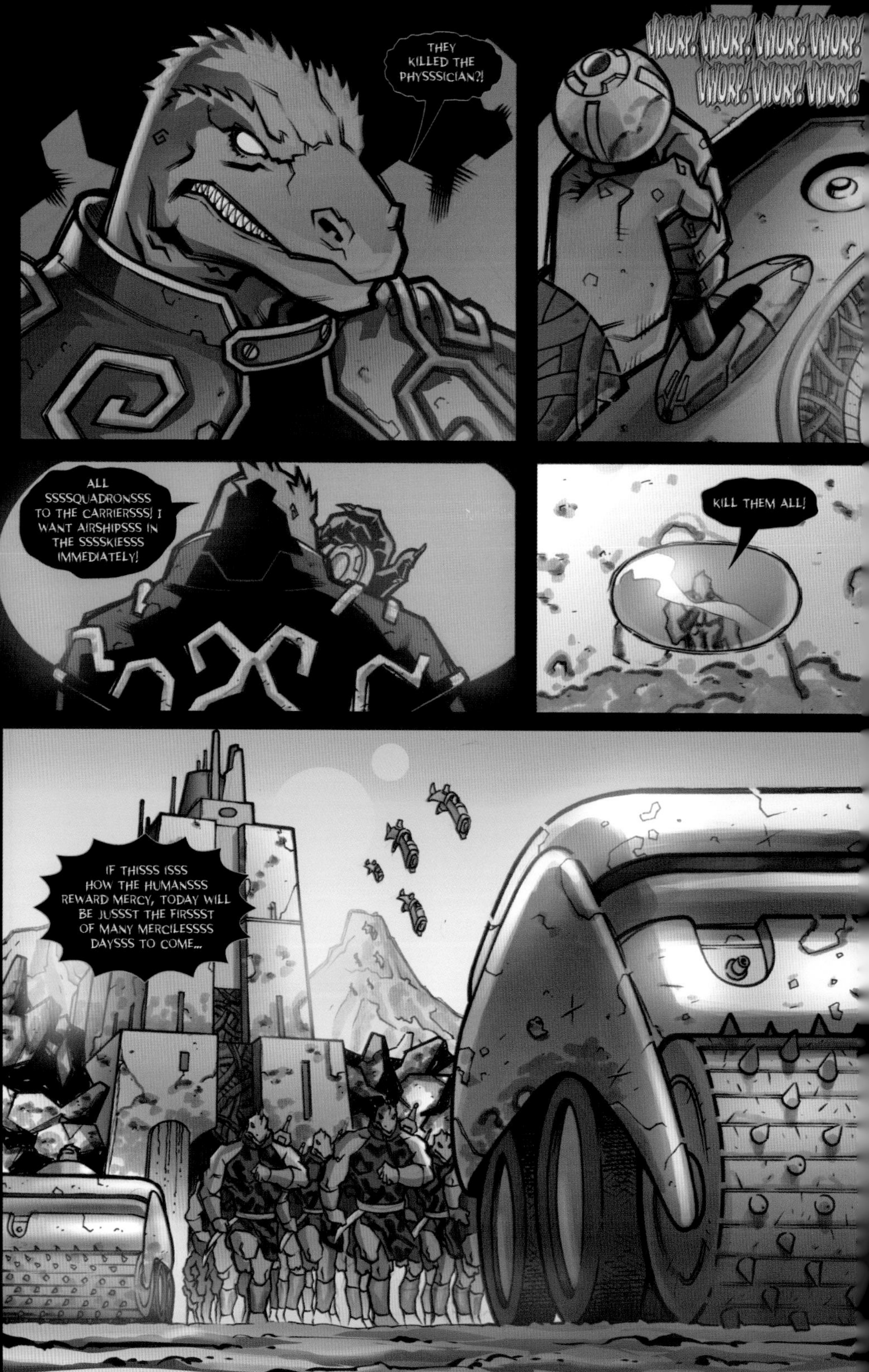
THEY KILLED THE PHYSSSICIAN?!
VWORP! VWORP! VWORP! VWORP! VWORP! VWORP! VWORP!
ALL SSSSQUADRONSSS TO THE CARRIERSSS! I WANT AIRSHIPSSS IN THE SSSSKIESSS IMMEDIATELY!
KILL THEM ALL!
IF THISSS ISSS HOW THE HUMANSSS REWARD MERCY, TODAY WILL BE JUSSST THE FIRSSST OF MANY MERCILESSSS DAYSSS TO COME...

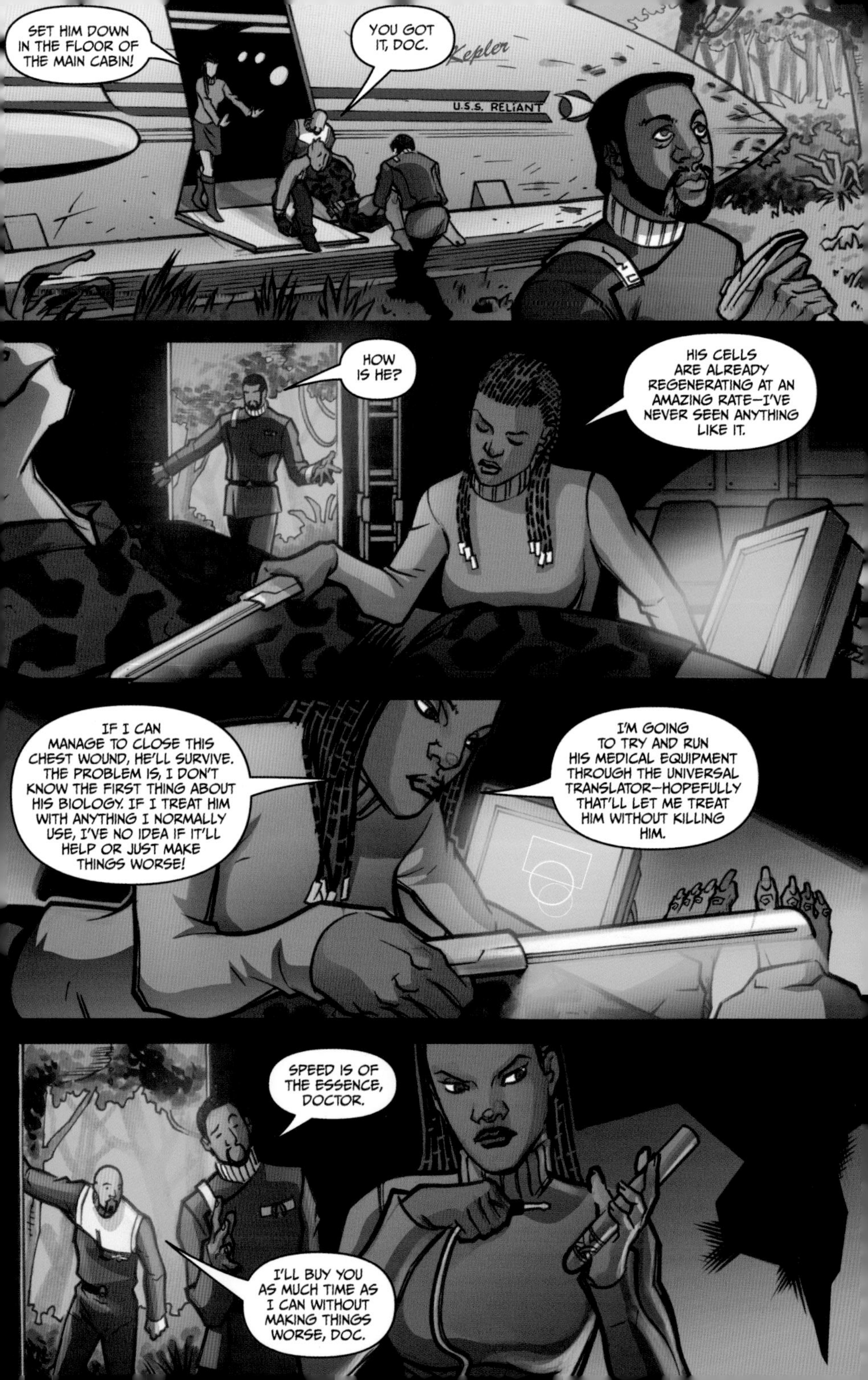
SET HIM DOWN IN THE FLOOR OF THE MAIN CABIN!
YOU GOT IT, DOC.
Kepler
U.S.S. RELIANT
HOW IS HE?
HIS CELLS ARE ALREADY REGENERATING AT AN AMAZING RATE—I'VE NEVER SEEN ANYTHING LIKE IT.
IF I CAN MANAGE TO CLOSE THIS CHEST WOUND, HE'LL SURVIVE. THE PROBLEM IS, I DON'T KNOW THE FIRST THING ABOUT HIS BIOLOGY. IF I TREAT HIM WITH ANYTHING I NORMALLY USE, I'VE NO IDEA IF IT'LL HELP OR JUST MAKE THINGS WORSE!
I'M GOING TO TRY AND RUN HIS MEDICAL EQUIPMENT THROUGH THE UNIVERSAL TRANSLATOR—HOPEFULLY THAT'LL LET ME TREAT HIM WITHOUT KILLING HIM.
SPEED IS OF THE ESSENCE, DOCTOR.
I'LL BUY YOU AS MUCH TIME AS I CAN WITHOUT MAKING THINGS WORSE, DOC.

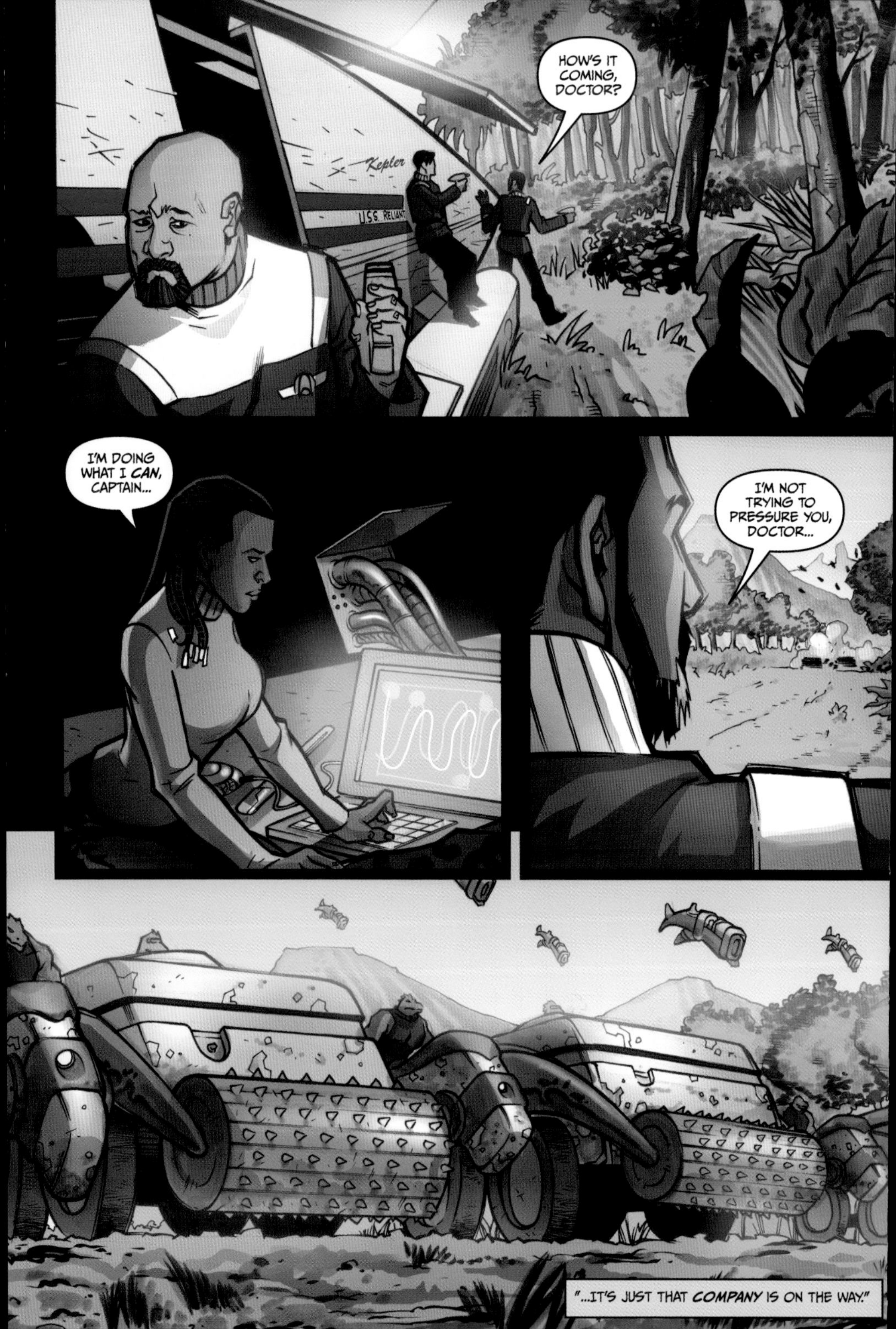
Kepler
U.S.S. RELIANT
HOW'S IT COMING, DOCTOR?
I'M DOING WHAT I *CAN*, CAPTAIN...
I'M NOT TRYING TO PRESSURE YOU, DOCTOR...
"...IT'S JUST THAT *COMPANY* IS ON THE WAY."

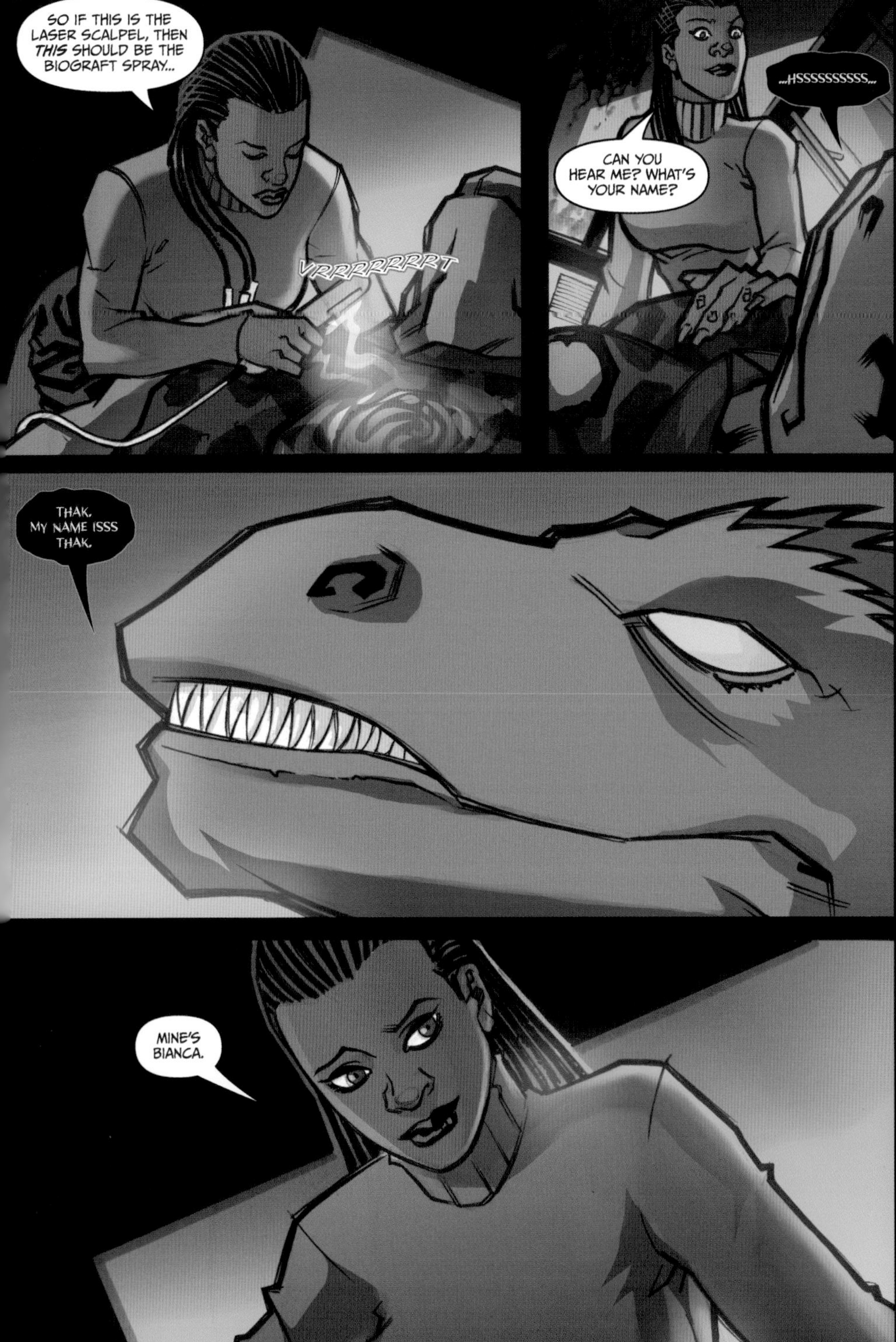
SO IF THIS IS THE LASER SCALPEL, THEN *THIS* SHOULD BE THE BIOGRAFT SPRAY...
VRRRRRRRRT
CAN YOU HEAR ME? WHAT'S YOUR NAME?
...HSSSSSSSSSS...
THAK. MY NAME ISSS THAK.
MINE'S BIANCA.

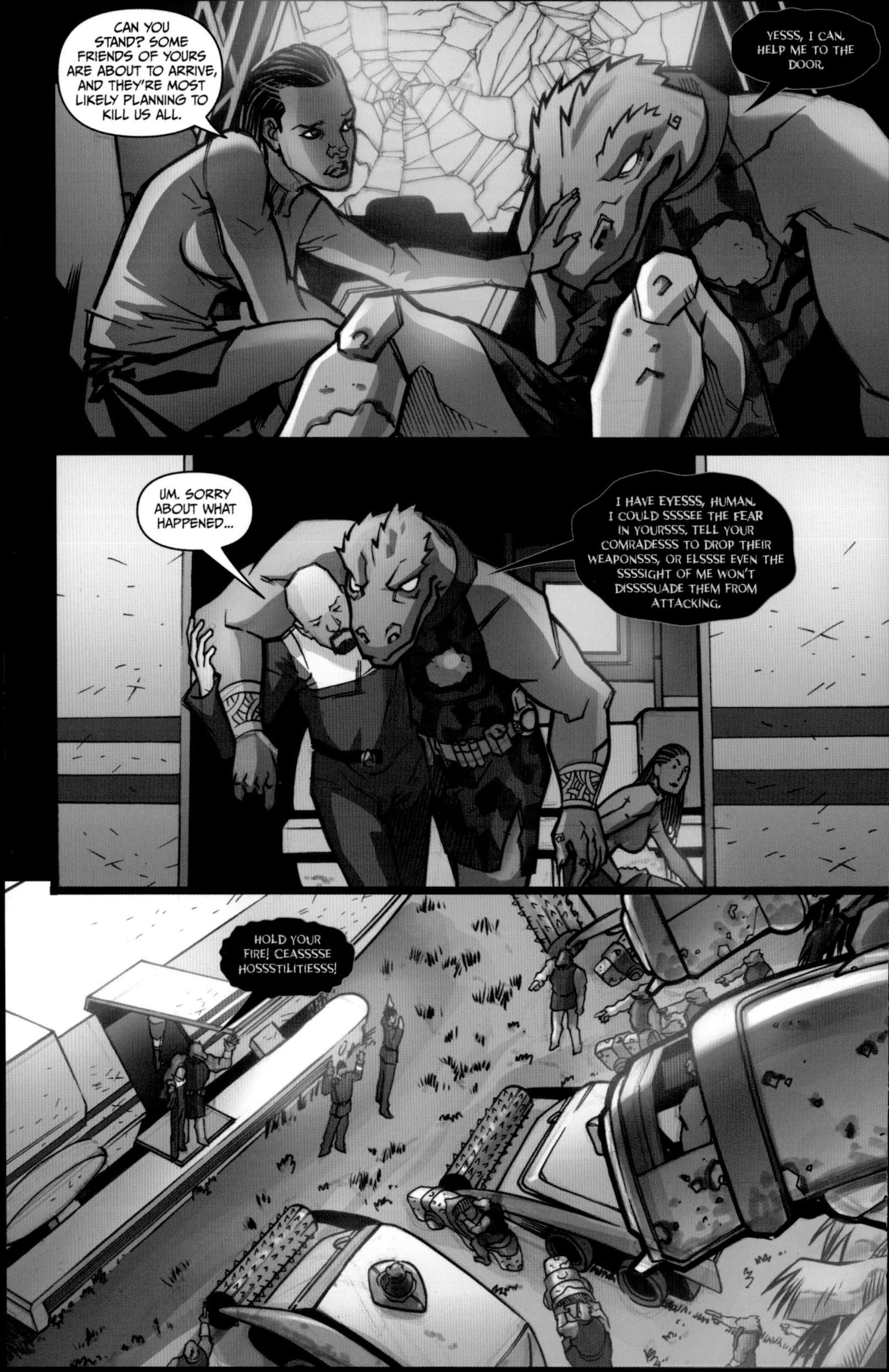
CAN YOU STAND? SOME FRIENDS OF YOURS ARE ABOUT TO ARRIVE, AND THEY'RE MOST LIKELY PLANNING TO KILL US ALL.
YESSS, I CAN. HELP ME TO THE DOOR.
UM. SORRY ABOUT WHAT HAPPENED...
I HAVE EYESSS, HUMAN. I COULD SSSSEE THE FEAR IN YOURSSS. TELL YOUR COMRADESSS TO DROP THEIR WEAPONSSS, OR ELSSSE EVEN THE SSSSIGHT OF ME WON'T DISSSSUADE THEM FROM ATTACKING.
HOLD YOUR FIRE! CEASSSSE HOSSSTILITIESSS!

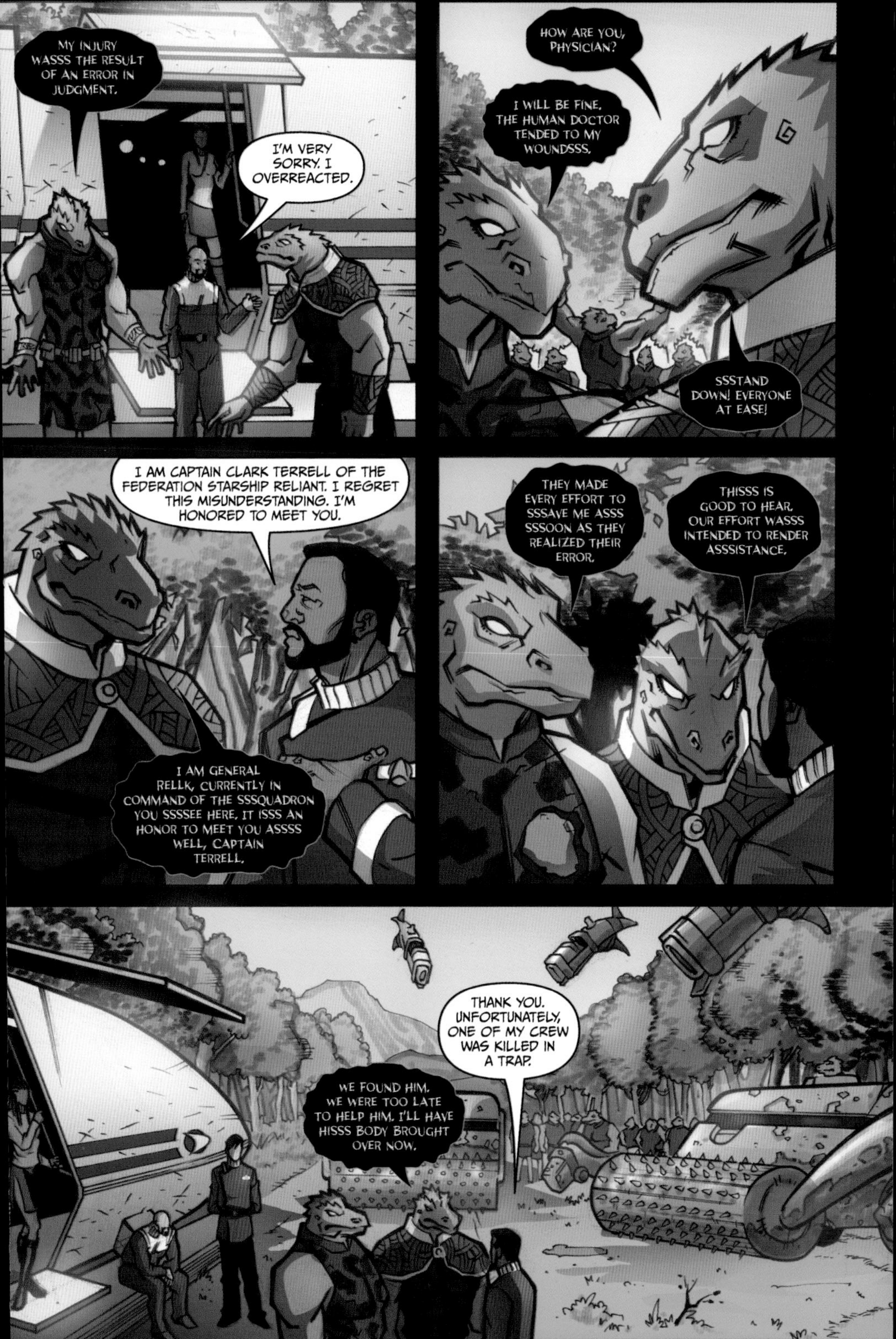
MY INJURY WASSS THE RESULT OF AN ERROR IN JUDGMENT.
I'M VERY SORRY. I OVERREACTED.
HOW ARE YOU, PHYSICIAN?
I WILL BE FINE. THE HUMAN DOCTOR TENDED TO MY WOUNDSSS.
SSSTAND DOWN! EVERYONE AT EASE!
I AM CAPTAIN CLARK TERRELL OF THE FEDERATION STARSHIP RELIANT. I REGRET THIS MISUNDERSTANDING. I'M HONORED TO MEET YOU.
I AM GENERAL RELLK, CURRENTLY IN COMMAND OF THE SSSQUADRON YOU SSSSEE HERE. IT ISSS AN HONOR TO MEET YOU ASSSS WELL, CAPTAIN TERRELL.
THEY MADE EVERY EFFORT TO SSSAVE ME ASSS SSSOON AS THEY REALIZED THEIR ERROR.
THISSS IS GOOD TO HEAR. OUR EFFORT WASSS INTENDED TO RENDER ASSSISTANCE.
THANK YOU. UNFORTUNATELY, ONE OF MY CREW WAS KILLED IN A TRAP.
WE FOUND HIM. WE WERE TOO LATE TO HELP HIM. I'LL HAVE HISSS BODY BROUGHT OVER NOW.

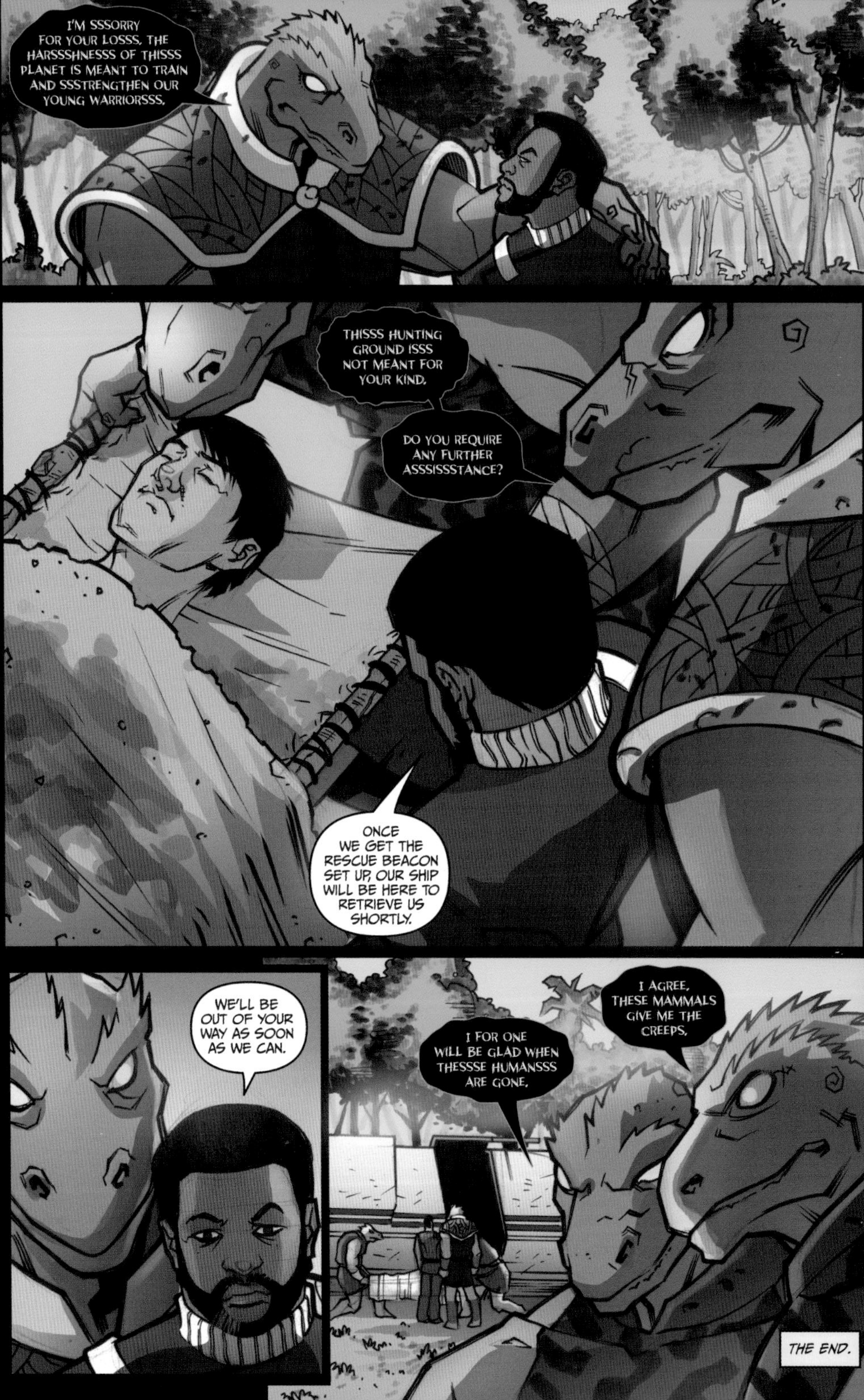
I'M SSSORRY FOR YOUR LOSSS, THE HARSSSHNESSS OF THISSS PLANET IS MEANT TO TRAIN AND SSSTRENGTHEN OUR YOUNG WARRIORSSS.
THISSS HUNTING GROUND ISSS NOT MEANT FOR YOUR KIND.
DO YOU REQUIRE ANY FURTHER ASSSISSSTANCE?
ONCE WE GET THE RESCUE BEACON SET UP, OUR SHIP WILL BE HERE TO RETRIEVE US SHORTLY.
WE'LL BE OUT OF YOUR WAY AS SOON AS WE CAN.
I FOR ONE WILL BE GLAD WHEN THESSSE HUMANSSS ARE GONE.
I AGREE, THESE MAMMALS GIVE ME THE CREEPS.
THE END.

STAR TREK®

THE ORIGINAL SERIES

OMNIBUS

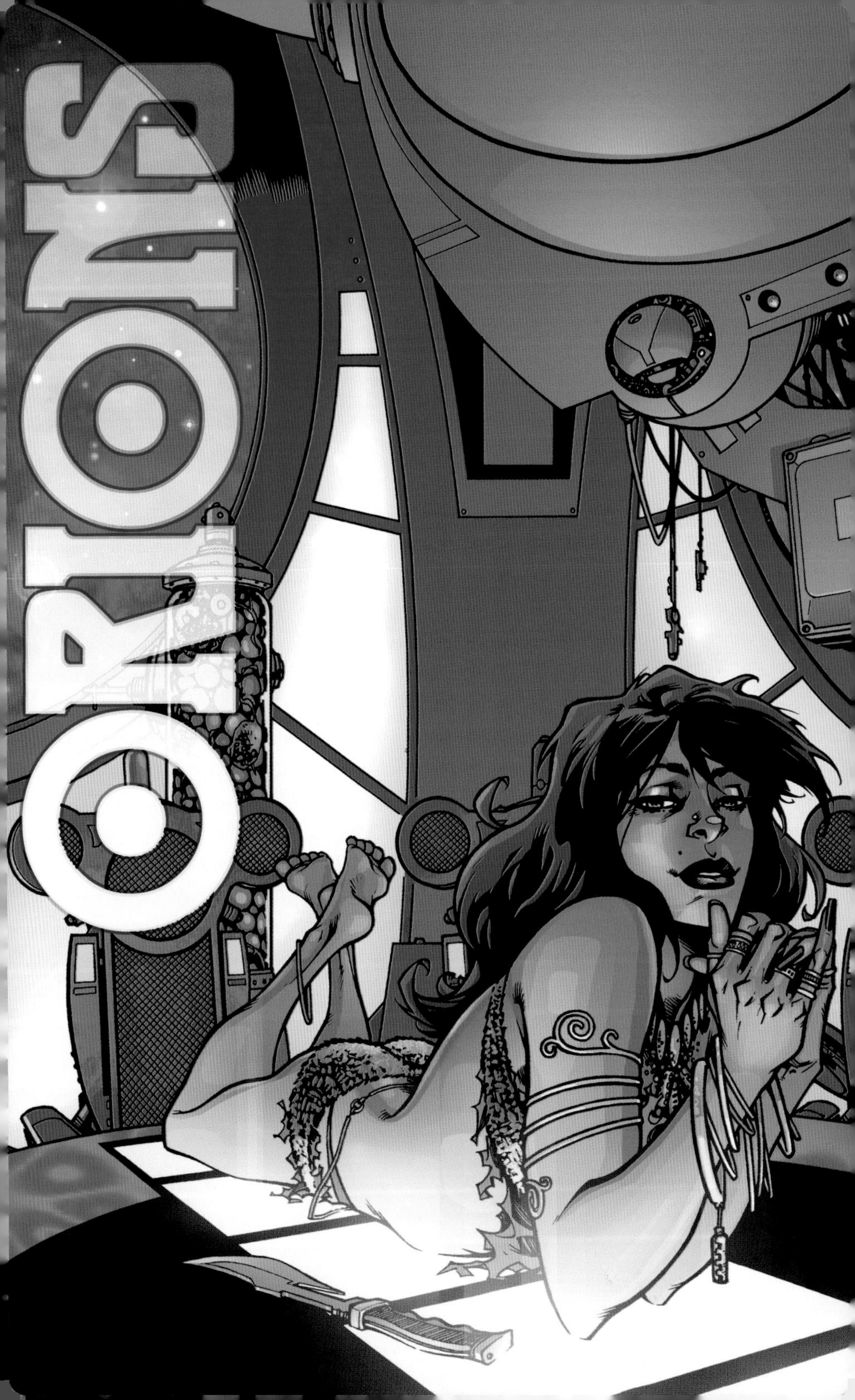
ORIONS

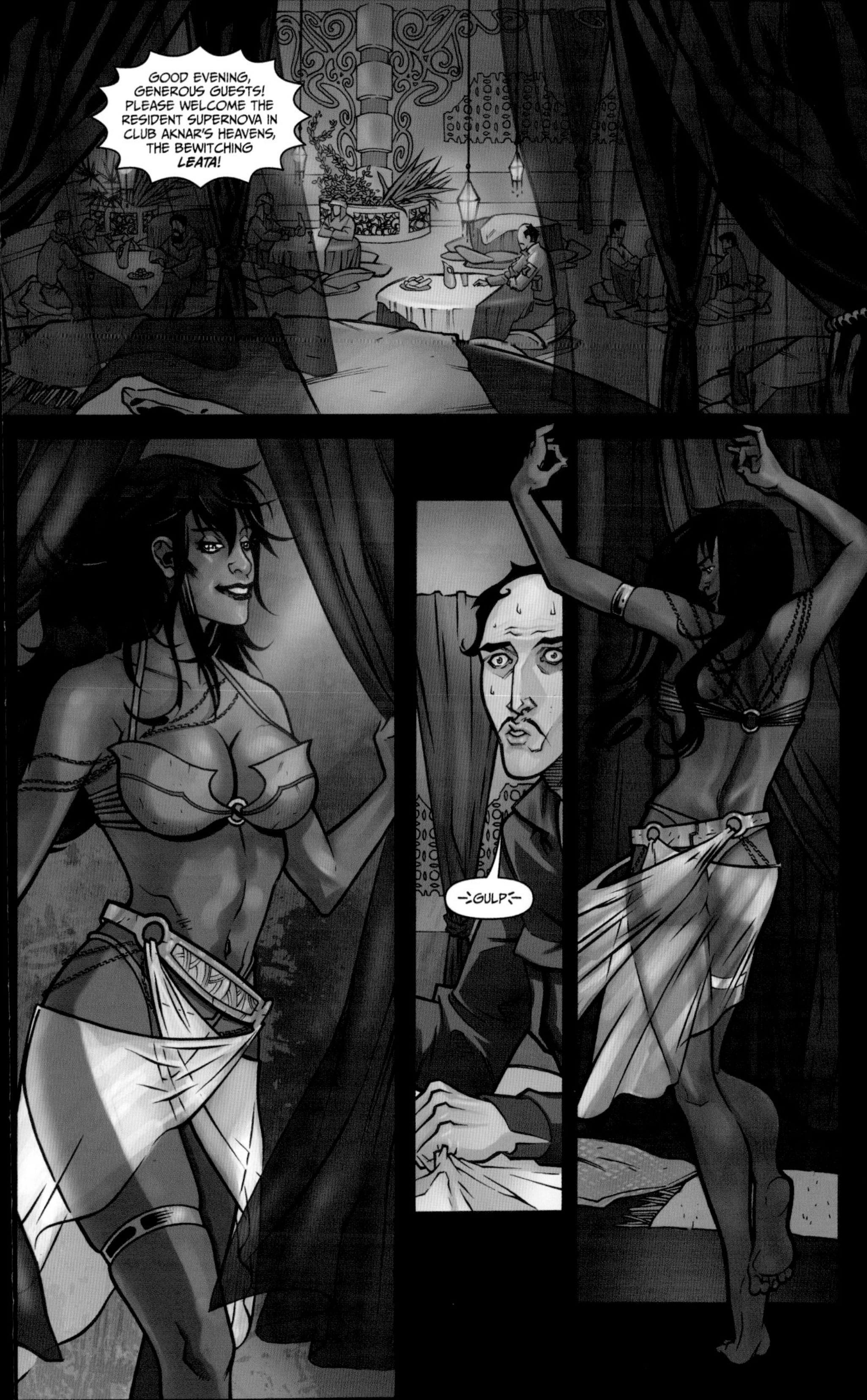
GOOD EVENING, GENEROUS GUESTS! PLEASE WELCOME THE RESIDENT SUPERNOVA IN CLUB AKNAR'S HEAVENS, THE BEWITCHING *LEATA*!
-GULP-

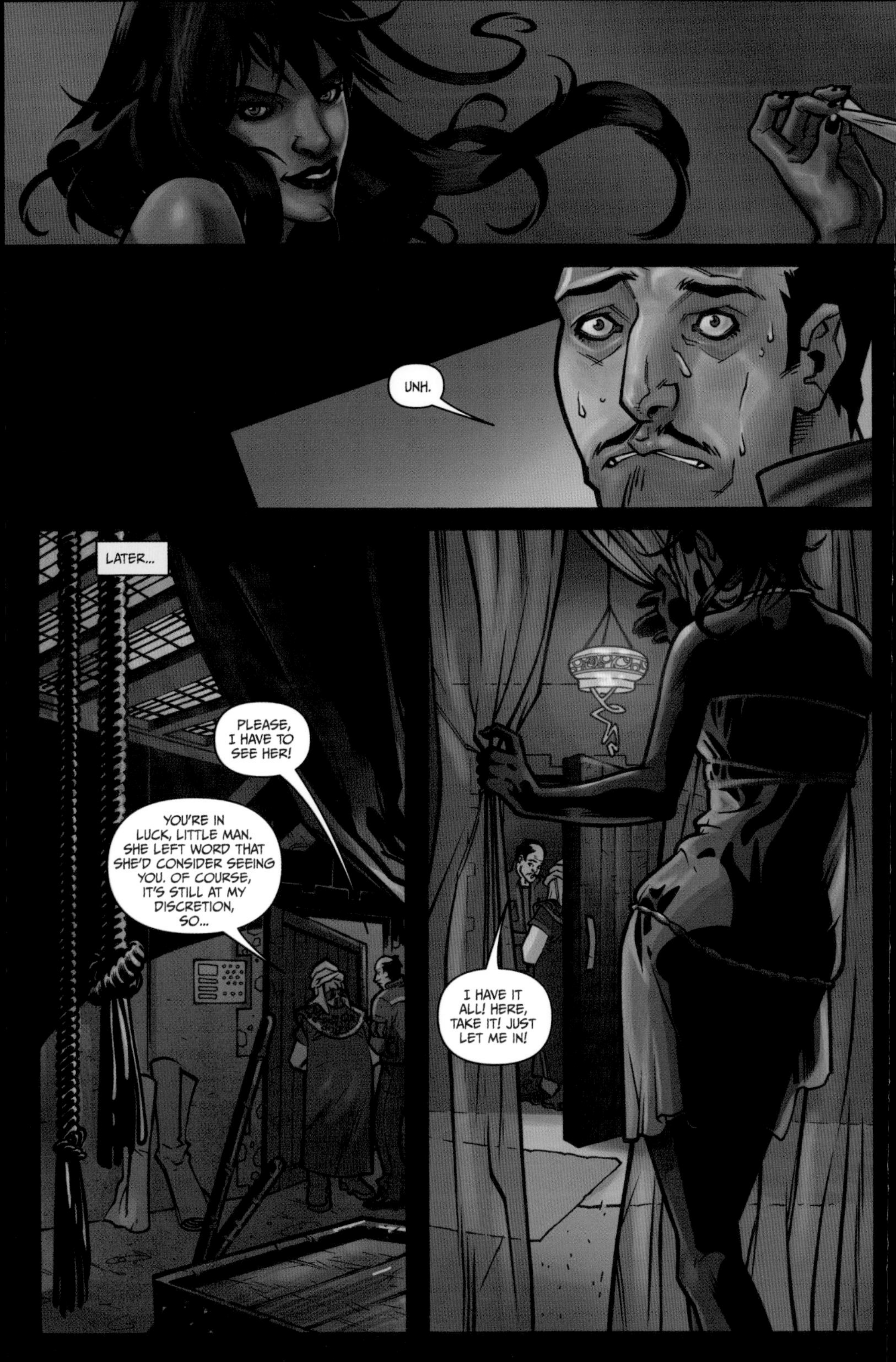
UNH.
LATER...
PLEASE, I HAVE TO SEE HER!
YOU'RE IN LUCK, LITTLE MAN. SHE LEFT WORD THAT SHE'D CONSIDER SEEING YOU. OF COURSE, IT'S STILL AT MY DISCRETION, SO...
I HAVE IT ALL! HERE, TAKE IT! JUST LET ME IN!

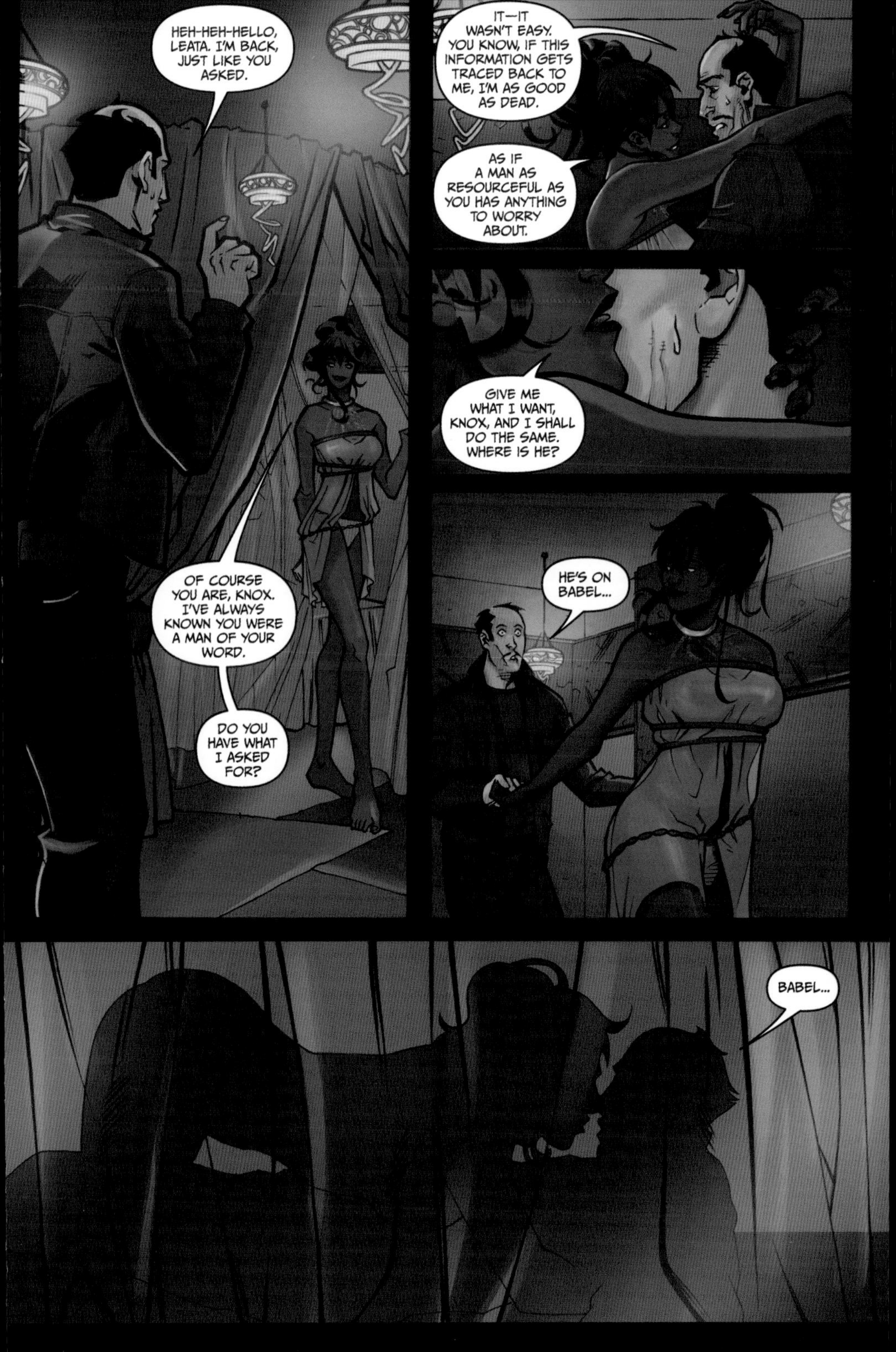
HEH-HEH-HELLO, LEATA. I'M BACK, JUST LIKE YOU ASKED.
OF COURSE YOU ARE, KNOX. I'VE ALWAYS KNOWN YOU WERE A MAN OF YOUR WORD.
DO YOU HAVE WHAT I ASKED FOR?
IT—IT WASN'T EASY. YOU KNOW, IF THIS INFORMATION GETS TRACED BACK TO ME, I'M AS GOOD AS DEAD.
AS IF A MAN AS RESOURCEFUL AS YOU HAS ANYTHING TO WORRY ABOUT.
GIVE ME WHAT I WANT, KNOX, AND I SHALL DO THE SAME. WHERE IS HE?
HE'S ON BABEL...
BABEL...

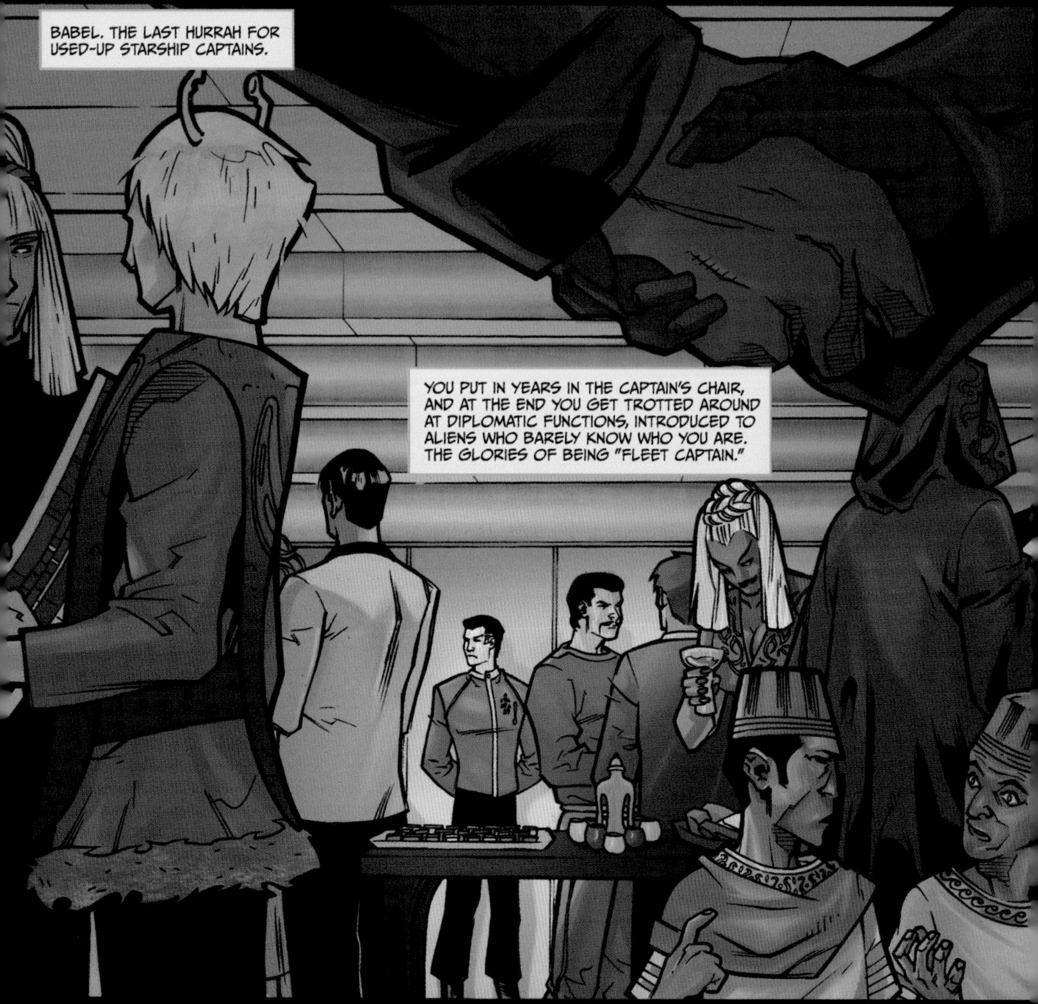
BABEL. THE LAST HURRAH FOR USED-UP STARSHIP CAPTAINS.
YOU PUT IN YEARS IN THE CAPTAIN'S CHAIR, AND AT THE END YOU GET TROTTED AROUND AT DIPLOMATIC FUNCTIONS, INTRODUCED TO ALIENS WHO BARELY KNOW WHO YOU ARE. THE GLORIES OF BEING "FLEET CAPTAIN."

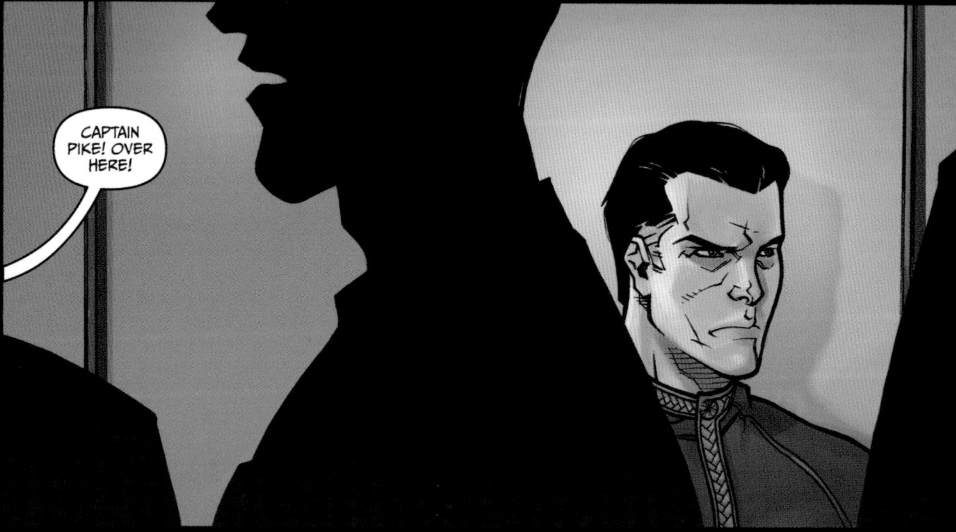
CAPTAIN PIKE! OVER HERE!

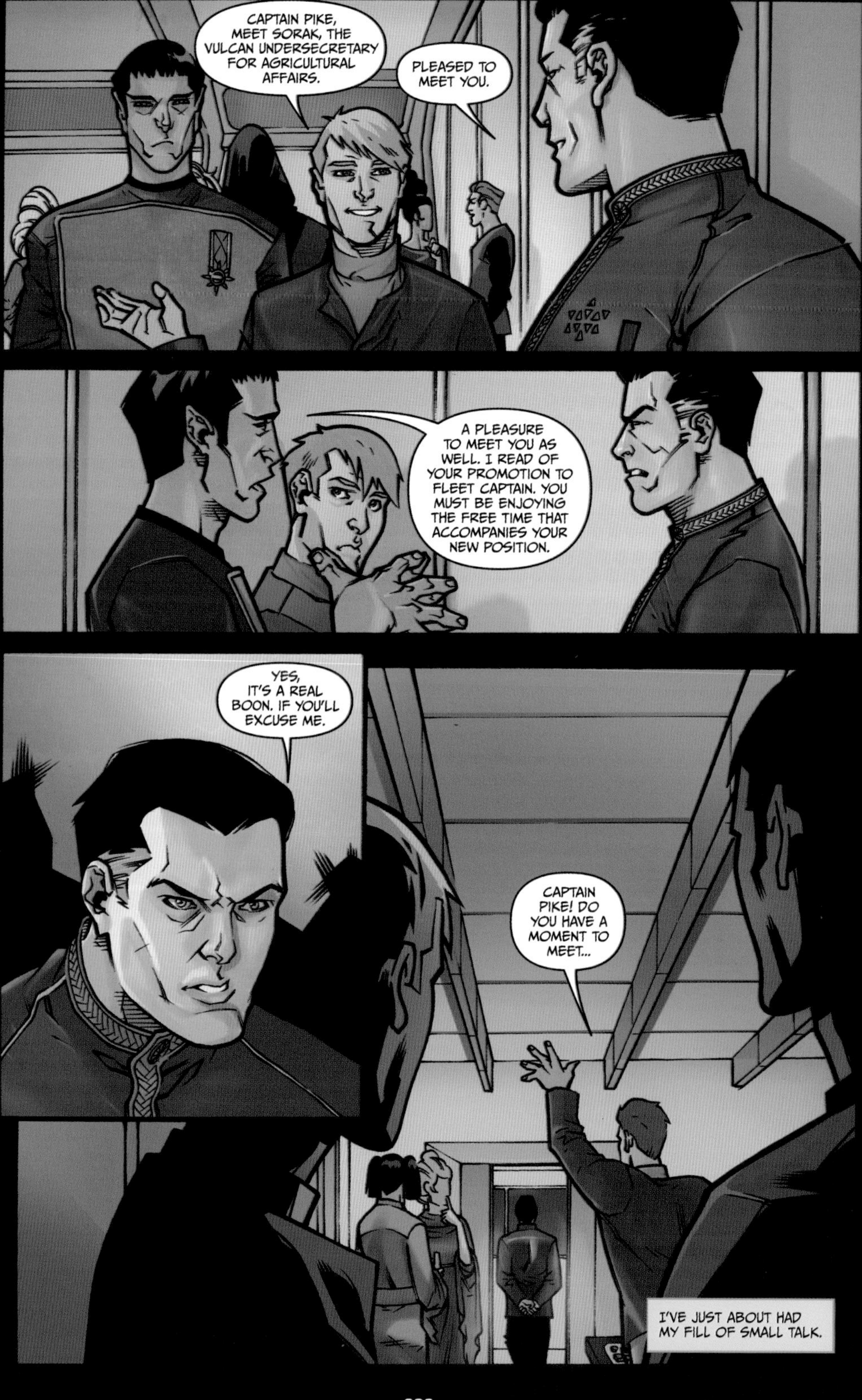
CAPTAIN PIKE, MEET SORAK, THE VULCAN UNDERSECRETARY FOR AGRICULTURAL AFFAIRS.
PLEASED TO MEET YOU.
A PLEASURE TO MEET YOU AS WELL. I READ OF YOUR PROMOTION TO FLEET CAPTAIN. YOU MUST BE ENJOYING THE FREE TIME THAT ACCOMPANIES YOUR NEW POSITION.
YES, IT'S A REAL BOON. IF YOU'LL EXCUSE ME.
CAPTAIN PIKE! DO YOU HAVE A MOMENT TO MEET...
I'VE JUST ABOUT HAD MY FILL OF SMALL TALK.

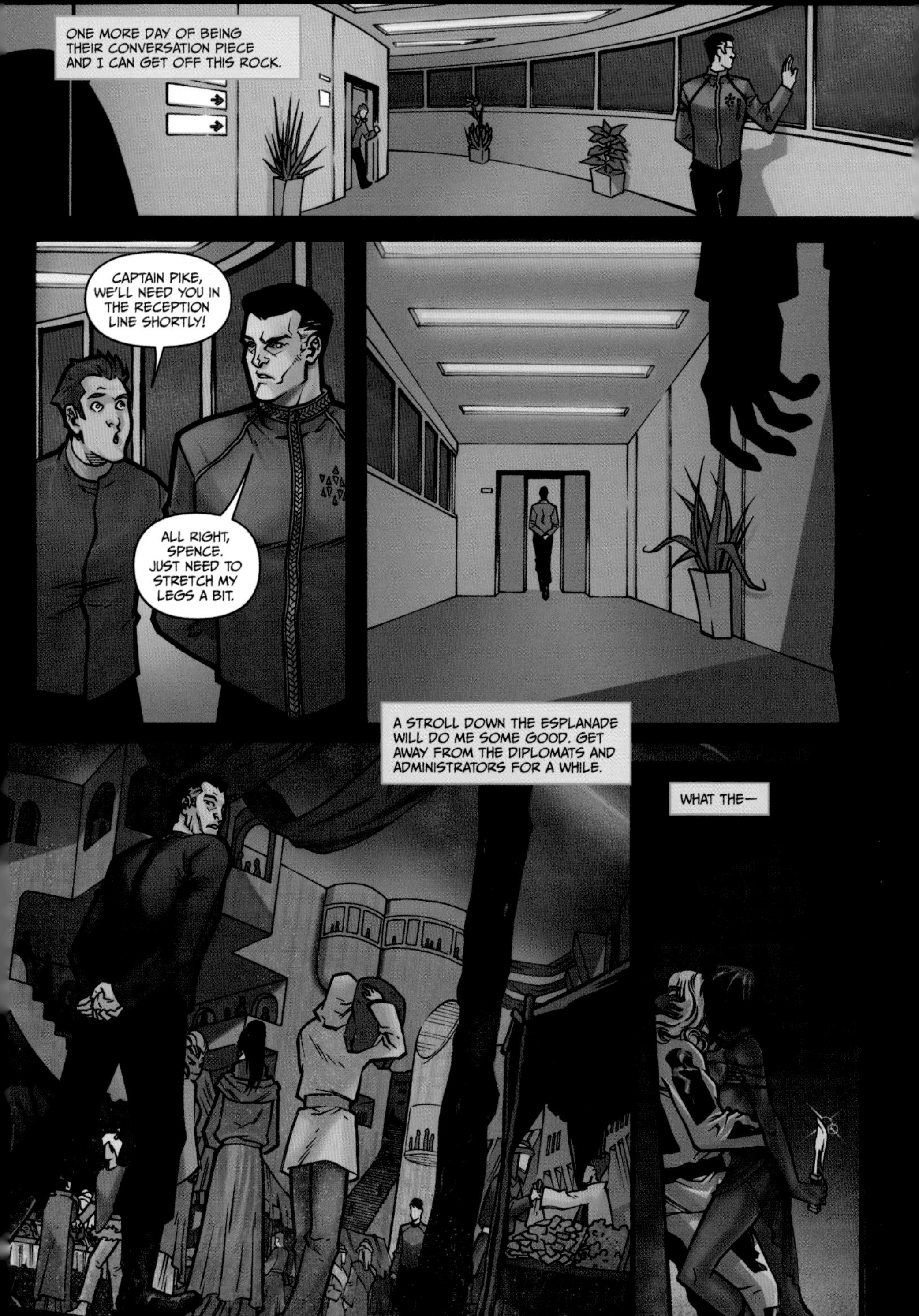
ONE MORE DAY OF BEING THEIR CONVERSATION PIECE AND I CAN GET OFF THIS ROCK.
CAPTAIN PIKE, WE'LL NEED YOU IN THE RECEPTION LINE SHORTLY!
ALL RIGHT, SPENCE. JUST NEED TO STRETCH MY LEGS A BIT.
A STROLL DOWN THE ESPLANADE WILL DO ME SOME GOOD. GET AWAY FROM THE DIPLOMATS AND ADMINISTRATORS FOR A WHILE.
WHAT THE—

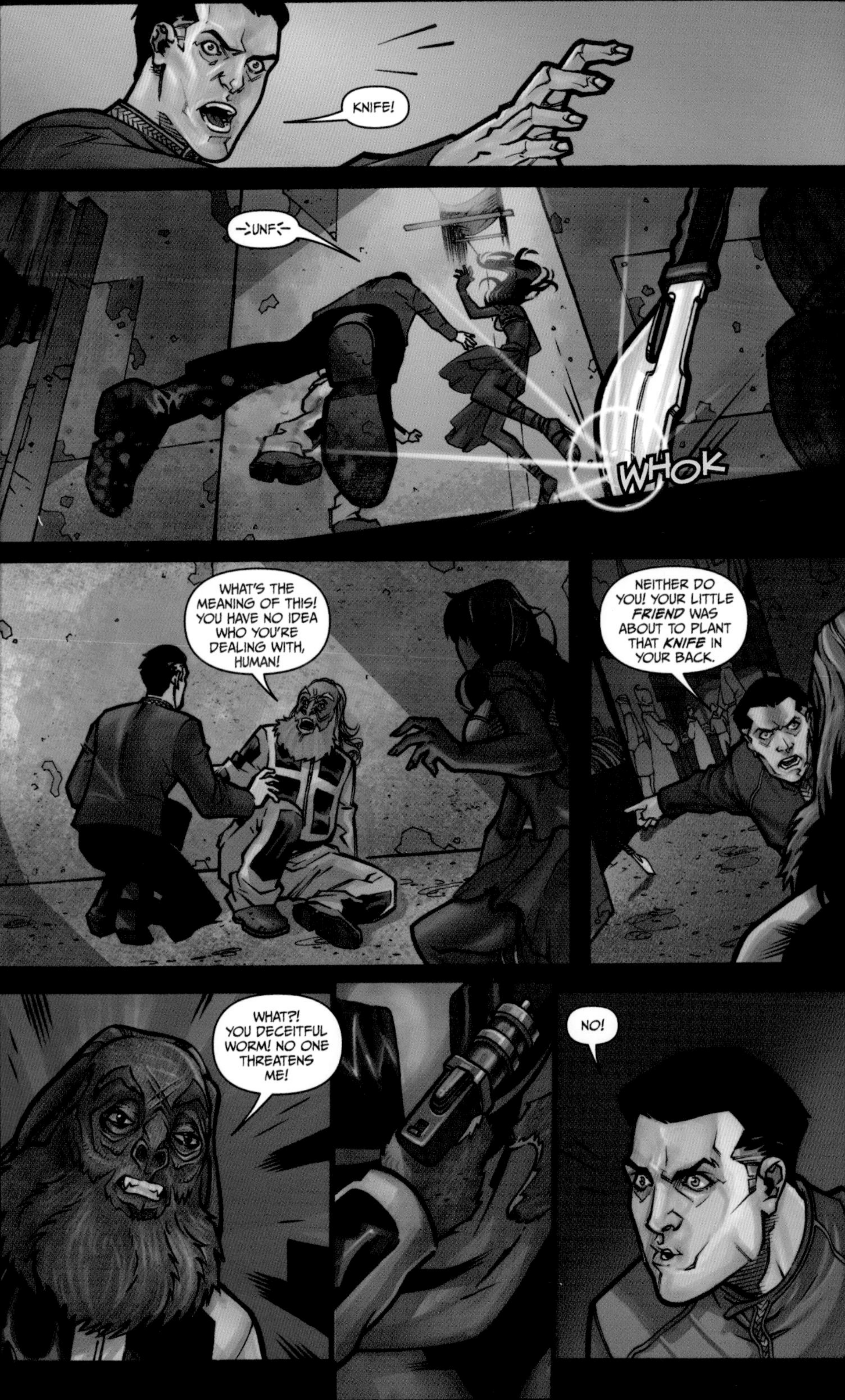
KNIFE!
-UNF-
WHOK
WHAT'S THE MEANING OF THIS! YOU HAVE NO IDEA WHO YOU'RE DEALING WITH, HUMAN!
NEITHER DO YOU! YOUR LITTLE FRIEND WAS ABOUT TO PLANT THAT KNIFE IN YOUR BACK.
WHAT?! YOU DECEITFUL WORM! NO ONE THREATENS ME!
NO!

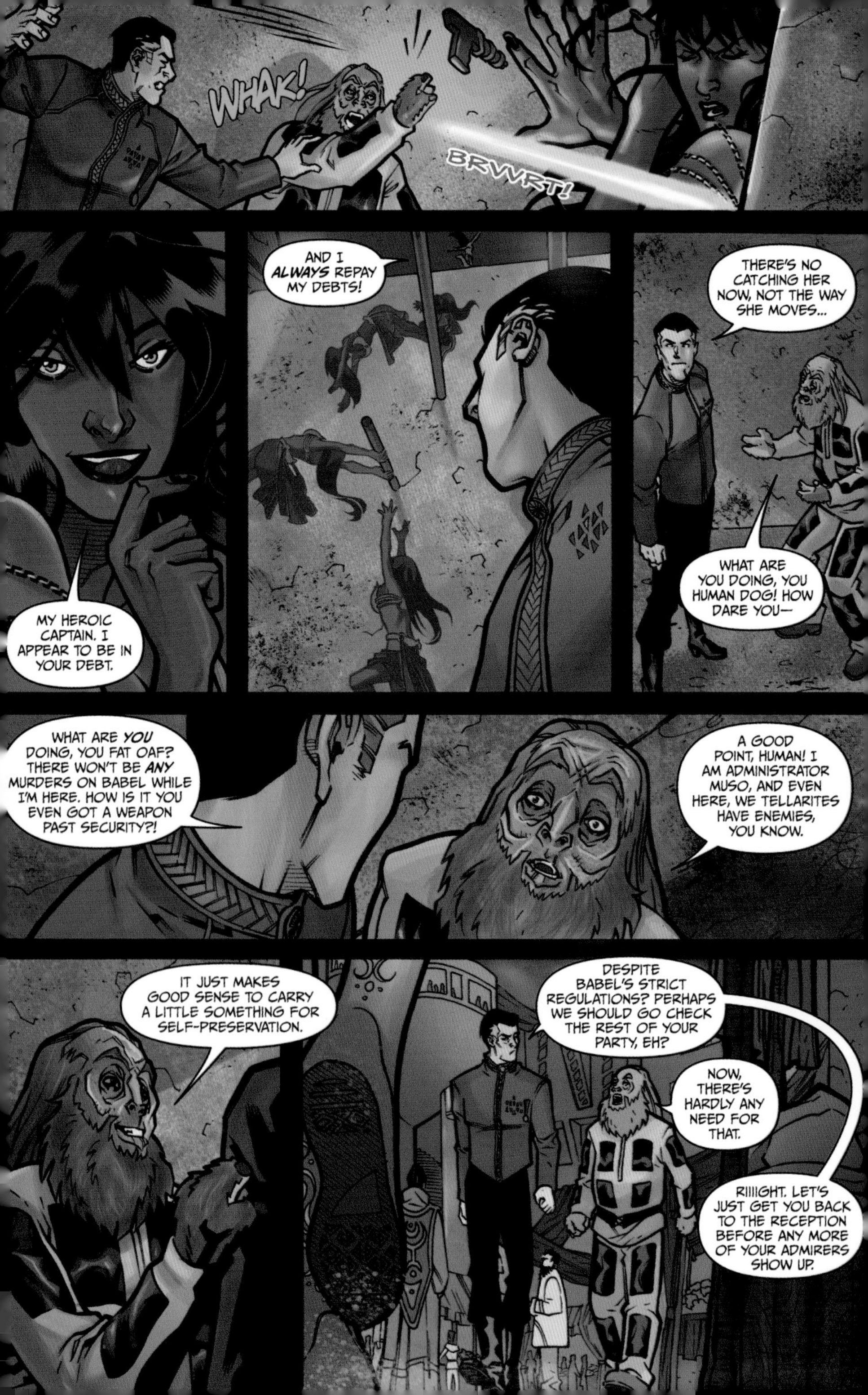
WHAK!
BRVVRT!
MY HEROIC CAPTAIN. I APPEAR TO BE IN YOUR DEBT.
AND I ALWAYS REPAY MY DEBTS!
THERE'S NO CATCHING HER NOW, NOT THE WAY SHE MOVES...
WHAT ARE YOU DOING, YOU HUMAN DOG! HOW DARE YOU—
WHAT ARE YOU DOING, YOU FAT OAF? THERE WON'T BE ANY MURDERS ON BABEL WHILE I'M HERE. HOW IS IT YOU EVEN GOT A WEAPON PAST SECURITY?!
A GOOD POINT, HUMAN! I AM ADMINISTRATOR MUSO, AND EVEN HERE, WE TELLARITES HAVE ENEMIES, YOU KNOW.
IT JUST MAKES GOOD SENSE TO CARRY A LITTLE SOMETHING FOR SELF-PRESERVATION.
DESPITE BABEL'S STRICT REGULATIONS? PERHAPS WE SHOULD GO CHECK THE REST OF YOUR PARTY, EH?
NOW, THERE'S HARDLY ANY NEED FOR THAT.
RIIIIGHT. LET'S JUST GET YOU BACK TO THE RECEPTION BEFORE ANY MORE OF YOUR ADMIRERS SHOW UP.

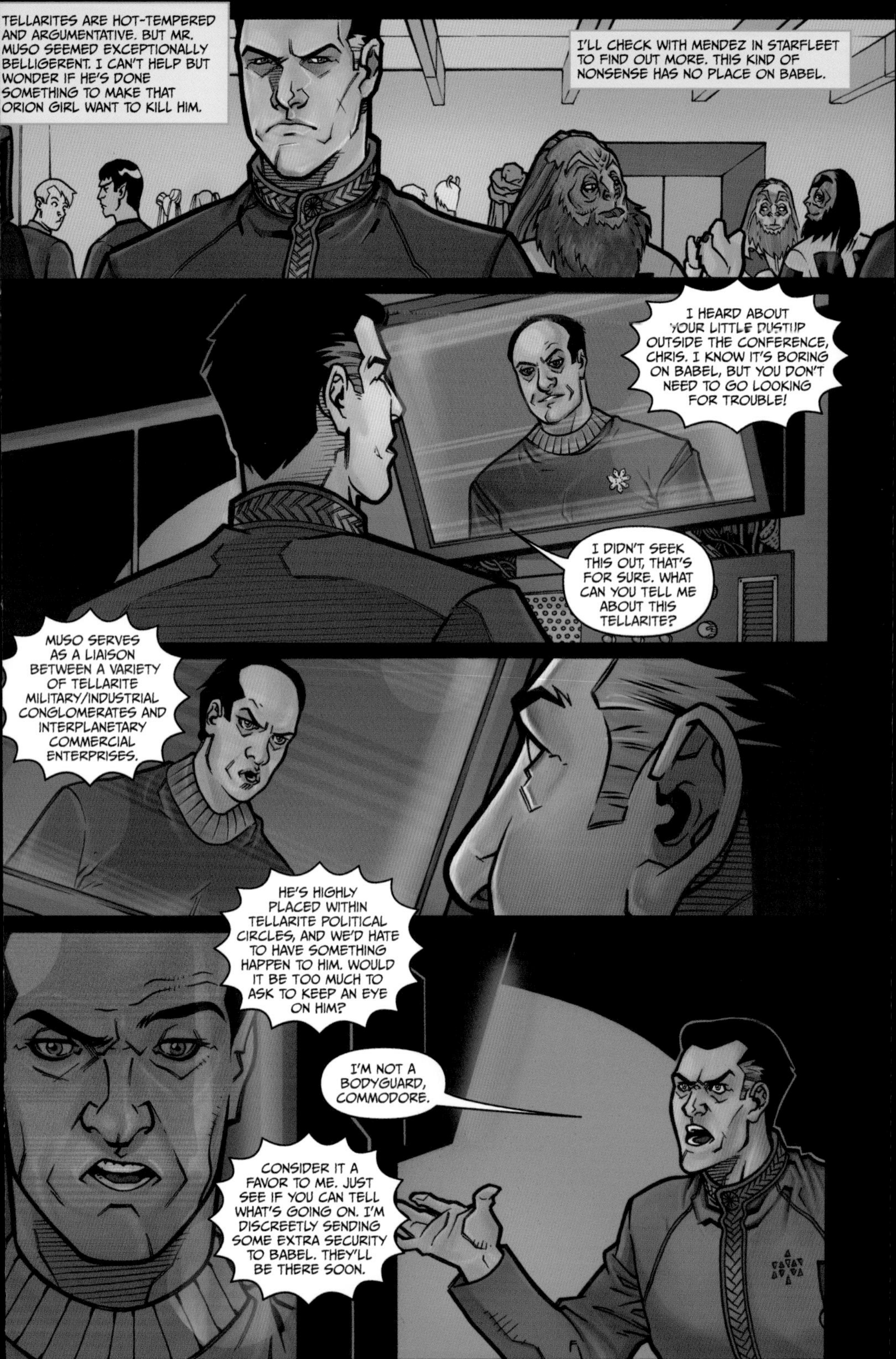
TELLARITES ARE HOT-TEMPERED AND ARGUMENTATIVE. BUT MR. MUSO SEEMED EXCEPTIONALLY BELLIGERENT. I CAN'T HELP BUT WONDER IF HE'S DONE SOMETHING TO MAKE THAT ORION GIRL WANT TO KILL HIM.
I'LL CHECK WITH MENDEZ IN STARFLEET TO FIND OUT MORE. THIS KIND OF NONSENSE HAS NO PLACE ON BABEL.
I HEARD ABOUT YOUR LITTLE DUSTUP OUTSIDE THE CONFERENCE, CHRIS. I KNOW IT'S BORING ON BABEL, BUT YOU DON'T NEED TO GO LOOKING FOR TROUBLE!
I DIDN'T SEEK THIS OUT, THAT'S FOR SURE. WHAT CAN YOU TELL ME ABOUT THIS TELLARITE?
MUSO SERVES AS A LIAISON BETWEEN A VARIETY OF TELLARITE MILITARY/INDUSTRIAL CONGLOMERATES AND INTERPLANETARY COMMERCIAL ENTERPRISES.
HE'S HIGHLY PLACED WITHIN TELLARITE POLITICAL CIRCLES, AND WE'D HATE TO HAVE SOMETHING HAPPEN TO HIM. WOULD IT BE TOO MUCH TO ASK TO KEEP AN EYE ON HIM?
I'M NOT A BODYGUARD, COMMODORE.
CONSIDER IT A FAVOR TO ME. JUST SEE IF YOU CAN TELL WHAT'S GOING ON. I'M DISCREETLY SENDING SOME EXTRA SECURITY TO BABEL. THEY'LL BE THERE SOON.

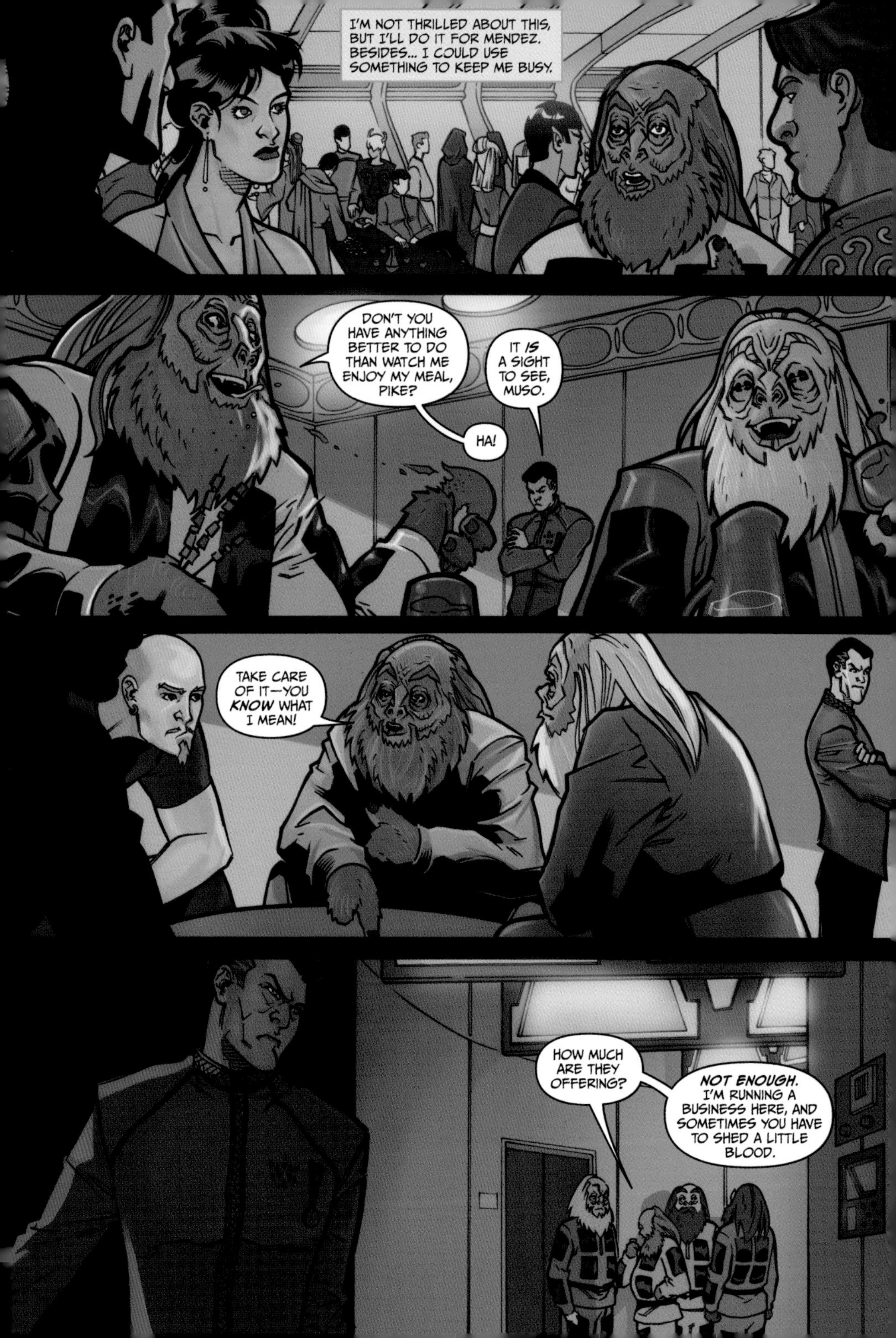
I'M NOT THRILLED ABOUT THIS, BUT I'LL DO IT FOR MENDEZ. BESIDES... I COULD USE SOMETHING TO KEEP ME BUSY.
DON'T YOU HAVE ANYTHING BETTER TO DO THAN WATCH ME ENJOY MY MEAL, PIKE?
HA!
IT *IS* A SIGHT TO SEE, MUSO.
TAKE CARE OF IT—YOU ***KNOW*** WHAT I MEAN!
HOW MUCH ARE THEY OFFERING?
NOT ENOUGH. I'M RUNNING A BUSINESS HERE, AND SOMETIMES YOU HAVE TO SHED A LITTLE BLOOD.

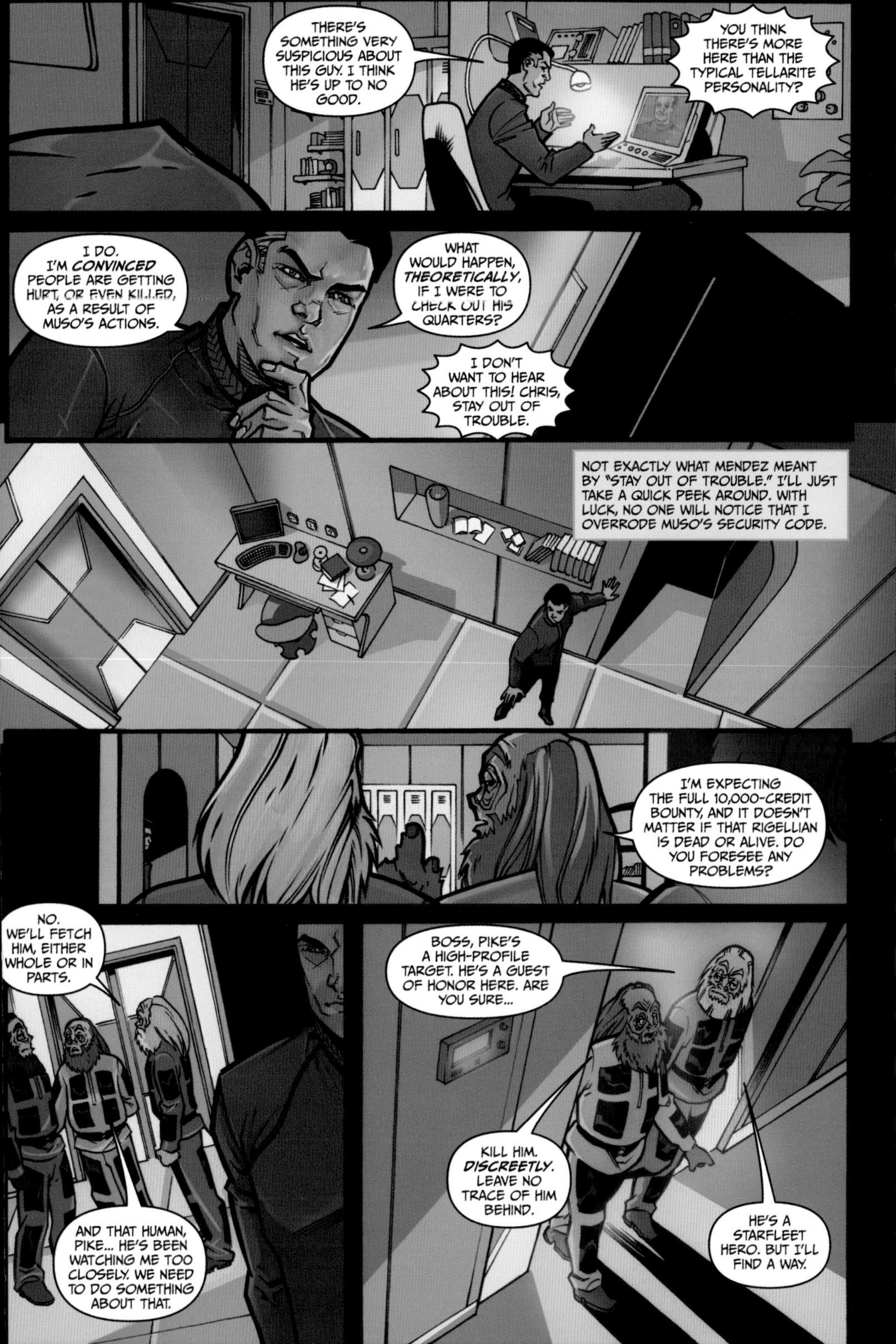
THERE'S SOMETHING VERY SUSPICIOUS ABOUT THIS GUY. I THINK HE'S UP TO NO GOOD.
YOU THINK THERE'S MORE HERE THAN THE TYPICAL TELLARITE PERSONALITY?
I DO. I'M CONVINCED PEOPLE ARE GETTING HURT, OR EVEN KILLED, AS A RESULT OF MUSO'S ACTIONS.
WHAT WOULD HAPPEN, THEORETICALLY, IF I WERE TO CHECK OUT HIS QUARTERS?
I DON'T WANT TO HEAR ABOUT THIS! CHRIS, STAY OUT OF TROUBLE.
NOT EXACTLY WHAT MENDEZ MEANT BY "STAY OUT OF TROUBLE." I'LL JUST TAKE A QUICK PEEK AROUND. WITH LUCK, NO ONE WILL NOTICE THAT I OVERRODE MUSO'S SECURITY CODE.
I'M EXPECTING THE FULL 10,000-CREDIT BOUNTY, AND IT DOESN'T MATTER IF THAT RIGELLIAN IS DEAD OR ALIVE. DO YOU FORESEE ANY PROBLEMS?
NO. WE'LL FETCH HIM, EITHER WHOLE OR IN PARTS.
AND THAT HUMAN, PIKE... HE'S BEEN WATCHING ME TOO CLOSELY. WE NEED TO DO SOMETHING ABOUT THAT.
BOSS, PIKE'S A HIGH-PROFILE TARGET. HE'S A GUEST OF HONOR HERE. ARE YOU SURE...
KILL HIM. DISCREETLY. LEAVE NO TRACE OF HIM BEHIND.
HE'S A STARFLEET HERO. BUT I'LL FIND A WAY.

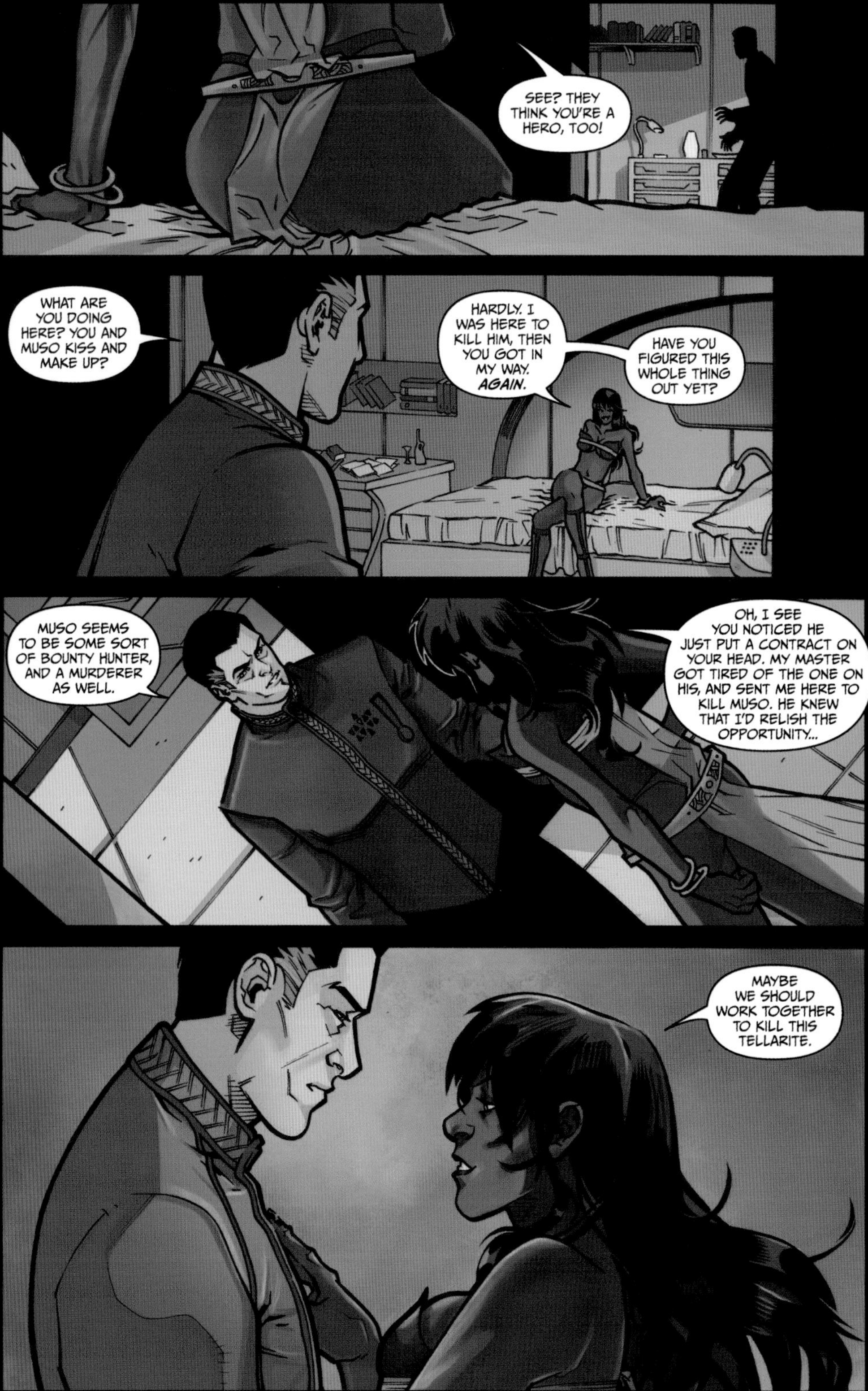
SEE? THEY THINK YOU'RE A HERO, TOO!
WHAT ARE YOU DOING HERE? YOU AND MUSO KISS AND MAKE UP?
HARDLY. I WAS HERE TO KILL HIM, THEN YOU GOT IN MY WAY. ***AGAIN.***
HAVE YOU FIGURED THIS WHOLE THING OUT YET?
MUSO SEEMS TO BE SOME SORT OF BOUNTY HUNTER, AND A MURDERER AS WELL.
OH, I SEE YOU NOTICED HE JUST PUT A CONTRACT ON YOUR HEAD. MY MASTER GOT TIRED OF THE ONE ON HIS, AND SENT ME HERE TO KILL MUSO. HE KNEW THAT I'D RELISH THE OPPORTUNITY...
MAYBE WE SHOULD WORK TOGETHER TO KILL THIS TELLARITE.

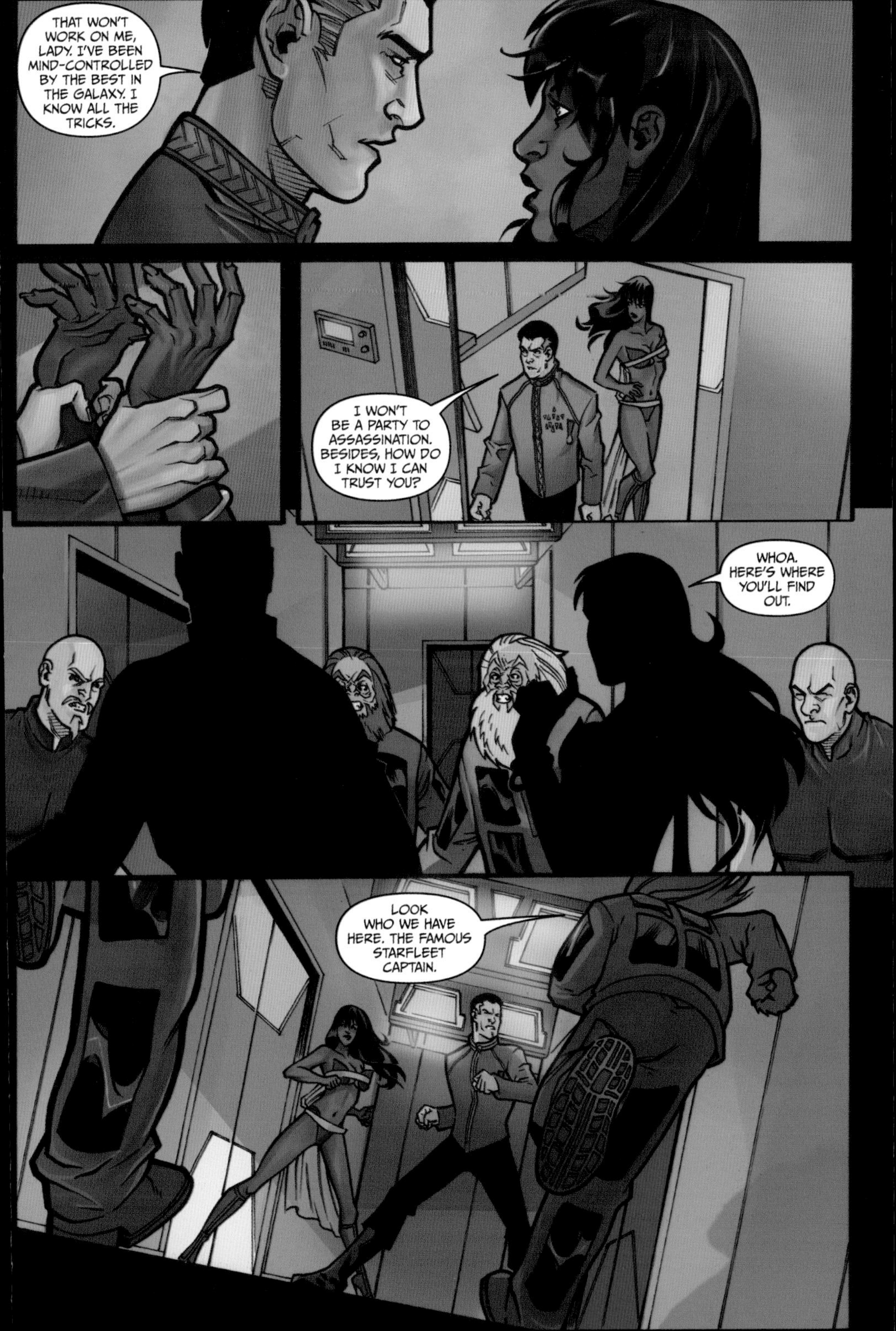
THAT WON'T WORK ON ME, LADY. I'VE BEEN MIND-CONTROLLED BY THE BEST IN THE GALAXY. I KNOW ALL THE TRICKS.
I WON'T BE A PARTY TO ASSASSINATION. BESIDES, HOW DO I KNOW I CAN TRUST YOU?
WHOA. HERE'S WHERE YOU'LL FIND OUT.
LOOK WHO WE HAVE HERE. THE FAMOUS STARFLEET CAPTAIN.

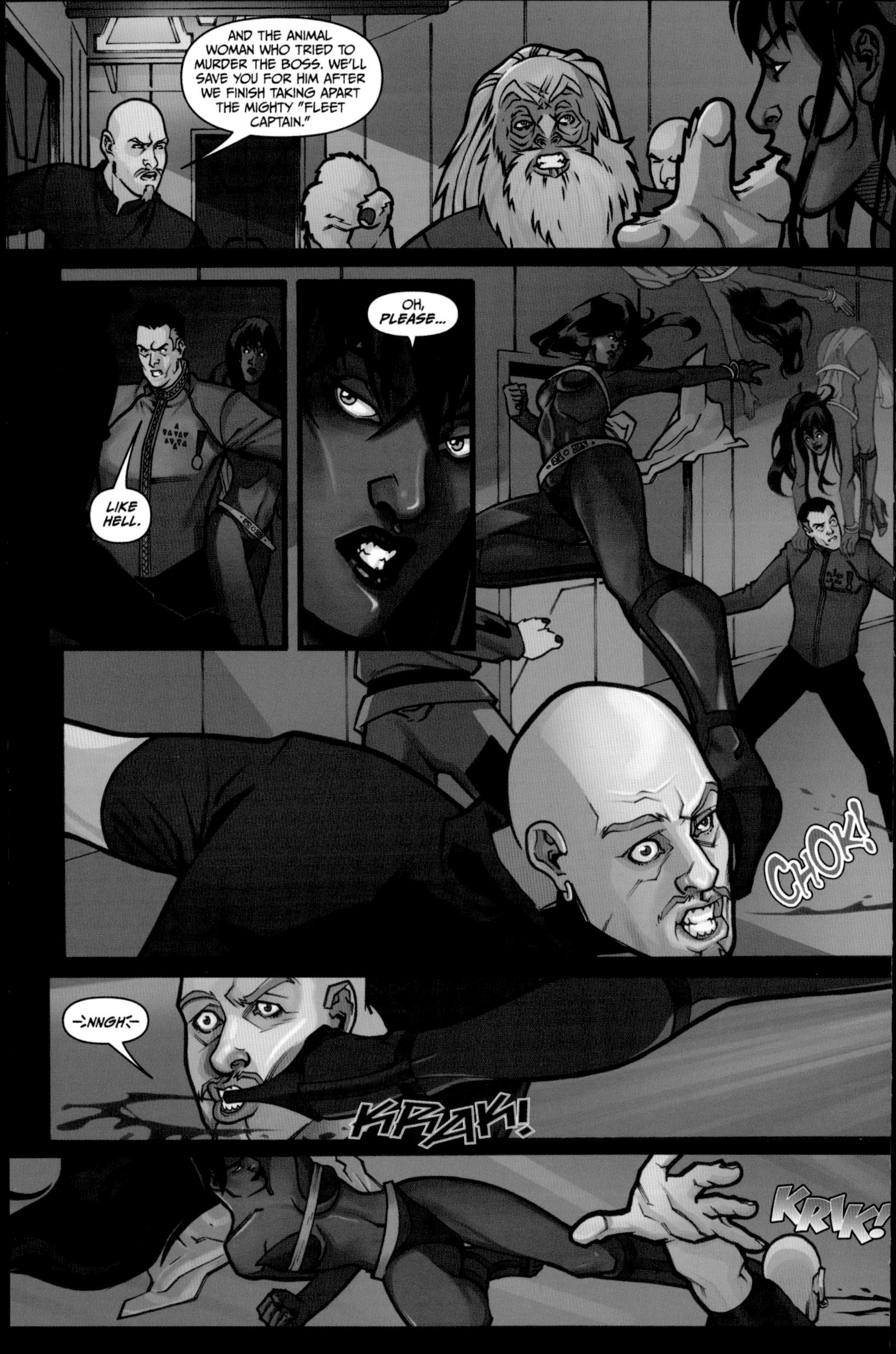
AND THE ANIMAL WOMAN WHO TRIED TO MURDER THE BOSS. WE'LL SAVE YOU FOR HIM AFTER WE FINISH TAKING APART THE MIGHTY "FLEET CAPTAIN."
LIKE HELL.
OH, PLEASE...
CHOK!
-NNGH-
KRAK!
KRIK!

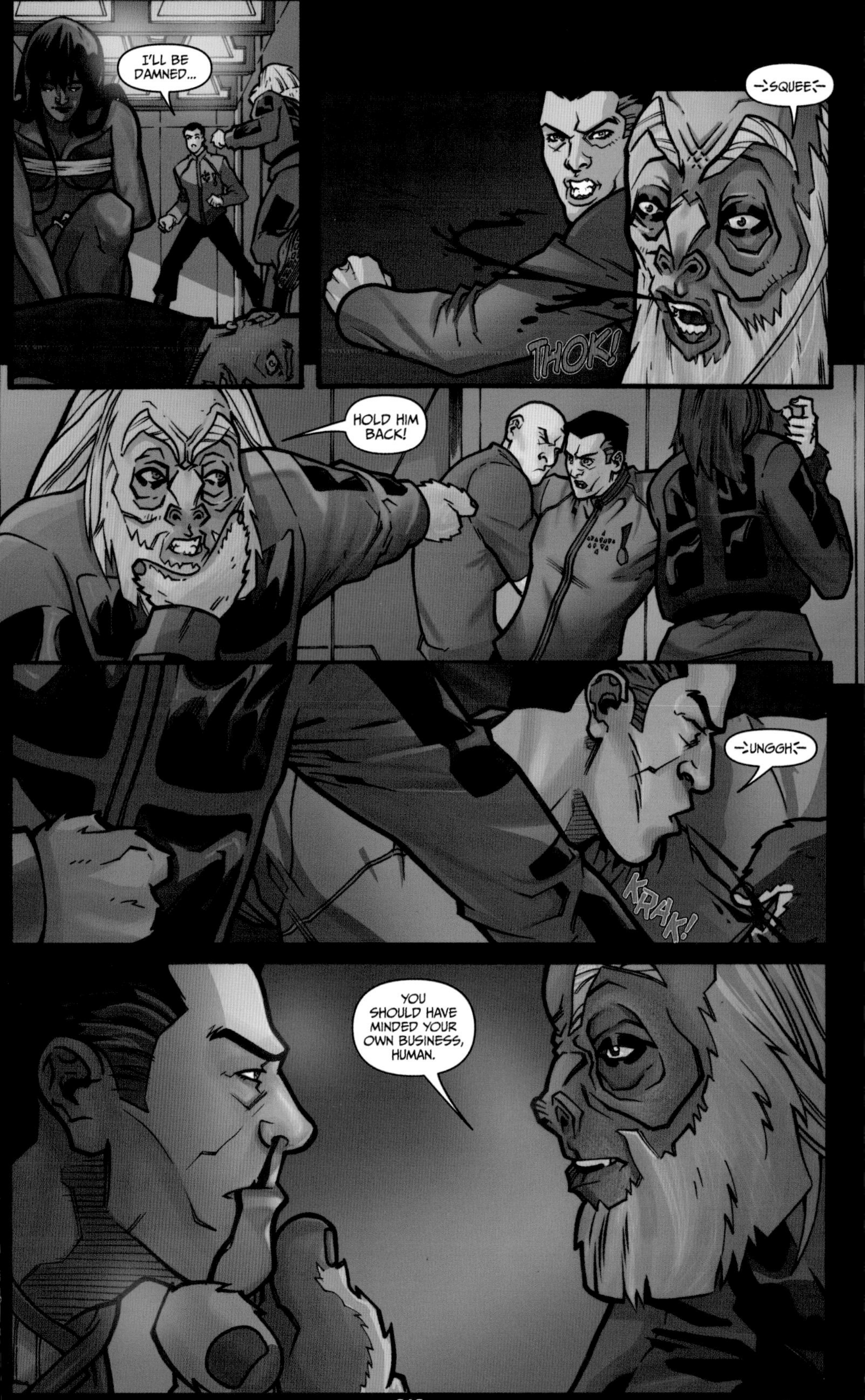
I'LL BE DAMNED...
-SQUEE-
THOK!
HOLD HIM BACK!
-UNGGH-
KRAK!
YOU SHOULD HAVE MINDED YOUR OWN BUSINESS, HUMAN.

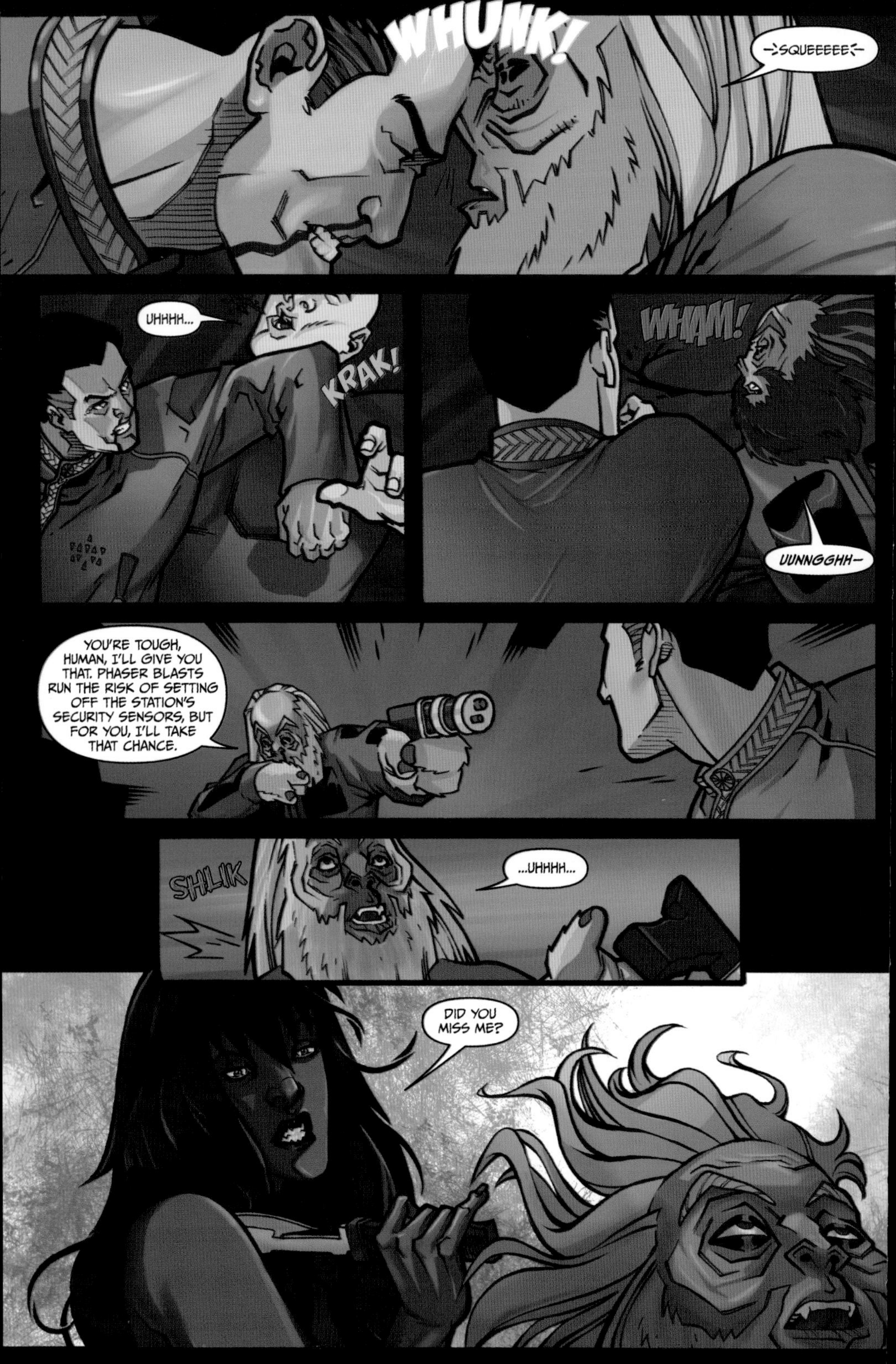
WHUNK!
SQUEEEEEE
UHHHH...
KRAK!
WHAM!
UUNNGGHH—
YOU'RE TOUGH, HUMAN, I'LL GIVE YOU THAT. PHASER BLASTS RUN THE RISK OF SETTING OFF THE STATION'S SECURITY SENSORS, BUT FOR YOU, I'LL TAKE THAT CHANCE.
SHLIK
...UHHHH...
DID YOU MISS ME?

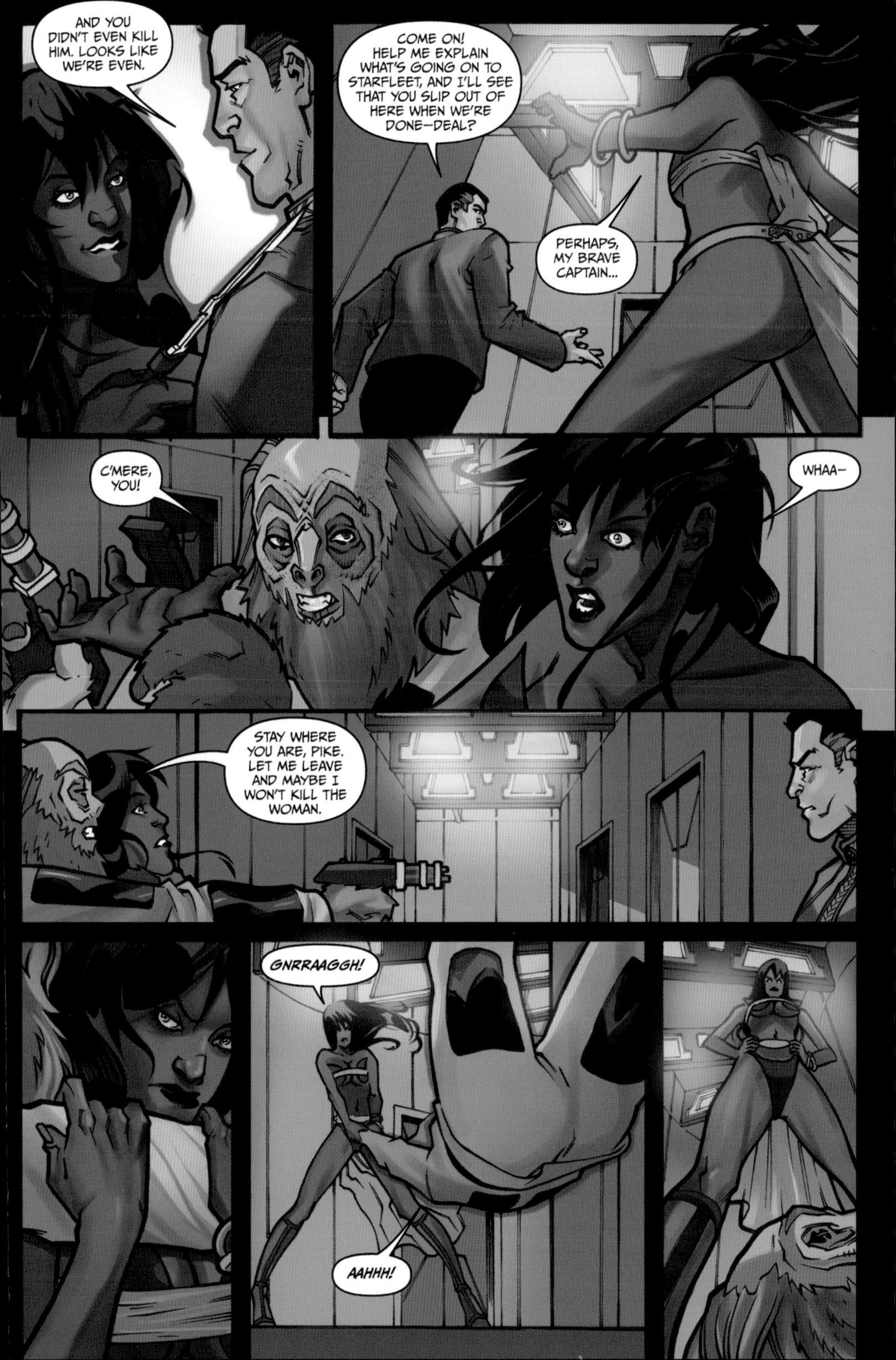
AND YOU DIDN'T EVEN KILL HIM. LOOKS LIKE WE'RE EVEN.
COME ON! HELP ME EXPLAIN WHAT'S GOING ON TO STARFLEET, AND I'LL SEE THAT YOU SLIP OUT OF HERE WHEN WE'RE DONE—DEAL?
PERHAPS, MY BRAVE CAPTAIN...
C'MERE, YOU!
WHAA-
STAY WHERE YOU ARE, PIKE. LET ME LEAVE AND MAYBE I WON'T KILL THE WOMAN.
GNRRAAGGH!
AAHHH!

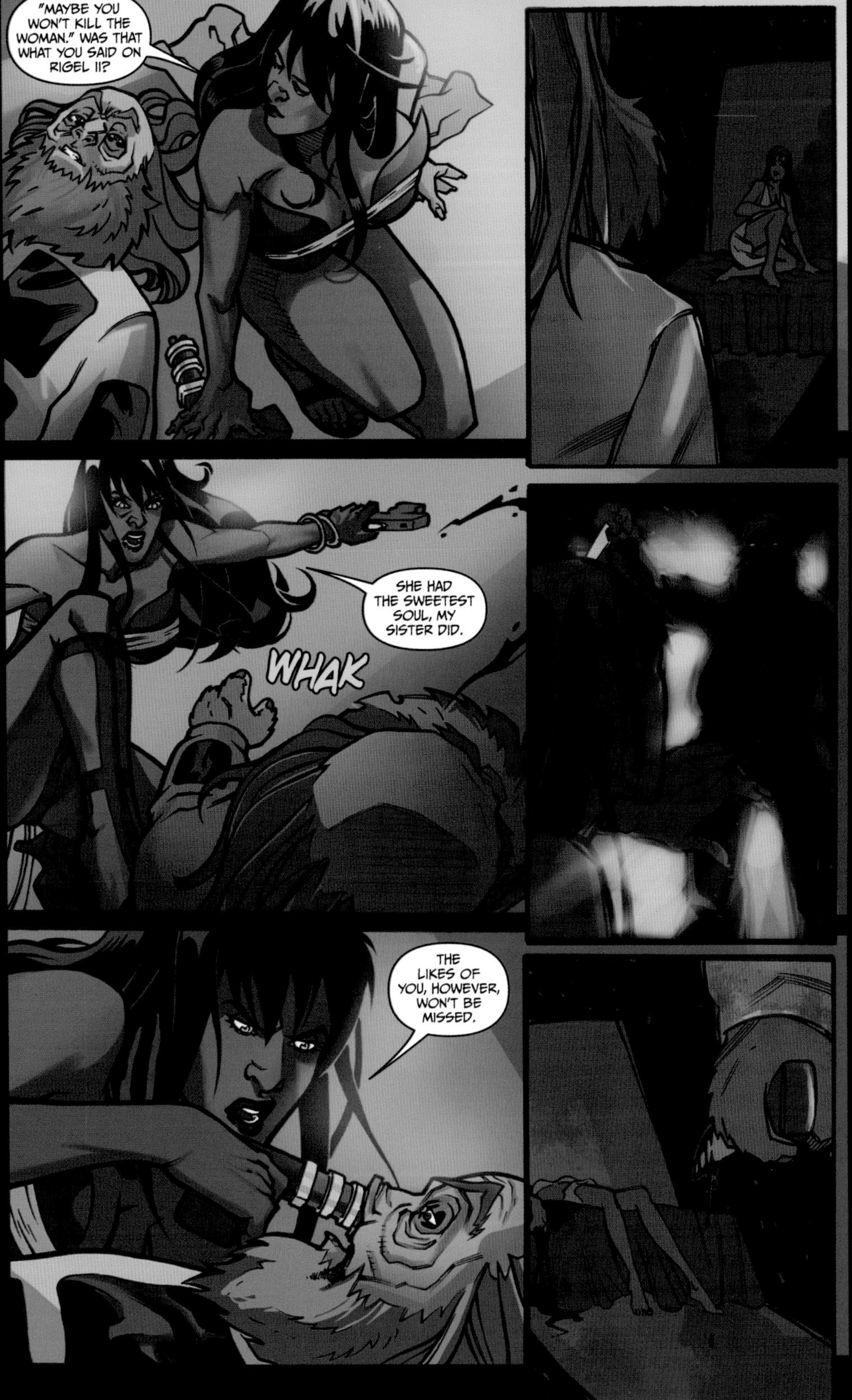
"MAYBE YOU WON'T KILL THE WOMAN." WAS THAT WHAT YOU SAID ON RIGEL II?
SHE HAD THE SWEETEST SOUL, MY SISTER DID.
WHAK
THE LIKES OF YOU, HOWEVER, WON'T BE MISSED.

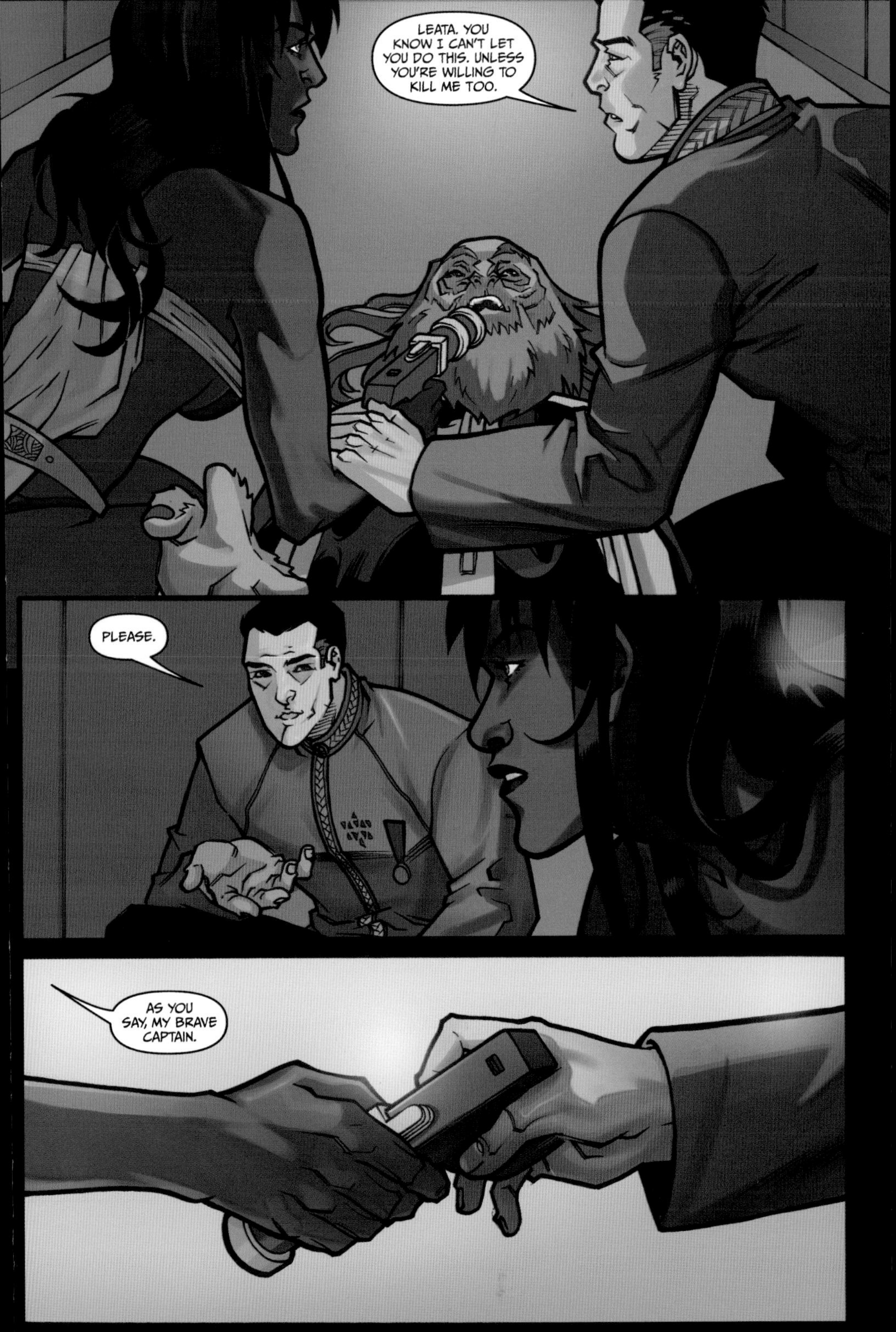
LEATA. YOU KNOW I CAN'T LET YOU DO THIS. UNLESS YOU'RE WILLING TO KILL ME TOO.
PLEASE.
AS YOU SAY, MY BRAVE CAPTAIN.

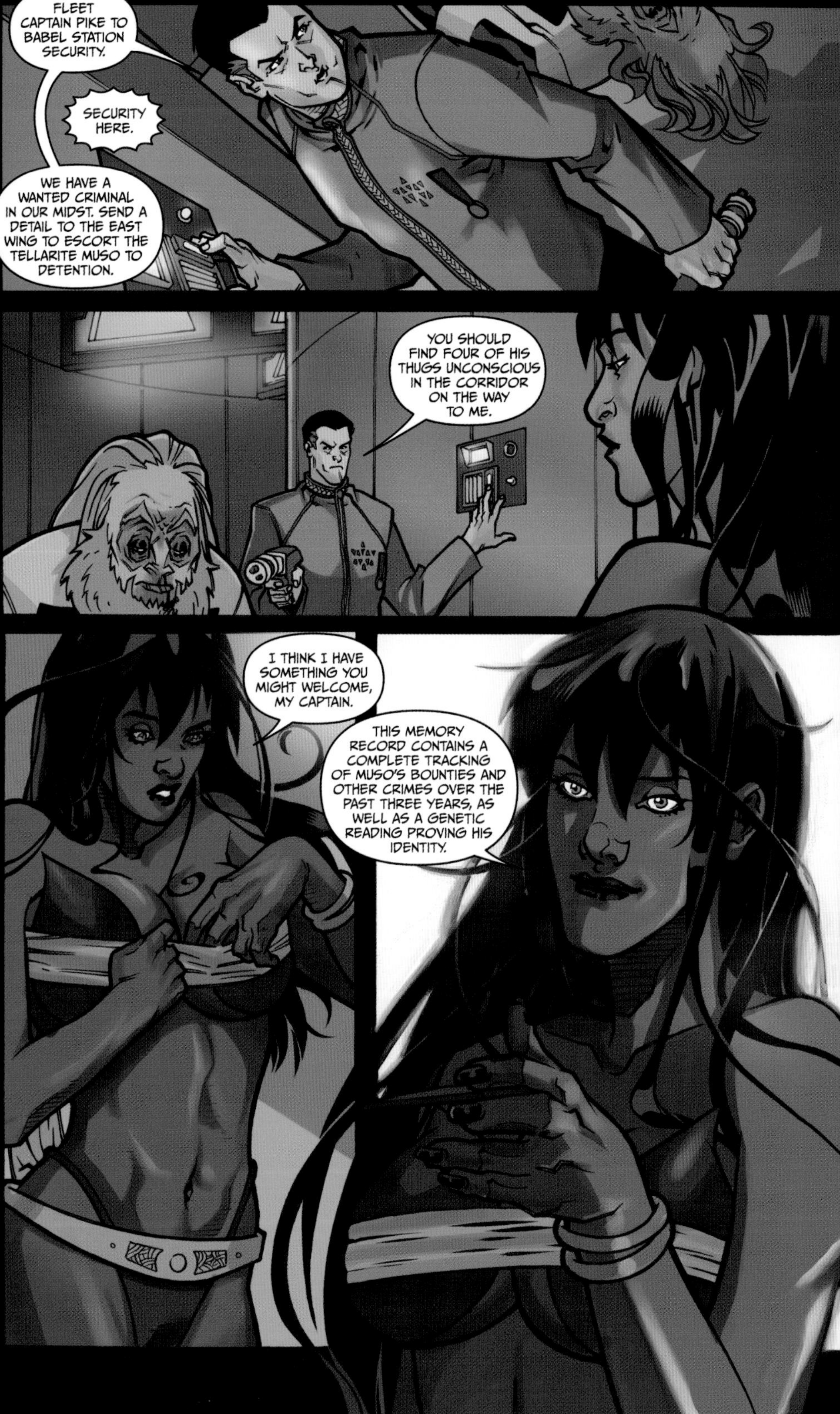

FLEET CAPTAIN PIKE TO BABEL STATION SECURITY.
SECURITY HERE.
WE HAVE A WANTED CRIMINAL IN OUR MIDST. SEND A DETAIL TO THE EAST WING TO ESCORT THE TELLARITE MUSO TO DETENTION.
YOU SHOULD FIND FOUR OF HIS THUGS UNCONSCIOUS IN THE CORRIDOR ON THE WAY TO ME.
I THINK I HAVE SOMETHING YOU MIGHT WELCOME, MY CAPTAIN.
THIS MEMORY RECORD CONTAINS A COMPLETE TRACKING OF MUSO'S BOUNTIES AND OTHER CRIMES OVER THE PAST THREE YEARS, AS WELL AS A GENETIC READING PROVING HIS IDENTITY.

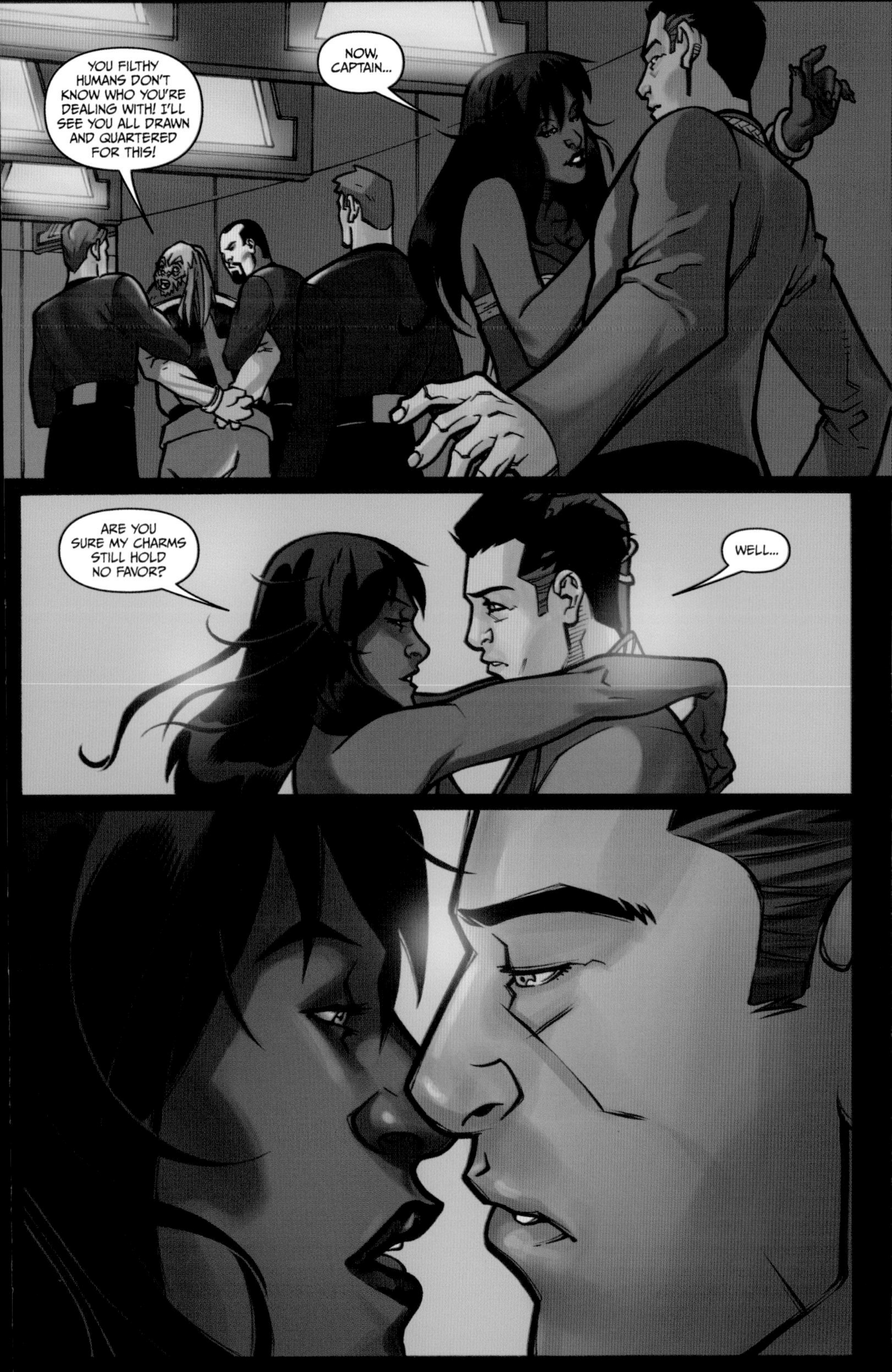
YOU FILTHY HUMANS DON'T KNOW WHO YOU'RE DEALING WITH! I'LL SEE YOU ALL DRAWN AND QUARTERED FOR THIS!
NOW, CAPTAIN...
ARE YOU SURE MY CHARMS STILL HOLD NO FAVOR?
WELL...

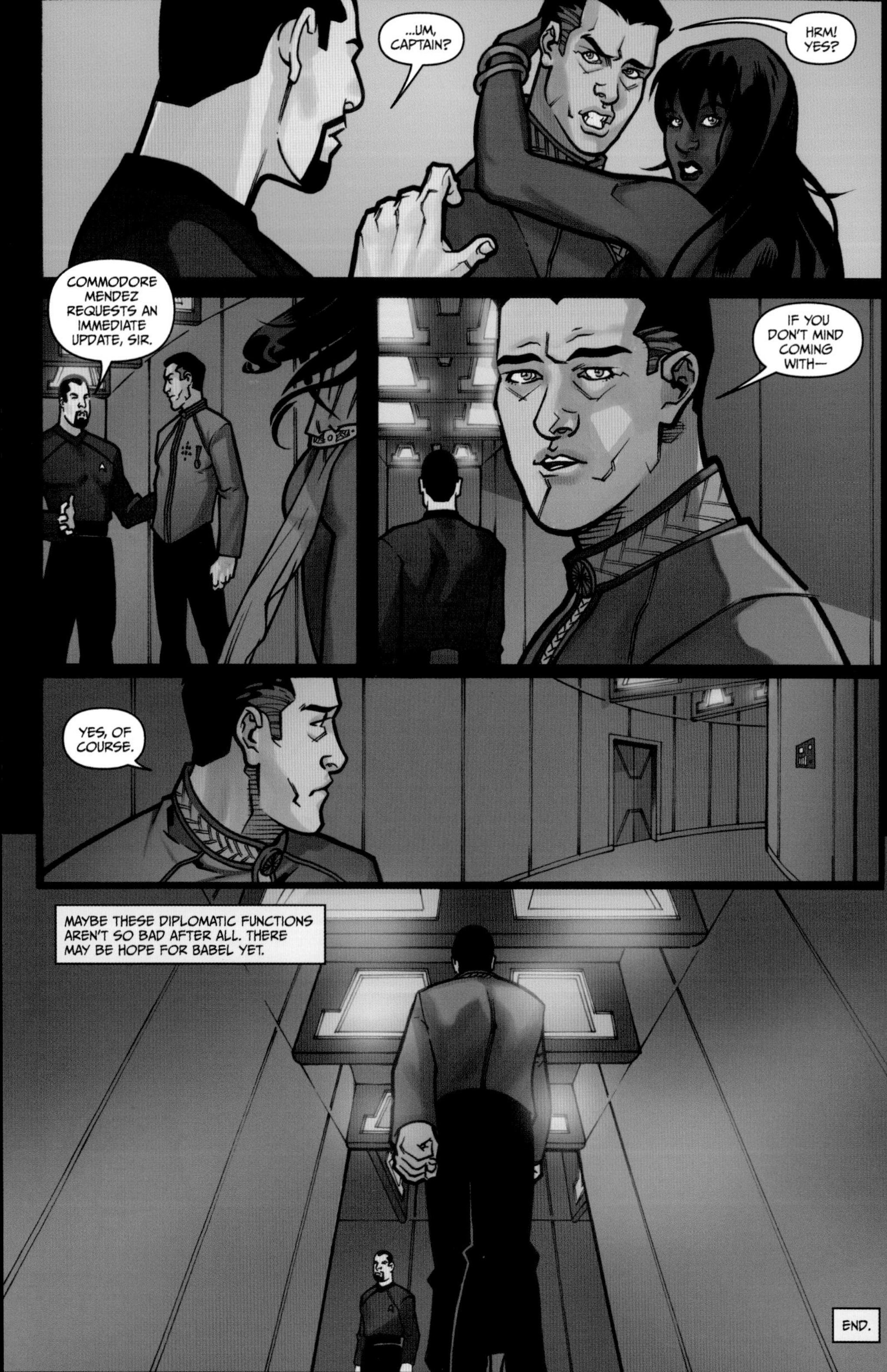
...UM, CAPTAIN?
HRM! YES?
COMMODORE MENDEZ REQUESTS AN IMMEDIATE UPDATE, SIR.
IF YOU DON'T MIND COMING WITH—
YES, OF COURSE.
MAYBE THESE DIPLOMATIC FUNCTIONS AREN'T SO BAD AFTER ALL. THERE MAY BE HOPE FOR BABEL YET.
END.

STAR TREK ®

THE ORIGINAL SERIES

OMNIBUS

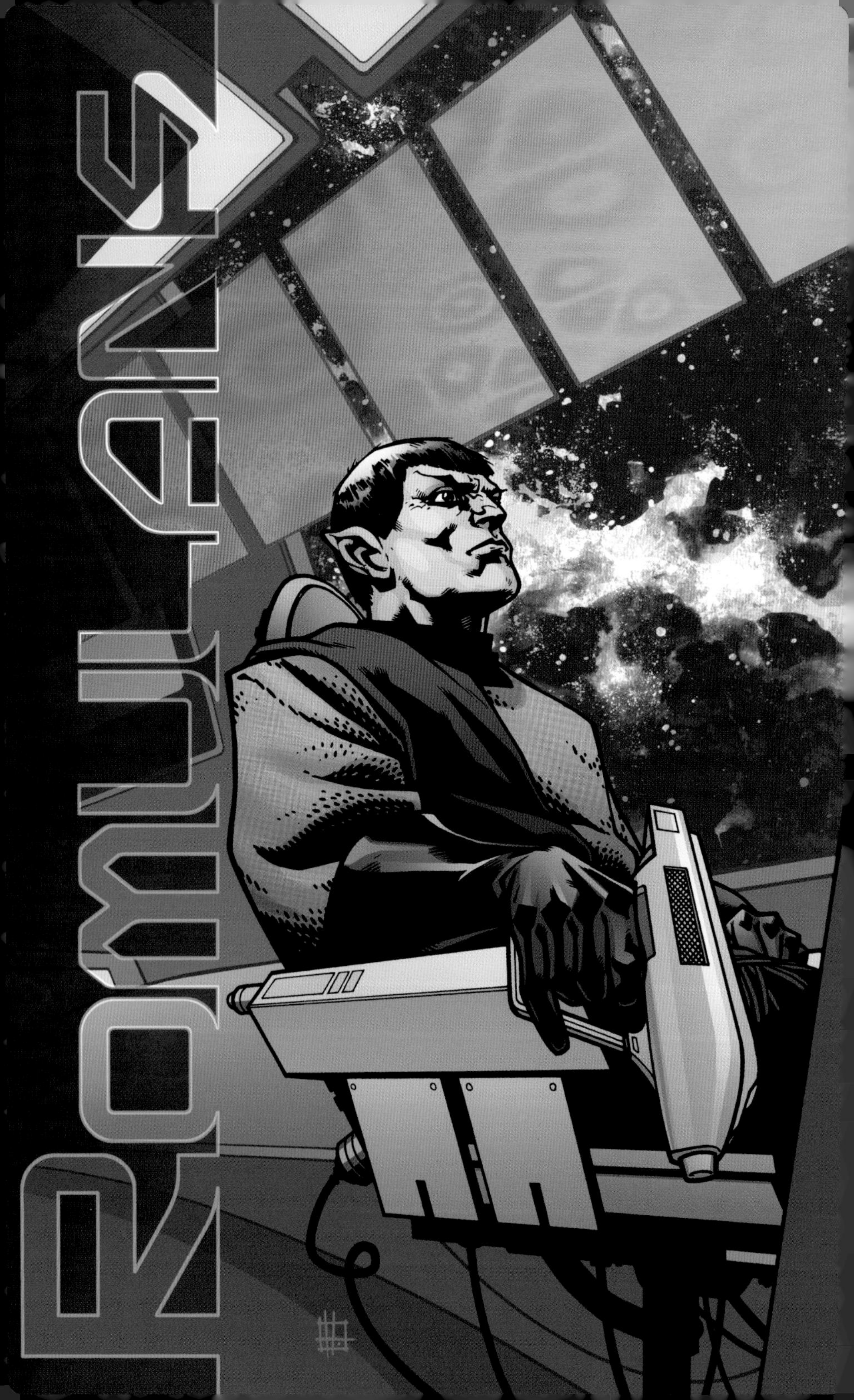
ROMULANS

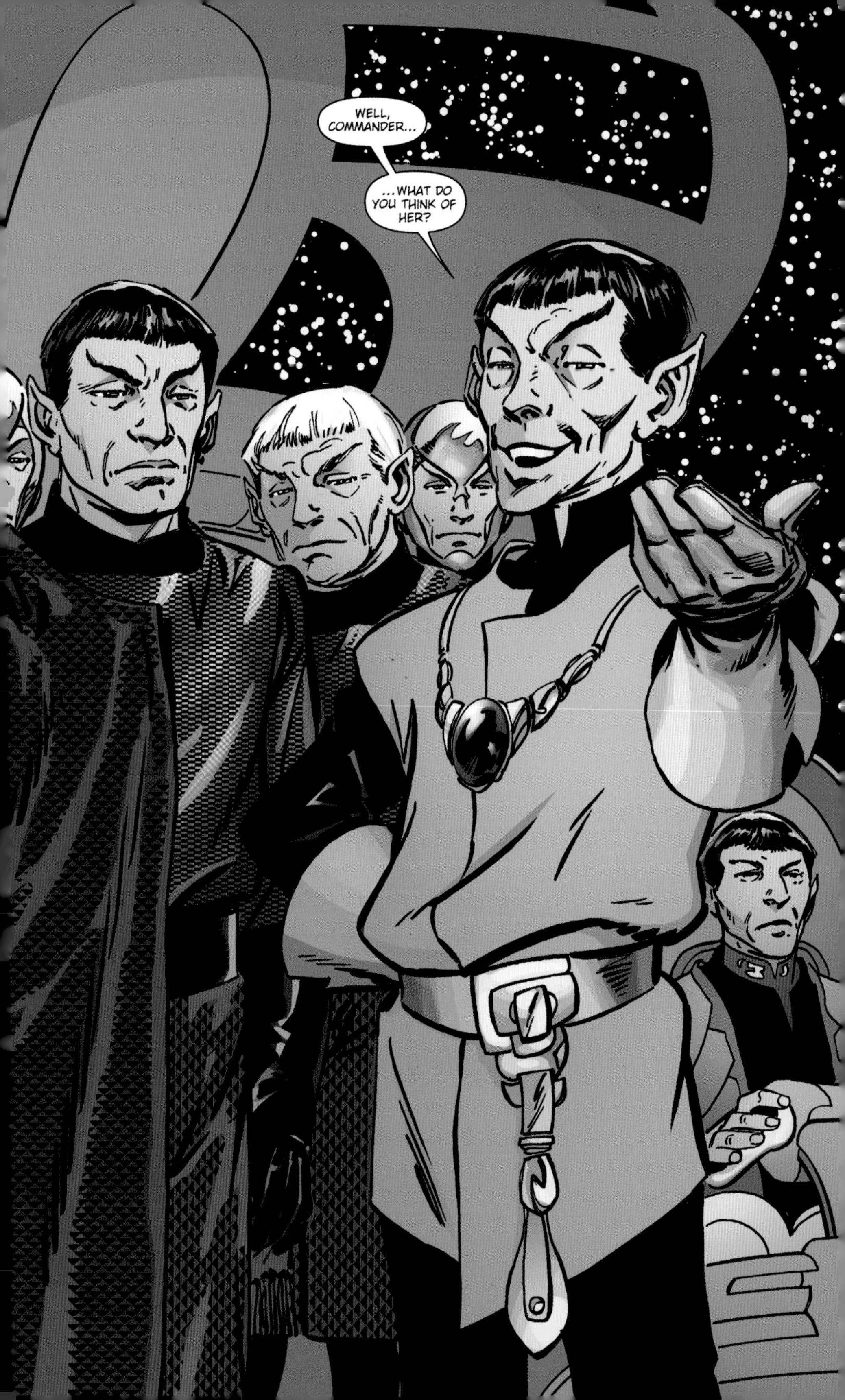
WELL, COMMANDER...
...WHAT DO YOU THINK OF HER?

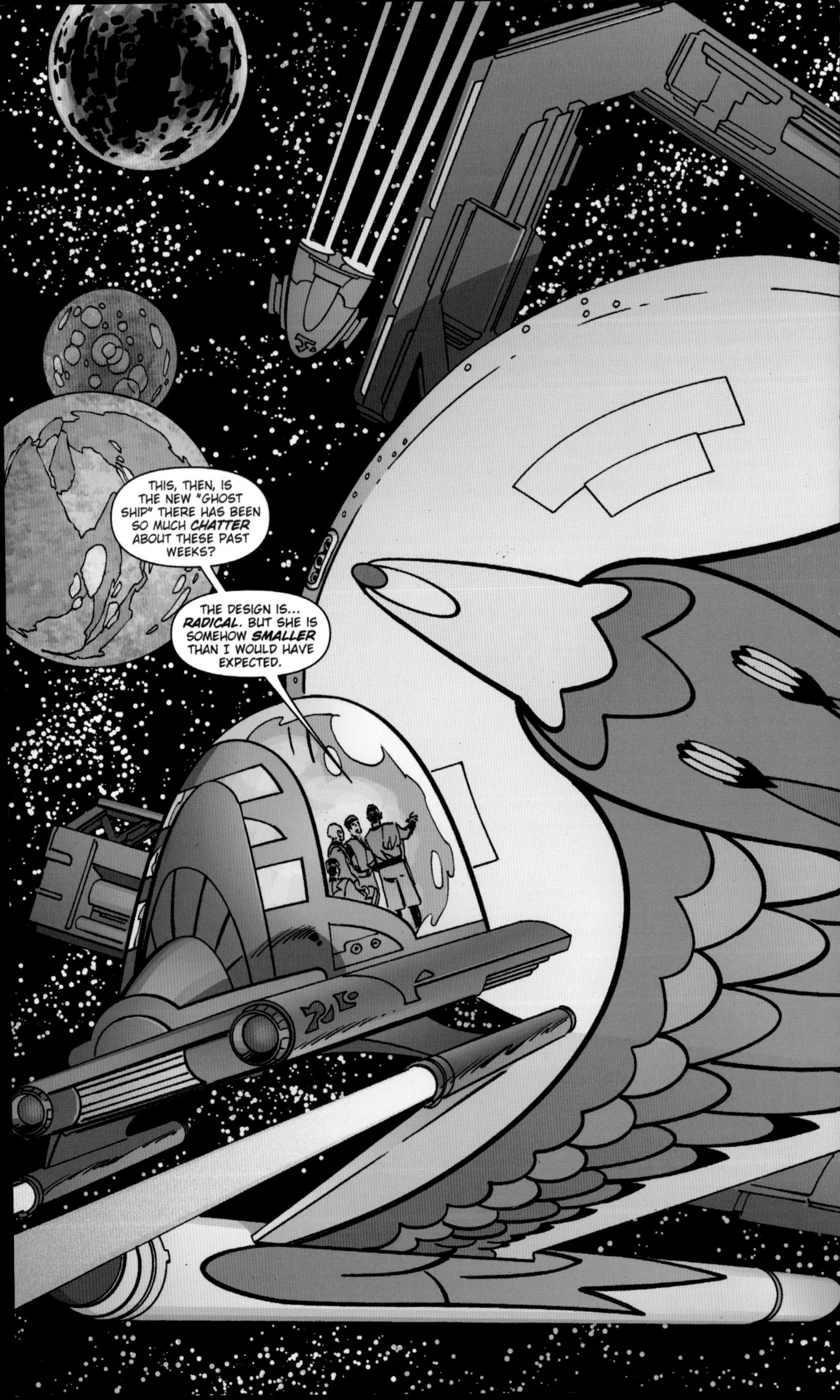
THIS, THEN, IS THE NEW "GHOST SHIP" THERE HAS BEEN SO MUCH *CHATTER* ABOUT THESE PAST WEEKS?
THE DESIGN IS... *RADICAL*. BUT SHE IS SOMEHOW *SMALLER* THAN I WOULD HAVE EXPECTED.

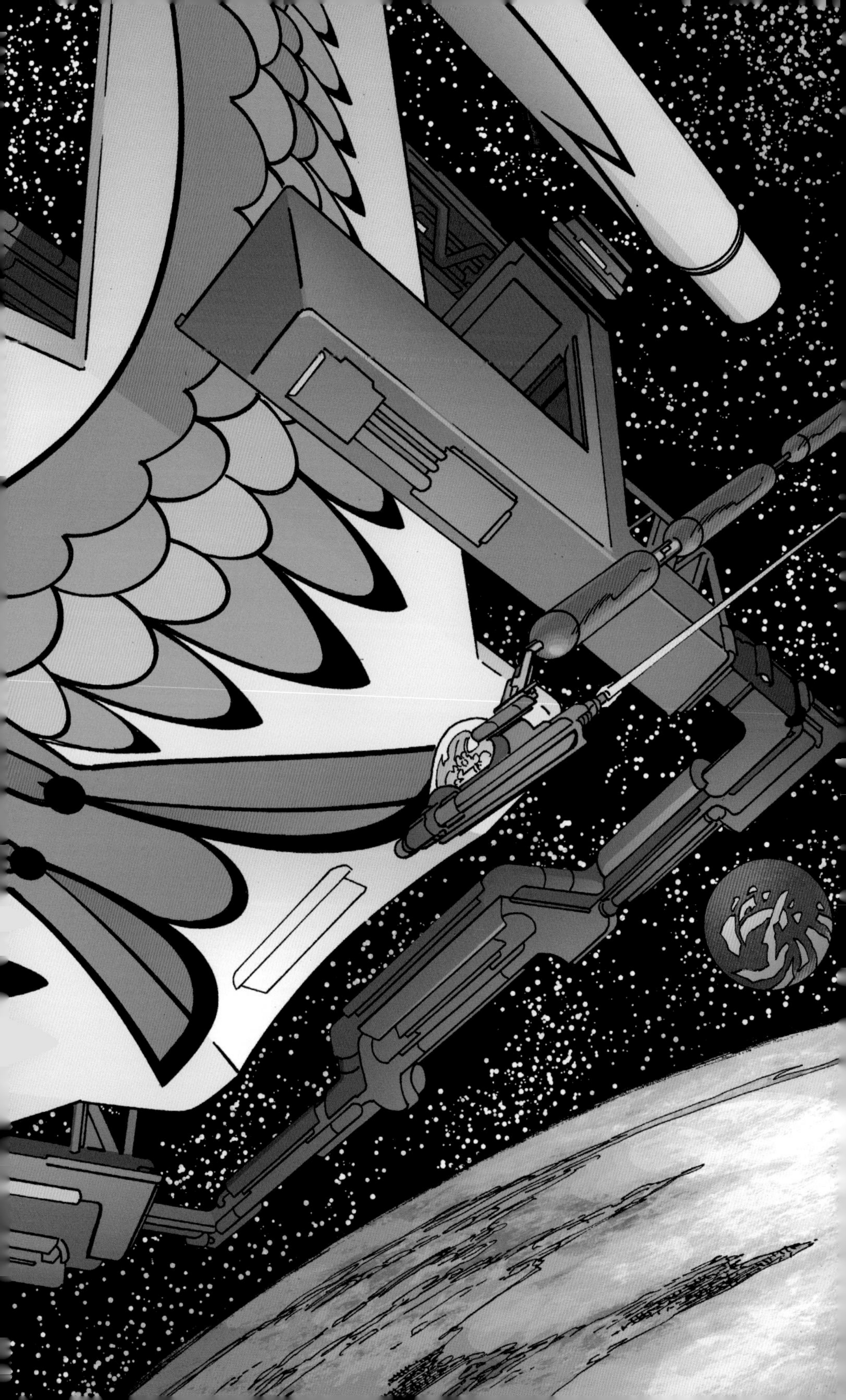

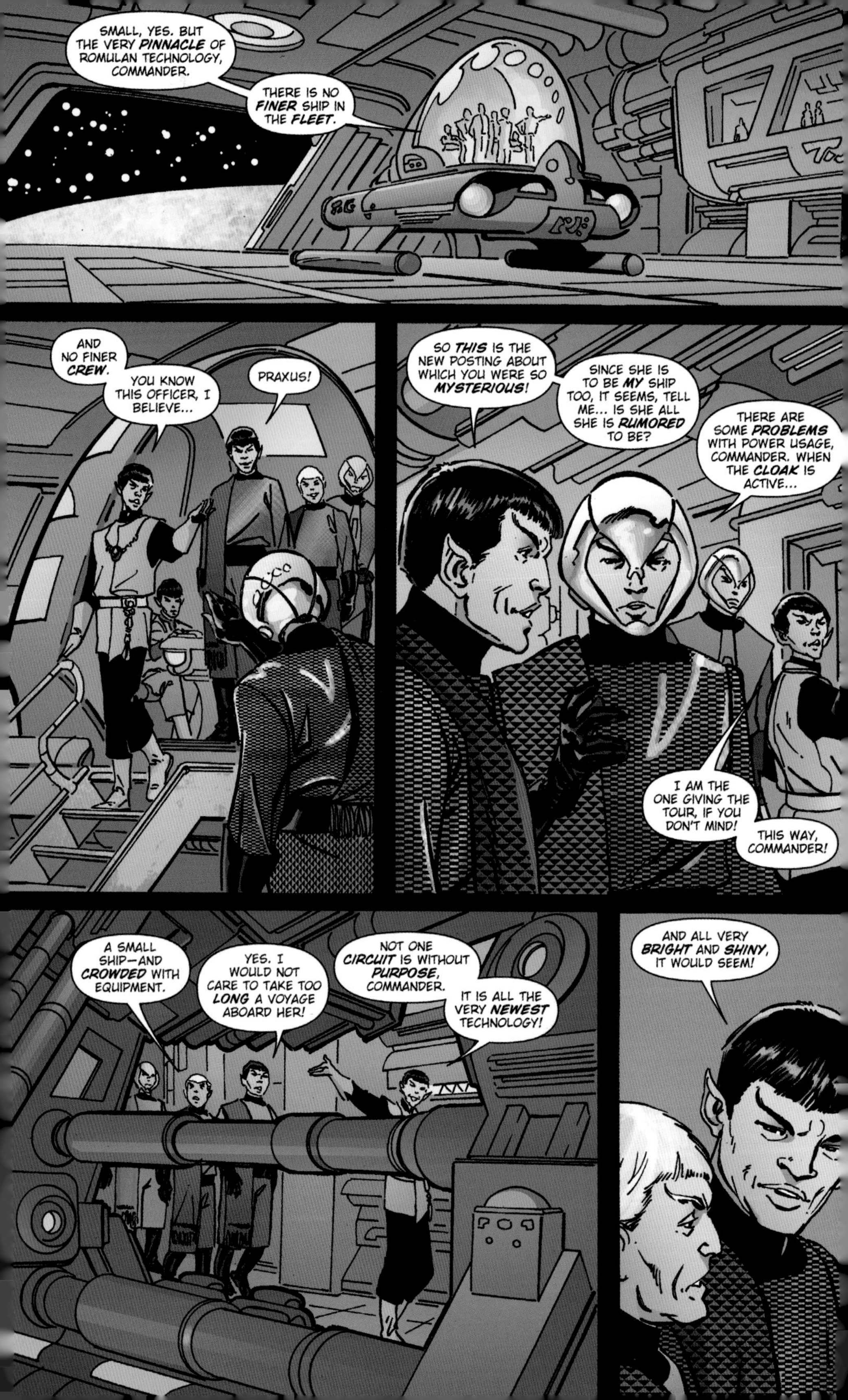
SMALL, YES. BUT THE VERY PINNACLE OF ROMULAN TECHNOLOGY, COMMANDER.
THERE IS NO FINER SHIP IN THE FLEET.
AND NO FINER CREW.
YOU KNOW THIS OFFICER, I BELIEVE...
PRAXUS!
SO THIS IS THE NEW POSTING ABOUT WHICH YOU WERE SO MYSTERIOUS!
SINCE SHE IS TO BE MY SHIP TOO, IT SEEMS, TELL ME... IS SHE ALL SHE IS RUMORED TO BE?
THERE ARE SOME PROBLEMS WITH POWER USAGE, COMMANDER. WHEN THE CLOAK IS ACTIVE...
I AM THE ONE GIVING THE TOUR, IF YOU DON'T MIND!
THIS WAY, COMMANDER!
A SMALL SHIP—AND CROWDED WITH EQUIPMENT.
YES. I WOULD NOT CARE TO TAKE TOO LONG A VOYAGE ABOARD HER!
NOT ONE CIRCUIT IS WITHOUT PURPOSE, COMMANDER.
IT IS ALL THE VERY NEWEST TECHNOLOGY!
AND ALL VERY BRIGHT AND SHINY, IT WOULD SEEM!

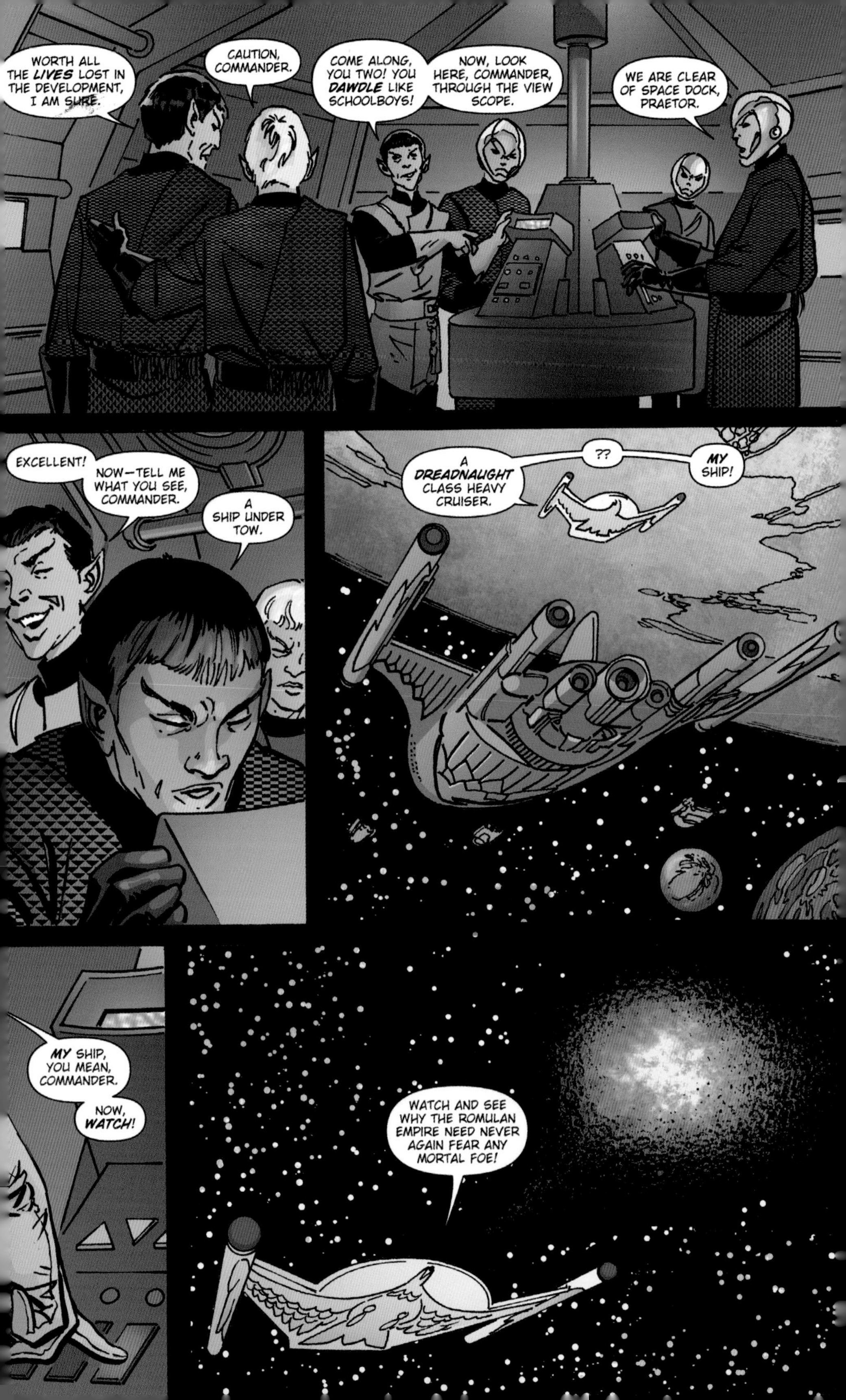
WORTH ALL THE LIVES LOST IN THE DEVELOPMENT, I AM SURE.
CAUTION, COMMANDER.
COME ALONG, YOU TWO! YOU DAWDLE LIKE SCHOOLBOYS!
NOW, LOOK HERE, COMMANDER, THROUGH THE VIEW SCOPE.
WE ARE CLEAR OF SPACE DOCK, PRAETOR.
EXCELLENT!
NOW—TELL ME WHAT YOU SEE, COMMANDER.
A SHIP UNDER TOW.
A DREADNAUGHT CLASS HEAVY CRUISER.
??
MY SHIP!
MY SHIP, YOU MEAN, COMMANDER.
NOW, WATCH!
WATCH AND SEE WHY THE ROMULAN EMPIRE NEED NEVER AGAIN FEAR ANY MORTAL FOE!

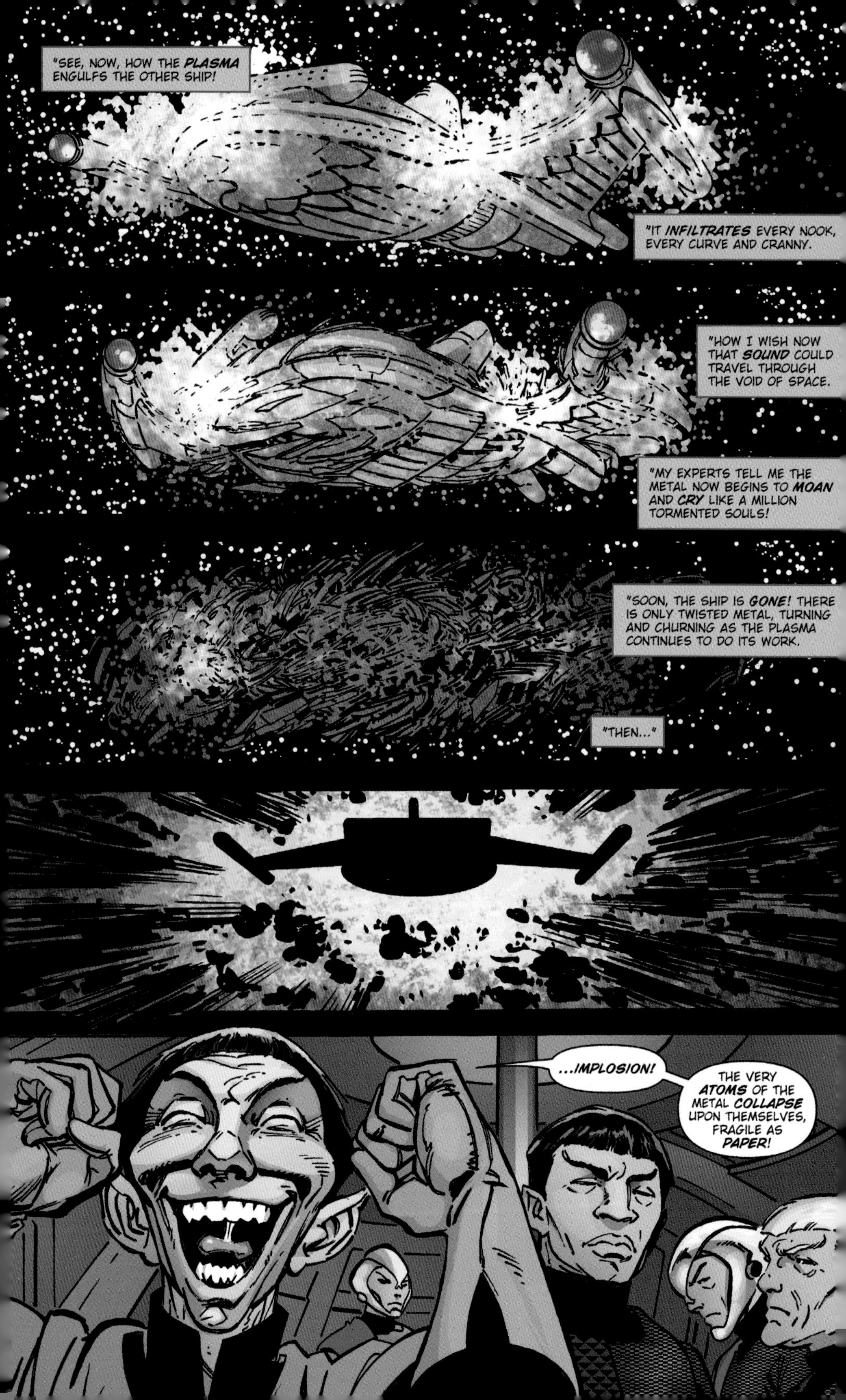
"SEE, NOW, HOW THE PLASMA ENGULFS THE OTHER SHIP!
"IT INFILTRATES EVERY NOOK, EVERY CURVE AND CRANNY.
"HOW I WISH NOW THAT SOUND COULD TRAVEL THROUGH THE VOID OF SPACE.
"MY EXPERTS TELL ME THE METAL NOW BEGINS TO MOAN AND CRY LIKE A MILLION TORMENTED SOULS!
"SOON, THE SHIP IS GONE! THERE IS ONLY TWISTED METAL, TURNING AND CHURNING AS THE PLASMA CONTINUES TO DO ITS WORK.
"THEN..."
...IMPLOSION!
THE VERY ATOMS OF THE METAL COLLAPSE UPON THEMSELVES, FRAGILE AS PAPER!

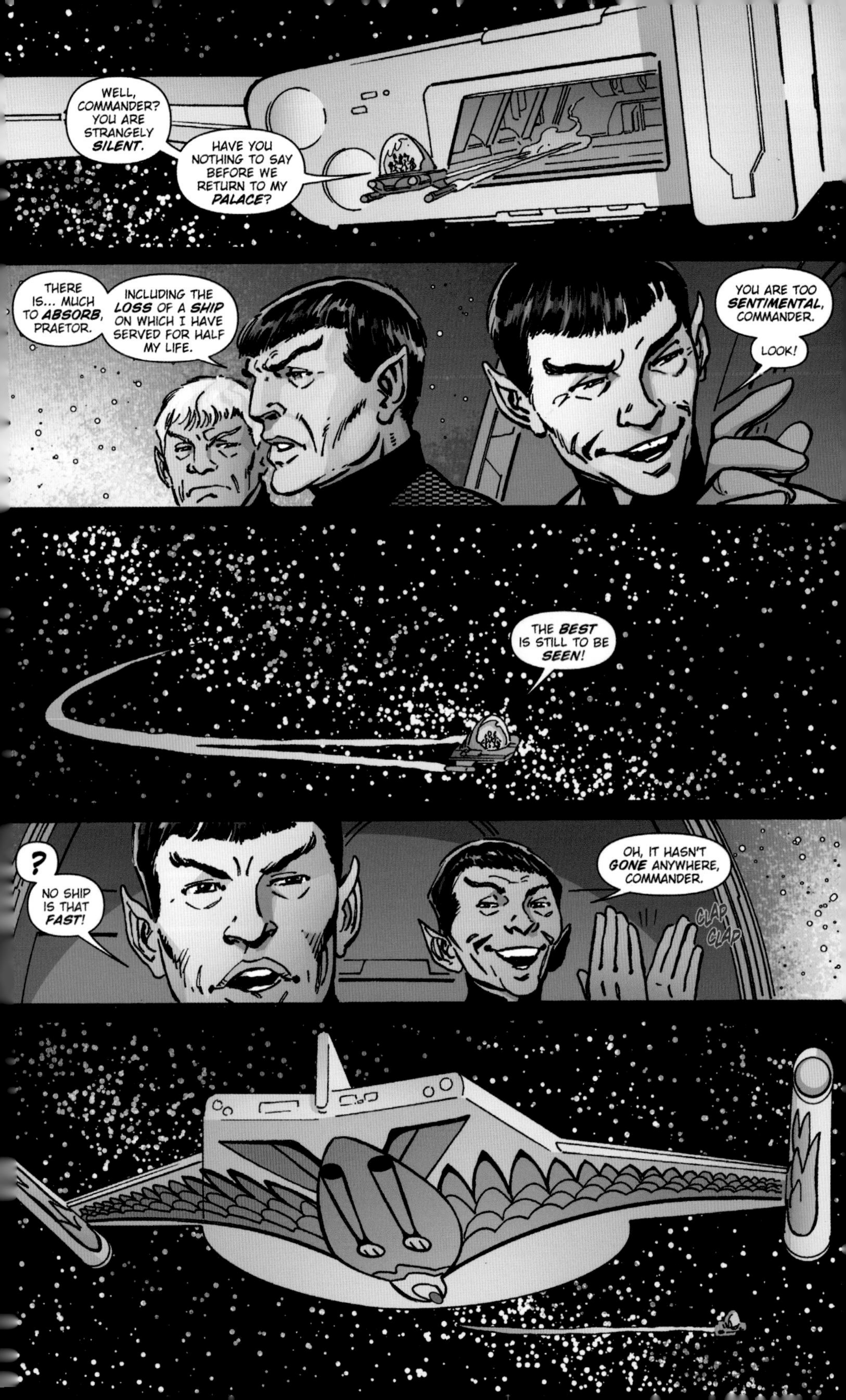
WELL, COMMANDER? YOU ARE STRANGELY SILENT.
HAVE YOU NOTHING TO SAY BEFORE WE RETURN TO MY PALACE?
THERE IS... MUCH TO ABSORB, PRAETOR.
INCLUDING THE LOSS OF A SHIP ON WHICH I HAVE SERVED FOR HALF MY LIFE.
YOU ARE TOO SENTIMENTAL, COMMANDER.
LOOK!
THE BEST IS STILL TO BE SEEN!
?
NO SHIP IS THAT FAST!
OH, IT HASN'T GONE ANYWHERE, COMMANDER.
CLAP CLAP

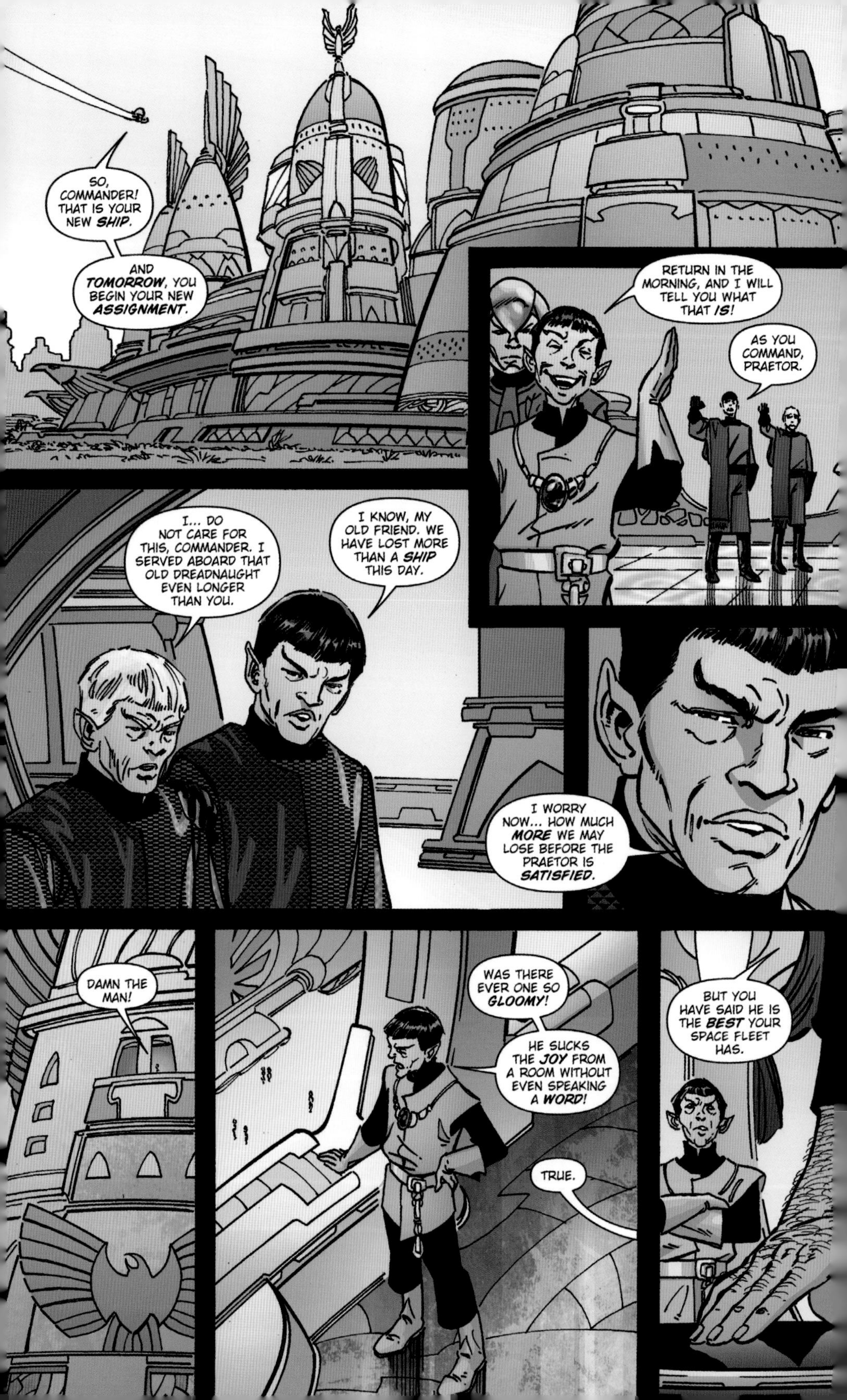
SO, COMMANDER! THAT IS YOUR NEW SHIP.
AND TOMORROW, YOU BEGIN YOUR NEW ASSIGNMENT.
RETURN IN THE MORNING, AND I WILL TELL YOU WHAT THAT IS!
AS YOU COMMAND, PRAETOR.
I... DO NOT CARE FOR THIS, COMMANDER. I SERVED ABOARD THAT OLD DREADNAUGHT EVEN LONGER THAN YOU.
I KNOW, MY OLD FRIEND. WE HAVE LOST MORE THAN A SHIP THIS DAY.
I WORRY NOW... HOW MUCH MORE WE MAY LOSE BEFORE THE PRAETOR IS SATISFIED.
DAMN THE MAN!
WAS THERE EVER ONE SO GLOOMY!
HE SUCKS THE JOY FROM A ROOM WITHOUT EVEN SPEAKING A WORD!
BUT YOU HAVE SAID HE IS THE BEST YOUR SPACE FLEET HAS.
TRUE.

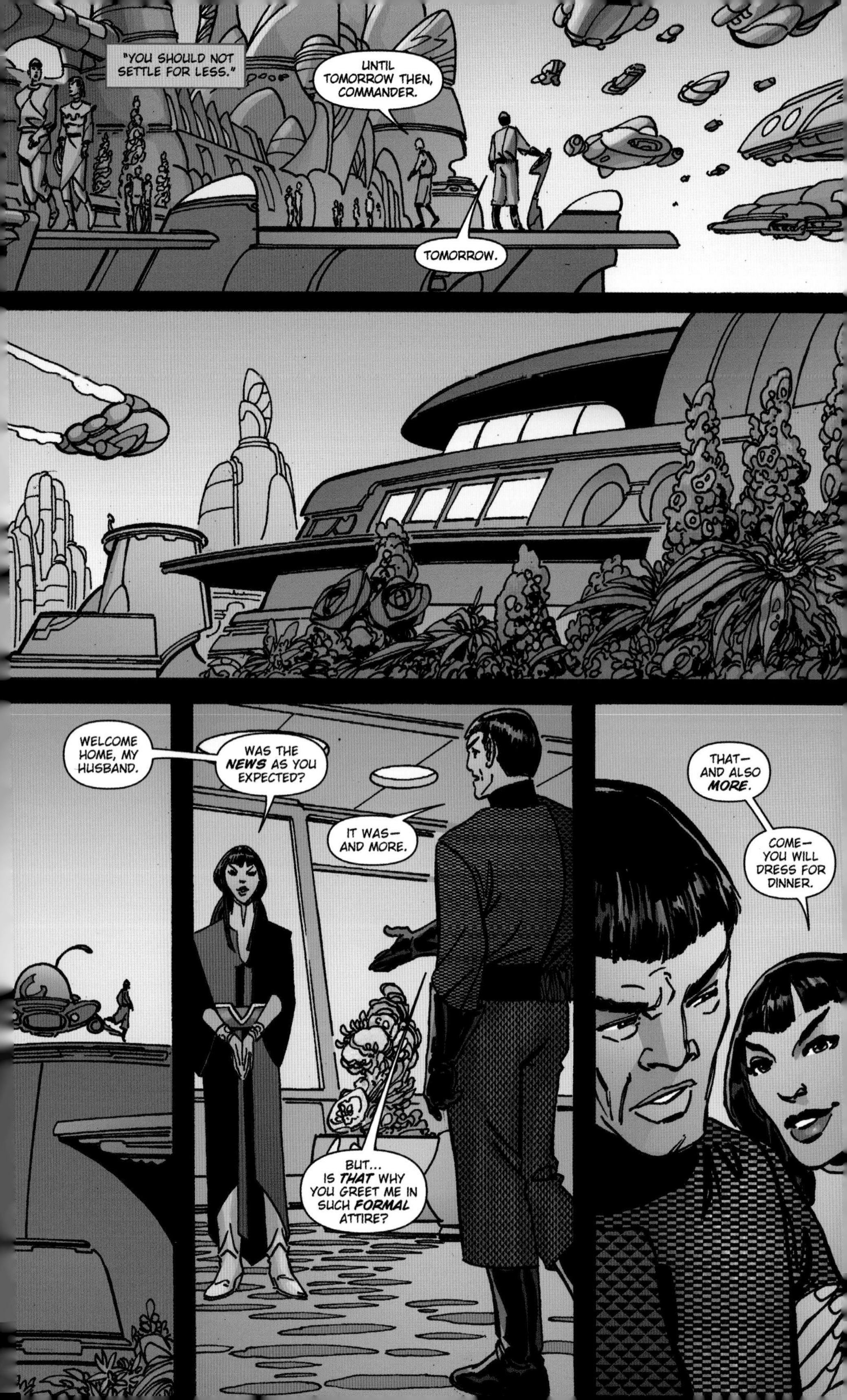
"YOU SHOULD NOT SETTLE FOR LESS."
UNTIL TOMORROW THEN, COMMANDER.
TOMORROW.
WELCOME HOME, MY HUSBAND.
WAS THE NEWS AS YOU EXPECTED?
IT WAS— AND MORE.
BUT... IS THAT WHY YOU GREET ME IN SUCH FORMAL ATTIRE?
THAT— AND ALSO MORE.
COME— YOU WILL DRESS FOR DINNER.

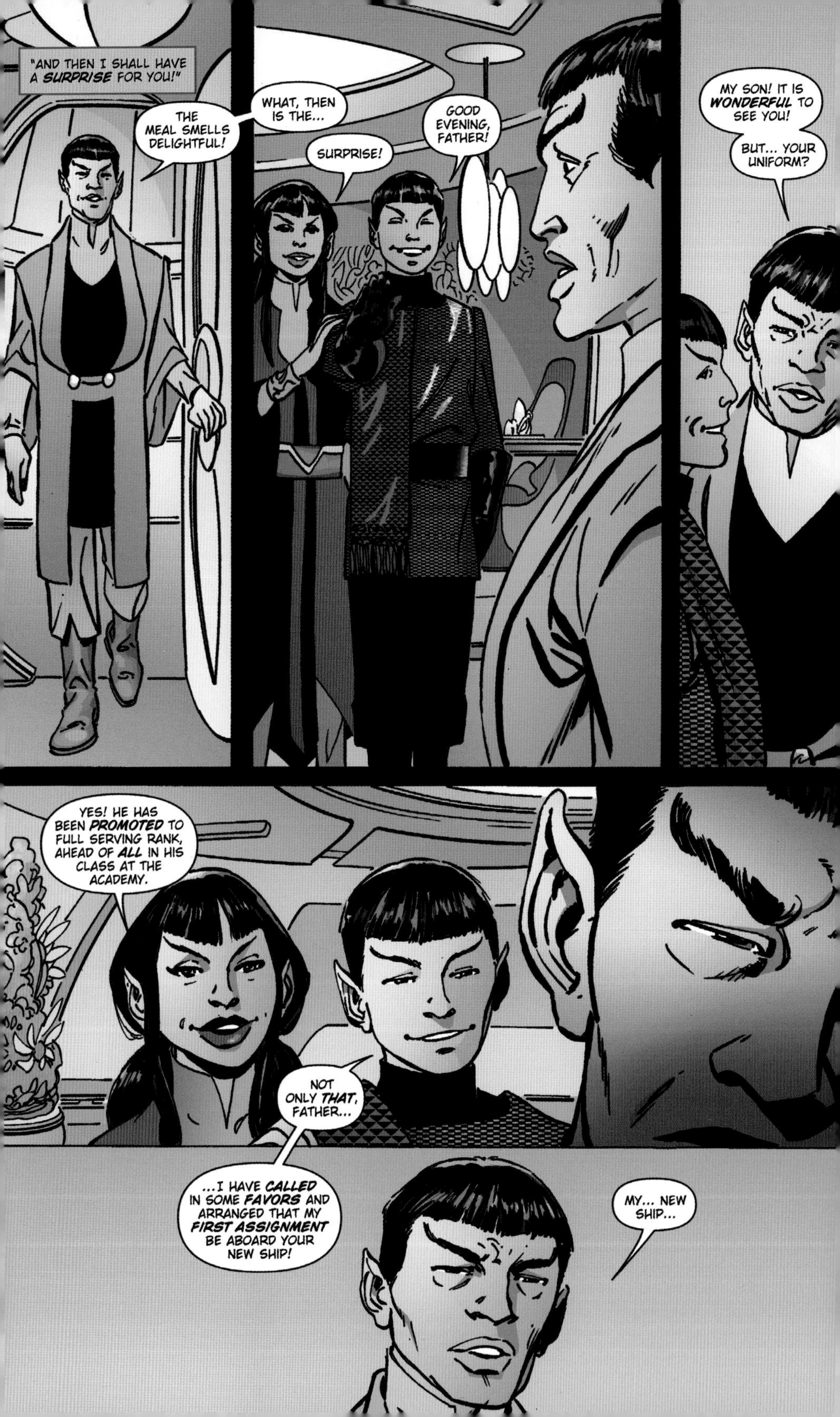

"AND THEN I SHALL HAVE A SURPRISE FOR YOU!"
THE MEAL SMELLS DELIGHTFUL!
WHAT, THEN IS THE...
SURPRISE!
GOOD EVENING, FATHER!
MY SON! IT IS WONDERFUL TO SEE YOU!
BUT... YOUR UNIFORM?
YES! HE HAS BEEN PROMOTED TO FULL SERVING RANK, AHEAD OF ALL IN HIS CLASS AT THE ACADEMY.
NOT ONLY THAT, FATHER...
...I HAVE CALLED IN SOME FAVORS AND ARRANGED THAT MY FIRST ASSIGNMENT BE ABOARD YOUR NEW SHIP!
MY... NEW SHIP...

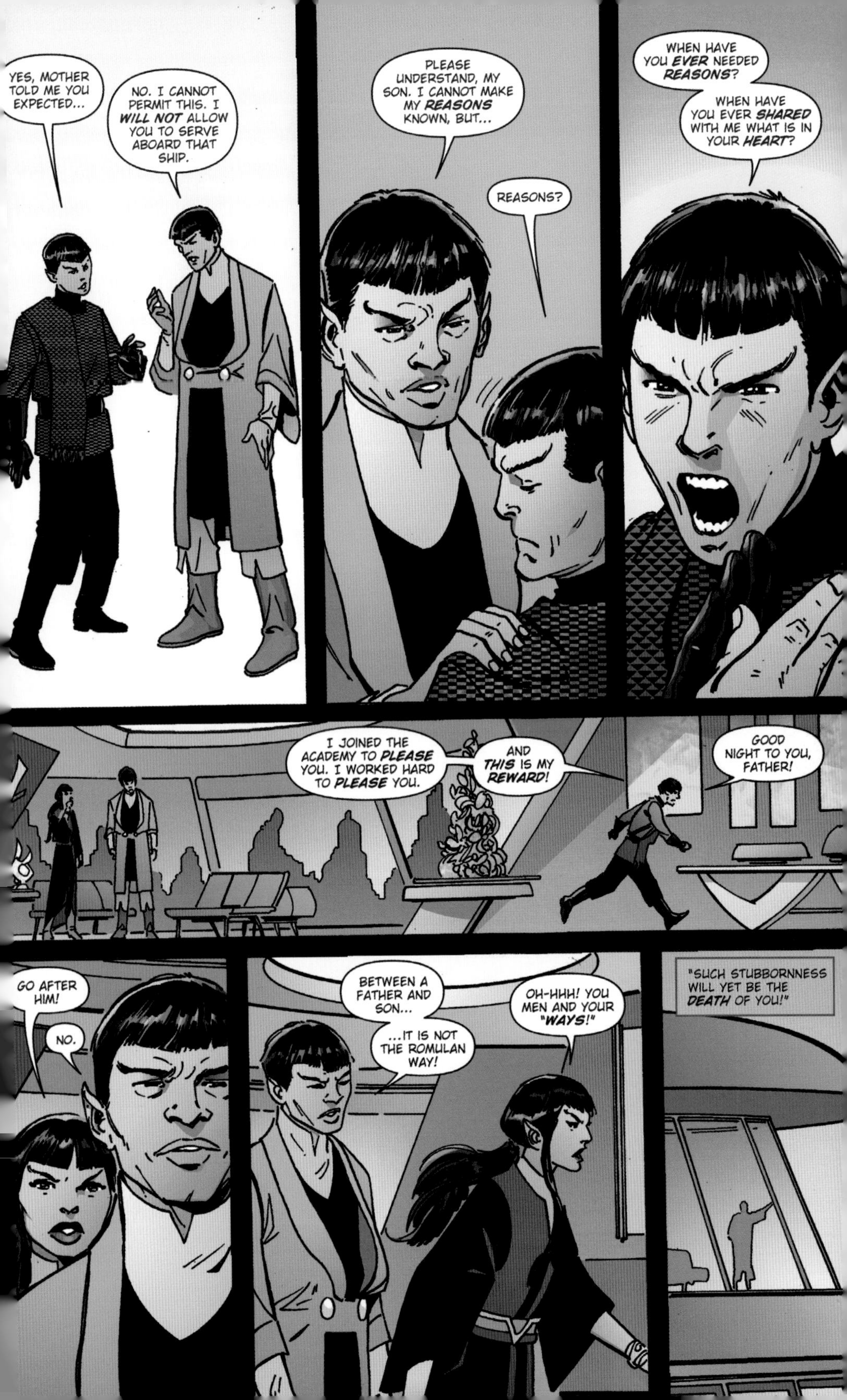
YES, MOTHER TOLD ME YOU EXPECTED...
NO. I CANNOT PERMIT THIS. I WILL NOT ALLOW YOU TO SERVE ABOARD THAT SHIP.
PLEASE UNDERSTAND, MY SON. I CANNOT MAKE MY REASONS KNOWN, BUT...
REASONS?
WHEN HAVE YOU EVER NEEDED REASONS?
WHEN HAVE YOU EVER SHARED WITH ME WHAT IS IN YOUR HEART?
I JOINED THE ACADEMY TO PLEASE YOU. I WORKED HARD TO PLEASE YOU.
AND THIS IS MY REWARD!
GOOD NIGHT TO YOU, FATHER!
GO AFTER HIM!
NO.
BETWEEN A FATHER AND SON...
...IT IS NOT THE ROMULAN WAY!
OH-HHH! YOU MEN AND YOUR "WAYS!"
"SUCH STUBBORNNESS WILL YET BE THE DEATH OF YOU!"

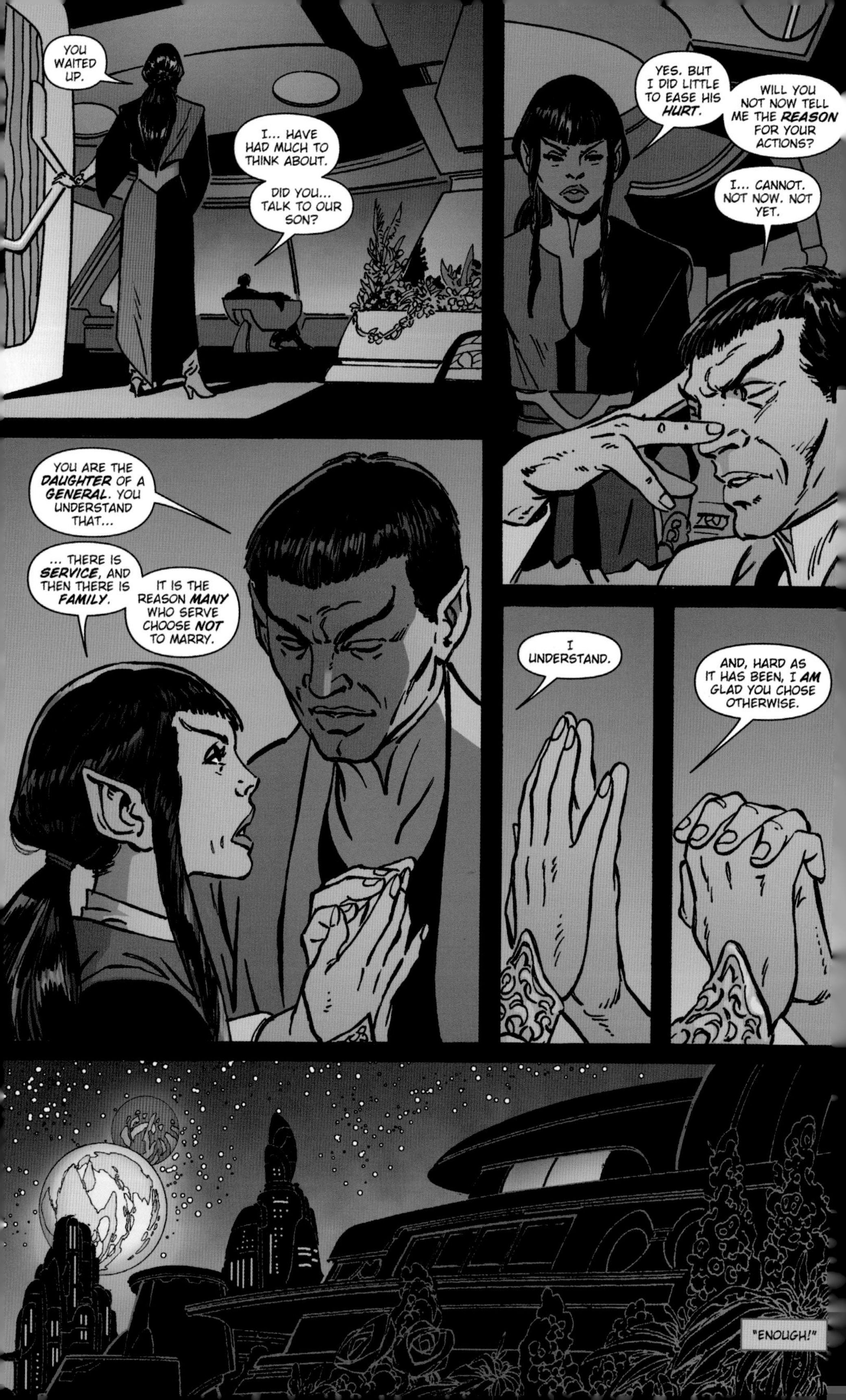
YOU WAITED UP.
I... HAVE HAD MUCH TO THINK ABOUT.
DID YOU... TALK TO OUR SON?
YES. BUT I DID LITTLE TO EASE HIS HURT.
WILL YOU NOT NOW TELL ME THE REASON FOR YOUR ACTIONS?
I... CANNOT. NOT NOW. NOT YET.
YOU ARE THE DAUGHTER OF A GENERAL. YOU UNDERSTAND THAT...
... THERE IS SERVICE, AND THEN THERE IS FAMILY.
IT IS THE REASON MANY WHO SERVE CHOOSE NOT TO MARRY.
I UNDERSTAND.
AND, HARD AS IT HAS BEEN, I AM GLAD YOU CHOSE OTHERWISE.
"ENOUGH!"

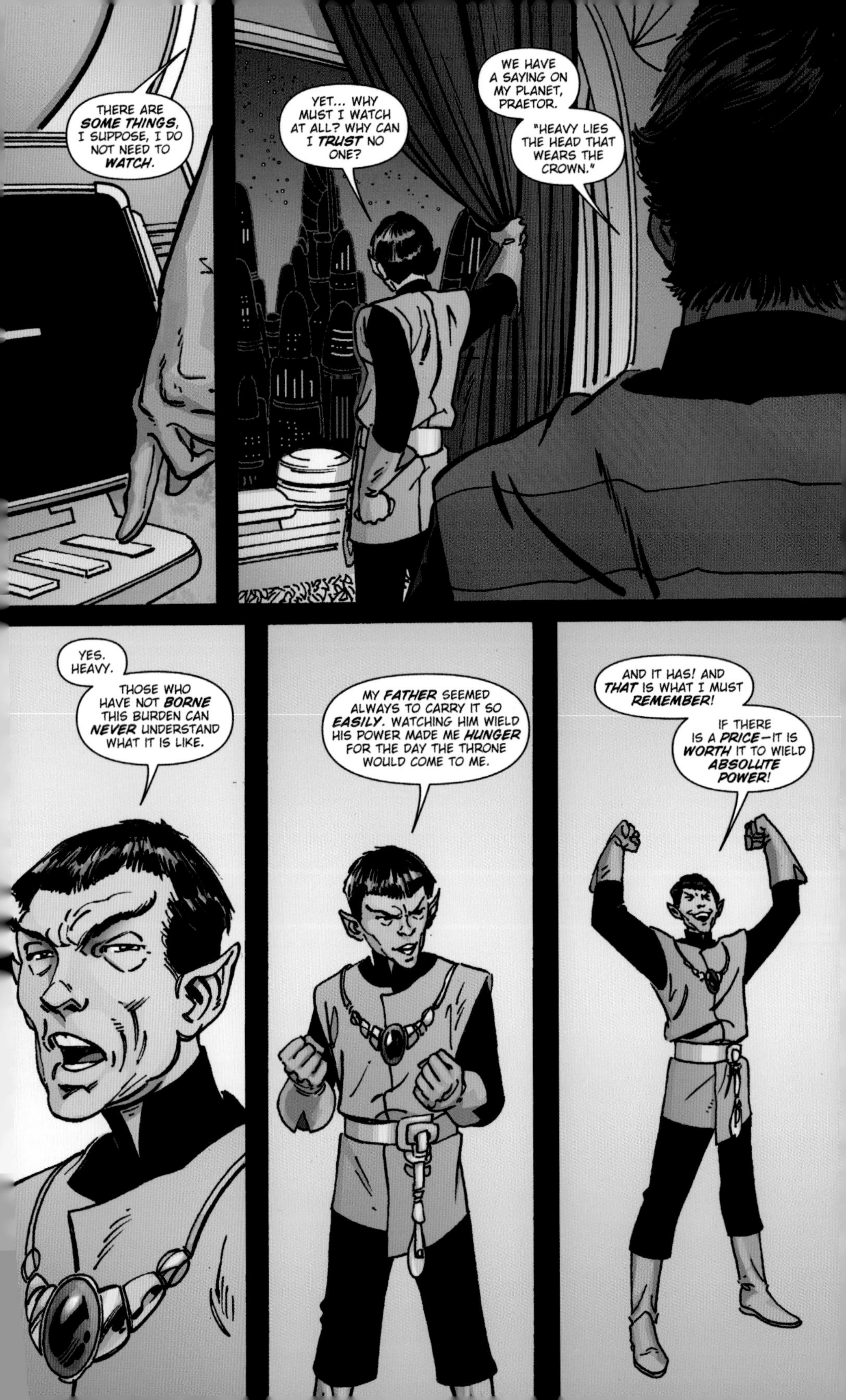
THERE ARE SOME THINGS, I SUPPOSE, I DO NOT NEED TO WATCH.
YET... WHY MUST I WATCH AT ALL? WHY CAN I TRUST NO ONE?
WE HAVE A SAYING ON MY PLANET, PRAETOR.
"HEAVY LIES THE HEAD THAT WEARS THE CROWN."
YES. HEAVY.
THOSE WHO HAVE NOT BORNE THIS BURDEN CAN NEVER UNDERSTAND WHAT IT IS LIKE.
MY FATHER SEEMED ALWAYS TO CARRY IT SO EASILY. WATCHING HIM WIELD HIS POWER MADE ME HUNGER FOR THE DAY THE THRONE WOULD COME TO ME.
AND IT HAS! AND THAT IS WHAT I MUST REMEMBER!
IF THERE IS A PRICE—IT IS WORTH IT TO WIELD ABSOLUTE POWER!

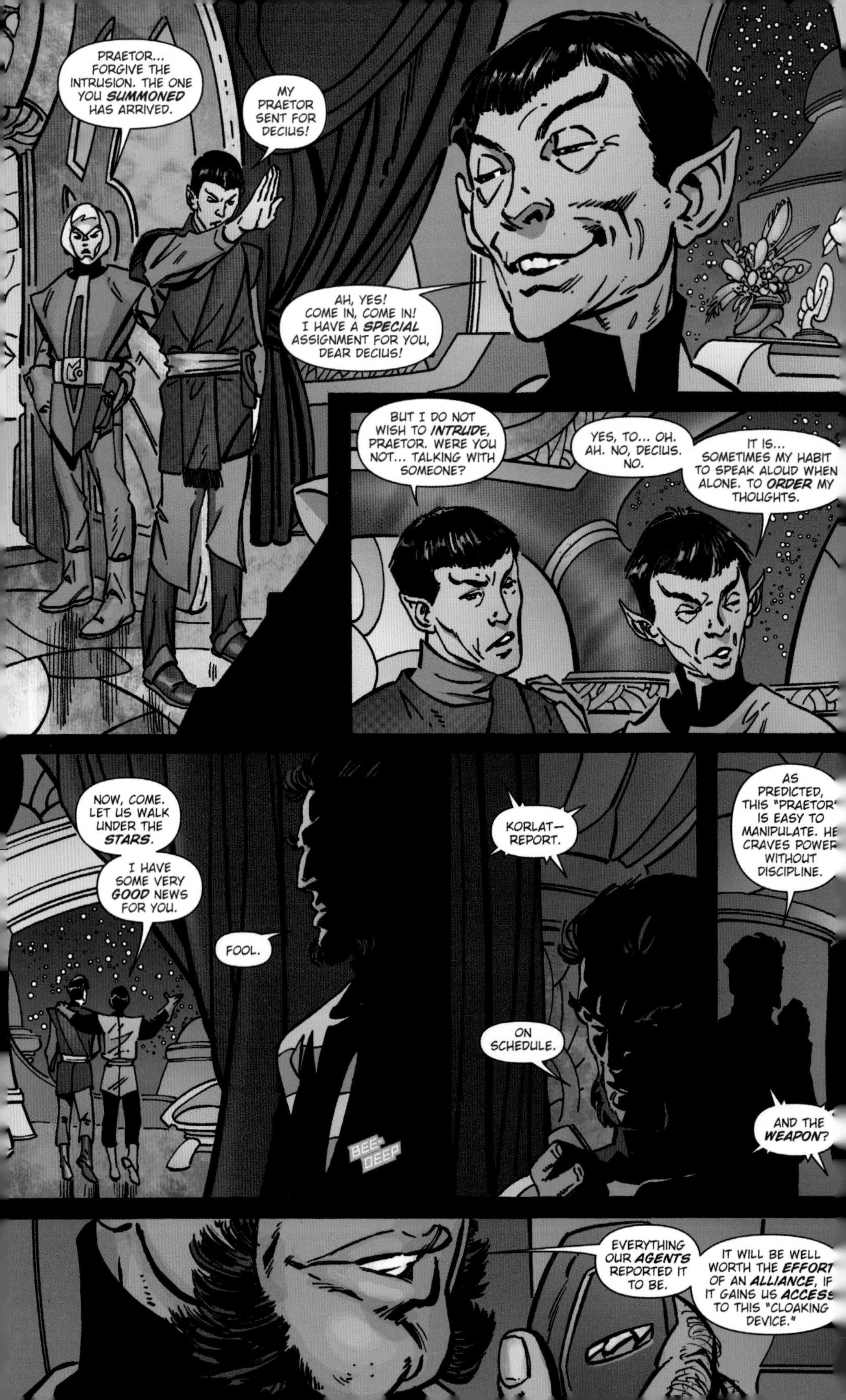
PRAETOR... FORGIVE THE INTRUSION. THE ONE YOU SUMMONED HAS ARRIVED.
MY PRAETOR SENT FOR DECIUS!
AH, YES! COME IN, COME IN! I HAVE A SPECIAL ASSIGNMENT FOR YOU, DEAR DECIUS!
BUT I DO NOT WISH TO INTRUDE, PRAETOR. WERE YOU NOT... TALKING WITH SOMEONE?
YES, TO... OH. AH. NO, DECIUS. NO.
IT IS... SOMETIMES MY HABIT TO SPEAK ALOUD WHEN ALONE. TO ORDER MY THOUGHTS.
NOW, COME. LET US WALK UNDER THE STARS.
I HAVE SOME VERY GOOD NEWS FOR YOU.
FOOL.
BEE-DEEP
KORLAT— REPORT.
AS PREDICTED, THIS "PRAETOR" IS EASY TO MANIPULATE. HE CRAVES POWER WITHOUT DISCIPLINE.
ON SCHEDULE.
AND THE WEAPON?
EVERYTHING OUR AGENTS REPORTED IT TO BE.
IT WILL BE WELL WORTH THE EFFORT OF AN ALLIANCE, IF IT GAINS US ACCESS TO THIS "CLOAKING DEVICE."

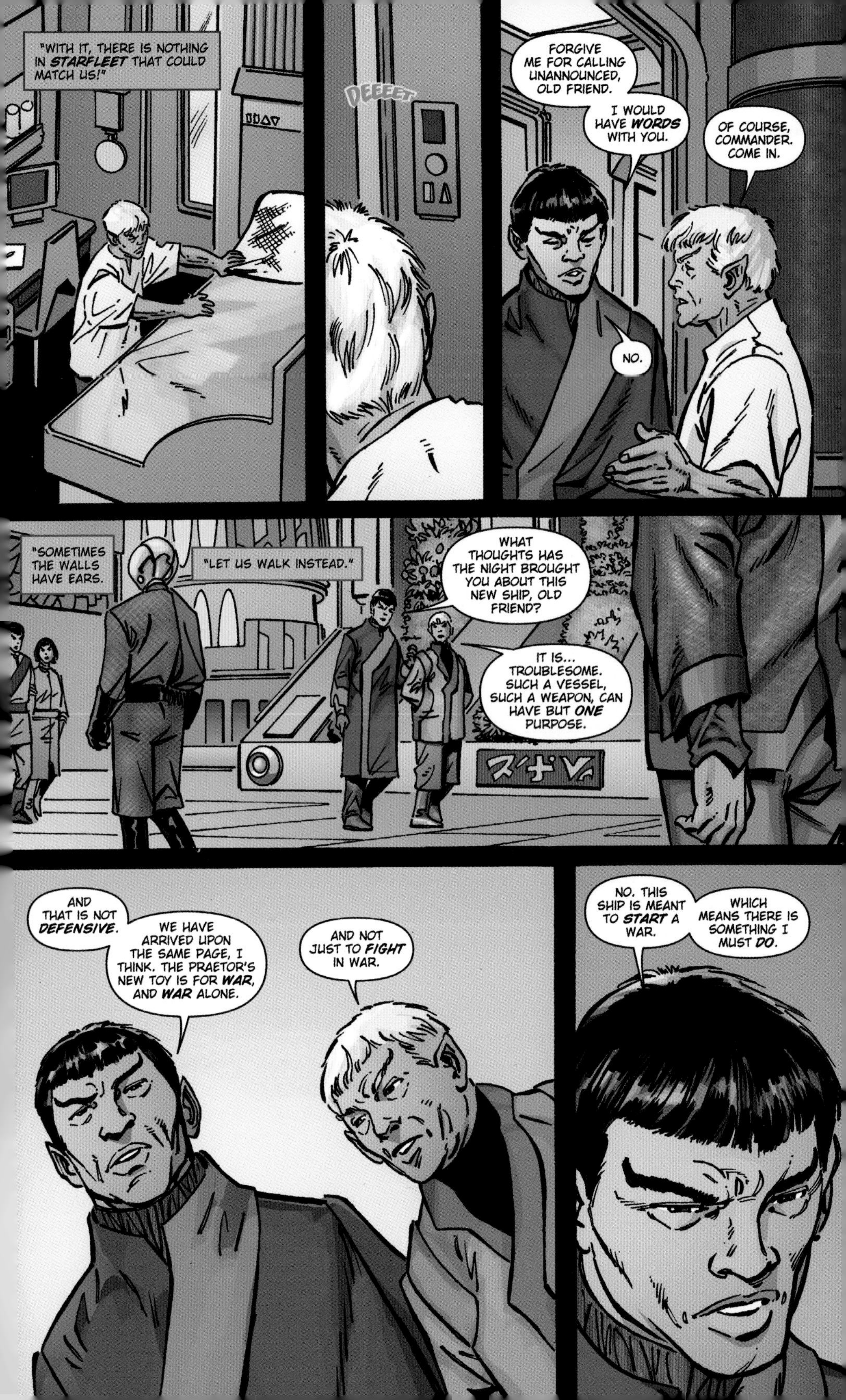
"WITH IT, THERE IS NOTHING IN STARFLEET THAT COULD MATCH US!"
DEEEEET
FORGIVE ME FOR CALLING UNANNOUNCED, OLD FRIEND.
I WOULD HAVE WORDS WITH YOU.
OF COURSE, COMMANDER. COME IN.
NO.
"SOMETIMES THE WALLS HAVE EARS.
"LET US WALK INSTEAD."
WHAT THOUGHTS HAS THE NIGHT BROUGHT YOU ABOUT THIS NEW SHIP, OLD FRIEND?
IT IS... TROUBLESOME. SUCH A VESSEL, SUCH A WEAPON, CAN HAVE BUT ONE PURPOSE.
AND THAT IS NOT DEFENSIVE.
WE HAVE ARRIVED UPON THE SAME PAGE, I THINK. THE PRAETOR'S NEW TOY IS FOR WAR, AND WAR ALONE.
AND NOT JUST TO FIGHT IN WAR.
NO. THIS SHIP IS MEANT TO START A WAR.
WHICH MEANS THERE IS SOMETHING I MUST DO.

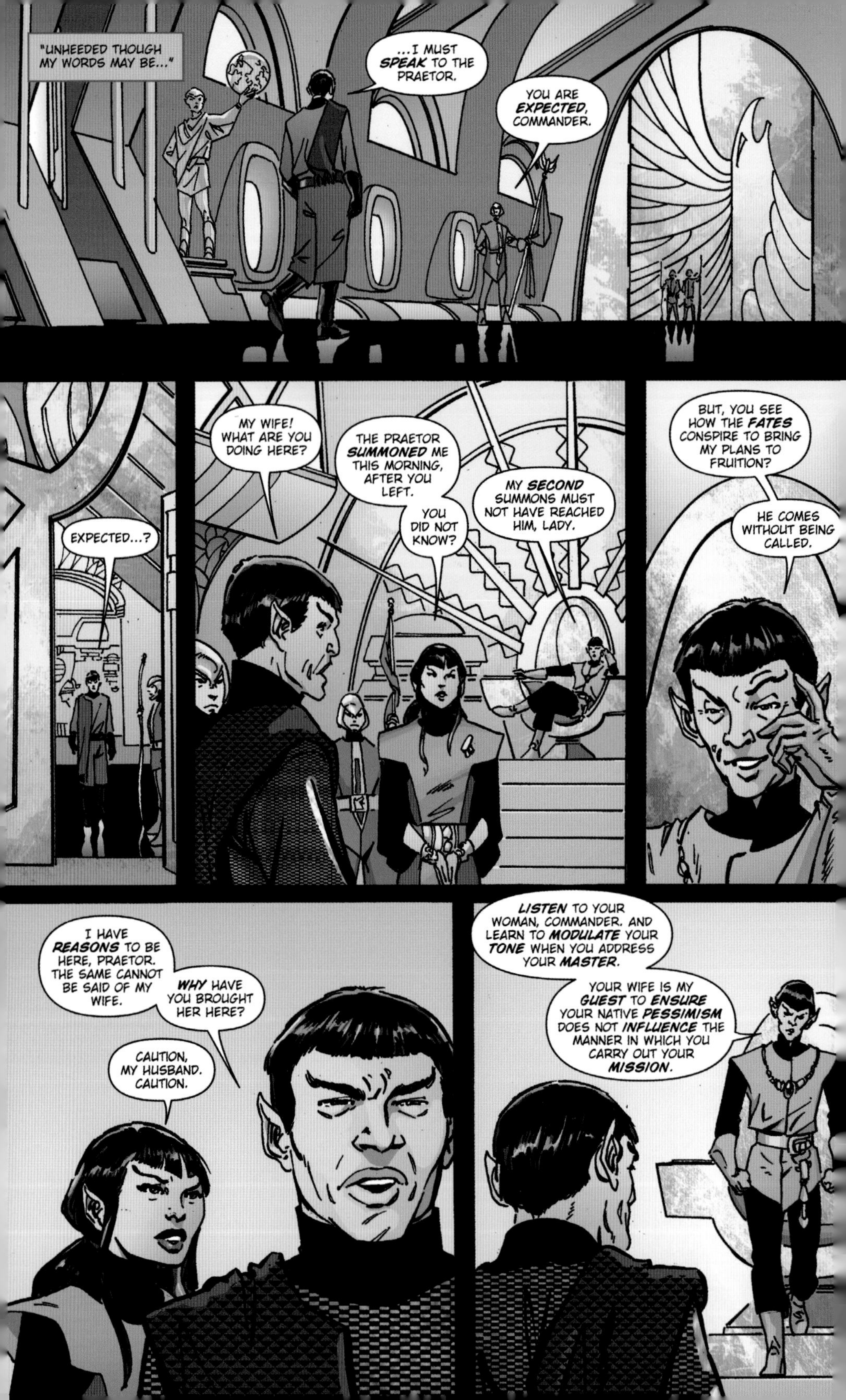
"UNHEEDED THOUGH MY WORDS MAY BE..."
...I MUST SPEAK TO THE PRAETOR.
YOU ARE EXPECTED, COMMANDER.
EXPECTED...?
MY WIFE! WHAT ARE YOU DOING HERE?
THE PRAETOR SUMMONED ME THIS MORNING, AFTER YOU LEFT.
YOU DID NOT KNOW?
MY SECOND SUMMONS MUST NOT HAVE REACHED HIM, LADY.
BUT, YOU SEE HOW THE FATES CONSPIRE TO BRING MY PLANS TO FRUITION?
HE COMES WITHOUT BEING CALLED.
I HAVE REASONS TO BE HERE, PRAETOR. THE SAME CANNOT BE SAID OF MY WIFE.
WHY HAVE YOU BROUGHT HER HERE?
CAUTION, MY HUSBAND. CAUTION.
LISTEN TO YOUR WOMAN, COMMANDER. AND LEARN TO MODULATE YOUR TONE WHEN YOU ADDRESS YOUR MASTER.
YOUR WIFE IS MY GUEST TO ENSURE YOUR NATIVE PESSIMISM DOES NOT INFLUENCE THE MANNER IN WHICH YOU CARRY OUT YOUR MISSION.

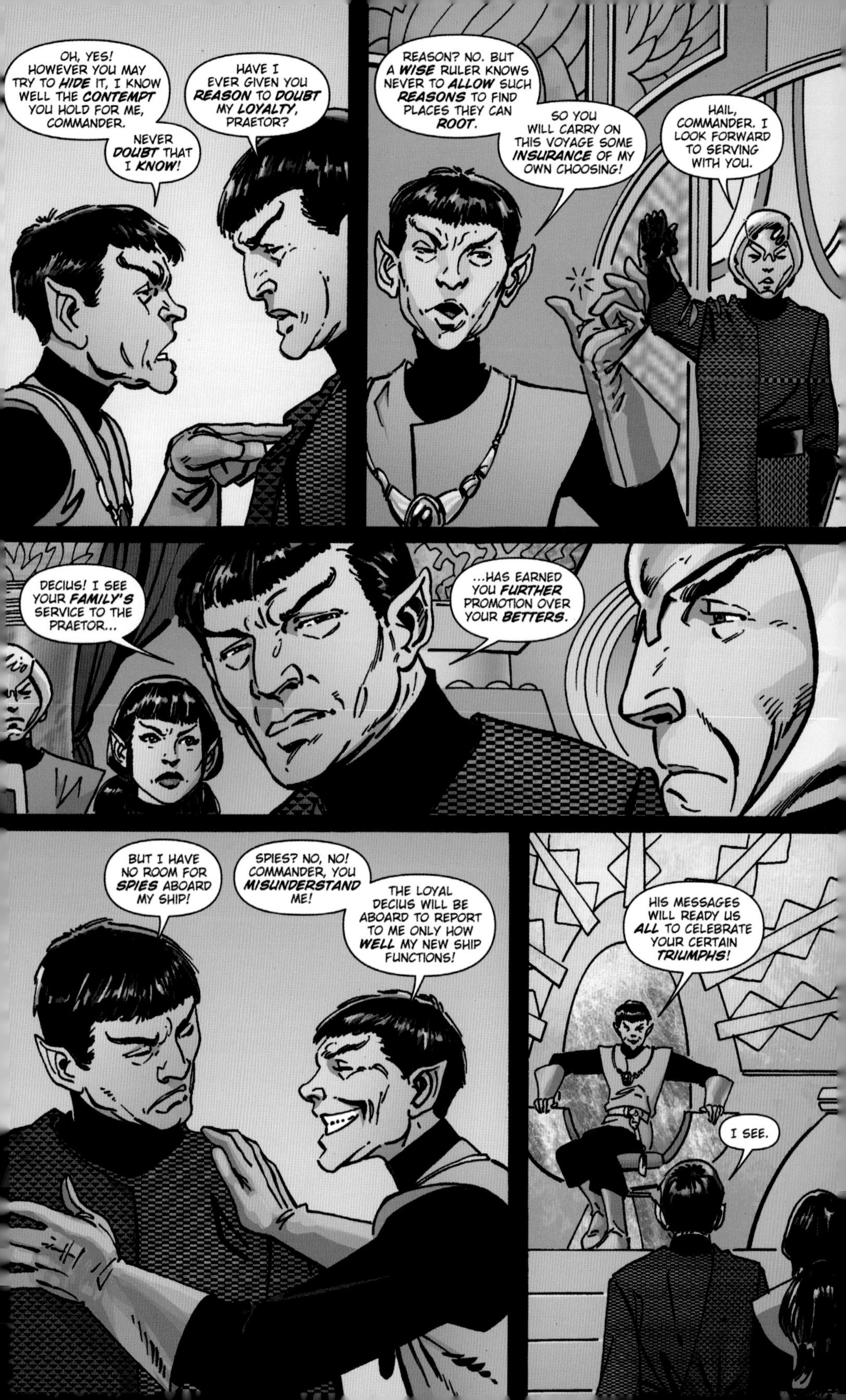
OH, YES! HOWEVER YOU MAY TRY TO HIDE IT, I KNOW WELL THE CONTEMPT YOU HOLD FOR ME, COMMANDER.
NEVER DOUBT THAT I KNOW!
HAVE I EVER GIVEN YOU REASON TO DOUBT MY LOYALTY, PRAETOR?
REASON? NO. BUT A WISE RULER KNOWS NEVER TO ALLOW SUCH REASONS TO FIND PLACES THEY CAN ROOT.
SO YOU WILL CARRY ON THIS VOYAGE SOME INSURANCE OF MY OWN CHOOSING!
HAIL, COMMANDER. I LOOK FORWARD TO SERVING WITH YOU.
DECIUS! I SEE YOUR FAMILY'S SERVICE TO THE PRAETOR...
...HAS EARNED YOU FURTHER PROMOTION OVER YOUR BETTERS.
BUT I HAVE NO ROOM FOR SPIES ABOARD MY SHIP!
SPIES? NO, NO! COMMANDER, YOU MISUNDERSTAND ME!
THE LOYAL DECIUS WILL BE ABOARD TO REPORT TO ME ONLY HOW WELL MY NEW SHIP FUNCTIONS!
HIS MESSAGES WILL READY US ALL TO CELEBRATE YOUR CERTAIN TRIUMPHS!
I SEE.

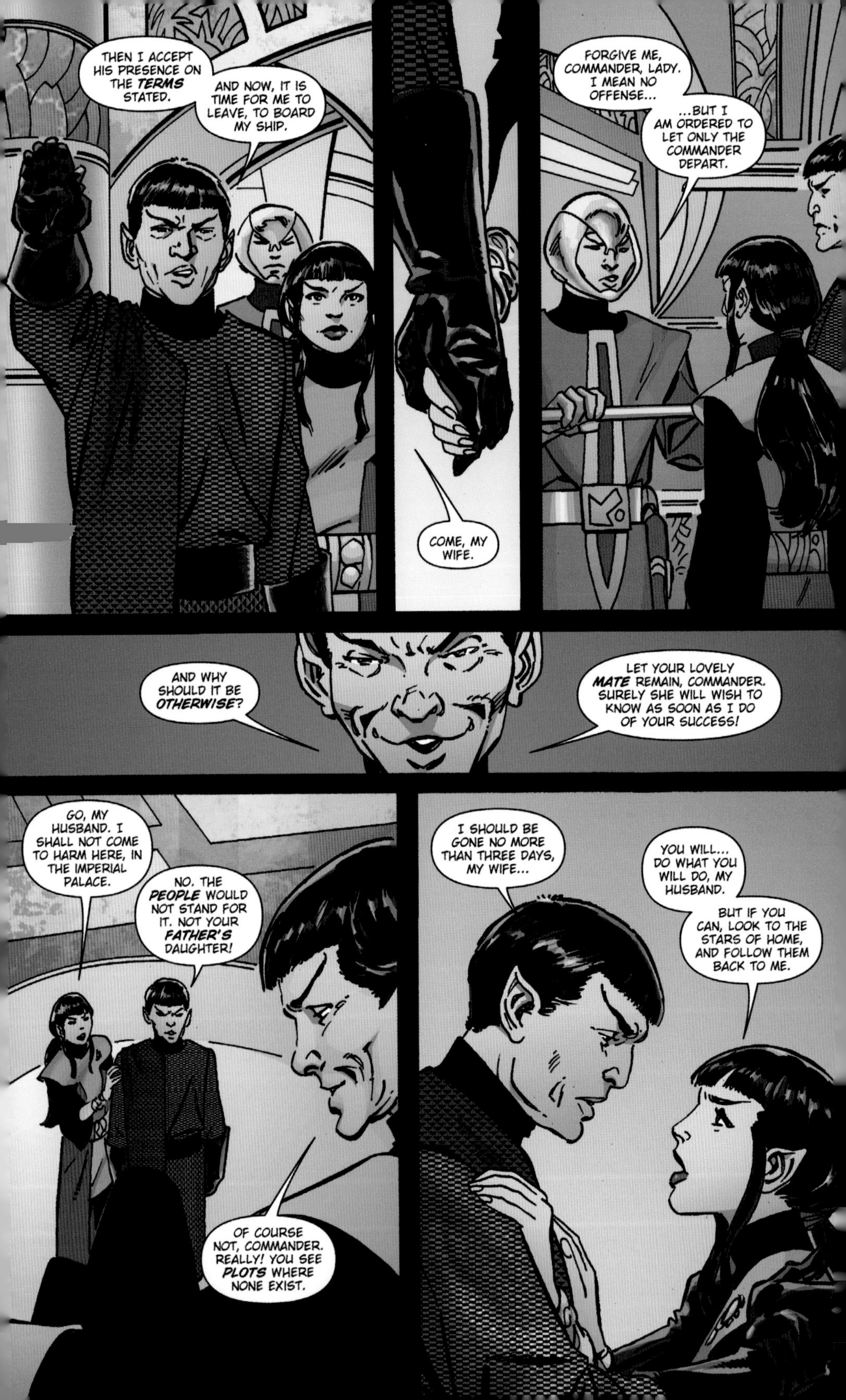

THEN I ACCEPT HIS PRESENCE ON THE *TERMS* STATED.
AND NOW, IT IS TIME FOR ME TO LEAVE, TO BOARD MY SHIP.
COME, MY WIFE.
FORGIVE ME, COMMANDER, LADY. I MEAN NO OFFENSE...
...BUT I AM ORDERED TO LET ONLY THE COMMANDER DEPART.
AND WHY SHOULD IT BE *OTHERWISE*?
LET YOUR LOVELY *MATE* REMAIN, COMMANDER. SURELY SHE WILL WISH TO KNOW AS SOON AS I DO OF YOUR SUCCESS!
GO, MY HUSBAND. I SHALL NOT COME TO HARM HERE, IN THE IMPERIAL PALACE.
NO. THE *PEOPLE* WOULD NOT STAND FOR IT. NOT YOUR *FATHER'S* DAUGHTER!
OF COURSE NOT, COMMANDER. REALLY! YOU SEE *PLOTS* WHERE NONE EXIST.
I SHOULD BE GONE NO MORE THAN THREE DAYS, MY WIFE...
YOU WILL... DO WHAT YOU WILL DO, MY HUSBAND.
BUT IF YOU CAN, LOOK TO THE STARS OF HOME, AND FOLLOW THEM BACK TO ME.

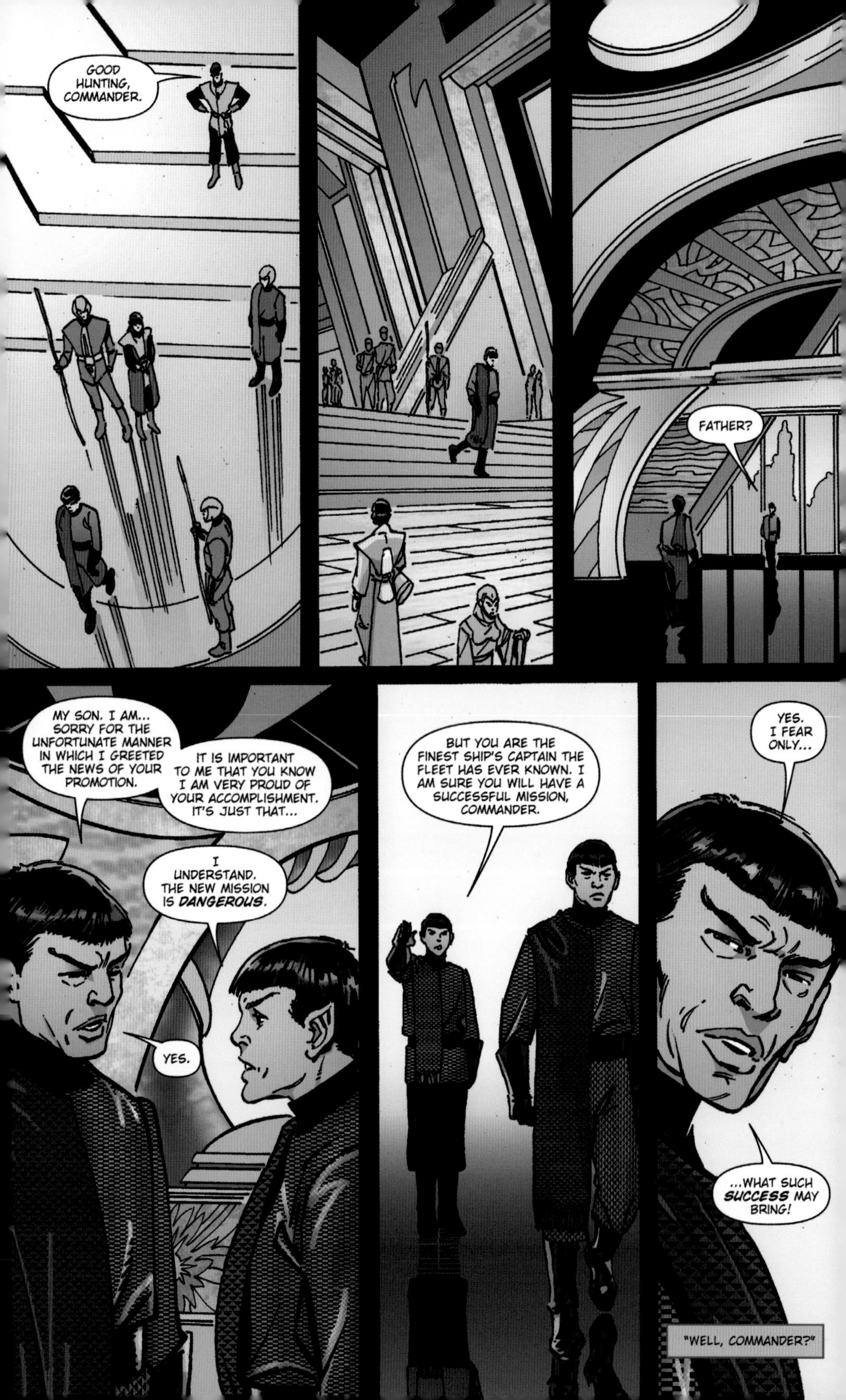
GOOD HUNTING, COMMANDER.
FATHER?
MY SON. I AM... SORRY FOR THE UNFORTUNATE MANNER IN WHICH I GREETED THE NEWS OF YOUR PROMOTION.
IT IS IMPORTANT TO ME THAT YOU KNOW I AM VERY PROUD OF YOUR ACCOMPLISHMENT. IT'S JUST THAT...
I UNDERSTAND. THE NEW MISSION IS DANGEROUS.
YES.
BUT YOU ARE THE FINEST SHIP'S CAPTAIN THE FLEET HAS EVER KNOWN. I AM SURE YOU WILL HAVE A SUCCESSFUL MISSION, COMMANDER.
YES. I FEAR ONLY...
...WHAT SUCH SUCCESS MAY BRING!
"WELL, COMMANDER?"

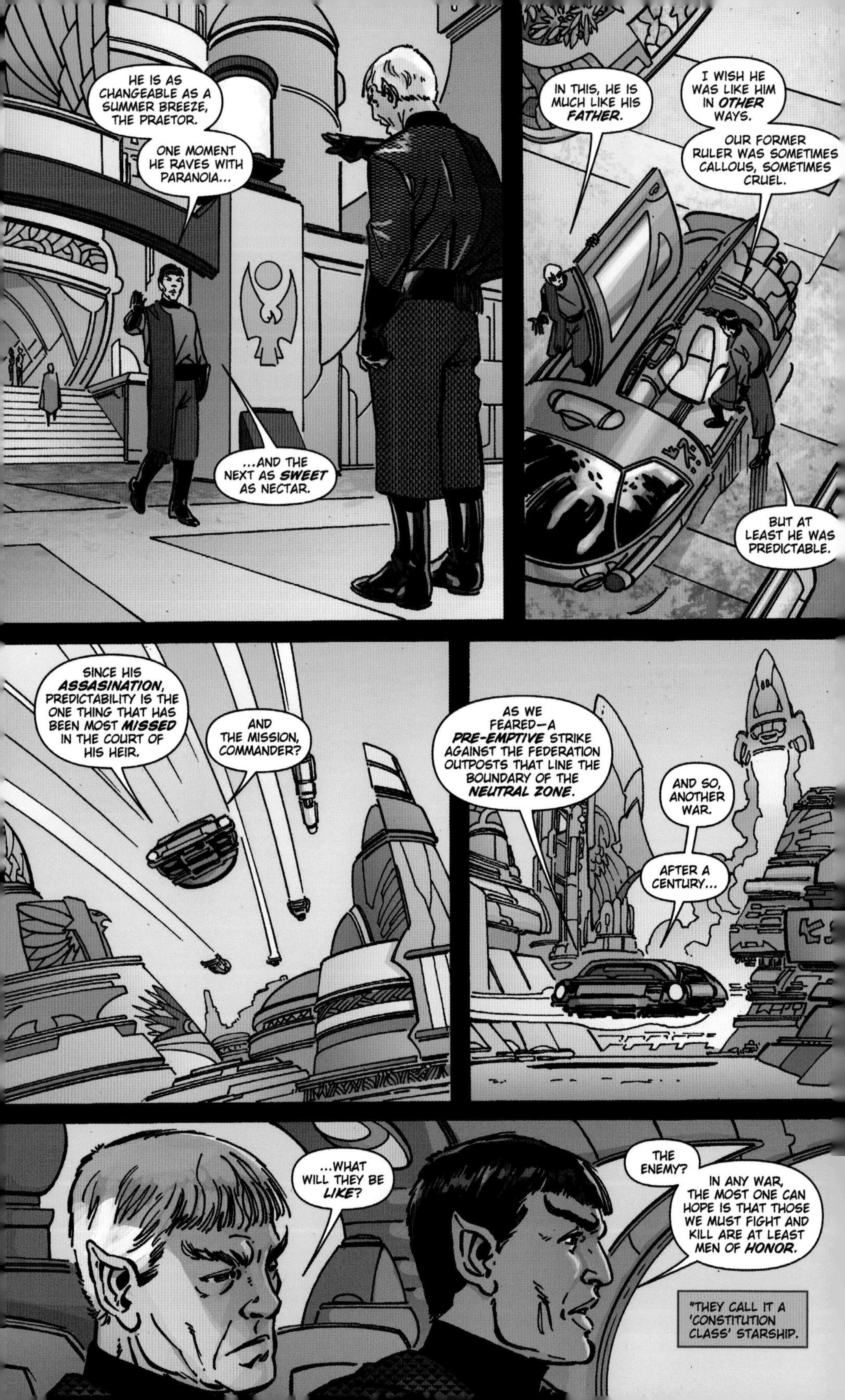
HE IS AS CHANGEABLE AS A SUMMER BREEZE, THE PRAETOR.
ONE MOMENT HE RAVES WITH PARANOIA...
...AND THE NEXT AS SWEET AS NECTAR.
IN THIS, HE IS MUCH LIKE HIS FATHER.
I WISH HE WAS LIKE HIM IN OTHER WAYS.
OUR FORMER RULER WAS SOMETIMES CALLOUS, SOMETIMES CRUEL.
BUT AT LEAST HE WAS PREDICTABLE.
SINCE HIS ASSASINATION, PREDICTABILITY IS THE ONE THING THAT HAS BEEN MOST MISSED IN THE COURT OF HIS HEIR.
AND THE MISSION, COMMANDER?
AS WE FEARED—A PRE-EMPTIVE STRIKE AGAINST THE FEDERATION OUTPOSTS THAT LINE THE BOUNDARY OF THE NEUTRAL ZONE.
AND SO, ANOTHER WAR.
AFTER A CENTURY...
...WHAT WILL THEY BE LIKE?
THE ENEMY?
IN ANY WAR, THE MOST ONE CAN HOPE IS THAT THOSE WE MUST FIGHT AND KILL ARE AT LEAST MEN OF HONOR.
"THEY CALL IT A 'CONSTITUTION CLASS' STARSHIP.

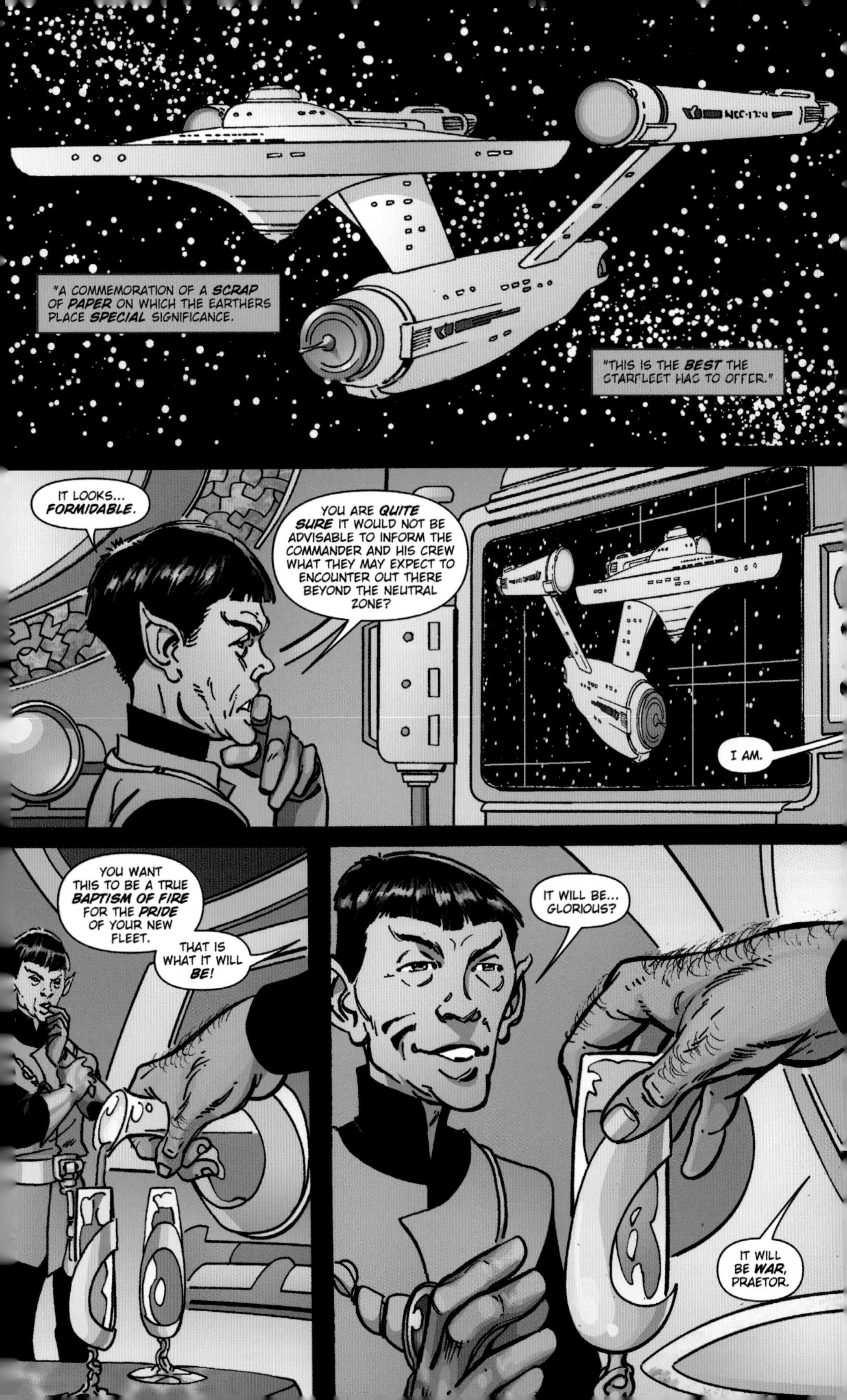
"A COMMEMORATION OF A SCRAP OF PAPER ON WHICH THE EARTHERS PLACE SPECIAL SIGNIFICANCE.
"THIS IS THE BEST THE STARFLEET HAS TO OFFER."
IT LOOKS... FORMIDABLE.
YOU ARE QUITE SURE IT WOULD NOT BE ADVISABLE TO INFORM THE COMMANDER AND HIS CREW WHAT THEY MAY EXPECT TO ENCOUNTER OUT THERE BEYOND THE NEUTRAL ZONE?
I AM.
YOU WANT THIS TO BE A TRUE BAPTISM OF FIRE FOR THE PRIDE OF YOUR NEW FLEET.
THAT IS WHAT IT WILL BE!
IT WILL BE... GLORIOUS?
IT WILL BE WAR, PRAETOR.

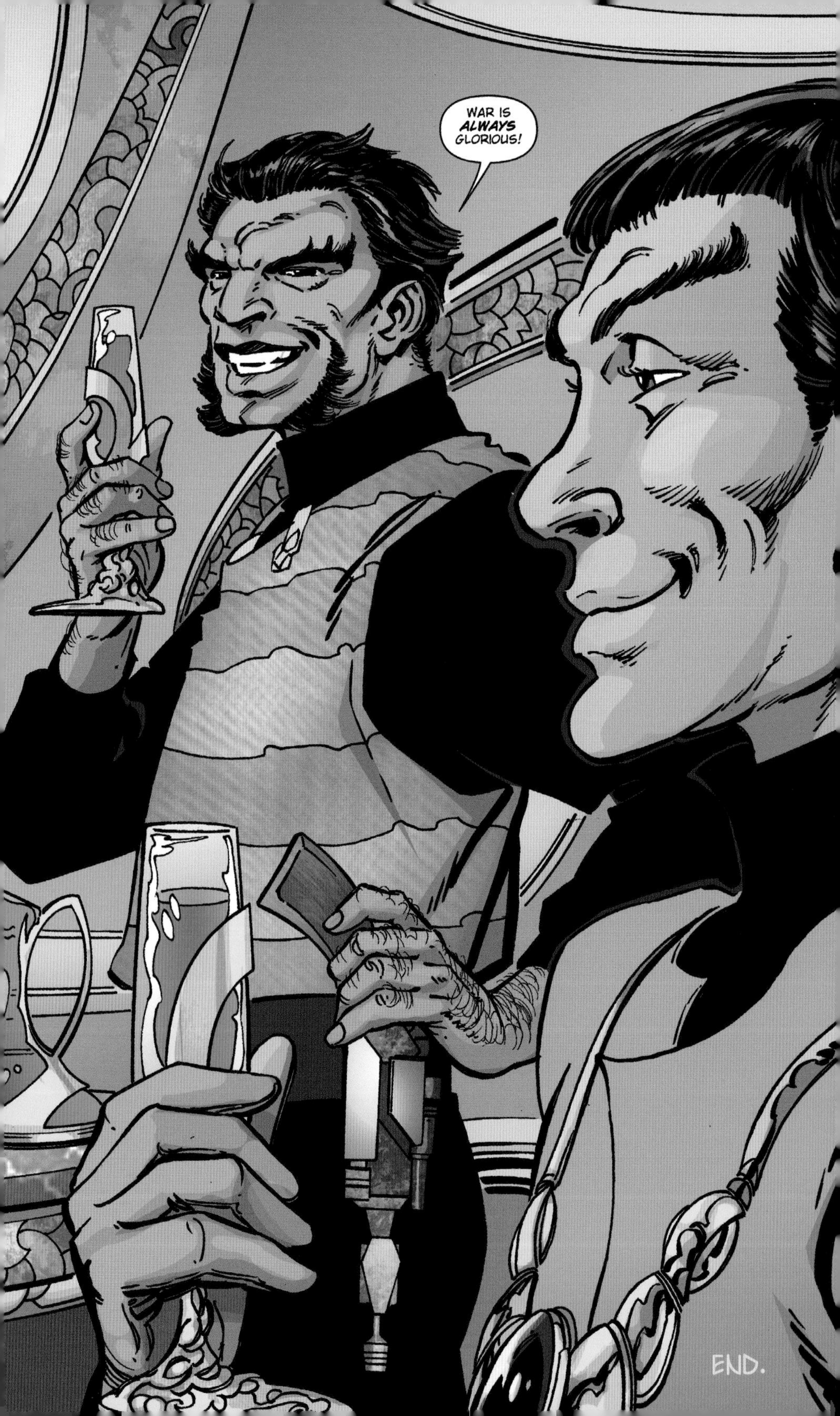
WAR IS ALWAYS GLORIOUS!
END.

STAR TREK®

THE ORIGINAL SERIES

OMNIBUS

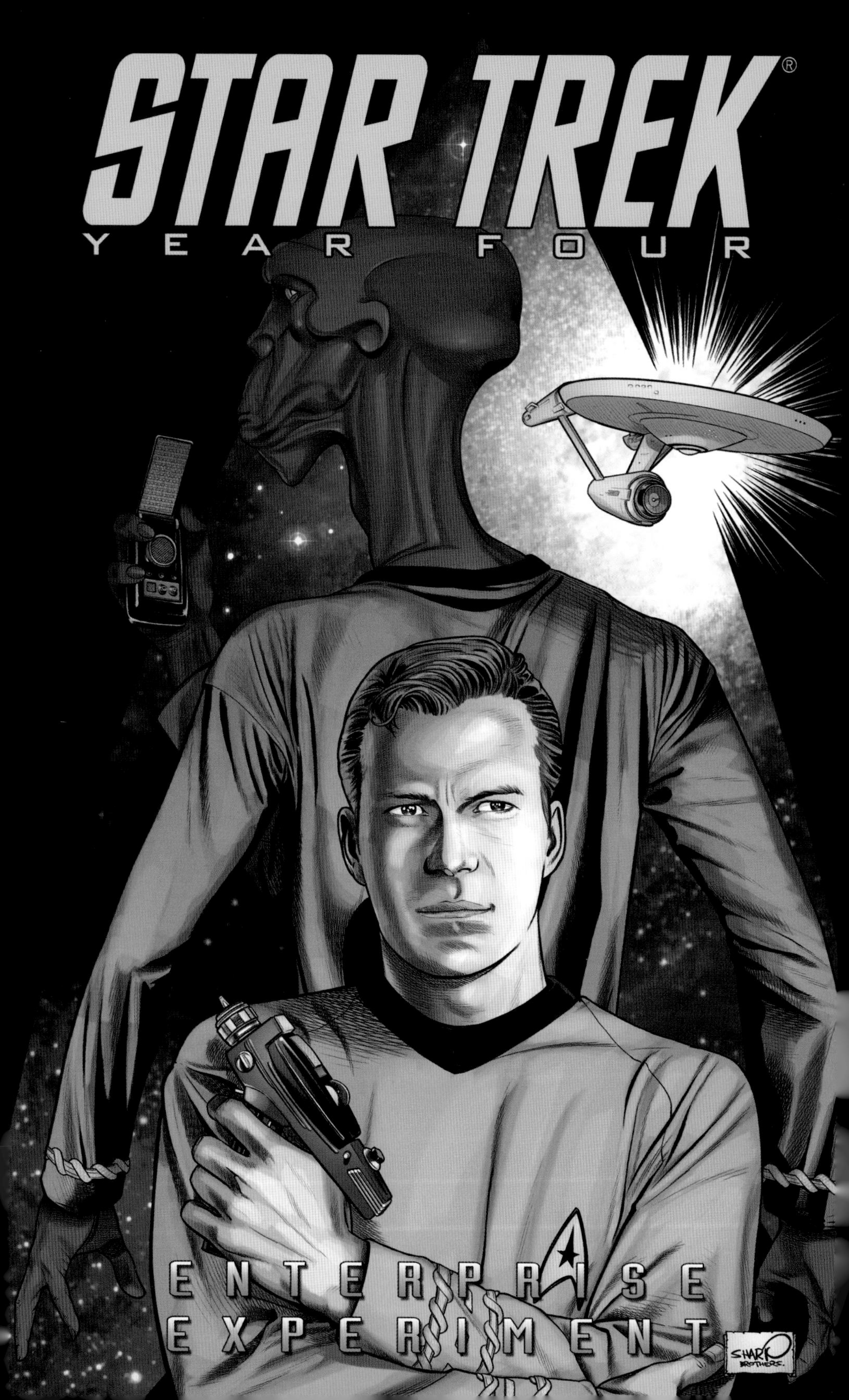
STAR TREK®
YEAR FOUR
ENTERPRISE EXPERIMENT
SHARP BROTHERS.

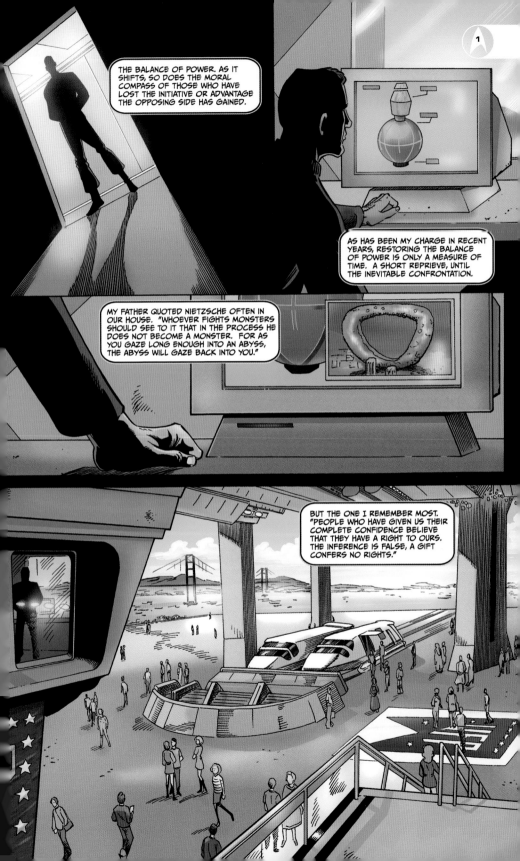

THE BALANCE OF POWER. AS IT SHIFTS, SO DOES THE MORAL COMPASS OF THOSE WHO HAVE LOST THE INITIATIVE OR ADVANTAGE THE OPPOSING SIDE HAS GAINED.

AS HAS BEEN MY CHARGE IN RECENT YEARS, RESTORING THE BALANCE OF POWER IS ONLY A MEASURE OF TIME. A SHORT REPRIEVE, UNTIL THE INEVITABLE CONFRONTATION.

MY FATHER QUOTED NIETZSCHE OFTEN IN OUR HOUSE. "WHOEVER FIGHTS MONSTERS SHOULD SEE TO IT THAT IN THE PROCESS HE DOES NOT BECOME A MONSTER. FOR AS YOU GAZE LONG ENOUGH INTO AN ABYSS, THE ABYSS WILL GAZE BACK INTO YOU."

BUT THE ONE I REMEMBER MOST. "PEOPLE WHO HAVE GIVEN US THEIR COMPLETE CONFIDENCE BELIEVE THAT THEY HAVE A RIGHT TO OURS. THE INFERENCE IS FALSE, A GIFT CONFERS NO RIGHTS."

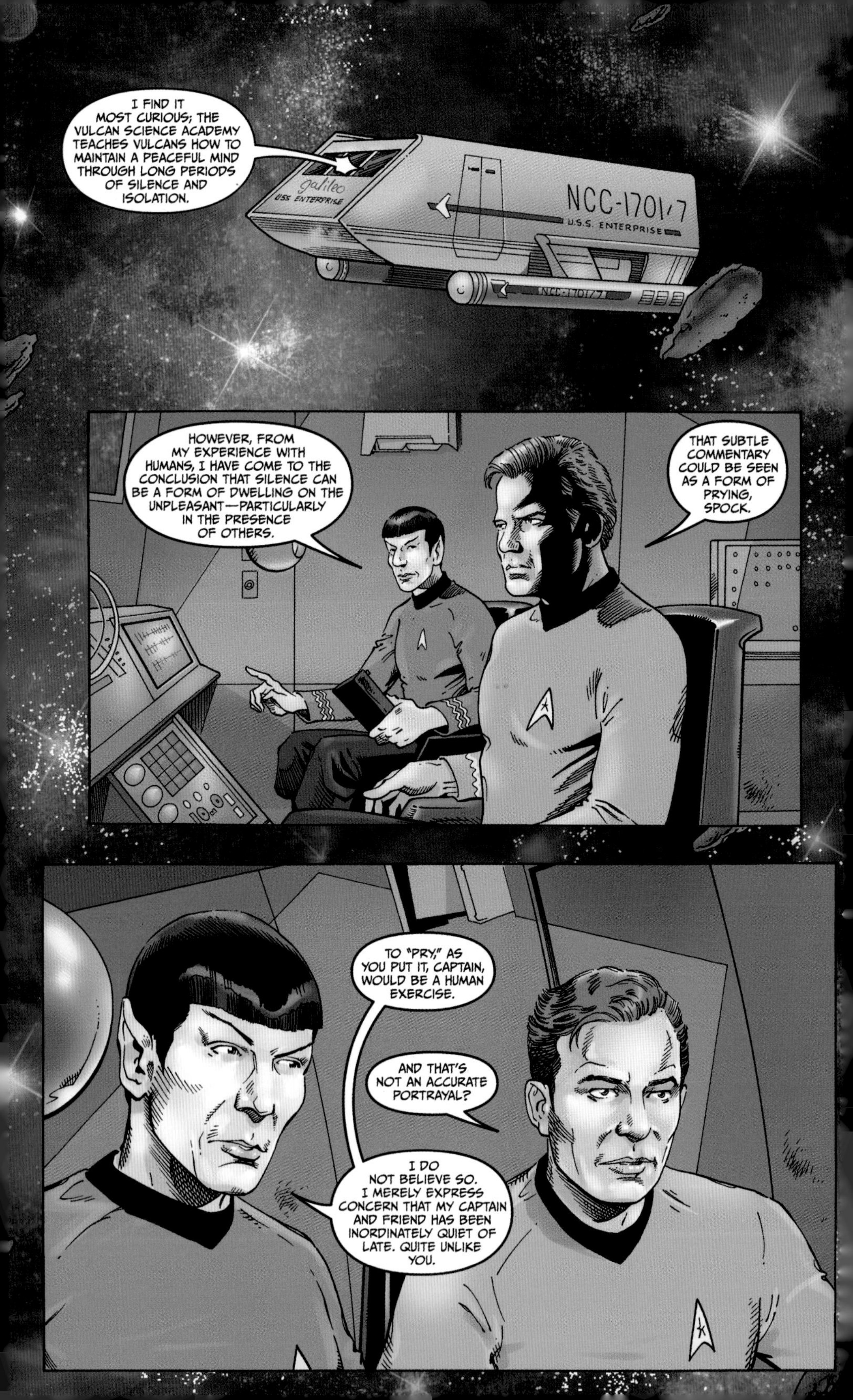
I FIND IT MOST CURIOUS; THE VULCAN SCIENCE ACADEMY TEACHES VULCANS HOW TO MAINTAIN A PEACEFUL MIND THROUGH LONG PERIODS OF SILENCE AND ISOLATION.
galileo U.S.S. ENTERPRISE
NCC-1701/7
U.S.S. ENTERPRISE
HOWEVER, FROM MY EXPERIENCE WITH HUMANS, I HAVE COME TO THE CONCLUSION THAT SILENCE CAN BE A FORM OF DWELLING ON THE UNPLEASANT—PARTICULARLY IN THE PRESENCE OF OTHERS.
THAT SUBTLE COMMENTARY COULD BE SEEN AS A FORM OF PRYING, SPOCK.
TO "PRY," AS YOU PUT IT, CAPTAIN, WOULD BE A HUMAN EXERCISE.
AND THAT'S NOT AN ACCURATE PORTRAYAL?
I DO NOT BELIEVE SO. I MERELY EXPRESS CONCERN THAT MY CAPTAIN AND FRIEND HAS BEEN INORDINATELY QUIET OF LATE. QUITE UNLIKE YOU.

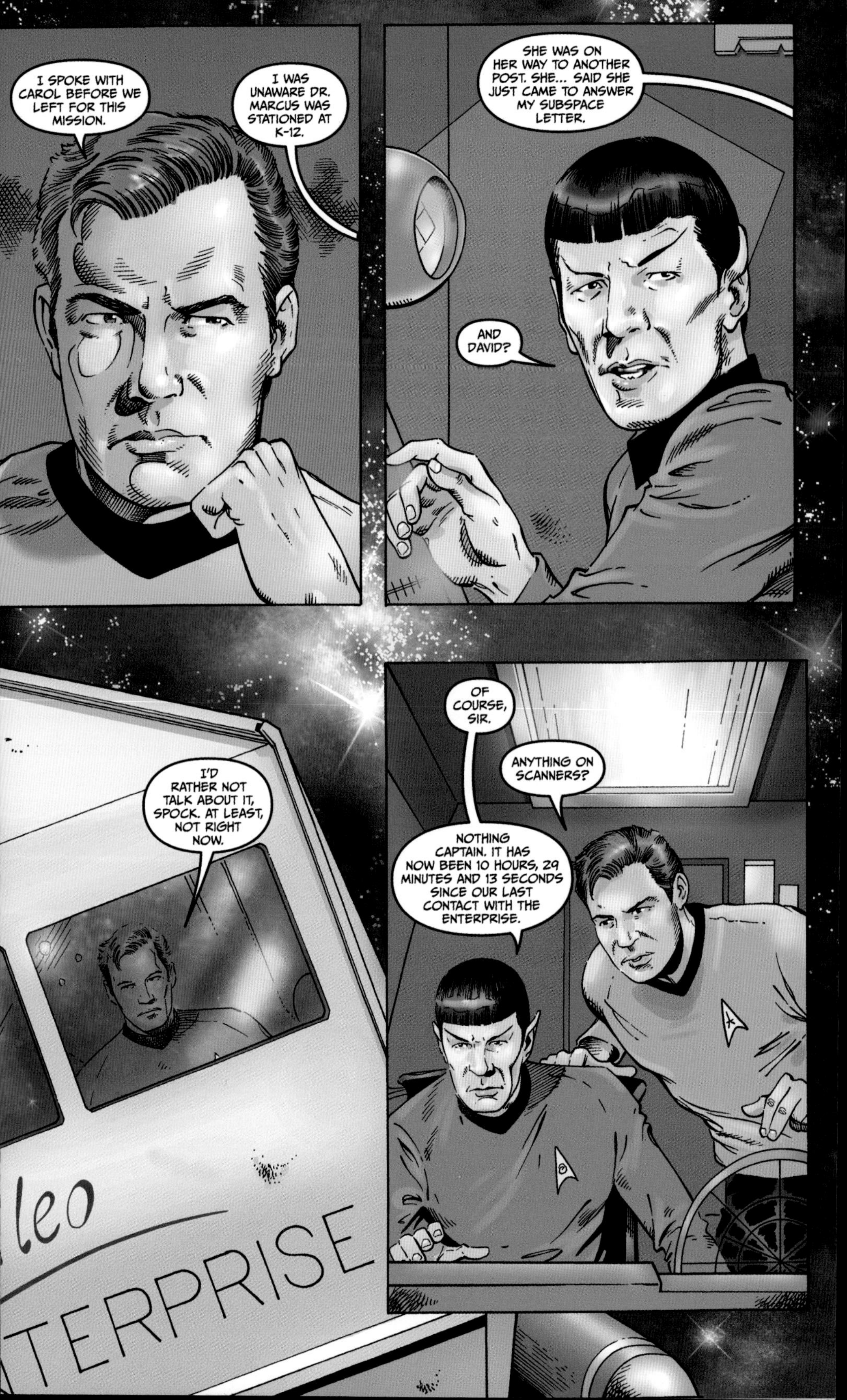
I SPOKE WITH CAROL BEFORE WE LEFT FOR THIS MISSION.
I WAS UNAWARE DR. MARCUS WAS STATIONED AT K-12.
SHE WAS ON HER WAY TO ANOTHER POST. SHE... SAID SHE JUST CAME TO ANSWER MY SUBSPACE LETTER.
AND DAVID?
I'D RATHER NOT TALK ABOUT IT, SPOCK. AT LEAST, NOT RIGHT NOW.
leo
ENTERPRISE
OF COURSE, SIR.
ANYTHING ON SCANNERS?
NOTHING CAPTAIN. IT HAS NOW BEEN 10 HOURS, 29 MINUTES AND 13 SECONDS SINCE OUR LAST CONTACT WITH THE ENTERPRISE.

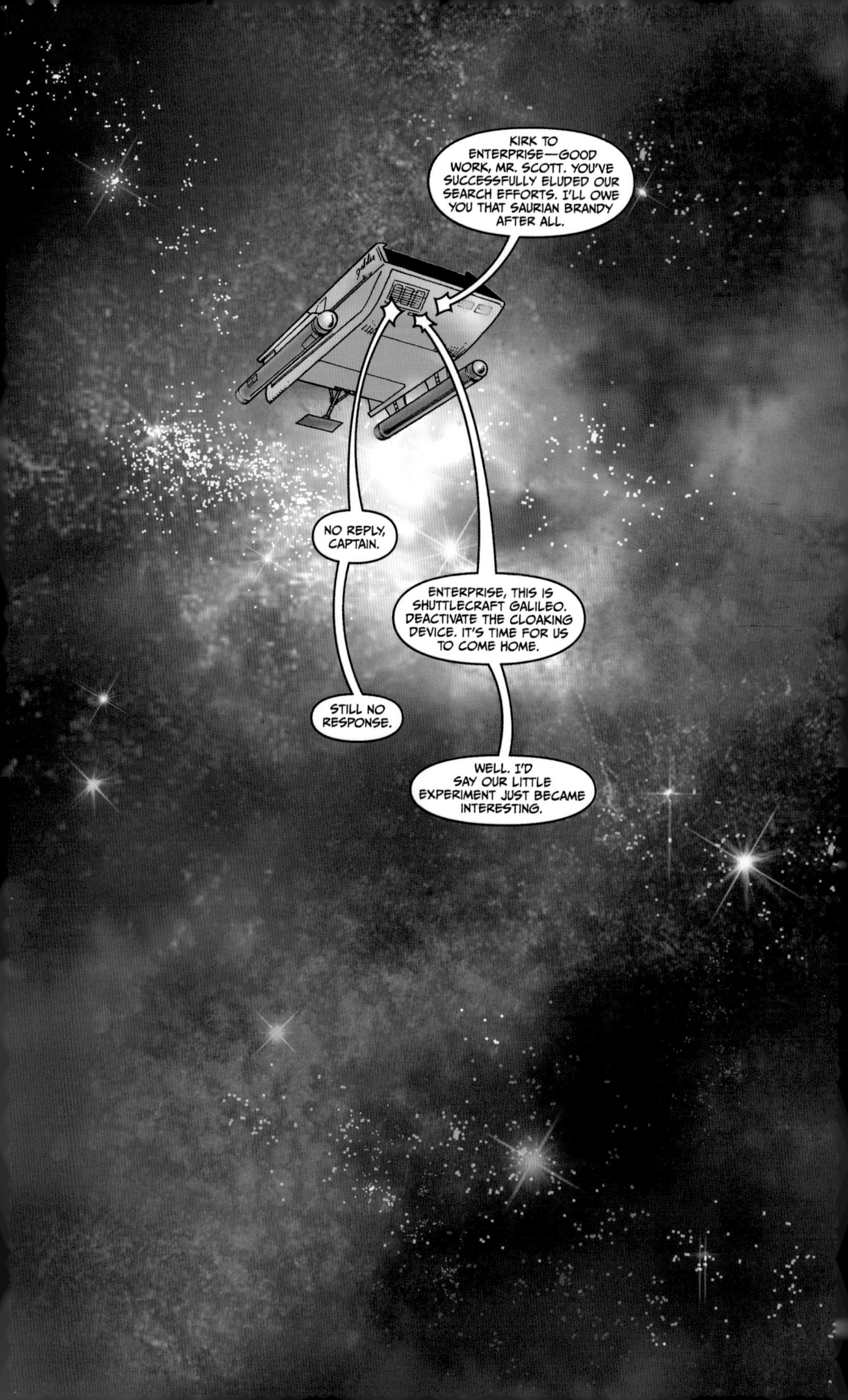
KIRK TO ENTERPRISE—GOOD WORK, MR. SCOTT. YOU'VE SUCCESSFULLY ELUDED OUR SEARCH EFFORTS. I'LL OWE YOU THAT SAURIAN BRANDY AFTER ALL.
NO REPLY, CAPTAIN.
ENTERPRISE, THIS IS SHUTTLECRAFT GALILEO. DEACTIVATE THE CLOAKING DEVICE. IT'S TIME FOR US TO COME HOME.
STILL NO RESPONSE.
WELL. I'D SAY OUR LITTLE EXPERIMENT JUST BECAME INTERESTING.

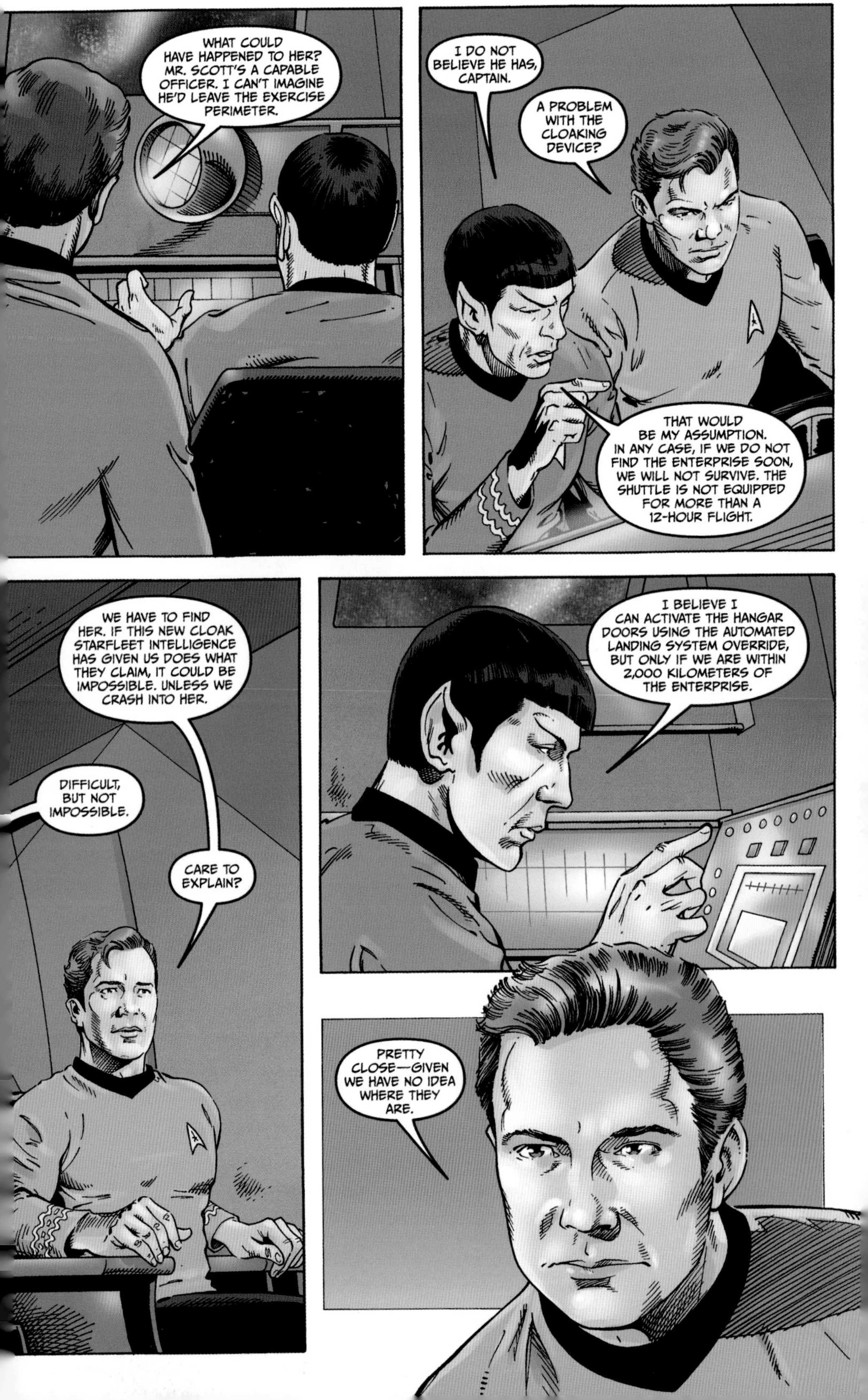
WHAT COULD HAVE HAPPENED TO HER? MR. SCOTT'S A CAPABLE OFFICER. I CAN'T IMAGINE HE'D LEAVE THE EXERCISE PERIMETER.
I DO NOT BELIEVE HE HAS, CAPTAIN.
A PROBLEM WITH THE CLOAKING DEVICE?
THAT WOULD BE MY ASSUMPTION. IN ANY CASE, IF WE DO NOT FIND THE ENTERPRISE SOON, WE WILL NOT SURVIVE. THE SHUTTLE IS NOT EQUIPPED FOR MORE THAN A 12-HOUR FLIGHT.
WE HAVE TO FIND HER. IF THIS NEW CLOAK STARFLEET INTELLIGENCE HAS GIVEN US DOES WHAT THEY CLAIM, IT COULD BE IMPOSSIBLE. UNLESS WE CRASH INTO HER.
DIFFICULT, BUT NOT IMPOSSIBLE.
CARE TO EXPLAIN?
I BELIEVE I CAN ACTIVATE THE HANGAR DOORS USING THE AUTOMATED LANDING SYSTEM OVERRIDE, BUT ONLY IF WE ARE WITHIN 2,000 KILOMETERS OF THE ENTERPRISE.
PRETTY CLOSE—GIVEN WE HAVE NO IDEA WHERE THEY ARE.

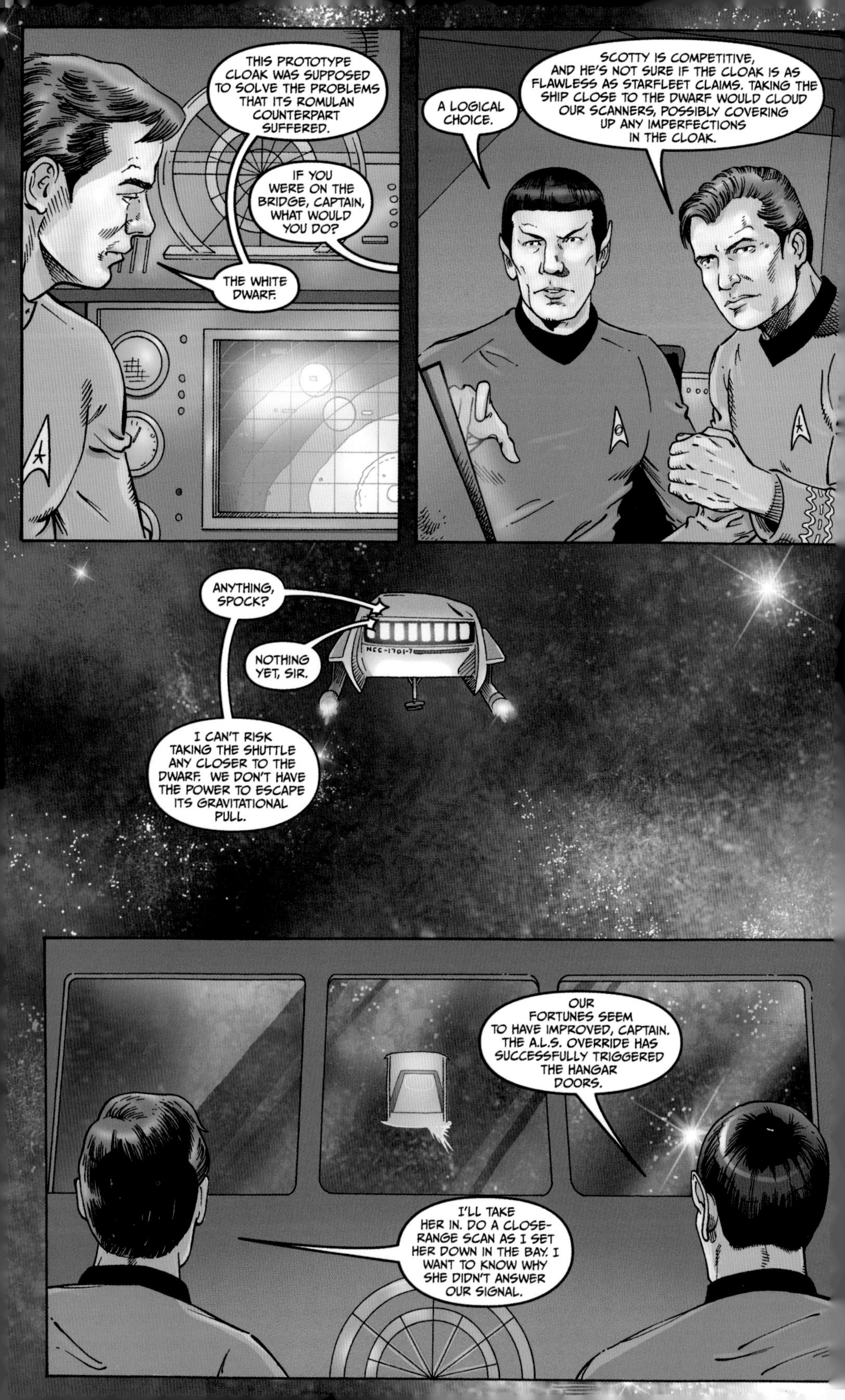
THIS PROTOTYPE CLOAK WAS SUPPOSED TO SOLVE THE PROBLEMS THAT ITS ROMULAN COUNTERPART SUFFERED.
IF YOU WERE ON THE BRIDGE, CAPTAIN, WHAT WOULD YOU DO?
THE WHITE DWARF.
A LOGICAL CHOICE.
SCOTTY IS COMPETITIVE, AND HE'S NOT SURE IF THE CLOAK IS AS FLAWLESS AS STARFLEET CLAIMS. TAKING THE SHIP CLOSE TO THE DWARF WOULD CLOUD OUR SCANNERS, POSSIBLY COVERING UP ANY IMPERFECTIONS IN THE CLOAK.
ANYTHING, SPOCK?
NOTHING YET, SIR.
NCC-1701-7
I CAN'T RISK TAKING THE SHUTTLE ANY CLOSER TO THE DWARF. WE DON'T HAVE THE POWER TO ESCAPE ITS GRAVITATIONAL PULL.
OUR FORTUNES SEEM TO HAVE IMPROVED, CAPTAIN. THE A.L.S. OVERRIDE HAS SUCCESSFULLY TRIGGERED THE HANGAR DOORS.
I'LL TAKE HER IN. DO A CLOSE-RANGE SCAN AS I SET HER DOWN IN THE BAY. I WANT TO KNOW WHY SHE DIDN'T ANSWER OUR SIGNAL.

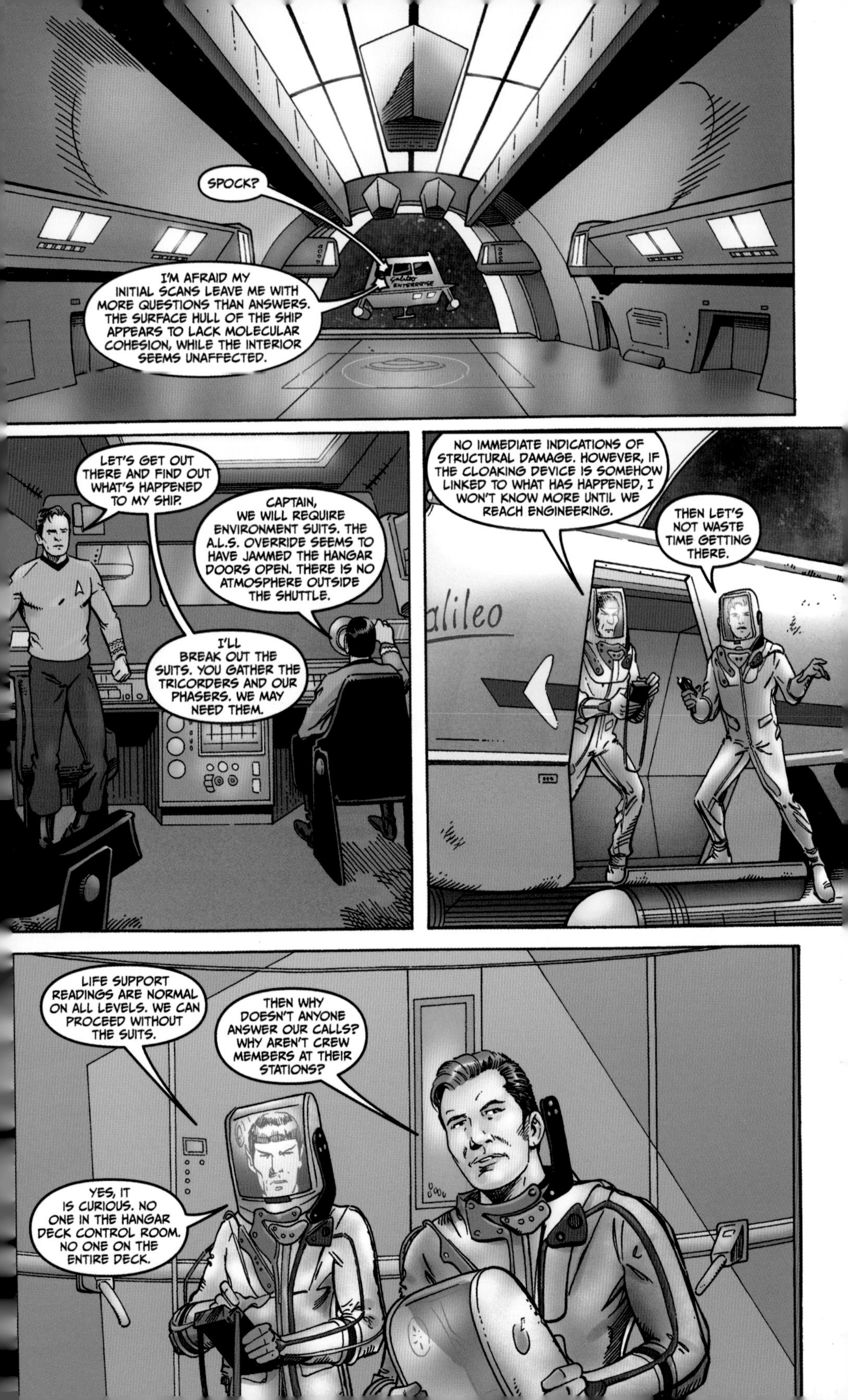

SPOCK?
I'M AFRAID MY INITIAL SCANS LEAVE ME WITH MORE QUESTIONS THAN ANSWERS. THE SURFACE HULL OF THE SHIP APPEARS TO LACK MOLECULAR COHESION, WHILE THE INTERIOR SEEMS UNAFFECTED.
LET'S GET OUT THERE AND FIND OUT WHAT'S HAPPENED TO MY SHIP.
CAPTAIN, WE WILL REQUIRE ENVIRONMENT SUITS. THE A.L.S. OVERRIDE SEEMS TO HAVE JAMMED THE HANGAR DOORS OPEN. THERE IS NO ATMOSPHERE OUTSIDE THE SHUTTLE.
I'LL BREAK OUT THE SUITS. YOU GATHER THE TRICORDERS AND OUR PHASERS. WE MAY NEED THEM.
NO IMMEDIATE INDICATIONS OF STRUCTURAL DAMAGE. HOWEVER, IF THE CLOAKING DEVICE IS SOMEHOW LINKED TO WHAT HAS HAPPENED, I WON'T KNOW MORE UNTIL WE REACH ENGINEERING.
THEN LET'S NOT WASTE TIME GETTING THERE.
LIFE SUPPORT READINGS ARE NORMAL ON ALL LEVELS. WE CAN PROCEED WITHOUT THE SUITS.
THEN WHY DOESN'T ANYONE ANSWER OUR CALLS? WHY AREN'T CREW MEMBERS AT THEIR STATIONS?
YES, IT IS CURIOUS. NO ONE IN THE HANGAR DECK CONTROL ROOM. NO ONE ON THE ENTIRE DECK.

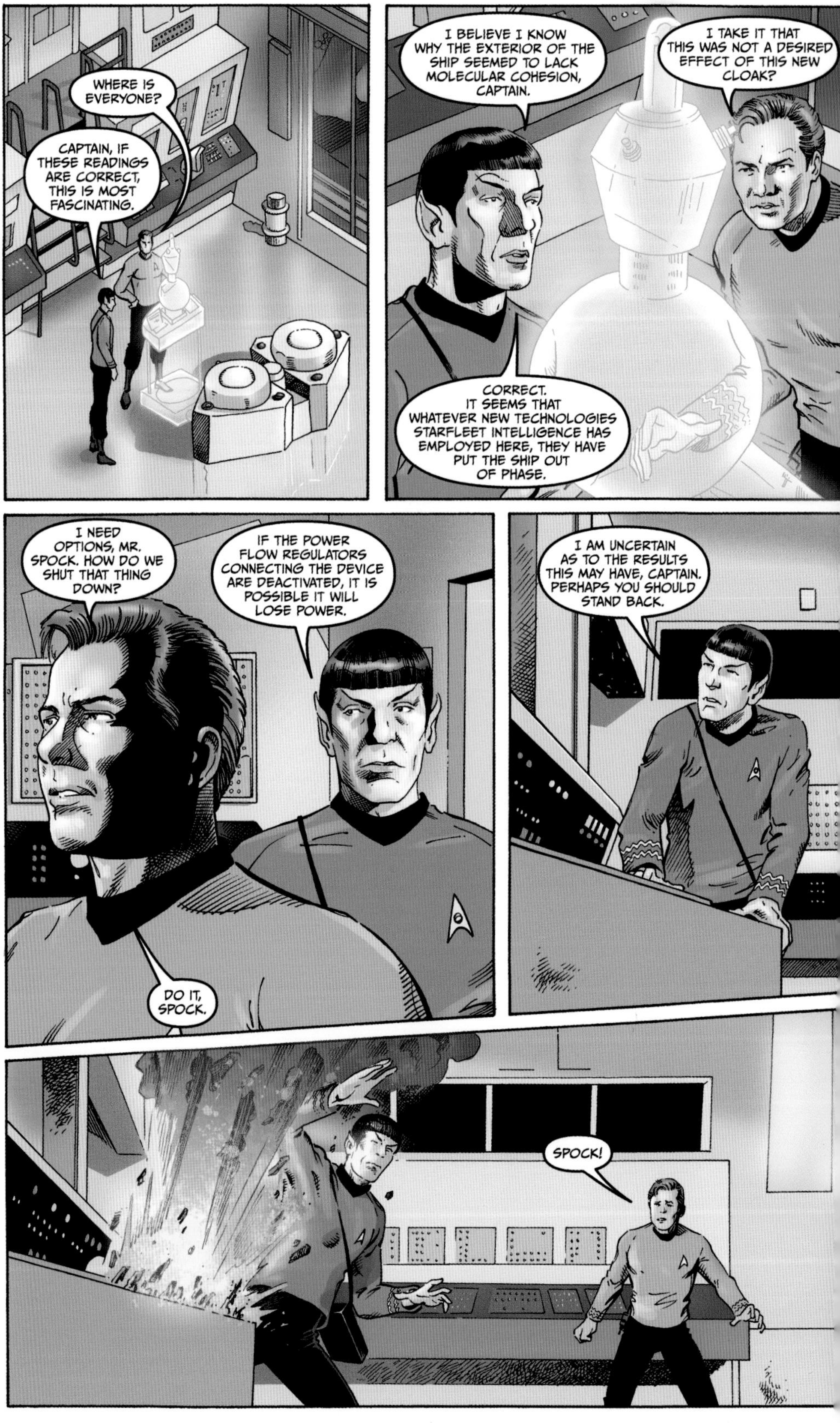
WHERE IS EVERYONE?
CAPTAIN, IF THESE READINGS ARE CORRECT, THIS IS MOST FASCINATING.
I BELIEVE I KNOW WHY THE EXTERIOR OF THE SHIP SEEMED TO LACK MOLECULAR COHESION, CAPTAIN.
I TAKE IT THAT THIS WAS NOT A DESIRED EFFECT OF THIS NEW CLOAK?
CORRECT. IT SEEMS THAT WHATEVER NEW TECHNOLOGIES STARFLEET INTELLIGENCE HAS EMPLOYED HERE, THEY HAVE PUT THE SHIP OUT OF PHASE.
I NEED OPTIONS, MR. SPOCK. HOW DO WE SHUT THAT THING DOWN?
IF THE POWER FLOW REGULATORS CONNECTING THE DEVICE ARE DEACTIVATED, IT IS POSSIBLE IT WILL LOSE POWER.
DO IT, SPOCK.
I AM UNCERTAIN AS TO THE RESULTS THIS MAY HAVE, CAPTAIN. PERHAPS YOU SHOULD STAND BACK.
SPOCK!

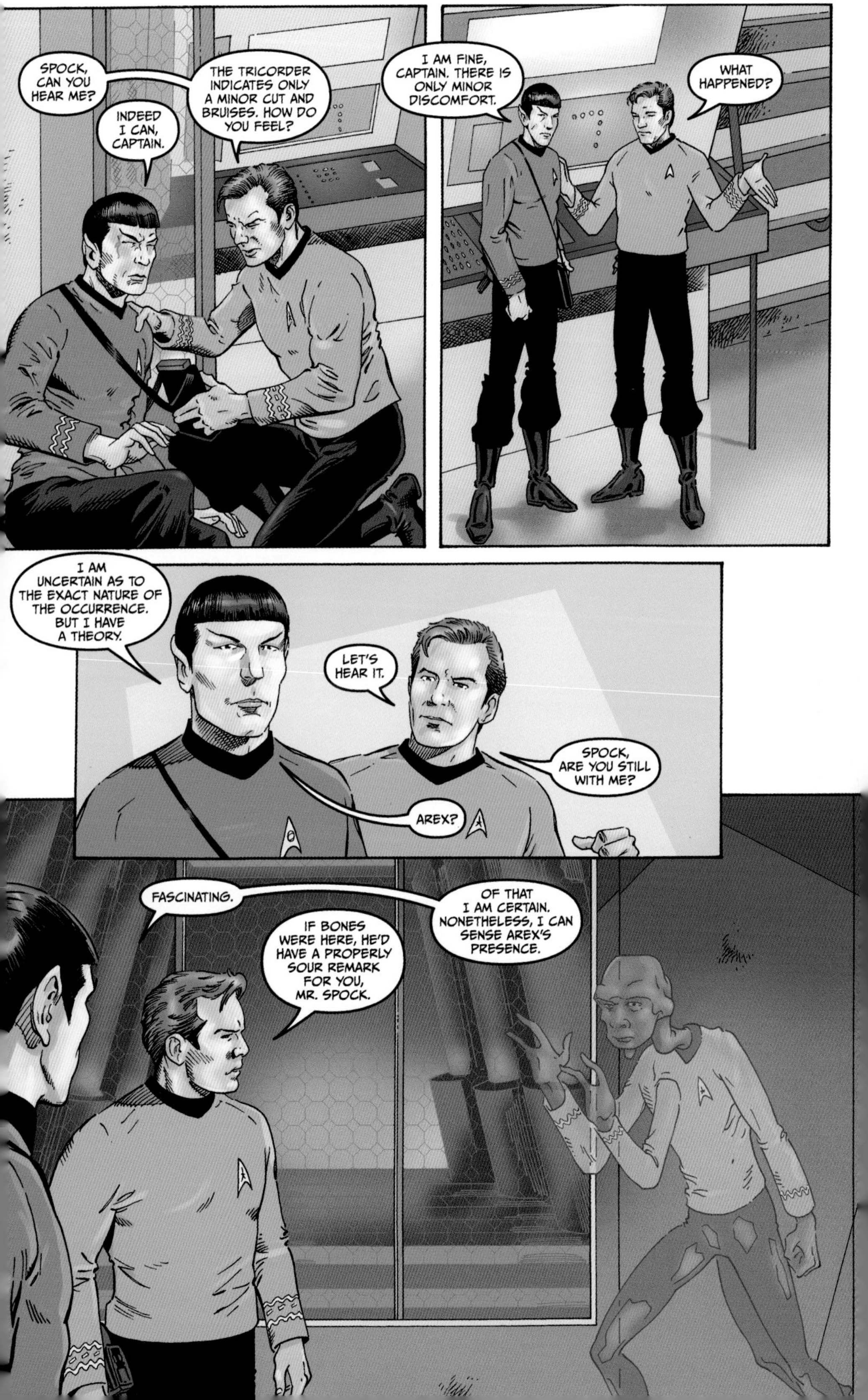
SPOCK, CAN YOU HEAR ME?
INDEED I CAN, CAPTAIN.
THE TRICORDER INDICATES ONLY A MINOR CUT AND BRUISES. HOW DO YOU FEEL?
I AM FINE, CAPTAIN. THERE IS ONLY MINOR DISCOMFORT.
WHAT HAPPENED?
I AM UNCERTAIN AS TO THE EXACT NATURE OF THE OCCURRENCE. BUT I HAVE A THEORY.
LET'S HEAR IT.
SPOCK, ARE YOU STILL WITH ME?
AREX?
FASCINATING.
OF THAT I AM CERTAIN. NONETHELESS, I CAN SENSE AREX'S PRESENCE.
IF BONES WERE HERE, HE'D HAVE A PROPERLY SOUR REMARK FOR YOU, MR. SPOCK.

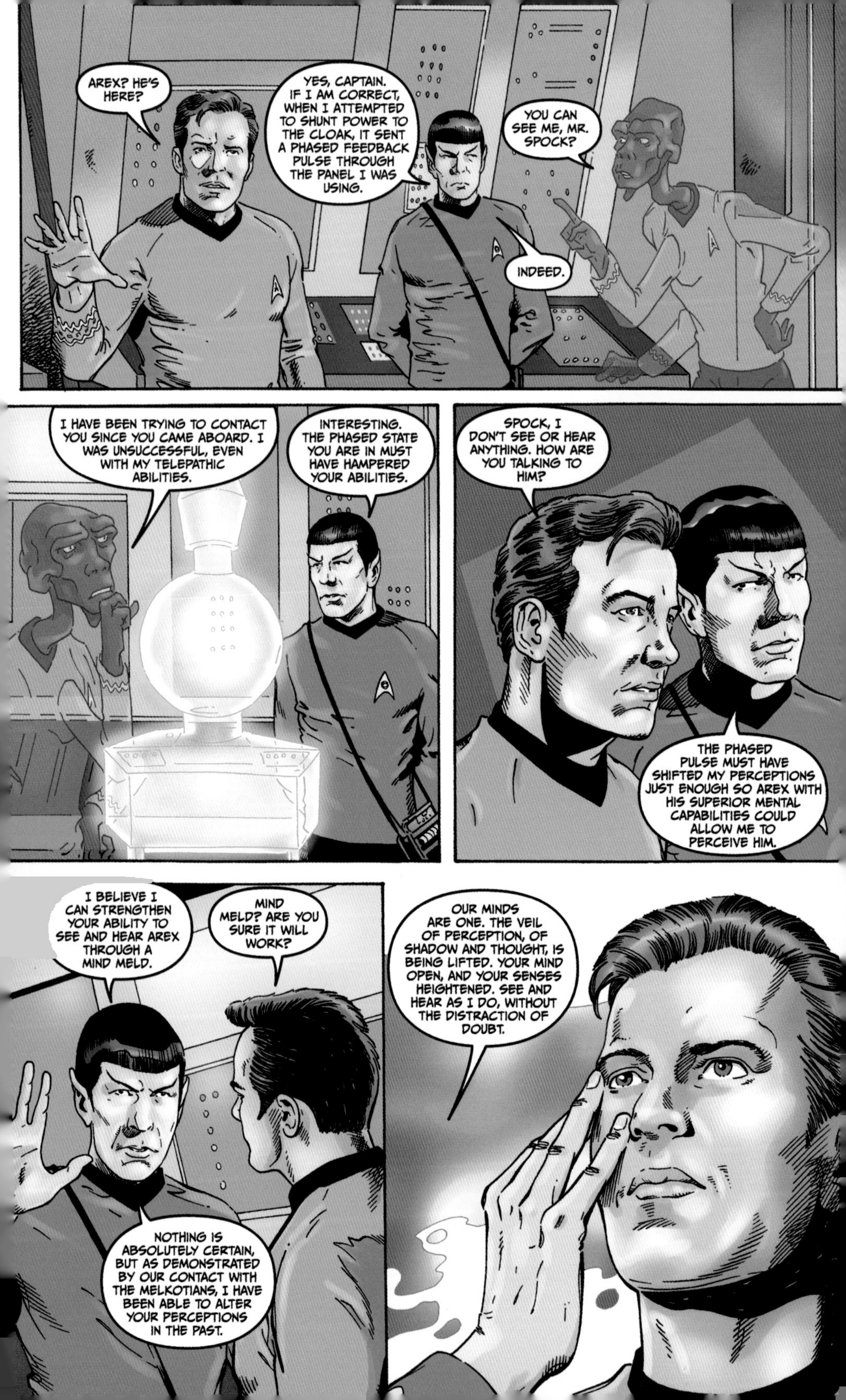
AREX? HE'S HERE?
YES, CAPTAIN. IF I AM CORRECT, WHEN I ATTEMPTED TO SHUNT POWER TO THE CLOAK, IT SENT A PHASED FEEDBACK PULSE THROUGH THE PANEL I WAS USING.
YOU CAN SEE ME, MR. SPOCK?
INDEED.
I HAVE BEEN TRYING TO CONTACT YOU SINCE YOU CAME ABOARD. I WAS UNSUCCESSFUL, EVEN WITH MY TELEPATHIC ABILITIES.
INTERESTING. THE PHASED STATE YOU ARE IN MUST HAVE HAMPERED YOUR ABILITIES.
SPOCK, I DON'T SEE OR HEAR ANYTHING. HOW ARE YOU TALKING TO HIM?
THE PHASED PULSE MUST HAVE SHIFTED MY PERCEPTIONS JUST ENOUGH SO AREX WITH HIS SUPERIOR MENTAL CAPABILITIES COULD ALLOW ME TO PERCEIVE HIM.
I BELIEVE I CAN STRENGTHEN YOUR ABILITY TO SEE AND HEAR AREX THROUGH A MIND MELD.
MIND MELD? ARE YOU SURE IT WILL WORK?
NOTHING IS ABSOLUTELY CERTAIN, BUT AS DEMONSTRATED BY OUR CONTACT WITH THE MELKOTIANS, I HAVE BEEN ABLE TO ALTER YOUR PERCEPTIONS IN THE PAST.
OUR MINDS ARE ONE. THE VEIL OF PERCEPTION, OF SHADOW AND THOUGHT, IS BEING LIFTED. YOUR MIND OPEN, AND YOUR SENSES HEIGHTENED. SEE AND HEAR AS I DO, WITHOUT THE DISTRACTION OF DOUBT.

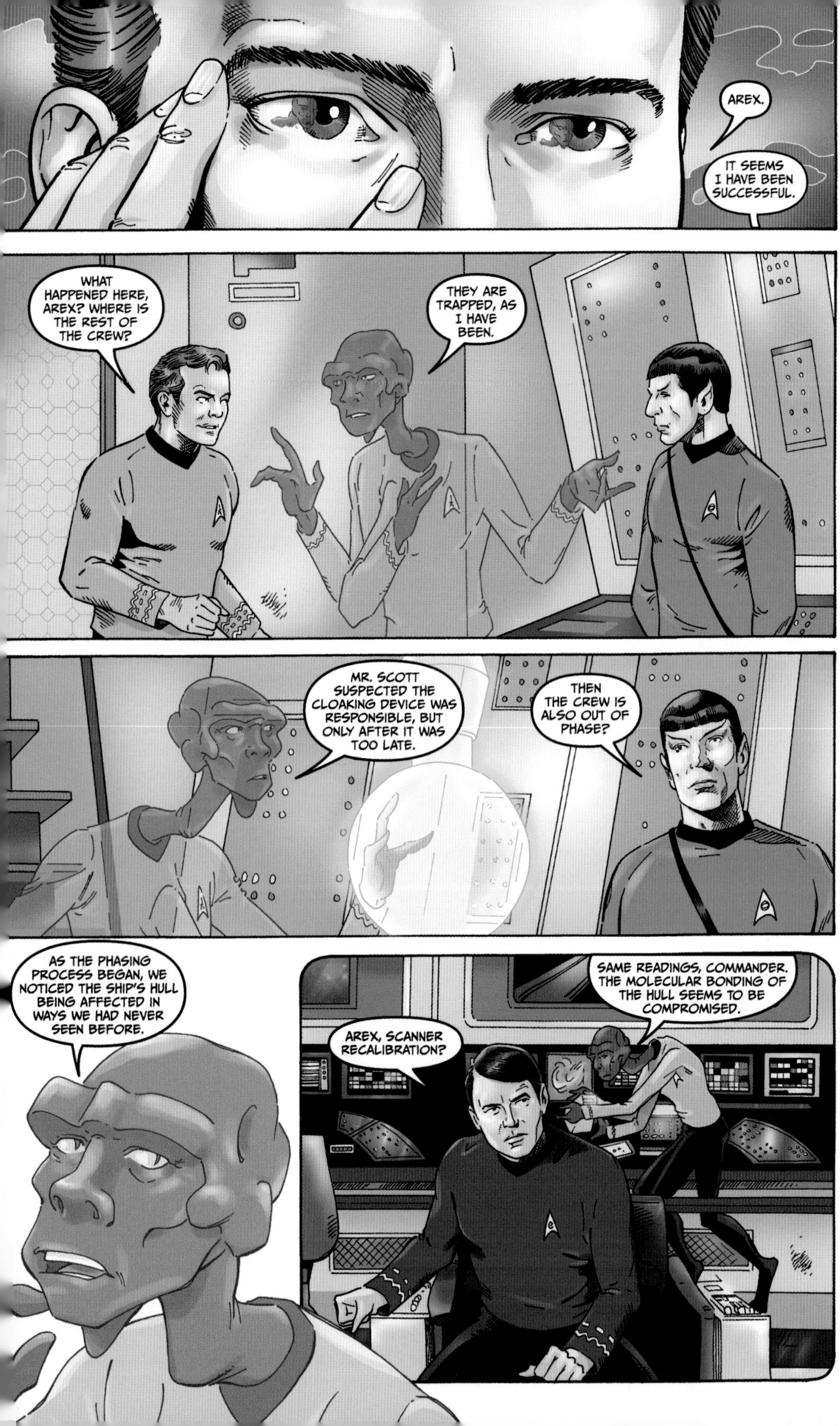
AREX.
IT SEEMS I HAVE BEEN SUCCESSFUL.
WHAT HAPPENED HERE, AREX? WHERE IS THE REST OF THE CREW?
THEY ARE TRAPPED, AS I HAVE BEEN.
MR. SCOTT SUSPECTED THE CLOAKING DEVICE WAS RESPONSIBLE, BUT ONLY AFTER IT WAS TOO LATE.
THEN THE CREW IS ALSO OUT OF PHASE?
AS THE PHASING PROCESS BEGAN, WE NOTICED THE SHIP'S HULL BEING AFFECTED IN WAYS WE HAD NEVER SEEN BEFORE.
AREX, SCANNER RECALIBRATION?
SAME READINGS, COMMANDER. THE MOLECULAR BONDING OF THE HULL SEEMS TO BE COMPROMISED.

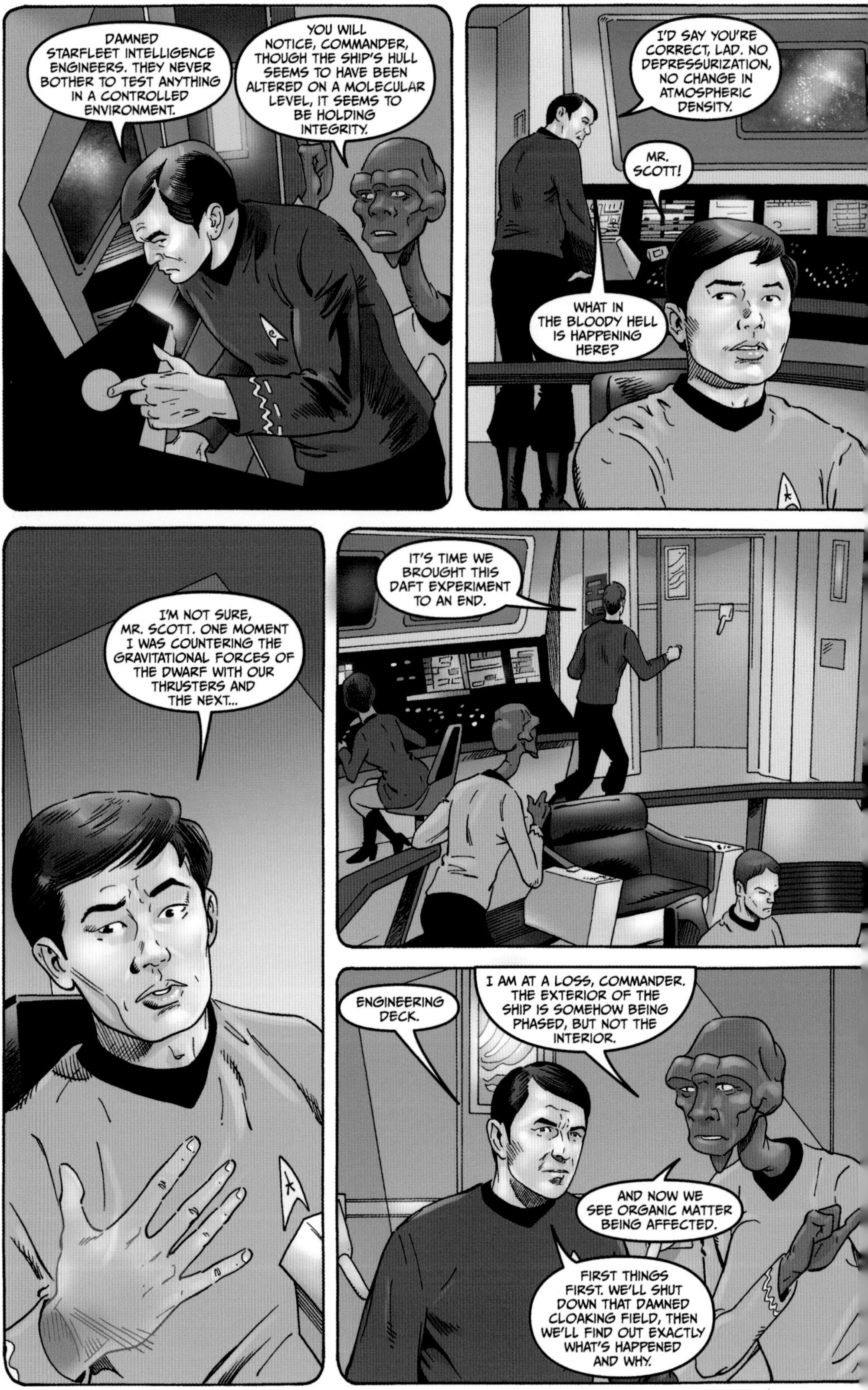
DAMNED STARFLEET INTELLIGENCE ENGINEERS. THEY NEVER BOTHER TO TEST ANYTHING IN A CONTROLLED ENVIRONMENT.
YOU WILL NOTICE, COMMANDER, THOUGH THE SHIP'S HULL SEEMS TO HAVE BEEN ALTERED ON A MOLECULAR LEVEL, IT SEEMS TO BE HOLDING INTEGRITY.
I'D SAY YOU'RE CORRECT, LAD. NO DEPRESSURIZATION, NO CHANGE IN ATMOSPHERIC DENSITY.
MR. SCOTT!
WHAT IN THE BLOODY HELL IS HAPPENING HERE?
I'M NOT SURE, MR. SCOTT. ONE MOMENT I WAS COUNTERING THE GRAVITATIONAL FORCES OF THE DWARF WITH OUR THRUSTERS AND THE NEXT...
IT'S TIME WE BROUGHT THIS DAFT EXPERIMENT TO AN END.
ENGINEERING DECK.
I AM AT A LOSS, COMMANDER. THE EXTERIOR OF THE SHIP IS SOMEHOW BEING PHASED, BUT NOT THE INTERIOR.
AND NOW WE SEE ORGANIC MATTER BEING AFFECTED.
FIRST THINGS FIRST. WE'LL SHUT DOWN THAT DAMNED CLOAKING FIELD, THEN WE'LL FIND OUT EXACTLY WHAT'S HAPPENED AND WHY.

IF THESE READINGS ARE CORRECT, MR. SCOTT, THE POWER FLOW FROM THE MAIN DRIVE SYSTEMS HAS INCREASED.

AYE, I NOTICED IT WHILE WE WERE STILL ON THE BRIDGE. WHATEVER THIS THING IS DOING, IT'S DRAINING MORE POWER FROM OUR ENGINES TO MAKE IT HAPPEN.

IF I CAN JUST CLOSE THE FUEL REACTION VALVES, WE MIGHT BE ABLE TO STARVE OUR LITTLE FRIEND HERE.

ANTI-MATTER REACTION IS STILL INCREASING.

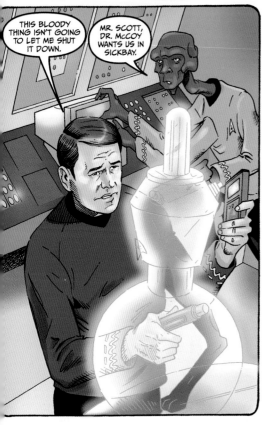

THIS BLOODY THING ISN'T GOING TO LET ME SHUT IT DOWN.

MR. SCOTT, DR. McCOY WANTS US IN SICKBAY.

SICKBAY.

IF WE CANNOT SHUT DOWN THE CLOAK, HOW WILL WE STOP THE PHASING EFFECT?

I DON'T KNOW, BUT WE NEED ANSWERS.

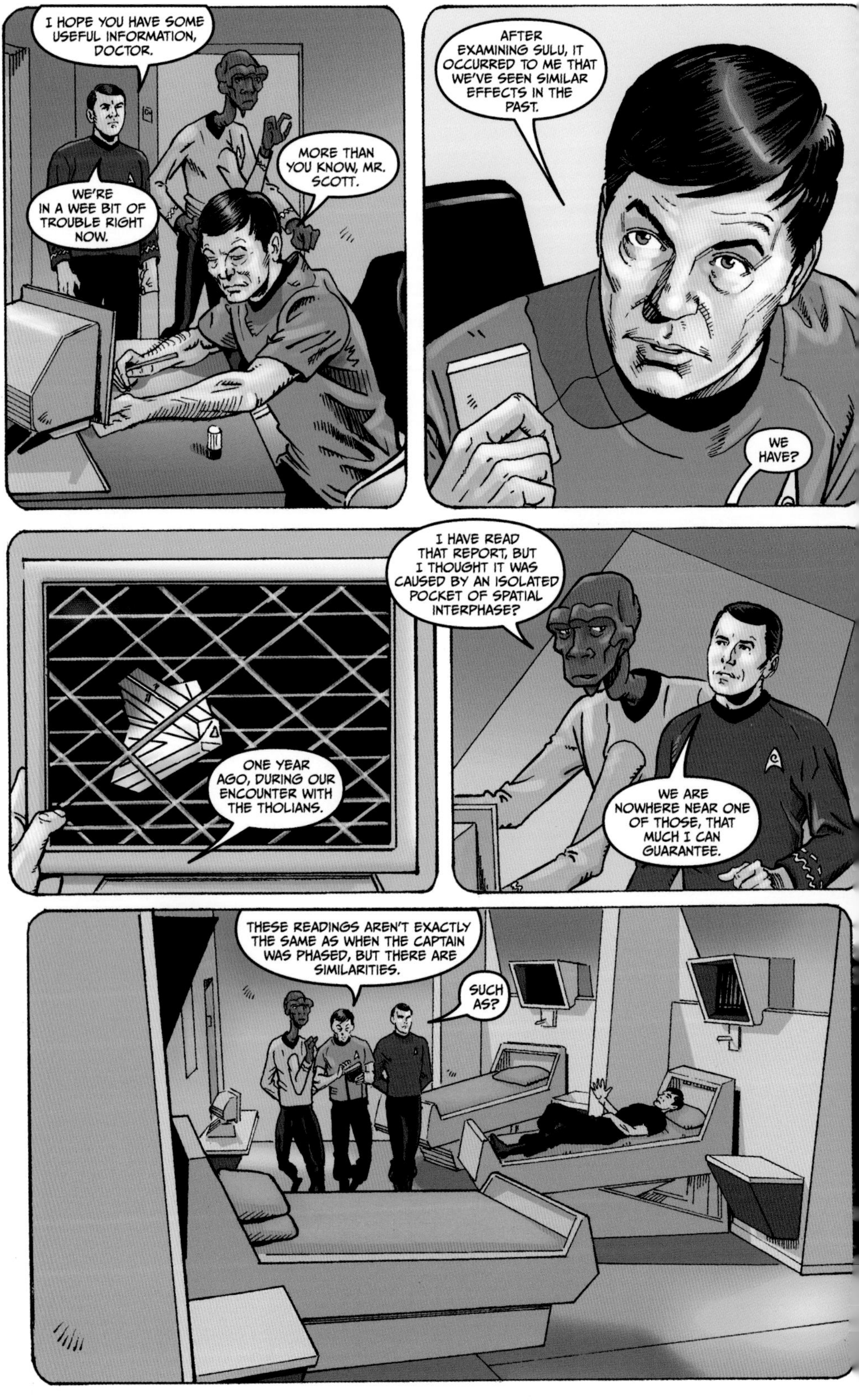
I HOPE YOU HAVE SOME USEFUL INFORMATION, DOCTOR.
WE'RE IN A WEE BIT OF TROUBLE RIGHT NOW.
MORE THAN YOU KNOW, MR. SCOTT.
AFTER EXAMINING SULU, IT OCCURRED TO ME THAT WE'VE SEEN SIMILAR EFFECTS IN THE PAST.
WE HAVE?
ONE YEAR AGO, DURING OUR ENCOUNTER WITH THE THOLIANS.
I HAVE READ THAT REPORT, BUT I THOUGHT IT WAS CAUSED BY AN ISOLATED POCKET OF SPATIAL INTERPHASE?
WE ARE NOWHERE NEAR ONE OF THOSE, THAT MUCH I CAN GUARANTEE.
THESE READINGS AREN'T EXACTLY THE SAME AS WHEN THE CAPTAIN WAS PHASED, BUT THERE ARE SIMILARITIES.
SUCH AS?

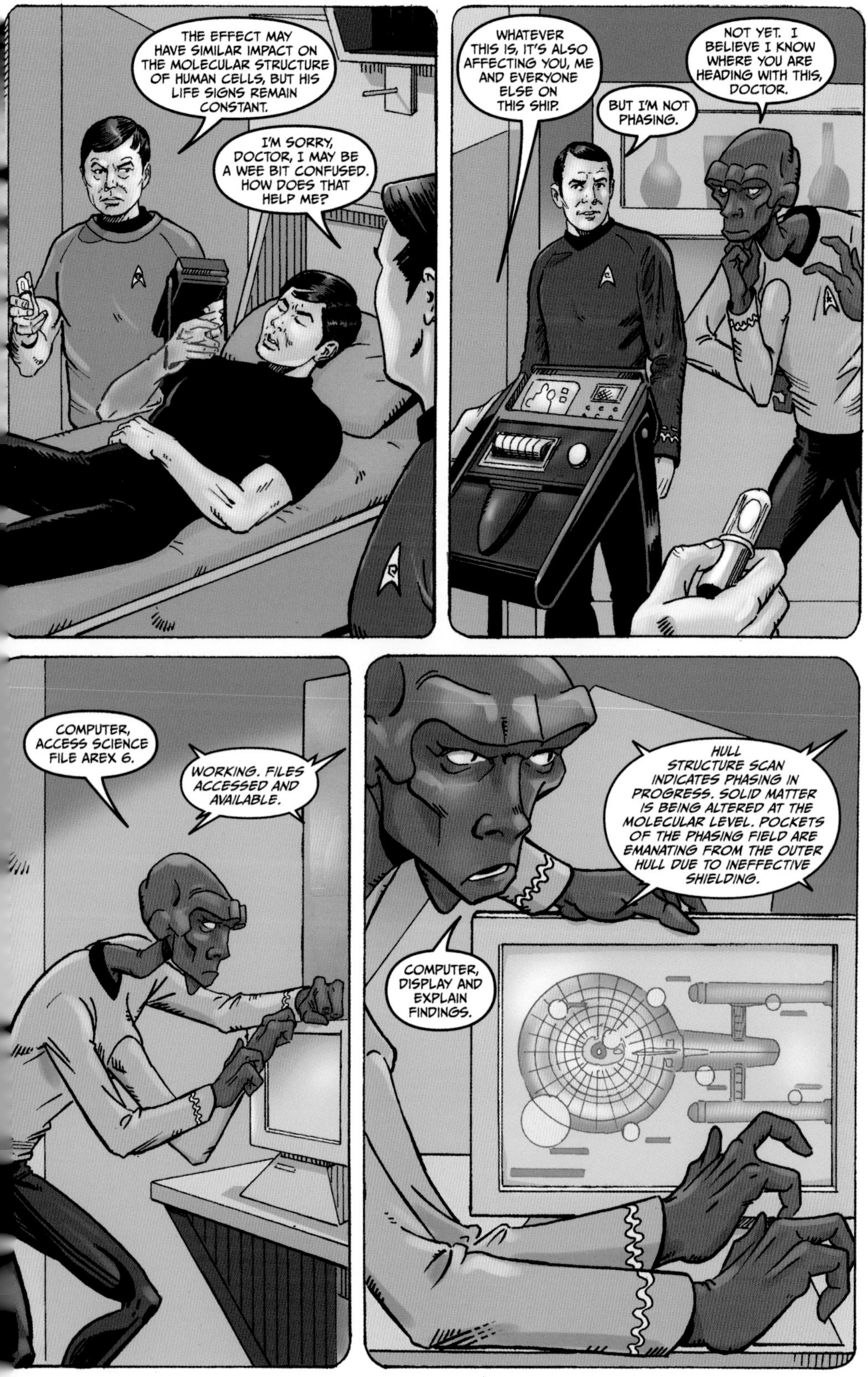
THE EFFECT MAY HAVE SIMILAR IMPACT ON THE MOLECULAR STRUCTURE OF HUMAN CELLS, BUT HIS LIFE SIGNS REMAIN CONSTANT.
I'M SORRY, DOCTOR, I MAY BE A WEE BIT CONFUSED. HOW DOES THAT HELP ME?
WHATEVER THIS IS, IT'S ALSO AFFECTING YOU, ME AND EVERYONE ELSE ON THIS SHIP.
BUT I'M NOT PHASING.
NOT YET. I BELIEVE I KNOW WHERE YOU ARE HEADING WITH THIS, DOCTOR.
COMPUTER, ACCESS SCIENCE FILE AREX 6.
WORKING. FILES ACCESSED AND AVAILABLE.
COMPUTER, DISPLAY AND EXPLAIN FINDINGS.
HULL STRUCTURE SCAN INDICATES PHASING IN PROGRESS. SOLID MATTER IS BEING ALTERED AT THE MOLECULAR LEVEL. POCKETS OF THE PHASING FIELD ARE EMANATING FROM THE OUTER HULL DUE TO INEFFECTIVE SHIELDING.

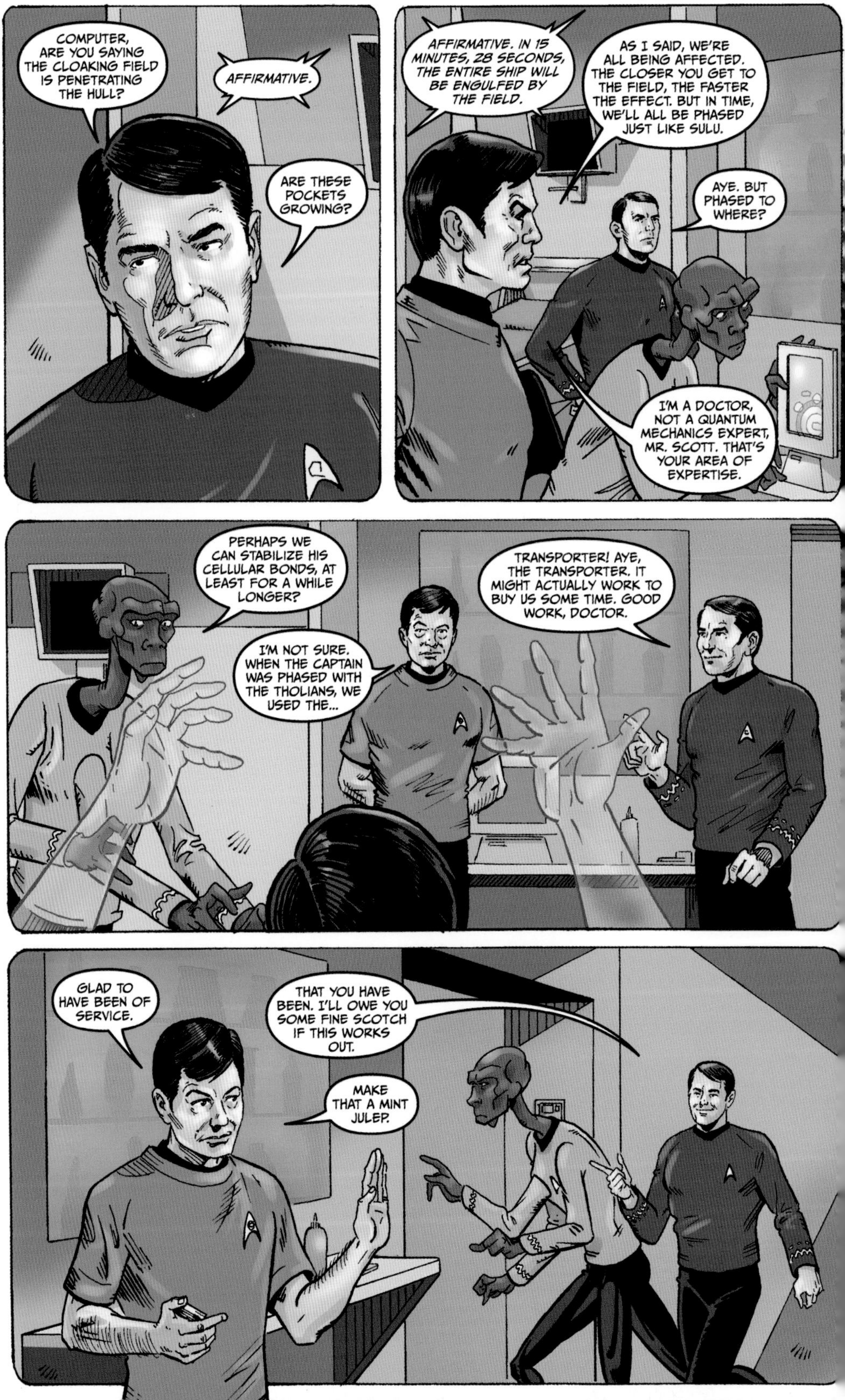
COMPUTER, ARE YOU SAYING THE CLOAKING FIELD IS PENETRATING THE HULL?
AFFIRMATIVE.
ARE THESE POCKETS GROWING?
AFFIRMATIVE. IN 15 MINUTES, 28 SECONDS, THE ENTIRE SHIP WILL BE ENGULFED BY THE FIELD.
AS I SAID, WE'RE ALL BEING AFFECTED. THE CLOSER YOU GET TO THE FIELD, THE FASTER THE EFFECT. BUT IN TIME, WE'LL ALL BE PHASED JUST LIKE SULU.
AYE. BUT PHASED TO WHERE?
I'M A DOCTOR, NOT A QUANTUM MECHANICS EXPERT, MR. SCOTT. THAT'S YOUR AREA OF EXPERTISE.
PERHAPS WE CAN STABILIZE HIS CELLULAR BONDS, AT LEAST FOR A WHILE LONGER?
I'M NOT SURE. WHEN THE CAPTAIN WAS PHASED WITH THE THOLIANS, WE USED THE...
TRANSPORTER! AYE, THE TRANSPORTER. IT MIGHT ACTUALLY WORK TO BUY US SOME TIME. GOOD WORK, DOCTOR.
GLAD TO HAVE BEEN OF SERVICE.
THAT YOU HAVE BEEN. I'LL OWE YOU SOME FINE SCOTCH IF THIS WORKS OUT.
MAKE THAT A MINT JULEP.

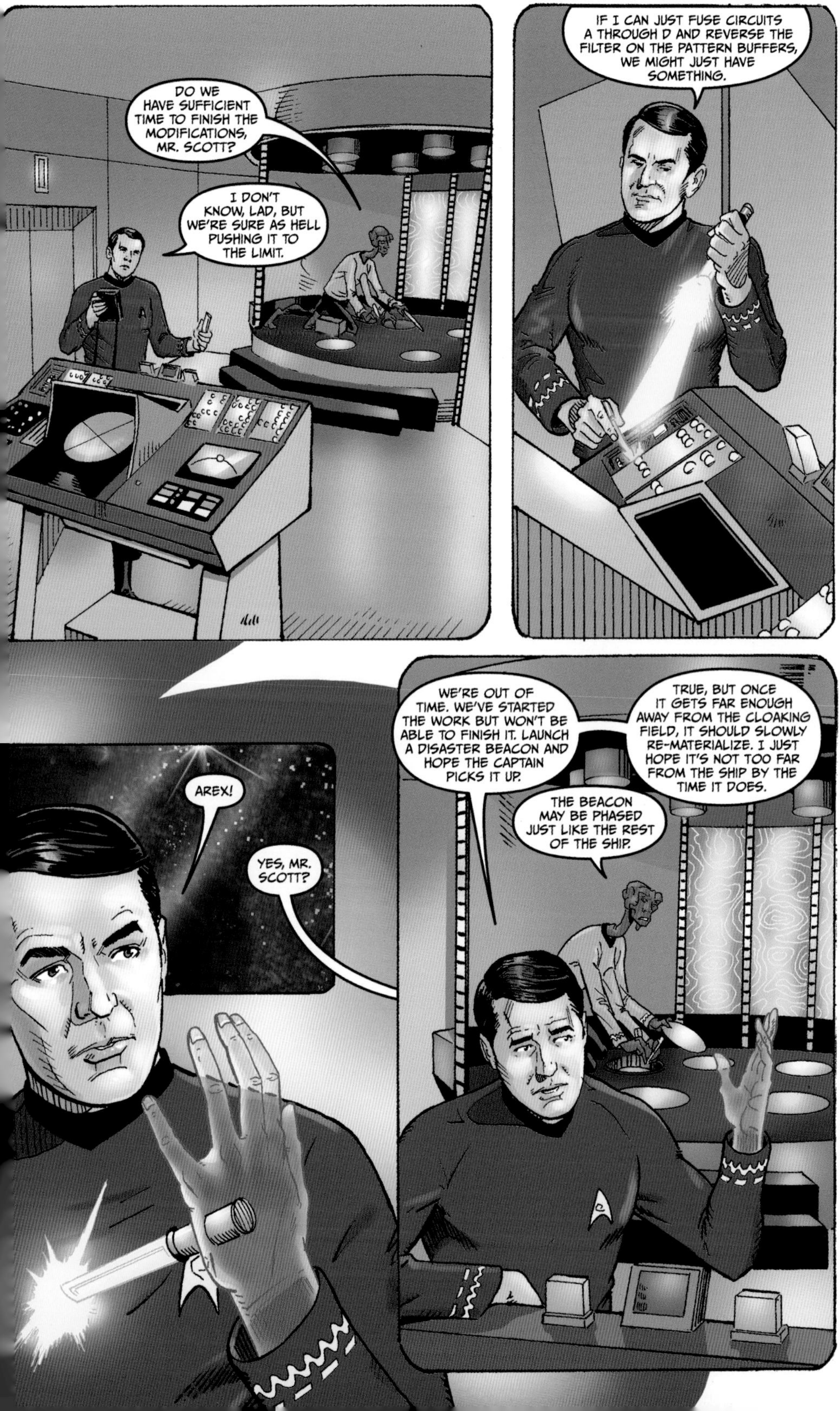
DO WE HAVE SUFFICIENT TIME TO FINISH THE MODIFICATIONS, MR. SCOTT?
I DON'T KNOW, LAD, BUT WE'RE SURE AS HELL PUSHING IT TO THE LIMIT.
IF I CAN JUST FUSE CIRCUITS A THROUGH D AND REVERSE THE FILTER ON THE PATTERN BUFFERS, WE MIGHT JUST HAVE SOMETHING.
AREX!
YES, MR. SCOTT?
WE'RE OUT OF TIME. WE'VE STARTED THE WORK BUT WON'T BE ABLE TO FINISH IT. LAUNCH A DISASTER BEACON AND HOPE THE CAPTAIN PICKS IT UP.
THE BEACON MAY BE PHASED JUST LIKE THE REST OF THE SHIP.
TRUE, BUT ONCE IT GETS FAR ENOUGH AWAY FROM THE CLOAKING FIELD, IT SHOULD SLOWLY RE-MATERIALIZE. I JUST HOPE IT'S NOT TOO FAR FROM THE SHIP BY THE TIME IT DOES.

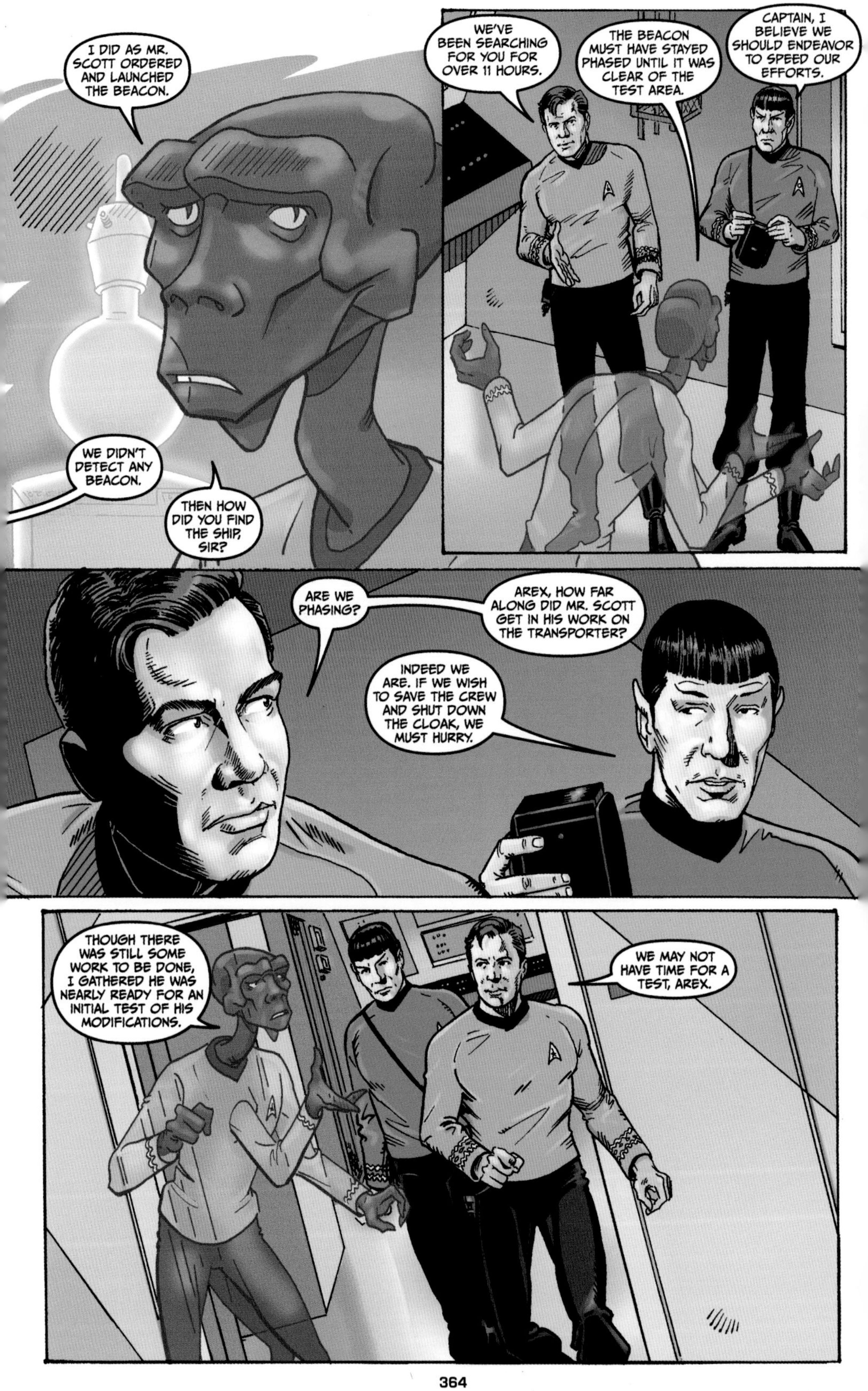
I DID AS MR. SCOTT ORDERED AND LAUNCHED THE BEACON.
WE'VE BEEN SEARCHING FOR YOU FOR OVER 11 HOURS.
THE BEACON MUST HAVE STAYED PHASED UNTIL IT WAS CLEAR OF THE TEST AREA.
CAPTAIN, I BELIEVE WE SHOULD ENDEAVOR TO SPEED OUR EFFORTS.
WE DIDN'T DETECT ANY BEACON.
THEN HOW DID YOU FIND THE SHIP, SIR?
ARE WE PHASING?
INDEED WE ARE. IF WE WISH TO SAVE THE CREW AND SHUT DOWN THE CLOAK, WE MUST HURRY.
AREX, HOW FAR ALONG DID MR. SCOTT GET IN HIS WORK ON THE TRANSPORTER?
THOUGH THERE WAS STILL SOME WORK TO BE DONE, I GATHERED HE WAS NEARLY READY FOR AN INITIAL TEST OF HIS MODIFICATIONS.
WE MAY NOT HAVE TIME FOR A TEST, AREX.

AREX, DID YOU COMPLETE THE MODIFICATIONS TO THE TRANSPORTER PLATFORM?
EVERYTHING THAT MR. SCOTT ASKED OF ME, YES.
THEN LET'S SEE WHAT REMAINS TO BE DONE HERE.
IT APPEARS MR. SCOTT WAS IN THE PROCESS OF FUSING CIRCUITS A THROUGH D WHEN HE BEGAN TO PHASE.
HE ALSO SAID SOMETHING REGARDING THE PATTERN BUFFERS.
YES, REVERSING THE POLARITY OF THE BUFFERS FILTER WOULD IN THEORY ADD TO PATTERN RESTORATION.
SPOCK, HOW MUCH TIME?
UNKNOWN, CAPTAIN. WE COULD BEGIN PHASING AT ANY MOMENT.
CAN WE DO ANYTHING TO SLOW DOWN THE PROCESS?
A SLIGHT POSSIBILITY, CAPTAIN. AREX MENTIONED THAT THE COMPUTER ANALYZED THE HULL SHIELDING AS INSUFFICIENT TO KEEP THE CLOAKING FIELD FROM PENETRATING IT.
WE COULD USE THE ENVIRONMENT SUITS.
THEY *ARE* SHIELDED AGAINST MOST FORMS OF RADIATION. PERHAPS IT IS ENOUGH TO IMPEDE THE PROCESS FOR A LIMITED TIME.

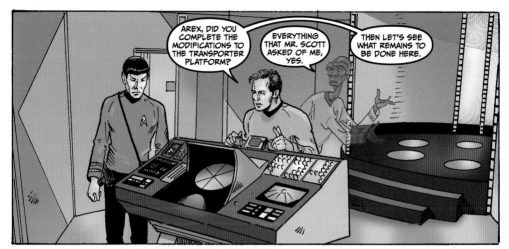

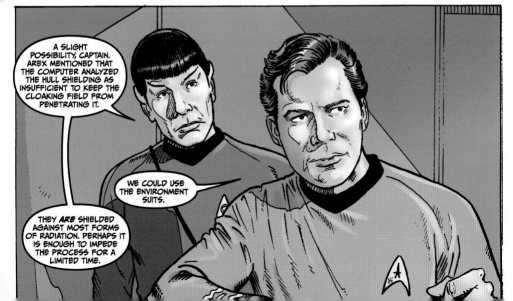

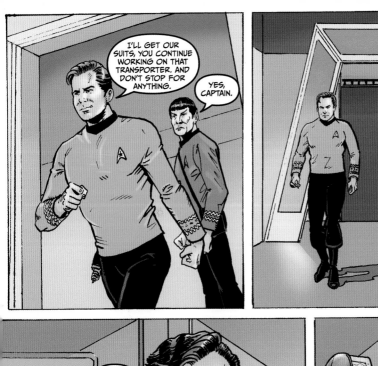

I'LL GET OUR SUITS, YOU CONTINUE WORKING ON THAT TRANSPORTER. AND DON'T STOP FOR ANYTHING.

YES, CAPTAIN.

PROXIMITY ALERT

KIRK TO SPOCK.

SPOCK HERE, CAPTAIN.

PHASER CONTROL SENSORS ARE INDICATING A PROXIMITY ALERT. I CAN'T GET AN EXTERIOR VISUAL FROM HERE, CAN'T TELL IF IT'S ANOTHER VESSEL OR SOMETHING ELSE, BUT WE MAY NEED TO MOVE THE SHIP.

AGREED.

PROGRESS, SPOCK?

A FEW MORE ADJUSTMENTS, AND I BELIEVE IT MAY BE POSSIBLE TO TEMPORARILY RECONSTITUTE MEMBERS OF THE CREW TO ASSIST US IN SHUTTING DOWN THE CLOAKING FIELD.

FINISH YOUR WORK. I'M GOING TO THE BRIDGE TO FIND OUT WHAT'S HAPPENING. KEEP ME INFORMED.

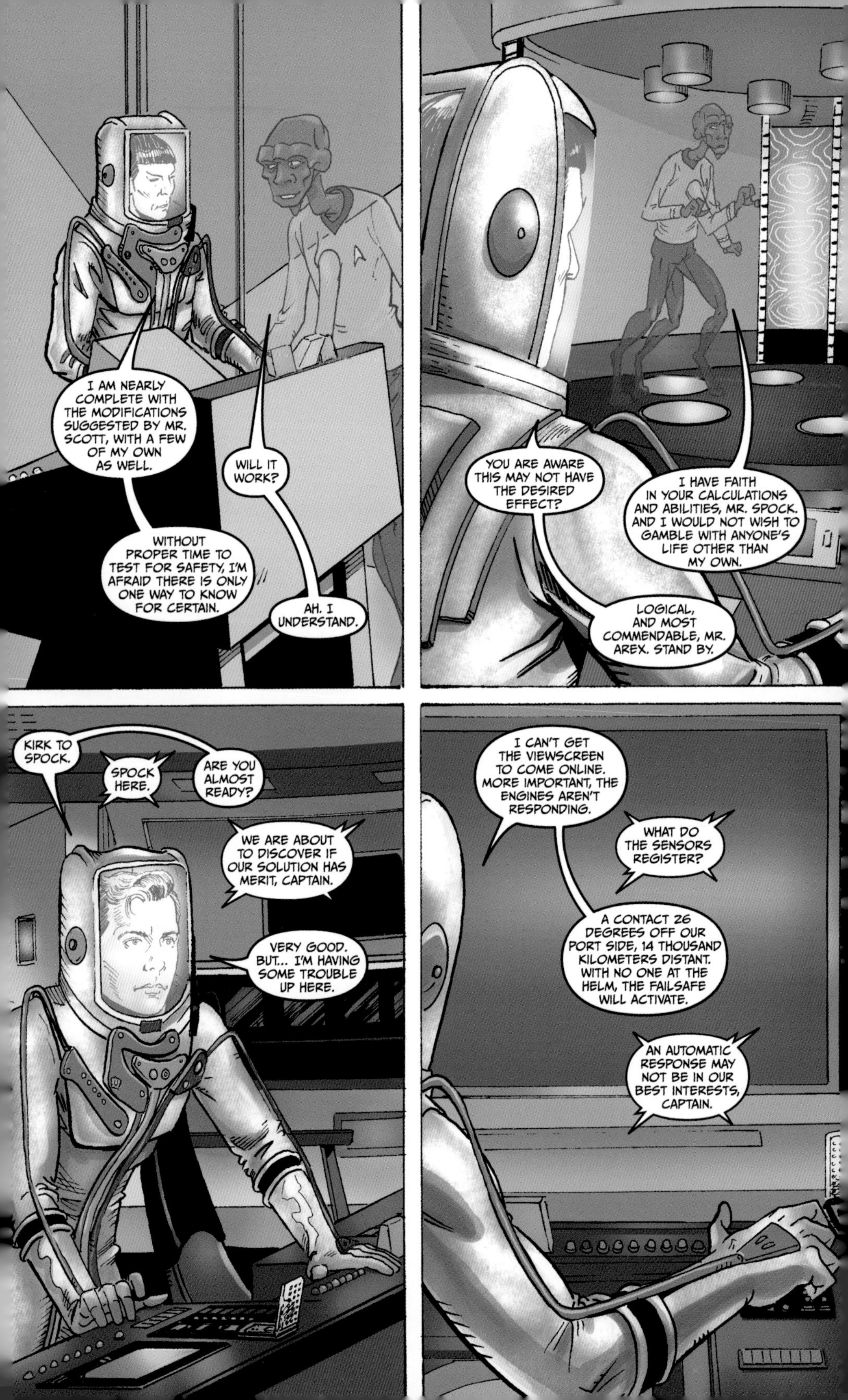
I AM NEARLY COMPLETE WITH THE MODIFICATIONS SUGGESTED BY MR. SCOTT, WITH A FEW OF MY OWN AS WELL.
WILL IT WORK?
WITHOUT PROPER TIME TO TEST FOR SAFETY, I'M AFRAID THERE IS ONLY ONE WAY TO KNOW FOR CERTAIN.
AH. I UNDERSTAND.
YOU ARE AWARE THIS MAY NOT HAVE THE DESIRED EFFECT?
I HAVE FAITH IN YOUR CALCULATIONS AND ABILITIES, MR. SPOCK. AND I WOULD NOT WISH TO GAMBLE WITH ANYONE'S LIFE OTHER THAN MY OWN.
LOGICAL, AND MOST COMMENDABLE, MR. AREX. STAND BY.
KIRK TO SPOCK.
SPOCK HERE.
ARE YOU ALMOST READY?
WE ARE ABOUT TO DISCOVER IF OUR SOLUTION HAS MERIT, CAPTAIN.
VERY GOOD. BUT... I'M HAVING SOME TROUBLE UP HERE.
I CAN'T GET THE VIEWSCREEN TO COME ONLINE. MORE IMPORTANT, THE ENGINES AREN'T RESPONDING.
WHAT DO THE SENSORS REGISTER?
A CONTACT 26 DEGREES OFF OUR PORT SIDE, 14 THOUSAND KILOMETERS DISTANT. WITH NO ONE AT THE HELM, THE FAILSAFE WILL ACTIVATE.
AN AUTOMATIC RESPONSE MAY NOT BE IN OUR BEST INTERESTS, CAPTAIN.

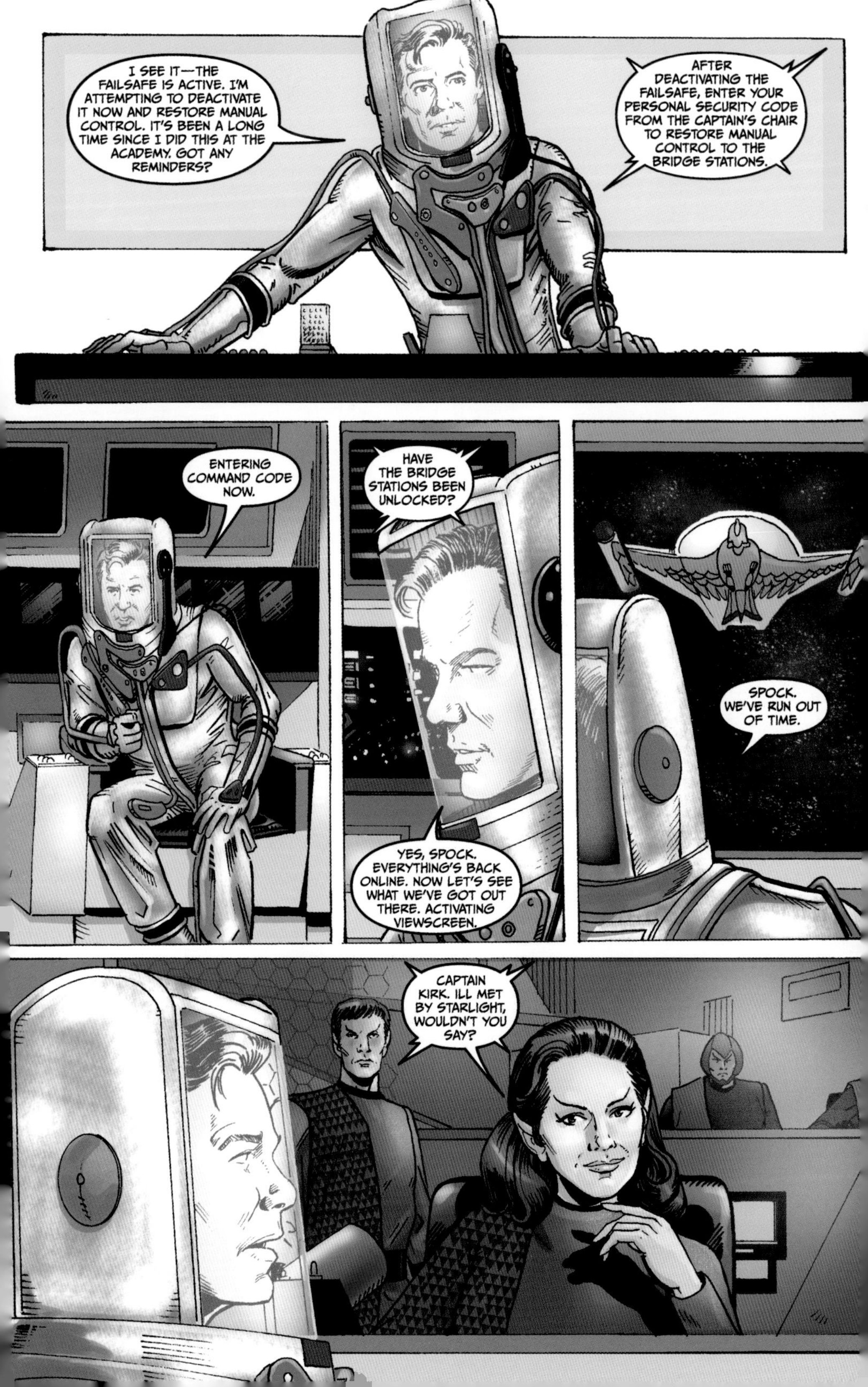
I SEE IT—THE FAILSAFE IS ACTIVE. I'M ATTEMPTING TO DEACTIVATE IT NOW AND RESTORE MANUAL CONTROL. IT'S BEEN A LONG TIME SINCE I DID THIS AT THE ACADEMY. GOT ANY REMINDERS?
AFTER DEACTIVATING THE FAILSAFE, ENTER YOUR PERSONAL SECURITY CODE FROM THE CAPTAIN'S CHAIR TO RESTORE MANUAL CONTROL TO THE BRIDGE STATIONS.
ENTERING COMMAND CODE NOW.
HAVE THE BRIDGE STATIONS BEEN UNLOCKED?
YES, SPOCK. EVERYTHING'S BACK ONLINE. NOW LET'S SEE WHAT WE'VE GOT OUT THERE. ACTIVATING VIEWSCREEN.
SPOCK. WE'VE RUN OUT OF TIME.
CAPTAIN KIRK. ILL MET BY STARLIGHT, WOULDN'T YOU SAY?

IT SHOULD BE UNDERSTOOD, I AM A PATRIOT, SPOCK. I WILL SHARE THE KNOWLEDGE OF MY EXPERIENCES HERE.

I WOULD EXPECT NOTHING LESS.

AS OUR AGREEMENT WITH THE FEDERATION STIPULATED, I HAVE BROUGHT AMBASSADOR SAREK.

IT SHOULD BE NOTED THAT ALTHOUGH YOU HAVE USED THIS OPPORTUNITY TO REGAIN YOUR FORMER COMMANDER, THE AMBASSADOR WAS FULLY PROTECTED BY HIS DIPLOMATIC CREDENTIALS.

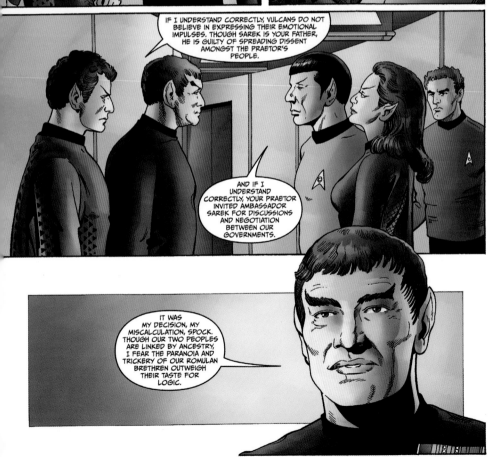

IF I UNDERSTAND CORRECTLY, VULCANS DO NOT BELIEVE IN EXPRESSING THEIR EMOTIONAL IMPULSES. THOUGH SAREK IS YOUR FATHER, HE IS GUILTY OF SPREADING DISSENT AMONGST THE PRAETOR'S PEOPLE.

AND IF I UNDERSTAND CORRECTLY, YOUR PRAETOR INVITED AMBASSADOR SAREK FOR DISCUSSIONS AND NEGOTIATION BETWEEN OUR GOVERNMENTS.

IT WAS MY DECISION, MY MISCALCULATION, SPOCK. THOUGH OUR TWO PEOPLES ARE LINKED BY ANCESTRY, I FEAR THE PARANOIA AND TRICKERY OF OUR ROMULAN BRETHREN OUTWEIGH THEIR TASTE FOR LOGIC.

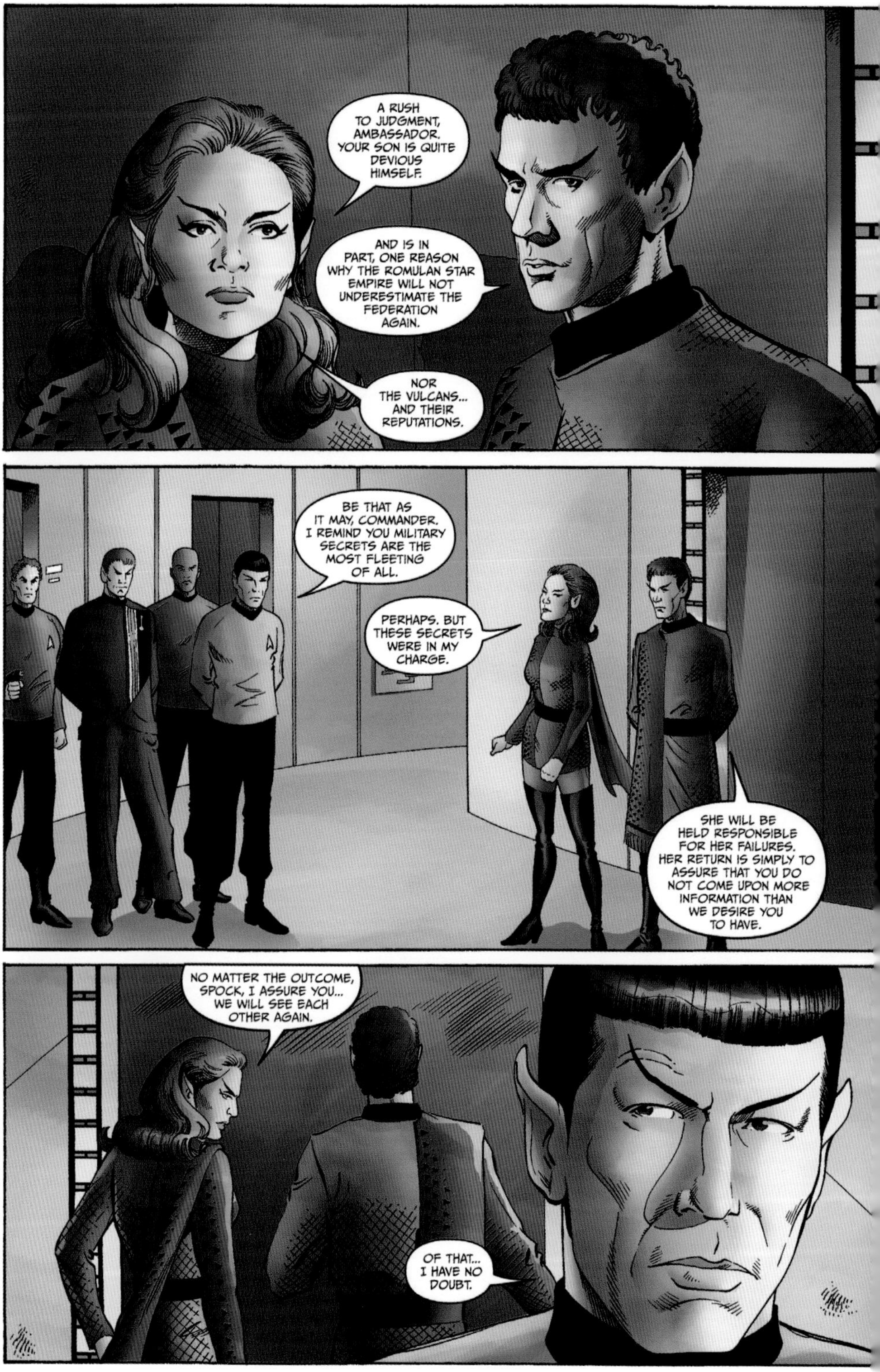
A RUSH TO JUDGMENT, AMBASSADOR. YOUR SON IS QUITE DEVIOUS HIMSELF.
AND IS IN PART, ONE REASON WHY THE ROMULAN STAR EMPIRE WILL NOT UNDERESTIMATE THE FEDERATION AGAIN.
NOR THE VULCANS... AND THEIR REPUTATIONS.
BE THAT AS IT MAY, COMMANDER. I REMIND YOU MILITARY SECRETS ARE THE MOST FLEETING OF ALL.
PERHAPS. BUT THESE SECRETS WERE IN MY CHARGE.
SHE WILL BE HELD RESPONSIBLE FOR HER FAILURES. HER RETURN IS SIMPLY TO ASSURE THAT YOU DO NOT COME UPON MORE INFORMATION THAN WE DESIRE YOU TO HAVE.
NO MATTER THE OUTCOME, SPOCK, I ASSURE YOU... WE WILL SEE EACH OTHER AGAIN.
OF THAT... I HAVE NO DOUBT.

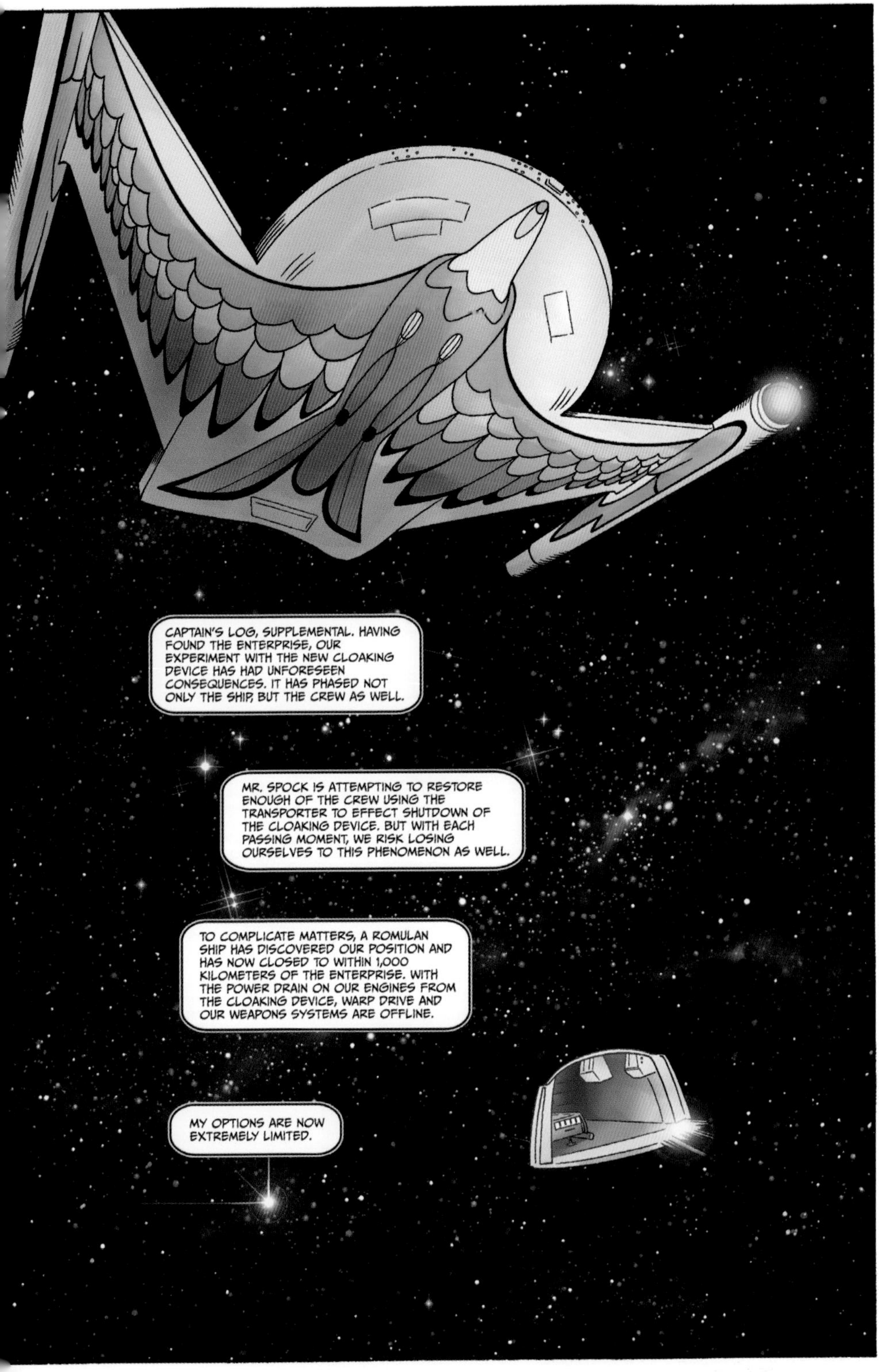
CAPTAIN'S LOG, SUPPLEMENTAL. HAVING FOUND THE ENTERPRISE, OUR EXPERIMENT WITH THE NEW CLOAKING DEVICE HAS HAD UNFORESEEN CONSEQUENCES. IT HAS PHASED NOT ONLY THE SHIP, BUT THE CREW AS WELL.
MR. SPOCK IS ATTEMPTING TO RESTORE ENOUGH OF THE CREW USING THE TRANSPORTER TO EFFECT SHUTDOWN OF THE CLOAKING DEVICE. BUT WITH EACH PASSING MOMENT, WE RISK LOSING OURSELVES TO THIS PHENOMENON AS WELL.
TO COMPLICATE MATTERS, A ROMULAN SHIP HAS DISCOVERED OUR POSITION AND HAS NOW CLOSED TO WITHIN 1,000 KILOMETERS OF THE ENTERPRISE. WITH THE POWER DRAIN ON OUR ENGINES FROM THE CLOAKING DEVICE, WARP DRIVE AND OUR WEAPONS SYSTEMS ARE OFFLINE.
MY OPTIONS ARE NOW EXTREMELY LIMITED.

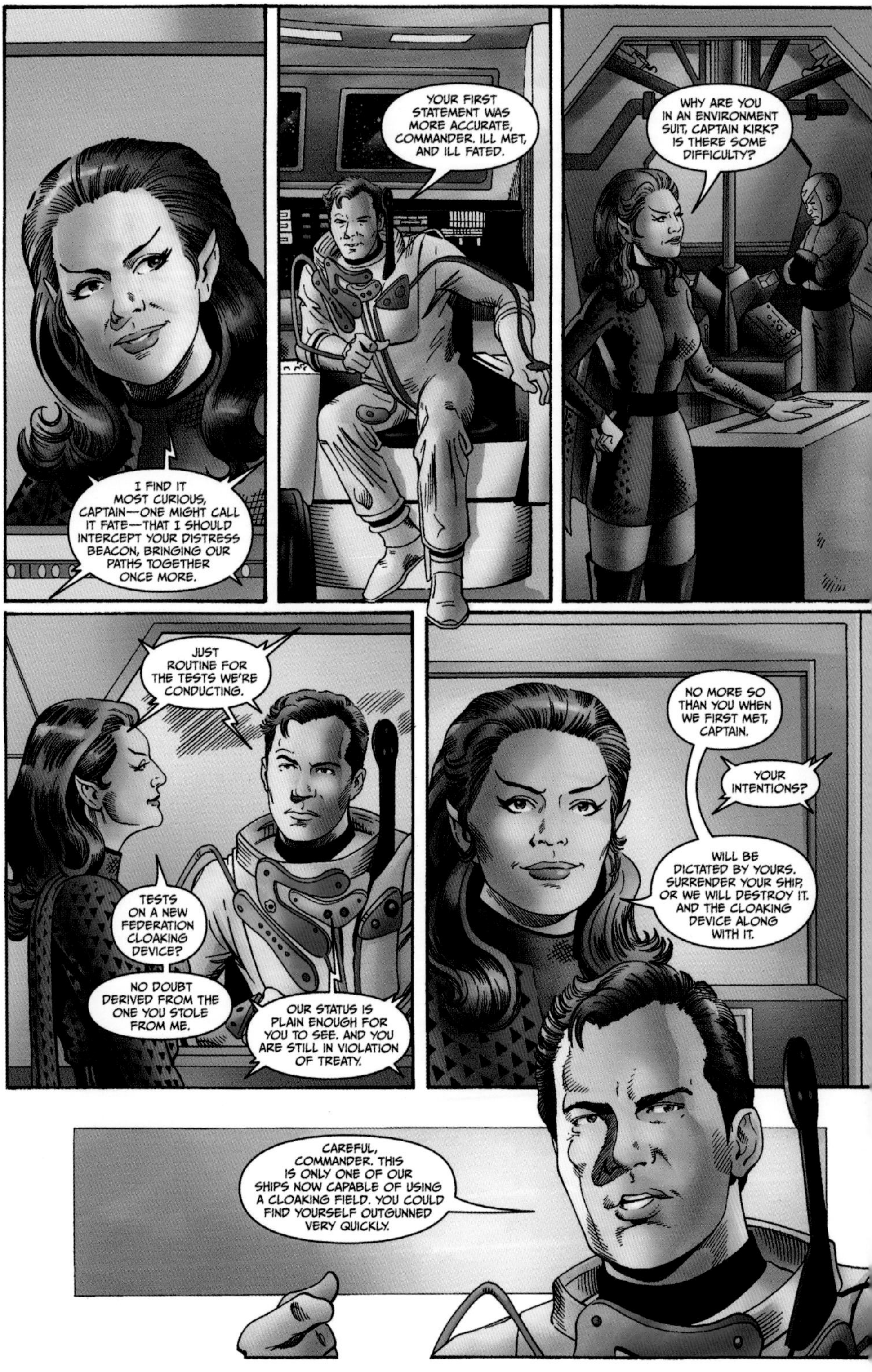
I FIND IT MOST CURIOUS, CAPTAIN—ONE MIGHT CALL IT FATE—THAT I SHOULD INTERCEPT YOUR DISTRESS BEACON, BRINGING OUR PATHS TOGETHER ONCE MORE.
YOUR FIRST STATEMENT WAS MORE ACCURATE, COMMANDER. ILL MET, AND ILL FATED.
WHY ARE YOU IN AN ENVIRONMENT SUIT, CAPTAIN KIRK? IS THERE SOME DIFFICULTY?
JUST ROUTINE FOR THE TESTS WE'RE CONDUCTING.
TESTS ON A NEW FEDERATION CLOAKING DEVICE?
NO DOUBT DERIVED FROM THE ONE YOU STOLE FROM ME.
OUR STATUS IS PLAIN ENOUGH FOR YOU TO SEE. AND YOU ARE STILL IN VIOLATION OF TREATY.
NO MORE SO THAN YOU WHEN WE FIRST MET, CAPTAIN.
YOUR INTENTIONS?
WILL BE DICTATED BY YOURS. SURRENDER YOUR SHIP, OR WE WILL DESTROY IT. AND THE CLOAKING DEVICE ALONG WITH IT.
CAREFUL, COMMANDER. THIS IS ONLY ONE OF OUR SHIPS NOW CAPABLE OF USING A CLOAKING FIELD. YOU COULD FIND YOURSELF OUTGUNNED VERY QUICKLY.

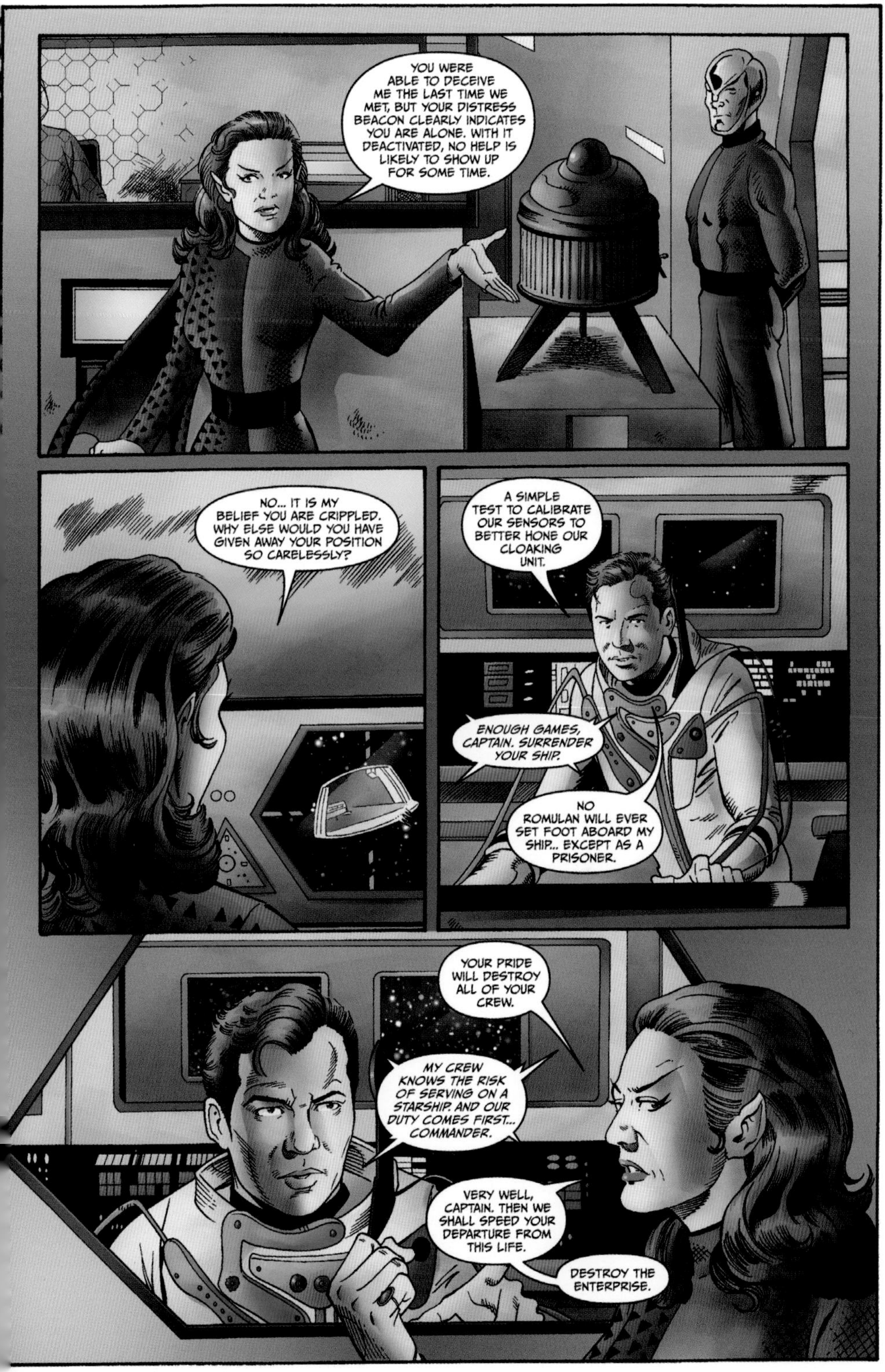
YOU WERE ABLE TO DECEIVE ME THE LAST TIME WE MET, BUT YOUR DISTRESS BEACON CLEARLY INDICATES YOU ARE ALONE. WITH IT DEACTIVATED, NO HELP IS LIKELY TO SHOW UP FOR SOME TIME.
NO... IT IS MY BELIEF YOU ARE CRIPPLED. WHY ELSE WOULD YOU HAVE GIVEN AWAY YOUR POSITION SO CARELESSLY?
A SIMPLE TEST TO CALIBRATE OUR SENSORS TO BETTER HONE OUR CLOAKING UNIT.
ENOUGH GAMES, CAPTAIN. SURRENDER YOUR SHIP.
NO ROMULAN WILL EVER SET FOOT ABOARD MY SHIP... EXCEPT AS A PRISONER.
YOUR PRIDE WILL DESTROY ALL OF YOUR CREW.
MY CREW KNOWS THE RISK OF SERVING ON A STARSHIP. AND OUR DUTY COMES FIRST... COMMANDER.
VERY WELL, CAPTAIN. THEN WE SHALL SPEED YOUR DEPARTURE FROM THIS LIFE.
DESTROY THE ENTERPRISE.

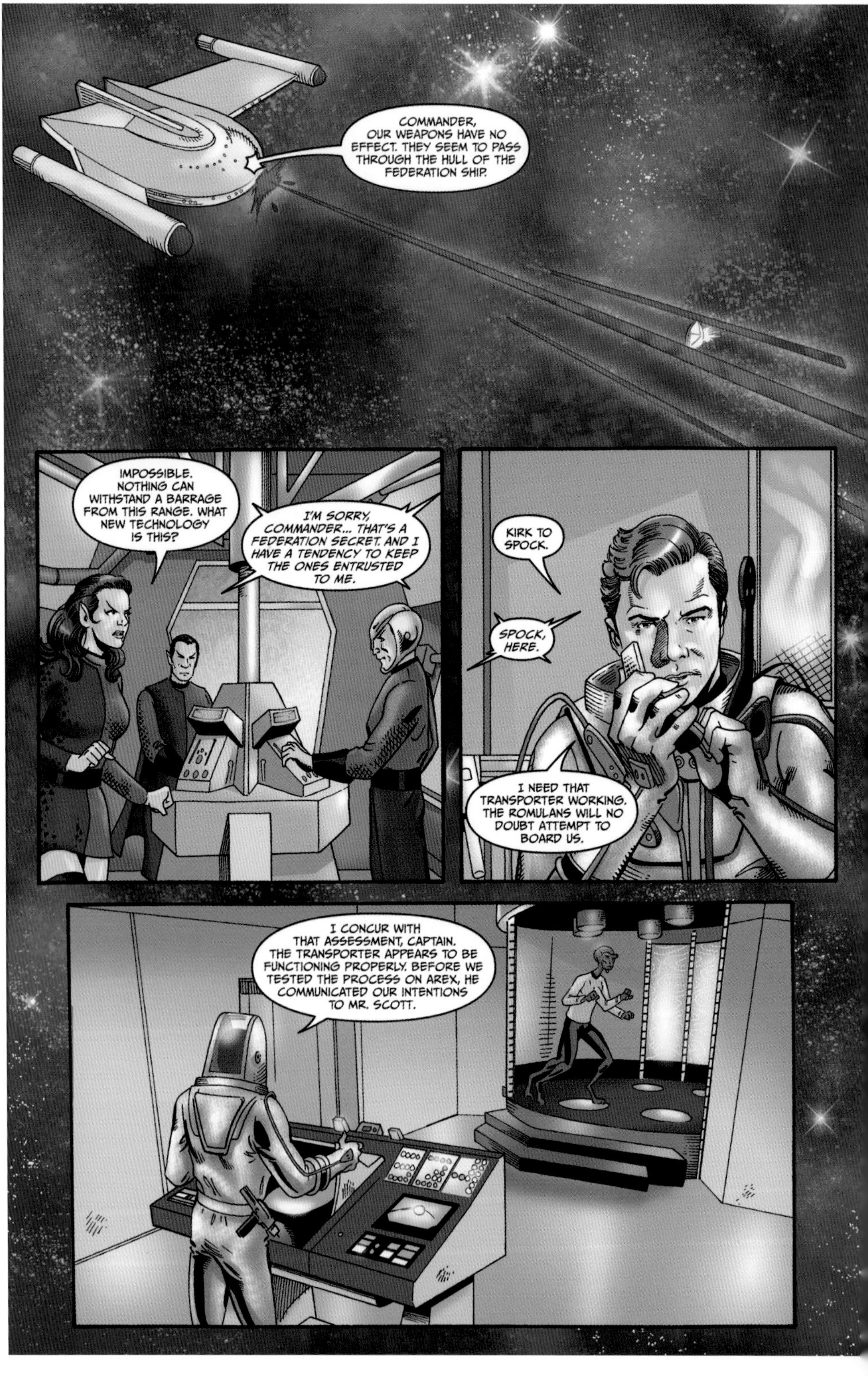
COMMANDER, OUR WEAPONS HAVE NO EFFECT. THEY SEEM TO PASS THROUGH THE HULL OF THE FEDERATION SHIP.
IMPOSSIBLE. NOTHING CAN WITHSTAND A BARRAGE FROM THIS RANGE. WHAT NEW TECHNOLOGY IS THIS?
I'M SORRY, COMMANDER... THAT'S A FEDERATION SECRET. AND I HAVE A TENDENCY TO KEEP THE ONES ENTRUSTED TO ME.
KIRK TO SPOCK.
SPOCK, HERE.
I NEED THAT TRANSPORTER WORKING. THE ROMULANS WILL NO DOUBT ATTEMPT TO BOARD US.
I CONCUR WITH THAT ASSESSMENT, CAPTAIN. THE TRANSPORTER APPEARS TO BE FUNCTIONING PROPERLY. BEFORE WE TESTED THE PROCESS ON AREX, HE COMMUNICATED OUR INTENTIONS TO MR. SCOTT.

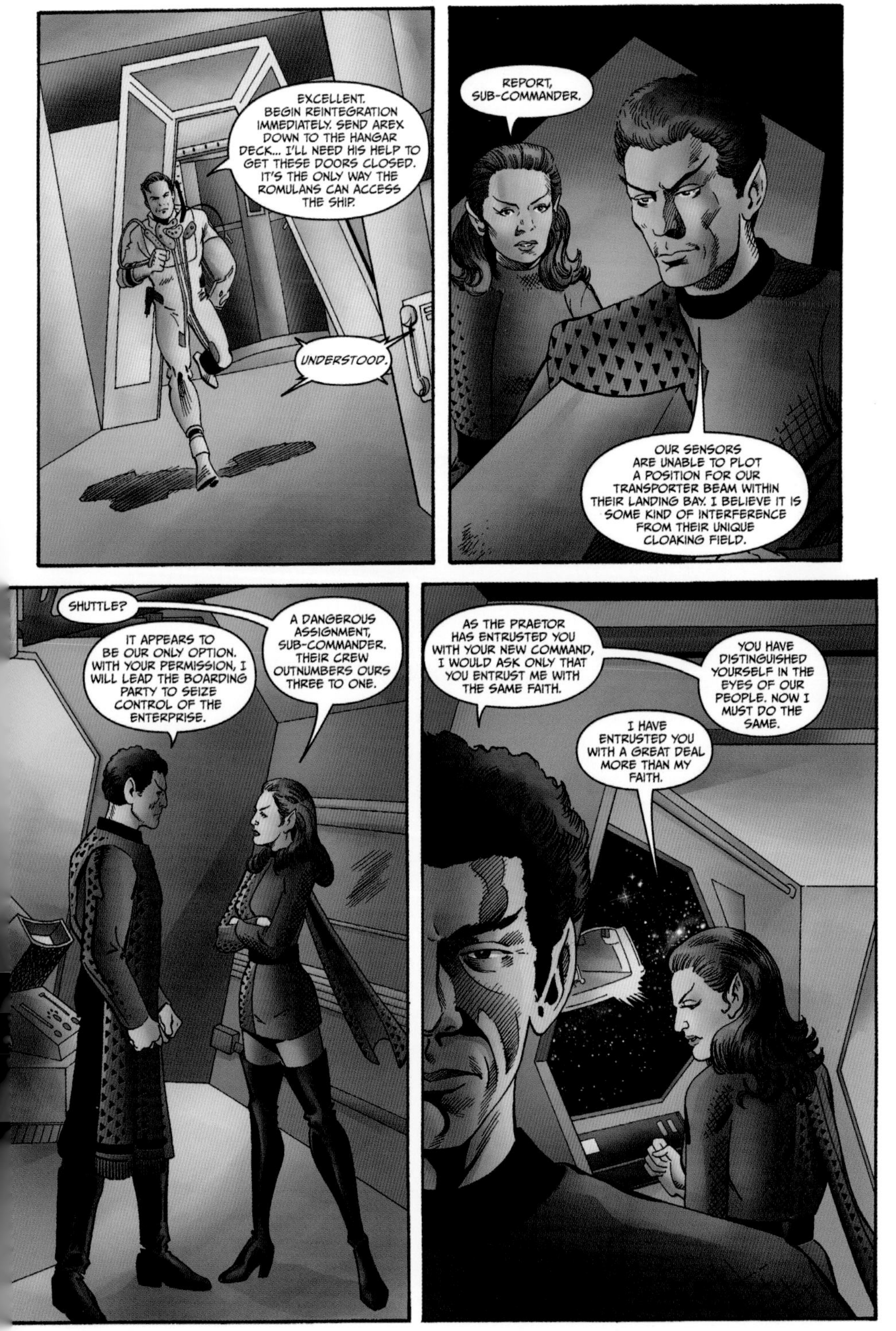
EXCELLENT. BEGIN REINTEGRATION IMMEDIATELY. SEND AREX DOWN TO THE HANGAR DECK... I'LL NEED HIS HELP TO GET THESE DOORS CLOSED. IT'S THE ONLY WAY THE ROMULANS CAN ACCESS THE SHIP.
UNDERSTOOD.
REPORT, SUB-COMMANDER.
OUR SENSORS ARE UNABLE TO PLOT A POSITION FOR OUR TRANSPORTER BEAM WITHIN THEIR LANDING BAY. I BELIEVE IT IS SOME KIND OF INTERFERENCE FROM THEIR UNIQUE CLOAKING FIELD.
SHUTTLE?
IT APPEARS TO BE OUR ONLY OPTION. WITH YOUR PERMISSION, I WILL LEAD THE BOARDING PARTY TO SEIZE CONTROL OF THE ENTERPRISE.
A DANGEROUS ASSIGNMENT, SUB-COMMANDER. THEIR CREW OUTNUMBERS OURS THREE TO ONE.
AS THE PRAETOR HAS ENTRUSTED YOU WITH YOUR NEW COMMAND, I WOULD ASK ONLY THAT YOU ENTRUST ME WITH THE SAME FAITH.
YOU HAVE DISTINGUISHED YOURSELF IN THE EYES OF OUR PEOPLE. NOW I MUST DO THE SAME.
I HAVE ENTRUSTED YOU WITH A GREAT DEAL MORE THAN MY FAITH.

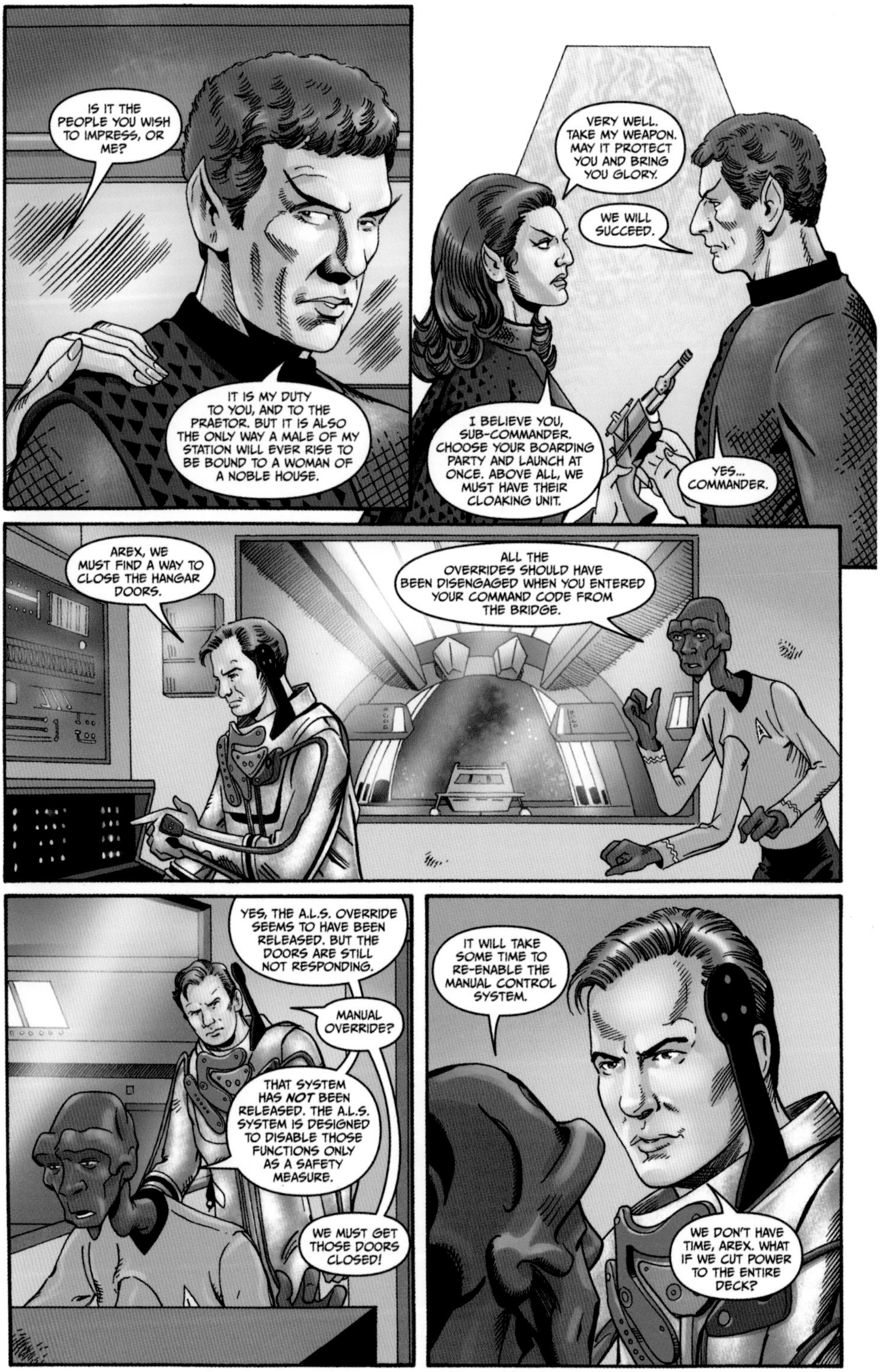
IS IT THE PEOPLE YOU WISH TO IMPRESS, OR ME?
IT IS MY DUTY TO YOU, AND TO THE PRAETOR. BUT IT IS ALSO THE ONLY WAY A MALE OF MY STATION WILL EVER RISE TO BE BOUND TO A WOMAN OF A NOBLE HOUSE.
VERY WELL. TAKE MY WEAPON. MAY IT PROTECT YOU AND BRING YOU GLORY.
WE WILL SUCCEED.
I BELIEVE YOU, SUB-COMMANDER. CHOOSE YOUR BOARDING PARTY AND LAUNCH AT ONCE. ABOVE ALL, WE MUST HAVE THEIR CLOAKING UNIT.
YES... COMMANDER.
AREX, WE MUST FIND A WAY TO CLOSE THE HANGAR DOORS.
ALL THE OVERRIDES SHOULD HAVE BEEN DISENGAGED WHEN YOU ENTERED YOUR COMMAND CODE FROM THE BRIDGE.
YES, THE A.L.S. OVERRIDE SEEMS TO HAVE BEEN RELEASED. BUT THE DOORS ARE STILL NOT RESPONDING.
MANUAL OVERRIDE?
THAT SYSTEM HAS *NOT* BEEN RELEASED. THE A.L.S. SYSTEM IS DESIGNED TO DISABLE THOSE FUNCTIONS ONLY AS A SAFETY MEASURE.
WE MUST GET THOSE DOORS CLOSED!
IT WILL TAKE SOME TIME TO RE-ENABLE THE MANUAL CONTROL SYSTEM.
WE DON'T HAVE TIME, AREX. WHAT IF WE CUT POWER TO THE ENTIRE DECK?

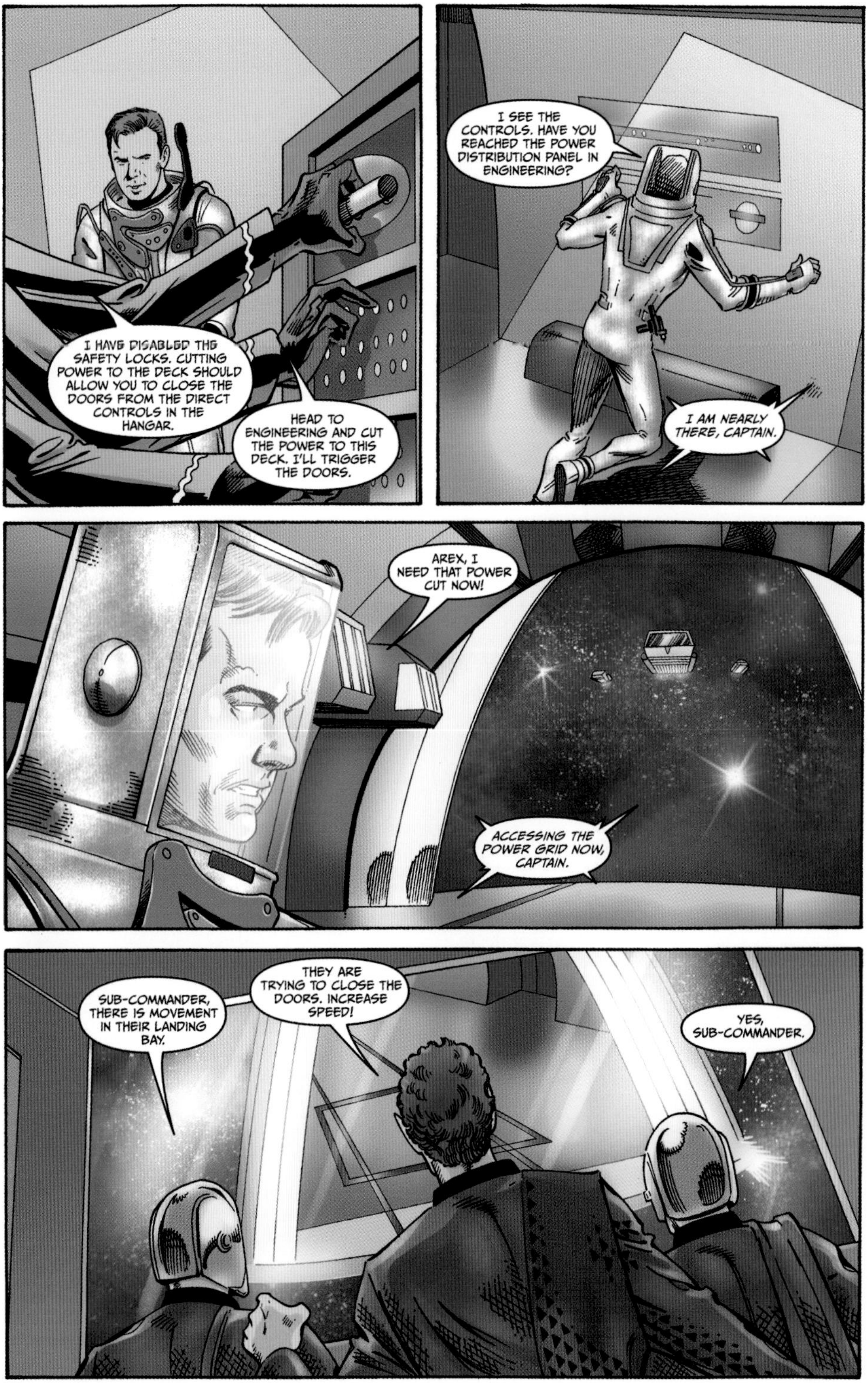
I HAVE DISABLED THE SAFETY LOCKS. CUTTING POWER TO THE DECK SHOULD ALLOW YOU TO CLOSE THE DOORS FROM THE DIRECT CONTROLS IN THE HANGAR.
HEAD TO ENGINEERING AND CUT THE POWER TO THIS DECK. I'LL TRIGGER THE DOORS.
I SEE THE CONTROLS. HAVE YOU REACHED THE POWER DISTRIBUTION PANEL IN ENGINEERING?
I AM NEARLY THERE, CAPTAIN.
AREX, I NEED THAT POWER CUT NOW!
ACCESSING THE POWER GRID NOW, CAPTAIN.
SUB-COMMANDER, THERE IS MOVEMENT IN THEIR LANDING BAY.
THEY ARE TRYING TO CLOSE THE DOORS. INCREASE SPEED!
YES, SUB-COMMANDER.

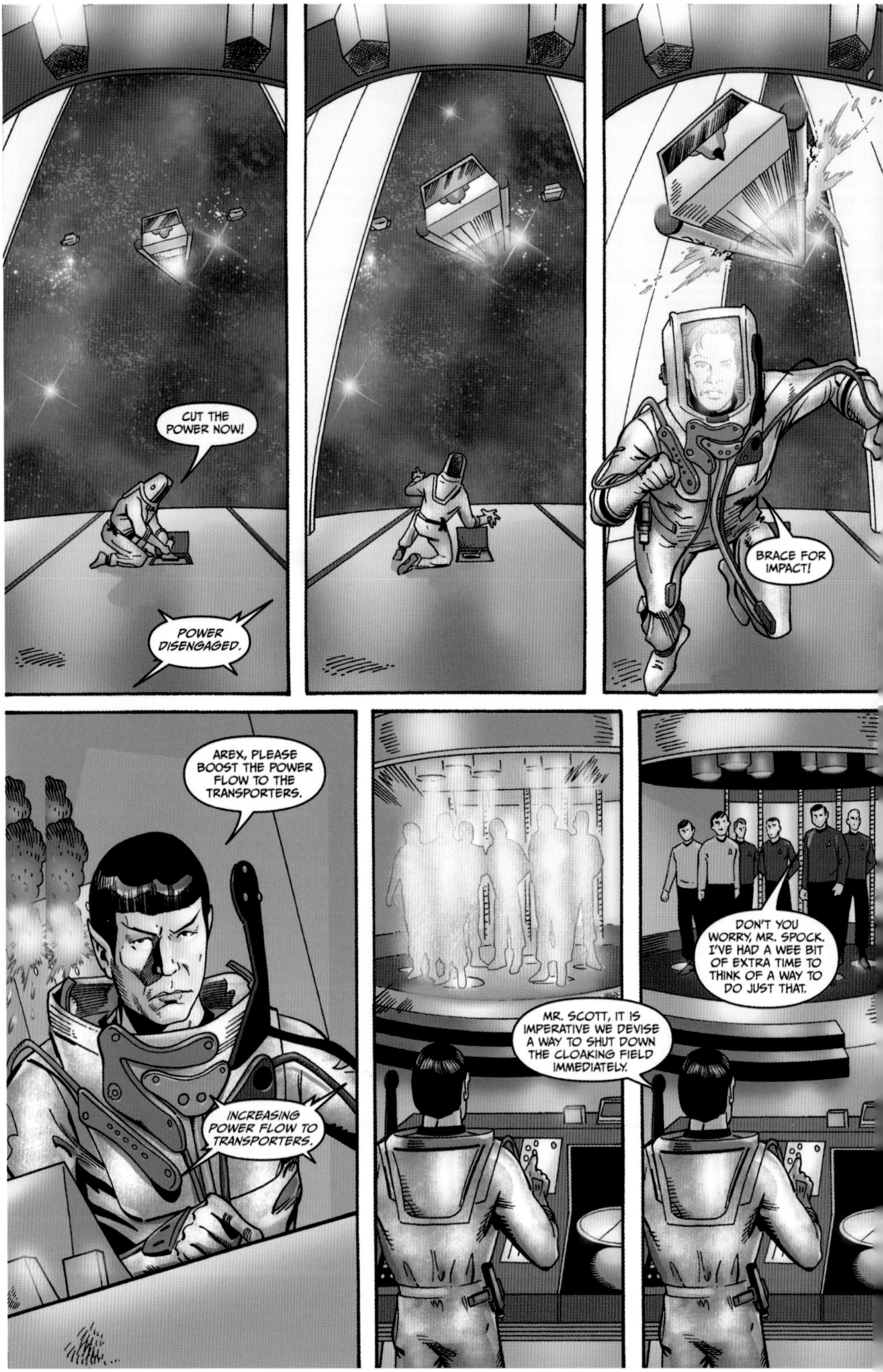
CUT THE POWER NOW!
POWER DISENGAGED.
BRACE FOR IMPACT!
AREX, PLEASE BOOST THE POWER FLOW TO THE TRANSPORTERS.
INCREASING POWER FLOW TO TRANSPORTERS.
MR. SCOTT, IT IS IMPERATIVE WE DEVISE A WAY TO SHUT DOWN THE CLOAKING FIELD IMMEDIATELY.
DON'T YOU WORRY, MR. SPOCK. I'VE HAD A WEE BIT OF EXTRA TIME TO THINK OF A WAY TO DO JUST THAT.

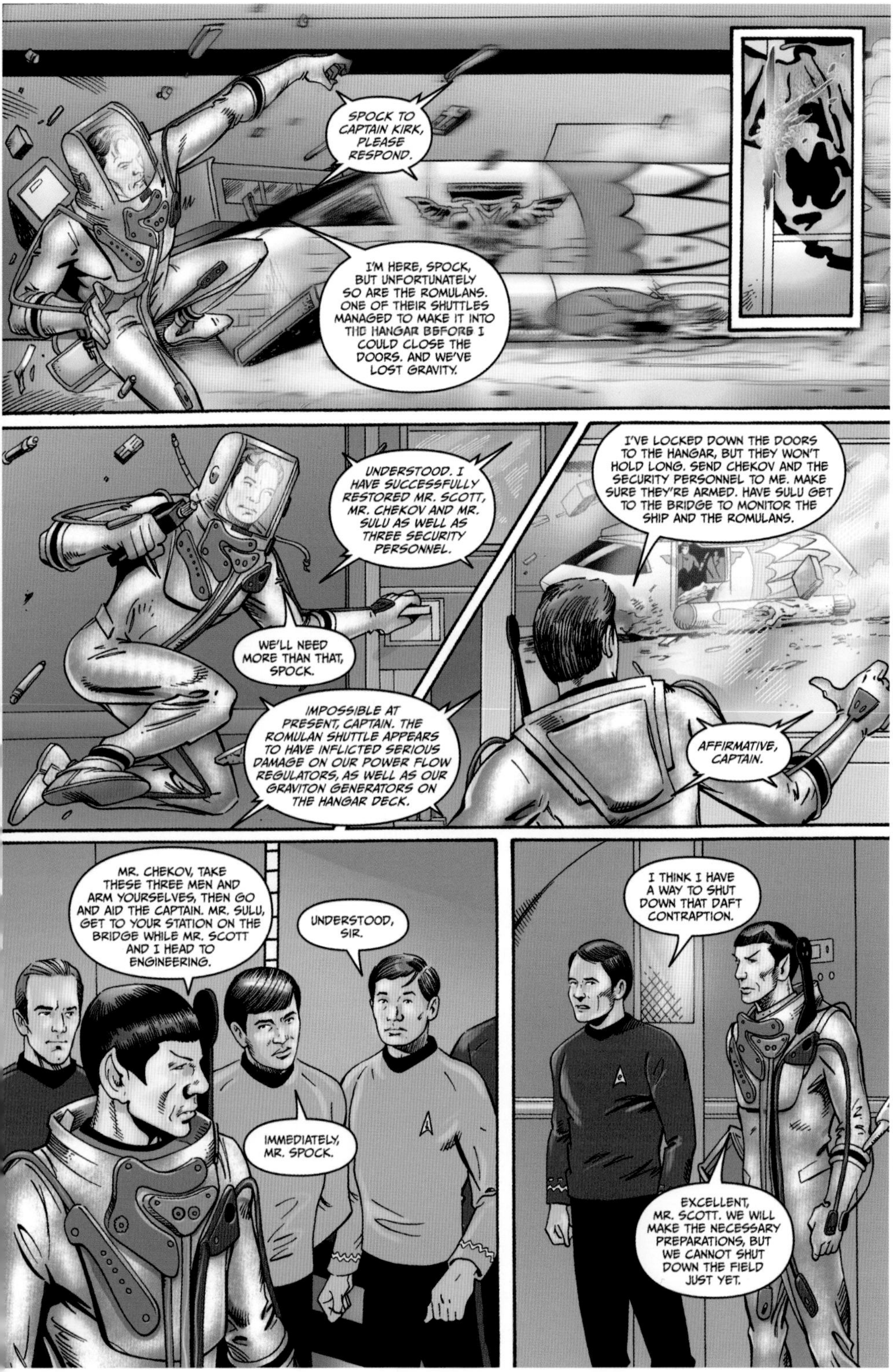
SPOCK TO CAPTAIN KIRK, PLEASE RESPOND.
I'M HERE, SPOCK, BUT UNFORTUNATELY SO ARE THE ROMULANS. ONE OF THEIR SHUTTLES MANAGED TO MAKE IT INTO THE HANGAR BEFORE I COULD CLOSE THE DOORS. AND WE'VE LOST GRAVITY.
UNDERSTOOD. I HAVE SUCCESSFULLY RESTORED MR. SCOTT, MR. CHEKOV AND MR. SULU AS WELL AS THREE SECURITY PERSONNEL.
WE'LL NEED MORE THAN THAT, SPOCK.
IMPOSSIBLE AT PRESENT, CAPTAIN. THE ROMULAN SHUTTLE APPEARS TO HAVE INFLICTED SERIOUS DAMAGE ON OUR POWER FLOW REGULATORS, AS WELL AS OUR GRAVITON GENERATORS ON THE HANGAR DECK.
I'VE LOCKED DOWN THE DOORS TO THE HANGAR, BUT THEY WON'T HOLD LONG. SEND CHEKOV AND THE SECURITY PERSONNEL TO ME. MAKE SURE THEY'RE ARMED. HAVE SULU GET TO THE BRIDGE TO MONITOR THE SHIP AND THE ROMULANS.
AFFIRMATIVE, CAPTAIN.
MR. CHEKOV, TAKE THESE THREE MEN AND ARM YOURSELVES, THEN GO AND AID THE CAPTAIN. MR. SULU, GET TO YOUR STATION ON THE BRIDGE WHILE MR. SCOTT AND I HEAD TO ENGINEERING.
UNDERSTOOD, SIR.
IMMEDIATELY, MR. SPOCK.
I THINK I HAVE A WAY TO SHUT DOWN THAT DAFT CONTRAPTION.
EXCELLENT, MR. SCOTT. WE WILL MAKE THE NECESSARY PREPARATIONS, BUT WE CANNOT SHUT DOWN THE FIELD JUST YET.

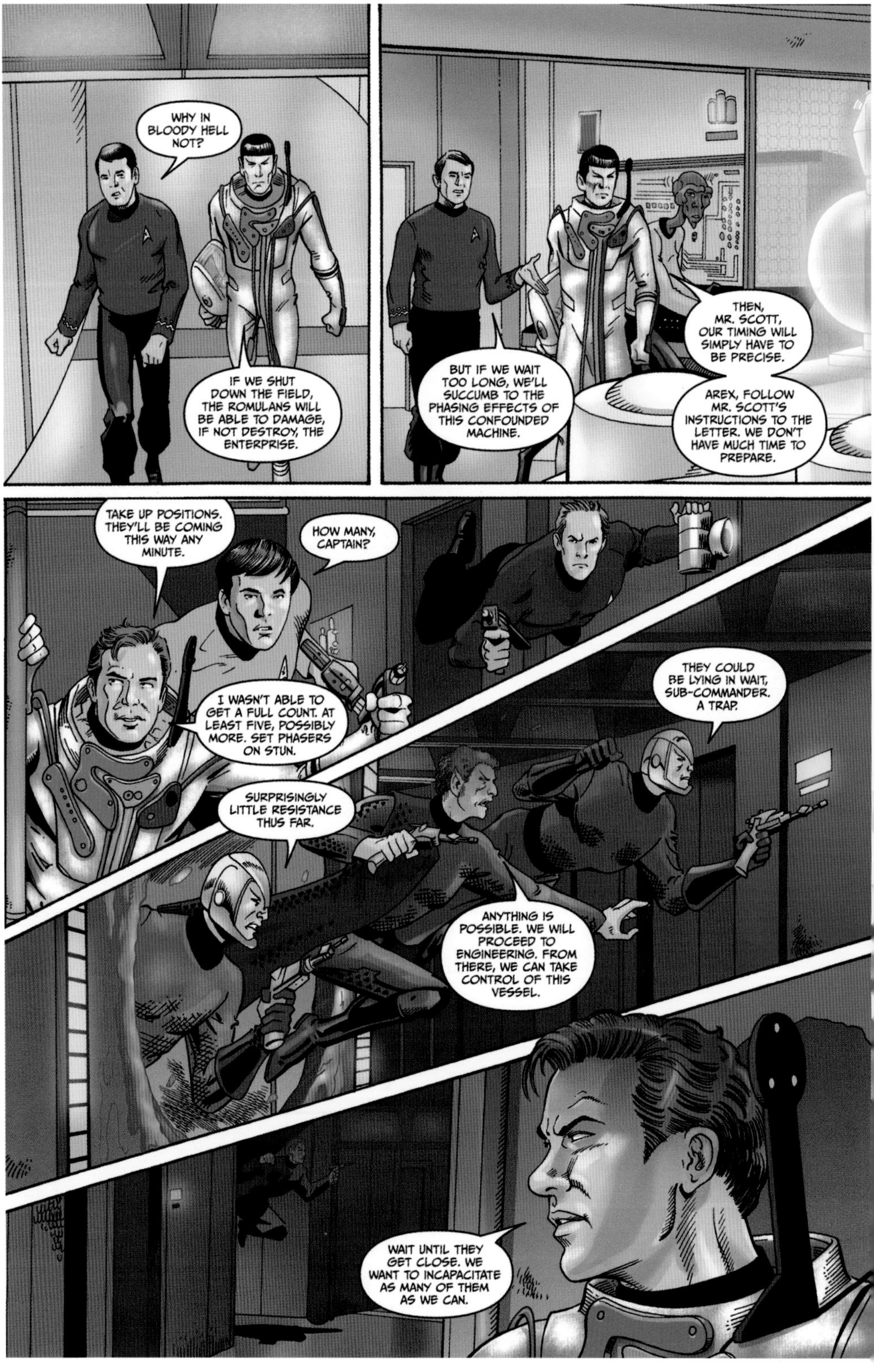
WHY IN BLOODY HELL NOT?
IF WE SHUT DOWN THE FIELD, THE ROMULANS WILL BE ABLE TO DAMAGE, IF NOT DESTROY, THE ENTERPRISE.
BUT IF WE WAIT TOO LONG, WE'LL SUCCUMB TO THE PHASING EFFECTS OF THIS CONFOUNDED MACHINE.
THEN, MR. SCOTT, OUR TIMING WILL SIMPLY HAVE TO BE PRECISE.
AREX, FOLLOW MR. SCOTT'S INSTRUCTIONS TO THE LETTER. WE DON'T HAVE MUCH TIME TO PREPARE.
TAKE UP POSITIONS. THEY'LL BE COMING THIS WAY ANY MINUTE.
HOW MANY, CAPTAIN?
I WASN'T ABLE TO GET A FULL COUNT. AT LEAST FIVE, POSSIBLY MORE. SET PHASERS ON STUN.
THEY COULD BE LYING IN WAIT, SUB-COMMANDER. A TRAP.
SURPRISINGLY LITTLE RESISTANCE THUS FAR.
ANYTHING IS POSSIBLE. WE WILL PROCEED TO ENGINEERING. FROM THERE, WE CAN TAKE CONTROL OF THIS VESSEL.
WAIT UNTIL THEY GET CLOSE. WE WANT TO INCAPACITATE AS MANY OF THEM AS WE CAN.

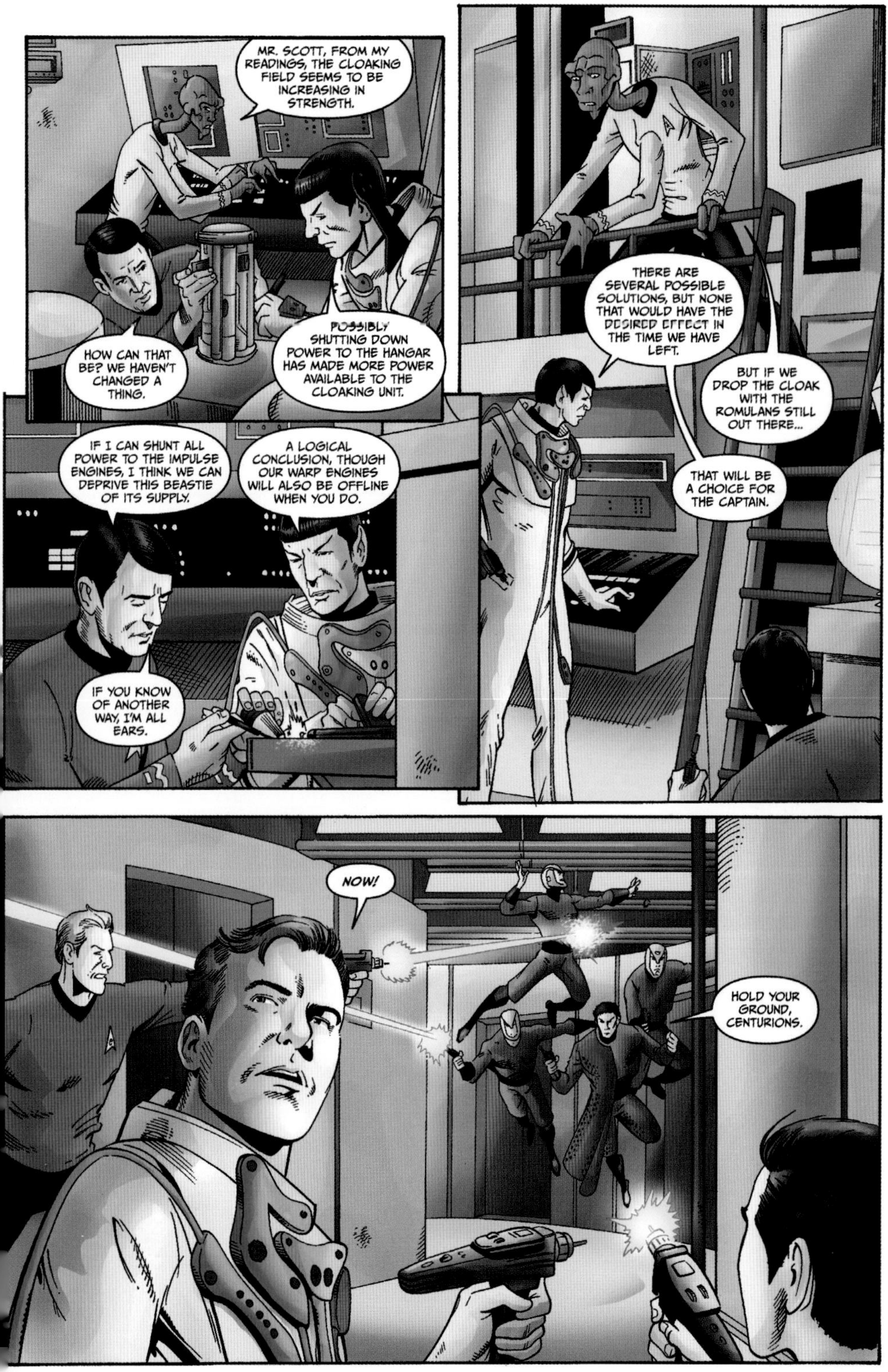
MR. SCOTT, FROM MY READINGS, THE CLOAKING FIELD SEEMS TO BE INCREASING IN STRENGTH.
HOW CAN THAT BE? WE HAVEN'T CHANGED A THING.
POSSIBLY SHUTTING DOWN POWER TO THE HANGAR HAS MADE MORE POWER AVAILABLE TO THE CLOAKING UNIT.
IF I CAN SHUNT ALL POWER TO THE IMPULSE ENGINES, I THINK WE CAN DEPRIVE THIS BEASTIE OF ITS SUPPLY.
A LOGICAL CONCLUSION, THOUGH OUR WARP ENGINES WILL ALSO BE OFFLINE WHEN YOU DO.
IF YOU KNOW OF ANOTHER WAY, I'M ALL EARS.
THERE ARE SEVERAL POSSIBLE SOLUTIONS, BUT NONE THAT WOULD HAVE THE DESIRED EFFECT IN THE TIME WE HAVE LEFT.
BUT IF WE DROP THE CLOAK WITH THE ROMULANS STILL OUT THERE...
THAT WILL BE A CHOICE FOR THE CAPTAIN.
NOW!
HOLD YOUR GROUND, CENTURIONS.

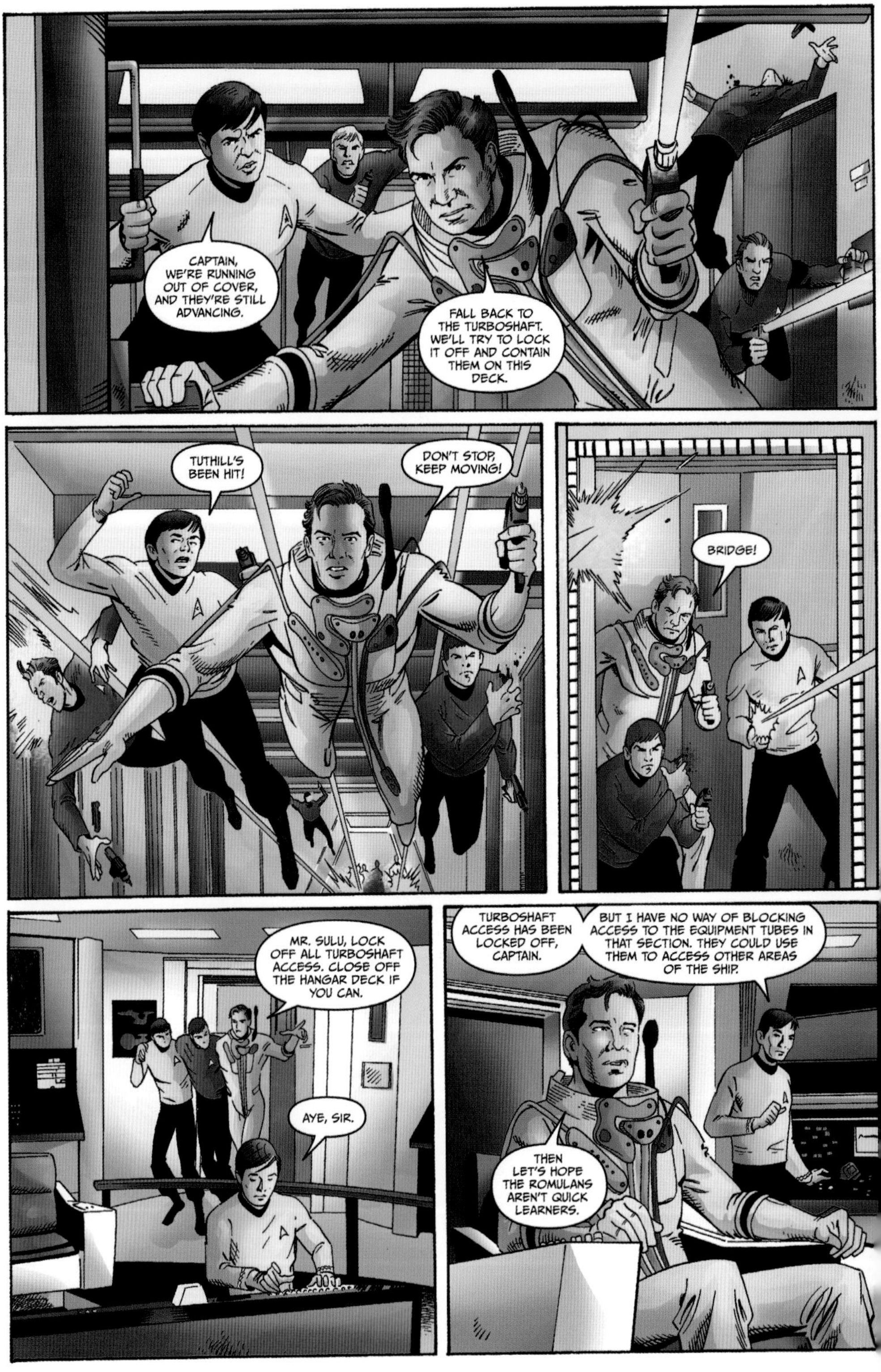
CAPTAIN, WE'RE RUNNING OUT OF COVER, AND THEY'RE STILL ADVANCING.
FALL BACK TO THE TURBOSHAFT. WE'LL TRY TO LOCK IT OFF AND CONTAIN THEM ON THIS DECK.
TUTHILL'S BEEN HIT!
DON'T STOP, KEEP MOVING!
BRIDGE!
MR. SULU, LOCK OFF ALL TURBOSHAFT ACCESS. CLOSE OFF THE HANGAR DECK IF YOU CAN.
AYE, SIR.
TURBOSHAFT ACCESS HAS BEEN LOCKED OFF, CAPTAIN.
BUT I HAVE NO WAY OF BLOCKING ACCESS TO THE EQUIPMENT TUBES IN THAT SECTION. THEY COULD USE THEM TO ACCESS OTHER AREAS OF THE SHIP.
THEN LET'S HOPE THE ROMULANS AREN'T QUICK LEARNERS.

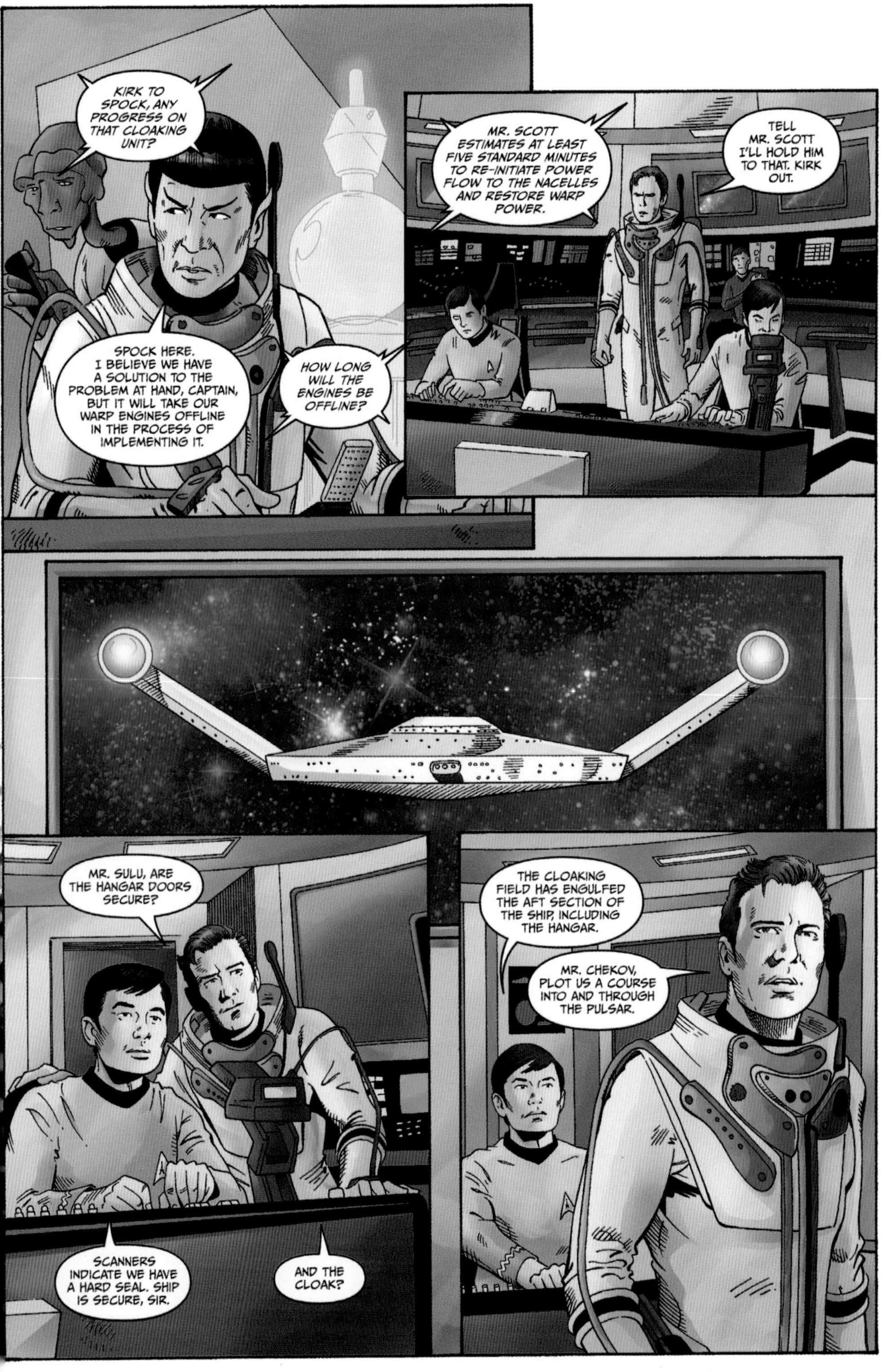
KIRK TO SPOCK, ANY PROGRESS ON THAT CLOAKING UNIT?
SPOCK HERE. I BELIEVE WE HAVE A SOLUTION TO THE PROBLEM AT HAND, CAPTAIN, BUT IT WILL TAKE OUR WARP ENGINES OFFLINE IN THE PROCESS OF IMPLEMENTING IT.
HOW LONG WILL THE ENGINES BE OFFLINE?
MR. SCOTT ESTIMATES AT LEAST FIVE STANDARD MINUTES TO RE-INITIATE POWER FLOW TO THE NACELLES AND RESTORE WARP POWER.
TELL MR. SCOTT I'LL HOLD HIM TO THAT. KIRK OUT.
MR. SULU, ARE THE HANGAR DOORS SECURE?
SCANNERS INDICATE WE HAVE A HARD SEAL. SHIP IS SECURE, SIR.
AND THE CLOAK?
THE CLOAKING FIELD HAS ENGULFED THE AFT SECTION OF THE SHIP, INCLUDING THE HANGAR.
MR. CHEKOV, PLOT US A COURSE INTO AND THROUGH THE PULSAR.

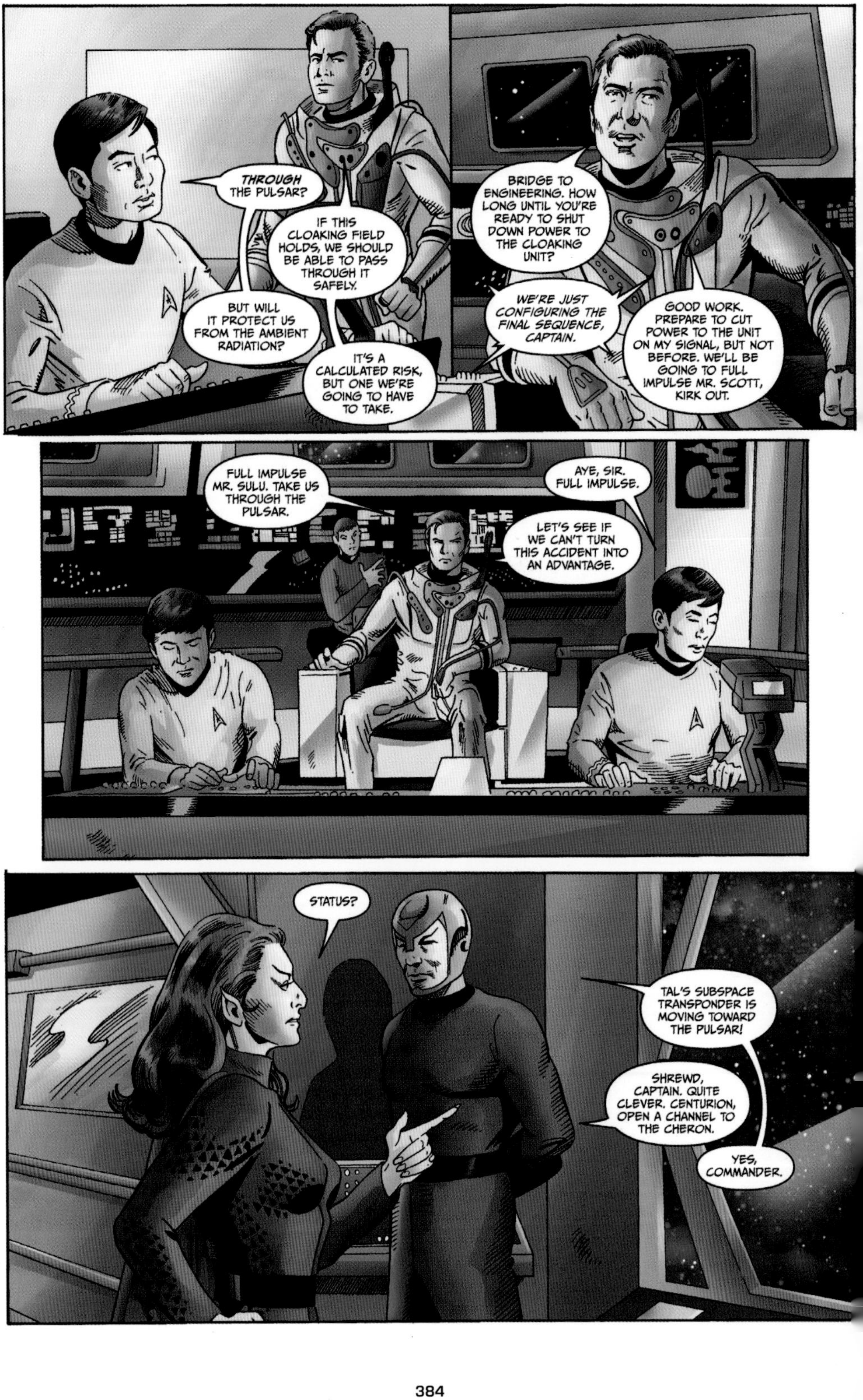
THROUGH THE PULSAR?
IF THIS CLOAKING FIELD HOLDS, WE SHOULD BE ABLE TO PASS THROUGH IT SAFELY.
BUT WILL IT PROTECT US FROM THE AMBIENT RADIATION?
IT'S A CALCULATED RISK, BUT ONE WE'RE GOING TO HAVE TO TAKE.
BRIDGE TO ENGINEERING. HOW LONG UNTIL YOU'RE READY TO SHUT DOWN POWER TO THE CLOAKING UNIT?
WE'RE JUST CONFIGURING THE FINAL SEQUENCE, CAPTAIN.
GOOD WORK. PREPARE TO CUT POWER TO THE UNIT ON MY SIGNAL, BUT NOT BEFORE. WE'LL BE GOING TO FULL IMPULSE MR. SCOTT, KIRK OUT.
FULL IMPULSE MR. SULU. TAKE US THROUGH THE PULSAR.
AYE, SIR. FULL IMPULSE.
LET'S SEE IF WE CAN'T TURN THIS ACCIDENT INTO AN ADVANTAGE.
STATUS?
TAL'S SUBSPACE TRANSPONDER IS MOVING TOWARD THE PULSAR!
SHREWD, CAPTAIN. QUITE CLEVER. CENTURION, OPEN A CHANNEL TO THE CHERON.
YES, COMMANDER.

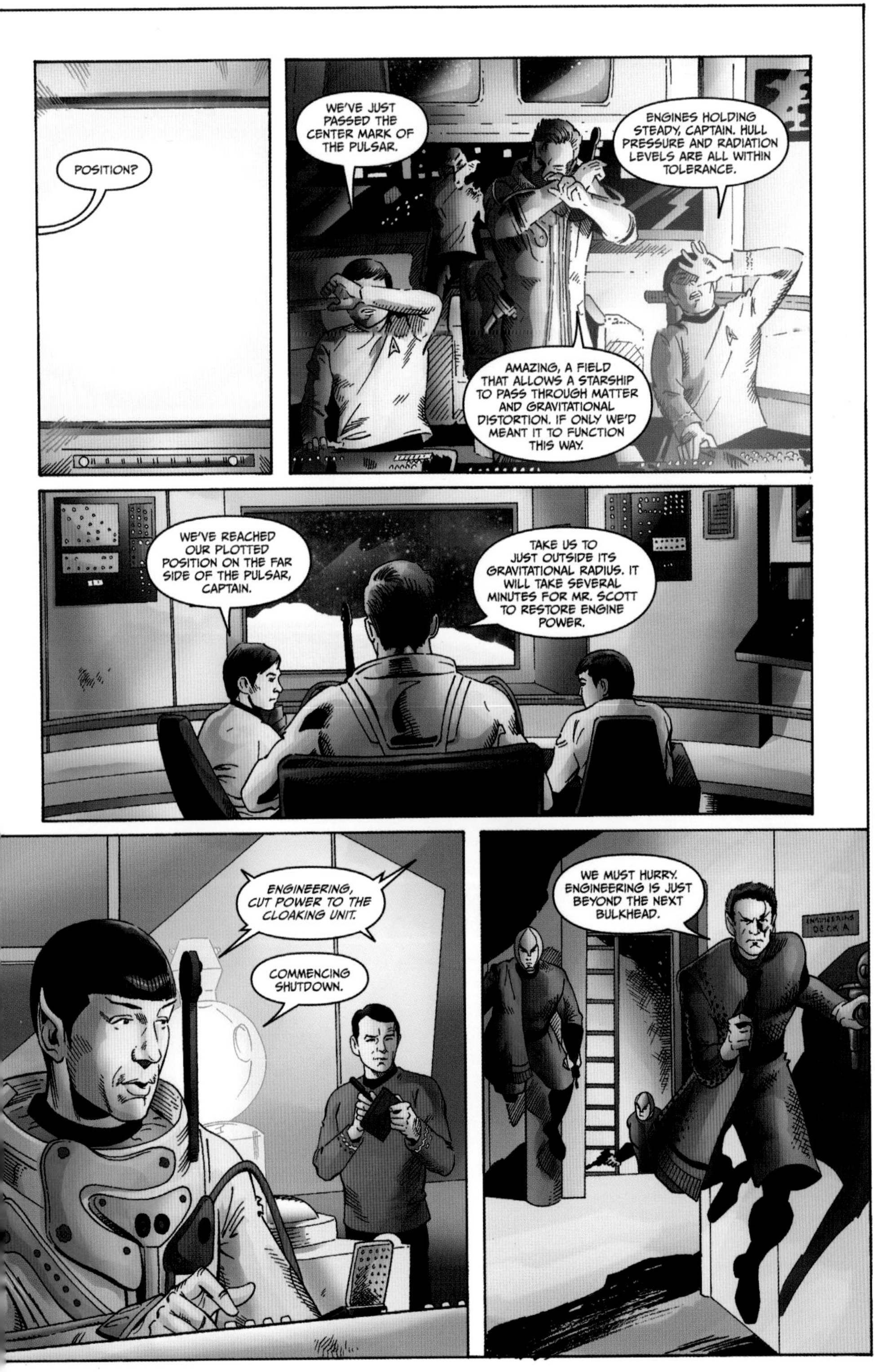
POSITION?
WE'VE JUST PASSED THE CENTER MARK OF THE PULSAR.
ENGINES HOLDING STEADY, CAPTAIN. HULL PRESSURE AND RADIATION LEVELS ARE ALL WITHIN TOLERANCE.
AMAZING, A FIELD THAT ALLOWS A STARSHIP TO PASS THROUGH MATTER AND GRAVITATIONAL DISTORTION. IF ONLY WE'D MEANT IT TO FUNCTION THIS WAY.
WE'VE REACHED OUR PLOTTED POSITION ON THE FAR SIDE OF THE PULSAR, CAPTAIN.
TAKE US TO JUST OUTSIDE ITS GRAVITATIONAL RADIUS. IT WILL TAKE SEVERAL MINUTES FOR MR. SCOTT TO RESTORE ENGINE POWER.
ENGINEERING, CUT POWER TO THE CLOAKING UNIT.
COMMENCING SHUTDOWN.
WE MUST HURRY. ENGINEERING IS JUST BEYOND THE NEXT BULKHEAD.

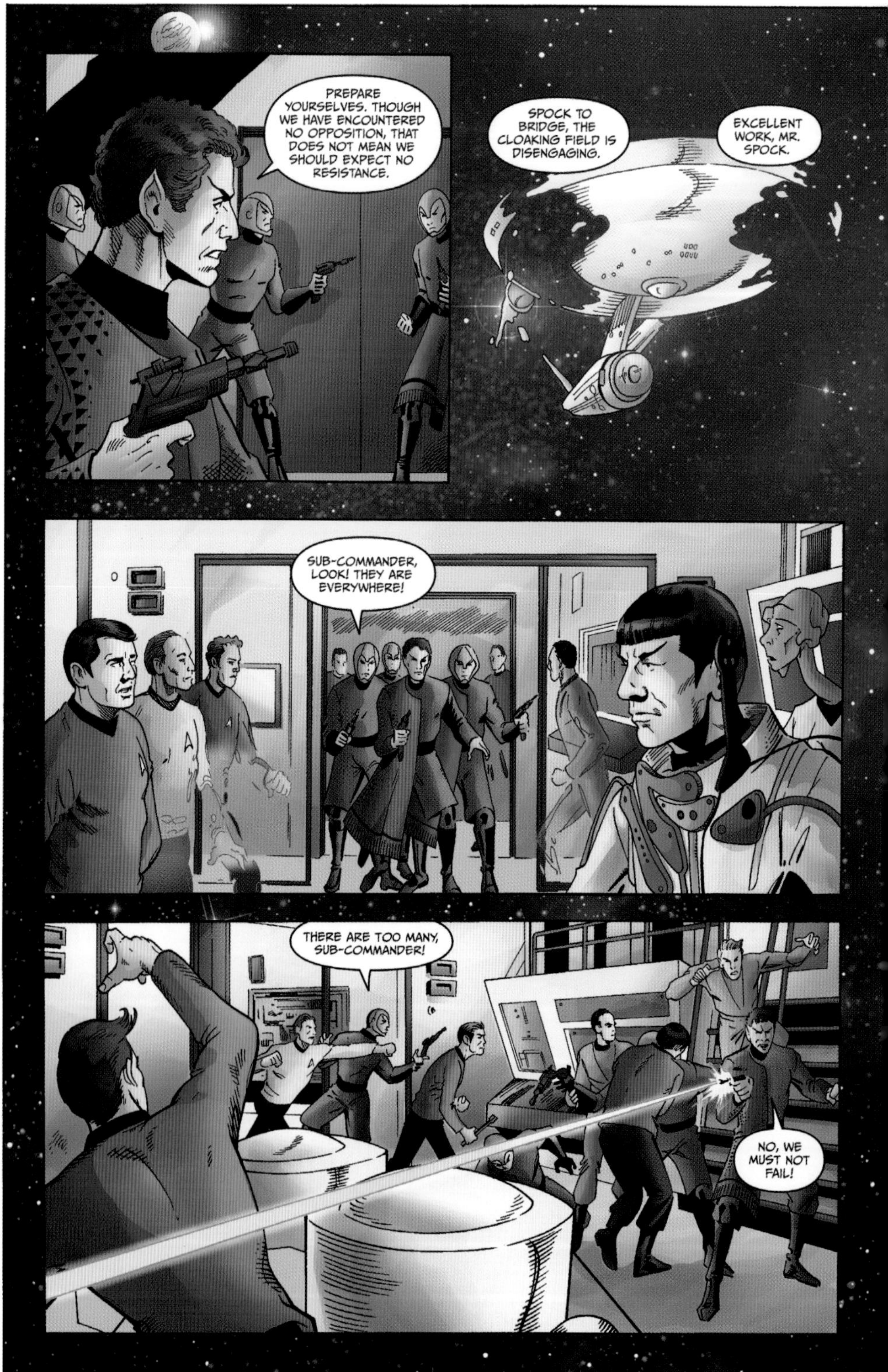
PREPARE YOURSELVES. THOUGH WE HAVE ENCOUNTERED NO OPPOSITION, THAT DOES NOT MEAN WE SHOULD EXPECT NO RESISTANCE.
SPOCK TO BRIDGE, THE CLOAKING FIELD IS DISENGAGING.
EXCELLENT WORK, MR. SPOCK.
SUB-COMMANDER, LOOK! THEY ARE EVERYWHERE!
THERE ARE TOO MANY, SUB-COMMANDER!
NO, WE MUST NOT FAIL!

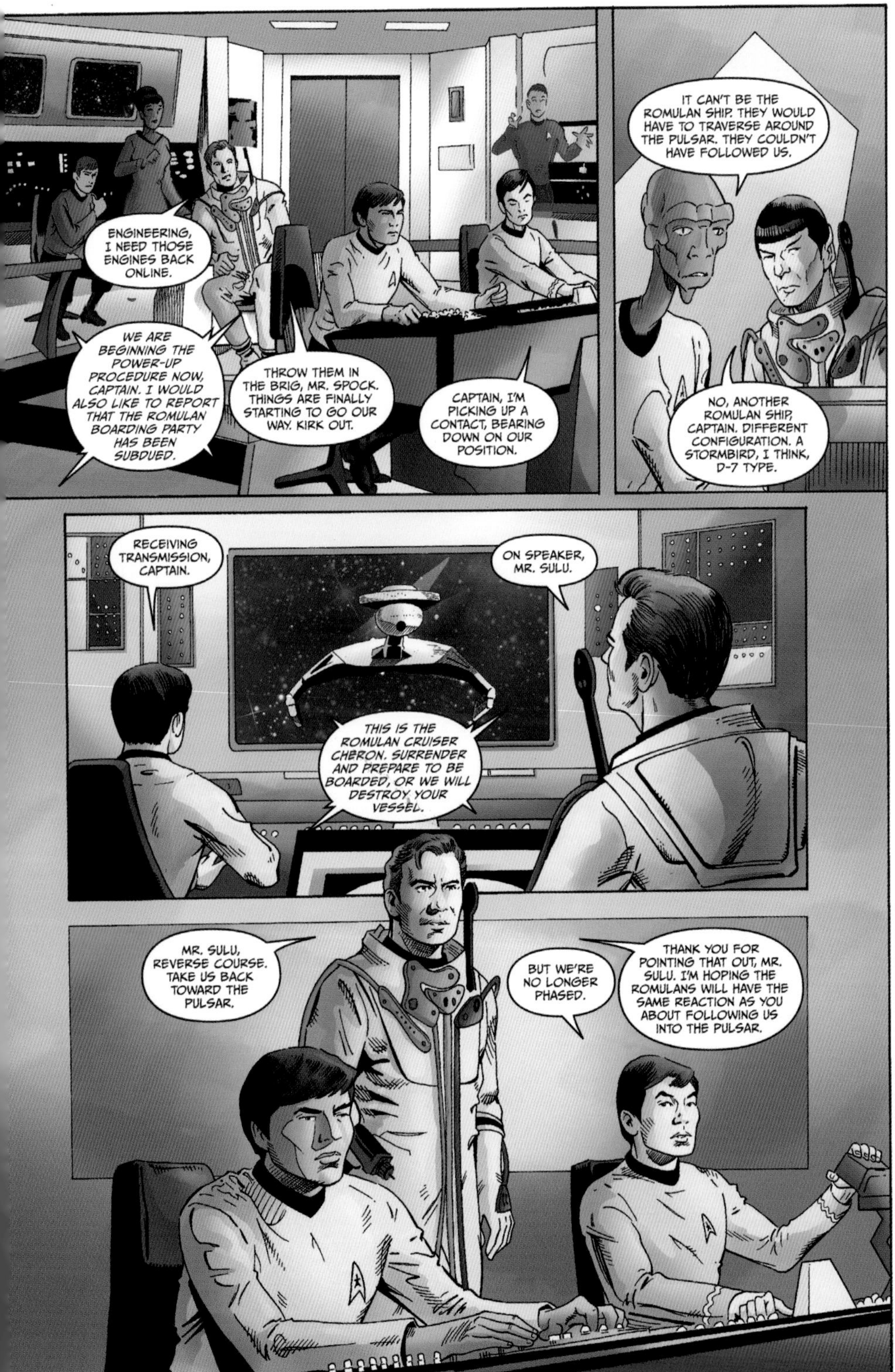
ENGINEERING, I NEED THOSE ENGINES BACK ONLINE.
WE ARE BEGINNING THE POWER-UP PROCEDURE NOW, CAPTAIN. I WOULD ALSO LIKE TO REPORT THAT THE ROMULAN BOARDING PARTY HAS BEEN SUBDUED.
THROW THEM IN THE BRIG, MR. SPOCK. THINGS ARE FINALLY STARTING TO GO OUR WAY. KIRK OUT.
CAPTAIN, I'M PICKING UP A CONTACT, BEARING DOWN ON OUR POSITION.
IT CAN'T BE THE ROMULAN SHIP. THEY WOULD HAVE TO TRAVERSE AROUND THE PULSAR. THEY COULDN'T HAVE FOLLOWED US.
NO, ANOTHER ROMULAN SHIP, CAPTAIN. DIFFERENT CONFIGURATION. A STORMBIRD, I THINK, D-7 TYPE.
RECEIVING TRANSMISSION, CAPTAIN.
ON SPEAKER, MR. SULU.
THIS IS THE ROMULAN CRUISER CHERON. SURRENDER AND PREPARE TO BE BOARDED, OR WE WILL DESTROY YOUR VESSEL.
MR. SULU, REVERSE COURSE. TAKE US BACK TOWARD THE PULSAR.
BUT WE'RE NO LONGER PHASED.
THANK YOU FOR POINTING THAT OUT, MR. SULU. I'M HOPING THE ROMULANS WILL HAVE THE SAME REACTION AS YOU ABOUT FOLLOWING US INTO THE PULSAR.

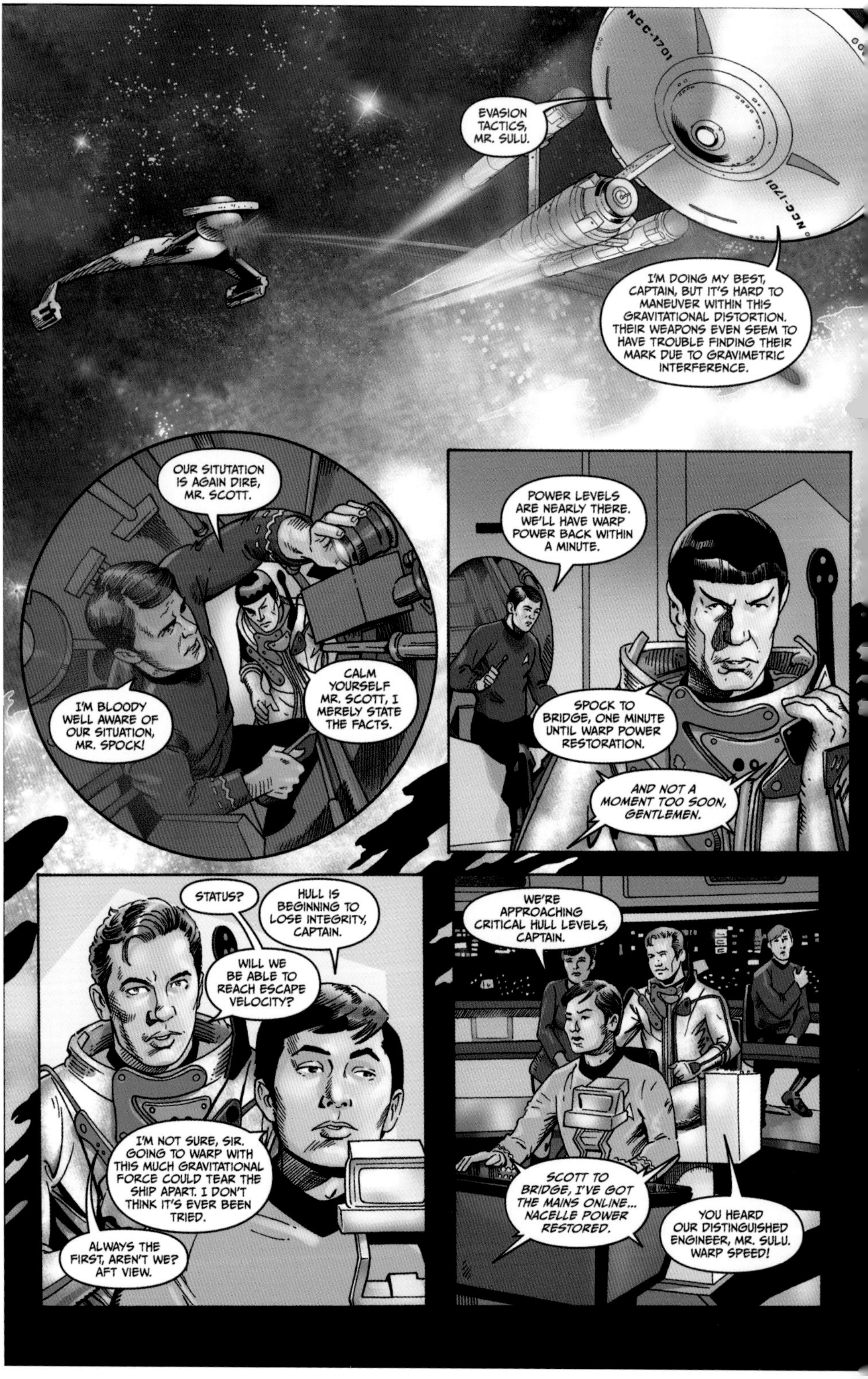
NCC-1701
EVASION TACTICS, MR. SULU.
NCC-1701
I'M DOING MY BEST, CAPTAIN, BUT IT'S HARD TO MANEUVER WITHIN THIS GRAVITATIONAL DISTORTION. THEIR WEAPONS EVEN SEEM TO HAVE TROUBLE FINDING THEIR MARK DUE TO GRAVIMETRIC INTERFERENCE.
OUR SITUTATION IS AGAIN DIRE, MR. SCOTT.
CALM YOURSELF MR. SCOTT, I MERELY STATE THE FACTS.
I'M BLOODY WELL AWARE OF OUR SITUATION, MR. SPOCK!
POWER LEVELS ARE NEARLY THERE. WE'LL HAVE WARP POWER BACK WITHIN A MINUTE.
SPOCK TO BRIDGE, ONE MINUTE UNTIL WARP POWER RESTORATION.
AND NOT A MOMENT TOO SOON, GENTLEMEN.
STATUS?
HULL IS BEGINNING TO LOSE INTEGRITY, CAPTAIN.
WILL WE BE ABLE TO REACH ESCAPE VELOCITY?
I'M NOT SURE, SIR. GOING TO WARP WITH THIS MUCH GRAVITATIONAL FORCE COULD TEAR THE SHIP APART. I DON'T THINK IT'S EVER BEEN TRIED.
ALWAYS THE FIRST, AREN'T WE? AFT VIEW.
WE'RE APPROACHING CRITICAL HULL LEVELS, CAPTAIN.
SCOTT TO BRIDGE, I'VE GOT THE MAINS ONLINE... NACELLE POWER RESTORED.
YOU HEARD OUR DISTINGUISHED ENGINEER, MR. SULU. WARP SPEED!

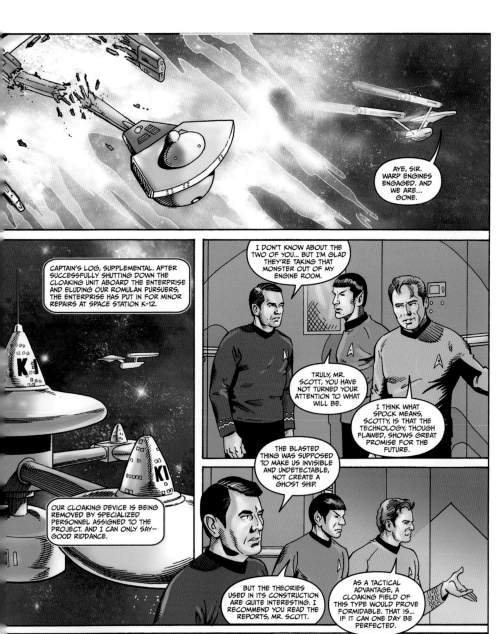

AYE, SIR. WARP ENGINES ENGAGED. AND WE ARE... GONE.

CAPTAIN'S LOG, SUPPLEMENTAL. AFTER SUCCESSFULLY SHUTTING DOWN THE CLOAKING UNIT ABOARD THE ENTERPRISE AND ELUDING OUR ROMULAN PURSUERS, THE ENTERPRISE HAS PUT IN FOR MINOR REPAIRS AT SPACE STATION K-12.

I DON'T KNOW ABOUT THE TWO OF YOU... BUT I'M GLAD THEY'RE TAKING THAT MONSTER OUT OF MY ENGINE ROOM.

TRULY, MR. SCOTT, YOU HAVE NOT TURNED YOUR ATTENTION TO WHAT WILL BE.

I THINK WHAT SPOCK MEANS, SCOTTY, IS THAT THE TECHNOLOGY, THOUGH FLAWED, SHOWS GREAT PROMISE FOR THE FUTURE.

THE BLASTED THING WAS SUPPOSED TO MAKE US INVISIBLE AND UNDETECTABLE, NOT CREATE A GHOST SHIP.

OUR CLOAKING DEVICE IS BEING REMOVED BY SPECIALIZED PERSONNEL ASSIGNED TO THE PROJECT. AND I CAN ONLY SAY— GOOD RIDDANCE.

BUT THE THEORIES USED IN ITS CONSTRUCTION ARE QUITE INTERESTING. I RECOMMEND YOU READ THE REPORTS, MR. SCOTT.

AS A TACTICAL ADVANTAGE, A CLOAKING FIELD OF THIS TYPE WOULD PROVE FORMIDABLE. THAT IS... IF IT CAN ONE DAY BE PERFECTED.

IF THE INDIVIDUAL MOST RESPONSIBLE FOR THIS PROTOTYPE IS ANY INDICATION, I BELIEVE ONE DAY THE WORK WILL BE SUCCESSFULLY IMPLEMENTED.

I KNOW EVERY ENGINEER AT STARFLEET DEVELOPMENT, AND THIS IS FAR BEYOND ANY OF THEM.

PROBABLY BECAUSE IT WASN'T DEVELOPED THERE.

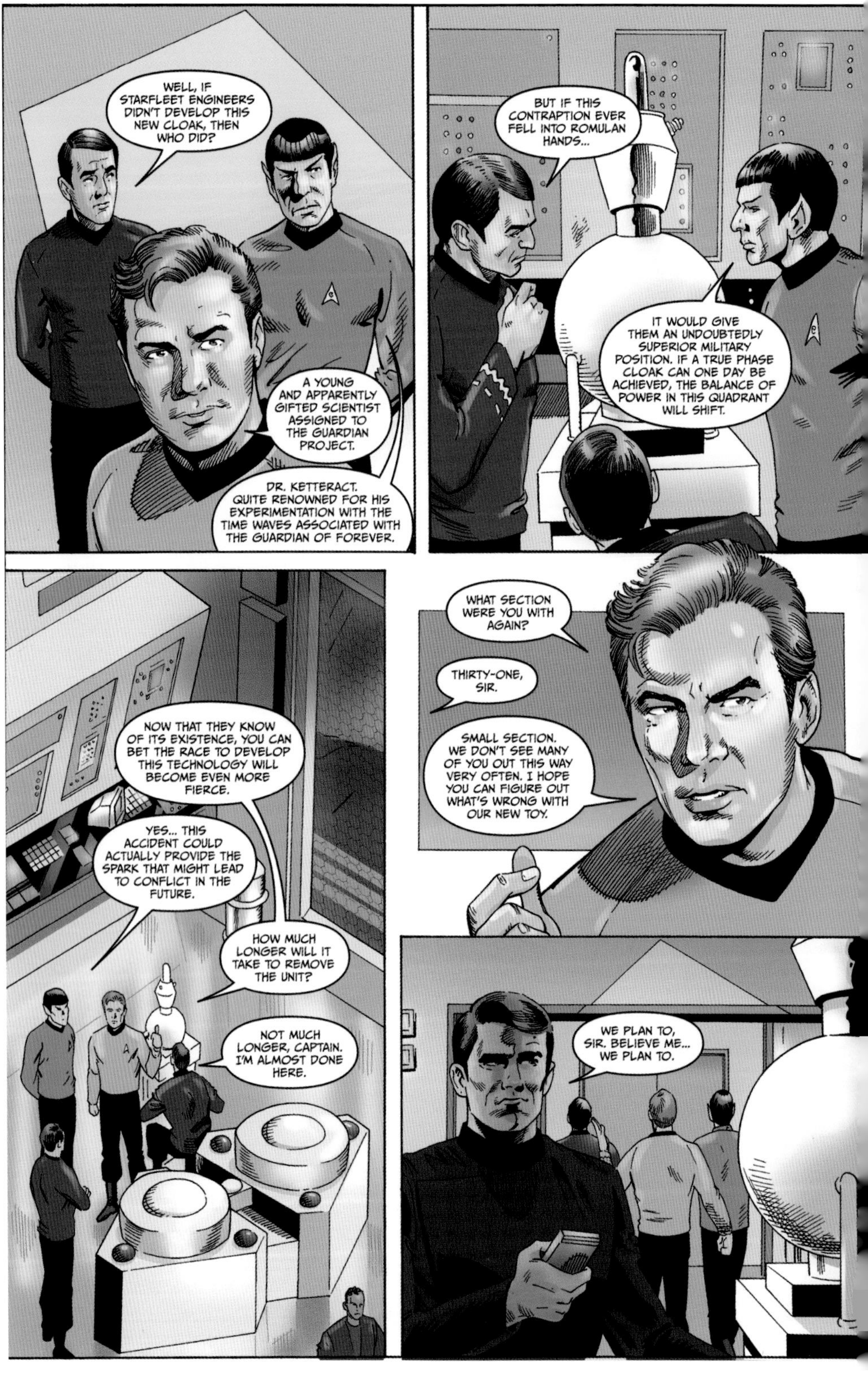
WELL, IF STARFLEET ENGINEERS DIDN'T DEVELOP THIS NEW CLOAK, THEN WHO DID?
A YOUNG AND APPARENTLY GIFTED SCIENTIST ASSIGNED TO THE GUARDIAN PROJECT.
DR. KETTERACT. QUITE RENOWNED FOR HIS EXPERIMENTATION WITH THE TIME WAVES ASSOCIATED WITH THE GUARDIAN OF FOREVER.
BUT IF THIS CONTRAPTION EVER FELL INTO ROMULAN HANDS...
IT WOULD GIVE THEM AN UNDOUBTEDLY SUPERIOR MILITARY POSITION. IF A TRUE PHASE CLOAK CAN ONE DAY BE ACHIEVED, THE BALANCE OF POWER IN THIS QUADRANT WILL SHIFT.
NOW THAT THEY KNOW OF ITS EXISTENCE, YOU CAN BET THE RACE TO DEVELOP THIS TECHNOLOGY WILL BECOME EVEN MORE FIERCE.
YES... THIS ACCIDENT COULD ACTUALLY PROVIDE THE SPARK THAT MIGHT LEAD TO CONFLICT IN THE FUTURE.
HOW MUCH LONGER WILL IT TAKE TO REMOVE THE UNIT?
NOT MUCH LONGER, CAPTAIN. I'M ALMOST DONE HERE.
WHAT SECTION WERE YOU WITH AGAIN?
THIRTY-ONE, SIR.
SMALL SECTION. WE DON'T SEE MANY OF YOU OUT THIS WAY VERY OFTEN. I HOPE YOU CAN FIGURE OUT WHAT'S WRONG WITH OUR NEW TOY.
WE PLAN TO, SIR. BELIEVE ME... WE PLAN TO.

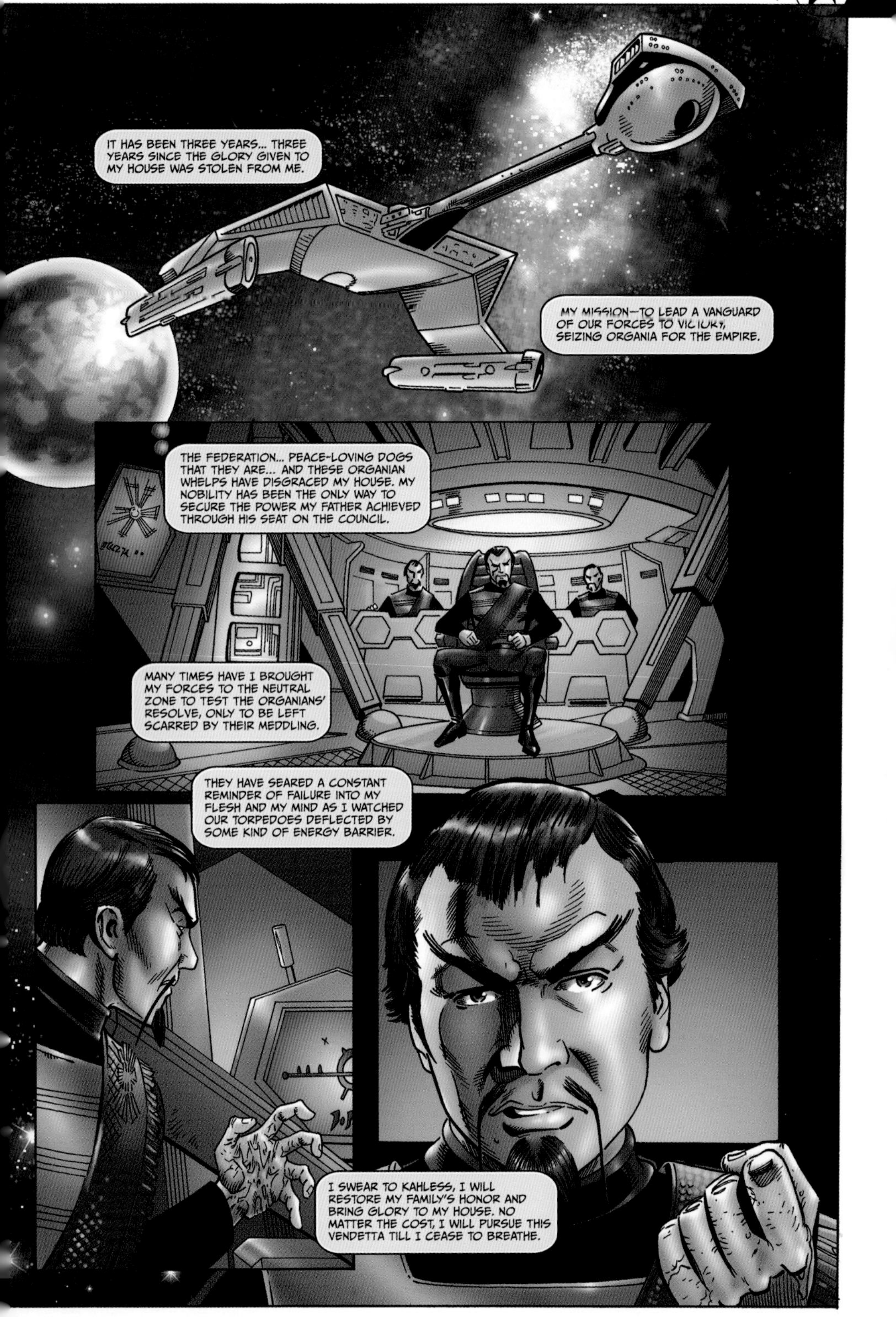
IT HAS BEEN THREE YEARS... THREE YEARS SINCE THE GLORY GIVEN TO MY HOUSE WAS STOLEN FROM ME.
MY MISSION—TO LEAD A VANGUARD OF OUR FORCES TO VICTORY, SEIZING ORGANIA FOR THE EMPIRE.
THE FEDERATION... PEACE-LOVING DOGS THAT THEY ARE... AND THESE ORGANIAN WHELPS HAVE DISGRACED MY HOUSE. MY NOBILITY HAS BEEN THE ONLY WAY TO SECURE THE POWER MY FATHER ACHIEVED THROUGH HIS SEAT ON THE COUNCIL.
MANY TIMES HAVE I BROUGHT MY FORCES TO THE NEUTRAL ZONE TO TEST THE ORGANIANS' RESOLVE, ONLY TO BE LEFT SCARRED BY THEIR MEDDLING.
THEY HAVE SEARED A CONSTANT REMINDER OF FAILURE INTO MY FLESH AND MY MIND AS I WATCHED OUR TORPEDOES DEFLECTED BY SOME KIND OF ENERGY BARRIER.
I SWEAR TO KAHLESS, I WILL RESTORE MY FAMILY'S HONOR AND BRING GLORY TO MY HOUSE. NO MATTER THE COST, I WILL PURSUE THIS VENDETTA TILL I CEASE TO BREATHE.

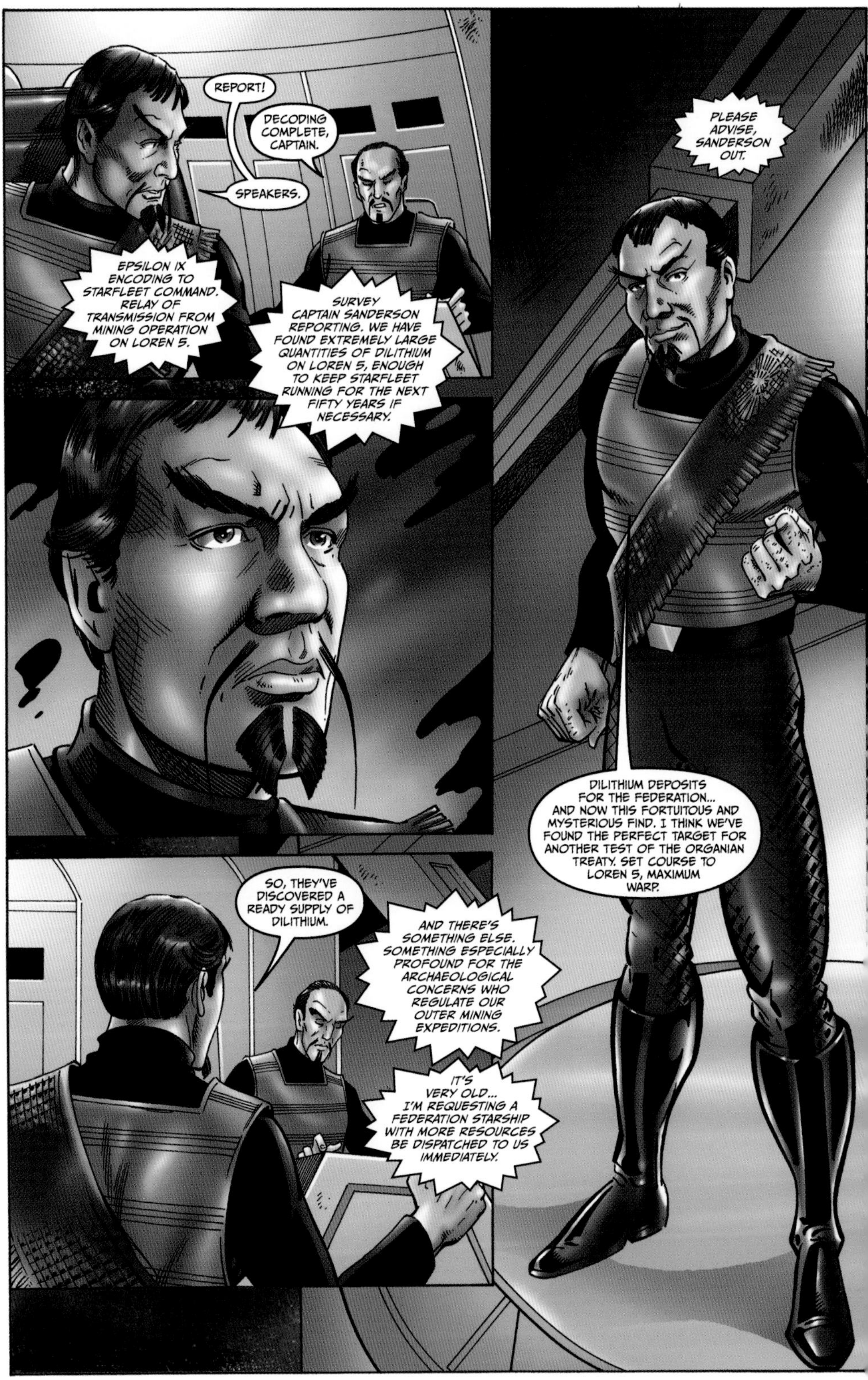
REPORT!
DECODING COMPLETE, CAPTAIN.
SPEAKERS.
EPSILON IX ENCODING TO STARFLEET COMMAND. RELAY OF TRANSMISSION FROM MINING OPERATION ON LOREN 5.
SURVEY CAPTAIN SANDERSON REPORTING. WE HAVE FOUND EXTREMELY LARGE QUANTITIES OF DILITHIUM ON LOREN 5, ENOUGH TO KEEP STARFLEET RUNNING FOR THE NEXT FIFTY YEARS IF NECESSARY.
SO, THEY'VE DISCOVERED A READY SUPPLY OF DILITHIUM.
AND THERE'S SOMETHING ELSE. SOMETHING ESPECIALLY PROFOUND FOR THE ARCHAEOLOGICAL CONCERNS WHO REGULATE OUR OUTER MINING EXPEDITIONS.
IT'S VERY OLD... I'M REQUESTING A FEDERATION STARSHIP WITH MORE RESOURCES BE DISPATCHED TO US IMMEDIATELY.
PLEASE ADVISE, SANDERSON OUT.
DILITHIUM DEPOSITS FOR THE FEDERATION... AND NOW THIS FORTUITOUS AND MYSTERIOUS FIND. I THINK WE'VE FOUND THE PERFECT TARGET FOR ANOTHER TEST OF THE ORGANIAN TREATY. SET COURSE TO LOREN 5, MAXIMUM WARP.

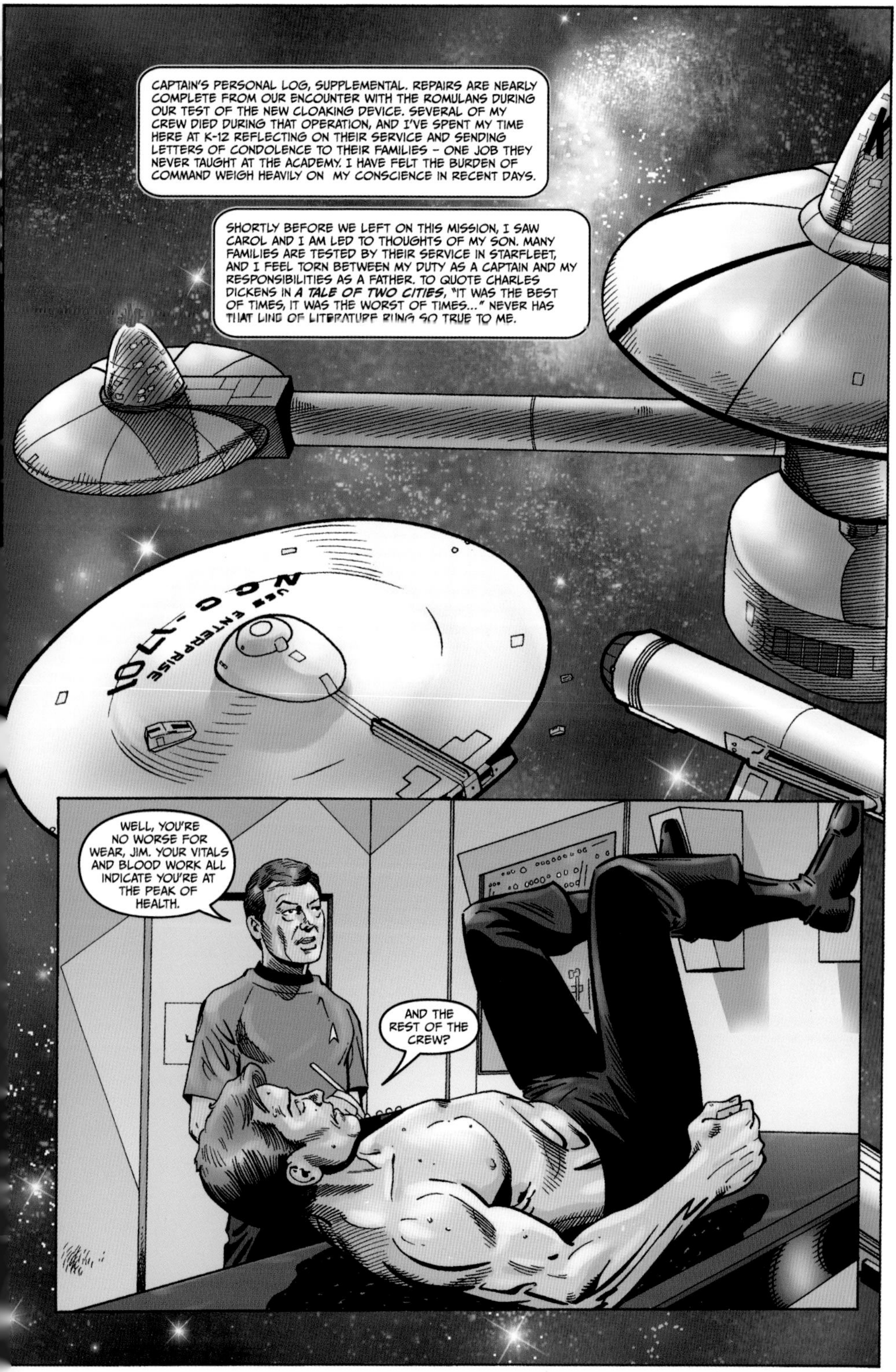
CAPTAIN'S PERSONAL LOG, SUPPLEMENTAL. REPAIRS ARE NEARLY COMPLETE FROM OUR ENCOUNTER WITH THE ROMULANS DURING OUR TEST OF THE NEW CLOAKING DEVICE. SEVERAL OF MY CREW DIED DURING THAT OPERATION, AND I'VE SPENT MY TIME HERE AT K-12 REFLECTING ON THEIR SERVICE AND SENDING LETTERS OF CONDOLENCE TO THEIR FAMILIES – ONE JOB THEY NEVER TAUGHT AT THE ACADEMY. I HAVE FELT THE BURDEN OF COMMAND WEIGH HEAVILY ON MY CONSCIENCE IN RECENT DAYS.
SHORTLY BEFORE WE LEFT ON THIS MISSION, I SAW CAROL AND I AM LED TO THOUGHTS OF MY SON. MANY FAMILIES ARE TESTED BY THEIR SERVICE IN STARFLEET, AND I FEEL TORN BETWEEN MY DUTY AS A CAPTAIN AND MY RESPONSIBILITIES AS A FATHER. TO QUOTE CHARLES DICKENS IN *A TALE OF TWO CITIES*, "IT WAS THE BEST OF TIMES, IT WAS THE WORST OF TIMES..." NEVER HAS THAT LINE OF LITERATURE RUNG SO TRUE TO ME.
NCC-1701
U.S.S. ENTERPRISE
WELL, YOU'RE NO WORSE FOR WEAR, JIM. YOUR VITALS AND BLOOD WORK ALL INDICATE YOU'RE AT THE PEAK OF HEALTH.
AND THE REST OF THE CREW?

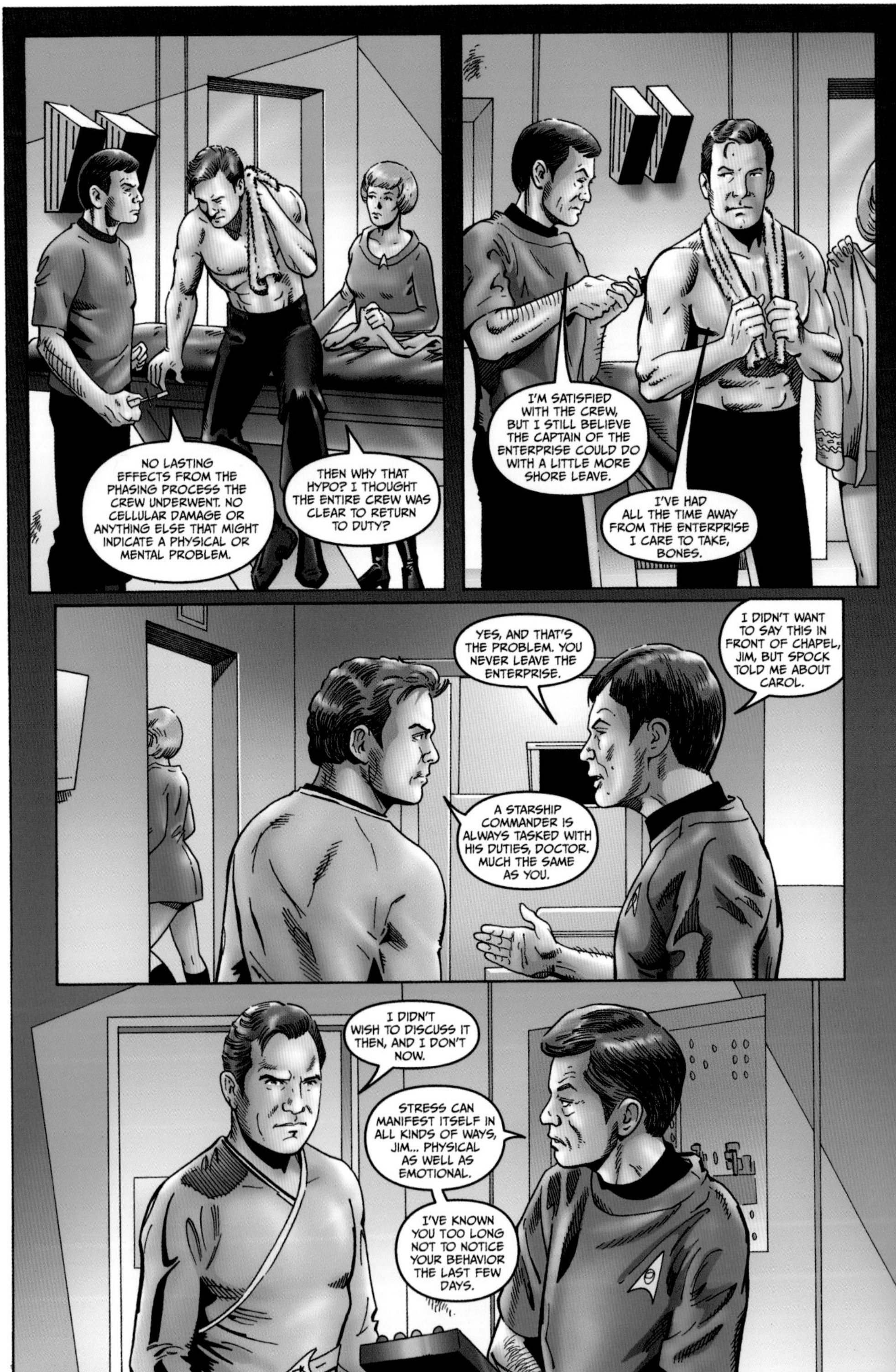
NO LASTING EFFECTS FROM THE PHASING PROCESS THE CREW UNDERWENT. NO CELLULAR DAMAGE OR ANYTHING ELSE THAT MIGHT INDICATE A PHYSICAL OR MENTAL PROBLEM.
THEN WHY THAT HYPO? I THOUGHT THE ENTIRE CREW WAS CLEAR TO RETURN TO DUTY?
I'M SATISFIED WITH THE CREW, BUT I STILL BELIEVE THE CAPTAIN OF THE ENTERPRISE COULD DO WITH A LITTLE MORE SHORE LEAVE.
I'VE HAD ALL THE TIME AWAY FROM THE ENTERPRISE I CARE TO TAKE, BONES.
YES, AND THAT'S THE PROBLEM. YOU NEVER LEAVE THE ENTERPRISE.
I DIDN'T WANT TO SAY THIS IN FRONT OF CHAPEL, JIM, BUT SPOCK TOLD ME ABOUT CAROL.
A STARSHIP COMMANDER IS ALWAYS TASKED WITH HIS DUTIES, DOCTOR. MUCH THE SAME AS YOU.
I DIDN'T WISH TO DISCUSS IT THEN, AND I DON'T NOW.
STRESS CAN MANIFEST ITSELF IN ALL KINDS OF WAYS, JIM... PHYSICAL AS WELL AS EMOTIONAL.
I'VE KNOWN YOU TOO LONG NOT TO NOTICE YOUR BEHAVIOR THE LAST FEW DAYS.

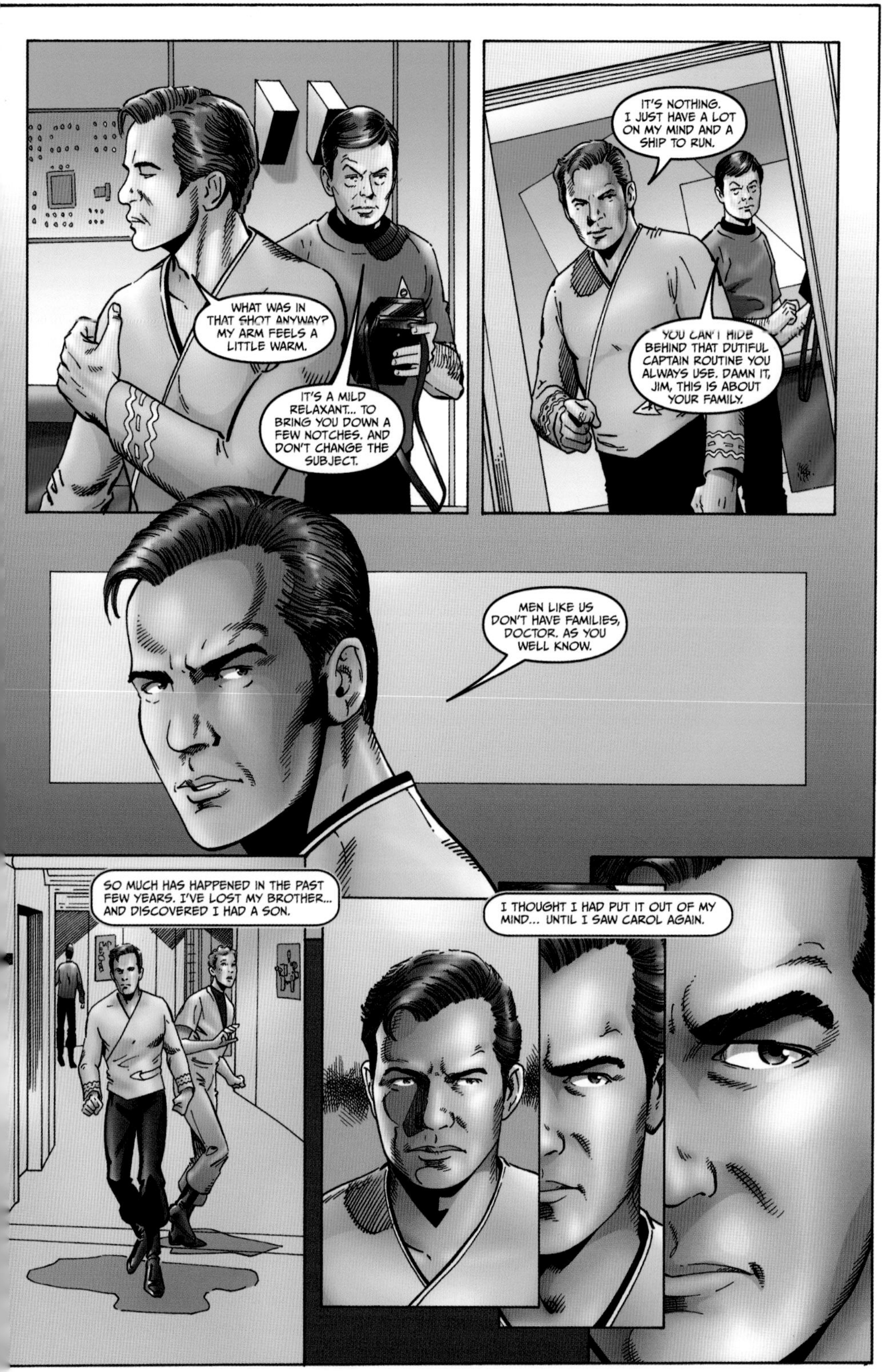
WHAT WAS IN THAT SHOT ANYWAY? MY ARM FEELS A LITTLE WARM.
IT'S A MILD RELAXANT... TO BRING YOU DOWN A FEW NOTCHES. AND DON'T CHANGE THE SUBJECT.
IT'S NOTHING. I JUST HAVE A LOT ON MY MIND AND A SHIP TO RUN.
YOU CAN'T HIDE BEHIND THAT DUTIFUL CAPTAIN ROUTINE YOU ALWAYS USE. DAMN IT, JIM, THIS IS ABOUT YOUR FAMILY.
MEN LIKE US DON'T HAVE FAMILIES, DOCTOR. AS YOU WELL KNOW.
SO MUCH HAS HAPPENED IN THE PAST FEW YEARS. I'VE LOST MY BROTHER... AND DISCOVERED I HAD A SON.
I THOUGHT I HAD PUT IT OUT OF MY MIND... UNTIL I SAW CAROL AGAIN.

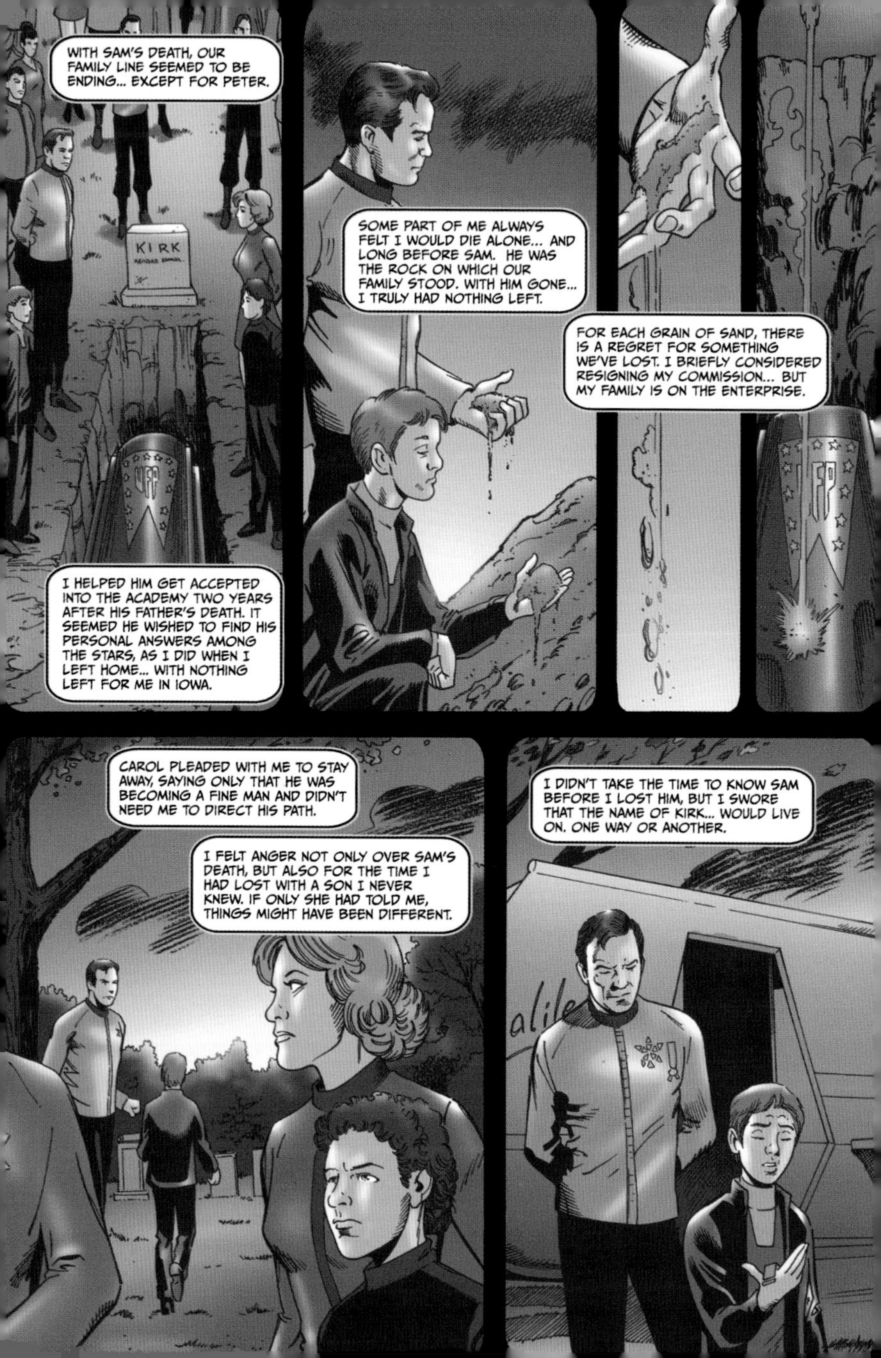
WITH SAM'S DEATH, OUR FAMILY LINE SEEMED TO BE ENDING... EXCEPT FOR PETER.
KIRK
I HELPED HIM GET ACCEPTED INTO THE ACADEMY TWO YEARS AFTER HIS FATHER'S DEATH. IT SEEMED HE WISHED TO FIND HIS PERSONAL ANSWERS AMONG THE STARS, AS I DID WHEN I LEFT HOME... WITH NOTHING LEFT FOR ME IN IOWA.
SOME PART OF ME ALWAYS FELT I WOULD DIE ALONE... AND LONG BEFORE SAM. HE WAS THE ROCK ON WHICH OUR FAMILY STOOD. WITH HIM GONE... I TRULY HAD NOTHING LEFT.
FOR EACH GRAIN OF SAND, THERE IS A REGRET FOR SOMETHING WE'VE LOST. I BRIEFLY CONSIDERED RESIGNING MY COMMISSION... BUT MY FAMILY IS ON THE ENTERPRISE.
CAROL PLEADED WITH ME TO STAY AWAY, SAYING ONLY THAT HE WAS BECOMING A FINE MAN AND DIDN'T NEED ME TO DIRECT HIS PATH.
I FELT ANGER NOT ONLY OVER SAM'S DEATH, BUT ALSO FOR THE TIME I HAD LOST WITH A SON I NEVER KNEW. IF ONLY SHE HAD TOLD ME, THINGS MIGHT HAVE BEEN DIFFERENT.
I DIDN'T TAKE THE TIME TO KNOW SAM BEFORE I LOST HIM, BUT I SWORE THAT THE NAME OF KIRK... WOULD LIVE ON. ONE WAY OR ANOTHER.

ARE WE CLEARED TO DISEMBARK?

MR. SCOTT HAS INDICATED THE LAST OF OUR REPAIRS HAVE BEEN COMPLETED. WE ARE FREE TO LEAVE THE STATION ON YOUR ORDERS, SIR.

DR. MCCOY SEEMED VERY CONCERNED ABOUT SOME PERSONAL MATTERS OF MINE, MR. SPOCK. YOU WOULDN'T KNOW ANYTHING ABOUT THAT, WOULD YOU?

ONLY THAT I ALSO SHARE CONCERN FOR YOUR WELLBEING, CAPTAIN.

AND IT IS MY DUTY TO ANSWER THE CHIEF MEDICAL OFFICER'S QUESTIONS REGARDING MATTERS OF FITNESS OF THE SHIP'S CREW... EVEN THAT OF THE CAPTAIN.

YOUR LOGIC SEEMS TO JUSTIFY YOUR EVERY ACTION, AS ALWAYS, SPOCK.

INDEED. THANK YOU FOR NOTICING, CAPTAIN.

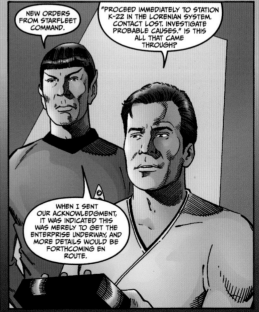

NEW ORDERS FROM STARFLEET COMMAND.

"PROCEED IMMEDIATELY TO STATION K-22 IN THE LORENIAN SYSTEM. CONTACT LOST. INVESTIGATE PROBABLE CAUSES." IS THIS ALL THAT CAME THROUGH?

WHEN I SENT OUR ACKNOWLEDGMENT, IT WAS INDICATED THIS WAS MERELY TO GET THE ENTERPRISE UNDERWAY, AND MORE DETAILS WOULD BE FORTHCOMING EN ROUTE.

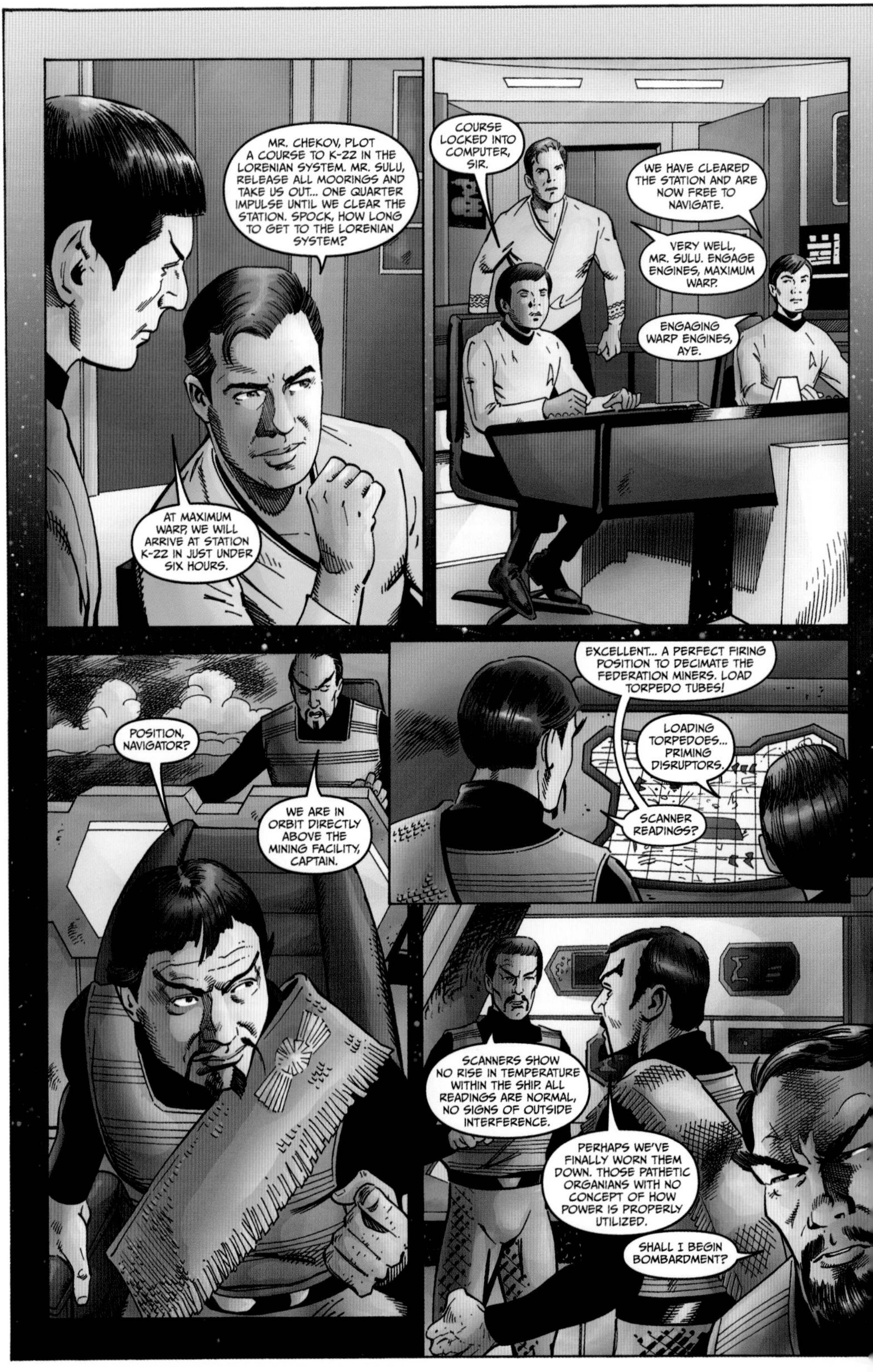
MR. CHEKOV, PLOT A COURSE TO K-22 IN THE LORENIAN SYSTEM. MR. SULU, RELEASE ALL MOORINGS AND TAKE US OUT... ONE QUARTER IMPULSE UNTIL WE CLEAR THE STATION. SPOCK, HOW LONG TO GET TO THE LORENIAN SYSTEM?
AT MAXIMUM WARP, WE WILL ARRIVE AT STATION K-22 IN JUST UNDER SIX HOURS.
COURSE LOCKED INTO COMPUTER, SIR.
WE HAVE CLEARED THE STATION AND ARE NOW FREE TO NAVIGATE.
VERY WELL, MR. SULU. ENGAGE ENGINES, MAXIMUM WARP.
ENGAGING WARP ENGINES, AYE.
POSITION, NAVIGATOR?
WE ARE IN ORBIT DIRECTLY ABOVE THE MINING FACILITY, CAPTAIN.
EXCELLENT... A PERFECT FIRING POSITION TO DECIMATE THE FEDERATION MINERS. LOAD TORPEDO TUBES!
LOADING TORPEDOES... PRIMING DISRUPTORS.
SCANNER READINGS?
SCANNERS SHOW NO RISE IN TEMPERATURE WITHIN THE SHIP. ALL READINGS ARE NORMAL, NO SIGNS OF OUTSIDE INTERFERENCE.
PERHAPS WE'VE FINALLY WORN THEM DOWN. THOSE PATHETIC ORGANIANS WITH NO CONCEPT OF HOW POWER IS PROPERLY UTILIZED.
SHALL I BEGIN BOMBARDMENT?

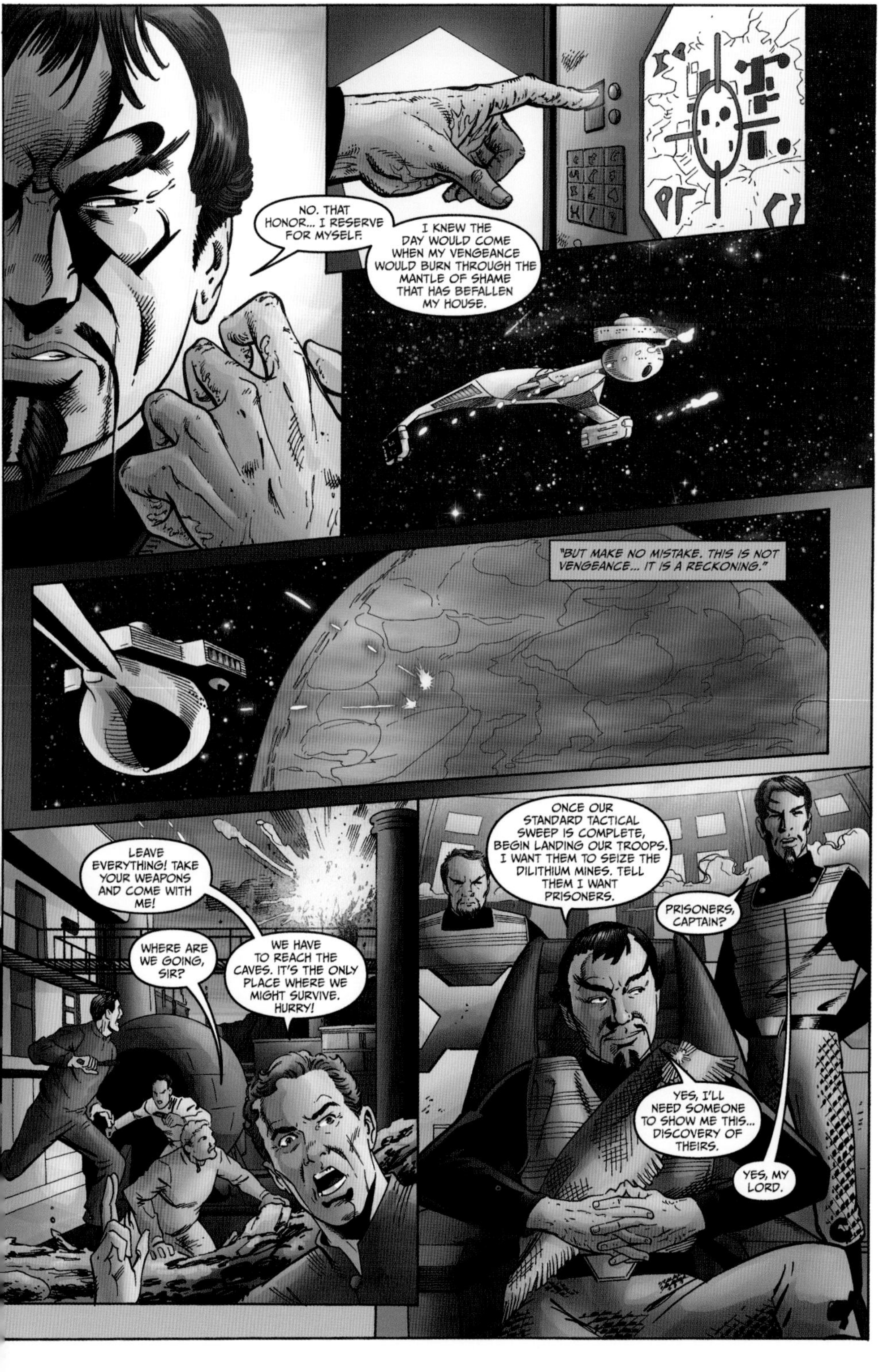
NO. THAT HONOR... I RESERVE FOR MYSELF.
I KNEW THE DAY WOULD COME WHEN MY VENGEANCE WOULD BURN THROUGH THE MANTLE OF SHAME THAT HAS BEFALLEN MY HOUSE.
"BUT MAKE NO MISTAKE. THIS IS NOT VENGEANCE... IT IS A RECKONING."
LEAVE EVERYTHING! TAKE YOUR WEAPONS AND COME WITH ME!
WHERE ARE WE GOING, SIR?
WE HAVE TO REACH THE CAVES. IT'S THE ONLY PLACE WHERE WE MIGHT SURVIVE. HURRY!
ONCE OUR STANDARD TACTICAL SWEEP IS COMPLETE, BEGIN LANDING OUR TROOPS. I WANT THEM TO SEIZE THE DILITHIUM MINES. TELL THEM I WANT PRISONERS.
PRISONERS, CAPTAIN?
YES, I'LL NEED SOMEONE TO SHOW ME THIS... DISCOVERY OF THEIRS.
YES, MY LORD.

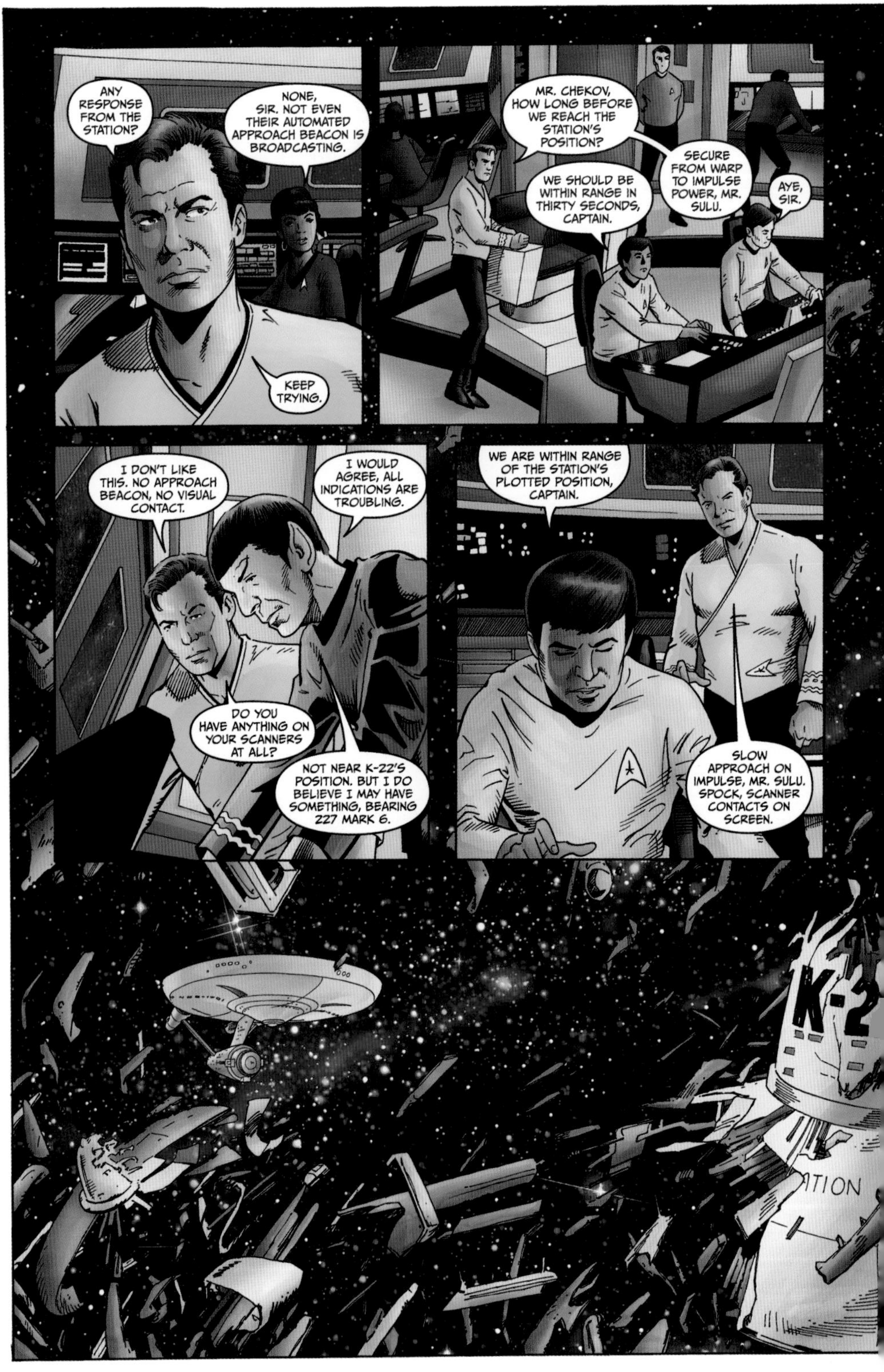
ANY RESPONSE FROM THE STATION?
NONE, SIR. NOT EVEN THEIR AUTOMATED APPROACH BEACON IS BROADCASTING.
KEEP TRYING.
MR. CHEKOV, HOW LONG BEFORE WE REACH THE STATION'S POSITION?
WE SHOULD BE WITHIN RANGE IN THIRTY SECONDS, CAPTAIN.
SECURE FROM WARP TO IMPULSE POWER, MR. SULU.
AYE, SIR.
I DON'T LIKE THIS. NO APPROACH BEACON, NO VISUAL CONTACT.
I WOULD AGREE, ALL INDICATIONS ARE TROUBLING.
DO YOU HAVE ANYTHING ON YOUR SCANNERS AT ALL?
NOT NEAR K-22'S POSITION. BUT I DO BELIEVE I MAY HAVE SOMETHING, BEARING 227 MARK 6.
WE ARE WITHIN RANGE OF THE STATION'S PLOTTED POSITION, CAPTAIN.
SLOW APPROACH ON IMPULSE, MR. SULU. SPOCK, SCANNER CONTACTS ON SCREEN.
K-2
TION

K-22?

THE DEBRIS FIELD CONTAINS SUFFICIENT MASS, AND THE MARKINGS LEAVE LITTLE DOUBT THE STATION HAS BEEN DESTROYED.

THERE WERE OVER SEVEN HUNDRED PEOPLE ON THAT STATION. ANY LIFE PODS OR DISASTER BEACONS?

NEGATIVE, CAPTAIN.

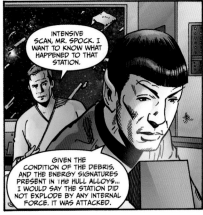

INTENSIVE SCAN, MR. SPOCK. I WANT TO KNOW WHAT HAPPENED TO THAT STATION.

GIVEN THE CONDITION OF THE DEBRIS, AND THE ENERGY SIGNATURES PRESENT IN THE HULL ALLOYS... I WOULD SAY THE STATION DID NOT EXPLODE BY ANY INTERNAL FORCE. IT WAS ATTACKED.

ATTACKED!?

YES, CAPTAIN. THE ENERGY SIGNATURE LEFT BEHIND IN THE DEBRIS IS CONSISTENT WITH KLINGON DISRUPTORS.

BUT THE ORGANIANS HAVE KEPT THE BORDER QUIET FOR OVER TWO YEARS. NEITHER SIDE HAS BEEN ABLE TO TAKE ANY OFFENSIVE ACTION. THIS SHOULD NOT HAVE HAPPENED.

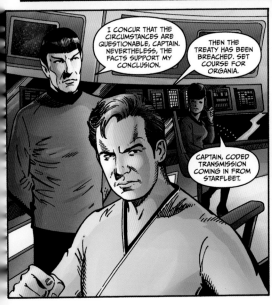

I CONCUR THAT THE CIRCUMSTANCES ARE QUESTIONABLE, CAPTAIN. NEVERTHELESS, THE FACTS SUPPORT MY CONCLUSION.

THEN THE TREATY HAS BEEN BREACHED. SET COURSE FOR ORGANIA.

CAPTAIN, CODED TRANSMISSION COMING IN FROM STARFLEET.

COMMAND DIRECTIVE?

AFFIRMATIVE, SIR. IT'S BEING ROUTED THROUGH EPSILON IX. AT LEAST A TWO-HOUR DELAY SINCE IT WAS TRANSMITTED.

TWO HOURS... LET'S HEAR IT.

ON SPEAKERS NOW, SIR.

COMMAND DIRECTIVE, STARFLEET TACTICAL ORDER. OUR LISTENING POSTS ALONG THE KLINGON NEUTRAL ZONE HAVE REPORTED MULTIPLE KLINGON WARSHIPS.

WE HAVE OUR ORDERS. MR. CHEKOV, LAY IN OUR COURSE TO LOREN 5. UHURA, SEND OUR UPDATED LOGS AND SITUATION TO STARFLEET COMMAND.

AYE, SIR.

THE ENTERPRISE IS ORDERED TO LOREN 5... WE BELIEVE IT TO BE THEIR TARGET. INVESTIGATE IMMEDIATELY.

LAYING IN COURSE NOW.

MR. SULU, TAKE US TO THAT POSITION, BEST POSSIBLE SPEED. SPOCK... COME WITH ME.

AYE, SIR.

RULES OF ENGAGEMENT ARE CAPTAIN'S DISCRETION. EXPECT REINFORCEMENTS IN TWENTY-TWO STANDARD HOURS. TACTICAL INFORMATION ON LOREN 5 INCLUDED IN THIS TRANSMISSION. STARFLEET OUT.

WE WON'T KNOW THEIR SIZE OR DISPOSITION UNTIL WE GET CLOSER.

ALL RIGHT, I'M HERE. WILL SOMEONE PLEASE TELL ME WHAT THE HELL IS GOING ON? SOMEONE SAID WE'RE AT WAR.

THERE IS A VERY HIGH PROBABILITY THAT WE ARE, DOCTOR.

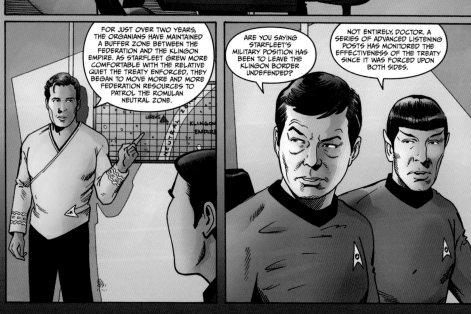

FOR JUST OVER TWO YEARS, THE ORGANIANS HAVE MAINTAINED A BUFFER ZONE BETWEEN THE FEDERATION AND THE KLINGON EMPIRE. AS STARFLEET GREW MORE COMFORTABLE WITH THE RELATIVE QUIET THE TREATY ENFORCED, THEY BEGAN TO MOVE MORE AND MORE FEDERATION RESOURCES TO PATROL THE ROMULAN NEUTRAL ZONE.

ARE YOU SAYING STARFLEET'S MILITARY POSITION HAS BEEN TO LEAVE THE KLINGON BORDER UNDEFENDED?

NOT ENTIRELY, DOCTOR. A SERIES OF ADVANCED LISTENING POSTS HAS MONITORED THE EFFECTIVENESS OF THE TREATY SINCE IT WAS FORCED UPON BOTH SIDES.

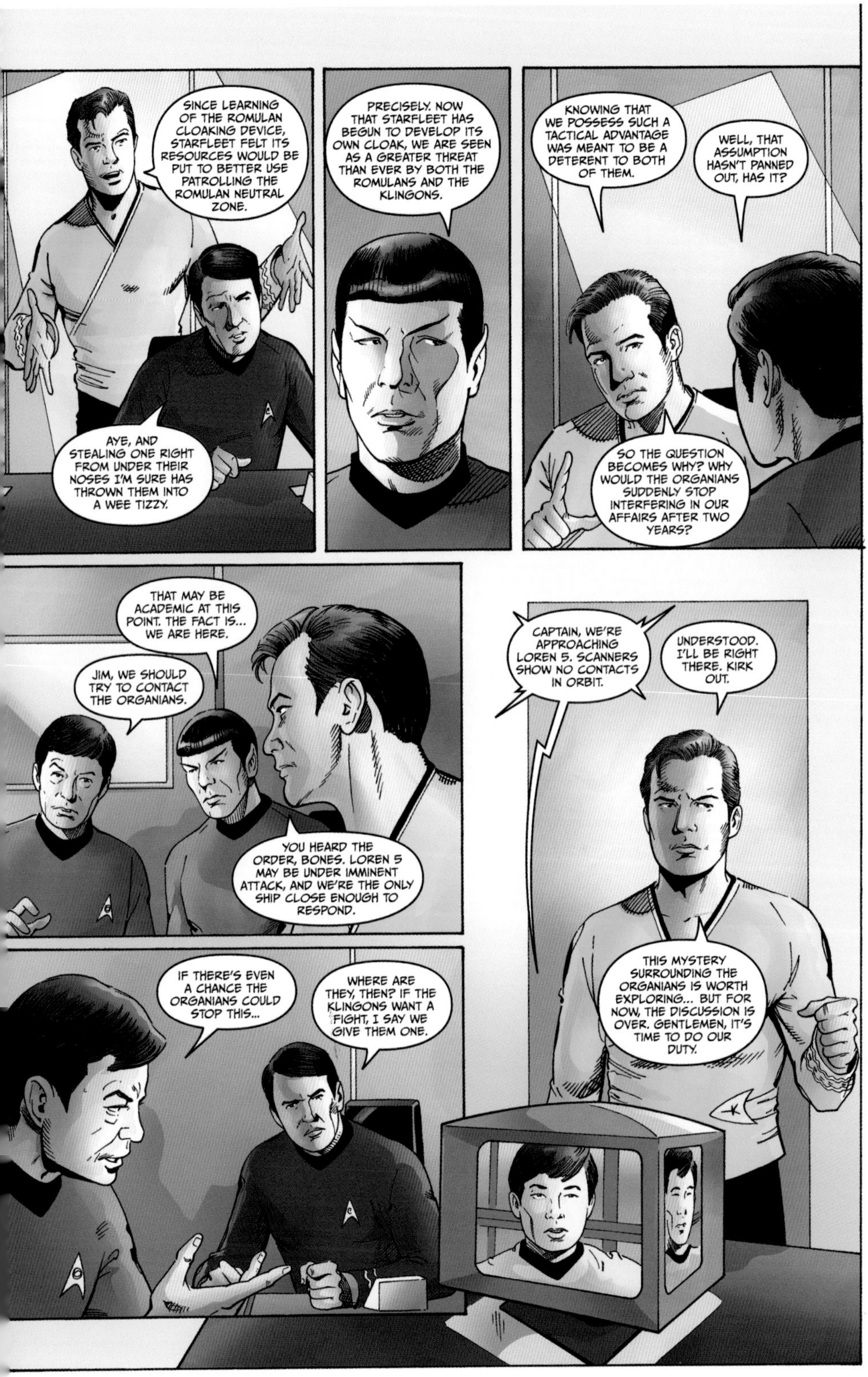
SINCE LEARNING OF THE ROMULAN CLOAKING DEVICE, STARFLEET FELT ITS RESOURCES WOULD BE PUT TO BETTER USE PATROLLING THE ROMULAN NEUTRAL ZONE.
AYE, AND STEALING ONE RIGHT FROM UNDER THEIR NOSES I'M SURE HAS THROWN THEM INTO A WEE TIZZY.
PRECISELY. NOW THAT STARFLEET HAS BEGUN TO DEVELOP ITS OWN CLOAK, WE ARE SEEN AS A GREATER THREAT THAN EVER BY BOTH THE ROMULANS AND THE KLINGONS.
KNOWING THAT WE POSSESS SUCH A TACTICAL ADVANTAGE WAS MEANT TO BE A DETERENT TO BOTH OF THEM.
WELL, THAT ASSUMPTION HASN'T PANNED OUT, HAS IT?
SO THE QUESTION BECOMES WHY? WHY WOULD THE ORGANIANS SUDDENLY STOP INTERFERING IN OUR AFFAIRS AFTER TWO YEARS?
THAT MAY BE ACADEMIC AT THIS POINT. THE FACT IS... WE ARE HERE.
JIM, WE SHOULD TRY TO CONTACT THE ORGANIANS.
YOU HEARD THE ORDER, BONES. LOREN 5 MAY BE UNDER IMMINENT ATTACK, AND WE'RE THE ONLY SHIP CLOSE ENOUGH TO RESPOND.
IF THERE'S EVEN A CHANCE THE ORGANIANS COULD STOP THIS...
WHERE ARE THEY, THEN? IF THE KLINGONS WANT A FIGHT, I SAY WE GIVE THEM ONE.
CAPTAIN, WE'RE APPROACHING LOREN 5. SCANNERS SHOW NO CONTACTS IN ORBIT.
UNDERSTOOD. I'LL BE RIGHT THERE. KIRK OUT.
THIS MYSTERY SURROUNDING THE ORGANIANS IS WORTH EXPLORING... BUT FOR NOW, THE DISCUSSION IS OVER. GENTLEMEN, IT'S TIME TO DO OUR DUTY.

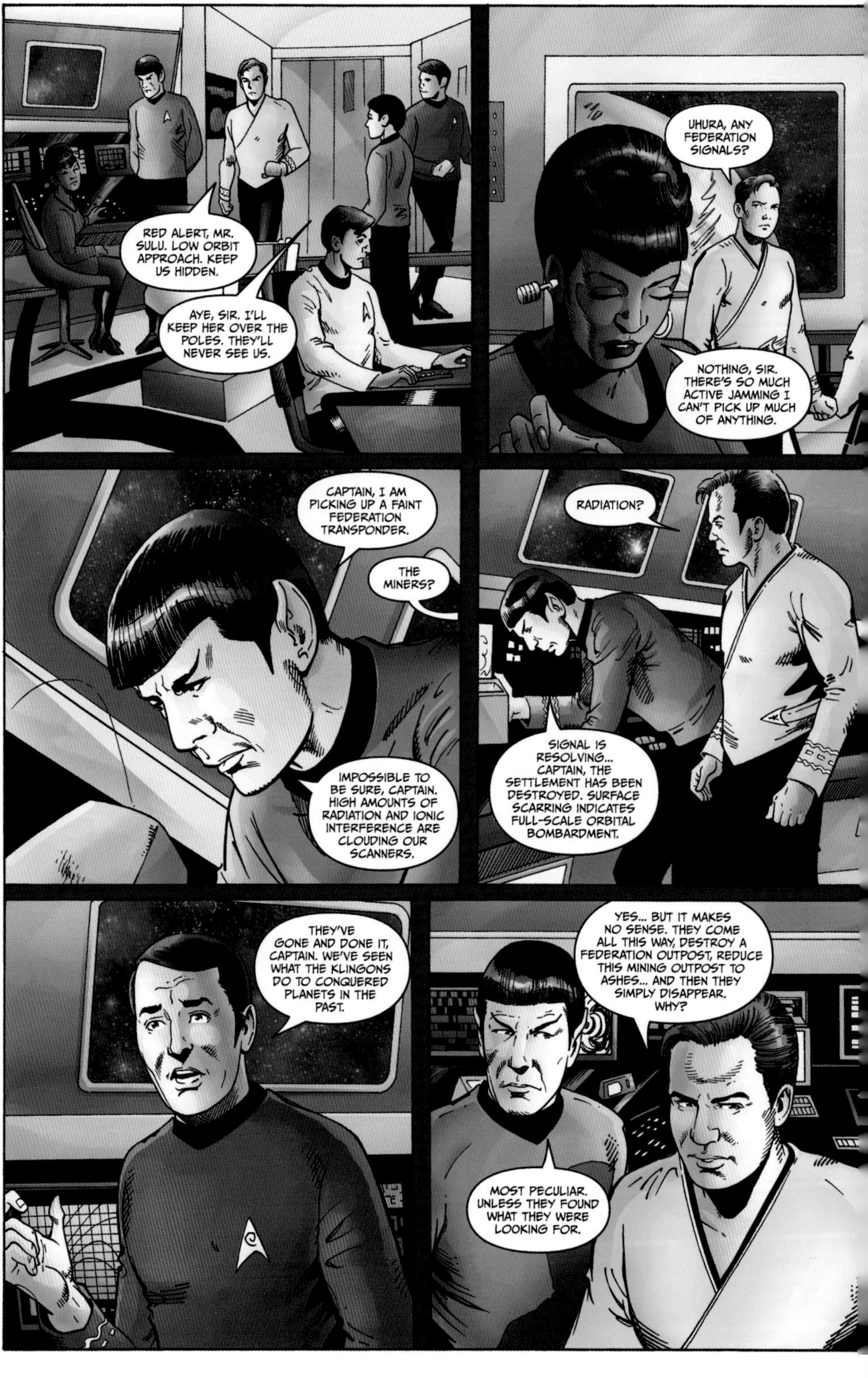
RED ALERT, MR. SULU. LOW ORBIT APPROACH. KEEP US HIDDEN.
AYE, SIR. I'LL KEEP HER OVER THE POLES. THEY'LL NEVER SEE US.
UHURA, ANY FEDERATION SIGNALS?
NOTHING, SIR. THERE'S SO MUCH ACTIVE JAMMING I CAN'T PICK UP MUCH OF ANYTHING.
CAPTAIN, I AM PICKING UP A FAINT FEDERATION TRANSPONDER.
THE MINERS?
IMPOSSIBLE TO BE SURE, CAPTAIN. HIGH AMOUNTS OF RADIATION AND IONIC INTERFERENCE ARE CLOUDING OUR SCANNERS.
RADIATION?
SIGNAL IS RESOLVING... CAPTAIN, THE SETTLEMENT HAS BEEN DESTROYED. SURFACE SCARRING INDICATES FULL-SCALE ORBITAL BOMBARDMENT.
THEY'VE GONE AND DONE IT, CAPTAIN. WE'VE SEEN WHAT THE KLINGONS DO TO CONQUERED PLANETS IN THE PAST.
YES... BUT IT MAKES NO SENSE. THEY COME ALL THIS WAY, DESTROY A FEDERATION OUTPOST, REDUCE THIS MINING OUTPOST TO ASHES... AND THEN THEY SIMPLY DISAPPEAR. WHY?
MOST PECULIAR. UNLESS THEY FOUND WHAT THEY WERE LOOKING FOR.

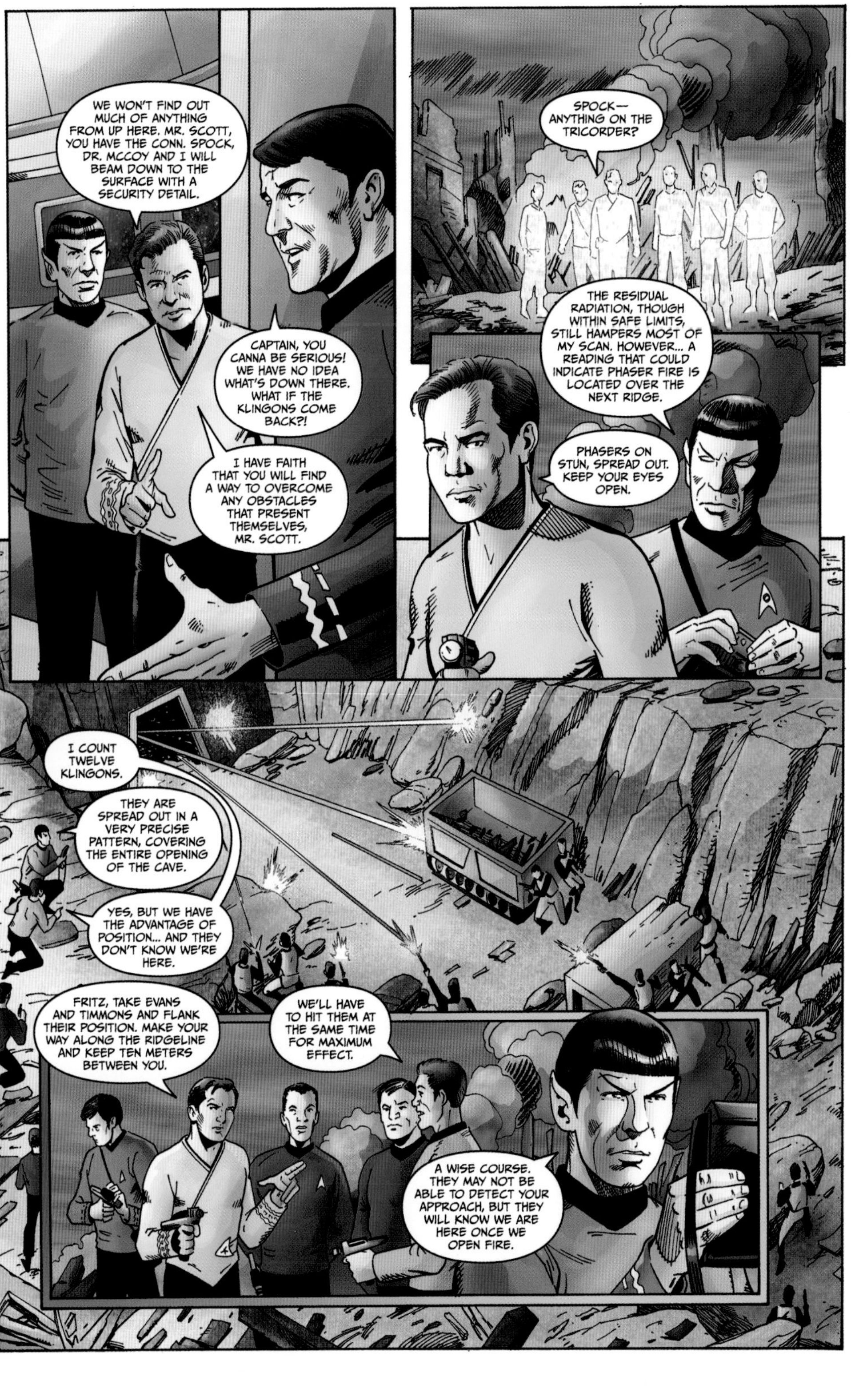
WE WON'T FIND OUT MUCH OF ANYTHING FROM UP HERE. MR. SCOTT, YOU HAVE THE CONN. SPOCK, DR. MCCOY AND I WILL BEAM DOWN TO THE SURFACE WITH A SECURITY DETAIL.
CAPTAIN, YOU CANNA BE SERIOUS! WE HAVE NO IDEA WHAT'S DOWN THERE. WHAT IF THE KLINGONS COME BACK?!
I HAVE FAITH THAT YOU WILL FIND A WAY TO OVERCOME ANY OBSTACLES THAT PRESENT THEMSELVES, MR. SCOTT.
SPOCK— ANYTHING ON THE TRICORDER?
THE RESIDUAL RADIATION, THOUGH WITHIN SAFE LIMITS, STILL HAMPERS MOST OF MY SCAN. HOWEVER... A READING THAT COULD INDICATE PHASER FIRE IS LOCATED OVER THE NEXT RIDGE.
PHASERS ON STUN, SPREAD OUT. KEEP YOUR EYES OPEN.
I COUNT TWELVE KLINGONS.
THEY ARE SPREAD OUT IN A VERY PRECISE PATTERN, COVERING THE ENTIRE OPENING OF THE CAVE.
YES, BUT WE HAVE THE ADVANTAGE OF POSITION... AND THEY DON'T KNOW WE'RE HERE.
FRITZ, TAKE EVANS AND TIMMONS AND FLANK THEIR POSITION. MAKE YOUR WAY ALONG THE RIDGELINE AND KEEP TEN METERS BETWEEN YOU.
WE'LL HAVE TO HIT THEM AT THE SAME TIME FOR MAXIMUM EFFECT.
A WISE COURSE. THEY MAY NOT BE ABLE TO DETECT YOUR APPROACH, BUT THEY WILL KNOW WE ARE HERE ONCE WE OPEN FIRE.

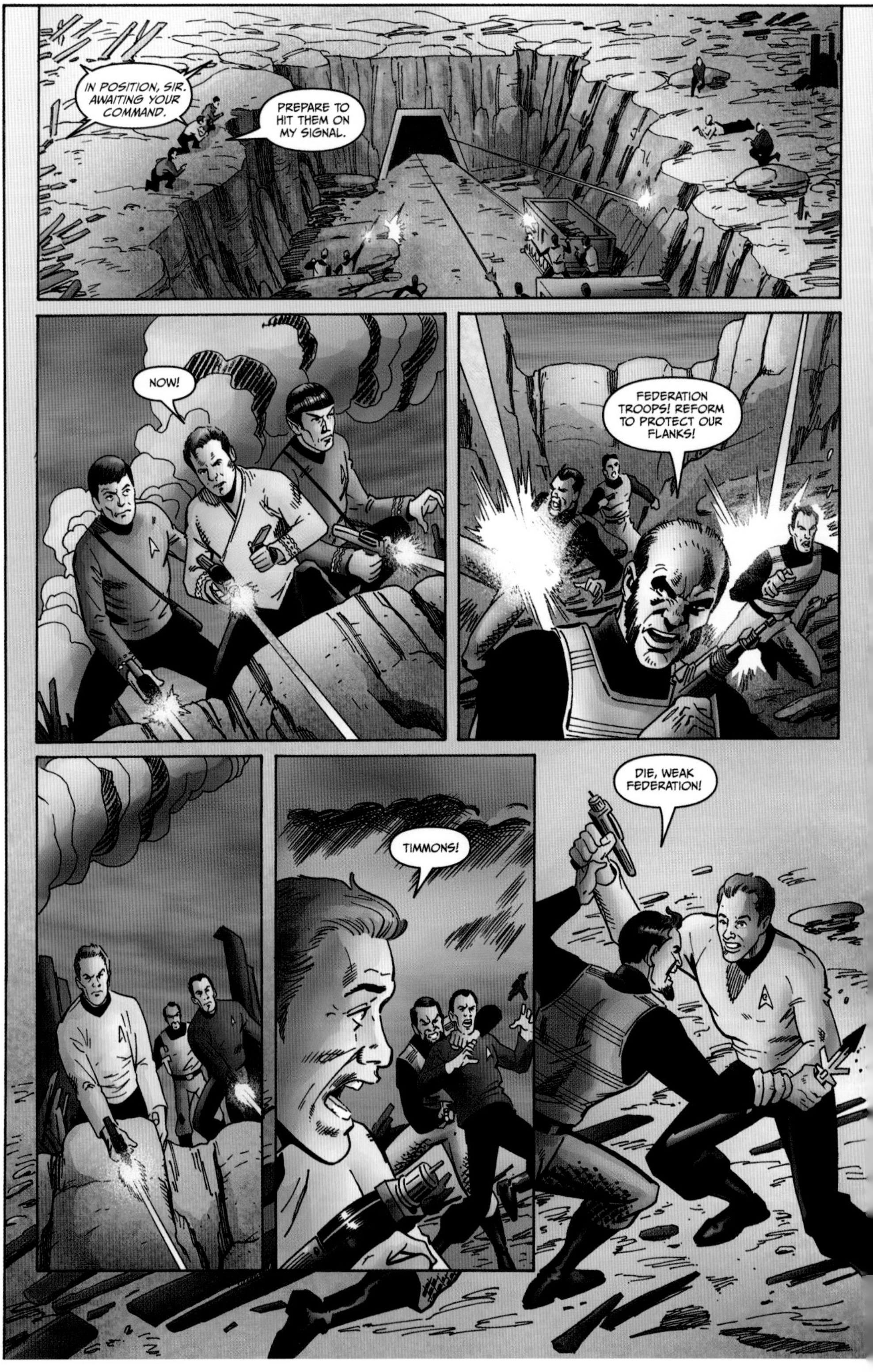
IN POSITION, SIR. AWAITING YOUR COMMAND.
PREPARE TO HIT THEM ON MY SIGNAL.
NOW!
FEDERATION TROOPS! REFORM TO PROTECT OUR FLANKS!
TIMMONS!
DIE, WEAK FEDERATION!

THERE! MOVE TO THE TOP OF THE RIDGE. THEIR ATTACK IS COLLAPSING!

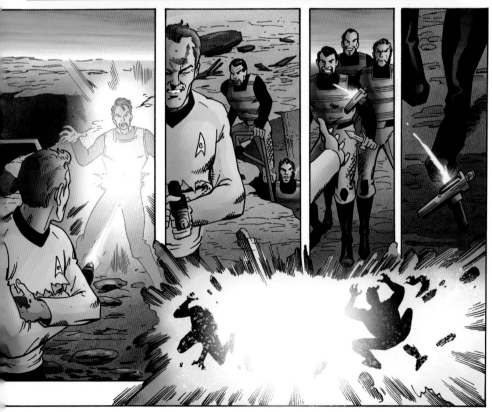

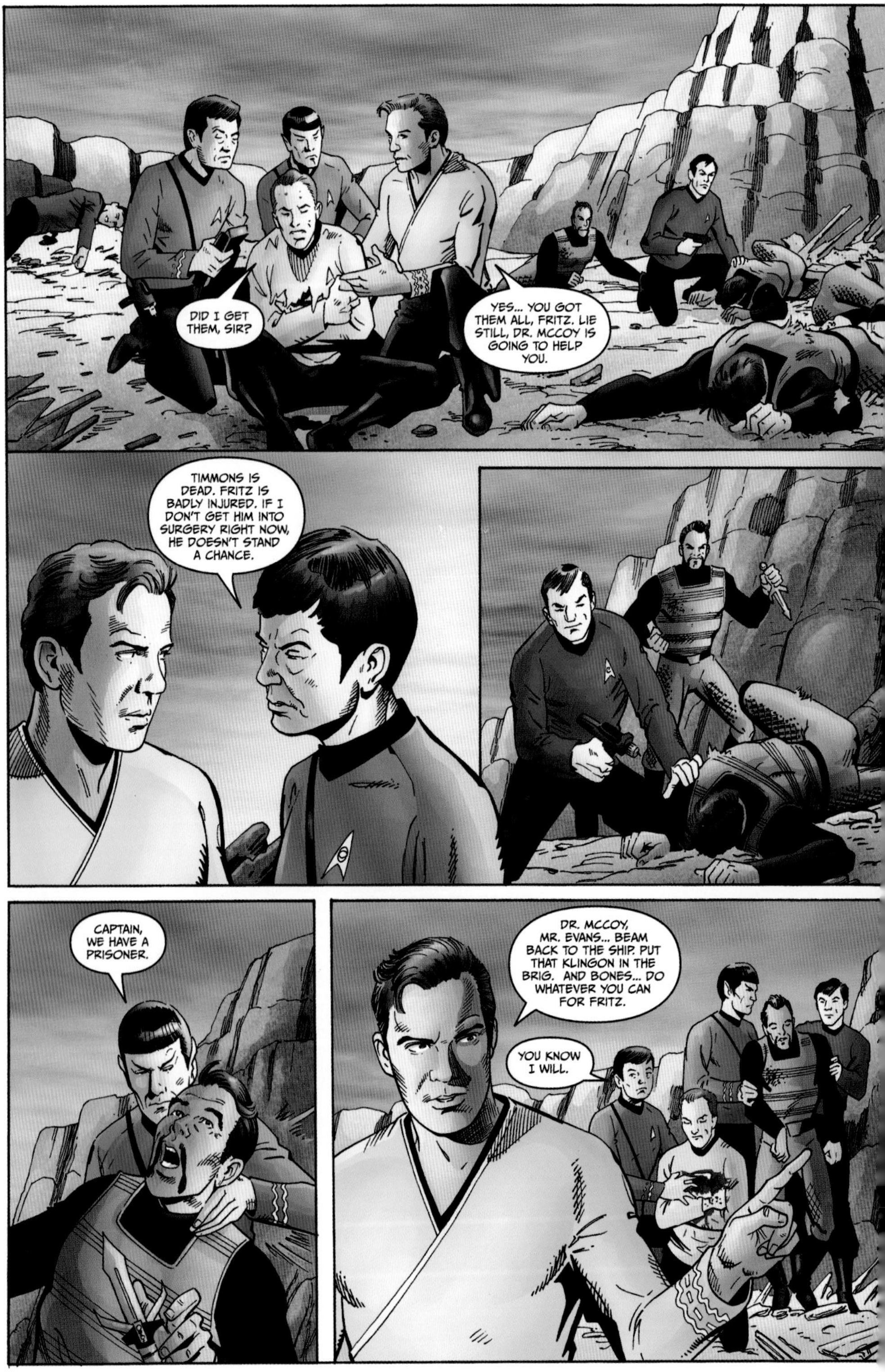
DID I GET THEM, SIR?
YES... YOU GOT THEM ALL, FRITZ. LIE STILL, DR. MCCOY IS GOING TO HELP YOU.
TIMMONS IS DEAD. FRITZ IS BADLY INJURED. IF I DON'T GET HIM INTO SURGERY RIGHT NOW, HE DOESN'T STAND A CHANCE.
CAPTAIN, WE HAVE A PRISONER.
DR. MCCOY, MR. EVANS... BEAM BACK TO THE SHIP. PUT THAT KLINGON IN THE BRIG. AND BONES... DO WHATEVER YOU CAN FOR FRITZ.
YOU KNOW I WILL.

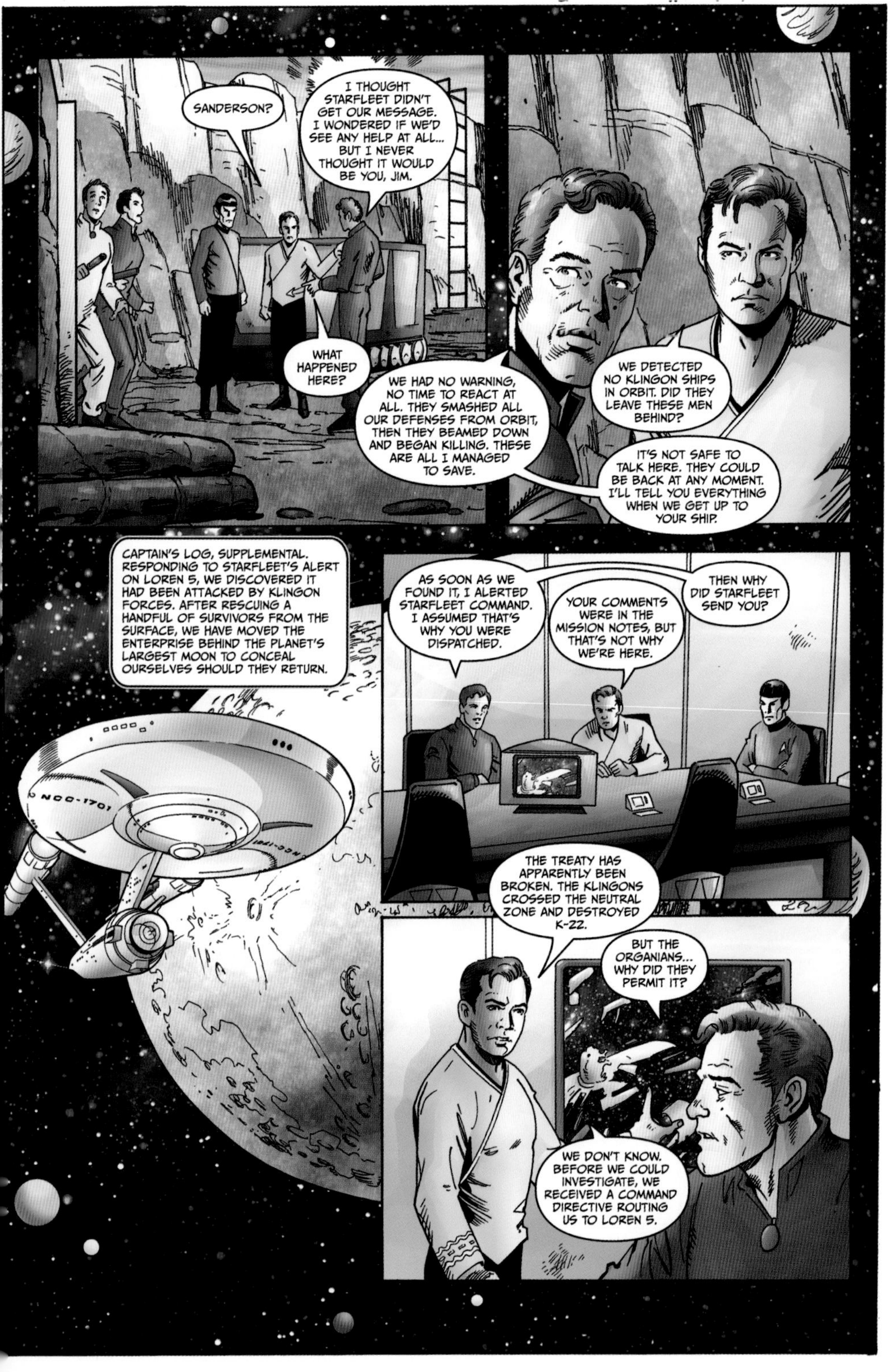
SANDERSON?
I THOUGHT STARFLEET DIDN'T GET OUR MESSAGE. I WONDERED IF WE'D SEE ANY HELP AT ALL... BUT I NEVER THOUGHT IT WOULD BE YOU, JIM.
WHAT HAPPENED HERE?
WE HAD NO WARNING, NO TIME TO REACT AT ALL. THEY SMASHED ALL OUR DEFENSES FROM ORBIT, THEN THEY BEAMED DOWN AND BEGAN KILLING. THESE ARE ALL I MANAGED TO SAVE.
WE DETECTED NO KLINGON SHIPS IN ORBIT. DID THEY LEAVE THESE MEN BEHIND?
IT'S NOT SAFE TO TALK HERE. THEY COULD BE BACK AT ANY MOMENT. I'LL TELL YOU EVERYTHING WHEN WE GET UP TO YOUR SHIP.
CAPTAIN'S LOG, SUPPLEMENTAL. RESPONDING TO STARFLEET'S ALERT ON LOREN 5, WE DISCOVERED IT HAD BEEN ATTACKED BY KLINGON FORCES. AFTER RESCUING A HANDFUL OF SURVIVORS FROM THE SURFACE, WE HAVE MOVED THE ENTERPRISE BEHIND THE PLANET'S LARGEST MOON TO CONCEAL OURSELVES SHOULD THEY RETURN.
NCC-1701
AS SOON AS WE FOUND IT, I ALERTED STARFLEET COMMAND. I ASSUMED THAT'S WHY YOU WERE DISPATCHED.
YOUR COMMENTS WERE IN THE MISSION NOTES, BUT THAT'S NOT WHY WE'RE HERE.
THEN WHY DID STARFLEET SEND YOU?
THE TREATY HAS APPARENTLY BEEN BROKEN. THE KLINGONS CROSSED THE NEUTRAL ZONE AND DESTROYED K-22.
BUT THE ORGANIANS... WHY DID THEY PERMIT IT?
WE DON'T KNOW. BEFORE WE COULD INVESTIGATE, WE RECEIVED A COMMAND DIRECTIVE ROUTING US TO LOREN 5.

THAT CHANGES EVERYTHING. IF THE ORGANIANS ARE NO LONGER ENFORCING THE PEACE, THE KLINGONS COULD TAKE THE FIND BY FORCE.

SANDERSON? WHAT IS THIS FIND—WHAT'S SO IMPORTANT ABOUT IT?

WE WEREN'T COMPLETELY SURE. THAT'S WHY WE REQUESTED A STARSHIP. BUT IT'S BIG, WHATEVER IT IS... AND IT'S THE REASON THE KLINGONS LEFT THEIR TROOPS BEHIND.

THEN YOU EXPECT THEM TO RETURN.

I KNOW THEY WILL. THEY LEFT THEIR TROOPS TO SECURE THE PLANET WHILE THEY WENT OFF TO HELL-KNOWS-WHERE.

I KNOW YOU'VE BEEN THROUGH A LOT, BUT... THINK. WHERE WAS THE FIND LOCATED?

ABOUT... TEN KILOMETERS NORTHEAST OF THE SETTLEMENT.

IT IS LIKELY WE COULD PINPOINT ITS LOCATION WITH OUR SCANNERS.

ANYTHING?

THE SAME INTERFERENCE AS BEFORE, CAPTAIN. HOWEVER, THERE IS A HIGHER CONCENTRATION OF NEUTRINO PARTICLES AT THE COORDINATES CAPTAIN SANDERSON INDICATED.

THEN WE'RE GOING TO HAVE TO GO DOWN THERE.

SO IT SEEMS.

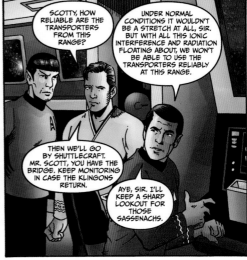

SCOTTY, HOW RELIABLE ARE THE TRANSPORTERS FROM THIS RANGE?

UNDER NORMAL CONDITIONS IT WOULDN'T BE A STRETCH AT ALL, SIR. BUT WITH ALL THIS IONIC INTERFERENCE AND RADIATION FLOATING ABOUT, WE WON'T BE ABLE TO USE THE TRANSPORTERS RELIABLY AT THIS RANGE.

THEN WE'LL GO BY SHUTTLECRAFT. MR. SCOTT, YOU HAVE THE BRIDGE. KEEP MONITORING IN CASE THE KLINGONS RETURN.

AYE, SIR. I'LL KEEP A SHARP LOOKOUT FOR THOSE SASSENACHS.

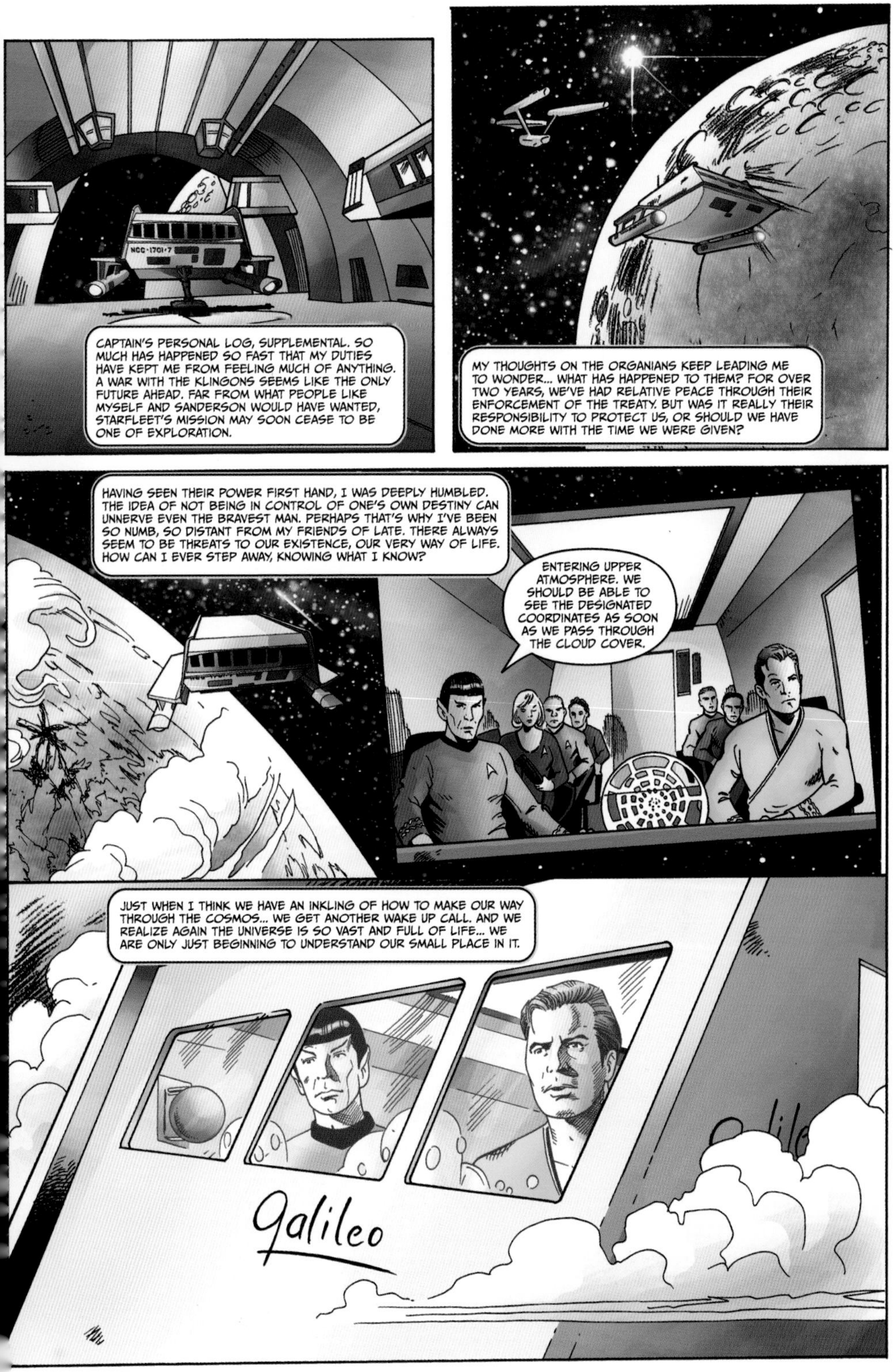
CAPTAIN'S PERSONAL LOG, SUPPLEMENTAL. SO MUCH HAS HAPPENED SO FAST THAT MY DUTIES HAVE KEPT ME FROM FEELING MUCH OF ANYTHING. A WAR WITH THE KLINGONS SEEMS LIKE THE ONLY FUTURE AHEAD. FAR FROM WHAT PEOPLE LIKE MYSELF AND SANDERSON WOULD HAVE WANTED, STARFLEET'S MISSION MAY SOON CEASE TO BE ONE OF EXPLORATION.
NCC-1701-7
MY THOUGHTS ON THE ORGANIANS KEEP LEADING ME TO WONDER... WHAT HAS HAPPENED TO THEM? FOR OVER TWO YEARS, WE'VE HAD RELATIVE PEACE THROUGH THEIR ENFORCEMENT OF THE TREATY. BUT WAS IT REALLY THEIR RESPONSIBILITY TO PROTECT US, OR SHOULD WE HAVE DONE MORE WITH THE TIME WE WERE GIVEN?
HAVING SEEN THEIR POWER FIRST HAND, I WAS DEEPLY HUMBLED. THE IDEA OF NOT BEING IN CONTROL OF ONE'S OWN DESTINY CAN UNNERVE EVEN THE BRAVEST MAN. PERHAPS THAT'S WHY I'VE BEEN SO NUMB, SO DISTANT FROM MY FRIENDS OF LATE. THERE ALWAYS SEEM TO BE THREATS TO OUR EXISTENCE, OUR VERY WAY OF LIFE. HOW CAN I EVER STEP AWAY, KNOWING WHAT I KNOW?
ENTERING UPPER ATMOSPHERE. WE SHOULD BE ABLE TO SEE THE DESIGNATED COORDINATES AS SOON AS WE PASS THROUGH THE CLOUD COVER.
JUST WHEN I THINK WE HAVE AN INKLING OF HOW TO MAKE OUR WAY THROUGH THE COSMOS... WE GET ANOTHER WAKE UP CALL. AND WE REALIZE AGAIN THE UNIVERSE IS SO VAST AND FULL OF LIFE... WE ARE ONLY JUST BEGINNING TO UNDERSTAND OUR SMALL PLACE IN IT.
Galileo

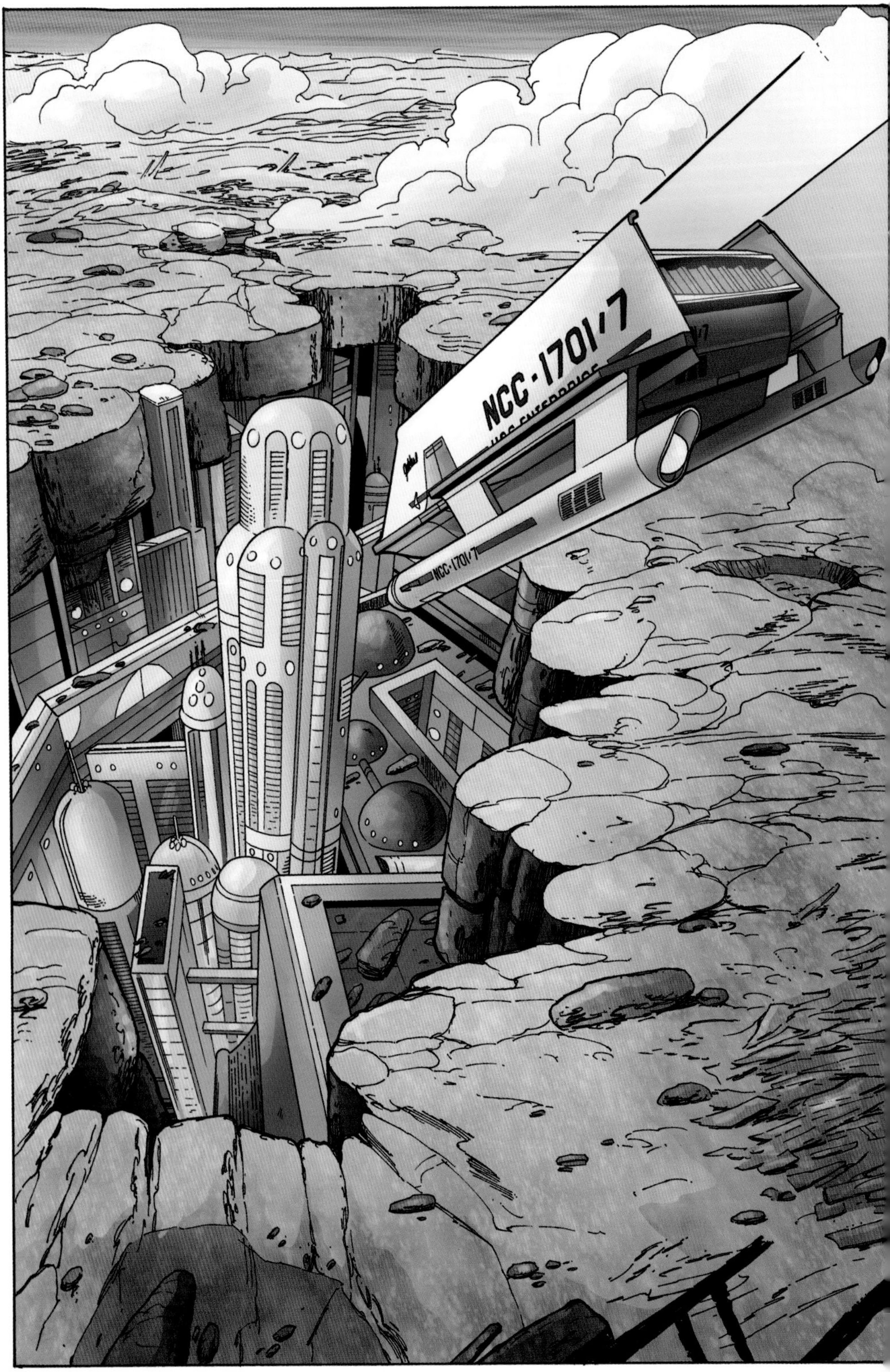
NCC-1701/7
NCC-1701/7

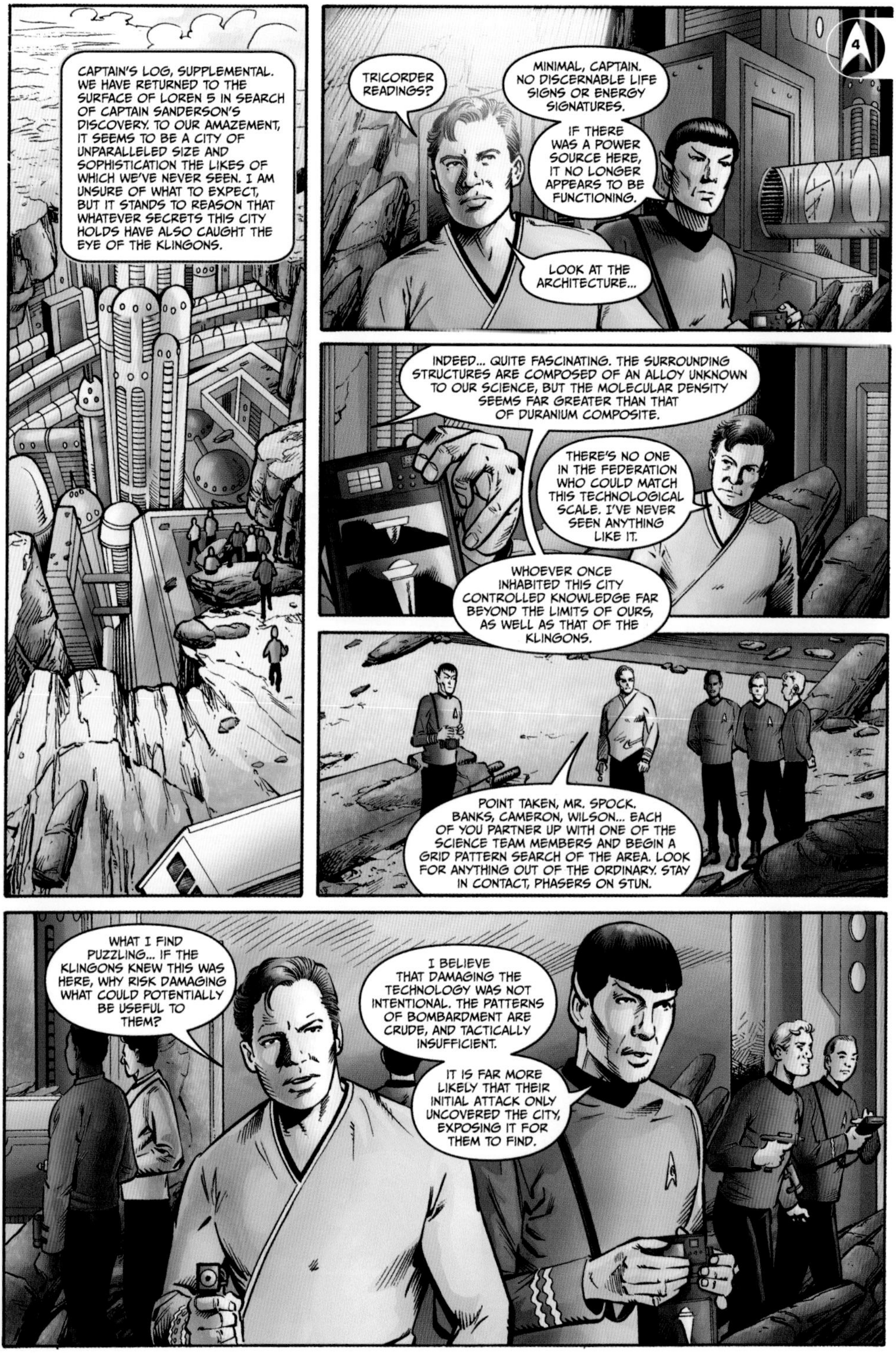
4
CAPTAIN'S LOG, SUPPLEMENTAL. WE HAVE RETURNED TO THE SURFACE OF LOREN 5 IN SEARCH OF CAPTAIN SANDERSON'S DISCOVERY. TO OUR AMAZEMENT, IT SEEMS TO BE A CITY OF UNPARALLELED SIZE AND SOPHISTICATION THE LIKES OF WHICH WE'VE NEVER SEEN. I AM UNSURE OF WHAT TO EXPECT, BUT IT STANDS TO REASON THAT WHATEVER SECRETS THIS CITY HOLDS HAVE ALSO CAUGHT THE EYE OF THE KLINGONS.
TRICORDER READINGS?
MINIMAL, CAPTAIN. NO DISCERNABLE LIFE SIGNS OR ENERGY SIGNATURES.
IF THERE WAS A POWER SOURCE HERE, IT NO LONGER APPEARS TO BE FUNCTIONING.
LOOK AT THE ARCHITECTURE...
INDEED... QUITE FASCINATING. THE SURROUNDING STRUCTURES ARE COMPOSED OF AN ALLOY UNKNOWN TO OUR SCIENCE, BUT THE MOLECULAR DENSITY SEEMS FAR GREATER THAN THAT OF DURANIUM COMPOSITE.
THERE'S NO ONE IN THE FEDERATION WHO COULD MATCH THIS TECHNOLOGICAL SCALE. I'VE NEVER SEEN ANYTHING LIKE IT.
WHOEVER ONCE INHABITED THIS CITY CONTROLLED KNOWLEDGE FAR BEYOND THE LIMITS OF OURS, AS WELL AS THAT OF THE KLINGONS.
POINT TAKEN, MR. SPOCK. BANKS, CAMERON, WILSON... EACH OF YOU PARTNER UP WITH ONE OF THE SCIENCE TEAM MEMBERS AND BEGIN A GRID PATTERN SEARCH OF THE AREA. LOOK FOR ANYTHING OUT OF THE ORDINARY. STAY IN CONTACT, PHASERS ON STUN.
WHAT I FIND PUZZLING... IF THE KLINGONS KNEW THIS WAS HERE, WHY RISK DAMAGING WHAT COULD POTENTIALLY BE USEFUL TO THEM?
I BELIEVE THAT DAMAGING THE TECHNOLOGY WAS NOT INTENTIONAL. THE PATTERNS OF BOMBARDMENT ARE CRUDE, AND TACTICALLY INSUFFICIENT.
IT IS FAR MORE LIKELY THAT THEIR INITIAL ATTACK ONLY UNCOVERED THE CITY, EXPOSING IT FOR THEM TO FIND.

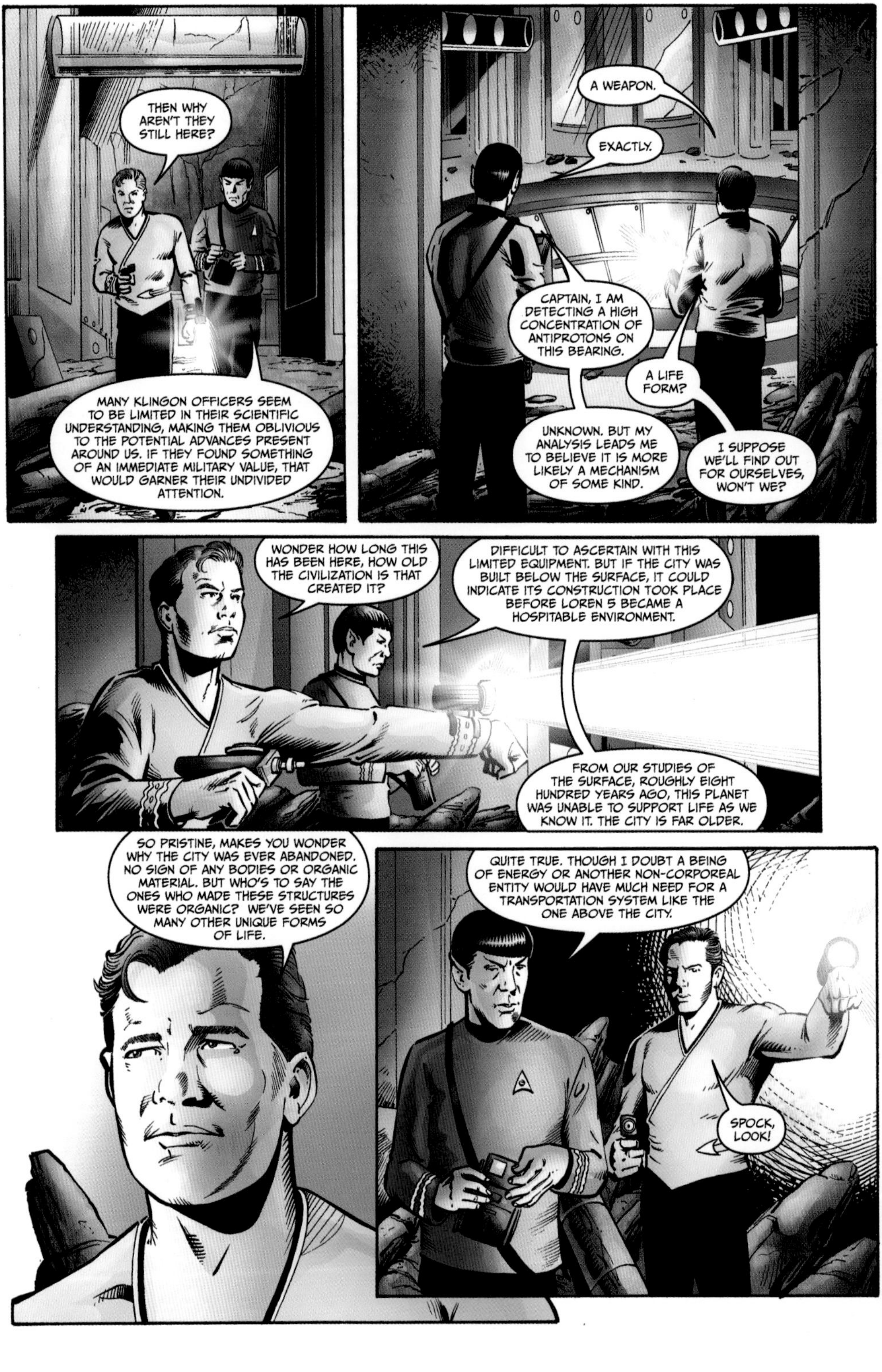
THEN WHY AREN'T THEY STILL HERE?
MANY KLINGON OFFICERS SEEM TO BE LIMITED IN THEIR SCIENTIFIC UNDERSTANDING, MAKING THEM OBLIVIOUS TO THE POTENTIAL ADVANCES PRESENT AROUND US. IF THEY FOUND SOMETHING OF AN IMMEDIATE MILITARY VALUE, THAT WOULD GARNER THEIR UNDIVIDED ATTENTION.
A WEAPON.
EXACTLY.
CAPTAIN, I AM DETECTING A HIGH CONCENTRATION OF ANTIPROTONS ON THIS BEARING.
A LIFE FORM?
UNKNOWN. BUT MY ANALYSIS LEADS ME TO BELIEVE IT IS MORE LIKELY A MECHANISM OF SOME KIND.
I SUPPOSE WE'LL FIND OUT FOR OURSELVES, WON'T WE?
WONDER HOW LONG THIS HAS BEEN HERE, HOW OLD THE CIVILIZATION IS THAT CREATED IT?
DIFFICULT TO ASCERTAIN WITH THIS LIMITED EQUIPMENT. BUT IF THE CITY WAS BUILT BELOW THE SURFACE, IT COULD INDICATE ITS CONSTRUCTION TOOK PLACE BEFORE LOREN 5 BECAME A HOSPITABLE ENVIRONMENT.
FROM OUR STUDIES OF THE SURFACE, ROUGHLY EIGHT HUNDRED YEARS AGO, THIS PLANET WAS UNABLE TO SUPPORT LIFE AS WE KNOW IT. THE CITY IS FAR OLDER.
SO PRISTINE, MAKES YOU WONDER WHY THE CITY WAS EVER ABANDONED. NO SIGN OF ANY BODIES OR ORGANIC MATERIAL. BUT WHO'S TO SAY THE ONES WHO MADE THESE STRUCTURES WERE ORGANIC? WE'VE SEEN SO MANY OTHER UNIQUE FORMS OF LIFE.
QUITE TRUE. THOUGH I DOUBT A BEING OF ENERGY OR ANOTHER NON-CORPOREAL ENTITY WOULD HAVE MUCH NEED FOR A TRANSPORTATION SYSTEM LIKE THE ONE ABOVE THE CITY.
SPOCK, LOOK!

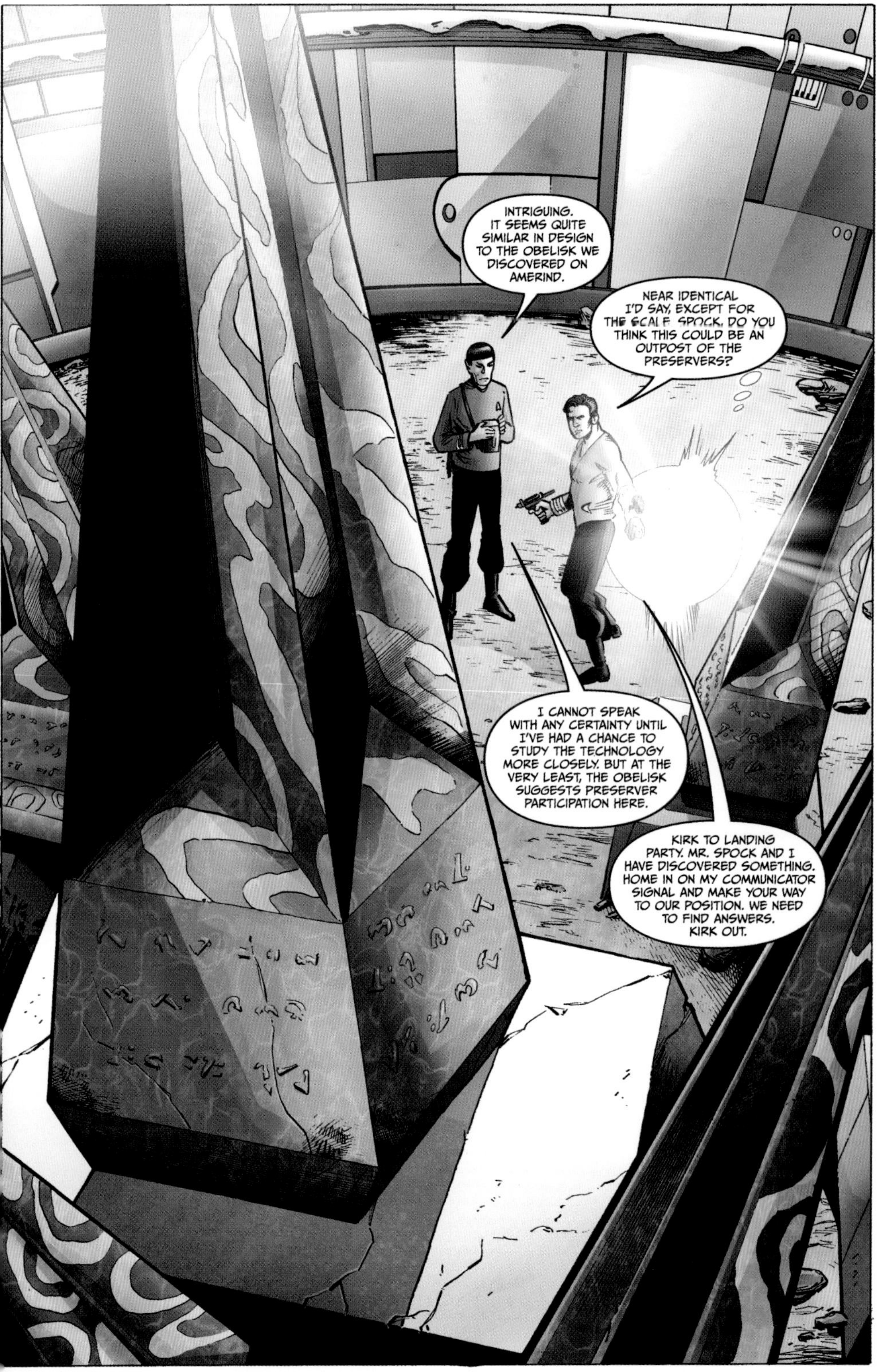
INTRIGUING. IT SEEMS QUITE SIMILAR IN DESIGN TO THE OBELISK WE DISCOVERED ON AMERIND.
NEAR IDENTICAL I'D SAY, EXCEPT FOR THE SCALE. SPOCK, DO YOU THINK THIS COULD BE AN OUTPOST OF THE PRESERVERS?
I CANNOT SPEAK WITH ANY CERTAINTY UNTIL I'VE HAD A CHANCE TO STUDY THE TECHNOLOGY MORE CLOSELY. BUT AT THE VERY LEAST, THE OBELISK SUGGESTS PRESERVER PARTICIPATION HERE.
KIRK TO LANDING PARTY. MR. SPOCK AND I HAVE DISCOVERED SOMETHING. HOME IN ON MY COMMUNICATOR SIGNAL AND MAKE YOUR WAY TO OUR POSITION. WE NEED TO FIND ANSWERS. KIRK OUT.

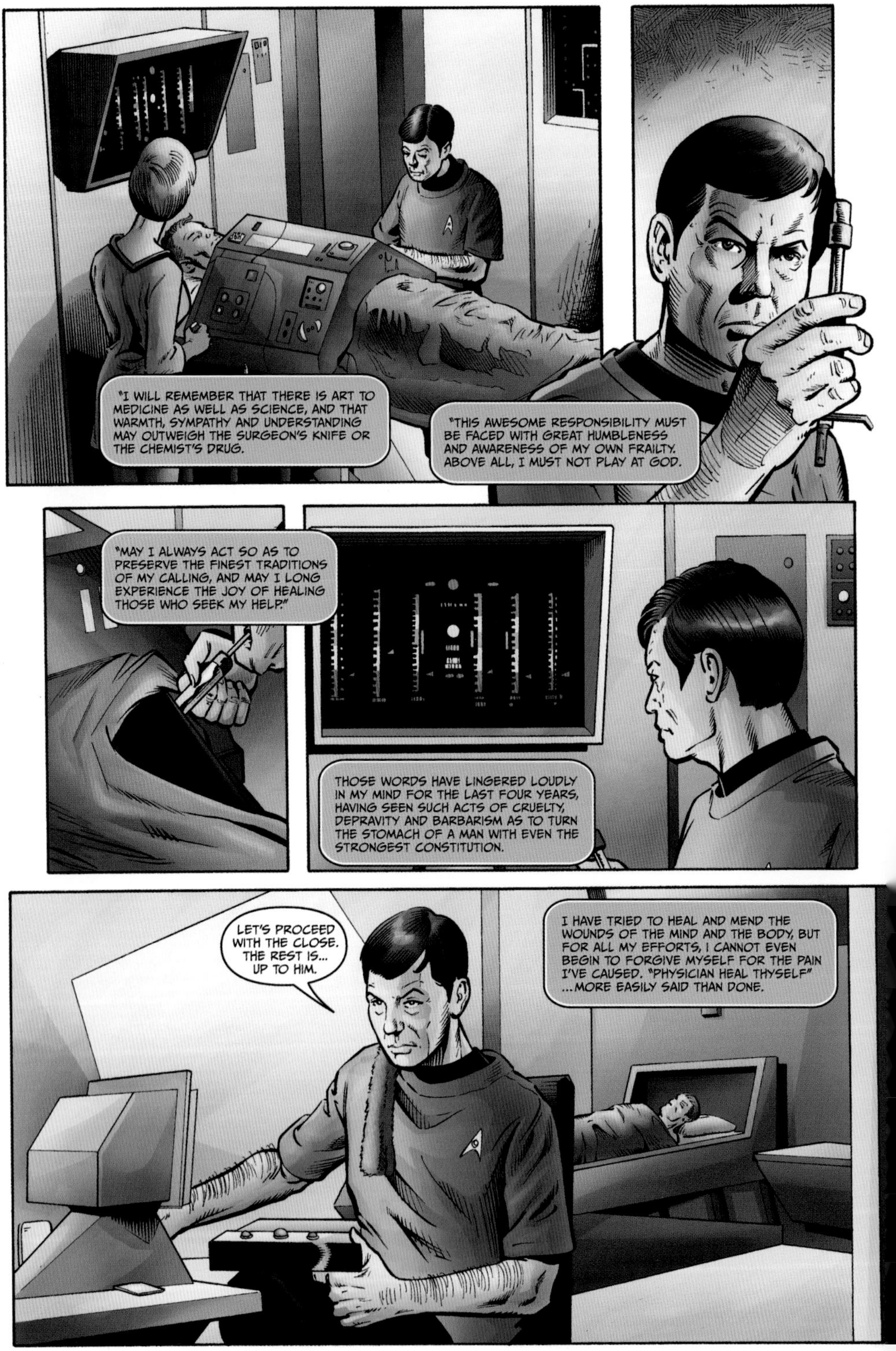
"I WILL REMEMBER THAT THERE IS ART TO MEDICINE AS WELL AS SCIENCE, AND THAT WARMTH, SYMPATHY AND UNDERSTANDING MAY OUTWEIGH THE SURGEON'S KNIFE OR THE CHEMIST'S DRUG.
"THIS AWESOME RESPONSIBILITY MUST BE FACED WITH GREAT HUMBLENESS AND AWARENESS OF MY OWN FRAILTY. ABOVE ALL, I MUST NOT PLAY AT GOD.
"MAY I ALWAYS ACT SO AS TO PRESERVE THE FINEST TRADITIONS OF MY CALLING, AND MAY I LONG EXPERIENCE THE JOY OF HEALING THOSE WHO SEEK MY HELP."
THOSE WORDS HAVE LINGERED LOUDLY IN MY MIND FOR THE LAST FOUR YEARS, HAVING SEEN SUCH ACTS OF CRUELTY, DEPRAVITY AND BARBARISM AS TO TURN THE STOMACH OF A MAN WITH EVEN THE STRONGEST CONSTITUTION.
LET'S PROCEED WITH THE CLOSE. THE REST IS... UP TO HIM.
I HAVE TRIED TO HEAL AND MEND THE WOUNDS OF THE MIND AND THE BODY, BUT FOR ALL MY EFFORTS, I CANNOT EVEN BEGIN TO FORGIVE MYSELF FOR THE PAIN I'VE CAUSED. "PHYSICIAN HEAL THYSELF" ...MORE EASILY SAID THAN DONE.

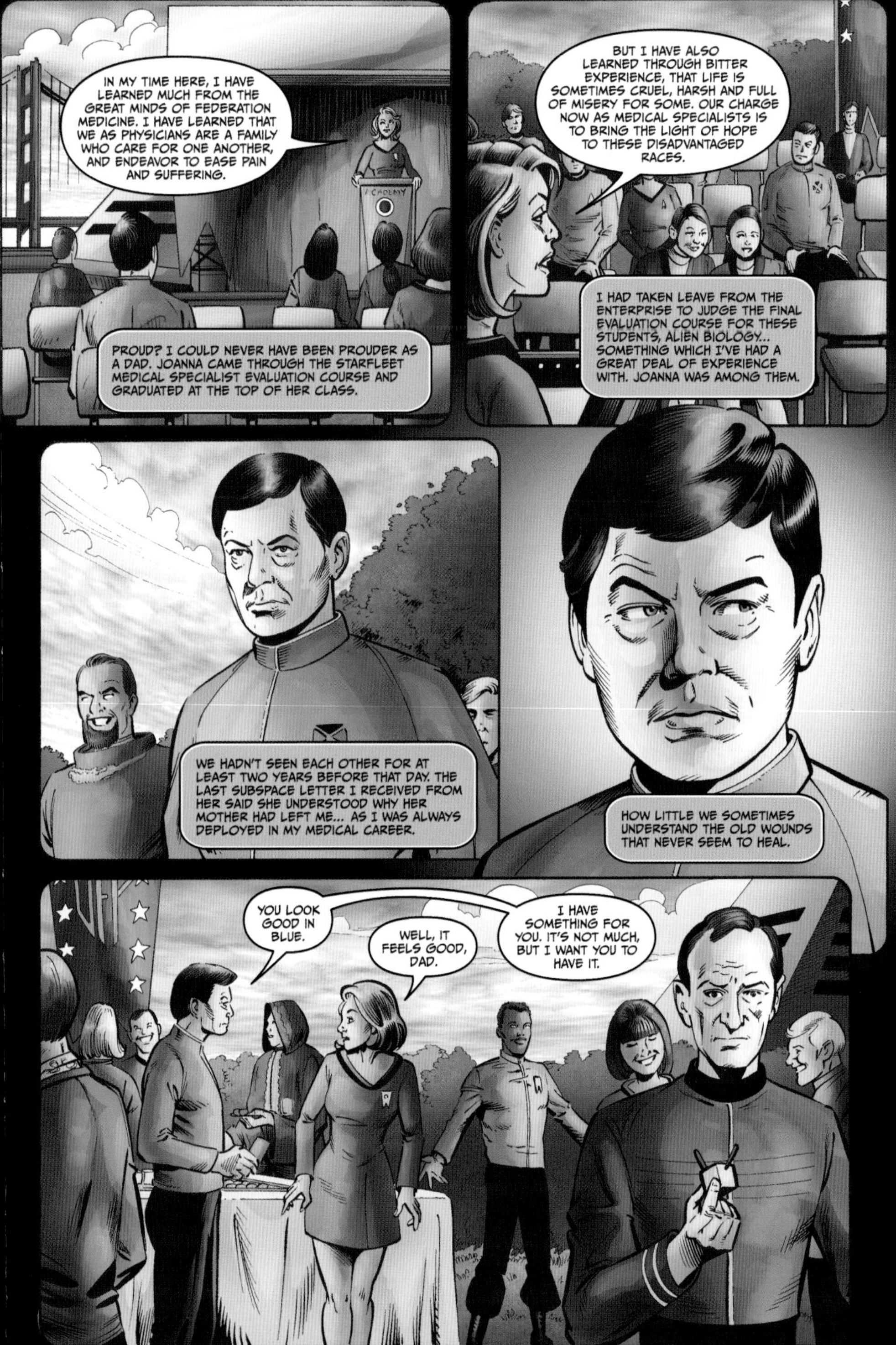
IN MY TIME HERE, I HAVE LEARNED MUCH FROM THE GREAT MINDS OF FEDERATION MEDICINE. I HAVE LEARNED THAT WE AS PHYSICIANS ARE A FAMILY WHO CARE FOR ONE ANOTHER, AND ENDEAVOR TO EASE PAIN AND SUFFERING.
PROUD? I COULD NEVER HAVE BEEN PROUDER AS A DAD. JOANNA CAME THROUGH THE STARFLEET MEDICAL SPECIALIST EVALUATION COURSE AND GRADUATED AT THE TOP OF HER CLASS.
BUT I HAVE ALSO LEARNED THROUGH BITTER EXPERIENCE, THAT LIFE IS SOMETIMES CRUEL, HARSH AND FULL OF MISERY FOR SOME. OUR CHARGE NOW AS MEDICAL SPECIALISTS IS TO BRING THE LIGHT OF HOPE TO THESE DISADVANTAGED RACES.
I HAD TAKEN LEAVE FROM THE ENTERPRISE TO JUDGE THE FINAL EVALUATION COURSE FOR THESE STUDENTS, ALIEN BIOLOGY... SOMETHING WHICH I'VE HAD A GREAT DEAL OF EXPERIENCE WITH. JOANNA WAS AMONG THEM.
WE HADN'T SEEN EACH OTHER FOR AT LEAST TWO YEARS BEFORE THAT DAY. THE LAST SUBSPACE LETTER I RECEIVED FROM HER SAID SHE UNDERSTOOD WHY HER MOTHER HAD LEFT ME... AS I WAS ALWAYS DEPLOYED IN MY MEDICAL CAREER.
HOW LITTLE WE SOMETIMES UNDERSTAND THE OLD WOUNDS THAT NEVER SEEM TO HEAL.
YOU LOOK GOOD IN BLUE.
WELL, IT FEELS GOOD, DAD.
I HAVE SOMETHING FOR YOU. IT'S NOT MUCH, BUT I WANT YOU TO HAVE IT.

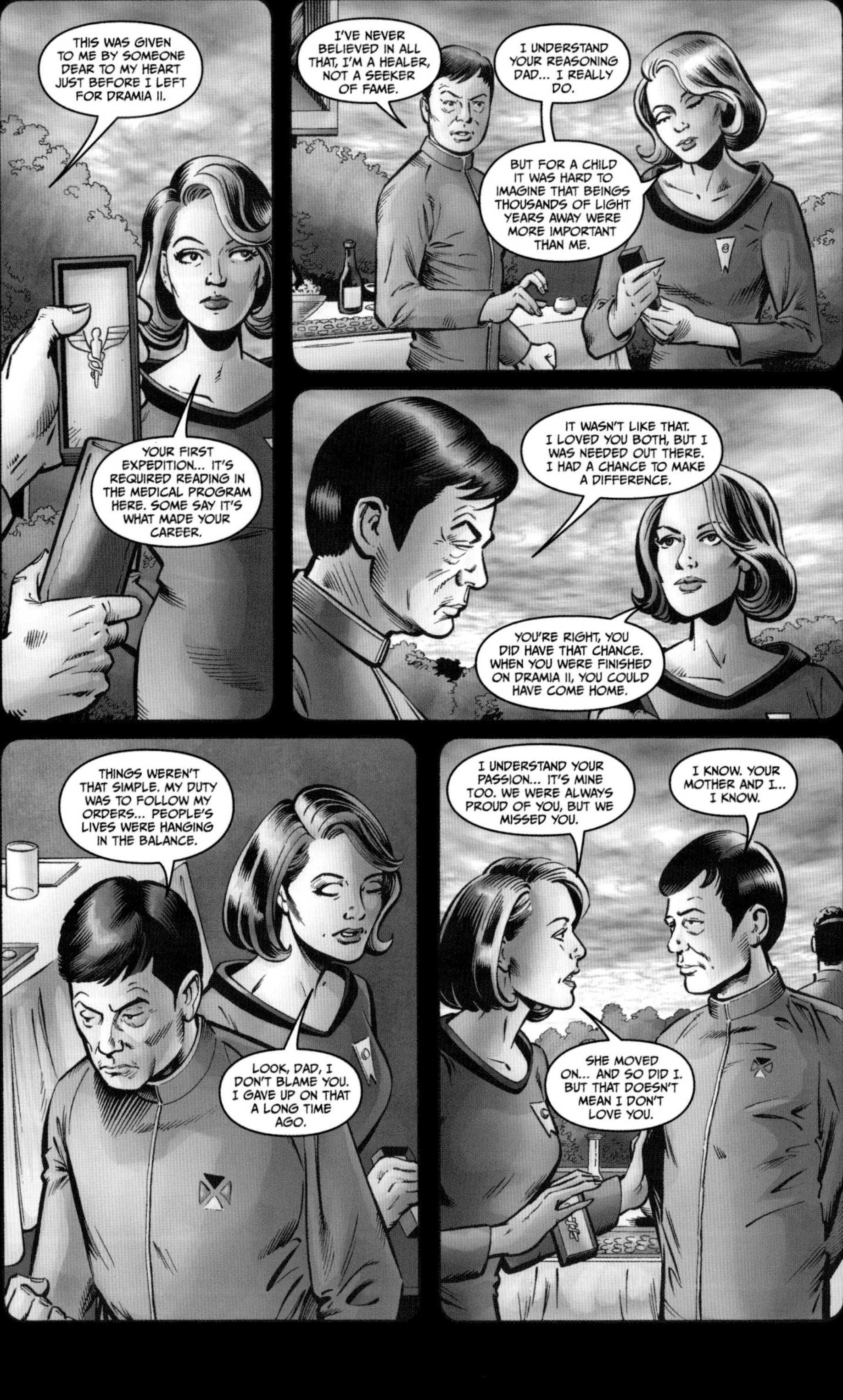

THIS WAS GIVEN TO ME BY SOMEONE DEAR TO MY HEART JUST BEFORE I LEFT FOR DRAMIA II.
YOUR FIRST EXPEDITION... IT'S REQUIRED READING IN THE MEDICAL PROGRAM HERE. SOME SAY IT'S WHAT MADE YOUR CAREER.
I'VE NEVER BELIEVED IN ALL THAT, I'M A HEALER, NOT A SEEKER OF FAME.
I UNDERSTAND YOUR REASONING DAD... I REALLY DO.
BUT FOR A CHILD IT WAS HARD TO IMAGINE THAT BEINGS THOUSANDS OF LIGHT YEARS AWAY WERE MORE IMPORTANT THAN ME.
IT WASN'T LIKE THAT. I LOVED YOU BOTH, BUT I WAS NEEDED OUT THERE. I HAD A CHANCE TO MAKE A DIFFERENCE.
YOU'RE RIGHT, YOU DID HAVE THAT CHANCE. WHEN YOU WERE FINISHED ON DRAMIA II, YOU COULD HAVE COME HOME.
THINGS WEREN'T THAT SIMPLE. MY DUTY WAS TO FOLLOW MY ORDERS... PEOPLE'S LIVES WERE HANGING IN THE BALANCE.
LOOK, DAD, I DON'T BLAME YOU. I GAVE UP ON THAT A LONG TIME AGO.
I UNDERSTAND YOUR PASSION... IT'S MINE TOO. WE WERE ALWAYS PROUD OF YOU, BUT WE MISSED YOU.
I KNOW. YOUR MOTHER AND I... I KNOW.
SHE MOVED ON... AND SO DID I. BUT THAT DOESN'T MEAN I DON'T LOVE YOU.

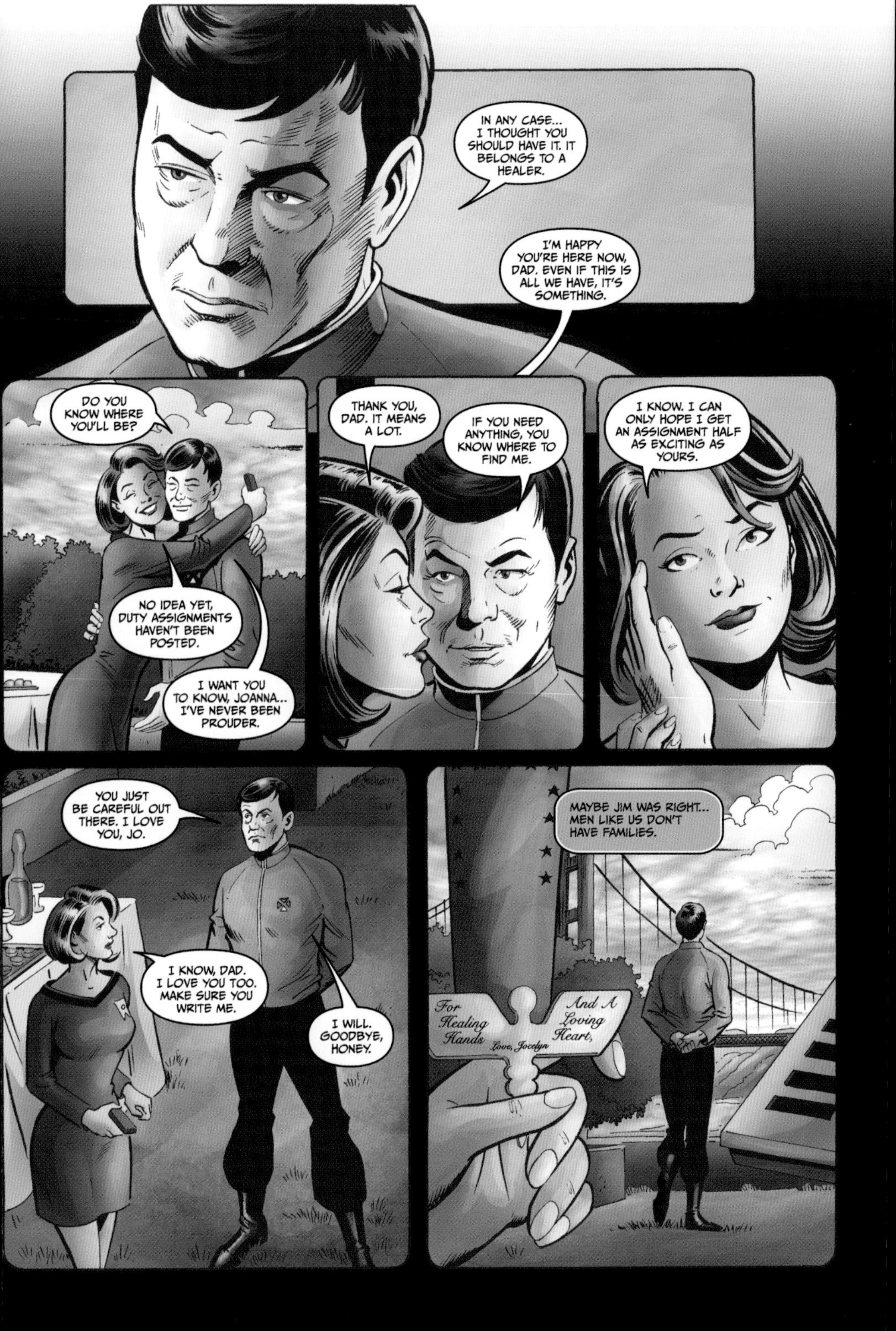
IN ANY CASE... I THOUGHT YOU SHOULD HAVE IT. IT BELONGS TO A HEALER.
I'M HAPPY YOU'RE HERE NOW, DAD. EVEN IF THIS IS ALL WE HAVE, IT'S SOMETHING.
DO YOU KNOW WHERE YOU'LL BE?
NO IDEA YET, DUTY ASSIGNMENTS HAVEN'T BEEN POSTED.
I WANT YOU TO KNOW, JOANNA... I'VE NEVER BEEN PROUDER.
THANK YOU, DAD. IT MEANS A LOT.
IF YOU NEED ANYTHING, YOU KNOW WHERE TO FIND ME.
I KNOW. I CAN ONLY HOPE I GET AN ASSIGNMENT HALF AS EXCITING AS YOURS.
YOU JUST BE CAREFUL OUT THERE. I LOVE YOU, JO.
I KNOW, DAD. I LOVE YOU TOO. MAKE SURE YOU WRITE ME.
I WILL. GOODBYE, HONEY.
MAYBE JIM WAS RIGHT... MEN LIKE US DON'T HAVE FAMILIES.
For Healing Hands And A Loving Heart, Love, Jocelyn

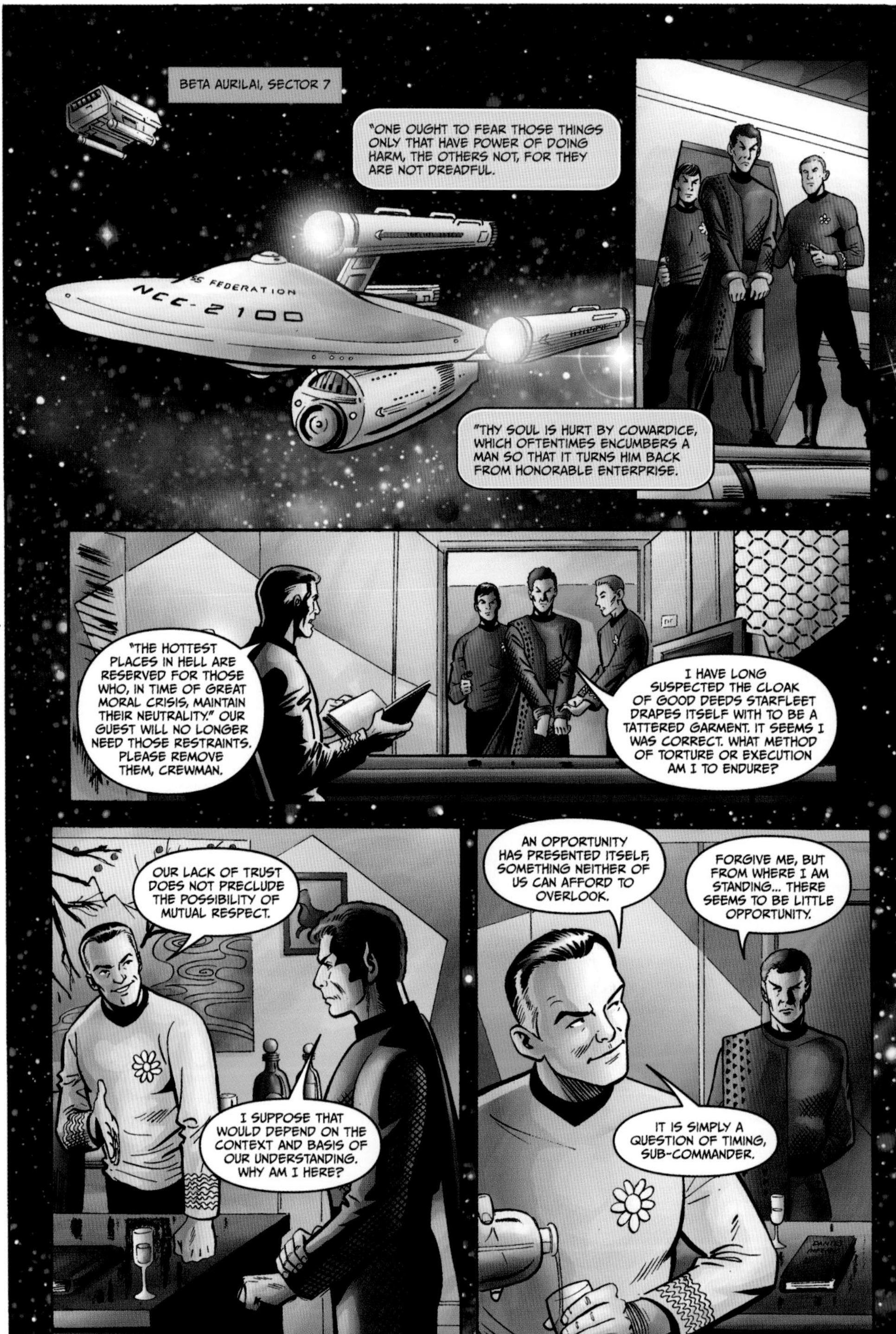
BETA AURILAI, SECTOR 7
"ONE OUGHT TO FEAR THOSE THINGS ONLY THAT HAVE POWER OF DOING HARM, THE OTHERS NOT, FOR THEY ARE NOT DREADFUL.
USS FEDERATION NCC-2100
"THY SOUL IS HURT BY COWARDICE, WHICH OFTENTIMES ENCUMBERS A MAN SO THAT IT TURNS HIM BACK FROM HONORABLE ENTERPRISE.
"THE HOTTEST PLACES IN HELL ARE RESERVED FOR THOSE WHO, IN TIME OF GREAT MORAL CRISIS, MAINTAIN THEIR NEUTRALITY." OUR GUEST WILL NO LONGER NEED THOSE RESTRAINTS. PLEASE REMOVE THEM, CREWMAN.
I HAVE LONG SUSPECTED THE CLOAK OF GOOD DEEDS STARFLEET DRAPES ITSELF WITH TO BE A TATTERED GARMENT. IT SEEMS I WAS CORRECT. WHAT METHOD OF TORTURE OR EXECUTION AM I TO ENDURE?
OUR LACK OF TRUST DOES NOT PRECLUDE THE POSSIBILITY OF MUTUAL RESPECT.
I SUPPOSE THAT WOULD DEPEND ON THE CONTEXT AND BASIS OF OUR UNDERSTANDING. WHY AM I HERE?
AN OPPORTUNITY HAS PRESENTED ITSELF, SOMETHING NEITHER OF US CAN AFFORD TO OVERLOOK.
FORGIVE ME, BUT FROM WHERE I AM STANDING... THERE SEEMS TO BE LITTLE OPPORTUNITY.
IT IS SIMPLY A QUESTION OF TIMING, SUB-COMMANDER.

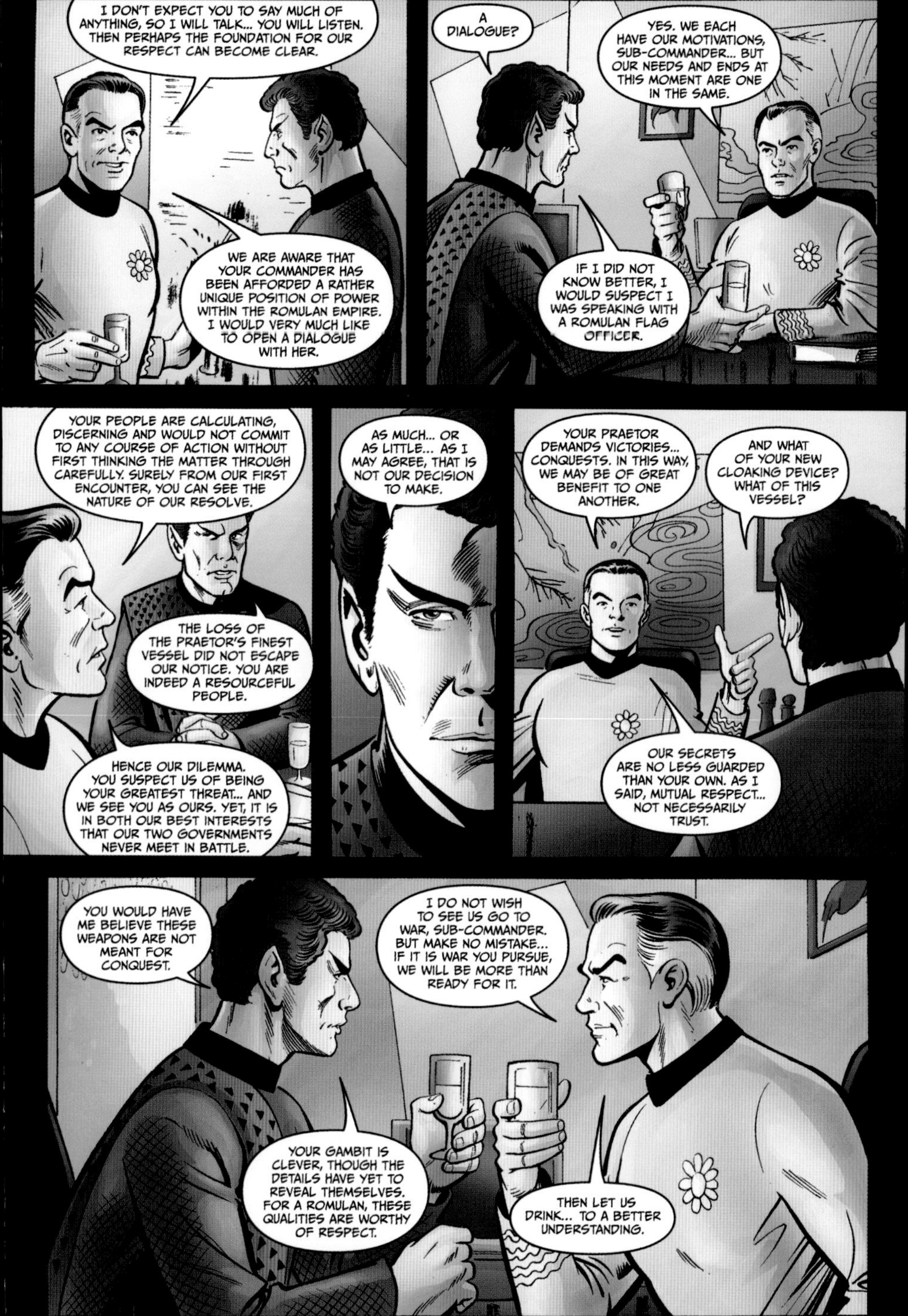
I DON'T EXPECT YOU TO SAY MUCH OF ANYTHING, SO I WILL TALK... YOU WILL LISTEN. THEN PERHAPS THE FOUNDATION FOR OUR RESPECT CAN BECOME CLEAR.
WE ARE AWARE THAT YOUR COMMANDER HAS BEEN AFFORDED A RATHER UNIQUE POSITION OF POWER WITHIN THE ROMULAN EMPIRE. I WOULD VERY MUCH LIKE TO OPEN A DIALOGUE WITH HER.
A DIALOGUE?
YES. WE EACH HAVE OUR MOTIVATIONS, SUB-COMMANDER... BUT OUR NEEDS AND ENDS AT THIS MOMENT ARE ONE IN THE SAME.
IF I DID NOT KNOW BETTER, I WOULD SUSPECT I WAS SPEAKING WITH A ROMULAN FLAG OFFICER.
YOUR PEOPLE ARE CALCULATING, DISCERNING AND WOULD NOT COMMIT TO ANY COURSE OF ACTION WITHOUT FIRST THINKING THE MATTER THROUGH CAREFULLY. SURELY FROM OUR FIRST ENCOUNTER, YOU CAN SEE THE NATURE OF OUR RESOLVE.
THE LOSS OF THE PRAETOR'S FINEST VESSEL DID NOT ESCAPE OUR NOTICE. YOU ARE INDEED A RESOURCEFUL PEOPLE.
HENCE OUR DILEMMA. YOU SUSPECT US OF BEING YOUR GREATEST THREAT... AND WE SEE YOU AS OURS. YET, IT IS IN BOTH OUR BEST INTERESTS THAT OUR TWO GOVERNMENTS NEVER MEET IN BATTLE.
AS MUCH... OR AS LITTLE... AS I MAY AGREE, THAT IS NOT OUR DECISION TO MAKE.
YOUR PRAETOR DEMANDS VICTORIES... CONQUESTS. IN THIS WAY, WE MAY BE OF GREAT BENEFIT TO ONE ANOTHER.
AND WHAT OF YOUR NEW CLOAKING DEVICE? WHAT OF THIS VESSEL?
OUR SECRETS ARE NO LESS GUARDED THAN YOUR OWN. AS I SAID, MUTUAL RESPECT... NOT NECESSARILY TRUST.
YOU WOULD HAVE ME BELIEVE THESE WEAPONS ARE NOT MEANT FOR CONQUEST.
I DO NOT WISH TO SEE US GO TO WAR, SUB-COMMANDER. BUT MAKE NO MISTAKE... IF IT IS WAR YOU PURSUE, WE WILL BE MORE THAN READY FOR IT.
YOUR GAMBIT IS CLEVER, THOUGH THE DETAILS HAVE YET TO REVEAL THEMSELVES. FOR A ROMULAN, THESE QUALITIES ARE WORTHY OF RESPECT.
THEN LET US DRINK... TO A BETTER UNDERSTANDING.

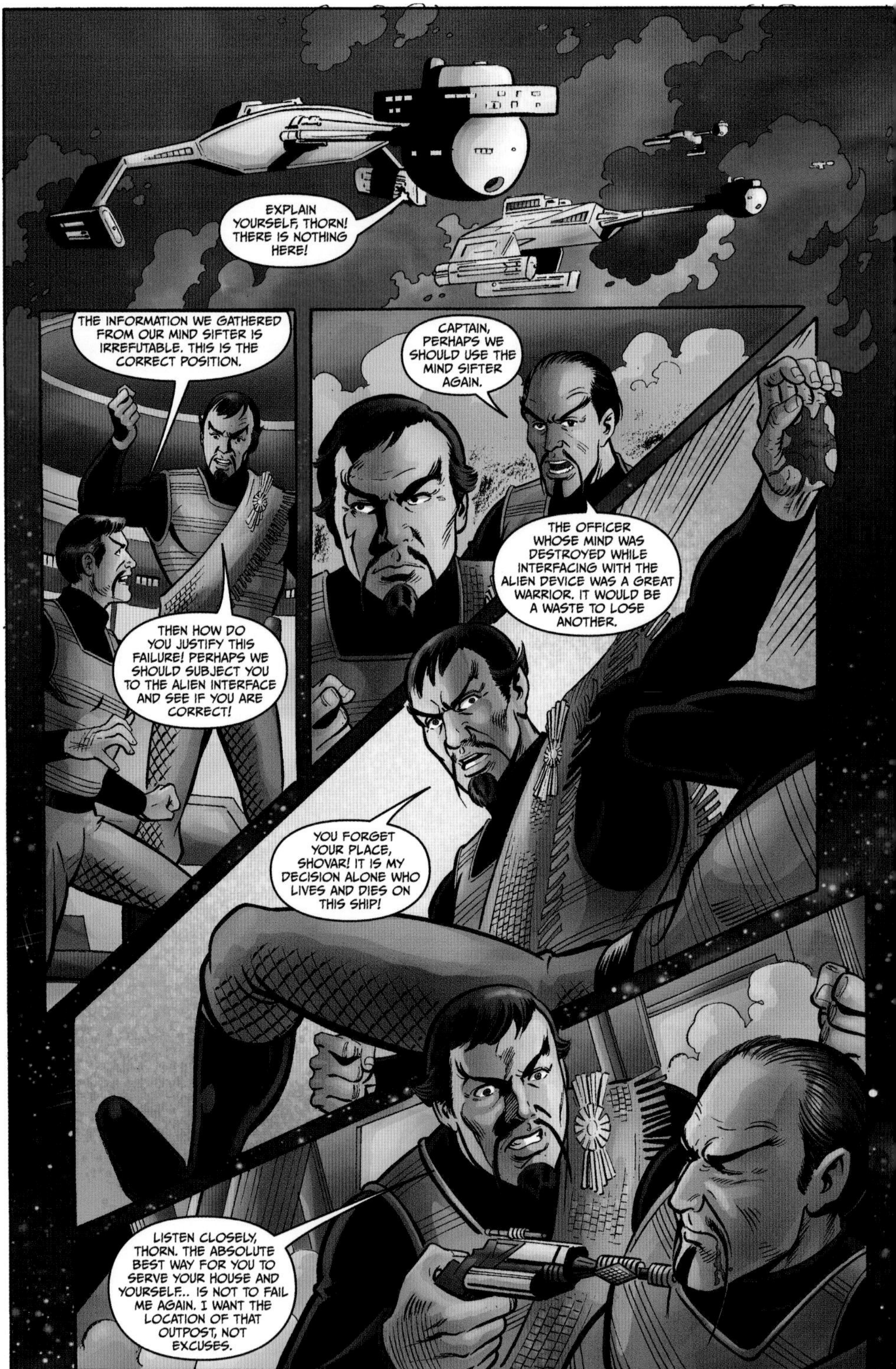
EXPLAIN YOURSELF, THORN! THERE IS NOTHING HERE!
THE INFORMATION WE GATHERED FROM OUR MIND SIFTER IS IRREFUTABLE. THIS IS THE CORRECT POSITION.
THEN HOW DO YOU JUSTIFY THIS FAILURE! PERHAPS WE SHOULD SUBJECT YOU TO THE ALIEN INTERFACE AND SEE IF YOU ARE CORRECT!
CAPTAIN, PERHAPS WE SHOULD USE THE MIND SIFTER AGAIN.
THE OFFICER WHOSE MIND WAS DESTROYED WHILE INTERFACING WITH THE ALIEN DEVICE WAS A GREAT WARRIOR. IT WOULD BE A WASTE TO LOSE ANOTHER.
YOU FORGET YOUR PLACE, SHOVAR! IT IS MY DECISION ALONE WHO LIVES AND DIES ON THIS SHIP!
LISTEN CLOSELY, THORN. THE ABSOLUTE BEST WAY FOR YOU TO SERVE YOUR HOUSE AND YOURSELF... IS NOT TO FAIL ME AGAIN. I WANT THE LOCATION OF THAT OUTPOST, NOT EXCUSES.

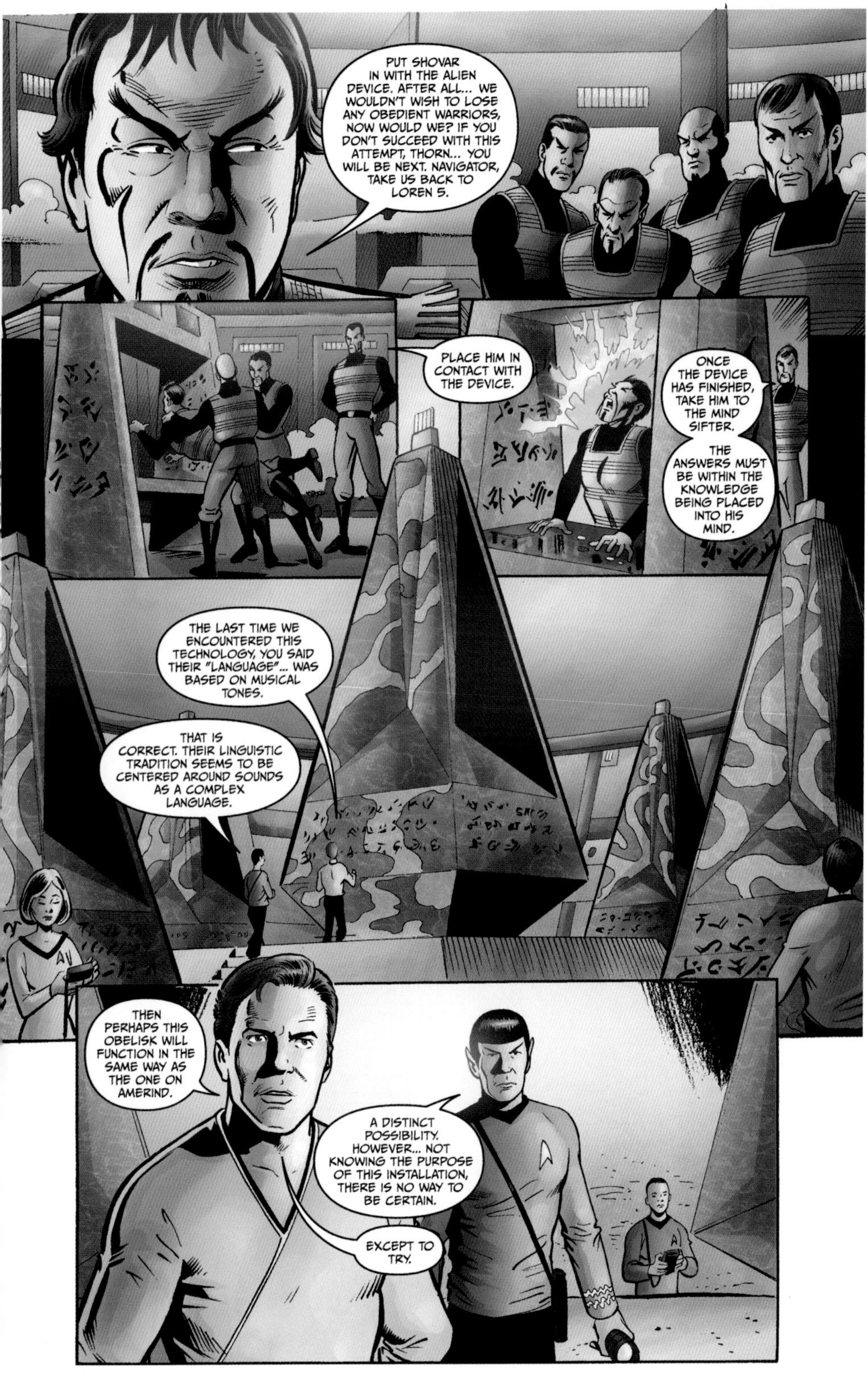
PUT SHOVAR IN WITH THE ALIEN DEVICE. AFTER ALL... WE WOULDN'T WISH TO LOSE ANY OBEDIENT WARRIORS, NOW WOULD WE? IF YOU DON'T SUCCEED WITH THIS ATTEMPT, THORN... YOU WILL BE NEXT. NAVIGATOR, TAKE US BACK TO LOREN 5.
PLACE HIM IN CONTACT WITH THE DEVICE.
ONCE THE DEVICE HAS FINISHED, TAKE HIM TO THE MIND SIFTER.
THE ANSWERS MUST BE WITHIN THE KNOWLEDGE BEING PLACED INTO HIS MIND.
THE LAST TIME WE ENCOUNTERED THIS TECHNOLOGY, YOU SAID THEIR "LANGUAGE"... WAS BASED ON MUSICAL TONES.
THAT IS CORRECT. THEIR LINGUISTIC TRADITION SEEMS TO BE CENTERED AROUND SOUNDS AS A COMPLEX LANGUAGE.
THEN PERHAPS THIS OBELISK WILL FUNCTION IN THE SAME WAY AS THE ONE ON AMERIND.
A DISTINCT POSSIBILITY. HOWEVER... NOT KNOWING THE PURPOSE OF THIS INSTALLATION, THERE IS NO WAY TO BE CERTAIN.
EXCEPT TO TRY.

EITHER THIS OBELISK WORKS ON A DIFFERENT PRINCIPLE, OR IT'S NOT OPERATIONAL.

LOGICALLY THE LATTER, CAPTAIN. BUT I SUSPECT THE ANTIPROTON READINGS MAY FACTOR INTO THIS EQUATION.

IF I AM CORRECT, THE RESIDUAL RADIATION MAY EXPLAIN WHY MY TRICORDER DIDN'T DETECT THIS EARLIER.

WITH THE SCALE OF THE KLINGON ATTACK, I'M SURPRISED OUR TRICORDERS FUNCTION AT ALL.

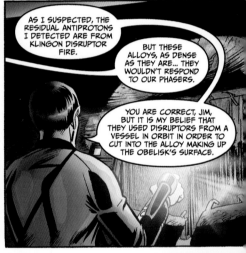

AS I SUSPECTED, THE RESIDUAL ANTIPROTONS I DETECTED ARE FROM KLINGON DISRUPTOR FIRE.

BUT THESE ALLOYS, AS DENSE AS THEY ARE... THEY WOULDN'T RESPOND TO OUR PHASERS.

YOU ARE CORRECT, JIM, BUT IT IS MY BELIEF THAT THEY USED DISRUPTORS FROM A VESSEL IN ORBIT IN ORDER TO CUT INTO THE ALLOY MAKING UP THE OBELISK'S SURFACE.

LOOK AT THE DAMAGE. DEFINITELY AN EXAMPLE OF KLINGON SUBTLETY.

THE MEASURE OF LOST KNOWLEDGE FROM THIS DESTRUCTION IS APPARENT, BUT THE KLINGONS SEEM TO CARE LITTLE FOR SCIENTIFIC OR PHILOSOPHICAL DISCOVERY.

SPOCK, THE DEVICE THAT MADE ME FORGET... ON AMERIND. IT WAS IN THIS POSITION.

YES, THE NEURAL INTERFACE WAS LOCATED IN ALMOST THE EXACT SAME POSITION AS WHATEVER WAS HERE PREVIOUSLY.

THEY TOOK IT, SPOCK. DAMN! THEY TOOK IT.

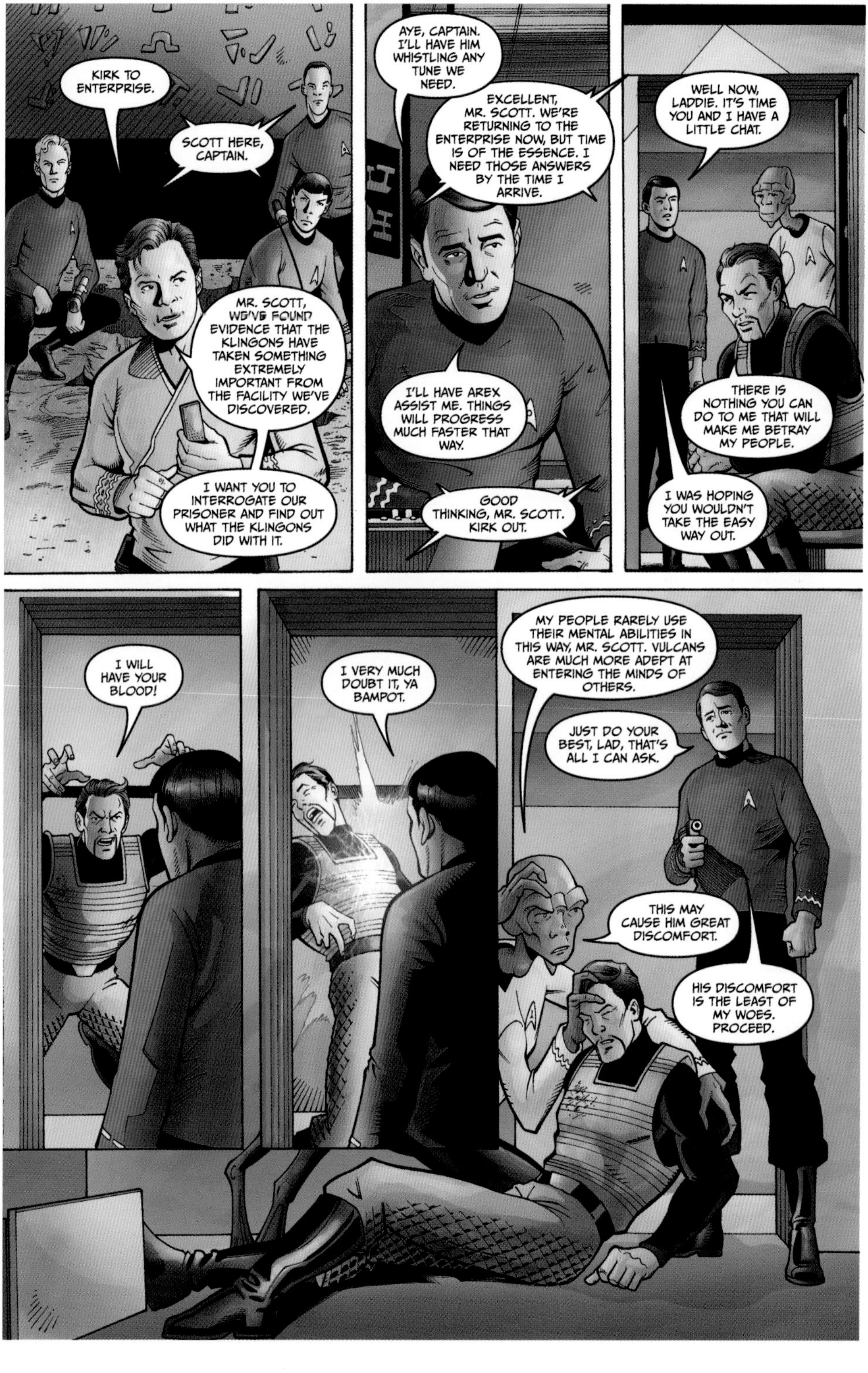
KIRK TO ENTERPRISE.
SCOTT HERE, CAPTAIN.
MR. SCOTT, WE'VE FOUND EVIDENCE THAT THE KLINGONS HAVE TAKEN SOMETHING EXTREMELY IMPORTANT FROM THE FACILITY WE'VE DISCOVERED.
I WANT YOU TO INTERROGATE OUR PRISONER AND FIND OUT WHAT THE KLINGONS DID WITH IT.
AYE, CAPTAIN. I'LL HAVE HIM WHISTLING ANY TUNE WE NEED.
EXCELLENT, MR. SCOTT. WE'RE RETURNING TO THE ENTERPRISE NOW, BUT TIME IS OF THE ESSENCE. I NEED THOSE ANSWERS BY THE TIME I ARRIVE.
I'LL HAVE AREX ASSIST ME. THINGS WILL PROGRESS MUCH FASTER THAT WAY.
GOOD THINKING, MR. SCOTT. KIRK OUT.
WELL NOW, LADDIE. IT'S TIME YOU AND I HAVE A LITTLE CHAT.
THERE IS NOTHING YOU CAN DO TO ME THAT WILL MAKE ME BETRAY MY PEOPLE.
I WAS HOPING YOU WOULDN'T TAKE THE EASY WAY OUT.
I WILL HAVE YOUR BLOOD!
I VERY MUCH DOUBT IT, YA BAMPOT.
MY PEOPLE RARELY USE THEIR MENTAL ABILITIES IN THIS WAY, MR. SCOTT. VULCANS ARE MUCH MORE ADEPT AT ENTERING THE MINDS OF OTHERS.
JUST DO YOUR BEST, LAD, THAT'S ALL I CAN ASK.
THIS MAY CAUSE HIM GREAT DISCOMFORT.
HIS DISCOMFORT IS THE LEAST OF MY WOES. PROCEED.

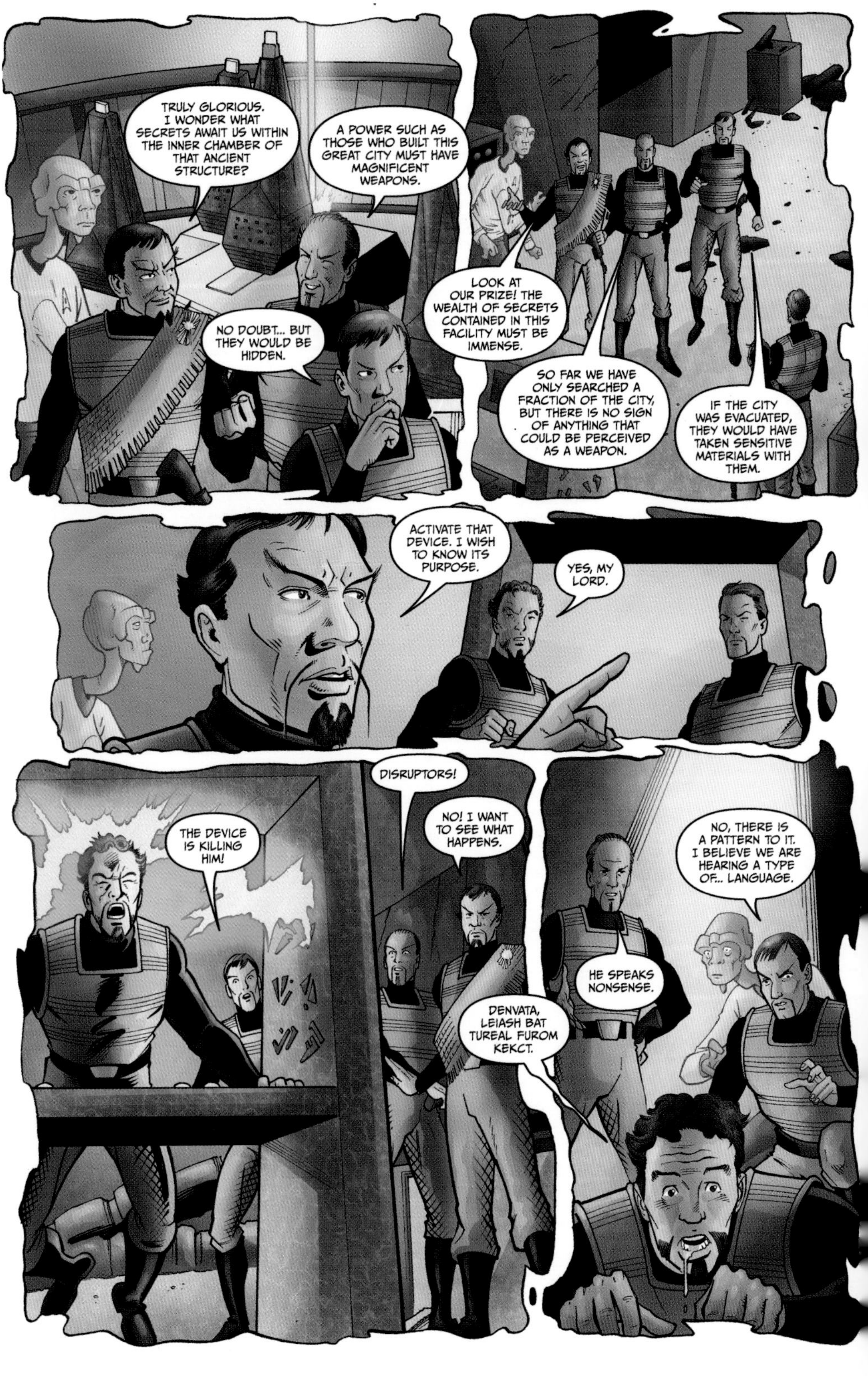
TRULY GLORIOUS. I WONDER WHAT SECRETS AWAIT US WITHIN THE INNER CHAMBER OF THAT ANCIENT STRUCTURE?
A POWER SUCH AS THOSE WHO BUILT THIS GREAT CITY MUST HAVE MAGNIFICENT WEAPONS.
NO DOUBT... BUT THEY WOULD BE HIDDEN.
LOOK AT OUR PRIZE! THE WEALTH OF SECRETS CONTAINED IN THIS FACILITY MUST BE IMMENSE.
SO FAR WE HAVE ONLY SEARCHED A FRACTION OF THE CITY, BUT THERE IS NO SIGN OF ANYTHING THAT COULD BE PERCEIVED AS A WEAPON.
IF THE CITY WAS EVACUATED, THEY WOULD HAVE TAKEN SENSITIVE MATERIALS WITH THEM.
ACTIVATE THAT DEVICE. I WISH TO KNOW ITS PURPOSE.
YES, MY LORD.
THE DEVICE IS KILLING HIM!
DISRUPTORS!
NO! I WANT TO SEE WHAT HAPPENS.
NO, THERE IS A PATTERN TO IT. I BELIEVE WE ARE HEARING A TYPE OF... LANGUAGE.
HE SPEAKS NONSENSE.
DENVATA, LEIASH BAT TUREAL FUROM KEKCT.

AS SOON AS YOU HAVE FINISHED CUTTING IT FREE, HAVE IT TRANSPORTED UP TO THE KLOTHOS. EXAMINE IT CAREFULLY, THORN... I WANT ANSWERS.

YES, CAPTAIN KOR.

I WANT TO KNOW WHAT KNOWLEDGE IS BURIED WITHIN THIS MACHINE.

THAT IS ALL I WAS ABLE TO DIVINE FROM MY INTRUSION INTO THE PRISONER'S MIND.

FASCINATING.

KOR... I WONDERED WHEN I'D BE HEARING THAT NAME AGAIN.

DID THE KLINGON PRISONER HAVE ANY SENSE AS TO WHERE KOR MIGHT HAVE GONE?

NO, SIR. BUT I DID HAVE THE DISTINCT IMPRESSION THAT KOR WILL RETURN.

IF HE'S GOT ACCESS TO PRESERVER KNOWLEDGE, THAT COULD MAKE THINGS VERY BAD FOR THE FEDERATION.

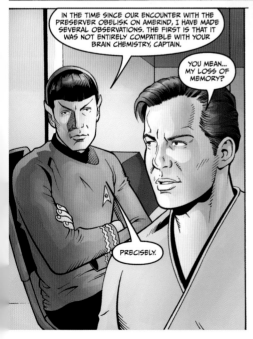

IN THE TIME SINCE OUR ENCOUNTER WITH THE PRESERVER OBELISK ON AMERIND, I HAVE MADE SEVERAL OBSERVATIONS. THE FIRST IS THAT IT WAS NOT ENTIRELY COMPATIBLE WITH YOUR BRAIN CHEMISTRY, CAPTAIN.

YOU MEAN... MY LOSS OF MEMORY?

PRECISELY.

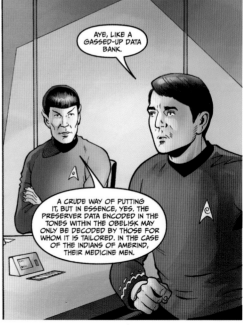

AYE, LIKE A GASSED-UP DATA BANK.

A CRUDE WAY OF PUTTING IT, BUT IN ESSENCE, YES. THE PRESERVER DATA ENCODED IN THE TONES WITHIN THE OBELISK MAY ONLY BE DECODED BY THOSE FOR WHOM IT IS TAILORED. IN THE CASE OF THE INDIANS OF AMERIND, THEIR MEDICINE MEN.

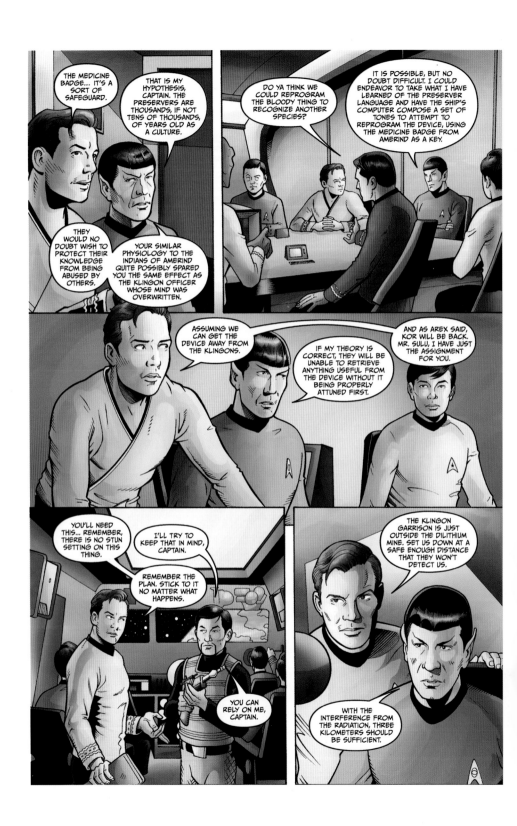

THE MEDICINE BADGE... IT'S A SORT OF SAFEGUARD.

THAT IS MY HYPOTHESIS, CAPTAIN. THE PRESERVERS ARE THOUSANDS, IF NOT TENS OF THOUSANDS, OF YEARS OLD AS A CULTURE.

DO YA THINK WE COULD REPROGRAM THE BLOODY THING TO RECOGNIZE ANOTHER SPECIES?

IT IS POSSIBLE, BUT NO DOUBT DIFFICULT. I COULD ENDEAVOR TO TAKE WHAT I HAVE LEARNED OF THE PRESERVER LANGUAGE AND HAVE THE SHIP'S COMPUTER COMPOSE A SET OF TONES TO ATTEMPT TO REPROGRAM THE DEVICE, USING THE MEDICINE BADGE FROM AMERIND AS A KEY.

THEY WOULD NO DOUBT WISH TO PROTECT THEIR KNOWLEDGE FROM BEING ABUSED BY OTHERS.

YOUR SIMILAR PHYSIOLOGY TO THE INDIANS OF AMERIND QUITE POSSIBLY SPARED YOU THE SAME EFFECT AS THE KLINGON OFFICER WHOSE MIND WAS OVERWRITTEN.

ASSUMING WE CAN GET THE DEVICE AWAY FROM THE KLINGONS.

IF MY THEORY IS CORRECT, THEY WILL BE UNABLE TO RETRIEVE ANYTHING USEFUL FROM THE DEVICE WITHOUT IT BEING PROPERLY ATTUNED FIRST.

AND AS AREX SAID, KOR WILL BE BACK. MR. SULU, I HAVE JUST THE ASSIGNMENT FOR YOU.

YOU'LL NEED THIS... REMEMBER, THERE IS NO STUN SETTING ON THIS THING.

I'LL TRY TO KEEP THAT IN MIND, CAPTAIN.

REMEMBER THE PLAN. STICK TO IT NO MATTER WHAT HAPPENS.

YOU CAN RELY ON ME, CAPTAIN.

THE KLINGON GARRISON IS JUST OUTSIDE THE DILITHIUM MINE. SET US DOWN AT A SAFE ENOUGH DISTANCE THAT THEY WON'T DETECT US.

WITH THE INTERFERENCE FROM THE RADIATION, THREE KILOMETERS SHOULD BE SUFFICIENT.

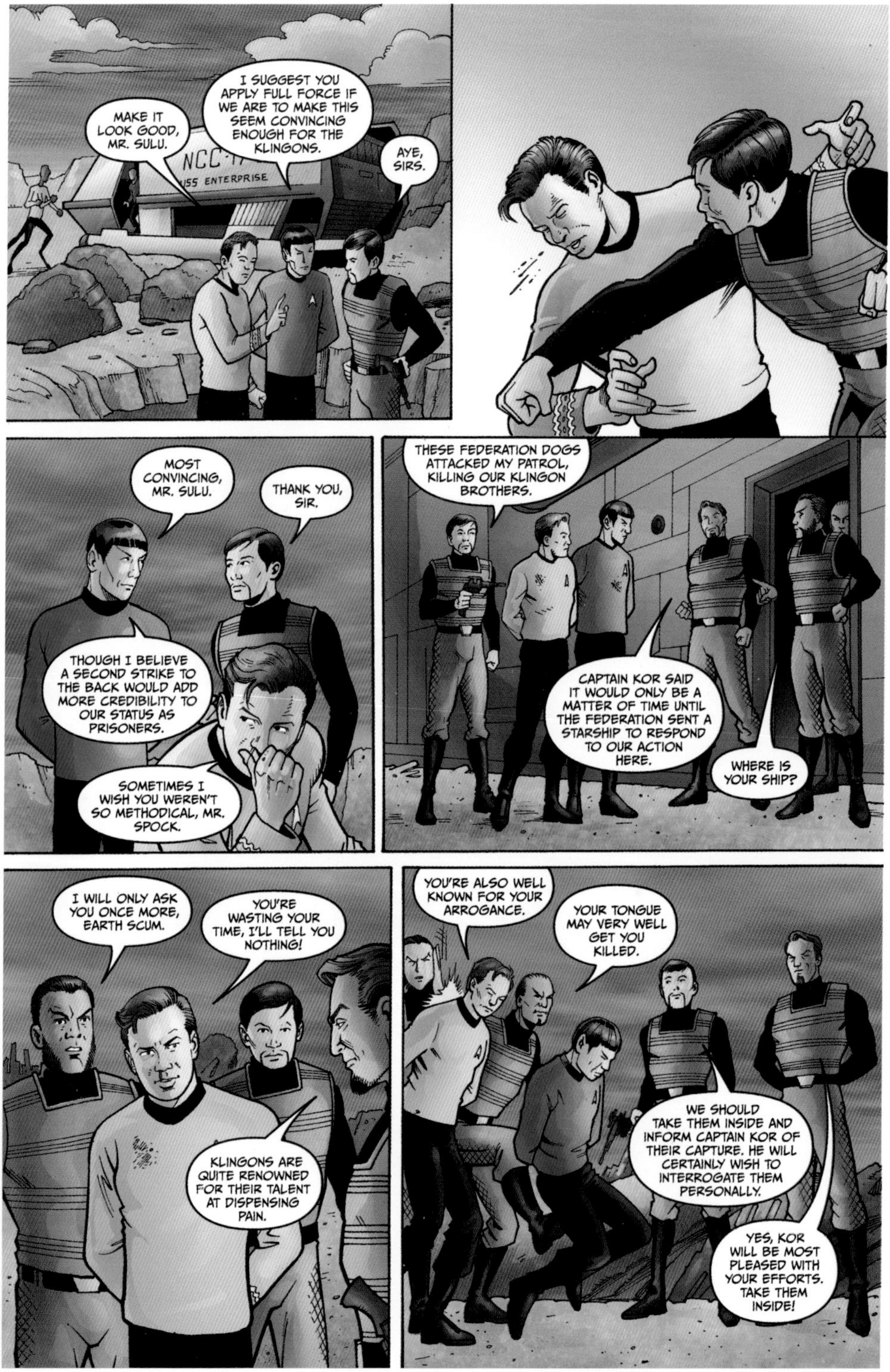
MAKE IT LOOK GOOD, MR. SULU.
I SUGGEST YOU APPLY FULL FORCE IF WE ARE TO MAKE THIS SEEM CONVINCING ENOUGH FOR THE KLINGONS.
AYE, SIRS.
USS ENTERPRISE
MOST CONVINCING, MR. SULU.
THANK YOU, SIR.
THOUGH I BELIEVE A SECOND STRIKE TO THE BACK WOULD ADD MORE CREDIBILITY TO OUR STATUS AS PRISONERS.
SOMETIMES I WISH YOU WEREN'T SO METHODICAL, MR. SPOCK.
THESE FEDERATION DOGS ATTACKED MY PATROL, KILLING OUR KLINGON BROTHERS.
CAPTAIN KOR SAID IT WOULD ONLY BE A MATTER OF TIME UNTIL THE FEDERATION SENT A STARSHIP TO RESPOND TO OUR ACTION HERE.
WHERE IS YOUR SHIP?
I WILL ONLY ASK YOU ONCE MORE, EARTH SCUM.
YOU'RE WASTING YOUR TIME, I'LL TELL YOU NOTHING!
KLINGONS ARE QUITE RENOWNED FOR THEIR TALENT AT DISPENSING PAIN.
YOU'RE ALSO WELL KNOWN FOR YOUR ARROGANCE.
YOUR TONGUE MAY VERY WELL GET YOU KILLED.
WE SHOULD TAKE THEM INSIDE AND INFORM CAPTAIN KOR OF THEIR CAPTURE. HE WILL CERTAINLY WISH TO INTERROGATE THEM PERSONALLY.
YES, KOR WILL BE MOST PLEASED WITH YOUR EFFORTS. TAKE THEM INSIDE!

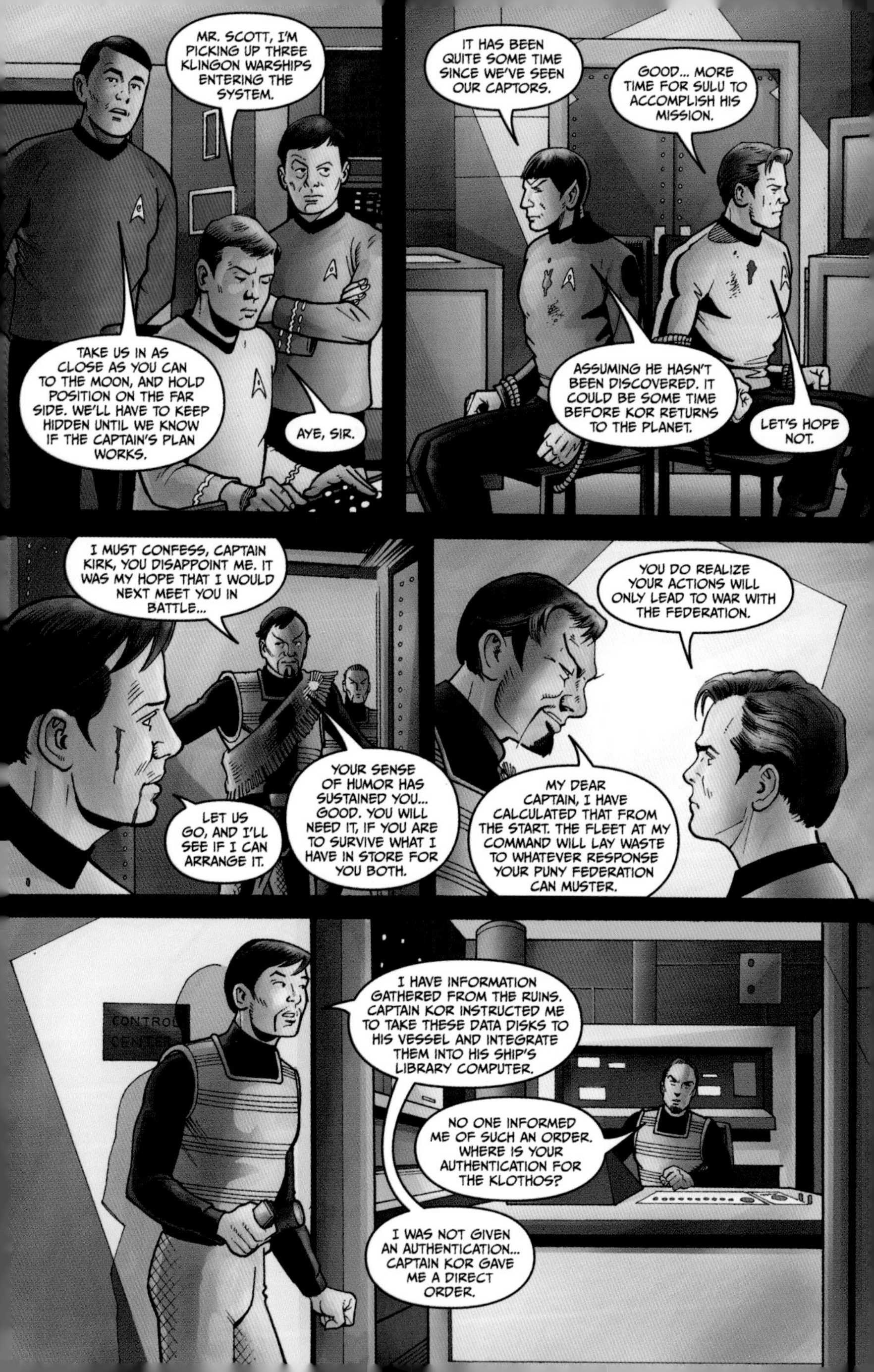
MR. SCOTT, I'M PICKING UP THREE KLINGON WARSHIPS ENTERING THE SYSTEM.
TAKE US IN AS CLOSE AS YOU CAN TO THE MOON, AND HOLD POSITION ON THE FAR SIDE. WE'LL HAVE TO KEEP HIDDEN UNTIL WE KNOW IF THE CAPTAIN'S PLAN WORKS.
AYE, SIR.
IT HAS BEEN QUITE SOME TIME SINCE WE'VE SEEN OUR CAPTORS.
GOOD... MORE TIME FOR SULU TO ACCOMPLISH HIS MISSION.
ASSUMING HE HASN'T BEEN DISCOVERED. IT COULD BE SOME TIME BEFORE KOR RETURNS TO THE PLANET.
LET'S HOPE NOT.
I MUST CONFESS, CAPTAIN KIRK, YOU DISAPPOINT ME. IT WAS MY HOPE THAT I WOULD NEXT MEET YOU IN BATTLE...
LET US GO, AND I'LL SEE IF I CAN ARRANGE IT.
YOUR SENSE OF HUMOR HAS SUSTAINED YOU... GOOD. YOU WILL NEED IT, IF YOU ARE TO SURVIVE WHAT I HAVE IN STORE FOR YOU BOTH.
YOU DO REALIZE YOUR ACTIONS WILL ONLY LEAD TO WAR WITH THE FEDERATION.
MY DEAR CAPTAIN, I HAVE CALCULATED THAT FROM THE START. THE FLEET AT MY COMMAND WILL LAY WASTE TO WHATEVER RESPONSE YOUR PUNY FEDERATION CAN MUSTER.
CONTROL CENTER
I HAVE INFORMATION GATHERED FROM THE RUINS. CAPTAIN KOR INSTRUCTED ME TO TAKE THESE DATA DISKS TO HIS VESSEL AND INTEGRATE THEM INTO HIS SHIP'S LIBRARY COMPUTER.
NO ONE INFORMED ME OF SUCH AN ORDER. WHERE IS YOUR AUTHENTICATION FOR THE KLOTHOS?
I WAS NOT GIVEN AN AUTHENTICATION... CAPTAIN KOR GAVE ME A DIRECT ORDER.

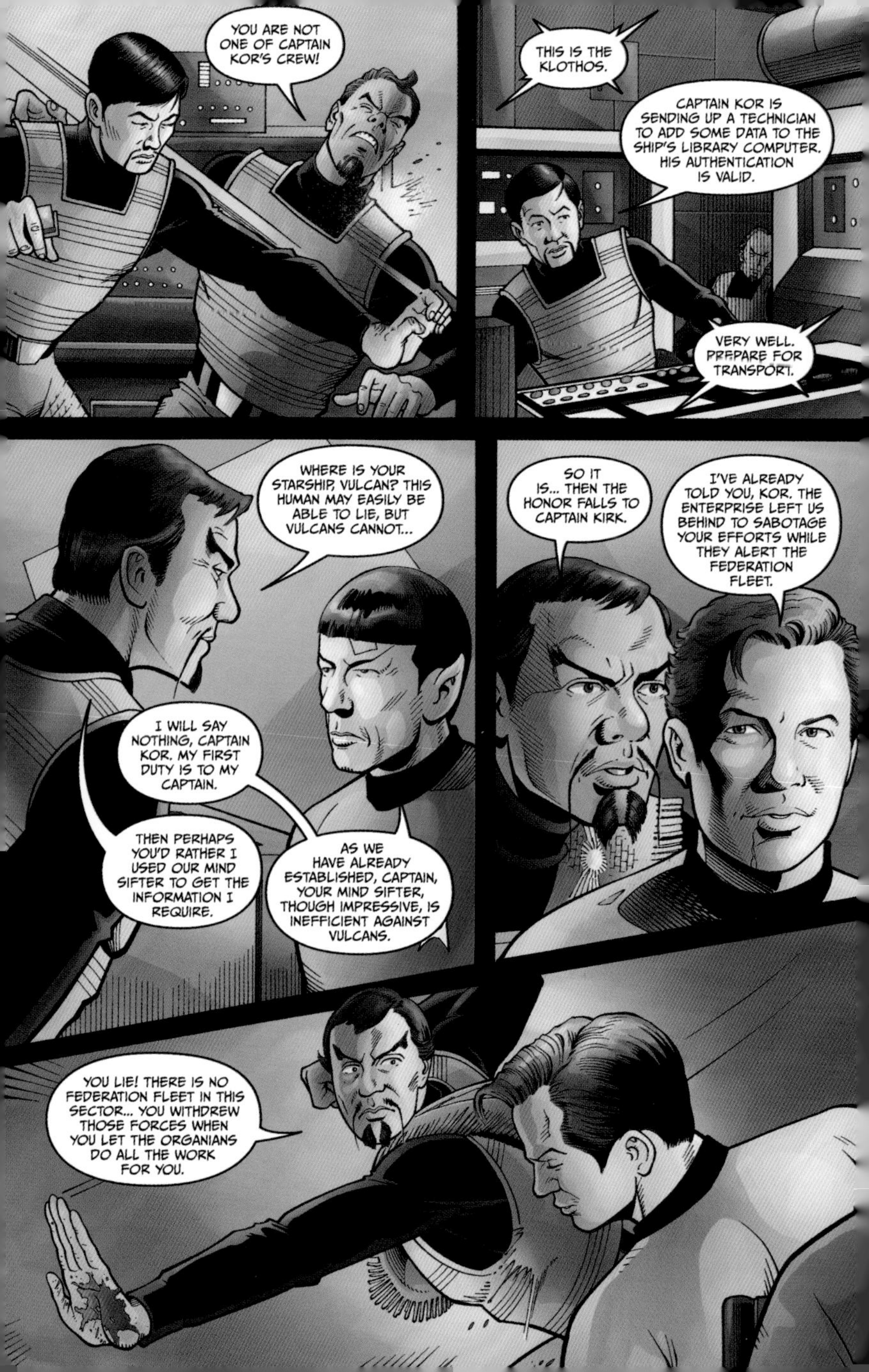
YOU ARE NOT ONE OF CAPTAIN KOR'S CREW!
THIS IS THE KLOTHOS.
CAPTAIN KOR IS SENDING UP A TECHNICIAN TO ADD SOME DATA TO THE SHIP'S LIBRARY COMPUTER. HIS AUTHENTICATION IS VALID.
VERY WELL. PREPARE FOR TRANSPORT.
WHERE IS YOUR STARSHIP, VULCAN? THIS HUMAN MAY EASILY BE ABLE TO LIE, BUT VULCANS CANNOT...
I WILL SAY NOTHING, CAPTAIN KOR. MY FIRST DUTY IS TO MY CAPTAIN.
THEN PERHAPS YOU'D RATHER I USED OUR MIND SIFTER TO GET THE INFORMATION I REQUIRE.
AS WE HAVE ALREADY ESTABLISHED, CAPTAIN, YOUR MIND SIFTER, THOUGH IMPRESSIVE, IS INEFFICIENT AGAINST VULCANS.
SO IT IS... THEN THE HONOR FALLS TO CAPTAIN KIRK.
I'VE ALREADY TOLD YOU, KOR. THE ENTERPRISE LEFT US BEHIND TO SABOTAGE YOUR EFFORTS WHILE THEY ALERT THE FEDERATION FLEET.
YOU LIE! THERE IS NO FEDERATION FLEET IN THIS SECTOR... YOU WITHDREW THOSE FORCES WHEN YOU LET THE ORGANIANS DO ALL THE WORK FOR YOU.

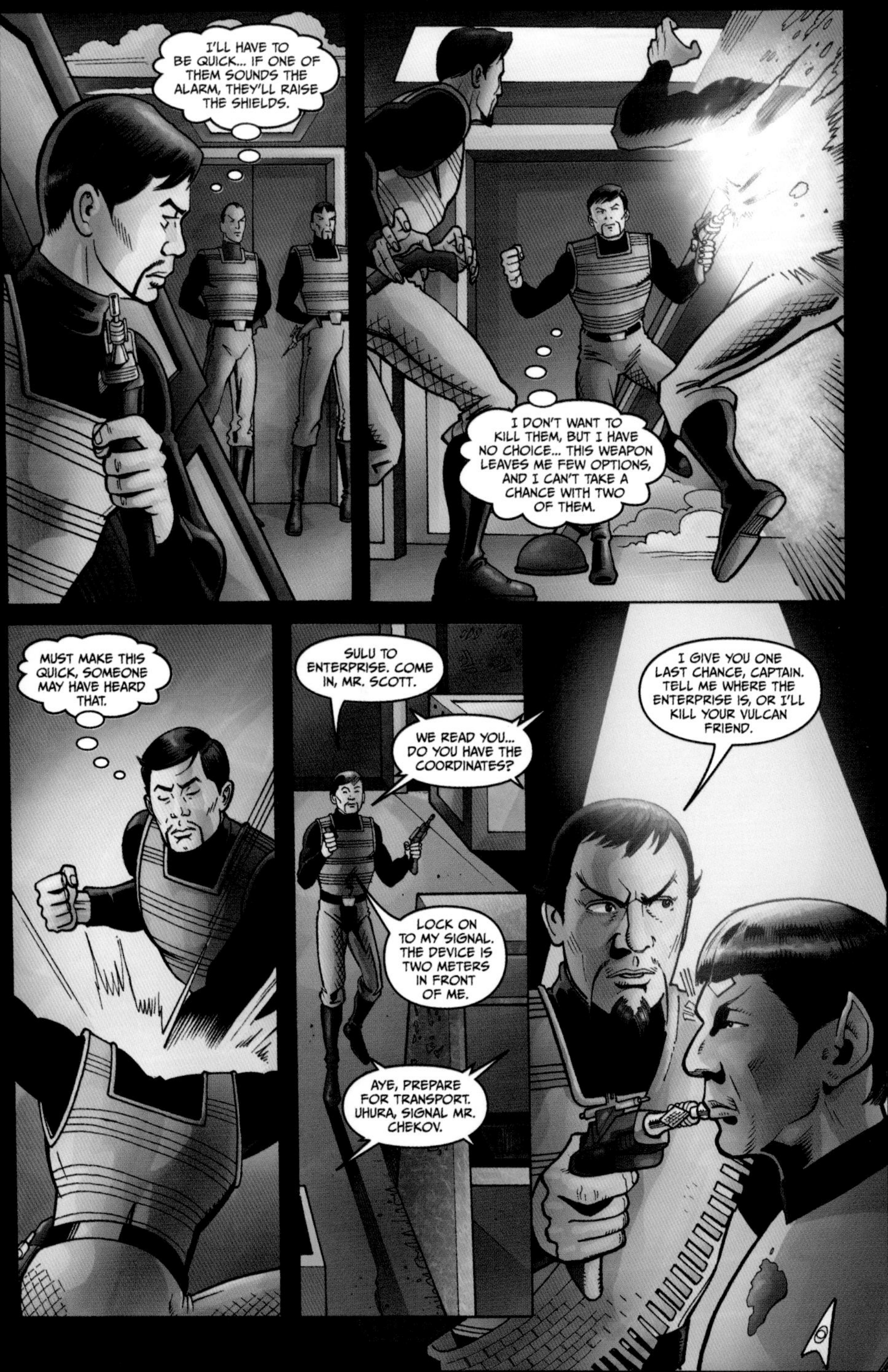
I'LL HAVE TO BE QUICK... IF ONE OF THEM SOUNDS THE ALARM, THEY'LL RAISE THE SHIELDS.
I DON'T WANT TO KILL THEM, BUT I HAVE NO CHOICE... THIS WEAPON LEAVES ME FEW OPTIONS, AND I CAN'T TAKE A CHANCE WITH TWO OF THEM.
MUST MAKE THIS QUICK, SOMEONE MAY HAVE HEARD THAT.
SULU TO ENTERPRISE. COME IN, MR. SCOTT.
WE READ YOU... DO YOU HAVE THE COORDINATES?
LOCK ON TO MY SIGNAL. THE DEVICE IS TWO METERS IN FRONT OF ME.
AYE, PREPARE FOR TRANSPORT. UHURA, SIGNAL MR. CHEKOV.
I GIVE YOU ONE LAST CHANCE, CAPTAIN. TELL ME WHERE THE ENTERPRISE IS, OR I'LL KILL YOUR VULCAN FRIEND.

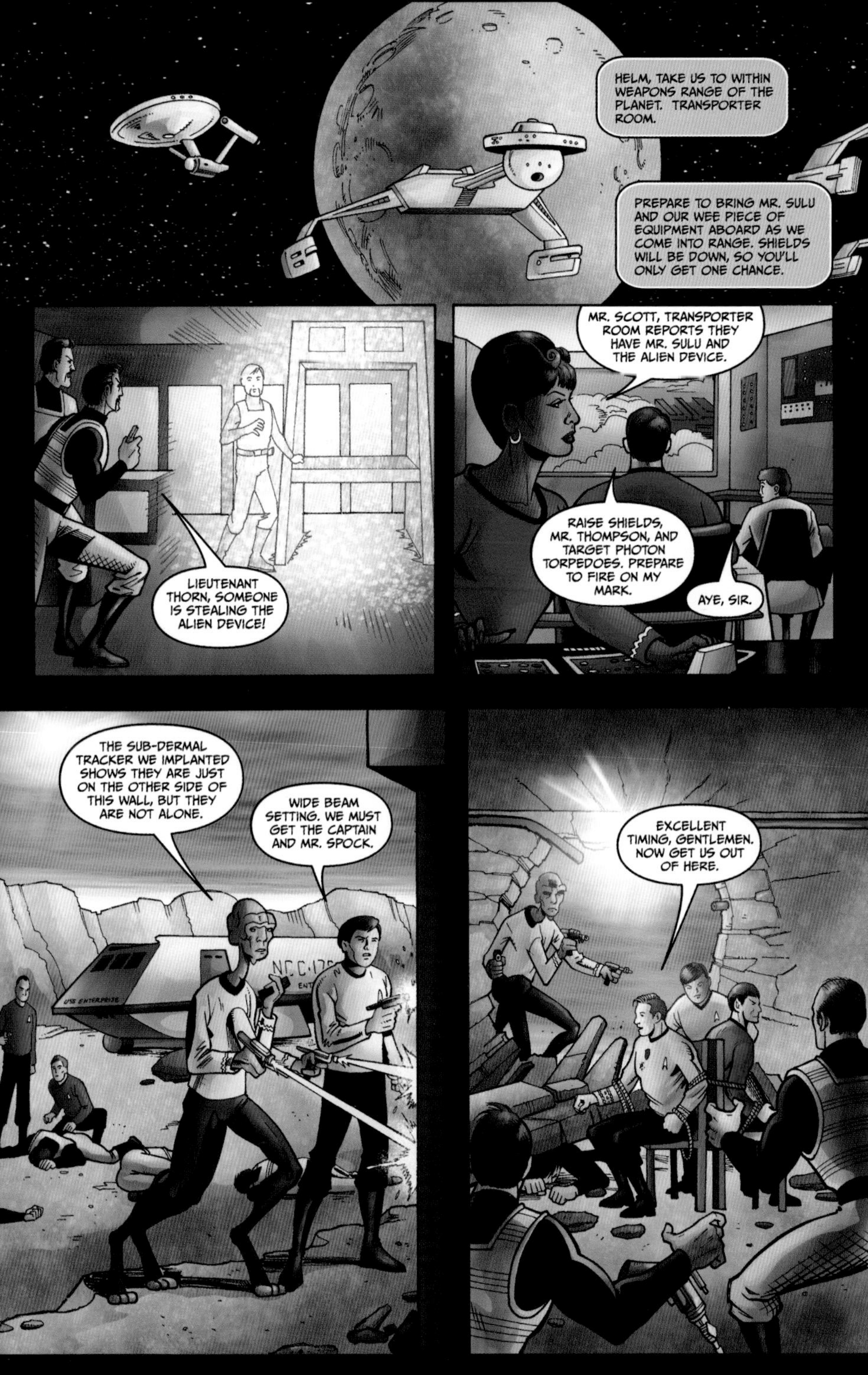
HELM, TAKE US TO WITHIN WEAPONS RANGE OF THE PLANET. TRANSPORTER ROOM.
PREPARE TO BRING MR. SULU AND OUR WEE PIECE OF EQUIPMENT ABOARD AS WE COME INTO RANGE. SHIELDS WILL BE DOWN, SO YOU'LL ONLY GET ONE CHANCE.
LIEUTENANT THORN, SOMEONE IS STEALING THE ALIEN DEVICE!
MR. SCOTT, TRANSPORTER ROOM REPORTS THEY HAVE MR. SULU AND THE ALIEN DEVICE.
RAISE SHIELDS, MR. THOMPSON, AND TARGET PHOTON TORPEDOES. PREPARE TO FIRE ON MY MARK.
AYE, SIR.
THE SUB-DERMAL TRACKER WE IMPLANTED SHOWS THEY ARE JUST ON THE OTHER SIDE OF THIS WALL, BUT THEY ARE NOT ALONE.
WIDE BEAM SETTING. WE MUST GET THE CAPTAIN AND MR. SPOCK.
EXCELLENT TIMING, GENTLEMEN. NOW GET US OUT OF HERE.

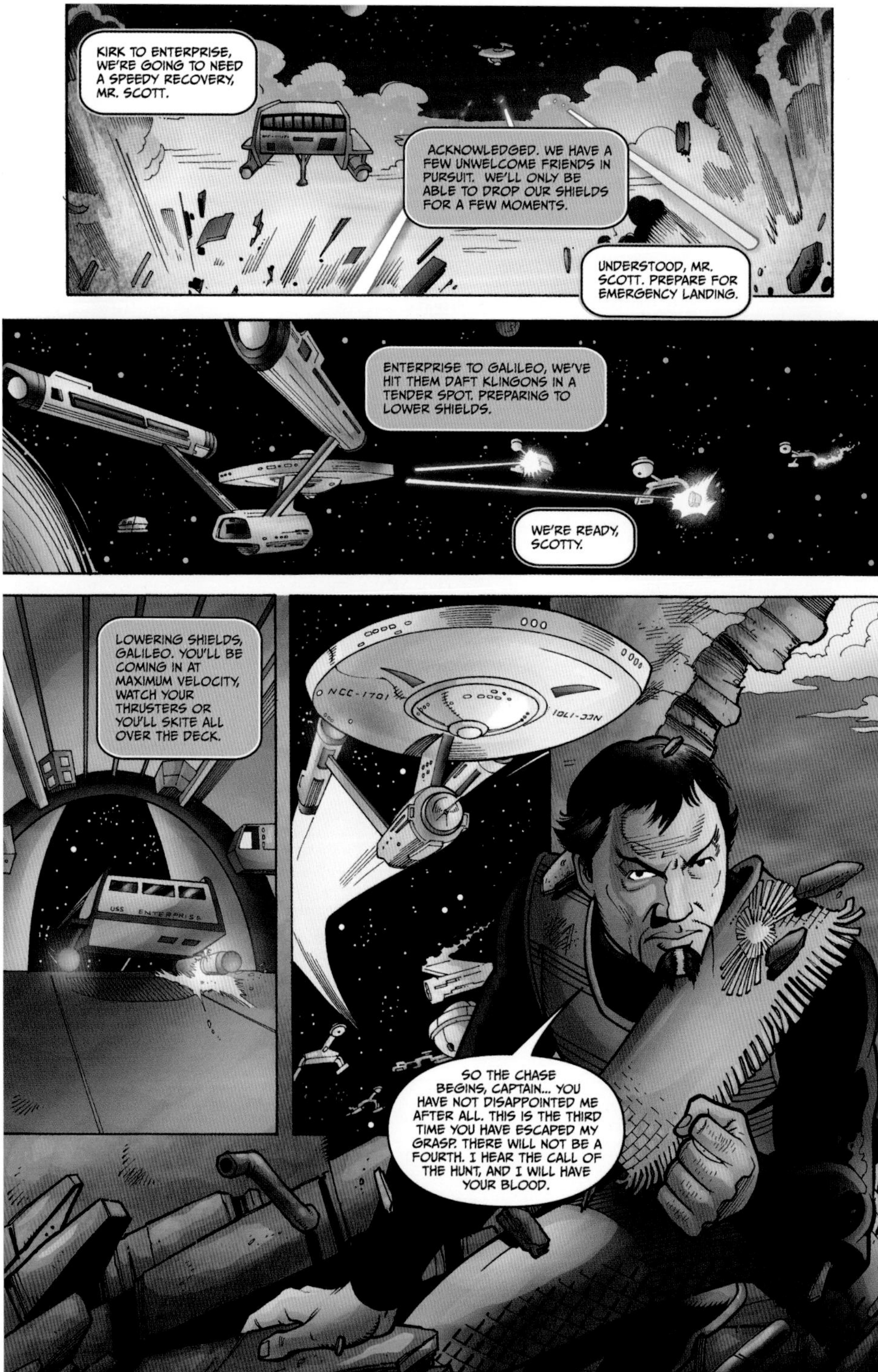
KIRK TO ENTERPRISE, WE'RE GOING TO NEED A SPEEDY RECOVERY, MR. SCOTT.
ACKNOWLEDGED. WE HAVE A FEW UNWELCOME FRIENDS IN PURSUIT. WE'LL ONLY BE ABLE TO DROP OUR SHIELDS FOR A FEW MOMENTS.
UNDERSTOOD, MR. SCOTT. PREPARE FOR EMERGENCY LANDING.
ENTERPRISE TO GALILEO, WE'VE HIT THEM DAFT KLINGONS IN A TENDER SPOT. PREPARING TO LOWER SHIELDS.
WE'RE READY, SCOTTY.
LOWERING SHIELDS, GALILEO. YOU'LL BE COMING IN AT MAXIMUM VELOCITY, WATCH YOUR THRUSTERS OR YOU'LL SKITE ALL OVER THE DECK.
USS ENTERPRISE
NCC-1701
SO THE CHASE BEGINS, CAPTAIN... YOU HAVE NOT DISAPPOINTED ME AFTER ALL. THIS IS THE THIRD TIME YOU HAVE ESCAPED MY GRASP. THERE WILL NOT BE A FOURTH. I HEAR THE CALL OF THE HUNT, AND I WILL HAVE YOUR BLOOD.

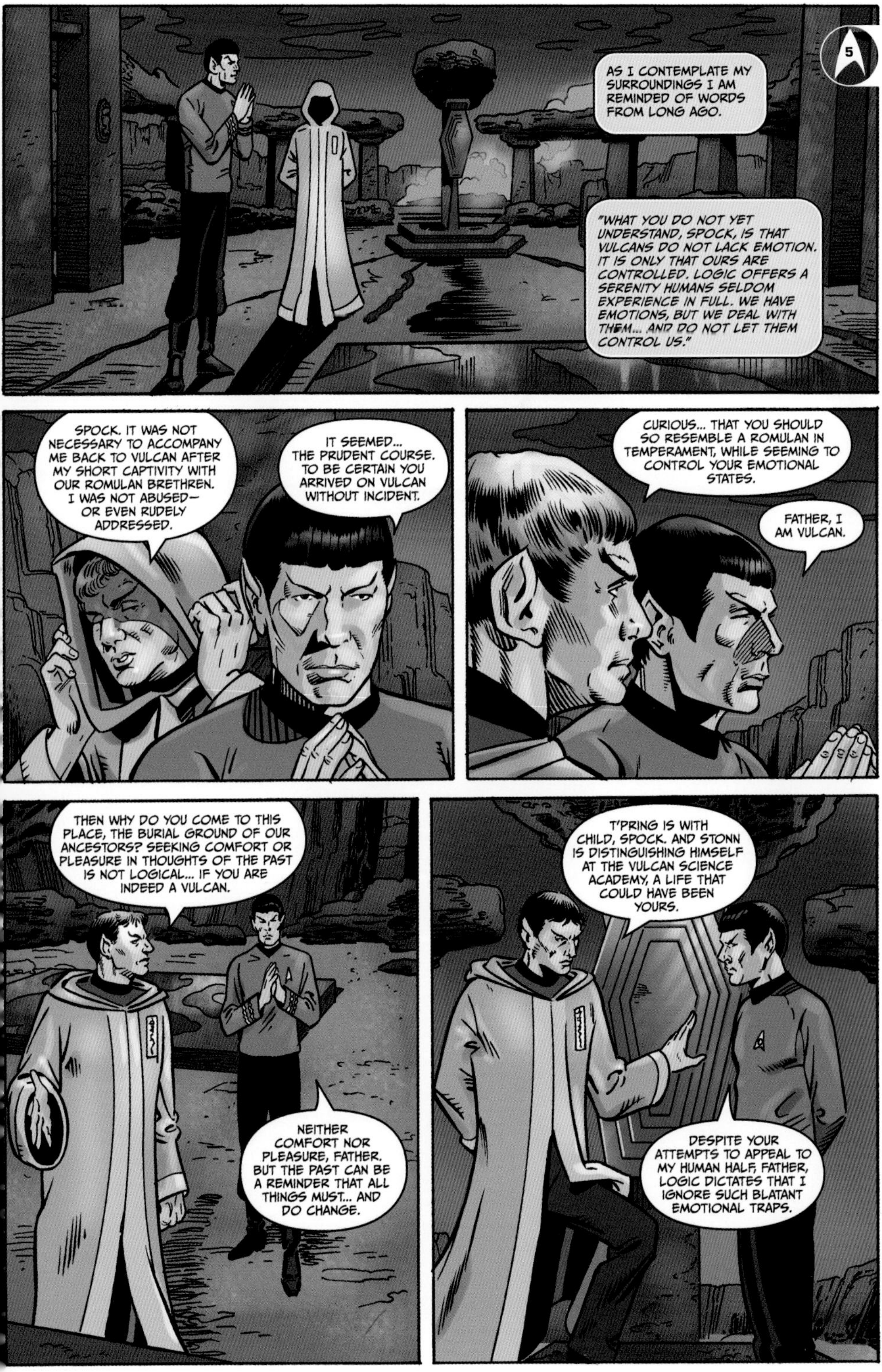
5
AS I CONTEMPLATE MY SURROUNDINGS I AM REMINDED OF WORDS FROM LONG AGO.
"WHAT YOU DO NOT YET UNDERSTAND, SPOCK, IS THAT VULCANS DO NOT LACK EMOTION. IT IS ONLY THAT OURS ARE CONTROLLED. LOGIC OFFERS A SERENITY HUMANS SELDOM EXPERIENCE IN FULL. WE HAVE EMOTIONS, BUT WE DEAL WITH THEM... AND DO NOT LET THEM CONTROL US."
SPOCK. IT WAS NOT NECESSARY TO ACCOMPANY ME BACK TO VULCAN AFTER MY SHORT CAPTIVITY WITH OUR ROMULAN BRETHREN. I WAS NOT ABUSED— OR EVEN RUDELY ADDRESSED.
IT SEEMED... THE PRUDENT COURSE. TO BE CERTAIN YOU ARRIVED ON VULCAN WITHOUT INCIDENT.
CURIOUS... THAT YOU SHOULD SO RESEMBLE A ROMULAN IN TEMPERAMENT, WHILE SEEMING TO CONTROL YOUR EMOTIONAL STATES.
FATHER, I AM VULCAN.
THEN WHY DO YOU COME TO THIS PLACE, THE BURIAL GROUND OF OUR ANCESTORS? SEEKING COMFORT OR PLEASURE IN THOUGHTS OF THE PAST IS NOT LOGICAL... IF YOU ARE INDEED A VULCAN.
NEITHER COMFORT NOR PLEASURE, FATHER. BUT THE PAST CAN BE A REMINDER THAT ALL THINGS MUST... AND DO CHANGE.
T'PRING IS WITH CHILD, SPOCK. AND STONN IS DISTINGUISHING HIMSELF AT THE VULCAN SCIENCE ACADEMY, A LIFE THAT COULD HAVE BEEN YOURS.
DESPITE YOUR ATTEMPTS TO APPEAL TO MY HUMAN HALF, FATHER, LOGIC DICTATES THAT I IGNORE SUCH BLATANT EMOTIONAL TRAPS.

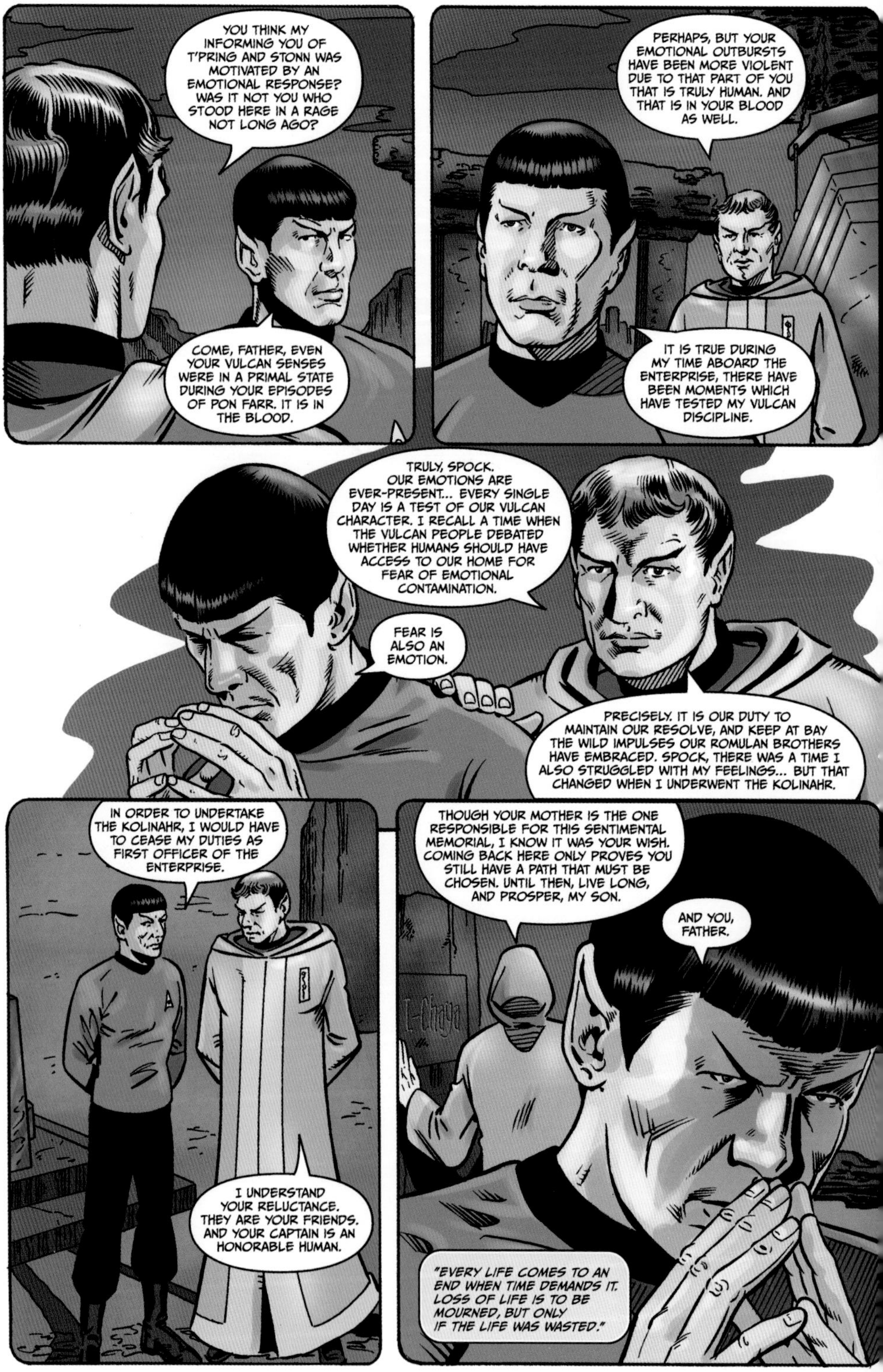
YOU THINK MY INFORMING YOU OF T'PRING AND STONN WAS MOTIVATED BY AN EMOTIONAL RESPONSE? WAS IT NOT YOU WHO STOOD HERE IN A RAGE NOT LONG AGO?
COME, FATHER, EVEN YOUR VULCAN SENSES WERE IN A PRIMAL STATE DURING YOUR EPISODES OF PON FARR. IT IS IN THE BLOOD.
PERHAPS, BUT YOUR EMOTIONAL OUTBURSTS HAVE BEEN MORE VIOLENT DUE TO THAT PART OF YOU THAT IS TRULY HUMAN. AND THAT IS IN YOUR BLOOD AS WELL.
IT IS TRUE DURING MY TIME ABOARD THE ENTERPRISE, THERE HAVE BEEN MOMENTS WHICH HAVE TESTED MY VULCAN DISCIPLINE.
TRULY, SPOCK. OUR EMOTIONS ARE EVER-PRESENT... EVERY SINGLE DAY IS A TEST OF OUR VULCAN CHARACTER. I RECALL A TIME WHEN THE VULCAN PEOPLE DEBATED WHETHER HUMANS SHOULD HAVE ACCESS TO OUR HOME FOR FEAR OF EMOTIONAL CONTAMINATION.
FEAR IS ALSO AN EMOTION.
PRECISELY. IT IS OUR DUTY TO MAINTAIN OUR RESOLVE, AND KEEP AT BAY THE WILD IMPULSES OUR ROMULAN BROTHERS HAVE EMBRACED. SPOCK, THERE WAS A TIME I ALSO STRUGGLED WITH MY FEELINGS... BUT THAT CHANGED WHEN I UNDERWENT THE KOLINAHR.
IN ORDER TO UNDERTAKE THE KOLINAHR, I WOULD HAVE TO CEASE MY DUTIES AS FIRST OFFICER OF THE ENTERPRISE.
I UNDERSTAND YOUR RELUCTANCE. THEY ARE YOUR FRIENDS. AND YOUR CAPTAIN IS AN HONORABLE HUMAN.
THOUGH YOUR MOTHER IS THE ONE RESPONSIBLE FOR THIS SENTIMENTAL MEMORIAL, I KNOW IT WAS YOUR WISH. COMING BACK HERE ONLY PROVES YOU STILL HAVE A PATH THAT MUST BE CHOSEN. UNTIL THEN, LIVE LONG, AND PROSPER, MY SON.
AND YOU, FATHER.
"EVERY LIFE COMES TO AN END WHEN TIME DEMANDS IT. LOSS OF LIFE IS TO BE MOURNED, BUT ONLY IF THE LIFE WAS WASTED."

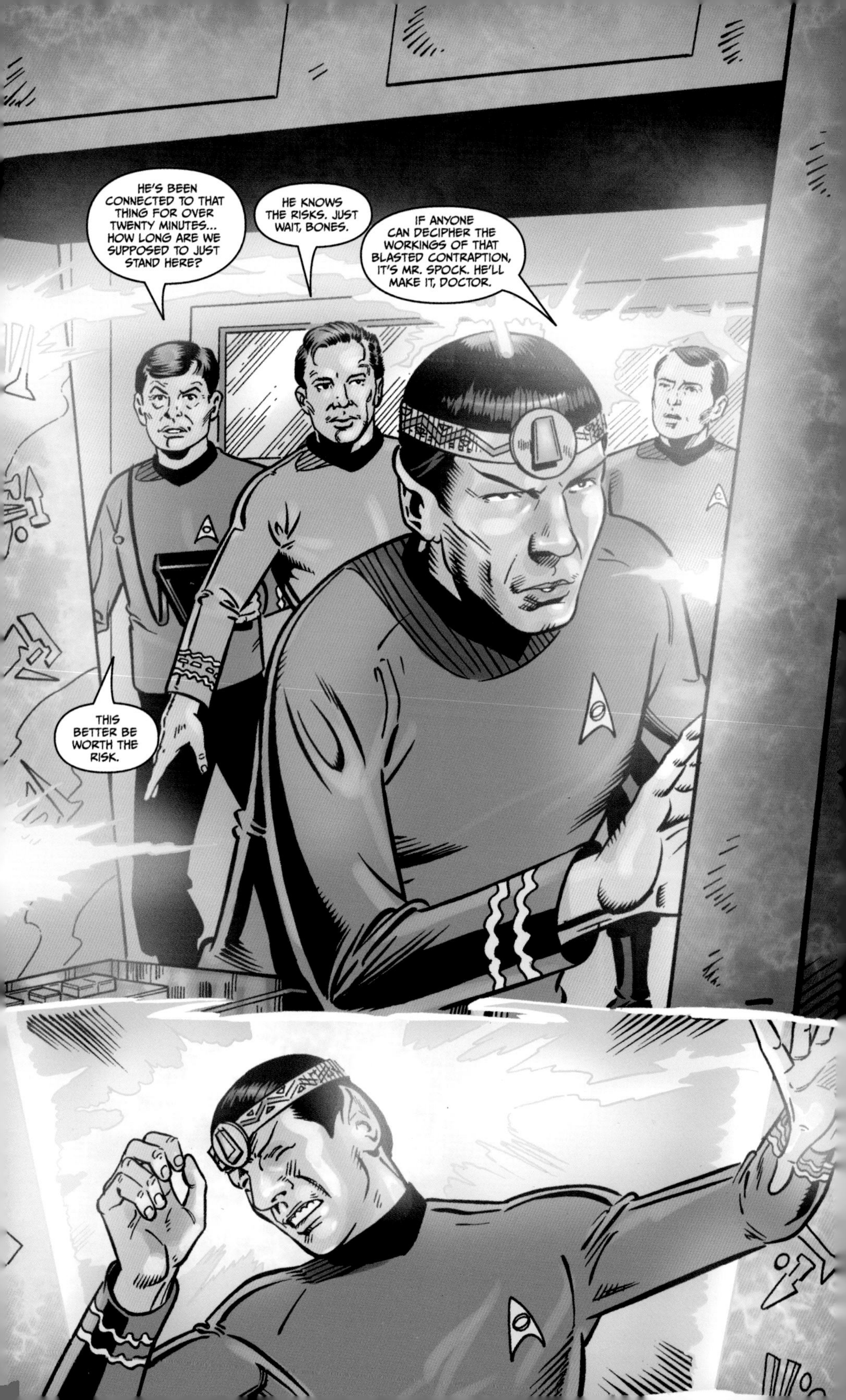
HE'S BEEN CONNECTED TO THAT THING FOR OVER TWENTY MINUTES... HOW LONG ARE WE SUPPOSED TO JUST STAND HERE?
HE KNOWS THE RISKS. JUST WAIT, BONES.
IF ANYONE CAN DECIPHER THE WORKINGS OF THAT BLASTED CONTRAPTION, IT'S MR. SPOCK. HE'LL MAKE IT, DOCTOR.
THIS BETTER BE WORTH THE RISK.

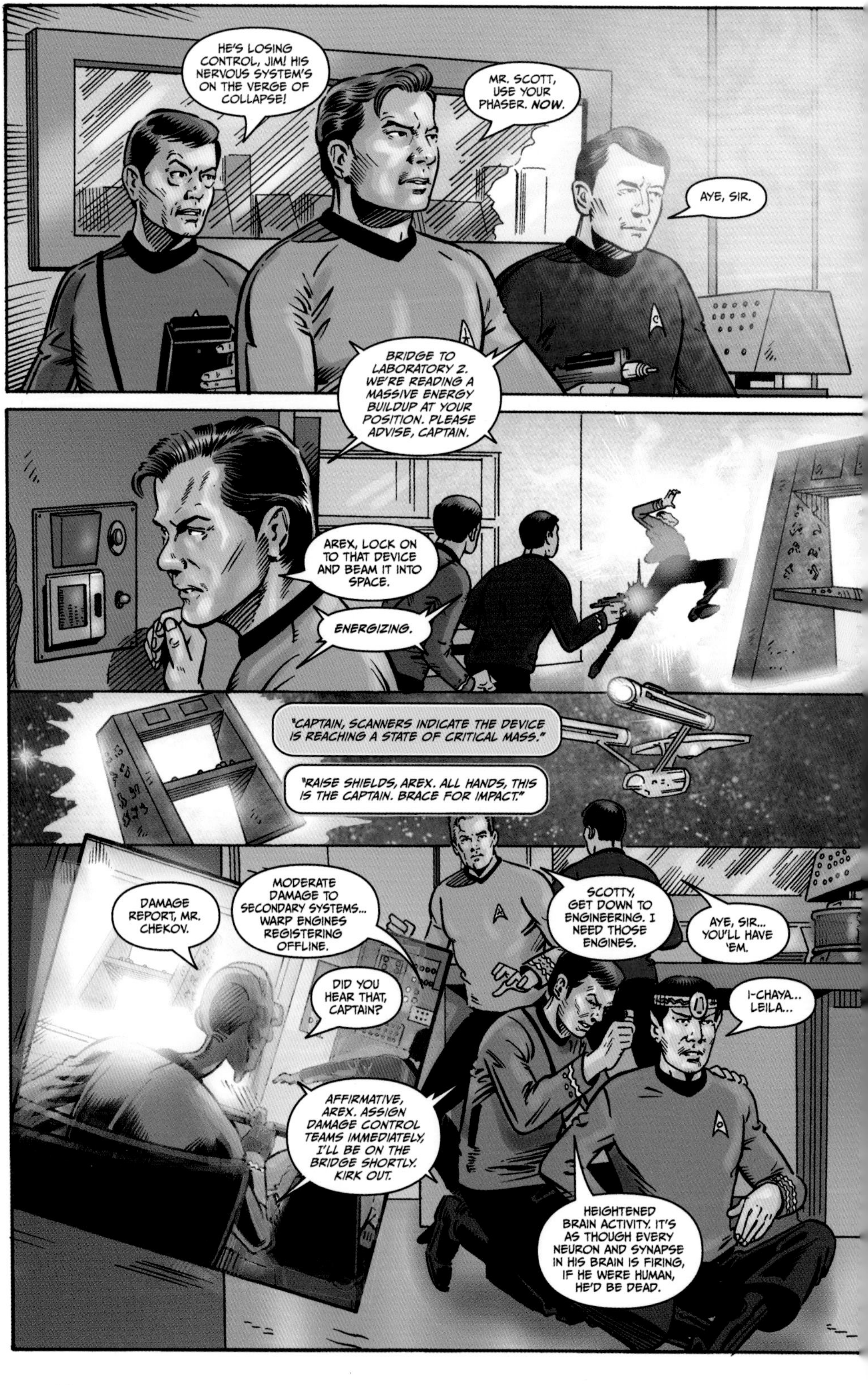

HE'S LOSING CONTROL, JIM! HIS NERVOUS SYSTEM'S ON THE VERGE OF COLLAPSE!
MR. SCOTT, USE YOUR PHASER. NOW.
AYE, SIR.
BRIDGE TO LABORATORY 2. WE'RE READING A MASSIVE ENERGY BUILDUP AT YOUR POSITION. PLEASE ADVISE, CAPTAIN.
AREX, LOCK ON TO THAT DEVICE AND BEAM IT INTO SPACE.
ENERGIZING.
"CAPTAIN, SCANNERS INDICATE THE DEVICE IS REACHING A STATE OF CRITICAL MASS."
"RAISE SHIELDS, AREX. ALL HANDS, THIS IS THE CAPTAIN. BRACE FOR IMPACT."
DAMAGE REPORT, MR. CHEKOV.
MODERATE DAMAGE TO SECONDARY SYSTEMS... WARP ENGINES REGISTERING OFFLINE.
SCOTTY, GET DOWN TO ENGINEERING. I NEED THOSE ENGINES.
AYE, SIR... YOU'LL HAVE 'EM.
DID YOU HEAR THAT, CAPTAIN?
I-CHAYA.. LEILA...
AFFIRMATIVE, AREX. ASSIGN DAMAGE CONTROL TEAMS IMMEDIATELY, I'LL BE ON THE BRIDGE SHORTLY. KIRK OUT.
HEIGHTENED BRAIN ACTIVITY. IT'S AS THOUGH EVERY NEURON AND SYNAPSE IN HIS BRAIN IS FIRING, IF HE WERE HUMAN, HE'D BE DEAD.

SPOCK. SPOCK!

I AM... HAVING DIFFICULTY CONCENTRATING, JIM.

WHAT'S THAT, BONES?

ACETYLCHOLINE INJECTION, TO STABILIZE HIS SYNAPSE FUNCTION.

SPOCK, ARE YOU ALL RIGHT? TALK TO ME.

JIM... THE VOLUME OF KNOWLEDGE IS ASTOUNDING. IT TOOK ALL MY MENTAL DISCIPLINES TO DECIPHER EVEN A SMALL FRACTION OF WHAT IT CONTAINS.

FORGIVE ME, I MUST CENTER MYSELF.

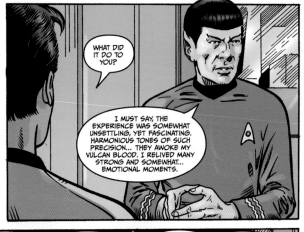

WHAT DID IT DO TO YOU?

I MUST SAY, THE EXPERIENCE WAS SOMEWHAT UNSETTLING, YET FASCINATING. HARMONIOUS TONES OF SUCH PRECISION... THEY AWOKE MY VULCAN BLOOD. I RELIVED MANY STRONG AND SOMEWHAT... EMOTIONAL MOMENTS.

I'M SORRY, SPOCK. THAT MUST HAVE BEEN DIFFICULT FOR YOU.

THERE IS NO NEED FOR ANY APOLOGIES, CAPTAIN.

I BELIEVE MY REPROGRAMMING OF THE DEVICE WAS MODERATELY SUCCESSFUL.

I HOPE YOU MANAGED TO GLIMPSE SOMETHING USEFUL. OTHERWISE WE'RE AT A DEAD END. THE DEVICE WAS DESTROYED.

MY EFFORTS TO REPROGRAM THE DEVICE DID ALLOW ME TO ACCESS THE RESERVOIR OF KNOWLEDGE IT CONTAINED, BUT I FEAR THAT DOING SO MAY HAVE TRIGGERED A SORT OF COUNTERMEASURE.

A SELF-DESTRUCT.

SO IT WOULD SEEM.

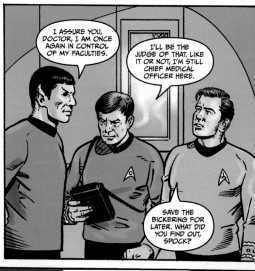

I ASSURE YOU, DOCTOR, I AM ONCE AGAIN IN CONTROL OF MY FACULTIES.

I'LL BE THE JUDGE OF THAT. LIKE IT OR NOT, I'M STILL CHIEF MEDICAL OFFICER HERE.

SAVE THE BICKERING FOR LATER. WHAT DID YOU FIND OUT, SPOCK?

IT APPEARS THE STRUCTURE WE DISCOVERED ON LOREN 5 WAS INDEED AN OUTPOST OF THE PRESERVERS SOME MILLIONS OF YEARS AGO.

PURPOSE?

THEIR PRIMARY MISSION TO PRESERVE CULTURES ON THE VERGE OF EXTINCTION WAS BEING THREATENED BY AN OUTSIDE FORCE.

THREATENED? WHAT COULD POSSIBLY THREATEN SUCH AN ADVANCED CIVILIZATION?

I WAS NOT ABLE TO PROCURE THAT INFORMATION. HOWEVER, IT WAS THIS THREAT THAT DROVE THEM TO CREATE THE GALACTIC BARRIER.

THE BARRIER... WAS CREATED BY THE PRESERVERS?

THAT IS CORRECT.

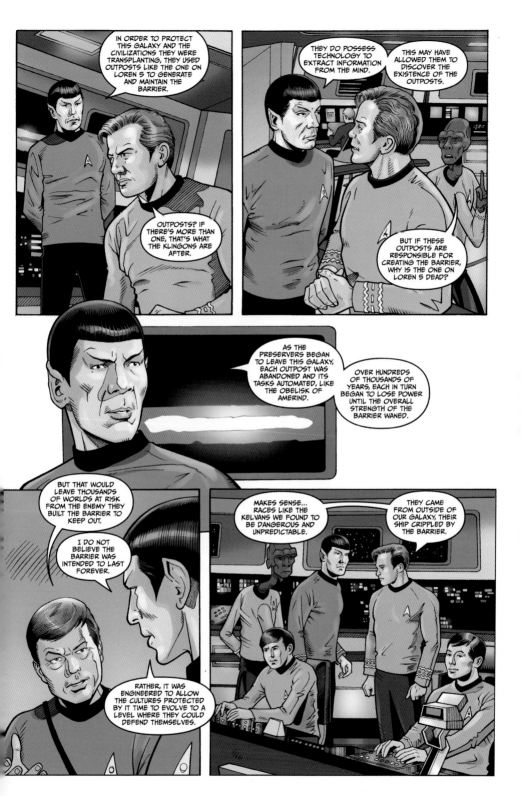

IN ORDER TO PROTECT THIS GALAXY AND THE CIVILIZATIONS THEY WERE TRANSPLANTING, THEY USED OUTPOSTS LIKE THE ONE ON LOREN 5 TO GENERATE AND MAINTAIN THE BARRIER.

OUTPOSTS? IF THERE'S MORE THAN ONE, THAT'S WHAT THE KLINGONS ARE AFTER.

THEY DO POSSESS TECHNOLOGY TO EXTRACT INFORMATION FROM THE MIND.

THIS MAY HAVE ALLOWED THEM TO DISCOVER THE EXISTENCE OF THE OUTPOSTS.

BUT IF THESE OUTPOSTS ARE RESPONSIBLE FOR CREATING THE BARRIER, WHY IS THE ONE ON LOREN 5 DEAD?

AS THE PRESERVERS BEGAN TO LEAVE THIS GALAXY, EACH OUTPOST WAS ABANDONED AND ITS TASKS AUTOMATED, LIKE THE OBELISK OF AMERIND.

OVER HUNDREDS OF THOUSANDS OF YEARS, EACH IN TURN BEGAN TO LOSE POWER UNTIL THE OVERALL STRENGTH OF THE BARRIER WANED.

BUT THAT WOULD LEAVE THOUSANDS OF WORLDS AT RISK FROM THE ENEMY THEY BUILT THE BARRIER TO KEEP OUT.

I DO NOT BELIEVE THE BARRIER WAS INTENDED TO LAST FOREVER.

RATHER, IT WAS ENGINEERED TO ALLOW THE CULTURES PROTECTED BY IT TIME TO EVOLVE TO A LEVEL WHERE THEY COULD DEFEND THEMSELVES.

MAKES SENSE... RACES LIKE THE KELVANS WE FOUND TO BE DANGEROUS AND UNPREDICTABLE.

THEY CAME FROM OUTSIDE OF OUR GALAXY, THEIR SHIP CRIPPLED BY THE BARRIER.

THOSE COORDINATES ARE ON THE EDGE OF GORN SPACE, MR. SPOCK.

CORRECT, MR. CHEKOV. THERE WAS AN INDICATION AS TO THE LOCATION OF ONE OTHER OUTPOST, REFERENCED ONLY BY A SERIES OF CONSTELLATIONS.

YOU'RE USING THEM AS A BASIS FOR TRIANGULATION?

PRECISELY.

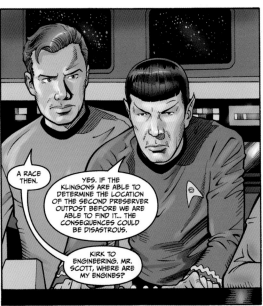

A RACE THEN.

YES. IF THE KLINGONS ARE ABLE TO DETERMINE THE LOCATION OF THE SECOND PRESERVER OUTPOST BEFORE WE ARE ABLE TO FIND IT... THE CONSEQUENCES COULD BE DISASTROUS.

KIRK TO ENGINEERING. MR. SCOTT, WHERE ARE MY ENGINES?

SCOTT HERE, CAPTAIN. THE ANTIMATTER PODS TOOK A BIT OF A JOLT FROM THAT EXPLOSION. I'M GOING TO RE-INITIALIZE THEM NOW.

BUT THE BEST I CAN GIVE YOU FOR THE MOMENT IS WARP FIVE.

IT WILL HAVE TO DO. PREPARE TO ENGAGE WARP ENGINES.

AYE, SIR.

OUR SCANNERS HAVE REGISTERED AN EXPLOSION IN QUADRANT NINE, MAGNITUDE SEVEN.

GOOD... TAKE US TO THAT POSITION, BUT KEEP US AT THE EDGE OF SCANNER RANGE.

I DON'T WANT OUR QUARRY TO KNOW OF OUR PRESENCE.

CAPTAIN KOR, I MUST POINT OUT... IT COULD SIMPLY BE A NATURALLY OCCURRING PHENOMENA.

IF WE ARE TAKEN IN THE WRONG DIRECTION...

THORN, MY INSTINCTS AS A HUNTER HAVE MADE ME THE WARRIOR I AM TODAY.

TRUST ME... WE HAVE FOUND THEM.

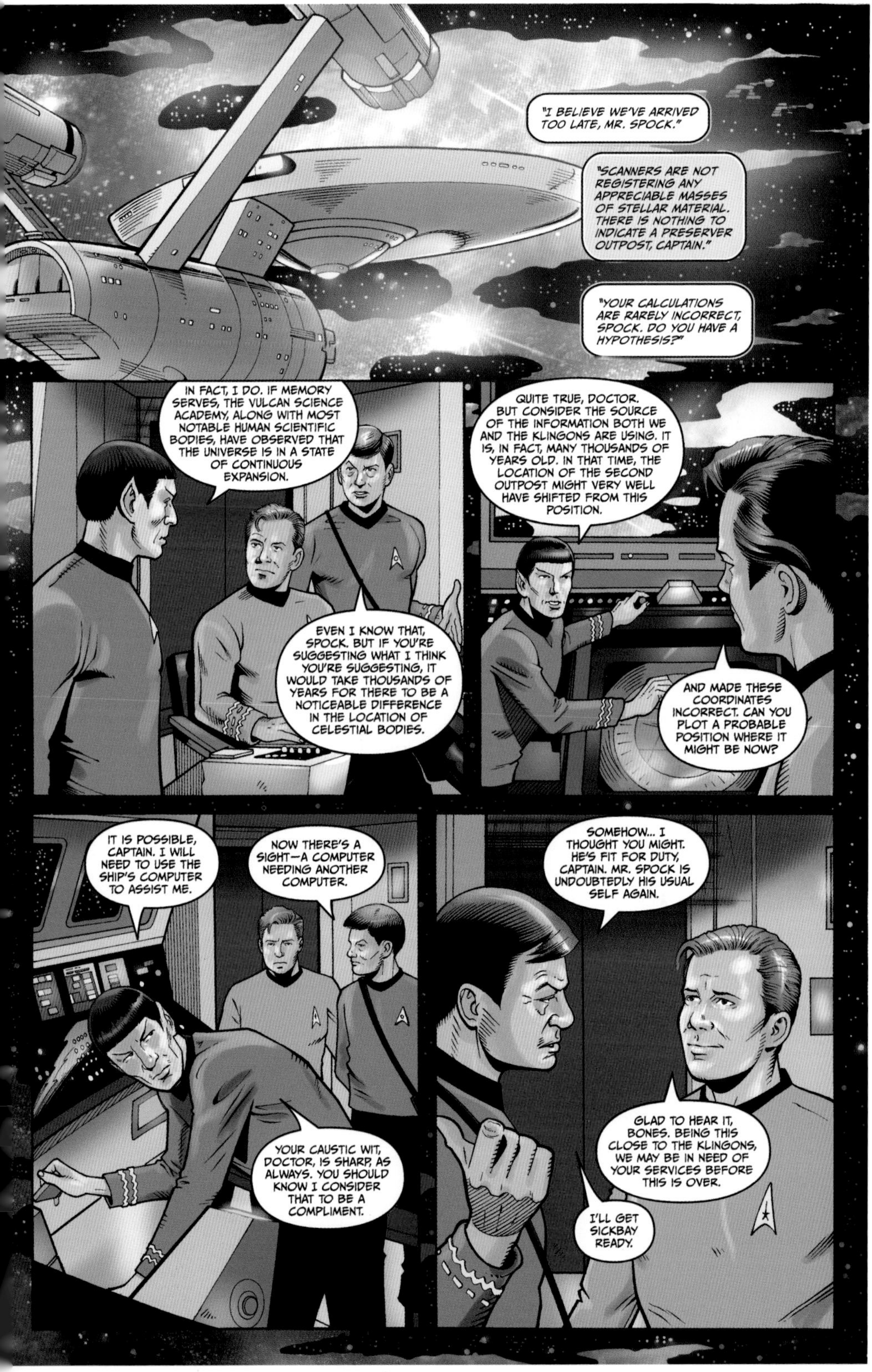
"I BELIEVE WE'VE ARRIVED TOO LATE, MR. SPOCK."
"SCANNERS ARE NOT REGISTERING ANY APPRECIABLE MASSES OF STELLAR MATERIAL. THERE IS NOTHING TO INDICATE A PRESERVER OUTPOST, CAPTAIN."
"YOUR CALCULATIONS ARE RARELY INCORRECT, SPOCK. DO YOU HAVE A HYPOTHESIS?"
IN FACT, I DO. IF MEMORY SERVES, THE VULCAN SCIENCE ACADEMY, ALONG WITH MOST NOTABLE HUMAN SCIENTIFIC BODIES, HAVE OBSERVED THAT THE UNIVERSE IS IN A STATE OF CONTINUOUS EXPANSION.
EVEN I KNOW THAT, SPOCK. BUT IF YOU'RE SUGGESTING WHAT I THINK YOU'RE SUGGESTING, IT WOULD TAKE THOUSANDS OF YEARS FOR THERE TO BE A NOTICEABLE DIFFERENCE IN THE LOCATION OF CELESTIAL BODIES.
QUITE TRUE, DOCTOR. BUT CONSIDER THE SOURCE OF THE INFORMATION BOTH WE AND THE KLINGONS ARE USING. IT IS, IN FACT, MANY THOUSANDS OF YEARS OLD. IN THAT TIME, THE LOCATION OF THE SECOND OUTPOST MIGHT VERY WELL HAVE SHIFTED FROM THIS POSITION.
AND MADE THESE COORDINATES INCORRECT. CAN YOU PLOT A PROBABLE POSITION WHERE IT MIGHT BE NOW?
IT IS POSSIBLE, CAPTAIN. I WILL NEED TO USE THE SHIP'S COMPUTER TO ASSIST ME.
NOW THERE'S A SIGHT—A COMPUTER NEEDING ANOTHER COMPUTER.
YOUR CAUSTIC WIT, DOCTOR, IS SHARP, AS ALWAYS. YOU SHOULD KNOW I CONSIDER THAT TO BE A COMPLIMENT.
SOMEHOW... I THOUGHT YOU MIGHT. HE'S FIT FOR DUTY, CAPTAIN. MR. SPOCK IS UNDOUBTEDLY HIS USUAL SELF AGAIN.
GLAD TO HEAR IT, BONES. BEING THIS CLOSE TO THE KLINGONS, WE MAY BE IN NEED OF YOUR SERVICES BEFORE THIS IS OVER.
I'LL GET SICKBAY READY.

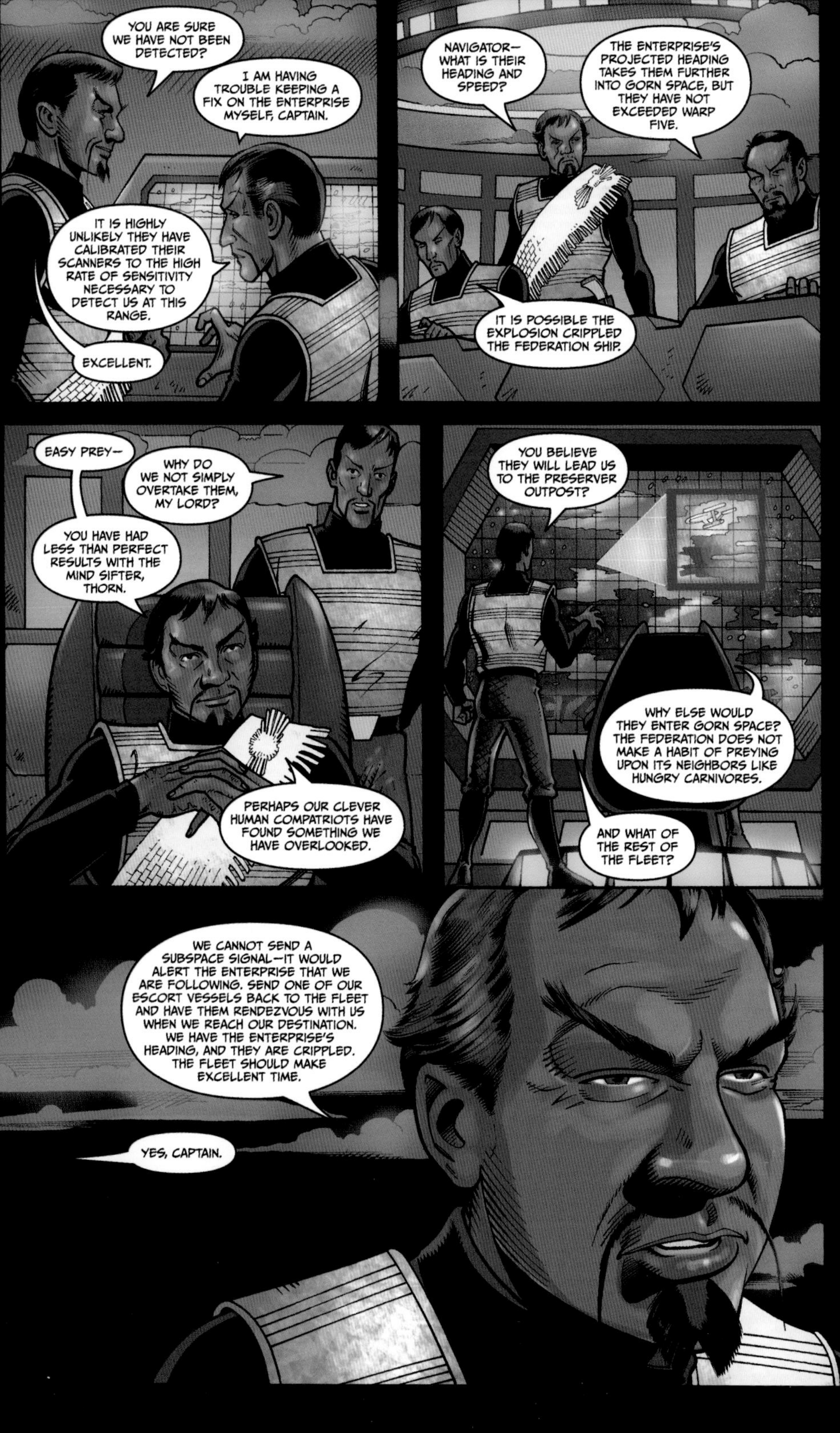
YOU ARE SURE WE HAVE NOT BEEN DETECTED?
I AM HAVING TROUBLE KEEPING A FIX ON THE ENTERPRISE MYSELF, CAPTAIN.
IT IS HIGHLY UNLIKELY THEY HAVE CALIBRATED THEIR SCANNERS TO THE HIGH RATE OF SENSITIVITY NECESSARY TO DETECT US AT THIS RANGE.
EXCELLENT.
NAVIGATOR— WHAT IS THEIR HEADING AND SPEED?
THE ENTERPRISE'S PROJECTED HEADING TAKES THEM FURTHER INTO GORN SPACE, BUT THEY HAVE NOT EXCEEDED WARP FIVE.
IT IS POSSIBLE THE EXPLOSION CRIPPLED THE FEDERATION SHIP.
EASY PREY—
WHY DO WE NOT SIMPLY OVERTAKE THEM, MY LORD?
YOU HAVE HAD LESS THAN PERFECT RESULTS WITH THE MIND SIFTER, THORN.
PERHAPS OUR CLEVER HUMAN COMPATRIOTS HAVE FOUND SOMETHING WE HAVE OVERLOOKED.
YOU BELIEVE THEY WILL LEAD US TO THE PRESERVER OUTPOST?
WHY ELSE WOULD THEY ENTER GORN SPACE? THE FEDERATION DOES NOT MAKE A HABIT OF PREYING UPON ITS NEIGHBORS LIKE HUNGRY CARNIVORES.
AND WHAT OF THE REST OF THE FLEET?
WE CANNOT SEND A SUBSPACE SIGNAL—IT WOULD ALERT THE ENTERPRISE THAT WE ARE FOLLOWING. SEND ONE OF OUR ESCORT VESSELS BACK TO THE FLEET AND HAVE THEM RENDEZVOUS WITH US WHEN WE REACH OUR DESTINATION. WE HAVE THE ENTERPRISE'S HEADING, AND THEY ARE CRIPPLED. THE FLEET SHOULD MAKE EXCELLENT TIME.
YES, CAPTAIN.

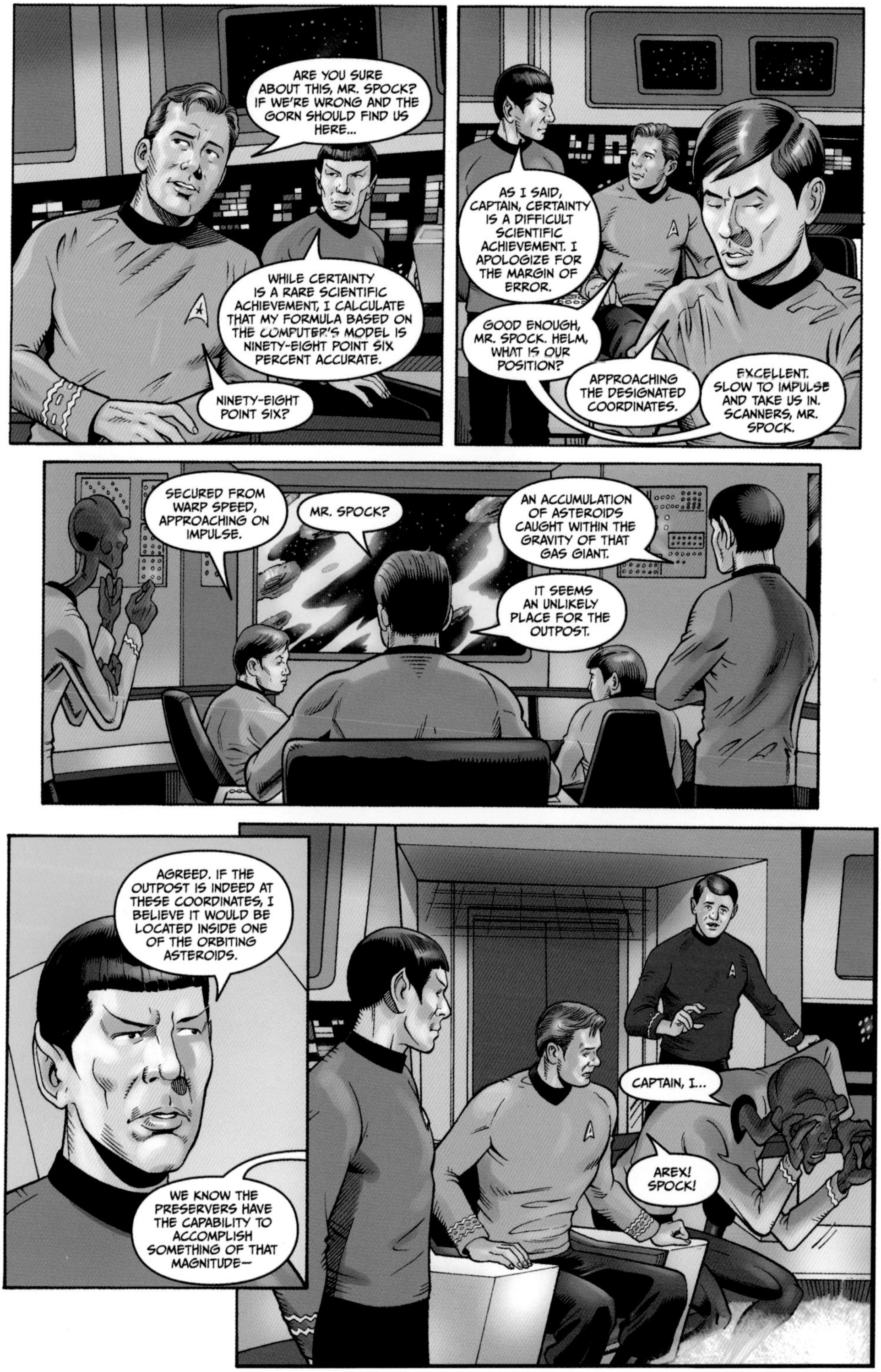
ARE YOU SURE ABOUT THIS, MR. SPOCK? IF WE'RE WRONG AND THE GORN SHOULD FIND US HERE...
WHILE CERTAINTY IS A RARE SCIENTIFIC ACHIEVEMENT, I CALCULATE THAT MY FORMULA BASED ON THE COMPUTER'S MODEL IS NINETY-EIGHT POINT SIX PERCENT ACCURATE.
NINETY-EIGHT POINT SIX?
AS I SAID, CAPTAIN, CERTAINTY IS A DIFFICULT SCIENTIFIC ACHIEVEMENT. I APOLOGIZE FOR THE MARGIN OF ERROR.
GOOD ENOUGH, MR. SPOCK. HELM, WHAT IS OUR POSITION?
APPROACHING THE DESIGNATED COORDINATES.
EXCELLENT. SLOW TO IMPULSE AND TAKE US IN. SCANNERS, MR. SPOCK.
SECURED FROM WARP SPEED, APPROACHING ON IMPULSE.
MR. SPOCK?
AN ACCUMULATION OF ASTEROIDS CAUGHT WITHIN THE GRAVITY OF THAT GAS GIANT.
IT SEEMS AN UNLIKELY PLACE FOR THE OUTPOST.
AGREED. IF THE OUTPOST IS INDEED AT THESE COORDINATES, I BELIEVE IT WOULD BE LOCATED INSIDE ONE OF THE ORBITING ASTEROIDS.
WE KNOW THE PRESERVERS HAVE THE CAPABILITY TO ACCOMPLISH SOMETHING OF THAT MAGNITUDE—
CAPTAIN, I...
AREX! SPOCK!

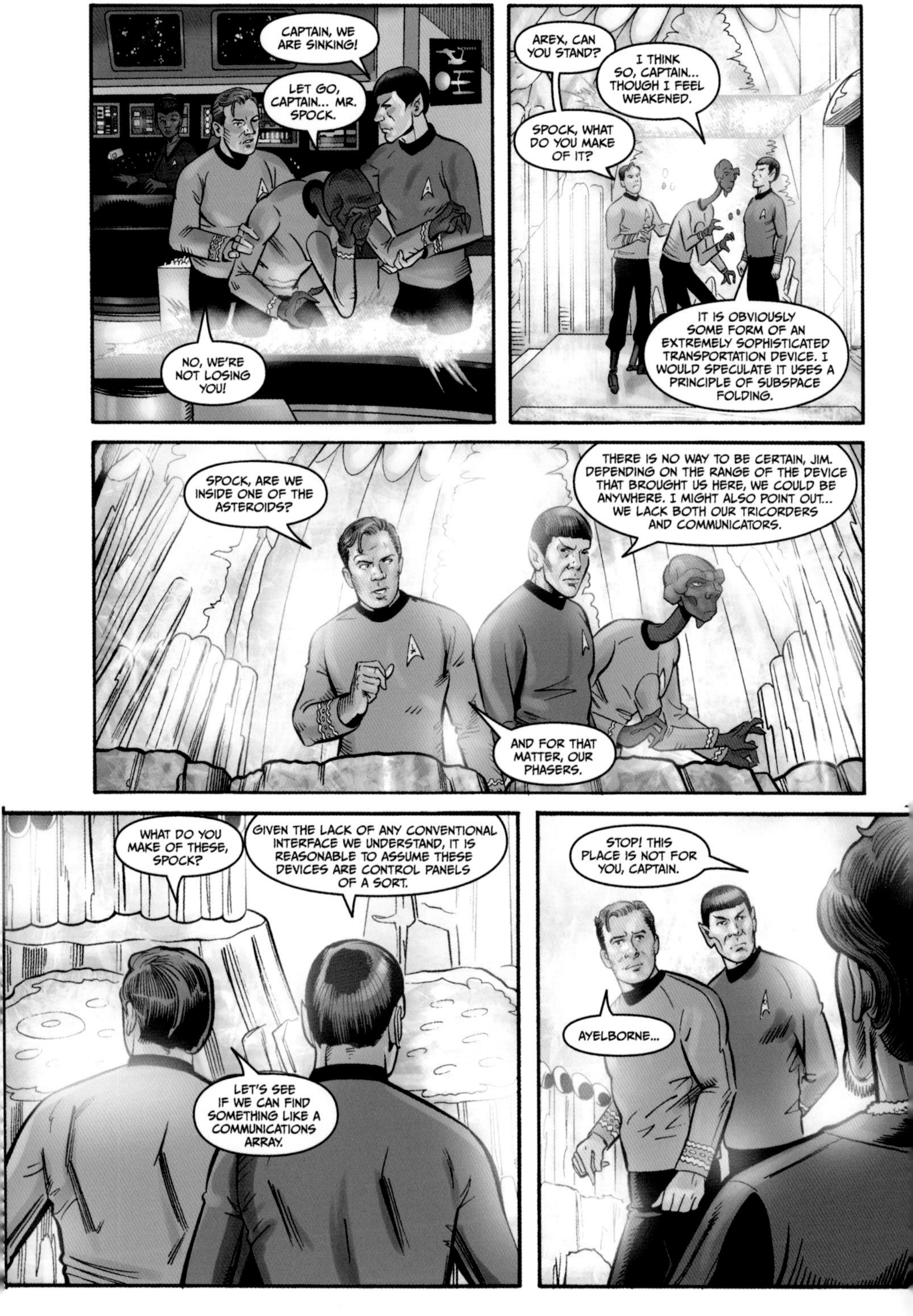
CAPTAIN, WE ARE SINKING!
LET GO, CAPTAIN... MR. SPOCK.
NO, WE'RE NOT LOSING YOU!
AREX, CAN YOU STAND?
I THINK SO, CAPTAIN... THOUGH I FEEL WEAKENED.
SPOCK, WHAT DO YOU MAKE OF IT?
IT IS OBVIOUSLY SOME FORM OF AN EXTREMELY SOPHISTICATED TRANSPORTATION DEVICE. I WOULD SPECULATE IT USES A PRINCIPLE OF SUBSPACE FOLDING.
SPOCK, ARE WE INSIDE ONE OF THE ASTEROIDS?
THERE IS NO WAY TO BE CERTAIN, JIM. DEPENDING ON THE RANGE OF THE DEVICE THAT BROUGHT US HERE, WE COULD BE ANYWHERE. I MIGHT ALSO POINT OUT... WE LACK BOTH OUR TRICORDERS AND COMMUNICATORS.
AND FOR THAT MATTER, OUR PHASERS.
WHAT DO YOU MAKE OF THESE, SPOCK?
GIVEN THE LACK OF ANY CONVENTIONAL INTERFACE WE UNDERSTAND, IT IS REASONABLE TO ASSUME THESE DEVICES ARE CONTROL PANELS OF A SORT.
LET'S SEE IF WE CAN FIND SOMETHING LIKE A COMMUNICATIONS ARRAY.
STOP! THIS PLACE IS NOT FOR YOU, CAPTAIN.
AYELBORNE...

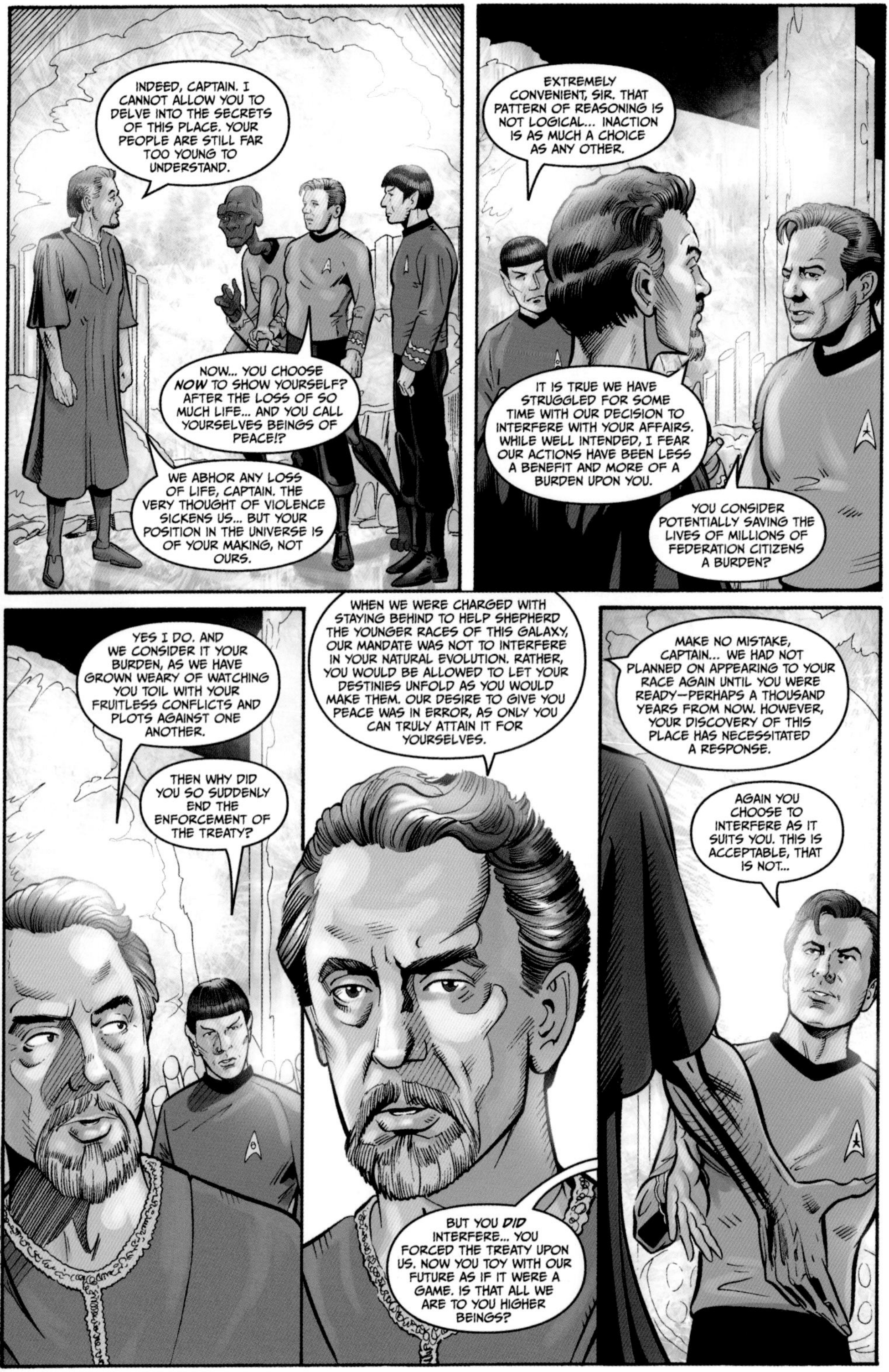
INDEED, CAPTAIN. I CANNOT ALLOW YOU TO DELVE INTO THE SECRETS OF THIS PLACE. YOUR PEOPLE ARE STILL FAR TOO YOUNG TO UNDERSTAND.
NOW... YOU CHOOSE *NOW* TO SHOW YOURSELF? AFTER THE LOSS OF SO MUCH LIFE... AND YOU CALL YOURSELVES BEINGS OF PEACE!?
WE ABHOR ANY LOSS OF LIFE, CAPTAIN. THE VERY THOUGHT OF VIOLENCE SICKENS US... BUT YOUR POSITION IN THE UNIVERSE IS OF YOUR MAKING, NOT OURS.
EXTREMELY CONVENIENT, SIR. THAT PATTERN OF REASONING IS NOT LOGICAL... INACTION IS AS MUCH A CHOICE AS ANY OTHER.
IT IS TRUE WE HAVE STRUGGLED FOR SOME TIME WITH OUR DECISION TO INTERFERE WITH YOUR AFFAIRS. WHILE WELL INTENDED, I FEAR OUR ACTIONS HAVE BEEN LESS A BENEFIT AND MORE OF A BURDEN UPON YOU.
YOU CONSIDER POTENTIALLY SAVING THE LIVES OF MILLIONS OF FEDERATION CITIZENS A BURDEN?
YES I DO. AND WE CONSIDER IT YOUR BURDEN, AS WE HAVE GROWN WEARY OF WATCHING YOU TOIL WITH YOUR FRUITLESS CONFLICTS AND PLOTS AGAINST ONE ANOTHER.
THEN WHY DID YOU SO SUDDENLY END THE ENFORCEMENT OF THE TREATY?
WHEN WE WERE CHARGED WITH STAYING BEHIND TO HELP SHEPHERD THE YOUNGER RACES OF THIS GALAXY, OUR MANDATE WAS NOT TO INTERFERE IN YOUR NATURAL EVOLUTION. RATHER, YOU WOULD BE ALLOWED TO LET YOUR DESTINIES UNFOLD AS YOU WOULD MAKE THEM. OUR DESIRE TO GIVE YOU PEACE WAS IN ERROR, AS ONLY YOU CAN TRULY ATTAIN IT FOR YOURSELVES.
BUT YOU *DID* INTERFERE... YOU FORCED THE TREATY UPON US. NOW YOU TOY WITH OUR FUTURE AS IF IT WERE A GAME. IS THAT ALL WE ARE TO YOU HIGHER BEINGS?
MAKE NO MISTAKE, CAPTAIN... WE HAD NOT PLANNED ON APPEARING TO YOUR RACE AGAIN UNTIL YOU WERE READY—PERHAPS A THOUSAND YEARS FROM NOW. HOWEVER, YOUR DISCOVERY OF THIS PLACE HAS NECESSITATED A RESPONSE.
AGAIN YOU CHOOSE TO INTERFERE AS IT SUITS YOU. THIS IS ACCEPTABLE, THAT IS NOT...

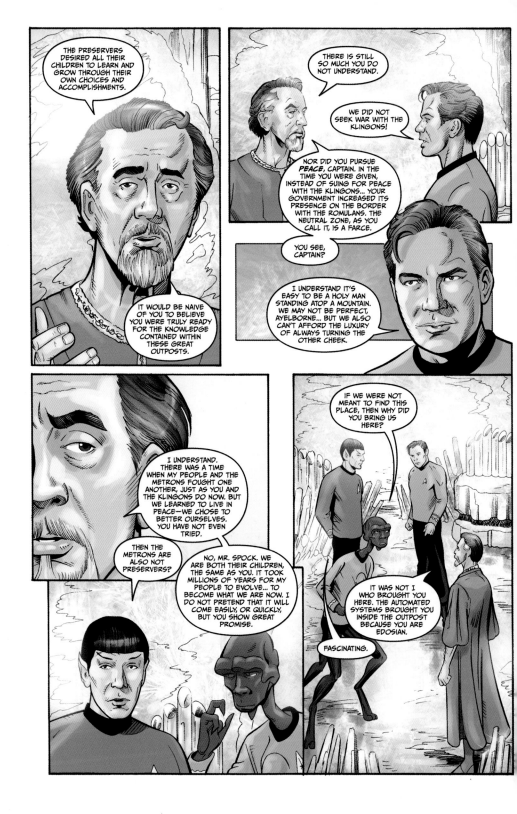

THE PRESERVERS DESIRED ALL THEIR CHILDREN TO LEARN AND GROW THROUGH THEIR OWN CHOICES AND ACCOMPLISHMENTS.

THERE IS STILL SO MUCH YOU DO NOT UNDERSTAND.

WE DID NOT SEEK WAR WITH THE KLINGONS!

NOR DID YOU PURSUE *PEACE*, CAPTAIN. IN THE TIME YOU WERE GIVEN, INSTEAD OF SUING FOR PEACE WITH THE KLINGONS... YOUR GOVERNMENT INCREASED ITS PRESENCE ON THE BORDER WITH THE ROMULANS. THE NEUTRAL ZONE, AS YOU CALL IT, IS A FARCE.

YOU SEE, CAPTAIN?

I UNDERSTAND IT'S EASY TO BE A HOLY MAN STANDING ATOP A MOUNTAIN. WE MAY NOT BE PERFECT, AYELBORNE... BUT WE ALSO CAN'T AFFORD THE LUXURY OF ALWAYS TURNING THE OTHER CHEEK.

IT WOULD BE NAIVE OF YOU TO BELIEVE YOU WERE TRULY READY FOR THE KNOWLEDGE CONTAINED WITHIN THESE GREAT OUTPOSTS.

I UNDERSTAND. THERE WAS A TIME WHEN MY PEOPLE AND THE METRONS FOUGHT ONE ANOTHER, JUST AS YOU AND THE KLINGONS DO NOW. BUT WE LEARNED TO LIVE IN PEACE—WE CHOSE TO BETTER OURSELVES. YOU HAVE NOT EVEN TRIED.

IF WE WERE NOT MEANT TO FIND THIS PLACE, THEN WHY DID YOU BRING US HERE?

THEN THE METRONS ARE ALSO NOT PRESERVERS?

NO, MR. SPOCK. WE ARE BOTH THEIR CHILDREN, THE SAME AS YOU. IT TOOK MILLIONS OF YEARS FOR MY PEOPLE TO EVOLVE... TO BECOME WHAT WE ARE NOW. I DO NOT PRETEND THAT IT WILL COME EASILY, OR QUICKLY, BUT YOU SHOW GREAT PROMISE.

IT WAS NOT I WHO BROUGHT YOU HERE. THE AUTOMATED SYSTEMS BROUGHT YOU INSIDE THE OUTPOST BECAUSE YOU ARE EDOSIAN.

FASCINATING.

I DO NOT UNDERSTAND.

YOU ARE NOT MEANT TO... UNTIL THE PROPER TIME.

THE AEGIS, THE GREAT SHIELD OF THIS GALAXY, WAS BUILT BY THE PRESERVERS TO PROTECT ALL LIFE WITHIN, BUT YOUR PEOPLE HAVE AN ESSENTIAL ROLE TO PLAY IN THE YEARS TO COME.

ARE YOU IMPLYING THE EDOSIANS HAVE HAD SOME PAST CONTACT WITH THE PRESERVERS?

WHILE IT WOULD NOT BE WISE FOR ME TO TELL YOU EVERYTHING, I WILL SAY AREX'S PEOPLE HAVE A SPECIAL DESTINY. ONE THAT WILL HELP ALL THE CIVILIZATIONS OF THIS GALAXY. IF YOU DO NOT DESTROY EACH OTHER IN THE MEANTIME.

YOU SPEAK IN RIDDLES, NEVER A CLEAR ANSWER. IS THAT TOO MUCH TO ASK?

WE DO NOT EXPECT YOU TO ATTAIN TOTAL UNDERSTANDING, AS THESE EVENTS WERE NEVER INTENDED TO TRANSPIRE. YOUR CURIOSITY AND FASCINATION FOR DISCOVERY ARE ONE OF YOUR RACE'S GREATEST TRAITS. BUT KNOWLEDGE COMES WITH A PRICE.

AS YOU GO DEEPER INTO THIS GALAXY, YOU WILL DISCOVER MANY GREAT *AND* TERRIBLE THINGS. WE CANNOT ALWAYS BE THERE TO PROTECT YOU, NOR CAN WE FORCE YOUR EVOLUTION TOWARD A SPECIFIC OUTCOME. YOUR CHOICES WILL DECIDE YOUR FATE, CAPTAIN. AS THEY ALWAYS HAVE.

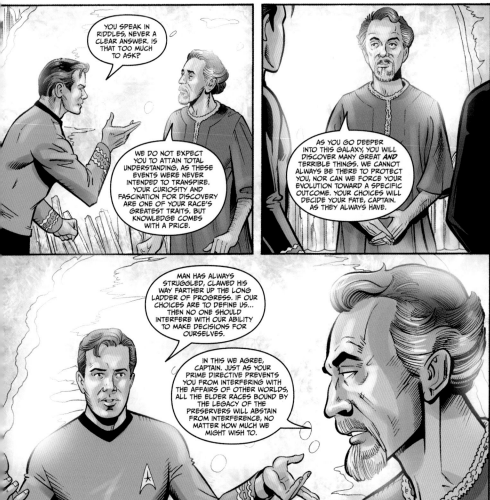

MAN HAS ALWAYS STRUGGLED, CLAWED HIS WAY FARTHER UP THE LONG LADDER OF PROGRESS. IF OUR CHOICES ARE TO DEFINE US... THEN NO ONE SHOULD INTERFERE WITH OUR ABILITY TO MAKE DECISIONS FOR OURSELVES.

IN THIS WE AGREE, CAPTAIN. JUST AS YOUR PRIME DIRECTIVE PREVENTS YOU FROM INTERFERING WITH THE AFFAIRS OF OTHER WORLDS, ALL THE ELDER RACES BOUND BY THE LEGACY OF THE PRESERVERS WILL ABSTAIN FROM INTERFERENCE, NO MATTER HOW MUCH WE MIGHT WISH TO.

AND WHAT OF THIS PLACE? THE KLINGONS SEEK ITS KNOWLEDGE TO USE AGAINST US. IF WE CANNOT STOP THEM AND YOU WILL NO LONGER INTERFERE...

YOU WILL UNDERSTAND SHORTLY, CAPTAIN.

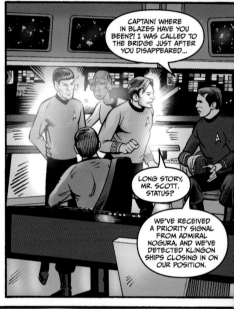

CAPTAIN! WHERE IN BLAZES HAVE YOU BEEN?! I WAS CALLED TO THE BRIDGE JUST AFTER YOU DISAPPEARED...

LONG STORY, MR. SCOTT. STATUS?

WE'VE RECEIVED A PRIORITY SIGNAL FROM ADMIRAL NOGURA, AND WE'VE DETECTED KLINGON SHIPS CLOSING IN ON OUR POSITION.

THE KLINGONS?! IT DIDN'T TAKE THEM LONG TO FIND US.

SCOTTY, I'LL NEED AS MUCH WARP POWER AS YOU CAN GIVE ME.

I'LL COAX ENOUGH POWER OUT OF MY BAIRNS TO OUTRUN THE DEVIL HIMSELF.

WE'RE GOING TO NEED IT.

MR. SULU, PREPARE...

AS YOU SEE ME AT THIS MOMENT, I ALSO APPEAR TO THE LEADERS OF YOUR GOVERNMENTS. WE HAVE WATCHED FOR TOO LONG AS YOU SOUGHT TO DO ONE ANOTHER HARM, IGNORING THE GREAT POSSIBILITIES AN ALLIANCE BETWEEN YOUR PEOPLES WOULD BRING.

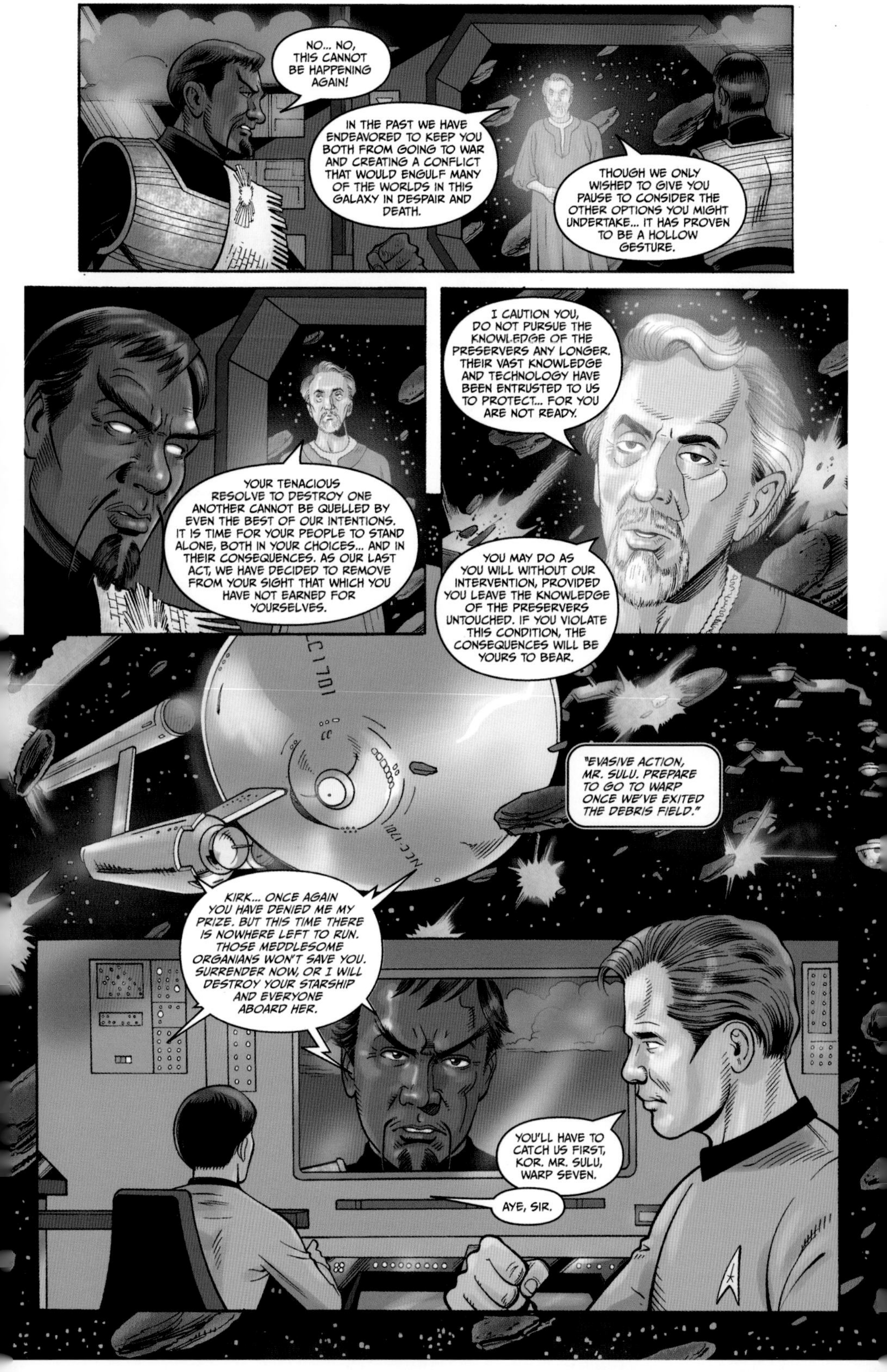
NO... NO, THIS CANNOT BE HAPPENING AGAIN!
IN THE PAST WE HAVE ENDEAVORED TO KEEP YOU BOTH FROM GOING TO WAR AND CREATING A CONFLICT THAT WOULD ENGULF MANY OF THE WORLDS IN THIS GALAXY IN DESPAIR AND DEATH.
THOUGH WE ONLY WISHED TO GIVE YOU PAUSE TO CONSIDER THE OTHER OPTIONS YOU MIGHT UNDERTAKE... IT HAS PROVEN TO BE A HOLLOW GESTURE.
YOUR TENACIOUS RESOLVE TO DESTROY ONE ANOTHER CANNOT BE QUELLED BY EVEN THE BEST OF OUR INTENTIONS. IT IS TIME FOR YOUR PEOPLE TO STAND ALONE, BOTH IN YOUR CHOICES... AND IN THEIR CONSEQUENCES. AS OUR LAST ACT, WE HAVE DECIDED TO REMOVE FROM YOUR SIGHT THAT WHICH YOU HAVE NOT EARNED FOR YOURSELVES.
I CAUTION YOU, DO NOT PURSUE THE KNOWLEDGE OF THE PRESERVERS ANY LONGER. THEIR VAST KNOWLEDGE AND TECHNOLOGY HAVE BEEN ENTRUSTED TO US TO PROTECT... FOR YOU ARE NOT READY.
YOU MAY DO AS YOU WILL WITHOUT OUR INTERVENTION, PROVIDED YOU LEAVE THE KNOWLEDGE OF THE PRESERVERS UNTOUCHED. IF YOU VIOLATE THIS CONDITION, THE CONSEQUENCES WILL BE YOURS TO BEAR.
NCC 1701
"EVASIVE ACTION, MR. SULU. PREPARE TO GO TO WARP ONCE WE'VE EXITED THE DEBRIS FIELD."
KIRK... ONCE AGAIN YOU HAVE DENIED ME MY PRIZE. BUT THIS TIME THERE IS NOWHERE LEFT TO RUN. THOSE MEDDLESOME ORGANIANS WON'T SAVE YOU. SURRENDER NOW, OR I WILL DESTROY YOUR STARSHIP AND EVERYONE ABOARD HER.
YOU'LL HAVE TO CATCH US FIRST, KOR. MR. SULU, WARP SEVEN.
AYE, SIR.

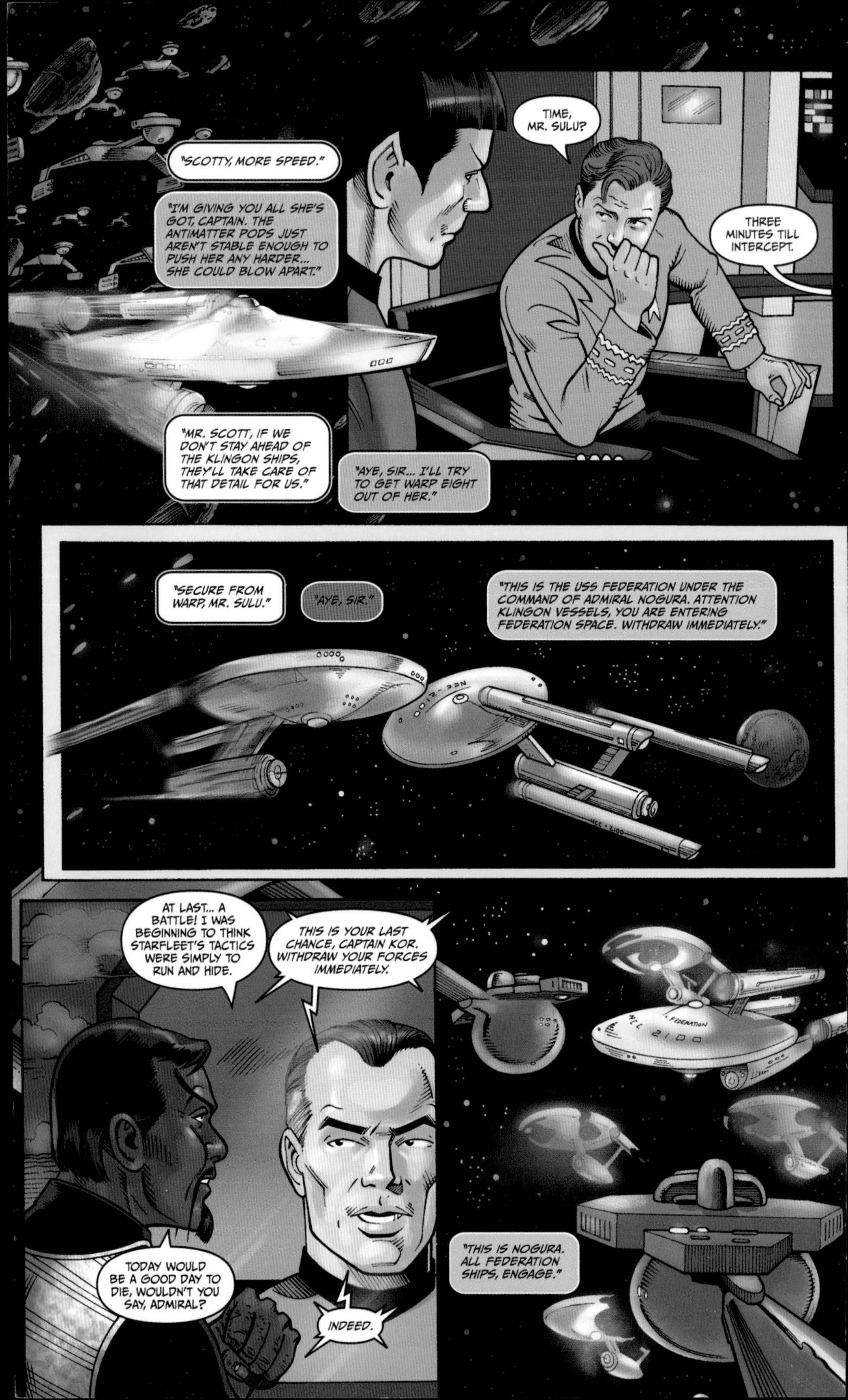
"SCOTTY, MORE SPEED."
TIME, MR. SULU?
"I'M GIVING YOU ALL SHE'S GOT, CAPTAIN. THE ANTIMATTER PODS JUST AREN'T STABLE ENOUGH TO PUSH HER ANY HARDER... SHE COULD BLOW APART."
THREE MINUTES TILL INTERCEPT.
"MR. SCOTT, IF WE DON'T STAY AHEAD OF THE KLINGON SHIPS, THEY'LL TAKE CARE OF THAT DETAIL FOR US."
"AYE, SIR... I'LL TRY TO GET WARP EIGHT OUT OF HER."
"SECURE FROM WARP, MR. SULU."
"AYE, SIR."
"THIS IS THE USS FEDERATION UNDER THE COMMAND OF ADMIRAL NOGURA. ATTENTION KLINGON VESSELS, YOU ARE ENTERING FEDERATION SPACE. WITHDRAW IMMEDIATELY."
AT LAST... A BATTLE! I WAS BEGINNING TO THINK STARFLEET'S TACTICS WERE SIMPLY TO RUN AND HIDE.
THIS IS YOUR LAST CHANCE, CAPTAIN KOR. WITHDRAW YOUR FORCES IMMEDIATELY.
TODAY WOULD BE A GOOD DAY TO DIE, WOULDN'T YOU SAY, ADMIRAL?
INDEED.
"THIS IS NOGURA. ALL FEDERATION SHIPS, ENGAGE."

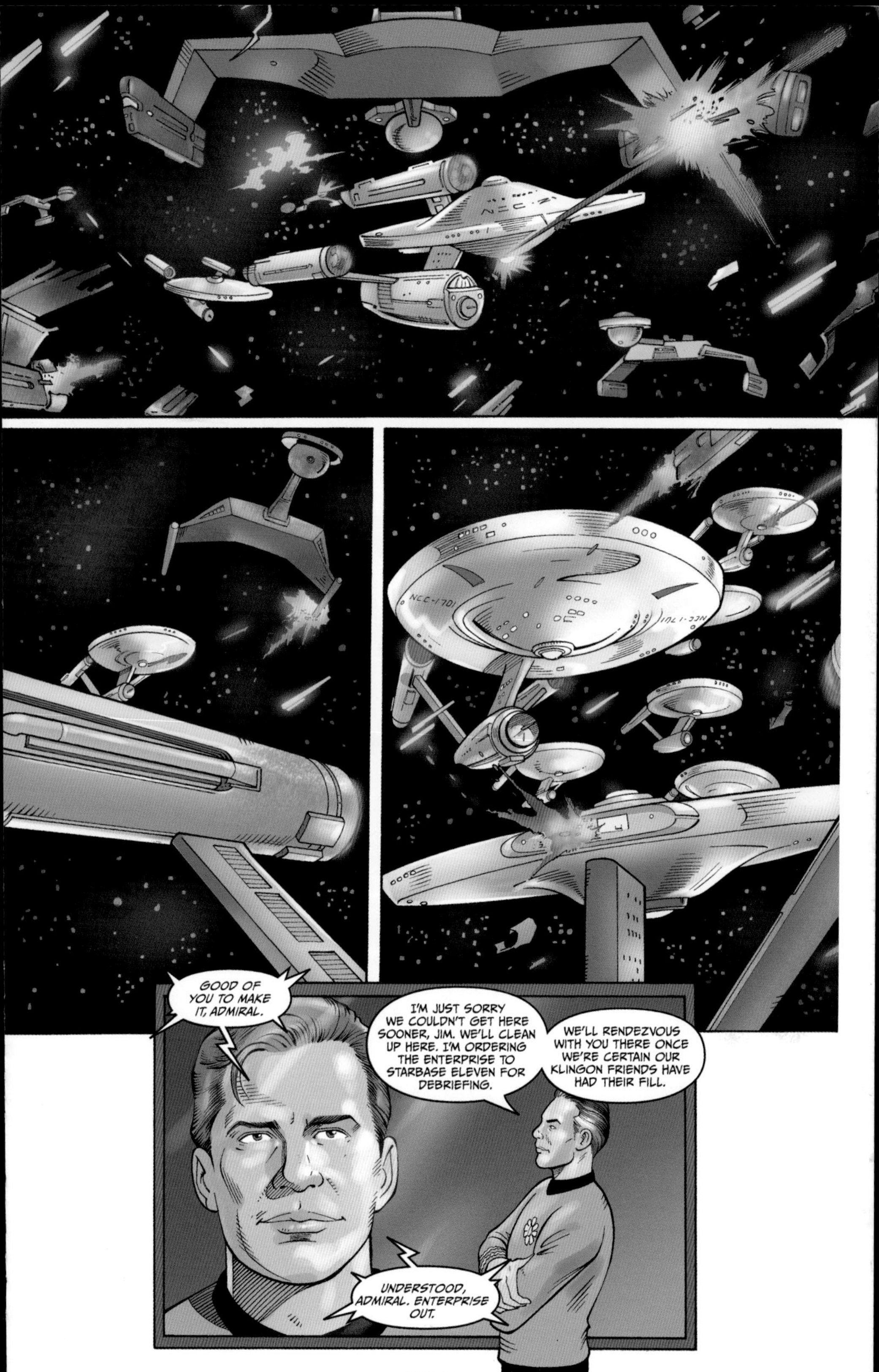
NCC-1701
NCC-1701
GOOD OF YOU TO MAKE IT, ADMIRAL.
I'M JUST SORRY WE COULDN'T GET HERE SOONER, JIM. WE'LL CLEAN UP HERE. I'M ORDERING THE ENTERPRISE TO STARBASE ELEVEN FOR DEBRIEFING.
WE'LL RENDEZVOUS WITH YOU THERE ONCE WE'RE CERTAIN OUR KLINGON FRIENDS HAVE HAD THEIR FILL.
UNDERSTOOD, ADMIRAL. ENTERPRISE OUT.

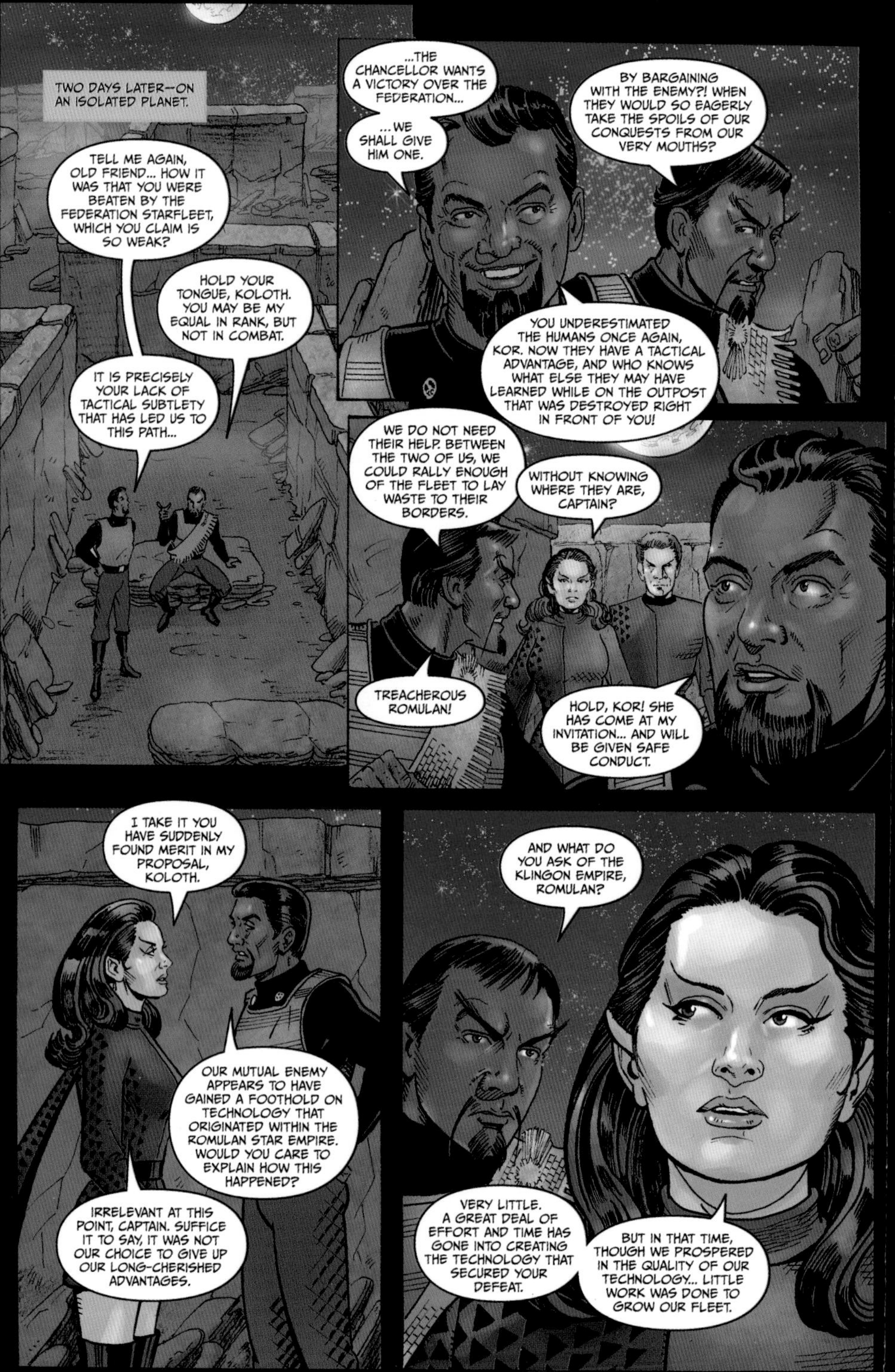

TWO DAYS LATER—ON AN ISOLATED PLANET.
TELL ME AGAIN, OLD FRIEND... HOW IT WAS THAT YOU WERE BEATEN BY THE FEDERATION STARFLEET, WHICH YOU CLAIM IS SO WEAK?
HOLD YOUR TONGUE, KOLOTH. YOU MAY BE MY EQUAL IN RANK, BUT NOT IN COMBAT.
IT IS PRECISELY YOUR LACK OF TACTICAL SUBTLETY THAT HAS LED US TO THIS PATH...
...THE CHANCELLOR WANTS A VICTORY OVER THE FEDERATION...
...WE SHALL GIVE HIM ONE.
BY BARGAINING WITH THE ENEMY?! WHEN THEY WOULD SO EAGERLY TAKE THE SPOILS OF OUR CONQUESTS FROM OUR VERY MOUTHS?
YOU UNDERESTIMATED THE HUMANS ONCE AGAIN, KOR. NOW THEY HAVE A TACTICAL ADVANTAGE, AND WHO KNOWS WHAT ELSE THEY MAY HAVE LEARNED WHILE ON THE OUTPOST THAT WAS DESTROYED RIGHT IN FRONT OF YOU!
WE DO NOT NEED THEIR HELP. BETWEEN THE TWO OF US, WE COULD RALLY ENOUGH OF THE FLEET TO LAY WASTE TO THEIR BORDERS.
WITHOUT KNOWING WHERE THEY ARE, CAPTAIN?
TREACHEROUS ROMULAN!
HOLD, KOR! SHE HAS COME AT MY INVITATION... AND WILL BE GIVEN SAFE CONDUCT.
I TAKE IT YOU HAVE SUDDENLY FOUND MERIT IN MY PROPOSAL, KOLOTH.
OUR MUTUAL ENEMY APPEARS TO HAVE GAINED A FOOTHOLD ON TECHNOLOGY THAT ORIGINATED WITHIN THE ROMULAN STAR EMPIRE. WOULD YOU CARE TO EXPLAIN HOW THIS HAPPENED?
IRRELEVANT AT THIS POINT, CAPTAIN. SUFFICE IT TO SAY, IT WAS NOT OUR CHOICE TO GIVE UP OUR LONG-CHERISHED ADVANTAGES.
AND WHAT DO YOU ASK OF THE KLINGON EMPIRE, ROMULAN?
VERY LITTLE. A GREAT DEAL OF EFFORT AND TIME HAS GONE INTO CREATING THE TECHNOLOGY THAT SECURED YOUR DEFEAT.
BUT IN THAT TIME, THOUGH WE PROSPERED IN THE QUALITY OF OUR TECHNOLOGY... LITTLE WORK WAS DONE TO GROW OUR FLEET.

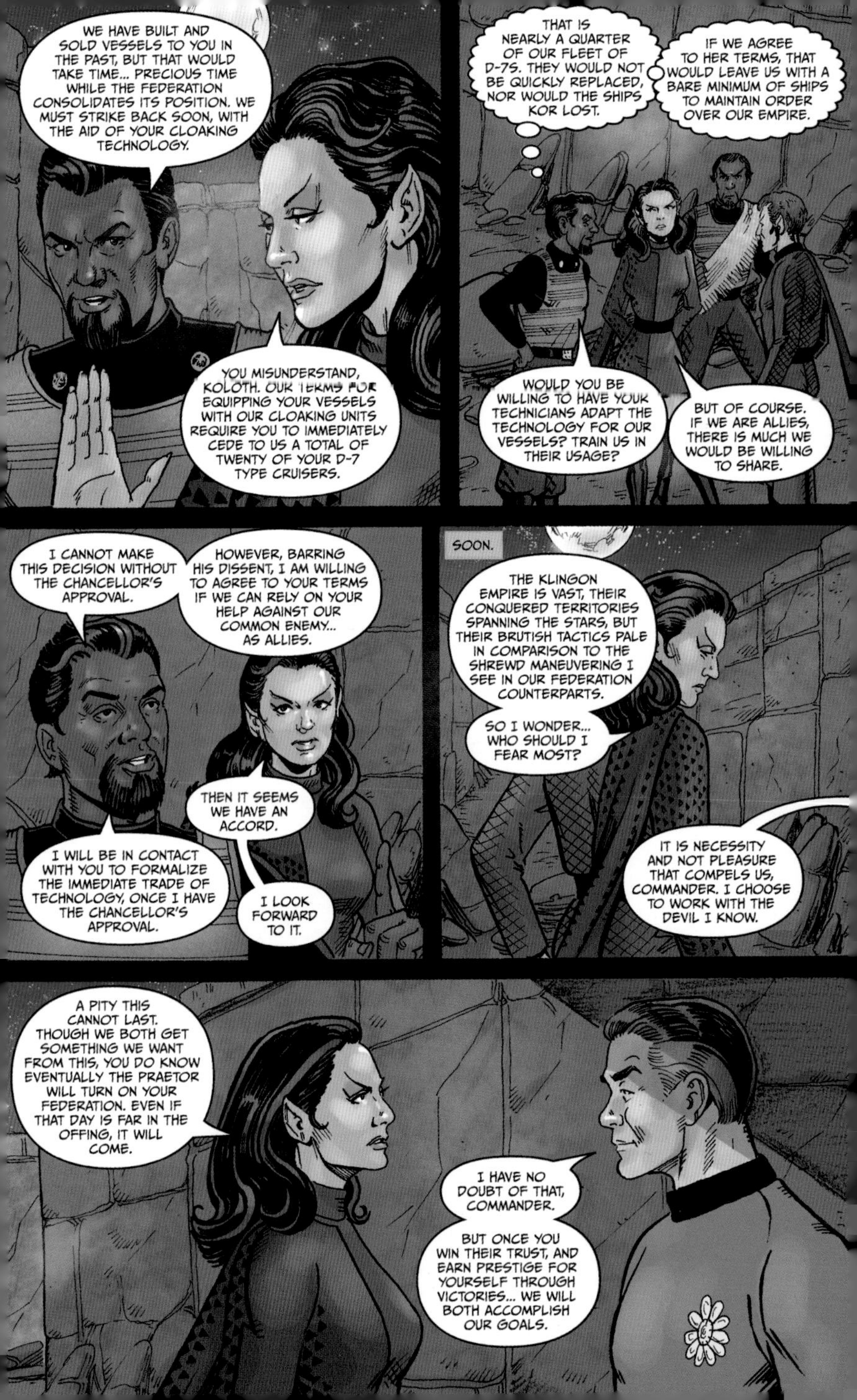
WE HAVE BUILT AND SOLD VESSELS TO YOU IN THE PAST, BUT THAT WOULD TAKE TIME... PRECIOUS TIME WHILE THE FEDERATION CONSOLIDATES ITS POSITION. WE MUST STRIKE BACK SOON, WITH THE AID OF YOUR CLOAKING TECHNOLOGY.
YOU MISUNDERSTAND, KOLOTH. OUR TERMS FOR EQUIPPING YOUR VESSELS WITH OUR CLOAKING UNITS REQUIRE YOU TO IMMEDIATELY CEDE TO US A TOTAL OF TWENTY OF YOUR D-7 TYPE CRUISERS.
THAT IS NEARLY A QUARTER OF OUR FLEET OF D-7S. THEY WOULD NOT BE QUICKLY REPLACED, NOR WOULD THE SHIPS KOR LOST.
IF WE AGREE TO HER TERMS, THAT WOULD LEAVE US WITH A BARE MINIMUM OF SHIPS TO MAINTAIN ORDER OVER OUR EMPIRE.
WOULD YOU BE WILLING TO HAVE YOUR TECHNICIANS ADAPT THE TECHNOLOGY FOR OUR VESSELS? TRAIN US IN THEIR USAGE?
BUT OF COURSE. IF WE ARE ALLIES, THERE IS MUCH WE WOULD BE WILLING TO SHARE.
I CANNOT MAKE THIS DECISION WITHOUT THE CHANCELLOR'S APPROVAL.
HOWEVER, BARRING HIS DISSENT, I AM WILLING TO AGREE TO YOUR TERMS IF WE CAN RELY ON YOUR HELP AGAINST OUR COMMON ENEMY... AS ALLIES.
THEN IT SEEMS WE HAVE AN ACCORD.
I WILL BE IN CONTACT WITH YOU TO FORMALIZE THE IMMEDIATE TRADE OF TECHNOLOGY, ONCE I HAVE THE CHANCELLOR'S APPROVAL.
I LOOK FORWARD TO IT.
SOON.
THE KLINGON EMPIRE IS VAST, THEIR CONQUERED TERRITORIES SPANNING THE STARS, BUT THEIR BRUTISH TACTICS PALE IN COMPARISON TO THE SHREWD MANEUVERING I SEE IN OUR FEDERATION COUNTERPARTS.
SO I WONDER... WHO SHOULD I FEAR MOST?
IT IS NECESSITY AND NOT PLEASURE THAT COMPELS US, COMMANDER. I CHOOSE TO WORK WITH THE DEVIL I KNOW.
A PITY THIS CANNOT LAST. THOUGH WE BOTH GET SOMETHING WE WANT FROM THIS, YOU DO KNOW EVENTUALLY THE PRAETOR WILL TURN ON YOUR FEDERATION. EVEN IF THAT DAY IS FAR IN THE OFFING, IT WILL COME.
I HAVE NO DOUBT OF THAT, COMMANDER.
BUT ONCE YOU WIN THEIR TRUST, AND EARN PRESTIGE FOR YOURSELF THROUGH VICTORIES... WE WILL BOTH ACCOMPLISH OUR GOALS.

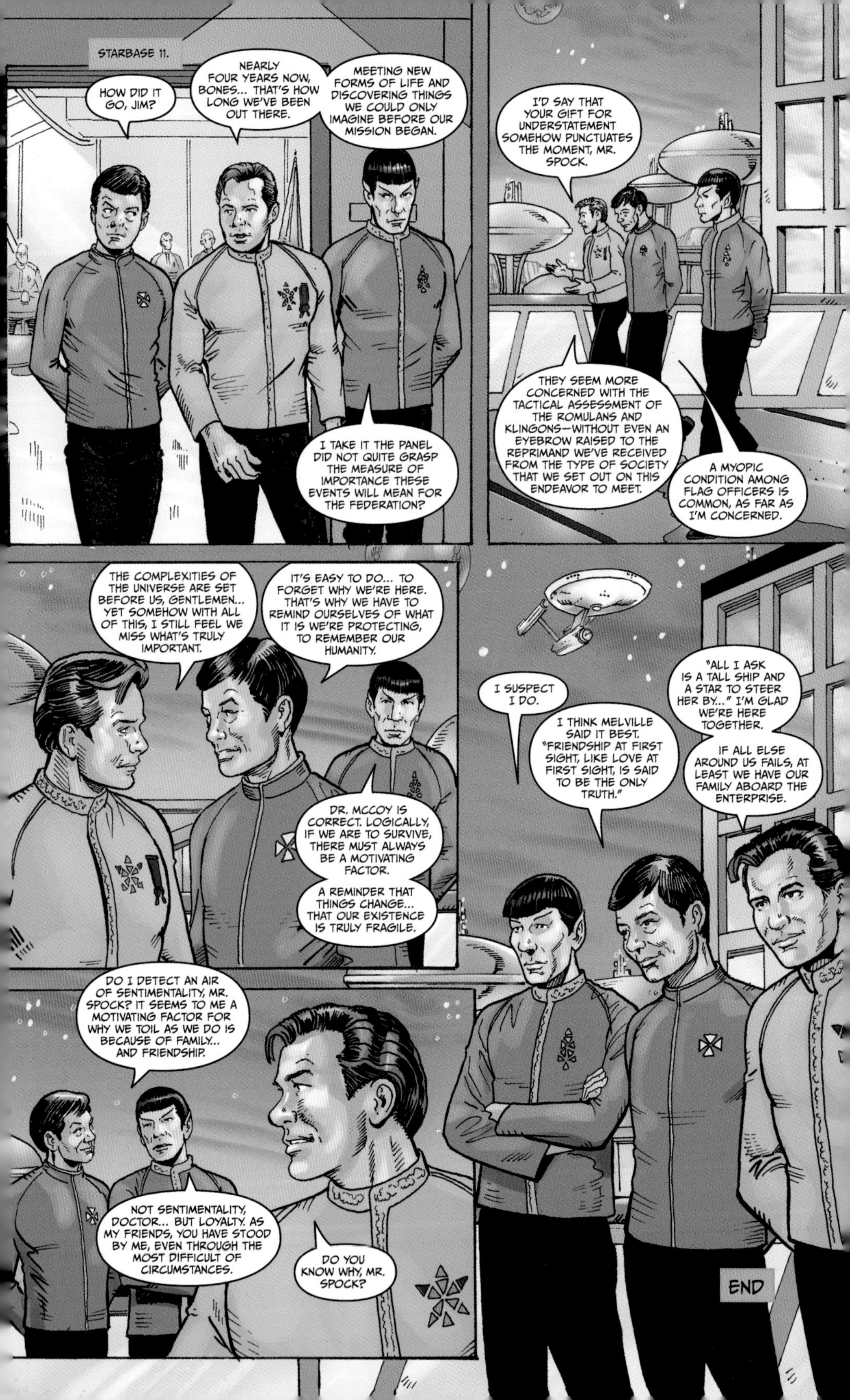
STARBASE 11.
HOW DID IT GO, JIM?
NEARLY FOUR YEARS NOW, BONES... THAT'S HOW LONG WE'VE BEEN OUT THERE.
MEETING NEW FORMS OF LIFE AND DISCOVERING THINGS WE COULD ONLY IMAGINE BEFORE OUR MISSION BEGAN.
I TAKE IT THE PANEL DID NOT QUITE GRASP THE MEASURE OF IMPORTANCE THESE EVENTS WILL MEAN FOR THE FEDERATION?
I'D SAY THAT YOUR GIFT FOR UNDERSTATEMENT SOMEHOW PUNCTUATES THE MOMENT, MR. SPOCK.
THEY SEEM MORE CONCERNED WITH THE TACTICAL ASSESSMENT OF THE ROMULANS AND KLINGONS—WITHOUT EVEN AN EYEBROW RAISED TO THE REPRIMAND WE'VE RECEIVED FROM THE TYPE OF SOCIETY THAT WE SET OUT ON THIS ENDEAVOR TO MEET.
A MYOPIC CONDITION AMONG FLAG OFFICERS IS COMMON, AS FAR AS I'M CONCERNED.
THE COMPLEXITIES OF THE UNIVERSE ARE SET BEFORE US, GENTLEMEN... YET SOMEHOW WITH ALL OF THIS, I STILL FEEL WE MISS WHAT'S TRULY IMPORTANT.
IT'S EASY TO DO... TO FORGET WHY WE'RE HERE. THAT'S WHY WE HAVE TO REMIND OURSELVES OF WHAT IT IS WE'RE PROTECTING, TO REMEMBER OUR HUMANITY.
DR. MCCOY IS CORRECT. LOGICALLY, IF WE ARE TO SURVIVE, THERE MUST ALWAYS BE A MOTIVATING FACTOR.
A REMINDER THAT THINGS CHANGE... THAT OUR EXISTENCE IS TRULY FRAGILE.
DO I DETECT AN AIR OF SENTIMENTALITY, MR. SPOCK? IT SEEMS TO ME A MOTIVATING FACTOR FOR WHY WE TOIL AS WE DO IS BECAUSE OF FAMILY... AND FRIENDSHIP.
NOT SENTIMENTALITY, DOCTOR... BUT LOYALTY. AS MY FRIENDS, YOU HAVE STOOD BY ME, EVEN THROUGH THE MOST DIFFICULT OF CIRCUMSTANCES.
DO YOU KNOW WHY, MR. SPOCK?
I SUSPECT I DO.
I THINK MELVILLE SAID IT BEST. "FRIENDSHIP AT FIRST SIGHT, LIKE LOVE AT FIRST SIGHT, IS SAID TO BE THE ONLY TRUTH."
"ALL I ASK IS A TALL SHIP AND A STAR TO STEER HER BY..." I'M GLAD WE'RE HERE TOGETHER.
IF ALL ELSE AROUND US FAILS, AT LEAST WE HAVE OUR FAMILY ABOARD THE ENTERPRISE.
END

STAR TREK®

THE ORIGINAL SERIES

OMNIBUS

ART GALLERY

ART BY JOE CORRONEY

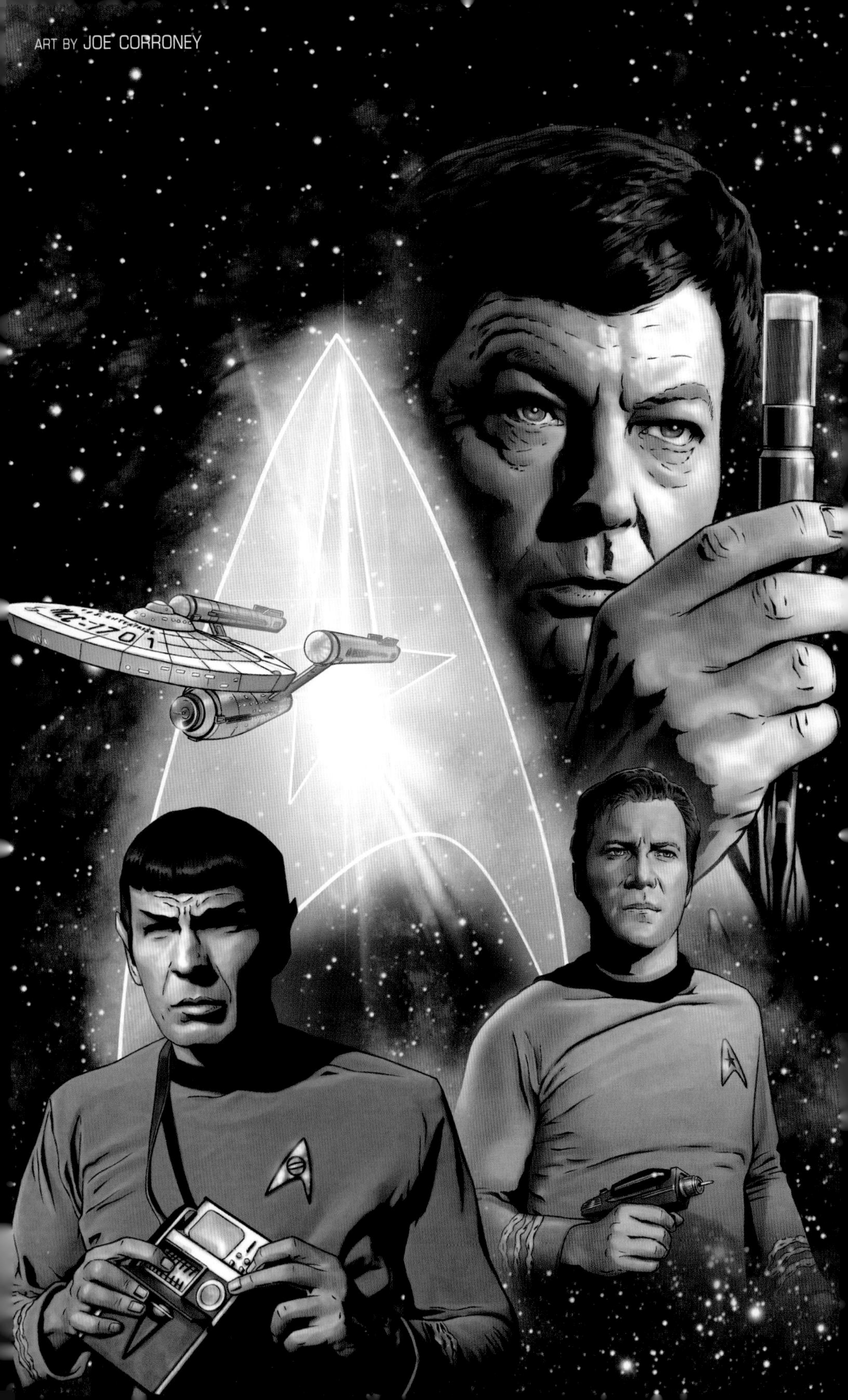
NCC-1701

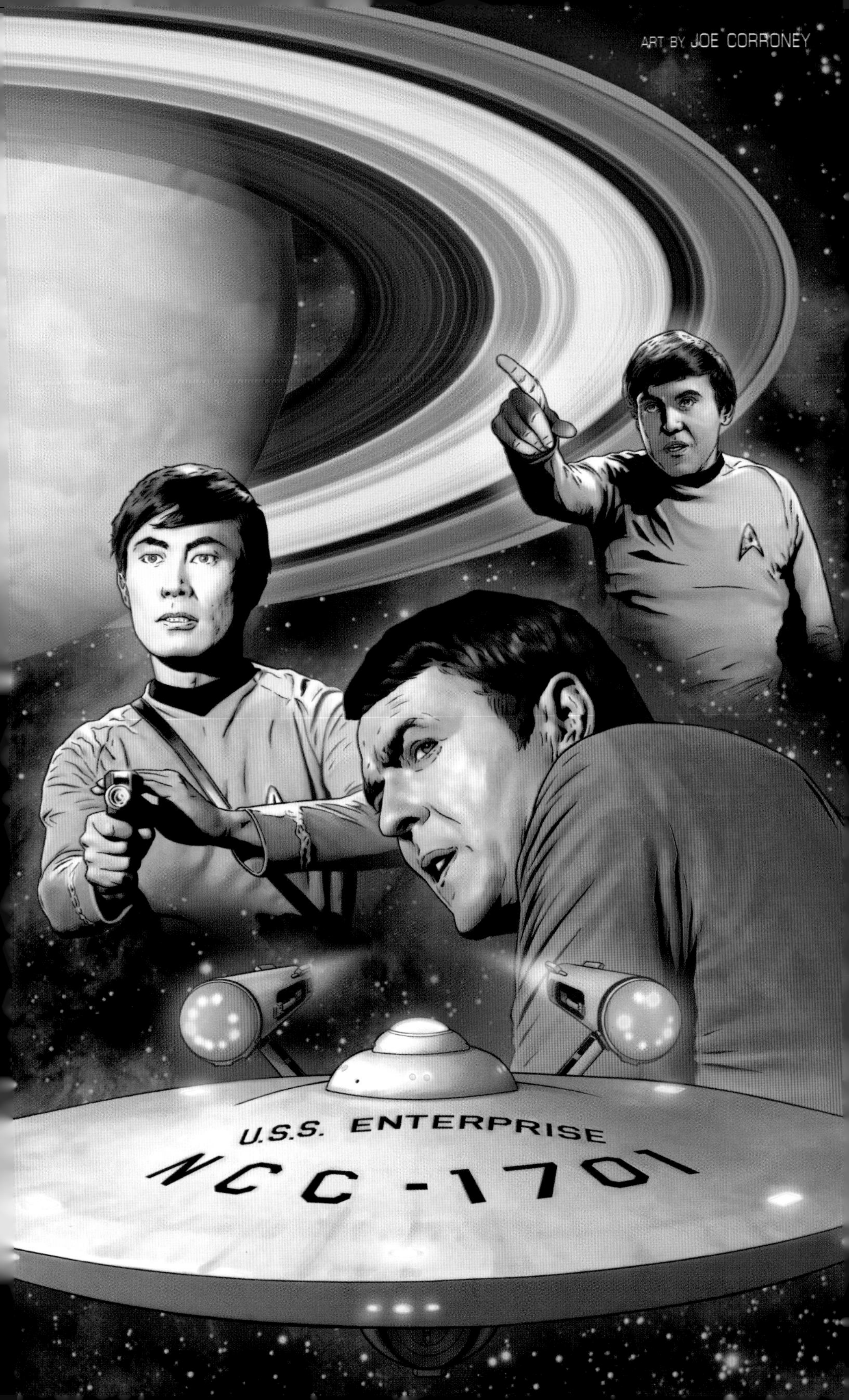
U.S.S. ENTERPRISE
NCC-1701
ART BY JOE CORRONEY

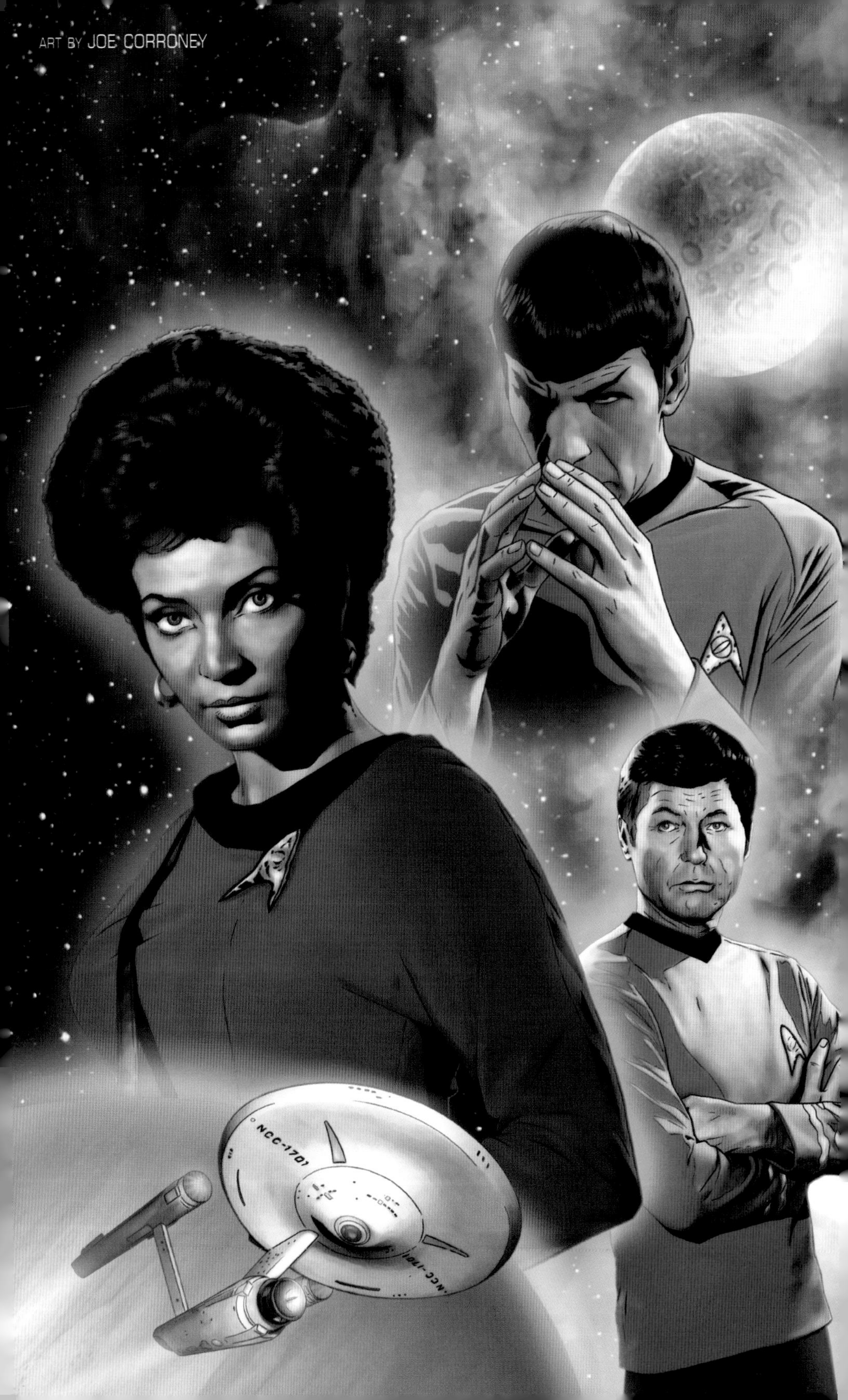
NCC-1701
NCC-1701

ART BY JOE CORRONEY

ART BY JOE CORRONEY

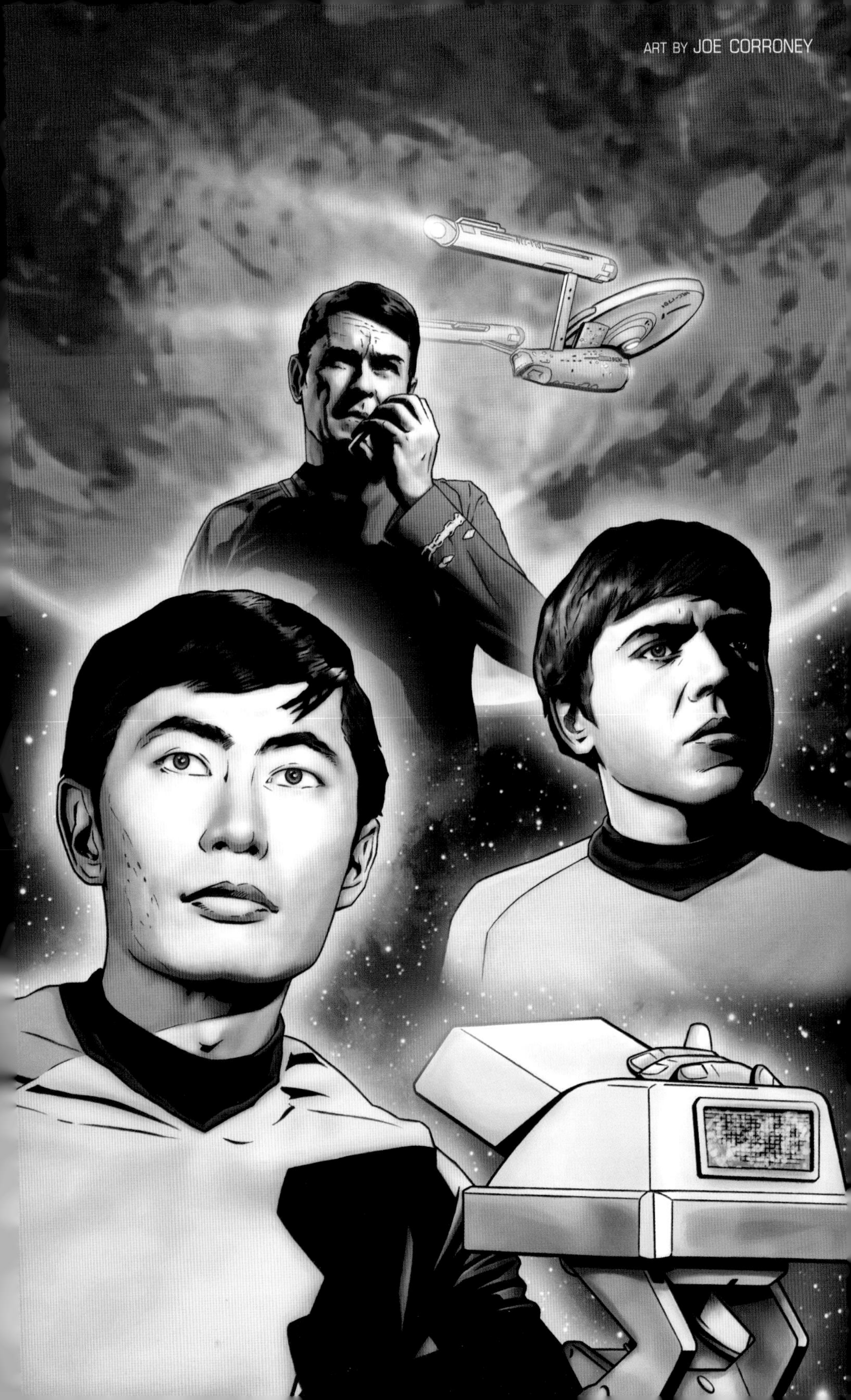

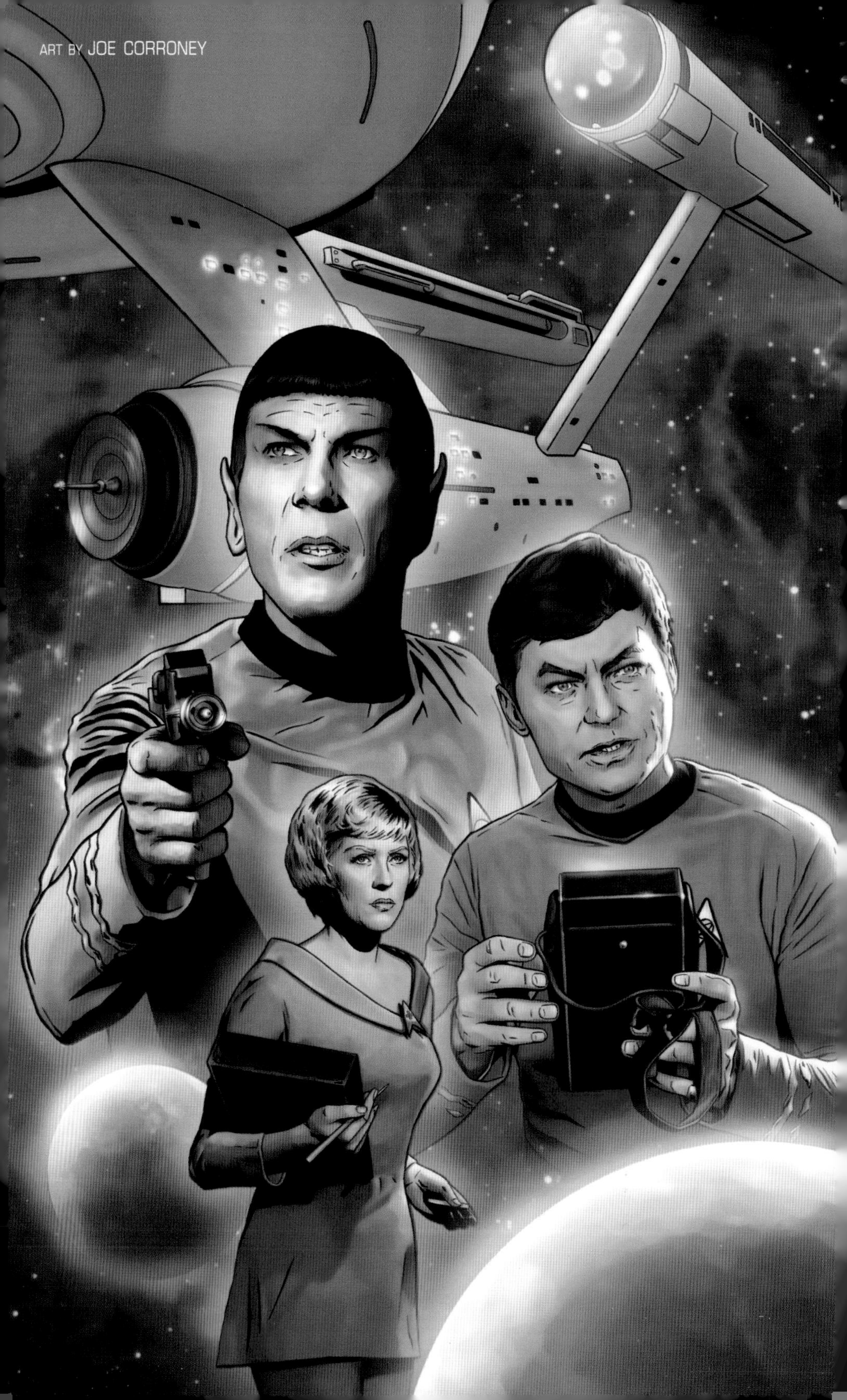
ART BY JOE CORRONEY

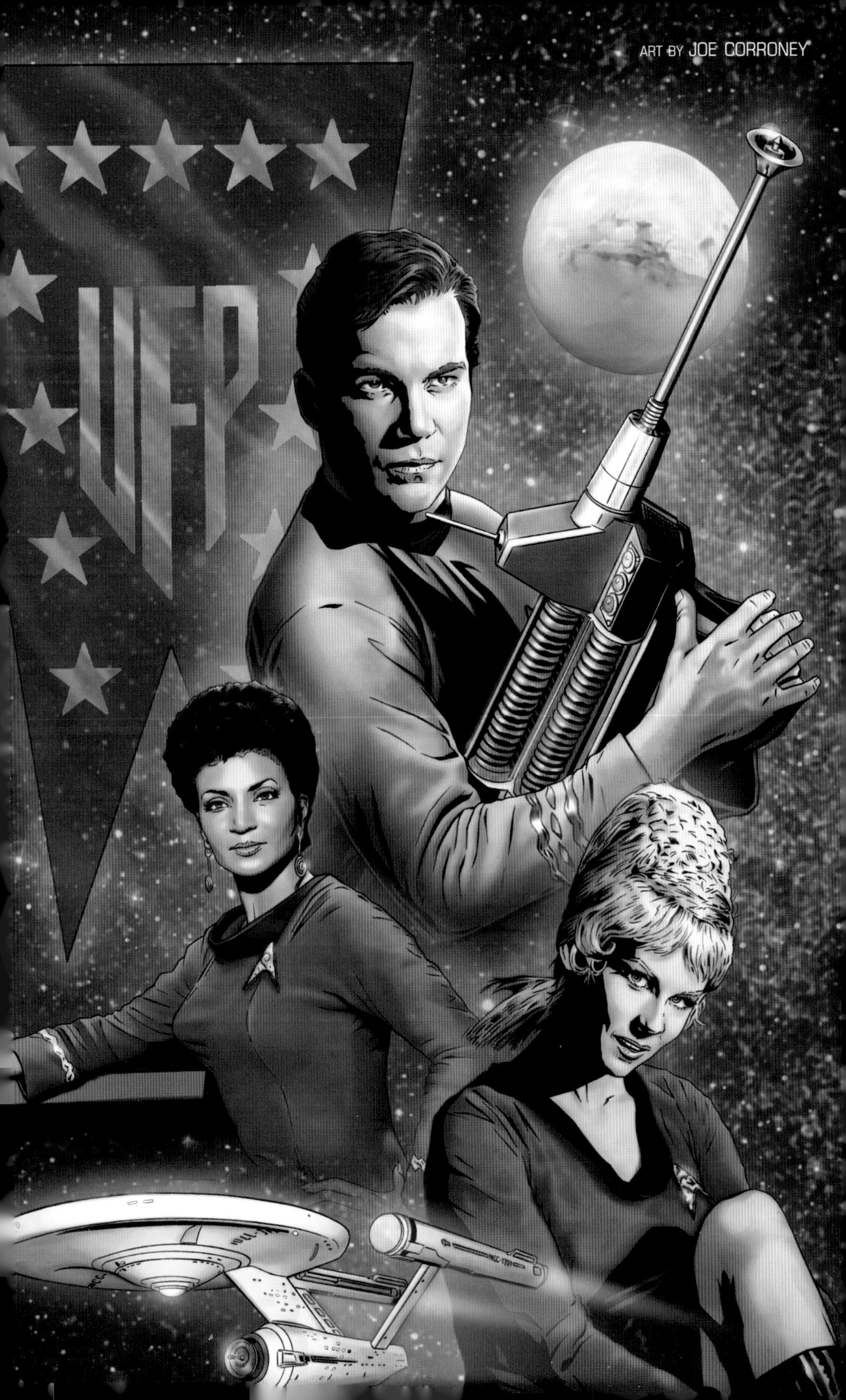
UFP
NCC-1701
ART BY JOE CORRONEY

STAR TREK®

THE ORIGINAL SERIES

OMNIBUS